D1202367

A STRANGE STORY.

THE WORKS

OF

EDWARD BULWER LYTTON

(LORD LYTTON)

A STRANGE STORY.

THE HAUNTED AND THE HAUNTERS,

THE LAST OF THE BARONS.

RIENZI.

VOLUME VII.

NEW YORK:

P. F. COLLIER, PUBLISHER.

CONTENTS.

BOOK FIFTH.

BOOK SIXTH.

BOOK SEVENTH.

BOOK EIGHTH.

BOOK NINTH.

BOOK TENTH.

BOOK ELEVENTH.

BOOK TWELFTH.

RIENZI, THE LAST OF THE TRIBUNES.

BOOK FIRST.

BOOK SECOND.

BOOK THIRD.

BOOK FOURTH.

BOOK FIFTH.

BOOK SIXTH.

BOOK SEVENTH.

BOOK EIGHTH.

BOOK NINTH.

BOOK TENTH.

A STRANGE STORY

PREFACE.

Of the many illustrious thinkers whom the schools of France have contributed to the intellectual philosophy of our age, Victor Cousin, the most accomplished, assigns to Maine de Biran the rank of the most original.

In the successive developments of his own mind, Maine de Biran may, indeed, be said to represent the change that has been silently at work throughout the general mind of Europe since the close of the last century. He begins his career of philosopher with blind faith in Condillac and Materialism. As an intellect severely conscientious in the pursuit of truth, expands amidst the perplexities it revolves, phenomena which cannot be accounted for by Condillac's sensuous theories open to his eye. To the first rudimentary life of man, the animal life, "characterized by impressions, appetites, movements, organic in their origin and ruled by the Law of Necessity," * he is compelled to add "the second or human life, from which Free-will and Self-consciousness emerge." He thus arrives at the union of mind and matter; but still a something is wanted—some key to the marvels which neither of these conditions of vital being suffices to explain. And at last the grand self-completing Thinker attains to the Third Life of Man in Man's Soul.

"There are not," says this philosopher, towards the close of his last and loftiest work—"There are not only two principles opposed to each other in Man, there are three. For there are, in him, three lives and three orders of faculties. Though all should be in accord and in harmony between the sensitive and the active faculties which constitute Man, there would still be a nature superior, a third life which would not be satisfied; which would make felt (*ferait sentir*) the truth that there is another happiness, another wisdom, another perfection, at once above the greatest human happiness, above the highest wisdom, or intellectual and moral perfection of which the human being is susceptible." *

Now, as Philosophy and Romance both take their origin in the Principle of Wonder, so in the Strange Story submitted to the Public, it will be seen that Romance, through the freest exercise of its wildest vagaries, conducts its bewildered hero towards the same goal to which Philosophy leads its luminous Student, through far grander portents of Nature, far higher visions of Supernatural Power, than Fable can yield to Fancy. That goal is defined in these noble words: "The relations (*rapports*) which exist between the elements and the products of the three lives of Man are the subjects of meditation, the fairest and finest, but also the most difficult. The Stoic Philosophy shows us all which can be most elevated in active life; but it makes abstraction of the animal nature, and absolutely fails to recognize all which belongs to the life of

* Œuvres inédites de Maine de Biran, vol. i. See Introduction.

* Œuvres inédites de Maine de Biran, vol. iii. p. 546 (Anthropologie).

the spirit. Its practical morality is beyond the forces of humanity. Christianity alone embraces the whole Man. It dissimulates none of the sides of his nature, and avails itself of his miseries and his weakness in order to conduct him to his end in showing him all the want that he has of a succor more exalted." *

In the passages thus quoted, I imply one of the objects for which this tale has been written; and I cite them, with a wish to acknowledge one of those priceless obligations which writings the lightest and most fantastic often incur to reasoners the most serious and profound.

But I here construct a romance which should have, as a romance, some interest for the general reader. I do not elaborate a treatise submitted to the logic of sages. And it is only when "in fairy fiction drest" that Romance give admission to "truths severe."

I venture to assume that none will question my privilege to avail myself of the marvellous agencies which have ever been at the legitimate command of the fabulist.

To the highest form of romantic narrative, the Epic, critics, indeed, have declared that a supernatural machinery is indispensable. That the Drama has availed itself of the same licence as the Epic, it would be unnecessary to say to the countrymen of Shakespeare, or to the generation that is yet studying the enigmas of Goethe's Faust. Prose Romance has immemorially asserted, no less than the Epic or the Drama, its heritage in the Realm of the Marvellous. The interest which attaches to the supernatural is sought in the earliest Prose Romance which modern times take from the ancient, and which, perhaps, and its origin in the lost Novels of Miletus; † and the right to invoke such interest has, ever since, been maintained by Romance through all varieties of form and fancy—from the majestic epopee of Télémeque to the graceful phantasies of Undine, or the mighty mockeries of Gulliver's Travels, down to such comparatively commonplace elements of wonder as yet preserve from oblivion the Castle of Otranto and the Old English Baron.

Now, to my mind, the true reason why a supernatural agency is indispensable to the conception of the Epic, is that the Epic is the highest and the completest form in which Art can express either Man or Nature, and that without some gleams of the supernatural, Man is not man, nor Nature, nature.

It is said, by a writer to whom an eminent philosophical critic justly applies the epithets of "pious and profound:" *—"Is it unreasonable to confess that we believe in God, not by reason of the Nature which conceals Him, but by reason of the Supernatural in Man which alone reveals and proves Him to exist? * * * Man reveals God: for Man, by his intelligence, rises above Nature: and in virtue of this intelligence is conscious of himself as a power not only independent of, but opposed to, Nature, and capable of resisting, conquering, and controlling her." †

If the meaning involved in the argument of which I have here made but scanty extracts be carefully studied, I think that we shall find deeper reasons than the critics who dictated canons of taste to the last century discovered—why the supernatural is indispensable to the Epic, and why it is allowable to all works of imagination, in which Art looks on Nature with Man's inner sense of a something beyond and above her.

But the Writer who, whether in verse or prose, would avail himself of such sources of pity or terror as flow from the Marvellous, can only attain his object in proportion as the wonders he narrates are of a kind to excite the curiosity of the age he addresses.

In the brains of our time, the faculty of *Causation* is very markedly developed. People, nowadays, do not delight in the Marvellous according to the old childlike spirit. They say in one breath "Very extraordinary!" and in the next breath, ask, "How do you account for it?" If the Author of this work has presumed to borrow from science some elements of interest for Romance, he ventures to hope that no thoughtful reader—and certainly no true son of science—will be disposed to reproach him. In fact, such illustrations from the masters of Thought were essential to the completion of the purpose which pervades the work.

* Œuvres inédits de Maine de Biran, vol. iii. p. 524.
† The Golden Ass of Apuleius.

* Sir William Hamilton. Lectures on Metaphysics p. 40.
† Jacobi—*Von der Gottlichen Dingen; Werke*, p. 424–6.

That purpose, I trust, will develop itself in proportion as the story approaches the close; and whatever may appear violent or melodramatic in the catastrophe, will perhaps be found, by a reader capable of perceiving the various symbolical meanings conveyed in the story, essential to the end in which those meanings converge, and towards which the incidents that give them the character and interest of fiction have been planned and directed from the commencement.

Of course, according to the most obvious principles of art, the narrator of a fiction must be as thoroughly in earnest as if he were the narrator of facts. One could not tell the most extravagant fairy-tale so as to rouse and sustain the attention of the most infantine listener, if the tale were told as if the tale-teller did not believe in it. But when the reader lays down this Strange Story, perhaps he will detect, through all the haze of Romance, the outlines of these images suggested to his reason: Firstly, the image of sensuous, soulless Nature, such as the Materialist had conceived it. Secondly, the image of Intellect, obstinately separating all its inquiries from the belief in the spiritual essence and destiny of man, and incurring all kinds of perplexity and resorting to all kinds of visionary speculation before it settles at last into the simple faith which unites the philosopher and the infant. And, Thirdly, the image of the erring but pure-thoughted visionary, seeking overmuch on this earth to separate soul from mind, till innocence itself is led astray by a phantom, and reason is lost in the space between earth and the stars. Whether in these pictures there be any truth worth the implying, every reader must judge for himself; and if he doubt or deny that there be any such truth, still, in that process of thought which the doubt or denial enforces, he may chance on a truth which it pleases himself to discover.

"Most of the Fables of Æsop"—thus says Montaigne in his charming essay "Of Books" *—"have several senses and meanings, of which the Mythologists choose some one that tallies with the fable. But for the most part 'tis only what presents itself at the first view, and is superficial; there being others more lively, essential, and internal into which they have not been able to penetrate; and"—adds Montaigne—"the case is the very same with me."

* Translation 1776, vol. ii. p. 103.

A STRANGE STORY.

CHAPTER I.

In the year 18— I settled as a physician at one of the wealthiest of our great English towns, which I will designate by the initial L——. I was yet young, but I had acquired some reputation by a professional work, which is, I believe, still amongst the received authorities on the subject of which it treats. I had studied at Edinburgh and at Paris, and had borne away from both those illustrious schools of medicine whatever guarantees for future distinction the praise of professors may concede to the ambition of students. On becoming a member of the College of Physicians, I made a tour of the principal cities of Europe, taking letters of introductions to eminent medical men; and gathering from many theories and modes of treatment, hints to enlarge the foundations of unprejudiced and comprehensive practice. I had resolved to fix my ultimate residence in London. But before this preparatory tour was completed, my resolve was changed by one of those unexpected events which determine the fate man in vain would work out for himself. In passing through the Tyrol, on my way into the north of Italy. I found in a small inn, remote from medical attendance, an English traveller, seized with acute inflammation of the lungs, and in a state of imminent danger. I devoted myself to him night and day; and, perhaps, more through careful nursing than active remedies, I had the happiness to effect his complete recovery.

The traveller proved to be Julius Faber, a physician of great distinction, contented to reside, where he was born, in the provincial city of L——, but whose reputation as a profound and original pathologist was widely spread; and whose writings had formed no unimportant part of my special studies. It was during a short holiday excursion, from which he was about to return with renovated vigor, that he had been thus stricken down. The patient so accidentally met with, became the founder of my professional fortunes. He conceived a warm attachment for me; perhaps the more affectionate because he was a childless bachelor, and the nephew who would succeed to his wealth evinced no desire to succeed to to the toils by which the wealth had been acquired. Thus, having an heir for the the one, he had long looked about for an heir to the other, and now resolved in finding that heir in me, So when we parted, Dr. Faber made me promise to correspond with him regularly, and it was not long before he disclosed by letter the plans he had formed in my favor. He said that he was growing old; his practice was beyond his strength; he needed a partner; he was not disposed to put up to sale the health of patients whom he had learned to regard as his children; money was no object to him, but it was an object close at his heart that the humanity he had served, and the reputation he had acquired, should suffer no loss in his choice of a successor. In fine, he proposed that I should at once come to L—— as his partner, with the view of succeeding to his entire practice at the end of two years, when it was his intention to retire.

The opening into fortune thus afforded to me was one that rarely presents itself to a young man entering upon an overcrowded profession. And to an aspirant less allured by the desire of fortune than the hope of distinction, the fame of the physician who thus generously offered to me the inestimable benefits of his long experience and his cordial introduction, was in itself an assurance that a metropolitan practice is not essential to a national renown.

I went, then, to L——, and before the two years of my partenership had expired, my success justified my kind friend's selection, and far more than realized my own expectations. I was fortunate in affecting some notable cures in the earliest cases submitted to me, and it is everything in the career of a physician when good luck wins betimes for him that confidence which patients rarely accord except to lengthened experience. To the rapid facility with which my way was made, some circumstances apart from professional skill probably contributed. I was saved from the suspicion of a medical adventurer by the accidents of birth and fortune. I belonged to an ancient family (a branch of the once powerful border clan of the Fenwicks) that had for many generations held a fair estate in the neighborhood of Windermere. As an only son I had succeeded to that estate on attaining my majority, and had sold it to pay off the debts which had been made by my father, who had the costly tastes of an antiquary and collector. The residue on the sale insured me a modest independence apart from the profits of a profession; and as I had not been legally bound to defray my father's debts, so I obtained that character for disinterestedness and integrity which always in England tends to propitiate the public to the successes achieved by industry or talent. Perhaps, too, any professional ability I might possess was the more readily conceded, because I had cultivated with assiduity the sciences and the scholarship which are collaterally connected with the study of medicine. Thus, in a word, I established a social position which came in aid of my professional repute, and silenced much of that envy which usually embitters and sometimes impedes success.

Dr. Faber retired at the end of the two years agreed upon. He went abroad; and being, though advanced in years, of a frame still robust, and habits of mind still inquiring and eager, he commenced a lengthened course of foreign travel, during which our correspondence, at first frequent, gradually languished, and finally died away.

I succeeded at once to the larger part of the practice which the labors of thirty years had secured to my predecessor. My chief rival was a Dr. Lloyd, a benevolent, a fervid man, not without genius—if genius be present where judgment is absent; not without science, if that may be science which fails in precision. One of those clever desultory men who, in adopting a profession, do not give up to it the whole force and heat of their minds. Men of that kind habitually accept a mechanical routine, because in the exercise of the ostensible calling their imaginative faculties are drawn away to pursuits more alluring. Therefore, in their proper vocation they are seldom bold or inventive—out of it they are sometimes both to excess. And when they do take up a novelty in their own profession they cherish it with an obstinate tenacity, and an extravagant passion, unknown to those quiet philosophers who take up novelties every day, examine them with the sobriety of practised eyes, to lay down altogether, modify in part, or accept in whole, according as inductive experiment supports or destroys conjecture.

Dr. Lloyd had been esteemed a learned naturalist long before he was admitted to be a tolerable physician. Amidst the privations of his youth he had contrived to form, and with each succeeding year he had perseveringly increased, a zoological collection of creatures, not alive, but, happily for the beholder, stuffed or embalmed. From what I have said, it will be truly inferred that Dr. Lloyd's earlier career as a physician had not been brilliant; but of late years he had gradually rather *aged*, than worked himself, into that professional authority and station, which time confers on a thoroughly respectable man, whom no one is disposed to envy, and all are disposed to like.

Now in L—— there were two distinct social circles. That of the wealthy merchants and traders, and that of a few privileged families inhabiting a part of the town aloof from the marts of commerce, and called the Abbey Hill. These superb Areopagites exercised over the wives and daughters of the inferior citizens to whom all of L——, except the Abbey Hill, owed its prosperity, the same kind of mysterious influence which the fine ladies of May Fair and Belgravia are reported to hold over the female denizens of Bloomsbury and Marylebone.

Abbey Hill was not opulent; but it was powerful by a concentration of its resources in all matters of patronage. Abbey Hill had its own milliner and its own draper, its own confectioner, butcher, baker, and tea-dealer; and the patronage of Abbey Hill was like the patronage of royalty, less lucrative in itself than as a solemn certificate of general merit.

The shops on which Abbey Hill conferred its custom were certainly not the cheapest, possibly not the best. But they were undeniably the most imposing. The proprietors were decorously pompous—the shopmen superciliously polite. They could not be more so if they had belonged to the State, and been paid by a public which they benefited and despised. The ladies of Low Town (as the city subjacent to the Hill had been styled from a date remote in the feudal ages) entered those shops with a certain awe, and left them with a certain pride. There they had learned what the Hill approved. There they had bought what the Hill had purchased. It is much in this life to be quite sure that we are in the right, whatever that conviction may cost us. Abbey Hill had been in the habit of appointing, amongst other objects of patronage, its own physician. But that habit had fallen into disuse during the latter years of my predecessor's practice. His superiority over all other medical men in the town had become so incontestable, that, though he was emphatically the doctor of Low Town, the heads of its hospitals and infirmaries, and by birth related to its principal traders, still as Abbey Hill was occasionally subject to the physical infirmities of meaner mortals, so on those occasions it deemed it best not to push the point of honor to the wanton sacrifice of life. Since Low Town possessed one of the most famous physicians in England, Abbey Hill magnanimously resolved not to crush him by a rival. Abbey Hill let him feel its pulse.

When my predecessors retired, I had presumptuously expected that the Hill would have continued to suspend its normal right to a special physician, and shown to me the same generous favor it had shown to him, who had declared me worthy to succeed to his honors. I had the more excuse for this presumption because the Hill had already allowed me to visit a fair proportion of its invalids, had said some very gracious things to me about the great respectability of the Fenwick family, and sent me some invitations to dinner, and a great many invitations to tea.

But my self-conceit received a notable check. Abbey Hill declared that the time had come to reassert its dormant privilege—it must have a doctor of its own choosing—a doctor who might, indeed, be permitted to visit Low Town from motives of humanity or gain, but who must emphatically assert his special allegiance to Abbey Hill by fixing his home on that venerable promontory. Miss Brabazon, a spinster of uncertain age, but undoubted pedigree, with small fortune, but high nose, which she would pleasantly observe was a proof of her descent from Humphrey Duke of Gloucester (with whom, indeed, I have no doubt, in spite of chronology, that she very often dined), was commissioned to inquire of me diplomatically, and without committing Abbey Hill too much by the overture, whether I would take a large and antiquated mansion, in which abbots were said to have lived many centuries ago, and which was still popularly styled Abbots' House, situated on the verge of the Hill, as in that case the "Hill" would think of me.

"It is a large house for a single man, I allow," said Miss Brabazon, candidly; and then added, with a sidelong glance of alarming sweetness, "But when Dr. Fenwick has taken his true position (so old a family)! amongst us, he need not long remain single, unless he prefer it."

I replied, with more asperity than the occasion called for, that I had no thought of changing my residence at present. And if the Hill wanted me, the Hill must send for me.

Two days afterwards Dr. Lloyd took Abbots' House, and in less than a week was proclaimed medical adviser to the Hill. The election had been decided by the fiat of a great lady, who reigned supreme on the sacred eminence, under the name and title of Mrs. Colonel Poyntz.

"Dr. Fenwick," said this lady, "is a clever young man and a gentleman, but he gives himself airs—the Hill does not allow any airs but its own. Besides, he is a new comer: resistance to new comers, and, indeed, to all things new, except caps and novels, is one of the bonds that keep old established societies together. Accordingly, it is by my advice that Dr. Lloyd has taken Abbots' House; the rent would be too high for his means if the Hill did not feel bound in honor to justify the trust he has placed in its patronage. I told him that all my friends, when they were in want of a doctor, would send for him; those who are my friends will do so. What the Hill does, plenty of common people down *there* will do also:—so that question is settled!" And it was settled.

Dr. Lloyd, thus taken by the hand, soon extended the range of his visits beyond the Hill, which was not precisely a mountain of gold to doctors, and shared with myself, though in a comparatively small degree, the much more lucrative practice of Low Town.

I had no cause to grudge his success, nor did I. But to my theories of medicine his diagnosis was shallow, and his prescriptions obsolete. When we were summoned to a joint consultation, our views as to the proper course of treatment seldom agreed. Doubtless he thought I ought to have deferred to his seniority in years; but I held the doctrine which youth deems a truth and age a paradox, namely, that in science the young men are the practical elders, inasmuch as they are schooled in the latest experiences science has gathered up, while their seniors are cramped by the dogmas they were schooled to believe when the world was some decades the younger.

Meanwhile my reputation continued rapidly to advance; it became more than local; my advice was sought even by patients from the metropolis. That ambition which, conceived in early youth, had decided my career and sweetened all its labors—the ambition to take a rank and leave a name as one of the great pathologists, to whom humanity accords a grateful, if calm, renown—saw before it a level field and a certain goal.

I know not whether a success far beyond that unusally attained at the age I had reached served to increase, but it seemed to myself to justify, the main characteristic of my moral organization—intellectual pride.

Though mild and gentle to the sufferers under my care, as a necessary element of professional duty, I was intolerant of contradiction from those who belonged to my calling, or even from those who, in general opinion, opposed my favorite theories.

I had espoused a school of medical philosophy severely rigid in its inductive logic. My creed was that of stern materialism. I had a contempt for the understanding of men who accepted with credulity what they could not explain by reason. My favorite phrase was "common sense." At the same time I had no prejudice againt bold discovery, and discovery necessitates conjecture, but I dismissed as idle all conjecture that could not be brought to a practical test.

As in medicine I had been the pupil of Broussais, so in metaphysics I was the disciple of Condillac. I believed with that philosopher that "all our knowledge we owe to Nature, that in the beginning we can only instruct ourselves through her lessons, and that the whole art of reasoning consists in continuing as she has compelled us to commence." Keeping natural philosophy apart from the doctrines of revelation, I never assailed the last, but I contended that by the first no accurate reasoner could arrive at the existence of the soul as a third principle of being equally distinct from mind and body. That by a miracle man might live again, was a question of faith and not of understanding. I left faith to religion, and banished it from philosophy. How define with a precision to satisfy the logic of philosophy what was to live again? The body? We know that the body rests in its grave till by the process of decomposition its elemental parts enter into other forms of matter. The mind? But the mind was as clearly the result of the bodily organization as the music of the harpsichord is the result of the instrumental mechanism.

The mind shared the decrepitude of the body in extreme old age, and in the full vigor of youth a sudden injury to the brain might for ever destroy the intellect of a Plato or a Shakspeare. But the third principle—the soul—the something lodged within the body, which yet was to survive it? Where was that soul hidden out of the ken of the anatomist? When philosophers attempted to define it, were they not compelled to confound its nature and its actions with those of the mind? Could they reduce it to the mere moral sense, varying according to education, circumstances, and physical constitution? But even the moral sense in the most virtuous of men may be swept away by a fever. Such at the time I now speak of were the views I held. Views certainly not original nor pleasing; but I cherished them with as fond a tenacity as if they had been consolatory truths of which I was the first discoverer. I was intolerant to those who maintained opposite doctrines—despised them as irrational, or disliked them as insincere. Certainly if I had fulfilled the career which my ambition predicted—become the founder of a new school in pathology, and summed up my theories in academical lectures, I should have added another authority, however feeble, to the sects which circumscribe the interest of man to the life that has its close in his grave.

Possibly that which I have called my intellectual pride was more nourished than I should have been willing to grant by the self-reliance which an unusual degree of physical power is apt to bestow. Nature had blessed me with the thews of an athlete. Among the hardy youths of the Northern Athens I had been pre-eminently distinguished for feats of activity and strength. My mental labors, and the anxiety which is inseparable from the conscientious responsibilities of the medical profession, kept my health below the par of keen enjoyment, but had in no way diminished my rare muscular force. I walked through the crowd with the firm step and lofty crest of the mailed knight of old, who felt himself, in his casement of iron, a match against numbers. Thus the sense of a robust individuality, strong alike in disciplined reason and animal vigor—habituated to aid others, needing no aid for itself—contributed to render me imperious in will and arrogant in opinion. Nor were such defects injurious to me in my profession; on the contrary, aided as they were by a calm manner, and a presence not without that kind of dignity which is the livery of self-esteem, they served to impose respect and to inspire trust.

CHAPTER II.

I HAD been about six years at L—— when I became suddenly involved in a controversy with Dr. Lloyd. Just as this ill-fated man appeared at the culminating point of his professional fortunes, he had the imprudence to proclaim himself not only an enthusiastic advocate of mesmerism, as a curative process but an ardent believer of the reality of somnambular chairvoyance as an invaluable gift of certain privileged organizations. To these doctrines I sternly opposed myself—the more sternly, perhaps, became on these doctrines Dr. Lloyd founded an argument for the existence of soul, independent of mind, as of matter, and built thereon a superstructure of physiological fantasies, which, could it be substantiated, would replace every system of metaphysics on which recognized philosophy condescends to dispute.

About two years before he became a disciple rather of Puysegur than Mesmer (for Mesmer had little faith in that gift of clairvoyance of which Puysegur was, I believe, at least in modern times, the first audacious asserter), Dr. Lloyd had been afflicted with the loss of a wife many years younger than himself, and to whom he had been tenderly attached. And this bereavement, in directing the hopes that consoled him to a world beyond the grave, had served perhaps to render him more credulous of the phenomena in which he greeted additional proofs of purely spiritual existence. Certainly, if, in controverting the notions of another physiologist, I had restricted myself to that fair antagonism which belongs to scientific disputants, anxious only for the truth, I should need no apology for sincere conviction and honest argument; but when, with condescending good nature, as if to a man much younger than himself, who was ignorant of the phenomena which he nevertheless denied, Dr. Lloyd invited me to attend his *séances* and witness his cures, my *amour propre* became roused and nettled, and it seemed to me necessary to put down what I asserted to be too gross an outrage on common sense to justify the ceremony of examination. I wrote, therefore, a small pamphlet on the subject, in which I exhausted all the weapons that irony can lend to contempt. Dr. Lloyd replied, and as he was no very skilful arguer, his reply injured him perhaps more than my assault. Meanwhile, I had made some inquiries as to the moral character of his favorite clairvoyants. I imagined that I had learned enough to justify me in treating them as flagrant cheats—and himself as their egregious dupe.

Low Town soon ranged itself, with very few exceptions, on my side. The Hill at first at first seemed disposed to rally round its insulted physician, and to make the dispute a party question, in which the Hill would have been signally worsted, when suddenly the same lady paramount, who had secured to Dr. Lloyd the smile of the Eminence, spoke forth against him, and the Eminence frowned.

"Dr. Lloyd," said the Queen of the Hill

"is an amiable creature, but on this subject decidedly cracked. Cracked poets may be all the better for being cracked;—cracked doctors are dangerous. Besides, in deserting that old-fashioned routine, his adherence to which made his claim to the Hill's approbation—and unsettling the mind of the Hill with wild revolutionary theories—Dr. Lloyd has betrayed the principles on which the Hill itself rests its social foundations. Of those principles Dr. Fenwick has made himself champion; and the Hill is bound to support him. There, the question is settled!"

And it was settled.

From the moment Mrs. Colonel Poyntz thus issued the word of command, Dr. Lloyd was demolished. His practice was gone, as well as his repute. Mortification or anger brought on a stroke of paralysis which, disabling my opponent, put an end to our controversy. An obscure Dr. Jones, who had been the special pupil and *protégé* of Dr Lloyd, offered himself as a candidate for the Hill's tongues and pulses. The Hill gave him little encouragement. It once more suspended its electoral privileges, and without insisting on calling me up to it, the Hill quietly called me in whenever its health needed other advice than that of its visiting apothecary. Again it invited me sometimes to dinner, often to tea. And again, Miss Brabazon assured me by a sidelong glance that it was no fault of hers if I were still single.

I had almost forgotten the dispute which had obtained for me so conspicuous a triumph, when one winter's night I was roused from sleep by a summons to attend Dr. Lloyd, who, attacked by a second stroke a few hours previously, had, on recovering sense, expressed a vehement desire to consult the rival by whom he had suffered so severely. I dressed myself in haste and hurried to his house.

A February night, sharp and bitter. An iron-gray frost below—a spectral melancholy moon above. I had to ascend the Abbey Hill by a steep, blind lane between high walls. I passed through stately gates, which stood wide open, into the garden ground that surrounded the old Abbots' House. At the end of a short carriage-drive, the dark and gloomy building cleared itself from leafless skeleton trees; the moon resting keen and cold on its abrupt gables and lofty chimney-stacks. An old woman-servant received me at the door, and, without saying a word, led me through a long low hall, and up dreary oak stairs, to a broad landing, at which she paused for a moment, listening. Round and about hall, staircase, and landing were ranged the dead specimens of the savage world which it had been the pride of the naturalist's life to collect. Close where I stood yawned the open jaws of the fell anaconda—its lower coils hidden, as they rested on the floor below, by the winding of the massive stairs. Against the dull wainscot walls were pendent cases stored with grotesque unfamiliar mummies, seen imperfectly by the moon that shot through the window-panes, and the candle in the old woman's hand. And as now she turned towards me, nodding her signal to follow, and went on up the shadowy passage, rows of gigantic birds—ibis and vulture, and huge sea glaucus—glared at me in the false light of their hungry eyes.

So I entered the sick-room, and the first glance told me that my art was powerless there.

The children of the stricken widower were grouped round his bed, the eldest apparently about fifteen, the youngest four; one little girl—the only female child—was clinging to her father's neck, her face pressed to his bosom, and in that room her sobs alone were loud.

As I passed the threshold, Dr. Lloyd lifted his face, which had been bent over the weeping child, and gazed on me with an aspect of strange glee, which I failed to interpret. Then, as I stole towards him softly and slowly, he pressed the lips on his long fair tresses that streamed wild over his breast, motioned to a nurse who stood beside his pillow to take the child away, and in a voice clearer than I could have expected in one on whose brow lay the unmistakable hand of death, he bade the nurse and the children quit the room. All went sorrowfully, but silently, save the little girl, who, borne off in the nurse's arms, continued to sob as if her heart were breaking.

I was not prepared for a scene so affecting; it moved me to the quick. My eyes wistfully followed the children so soon to be orphans, as one after one went out into the dark, chill shadow, and amidst the bloodless forms of the dumb brute nature, ranged in grisly vista beyond the death-room of man. And when the last infant shape had vanished, and the door closed with a jarring click, my sight wandered loiteringly around the chamber before I could bring myself to fix it on the broken form, beside which I now stood in all that glorious vigor of frame which had fostered the pride of my mind.

In the moment consumed by my mournful survey, the whole aspect of the place impressed itself ineffaceable on life-long remembrance. Through the high, deep sunken casement, across which the thin, faded curtain was but half drawn, the moonlight rushed, and then settled on the floor in one shroud of white glimmer, lost under the gloom of the death-bed. The roof was low, and seemed lower still by heavy intersecting beams, which I might have touched with my lifted hand. And the tall guttering candle by the bedside, and the flicker from the fire struggling out through the fuel but newly heaped on it, threw their reflection on the ceiling just over my head in a reek of quivering blackness, like an angry cloud.

Suddenly I felt my arm grasped: with his left hand (the right side was already lifeless) the dying man drew me towards him nearer and nearer, till his lips almost touched my ear. And, in a voice now firm, now splitting into gasp and hiss, thus he said:—

"I have summoned you to gaze on your own work! You have stricken down my life at the moment when it was most needed by my children, and most serviceable to mankind. Had I lived a few years longer, my children would have entered on manhood, safe from the temptations of want and undejected by the charity of strangers. Thanks to you, they will be penniless orphans. Fellow-creatures afflicted by maladies your pharmacopœia had failed to reach, came to me for relief, and they found it. 'The effect of imagination,' you say. What matters, if I directed the imagination to cure? Now you have mocked the unhappy ones out of their last chance of life. They will suffer and perish. Did you believe me in error? Still you knew that my object was research into truth. You employed against your brother in art venomous drugs and a poisoned probe. Look at me! Are you satisfied with your work?"

I sought to draw back and pluck my arm from the dying man's grasp. I could not do so without using a force that would have been inhuman. His lips drew nearer still to my ear.

"Vain pretender, do not boast that you brought a genius for epigram to the service of science. Science is lenient to all who offer experiment as the test of conjecture. You are of the stuff of which inquisitors are made. You cry that truth is profaned when your dogmas are questioned. In your shallow presumption you have meted the dominions of nature, and where your eye halts its vision, you say, 'There, nature must close;' in the bigotry which adds crime to presumption, you would stone the discoverer who, in annexing new realms to her chart, unsettles your arbitrary landmarks. Verily, retribution shall await you. In those spaces which your sight has disdained to explore you shall yourself be a lost and bewildered straggler. Hist! I see them already! The gibbering phantoms are gathering round you!"

The man's voice stopped abruptly; his eye fixed in a glazing stare; his hand relaxed its hold; he fell back on his pillow. I stole from the room; on the landing-place I met the nurse and the old woman-servant. Happily the children were not there. But I heard the wail of the female child from some room not far distant.

I whispered hurriedly to the nurse, "All is over!"—passed again under the jaws of the vast anaconda—and, on through the blind lane between the dead walls—on through the ghastly streets, under the ghastly moon—went back to my solitary home.

CHAPTER III.

It was some time before I could shake off the impression made on me by the words and the look of that dying man.

It was not that my conscience upbraided me. What had I done? Denounced that which I held, in common with most men of sense in or out of my profession, to be one of those illusions by which quackery draws profit from the wonder of ignorance. Was I to blame if I refused to treat with the grave respect due to asserted discovery in legitimate science pretensions to powers akin to the fables of wizards? was I to descend from the

Academe of decorous science to examine whether a slumbering sibyl could read from a book placed at her back, or tell me at L —— what at that moment was being done by my friend at the Antipodes?

And what though Dr. Lloyd himself might be a worthy and honest man, and a sincere believer in the extravagances for which he demanded an equal credulity in others, do not honest men every day incur the penalty of ridicule if, from a defect of good sense, they make themselves ridiculous? Could I have foreseen that a satire so justly provoked would inflict so deadly a wound? Was I inhumanly barbarous because the antagonist destroyed was morbidly sensitive? My conscience, therefore, made me no reproach, and the public was as little severe as my conscience. The public had been with me in our contest—the public knew nothing of my opponent's death-bed accusations—the public knew only that I had attended him in his last moments—it saw me walk beside the bier that bore him to his grave—it admired the respect to his memory which I evinced in the simple tomb that I placed over his remains, inscribed with an epitaph that did justice to his unquestionable benevolence and integrity;—above all, it praised the energy with which I set on foot a subscription for his orphan children, and the generosity with which I headed that subscription by a sum that was large in proportion to my means.

To that sum I did not, indeed, limit my contribution. The sobs of the poor female child rang still on my heart. As her grief had been keener than that of her brothers, so she might be subjected to sharper trials than they, when the time came for her to fight her own way through the world; therefore I secured to her, but with such precautions that the gift could not be traced to my hand, a sum to accumulate till she was of marriageable age, and which then might suffice for a small wedding portion; or if she remained single, for an income that would place her beyond the temptation of want, or the bitterness of a servile dependence.

That Dr. Lloyd should have died in poverty was a matter of surprise at first, for his profits during the last few years had been considerable, and his mode of life far from extravagant. But just before the date of our controversy he had been induced to assist the brother of his lost wife, who was a junior partner in a London Bank, with the loan of his accumulated savings. This man proved dishonest; he embezzled that and other sums intrusted to him, and fled the country. The same sentiment of conjugal affection which had cost Dr. Lloyd his fortune kept him silent as to the cause of the loss. It was reserved for his executors to discover the treachery of the brother-in-law whom he, poor man, would have generously screened from additional disgrace.

The Mayor of L——, a wealthy and public-spirited merchant, purchased the museum, which Dr. Lloyd's passion for natural history had induced him to form; and the sum thus obtained, together with that raised by subscription, sufficed, not only to discharge all debts due by the deceased, but to insure to the orphans the benefits of an education that might fit at least the boys to enter fairly armed into that game, more of skill than of chance, in which Fortune is really so little blinded that we see, in each turn of her wheel, wealth and its honors pass away from the lax fingers of ignorance and sloth, to the resolute grasp of labor and knowledge.

Meanwhile, a relation in a distant county undertook the charge of the orphans; they disappeared from the scene, and the tides of life in a commercial community soon flowed over the place which the dead man had occupied in the thoughts of his bustling townsfolk.

One person at L——, and only one, appeared to share and inherit the rancour with which the poor physician had denounced me on his death-bed. It was a gentleman named Vigors, distantly related to the deceased, and who had been, in point of station, the most eminent of Dr. Lloyd's partisans in the controversy with myself; a man of no great scholastic acquirements, but of respectable abilities. He had that kind of power which the world concedes to respectable abilities, when accompanied with a temper more than usually stern, and a moral character more than usually austere. His ruling passion was to sit in judgment upon others; and, being a magistrate, he was the most active and the most rigid of all the magistrates L—— had ever known.

Mr. Vigors at first spoke of me with great bitterness, as having ruined, and in fact killed, his friend, by the uncharitable and unfair acerbity which he declared I had brought into what ought to have been an unprejudiced examination of simple matter of fact. But finding no sympathy in these charges, he had the discretion to cease from making them, contenting himself with a solemn shake of his head if he heard my name mentioned in terms of praise, and an oracular sentence or two, such as "Time will show;" "All's well that ends well," etc. Mr. Vigors, however, mixed very little in the more convival intercourse of the townspeople. He called himself domestic; but, in truth, he was ungenial. A stiff man, starched with self-esteem. He thought that his dignity of station was not sufficiently acknowledged by the merchants of Low Town, and his superiority of intellect not sufficiently recognized by the exclusives of the Hill. His visits were, therefore, chiefly confined to the houses of neighboring squires, to whom his reputation as a magistrate, conjoined with his solemn exterior, made him one of those oracles by which men consent to be awed on condition that the awe is not often inflicted. And though he opened his house three times a week, it was only to a select few, whom he first fed and then biologized. Electrobiology was very naturally the special entertainment of a man whom no intercourse ever pleased in which his will was not imposed upon others. Therefore he only invited to his table persons whom he could stare into the abnegation of their senses, willing to say that beef was lamb, or brandy was coffee, according as he willed them to say. And, no doubt, the persons asked would have said anything he willed, so long as they had, in substance, as well as in idea, the beef and the brandy, the lamb and the coffee. I did not, then, often meet Mr. Vigors at the houses in which I occasionally spent my evenings. I heard of his enmity as a man safe in his home hears the sough of a wind on a common without. If now and then we chanced to pass in the streets, he looked up at me (he was a small man walking on tiptoe) with the sullen scowl of dislike. And, from the height of my stature, I dropped upon the small man and sullen scowl the affable smile of supreme indifference.

CHAPTER IV.

I HAD now arrived at that age when an ambitious man, satisfied with his progress in the world without, begins to feel, in the cravings of unsatisfied affection, the void of a solitary hearth. I resolved to marry, and looked out for a wife. I had never hitherto admitted in to my life the passion of love. In fact, I had regarded that passion, even in my earlier youth, with a certain superb contempt—as a malady engendered by an effeminate idleness, and fostered by a sickly imagination.

I wished to find in a wife a rational companion, an affectionate and trustworthy friend. No views of matrimony could be less romantic, more soberly sensible, than those which I conceived. Nor were my requirements mercenary or presumptuous. I cared not for fortune; I asked nothing from connections. My ambition was exclusively professional; it could be served by no titled kindred, accelerated by no wealthy dower. I was no slave to beauty. I did not seek in a wife the accomplishments of a finishing school-teacher.

Having decided that the time had come to select my helpmate, I imagined that I should find no difficulty in a choice that my reason would approve. But day upon day, week upon week, passed away, and though among the families I visited there were many young ladies who possessed more than the qualifications with which I conceived that I should be amply contented, and by whom I might flatter myself that my proposals would not be disdained, I saw not one to whose lifelong companionship I should not infinitely have preferred the solitude I found so irksome.

One evening, in returning home from visiting a poor female patient whom I attended gratuitously, and whose case demanded more thought than that of any other in my list—for though it had been considered hopeless in the hospital, and she had come home to die, I felt certain that I could save her, and she seemed recovering under my care;—one evening, it was the fifteenth of May, I found myself just before the gates of the house that had been inhabited by Dr. Lloyd. Since his death the house had been unoccupied: the rent asked for it by the proprietor was considered high; and from the sacred Hill on which it was situated, shyness or pride banished the wealthier traders. The garden gates stood wide open, as they had stood in the winter night on which I had passed through them to the chamber of death. The remembrance of that death-bed came vividly before me, and the dying man's fantastic threat rang again in my startled ears. An irresistible impulse, which I could not then account for, and which I cannot account for now—an impulse the reverse of that which usually makes us turn away with quickened step from a spot that recalls associations of pain—urged me on through the open gates up the neglected grass-grown road, urged me to look, under the westering sun of the joyous spring, at that house which I had never seen but in the gloom of a winter night, under the melancholy moon. As the building came in sight, with dark-red bricks, partially overgrown with ivy, I perceived that it was no longer unoccupied. I saw forms passing athwart the open windows; a van laden with articles of furniture stood before the door; a servant in livery was beside it giving directions to the men who were unloading.

Evidently some family was just entering into possession. I felt somewhat ashamed of my tresspass, and turned round quickly to retrace my steps. I had retreated but a few yards, when I saw before me, at the entrance gates, Mr. Vigors, walking beside a lady apparently of middle age; while, just at hand, a path cut through the shrubs gave view of a small wicket-gate at the end of the grounds. I felt unwilling not only to meet the lady, whom I guessed to be the new occupier, and to whom I should have to make a somewhat awkward apology for intrusion, but still more to encounter the scornful look of Mr. Vigors, in what appeared to my pride a false or undignified position. Involuntarily, therefore, I turned down the path which would favor my escape unobserved. When about half way between the house and the wicketgate, the shrubs that had clothed the path on either side suddenly opened to the left, bringing into view a circle of sward, surrounded by irregular fragments of old brick-work partially covered with ferns, creepers, or rock-plants, weeds, or wild flowers; and, in the centre of the circle, a fountain, or rather well, over which was built a Gothic monastic dome, or canopy, resting on small Norman columns, time-worn, dilapidated. A large willow overhung this unmistakable relic of the ancient abbey. There was an air of antiquity, romance, legend about this spot, so abruptly disclosed amidst the delicate green of the young shrubberies. But it was not the ruined wall nor the Gothic well that chained my footstep and charmed my eye.

It was a solitary human form, seated amidst the mournful ruins.

The form was so slight, the face so young, that at the first glance I murmured to myself, "What a lovely child!" But as my eye lingered it recognized in the upturned thoughtful brow, in the sweet serious aspect, in the rounded outlines of that slender shape, the inexpressible dignity of virgin woman.

A book was on her lap, at her feet a little basket, half filled with violets and blossoms culled from the rock-plants that nestled amidst the ruins. Behind her, the willow, like an emerald waterfall, showered down its arching abundant green, bough after bough, from the tree-top to the sward, descending in wavy verdure, bright towards the summit, in the smile of the setting sun, and darkening into shadow as it neared the earth.

She did not notice, she did not see me; her eyes were fixed upon the horizon, where it sloped farthest into space, above the tree-tops and the ruins; fixed so intently that mechanically I turned my own gaze to follow the flight of hers. It was as if she watched for some expected, familiar sign to grow out from the depths of heaven; perhaps to greet, before other eyes beheld it, the ray of the earliest star.

The birds dropped from the boughs on the turf around her, so fearlessly that one alighted amidst the flowers in the little basket at her feet. There is a famous German poem, which I had read in my youth, called the Maiden from Abroad, variously supposed to be an allegory of Spring, or of Poetry, according to the choice of commentators: it seemed to me as if the poem had been made for her. Verily, indeed, in her, poet or painter might have seen an image equally true to either of those adorners of the earth; both outwardly a delight to sense, yet both wakening up thoughts within us, not sad, but akin to sadness.

I heard now a step behind me, and a voice which I recognized to be that of Mr. Vigors. I broke from the charm by which I had been so lingeringly spell-bound, hurried on confusedly, gained the wicket-gate, from which a short flight of stairs descended into the common thoroughfare. And there the every-day life lay again before me. On the opposite side, houses, shops, church-spires; a few steps more, and the bustling streets! How immeasurably far from, yet how familiarly near to, the world in which we move and have being is that fairy land of romance which opens out from the hard earth before us, when Love steals at first to our side; fading back into the hard earth again as Love smiles or sighs its farewell!

CHAPTER V.

AND before that evening I had looked on Mr. Vigors with supreme indifference!—what importance he now assumed in my eyes! The lady with whom I had seen him was doubtless the new tenant of that house in which the young creature by whom my heart was so strangely moved evidently had her home. Most probably the relation between the two ladies was that of mother and daughter. Mr. Vigors, the friend of one, might himself be related to both—might prejudice them against me—might—here, starting up, I snapped the thread of conjecture, for right before my eyes, on the table beside which I had seated myself on entering my room, lay a card of invitation:—

MRS. POYNTZ.
At Home,
Wednesday, May 15th.
Early.

Mrs. Poyntz—Mrs. Colonel Poyntz? the Queen of the Hill. There, at her house, I could not fail to learn all about the new comers, who could never without her sanction have settled on her domain.

I hastily changed my dress, and, with beating heart, wound my way up the venerable eminence.

I did not pass through the lane which led direct to Abbot's House (for that old building stood solitary amidst its grounds, a little apart from the spacious platform on which the society of the Hill was concentrated), but up the broad causeway, with vistaed gas-lamps; the gayer shops still unclosed, the tide of busy life only slowly ebbing from the still animated street, on to a square, in which the four main thoroughfares of the city converged, and which formed the boundary of Low Town. A huge dark archway, popularly called Monk's Gate, at the angle of this square, made the entrance to Abbey Hill. When the arch was passed, one felt at once that one was in the town of a former day. The pavement was narrow, and rugged; the shops small, their upper stories projecting, with, here and there, plastered fronts, quaintly arabesqued. An ascent, short, but steep and tortuous, conducted at once to the old Abbey Church, nobly situated in a vast quadrangle, round which were the genteel and gloomy dwellings of the Areopagites of the Hill. More genteel and less gloomy than the rest—lights at the windows and flowers on the balcony—stood forth, flanked by a garden wall at either side, the mansion of Mrs. Colonel Poyntz.

As I entered the drawing-room, I heard the voice of the hostess; it was a voice clear, decided, metallic, bell-like, uttering these words: "Taken Abbot's House? I will tell you."

CHAPTER VI.

MRS. POYNTZ was seated on the sofa; at her right sat fat Mrs. Bruce, who was a Scotch lord's grand-daughter; at her left thin Miss Brabazon, who was an Irish baronet's niece. Around her—a few seated, many standing—had grouped all the guests, save two old gentlemen, who remained aloof with Colonel Poyntz near the whist-table, waiting for the fourth old gentleman, who was to make up the rubber, bnt who was at that moment spell-bound in the magic circle, which curiosity, that strongest of social demons, had attracted round the hostess.

"Taken Abbot's House? I will tell you. —Ah, Dr. Fenwick, charmed to see you. You know Abbot's house is let at last? Well, Miss Brabazon, dear, you ask who has taken it. I will inform you—a particular friend of mine."

"Indeed! Dear me!" said Miss Brabazon, looking confused. "I hope I did not say anything to—"

"Wound my feelings. Not in the least.

You said your uncle, Sir Phelim, employed a coachmaker named Ashleigh; that Ashleigh was an uncommon name, though Ashley was a common one; you intimated an appalling suspicion that the Mrs. Ashleigh who had come to the Hill was the coachmaker's widow. I relieve your mind—she is not; she is the widow of Gilbert Ashleigh, of Kirby Hall."

"Gilbert Ashleigh," said one of the guests, a bachelor, whose parents had reared him for the Church, but who, like poor Goldsmith, did not think himself good enough for it,—a mistake of over-modesty, for he matured into a very harmless creature. "Gilbert Ashleigh. I was at Oxford with him—a gentleman commoner of Christ Church. Good-looking man—very *sapped*—"

"Sapped! what's that?—Oh, studied. That he did all his life. He married young—Anne Chaloner; she and I were girls together: married the same year. They settled at Kirby Hall—nice place, but dull. Poyntz and I spent a Christmas there. Ashleigh when he talked was charming, but he talked very little. Anne, when she talked, was commonplace, and she talked very much. Naturally, poor thing, she was so happy. Poyntz and I did not spend another Christmas there. Friendship is long, but life is short. Gilbert Ashleigh's life was short indeed; he died in the seventh year of his marriage, leaving only one child, a girl. Since then, though I never spent another Christmas at Kirby Hall, I have frequently spent a day there, doing my best to cheer up Anne. She was no longer talkative, poor dear. Wrapt up in her child, who has now grown into a beautiful girl of eigeteen—such eyes, her father's—the real dark blue—rare; sweet creature, but delicate; not, I hope, consumptive, but delicate; quiet—wants life. My girl Jane adores her. Jane has life enough for two."

"Is Miss Ashleigh the heiress to Kirby Hall?" asked Mrs. Bruce, who had an unmarried son.

"No. Kirby Hall passed to Ashleigh Sumner, the male heir, a cousin. And the luckiest of cousins! Gilbert's sister, showy woman (indeed all show), had contrived to marry her kinsman, Sir Walter Ashleigh Haughton, the head of the Ashleigh family,—just the man made to be the reflector of a showy woman! He died years ago, leaving an only son, Sir James, who was killed last winter, by a fall from his horse. And here, again, Ashleigh Sumner proved to be the male heir-at-law. During the minority of this fortunate youth, Mrs. Ashleigh had rented Kirby Hall of his guardian. He is now just coming of age, and that is why she leaves. Lilian Ashleigh will have, however, a very good fortune—is what we genteel paupers call an heiress. Is there anything more you want to know?"

Said thin Miss Brabazon, who took advantage of her thinness to wedge herself into every one's affairs, "A most interesting account. What a nice place Abbots' House could be made with a little taste! So aristocratic! Just what I should like if I could afford it! The drawing-room should be done up in the Moorish style, with geranium-colored silk curtains like dear Lady L——'s boudoir at Twickenham. And Mrs. Ashleigh has taken the house! on lease too, I suppose!" Here Miss Brabazon fluttered her fan angrily, and then exclaimed "But what on earth brings Mrs. Ashleigh here?"

Answered Mrs. Colonel Poyntz, with the military frankness by which she kept her company in good humor, as well as awe:

"Why do any of us come here? Can any one tell me?"

There was a blank silence, which the hostess herself was the first to break.

"None of us present can say why we came here. I can tell you why Mrs. Ashleigh came. Our neighbor, Mr. Vigors, is a distant connection of the late Gilbert Ashleigh, one of the executors to his will, and the guardian to the hair-at-law. About ten days ago, Mr. Vigors called on me, for the first time since I felt it my duty to express my disapprobation of the strange vagaries so unhappily conceived by our poor dear friend Dr. Lloyd. And when he had taken his chair, just where you now sit, Dr. Fenwick, he said, in a sepulchral voice, stretching out two fingers, so,—as if I were one of the what-do-call-'ems who go to sleep when he bids them, "Marm, you know Mrs. Ashleigh? You correspond with.' 'Yes, Mr. Vigors; is there any crime in that? You look as if there were.' 'No crime, marm,' said the man, quite seriously. 'Mrs. Ashleigh is a lady of amiable temper, and you are a woman of masculine understanding.'"

Here there was a general titter. Mrs. Colonel Poyntz hushed with a look of severe surprise. "What is there to laugh at? All women would be men if they could. If my understanding is masculine, so much the better for me. I thanked Mr. Vigors for his very handsome compliment, and he then went on to say, 'that though Mrs. Ashleigh would now have to leave Kirby Hall in a very few weeks, she seemed quite unable to make up her mind where to go; that it had occurred to him that, as Miss Ashleigh was of an age to see a little of the world, she ought not to remain buried in the country; while, being of quiet mind, she recoiled from the dissipation of London. Between the seclusion of the one and the turmoil of the other, the society of L—— was a happy medium. He should be glad of my opinion. He had put off asking for it, because he owned his belief that I had behaved unkindly to his lamented friend, Dr. Lloyd; but he now found himself in rather an awkward position. His ward, young Sumner had prudently resolved on fixing his country residence at Kirby Hall, rather than at Haughton Park, the much larger seat, which had so suddenly passed to his inheritance, and which he could not occupy without a vast establishment, that to a single man, so young, would be but a cumbersome and costly trouble. Mr. Vigors was pledged to his ward to obtain him possession of Kirby Hall, the precise day agreed upon, but Mrs. Ashleigh did not seem disposed to stir—could not decide where else to go. Mr. Vigors was loth to press hard on his old friends's widow and child. It was a thousand pities Ashleigh could not make up her mind; she had had ample time for preparation.

A word from me at this moment, would be an effective kindness. Abbots' House was vacant, with a garden so extensive that the ladies would not miss the country. Another party was after it, but—' 'Say no more,' I cried; 'no party but my dear old friend Anne Ashleigh shall have Abbots' House. So that question is settled.' I dismissed Mr. Vigors, sent for my carriage—that is, for Mr. Barker's yellow fly and his best horses—and drove that very day to Kirby Hall, which, though not in this county, is only twenty-five miles distant. I slept there that night. By nine o'clock the next morning I had secured Mrs. Ashleigh's consent, on the promise to save her all trouble; came back, sent for the landlord, settled the rent, lease, agreement; engaged Forbes' vans to remove the furniture from Kirby Hall, told Forbes to begin with the beds. When her own bed came, which was last night, Anne Ashleigh came too. I have seen her this morning. She likes the place, so does Lilian. I asked them to meet you all here to-night; but Mrs. Ashleigh was tired. The last of the furniture was to arrive to-day; and though dear Mrs. Ashleigh is an undecided character, she is not inactive. But it is not only the planning where to put tables and chairs that would have tired her to-day; she has had Mr. Vigors on her hands all the afternoon, and he has been—here's her little note—what are the words? no doubt, 'most overpowering and oppressive'—no, 'most kind and attentive'—different words, but, as applied to Mr. Vigors, they mean the same thing.

"And now, next Monday—we must leave them in peace till then—you will all call on the Ashleighs. The Hill knows what is due to itself; it cannot delegate to Mr. Vigors, a respectable man indeed, but who does not belong to its set, its own proper course of action towards those who would shelter themselves on its bosom. The Hill cannot be kind and attentive, overpowering or oppressive by proxy. To those newborn, into its family circle it cannot be an indifferent godmother; it has towards them all the feelings of a mother,—or of a stepmother, as the case may be. Where it says, 'This can be no child of mine,' it is a stepmother indeed; but, in all those whom I have presented to its arms, it has hitherto, I am proud to say, recognized desirable acquaintances, and to them the Hill has been a mother. And now, my dear Mr. Sloman, go to your rubber: Poyntz is impatient, though he don't show it. Miss Brabazon, love, we all long to see you seated at the piano—you play so divinely! Something gay, if you please; something gay, but not very noisy—Mr. Leopold Smythe will turn the leaves for you. Mrs. Bruce, your own favorite set at vingt-un, with four new recruits. Dr. Fenwick, you are like me, don't play cards, and don't care for music: sit here, and talk or not, as you please, while I knit."

The other guests thus disposed of, some at the card-tables, some round the piano, I placed myself at Mrs. Poyntz's side, on a seat niched in the recess of a window which an evening unusually warm for the month of May permitted to be left open. I was next to one who had known Lillian as a child, one from whom I had learned by what sweet name to call the image which my thoughts had already shrined. How much that I still longed to know she could tell me! But in what form of question could I lead to the subject, yet not betray my absorbing interest in it? Longing to speak, I felt as if stricken dumb; stealing an unquiet glance towards the face beside me, and deeply impressed with that truth which the Hill had long ago reverently acknowledged, viz., that Mrs. Colonel Poyntz was a very superior woman—a very powerful creature.

And there she sat knitting—rapidly, firmly; a woman somewhat on the other side of forty, complexion a bronzed paleness, hair a bronzed brown, in strong ringlets cropped short behind—handsome hair for a man; lips that, when closed, showed inflexible decision, when speaking, became supple and flexile with an easy humor and a vigilant fineness; eyes of a red hazel, quick but steady; observant, piercing, dauntless eyes; altogether a fine countenance—would have been a very fine countenance in a man; profile sharp, straight, clear-cut, with an expression, when in repose, like that of a sphinx; a frame robust, not corpulent, of middle height, but with an air and carriage that made her appear tall; peculiarly white firm hands, indicative of vigorous health, not a vein visible on the surface.

There she sat knitting, knitting, and I by her side, gazing now on herself, now on her work, with a vague idea that the threads in the skein of my own web of love or of life were passing quick through those noiseless fingers. And, indeed, in every web of romance, the fondest, one of the Parcæ is sure to be some matter of fact She, Social Destiny, as little akin to romance herself—as was this worldly Queen of the Hill.

CHAPTER VII.

I HAVE given a sketch of the outward woman of Mrs. Colonel Poyntz. The inner woman was a recondite mystery, deep as that of the sphinx, whose features her own resembled. But between the outward and the inward woman there is ever a third woman—the conventional woman—such as the whole human being appears to the world—always mantled, sometimes masked.

I am told that the fine people of London do not recognize the title of "Mrs. Colonel." If that be true, the fine people of London must be clearly in the wrong, for no people in the universe could be finer than the fine people of Abbey Hill; and they considered their sovereign had as good a right to the title of Mrs. Colonel as the Queen of England has to that of "our Gracious Lady." But Mrs. Poyntz, herself never assumed the title of Mrs. Colonel; it never appeared on her cards any more than the title of "Gracious Lady" appears on the cards which convey the invitation that a Lord Steward or Lord Chamberlain is commanded by her Majesty to issue. To titles, indeed, Mrs. Poyntz evinced no superstitious reverence. Two peeresses, related to her, not distantly, were in the habit of paying her a yearly visit, which lasted two or three days. The Hill considered these visits an honor to its eminence. Mrs. Poyntz never seemed to esteem them an honor to herself; never boasted of them; never sought to show off her grand relations, nor put herself the least out of the way to receive them. Her mode of life was free from ostentation. She had the advantage of being a few hundreds a year richer than any other inhabitant of the Hill; but she did not devote her superior resources to the invidious exhibition of superior splendor.

Like a wise sovereign the revennes of her exchequer were applied to the benefit of her subjects, and not to the vanity of egotistical parade. As no one else on the Hill kept a carriage, she declined to keep one. Her entertainments were simple, but numerous. Twice a week she received the Hill, and was genuinely at home to it. She contrived to make her parties proverbially agreeable. The refreshments were of the same kind as those which the poorest of her old maids of honor might proffer; but they were better of their kind, the best of their kind—the best tea, the best lemonade, the best cakes. Her rooms had an air of comfort, which was peculiar to them. They looked like rooms accustomed to receive, and receive in a friendly way; well warmed, well lighted, card-tables and piano each in the place that made cards and music inviting. On the walls a few old family portraits, and three or four other pictures said to be valuable and certainly pleasing—two Watteaus, a Canaletti, a Weenix—plenty of easy-chairs and settees covered with a cheerful chintz. In the arrangement of the furniture generally, and indescribable careless elegançe.

She herself was studiously plain in dress, more conspicuously free from jewellery and trinkets than any married lady on the Hill. But I have heard from those who were authorities on such a subject, that she was never seen in a dress of the last year's fashion. She adopted the mode as it came out, just enough to show that she was aware it was out; but with a sober reserve, as much as as to say, "I adopt the fashion as far as it suits myself; I do not permit the fashion to adopt me." In short, Mrs. Colonel Poyntz was sometimes rough, sometimes coarse, always masculine, and yet somehow or other masculine in a womanly way; but she was never vulgar because never affected. It was impossible not to allow that she was a thorough gentlewoman, and she could do things that lower other gentlewomen, without any loss of dignity. Thus she was an admirable mimic, certainly in itself the least ladylike condescension of humor. But when she mimicked, it was with so tranquil a gravity, or so royal a good humor, that one could only say, "What talents for society dear Mrs. Colonel has!" As she was a gentlewoman emphatically, so the other colonel, the he-colonel, was emphatically a gentleman; rather shy, but not cold; hating trouble of every kind, pleased to seem a cipher in his own house. If the sole study of Mrs. Colonel had been to make her husband comfortable, she could not have succeeded better than by bringing friends about him and then taking them off his hands.

Colonel Poyntz, the he-colonel, had seen, in his youth, actual service; but had retired from his profession many years ago, shortly after his marriage. He was a younger brother of one of the principal squires in the county; inherited the house he lived in, with some other valuable property in and about L——, from an uncle; was considered a good landlord; and popular in Low Town, though he never interfered in its affairs. He was punctiliously neat in his dress; a thin youthful figure, crowned with a thick youthful wig. He never seemed to read anything but the newspapers and the Meteorological Journal: was supposed to be the most weather-wise man in all L——. He had another intellectual predilection—whist. But in that he had less reputation for wisdom. Perhaps it requires a rarer combination of mental faculties to win an odd trick than to divine a fall in the glass. For the rest, the he-colonol, many years older than his wife, despite the thin youthful figure, was an admirable aide-de-camp to the general in command, Mrs. Colonel; and she could not have found one more obedient, more devoted, or more proud of a distinguished chief.

In giving to Mrs. Colonel Poyntz the appellation of Queen of the Hill, let there be no mistake. She was not a constitutional sovereign; her monarchy was absolute. All her proclamations had the force of laws.

Such ascendancy could not have been attained without considerable talents for acquiring and keeping it. Amidst all her off-hand, brisk, imperious frankness, she had the ineffable discrimination of tact. Whether civil or rude, she was never civil or rude but what she carried public opinion along with her. Her knowledge of general society must have been limited, as must be that of all female sovereigns. But she seemed gifted with an intuitive knowledge of human nature, which she applied to her special ambition of ruling it. I have not a doubt that if she had been suddenly transferred, a perfect stranger, to the world of London, she would have soon forced her way to its selectest circles, and, when once there, held her own against a duchess.

I have said that she was not affected: this might be one cause of her sway over a set in which nearly every other woman was trying rather to seem, than to be, a somebody.

But if Mrs. Colonel Poyntz was not artificial, she was artful, or perhaps I might more justly say—artistic. In all she said and did there were conduct, system, plan. She could be a most serviceable friend, a most damaging enemy; yet I believe she seldom indulged in strong likings or strong hatreds. All was policy—a policy akin to that of a grand party chief, determined to raise up those whom, for any reason, of state, it was prudent to favor, and to put down those whom, for any reason of state, it was expedient to humble or to crush.

Ever since the controversy with Dr. Lloyd, this lady had honored me with her benignest countenance. And nothing could be more adroit than the manner in which, while imposing me on others as an oracular authority, she sought to subject to her will the oracle itself.

She was in the habit of addressing me in a sort of motherly way, as if she had the deepest interest in my welfare, happiness, and reputation. And thus, in every compliment, in every seeming mark of respect, she maintained the superior dignity of one who takes from responsible station the duty to encourage rising merit: so that somehow or other, despite all that pride which made me believe that I needed no helping hand to advance or to clear my way through the world, I could not shake off from my mind the impression that I was mysteriously patronized by Mrs. Colonel Poyntz.

We might have sat together five minutes, side by side—in silence as complete as if in the cave of Trophonius—when, without looking up from her work, Mrs. Poyntz said abruptly,

"I am thinking about you, Dr. Fenwick. And you—are thinking about some other woman. Ungrateful man!"

"Unjust accusation! My very silence should prove how intently my thoughts were fixed on you, and on the weird web which springs under your hand in meshes that bewilder the gaze and snare the attention."

Mrs. Poyntz looked up at me for a moment—one rapid glance of the bright red hazel eye and said,

"Was I really in your thoughts? Answer truly."

"Truly, I answer, you were."

"That is strange! Who can it be?"

"Who can it be? What do you mean?"

"If you were thinking of me, it was in connection with some other person—some other person of my own sex. It is certainly not poor dear Miss Brabazon. Who else can it be?"

Again the red eye shot over me, and I felt my cheek redden beneath it.

"Hush!" she said, lowering her voice; "you are in love!"

"In love!—I! Permit me to ask you why you think so?"

"The signs are unmistakable; you are altered in your manner, even in the expression of your face, since I last saw you; your manner is generally quiet and observant, it is now restless and distracted; your expression of face is generally proud and serene, it is now humbled and troubled. You have something on your mind! It is not anxiety for your reputation, that is established; nor for your fortune, that is made; it is not anxiety for a patient, or you would scarcely be here. But anxiety it is, an anxiety that is remote from your profession, that touches your heart and is new to it!"

I was startled, almost awed. But I tried to cover my confusion with a forced laugh.

"Profound observer! Subtle analyst! You have convinced me that I must be in love, though I did not suspect it before. But when I strive to conjecture the object, I am as much perplexed as yourself; and with you, I ask, who can it be?"

"Whoever it be," said Mrs. Poyntz, who had paused, while I spoke, from her knitting, and now resumed it very slowly and very carefully, as if her mind and her knitting worked in unison together; "Whoever it be, love in you would be serious; and, with or without love, marriage is a serious think to us all. It is not every pretty girl that would suit Allen Fenwick."

"Alas! is there any pretty girl whom Allen Fenwick would suit?"

"Tut! You should be above the fretful vanity that lays traps for a compliment. Yes; the time has come in your life and your career when you would do well to marry. I give my consent to that," she added with a smile as if in jest, and a slight nod as if in earnest. The knitting here went on more decidely, more quickly. "But I do not yet see the person. No! 'Tis a pity, Allen Fenwick" (whenever Mrs. Poyntz called me by my Christian name, she always assumed her majestic motherly manner),—"a pity that, with your birth, energies, perseverance, talents, and, let me add, your advantages of manner and person,—a pity that you did not choose a career that might achieve higher fortunes and louder fame than the most brilliant success can give to a provincial physician. But in that very choice you interest me. My choice has been much the same. A small circle, but the first in it. Yet, had I been a man, or had my dear colonel been a man whom it was in the power of a woman's art to raise one step higher in that metaphorical ladder which is not the ladder of the angels, why, then—what then? No matter! I am contented. I transfer my ambition to Jane. Do you not think her handsome?"

"There can be no doubt of that," said I, carelessly and naturally.

"I have settled Jane's lot in my own mind," resumed Mrs. Poyntz, striking firm into another row of knitting. "She will marry a country gentleman of large estate. He will go into parliament. She will study his advancement as I study Poyntz's comfort. If he be clever, she will help to make him a minister; if he be not clever, his wealth will make her a personage, and lift him into a personage's husband. And, now that you see I have no matrimonial designs on you, Allen Fenwick, think if it will be worth while to confide in me. Possibly I may be useful—"

"I know not how to thank you. But, as yet, I have nothing to confide."

While thus saying, I turned my eyes towards the open window beside which I sat. It was a beautiful soft night. The May moon in all her splendor. The town stretched, far and wide, below with all its numberless lights; below—but somewhat distant; an intervening space was covered, here, by the broad quadrangle (in the the midst of which stood, massive and lonely, the grand old church); and, there, by the gardens and scattered cottages or mansions that clothed the sides of the hill.

"Is not that house," I said, after a short pause, "yonder, with the three gables, the one in which—in which poor Dr. Loyld lived—Abbots' House?"

I spoke abruptly, as if to intimate my desire to change the subject of conversation. My hostess stopped her knitting, half rose, looked forth.

"Yes. But what a lovely night! How is it that the moon blends into harmony things of which the sun only marks the contrast? That stately old church tower, gray with its thousand years—those vulgar tile-roofs and chimney-pots raw in the freshness of yesterday: now, under the moonlight, all melt into one indivisible charm!"

As my hostess thus spoke, she had left her seat, taking her work with her, and passed from the window into the balcony. It was not often that Mrs. Poyntz condescended to admit what is called "sentiment" into the range of her sharp practical, worldly talk, but she did so at times; always, when she did, giving me the notion of an intellect much too comprehensive not to allow that sentiment has a place in this life, but keeping it in its proper place, by that mixture of affability and indifference with which some high-born beauty allows the genius, but checks the presumption, of a charming and penniless poet. For a few minutes her eyes roved over the scene in evident enjoyment; then, as they slowly settled upon the three gables of Abbots' House, her face regained that something of hardness which belonged to its decided character; her fingers again mechanically resumed her knitting, and she said, in her clear, unsoftened metallic chime of voice, "Can you guess why I took so much trouble to oblige Mr. Vigors and locate Mrs. Ashleigh yonder?"

"You favored us with a full explanation of your reasons."

"Some of my reasons; not the main one. People who undertake the task of governing others, as I do, be their rule a kingdom or a hamlet, must adopt a principle of government and adhere to it. The principle that suits best with the Hill is respect for the Proprieties. We have not much money; *entre nous*, we have no great rank. Our policy is, then, to set up the Proprieties as an influence which money must court and rank is afraid of. I had learned just befere Mr. Vigors called on me that Lady Sarah Bellasis entertained the idea of hiring Abbots' house. London has set its face against her; a provincial town would be more charitable. An earl's daughter, with a good income and an awfully bad name, of the best manners and of the worst morals, would have made sad havoc among the Proprieties. How many of our primmest old maids would have deserted tea and Mrs. Poyntz for champagne and her ladyship? The Hill was never in so imminent a danger. Rather tnan Lady Sarah Bellasis should have had that house, I would have taken it myself, and stocked it with owls.

"Mrs. Ashleigh turned up just in the critical moment. Lady Sarah is foiled, the Proprieties safe, and so that question is settled."

"And it will be pleasant to have your early friend so near you."

Mrs. Poyntz. lifted her eyes full upon me. "Do you know Mrs. Ashleigh?"

"Not in the least."

"She has many virtues and few ideas. She is commonplace weak, as I am commonplace. strong. But commonplace weak can be very lovable. Her husband, a man of genius and learning, gave her his whole heart—a heart worth having, but he was not ambitious, and he despised the world."

"I think you said your daughter was very much attached to Miss Ashleigh? Does her character resemble her mother's?"

I was afraid while I spoke that I should again meet Mrs. Poyntz's searching gaze, but she did not this time look up from her work.

"No; Lilian is anything but commonplace."

"You described her as having delicate health; you implied a hope that she was not consumptive. I trust that there is no serious reason for apprehending a constitutional tendency which at her age would require the most careful watching!"

"I trust not. If she were to die—Dr. Fenwick, what is the matter?"

So terrible had been the picture which this woman's words had brought before me, that I started as if my own life had received a shock.

"I beg pardon," I said, falteringly, pressing my hand to my heart; "a sudden spasm here—it is over now. You were saying that—that—"

"I was about to say—" and here Mrs. Poyntz laid her hand lightly on mine. "I was about to say, that if Lilian Ashleigh were to die, I should mourn for her less than I might for one who valued the things of the earth more. But I believe there is no cause for the alarm my words so inconsiderately excited in you. Her mother is watchful and dovoted; and if the least thing ailed Lilian, she would call in medical advice. Mr. Vigors would, I know, recommend Dr. Jones."

Closing our conference with those stinging words, Mrs. Poyntz here turned back into the drawing-room.

I remained some minutes on the balcony, disconcerted, enraged. With what consummate art had this practised diplomatist wound herself into my secret! That she had read my heart better than myself was evident from that Parthian shaft, barbed with Dr. Jones, which she had shot over her shoulder in retreat. That from the first moment in which she had decoyed me to her side, she had detected "the something" on my mind, was perhaps but the ordinary quickness of female penetration. But it was with no ordinary craft that her whole conversation afterwards had been so shaped as to learn the something, and lead me to reveal the some one to whom the somethihg was linked. For what purpose? What was it to her? What motive could she have beyond the mere gratification of curiosity? Perhaps, at first, she thought I had been caught by her daughter's showy beauty, and hence the half-friendly, half-cynical frankness with which she had avowed her ambitious projects for that young lady's matrimonial advancement. Satisfied by my manner that I cherished no presumptuous hopes in that quarter, her scrutiny was doubtless continued from that pleasure in the exercise of a wily intellect which impels schemers and politicians to an activity for which, without that pleasure itself, there would seem no adequate inducement; and besides, the ruling passion of this petty sovereign was power. And if knowledge be power, there is no better instrument of power over a contumacious subject than that hold on his heart which is gained in the knowledge of its secret.

But "secret!" Had it really come to this? Was it possible that the mere sight of a human face, never beheld before, could disturb the whole tenor of my life—a stranger of whose mind and character I knew nothing, whose very voice I had never heard? It was only by the intolerable pang of anguish that had rent my heart in the words, carelessly, abruptly spoken, "if she were to die," that I had felt how the world would be changed to me, if indeed that face were seen in it no more! Yes, secret it was no longer to myself—I loved! And like all on whom love descends, sometimes softly, slowly, with the gradual wing of the cushat settling down into its nest, sometimes with the swoop of the eagle on his unsuspecting quarry, I believed that none ever before loved as I loved; that such love was an abnormal wonder, made solely for me, and I for it. Then my mind insensibly hushed its angrier and more turbulent thoughts, as my gaze rested upon the roof-tops of Lilian's home, and the shimmering silver of the moonlit willow, under which I had seen her gazing into the roseate heavens.

CHAPTER VIII.

When I returned to the drawing-room, the party was evidently about to break up. Those who had grouped round the piano were now assembled round the refreshment-table. The card-players had risen, and were settling or discussing gains and losses. While I was searching for my hat, which I had somewhere mislaid, a poor gentleman, tormented by tic-douloreux, crept timidly up to me—the proudest and the poorest of all the hidalgoes settled on the Hill. He could not afford a fee for a physician's advice, but pain had humbled his pride, and I saw at a glance that he was considering how to take a surreptitious advantage of social intercourse, and obtain the advice without paying the fee. The old man discovered the hat before I did, stooped, took it up, extended it to me with the profound bow of the old school, while the other hand, clenched and quivering, was pressed into the hollow of his cheek, and his eyes met mine with wistful mute entreaty. The instinct of my profession seized me at once. I could never behold suffering, without forgetting all else in the desire to relieve it."

"You are in pain," said I, softly. "Sit down and describe the symptoms. Here, it is true, I am no professional doctor, but I am a friend who is fond of doctoring, and knows something about it."

So we sat down a little apart from the other guests, and after a few questions and answers, I was pleased to find that his "tic" did not belong to the less curable kind of that agonizing neuralgia. I was especially successful in my treatment of similar sufferings, for which I had discovered an anodyne that was almost specific. I wrote on a leaf of my pocket-book a prescription which I felt sure would be efficacious, and as I tore it out and placed it in his hand, I chanced to look up, and saw the hazel eyes of my hostess fixed upon me with a kinder and softer expression than they often condescended to admit into their cold and penetrating lustre. At that moment, however, her attention was drawn from me to a servant, who entered with a note, and I heard him say, though in an under tone, "From Mrs. Ashleigh."

She opened the note, read it hastily, ordered the servant to wait without the door, retired to her writing-table, which stood near the place at which I still lingered, rested her face on her hand, and seemed musing. Her meditation was very soon over. She turned her head, and, to my surprise, beckoned to me. I approached.

"Sit here," she whispered; "turn your back towards those people, who are no doubt watching us. Read this."

She placed in my hand the note she had just received. It contained but a few words to this effect:

"Dear Margaret,—I am so distressed. Since I wrote to you, a few hours ago, Lilian is taken suddenly ill, and I fear seriously. What medical man should I send for? Let my servant have his name and address.
"A. A."

I sprang from my seat.

"Stay," said Mrs. Poyntz. "Would you much care if I sent the servant to Dr. Jones?"

"Ah, madam, you are cruel! What have I done that you should become my enemy?"

"Enemy! No. You have just befriended one of my freinds. In this world of fools intellect should ally itself with intellect. No; I am not your enemy! But you have not yet asked me to be your friend."

Here she put into my hands a note she had written while thus speaking. "Receive your credentials. If there be any cause for alarm, or if I can be of use, send for me." Resuming the work she had suspended, but with lingering, uncertain fingers, she added, "So far, then, this is settled. Nay, no thanks; it is but little that is settled as yet."

CHAPTER IX.

In a very few minutes I was once more in the grounds of that old gable house; the servant, who went before me, entered them by the stairs and the wicket-gate of the private entrance; that way was the shortest. So again I passed by the circling glade and the monastic well—sward, trees, and ruins, all suffused in the limpid moonlight.

And now I was in the house; the servant took upstairs the note with which I was charged and a minute or two afterwards returned and conducted me to the corridor above, in which Mrs. Ashleigh received me. I was the first to speak. "Your daughter—is—is—not seriously ill, I hope. What is it?"

"Hush!" she said, under her breath. "Will you step this way for a moment?" She passed through a doorway to the right. I followed her, and as she placed on the table the light she had been holding, I looked round with a chill at the heart—it was the room in which Dr. Lloyd had died. Impossible to mistake. The furniture, indeed, was changed—there was no bed in the chamber; but the shape of the room, the position of the high casement, which was now wide open, and through which the moonlight streamed more softly than on that drear winter night, the great square beams intersecting the low ceiling—all were impressed vividly on my memory. The chair to which Mrs. Ashleigh beckoned me was placed just on the spot where I had stood by the bed-head of the dying man.

I shrank back—I could not have seated myself there. So, I remained leaning against the chimney-piece, while Mrs. Ashleigh told her story.

She said that on their arrival the day before, Lilian had been in more than usually good health and spirits, delighted with the old house, the grounds, and especially the nook by the Monk's Well, at which Mrs. Ashleigh had left her that evening in order to make some purchases in the town, in company with Mr. Vigors. When Mrs. Ashleigh returned, she and Mr. Vigors had sought Lilian in that nook, and Mrs. Ashleigh then detected, with a mother's eye some change in Lilian, which alarmed her. She seemed listless and dejected. and was very pale; but she denied that she felt unwell. On regaining the house she had sat down in the room in which we then were—"which," said Mrs. Ashleigh, "as it is not required for a sleeping-room, my daughter, who is fond of reading, wished to fit up as her own morning-room, or study. I left her here and went into the drawing-room below with Mr. Vigors. When he quitted me, which he did very soon, I remained for nearly an hour giving directions about the placing of furniture, which had just arrived from our late residence. I then went upstairs to join my daughter, and to my terror found her apparently lifeless in her chair. She had fainted away."

I interrupted Mrs. Ashleigh here. "Has Miss Ashleigh been subject to fainting fits?"

"No, never. When she recovered she seemed bewildered—disinclined to speak. I got her to bed, and as she then fell quietly to sleep, my mind was relieved. I thought it only a passing effect of excitement, in a change of abode; or caused by something like malaria in the atmosphere of that part of the grounds in which I had found her seated."

"Very likely. The hour of sunset at this time of year is trying to delicate constitutions. Go on."

"About three-quarters of an hour ago she woke up with a loud cry, and has been ever since in a state of great agitation, weeping violently, and answering none of my questions. Yet she does not seem light-headed, but rather what we call hysterical."

"You will permit me now to see her. Take comfort—in all you tell me I see nothing to warrant serious alarm."

CHAPTER X.

To the true physician there is an inexpressible sanctity in the sick-chamber. At its threshold the more human passions quit their hold on his heart. Love there would be profanation. Even the grief permitted to others he must put aside. He must enter that room—a calm intelligence. He is disabled for his mission if he suffer aught to obscure the keen quiet glance of his science. Age or youth, beauty or deformity, innocence or guilt, merge their distinctions in one common attribute—human suffering appealing to human skill.

Woe to the households in which the trusted Healer feels not on his conscience the solemn obligations of his glorious art. Reverently, as in a temple, I stood in the virgin's chamber. When her mother placed her hand in mine, and I felt the throb of its pulse, I was aware of no quicker beat of my own heart. I looked with a steady eye on the face, more beautiful from the flush that deepened the delicate hues of the young cheek, and the lustre that brightened the dark blue of the wandering eyes. She did not at first heed me; did not seem aware of my presence; but kept murmuring to herself words which I could not distinguish.

At length, when I spoke to her, in that low, soothing tone which we learn at the sick-bed, the expression of her face altered suddenly; she passed the hand I did not hold over her forehead, turned round, looked at me full and long, with unmistakable surprise, yet not as if the surprise displeased her; less the surprise which recoils from the sight of a stranger than that which seems doubtfully to recognize an unexpected friend. Yet on the surprise there seemed to creep something of apprehension—of fear;—her hand trembled, her voice quivered, as she said,—

"Can it be, can it be? Am I awake? Mother, who is this?"

"Only a kind visitor, Dr. Fenwick, sent by Mrs. Poyntz, for I was uneasy about you, darling. How are you now?"

"Better. Strangely better."

She removed her hand gently from mine, and with an involuntary modest shrinking, turned towards Mrs. Ashleigh, drawing her mother towards herself so that she became at once hidden from me.

Satisfied that there was here no delirium, nor even more than the slight and temporary fever which often accompanies a sudden nervous attack in constitutions peculiarly sensitive, I retired noiselessly from the room, and went, not into that which had been occupied by the ill-fated Naturalist, but downstairs into the drawing-room, to write my prescription. I had already sent the servant off with it to the chemist's before Mrs. Ashleigh joined me.

"She seems recovering surprisingly; her forehead is cooler; she is perfectly self-possessed, only she cannot account for her own seizure, cannot account either for the fainting or the agitation with which she awoke from sleep."

"I think I can account for both. The first room in which she entered—that in which she fainted—had its window open; the sides of the window are overgrown with rank creeping plants in full blosom. Miss Ashleigh had already predisposed herself to injurious effects from the effluvia, by fatigue, excitement, imprudence in sitting out at the fall of a heavy dew. The sleep after the fainting fit was the more disturbed, because Nature, always alert and active in subjects so young, was making its own effort to right itself from an injury. Nature has nearly succeeded. What I have prescribed will a little aid and accelerate that which Nature has yet to do, and in a day or two I do not doubt that your daughter will be perfectly restored. Only let me recommend care to avoid exposure to the open air during the close of the day. Let her avoid also the room in which she was first seized, for it is a strange phenomenon in nervous temperaments that a nervous attack may, without visible cause, be repeated in the same place where it was first experienced. You had better shut up the chamber for at least some weeks, burn fires in it, repaint and paper it, sprinkle chloroform. You are not, perhaps, aware that Dr. Llyod died in that room after a prolonged illness. Suffer me to wait till your servant returns with the medicine, and let me employ the interval in asking you a few questions. Miss Ashleigh, you say, never had a fainting fit before. I should presume that she is not what we call strong. But has she ever had any illness that alarmed you?"

"Never."

"No great liability to cold and cough, to attacks of the chest or lungs?"

"Certainly not. Still I have feared that she may have a tendency to consumption. Do you think so? Your questions alarm me!"

"I do not think so; but before I pronounce a positive opinion, one question more. You say you have feared a tendency to consumption. Is that disease in her family? She certainly did not inherit it from you. But on her father's side?"

"Her father," said Mrs. Ashleigh, with tears in her eyes, "died young, but of brain fever, which the medical men said was brought on by over study."

"Enough, my dear madam. What you say confirms my belief that your daughter's constitution is the very opposite to that in which the seeds of consumption lurk. It is rather that far nobler constitution, which the keenness of the nervous susceptible renders delicate but elastic—as quick to recover as it is to suffer."

"Thank you, thank you, Dr. Fenwick, for what you say. You take a load from my heart. For Mr. Vigors, I know, thinks Lilian consumptive, and Mrs. Poyntz has rather frightened me at times by hints to the same effect. But when you speak of nervous susceptibility, I do not quite understand you. My daughter is not what is commonly called nervous. Her temper is singularly even."

"But if not excitable, should you also say that she is not impressionable? The things which do not disturb her temper, may, perhaps, deject her spirits. Do I make myself understood?"

"Yes, I think I understand your distinction. But I am not quite sure if it applies. To most things that affect the spirits she is not more sensitive than other girls, perhaps less so. But she is certainly very impressionable in some things."

"In what?"

"She is more moved than any one I ever knew by objects in external nature, rural scenery, rural sounds, by music, by the books that she reads—even books that are not works of imagination. Perhaps in all this she takes after her poor father, but in a more marked degree—at least, I observe it more in her. For he was very silent and reserved. And perhaps also her peculiarities have been fostered by the seclusion in which she has been brought up. It was with a view to make her a little more like girls of her own age that our friend, Mrs. Poyntz induced me to come here. Lilian was reconciled to this change; but she shrank from the thoughts of London, which I should have preferred. Her poor father could not endure London."

"Miss Ashleigh is fond of reading?"

"Yes, she is fond of reading, but more fond of musing. She will sit by herself for hours without book or work, and seem as abstracted as if in a dream. She was so even in her earliest childhood. Then she would tell me what she had been conjuring up to herself. She would say that she had seen—positively seen—beautiful lands far away from earth; flowers and trees not like ours. As she grew older this visionary talk displeased me, and I scolded her, and said that if others heard her, they would think that she was not only silly but very untruthful. So of late years she never ventures to tell me what, in such dreamy moments, she suffers herself to imagine; but the habit of musing continues still. Do you not agree with Mrs. Poyntz, that the best cure would be a little cheerful society amongst other young people?"

"Certainly," said I, honestly, though with a jealous pang. "But here comes the medicine. Will you take it up to her, and then sit with her a half an hour or so? By that time I expect she will be asleep. I will wait here till you return. Oh, I can amuse myself with the newspapers and books on your table. Stay! one caution: be sure there are no flowers in Miss Ashleigh's sleeping-room. I think I saw a treacherous rose-tree in a stand by the window. If so, banish it."

Left alone, I examined the room in which, oh thought of joy! I had surely now won the claim to become a privileged guest. I touched the books Lilian must have touched; in the articles of furniture, as yet so hastily disposed that the settled look of home was not about them, I still knew that I was gazing on things which her mind must associate with the history of her young life. That lute-harp—must be surely hers, and the scarf, with a girl's favorite colors—pure white and pale blue,—and the bird-cage, and the childish ivory work-case, with implements too pretty for use, all spoke of her.

It was a blissful intoxicating reverie, which Mrs. Ashleigh's entrance disturbed.

Lilian was sleeping calmly. I had no excuse to linger there any longer.

"I leave you, I trust, with your mind quite at ease," said I. "You will allow me to call to-morrow, in the afternoon?"

"Oh yes, gratefully."

Mrs. Ashleigh held out her hand as I made towards the door.

Is there a physician who has not felt at times how that ceremonious fee throws him back from the garden-land of humanity into the market-place of money—seems to put him out of the pale of equal friendship, and say, "True, you have given health and life. Adieu! there, you are paid for it." With a poor person there would have been no dilemma, but Mrs. Ashleigh was affluent: to depart from custom here was almost impertinence. But had the penalty of my refusal been the doom of never again beholding Lilian, I could not have taken her mother's gold. So I did not appear to notice the hand held out to me, and passed by with a quickened step.

"But Dr. Fenwick, stop!"

"No, ma'am, no! Miss Ashleigh would have recovered as soon without me. Whenever my aid is really wanted, then—but heaven grant that time may never come! We will talk again about her to-morrow."

I was gone. Now in the garden ground, odorous with blossoms; now in the lane, enclosed by the narrow walls; now in the deserted streets, over which the moon shone full as in that winter night when I hurried from the chamber of death. But the streets were not ghastly now, and the moon was no longer Hecate, that dreary goddess of awe and spectres, but the sweet, simple Lady of the Stars, on whose gentle face lovers have gazed ever since (if that guess of astronomers be true) she was parted from earth to rule the tides of its deeps from afar, even as love, from love divided, rules the heart, that yearns towards it, with mysterious law!

CHAPTER XI.

WITH what increased benignity I listened to the patients who visited me the next morning. The whole human race seemed to be worthier of love, and I longed to diffuse amongst all some rays of the glorious hope that had dawned upon my heart. My first call, when I went forth, was on the poor young woman from whom I had been returning the day before, when an impulse, which seemed like a fate, had lured me into the grounds where I had first seen Lilian. I felt grateful to this poor patient; without her Lilian herself might be yet unknown to me.

The girl's brother, a young man employed in the police, and whose pay supported a widowed mother and the suffering sister, received me at the threshold of the cottage.

"Oh, sir! she is so much better to-day; almost free from pain. Will she live now? can she live?"

"If my treatment has really done the good you say; if she be really better under it, I think her recovery may be pronounced. But I must first see her."

The girl was indeed wonderfully better. I felt that my skill was achieving a signal triumph; but that day even my intellectual pride was forgotten in the luxurious unfolding of that sense of heart which had so newly waked into blossom.

As I recrossed the threshold, I smiled on the brother, who was still lingering there:

"Your sister is saved, Waby. She needs now chiefly wine, and good though light nourishment; these you will find at my house: call there for them every day."

"God bless you, sir! If ever I can serve you——" His tongue faltered—he could say no more.

Serve me—Allen Fenwick—that poor policeman! Me, whom a king could not serve! What did I ask from earth but Fame and Lilian's heart? Thrones and bread man wins from the aid of others. Fame and woman's heart he can only gain through himself.

So I strode gaily up the hill, through the iron gates, into the fairy ground, and stood before Lilian s home.

The man-servant, on opening the door, seemed somewhat confused; and said hastily, before I spoke,

"Not at home, sir; a note for you."

I turned the note mechanically in my hand; I felt stunned.

"Not at home! Miss Ashleigh cannot be out. How is she?"

"Better, sir, thank you."

I still could not open the note; my eyes turned wistfully towards the windows of the house, and there—at the drawing-room window—I encountered the scowl of Mr. Vigors. I colored with resentment, divined that I was dismissed, and walked away with a proud crest and a firm step.

When I was out of the gates, in the blind lane, I opened the note. It began formally. "Mrs Ashleigh presents her compliments," and went on to thank me, civilly enough, for my attendance the night before, would not give me the trouble to repeat my visit, and enclosed a fee, double the amount of the fee prescribed by custom. I flung the money, as an asp that had stung me over the high wall, and tore the note into shreds. Having thus idly vented my rage, a dull gnawing sorrow came heavily down upon all other emotions, stifling and replacing them. At the mouth of the lane I halted. I shrank from the thought of the crowded streets beyond. I shrank yet more from the routine of duties, which stretched before me in the desert into which daily life was so suddenly smitten. I sat down by the roadside, shading my dejected face with a nerveless hand. I looked up as the sound of steps reached my ear, and saw Dr. Jones coming briskly along the lane, evidently from Abbots' House. He must have been there at the very time I had called. I was not only dismissed but supplanted. I rose before he reached the spot on which I had seated myself, and went my way into the town, went through my allotted round of professional visits; but my attentions was not so tenderly devoted, my skill so genially quickened by the glow of benevolence, as my poorer patients had found them in the morning. I have said how the physician should enter the sick-room. "A Calm Intelligence!" But if you strike a blow on the heart, the intellect suffers. Little worth, I suspect, was my "calm intelligence" that day. Bichat, in his famous book upon Life and Death, divides life into two classes—animal and organic. Man's intellect, with the brain for its centre, belongs to life animal; his passions to life organic, centered in the heart, in the viscera. Alas! if the noblest passions through which alone we lift ourselves into the moral realm of the sublime and beautiful really have their centre in the life which the very vegetable, that lives organically, shares with us? And, alas! if it be that life which we share with the vegetable, that can cloud, obstruct, suspend, annul that life centered in the brain, which we share with every being howsoever angelic, in every star howsoever remote, on whom the Creator bestows the faculty of thought!

CHAPTER XII.

BUT suddenly I remembered Mrs. Poyntz. I ought to call on her. So I closed my round of visits at her door. The day was then far advanced, and the servant politely informed me that Mrs. Pointz was at dinner. I could only leave my card, with a message that I would pay my respects to her the next day. That evening I received from her this note:—

"DEAR DR. FENWICK,—I regret much that I cannot have the pleasure of seeing you to-morrow. Poyntz and I are going to visit his brother, at the other end of the county, and we start early. We shall be away some days. Sorry to hear from Mrs. Ashleigh that she has been persuaded by Mr. Vigors to consult Dr. Jones about Lilian. Vigors and Jones both frighten the poor mother, and insist upon consumptive tendencies. Unluckily, you seem to have said there was little the matter. Some doctors gain their practice, as some preachers fill their churches, by adoit use of the appeals to terror. You do not want patients, Dr. Jones does. And, after all, better perhaps as it is.—Yours, &c. "M. POYNTZ."

To my more selfish grief anxiety for Lilian was now added. I had seen many more patients die from being mistreated for consumption than from consumption itself. And Dr. Jones was a mercenary, cunning, needy man, with much crafty knowledge of human foibles, but very little skill in the treatment of human maladies. My fears were soon confirmed. A few days after I heard from Miss Brabazon that Miss Ashleigh was seriously ill, kept her room. Mrs. Ashleigh made this excuse for not immediately returning the visits which the Hill had showered upon her. Miss Brabazon had seen Dr. Jones, who had shaken his head, said it was a serious case; but that time and care (his time and his care!) might effect wonders.

How stealthily at the dead of the night I would climb the Hill, and look towards the windows of the old sombre house—one window, in which a light burnt dim and mournful, the light of a sick-room—of hers!

At length Mrs. Poyntz came back, and I entered her house, having fully resolved beforehand on the line of policy to be adopted towards the potentate whom I hoped to secure as an ally. It was clear that neither disguise nor half-confidence would baffle the penetration of so keen an intellect, nor propitiate the goodwill of so imperious and resolute a temper. Perfect frankness here was the wisest prudence; and, after all, it was most agreeable to my own nature, and most worthy of my own honor.

Luckily, I found Mrs. Poyntz alone, and taking in both mine the hand she somewhat coldly extended to me, I said, with the earnestness of suppressed emotion:

"You observed when I last saw you, that I had not yet asked you to be my friend. I ask it now. Listen to me with all the indulgence you can vouchsafe, and let me at least profit by your counsel if you refuse to give me your aid."

Rapidly, briefly, I went on to say how I had first seen Lilian, and how sudden, how strange to myself, had been the impression which that first sight of her had produced.

"You remarked the change that had come over me," said I; "you divined the cause before I divined it myself; divined it as I sat there beside you, thinking that through you I might see, in the freedom of social intercourse, the face that was then haunting me. You know what has since passed. Miss Ashleigh is ill: her case is I am convinced, wholly misunderstood. All other feelings are merged in one sense of anxiety—of alarm. But it has become due to me, due to all, to incur the risk of your ridicule even more than of your reproof, by stating to you thus candidly, plainly, bluntly, the sentiment which renders alarm so poignant, and which, if scarcely admissible to the romance of some wild dreamy boy, may seem an unpardonable folly in a man of my years and my sober calling; due to me, to you, to Mrs. Ashleigh; because still the dearest thing in life to me is honor. And if you who know Mrs. Ashleigh so intimately, who must be more or less aware of her plans or wishes for her daughter's future; if you believe that those plans or wishes lead to a lot far more ambitious than an alliance with me could offer to Miss Ashleigh, then aid Mr. Vigors in excluding me from the house; aid me in suppressing a presumptuous, visionary passion. I cannot enter that house without love and hope at my heart. And the threshold of that house I must not cross if such love and such hope would be a sin and a treachery in the eyes of its owner. I might restore Miss Ashleigh to health; her gratitude might—I cannot continue. This danger must not be to me nor to her, if her mother has views far above such a son-in-law. And I am the more bound to consider all this while it is yet time, because I heard you state that Miss Ashleigh had a fortune—was what would be here termed an heiress. And the full consciousness that whatever fame one in my profession may live to acquire, does not open those vistas of social power and grandeur which are opened by professions to my eyes less noble in themselves—that full consciousness, I say, was forced upon me by certain words of your own. For the rest, you know my descent is sufficiently recognized as that amidst well-born gentry to have rendered me no mésalliance to families the most proud of their ancestry, if I had kept my hereditary estate and avoided the career that makes me useful to man. But I acknowledge that on entering a profession such as mine—entering any profession except that of arms or the senate—all leave their pedigree at its door, an erased or dead letter. All must come as equals, high-born or low-born, into that arena in which men ask aid from a man as he makes himself; to them his dead forefathers are idle dust. Therefore, to the advantage of birth I cease to have a claim. I am but a provincial physician, whose station would be the same had he been a cobbler's son. But gold retains its grand privilege in all ranks. He who has gold is removed from the suspicion that attaches to the greedy fortune-hunter. My private fortune, swelled by my savings, is sufficient to secure to any one I married a larger settlement than many a wealthy squire can make. I need no fortune with a wife; if she have one, it would be settled on herself. Pardon these vulgar details. Now, have I made myself understood?"

"Fully," answered the Queen of the Hill, who had listened to me quietly, watchfully, and without one interruption. "Fully. And you have done well to confide in me with so generous an unreserve. But before I say further, let me ask, what would be your advice for Lilian, supposing that you ought not to attend her? You have no trust in Dr. Jones; neither have I. And Anne Ashleigh's note received to-day, begging me to call, justifies your alarm. Still you think there is no tendency to consumption?"

"Of that I am certain so far as my slight glimpse of a case that to me, however, seems a simple and not uncommon one, will permit. But in the alternative you put—that my own skill, whatever its worth, is forbidden—my earnest advice is, that Mrs. Ashleigh should take her daughter at once to London, and consult there those great authorities to whom I cannot compare my own opinion or experience; and by their counsel abide."

Mrs. Poyntz shaded her eyes with her hand for a few moments, and seemed in deliberation with herself. Then she said, with her peculiar smile, half grave, half ironical:

"In matters more ordinary you would have won me to your side long ago. That Mr. Vigors should have presumed to cancel my recommendation to a settler on the Hill, was an act of rebellion, and involved the honor of my prerogative. But I suppressed my indignation at an affront so unusual, partly out of pique against yourself, but much more, I think, out of regard for you."

"I understand. You detected the secret of my heart; you knew that Mrs. Ashleigh would not wish to see her daughter the wife of a provincial physician."

"Am I sure, or are you sure, that the daughter herself would accept that fate; or if she accepted it, would not repent?"

"Do not think me the vainest of men when I say this—that I cannot believe I should be so enthralled by a feeling at war with my reason, unfavored by anything I can detect in my habits of mind, or even by the dreams of a youth which exalted science and excluded love, unless I was intimately convinced that Miss Ashleigh's heart was free—that I could win, and that I could keep it! Ask me why I am convinced of this, and I can tell you no more why I think that she could love me, than I can tell you why I love her!"

"I am of the world, worldly. But I am a woman, womanly—though I may not care to be thought it. And, therefore, though what you say is, regarded in a worldly point of view, sheer nonsense, regarded in a womanly point of view, it is logically sound. But still you cannot know Lilian as I do. Your nature and hers are in strong contrast. I do not think she is a safe wife for you. The purest, the most innocent creature imaginable, certainly that, but always in the seventh heaven. And you in the seventh heaven, just at this moment, but with an irresistible gravitation to the solid earth, which will have its way again when the honey-moon is over. I do not believe you two would harmonize by intercourse. I do not believe Lilian would sympathize with you, and I am sure you could not sympathize with her throughout the long dull course of this work-day life. And, therefore, for your sake as well as hers, I was not displeased to find that Dr. Jones had replaced you; and now, in return for your frankness, I say frankly—do not go again to that house. Conquer this sentiment, fancy, passion, whatever it be. And I will advise Mrs. Ashleigh to take Lilian to town. Shall it be so settled?"

I could not speak. I buried my face in my hands—misery, misery, desolation!

I know not how long I remained thus silent, perhaps many minutes. At length I felt a cold, firm, but not ungentle hand placed upon mine; and a clear, full, but not discouraging voice said to me:—

"Leave me to think well over this conversation, and to ponder well the value of all you have shown that you so deeply feel. The interests of life do not fill both scales of the balance. The heart which does not always go in the same scale with the interests, still has its weight in the scale opposed to them. I have heard a few wise men say, as many a silly woman says, 'Better be unhappy with one we love, than be happy with one we love not.' Do you say that, too?"

"With every thought of my brain, every beat of my pulse, I say it."

"After that answer, all my questionings cease. You shall hear from me to-morrow. By that time, I shall have seen Anne and Lilian. I shall have weighed both scales of the balance, and the heart here, Allen Fenwick, seems very heavy. Go, now. I hear feet on the stairs, Poyntz bringing up some friendly gossiper; gossipers are spies."

I passed my hand over my eyes, tearless, but how tears would have relieved the anguish that burdened them! and, without a word, went down the stairs, meeting at the landing-place Colonel Pontyz and the old man whose pain my prescription had cured. The old man was whistling a merry tune, perhaps first learned on the playground. He broke from it to thank, almost to embrace me, as I slid by by him. I seized his jocund blessing as a good omen, and carried it with me as I passed into the broad sunlight. Solitary—solitary! Should I be so evermore?

CHAPTER XIII.

THE next day I had just dismissed the last of my visiting patients, and was about to enter my carriage and commence my round, when

I received a twisted note containing but these words:—

"Call on me to-day, as soon as you can.
"M. POYNTZ."

A few minitues afterwards I was in Mrs. Poyntz's drawing-room.

"Well, Allen Fenwick," said she, "I do not serve friends by halves. No thanks! I but adhere tò a principle I have laid down for myself. I spent last evening with the Ashleighs. Lilian is certainly much altered—very weak, I fear very ill, and I believe very unskilfully treated by Dr. Jones. I felt that it was my duty to insist on a change of physician, but there was something else to consider before deciding who that physician should be. I was bound, as your confidante, to consult your own scruples of honor. Of course I could not say point-blank to Mrs. Ashleigh, 'Dr. Fenwick admires your daughter, would you object to him as a son-in-law?' Of course I could not touch at all on the secret with which you intrusted me; but I have not the less arrived at a conclusion, in agreement with my previous belief, that not being a woman of the world, Anne Ashleigh has none of the ambition which women of the world would conceive for a daughter who has a good fortune and considerable beauty; that her predominant anxiety is for her child's happiness, and her predominant fear is that her child will die. She would never oppose any attachment which Lilian might form; and if that attachment were for one who had preserved her daughter's life, I believe her own heart would gratefully go with her daughter's. So far, then, as honor is concerned, all scruples vanish."

I sprang from my seat, radiant with joy. Mrs. Poyntz dryly continued: "You value yourself on your common sense, and to that I address a few words of counsel which may not be welcome to your romance. I said that I did not think you and Lilian would suit each other in the long run; reflection confirms me in that supposition. Do not look at me so increduously and so sadly. Listen, and take heed. Ask yourself what, as a man whose days are devoted to a laborious profession, whose ambition is entwined with its success, whose mind must be absorbed in its pursuits—ask yourself what kind of a wife you would have sought to win, had not this sudden fancy for a charming face rushed over your better reason, and obliterated all previous plans and resolutions. Surely some one with whom your heart would have been quite at rest; by whom your thoughts would have been undistracted from the channels into which your calling should concentrate their flow; in short, a serene companion in the quiet holiday of a trustful home! Is it not so?"

"You interpret my own thoughts when they have turned towards marriage. But what is there in Lilian Ashleigh that should mar the picture you have drawn?"

"What is there in Lilian Ashleigh which in the least accords with the picture? In the first place, the wife of a young physician should not be his perpetual patient. The more he loves her, and the more worthy she may be of love, the more her case will haunt him wherever he goes. When he returns home, it is not to a holiday; the patient he most cares for, the anxiety that most gnaws him awaits him there."

"But, good Heavens! why should Lilian Ashleigh be a perpetual patient? The sanitary resources of youth are incalcuable. And——"

"Let me stop you; I cannot argue against a physician in love! I will give up that point in dispute, remaining convinced that there is somthing in Lilian's constitution which will perplex, torment, and baffle you. It was so with her father, whom she resembles in face and in character. He showed no symptoms of any grave malady. His outward form was, like Lilian's, a model of symmetry, except in this, that, like hers, it was too exquisitely delicate; but, when seemingly in the midst of perfect health, at any slight jar on the nerves he would become alarmingly ill. I was sure that he would die young, and he did so."

"Ay, but Mrs. Ashleigh said that his death was from brain-fever, brought on by overstudy. Rarely, indeed, do women so fatigue the brain. No female patient, in the range of my practice, ever died of purely mental exertion."

"Of purely mental exertion, no; but of *heart* emotion, many female patients, perhaps? Oh, you own that! I know nothing about nerves. But I suppose that, whether they act on the brain or the heart, the result to life is much the same if the nerves be too finely strung for life's daily wear and tear. And this is what I mean, when I say you and Lilian will not suit. As yet, she is a mere child; her nature undeveloped, and her affections, therefore, untried. You might suppose that you had won her heart; she might believe that she gave it to you, and both be deceived. If fairies nowadays condescend to exchange their offspring with those of mortals, and if the popular tradition did not represent a fairy changeling as an ugly peevish creature, with none of the grace of its parents, I should be half inclined to suspect that Lilian was one of the elfin people. She never seems at home on earth; and I do not think she will ever be contented with a prosaic earthly lot. Now I have told you why I do not think she will suit you. I must leave it to yourself to conjecture how far you would suit her. I say this in due season, while you may set a guard upon your impulse; while you may yet watch, and weigh, and meditate; and from this moment on that subject I say no more. I lend advice, but I never throw it away."

She came here to a dead pause, and began putting on her bonnet and scarf, which lay on the table beside her. I was a little chilled by her words, and yet more by the blunt, shrewd, hard look and manner which aided the effect of their delivery. But the chill melted away in the sudden glow of my heart when she again turned towards me and said:

"Of course you guess, from these preliminary cautions, that you are going into danger? Mrs. Ashleigh wishes to consult you about Lilian, and I propose to take you to her house."

"Oh, my friend, my dear friend, how can I ever repay you?" I caught her hand, the white firm hand, and lifted it to my lips.

She drew it somewhat hastily away, and laying it gently on my shoulder, said, in a soft voice, "Poor Allen, how little the world knows either of us! But how little perhaps we know ourselves! Come, your carriage is here? That is right; we must put down Dr. Jones publicly and in all our state."

In the carriage Mrs. Poyntz told me the purport of that conversation with Mrs. Ashleigh to which I owed my re-introduction to Abbots' House. It seems that Mr. Vigors had called early the morning after my first visit; had evinced much discomposure on hearing that I had been summoned; dwelt much on my injurious treatment of Dr. Lloyd, whom, as distantly related to himself, and he (Mr. Vigors) being distantly connected with the late Gilbert Ashleigh, he endeavored to fasten upon his listener as one of her husband's family, whose quarrel she was bound in honor to take up. He spoke of me as an infidel "tainted with French doctrines," and as a practitioner rash and presumptuous; proving his own freedom from presumption and rashness by flatly deciding that my opinion must be wrong. Previously to Mrs. Ashleigh's migration to L——, Mr. Vigors had interested her in the pretended phenomena of mesmerism. He had consulted a clairvoyante, much esteemed by poor Dr. Lloyd, as to Lilian's health, and the clairvoyante had declared her to be constitutionally predisposed to consumption. Mr. Vigors persuaded Mrs. Ashleigh to come at once with him and see this clairvoyante herself, armed with a lock of Lilian's hair and a glove she had worn, as the media of mesmerical *rapport.*

The clairvoyante, one of those I had publicly denounced as an impostor, naturally enough denounced me in return. On being asked solemnly by Mr. Vigors "to look at Dr. Fenwick and see if his influence would be beneficial to the subject," the sibyl had become violently agitated, and said that, "when she looked at us together, we were enveloped in a black cloud; that this portended affliction and sinister consequences; that our *rapport* was antagonistic." Mr. Vigors then told her to dismiss my image, and conjure up that of Dr. Jones. Therewith the somnambule became more tranquil and said: "Dr. Jones would do well if he would be guided by higher lights than his own skill, and consult herself daily as to the proper remedies. The best remedy of all would be mesmerism. But since Dr. Lloyd's death, she did not know of a mesmerist, sufficiently gifted, in affinity with the patient." In fine, she impressed and awed Mrs. Ashleigh, who returned in haste, summoned Dr. Jones, and dismissed myself.

"I could not have conceived Mrs. Ashleigh to be so utterly wanting in common sense," said I. "She talked rationally enough when I saw her."

"She has common sense in general, and

plenty of the sense most common," answered Mrs. Poyntz. "But she is easily led and easily frightened wherever her affections are concerned, and therefore, just as easily as she had been persuaded by Mr. Vigors and terrified by the somnambule, I persuaded her against the one, and terrified her against the other. I had positive experience on my side, since it was clear that Lilian had been getting rapidly worse under Dr. Jones's care. The main obstacles I had to encounter in inducing Mrs. Ashleigh to consult you again, were, first, her reluctance to disoblige Mr. Vigors, as a friend and connection of Lilian's father; and, secondly, her sentiment of shame in reinviting your opinion after having treated you with so little respect. Both these difficulties I took on myself. I bring you to her house, and, on leaving you, I shall go on to Mr. Vigors, and tell him what is done is my doing, and not to be undone by him; so that matter is settled. Indeed, if you were out of the question, I should not suffer Mr. Vigors to reintroduce all these mummeries of clairvoyance and mesmerism into the precincts of the Hill. I did not demolish a man I really liked in Dr. Lloyd, to set up a Dr. Jones, whom I despise, in his stead. Clairvoyance on Abbey Hill, indeed ! I saw enough of it before."

"True; your strong intellect detected at once the absurdity of the whole pretence—the falsity of mesmerism—the impossibility of clairvoyance."

"No, my strong intellect did nothing of the kind. I do not know whether mesmerism be false or clairvoyance impossible; and I don't wish to know. All I do know is, that I saw the Hill in great danger; young ladies allowing themselves to be put to sleep by gentlemen, and pretending they had no will of their own against such fascination ! Improper and shocking ! And Miss Brabazon beginning to prophesy, and Mrs. Leopold Smythe questioning her maid (whom Dr. Lloyd declared to be highly gifted) as to all the secrets of her friends. When I saw this, I said, 'The Hill is becoming demoralized; the Hill is making itself ridiculous; the Hill must be saved !' I remonstrated with Dr. Lloyd, as a friend; he remained obdurate. I annihilated him as an enemy, not to me but to the State. I slew my best lover for the good of Rome. Now you know why I took your part—not because I have any opinion, one way or the other, as to the truth or falsehood of what Dr. Lloyd ascertained; but I have a strong opinion that, whether they be true or false, his notions were those which are not to be allowed on the Hill. And so, Allen Fenwick, that matter was settled."

Perhaps at another time I might have felt some little humiliation to learn that I had been honored with the influence of this great potentate not as a champion of truth, but as an instrument of policy; and I might have owned to some twinge of conscience in having assisted to sacrifice a fellow-seeker after science—misled, no doubt, but preferring his independent belief to his worldly interest—and sacrifice him to those deities with whom science is ever at war—the Prejudices of a Clique sanctified into the Proprieties of the World. But at that moment the words I heard made no perceptible impression on my mind. The gables of Abbots' House were visible above the evergreens and lilacs; another moment, and the carriage stopped at the door.

CHAPTER XIV.

MRS. ASHLEIGH received us in the dining-room. Her manner to me, at first, was a little confused and shy. But my companion soon communicated something of her own happy ease to her gentler friend. After a short conversation we all three went to Lilian, who was in a little room on the ground-floor, fitted up as her study. I was glad to perceive that my interdict of the death-chamber had been respected.

She reclined on a sofa near the window, which was, however, jealously closed; the light of the bright May-day obscured by blinds and curtains; a large fire on the hearth; the air of the room that of a hot-house—the ignorant, senseless, exploded system of nursing into consumption those who are confined on suspicion of it ! She did not heed us as we entered noiselessly; her eyes were drooped languidly on the floor, and with difficulty I suppressed the exclamation that rose to my lips on seeing her. She seemed within the last few days so changed, and on the aspect of the countenance there was so profound a melancholy! But as she slowly turned at the sound of our footsteps, and her eyes met mine, a quick blush came into the wan cheek, and she half rose, but sank back as if the effort exhausted her. There was a struggle for breath, and a low hollow cough. Was it possible that I had been mistaken, and that in that cough was heard the warning knell of the most insidious enemy to youthful life?

I sat down by her side, I lured her on to talk of indifferent subjects—the weather, the gardens, the bird in the cage, which was placed on the table near her. Her voice, at first low and feeble, became gradually stronger, and her face lighted up with a child's innocent, playful smile. No, I had not been mistaken! That was no lymphatic nerveless temperament, on which consumptions fastens as its lawful prey—here there was no hectic pulse, no hurried waste of the vital flame. Quietly and gently I made my observations, addressed my questions, applied my stethoscope; and when I turned my face towards her mother's anxious, eager eyes, that face told my opinion; for her mother sprang forward, clasped my hand, and said, through her struggling tears,—

"You smile! You see nothing to fear?"

"Fear! No, indeed! You will soon be again yourself, Miss Ashleigh, will you not?"

"Yes," she said, with her sweet laugh, "I shall be well now very soon. But may I not have the window open—may I not go into the garden? I so long for fresh air."

"No, no, darling," exclaimed Mrs. Ashleigh, "not while the east winds last. Dr. Jones said on no account. On no account, Dr. Fenwick, eh?"

"Will you take my arm, Miss Ashleigh, for a few turns up and down the room?" said I. "We will then see how far we may rebel against Dr. Jones."

She rose with some little effort, but there was no cough. At first her step was languid—it became lighter and more elastic after a few moments.

"Let her come out," said I to Mrs. Ashleigh. "The wind is not in the east, and, while are out, pray bid your servant lower to the last bar in the grate that fire—only fit for Christmas."

"But—"

"Ah, no buts! He is a poor doctor who is not a stern despot."

So the straw hat and mantle were sent for Lilian was wrapped with unnecessary care, and we all went forth into the garden. Involuntarily we took the way to the Monk's Well, and at every step Lilian seemed to revive under the bracing air and temperate sun. We paused by the well.

"You do not feel fatigued, Miss Ashleigh?"

"No."

"But your face seems changed. It is grown sadder."

"Not sadder."

"Sadder than when I first saw it—saw it when you were seated here!" I said this in a whisper. I felt her hand tremble as it lay on my arm.

"You saw me seated here!"

"Yes. I will tell you how some day."

Lilian lifted her eyes to mine, and there was int hem that same surprise which I had noticed on my first visit—a surprise that perplexed me, blended with no displeasure, but yet with a something of vague alarm.

We soon returned to the house.

"Mrs. Ashley made me a sign to follow her into the drawing-room, leaving Mrs. Poyntz with Lilian.

"Well?" said she, tremblingly.

"Permit me to see Dr. Jones's prescriptions. Thank you. Ay, I thought so. My dear madam, the mistake here has been in depressing nature instead of strengthening; in narcotics instead of stimulants. The main stimulants which leave no reaction are air and light. Promise me that I may have my own way for a week—that all I recommend will be implicitly heeded?"

"I promise. But that cough; you noticed it?"

"Yes. The nervous system is terribly lowered, and nervous exhaustion is a strange impostor; it imitates all manner of complaints with which it has no connection. The cough will soon disappear! But pardon my question. Mrs. Poyntz tells me that you consulted a clairvoyante about your daughter. Does Miss Ashleigh know that you did so?"

"No; I did not tell her."

"I am glad of that. And pray for Heaven's sake, guard her against all that may set her thinking on such subjects. Above all, guard her against concentring attention on any malady that your fears erroneously ascribe to her. It is amongst the phenomena of our organization that you cannot closely rivet your consciousness on any part of the frame, however healthy, but it will soon begin to exhibit morbid sensibility. Try to fix all your attention on your little finger for half an hour, and before the half-hour is over the little finger will be uneasy, probably even painful. How serious, then, is the danger to a young girl, at the age in which imagination is most active, most intense, if you force upon her a belief that she is in danger of a mortal disease; it is a peculiarity of youth to brood over the thought of early death much more resignedly, much more complacently, than we do in maturer years. Impress on a young imaginative girl, as free from pulmonary tendencies as you and I are, the conviction that she must fade away into the grave, and though she may not actually die of consumption, you instil slow poison into her system. Hope is the natural aliment of youth. You impoverish nourishment where you discourage hope. As soon as this temporary illness is over, reject for your daughter the melancholy care which seems to her own mind to mark her out from others of her age. Rear her for the air—which is the kindest life-giver; to sleep with open windows; to be out at sunrise. Nature will do more for her than all our drugs can do. You have been hitherto fearing Nature; now trust to her."

Here Mrs. Poyntz joined us, and having, while I had been speaking, written my prescription and some general injunctions, I closed my advice with an appeal to that powerful protectress.

"This, my dear madam, is a case in which I need your aid, and I ask it. Miss Ashleigh should not be left with no other companion than her mother. A change of faces is often as salutary as a change of air. If you could devote an hour or two this very evening to sit with Miss Ashleigh, to talk to her with your usual cheerfulness, and—"

"Anne," interrupted Mrs. Poyntz, 'I will come and drink tea with you at half-past seven, and bring my knitting; and perhaps, if you ask him, Dr. Fenwick will come too! He can be tolerably entertaining when he likes it."

"It is too great for a tax on his kindness, I fear," said Mrs. Ashleigh. "But," she added cordially, "I should be grateful indeed if he would spare us an hour of his time."

I murmured an assent, which I endeavored to make not too joyous.

"So that matter is settled," said Mrs. Poyntz; "and now I shall go to Mr. Vigors and prevent his further interference."

"Oh! but, Margaret, pray don't offend him—a connection of my poor dear Gilbert's. And so tetchy! I am sure I do not know how you will manage to—"

"To get rid of him? Never fear. As I manage everything and everybody," said Mrs. Poyntz, bluntly. So she kissed her friend on the forehead, gave me a gracious nod, and, declining the offer of my carriage, walked with her usual brisk, decided tread down the short path towards the town.

Mrs. Ashleigh timidly approached me, and again the furtive hand bashfully insinuated the hateful fee.

"Stay," said I; "this is a case which needs the most constant watching. I wish to call so often that I should seem the most greedy of doctors if my visits were to be computed at guineas. Let me be at ease to effect my cure; my pride of science is involved in it. And when amongst all the young ladies of the Hill you can point to none with a fresher bloom, or a fairer promise of healthful life, than the patient you intrust to my care, why, then the fee and the dismissal. Nay, nay; I must refer you to our friend Mrs. Poyntz. It was so settled with her before she brought me here to displace Dr. Jones." Therewith I escaped.

CHAPTER XV.

In less than a week Lilian was convalescent; in less than a fortnight she regained her usual health; nay, Mrs. Ashleigh declared that she had never known her daughter appear so cheerful and look so well. I had established a familiar intimacy at Abbots' House; most of my evenings were spent there. As horse exercise formed an important part of my advice, Mrs. Ashleigh had purchased a pretty and quiet horse for her daughter; and, except the weather was very unfavorable, Lilian now rode daily with Colonel Poyntz, who was a notable equestrian, and often accompanied by Miss

Jane Poyntz, and other young ladies of the Hill. I was generally relieved from my duties in time to join her as she returned homewards. Thus we made innocent appointments, openly, frankly, in her mother's presence, she telling me beforehand in what direction excursions had been planned with Colonel Poyntz, and I promising to fall in with the party—if my avocations would permit. At my suggestion, Mrs. Ashleigh now opened her house almost every evening to some of the neighboring families; Lilian was thus habituated to the intercourse of young persons of her own age. Music and dancing and childiike games made the old house gay. And the Hill gratefully acknowledged to Mrs. Poyntz, "that the Ashleighs were indeed a great acquisition."

But my happiness was not unchequered. In thus unselfishly surrounding Lilian with others, I felt the anguish of that jealousy which is inseparable from those earlier stages of love, when the lover as yet has won no right to that self-confidence which can only spring from the assurance that he is loved.

In these social reunions I remained aloof from Lilian. I saw her courted by the gay young admirers whom her beauty and her fortune drew around her: her soft face brightening in the exercise of the dance, which the gravity of my profession rather than my years forbade me to join—and her laugh, so musically subdued, ravishing my ear and fretting my heart as if the laugh were a mockery on my sombre self and my presumptuous dreams. But no, suddenly, shyly, her eyes would steal away from those about her, steal to the corner in which I sat, as if they missed me, and, meeting my own gaze, their light softened before they turned away; and the color on her cheek would deepen, and to her lip there came a smile different from the smile that it shed on others. And then—and then—all jealousy, all sadness vanished, and I felt the glory which blends with the growing belief that we are loved.

In that diviner epoch of man's mysterious passion, when ideas of perfection and purity, vague and fugitive before, start forth and concentre themselves round one virgin shape—that rises out from the sea of creation, welcomed by the Hours and adorned by the Graces—how the thought that this archetype of sweetness and beauty singles himself from the millions, singles himself for her choice, ennobles and lifts up his being! Though after-experience may rebuke the mortal's illusion, that mistook for a daughter of Heaven a creature of clay like himself, yet for a while the illusion has grandeur. Though it comes from the senses which shall later oppress and profane it, the senses at first shrink into shade, awed and hushed by the presence that charms them. All that is brightest and best in the man has soared up like long-dormant instincts of Heaven, to greet and to hallow what to him seems life's fairest dream of the heavenly! Take the wings from the image of Love, and the god disappears from the form!

Thus, if at moments jealous doubt made my torture, so the moment's relief from it sufficed for my rapture. But I had a cause for disquiet less acute but less varying than jealousy.

Despite Lilian's recovery from the special illness which had more immediately absorbed my care, I remained perplexed as to its cause and true nature. To her mother I gave it the convenient epithet of "nervous." But the epithet did not explain to myself all the symptoms I classified by it. There was still, at times, when no cause was apparent or conjecturable, a sudden change in the expression of her countenance; in the beat of her pulse: the eyes would become fixed, the bloom would vanish, the pulse would sink feebler and feebler till it could be scarcely felt; yet there was no indication of heart disease, of which such sudden lowering of life is in itself sometimes a warning indication.

The change would pass away after a few minutes, during which she seemed unconscious, or, at least, never spoke—never appeared to heed what was said to her. But in the expression of her countenance there was no character of suffering or distress; on the contrary a wondrous serenity, that made her beauty more beauteous, her very youthfulness younger; and when this spurious or partial kind of syncope passed, she recovered at once without effort, without acknowledging that she had felt faint or unwell, but rather with a sense of recruited vitality, as the weary obtain from a sleep. For the rest her spirits were more generally light and joyous than I should have premised from her mother's previous description. She would enter mirthfully into the mirth of young companions round her: she had evidently quick perception of the sunny sides of life; an infantine gratitude for kindness; an infatine joy in the trifles that amuse only those who delight in tastes pure and simple. But when talk rose into graver and more contemplative topics, her attention became earnest and absorbed; and, sometimes, a rich eloquence, such as I have never before nor since heard from lips so young, would startle me first into a wondering silence, and soon into a disapproving alarm: for the thoughts she then uttered seemed to me too fantastic, too visionary, too much akin to the vagaries of a wild though beautiful imagination. And then I would seek to check, to sober, to distract fancies with which my reason had no sympathy, and the indulgence of which I regarded as injurious to the normal functions of the brain.

When thus, sometimes with a chilling sentence, sometimes with a half-sarcastic laugh, I would repress outpourings frank and musical as the songs of a forest-bird, she would look at me with a kind of plaintive sorrow—often sigh and shiver as she turned away. Only in those modes did she show displeasure; otherwise ever sweet and docile, and ever, if, seeing that I had pained her, I asked forgiveness, humbling herself rather to ask mine, and brightening our reconciliation with her angel smile. As yet I had not dared to speak of love; as yet I gazed on her as the captive gazes on the flowers and the stars through the gratings of his cell, murmuring to himself, "When shall the doors unclose?"

CHAPTER XVI.

It was with a wrath suppressed in the presence of the fair ambassadress, that Mr. Vigors had received from Mrs. Poyntz the intelligence that I had replaced Dr. Jones at Abbots' House, not less abruptly than Dr. Jones had previously supplanted me. As Mrs. Poyntz took upon herself the whole responsibility of this change, Mr. Vigors did not venture to condemn it to her face; for the Administrator of Laws was at heart no little in awe of the Autocrat of Proprieties; as Authority, howsoever established, is in awe of Opinion, howsoever capricious.

To the mild Mrs. Ashleigh the magistrate's anger was more decidedly manifested. He ceased his visits; and in answer to a long and deprecatory letter with which she endeavored to soften his resentment and win him back to the house, he replied by an elaborate combination of homily and satire. He began by excusing himself from accepting her invitations, on the ground that *his* time was valuable, *his* habits domestic; and though ever willing to sacrifice both time and habits where he could do good, he owed it to himself and to mankind to sacrifice neither where his advice was rejected and his opinion contemned. He glanced briefly, but not hastily, at the respect with which her late husbahd had deferred to his judgment, and the benefits which that deference had enabled him to bestow. He contrasted the husband's deference with the widow's contumely, and hinted at the evils which the contumely would not permit him to prevent. He could not presume to say what women of the world might think due to deceased husbands, but even women of the world generally allowed the claims of living children, and did not act with levity where their interests were concerned, still less where their lives were at stake. As to Dr. Jones, he, Mr. Vigors, had the fullest confidence in his skill. Mrs. Ashleigh must judge for herself whether Mrs. Poyntz was as good an authority upon medical science as he had no doubt she was upon shawls and ribbons. Dr. Jones was a man of caution and modesty; he did not indulge in the hollow boasts by which charlatans decoy their dupes; but Dr. Jones had privately assured him that though the case was one that admitted of no rash experiments, he had no fear of the result if his own prudent system were persevered in. What might be the consequences of any other system, Dr. Jones would not say, because he was too high-minded to express his distrust of the rival who had made use of underhand arts to supplant him.

But Mr. Vigors was convinced, from other sources of information (meaning, I presume, the oracular prescience of his clairvoyants), that the time would come when the poor young lady would herself insist on discarding Dr. Fenwick, and when "that person" would appear in a very different light to many who now so fondly admired and so reverentially trusted him. When that time arrived, he, Mr. Vigors, might again be of use; but, meanwhile, though he declined to renew his intimacy at Abbots' House, or to pay unavailing visits of mere ceremony, his interest in the daughter of his old friend remained undiminished, nay, was rather increased by compassion; that he should silently keep his eye upon her; and whenever anything to her advantage suggested itself to him, he should not be deterred by the slight with which Mrs. Ashleigh had treated his judgment, from calling on her, and placing before her conscience as a mother his ideas for a child's benefit, leaving to herself then, as now, the entire responsibility of rejecting the advice which he might say, without vanity, was deemed of some value by those who could distinguish between sterling qualities and specious pretences.

Mrs. Ashleigh's was that thoroughly womanly nature which instinctively leans upon others. She was diffident, trustful, meek, affectionate. Not quite justly had Mrs. Poyntz described her as "commonplace weak," for though she might be called weak, it was not because she was commonplace; she had a goodness of heart, a sweetness of disposition, to which that disparaging definition could not apply, She could only be called commonplace, inasmuch as in the ordinary daily affairs of life she had a great deal of ordinary daily commonplace good sense. Give her a routine to follow, and no routine could be better adhered to. In the allotted sphere of a woman's duties she never seem in fault. No household, not even Mrs. Poyntz's was more happily managed. The old Abbot's House had merged its original antique gloom in the softer character of pleasing repose. All her servants adored Mrs. Ashleigh; all found it a pleasure to please her; her establishment had the harmony of clock-work; comfort diffused itself round her like quiet sunshine round a sheltered spot. To gaze on her pleasing countenance, to listen to the simple talk that lapsed from her guiless lips, in even, slow, and lulling murmur, was in itself a respite from "eating cares." She was to the mind what the color of green is to the eye. She had, therefore, excellent sense in all that relates to every-day life. There, she needed not to consult another; there, the wisest might have consulted her with profit.

But the moment anything, however trivial in itself, jarred on the routine to which her mind had grown wedded; the moment an incident hurried her out of the beaten track of woman's daily life, then her confidence forsook her: then she needed a confidant, an adviser; and by that confidant or adviser she could be credulously lured or submissively controlled. Therefore when she lost, in Mr. Vigors, the guide she had been accustomed to consult whenever she needed guidance, she turned, helplessly and piteously, first to Mrs. Poyntz, and then yet more imploringly to me, because a woman of that character is never quite satisfied without the advice of a man. And where an intimacy more familiar than that of his formal visits is once established with a physician, confidence in him grows fearless and rapid, as the natural result of sympathy concentred on an object of anxiety in common between himself and the home which opens its sacred recess to his observant but tender eye. Thus Mrs. Ashleigh had shown me Mr. Vigors's letter, and, forgetting that I might not be so amiable as herself, besought me to counsel her how to concilitate and soften her lost husband's friend and connection. That character clothed him with dignity and awe in her soft forgiving eyes. So, smothering my own resentment, less perhaps at the tone of offensive insinuation against myself than at the arrogance with which this prejudiced intermeddler implied to a mother the necessity of his guardian watch over a child under her own care, I sketched a reply which seemed to me both dignified and placatory, abstaining from all discussion, and conveying the assurance that Mrs. Ashliegh would be at all times glad to hear, and disposed to respect, whatever suggestion so esteemed a friend of her husband's would kindly submit to her for the welfare of her daughter.

There all communication had stopped for about a month since the date of my reintroduction to Abbots' House. One afternoon I unexpectedly met Mr. Vigors at the entrance of the blind lane, I on my way to Abbots' House, and my first glance at his face told me that he was coming from it, for the expression of that face was more than usually sinister; the sullen scowl was lit into significant menace by a sneer of unmistakable triumph. I felt at once that he had succeeded in some machination against me, and with ominous misgivings quickened my steps.

I found Mrs. Ashleigh seated alone in front of the house, under a large cedar-tree that formed a natural arbor in the centre of the sunny lawn. She was perceptibly embarrassed as I took my seat beside her.

"I hope," said I, forcing a smile, "that Mr. Vigors has not been telling you that I shall kill my patient, or that she looks much worse than she did under Dr. Jones's care?"

"No," she said. "He owned cheerfully that Lilian had grown quite strong, and said, without any displeasure, that he had heard how gay she had been, riding out and even dancing—which is very kind in him, for he disapproves of dancing, on principle."

"But still, I can see he has said something to vex or annoy you; and, to judge by his countenance when I met him in the lane, I should conjecture that that something was intended to lower the confidence you so kindly repose in me."

"I assure you not; he did not mention your name, either to me or to Lilian. I never knew him more friendly; quite like old times. He is a good man at heart, very, and was much attached to my poor husband."

"Did Mr. Ashleigh profess a very high opinion of Mr. Vigors?"

"Well, I don't quite know that, because my dear Gilbert never spoke to me much about him. Gilbert was naturally very silent. But he shrank from all trouble—all worldly affairs—and Mr. Vigors managed his estate, and inspected his steward's books, and protected him through a long lawsuit which he had inherited from his father. It killed his father. I don't know what we should have done without Mr. Vigors, and I am so glad he has forgiven me."

"Hem! Where is Miss Ashleigh? Indoors?"

"No; somewhere in the grounds. But, my dear Dr. Fenwick, do not leave me yet; you are so very, very kind, and somehow I have grown to look upon you quite as an old friend. Something has happened which has put me out—quite put me out."

She said this wearily and feebly, closing her eyes as if she were indeed put out in the sense of extinguished.

"The feeling of friendship you express," said I, with earnestness, "is reciprocal. On my side it is accompanied by a peculiar gratitude. I am a lonely man, by a lonely fire-side—no parents, no near kindred, and in this town, since Dr. Faber left it, without cordial intimacy till I knew you. In admitting me so familiarly to your hearth, you have given me what I have never known before since I come to man's estate—a glimpse of the happy domestic life; the charm and relief to eye, heart, and spirit which is never known but in households cheered by the face of woman; thus my sentiment for you and yours is indeed that of an old friend; and in any private confidence you show me, I feel as if I were no longer a lonely man, without kindred, without home."

Mrs. Ashleigh seemed much moved by these words, which my heart had forced from my lips, and, after replying to me with simple unaffected warmth of kindness, she rose, took my arm, and continued thus as we walked slowly to and fro the lawn:

"You know, perhaps, that my poor husband left a sister, now a widow like myself, Lady Haughton."

"I remember that Mrs. Poyntz said you had such a sister-in-law, but I never heard you mention Lady Haughton till now. Well!"

"Well, Mr. Vigors has brought me a letter from her, and it is that which has put me out. I dare say you have not heard me speak before of Lady Haughton, for I am ashamed to say I had almost forgotten her existence. She is many years older than my husband was; of a very different character. Only came once to see him after our marriage. Hurt me by ridiculing him as a bookworm. Offended him by looking a little down on me, as a nobody without spirit and fashion, which was quiet true. And, except by a cold and unfeeling letter of formal condolence after I lost my dear Gilbert, I have never heard from her since I have been a widow, till to-day. But, after all, she is my poor husband's sister, and his eldest sister, and Lilian's aunt; and as Mr. Vigors says, 'Duty is duty.'"

Had Mrs. Ashleigh said "Duty is torture," she could not have uttered the maxim with more mournful and despondent resignation.

"And what does this lady require of you, which Mr. Vigors deems it your duty to comply with?"

"Dear me! What penetration! You have guessed the exact truth. But I think you will agree with Mr. Vigors. Certainly I have no option; yes, I must do it."

"My penetration is in fault now. Do what? Pray explain."

"Poor Lady Haughton, six months ago, lost her only son, Sir James. Mr. Vigors says he was a very fine young man, of whom any mother would have been proud. I had heard he was wild; Mr. Vigors says, however, that he was just going to reform, and marry a young lady whom his mother chose for him, when, unluckily, he would ride a steeplechase, not being quite sober at the time, and broke his neck. Lady Haughton has been, of course, in great grief. She has retired to Brighton; and she wrote to me from thence, and Mr. Vigors brought the letter. He will go back to her to-day."

"Will go back to Lady Haughton? What! Has he been to her? Is he, then, as intimate with Lady Haughton as he was with her brother?"

"No; but there has been a long and constant correspondence. She had a settlement on the Kirby Estate—a sum which was not paid off during Gilbert's life; and a very small part of the property went to Sir James, which part Mr. Ashleigh Sumner, the heir-at-law to the rest of the estate, wished Mr. Vigors, as his guardian, to buy during his minority, and as it was mixed up with Lady Haughton's settlement her consent was necessary as well as Sir James's. So there was much negotiation, and, since then, Ashleigh Sumner has come into the Haughton property, on poor St. James's decease; so that complicated all affairs between Mr. Vigors and Lady Haughton, and he has just been to Brighton to see her. And poor Lady Haughton, in short, wants me and Lilian to go and visit her. I don't like it at all. But you said the other day you thought sea air might be good for Lilian during the heat of the summer, and she seems well enough now for the change. What do you think?"

"She is well enough, certainly. But Brighton is not the place I would recommend for the summer; it wants shade, and is much hotter than L——."

"Yes, but unluckily Lady Haughton foresaw that objection, and she has a jointure-house some miles from Brighton, and near the sea. She says the grounds are well wooded, and the place is proverbially cool and healthy, not far from St. Leonard's Forest. And, in short, I have written to say we will come. So we must, unless, indeed, you positively forbid it."

"When do you think of going?"

"Next Monday. Mr. Vigors would make me fix the day. If you knew how I dislike moving when I am once settled; and I do so dread Lady Haughton, she is so fine, and so satirical! But Mr. Vigors says she is very much altered, poor thing! I should like to show you her letter, but I had just sent it to Margaret—Mrs. Poyntz—a minute or two before you came. She knows something of Lady Haughton. Margaret knows everybody. And we shall have to go in mourning for poor Sir James, I suppose; and Margaret will choose it, for I am sure I can't guess to what extent we should be supposed to mourn. I ought to have gone in mourning before—poor Gilbert's nephew—but I am so stupid, and I had never seen him. And —— but oh, this *is* kind! Margaret herself—my dear Margaret!"

We had just turned away from the house, in our up-and-down walk; and Mrs. Poyntz stood immediately fronting us.

"So, Anne, you have actually accepted this invitation—and for Monday next?"

"Yes. Did I do wrong?"

"What does Dr. Fenwick say? Can Lilian go with safety?"

I could not honestly say she might not go with safety, but my heart sank like lead as I answered:

"Miss Ashleigh does not now need merely medical care; but more than half her cure has depended on keeping her spirits free from depression. She may miss the cheerful companionship of your daughter, and other young ladies of her own age. A very melancholy house, saddened by a recent bereavement, without other guests; a hostess to whom she is a stranger, and whom Mrs. Ashleigh herself appears to deem formidable—certainly these do not make that change of scene which a physician would recommend. When I spoke of sea air being good for Miss Ashleigh, I thought of our own northern coasts at a later time of the year, when I could escape myself for a few weeks and attend her. The journey to a northern watering-place would be also shorter and less fatiguing; the air there more invigorating."

"No doubt that would be better," said Mrs. Poyntz, dryly; "but so far as your objections to visiting Lady Haughton have been stated, they are groundless. Her house will not be melancholy; she will have other guests, and Lilian will find companions, young like herself—young ladies—and young gentlemen too!"

There was something ominous, something compassionate, in the look which Mrs. Poyntz cast upon me, in concluding her speech, which in itself was calculated to rouse the fears of a lover. Lilian away from me, in the house of a worldly-fine lady—such as I judged Lady Haughton to be—surrounded by young gentlemen, as well as young ladies—by admirers, no doubt, of a higher rank and more brilliant fashion than she had yet known! I closed my eyes, and with strong effort suppressed a groan.

"My dear Anne, let me satisfy myself that Dr. Fenwick really *does* consent to this journey. He will say to me what he may not to you. Pardon me, then, if I take him aside for a few minutes. Let me find you here again under this cedar-tree."

Placing her arm in mine, and without waiting for Mrs. Ashleigh's answer, Mrs. Poyntz drew me into the more sequestered walk that belted the lawn; and, when we out out of Mrs. Ashleigh's sight and hearing, said:

"From what you have now seen of Lilian Ashleigh, do you still desire to gain her as your wife?"

"Still? Oh! with an intensity proportioned to the fear with which I now dread that she is about to pass away from my eyes—from my life!"

Does your judgment confirm the choice of your heart? Reflect before you answer."

"Such selfish judgment as I had before I knew her would not confirm, but oppose it. The nobler judgment that now expands all my reasonings, approves and seconds my heart. No, no; do not smile so sarcastically. This is not the voice of a blind and egotistical passion. Let me explain myself if I can. I concede to you that Lilian's character is undeveloped. I concede to you that, amidst the childlike freshness and innocence of her nature, there is at times a strangeness, a mystery, which I have not yet traced to its cause. But I am certain that the intellect is organically as sound as the heart, and that intellect and heart will ultimately—if under happy auspices—bend in that felicitous union which constitutes the perfection of woman. But it is because she does, and may for years, may perhaps always, need a more devoted, thoughtful care than natures less tremulously sensitive, that my judgment sanctions my choice; for whatever is best for her is best for me. And who would watch over her as I should?"

"You have never yet spoken to Lilian as lovers speak?"

"Oh, no, indeed."

"And, nevertheless, you believe that your affection would not be unreturned?"

"I thought so once—I doubt now—yet, in doubting, hope. But why do you alarm me with these questions? You, too, forebode that in this visit I may lose her for ever?"

"If you fear that, tell her so, and perhaps her answer may dispel your fear."

"What now, already, when she has scarcely known me a month. Might I not risk all if too premature?"

"There is no almanack for love. With many women love is born the moment they know they are beloved. All wisdom tells us that a moment once gone is irrevocable. Were I in your place, I should feel that I approached a moment that I must not lose. I have said enough; now I shall rejoin Mrs. Ashleigh."

"Stay—tell me first what Lady Haughton's letter really contains to prompt the advice with which you so transport, and yet so daunt, me when you proffer it."

"Not now—later, perhaps—not now. If you wish to see Lilian alone, she is by the Old Monk's Well; I saw her seated there as I passed that way to the house."

"One word more—only one. Answer this question frankly, for it is one of honor. Do you still believe that my suit to her daughter would not be disapproved of by Mrs. Ashleigh?"

"At this moment, I am sure it would not; a week hence I might not give you the same answer."

So she passed on with her quick but measured tread, back through the shady walk, on to the open lawn, till the last glimpse of her pale gray robe disappeared under the boughs of the cedar-tree. Then, with a start, I broke the irresolute, tremulous suspense in which I had vainly endeavored to analyze my own mind, solve my own doubts, concentrate my own will, and went the opposlte way, skirting the circle of that haunted ground; as now, on one side its lofty terrace, the houses of the neighboring city came full and close into view divided from my fairyland of life but by the trodden murmurous thoroughfare winding low beneath the ivied parapets; and as now, again the world of men abruptly vanished behind the screening foliage of luxuriant June.

At last the enchanted glade opened out from the verdure, its borders fragrant with syringa, and rose, and woodbine; and there, by the grey memorial of the gone Gothic, age, my eyes seemed to close their unquiet wanderings, resting spell-bound on that image which had become to me the incarnation of earth's bloom and youth.

She stood amidst the Past, backed by the fragments of walls which man had raised to seclude him from human passion, locking, under those lids so downcast, the secret of the only knowledge I asked from the boundless Future.

Ah! what mockery there is in that grand word, the world's fierce war-cry—Freedom! Who has not known one period of life, and that so solemn that its shadows may rest over all life hereafter, when one human creature has over him a sovereignity more supreme and absolute than Orient servitude adores in the symbols of diadem and sceptre? What crest so haughty that has not bowed before a hand which could exalt or humble! What heart so dauntless that has not trembled to call forth the voice at whose sound ope the gates of rapture or despair! That life alone is free which rules, and suffices for itself. That life we forfeit when we love!

CHAPTER XVII

How did I utter it? By what words did my heart make itself known? I remember not. All was as a dream that falls upon a restless, feverish night, and fades away as the eyes unclose on the peace of a cloudless heaven, on the bliss of a golden sun. A new morrow seemed indeed upon the earth when I woke from a life-long yesterday;—her dear hand in mine, her sweet face bowed upon my breast.

And then there was that melodious silence in which there is no sound audible from without; yet within us there is heard a lulling celestial music, as if our whole being, grown harmonious wlth the universe, joined from its happy deeps in the hymn that unites the stars.

In that silence our two hearts seemed to make each other understood, to be drawing nearer and nearer, blending by mysterious concord into the completeness of a solemn union, never henceforth to be rent asunder.

At length I said softly: "And it was here on this spot that I first saw you—here that I for the first time knew what power to change our world and to rule our future goes forth from the charm of a human face!"

Then Lilian asked me timidly, and without lifting her eyes, how I had so seen her, reminding me that I promised to tell her, and had never yet done so.

And then I told her of the strange impulse that had led me into the grounds, and by what chance my steps had been diverted down the path that wound to the glade; how suddenly her form had shone upon my eyes, gathering round itself the rose hues of the setting sun, and how wistfully those eyes had followed her own silent gaze into the distant heaven.

As I spoke, her hand pressed mine eagerly, convulsively, and, raising her face from my breast, she looked at me with an intent, anxious earnestness. That look!—twice before it had thrilled and perplexed me.

"What is there in that look, oh! my Lilian, which tells me that there is something that startles you—something you wish to confide, and yet shrink from explaining? See how, already, I study the fair book from which the seal has been lifted, but as yet you must aid me to construe its language."

"If I shrink from explaining, it is only because I fear that I cannot explain so as to be understood or believed. But you have a right to know the secrets of a life which you would link to your own. Turn your face aside from me; a reproving look, an incredulous smile, chill—oh! you cannot guess how they chill me, when I would approach that which to me is so serious and so solemnly strange."

I turned my face away, and her voice grew firmer as, after a brief pause, she resumed:

"As far back as I can remember in my infancy, there have been moments when there seems to fall a soft hazy veil between my sight and the things around it, thickening and deepening till it has the likeness of one of those white fleecy clouds which gather on the verge of the horizon when the air is yet still, but the winds are about to rise; and then this vapor or veil will suddenly open, as clouds open and let in the blue sky."

"Go on," I said gently, for here she came to a stop.

She continued, speaking somewhat more hurriedly:

"Then, in that opening, strange appearances present themselves to me, as in a vision. In my childhood these were chiefly landscapes of wonderful beauty. I could but faintly describe them then; I could not attempt to describe them now, for they are almost gone from my memory. My dear mother chid me for telling her what I saw, so I did not impress it on my mind by repeating it. As I grew up, this kind of vision—if I may so call it—became much less frequent, or much less distinct; I still saw the soft veil fall, the pale cloud form and open, but often what may then have appeared was entirely forgotten when I recovered myself, waking as from a sleep. Sometimes, however, the recollection would be vivid and complete; sometimes I saw the face of my lost father; sometimes I heard his very voice, as I had seen and heard him in my early childhood, when he would let me rest for hours beside him as he mused or studied, happy to be so quietly near him—for I loved him, oh, so dearly! and I remember him so distinctly, though I was only in my sixth year when he died. Much more recently—indeed, within the last few months—the images of things to come are reflected on the space that I gaze into as clearly as in a glass. Thus, for weeks before I came hither, or knew that such a place existed, I saw distinctly the old House, yon trees, this sward, this moss-grown Gothic fount, and, with the sight, an impression was conveyed to me that in the scene before me my old childlike life would pass into some solemn change. So that when I came here, and recognized the picture in my vision, I took an affection for the spot—an affection not without awe—a powerful, perplexing interest, as one who feels under the influence of a fate of which a prophetic glimpse has been vouchsafed. And in that evening, when you first saw me, seated here——"

"Yes, Lilian, on that evening——?"

"I saw you also, but in my vision—yonder, far in the deeps of space—and—and my heart was stirred as it had never been before; and near where your image grew out from the cloud I saw my father's face, and I heard his voice, not in my ear, but as in my heart, whispering—"

"Yes, Lilian—whispering—what?"

"These words—only these—'Ye will need one another.' But then, suddenly, between my upward eyes and the two forms they had beheld, there rose from the earth, obscuring the skies, a vague, dusty vapor, undulous, and coiling like a vast serpent, nothing, indeed, of its shape and figure definite, but of its face one abrupt glare; a flash from two dread luminous eyes, and a young head, like the Medusa's changing, more rapidly than I could have drawn breath, into a grinning skull. Then my terror made me bow my head, and when I raised it again, all that I had seen was vanished. But the terror still remained, even when I felt my mother's arm round me and heard her voice. And then, when I entered the house, and sat down again alone, the recollection of what I had seen—those eyes—that face—that skull—grew on me stronger and stronger till I fainted, and remember no more, until my eyes, opening, saw you by my side, and in my wonder there was not terror. No, a sense of joy, protection, hope, yet still shadowed by a kind of fear or awe, in recognizing the countenance which had gleamed on me from the skies before the dark vapor had risen, and while my father's voice had murmured, 'Ye will need one another.' And now—and now—will you love me less that you know a secret in my being which I have told to no other—cannot construe to myself? Only—only, at least, do not mock me—do not disbelieve me! Nay, turn from me no longer now:—now I ask to meet your eyes. Now, before our hands can join again, tell me that you do not despise me as untruthful, do not pity me as insane."

"Hush—hush!" I said, drawing her to my breast. "Of all you tell me we will talk hereafter. The scales of our science have no weights fine enough for the gossamer threads of a maiden's pure fancies. Enough for me—for us both—if out from all such allusions start one truth, told to you, lovely child, from the heavens; told to me, ruder man, on the earth; repeated by each pulse of this heart that woos you to hear and to trust;—now and henceforth through life unto death—'Each has need of the other'—I of you—I of you! my Lilian—my Lilian!"

CHAPTER XVIII.

In spite of the previous assurance of Mrs. Poyntz, it was not without an uneasy apprehension that I approached the cedar-tree, under which Mrs. Ashleigh still sat, her friend beside her. I looked on the fair creature whose arm was linked in mine. So young, so singularly lovely, and with all the gifts of birth and fortune which bend avarice and ambition the more submissively to youth and beauty, I felt as if I had wronged what a parent might justly deem her natural lot.

"Oh, if your mother should disapprove!" said I, faltering.

Lilian leant on my arm less lightly: "If I had thought so," she said with her soft blush, "should I be thus by your side?"

So we passed under the boughs of the dark tree, and Lilian left me, and kissed Mrs. Ashleigh's cheek; then, seating herself on the turf, laid her head on her mother's lap. I looked on the Queen of the Hill, whose keen eye shot over me. I thought there was a momentary expression of pain or displeasure on her countenance; but it passed. Still there seemed to me something of irony, as well as of triumph or congratulation, in the half-smile with which she quitted her seat, and in the tone with which she whispered, as she glided by me to the open sward, "So, then, it is settled."

She walked lightly and quickly down the lawn. When she was out of sight I breathed more freely. I took the seat which she had left, by Mrs. Ashleigh's side, and said, "A little while ago I spoke of myself as a man without kindred, without home, and now I come to you and ask for both."

Mrs. Ashleigh looked at me benignly, then raised her daughter's face from her lap, and whispered "Lilian;" and Lilian's lips moved, but I did not hear her answer. Her mother did. She took Lilian's hand, simply placed it in mine, and said, "As she chooses, I choose; whom she loves, I love."

CHAPTER XIX.

From that evening till the day Mrs. Ashleigh and Lilian went on their dreaded visit, I was always at their house, when my avocations allowed me to steal to it; and during those few days, the happiest I had ever know, it seemed to me that years could not have more deepened my intimacy with Lilian's exquisite nature—made me more reverential of its purity, or more enamoured of its sweetness. I could detect in her but one fault, and I rebuked myself for believing that it was a fault. We see many who neglect the minor duties of life, who lack watchfull forethought and considerate care for others, and we recognize the cause of this failing in levity or egotism. Certainly, neither of those tendencies of character could be ascribed to Lilian. Yet still in daily trifles there was something of that neglect, some lack of that care and forethought. She loved her mother with fondness and devotion, yet it never occurred to her to aid in those petty household cares in which her mother centred so much of habitual interest. She was full of tenderness and pity to all want and suffering, yet many a young lady on the Hill was more actively beneficent—visiting the poor in their sickness, or instructing their children in the Infant Schools.

I was persuaded that her love for me was deep and truthful; it was clearly void of all ambition; doubtless she would have borne, unflinching and contented, whatever the world considers to be sacrifice and privation,—yet I should never have expected her to take her share in the troubles of ordinary life. I could never have applied to her the homely but significant name of helpmate. I reproach myself while I write for noticing such defect—if defect it were—in what may be called the practical routine of our postive, trivial, human existence. No doubt it was this that had caused Mrs. Poyntz's harsh judgment against the wisdom of my choice. But such chillier shape upon Lilian's charming nature was reflected from no inert, unamiable self-love. It was but the consequence of that self-absorption which the habit of reverie had fostered. I cautiously abstained from all allusion to those visionary deceptions, which she had confined to me as the truthful impressions of spirit, if not of sense. To me any approach to what I termed superstition was displeasing; any indulgence of phantasies not within the measured and beaten tracks of imagination, more than displeased me in her—it alarmed. I would not by a word encourage her in persuasions which I felt it would be at present premature to reason against, and cruel indeed to ridicule. I was convinced that of themselves these mists round her native intelligence, engendered by a solitary and musing childhood, would subside in the fuller daylight of wedded life.

She seemed pained when she saw how resolutely I shunned a subject dear to her thoughts. She made one or two timid attempts to renew it, but my grave looks sufficed to check her. Once or twice indeed, on such occasions, she would turn away and leave me, but she soon came back; that gentle heart could not bear one unkindlier shade between itself and what it loved. It was agreed that our engagement should be, for the present, confided only to Mrs. Poyntz. When Mrs. Ashleigh and Lilian returned, which would be in a few weeks at furthest, it should be proclaimed; and our marriage could take place in the autumn, when I should be most free for a brief holiday from professional toils.

So we parted—as lovers part. I felt none of those jealous fears which, before we were affianced, had made me tremble at the thought of separation, and had conjured up irresistible rivals. But it was with a settled heavy gloom that I saw her depart. From earth was gone a glory; from life a blessing!

CHAPTER XX.

DURING the busy years of my professional career, I had snatched leisure for some professional treatises, which had made more or less sensation, and one of them entitled The Vital Principle; its Waste and Supply, had gained a wide circulation among the general public. This last treatise contained the results of certain experiments, then new in chemistry, which were adduced in support of a theory I entertained as to the reinvigoration of the human system by principles similar to those which Liebig has applied to the replenishment of an exhausted soil—viz., the giving back to the frame those essentials to its nutrition, which it has lost by the action or accident of time; or supplying that special pabulum or energy in which the individual organism is constitutionally deficient; and neutralizing or counterbalancing that in which it superabounds—a theory upon which some eminent physicians have more recently improved with signal success. But on these essays, slight and suggestive, rather than dogmatic, I set no value. I had been for the last two years engaged on a work of much wider range, endeared to me by a far bolder ambition—a work upon which I fondly hoped to found an enduring reputation as a severe and original physiologist. It was an Inquiry into Organic Life, similar in comprehensiveness of survey to that by which the illustrious Müller, of Berlin, has enriched the science of our age; however inferior, alas! to that august combination of thought and learning, in the judgment which checks presumption, and the genius which adorns speculation. But at that day I was carried away by the ardor of composition, and I admired my performance because I loved my labor. This work had been entirely laid aside for the last agitated month. now that Lilian was gone, I resumed it earnestly, as the sole occupation that had power and charm enough to rouse me from the aching sense of void and loss.

The very night of the day she went, I reopened my MS. I had left off at the commencement of a chapter "Upon Knowledge as derived from our Senses." As my convictions on this head were founded on the well-known arguments of Locke and Condillac against innate ideas, and on the reasonings by which Hume has resolved the combination of sensations into a general idea to an impulse arising merely out of habit, so I set myself to oppose, as a dangerous concession to the sentimentalities or mysticism of a pseudo-philosophy, the doctrine favored by most of our recent physiologists, and of which some of the most eminent of German metaphysicians have accepted the substance, though refining into a subtlety its positive form—I mean the doctrine which Müller himself has expressed in these words:—

"That innate ideas may exist, cannot in the slightest degree be denied; it is, indeed, a fact. All the ideas of animals, which are induced by instinct, are innate and immediate: something presented to the mind, a desire to attain which is at the same time given. The new-born lamb and foal have such innate ideas, which lead them to follow their mother and suck the teats. Is it not in some measure the same with the intellectual ideas of man?"*

To this question I answered with an indignant "No!" A "Yes" would have shaken my creed of materialism to the dust. I wrote on rapidly, warmly. I defined the properties and meted the limits of natural laws, which I would not admit that a Deity himself could alter. I clamped and soldered dogma to dogma in the links of my tinkered logic, till out from my page, to my own complacent eye, grew Intellectual Man, as the pure formation of his material senses; mind, or what is called soul, born from and nurtured by them alone; through them to act, and to perish with the machine they moved. Strange, that at the very time my love for Lilian might have taught me that there are mysteries in the core of the feelings which my analysis of ideas could not solve, I should so stubbornly have opposed as unreal all that could be referred to the spiritual! Strange, that at the very time when the thought that I might lose from this life the being I had known scarce a month, had just before so appalled me, I should thus complacently sit down to prove that, according to the laws of the nature which my passion obeyed, I must lose for eternity the blessing I now hoped I had won to my life! But how distinctly dissimilar is man in his conduct from man in his systems! See the poet reclined under forest-boughs, conning odes to his mistress; follow him out into the world; no mistress ever lived for him there!* See the hard man of science, so austere in his passionless problems; follow him now where the brain rests from its toil, where the heart finds its Sabbath—what child is so tender, so yielding and soft?

But I had proved to my own satisfaction that poet and sage are dust, and no more, when the pulse ceases to beat. And on that consolatory conclusion my pen stopped.

Suddenly, beside me I distinctly heard a sigh—a compassionate, mournful sigh. The sound was unmistakeable. I started from my seat, looked round, amazed to discover no one—no living thing! The windows were closed, the night was still. That sigh was not the wail of the wind. But there, in the darker angle of the room, what was that? A silvery whiteness—vaguely shaped as a human form—receding, fading, gone! Why, I know not—for no face was visible, no form, if form it were, more distinct than the colorless outline;—why, I know not, but I cried aloud, "Lilian! Lilian!" My voice came strangely back to my own ear—I paused, then smiled and blushed at my folly. "So I, too, have learned what is superstition," I muttered to myself. "And here is an anecdote at my own expense (as Müller frankly tells us anecdotes of the illusions which would haunt his eyes, shut or open)—an anecdote I may quote when I come to my Chapter on the Cheats of the Senses and Spectral Phantasms." I went on with my book, and wrote till the lights waned in the grey of dawn. And I said then, in the triumph of my pride, as I laid myself down to rest, "I have written that which allots with precision man's place in the region of natnre; written that which will found a school—form disciples; and race after race of those who cultivate truth through pure reason, shall accept my bases if they enlarge my building." And again I heard the sigh, but this time it caused no surarise. "Certainly," I murmured, "a very strange thing is the nervous system!" So I turned on my pillow, and, wearied out, fell asleep.

* Müller's Elements of Physiology, vol. ii., p. 134. Translated by Dr. Baley.

* Cowley, who wrote so elaborate a series of amatory poems, is said "never to have been in love but once, and then he never had resolution to tell his passion."—Johnson's Lives of the Poets: COWLEY.

CHAPTER XXI.

THE next day, the last of the visiting patients to whom my forenoons were devoted, had just quitted me, when I was summoned in haste to attend the steward of a Sir Philip Derval, not residing at his family seat, which was about five miles from L——. It was rarely indeed that persons so far from the town, when of no higher rank than this applicant, asked my services. But it was my principle to go wherever I was summoned; my profession was not gain, it was healing, to which gain was the incident, not the essential. This case the messenger reported as urgent. I went on horseback, and rode fast; but swiftly as I cantered through the village that skirted the approach to Sir Philip Derval's park, the evident care bestowed on the accomodation of the cottagers forcibly struck me. I felt that I was on the lands of a rich, intelligent, and beneficient proprietor. Entering the park, and passing before the manor-house, the contrast between the neglect and decay of the absentee's stately hall and the smiling homes of his villagers was disconsolately mournful.

An imposing pile, built apparently by Vanburgh, with decorated pilasters, pompous portico, and grand perron (or double flight of stairs to the entrance), enriched with urns and statues, but discolored, mildewed, chipped, half-hidden with unpruned creepers and ivy. Most of the windows were closed with shutters, decaying for want of paint; in some of the casements the panes were broken; the peacock perched on the shattered balustrade, that fenced a garden overgrown with weeds. The sun glared hotly on the place, and made its ruinous condition still more painfully apparent. I was glad when a winding in the pard-road shut the house from my sight. Suddenly I emerged through a copse of ancient yew-trees, and before me there gleamed, in abrupt whiteness, a building evidently designed for the family mausoleum—classical in its outline, with the blind iron door niched into stone walls of massive thickness, and surrounded by a funereal garden of roses and evergreens fenced with an iron rail, parti-gilt.

The suddenness with which this House of the Dead came upon me heightened almost into pain, if not into awe, the dismal impression which the aspect of the deserted home in its neighborhood had made. I spurred my horse and soon arrived at the door of my patient, who lived in a fair brick house at the other extremity of the park.

I found my patient, a man somewhat advanced in years, but of a robust conformation, in bed: he had been seized with a fit, which was supposed to be apoplectic, a few hours before; but was already sensible, and out of immediate danger. After I had prescribed a few simple remedies, I took aside the patient's wife, and went with her to the parlor below stairs, to make some inquiry about her husband's ordinary regimen and habits of life. These seemed sufficiently regular; I could discover no apparent cause for the attack, which presented symptoms not familiar to my experience. "Has your husband ever had such fits before?"

"Never!"

"Had he experienced any sudden emotion? Had he heard any unexpected news? or had anything happened to put him out?"

The womam looked much disturbed at these inquiries. I pressed them more urgently. At last she burst into tears, and clasping my hand, said, "Oh! doctor, I ought to tell you—I sent for you on purpose—yet I fear you will not believe me: my good man has seen a ghost!"

"A ghost!" said I, repressing a smile. "Well, tell me all, that I may prevent the ghost coming again."

The woman's story was prolix. Its substance was this: Her husband, habitually an early riser, had left his bed that morning still earlier than usual, to give directions about some cattle that were to be sent for sale to a neighboring fair. An hour afterwards he had been found by a shepherd, near the mausoleum, apparently lifeless. On being removed to his own house, he had recovered speech, and bidding all except his wife leave the room, he then told her that on walking across the park towards the cattle-sheds, he had seen, what appeared to him at first, a pale light by the iron door of the mausoleum. On approaching nearer, this light changed into the distinct and visible form of his master, Sir Philip Derval, who was then abroad—supposed to be in the East, where he had resided for many years. The impression on the steward's mind was so strong, that he called out, "Oh! Sir Philip!" when looking still more intently, he perceived that the face was that of a corpse. As he continued to gaze, the apparition seemed gradually to recede as if vanishing into the sepulchre itself. He knew no more; he became ununconscious. It was the excess of the poor woman's alarm, on hearing this strange tale, that made her resolve to send for me instead of the parish apothecary. She fancied so astounding a cause for her husband's seizure could only be properly dealt with by some medical man reputed to have more than ordinary learning. And the steward himself objected to the apothecary in the immediate neighborhood, as more likely to annoy him by gossip than a physician from a comparative distance.

I took care not to lose the confidence of the good wife by parading too quickly my disbelief in the phantom her husband declared that he had seen; but as the story itself seemed at once to decide the nature of the fit to be epileptic, I began to tell her of similar delusions which, in my experience, had occurred to those subjected to epilepsy, and finally soothed her into the conviction that the apparition was clearly reducible to natural causes. Afterwards, I led her on to talk about Sir Philip Derval, less from any curiosity I felt about the absent proprietor than from a desire to re-familiarize her own mind to his image as a living man. The steward had been in the service of Sir Philip's father, and known Sir Philip himself from a child. He was warmly attached to his master, whom the old woman described as a man of rare benevolence and great eccentricity, which last she imputed to his studious habits. He had succeeded to the title and estates as a minor. For the first few years after attaining his majority, he had mixed much in the world. When at Derval Court his house had been filled with gay companions, and was the scene of lavish hospitality. But the estate was not in proportion to the grandeur of the mansion, still less to the expenditure of the owner.

He had become greatly embarrassed; and some love disappointment (so it was rumored) occurring simultaneously with his pecuniary difficulties, he had suddenly changed his way of life, shut himself up from his old friends, lived in seclusion, taking to books and scientific pursuits, and as the old woman said, vaguely and expressively, "to odd ways." He had gradually by an economy that, towards himself, was penurious, but which did not preclude much judicious generosity to others cleared off his debts, and once more rich, he had suddenly quitted the country, and taken to a life of travel. He was now about forty-eight years old, and had been eighteen years abroad. He wrote frequently to his steward, giving him minute and thoughtful instructions in regard to the employment, comforts, and homes of the peasantry, but peremptorily ordering him to spend no money on the grounds and mansion, stating as a reason why the latter might be allowed to fall into decay, his intention to pull it down whenever he returned to England.

I stayed some time longer than my engagements well warranted at my patient's house, not leaving till the sufferer, after a quiet sleep, had removed from his bed to his arm-chair, taken food, and seemed perfectly recovered from his attack.

Riding homeward, I mused on the difference that education makes, even pathologically, between man and man. Here was a brawny inhabitant of rural fields, leading the healthiest of lives, not conscious of the faculty we call imagination, stricken down almost to Death's door by his fright at an optical illusion, explicable, if examined, by the same simple causes which had impressed me the night before with a moment's belief in a sound and a spectre—me who, thanks to sublime education, went so quietly to sleep a few minutes after, convinced that no phantom, the ghostliest that ear ever heard or eye ever saw, can be anything else but a nervous phenomenon.

CHAPTER XXII.

THAT evening I went to Mrs. Poyntz's: it was one of her ordinary "reception nights," and I felt that she would naturally expect my attendance as "a proper attention."

I joined a group engaged in general conversation, of which Mrs. Poyntz herself made the centre, knitting as usual—rapidly while she talked, slowly when she listened.

Without mentioning the visit I had paid that morning, I turned the conversation on the different country places in the neighborhood, and then incidentally asked, "What sort of a man is Sir Philip Derval? Is it not strange that he should suffer so fine a place to fall into decay?" The answers I received added little to the information I had already obtained. Mrs. Poyntz knew nothing of Sir Philip Derval, except as a man of large estates, whose rental had been greatly increased by a rise in the value of property he possessed in the town of L——, and which lay contiguous to that of her husband. Two or three of the older inhabitants of the Hill had remembered Sir Philip in his early days, when he was gay, high-spirited, hospitable, lavish. One observed that the only person in L—— whom he had admitted to his subsequent seclusion was Dr. Lloyd, who was then without practice, and whom he had employed as an assistant in certain chemical experiments.

Here a gentleman struck into the conversation. He was a stranger to me and to L——, a visitor to one of the dwellers on the Hill who had asked leave to present him to its queen as a great traveller and an accomplished antiquary.

Said this gentleman: "Sir Philip Derval! I know him. I met him in the East. He was then still, I believe, very fond of chemical science; a clever, odd, philanthropical man; had studied medicine, or at least practised it; was said to have made many marvellous cures. I became acquainted with him in Aleppo. He had come to that town, not much frequented by English travellers, in order to inquire into the murder of two men, of whom one was his friend and the other his countryman.

"This is interesting," said Miss Poyntz, dryly, "We who live on this innocent Hill all love stories of crime; murder is the pleasantest subject subject you could have hit on. Pray give us the details."

"So encouraged," said the traveller, good-humoredly, "I will not hesitate to communicate the little I know. In Aleppo, there had lived for some years a man who was held by the natives in great reverence. He had the reputation of extraordinary wisdom, but was difficult of access; the lively imagination of the Orientals invested his character with the fascinations of fable; in short, Haroun of Aleppo was popularly considered a magician. Wild stories were told of his powers, of his preternatural age, of his hoarded treasures. Apart from such disputable titles to homage, there seemed no question, from all I heard, that his learning was considerable, his charities entensive, his manner of life irreproachably ascetic. He appears to have resembled those Arabian sages of the Gothic age to whom modern science is largely indebted—a mystic enthusiast, but an earnest scholar. A wealthy and singular Englishman, long resident in another part of the East, afflicted by some languishing disease, took a journey to Aleppo to consult this sage, who, among his other acquirements, was held to have discovered rare secrets in medicine—his countrymen said in 'charms.' One morning, not long after the Englishman's arrival, Haroun was found dead in his bed, apparently strangled, and the Englishman, who lodged in another part of the town, had disappeared; but some of his clothes, and a crutch on which he habitually supported himself, were found a few miles distant from Aleppo, near the roadside. There appeared no doubt that he, too, had been murdered, but his corpse could not be discovered. Sir Philip Derval had been a loving disciple of this Sage of Aleppo, to whom he assured me he owed not only that knowledge of medicine which, by report, Sir Philip possessed, but the insight into various truths of nature, on the promulgation of which, it was evident, Sir Philip cherished the ambition to found a philosophical celebrity for himself."

"Of what description were those truths of nature?" I asked, somewhat sarcastically.

"Sir, I am unable to tell you, for Sir Philip did not inform me, nor did I much care to ask; for what may be revered as truths in Asia are usually despised as dreams in Europe. To return to my story. Sir Philip had been in Aleppo a little time before the murder; had left the Englishman under the care of Haroun; he returned to Aleppo on hearing the tragic events I have related, and was busied in collecting such evidence as could be gleaned, and instituting inquiries after our missing countryman, at the time I myself chanced to arrive in the city. I assisted in his researches, but without avail. The assassins remained undiscovered. I do not myself doubt that they were mere vulgar robbers. Sir Philip had a darker suspicion, of which he made no secret to me; but as I confess that I thought the suspicion groundless, you will pardon me if I do not repeat it. Whether, since I left the East, the Englishman's remains have been discovered, I know not. Very probably; for I understand that his heirs got hold of what fortune he left—less than was generally supposed. But it was reported that he had buried great treasures, a rumor, however absurd, not altogether inconsistent with his character."

"What was his character?" asked Mrs. Poyntz.

"One of evil and sinister repute. He was regarded with terror by the attendants who had accompanied him to Aleppo. But he had lived in a very remote part of the East, little known to Europeans, and, from all I could learn, had there established an extraordinary power, strengthened by superstitious awe. He was said to have studied deeply that knowledge which the philosophers of old called 'occult,' not, like the Sage of Aleppo, for benevolent, but for malignant ends. He was accused of conferring with evil spirits, and filling his barbaric court (for he lived in a kind of savage royalty) with charmers and sorcerers. I suspect, after all, that he was only, like myself, an ardent antiquary, and cunningly made use of the fear he inspired in order to secure his authority, and prosecute in safety researches into ancient sepulchres or temples. His great passion was, indeed, in excavating such remains, in his neighborhood; with what result I know not, never having penetrated so far into regions infested by robbers and pestiferous with malaria. He wore the Eastern dress, and always carried jewels about him. I came to the conclusion that for the sake of these jewels he was murdered, perhaps by some of his own servants (and, indeed, two at least of his suite were missing), who then at once buried his body, and kept their own secret. He was old, very infirm; could never have got far from the town without assistance."

"You have not yet told us his name," said Mrs. Poyntz.

"His name was Grayle."

"Grayle!" exclaimed Mrs. Poyntz, dropping her work, "Louis Grayle?"

"Yes; Louis Grayle. You could not have known him?"

"Known him! No. But I have often heard my father speak of him. Such, then, was the tragic end of that strong dark creature, for whom, as a young girl in the nursery, I used to feel a kind of fearful admiring interest?"

"It is your turn to narrate now," said the traveller.

And we drew closer round our hostess, who remained silent some moments, her brow thoughtful, her work suspended.

"Well," said she at last, looking round us with a lofty air, which seemed half defying, "force and courage are always fascinating, even when they are quite in the wrong. I go with the world, because the world goes with me; if it did not——." Here she stopped for a moment, clenched the firm white hand, and then scornfully waved it, left the sentence unfinished, and broke into another:

"Going with the world, of course we must march over those who stand against it. But when one man stands single-handed against our march, we do not despise him; it is enough to crush. I am very glad I did not see Louis Grayle when I was a girl of sixteen." Again she paused a moment—and resumed: "Louis Grayle was the only son of a usurer, infamous for the rapacity with which he had acquired enormous wealth. Old Grayle desired to rear his heir as a gentleman; sent him to Eton; boys are always aristocratic; his birth was soon thrown in his teeth; he was fierce; he struck boys bigger than himself—fought till he was half killed. My father was at school with him; described him as a tiger-whelp. One day he—still a fag—struck a sixth-form boy. Sixth-form boys do not fight fags; they punish them. Louis Grayle was ordered to hold out his hand to the cane; he received the blow, drew forth his schoolboy knife, and stabbed the punisher. After that, he left Eton. I don't think he was publicly expelled—too mere a child for that honor—but he was taken or sent away: educated with great care under the first masters at home: when he was of age to enter the University, old Grayle was dead. Louis was sent by his guardians to Cambridge, with acquirements far exceeding the average of young men, and with unlimited command of money. My father was at the same college, and described him again—haughty, quarrelsome, reckless, handsome, aspiring, brave. Does that kind of creature interest you, my dears?" (appealing to the ladies).

"La!" said Miss Babazon; "a horrid usurer's son!"

"Ay, true; the vulgar proverb says it is good to be born with a silver spoon in one's mouth; so it is when one has one's own family crest on it; but when it is a spoon on which people recognize their family crest, and cry out, 'Stolen from our plate-chest,' it is a heritage that outlaws a babe in his cradle. However, young men at college who want money are less scrupulous about descent than boys at Eton are. Louis Grayle found, while at college, plenty of well-born acquaintances willing to recover from him some of the plunder his father had extorted from theirs. He was too wild to distinguish himself by academical honors, but my father said that the tutors of the college declared that there were not six undergraduates in the University who knew as much hard and dry science as wild Louis Grayle. He went into the world, no doubt, hoping to shine; but his father's name was too notorious to admit the son into good society. The Polite World, it is true, does not examine a scutcheon with the nice eye of a herald, nor look upon riches with the stately contempt of a stoic—still the Polite World has its family pride and its moral sentiment. It does not like to be cheated—I mean, in money matters; and when the son of the man who has emptied its purse and foreclosed on its acres, rides by its club-windows, hand on haunch, and head in the air, no lion has a scowl more awful, no hyæna a laugh more dread than that same easy, good-tempered, tolerant, polite, well-bred World which is so pleasant an acquaintance, so languid a friend, and—so remorseless an enemy.

"In short, Louis Grayle claimed the right to be courted—he was shunned; to be admired—he was loathed. Even his old college acquaintances were shamed out of knowing him. Perhaps he could have lived through all this had he sought to glide quietly into position; but he wanted the tact of the well-bred, and strove to storm his way, not to steal it. Reduced for companions to needy parasites, he braved and he shocked all decorous opinion by that ostentation of excess, which made Richelieus and Lauzuns the rage. But then Richelieus and Lauzuns were dukes! He now very naturally took the Polite World into hate gave it scorn for scorn. He would ally himself with Democracy; his wealth could not get him into a club, but it would buy him into parliament; he could not be a Lauzun, nor, perhaps, a Mirabeau, but he might be a Danton. He had plenty of knowledge and audacity, and with knowledge and audacity a good hater is sure to be eloquent. Possibly, then, this poor Louis Grayle might have made a great figure, left his mark on his age and his name in history; but in contesting the borough, which he was sure to carry, he had to face an opponent in a real fine gentleman whom his father had ruined, cool and high-bred, with a tongue like a rapier, a sneer like an adder. A quarrel of course; Louis Grayle sent a challenge. The fine gentleman, known to be no coward (fine gentleman never are), was at first disposed to refuse with contempt. But Grayle had made himself the idol of the mob; and at a word from Grayle, the fine gentleman might have been ducked at a pump, or tossed in a blanket—that would have made him ridiculous;—to be shot at is a trifle, to be laughed at is serious. He therefore condescended to accept the challenge, and my father was his second.

"It was settled, of course, according to English custom, that both combatants should fire at the same time, and by signal. The antagonist fired at the right moment; his ball grazed Louis Grayle's temple. Louis Grayle had not fired. He now seemed to the seconds to take slow and deliberate aim. They called out to him not to fire—they were rushing to prevent him—when the trigger was pulled, and his opponent fell dead on the field. The fight was, therefore, considered unfair; Louis Grayle was tried for his life; he did not stand the trial in person.* He escaped to the Continent; hurried on to some distant uncivilized lands; could not be traced; reappeared in England no more. The lawyer who conducted his defence pleaded skilfully. He argued that the delay in firing was not intentional, therefore not criminal—the effect of the stun which the wound in the temple had occasioned. The judge was a gentleman, and summed up the evidence so as to direct the jury to a verdict against the low wretch who had murdered a gentleman. But the jurors were not gentlemen,

* Mrs. Poyntx here makes a mistake in law which, though very evident, her listeners do not seem to have noticed. Her mistake will be referred to later.

and Grayle's advocate had of course excited their sympathy for a son of the people whom a gentleman had wantonly insulted—the verdict was manslaughter. But the sentence emphatically marked the aggravated nature of the homicide—three years' imprisonment. Grayle eluded the prison, but he was a man disgraced and an exile—his ambition blasted, his career an outlaw's, and his age not yet twenty-three. My father said that he was supposed to have changed his name; none knew what had become of him. And so this creature, brilliant and daring, whom if born under better auspices we might now be all fawning on, cringing to—after living to old age, no one knows how—dies murdered at Aleppo, no one, you say, knows by whom."

"I saw some account of his death in the papers about three years ago," said one of the party; "but the name was misspelt, and I had no idea that it was the same man who had fought the duel which Mrs. Colonel Poyntz had so graphically described. I have a very vague recollection of the trial; it took place when I was a boy, more than forty years since. The affair made a stir at the time, but was soon forgotten."

"Soon forgotten," said Mrs. Poyntz; "ay, what is not? Leave your place in the world for ten minutes, and when you come back somebody else has taken it; but when you leave the world for good, who remembers that you had ever a place even in the parish register?"

"Nevertheless," said I, "a great poet has said, finely and truly.

"'The sun of Homer shines upon us still.'"

"But it does not shine upon Homer; and learned folks tell me that we know no more who and what Homer was, if there was ever a single Homer at all, or, rather a whole herd of Homers, than we know about the man in the moon—if there be one man there, or millions of men. Now, my dear Miss Brabazon, it will be very kind in you to divert our thoughts into channels less gloomy. Some pretty French air——Dr. Fenwick, I have something to say to you." She drew me towards the window. "So Anne Ashleigh writes me word that I am not to mention your engagement. Do you think it quite prudent to keep it a secret?"

"I do not see how prudence is concerned in keeping it secret one way or the other—it is a mere matter of feeling. Most people wish to abridge, as far as they can, the time in which their private arrangements are the topic of public gossip."

"Public gossip is sometimes the best security for the due completion of private arrangements. As long as a girl is not known to be engaged, her betrothed must be prepared for rivals. Announce the engagement and rivals are warned off."

"I fear no rivals."

"Do you not? Bold man! I suppose you will write to Lilian?"

"Certainly."

"Do so, and constantly. By-the-way, Mrs Ashleigh, before she went, asked me to send her back Lady Haughton's letter of invitation. What for? to show to you?"

"Very likely. Have you the letter still? May I see it?"

"Not just at present. When Lilian or Mrs. Ashleigh writes to you, come and tell me how they like their visit, and what other guests form the party."

Therewith she turned away and conversed apart with the traveller.

Her words disquieted me, and I felt that they were meant to do so—wherefore I could not guess. But there is no language on earth which has more words with a double meaning than that spoken by the Clever Woman, who is never so guarded as when she appears to be frank.

As I walked home thoughtfully, I was accosted by a young man, the son of one of the wealthiest merchants in the town. I had attended him with success, some months before, in a rheumatic fever: he and his family were much attached to me.

"Ah, my dear Fenwick, I am so glad to see you; I owe you an obligation of which you are not aware—an exceedingly pleasant travelling companion. I came to-day with him from London, where I have been sight-seeing and holiday-making for the last fortnight."

"I suppose you mean that you kindly bring me a patient?"

"No, only an admirer. I was staying at Fenton's Hotel. It so happened one day that I had left in the coffee-room your last work on the Vital Principle, which, by-the-by, the bookseller assures me is selling immensely among readers as non-professional as myself. Coming into the coffee-room again, I found a gentleman reading the book. I claimed it politely; he as politely tendered his excuse for taking it. We made acquaintance on the spot. The next day we were intimate. He expressed great interest and curiosity about your theory and your experiments. I told him I knew you. You may guess if I described you as less clever in your practice than you are in your writings. And, in short, he came with me to L——, partly to see our flourishing town, principally on my promise to introduce him to you. My mother, you know, has what she calls a *déjeuner* to-morrow—*déjeuner* and dance. You will be there?"

"Thank you for reminding me of her invitation. I will avail myself of it if I can. Your new friend will be present? Who and what is he? A medical student?"

"No, a mere gentleman at ease but seems to have a good deal of general information. Very young; apparently very rich; wonderfully good-looking. I am sure you will like him; everybody must."

"It is quite enough to prepare me to like him that he is a friend of yours." And so we shook hands and parted.

CHAPTER XXIII.

It was late in the afternoon of the following day before I was able to join the party assembled at the merchant's house; it was a villa about two miles out of the town, pleasantly situated, amidst flower-gardens celebrated in the neighborhood for their beauty. The breakfast had been long over; the company was scattered over the lawn; some formed into a dance on the smooth lawn; some seated under shady awnings; others gliding amidst parterres, in which all the glow of color took a glory yet more vivid under the flush of a brilliant sunshine, and the ripple of a soft western breeze. Music, loud and lively, mingled with the laughter of happy children, who formed much the larger number of the party.

Standing at the entrance of an arched trellis, that led from the hardier flowers of the lawn to a rare collection of tropical plants under a lofty glass dome (connecting, as it were, the familiar vegetation of the North with that of the remotest East), with a form that instantaneously caught and fixed my gaze. The entrance of the arcade was covered with parasite creepers, in prodigal luxuriance, of variegated gorgeous tints,—scarlet, golden, purple; and the form, an idealized picture of man's youth fresh from the hand of Nature, stood literally in a frame of blooms.

Never have I seen human face so radiant as that young man's. There was in the aspect an indiscribable something that literally dazzled. As one continued to gaze, it was with surprise; one was forced to acknowledge that in the features themselves there was no faultless regularity; nor was the young man's stature imposing—about the middle height. But the effect of the whole was not less transcendent. Large eyes, unspeakably lustrous; a most harmonious coloring; an expression of contagious animation and joyousness; and the form itself so critically fine, that the welded strength of its sinews was best shown in the lightness and grace of its movements.

He was resting one hand carelessly on the golden locks of a child that had nestled itself against his knees, looking up to his face in that silent loving wonder with which children regard something too strangely beautiful for noisy admiration; he himself was conversing with the host, an old gray-haired, gouty man, propped on his crutched stick, and listening with a look of mournful envy. To the wealth of the old man all the flowers in that garden owed their renewed delight in the summer air and sun. Oh! that his wealth could renew to himself one hour of the youth whose incarnation stood beside him, Lord, indeed, of Creation; its splendor woven into his crown of beauty, its enjoyments subject to his sceptre of hope and gladness.

I was startled by the hearty voice of the merchant's son: "Ah, my dear Fenwick, I was afraid you would not come—you are late. There is the new friend of whom I spoke to you last night; let me now make you acquainted with him." He drew my arm in his, and led me up to the young man, where he stood under the arching flowers, and whom he then introduced to me by the name of Margrave.

Nothing could be more frankly cordial than

Mr. Margrave's manner. In a few minutes I found myself conversing with him familiarly, as if we had been reared in the same home, and sported together in the same playground. His vein of talk was peculiar, off-hand, careless, shifting from topic to topic with a bright rapidity.

He said that he liked the place; proposed to stay in it some weeks; asked my address which I gave to him; promised to call soon at an early hour, while my time was yet free from professional visits. I endeavored, when I went away, to analyze to myself the fascination which this young stranger so notably exercised over all who approached him; and it seemed to me, ever seeking to find material causes for all moral effects, that it rose from the contagious vitality of that rarest of all rare gifts in highly-civilized circles—perfect health; that health which is in itself the most exquisite luxury; which finding happiness in the mere sense of existence, diffuses round it, like an atmosphere, the harmless hilarity of its bright animal being. Health, to the utmost perfection, is seldom known after childhood; health to the utmost cannot be enjoyed by those who overwork the brain, or admit the sure wear and tear of the passions. The creature I had just seen gave me the notion of youth in the golden age of the poets—the youth of the careless Arcadian, before nymph or shepherdess had vexed his heart with a sigh.

CHAPTER XXIV.

THE house I occupied at L—— was a quaint, old-fashioned building—a corner house. One side, in which was the front entrance, looked upon a street which, as there were no shops in it, and it was no direct thoroughfare to the busy centres of the town, was always quiet, and at some hours of the day almost deserted. The other side of the house fronted a lane; opposite to it was the long and high wall of the garden to a Young Ladies' Boarding-School. My stables adjoined the house, abutting on a row of smaller buildings, with little gardens before them, chiefly occupied by mercantile clerks and retired tradesmen. By the lane there was a short and ready access both to the high turnpike-road, and to some pleasant walks through green meadows and along the banks of a river.

This house I had inhabitated since my arrival at L——, and it had to me so many attractions, in a situation sufficiently central to be convenient for patients, and yet free from noise, and favorable to ready outlet into the country for such foot or horse exercise as my professional avocations would allow me to carve for myself out of what the Latin poet calls the "solid day," that I had refused to change it for one better suited to my increased income; but it was not a house which Mrs. Ashleigh would have liked for Lilian. The main objection to it in the eyes of the "genteel" was, that it had formerly belonged to a member of the healing profession, who united the shop of an apotecary to the diploma of a surgeon; but that shop had given the house a special attraction to me; for it had been built out on the side of the house which fronted the lane, occupying the greated portion of a small gravel court, fenced from the road by a low iron palisade, and separated from the body of the house itself by a short and narrow corridor that communicated with the entrance-hall. This shop I turned into a rude study for scientific experiments, in which I generally spent some early hours of the morning, before my visiting patients began to arrive. I enjoyed the stillness of its separation from the rest of the house; I enjoyed the glimpse of the great chest-nut trees, which over-topped the wall of the school-garden; I enjoyed the ease with which, by opening the glazed sash-door, I could get out, if disposed for a short walk, into the pleasant fields; and so completely had I made this sanctuary my own, that not only my man-servant knew that I was never to be disturbed when in it, except by the summons of a patient, but even the house maid was forbidden to enter it with broom or duster, except upon special invitation.

The last thing at night, before retiring to rest, it was the man-servant's business to see that the sash-window was closed, and the gate to the iron palisade locked; but during the daytime I so often went out of the house by that private way that the gate was then very seldom locked, nor the sash-door bolted from within. In the town of L—— there was little apprehension of house-robberies—especially in the daylight—and certainly in this room, cut off from the main building, there was nothing to attract a vulgar cupidity. A few of the apothecary's shelves and cases still remained on the walls, with, here and there, a bottle of some chemical preparation for experiment. Two or three worm-eaten, wooden chairs; two or three shabby old tables; an old walnut-tree bureau, without a lock, into which odds and ends were confusedly thrust, and sundry ugly-looking inventions of mechanical science, were, assuredly, not the articles which a timid proprietor would guard with jealous care from the chances of robbery. It will be seen later why I have been thus prolix in description.

The morning after I had met the young stranger by whom I had been so favorably impressed, I was up as usual, a little before the sun, and long before any of my servants were astir. I went first into the room I have mentioned, and which I shall henceforth designate as my study, opened the window, unlocked the gate, and sauntered for some minutes up and down the silent lane skirting the opposite wall, and overhung by the chestnut-trees rich in the garniture of a glorious summer; then, refreshed for work, I re-entered my study and was soon absorbed in the examination of that now well-known machine, which was then, to me at least, a novelty; invented, if I remember right, by Dubois-Reymond, so distinguished by his researches into the mysteries of organic electricity. It is a wooden cylinder fixed against the edge of a table; on the table two vessels filled with salt and water are so placed that, as you close your hands on the cylinder, the fore-finger of each hand can drop into the water; each of the vessels has a metallic plate, and communicates by wires with a galvanometer with its needle. Now the theory is, that if you clutch the cylinder firmly with the right hand, leaving the left perfectly passive, the needle in the galvanometer will move from west to south; if, in like manner, you exert the left arm, leaving the right arm passive, the needle will deflect from west to north. Hence, it is argued that the electric current is induced through the agency of the nervous system, and that, as human Will produces the muscular contraction requisite, so is it human Will that causes the deflection of the needle.

I imagined that if this theory were substantiated by experiment, the discovery might lead to some sublime and unconjectured secrets of science. For human Will, thus actively effective on the electric current, and all matter, animate or inanimate, having more or less of electricity, a vast field became opened to conjecture. By what series of patient experimental deduction might not science arrive at the solution of problems which the Newtonian law of gravitation does not suffice to solve; and—— But here I halt. At the date which my story has reached my mind never lost itself long in the Cloudland of Guess.

I was dissatisfied with my experiment. The needle stirred, indeed, but erratically, and not in directions which, according to the theory, should correspond to my movement. I was about to dismiss the trial with some uncharitable contempt of the foreign philosopher's dogmas, when I heard a loud ring at my street door. While I paused to conjecture whether my servant was yet up to attend to the door, and which of my patients was the most likely to summon me at so unseasonable an hour, a shadow darkened my window. I looked up, and to my astonishment beheld the brilliant face of Mr. Margrave. The sash to the door was already partially opened; he raised it higher, and walked into the room. "Was it you who rang at the street door, and at this hour?" said I.

"Yes; and observing, after I had rung, that all the shutters were still closed, I felt ashamed of my own rash action, and made off rather than brave the reproachful face of some injured housemaid, robbed of her morning dreams. I turned down that pretty lane—lured by the green of the chestnut-trees—caught sight of you through the window, took courage, and here I am. You forgive me?" While thus speaking he continued to move along the littered floor of the dingy room, with the undulating restlessness of some wild animal in the confines of its den, and he now went on, in short fragmentary sentences, very slightly linked together, but smoothed, as it were, into harmony by a voice musical and fresh as a sky-lark's warble. "Morning dreams, indeed! dreams that waste the life of such a morning. Rosy magnificence of a summer dawn! Do you not pity the fool who prefers to lie a-bed, and to dream rather than to live? What! and you, strong man, with those noble limbs, in this den! Do you not long for a rush through the green of the fields, a bath in the blue of the river?"

Here he came to a pause, standing, still in the grey light of the growing day, with eyes whose joyous lustre forstalled the sun's, and lips which seemed to laugh even in repose.

But presently those eyes, as quick as they were bright, glanced over the walls, the floor, the shelves, the phials, the mechanical inventions, and then rested full on my cylinder fixed to the table. He approached, examined it curiously, asked what it was? I explained. To gratify him, I sat down and renewed my experiment, with equally ill success. The needle, which should have moved from west to south, describing an angle of from 30 deg. to 40 or even 50 deg., only made a few troubled undecided oscillations.

"Tut," cried the young man, "I see what it is; you have a wound in your right hand."

That was true. I had burnt my hand a few days before in a chemical experiment, and the sore had not healed.

"Well," said I, "and what does that matter?"

"Everything; the least scratch in the skin of the hand produces chemical actions on the electric current, independently of your will. Let me try."

He took my place, and in a moment the needle in the galvanometer responded to his grasp on the cylinder, exactly as the inventive philosopher had stated to be the due result of the experiment.

I was startled.

"But how came you, Mr. Margrave, to be so well acquainted with a scientific process little known, and but recently discovered?"

"I well acquainted! not so. But I am fond of all experiments that relate to animal life. Electricity, especially, is full of interest."

On that I drew him out (as I thought), and he talked volubly. I was amazed to find this young man, in whose brain I had conceived thought kept one careless holiday, was evidently familiar with the physical sciences, and especially with chemistry, which was my own study by predilection. But never had I met with a student in whom a knowledge so extensive was mixed up with notions so obsolete or so crotchety. In one sentence he showed that he had mastered some late discovery by Faraday or Liebig; in the next sentence he was talking the wild fallacies of Cardan or Van Helmont. I burst out laughing at some paradox about some sympathetic powders, which he enounced as if it were a recognized truth.

"Pray tell me," said I, "who was your master in physics, for a cleverer pupil never had a more crack-brained teacher."

"No," he answered with his merry laugh, "it is not the teacher's fault. I am a mere parrot; just cry out a few scraps of learning picked up here and there. But, however, I am fond of all researches into Nature; all guesses at her riddles. To tell you the truth, one reason why I have taken to you so heartily is not only that your published work caught my fancy in the dip which I took into its contents (pardon me if I say dip, I never do more than dip into any book), but also because young * * * * tells me that which all whom I have met in this town confirm; viz. that you are one of those few practical chemists who are at once exceedingly cautious and exceedingly bold—willing to try every new experiment, but submitting experiment to rigid tests. Well, I have an experiment running wild in this giddy head of mine, and I want you, some day when at leisure, to catch it, fix it as you have fixed that cylinder: make something of it. I am sure you can."

"What is it?"

"Something akin to the theories in your work. You would replenish or preserve to each special constitution the special substance that may fail to the equilibrium of its health. But you own that in a large proportion of cases the best cure of disease is less to deal with the disease itself than to support and stimulate the whole system, so as to enable Nature to cure the disease and restore the impaired equilibrium by her own agencies. Thus, if you find that in certain cases of nervous debility a substance like nitric acid is efficacious, it is because the nitric acid has a virtue in locking up, as it were, the nervous energy—that is, preventing all undue waste. Again, in some cases of what is commonly called feverish cold, stimulants like ammonia assist Nature itself to get rid of the disorder that oppresses its normal action; and, on the same principle, I apprehend, it is contended that a large average of human lives is saved in those hospitals which have adopted the supporting system of ample nourishment and alcoholic stimulants."

"Your medical learning surprises me," said I, smiling, "and without pausing to notice where it deals somewhat superficially with disputable points in general, and my own theory in particular, I ask you for the deduction you draw from your premises."

"It is simply this: that to all animate bodies, however various, there must be one principle in common—the vital principle itself. What if there be one certain means of recruiting that principle? and what if that secret can be discovered?"

"Pshaw! The old illusion of the mediæval empirics."

"Not so. But the mediæval empirics were great discoverers. You sneer at Van Helmont, who sought, in water, the principle of all things; but Van Helmont discovered in his search those invisible bodies called gases. Now the principle of life must be certainly ascribed to a gas.* And whatever is a gas, chemistry should not despair of producing! But I can argue no longer now—never can argue long at a stretch—we are wasting the morning; and, joy! the sun is up! See! Out! come out! out! and greet the great Life-giver face to face."

I could not resist the young man's invitation. In a few minutes we were in the quiet lane under the glinting chestnut-trees. Margrave was chanting, low, a wild tune—words in a strange language.

"What words are those? no European language, I think; for I know a little of most of the languages which are spoken in our quarter of the globe, at least by its more civilized races."

"Civilized race! What is civilization? Those words were uttered by men who founded empires when Europe itself was not civilized! Hush, is it not a grand old air?" and lifting his eyes towards the sun, he gave vent to a voice clear and deep as a mighty bell! The air was grand—the words had a sonorous swell that suited it, and they seemed to me jubilant and yet solemn. He stopped abruptly, as a path from the lane had led us into the fields, already half-bathed in sunlight—dews glittering on the hedgerows.

"Your song," said I, "would go well with the clash of cymbals or the peal of the organ. I am no judge of melody, but this strikes me as that of a religious hymn."

"I compliment you on the guess. It is a Persian fire-worshipper's hymn to the sun. The dialect is very different from modern Persian. Cyrus the Great might have chanted it on his march upon Babylon."

"And where did you learn it?"

"In Persia itself."

"You have travelled much—learned much—and are so young and so fresh. Is it an impertinent question if I ask whether your

* "According to the views we have mentioned, we must ascribe life to a gas, that is, to an aëriform body."—Liebig, Organic Chemistry, Playfair's translation, p. 363. It is perhaps not less superfluous to add that Liebig does not support the views "according to which life must be ascribed to a gas," than it would be to state had Dugald Stewart been quoted as writing, "According to the views we have mentioned the mind is but a bundle of impressions," that Dugald Stewart was not supporting, but opposing, the views of David Hume. The quotation is merely meant to show, in the shortest possible compass, that there are views entertained by speculative reasoners of our day, which, according to Liebig, would lead to the inference at which Margrave so boldly arrives. Margrave is, however, no doubt, led to his belief by his reminiscences of Van Helmont, to whose discovery of gas he is referring. Van Helmont plainly affirms "that the arterial spirit of our life is of the nature of a gas;" and in the same chapter (on the fiction of elementary complexions and mixtures) says, "Seeing that the spirit of our life, since it is a gas, is most mightily and swiftly affected by any other gas," etc. He repeats the same dogma in his treatise on Long Life, and indeed very generally throughout his writings, observing, in his Chapter on the "Vital Air," that the spirit of life is a salt sharp vapor, made of the arterial blood, etc. Liebig, therefore, in confuting some modern notions as to the nature of contagion by miasma, is leading their reasonings back to that assumption in the dawn of physiological science by which the discoverer of gas exalted into the principle of life the substance to which he first gave the name now so familiarly known. It is nevertheless just to Van Helmont to add that his conception of the vital principle was very far from being as purely materialistic as it would seem to those unacquainted with his writings; for he carefully distinguishes that principle of life which he ascribes to a gas, and by which he means the sensuous animal life, from the intellectual immortal principle of soul. Van Helmont, indeed, was a sincere believer of Divine Revelation. "The Lord Jesus is the way, the truth, and the life," says with earnest humility this daring genius, in that noble Chapter "on the completing of the mind by the 'prayer of silence,' and the loving offering up of the heart, soul, and strength to the obedienee of the Divine will," from which some of the most eloquent of recent philosophers, arguing against materialism, have borrowed largely in support and in ornament of their lofty cause.

parents are yet living, or are you wholly lord of yourself?"

"Thank you for the question—pray make my answer known in the town. Parents I have not—never had."

"Never had parents!"

"Well, I ought rather to say that no parents ever owned me. I am a natural son—a vagabond—a nobody. When I came of age I received an anonymous letter, informing me that a sum—I need not say what—but more than enough for all I need, was lodged at an English banker's in my name; that my mother had died in my infancy; that my father was also dead—but recently; that as I was a child of love, and he was unwilling that the secret of my birth should ever be traced, he had provided for me, not by will, but in his life, by a sum consigned to the trust of the friend who now wrote to me; I need give myself no trouble to learn more; faith, I never did. I am young, healthy, rich—yes, rich! Now you know all, and you had better tell it, that I may win no man's courtesy and no maiden's love upon false pretences. I have not even a right, you see, to the name I bear. Hist! let me catch that squirrel."

With what a panther-like bound he sprang! The squirrel eluded his grasp, and was up the oak-tree; in a moment he was up the oak-tree too. In amazement I saw him rising from bough to bough;—saw his bright eyes and glittering teeth through the green leaves; presently I heard the sharp piteous cry of the squirrel—echoed by the youth's merry laugh—and down, through that maze of green, Margrave came, dropping on the grass and bounding up, as Mercury migh have bounded with his wings at his heels.

"I have caught him—what pretty brown eyes!"

Suddenly the gay expression of his face changed to that of a savage; the squirrel had wrenched itself half-loose, and bitten him. The poor brute! In an instant its neck was wrung—its body dashed on the ground; and that fair young creature, every feature quivering with rage, was stamping his foot on his victim again and again! it was horrible. I caught him by the arm indignantly. He turned round on me like a wild beast disturbed from its prey. His teeth set, his hand lifted, his eyes like balls of fire.

"Shame!" said I, calmly; "shame on you!"

He continued to gaze on me a moment or so; his eye glaring—his breath panting—and then, as if mastering himself with an involuntary effort, his arm dropped to his side, and he said quite humbly, "I beg your pardon; indeed I do. I was beside myself for a moment; I cannot bear pain;" and he looked in deep compassion for himself at his wounded hand. "Venomous brute!" And he stamped again on the body of the squirrel, already crushed out of shape.

I moved away in disgust, and walked on.

But presently I felt my arm softly drawn aside, and a voice, dulcet as the coo of a dove, stole its way into my ears. There was no resisting the charm with which this extraordinary mortal could fascinate even the hard and the cold; nor them, perhaps, the least. For as you see in extreme old age, when the heart seems to have shrunk into itself, and to leave but meagre and nipped affections for the nearest relations if grown up, the indurated egotism softens at once towards a playful child; or as you see in middle life, some misanthrope, whose nature has been soured by wrong and sorrow, shrink from his own species, yet make friends with inferior races and respond to the caress of a dog,—so, for the worldling or the cynic, there was an attraction in the freshness of this joyous favorite of Nature;—an attraction like that of a beautiful child, spoilt and wayward, or of a graceful animal, half docile, half fierce.

"But," said I, with a smile, as I felt all displeasure gone, "such indulgence of passion for such a trifle is surely unworthy a student of philosophy!"

"Trifle," he said, dolorously. "But I tell you it is pain; pain is no trifle. I suffer. Look!"

I looked at the hand, which I took in mine. The bite no doubt had been sharp; but the hand that lay in my own was that which the Greek sculptor gives to a gladiator; not large (the extremities are never large in persons whose strength comes from the just proportion of all the members, rather than the factitious and partial force which continued muscular exertion will give to one part of the frame, to the comparative weakening of the rest), but with the firm knit joints, the solid fingers, the finished nails the massive palm, the supple polished skin, in which we recognize what Natuure designs the human hand to be—the skilled, swift, mightier doer of those marvels which win Nature herself from the wilderness.

"It is strange," said I, thoughtfully; "but your susceptibility to suffering confirms my opinion, which is different from the popular belief, viz., that pain is most acutely felt by those in whom the animal organization being perfect, and the sense of vitality exquisitely keen, every injury or lesion finds the whole system rise, as it were, to repel the mischief and communicate the consciousness of it to all those nerves which are the sentinels to the garrison of life. Yet my theory is scarcely borne out by general fact. The Indian savages must have a health as perfect as yours; a nervous system as fine. Witness their marvellous accuracy of ear, of eye, of scent, probably also of touch, yet they are indifferent to physical pain; or must I mortify your pride by saying that they have some moral quality defective in you which enables them to rise superior to it?"

"The Indian savages," said Margrave, sullenly, "have not a health as perfect as mine, and in what you call vitality—the blissful consciousness of life—they are as sticks and stones compared to me."

"How do you know?"

"Because I have lived with them. It is a fallacy to suppose that the savage has a health superior to that of the civilized man,—if the civilized man be but temperate;—and even if not, he has the stamina but can resist for years the effect of excesses which would destroy the savage in a month. As to the savage's fine perceptions of sense, such do not come from exquisite equilibrium of system, but are hereditary attributes transmitted from race to race, and strengthened by training from infancy. But is a pointer stronger and healthier than a mastiff, because the pointer through long descent and early teaching creeps stealthily to his game and stands to it motionless? I will talk of this later; now I suffer! Pain, pain! Has life any ill but pain?"

It so happened that I had about me some roots of the white lily which I meant, before returning home, to leave with a patient suffering from one of those acute local inflammations, in which that simple remedy often affords great relief. I cut up one of these roots, and bound the cooling leaves to the wounded hand with my handkerchief.

"There," said I. "Fortunately, if you feel pain more sensibly than others, you will recover from it more quickly."

And in a few minutes my companion felt perfectly relieved, and poured out his gratitude with an extravagance of expression and a beaming delight of countenance which positively touched me.

"I almost feel," said I, "as I do when I have stilled an infant's wailing, and restored it smiling to its mother's breast."

"You have done so. I am an infant, and Nature is my mother. Oh, to be restored to the full joy of life, the scent of wild flowers, the song of birds, and this air—summer air—summer air!"

I know not why it was, but at that moment, looking at him and hearing him, I rejoiced that Lilian was not at L——.

"But I came out to bathe. Can we not bathe in that stream?"

"No. You would derange the bandage round your hand; and for all bodily ills, from the least to the gravest, there is nothing like leaving Nature at rest the moment we have hit on the means which assist her own efforts at cure."

"I obey, then; but I so love the water."

"You swim, of course?"

"Ask the fish if it swim. Ask the fish if it can escape me! I delight to dive down—down; to plunge after the startled trout, as an otter does; and then to get amongst those cool, fragrant reeds and bulrushes, or that forest of emerald weed which one sometimes find waving under clear rivers. Man! man! could you live but an hour of my life you would know how horrible a thing it is to die!"

"Yet the dying do not think so; they pass away calm and smiling, as you will one day."

"I—I! die one day—die!" and he sank on the grass, and buried his face amongst the herbage, sobbing aloud.

Before I could get through half a dozen words, meant to soothe, he had once more bounded up, dashed the tears from his eyes, and was again singing some wild, barbaric chant. Abstracting itself from the appeal to its outward sense by melodies of which the language was unknown, my mind soon grew absorbed in meditative conjectures on the singular nature, so wayward: so impulsive, which had forced intimacy on a man grave and practical as myself.

I was puzzled how to reconcile so passionate a childishness, so undisciplined a want of self-control, with an experience of mankind so extended by travel, with an education, desultory and irregular indeed, but which must, at some time or other, have been familiarized to severe reasonings and laborious studies. In Margrave there seemed to be wanting that mysterious something which is needed to keep our faculties, however severally brilliant, harmoniously linked together—as the string by which a child mechanically binds the wild flowers it gathers; shaping them at choice into the garland or the chain.

CHAPTER XXV.

My intercourse with Margrave grew habitual and familiar. He came to my house every morning before sunrise; in the evenings we were again brought together: sometimes in the houses to which we were both invited, sometimes at his hotel, sometimes in my own home.

Nothing more perplexed me than his aspect of extreme youthfulness, contrasted with the extent of the travels, which, if he were to be believed, had left little of the known world unexplored. One day I asked him, bluntly, how old he was?

"How old do I look? How old should you suppose me to be?"

"I should have guessed you to be about twenty, till you spoke of having come of age some years ago."

"Is it a sign of longevity when a man looks much younger than he is?"

"Conjoined with other signs, certainly!"

"Have I the other signs?"

"Yes, a magnificent, perhaps a matchless, constitutional organization. But you have evaded my question as to your age; was it an impertinence to put it?"

"No. I came of age—let me see—three years ago."

"So long since? Is it possible? I wish I had your secret!"

"Secret! What secret?"

"The secret of preserving so much of boyish freshness in the wear and tear of man-like passions and man-like thoughts."

"You are still young yourself — under forty?"

"Oh, yes! some years under forty."

"And Nature gave you a grander frame and a finer symmetry of feature than she bestowed on me."

"Pooh! pooh! You have the beauty that must charm the eyes of woman, and that beauty in its sunny forenoon of youth. Happy man! if you love—and wish to be sure that you are loved again."

"What you call love—the unhealthy sentiment, the feverish folly—I left behind me, I think for ever, when—"

"Ay, indeed—when?"

"I came of age!"

"Hoary cynic! and you despise love! So did I once. Your time may come."

"I think not. Does any animal, except man, love its fellow she-animal as man loves woman?"

"As man loves woman? No, I suppose not."

"And why should the subject animals be wiser than their king? But, to return—you would like to have my youth and my careless enjoyment of youth?"

"Can you ask—who would not?" Margrave looked at me for a moment with unusual seriousness, and then, in the abrupt changes common to his capricious temperament, began to sing softly one of those barbaric chants—a chant, different from any I had heard him sing before—made either by the modulation of his voice or the nature of the tune—so sweet that, little as music generally affected me, this thrilled to my very heart's core. I drew closer and closer to him, and murmured when he paused,

"Is not that a love-song?"

"No," said he, "it is the song by which the serpent-charmer charms the serpent."

CHAPTER XXVI.

Increased intimacy with my new acquaintance did not diminish the charm of his society, though it brought to light some startling defects, both in his mental and moral organization. I have before said that his knowledge, though it had swept over a wide circuit and dipped into curious, unfrequented recesses, was desultory and erratic. It certainly was not that knowledge, sustained and aspiring, which the poet assures us is "the wing on which we mount to heaven." So, in his faculties themselves there were singular inequalities, or contradictions. His power of memory in some things seemed prodigious, but when examined it was seldom accurate; it could apprehend, but did not hold together with a binding grasp what metaphysicians call "complex ideas." He thus seemed unable to put it to any steadfast purpose in the sciences of which it retained, vaguely and loosely, many recondite principles. For the sublime and beautiful in literature he had no taste whatever. A passionate lover of nature, his imagination had no response to the arts by which nature is expressed or idealized; wholly unaffected by poetry or painting. Of the fine arts, music alone attracted and pleased him. His conversation was often eminently suggestive, touching on much, whether in books or mankind, that set one thinking, but I never remember him to have uttered any of those lofty or tender sentiments which form the connecting links between youth and genius. For if poets sing to the young, and the young hail their own interpreters in poets, it is because the tendency of both is to idealize the realities of life; finding everywhere in the Real a something that is noble or fair, and making the fair yet fairer, and the noble nobler still.

In Margrave's character there seemed no special vices, no special virtues; but a wonderful vivacity, joyousness, animal good humor. He was singularly temperate, having a dislike to wine, perhaps from that purity of taste which belongs to health absolutely perfect. No healthful child likes alcohols, no animal, except man, prefers wine to water.

But his main moral defect seemed to me, in a want of sympathy, even where he professed attachment. He who could feel so acutely for himself, be unmanned by the bite of a squirrel, and sob at the thought that he should one day die, was as callous to the sufferings of another as a deer who deserts and butts from him a wounded comrade.

I give an instance of this hardness of heart where I should have least expected to find it in him.

He had met and joined me as I was walking to visit a patient on the outskirts of the town, when we fell in with a group of children, just let loose for an hour or two from their day-school. Some of these children joyously recognized him as having played with them at their homes; they ran up to him, and he seemed as glad as themselves at the meeting.

He suffered them to drag him along with them, and became as merry and sportive as the youngest of the troop.

"Well," said I, laughing, "if you are going to play at leap-frog, pray don't let it be on the high road, or you will be run over by carts and draymen; see that meadow just in front to the left—off with you there!"

"With all my heart," cried Margrave, "while you pay your visit. Come along, boys."

A little urchin, not above six years old, but who was lame, began to cry, he could not run,—he should be left behind.

Margrave stooped. "Climb on my shoulder little one, and I'll be your horse."

The child dried its tears, and delightedly obeyed.

"Certainly," said I to myself, "Margrave, after all, must have a nature as gentle as it is simple. What other young man, so courted by all the allurements that steal innocence from pleasure, would stop in the thoroughfares to play with children?"

The thought had scarcely passed through my mind when I heard a scream of agony. Margrave had leaped the railing that divided the meadow from the road, and, in so doing, the poor child, perched on his shoulder, had, perhaps from surprise or fright, loosened its hold and fallen heavily—its cries were piteous. Margrave clapped his hands to his ears—uttered an exclamation of anger—and not even stopping to lift up the boy, or examine what the hurt was, called to the other children to come on, and was soon rolling with them on the grass, and pelting them with daisies. When I came up, only one child remained by the sufferer—his little brother, a year older than himself. The child had fallen on his arm, which was not broken, but violently contused. The pain must have been intense. I carried the child to his home, and had to remain their some time. I did not see Margrave till the next morning. When he then called, I felt so indignant that I could scarcely speak to him. When at last I rebuked him for his inhumanity, he seemed surprised: with difficulty remembered the circumstance, and then merely said—as if it were the most natural confession in the world—

"Oh, nothing so discordant as a child's wail. I hate discords. I am pleased with the company of children; but they must be children who laugh and play. Well! why do you look at me so sternly? What have I said to shock you?"

"Shock me—you shock manhood itself! Go; I cannot talk to you now. I am busy."

But he did not go; and his voice was so sweet, and his ways so winning, that disgust insensibly melted into that sort of forgiveness one accords (let me repeat the illustration) to the deer that forsakes its comrade. The poor thing knows no better. And what a graceful beautiful thing *this* was!

The fascination—I can give it no other name—which Margrave exercised was not confined to me, it was universal—old, young, high, low, man, woman, child, all felt it. Never in Low Town had stranger, even the most distinguished by fame, met with a reception so cordial—so flattering. His frank confession that he was a natural son, far from being to his injury, served to interest people more in him, and to prevent all those inquiries in regard to his connections and antecedents, which would otherwise have been afloat. To be sure, he was evidently rich; at least he had plenty of money. He lived in the best rooms in the principal hotel; was very hospitable; entertained the families with whom he had grown intimate; made them bring their children—music and dancing after dinner.

Among the houses in which he had established familiar acquaintance was that of the mayor of the town, who had bought Dr. Lloyd's collection of subjects in natural history. To that collection the mayor had added largely by a very recent purchase. He had arranged these various specimens, which his last acquisitions had enriched by the interesting carcases of an elephant and a hippopotamus, in a large wooden building contiguous to his dwelling, which had been constructed by a former proprietor (a retired fox-hunter) as a riding-house. And being a man who much affected the diffusion of knowledge, he proposed to open this museum to the admiration of the general public, and at his death, to bequeath it to the Athenæum or Literary Institute of his native town. Margrave, seconded by the influence of the mayor's daughters, had been scarcely three days at L—— before he had persuaded this excellent and public-spirited faunctionary to inaugurate the opening of his museum by the popular ceremony of a ball. A temporary corridor should unite the drawing-rooms, which were on the ground floor, with the building that contained the collection; and thus the fête would be elevated above the frivolous character of a fashionable amusement, and consecrated to the solemnization of an intellectual institute.

Dazzled by the brilliancy of this idea, the mayor announced his intention to give a ball that should include the surrounding neighborhood, and be worthy, in all expensive respects, of the dignity of himself and the occasion. A night had been fixed for the ball—a night that became memorable indeed to me! The entertainment was anticipated with a lively interest, in which even the Hill condescended to share. The Hill did not much patronize mayors in general; but when a mayor gave a ball for a purpose so patriotic, and on a scale so splendid, the Hill liberally acknowledged that Commerce was, on the whole, a thing which the Eminence might, now and then, condescend to acknowledge without absolutely derogating from the rank which Providence had assigned to it amongst the High Places of earth. Accordingly, the Hill was permitted by its Queen to honor the first magistrate of Low Town by a promise to attend his ball. Now, as this festivity had originated in the suggestion of Margrave, so, by a natural association of ideas, every one, in talking of the ball, talked also of Margrave.

The Hill had at first affected to ignore a stranger whose début had been made in the mercantile circle of Low Town. But the Queen of the Hill now said, sententiously, "This new man in a few days has become a Celebrity. It is the policy of the Hill to adopt Celebrities, if the Celebrities pay respect to the Proprieties. Dr. Fenwick is requested to procure Mr. Margrave the advantage of being known to the Hill."

I found it somewhat difficult to persuade Margrave to accept the Hill's condescending overture. He seemed to have a dislike to all societies pretending to aristocratic distinction —a dislike expressed with a fierceness so unwonted, that it made one suppose he had, at some time or other, been subjected to mortification by the supercilious air that blow upon heights so elevated. However, he yielded to my instances, and accompanied me one evening to Mrs. Poyntz's house. The Hill was encamped there for the occasion. Mrs. Poyntz was exeeedingly civil to him, and after a few commonplace speeches, hearing that he was fond of music, consigned him to the caressing care of Miss Brabazon, who was at the head of the musical department in the Queen of the Hill's administration.

Mrs. Poyntz retired to her favorite seat near the window, inviting me to sit beside her; and while she knitted in silence, in silence my eye glanced toward Margrave in the midst of the group assembled round the piano.

Whether he was in more than usually high spirits, or whether he was actuated by a malign and impish desire to upset the established laws of decorum by which the gaieties of the Hill were habitually subdued into a serene and somewhat pensive pleasantness, I know not; but it was not many minutes before the orderly aspect of the place was grotesquely changed.

Miss Brabazon having come to the close of a complicated and dreary sonata, I heard Margrave abruptly ask her if she could play the Tarantella, that famous Neapolitan air which is founded on the legendary belief that the bite of the tarantula excites an irresistible desire to dance. On that high-bred spinster's confession that she was ignorant of the air, and had not even heard of the legend, Margrave said, "Let me play it to you, with variations of my own." Miss Brabazon graciously yielded her place at the instrument. Margrave seated himself—there was great curiosity to hear his performance. Margrave's fingers rushed over the keys, and there was a general start, the prelude was so unlike any known combination of harmonious sounds. Then he began a chant—song I can scarcely call it—words certainly not in Italian, perhaps in some uncivilized tongue, perhaps in impromptu gibberish. And the torture of the instrument now commenced in good earnest: it shrieked, it groaned, wilder and noisier. Beethoven's Storm, roused by the fell touch of a German pianist, were mild in comparison; and the mighty voice, dominating the anguish of the cracking keys, had the full diapason of a chorus. Certainly I am no judge of music, but to my ear the discord was terrific—to the ears of better informed amateurs it seemed ravishing. All were spell-bound; even Mrs. Poyntz paused from her knitting, as the Fates paused from their web at the lyre of Orpheus. To this breathless delight, however, soon succeeded a general desire for movement. To my amazement, I beheld these formal matrons and sober fathers of families forming themselves into a dance, turbulent as a children's ball at Christmas.

And when, suddenly desisting from his music, Margrave started up, caught the skeleton hand of lean Miss Brabazon, and whirled her into the centre of the dance, I could have fancied myself at a witch's sabbat. My eye turned in scandalized alarm towards Mrs. Poyntz. That great creature seemed as much astounded as myself. Her eyes were fixed on the scene in a stare of positive stupor. For the first time, no doubt, in her life, she was overcome, deposed, dethroned. The awe of her presence was literally whirled away. The dance ceased as suddenly as it had begun. Darting from the galvanized mummy whom he had selected as his partner, Margrave shot to Mrs. Poyntz's side, and said, "Ten thousand pardons for quitting you so soon, but the clock warns me that I have an engagement elsewhere." In another moment he was gone.

The dance halted, people seemed slowly returning to their senses, looking at each other bashfully and ashamed.

"I could not help it, dear," sighed Miss Brabazon at last, sinking into a chair, and casting her deprecating, fainting eyes upon the hostess.

"It is witchcraft," said fat Mrs. Bruce, wiping her forehead.

"Witchcraft!" echoed Mrs. Poyntz; "it does indeed look like it. An amazing and portentous exhibition of animal spirits, and not to be endured by the Proprieties. Where on earth can that young savage have come from?"

"From savage lands," said I. "So he says."

"Do not bring him here again," said Mrs. Poyntz. "He would soon turn the Hill topsy-turvy. But how charming! I should like to see more of him," she added, in an under voice, "if he would call on me some morning, and not in the presence of those for whose Proprieties I am responsible. Jane must be out in her ride with the Colonel."

Margrave never again attended the patrician festivities of the Hill. Invitations were poured upon him, especially by Miss Brabazon and the other old maids, but in vain.

"Those people," said he, "are too tamed and civilized for me; and so few young persons among them. Even that girl Jane is only young on the surface; inside, as old as the World or her mother. I like youth, real youth—I am young, I am young!"

"And, indeed, I observed he would attach himself to some young person, often to some child, as if with cordial and special favor, yet for not more than an hour or so, never distinguishing them by the same preference when he next met them. I made that remark to him, in rebuke of his fickleness, one evening when he had fonnd me at work on my Ambitious Book, reducing to rule and measure the Laws of Nature.

"It is not fickleness," said he, "it is necessity."

"Necessity! Explain yourself."

"I seek to find what I have not found," said he; "it is my necessity to seek it, and among the young; and disappointed in one, I turn to the other. Necessity again. But find it at last I must."

"I suppose you mean what the young usually seek in the young; and if, as you said the other day, you have left love behind you, you now wander back to re-find it."

"Tush! If I may judge by the talk of young fools, love may be found every day by him who looks out for it. What I seek is among the rarest of all discoveries. You might aid me to find it, and in so doing aid yourself to a knowledge far beyond all that your formal experiments can bestow."

"Prove your words, and command my services," said I, smiling somewhat disdainfully.

"You told me that you had examined into the alleged phenomena of animal magnetism, and proved some persons who pretend to the gift which the Scotch call second sight to be bungling impostors. You were right. I have seen the clairvoyants who drive their trade in this town; a common gipsy could beat them in their own calling. But your experience must have shown you that there are certain temperaments in which the gift of the Pythoness is stored, unknown to the possessor, undetected by the common observer; but the signs of which should be as apparent to the modern physiologists as they were to the ancient priest."

"I at least, as a physiologist, am ignorant of the signs—what are they?"

"I should despair of making you comprehend them by mere verbal description. I could guide your observation to distinguish them unerringly were living subjects before us. But not one in a million has the gift to an extent available for the purposes to which the wise would apply it. Many have imperfect glimpses, few, few indeed, the unveiled, lucent sight. They who have but the imperfect glimpses, mislead and dupe the minds that consult them, because, being sometimes marvellousľy right, they excite a credulous belief in their general accuracy; and as they are but translators of dreams in their own brain, their assurances are no more to be trusted than are the dreams of commonplace sleepers. But where the gift exists to perfection, he who knows how to direct and to profit by it should be able to discover all that he desires to know for the guidance and perservation of his own life. He will be forewarned of every danger, forearmed in the means by which danger is avoided. For the eye of the true Pythoness matter has no obstruction, space no confines, time no measurement."

"My dear Magrave, you may well say that creatures so gifted are rare; and, for my part, I would as soon search for a unicorn, as, to use your affected expression, for a Pythoness."

"Nevertheless, whenever there come across the course of your practice some young creature to whom all the evil of the world is as yet unknown, to whom the ordinary cares and duties of the world are strange and unwelcome; who from the earliest dawn of reason has loved to sit apart and to muse; before whose eyes visions pass unsolicited; who converses with those who are not dwellers on the earth, and beholds in the space landscapes which the earth does not reflect—"

"Margrave, Margrave! of whom do you speak?'

"Whose frame, though exquisitely sensitive, has still a health and a soundness in which you recognize no disease; whose mind has a truthfulness that you know cannot deceive you, and a simple intelligence too clear to deceive itself; who is moved to a mysterious degree by all the varying aspects of external nature—innocently joyous, or unaccountably sad;—when, I say, such a being comes across your experience, inform me; and the chances are that the true Pythoness is found."

I had listened with vague terror, and with more than one exclamatlon of amazement, to descriptions which brought Lilian Ashleigh before me; and I now sat mute, bewildered, breathless, gazing upon Margrave, and rejoicing that, at least, Lilian he had never seen.

He returned my own gaze steadily, searchingly, and then, breaking into a slight laugh, resumed:

"You call my word 'Pythoness' affected. I know of no better. My recollections of classic anecdote and history are confused and dim; but somewhere I have read or heard that the priests of Delphi were accustomed to travel chiefly into Thrace or Thessaly, in search of the virgins who might fitly administer their oracles, and that the oracles gradually ceased in repute as the priests became unable to discover the organization requisite in the priestesses, and supplied by craft and imposture, or by such imperfect fragmentary developments as belong now to professional clairvoyants, the gifts which Nature failed to afford. Indeed, the demand was one that must have rapidly exhausted so limited a supply. The constant strain upon faculties so wearing to the vital functions in their relentless exercise, under the artful stimulants by which the priests heightened their power, was mortal, and no Pythoness ever retained her life more than three years from the time that her gift was elaborately trained and developed."

"Pooh! I know of no classical authority for the details you so confidently cite. Perhaps some such legends may be found in the Alexandrian Platonists, but those mystics are no authority on such a subject. After all," I added, recovering from my first surprise, or awe, "the Delphic oracles were proverbially ambiguous, and their responses might be read either way; a proof that the priests dictated the verses, though their arts on the unhappy priestess might throw her into real convulsions, and the real convulsions, not the false gift, might shorten her life. Enough of such idle subjects! Yet no! one question more. If you found your Pythoness, what then?"

"What then? Why, through her aid I might discover the process of an experiment which your practical science would assist me to complete."

"Tell me of what kind is your experiment; and precisely because such little science as I possess is exclusively practical, I may assist you without the help of the Pythoness."

Margrave was silent for some minutes, passing his hand several times across his forehead, which was a frequent gesture of his, and then rising, he answered, in listless accents:

"I cannot say more now, my brain is fatigued; and you are not yet in the right mood to hear me. By the way, how close and reserved you are with me!"

"How so?"

"You never told me that you were engaged to be married. You leave me, who thought to have won your friendship, to hear what concerns you so intimately from a comparative stranger."

"Who told you?"

"That woman with eyes that pry and lips that scheme, to whose house you took me."

"Mrs. Poyntz! is it possible? When?"

"This afternoon. I met her in the street—she stopped me, and, after some unmeaning talk, asked 'if I had seen you lately; if I did not find you very absent and distracted; no wonder—you were in love. The young lady was away on a visit, and wooed by a dangerous rival.'"

"Wooed by a dangerous rival!"

"Very rich, good-looking, young. Do you fear him? You turn pale."

"I do not fear, except so far as he who loves truly, loves humbly, and fears not that another may be preferred, but that another may be worthier of preference than himself. But that Mrs. Poyntz should tell you all this does amaze me. Did she mention the name of the young lady?"

"Yes; Lilian Ashleigh. Henceforth be more frank with me. Who knows? I may help you. Adieu!"

CHAPTER XXVII.

WHEN Margrave had gone, I glanced at the clock—not yet nine. I resolved to go at once to Mrs. Poyntz. It was not an evening on which she received, but doubtless she would see me. She owed me an explanation. How thus carelessly divulge a secret she had been enjoined to keep? and this rival, of whom I was ignorant? It was no longer a matter of wonder that Margrave should have described Lilian's peculiar idiosyncrasies in his sketch of his fabulous Pythoness. Doubtless, Mrs. Poyntz had, with unpardonable levity of indiscretion, revealed all of which she disapproved in my choice. But for what object? Was this her boasted friendship for me? Was it consistent with the regard she professed for Mrs. Ashleigh and Lilian? Occupied by these perplexed and indignant thoughts, I arrived at Mrs. Poyntz's house, and was admitted to her presence. She was fortunately alone; her daughter and the Colonel had gone to some party on the Hill. I would not take the hand she held out to me on entrance; seated myself in stern displeasure, and proceeded at once to inquire if she had really betrayed to Mr. Margrave the secret of my engagement to Lilian.

"Yes, Allen Fenwick; I have this day told, not only Mr. Margrave, but every person I met who is likely to tell it to some one else, the secret of your engagement to Lilian Ashleigh. I never promised to conceal it; on the contrary, I wrote word to Anne Ashleigh that I would therein act as my own judgment counselled me. I think my words to you were that 'public gossip was sometimes the best security for the completion of private engagements.'"

"Do you mean that Mrs. or Miss Ashleigh recoils from the engagement with me, and that I should meanly compel them both to fulfil it by calling in the public to censure them—if—if——Oh, madam, this is worldly artifice indeed!"

"Be good enough to listen to me quietly. I have never yet showed you the letter to Mrs. Ashley, written by Lady Haughton, and delivered by Mr. Vigors. That letter I will now show to you; but before doing so I must enter into a preliminary explanation. Lady Haughton is one of those women who love power, and cannot obtain it except through wealth and station—by her own intellect never obtain it. When her husband died she was reduced from an income of twelve thousand a year to a jointure of twelve hundred, but with the exclusive guardianship of a young son, a minor, and adequate allowances for the charge; she continued, therefore, to preside as mistress over the establishments in town and country; still had the administration of her son's wealth and rank. She stinted his education, in order to maintain her ascendency over him. He became a brainless prodigal—spendthrift alike of health and fortune. Alarmed, she saw that, probably, he would die young and a beggar; his only hope of reform was in marriage. She reluctantly resolved to marry him to a penniless, well-born, soft-minded young lady whom she knew she could control; just before this marriage was to take place he was killed by a fall from his horse. The Haughton estate passed to his cousin, the luckiest young man alive; the same Ashleigh Sumner who had already succeeded, in default of male issue, to poor Gilbert Ashleigh's landed possessions. Over this young man Lady Haughton could expect no influence. She would be a stranger in his house. But she had a niece! Mr. Vigors assured her the niece was beautiful. And if the niece could become Mrs. Ashleigh Sumner, then Lady Haughton would be a less unimportant Nobody in the world, because she would still have her nearest relation in a Somebody at Haughton Park. Mr. Vigors had his own pompous reasons for approving an alliance which he might help to accomplish. The first step towards that alliance was obviously to bring into reciprocal attraction the natural charms of the young lady and the acquired merits of the young gentleman. Mr. Vigors could easily induce his ward to pay a visit to Lady Haughton, and Lady Haughton had only to extend her invitations to her niece; hence the letter to Mrs. Ashleigh, of which Mr. Vigors was the bearer, and hence my advice to you, of which you can now understand the motive. Since you thought Lilian Ashleigh the only woman you could love, and since I thought there were other women in the world who might do as well for Ashleigh Sumner, it seemed to me fair for all parties that Lilian should not go to Lady Haughton's in ignorance of the sentiments with which she had inspired you. A girl can seldom be sure that she loves until she is sure that she is loved. And now," added Mrs. Poyntz, rising and walking across the room to her bureau—"now I will show you Lady Haughton's invitation to Mrs. Ashleigh. Here it is!"

I ran my eye over the letter, which she thrust into my hand, resuming her knitwork while I read.

The letter was short, couched in conventional terms of hollow affection. The writer blamed herself for having so long neglected her brother's widow and child; her heart had been wrapped up too much in the son she had lost; that loss had made her turn to the ties of blood still left to her; she had heard much of Lilian from their common friend, Mr Vigors; she longed to embrace so charming a niece. Then followed the invitation and the postscript. The postscript ran thus, so far as I can remember: "Whatever my own grief at my irreparable bereavement, I am no egotist. I keep my sorrow to myself. You will find some pleasant guests at my house, among others our joint connection, young Ashleigh Sumner."

"Women's postscripts are proverbial for their significance," said Mrs. Poyntz, when I had concluded the letter and laid it on the table; "and if I did not at once show you this hypocritical effusion, it was simply because at the name Ashleigh Sumner its object became transparent, not perhaps to poor Anne Ashleigh nor to innocent Lilian, but to my knowledge of the parties concerned, as it ought to be to that shrewd intelligence which you derive partly from nature, partly from the insight into life which a true physician cannot fail to acquire And if I know anything of you, you would have romantically said, had you seen the letter at first, and understood its covet intentiou, 'Let me not shackle the choice of the woman I love, and to whom an alliance so coveted in the eyes of the world might, if she were left free, be proffered.'"

"I should not have gathered from the postscript all that you see in it, but had its purport been so suggested to me, you are right, I should have so said. Well, and as Mr. Margrave tells me that you informed him that I have a rival, I am now to conclude that the rival is Mr. Ashleigh Summer?"

"Has not Mrs. Ashleigh or Lilian mentioned him in writing to you?"

"Yes, both; Lilian very slightly; Mrs. Ashleigh with some praise, as a young man of high character and very courteous to her."

"Yet, though I asked you to come and tell me who were the guests at Lady Haughton's, you never did so."

"Pardon me; but of the guests I thought nothing, and letters addressed to my heart seemed to me too sacred to talk about. And Ashleigh Summer then courts Lilian! How do you know?"

"I know everything that concerns me; and here, the explanation is simple. My aunt, Lady Delafield, is staying with Lady Haughton. Lady Delafield is one of the women of fashion who shine by their own light; Lady Haughton shines by borrowed light, and borrows every ray she can find."

"And Lady Delafield writes you word——"

"That Ashleigh Summer is caught by Lilian's beauty."

"And Lilian herself——"

"Women like Lady Delafield do not readily believe that any girl could refuse Ashleigh Summer; considered in himself, he is steady and good-looking; considered as owner of Kirby Hall and Haughton Park, he has, in the eyes of any sensible mother, the virtues of Cato and the beauty of Antinous."

I pressed my hand to my heart—close to my heart lay a letter from Lilian—and there was no word in that letter which showed that *her* heart was gone from mine. I shook my head gently, and smiled in confiding triumph.

Mrs. Poyntz surveyed me with a bent brow and a compressed lip.

"I understand your smile," she said, ironically. "Very likely Lilian may be quite untouched by this young man's admiration, but Annie Ashleigh may be dazzled by so brilliant a prospect for her daughter. And, in short, I thought it desirable to let your engagement be publicly known throughout the town to-day; that information will travel—it will reach Ashleigh Summer through Mr. Vigors, or others in this neighborhood, with whom I know that he corresponds. It will bring affairs to a crisis, and before it may be too late. I think it well that Ashleigh Summer should leave that house; if he leave it for good, so much the better. And, perhaps, the sooner Lilian returns to L—— the lighter your own heart will be."

"And for these reasons you have published the secret of—— "

"Your engagement? Yes. Prepare to be congratulated wherever you go. And now, if you hear either from mother or daughter, that Ashleigh Summer has proposed, and been, let us say, refused, I do not doubt that, in the pride of your heart, you will come and tell me."

"Rely upon it, I will; but before I take leave, allow me to ask, why you described to a young man like Mr. Margrave—whose wild and strange humors you have witnessed and not approved—any of those traits of character in Miss Ashleigh which distinguish her from other girls of her age?"

"I? You mistake. I said nothing to him of her character. I mentioned her name, and said she was beautiful, that was all."

"Nay, you said that she was fond of musing, of solitude; that in her fancies she believed in the reality of visions which might flit before her eyes as they flit before the eyes of all imaginative dreamers."

"Not a word did I say to Mr. Margrave of such peculiarities in Lilian; not a word more than what I have told you, on my honor!"

Still incredulous, but disguising my incredulity with that convenient smile by which we accomplish so much of the polite dissimulation indispensable to the decencies of civilized life, I took my departure, returned home, and wrote to Lilian.

———

CHAPTER XXVIII.

The conversation with Mrs. Poyntz left my mind restless and disquieted, I had no doubt, indeed, of Lilian's truth, but could I be sure that the attentions of a young man, with advantages of fortune, so brilliant, would not force on her thoughts the contrast of the humbler lot and the duller walk of life in which she had accepted as companion a man removed from her romantic youth less by disparity of years than by gravity of pursuits? And would my suit now be as welcomed as it had been by a mother even so unworldly as Mrs. Ashleigh? Why, too, should both mother and daughter have left me so unprepared to hear that I had a rival? Why not have implied some consoling assurance that such rivalry need not cause me alarm? Lilian's letters, it is true, touched but little on any of the persons round her—they were filled with the outpourings of an ingenuous heart, colored by the glow of a golden fancy. They were written as if in the wide world we two stood apart alone, consecrated from the crowd by the love that, in linking us together, had hallowed each to the other. Mrs. Ashleigh's letters were more general and diffusive, detailed the habits of the household, sketched the guests, intimated her continued fear of Lady Haughton, but had said nothing more of Mr. Ashleigh Sumner than I had repeated to Mrs. Poyntz. However, in my letter to Lilian I related the intelligence that had reached me, and impatiently I awaited her reply.

Three days after the interview with Mrs. Poyntz, and two days before the long-anticipated event of the mayor's ball, I was summoned to attend a nobleman who had lately been added to my list of patients, and whose residence was about twelve miles from L——. The nearest way was through Sir Philip Derval's park. I went on horseback, and proposed to stop on the way to inquire after the steward, whom I had seen but once since his fit, and that was two days after it, when he called himself at my house to thank me for my attendance, and to declare that he was quite recovered.

As I rode somewhat fast through the park, I come, however, upon the steward, just in front of the house. I reined in my horse and accosted him. He looked very cheerful.

"Sir," said he, in a whisper, "I have heard from Sir Philip; his letter is dated since—since;—my good woman told you what I saw;—well, since then. So that it must have been all a delusion of mine, as you told her. And yet, well—well—we will not talk of it, doctor. But I hope you have kept the secret. Sir Philip would not like to hear of it, if he comes back."

"Your secret is quite safe with me. But is Sir Philip likely to come back?"

"I hope so, doctor. His letter is dated Paris, and that's nearer home than he has been for many years; and—but bless me—some one is coming out of the house? a young gentleman! Who can it be?"

I looked, and to my surprise I saw Margrave descending the stately stairs that led from the front door. The steward turned towards him, and I mechanically followed, for I was curious to know what had brought Margrave to the house of the long-absent traveller.

It was easily explained. Mr. Margrave had heard at L—— much of the pictures and internal decorations of the mansion. He had, by dint of coaxing (he said, with his enchanting laugh), persuaded the old housekeeper to show him the rooms.

"It is against Sir Philip's positive orders to show the house to any stranger, sir; and the housekeeper has done very wrong," said the steward.

"Pray don't scold her. I dare say Sir Philip would not have refused me a permission he might not give to every idle sight-seer. Fellow-travellers have a freemasonry with each other; and I have been much in the same far countries as himself. I heard of him there, and could tell you more about him, I dare say, than you know yourself."

"You, sir! pray do then."

"The next time I come," said Margrave, gaily; and, with a nod to me, he glided off through the trees of the neighboring grove, along the winding footpath that led to the lodge.

"A very cool gentleman," muttered the steward; "but what pleasant ways he has! You seem to know him, sir. Who is he—may I ask?"

"Mr. Margrave. A visitor at L——, and he has been a great traveller, as he says; perhaps he met Sir Philip abroad."

"I must go and hear what he said to Mrs. Gates; excuse me, sir, but I am so anxious about Sir Philip."

"If it be not too great a favor, may I be allowed the same privilege granted to Mr. Margrave? To judge by the outside of the house, the inside must be worth seeing; still, if it be against Sir Philip's positive orders—"

"His orders were, not to let the Court become a show-houss—to admit none without my consent—but I should be ungrateful indeed, doctor, if I refused that consent to you."

I tied my horse to the rusty gate of the terrace-walk, and followed the steward up the broad stairs of the terrace. The great doors were unlocked. We entered a lofty hall with a domed ceiling; at the back of the hall the grand staircase ascended by a double flight. The design was undoubtedly Vanbrugh's, an architect who, beyond all others, sought the effect of grandeur less in space than in proportion. But Vanbrugh's designs need the relief of costume and movement, and the forms of a more pompous generation, in the bravery of velvets and laces, glancing amid those gilded columns, or descending with stately tread those broad palatial stairs. His halls and chambers are so made for festival and throng, that they become like deserted theatres, inexpressibly desolate, as we miss the glitter of the lamps and the movement of the actors.

The housekeeper had now appeared; a quiet, timid old woman. She excused herself for admitting Margrave—not very intelligibly. It was plain to see that she had, in truth, been unable to resist what the steward termed his "pleasant ways."

As if to escape from a scolding, she talked volubly all the time, bustling nervously through the rooms, along which I followed her guidance with a hushed footstep. The principal apartments were on the ground floor, or rather, a floor raised some ten or fifteen feet above the ground; they had not been modernized since the date in which they were built. Hangings of faded silk; tables of rare marble, and mouldered gliding; comfortless chairs at drill against the walls; pictures, of which connoisseurs alone could estimate the value, darkened by dust or blistered by sun and damp, made a general character of discomfort. On not one room, on not one nook, still lingered some old smile of home.

Meanwhile, I gathered from the housekeeper's rambling answers to questions put to her by the steward, as I moved on, glancing at the pictures, that Margrave's visit that day was not his first. He had been to the house twice before; his ostensible excuse that he was an amateur in pictures (though, as I had before observed, for that department of art he had no taste); but each time he had talked much of Sir Philip. He said that though not personally known to him, he had resided in the same towns abroad, and had friends equally intimate with Sir Philip; but when the steward inquired if the visitor had given any information as to the absentee, it became very clear that Margrave had been rather asking questions than volunteering intelligence.

We had now come to the end of the state apartments, the last of which was a library. "And," said the old woman, "I don't wonder the gentleman knew Sir Philip, for he seemed a scholar, and looked very hard over the books, especially those old ones by the fire-place, which Sir Philip, Heaven bless him, was always poring into."

Mechanically I turned to the shelves by the fireplace, and examined the volumes ranged in that department. I found they contained the works of those writers whom we may class together under the title of mystics—Iamblichus and Plotinus; Swedenborg and Behmen; Sandivogius, Van Helmont, Paracelsus, Cardan. Works, too, were there, by writers less renowned, on astrology, geomancy, chiromancy, etc. I began to understand among what class of authors Margrave had picked up the strange notions with which he was apt to interpolate the doctrines of practical philosophy.

"I suppose this library was Sir Philip's usual sitting-room?" said I.

"No, sir; he seldom sat here. This was his study;" and the old woman opened a small door, masked by false book-backs. I followed her into a room of moderate size, and evidently of much earlier date than the rest of the house. "It is the only room left of an older mansion," said the steward, in answer to my remark. "I have heard it was spared on account of the chimney-piece. But there is a Latin inscription which will tell you all about it. I don't know Latin myself."

The chimney-piece reached to the ceiling. The frieze of the lower part rested on rude stone caryatides; the upper part was formed of oak panels very curiously carved in the geometrical designs favored by the taste prevalent in the reigns of Elizabeth and James, but different from any I have ever seen in the drawings of old houses. And I was not quite unlearned in such matters, for my poor father was a passionate antiquary in all that relates to mediæval art. The design in the oak panels was composed of triangles interlaced with varied ingenuity, and enclosed in circular bands inscribed with the signs of the Zodiac. On the stone frieze supported by the caryatides, immediately under the wood-work, was inserted a metal plate, on which was written, in Latin, a few lines to the effect that "in this room, Simon Forman, the seeker of hidden truth, taking refuge from unjust persecution, made those discoveries in nature which he committed, for the benefit of a wiser age, to the charge of his protector and patron, the worshipful Sir Miles Derval, knight."

Formal! The name was not quite unfamiliar to me; but it was not without an effort that my memory enabled me to assign it to one of the most notorious of those astrologers or soothsayers whom the superstition of an earlier age alternately persecuted and honored.

The general character of the room was more cheerful than the statelier chambers I had hitherto passed through, for it had still the look of habitation. The arm-chair by the fire-place; the knee-hole writing-table beside it; the sofa near the recess of a large bay-window, with book-prop and candlestick screwed to its back; maps, coiled in their cylinders, ranged under the cornice; low strong safes, skirting two sides of the room, and apparently intended to hold papers and title-deeds; seals carefully affixed to their jealous locks. Placed on the top of these old-fashioned receptacles were articles familiar to modern use; a fowling-piece here; fishing-rods there; two or three simple flower vases; a pile of music books; a box of crayons. All in this room seemed to speak of residence and ownership—of the idiosyncrasies of a lone single man, it is true, but of a man of one's own time—a country gentleman of plain habits but not uncultivated tastes.

I moved to the window; it opened by a sash upon a large balcony, from which a wooden stair wound to a little garden, not visible in front of the house, surrounded by a thick grove of evergreens, through which one broad vista was cut; and that vista was closed by a view of the mausoleum.

I stepped out into the garden—a patch of sward with a fountain in the centre—and parterres, now more filled with weeds than flowers. At the left corner was a tall wooden summer-house or pavilion—its door wide open. "Oh, that's where Sir Philip used to study many a long summer's night," said the steward.

"What! in that damp pavilion?"

"It was a pretty place enough then, sir; but it is very old. They say as old as the room you have just left."

"Indeed, I must look at it, then."

The walls of this summer-house had once

been painted in the arabesques of the Renaissance period; but the figures were now scarcely traceable. The wood-work had started in some places, and the sunbeams stole through the chinks and played on the floor, which was formed from old tiles quaintly tesselated and in triangular patterns, similar to those I had observed in the chimney-piece. The room in the pavillion was large, furnished with old worm-eaten tables and settles.

"It was not only here that Sir Philip studied, but sometimes in the room above," said the steward.

"How do you get to the room above? Oh! I see; a staircase in the angle." I ascended the stairs with some caution, for they were crooked and decayed; and, on entering the room above, comprehended at once why Sir Philip had favored it.

The cornice of the ceiling rested on pilasters, within which the compartments were formed into open unglazed arches, surrounded by a railed balcony, Through these arches, on three sides of the room, the eye commanded a magnificent extent of prospect. On the fourth side the view was bounded by the mausoleum. In this room was a large telescope, and on stepping into the balcony, I saw that a winding stair mounted thence to a platform on the top of the pavilion—perhaps once used as an observatory by Forman himself.

"The gentleman who was here to-day was very much pleased with this look-out, sir," said the house-keeper.

"Who would not be? I suppose Sir Philip has a taste for astronomy."

"I dare say, sir," said the steward, looking grave; ' he likes most out-of-the-way things."

The position of the sun now warned me that my time pressed, and that I should have to ride fast to reach my new patient at the hour appointed. I therefore hastened back to my horse, and spurred on, wondering whether, in the chain of association which so subtly links our pursuits in manhood to our impressions in childhood, it was the Latin inscription on the chimney-piece that had originally biassed Sir Philip Derval's literary taste towards the mystic jargon of the books at which I had contemptuously glanced.

CHAPTER XXIX.

I DID not see Margrave the following day, but the next morning, a little after sunrise, he walked into my study, according to his ordinary habit.

"So you know something about Sir Philip Derval?" said I. "What sort of a man is he?"

"Hateful!" cried Margrave; and then checking himself, burst out into his merry laugh. "Just like my exaggerations! I am not acquainted with anything to his prejudice. I came across his track once or twice in the East. Travellers are always apt to be jealous of each other."

"You are a strange compound of cynicism and credulity. But I should have fancied that you and Sir Philip would have been congenial spirits, when I found, among his favorite books, Van Helmont and Paracelsus. Perhaps you, too, study Swedenborg, or, worse still, Ptolemy and Lilly?"

"Astrologers? No! They deal with the future! I live for the day; only I wish the day never had a morrow!"

"Have you not, then, that vague desire for the *something beyond;* that not unhappy, but grand discontent with the limits of the immediate Present, from which man takes his passion for improvement and progress, and from which some sentimental philosophers have deduced an argument in favor of his destined immortality?"

"Eh!" said Margrave, with as vacant a stare as that of a peasant whom one has addressed in Hebrew. "What farago of words is this? I do not comprehend you."

"With your natural abilities," I asked with interest, "do you never feel a desire for fame?"

"Fame? Certainly not. I cannot even understand it!"

"Well, then, would you have no pleasure in the thought that you had rendered a service to humanity?"

Margrave looked bewildered: after a moment's pause, he took from the table a piece of bread that chanced to be there, opened the window, and threw the crumbs into the lane. The sparrows gathered round the crumbs.

"Now," said Margrave, "the sparrows come to that dull pavement for the bread that recruits their lives in this world; do you believe that one sparrow would be silly enough to fly to a house-top for the sake of some benefit to other sparrows, or to be chirruped about after he was dead? I care for science as the sparrow cares for bread; it may help me to something good for my own life; and as for fame and humanity, I care for them as the sparrow cares for the general interest and posthumous approbation of sparrows!"

"Margrave; there is one thing in you that perplexes me more than all else—human puzzle as you are—in your many eccentricities and self-contradictions."

"What is that one thing in me most perplexing?"

"This; that in your enjoyment of Nature you have all the freshness of a child, but when you speak of Man and his objects in the world, you talk in the vein of some worn-out and hoary cynic. At such times, were I to close my eyes, I should say to myself, 'What weary old man is thus venting his spleen against the ambition which has failed, and the love which has forsaken him?' Outwardly the very personation of youth, and revelling like a butterfly in the warmth of the sun and the tints of the herbage, why have you none of the golden passions of the young? their bright dreams of some impossible love—their sublime enthusiasm for some unattainable glory? The sentiment you have just clothed in the illustration by which you place yourself on a level with the sparrows is too mean and too gloomy to be genuine at your age. Misanthropy is among the dismal fallacies or graybeards. No man, till man's energies leave him, can divorce himself from the bonds of our social kind."

"Our kind--your kind, possibly! But I——." He swept his hand over his brow, and resumed, in strange, absent, and wistful accents: "I wonder what it is that is wanting here, and of which at moments I have a dim reminiscence." Again he paused, and gazing on me, said with more appearance of friendly interest than I had ever before remarked in his countenance, "You are not looking well. Despite your great physical strength, you suffer like your own sickly patients."

"True! I suffer at this moment, but not from bodily pain."

"You have some cause of mental disquietude?"

"Who in this world has not?"

"I never have."

"Because you own you have never loved; certainly, you never seem to care for any one but yourself; and in yourself you find an unbroken sunny holiday,—high spirits, youth, health, beauty, wealth. Happy boy!"

At that moment my heart was heavy within me.

Margrave resumed:—

"Among the secrets which your knowledge places at the command of your art, what would you give for one which would enable you to defy and to deride a rival where you place your affections, which could lock to yourself, and imperiously control, the will of the being whom you desire to fascinate, by an influence paramount, transcendent?"

"Love has that secret," said I, "and love alone."

"A power stronger than love can suspend, can change love itself. But if love be the object or dream of your life, love is the rosy associate of youth and beauty. Beauty soon fades, youth soon departs. What if in nature there were means by which beauty and youth can be fixed into blooming duration—means that could arrest the course, nay, repair the effects, of time on the elements that make up the human frame?"

"Silly boy! Have the Rosicrucians bequeathed to you a prescription for the elixir of life?"

"If I had the prescription I should not ask your aid to discover its ingredients."

"And is it in the hope of that notable discovery you have studied chemistry, electricity, and magnetism? Again I say, Silly boy!"

Margrave did not heed my reply. His face was overcast, gloomy, troubled.

"That the vital principle is a gas," said he, abruptly, "I am fully convinced. Can that gas be the one which combines caloric with oxygen?"

"Phosoxygen? Sir Humphry Davy demonstrates that gas not to be, as Lavoisier supposed, caloric, but light, combined with oxygen; and he suggests, not indeed that it is the vital principle itself, but the pabulum of life to organic beings." *

"Does he?" said Margrave, his face clear-

* See Sir Humphry Davy on Heat, Light, and the Combinations of Light.

ing up. "Possibly, possibly then, here we approach the great secret of secrets. Look you, Allen Fenwick, I promise to secure to you unfailing security from all the jealous fears that now torture your heart; if you care for that fame which to me is not worth the scent of a flower, the balm of a breeze, I will impart to you a knowledge which, in the hands of ambition, would dwarf into commonplace the boasted wonders of recognized science. I will do all this, if, in return, but for one month you will give yourself up to my guidance in whatever experiments I ask, no matter how wild they may seem to you."

"My dear Margrave, I reject your bribes as I would reject the moon and the stars which a child might offer to me in exchange for a toy. But I may give the child its toy for nothing, and I may test your experiments for nothing some day when I have leisure."

I did not hear Margrave's answer, for at that moment my servant entered with letters. Lilian's hand! Tremblingly, breathlessly, I broke the seal. Such a loving, bright, happy letter; so sweet in its gentle chiding of my wrongful fears. It was implied rather than said that Ashleigh Sumner had proposed and been refused. He had now left the House. Lilian and her mother were coming back; in a few days we should meet. In this letter were enclosed a few lines from Mrs. Ashleigh. She was more explicit about my rival than Lilian had been. If no allusion to his attentions had been made to me before, it was from a delicate consideration for myself. Mrs. Ashleigh said that "the young man had heard from L—— of our engagement, and—disbelieved it;" but, as Mrs. Poyntz had so shrewdly predicted, hurried at once to the avowal of his own attachment, and the offer of his own hand. On Lilian's refusal his pride had been deeply mortified. He had gone away manifestly in more anger than sorrow. "Lady Delafield, dear Margaret Poyntz's aunt, had been most kind in trying to soothe Lady Haughton's disappointment, which which was rudely expressed—so rudely," added Mrs. Ashleigh, "that it gives us an excuse to leave sooner than had been proposed—which I am very glad of. Lady Delafield feels much for Mr. Sumner; has invited him to visit her at a place she has near Worthing: she leaves to-morrow in order to receive him; promises to reconcile him to our rejection, which, as he was my poor Gilbert's heir, and was very friendly at first, would be a great relief to my mind. Lilian is well, and so happy at the thoughts of coming back."

When I lifted my eyes from these letters I was as a new man, and the earth seemed a new earth. I felt as if I *had* realized Margrave's idle dreams—as if youth could never fade, love could never grow cold.

"You care for no secrets of mine at this moment," said Vargrave, abruptly.

"Secrets," I murmured; "none now are worth knowing. I am loved—I am loved!"

"I bide my time," said Vargrave; and as my eyes met his, I saw there a look I had never seen in those eyes before—sinister, wrathful, menacing. He turned away, went out through the sash door of the study; and as he passed towards the fields under the luxuriant chestnut-trees, I heard his musical, barbaric chant—the song by which the serpent-charmer charms the serpent—sweet, so sweet—the very birds on the boughs hushed their carol as if to listen.

CHAPTER XXX.

I CALLED that day on Mrs. Poyntz, and communicated to her the purport of the glad news I had received.

She was still at work on the everlasting knitting, her firm fingers linking mesh into mesh as she listened; and when I had done, she laid her skein deliberately down, and said, in her favorite characteristic formula,

"So at last?—that is settled!"

She rose and paced the room as men are apt to do in reflection—women rarely need such movement to aid their thoughts—her eyes were fixed on the floor, and one hand was lightly pressed on the palm of the other—the gesture of a musing reasoner who is approaching the close of a difficult calculation.

At length she paused, fronting me, and said, dryly.

"Accept my congratulations—life smiles on you now—guard that smile, aud when we meet next, may we be even firmer friends than we are now!"

"When we meet next—that will be to-night

—you surely go to the mayor's great ball? All the Hill descends to Low Town to-night."

"No; we are obliged to leave L—— this afternoon—in less than two hours we shall be gone—a family engagement. We may be weeks away; you will excuse me, then, if I take leave of you so unceremoniously. Stay, a motherly word of caution. That friend of yours, Mr. Margrave! Moderate you intimacy with him; and especially after you are married. There is in that stranger, of whom so little is known, a something which I cannot comprehend—a something that captivates, and yet revolts. I find him disturbing my thoughts, perplexing my conjectures, haunting my fancies—I, plain women of the world! Lilian is imaginative; beware of her imagination, even when sure of her heart. Beware of Margrave. The sooner he quits L——, the better, believe me, for your peace of mind. Adieu! I must prepare for our journey."

"That woman," muttered I, on quitting her house, "seems to have some strange spite against my poor Lilian, ever seeking to rouse my own distrust of that exquisite nature which has just given me such proof of its truth. And yet—and yet—is that woman so wrong here? True! Margrave with his wild notions, his strange beauty!—true—true—he might dangerously encourage that turn for the mystic and visionary which distresses me in Lilian. Lilian should not know him. How induce him to leave L——? Ah—those experiments on which he asks my assistance! I might commence them when he comes again, and then invent some excuse to send him for completer tests to the famous chemists of Paris or Berlin."

CHAPTER XXXI.

It is the night of the mayor's ball! The guests are assembling fast; county families twelve miles round have been invited, as well as the principal families of the town. All, before proceeding to the room set apart for the dance, moved in procession through the museum—homage to science before pleasure! The building was brilliantly lighted, and the effect was striking, perhaps because singular and grotesque. There, amidst stands of flowers and evergreens, lit up with colored lamps, were grouped the dead representatives of races all inferior—some deadly—to man. The fancy of the ladies had been permitted to decorate and arrange these types of the animal world. The tiger glared with glass eyes from amidst artificial reeds and herbage, as from his native jungle; the grisly white bear peered from a mimic iceberg. There, in front, stood the sage elephant, facing a hideous hippopotamus; whilst an anaconda twined its long spire round the stem of some tropical tree in zinc. In glass cases, brought into full light by festooned lamps, were dread specimens of the reptile race—scorpion and vampire, and cobra capella, with insects of gorgeous hues, not a few of with venomed stings.

But the chief boast of the collection was in the varities of the Genus Simia—babooms and apes, chimpanzees, with their human visage, mockeries of man, from the dwarf monkeys perched on boughs lopped from the mayor's shrubberies, to the formidable ourang-outang, leaning on the huge club.

Every one expressed to the mayor admiration; to each other antipathy, for this unwonted and somewhat ghastly, though instructive, addition to the revels of a ball-room.

Margrave of course, was there, and seemingly quite at home, gliding from group to group of gaily-dressed ladies, and brilliant with a childish eagerness to play off the shownman. Many of these grim fellow-creatures he declared he had seen, played, or fought with. He had something true or false to say about each. In his high spirits he contrived to make the tiger move, and imitated the hiss of the terrible anaconda. All that he did had its grace, its charm; and the buzz of admiration and the flattering glances of ladies' eyes followed him wherever he moved.

However, there was a general feeling of relief when the mayor led the way from the museum into the ball-room. In provincial parties guests arrive pretty much within the same hour, and so few who had once paid their respects to the apes and serpents, the hippopotamus and the tiger, were disposed to repeat the visit, that long before eleven o'clock the museum was as free from the intrusion of human life as the wilderness in which its dead occupants had been born.

I had gone my round through the rooms,

and, little disposed to be social, had crept into the retreat of a window-niche, pleased to think myself screened by its draperies;—not that I was melancholy, far from it—for the letter I had received that morning from Lilian had raised my whole being into a sovereignty of happiness high beyond the reach of the young pleasure-hunters, whose voices and laughter blended with that vulgar music.

To read her letter again I had stolen to my nook—and, now, sure that none saw me kiss it, I replaced it in my bosom. I looked through the parted curtain; the room was comparatively empty; but there, through the open folding-doors, I saw the gay crowd gathered round the dancers, and there again, at right angles, a vista along the corridor afforded a glmpse of the great elephant in the deserted museum.

Presently I heard, close beside me, my host's voice.

"Here's a cool corner, a pleasant sofa, you can have it all to yourself: what an honor to receive you under my roof, and on this interesting occasion! Yes, as you say, there are great changes in L—— since you left us. Society has much improved. I must look about and find some persons to introduce to you. Clever! oh, I know your tastes. We have a wonderful man—a new doctor. Carries all before him—very high character, too—good old family—greatly looked up to, even apart from his profession. Dogmatic a little—a Sir Oracle—'Lets no dog bark;' you remember the quotation—Shakespeare. Where on earth is he? My dear Sir Philip, I am sure you would enjoy his conversation."

Sir Philip! Could it be Sir Philip Derval, to whom the mayor was giving a flattering, yet scarcely propitiatory, description of myself? Curiosity combined with a sense of propriety in not keeping myself an unsuspected listener: I emerged from the curtain, but silently, and reached the centre of the room before the mayor perceived me. He then came up to me eagerly, linked his arm in mine, and leading me to a gentleman seated on a sofa, close by the window I had quitted, said:

"Doctor, I must present you to Sir Philip Derval, just returned to England, and not six hours in L——. If you would like to see the museum again, Sir Philip, the doctor, I am sure, will accompany you."

"No, I thank you; it is painful to me at present, to see, even under your roof, the collection which my poor dear friend, Dr. Lloyd, was so proudly beginning to form when I left these parts."

"Ay, Sir Philip—Dr. Lloyd was a worthy man in his way, but sadly duped in his latter years; took to mesmerism, only think! But our young doctor here showed him up, I can tell you."

Sir Philip, who had acknowledged my first introduction to his acquaintance by the quiet courtesy with which a well-bred man goes through a ceremony that custom enables him to endure with equal ease and indifference, now evinced by a slight change of manner how little the mayor's reference to my dispute with Dr. Lloyd advanced me in his good opinion. He turned away with a bow more formal than his first one, and said calmly:

"I regret to hear that a man so simple-minded and so sensitive as Dr. Lloyd should have provoked an encounter in which I can well conceive him to have been worsted. With your leave Mr. Mayor, I will look into your ball-room. I may perhaps find there some old acquaintances."

He walked toward the dancers, and the mayor, linking his arm in mine, followed close behind, saying in his loud hearty tones:

"Come along, you too, Dr. Fenwick, my girls are there; you have not spoken to them yet."

Sir Philip, who was then half way across the room, turned round abruptly, and looking me full in the face, said:

"Fenwick, is your name Fenwick?—Allen Fenwick?"

"That is my name, Sir Philip."

"Then permit me to shake you by the hand; you are no stranger, and no mere acquaintance to me. Mr. Mayor, we will look into your ball-room later: do not let us keep you now from your other guests."

The mayor, not in the least offended by being thus summarily dismissed, smiled, walked on, and was soon lost amongst the crowd.

Sir Philip, still retaining my hand, reseated himself on the sofa, and I took my place by his side. The room was still deserted: now and then a straggler from the ball-room looked in for a moment, and then sauntered back to the central place of attraction.

"I am trying to guess," said I, "how my name should be known to you. Possibly you may, in some visit to the Lakes, have known my father?"

"No; I know none of your name but yourself—if, indeed, as I doubt not, you are the Allen Fenwick to whom I owe no small obligation. You were a medical student at Edinburgh in the year * * *?"

"Yes."

"So! At that time there was also at Edinburgh a young man, named Richard Strahan. He lodged in a fourth flat in the Old Town."

"I remember him very well."

"And you remember, also, that a fire broke out at night in the house in which he lodged; that when it was discovered, there seemed no hope of saving him. The flames wrapped the lower part of the house; the staircase had given way. A boy, scarcely so old as himself, was the only human being in the crowd who dared to scale the ladder, that even then scarcely reached the windows from which the smoke rolled in volumes; that boy penetrated into the room—found the inmate almost insensible—rallied, supported, dragged him to the window—got him on the ladder—saved his life then—and his life later, by nursing with a woman's tenderness, through the fever caused by terror and excitement, the fellow-creature he had rescued by a man's daring. The name of that gallant student was Allen Fenwick, and Richard Strahan is my nearest living relation. Are we friends now?"

I answered confusedly. I had almost forgotten the circumstances referred to. Richard Strahan had not been one of my more intimate companions; and I had never seen nor heard of him since leaving college. I inquired what had become of him.

"He is at the Scotch bar," said Sir Philip, "and of course without practice. I understand that he has fair average abilities, but no application. If I am rightly informed, he is, however, a thoroughly honorable, upright man, and of an affectionate and grateful disposition."

"I can answer for all you have said in his praise. He had the qualities you name too deeply rooted in youth to have lost them now."

Sir Philip remained for some moments in a musing silence. And I took advantage of that silence to examine him with more minute attention than I had done before, much as the first sight of him had struck me.

He was somewhat below the common height. So delicately formed that one might call him rather fragile than slight. But in his carriage and air there was remarkable dignity. His countenance was at direct variance with his figure. For as delicacy was the attribute of the last, so power was unmistakeably the characteristic of the first. He looked fully the age his steward had ascribed to him—about forty-eight; at a superficial glance, more; for his hair was prematurely white—not grey, but white as snow. But his eyebrows were still jet black, and his eyes, equally dark, were serenely bright. His forehead was magnificent; lofty, and spacious, and with only one slight wrinkle between the brows. His complexion was sunburnt, showing no sign of weak health. The outline of his lips was that which I have often remarked in men accustomed to great dangers, and contracting in such dangers the habit of self-reliance; firm and quiet, compressed without an effort. And the power of this very noble countenance was not intimidating, not aggressive; it was mild—it was benignant. A man oppressed by some formidable tyranny, and despairing to find a protector, would on seeing that face, have said, "Here is one who can protect me, and who will!"

Sir Philip was the first to break the silence.

"I have so many relations scattered over England, that fortunately not one of them can venture to calculate on my property if I die childless, and therefore not one of them can feel injured when, a few weeks hence, he shall read in the newspapers, that Philip Derval is married. But for Richard Strahan, at least, though I never saw him, I must do something before the newspapers make that announcement. His sister was very dear to me."

"Your neighbors, Sir Philip, will rejoice at your marriage, since, I presume, it may induce you to settle amongst them at Derval Court."

"At Derval Court! No! I shall not settle there." Again he paused a moment or so, and then went on: "I have long lived a wandering life, and in it learned much that the wisdom of cities cannot teach. I return to my native land with a profound conviction that the happiest life is the life most in common with all. I have gone out of my way to do what I deemed good, and to avert or mitigate what appeared to me evil. I pause now and ask myself, whether the most virtuous existence be not that in which virtue flows spontaneously from the springs of quiet everyday action;—when a man does good without restlessly seeking it, does good unconsciously, simply because he is good and he lives? Better, perhaps, for me, if I had thought so long ago! And now I come back to England with the intention of marrying, late in life though it be, and with such hopes of happiness as any matter-of-fact man may form. But my home will not be at Derval Court. I shall reside either in London or its immediate neighborhood, and seek to gather round me minds by which I can correct, if I cannot confide to them, the knowledge I myself have acquired."

"Nay, if, as I have accidentally heard, you are fond of scientific, pursuits, I cannot wonder that, after so long an absence from England, you should feel interest in learning what new discoveries have been made, what new ideas are unfolding the germs of discoveries yet to be. But, pardon me, if in answer to your concluding remark, I venture to say that no man can hope to correct any error in his own knowledge, unless he has the courage to confide the error to those who can correct. La Place has said, '*Tout se tient dans le chaîne immense des vérités;* and the mistake we make in some science we have specially cultivated is often only to be seen by the light of a separate science as specially cultivated by another. Thus in the investigation of truth, frank exposition to congenial minds is essential to the earnest seeker."

"I am pleased with what you say," said Sir Philip, "and I shall be still more pleased to find in you the very confidant I require. But what was your controversy with my old friend, Dr. Lloyd? Do I understand our host rightly, that it related to what in Europe has of late days obtained the name of mesmerism?"

I had conceived a strong desire to conciliate the good opinion of a man who had treated me with so singular and so familiar a kindness, and it was sincerely that I expressed my regret at the acerbity with which I had assailed Dr. Lloyd; but of his theories and pretensions I could not disguise my contempt. I enlarged on the extravagant fallacies involved in a fabulous "clairvoyance," which always failed when put to plain test by sober-minded examiners. I did not deny the effects of imagination on certain nervous constitutions. "Mesmerism could cure nobody; credulity could cure many. There was the well-known story of the old woman tried as a witch; she cured ague by a charm; she owned the impeachment, and was ready to endure gibbet or stake for the truth of her talisman; more than a mesmerist would for the truth of his passes! And the charm was a scroll of gibberish sewn in an old bag and given to the woman in a freak by the judge himself when a young scamp on the circuit. But the charm cured? Certainly; just as mesmerism cures. Fools believed in it. Faith, that moves mountains may well cure agues."

Thus I ran on, supporting my views with anecdote and facts, to which Sir Philip listened with placid gravity.

When I had come to an end, he said, "Of mesmerism, as practised in Europe, I know nothing, except by report. I can well understand that medical men may hesitate to admit it amongst the legitimate resources of orthodox pathology; because, as I gather from what you and others say of its practice, it must, at the best, be far too uncertain in its application to satisfy the requirements of science. Yet an examination of its pretensions may enable you to perceive the truth that lies hid in the powers ascribed to witchcraft; benevolence is but a weak agency compared to malignity; magnetism perverted to evil may solve half the riddles of sorcery. On this, however, I say no more at present. But as to that which you appear to reject as the most preposterous and incredible pretension of the mesmerists, and which you designate by the word 'clairvoyance,' it is clear to me that you have never yourself witnessed even those very imperfect exhibitions which you decide at once to be imposture. I say imperfect, because it is only a limited number of persons whom the eye or the passes of the mesmerist can affect, and by such means, unaided by other means, it is rarely indeed that the magnetic sleep advances beyond the first vague shadowy twilight dawn of that condition to which only in its fuller developments I would apply the name of 'trance.' But still trance is as essential a condition of being as sleep or as waking, having privileges peculiar to itself. By means within the range of the science that explores its nature and its laws, trance, unlike the clairvoyance you describe, is producible in every human being, however unimpressible to mere mesmerism."

"Producible in every human being! Pardon me if I say that I will give any enchanter his own terms who will produce that effect upon me."

"Will you? You consent to have the experiment tried on yourself?"

"Consent most readily."

"I will remember that promise. But to return to the subject. By the word trance I do not mean exclusively the spiritual trance of the Alexandrian Platonists. There is one kind of trance,—that to which all human beings are susceptible,—in which the soul has no share; for of this kind of trance, and it was of this I spoke, some of the inferior animals are susceptible; and, therefore, trance is no more a proof of soul than is the clairvoyance of the mesmerists, or the dream of our ordinary sleep, which last has been called a proof of soul, though any man who has kept a dog must have observed that dogs dream as vividly as we do. But in this trance there is an extraordinary cerebral activity—a projectile force given to the mind—distinct from the soul,—by which it sends forth its own emanations to a distance in spite of material obstacles, just as a flower, in an altered condition of atmosphere, sends forth the particles of its aroma. This should not surprise you. Your thought travels over land and sea in your waking state; thought, too, can travel in trance, and in trance may acquire an intensified force. There is, however, another kind of trance which is truly called spiritual, a trance much more rare, and in which the soul entirely supersedes the mere action of the mind."

"Stay," said I; "you speak of the soul as something distinct from the mind. What the soul may be, I cannot pretend to conjecture. But I cannot separate it from the intelligence!"

"Can you not? A blow on the brain can destroy the intelligence! Do you think it can destroy the soul?

'From Marlbro's eyes the tears of dotage flow,
And swift expires, a driveller and a show.'

Towards the close of his life even Kant's giant intellect left him. Do you suppose that in these various archetypes of intellectual man the soul was worn out by the years that loosened the strings, or made tuneless the keys, of the perishing instrument on which the mind must rely for all notes of its music? If you cannot distinguish the operations of the mind from the essence of the soul, I know not by what rational inductions you arrive at the conclusion that the soul is imperishable."

I remained silent. Sir Philip fixed on me his dark eyes quietly and searchingly, and, after a short pause, said:

"Almost every known body in nature is susceptible of three several states of existence—the solid, the liquid, the aëriform. These conditions depend on the quantity of heat they contain. The same object at one moment may be liquid; at the next moment solid; at the next, aëriform. The water that flows before your gaze may stop consolidated into ice, or ascend into air as a vapor. Thus is man suceptible of three states of existence—the animal, the mental, the spiritual—and according as he is brought into relation or affinity with that occult agency of the whole natural world, which we familiarly call HEAT, and which no science has yet explained; which no scale can weigh, and no eye discern; one or the other of these three states of being prevails, or is subjected."

I still continued silent, for I was unwilling discourteously to say to a stranger, so much older than myself, that he seemed to me to reverse all the maxims of the philosophy to which he made pretence, in founding speculations audacious and abstruse upon unanalogous comparisons that would have been fantastic even in a poet. And Sir Philip, after another pause, resumed with a half smile:

"After what I have said, it will perhaps not very much surprise you when I add that but for my belief in the powers I ascribe to trance, we should not be known to each other at this moment."

"How—pray explain!"

"Certain circumstances which I trust to relate to you in detail hereafter, have imposed on me the duty to discover, to bring human laws to bear upon, a creature armed with terrible powers of evil. This monster, for, without metaphor, monster it is, not man like ourselves, has, by arts superior to those of ordinary fugitives, however dexterous in concealment, hitherto for years eluded my research. Through the trance of an Arab child, who, in her waking state, never heard of his existence, I have learned that this being is in England—is in L——. I am here to encounter him. I expect to do so this very night, and under this very roof."

"Sir Philip!"

"And if you wonder, as you well may, why I have been talking to you with this startling unreserve, know that the same Arab child, on whom I thus implicitly rely, informs me that your life is mixed up with that of the being I seek to unmask and disarm—to be destroyed by his arts or his agents—or to combine in the causes by which the destroyer himself shall be brought to destruction."

"My life!—your Arab child named me, Allen Fenwick?"

"My Arab child told me that the person in whom I should thus naturally seek an ally was he who had saved the life of the man whom I then meant for my heir, if I died unmarried and childless. She told me that I should not be many hours in this town, which she described minutely, before you would be made known to me. She described this house, with yonder lights, and yon dancers. In her trance she saw us sitting together, as we now sit. I accepted the invitation of our host, when he suddenly accosted me on entering the town, confident that I should meet you here, without even asking whether a person of your name were a resident in the place; and now you know why I have so freely unbosomed myself of much that might well make you, a physician, doubt the soundness of my understanding. The same infant, whose vision has been realized up to this moment, has warned me also that I am here at great peril. What the peril may be I have declined to learn, as I have ever declined to ask from the future, what affects only my own life on this earth. That life I regard with supreme indifference, conscious that I have only to discharge, while it lasts, the duties for which it is bestowed on me, to the best of my imperfect power: and aware that minds the strongest and souls the purest may fall into the sloth habitual to predestinarians, if they suffer the action due to the present hour to be awed and paralyzed by some grim shadow on the future! It is only where, irrespectively of aught that can menace myself, a light not struck out of my own reason guile me to disarm evil or minister to good, that I feel privileged to avail myself of those mirrors on which things, near and far, reflect themselves calm and distinct as the banks and the mountain peak are reflected in the glass of a lake. Here, then, under this roof, and by your side, I shall behold him who—Lo! the moment has come—I behold him now!"

As he spoke these last words, Sir Philip had risen, and, startled by his action and voice, I involuntarily rose too.

Resting one hand on my shoulder, he pointed with the other towards the threshold of the ball-room. There, the prominent figure of a gay group—the sole male amidst a fluttering circle of silks and lawn, of flowery wreaths, of female loveliness, and female frippery—stood the radiant image of Margrave. His eyes were not turned towards us. He was looking down, and his light laugh came soft, yet ringing, through the general murmur.

I turned my astonished gaze back to Sir Philip—yes, unmistakeably it was on Margrave that his look was fixed.

Impossible to associate crime with the image of that fair youth! Eccentric notions—fantastic speculations—vicacious egotism—defective benevolence—yes. But crime!—No—impossible.

"Impossible," I said aloud. As I spoke, the group had moved on. Margrave was no longer in sight. At the same moment some other guests came from the ball-room, and seated themselves near us.

Sir Philip looked round, and, observing the deserted museum at the end of the corridor, drew me into it.

When we were alone, he said in a voice quick and low, but decided:

"It is of importance that I should convince you at once of the nature of that prodigy which is more hostile to mankind than the wolf is to the sheepfold. No words of mine could at present suffice to clear your sight from the deception which cheats it. I must enable you to judge for yourself. It must be now and here. He will learn this night, if he has not learned already, that I am in the town. Dim and confused though his memories of myself may be, they are memories still; and he well knows what cause he has to dread me. I must put another in possession of his secret. Another, and at once! For all his arts will be brought to bear against me, and I cannot fortell their issue. Go, then; enter that giddy crowd—select that seeming young man—bring him hither. Take care only not to mention my name; and when here, turn the key in the door, so as to prevent interruption—five minutes will suffice."

"Am I sure that I guess whom you mean? The young light-hearted man; known in this place, under the name of Margrave? The young man with the radiant eyes, and the curls of a Grecian statue?"

"The same; him whom I pointed out: quick, bring him hither."

My curiosity was too much roused to disobey. Had I conceived that Margrave, in the heat of youth, had committed some offence which placed him in danger of the law and in the power of Sir Philip Derval, I possessed enough of the old borderers' black-mail loyalty to have given the man whose hand I had familiarly clasped a hint and a help to escape. But all Sir Philip's talk had been so out of the reach of common sense, that I rather expected to see him confounded by some egregious illusion than Margrave exposed to any well-grounded accusation. All, then, that I felt as I walked into the ball-room and approached Margrave, was that curiousity which, I think, any one of my readers will acknowledge that, in my position, he himself would have felt.

Margrave was standing near the dancers, not joining them, but talking with a young couple in the ring. I drew him aside.

"Come with me for a few minutes into the museum; I wish to talk to you."

"What about?—an experiment?"

"Yes, an experiment."

"Then I am at your service."

In a minute more, he had followed me into the desolate dead museum. I looked round, but did not see Sir Philip.

CHAPTER XXXII.

MARGRAVE threw himself on a seat just under the great anaconda; I closed and locked the door. When I had done so, my eye fell on the young man's face, and I was surprised to see that it had lost its color; that it showed great anxiety, great distress; that his hands were visibly trembling.

"What is this?" he said in feeble tones, and raising himself half from his seat as if with great effort. "Help me up—come away! Something in this room is hostile to me—hostile, overpowering! What can it be?"

"Truth and my presence," answered a stern, low voice; and Sir Philip Derval, whose slight form the huge bulk of the dead elephant had before obscured from my view, came suddenly out from the shadow into the full rays of the lamps which lit up, as if for Man's revel, that mocking catacomb for the playmates of Nature which he enslaves for his service or slays for his sport. As Sir Philip spoke and advanced, Margrave sank back into his seat, shrinking, collapsing, nerveless; terror the most abject expressed in his staring eyes and parted lips. On the other hand, the simple dignity of Sir Philip Derval's bearing, and the mild power of his countenance, were alike inconceivably heightened. A change had come over the whole man, the more impressive because wholly undefinable.

Halting opposite Margrave he uttered some words in a language unknown to me, and stretched one hand over the young man's head. Margrave at once became stiff and rigid as if turned to stone. Sir Philip said to me:

"Place one of those lamps on the floor—there, by his feet."

I took down one of the colored lamps from the mimic tree round which the huge anaconda coiled its spires, and placed it as I was told.

"Take the seat opposite to him and watch."

I obeyed.

Meanwhile, Sir Philip had drawn from his breast-pocket a small steel casket, and I observed, as he opened it, that the interior was subdivided into several compartments, each with its separate lid; from one of these he took and sprinkled over the flame of the lamp a few grains of a powder, colorless and sparkling as diamond dust; in a second or so, a delicate perfume, wholly unfamiliar to my sense, rose from the lamp.

"You would test the condition of trance, test it, and in the spirit.'

And, as he spoke, his hand rested lightly on my head. Hitherto, amidst a surprise not unmixed with awe, I had preserved a certain defiance, a certain distrust. I had been, as it were, on my guard.

But as those words were spoken, as that hand rested on my head, as that perfume arose from the lamp, all power of will deserted me. My first sensation was that of passive subjugation; but soon I was aware of a strange intoxicating effect from the ordor of the lamp, round which there now played a dazzling vapor. The room swam before me. Like a man oppressed by a nightmare, I tried to move, to cry out; feeling that to do so would suffice to burst the thrall that bound me: in vain.

A time that seemed to me inexorably long, but which, as I found afterwards, could only have occupied a few seconds, elapsed in this preliminary state, which, however powerless, was not without a vague luxurious sense of delight. And then suddenly came pain—pain, that in rapid gradations passed into a rending agony. Every bone, sinew, nerve, fibre of the body, seemed as if wrenched open, and as if some hitherto unconjectured Presence in the vital organization were forcing itself to light with all the pangs of travail. The veins seemed swollen to bursting, the heart laboring to maintain its action by fierce spasms. I feel in this description how language fails me. Enough, that the anguish I then endured surpassed all that I have ever experienced of physical pain. This dreadful interval subsided as suddenly as it had commenced. I felt as if a something undefinable by any name had rushed from me, and in that rush that a struggle was over. I was sensible of the passive bliss which attends the release from torture, and then there grew on me a wonderful calm, and, in that calm, a consciousness of some lofty intelligence immeasurably beyond that which human memory gathers from earthly knowledge. I saw before me the still rigid form of Margrave, and my sight seemed, with ease, to penetrate through its covering of flesh, and to survey the mechanism of the whole interior being.

"View that tenement of clay which now seems so fair, as it was when I last beheld it, three years ago, in the house of Haroun of Aleppo?"

I looked, and gradually, and as shade after shade falls on the mountain-side, while the clouds gather, and the sun vanishes at last, so the form and face on which I looked changed from exuberant youth into infirm old age. The discolored wrinkled skin, the bleared dim eye, the flaccid muscles, the brittle sapless bones. Nor was the change that of age alone; the expression of the countenance had passed into gloomy discontent, and in every furrow a passion or a vice had sown the seeds of grief.

And the brain now opened on my sight, with all its labyrinth of cells. I seemed to have the clue to every winding in the maze.

I saw therein a moral world, charred and ruined, as, in some fable I have read, the world of the moon is described to be; yet withal it was a brain of magnificent formation. The powers abused to evil had been originally of rare order; imagination, and scope; the energies that dare; the faculties that discover. But the moral part of the brain had failed to dominate the mental. Defective veneration of what is good or great; cynical disdain of what is right and just; in fine, a great intellect first misguided, then perverted, and now falling with the decay of the body into ghastly but imposing ruins. Such was the world of that brain as it had been three years ago. And still continuing to gaze thereon, I observed three separate emanations of light; the one of a pale red hue, the second of a pale azure, the third a silvery spark.

The red light, which grew paler and paler as I looked, undulated from the brain along the arteries, the veins, the nerves. And I murmured to myself, "Is this the principle of animal life?"

The azure light equally permeated the frame, crossing and uniting with the red, but in a separate and distinct ray, exactly as, in the outer world, a ray of light crosses or unites with a ray of heat, though in itself a separate individual agency. And again I murmured to myself, "Is this the principle of intellectual being, directing or influencing that of animal life; with it, yet not of it?"

But the silvery spark! What was that? Its centre seemed the brain. But I could fix it to no single organ. Nay, wherever I looked through the system, it reflected itself as a star reflects itself upon water. And I observed that while the red light was growing feebler and feebler, and the azure light was confused, irregular—now obstructed, now hurrying, now almost lost—the silvery spark was unaltered, undisturbed. So independent of all which agitated and vexed the frame, that I became strangely aware that if the heart stopped in its action, and the red light died out, if the brain were paralyzed, that energetic mind smitten into idiotcy, and the azure light wandering objectless as a meteor wanders over the morass, still that silver spark would shine the same, indestructible by aught that shattered its tabernacle. And I murmured to myself, "Can that starry spark speak the presence of the soul? Does the silver light shine within creatures to which no life immortal has been promised by Divine Revelation?"

Involuntarily I turned my sight towards the dead forms in the motley collection, and lo, in my trance or my vision, life returned to them all! To the elephant and the serpent; to the tiger, the vulture, the beetle, the moth; to the fish and the polypus, and to yon mockery of man in the giant ape.

I seemed to see each as it lived in its native realm of earth, or of air, or of water; and the red light played more or less warm, through the structure of each, and the azure light, though duller of hue, seemed to shoot the red, and communicate to the creatures an intelligence far inferior indeed, to that of man, but sufficing to conduct the current of their will, and influence the cunning of their instincts. But in none, from the elephant to the moth, from the bird in which brain was the largest, to the hybrid in which life seemed to live as in plants,—in none was visible the starry silver spark. I turned my eyes from the creatures around, back again to the form cowering under the huge anaconda, and in terror at the animation which the carcases took in the awful illusions of that marvellous trance. For the tiger moved as if scenting blood, and to the eyes of the serpent the dread fascination seemed slowly returning.

Again I gazed on the starry spark in the form of the man. And I murmured to myself, "But if this be the soul, why is it so undisturbed and undarkened by the sins which have left such trace and such ravage in the world of the brain?" And gazing yet more intently on the spark, I became vaguely aware that it was not the soul, but the halo around the soul, as the star we see in heaven is not the star itself, but its circle of rays. And if the light itself was undisturbed and undarkened, it was because no sins done in the body could annihilate its essence, nor affect the eternity of its duration. The light was clear within the ruins of its lodgment, because it might pass away, but could not be extinguished.

But the soul itself in the heart of the light reflected back on my own soul within me its ineffable trouble, humiliation, and sorrow; for those ghastly wrecks of power placed at its sovereign command it was responsible; and, appalled by its own sublime fate of duration, was about to carry into eternity the account of its mission in time. Yet it seemed that while the soul was still there, though so forlorn and so guilty, even the wrecks around it were majestic. And the soul, whatever sentence it might merit, was not among the hopelessly lost. For in its remorse and its shame, it might still have retained what could serve for redemption. And I saw that the mind was storming the soul in some terrible rebellious war—all of thought, of passion, of desire, through which the azure light poured its restless flow, were surging up round the starry spark, as in siege. And I could not comprehend the war, nor guess what it was that the mind demanded the soul to yield. Only the distinction between the two was made intelligible by their antagonism. And I saw that the soul, sorely tempted, looked afar to escape from the subjects it had ever so ill controlled, and who sought to reduce to their vassal the power which had lost authority as their king. I could feel its terror in the sympathy of my own terror, the keenness of my own supplicating pity. I knew that it was imploring release from the perils it confessed its want of strength to encounter. And suddenly the starry spark rose from the ruins and the tumult around it, —rose into space and vanished. And where my soul had recognized the presence of soul, there was a void. But the red light burned still, becoming more and more vivid; and as it thus repaired and recruited its lustre, the whole animal form which had been so decrepit, grew restored, from decay, grew into vigor and youth: and I saw Margrave as I had seen him in the waking world, the radiant image of animal life in the beauty of its fairest bloom.

And over this rich vitality and this symmetric mechanism now reigned only, with the animal life, the mind. The starry light fled and the soul vanished, still was left visible the mind: mind, by which sensations convey and cumulate ideas, and muscles obey volition: mind, as in those animals that have more than the elementary instincts: mind, as it might be in men, were men not immortal. As my eyes, in the Vision, followed the azure light, undulating, as before, through the cells of the brain, and crossing the red amidst the labyrinth of the nerves, I perceived that the essence of that azure light had undergone a change; it had lost that faculty of continuous and concentred power by which man improves on the works of the past, and weaves schemes to be developed in the future of remote generations; it had lost all sympathy in the past, because it had lost all conception of a future beyond the grave; it had lost conscience, it had lost remorse; the being it informed was no longer accountable through eternity for the employment of time. The azure light was even more vivid in certain organs useful to the conservation of existence, as in those organs I had observed it more vivid among some of the inferior animals than it is in man—secretiveness, destructiveness, and the ready perception of things immediate to the wants of the day. And the azure light was brilliant in cerebral cells, where before it had been dark, such as those which harbor mirthfulness and hope, for there the light was recruited by the exuberant health of the joyous animal being. But it was lead-like, or dim, in the great social organs through which man subordinates his own interest to that of his species, and utterly lost in those through which man is reminded of his duties to the throne of his Maker.

In that marvellous penetration with which the Vision endowed me, I perceived that in this mind, though in energy far superior to many; though retaining, from memories of the former existence, the relics of a culture wide and in some things profound; though sharpened and quickened into formidable, if desultory, force whenever it schemed or aimed at the animal self-conservation which now made its master impulse or instinct; and though among the reminiscences of its state before its change were arts which I could not comprehend, but which I felt were dark and terrible, lending to a will never checked by remorse, arms that no healthful philosophy has placed in the arsenal of disciplined genius; though the mind in itself had an ally in a body as perfect in strength and elasticity as man can take from the favor of nature—still, I say, I felt that that mind wanted *the something*, without which men never could found cities, frame laws, bind together, beautify, exalt the elements of this world, by creeds that habitually subject them to a reference to another. The ant, and the bee, and the beaver congregate and construct; but they do not improve. Man improves because the future impels onward that which is not found in the ant, the bee, and the beaver—that which was gone from the being before me.

I shrank appalled into myself, covered my face with my hands, and groaned aloud: "Have I ever then doubted that soul is distinct from mind?"

A hand here again touched my forehead, the light in the lamp was extinguished, I became insensible, and when I recovered I found myself back in the room in which I had first conversed with Sir Philip Derval, and seated, as before, on this sofa, by his side.

CHAPTER XXXIII.

My recollections of all which I have just attempted to describe were distinct and vivid; except with respect to time, it seemed to me as if many hours must have elapsed since I had entered the museum with Margrave; but the clock on the mantelpiece met my eyes as I turned them wistfully round the room; and I was indeed amazed to perceive that five minutes had sufficed for all which it has taken me so long to narrate, and which in their transit had hurried me through ideas and emotions so remote from anterior experience.

To my astonishment now succeeded shame and indignation—shame that I, who had scoffed at the possibility of the comparatively credible influences of mesmeric action, should have been so helpless a puppet under the hand of the slight fellow-man beside me, and so morbidly impressed by phantasmagorical illusions; indignation that, by some fumes which had special potency over the brain, I had thus been, as it were, conjured out of my senses; and, looking full into the calm face at my side, I said, with a smile to which I sought to convey disdain:

"I congratulate you, Sir Philip Derval, on having learned in your travels in the East so expert a familiarity with the tricks of its jugglers."

"The East has a proverb," answered Sir Philip, quietly, "that the juggler may learn much from the dervish, but the dervish can learn nothing from the juggler. You will pardon me, however, for the effect produced on you for a few minutes, whatever the cause of it may be, since it may serve to guard your whole life from calamities, to which it might otherwise have been exposed. And however you may consider that which you have just experienced to be a mere optical illusion, or the figment of a brain super-excited by the fumes of a vapor, look within yourself and tell me if you do not feel an inward and unanswerable conviction that there is more reason to shun and to fear the creature you left asleep under the dead jaws of the giant serpent, than there would be in the serpent itself, could hunger again move its coils, and venom again arm its fangs."

I was silent, for I could not deny that that conviction had come to me.

"Henceforth, when you recover from the confusion or anger which now disturbs your impressions, you will be prepared to listen to my explanations and my recital, in a spirit far different from that with which you would have received them before you were subjected to the experiment, which, allow me to remind you, you invited and defied. You will now, I trust, be fitted to become my confidant and my assistant—you will advise with me how, for the sake of humanity, we should act together against the incarnate lie, the anomalous prodigy which glides through the crowd in the image of joyous beauty. For the present I quit you. I have an engagement, on worldly affairs, in the town this night. I am staying at L——, which I shall leave for Derval Court to-morrow evening. Come to me there the day after to-morrow; at any hour that may suit you the best. Adieu!"

Here, Sir Philip Daıval rose and left the room. I made no effort to detain him. My mind was too occupied in striving to recompose itself, and account for the phenomena that had scared it, and for the strength of the impressions it still retained.

I sought to find natural and accountable causes for effects so abnormal.

Lord Bacon suggests that the ointments with which witches anointed themselves might have had the effect of stopping the pores and congesting the brain, and thus impressing the sleep of the unhappy dupes of their own imagination with dreams so vivid that, on waking, they were firmly convinced that they had been borne through the air to the *Sabbat*.

I remember also having heard a distinguished French traveller—whose veracity was unquestionable—say, that he had witnessed extraordinary effects produced on the sensorium by certain fumigations used by an African pretender to magic. A person, of however healthy a brain, subjected to the influence of these fumigations, was induced to believe that he saw the most frightful apparitions.

However extraordinary such effects, they were not incredible—not at variance with our notions of the known laws of nature. And to the vapor or the odors which a powder applied to a lamp had called forth, I was, therefore, prepared to ascribe properties similar to those which Bacon's conjecture ascribed to the witches' ointment, and the French traveller to the fumigations of the African conjuror.

But, as I came to that conclusion, I was seized with an intense curiosity to examine for myself those chemical agencies with which Sir Philip Derval appeared so familiar;—to test the contents in that mysterious casket of steel. I also felt a curiosity no less eager, but more, in spite of myself, intermingled with fear, to learn all that Sir Philip had to communicate of the past history of Margrave. I could but suppose that the young man must indeed be a terrible criminal, for a person of years so grave, and a station so high, to intimate accusations so vaguely dark, and to use means so extraordinary, in order to enlist my imagination rather than my reason against a youth in whom there appeared none of the signs which suspicion interprets into guilt.

While thus musing, I lifted my eyes and saw Margrave himself there, at the threshold of the ball-room—there, where Sir Philip had first pointed him out as the criminal he had come to L—— to seek and disarm; and now, as then, Margrave was the radiant centre of a joyous group: not the young boy-god Iacchus, amidst his nymphs, could, in Grecian frieze or picture, have seemed more the type of the sportive, hilarious vitality of sensuous nature. He must have passed, unobserved by me in my preoccupation of thought, from the museum and across the room in which I sat; and now there was as little trace in that animated countenance of the terror it had exhibited at Sir Philip's approach, as of the change it had undergone in my trance or my phantasy.

But he caught sight of me—left his young companion—came gaily to my side.

"Did you not ask me to go with you into that museum about half an hour ago, or did I dream that I went with you?"

"Yes; you went with me into that museum."

"Then pray what dull theme did you select to set me asleep there?"

I looked hard at him, and made no reply. Somewhat to my relief, I now heard my host's voice:

"Why, Fenwick, what has become of Sir Philip Derval?"

"He has left; he had business." And, as I spoke, again I looked hard on Margrave.

His countenance now showed a change; not surprise, not dismay, but rather a play of the lip, a flash of the eye, that indicated complacency—even triumph.

"So! Sir Philip Derval! He is in L——; he has been here to-night? So! as I expected."

"Did you expect it?" said our host. "No one else did. Who could have told you?"

"The movements of men so distinguished need never take us by surprise. I knew he was in Paris the other day. It is natural eno' that he should come here. I was prepared for his coming."

Margrave here turned away towards the window, which he threw open and looked out.

"There is a storm in the air," said he, as he continued to gaze into the night.

Was it possible that Margrave was so wholly unconscious of what had passed in the museum, as to include in oblivion even the rememberance of Sir Philip Derval's presence before he had been rendered insensible, or laid asleep? Was it now only for the first time that he learned of Sir Philip's arrival in L——, and visit to that house? Was there any intimation of menace in his words and his aspect?

I felt that the trouble of my thoughts communicated itself to my countenance and manner; and, longing for solitude and fresh air, I quitted the house. When I found myself in the street, I turned round and saw Margrave still standing at the open window, but he did not appear to notice me; his eyes seemed fixed abstractedly on space.

CHAPTER XXXIV.

I WALKED on slowly and with the downcast brow of a man absorbed in meditation. I had gained the broad place in which the main streets of the town converged, when I was overtaken by a violent storm of rain. I sought shelter under the dark archway of that entrance to the district of Abbey Hill, which was still called Monk's Gate. The shadow within the arch was so deep that I was not aware that I had a companion till I heard my own name, close at my side. I recognized the voice before I could distinguish the form of Sir Philip Derval.

"The storm will soon be over," said he, quietly. "I saw it coming on in time. I fear you neglected the first warning of those sable clouds, and must be already drenched."

I made no reply, but moved involuntarily away towards the mouth of the arch.

"I see that you cherish a grudge against me!" resumed Sir Philip. "Are you, then, by nature vindictive?"

Somewhat softened by the friendly tone of this reproach, I answered, half in jest, half in earnest,—

"You must own, Sir Philip, that I have some little reason for the uncharitable anger your question imputes to me. But I can forgive you on one condition."

"What is that?"

"The possession, for half an hour, of that mysterious steel casket which you carry about with you, and full permission to analyze and test its contents."

"Your analysis of the contents," returned Sir Philip, dryly, "would leave you as ignorant as before of the uses to which they can be applied. But I will own to you frankly, that it is my intention to select some confident among men of science, to whom I may safely communicate the wonderful properties which certain essences in that casket possess. I invite your acquaintance, nay, your friendship, in the hope that I may find such a confidant in you. But the casket contains other combinations, which, if wasted, could not be re-supplied; at least by any process which the great Master from whom I received them placed within reach of my knowledge. In this they resemble the diamond; when the chemist has found that the diamond affords no other substance by its combustion than pure carbonic acid gas, and that the only chemical difference between the costliest diamond and a lump of pure charcoal is a proportion of hydrogen less than $\frac{1}{50000}$ part of the weight of the substance—can the chemist make you a diamond?

"These, then, the more potent, but also the more perilous of the casket's contents, shall be explored by no science, submitted to no test. They are the keys to masked doors in the ramparts of Nature, which no mortal can pass through without rousing dread sentries never seen upon this side her wall. The powers they confer are secrets locked in my breast, to be lost in my grave; as the casket which lies on my breast shall not be transferred to the hands of another, till all the rest of my earthly possessions pass away with my last breath in life, and my first in eternity."

"Sir Philip Derval," said I, struggling against the appeals to fancy or to awe, made in words so strange, uttered in a tone of earnest conviction, and heard amidst the glare of the lightning, the howl of the winds, and the roll of the thunder—"Sir Philip Derval, you accost me in language which, but for my experience of the powers at your command, I should hear with the contempt that is due to the vaunts of a mountebank, or the pity we give to the morbid beliefs of his dupe. As it is, I decline the confidence with which you would favor me, subject to the conditions which it seems you would impose. My profession abandons to quacks all drugs which may not be analyzed—all secrects which may not be fearlessly told. I cannot visit you at Derval Court. I cannot trust myself, voluntarily, again in the power of a man, who has arts of which I may not examine the nature, by which he can impose on my imagination and steal away my reason."

"Reflect well before you decide," said Sir Philip with a solemnity that was stern. "If you refuse to be warned and to be armed by me, your reason and your imagination will alike be subjected to influences which I can only explain by telling you that there is truth in those immemorial legends which depose to the existence of magic."

"Magic!"

"There is magic of two kinds—the dark and evil, appertaining to witchcraft or necromancy; the pure and beneficent, which is but philosophy, applied to certain mysteries in Nature remote from the beaten tracks of science, but which deepened the wisdom of ancient sages, and can yet unriddle the myths of departed races."

"Sir Philip," I said, with impatient and angry interruption, "If you think that a jargon of this kind be worthy a man of your acquirements and station, it is at least a waste of time to address it to me. I am led to conclude that your desire to make use of me for some purpose which I have a right to suppose honest and blameless, because all you know of me is, that I rendered to your relation services which cannot lower my character in your eyes. If your object be, as you have intimated, to aid you in exposing and disabling a man whose antecedents have been those of guilt, and who threatens with danger the society which receives him, you must give me proofs that are not reducible to magic; and you must prepossess me against the person you accuse, not by powders and and fumes that disorder the brain, but by substantial statements, such as justify one man in condemning another. And, since you have thought fit to convince me that there are chemical means at your disposal, by which the imagination can be so affected as to accept, temporarily, illusions for realities, so I again demand, and now still more decidedly than before, that while you address yourself to my reason, whether to explain your object or to vindicate your charges against a man whom I have admitted to my acquaintance, you will divest yourself of all means and agencies to warp my judgment, so illicit and fraudulent as those which you own yourself to possess. Let the casket, with all its contents, be transferred to my hands, and pledge me your word that, in giving that casket, you reserve to yourself no other means by which chemistry can be abused to those influences over physical organization, which ignorance or imposture may ascribe to—magic."

"I accept no conditions for my confidence, though I think the better of you for attempting to make them. If I live, you will seek me yourself, and implore my aid. Meanwhile, listen to me, and—"

"No; I prefer the rain and the thunder to the whispers that steal to my ear in the dark from one of whom I have reason to beware."

So saying, I stepped forth, and at that moment the lightning flashed through the arch, and brought into full view the face of the man beside me. Seen by that glare, it was pale as the face of a corpse, but its expression was compassionate and serene.

I hesitated, for the expression of that hueless countenance touched me; it was not the face which inspires distrust or fear.

"Come," said I, gently; "grant my demand. The casket—"

"It is no scruple of distrust that now makes that demand; it is a curiosity which in itself is a fearful tempter. Did you now possess what at this moment you desire, how bitterly you would repent!"

"Do you still refuse my demand?"

"I refuse."

"If then you really need me, it is you who will repent."

I passed from the arch into the open space. The rain had passed, the thunder was more distant. I looked back when I had gained the opposite side of the way, at the angle of a street which led to my own house. As I did so, again the skies lightened, but the flash was comparatively slight and evanescent; it did not penetrate the gloom of the arch; it did not bring the form of Sir Philip into view; but, just under the base of the outer buttress to the gateway, I described the outline of a dark figure, cowering down, huddled up for shelter, the outline so indistinct, and so soon lost to sight as the flash faded, that I could not distinguish if it were man or brute. If it were some chance passer-by, who had sought refuge from the rain, and overheard any part of our strange talk, "the listener," thought I, with a half-smile, "must have been mightily perplexed."

CHAPTER XXXV.

On reaching my own home, I found my servant sitting up for me with the information that my attendance was immediately required. The little boy whom Margrave's carelessness had so injured, and for whose injury he had shown so little feeling, had been weakened by the confinement which the nature of the injury required, and for the last few days had been generally ailing. The father had come to my house a few minutes before I reached it, in great distress of mind, saying that his child had been seized with fever, and had become delirious. Hearing that I was at the mayor's house, he had hurried thither in search of me.

I felt as if it were almost a relief to the troubled and haunting thoughts which tormented me, to be summoned to the exercise of a familiar knowledge. I hastened to the bedside of the little sufferer, and soon forgot all else in the anxious struggle for a human life. The struggle promised to be successful; the worst symptoms began to yield to remedies prompt and energetic, if simple. I remained at the house, rather to comfort and support the parents than because my continued attendance was absolutely needed, till the night was well-nigh gone; and all cause of immediate danger having subsided, I then found myself once more in the streets. An atmosphere palely clear in the grey of dawn had succeeded to the thunder-clouds of the stormy night; the street-lamps, here and there, burned wan and still. I was walking slowly and wearily, so tired out that I was scarcely conscious of my own thoughts, when in a narrow lane, my feet stopped almost mechanically before a human form stretched at full length in the centre of the road, right in my path. The form was dark in the shadow thrown from the neighboring houses. "Some poor drunkard," thought I, and the humanity inseparable from my calling not allowing me to leave a fellow-creature thus exposed to the risk of being run over by the first drowsy waggoner who might pass along the thoroughfare, I stooped to rouse and to lift the form. What was my horror when my eyes met the rigid stare of a dead man's. I started, looked again; it was the face of Sir Philip Derval! He was lying on his back, the countenance upturned, a dark stream oozing from the breast—murdered by two ghastly wounds—murdered not long since; the blood was still warm. Stunned and terror-stricken, I stood bending over the body. Suddenly I was touched on the shoulder.

"Hollo! what is this?" said a gruff voice.

"Murder!" I answered in hollow accents, which sounded strangely to my own ear.

"Murder! so it seems." And the policeman who had thus accosted me lifted the body.

"A gentleman by his dress. How did this happen? How did you come here?" and the policeman glanced suspiciously at me.

At this moment, however, there came up another policeman, in whom I recognized the young man whose sister I had attended and cured.

"Dr. Fenwick," said the last, lifting his hat respectfully, and at the sound of my name his fellow-policeman changed his manner, and muttered an apology.

I now collected myself sufficiently to state the name and rank of the murdered man. The policeman bore the body to their station, to which I accompanied them. I then returned to my own house, and had scarcely sunk on my bed when sleep came over me. But what a sleep! Never till then had I known how awfully distinct dreams can be. The phantasmagoria of the naturalist's collection revived. Life again awoke in the serpent and the tiger, the scorpion moved, and the vulture flapped its wings. And there was Margrave, and there Sir Philip; but there position of power was reversed. And Margrave's foot was on the breast of the dead man. Still I slept on till I was roused by the summons to attend on Mr. Vigors, the magistrate to whom the police had reported the murder.

I dressed hastily and went forth. As I passed through the street, I found that the dismal news had already spread. I was accosted on my way to the magistrate by a hundred eager, tremulous, inquiring tongues.

The scanty evidence I could impart was soon given.

My introduction to Sir Philip at the mayor's house, our acidental meeting under the arch, my discovery of the corpse some hours afterwards on my return from my patient, my professional belief that the deed must have been done a very short time, perhaps but a few minutes, before I chanced upon its victim. But, in that case, how account for the long interval that had elapsed between the time in which I had left Sir Philip under the arch, and the time in which the murder must have been committed? Sir Philip could not have been wandering through the streets all those hours. This doubt, however, was easily and speedily cleared up. A Mr. Jeeves, who was one of the principal solicitors in the town, stated that he had acted as Sir Philip's legal agent and adviser ever since Sir Philip came of age, and was charged with the exclusive management of some valuable house property which the deceased had possessed in L——; that when Sir Philip had arrived in the town late in the afternoon of the previous day, he had sent for Mr. Jeeves; informed him that he, Sir Philip, was engaged to be married; that he wished to have full and minute information as to the details of his house property (which had greatly increased in value since his absence from England), in connection with the settlements his marriage would render necessary; and that this information was also required by him in respect to a codical he desired to add to his will.

He had, accordingly, requested Mr. Jeeves to have all the books and statements concerning the property ready for his inspection that night, when he would call, after leaving the ball which he had promised the mayor, whom he had accidentally met on entering the town, to attend. Sir Philip had also asked Mr. Jeeves to detain one of his clerks in his office, in order to serve, conjointly with Mr. Jeeves, as a witness to the codicil he desired to add to his will. Sir Philip had accordingly come to Mr. Jeeves's house a little before midnight; had gone carefully through all the statements prepared for him, and had executed the fresh condicil to his testament, which testament he had in their previous interview given to Mr. Jeeves's care sealed up. Mr. Jeeves stated that Sir Philip, though a man of remarkable talents and great acquirements, was extremely eccentric, and of a very peremptory temper, and that the importance attached to a promptitude for which their seemed no pressing occasion, did not surprise him in Sir Philip as it might have done in an ordinary client. Sir Philip said, indeed, that he should devote the next morning to the draft for his wedding settlements, according to the information of his property which he had acquired; and after a visit of very brief duration to Derval Court, should quit the neighborhood and return to Paris, where his intended bride then was, and in which city it had been settled that the marriage ceremony should take place.

Mr. Jeeves had, however, observed to him, that if he were so soon to be married, it was better to postpone any revision of testamentary bequests, since after marriage he would have to make a new will altogether.

And Sir Philip had simply answered,

"Life is uncertain; who can be sure of the morrow?"

Sir Philip's visit to Mr. Jeeves's house had lasted some hours, for the conversation between them had branched off from actual business to various topics. Mr. Jeeves had not noticed the hour when Sir Philip went; he could only say that as he attended him to the street-door, he observed, rather to his own surprise, that it was close upon daybreak.

Sir Philip's body had been found not many yards distant from the hotel at which he had put up, and to which, therefore, he was evidently returning when he left Mr. Jeeves: an old-fashioned hotel, which had been the principal one at L—— when Sir Philip left England, though now outrivalled by the new and more central establishment in which Margrave was domiciled.

The primary and natural supposition was that Sir Philip had been murdered for the sake of plunder; and this supposition was borne out by the fact to which his valet deposed, viz.,—

That Sir Philip had about his person, on going to the mayor's house, a purse containing notes and sovereigns; and this purse was now missing.

The valet, who, though an Albanian, spoke English fluently, said that the purse had a gold clasp, on which Sir Philip's crest and initials were engraved. Sir Philip's watch was, however, not taken.

And now, it was not without a quick beat of the heart that I heard the valet declare that a steel casket, to which Sir Philip attached extraordinary value, and always carried about with him, was also missing.

The Albanian described this casket as of ancient Byzantine workmanship, opening with a peculiar spring, only known to Sir Philip, in whose possession it had been, so far as the servant knew, about three years; when, after a visit to Aleppo, in which the servant had not accompanied him, he had first observed it in his master's hands. He was asked if this casket contained articles to account for the value Sir Philip set on it—such as jewels, banknotes, letters of credit, etc. The man replied that it might possibly do so; he had never been allowed the opportunity of examining its contents; but that he was certain the casket held medicines, for he had seen Sir Philip take from it some small phials, by which he had performed great cures in the East, and especially during a pestilence which had visited Damascus, just after Sir Philip had arrived at that city on quitting Aleppo. Almost every European traveller is supposed to be a physician; and Sir Philip was a man of great benevolence, and the servant firmly believed him also to be of great medical skill. After this statement, it was very naturally and generally conjectured that Sir Philip was an amateur disciple of homœpathy, and that the casket contained the phials or globules in use among homœopathists.

Whether or not Mr. Vigors enjoyed a vindictive triumph in making me feel the weight of his authority, or whether his temper was ruffled in the excitement of so grave a case, I cannot say, but his manner was stern and his tone discourteous in the questions which he addressed to me. Nor did the questions themselves seem very pertinent to the object of the investigation.

"Pray, Dr. Fenwick," said he, knitting his brows, and fixing his eyes on me rudely, "did Sir Philip Derval, in his conversation with you, mention the steel casket which it seems he carried about with him?"

I felt my countenance change slightly as I answered, "Yes."

"Did he tell you what it contained?"

"He said it contained secrets."

"Secrets of what nature? medicinal or chemical? Secrets which a physician might be curious to learn and covetous to possess?"

This question seemed to me so offensively

significant that it roused my indignation, and I answered haughtily, that "a physician of any degree of merited reputation did not much believe in, and still less covet, those secrets in his art which were the boast of quacks and pretenders.

"My question need not offend you, Dr. Fenwick. I put it in another shape: Did Sir Philip Derval so boast of the secrets contained in his casket, that a quack or pretender might deem such secrets of use to him?"

"Possibly he might, if he believed in such a boast."

"Humph!—he might if he so believed. I have no more questions to put to you, at present, Dr. Fenwick."

Little of any importance in connection with the deceased, or his murder, transpired in the course of that day's examination and inquiries.

The next day, a gentleman distantly related to the young lady to whom Sir Philip was engaged, and who had been for some time in correspondence with the deceased, arrived at L——. He had been sent for at the suggestion of the Albanian servant, who said that Sir Philip had stayed a day at this gentleman's house in London, on his way to L——, from Dover.

The new comer, whose name was Danvers, gave a more touching pathos to the horror which the murder had excited. It seemed that the motives which had swayed Sir Philip in the choice of his betrothed, were singularly pure and noble. The young lady's father—an intimate college friend—had been visited by a sudden reverse of fortune, which had brought on a fever that proved mortal. He had died some years ago, leaving his only child penniless, and had bequeathed her to the care and guardianship of Sir Philip.

The orphan received her education at a convent near Paris; and when Sir Philip, a few weeks since, arrived in that city from the East, he offered her his hand and fortune.

"I know," said Mr. Danvers, "from the conversation I held with him when he came to me in London, that he was induced to this offer by the conscientious desire to discharge the trust consigned to him by his old friend. Sir Philip was still of an age that could not permit him to take under his own roof a female ward of eighteen, without injury to her good name. He could only get over that difficulty by making the ward his wife. 'She will be safer and happier with the man she will love and honor for her father's sake,' said the chivalrous gentleman, 'than she will be under any other roof I could find for her.'"

And now there arrived another stranger to L——, sent for by Mr. Jeeves, the lawyer;—a stranger to L——, but not to me; my old Edinburgh acquaintance, Richard Strahan.

The will in Mr. Jeeves's keeping. with its recent codicil, was opened and read. The will itself bore date about six years anterior to the testator's tragic death: it was very short, and, with the exception of a few legacies, of which the most important was ten thousand pounds to his ward, the whole of his property was left to Richard Strahan, on the condition that he took the name and arms of Derval within a year from the date of Sir Philip's decease. The codicil, added to the will the night before his death, increased the legacy to the young lady from ten to thirty thousand pounds, and bequeathed an annuity of one hundred pounds a year to his Albanian servant. Accompanying the will, and within the same envelope, was a sealed letter, addressed to Richard Strahan, and dated at Paris two weeks before Sir Philip's decease. Strahan brought that letter to me. It ran thus: "Richard Strahan, I advise you to pull down the house called Derval Court, and to build another on a better site, the plans of which, to be modified according to your own taste and requirements, will be found among my papers. This is a recommendation, not a command. But I strictly enjoin you entirely to demolish the more ancient part, which was chiefly occupied by myself, and to destroy by fire, without perusal, all the books and manuscripts found in the safes in my study. I have appointed you my sole executor, as well as my heir, because I have no personal friends in whom I can confide as I trust I may do in the man I have never seen, simply because he will bear my name and represent my lineage. There will be found in my writing-desk, which always accompanies me in my travels, an autobiographical work, a record of my own life, comprising discoveries, or hints at discovery, in science, through means little cultivated in our age. You will not be surprised that before selecting you as my heir and executor, from a crowd of relations not more distant, I should have made inquiries in order to justify my selection. The result of those inquiries informs me that you have not yourself the peculiar knowledge nor the habits of mind that could enable you to judge of matters which demand the attainments and the practice of science; but that you are of an honest, affectionate nature, and will regard as sacred the last injunctions of a benefactor. I enjoin you, then, to submit the aforesaid manuscript memoir to some man on whose character for humanity and honor you can place confidential reliance, and who is accustomed to the study of the positive sciences, more especially chemistry, in connection with electricity and magnetism. My desire is that he shall edit and arrange this memoir for publication; and that, wherever he feels a conscientious doubt whether any discovery, or hint of discovery, therein contained, would not prove more dangerous than useful to mankind, he shall consult with any other three men of science whose names are a guarantee for probity and knowledge, and according to the best of his judgment, after such consultation, suppress or publish the passage of which he has so doubted. I own the ambition which first directed me towards studies of a very unusual character, and which has encouraged me in their pursuit through many years of voluntary exile, in lands where they could be best facilitated or aided—the ambition of leaving behind me the renown of a bold discoverer in those recesses of nature which philosophy has hitherto abandoned to superstition. But I feel, at the moment in which I trace these lines, a fear lest, in the absorbing interest of researches which tend to increase to a marvellous degree the power of man over all matter, animate or inanimate, I may have blunted my own moral perceptions; and that there may be much in the knowledge which I sought and acquired from the pure desire of investigating hidden truths, that could be more abused to purposes of tremendous evil than be likely to conduce to benignant good. And of this a mind disciplined to severe reasoning, and uninfluenced by the enthusiasm which has probably obscured my own judgment, should be the unprejudiced arbiter. Much as I have coveted and still do covet that fame which makes the memory of one man the common inheritance of all, I would infinitely rather that my name should pass away with my breath, than that I should transmit to my fellow-men any portion of a knowledge which the good might forbear to exercise and the bad might unscrupulously pervert. I bear about with me, wherever I wander, a certain steel casket. I received this casket, with its contents, from a man whose memory I hold in profound veneration. Should I live to find a person whom, after minute and intimate trial of his character, I should deem worthy of such confidence, it is my intention to communicate to him the secret how to prepare and how to use such of the powders and essences stored within that casket as I myself have ventured to employ. Others I have never tested, nor do I know how they could be resupplied if lost or wasted. But as the contents of this casket, in the hands of any one not duly instructed as to the mode of applying them, would either be useless, or conduce, through inadvertent and ignorant misapplication, to the most dangerous consequences; so, if I die without having found, and in writing named, such a confidant as I have described above, I command you immediately to empty all the powders and essences found therein into any running stream of water, which will at once harmlessly dissolve them. On no account must they be cast into fire!

"This letter, Richard Strahan, will only come under your eyes in case the plans and the hopes which I have formed for my earthly future should be frustrated by the death on which I do not calculate, but against the chances of which this will and this letter provide. I am about to revisit England, in defiance of a warning that I shall be there subjected to some peril which I refuse to have defined, because I am unwilling that any mean apprehension of personal danger should enfeeble my nerves in the discharge of a stern and solemn duty. If I overcome that peril, you will not be my heir; my testament will be remodelled; this letter will be recalled and destroyed. I shall form ties which promise me the happiness I have never hitherto found, though it is common to all men—the affections of home, the caresses of children, among whom I may find one to whom hereafter I may bequeath, in my knowledge, a far noble heritage than my lands. In that case, however, my first care would be to assure your own fortunes. And the sum which this codicil assures to my betrothed, would be transferred to yourself on my wedding-day. Do you know why, never having seen you, I thus select you for preference, to all my other kindred?—why my heart, in writing thus, warms to your image? Richard Strahan, your only sister, many years older than yourself—you were then a child—was the object of my first love. We were to have been wedded, for her parents deceived me into the belief that she returned my affection. With a rare and noble candor, she herself informed me that her heart was given to another, who possessed not my worldly gifts of wealth and station. In resigning my claims to her hand, I succeeded in propitiating her parents to her own choice. I obtained for her husband the living which he held, and I settled on your sister the dower which, at her death, passed to you as the brother to whom she had shown a mother's love, and the interest of which has secured you a modest independence.

"If these lines ever reach you, recognize my title to reverential obedience to commands which may seem to you wild, perhaps irrational; and repay, as if a debt due from your own lost sister, the affection I have borne to you for her sake."

While I read this long and strange letter, Strahan sat by my side, covering his face with his hands, and weeping with honest tears for the man whose death had made him powerful and rich.

"You will undertake the trust ordained to me in this letter," said he, struggling to compose himself. "You will read and edit this memoir; you are the very man he himself would have selected. Of your honor and humanity there can be no doubt, and you have studied with success the sciences which he specifies as requisite for the discharge of the task he commands."

At this request, though I could not be wholly unprepared for it, my first impulse was that of a vague terror. It seemed to me as if I were becoming more and more entangled in a mysterious and fatal web. But this impulse soon faded in the eager yearnings of an ardent and irresistible curiosity.

I promised to read the manuscript, and in order that I might fully imbue my mind with the object and wish of the deceased, I asked leave to make a copy of the letter I had just read. To this, Strahan readily assented, and that copy I have transcribed in the preceding pages.

I asked Strahan if he had yet found the manuscript; he said, "No, he had not yet had the heart to inspect the papers left by the deceased. He would now do so. He should go in a day or two to Derval Gourt, and reside there till the murderer was discovered, as doubtless he soon must be through the vigilance of the police. Not till that discovery was made should Sir Philip's remains, though already placed in their coffin, he consigned to the family vault."

Strahan seemed to have some superstitious notion that the murderer might be more secure from justice if his victim were thrust, unavenged, into the tomb.

CHAPTER XXXVI.

THE belief prevalent in the town ascribed the murder of Sir Philip to the violence of some vulgar robber, probably not an inhabitant of L——. Mr. Vigors did not favor that belief. He intimated an opinion, which seemed extravagant and groundless, that Sir Philip had been murdered, for the sake not of the missing purse, but of the missing casket. It was currently believed that the solemn magistrate had consulted one of his pretended *clairvoyants*, and that this impostor had gulled him with assurances, to which he attached a credit that perverted into egregiously absurd directions his characteristic activity and zeal.

Be that as it may, the coroner's inquest closed without casting any light on so mysterious a tragedy.

What were my own conjectures I scarcely dared to admit—I certainly could not venture to utter them. But my suspicious centred upon Margrave. That for some reason or other he had cause to dread Sir Philip's presence in L—— was clear, even to my reason. And how could my reason reject all the influences which had been brought to bear on my imagination, whether by the scene in the museum or my conversation with the deceased? But it was impossible to act on such suspicions—impossible even to confide them. Could I have told to any man the effect produced on me in the museum, he would have considered me a liar or a madman. And in Sir Philip's accusations against Margrave, there was nothing tangible—nothing that could bear repetition. Those accusations, if analyzed, vanished into air. What did they imply?—that Margrave was a magician, a monstrous prodigy, a creature exceptional to the ordinary conditions of humanity. Would the most reckless of mortals have ventured to bring against the worst of characters such a charge, on the authority of a deceased witness, and to found on evidence so fantastic the awful accusation of murder? But of all men, certainly I—a sober, practical physician—was the last whom the public could excuse for such incredible implications—and certainly, of all men, the last against whom any suspicion of heinous crime would be readily entertained was that joyous youth in whose sunny aspect life and conscience alike seemed to keep careless holiday. But I could not overcome, nor did I attempt to reason against, the horror akin to detestation, that had succeeded to the fascinating attraction by which Margrave had before conciliated a liking founded rather on admiration than esteem.

In order to avoid his visits I kept away from the study in which I had habitually spent my mornings, and to which he had been accustomed to so ready an access. And if he called at the front door, I directed my servant to tell him that I was either from home or engaged. He did attempt for the first few days to visit me as before, but when my intention to shun him became thus manifest, desisted; naturally enough, as any other man so pointedly repelled would have done.

I abstained from all those houses in which I was likely to meet him; and went my professional round of visits in a close carriage; so that I might not be accosted by him in his walks.

One morning, a very few days after Strahan had shown me Sir Philip Derval's letter, I received a note from my old college acquaintance, stating that he was going to Derval Court that afternoon; that he should take with him the memoir which he had found, and begging me to visit him at his new home, the next day, and commence my inspection of the manuscript. I consented eagerly.

That morning, on going my round, my carriage passed by another drawn up to the pavement, and I recognized the figure of Margrave standing beside the vehicle, and talking to some one seated within it. I looked back, as my own carriage whirled rapidly by, and saw with uneasiness and alarm that it was Richard Strahan to whom Margrave was thus familiarly addressing himself. How had the two made acquaintance? Was it not an outrage on Sir Philip Derval's memory, that the heir he had selected should be thus apparently intimate with the man whom he had so sternly denounced? I became still more impatient to read the memoir—in all probality it would give such explanations with respect to Margrave's antecedents, as, if not sufficing to criminate him of legal offences, would at least effectually terminate any acquaintance between Sir Philip's successor and himself.

All my thoughts were, however, diverted to channels of far deeper interest even than those in which my mind had of late been so tumultuously whirled along; when, on returning home, I found a note from Mrs. Ashleigh. She and Lilian had just come back to L——, sooner than she had led me to anticipate. Lilian had not seemed quite well the last day or two, and had been anxious to return.

CHAPTER XXXVII.

LET me recall it—softly—softly! Let me recall that evening spent with her!—that evening, the last before darkness rose between us like a solid wall.

It was evening, at the close of summer. The sun had set, the twilight was lingering still. We were in the old monastic garden—garden so quiet, so cool, so fragrant. She was seated on a bench under the one great cedar-tree that rose sombre in the midst of the grassy lawn with its little paradise of flowers. I had thrown myself on the sward at her feet; her hand so confidingly lay in the clasp of mine. I see her still—how young, how fair, how innocent!

Strange, strange! So inexpressibly English; so thoroughly the creature of our sober, homely life! The pretty delicate white robe that I touch so timorously, and the ribbon-knots of blue that so well become the soft color of the fair cheek, the wavy silk of the brown hair! She is murmuring low her answer to my trembling question.

"As well as when last we parted? Do you love me as well still?"

"There is no 'still' written here," said she, softly pressing her hand to her heart. "Yesterday is as to-morrow in the For ever.

"Ah, Lilian! if I could reply to you in words as akin to poetry as your own."

"Fie! you who affect not to care for poetry!"

"That was before you went away—before I missed you from my eyes, from my life—before I was quite conscious how precious you were to me, more precious than common words can tell! Yes, there is one period in love when all men are poets, however the penury of their language may belie the luxuriance of their fancies. What would become of me if you ceased to love me?"

"Or of me, if you could cease to love?"

"And somehow it seems to me this evening as if my heart drew nearer to you—nearer as if for shelter."

"It is sympathy," said she, with tremulous eagerness; "that sort of mysterious sympathy which I have often heard you deny or deride; for I, too, feel drawn nearer to you, as if there were a storm at hand. I was oppressed by an indescribable terror in returning home, and the moment I saw you there came a sense of protection."

Her head sank on my shoulder; we were silent some moments; then we both rose by the same involuntary impulse, and round her slight form I twined my strong arm of man. And now we are winding slow under the lilacs and acacies that belt the lawn. Lilian has not yet heard of the murder, which forms the one topic of the town, for all tales of violence and blood affected her as they affect a fearful child. Mrs. Ashleigh, therefore, had judiciously concealed from her the letters and the journals by which the dismal news had been carried to herself. I need scarcely say that the grim subject was not broached by me. In fact, my own mind escaped from the events which had of late so perplexed and tormented it; the tranquillity of the scene, the bliss of Lilian's presence, had begun to chase away even that melancholy foreboding which had overshadowed me in the first moments of our reunion. So we came gradually to converse of the future—of the day, not far distant, when we two should be as one. We planned our bridal excursion. We would visit the scenes endeared to her by song, to me by childhood—the bank and waves of my native Windermere—our one brief holiday before life returned to labor, and hearts now so disquieted by hope and joy settled down to the calm serenity of home.

As we thus talked, the moon, nearly rounded to her full, rose amidst skies without a cloud. We paused to gaze on her solemn haunting beauty, as where are the lovers who have not paused to gaze? We were then on the terrace walk, which commanded a view of the town below. Before us was a parapet wall, low on the garden side, but inaccessible on the outer side, forming part of a straggling irregular street that made one of the boundaries dividing Abbey Hill from Low Town. The lamps of the thoroughfares, in many a line and row beneath us, stretched far away, obscured, here and there, by intervening roofs and tall church towers. The hum of the city came to our ears, low and mellowed into a lulling sound. It was not displeasing to be reminded that there was a world without, as close and closer we drew each to each—worlds to one another! Suddenly there carolled forth the song of a human voice—a wild, irregular, half-savage melody—foreign, uncomprehended words—air and words not new to me. I recognized the voice and chant of Margrave. I started, and uttered an angry exclamation.

"Hush!" whispered Lilian, and I felt her frame shiver within my encircling arm. "Hush! listen! Yes; I have heard that voice before—last night—"

"Last night! you were not here; you were more than a hundred miles away."

"I heard it in a dream! Hush, hush!"

The song rose louder; impossible to describe its effect, in the midst of the tranquil night, chiming over the serried roof-tops, and under the solitary moon. It was not like the artful song of man, for it was defective in the methodical harmony of tune; it was not like the song of the wild bird, for it had no monotony in its sweetness: it was wandering and various as the sounds from an Æolian harp. But it affected the senses to a powerful degree, as in remote lands and in vast solitudes I have since found the note of the mocking-bird, suddenly heard, affect the listener half with delight, half with awe, as if some demon creature of the desert were mimicking man for its own merriment. The chant now had changed into an air of defying glee, of menacing exultation; it might have been the triumphant war-song of some antique barbarian race. The note was sinister; a shadow passed through me, and Lilian had closed her eyes, and was sighing heavily; then with a rapid change, sweet as the coo with which an Arab mother lulls her babe to sleep, the melody died away. "There, there, look," murmured Lilian, moving from me, "the same I saw last night in sleep; the same I saw in the space above, on the evening I first knew you!"

Her eyes were fixed—her hand raised; my look followed hers, and rested on the face and form of Margrave. The moon shone full upon him, so full as if concentrating all its light upon his image. The place on which he stood (a balcony to the upper story of a house about fifty yards distant) was considerably above the level of the terrace from which we gazed on him. His arms were folded on his breast, and he appeared to be looking straight towards us. Even at that distance, the lustrous youth of his countenance appeared to me terribly distinct, and the light of his wonderous eye seemed to rest upon us in one lengthened, steady ray through the limpid moonshine. Involuntarily I seized Lilian's hand, and drew her away almost by force, for she was unwilling to move, and as I led her back, she turned her head to look round; I, too, turned in jealous rage! I breathed more freely. Margrave had disappeared!

"How came he there? It is not his hotel. Whose house is it?" I said aloud, though speaking to myself.

Lilian remained silent; her eyes fixed upon the ground as if in deep reverie. I took her hand; it did not return my pressure. I felt cut to the heart when she drew coldly from me that hand, till then so frankly cordial. I stopped short: "Lilian, what is this? you are chilled towards me. Can the mere sound of that man's voice, the mere glimpse of that man's face, have—" I paused; I did not dare to complete my question.

Lilian lifted her eyes to mine, and I saw at once in those eyes a change. Their look was cold; not haughty, but abstracted. "I do not understand you," she said, in a weary, listless accent. "It is growing late; I must go in."

So we walked on moodily, no longer arm in arm, nor hand in hand. Then it occurred to me that, the next day, Lilien would be in that narrow world of society; that there she could scarcely fail to hear of Margrave, to meet, to know him. Jealousy seized me with all its imaginary terrors, and amidst that jealousy, a nobler, purer apprehension for herself. Had I been Lilian's brother instead of her betrothed, I should not have been trembled less to foresee the shadow of Margrave's mysterious influence passing over a mind so predisposed to the charm which Mystery itself has for those whose thoughts find their outlines in fancies; —whose world melts away into Dreamland. Therefore I spoke.

"Lilian, at the risk of offending you—alas! I have never done so before this night—I must address to you a prayer which I implore you not to regard as the dictate of a suspicion unworthy you and myself. The person whom you have just heard and seen is, at present, much courted in the circles of this town. I entreat you not to permit any one to introduce him to you. I entreat you not to know him. I cannot tell you all my reasons for this petition; enough that I pledge you my honor that those reasons are grave. Trust, then, in my truth, as I trust in yours. Be assured that I stretch not the rights which your heart has bestowed upon mine in the promise that I ask, as I shall be freed from all fear by a promise which I know will be sacred when once it is given."

"What promise?" asked Lilian, absently, as if she had not heard my words.

"What promise? Why, to refuse all acquaintance with that man; his name is Margrave. Promise me, dearest, promise me."

"Why is your voice so changed?" said Lilian." "Its tone jars on my ear," she added with a peevishness so unlike her, that it startled me more than it offended; and, without a word further, she quickened her pace, and entered the house.

For the rest of the evening we were both taciturn and distant towards each other. In vain Mrs. Ashleigh kindly sought to break down our mutual reserve. I felt that I had the right to be resentful, and I clung to that right the more because Lilian made no attempt at reconciliation. This, too, was wholly unlike herself, for her temper was ordinarily sweet—sweet to the extreme of meekness; saddened if the slightest misunderstanding between us had ever vexed me, and yearning to ask forgiveness if a look or a word had pained me. I was in hopes that, before I went away, peace between us would be restored. But long ere her usual hour for retiring to rest, she rose abruptly, and, complaining of fatigue and headache, wished me good night, and avoided the hand I sorrowfully held out to her as I opened the door.

"You must have been very unkind to poor Lilian," said Mrs. Ashleigh, between jest and earnest, "for I never saw her so cross to you before. And the first day of her return, too!"

"The fault is not mine," said I, somewhat sullenly; "I did but ask Lilian, and that as a humble prayer, not to make the acquaintance of a stranger in this town against whom I have reasons for distrust and aversion. I know not why that prayer should displease her."

"Nor I. Who is the stranger?"

"A person who calls himself Margrave. Let me at least entreat you to avoid him!"

"Oh, I have no desire to make acquaintance with strangers. But, now Lilian is gone, do tell me all about this dreadful murder? The servants are full of it, and I cannot keep it long concealed from Lilian. I was in hopes that you would have broken it to her."

I rose impatiently; I could not bear to talk thus of an event the tragedy of which was associated in my mind with circumstances so mysterious. I became agitated and even angry when Mrs. Ashleigh persisted in rambling woman-like inquiries—"Who was suspected of the deed? Who did I think had committed it? What sort of a man was Sir Philip? What was that strange story about a casket?" Breaking from such interrogations, to which I could give but abrupt and evasive answers, I seized my hat, and took my departure.

CHAPTER XXXVIII.

LETTER FROM ALLEN FENWICK TO LILIAN ASHLEIGH.

"I HAVE promised to go to Derval Court to-day, and shall not return till to-morrow. I cannot bear the thought that so many hours should pass away with one feeling less kind than usual resting like a cloud upon you and me. Lilian, if I offended you, forgive me! Send me one line to say so!—one line which I can place next to my heart and cover with grateful kisses till we meet again!"

REPLY.

"I scarcely know what you mean, nor do I quite understand my own state of mind at this moment. It cannot be that I love you less—and yet—but I will not write more now. I feel glad that we shall not meet for the next day or so, and then I hope to be quite recovered. I am not well at this moment. Do not ask me to forgive you—but if it is I who am in fault—forgive me, oh forgive me, Allen."

And with this unsatisfactory note—not worn next to my heart, not covered with kisses, but thrust crumpled into my desk like a creditor's unwelcome bill, I flung myself on my horse and rode to Derval Court. I am naturally proud; my pride came now to my aid. I felt bitterly indignant against Lilian, so indignant that I resolved on my return to say to her, "If in those words, 'And yet,' you implied a doubt whether you loved me less, I cancel your vows I give you back your freedom." And I could have passed from her threshold with a firm foot, though with the certainity that I should never smile again.

Does her note seem to you who may read these pages to justify such resentment? Perhaps not. But there is an atmosphere in the letters of the one we love, which we alone—we who love—can feel, and in the atmosphere of that letter I felt the chill of the coming winter.

I reached the park lodge of Derval Court late in the day. I had occasion to visit some patients whose houses lay scattered many miles apart, and for that reason, as well as from the desire for some quick bodily exercise which is so natural an effect of irritable perturbation of mind, I had made the journey on horseback instead of using a carriage, that I could not have got through the lanes and field-paths by which alone the work set to myself could be accomplished in time.

Just as I entered the park, an uneasy thought seized hold of me with the strength which is ascribed to presentiments. I had passed through my study (which has been so elaborately described) to my stables, as I generally did when I wanted my saddle-horse, and, in so doing, had, doubtless, left open the gate to the iron palisade, and probably the window of the study itself. I had been in this careless habit for several years, without ever once having cause for self-reproach. As I before said, there was nothing in my study to tempt a thief; the study shut out from the body of the house, and the servant sure at nightfall both to close the window and lock the gate; yet now, for the first time, I felt an impulse, urgent, keen, and disquieting, to ride back to the town and see those precautions taken. I could not guess why, but something whispered to me that my neglect had exposed me to some great danger. I even checked my horse and looked at my watch; too late!—already just on the stroke of Strahan's dinner-hour as fixed in his note; my horse, too, was fatigued and spent: besides, what folly! what bearded man can believe in the warnings of a "presentiment?" I pushed on, and soon halted before the old-fashioned flight of stairs that led up to the hall. Here I was accosted by the old steward; he had just descended the stairs, and, as I dismounted, he thrust his arm into mine unceremoniously, and drew me a little aside.

"Doctor, I was right; it *was* his ghost that I saw by the iron door of the mausoleum. I saw it again at the same place last night, but I had no fit then. Justice on his murderer! Blood for blood!"

"Ay!" said I sternly; for if I suspected Margrave before, I felt convinced now that the inexpiable deed was his. Wherefore convinced? Simply because I now hated him more, and hate is so easily convinced! "Lilian! Lilian!" I murmured to myself that name; the flame of my hate was fed by my jealousy. "Ay!" said I, sternly, "murder will out."

"What are the police about?" said the old man, querulously; "days pass on days, and no nearer the truth, But what does the new owner care? He has the rents and acres; what does he care for the dead? I will never serve another master. I have just told Mr. Strahan so. How do I know whether he did not do the deed? Who else had an interest in it?"

"Hush, hush!" I cried; "you do not know how wildly you are talking."

The old man stared at me, shook his head, released my arm, and strode away.

A laboring man came out of the garden, and having unbuckled the saddle-bags, which contained the few things required for so short a visit, I consigned my horse to his care, and ascended the perron. The old housekeeper met me in the hall, conducted me up the great staircase, showed me into a bedroom prepared for me, and told me that Mr. Strahan was already waiting dinner for me. I should find him in the study. I hastened to join him. He began apologizing, very unnecessarily, for the state of his establishment. He had, as yet, engaged no new servants. The housekeeper, with the help of a housemaid, did all the work.

Richard Strahan at college had been as little distinguishable from other young men as a youth neither rich nor poor, neither clever nor stupid, neither handsome nor ugly, neither audacious sinner nor formal saint, possibly could be.

Yet, to those who understood him well, he was not without some of those moral qualities by which a youth of mediocre intellect often matures into a superior man.

He was, as Sir Philip had been righty informed, thoroughly honest and upright. But with a strong sense of duty, there was also a certain latent hardness. He was not indulgent. He had outward frankness with acquaintances, but was easily roused to suspicion. He had much of the thriftiness and self-denial of the North countryman, and I have no doubt that he had lived with calm content and systematic economy on an income which made him, as a bachelor, independent of his nominal profession, but would not have sufficed, in itself, for the fitting maintenance of a wife and family. He was, therefore, still single.

It seemed to me, even during the few minutes in which we conversed before dinner was announced, that his character showed a new phase with his new fortunes. He talked in a grandiose style of the duties of station and the woes of wealth. He seemed to be very much afraid of spending, and still more appalled at the idea of being cheated. His temper, too, was ruffled; the steward had given him notice to quit. Mr. Jeeves, who had spent the morning with him, had said the steward would be a great loss, and a steward, at once sharp and honest, was not to be easily found.

What trifles can embitter the posession of great goods! Strahan had taken a fancy to the old house; it was comfortable to his notions, both of comfort and pomp, and Sir Philip had expressed a desire that the old house should be pulled down. Strahan had inspected the plans for the new mansion to which Sir Philip had referred, and the plans did not please him; on the contrary, they terrified.

"Jeeves says that I could not build such a house under seventy or eighty thousand pounds, and then it will require twice the establishment which will suffice for this. I shall be ruined," cried the man who had just come into possession of at least ten thousand a year.

"Sir Philip did not enjoin you to pull down the old house; he only advised you to do so. Perhaps he thought the site less healthy than that which he proposes for a new building, or was aware of some other drawback to the house, which you may discover later. Wait a little and see before deciding."

"But, at all events, I suppose I must pull down this curious old room—the nicest part of the whole house!"

Strahan, as he spoke, looked wistfully round at the quaint oak chimney-piece; the carved ceiling; the well-built solid walls, with the large mullion casement, opening so pleasantly on the sequestered gardens. He had ensconced himself in Sir Philip's study, the chamber in which the once famous mystic, Forman, had found a refuge.

"So cozy a room for a single man!" sighed Strahan. "Near the stables and dog-kennels, too! But I suppose I must pull it down. I am not bound to do so legally; it is no condition of the will. But in honor and gratitude I ought not to disobey poor Sir Philip's positive injuction."

"Of that," said I, gravely, "there cannot be a doubt."

Here our conversation was interrupted by Mrs. Gates, who informed us that dinner was served in the library. Wine of great age was brought from the long-neglected cellars; Strahan filled and refilled his glass, and, warmed into hilarity, began to talk of bringing old college friends around him in the winter season, and making the roof-tree ring with laughter and song once more.

Time wore away, and night had long set in, when Strahan at last rose from the table, his speech thick and his tongue unsteady. We returned to the study, and I reminded my host of the special object of my visit to him, viz., the inspection of Sir Philip's manuscript.

"It is tough reading," said Strahan; "better put it off till to-morrow. You will stay here two or three days."

"No; I must return to L—— to-morrow. I cannot absent myself from my patients. And it is the more desirable that no time should be lost before examining the contents of the manuscript, because probably they may give some clue to the detection of the murderer."

"Why do you think that?" cried Strahan, startled from the drowsiness that was creeping over him.

"Because the manuscript may show that Sir Philip had some enemy—and who but an enemy could have had a motive for such a crime? Come, bring forth the book. You of all men are bound to be alert in every research that may guide the retribution of justice to the assassin of your benetactor."

"Yes, yes. I will offer a reward of five thousand pounds for the discovery. Allen, that wretched old steward had the insolence to tell me that I was the only man in the world who could have an interest in the death of his master; and he looked at me as if he thought that I had committed the crime. You are right; it becomes me, of all men, to be alert. The assassin must be found. He must hang."

While thus speaking, Strahan had risen, unlocked a desk which stood on one of the safes, and drawn forth a thick volume, the contents of which were protected by a clasp and lock. Strahan proceeded to open this lock by one of a bunch of keyes, which he said had been found on Sir Philip's person.

"There, Allen, this is the memoir. I need not tell you what store I place on it; not, between you and me, that I expect it will warrant poor Sir Philip's high opinion of his own scientific discoveries. That part of his letter seems to me very queer, and very flighty. But he evidently set his heart on the publication of his work, in part if not in whole. And, naturally, I must desire to comply with a wish so distinctly intimated by one to whom I owe so much. I beg you, therefore, not to be too fastidious. Some valuable hints in medicine, I have reason to believe, the manuscript will contain, and those may help you in your profession, Allen."

"You have reason to believe! Why?"

"Oh, a charming young fellow, who, with most of the other gentry resident at L——, called on me at my hotel, told me that he had travelled in the East, and had there heard much of Sir Philip's knowledge of chemistry, and the cures it had enabled him to perform."

"You speak of Mr. Margrave. He called on you?"

"Yes."

"You did not, I trust, mention to him the existence of Sir Philip's manuscript."

"Indeed I did; and I said you had promised to examine it. He seemed delighted at that, and spoke most highly of your peculiar fitness for the task."

"Give me the manuscript," said I, abruptly, "and, after I have looked at it to-night, I may have something to say to you to-morrow in reference to Mr. Margrave."

"There is the book," said Strahan; "I have just glanced at it, and find much of it written in Latin; and I am ashamed to say that I have so neglected the little Latin I learned in our college days, that I could not construe what I looked at."

I sat down and placed the book before me; Strahan fell into a doze, from which he was wakened by the housekeeper, who brought in the tea things.

"Well," said Strahan, languidly, "do you find much in the book that explains the many puzzling riddles in poor Sir Philip's eccentric life and pursuits?"

"Yes," said I. "Do not interrupt me."

Strahan again began to doze, and the housekeeper asked if we should want anything more that night, and if I thought I could find my way to my bedroom.

I dismissed her impatiently, and continued to read.

Strahan woke up again as the clock struck eleven, and finding me still absorbed in the manuscript, and disinclined to converse, lighted his candle, and telling me to replace the manurscript in the desk when I had done with it, and be sure to lock the desk and take charge of the key, which he took off the bunch and gave me, went upstairs, yawning.

I was alone in the wizard Forman's chamber, and bending over a stranger record than had ever excited my infant wonder, or, in later years, provoked my sceptic smile.

CHAPTER XXXIX.

THE Manuscript was written in a small and peculiar hand-writing, which, though evidently by the same person whose letter to Strahan I had read, was, whether from haste or some imperfection in the ink, much more hard to decipher. Those parts of the Memoir which related to experiments, or alleged secrets in Nature, that the writer intimated a desire to submit exclusively to scholars or men of science, were in Latin — and Latin which, though grammatically correct was frequently obscure. But all that detained the eye and attention on the page, necessarily served to impress the contents more deeply on remembrance.

The narrative commenced with the writer's sketch of his childhood. Both his parents had died before he attained his seventh year. The orphan had been sent by his guardians to a private school, and his holidays had been passed at Derval Court. Here, his earliest reminiscences were those of the quaint old room, in which I now sat, and of his childish wonder at the inscription on the chimney-piece—who and what was the Simon Forman who had there found a refuge from persecution? Of what nature were the studies he had cultivated, and the discoveries he boasted to have made?

When he was about sixteen, Philip Derval had begun to read the many mystic books which the library contained; but without other result on his mind than the sentiment of disappointment and disgust. The impressions produced on the credulous imagination of childhood vanished. He went to the university; was sent abroad to travel; and on his return took that place in the circles of London which is so readily conceded to a young idler of birth and fortune. He passed quickly over that period of his life, as one of extravagance and dissipation, from which he was first drawn by the attachment for his cousin to which his letter to Strahan referred. Disappointed in the hopes which that affection had conceived, and his fortune impaired, partly by some years of reckless profusion, and partly by the pecuniary sacrifices at which he had effected his cousin's marriage with another, he retired to Derval Court, to live there in solitude and seclusion. On searching for some old title-deeds required for a mortgage, he chanced upon a collection of manuscripts much discolored, and, in part, eaten away by moth or damp. These, on examination, proved to be the writings of Forman. Some of them were astrological observations and predictions; some were upon the nature of the Cabbala; some upon the invocation of spirits and the magic of the dark ages. All had a certain interest, for they were interspersed with personal remarks, anecdotes of eminent actors in a very stirring time, and were composed as Colloquies, in imitation of Erasmus; the second person in the dialogue being Sir Miles Derval, the patron and pupil; the first person being Formon, the philosopher and expounder.

But along with these shadowy lucubrations were treatises of a more uncommon and a more startling character; discussions on various occult laws of nature, and detailed accounts of analytical experiments. These opened a new, and what seemed to Sir Philip a practical, field of inquiry—a true border-land between natural science and imaginative speculation. Sir Philip had cultivated philosophical science at the university; he resumed the study, and tested himself the truth of various experiments suggested by Forman. Some, to his surpise, proved successful—some wholly failed. These lucubrations first tempted the writer of the memoir towards the studies in which the remainder of his life had been consumed. But he spoke of the lucubrations themselves as valuable only where suggestive of some truths which Forman had accidentally approached, without being aware of their true nature and importance. They were debased by absurd puerilities, and vitiated by the vain and presumptuous ignorance which characterized the astrology of the middle ages. For these reasons the writer intimated his intention (if he lived to return to England) to destroy Forman's manuscripts, together with sundry other books, and a few commentaries of his own upon studies which had for a while misled him—all now deposited in the safes of the room in which I sat.

After some years passed in the retirement of Derval Court, Sir Philip was seized with the desire to travel, and the taste he had imbibed for occult studies led him towards those Eastern lands in which they took their origin, and still retain their professors.

Several pages of the manuscript were now occupied with minute statements of the writer's earlier disappointment in the objects of his singular research. The so-called magicians, accessible to the curiosity of European travellers, were either but ingenious jugglers, or produced effects that perplexed him by practices they had mechanically learned, but of the rationale of which they were as ignorant as himself. It was not till he had resided some considerable time in the East, and acquired a familiar knowledge of its current languages and the social habits of its various populations, that he became acquainted with men in whom he recognized earnest cultivators of the lore which tradition ascribes to the colleges and priesthoods of the ancient world; men generally living remote from others, and seldom to be bribed by money to exhibit their marvels or divulge their secrets. In his intercourse with these sages, Sir Philip arrived at the conviction that there does evist an art of magic, distinct from the guile of the conjuror, and applying to certain latent powers and affinities in nature a philosophy akin to that which we receive in our acknowledged schools, inasmuch as it is equally based upon experiment, and produces from definite causes definite results.

In support of this startling proposition, Sir Philip now devoted more than half his volume to the detail of various experiments, to the process and result of which he pledged his guarantee as the actual operator. As most of these alleged experiments appeared to me wholly incredible, and as all of them were unfamiliar to my practical experience, and could only be verified or falsified by tests that would require no inconsiderable amount of time and care, I passed, with little heed, over the pages in which they were set forth. I was impatient to arrive at that part of the manuscript which might throw light on the mystery in which my interest was the keenest. What were the links which connected the existence of Margrave with the history of Sir Philip Derval? Thus hurrying on, page after page, I suddenly, towards the end of the volume, came upon a name that arrested all my attention—Haroun of Aleppo. He who has read the words addressed to me in my trance may well conceive the thrill that shot through my heart when I came upon that name, and will readily understand how much more vividly my memory retains that part of the manuscript to which I now proceed, than all which had gone before.

"It was," wrote Sir Philip, "in an obscure suburb of Aleppo that I at length met with the wonderful man from whom I have acquired a knowledge immeasurably more profound and occult than that which may be tested in the experiments to which I have devoted so large a share of this memoir. Haroun of Aleppo had, indeed, mastered every secret in nature which the nobler, or theurgic, magic seeks to fathom.

"He had discovered the great Principle of Animal Life, which had hitherto baffled the subtlest anatomist;—provided only that the great organs were not irreparably destroyed, there was no disease that he could not cure; no decrepitude to which he could not restore vigor; yet his science was based on the same theory as that espoused by the best professional practitioners of medicine—viz. that the true art of healing is to assist nature to throw off the disease—to summon, as it were, the whole system to eject the enemy that has fastened on a part. And thus his processes, though occasionally varying in the means employed, all combined in this—viz. the reinvigorating and recruiting of the principle of life."

No one knew the birth or origin of Haroun; no one knew his age. In outward appearance he was in the strength nnd prime of mature manhood. But, according to testimonies in which the writer of the memoir expressed a belief that, I need scarcely say, appeared to me egregiousiy credulous, Haroun's existence under the same name, and known by the same repute, could be tracked back to more than a hundred years. He told Sir Philip that he had thrice renewed his own life, and had resolved to do so no more—he had grown weary of living on. With all his gifts, Haroun owned himself to be consumed by a profound melancholy. He complained that there was nothing new to him under the sun; he said that, while he had at his command unlimited wealth, wealth had ceased to bestow enjoyment; and he preferred living as simply as a peasant: he had tired out all the affections and all the passions of the human heart; he was in the universe as in a solitude. In a word, Heroun would often repeat, with mournful solemnity, "The soul is not meant to inhabit this earth, and in fleshy tabernacle, for more than the period usually assigned to mortals; and when by art in repairing the walls of the body, we so retain it, the soul repines, becomes inert or dejected." "He only," said Haroun, "would feel continued joy in continued existence who could preserve in perfection the sensual part of man, with such mind or reason as may be independent of the spiritual essence; but whom soul itself has quitted! Man, in short, as the grandest of the animals, but without the sublime discontent of earth, which is the peculiar attribute of soul."

One evening Sir Philip was surprised to find at Haroun's house another European. He paused in his narrative to describe this man. He said that for three or four years previously he had heard frequent mention amongst the cultivators of magic, of an orientalized Englishman engaged in researches similar to his own and to whom was ascribed a terrible knowledge in those branches of the art which, even in the East, are condemned as instrumental to evil. Sir Philip here distinguished at length, as he had so briefly distinguished in his conversation with me, between the two kinds of magic—that which he alleged to be as pure from sin as any other species of experimental knowledge, and that by which the agencies of witchcraft are invoked for the purposes of guilt.

The Englishman, to whom the culture of this latter and darker kind of magic was ascribed, Sir Philip Derval had never hitherto come across. He now met him at the house of Haroun; decrepit, emaciated, bowed down with infirmities, and racked with pain. Though little more than sixty, his aspect was that of extreme old age, but still on his face there was seen the ruins of a once singular beauty; and still, in his mind, there was a force that contrasted the decay of the body. Sir Philip had never met with an intellect more powerful and more corrupt. The son of a notorious usurer heir to immense wealth, and endowed with the talents which justify ambition, he had entered upon life burdened with the odium of his father's name.

A duel, to which he had been provoked by an ungenerous taunt on his orgin, but in which a temperament fiercely vindictive had led him to violate the usages prescribed by the social laws that regulate such encounters, had subjected him to a trial in which he escaped conviction, either by a flaw in the technicalities of legal procedure, or by the compassion of the jury; * but the moral presumptions against him were sufficiently strong to set an indelible brand on his honor, and an insurmountable barrier to the hopes which his early ambition had conceived.

After this trial he has quitted his country to return to it no more. Thenceforth, much of his life had been passed out of sight or conjecture of civilized men in remote regions and amongst barbarous tribes. At intervals, however, he had reappeared in European capitals; shunned by and shunning his equals, surrounded by parasites, amongst whom were always to be found men of considerable learning, whom avarice or poverty subjected to the influences of his wealth. For the last nine or ten years he had settled in Persia, purchased extensive lands, maintained the retinue, and exercised more than the power, of an Oriental prince. Such was the man who, prematurely worn out, and assured by physicians that he had not six weeks of life, had come to Aleppo with the gaudy escort of an Eastern satrap, had caused himself to be borne in his litter to the mud-hut of Haroun the Sage, and now called on the magician, in whose art was his last hope, to reprieve him from the—grave.

He turned round to Sir Philip, when the latter entered the room, and exclaimed in English, "I am here because you are. Your intimacy with this man was known to me. I took your character as the guarantee of his own. Tell me that I am no credulous dupe. Tell him that I, Louis Grayle, am no need petitioner. Tell me of his wisdom; assure him of my wealth."

Sir Philip looked inquiringly at Haroun, who remained seated on his carpet in profound silence.

"What is it you ask of Haroun?"

"To live on—to live on. For every year of life he can give me, I will load these floors with gold."

"Gold will not tempt Haroun."

"What will?"

"Ask him yourself; you speak his language."

"I have asked him; he vouchsafes me no answer."

* The reader will here observe a discrepancy between Mrs. Poyntz's account and Sir Philip Derval's narrative. According to the former, Louis Grayle was tried in his absence from England, and sentenced to three years' imprisonment, which his flight enabled him to evade. According to the latter, Louis Grayle stood his trial, and obtained an acquittal. Sir Philip's account must, at least, be nearer the truth than the lady's, because Louis Grayle could not, according to English law, have been tried on a capital charge without being present in court. Mrs. Poyntz tells her story as a woman generally does tell a story—sure to make a mistake where she touches on a question of law; and—unconsciously perhaps to herself—the Woman of the World warps the facts in her narrative so as to save the personal dignity of the hero, who has captivated her interest, not from the moral odium of a great crime, but the debasing position of a prisoner at the bar. Allen Fenwick, no doubt, purposely omits to notice the discrepancy between these two statements, or to animadvert on the mistake which, in the eyes of a lawyer, would discredit Mrs. Poyntz's. It is consistent with some of the objects for which Allen Fenwick makes public his Strange Story, to invite the reader to draw his own inferences from the contradictions by which, even in the most commonplace matters (and how much more in any tale of wonder!), a fact stated by one person is made to differ from the same fact stated by another. The rapidity with which a truth becomes transformed into fable, when it is once sent on its travels from lip to lip, is illustrated by an amusement at this moment in fashion. The amusement is this: In a party of eight or ten persons, let one whisper to another an account of some supposed transaction, or a piece of invented gossip relating to absent persons, dead or alive; let the person, who thus first hears the story, proceed to whisper it, as exactly as he can remember what he has just heard, to the next; the next does the same to his neighbor, and so on, till the tale has run the round of the party. Each narrator, as soon as he has whsipered his version of the tale, writes down what he has whispered. And though, in this game, no one has any interest to misrepresent, but, on the contrary, each for his own credit's sake, strives to repeat what he has heard as faithfully as he can, it will be almost invariably found that the story told by the first person has received the most material alterations before it has reached the eighth or the tenth. Sometimes, the most important feature of the whole narrative is altogether omitted; sometimes, a feature altogether new and preposterously absurd has been added. At the close of the experiment one is tempted to exclaim, "How, after this, can any of those portions of history which the chronicler took from hearsay, be believed?" But, above all, does not every anecdote of scancal which has passed, not through ten lips, but perhaps through ten thousand, before it has reached us, become quite as perplexing to him who would get at the truth, as the marvels he recounts are to the bewildered reason of Fenwick the Sceptic?

Haroun here suddenly roused himself as from a reverie. He drew from under his robe a small phial, from which he let fall a single drop into a cup of water, and said, "Drink this. Send to me to-morrow for such medicaments as I may prescribe. Return hither yourself in three days; not before!"

When Grayle was gone, Sir Philip, moved to pity, asked Haroun if, indeed, it were within the compass of his art to preserve life in a frame that appeared so thoroughly exhausted. Haroun answered, "A fever may so waste the lamp of life that one ruder gust of air could extinguish the flame, yet the sick man recovers. This sick man's existence has been one long fever; this sick man can recover."

"You will aid him to do so?"

"Three days hence I will tell you."

On the third day Grayle revisited Haroun, and at Haroun's request, Sir Philip came also. Grayle declared that he had already derived unspeakable relief from the remedies administered; he was lavish in expressions of gratitude; pressed large gifts on Haroun, and seemed pained when they were refused. This time Haroun conversed freely, drawing forth Grayle's own irregular, perverted, stormy, but powerful intellect.

I can best convey the general nature of Grayle's share in the dialogue between himself, Haroun, and Derval—recorded in the narrative in words which I cannot trust my memory to repeat in detail—by stating the effect it produced on my own mind. It seemed, while I read, as if there passed before me some convulsion of Nature—a storm, an earthquake. Outcries of rage, of scorn, of despair; a despot's vehemence of will; a rebel's scoff at authority. Yet, ever and anon, some swell of lofty thought, some burst of passionate genius—abrupt variations from the vaunt of superb defiance to the wail of intense remorse.

The whole had in it, I know not what, of uncouth but colossal—like the chant, in the old lyrical tragedy, of one of those mythical giants, who, proud of descent from Night and Chaos, had held sway over the elements, while still crude and conflicting, to be crushed under the rocks, upheaved in their struggle, as Order and Harmony subjected a brightening Creation to the milder influences throned in Olympus. But it was not till the later passages of the dialogue in which my interest was now absorbed, that the language to this sinister personage lost a gloomy pathos not the less impressive for the awe with which it was mingled. For, till then, it seemed to me as if in that tempestuous nature there was still broken glimpses of starry light; that a character originally lofty, if irregular and fierce, had been embittered by early and continuous war with the social world, and had, in that war, become maimed and distorted; that, under happier circumstances, its fiery strength might have been disciplined to good; that even now, where remorse was so evidently poignant, evil could not be irredeemably confirmed.

At length all the dreary compassion previously inspired vanished in one unqualified abhorrence.

The subjects discussed changed from those which, relating to the common world of men, were within the scope of my reason. Haroun led his wild guest to boast of his own proficiency in magic, and despite my incredulity, I could not overcome the shudder with which fictions, however extravagant, that deal with that dark Unknown abandoned to the chimeras of poets, will at night and in solitude, send through the veins of men the least accessible to imaginary terrors.

Grayle spoke of the power he had exercised through the agency of evil spirits—a power to fascintate and to destroy. He spoke of the aid revealed to him, now too late, which such direful allies could afford, not only to a private revenge, but to a kingly ambition. Had he acquired the knowledge he declared himself to possess, before the feebleness of the decaying body made it valueless, how he could have triumphed over that world, which had expelled his youth from its pale! He spoke of means by which his influence could work undetected on the minds of others, control agencies that could never betray, and baffle the justice that could never discover. He spoke vaguely of a power by which a spectral reflection of the material body could be cast, like a shadow, to a distance; glide through the walls of a prison, elude the sentinels of a camp—a power that he asserted to be—when enforced by concentred will, and acting on the mind, where, in each individual temptation found mind the weakest—almost infallible in its effect to seduce or to appal. And he closed these and similar boasts of demoniacal arts, which I remember too obscurely to repeat, with a tumultuous imprecation on their nothingness to avail against the gripe of death. All this lore he would communicate to Haroun, in return for what? A boon shared by the meanest peasant—life, common-life; to breathe yet a while the air, feel yet a while the sun.

Then Haroun replied. He said, with a quiet disdain, that the dark art to which Grayle made such boastful pretence, was the meanest of all abuses of knowledge, rightly abandoned, in all ages, to the vilest natures. And then, suddenly changing his tone, he spoke, so far as I can remember the words assigned to him in the manuscript, to this effect:

"Fallen and unhappy wretch, and you ask me for prolonged life!—a prolonged curse to the world and to yourself. Shall I employ spells to lengthen the term of the Pestilence, or profane the secrets of Nature to restore vigor and youth to the failing energies of Crime?"

Grayle, as if stunned by the rebuke, fell on his knees with despairing entreaties that strangely contrasted his previous arrogance. "And it was," he said, "because his life had been evil that he dreaded death. If life could be renewed he would repent, he would change; he retracted his vaunts, he would forsake the arts he had boasted, he would re-enter the world as its benefactor."

"So ever the wicked man lies to himself when appalled by the shadow of death," answered Haroun. "But know, by the remorse which preys on thy soul, that it is not thy soul that addresses this prayer to me. Couldst thou hear, through the storms of the Mind, the Soul's melancholy whisper, it would dissuade thee from a wish to live on. While I speak, I behold it, that SOUL! Sad for the stains on its essence, awed by the account it must render, but dreading, as the direst calamity, a renewal of years below,—darker stains and yet heavier accounts? Whatever the sentence it may now undergo, it has a hope for mercy in the remorse which the mind vainly struggles to quell. But darker its doom if longer retained to earth, yoked to the mind that corrupts it, and enslaved to the senses which thou bidst me restore to their tyrannous forces."

And Grayle bowed his head and covered his face with his hands in silence and in trembling.

Then Sir Philip seized with compassion pleaded for him. "At least, could not the soul have longer time on earth for repentance?" And while Sir Philip was so pleading, Grayle fell prostrate in a swoon like that of death. When he recovered, his head was leaning on Haroun's knee, and his opening eyes fixed on the glittering phial which Haroun held, and from which his lips had been moistened.

"Wondrous!" he murmured; "how I feel like flowing back to me. And that, then, is the elixir! it is no fable!"

His hands stretched greedily as to seize the phial, and he cried imploringly, "More, more!" Haroun replaced the vessel in the folds of his robe, and answered:

"I will not renew thy youth, but I will release thee from bodily suffering: I will leave the mind and the soul free from the pangs of the flesh to reconcile, if yet possible, their long war. My skill may afford thee months yet for repentance; seek, in that interval, to atone for the evil of sixty years; apply thy wealth where it may most compensate for injury done, most relieve the indigent, and most aid the virtuous. Listen to thy remorse. Humble thyself in prayer."

Grayle departed, sighed heavily, and muttering to himself.

The next day Haroun summoned Sir Philip Derval, and said to him:

"Depart to Damascus. In that city the Pestilence has appeared. Go thither thou, to heal and to save. In this casket are stored the surest antidotes to the poison of the plague. Of that essence, undilated and pure, which tempts to the undue prolongation of soul in the prison of flesh, this casket contains not a drop. I curse not my friend with so mournful a boon. Thou hast learned enough of my art to know by what simples the health of the temperate is easily restored to its balance, and their path to the grave smoothed from pain. Not more should Man covet from Nature for the solace and weal of the body. Nobler gifts far than aught for the body this casket contains. Herein are the essences which quicken the life of those duplicate senses that lie dormant and coiled in their chrysalis web, awaiting the wings of a future development—the senses by which we can see, though not with the eye, and hear, but not by the ear. Herein are the links between Man's mind and Nature's; herein are secrets more precious even than these —those extracts of light which enable the Soul to distinguish itself from the Mind, and discriminate the spiritual life, not more from life carnal than life intellectual.

"Where thou seest some noble intellect, studious of Nature, intent upon Truth, yet ignoring the fact that all animal life has a mind, and Man alone on the earth ever asked, and has asked, from the hour his step trod the Earth and his eye sought the Heaven, 'Have I not a soul—can it perish!'—there, such aids to the soul, in the innermost vision vouchsafed to the mind, thou mayst lawfully use. But the treasures contained in this casket are like all which a mortal can win from the mines he explores;—good or ill in their uses as they pass to the hands of the good or the evil. Thou wilt never confide them but to those who will not abuse; and even then, thou art an adept too versed in the mysteries of Nature not to discriminate between the powers that may serve the good to good ends, and the powers that may tempt the good—where less wise than experience has made thee and me—to the ends that are evil; and not even to thy friend, the most virtuous—if less proof against passion, than thou and I have become—wilt thou confide such contents of the casket as may work on the fancy, to deafen the conscience, and imperil the soul."

Sir Philip took the casket, and with it directions for use, which he did not detail. He then spoke to Haroun about Louis Grayle, who had inspired him with a mingled sentiment of admiration and abhorrence; of pity and terror. And Haroun answered thus, repeating the words ascribed to him, so far as I can trust, in regard to them—as to all else in this marvellous narrative—to a memory habitually tenacious even in ordinary matters, and constrained to the utmost extent of his power, by the strangeness of the ideas presented to it, and the intensity of my personal interest in whatever admitted a ray into that cloud which, gathering fast over my reason, now threatened storm to my affections:

"When the mortal deliberately allies himself to the spirits of evil, he surrenders the citadel of his being to the guard of its enemies; and those who look from without can only dimly guess what passes within the precincts abandoned to Powers whose very nature we shrink to contemplate, lest our mere gaze should invite them. This man, whom thou pitiest, is not yet everlastingly consigned to the fiends; because his soul still struggles against them. His life has been one long war between his intellect which is mighty and his spirit which is feeble. The intellect, armed and winged by the passions, has besieged and oppressed the soul; but the soul has never ceased to repine and to repent. And at moments it has gained its inherent ascendency, persuaded revenge to drop the prey it had seized, turned the mind astray from hatred and wrath into unwonted paths of charity and love. In the long desert of guilt, there have been green spots and fountains of good. The fiends have occupied the intellect which invoked them, but they have never yet thoroughly mastered the soul which their presence appals. In the struggle that now passes within that breast, amidst the flickers of wanning mortality, only Allah, whose eye never slumbers, can aid."

Haroun then continued, in words yet more strange and yet more deeply graved in my memory:

"There have been men (thou mayst have known such), who, after an illness in which life itself seemed suspended, have arisen, as out of a sleep, with characters wholly changed. Before, perhaps gentle and good and truthful, they now become bitter, malignant, and false. To the persons and the things they had before love, they evince repugnance and loathing. Sometimes this change is so marked and irrational, that their kindred ascribe it to madness. Not the madness which affects them in the ordinary business of life, but that which turns into harshness and discord the moral harmony that results from natures whole and complete. But there are dervishes who hold that in that illness, which had for its time the likeness of death, the soul itself has passed away, and an evil genius has fixed itself into the body and the brain, thus left void of their former tenant, and animates them in the unaccountable change from the past to the present existence. Such mysteries have formed no part of my study, and I tell you the conjecture received in the East without hazarding a comment whether of incredulity or belief. But if, in this war between the mind which the fiends have seized, and the soul which implores refuge of Allah; if, while the mind of yon traveller now covets life lengthened on earth for the enjoyments it had perverted its faculties to seek and to find in sin, and covets so eagerly that it would shrink from no crime, and revolt from no fiend, that could promise the gift—the soul shudderingly implores to be saved from new guilt, and would rather abide by the judgment of Allah on the sins that have darkened it, than pass for ever irredeemably away to the demons: if this be so, what if the soul's petition be heard—what if it rise from the ruins around it—what if the ruins be left to the witchcraft that seeks to rebuild them? There, if demons might enter, that which they sought as their prize has escaped them; that which they find would mock them by its own incompleteness even in evil. In vain might animal life the most perfect be given to the machine of the flesh; in vain might the mind, freed from the check of the soul, be left to roam at will through a brain stored with memories of knowledge and skilled in the command of its faculties; in vain, in addition to all that body and brain bestow on the normal condition of man, might unhallowed reminiscences gather all the arts and the charms of the sorcery by which the fiends tempted the soul, before it fled, through the passions of flesh and the cravings of mind: the Thing, thus devoid of a soul, would be an instrument of evil, doubtless; but an instrument that of itself could not design, invent, and complete. The demons themselves could have no permanent hold on the perishable materials. They might enter it for some gloomy end which Allah permits in his inscrutable wisdom; but they could leave it no trace when they pass from it, because there is no conscience where soul is wanting. The human animal without soul, but otherwise made felicitously perfect in its mere vital organization, might ravage and destroy, as the tiger and the serpent may destroy and ravage, and, the moment after, would sport in the sunlight harmless and rejoicing, because, like the serpent and the tiger, it is incapable of remorse."

"Why startle my wonder," said Derval, "with so fantastic an image?"

"Because, possibly, the image may come into palable form! I know, while I speak to thee, that this miserable man is calling to his aid the evil sorcery over which he boasts his control. To gain the end he desires, he must pass through a crime. Sorcery whispers to him how to pass through it, secure from the detection of man. The soul resists, but in resisting, is weak against the tyranny of the mind to which it has submitted so long. Question me no more. But if I vanish from thine eyes, if thou hear that the death which, to my sorrow and in my foolishness I have failed to recognize as the merciful minister of Heaven, has removed me at last from the earth, believe that the Pale Visitant was welcome, and that I humbly accept as a blessed release the lot of our common humanity."

Sir Philip went to Damascus. There he found the pestilence raging—there, he devoted himself to the cure of the afflicted; in no single instance, so at least he declared, did the antidotes stored in the casket fail in their effect. The pestilence had passed; his medicaments were exhausted; when the news reached him that Haroun was no more. The Sage had been found, one morning, lifeless in his solitary home, and, according to popular rumor, marks on his throat betrayed the murderous hand of the strangler. Simultaneously, Louis Grayle had disappeared from the city, and was supposed to have shared the fate of Haroun, and been secretly buried by the assassins who had deprived him of life. Sir Philip hastened to Aleppo. There, he ascertained that on the night in which Haroun died, Grayle did not disappear alone; with him were also missing two of his numerous suite; the one, an Arab woman, named Ayesha, who had for some years been his constant companion, his pupil and associate in the mystic practices to which his intellect had been debased, and who was said to have acquired a singular influence over him, partly by her beauty and partly by the tenderness with which she had nursed him through his long decline; the other, an Indian, specially assigned to her service, of whom all the wild retainers of Grayle spoke with detestation and terror.

He was believed by them to belong to that murderous sect of fanatics whose existence as a community has only recently been made known to Europe, and who strangle their unsuspecting victim in the firm belief that they thereby propitiate the favor of the goddess they serve. The current opinion at Aleppo was, that if those two persons had conspired to murder Haroun, perhaps for the sake of the treasures he was said to possess, it was still more certain that they had made away with their own English lord, whether for the sake of the jewels he wore about him, or for the sake of treasures less doubtful than those imputed to Haroun—and of which the hiding-place would to them be much better known. "I did not share that opinion," wrote the narrator; for I assured myself that Ayesha sincerly loved her awful master; and that love need excite no wonder, for Louis Grayle was one whom if a woman, and especially a woman of the East, had once loved, before old age and infirmity fell on him, she would love and cherish still more devotedly when it became her task to protect the being who, in his day of power and command, had exalted his slave into the rank of his pupil and companion. And the Indian whom Grayle had assigned to her service, was allowed to have that brute kind of fidelity which, though it recoils from no crime for a master, refuses all crime against him.

"I came to the conclusion that Haroun had been murdered by order of Louis Grayle—for the sake of the elixir of life—murdered by Juma the Strangler; and that Grayle himself had been aided in his flight from Aleppo, and tended, through the effects of the life-giving drug thus murderously obtained, by the womanly love of the Arab woman, Ayesha. These convictions (since I could not—without being ridiculed as the wildest of dupes—even hint at the vital elixir) I failed to impress on the Eastern officials, or even on a countryman of my own whom I chanced to find at Aleppo. They only arrived at what seemed the common-sense verdict—viz. that Haroun might have been strangled, or might have died in a fit (the body, little examined, was buried long before I came to Aleppo); and that Louis Grayle was murdered by his own treacherous dependents. But all trace of the fugitives was lost.

"And now," wrote Sir Philip, "I will state by what means I discovered that Louis Grayle still lived—changed from age into youth; a new form, a new being; realizing, I verily believe, the image which Haroun's words had raised up, in what then seemed to me the metaphysics of phantasy; criminal, without consciousness of crime; the dreadest of the mere animal race; an incarnation of the blind powers of Nature—beautiful and joyous, wanton, and terrible, and destroying! Such as ancient myths have personified in the idols of Oriental creeds; such as Nature, of herself, might form man in her moments of favor, if man were wholly the animal, and spirit were no longer the essential distinction between himself and the races to which by superior formation and subtler perceptions he would still be the king.

"But *this* being is yet more dire and portentious than the mere animal man, for in him are not only the fragmentary memories of a priestine intelligence which no mind, unaided by the presence of soul, could have originally compassed, but amidst that intelligence are the secrets of the magic which is learned through the agencies of spirits the most hostile to our race. And who shall say whether the fiends do not enter at their will this void and deserted temple whence the soul has departed, and use as their tools, passive and unconscious, all the faculties which, skilful in sorcery, still place a mind at the control of their malice?

"It was in the interest excited in me by the strange and terrible fate that befel an Armenian family with which I was slightly acquainted, that I first traced, in the creature I am now about to describe, and whose course I devote myself to watch, and trust to bring to a close—the murderer of Haroun for the sake of the elixir of youth.

"In this Armenian family there were three daughters; one of them—"

I had just read thus far when a dim shadow fell over the page, and a cold air seemed to breathe on me. Cold—so cold, that my blood halted in my veins as if suddenly frozen! Involuntarily I started, and looked up, sure that some ghastly presence was in the room. And then, on the opposite side of the wall, I beheld an unsubstantial likeness of a human form. Shadow I call it, but the word is not strictly correct, for it was luminous, though with a pale shine. In some exhibition in London there is shown a curious instance of optical illusion; at the end of a corridor you see, apparently in strong light, a human skull. You are convinced it is there as you approach; it is, however, only a reflection from a skull at a distance.

The image before me was less vivid, less seemingly prominent than is the illusion I speak of. I was not deceived. I felt it was a spectrum, a phantasm, but I felt no less surely that it was a reflection from an animate form—the form and the face of Margrave; it was there, distinct, unmistakeable. Conceiving that he himself must be behind me, I sought to rise, to turn round, to examine. I could not move: limb and muscle were overmastered by some incomprehensible spell. Gradually my senses forsook me, I became unconscious as well as motionless. When I recovered, I heard the clock strike three. I must have been nearly two hours insensible; the candles before me were burning low; my eyes rested on the table; the dead man's manuscript was gone!

CHAPTER XL.

THE dead man's manuscript was gone. But how? A phantom might delude my eye, a human will, though exerted at a distance, might, if the tales of mesmerism be true, deprive me of movement and of consciousness; but neither phantom nor mesmeric will could surely remove from the table before me the material substance of the book that had vanished! Was I to seek explanation in the arts sorcery ascribed to Louis Grayle in the narrative?—I would not pursue that conjecture. Against it my reason rose up half alarmed, half disdainful. Some one must have entered the room—some one have removed the manuscript. I looked round. The windows were closed, the curtains partly drawn over the shutters, as they were before my consciousness had left me: all seemed undisturbed. Snatching up one of the candles, fast dying out, I went into the adjoining library, the desolate state-rooms, into the entrance hall, and examined the outer door. Barred and locked! The robber had left no vestige of his stealthy presence.

I resolved to go at once to Strahan's room and tell him of the loss sustained. A deposit had been confided to me, and I felt as if there were a slur on my honor every moment in which I kept its abstraction concealed from him to whom I was responsible for the trust. I hastily ascended the great staircase, grim with faded portraits, and found myself in a longer corridor opening on my own bed-room; no douht also on Strahan's. Which was his? I knew not. I opened rapidly door after door, peered into empty chambers, went blundering on, when, to the right, down a narrow passage, I recognized the signs of my host's whereabouts—signs familiarly commonplace and vulgar, signs by which the inmate of any chamber in lodging-house or inn makes himself known—a chair before a doorway, clothes negligently thrown on it, beside it a pair of shoes. And so ludicrous did such testimony of common every-day life, of the habits which Strahan would necessarily have contracted in his desultory unluxurious bachelor's existence—so ludicrous, I say, did these homely details seem to me, so grotesquely at variance with the wonders of which I had been reading, with the wonders yet more incredible of which I myself had been witness and victim, that as I turned down the passage, I heard my own unconscious half-hysterical laugh; and, startled by the sound of that laugh as if it came from some one else, I paused, my hand on the door, and asked myself: "Do I dream? Am I awake? And if awake, what am I to say to the commonplace mortal I am about to rouse? Speak to him of a phantom! Speak to him of some weird spell over this strong frame! Speak to him of a mystic trance in which has been stolen what he confided to me, without my knowledge! What will he say? What should I have said a few days ago to any man who told such a tale to me?" I did not wait to resolve these questions. I entered the room. There was Strahan sound asleep on his bed. I shook him roughly. He started up, rubbed his eyes—"You, Allen—you! What the deuce?—what's the matter?"

"Strahan, I have been robbed!—robbed of the manuscript you lent me. I could not rest till I had told you."

"Robbed, robbed! Are you serious?"

By this time Strahan had thrown off the bedclothes, and sat upright, staring at me.

And then those questions which my mind

had suggested while I was standing at his door repeated themselves with double force. Tell this man, this unimaginative, hard-headed, raw-boned, sandy-haired North-countryman—tell this man a story which the most credulous school-girl would have rejected as a fable! Impossible.

"I fell asleep," said I, coloring and stammering, for the slightest deviation from truth was painful to me, "and—and—when I woke—the manuscript was gone. Some one must have entered, and committed the theft—"

"Some one entered the house at this hour of the night, and then only stolen a manuscript which could be of no value to him! Absurd! If thieves have come in, it must be for other objects—for plate, for money. I will dress; we will see!"

Strahan hurried on his clothes, muttering to himself, and avoiding my eye. He was embarrassed. He did not like to say to an old friend what was on his mind, but I saw at once that he suspected I had resolved to deprive him of the manuscript, and had invented a wild tale in order to conceal my own dishonesty.

Nevertheless, he proceeded to search the house. I followed him in silence, oppressed with my own thoughts, and longing for solitude in my own chamber. We found no one, no trace of any one, nothing to excite suspicion. There was but two female servants sleeping in the house—the old housekeeper, and a country girl who assisted her. It was not possible to suspect either of these persons, but in the course of our search we opened the doors of their rooms. We saw that they were both in bed, both seemingly asleep: it seemed idle to wake and question them. When the formality of our futile investigation was concluded, Strahan stopped at the door of my bedroom, and for the first time fixing his eyes on me steadily, said:—

"Allen Fenwick, I would have given half the fortune I have come into rather than this had happened. The manuscript, as you know, was bequeathed to me as a sacred trust by a benefactor whose slightest wish it is my duty to observe religiously. If it contained aught valuable to a man of your knowledge and profession,—why, you were free to use its contents. Let me hope, Allen, that the book will reappear to-morrow."

He said no more, drew himself away from the hand I involuntarily extended, and walked quickly back towards his own room.

Alone once more, I sank on a seat, buried my face in my hands, and strove in vain to collect into some definite shape my own tumultuous and disordered thoughts. Could I attach serious credit to the marvellous narrative I had read? Were there, indeed, such powers given to man? such influences latent in the calm routine of Nature? I could not believe it; I must have some morbid affection of the brain; I must be under an hallucination. Hullucination? The phantom, yes — the trance, yes. But still, how came the book gone? That, at least, was not hallucination.

I left my room the next morning with a vague hope that I should find the manuscript somewhere in the study; that, in my own trance, I might have secreted it, as sleep-walkers are said to secrete things, without remembrance of their acts in their waking state.

I searched minutely in every conceivable place. Strahan found me still employed in that hopeless task. He had breakfasted in his own room, and it was past eleven o'clock when he joined me. His manner was now hard, cold, and distant, and his suspicion so bluntly shown, that my distress gave way to resentment.

"Is it possible," I cried indignantly, "that you who have known me so well can suspect me of an act so base, and so gratuitously base? Purloin, conceal a book confided to me, with full power to copy from it whatever I might desire, use its contents in any way that might seem to me serviceable to science, or useful to me in my own calling!"

"I have not accused you," answered Strahan, sullenly. "But what are we to say to Mr. Jeeves; to all others who know that this manuscript existed? Will they believe what you tell me?"

"Mr. Jeeves," I said, "cannot suspect a fellow-townsman, whose character is as high as mine, of untruth and theft. And to whom else have you communicated the facts connected with a memoir and a request of so extraordinary a nature!"

"To young Margrave; I told you so!"

"True, true. We need not go further to find the thief. Margrave has been in this house more than once. He knows the position of the rooms. You have named the robber!"

"Tut! what on earth could a gay young fellow like Margrave want with a work of such dry and recondite nature as I presume my poor kinsman's memoir must be?"

I was about to answer, when the door was abruptly opened, and the servant girl entered, followed by two men in whom I recognized the superintendent of the L—— police and the same subordinate who had found me by Sir Philip's corpse.

The superintendent came up to me with a grave face, and whispered in my ear. I did not at first comprehend him. "Come with you," I said, "and to Mr. Vigors, the magistrate? I thought my deposition was closed."

The superintendent shook his head. "I have the authority here, Dr. Fenwick."

"Well, I will come, of course. Has anything new transpired?"

The superintendent turned to the servant girl, who was standing with gaping mouth and staring eyes. "Show us Dr. Fenwick's room. You had better put up, sir, whatever things you have brought here. I will go upstairs with you," he whispered again. "Come, Dr. Fenwick, I am in the discharge of my duty."

Something in the man's manner was so sinister and menacing that I felt at once, that some new and strange calamity had befallen me. I turned towards Strahan. He was at the threshold, speaking in a low voice to the subordinate policeman, and there was an expression of amazement and horror in his countenance. As I came towards him he darted away without a word.

I went up the stairs, entered my bedroom, the superintendent close behind me. As I took up mechanically the few things I had brought with me, the police officer drew them from me with an abruptness that appeared insolent, and deliberately scarched the pockets of the coat which I had worn the evening before, then opened the drawers in the room, and even pried into the bed.

"What do you mean?" I asked haughtily.

"Excuse me, sir. Duty. You are—"

"Well, I am what?"

"My prisoner; here is the warrant."

"Warrant! on what charge?"

"The murder of Sir Philip Derval."

"I—I! Murder!' I could say no more.

I must hurry over this awful passage in my marvellous record. It is torture to dwell on the details, and indeed I have so sought to chase them from my recollection, that they only come back to me in hideous fragments, like the incoherent remains of a horrible dream.

All that I need state is as follows: Early on the very morning on which I had been arrested, a man, a stranger in the town, had privately sought Mr. Vigors, and deposed that on the night of the murder, he had been taking refuge from a sudden storm under shelter of the eaves and buttresses of a wall adjoining an old archway; that he had heard men talking within the archway; had heard one say to the other, "You still bear me a grudge." The other had replied, "I can forgive you on one condition." That he then lost much of the conversation that ensued, which was in a lower voice; but he gathered enough to know that the condition demanded by the one was the possession of a casket which the other carried about with him. That there seemed an altercation on this matter between the two men, which, to judge by the tones of voice, was angry on the part of the man demanding the casket; that, finally, this man said in a loud key, "Do you still refuse?" and on receiving the answer which the witness did not overhear, exclaimed threateningly, "It is you who will repent:" and then stepped forth from the arch into the street.

The rain had then ceased, but by a broad flash of lightning the witness saw distinctly the figure of the person thus quitting the shelter of the arch; a man of tall stature, powerful frame, erect carriage. A little time afterwards, witness saw a slighter and older man come forth from the arch, whom he could only examine by the flickering ray of the gas-lamp near the wall, the lightning having ceased, but whom he fully believed to be the person he afterwards discovered to be Sir Philip Derval.

He said that he himself had only arrived at the town a few hours before; a stranger to L——, and indeed to England; having come from the United States of America, where he had passed his life from childhood. He had journeyed on foot to L——, in the hope of finding there some distant relatives. He had put up at a small inn, after which he had strolled through the town, when the storm had driven him to seek shelter. He had then failed to find his way back to the inn, and after wandering about in vain, and seeing no one at that late hour of night of whom he could ask the way, he had crept under a portico and slept for two or three hours. Waking towards the dawn, he had then got up, and again sought to find his way to the inn, when he saw, in a narrow street before him, two men, one of whom he recognized as the taller of the two, to whose conversation he had listened under the arch, the other he did not recognize at the moment.

The taller man seemed angry and agitated, and he heard him say, "The casket; I will have it." There then seemed to be a struggle between these two persons, when the taller one struck down the shorter, knelt on his breast, and he caught distinctly the gleam of some steel instrument. That he was so frightened that he could not stir from the place, and that though he cried out, he believed his voice was not heard. He then saw the taller man rise, the other resting on the pavement motionless; and a minute or so afterwards beheld policemen coming to the place, on which he, the witness, walked away. He did not know that a murder had been committed; it might be only an assault; it was no business of his, he was a stranger. He thought it best not to interfere, the police having cognizance of the affair. He found out his inn; for the next few days he was absent from L—— in search of his relations, who had left the town, many years ago, to fix their residence in one of the neighboring villages.

He was, however, disappointed, none of these relations now survived. He had now returned to L——, heard of the murder, was in doubt what to do, might get himseif into trouble if, a mere stranger, he gave an unsupported testimony. But, on the day before the evidence was volunteered, as he was lounging in the streets, he had seen a gentleman pass by on horseback, in whom he immediately recognized the man, who, in his belief, was the murderer of Sir Philip Derval. He inquired of a bystander the name of the gentleman, the answer was "Dr. Fenwick." That, the rest of the day, he felt much disturbed in his mind, not liking to volunteer such a charge against a man of apparent respectability and station. But that his consciencce would not let him sleep that night, and he had resolved at morning to go to the magistrate and make a clean breast of it.

The story was in itself so improbable that any other magistrate but Mr. Vigors would perhaps have dismissed it in contempt. But Mr. Vigors, already so bitterly prejudiced against me, and not sorry, perhaps, to subject me to the humiliation of so horrible a charge, immediately issued his warrant to search my house. I was absent at Derval Court; the house was searched. In the bureau in my favorite study, which was unlocked, the steel casket was discovered, and a large case-knife, on the blade of which the stains of blood were still perceptible. On this discovery I was apprehended, and on these evidences, and on the deposition of this vagrant stranger, I was, not indeed committed to take my trial for murder, but placed in confinement; all bail for my appearance refused, and the examination adjourned to give time for further evidence and inquiries. I had requested the professional aid of Mr. Jeeves. To my surprise and dismay Mr. Jeeves begged me to excuse him. He said he was pre-engaged by Mr. Strahan to detect and prosecute the murderer of Sir P. Derval, and could not assist one accused of the murder.

I gathered from the little he said that Strahan had already been to him that morning and told him of the missing manuscript—that Strahan had ceased to be my friend. I engaged another solicitor, a young man of ability, and who professed personal esteem for me. Mr. Stanton (such was the lawyer's name) believed in my incocence; but he warned me that appearances were grave, he implored me to be perfectly frank with him. Had I held conversation with Sir Philip under the archway as reported by the witness? Had I used such or similiar words? Had the deceased said, "I had a grudge against him?" Had I demanded the casket? Had I threatened Sir Philip that he would repent? And of what? His refusal?

I felt myself grow pale as I answered, "Yes, I thought such or similiar expressions had occurred in my conversation with the deceased."

"What was the reason of the grudge? What was the nature of this casket, that I should so desire its possession?"

There, I became terribly embarrassed. What could I say to a keen, sensible, worldly man of law? Tell him of the power and the fumes, of the scene in the museum, of Sir Philip's tale, of the implied identity of the youthful Margrave with the aged Grayle, of the elixir of life, and of magic arts? I—I tell such a romance! I the noted adversary of all pretended mysticism. I—I a sceptical practitioner of medicine! Had that manuscript of Sir Philip's been available—a substantial record of marvellous events by a man of repute for intellect and learning—I might, perhaps, have ventured to startle the solicitor of L—— with my revelations. But the sole proof that all which the solicitor urged me to confide was not a monstrous fiction or an insane delusion had disappeared; and its disappearance was a part of the terrible mystery that enveloped the whole. I answered, therefore, as composedly as I could, that "I could have no serious grudge against Sir Philip, whom I had never seen before that evening; that the words, which applied to my supposed grudge, were lightly said by Sir Philip, in reference to a physiologcal dispute on matters connected with mesmerical phenomena, that the deceased had declared his casket, which he had shown me at the mayor's house, contained drugs of great potency in medicine; that I had asked permission to test those drugs myself; and that when I said he would repent of his refusal, I merely meant that he would repent of his reliance on drugs not warranted by the experiments of professional science.

My replies seemed to satisfy the lawyer so far, but "how could I account for the casket and the knife being found in my room?"

"In no way but this; the window of my study is a door-window opening on the lane, from which any one might enter the room. I was in the habit, not only of going out myself that way, but of admitting through that door any more familiar private acquaintance."

"Whom, for instance?"

I hesitated a moment, and then said, with a significance I could not forbear, "Mr. Margrave! He would know the *locale* perfectly; he would know that the door was rarely bolted from within during the day-time; he could enter at all hours; he could place, or instruct any one to deposit the knife and casket in my bureau, which he knew I never kept locked; it contained no secrets, no private correspondence—chiefly surgical implements, or such things as I might want for professional experiments."

"Mr. Margrave! But you cannot suspect him—a lively, charming young man, against whose character not a whisper was ever heard—of connivance with such a charge against you; a connivance that would implicate him in the murder itself, for if you are accused wrongfully, he who accuses you is either the criminal or the criminal's accomplice; his instigator or his tool."

"Mr. Stanton," I said firmly, after a moment's pause, "I do suspect Mr. Margrave of a hand in this crime. Sir Philip, on seeing him at the mayor's house, expressed a strong abhorrence of him, more than hinted at crimes he had committed; appointed me to come to Derval Court the day after that on which the murder was committed. Sir Philip had known something of this Margrave in the East—Margrave might dread exposure, revelations—of what I know not; but, strange as it may seem to you, it is my conviction that this young man, apparently so gay and so thoughtless, is the real criminal, and in some way, which I cannot conjecture, has employed this lying vagabond in the fabrication of a charge against myself. Reflect: of Mr. Margrave's antecedents we know nothing; of them nothing was known even by the young gentleman who first introduced him to the society of this town. If you would serve and save me, it is to that quarter that you will direct your vigilant and unrelaxing researches."

I had scarcely so said when I repented my candor, for I observed in the face of Mr. Stanton a sudden revulsion of feeling, an utter incredulity of the accusation I had thus hazarded, and for the first time a doubt of my own innocence. The fascination exercised by Margrave was universal; nor was it to be wondered at: for, besides the charm of his joyous presence, he seemed so singularly free from even the errors common enough with the young. So gay and boon a companion, yet a shunner of wine; so dazzling in aspect, so more than beautiful, so courted, so idolized by women, yet no tale of seduction, of profligacy, attached to his name! As to his antecedents, he had so frankly owned himself a natural son, a nobody, a traveller, an idler; his expenses, though lavish, were so unostentatious, so regularly defrayed. He was so wholly the reverse of the character assigned to criminals, that it seemed as absurd to bring a charge of homicide against a butterfly or a goldfinch as against this seemingly innocent and delightful favorite of humanity and nature.

However, Mr. Stanton said little or nothing, and shortly afterwards left me, with a dry expression of hope that my innocence would be cleared in spite of evidence that, he was bound to say, was of the most serious character.

I was exhausted. I fell into a profound sleep early that night; it might be a little after twelve when I woke, and woke as fully, as completely, as much restored to life and consciousness, as it was then my habit to be at the break of day. And, so waking, I saw, on the wall opposite my bed, the same luminous phantom I had seen in the wizard's study at Derval court. I have read in Scandinavian legends of an apparition called the Scin-Læca, or shining corpse. It is supposed, in the northern superstition, sometimes to haunt sepulchres, sometimes to fortel doom. It is the spectre of a human body seen in a phosporic light, and so exactly did this phantom correspond to the desccription of such an apparition in Scandinavian fable that I know not how to give it a better name than that of Scin-Læca—the shining corpse.

There it was before me, corpse-like, yet not dead; there, as in the haunted study of the wizard Forman!—the form and the face of Margrave. Constitutionally, my nerves are strong, and my temper hardy, and now I was resolved to battle against any impression which my senses might receive from my own deluding fancies. Things that witnessed for the first time daunt us, witnessed for the second time lose their terror. I rose from my bed with a bold aspect, I approached the phantom with a firm step; but when within two paces of it, and my hand outstretched to touch it, my arm became fixed in air, my feet locked to the ground. I did not experience fear; I felt that my heart beat regularly, but an invincible something opposed itself to me. I stood as if turned to stone, and then from the lips of this phantom there came a voice, but a voice which seemed borne from a great distance—very low, muffled, and yet distinct: I could not even be sure that my ear heard it, or whether the sound was not conveyed to me by an inner sense.

"I, and I alone, can save and deliver you," said the voice. "I will do so; and the conditions I ask, in return, are simple and easy."

"Fiend or spectre, or more delusion of my own brain," cried I, "there can be no compact between thee and me. I despise thy malice, I reject thy services; I accept no conditions to escape from the one or to obtain the other."

"You may give a different answer when I ask again."

The Scin-Læca slowly waned, and, fading first into a paler shadow, then vanished. I rejoiced at the reply I had given. Two days elapsed before Mr. Stanton again came to me; in the interval the Scin-Læca did not reappear. I had mustered ail my courage, all my common sense, noted down all the weak points of the false evidence against me, and felt calm and supported by the strength of my innocence.

The first few words of the solicitor dashed all my courage to the ground. For I was anxious to hear news of Lilian, anxious to have some message from her that might cheer and strengthen me, and my first question was this:

"Mr. Stanton, you are aware that I am engaged in marriage to Miss Ashleigh. Your family are not unacquainted with her. What says, what thinks she of this monstrous charge against her betrothed?"

"I was for two hours at Mrs. Ashleigh's house last evening," replied the lawyer; "she was naturally anxious to see me as employed in your defence. Who do you think was there? Who, eager to defend you, to express his persuasion of your innocence, to declare his conviction that the real criminal would soon be discovered—who but that same Mr. Margrave, whom, pardon me my frankness, you so rashly and groundlessly suspected."

"Heavens! Do you say that he is received in that house?—that he—*he* is familiarly admitted to *her* presence?"

"My good sir, why these unjust prepossessions against a true friend? It was as your friend that, as soon as the charge against you amazed and shocked the town of L——, Mr. Margrave called on Mrs. Ashleigh—presented to her by Miss Brabazon—and was so cheering and hopeful that—"

"Enough!" I exclaimed—"enough!"

I paced the room in a state of excitement and rage, which the lawyer in vain endeavored to calm, until at length I halted abruptly: "Well,—and you saw Miss Ashleigh? What message does she send to me—her betrothed?"

Mr. Stanton looked confused. "Message! Consider, sir—Miss Ashleigh's situation—the delicacy—and—and—"

"I understand! no message, no word, from a young lady so respectable to a man accused of murder."

Mr. Stanton was silent for some moments; and then said quietly, "Let us change this subject; let us think of what more immediately presses. I see you have been making some notes; may I look at them?"

I composed myself and sat down. "This accuser. Have inquiries really been made as to himself, and his statement of his own proceedings? He comes, he says, from America—in what ship? At what port did he land? Is there any evidence to corroborate his story of the relations he tried to discover—at the inn in which he first put up, and to which he could not find his way?"

"Your suggestions are sensible, Dr. Fenwick. I have forestalled them. It is true that the man lodged at a small inn—the Rising Sun — true that he made inquiries about some relations of the name of Walls, who formerly resided at L——, and afterwards removed to a village ten miles distant—two brothers—tradesmen of small means but respectable character. He at first refused to say at what sea-port he landed, in what ship he sailed. I suspect that he has now told a falsehood as to these matters. I have sent my clerk to Southampton—for it is there he said he was put on shore; we shall see—the man himself is detained in close custody. I hear that his manner is strange and excitable; but that he preserves silence as much as possible. It is generally believed that he is a bad character, perhaps a returned convict, and that this is the true reason why he so long delayed giving evidence, and has been since so reluctant to account for himself. But even if his testimony should be impugned, should break down, still we should have to account for the fact that the casket and the case-knife were found in your bureau. For, granting that a person could, in your absence, have entered your study and placed the articles in your bureau, it is clear that such a person must have been well acquainted with your house, and this stranger to L—— could not have possessed that knowledge."

"Of course not—Mr. Margrave did possess it!"

"Mr. Margrave again!—oh, sir."

I arose and moved away, with an impatient gesture. I could not trust myself to speak. That night I did not sleep; I watched impatiently, gazing on the opposite wall, for the gleam of the Scin-Læca. But the night passed away, and the spectre did not appear.

CHAPTER XLI.

The lawyer came the next day, and with something like a smile on his lips. He brought me a few lines in pencil from Mrs. Ashleigh; they were kindly expressed, bade me be of good cheer; "she never for a moment believed in my guilt; Lilian bore up wonderfully under so terrible a trial; it was an unspeakable comfort to both to receive the visits of a friend so attached to me, and so confident of a triumphant refutation of the hideous calumny—under which I now suffered—as Mr. Margrave!"

The lawyer had seen Margrave again—seen him in that house. Margrave seemed almost domiciled there!

I remained sullen and taciturn during this visit. I longed again for the night. Night came. I heard the distant clock strike twelve, when again the icy wind passed through my hair, and against the wall stood the Luminous Shadow.

"Have you considered?" whispered the voice, still as from afar. "I repeat it—I alone can save you."

"Is it among the conditions which you ask, in return, that I shall resign to you the woman I love?"

"No."

"Is it one of the conditions that I should commit some crime—a crime perhaps heinous as that of which I am accused?"

"No."

"With such reservations, I accept the conditions you may name, provided I, in my turn, may demand one condition from yourself."

"Name it."

"I ask you to quit this town. I ask you, meanwhile, to cease your visits to the house that holds the woman betrothed to me."

"I will cease those visits. And before many days are over, I will quit this town."

"Now, then, say what you ask from me. I am prepared to concede it. And not from fear for myself, but because I fear for the pure and innocent being who is under the spell of your deadly fascination. This is your power over me. You command me through my love for another. Speak."

"My conditions are simple. You will pledge yourself to desist from all charges of insinuation against myself, of what nature soever. You will not, when you meet me in the flesh, refer to what you have known of my likeness in the Shadow. You will be invited to the house at which I may be also a guest; you will come; you will meet and converse with me as guest speaks with guest in the house of a host."

"Is that all?"

"It is all."

"Then I pledge you my faith; keep your own."

"Fear not; sleep secure in the certainty that you will soon be released from these walls."

The shadow waned and faded. Darkness settled back, and a sleep, profound and calm, fell over me.

The next day Mr. Stanton again visited me. He had received that morning a note from Mr. Margrave, stating that he had left L—— to pursue, in person, an investigation which he had already commenced through another, affecting the man who had given evidence against me, and that, if his hope should prove well founded, he trusted to establish my innocence, and convict the real murderer of Sir Philip Derval. In the research he thus volunteered, he had asked for, and obtained, the assistance of the policeman Waby, who, grateful to me for saving the life of his sister, had expressed a strong desire to be employed in my service.

Meanwhile, my most cruel assailant was my old college friend Richard Strahan. For Jeeves had spread abroad Strahan's charge of purloining the memoir which had been intrusted to me; and that accusation had done me great injury in public opinion, because it seemed to give probability to the only motive which ingenuity could ascribe to the foul deed imputed to me. That motive had been first suggested by Mr. Vigors. Cases are on record of men whose life had been previously blameless, who have committed a crime, which seemed to belie their nature, in the monomania of some intense desire. In Spain, a scholar reputed of austere morals, murdered and robbed a traveller for money in order to purchase books; books written, too, by Fathers of his Church! He was intent on solving some problem of theological casuistry. In France, an antiquary esteemed not more for his learning than for amiable and gentle qualities, murdered his most intimate friend for the possession of a medal, without which his own collection was incomplete. These, and similar anecdotes, tending to prove how fatally any vehement desire, morbidly cherished, may suspend the normal operations of reason and conscience, were whispered about by Dr. Lloyd's vindictive partisan, and the inference drawn from them and applied to the assumptions against myself, was the more credulously received, because of that over-refining speculation on motive and act which the shallow accept, in their eagerness to show how readily they understand the profound.

I was known to be fond of scientific, especially of chemical experiments; to be eager in testing the truth of any novel invention. Strahan catching hold of the magistrate's fantastic hypothesis, went about repeating anecdotes of the absorbing passion for analysis and discovery which had characterized me in youth as a medical student, and to which, indeed, I owed the precocious reputation I had obtained.

Sir Philip Derval, according not only to report, but to the direct testimony of his servant, had acquired in the course of his travels many secrets in natural science, especially as connected with the healing art—his servant had deposed to the remarkable cures he had effected by the medicinals stored in the stolen casket—doubtless Sir Philip, in boasting of these medicinals in the course of our conversation, had excited my curiosity, inflamed my imagination, and thus, when I afterwards suddenly met him in a lone spot, a passionate impulse had acted on a brain heated into madness by curiosity and covetuous desire.

All these suppositions, reduced into system, were corroborated by Strahan's charge that I had made away with the manuscript supposed to contain the explanations of the medical agencies employed by Sir Philip, and had sought to shelter my theft by a tale so improbable, that a man of my reputed talent could not have hazarded it if in his sound senses. I saw the web, that had thus been spread around me by hostile prepossessions and ignorant gossip; how could the arts of Margrave scatter that web to the winds? I knew not, but I felt confidence in his promise and his power. Still, so great had been my alarm for Lilian, that the hope of clearing my own innocence was almost lost in my joy that Margrave, at least, was no longer in her presence, and that I had received his pledge to quit the town in which she lived.

Thus, hours rolled on hours, till, I think, on the third day from that night in which I had last beheld the mysterious shadow, my door was hastily thrown open, a confused crowd presented itself at the threshold—the governor of the prison, the police superintendent, Mr. Stanton, and other familiar faces shut out from me since my imprisonment. I knew at the first glance that I was no longer an outlaw beyond the pale of human friendship. And proudly, sternly, as I had supported myself hitherto in solitude and suspense, when I felt warm hands clasping mine, heard joyous voices proffering congratulations, saw in the eyes of all that my innocence had been cleared, the revulsion of emotion was too strong for me—the room reeled on my sight—I fainted. I pass, as quickly as I can, over the explanations that crowded on me when I recovered, and that were publicly given in evidence in Court next morning. I had owed all to Margrave. It seems that he had construed to my favor the very supposition which had been bruited abroad to my prejudice. "For," said he, "it is conjectured that Fenwick committed the crime of which he is accused in the impulse of a disordered reason. That conjecture is based upon the probability that a madman alone could have committed a crime without adequate motive.

But it seems quite clear that the accused is not mad; and I see cause to suspect that the accuser is." Grounding this assumption on the current reports of the witness's manner and bearing since he had been placed under official surveillance, Margrave had commissioned the policeman, Waby, to make inquiries in the village to which the accuser asserted he had gone in quest of his relations, and Waby had, there, found persons who remembered to have heard that the two brothers named Walls lived less by the gains of the petty shop which they kept than by the proceeds of some property consigned to them as the nearest of kin to a lunatic who had once been tried for his life. Margrave had then examined the advertisements in the daily newspapers. One of them, warning the public against a dangerous maniac, who had effected his escape from an asylum in the west of England, caught his attention. To that asylum he had repaired.

There he learned that the patient advertised was one whose propensity was homicide, consigned for life to the asylum on account of a murder, for which he had been tried. The description of this person exactly tallied with that of the pretented American. The medical superintendent of the asylum hearing all particulars from Margrave, expressed a strong persuasion that the witness was his missing patient, and had himself committed the crime of which he had accused another. If so, the superintendent undertook to coax from him the full confession of ail the circumstances. Like many other madmen, and not least those whose propensity is to crime, the fugitive maniac was exceedingly cunning, treacherous, secret, and habituated to trick and stratagem. More subtle than even the astute in possession of all their faculties, whether to achieve his purpose or to conceal it, and fabricate appearances against another. But while, in ordinary conversation, he seemed rational enough to those who were not accustomed to study him, he had one hallucication which, when humored, led him always, not only to betray himself, but to glory in any crime proposed or committed.

He was under the belief that he had made a bargain with Satan, who, in return for implicit obedience, would bear him harmless through all the consequences of such submission, and finally raise him to great power and authorlty. It is no unfrequent illusion of homicidal maniacs to suppose they are under the influence of the Evil One, or possessed by a Demon. Murderers have assigned as the only reason they themselves could give for their crime, that "the Devil got into them," and urged the deed. But the insane have, perhaps, no attribute more in common than that of superweening self-esteem. The maniac who has been removed from a garret sticks straws in his hair and calls them a crown. So much does inordinate arrogance characterize mental aberration, that, in the course of my own practice, I have detected, in that infirmity, the certain sympton of insanity, long before the brain had made its disease manifest even to the most familiar kindred.

Morbid self-esteem accordingly pervaded the dreadful illusion by which the man I now speak of was possessed. He was proud to be the protected agent of the Fallen Angel. And if that self-esteem were artfully appealed to, he would exult superbly in the evil he held himself ordered to perform, as if a special prerogative, an official rank and privilege; then he would be led on to boast gleefully of thoughts which the most cynical of criminals, in whom intelligence was not ruined, would shrink from owning. Then, he would reveal himself in all his deformity with as complacent and frank a self-glorying as some vain good man displays in parading his amiable sentiments and his beneficent deeds.

"If," said the superintendent, "this be the patient who has escaped from me, and if his propensity to homicide has been, in some way, directed towards the person who has been murdered, I shall not be with him a quarter of an hour before he will inform me how it happened, and detail the arts he employed in shifting his crime upon another—all will be told as minutely as a child tells the tale of some school-boy exploit, in which he counts on your sympathy, and feels sure of your applause."

Margrave brought this gentleman back to L——, took him to the mayor, who was one of my warmest supporters: the mayor had sufficient influence to dictate and arrange the rest. The superintendent was introduced to the room in which the pretended American was lodged. At his own desire a select number of witnesses were admitted with him—Margrave excused himself; he said candidly that he was too intimate a friend of mine to be an impartial listener to aught that concerned me so nearly.

The superintendent proved right in his suspicions, and verified his promises. My false accuser was his missing patient; the man recognized Dr. * * * with no apparent terror, rather with an air of condescension, and in a very few minutes was led to tell his own tale, with a gloating complacency both at the agency by which he deemed himself exalted, and at the dexterous cunning with which he had acquitted himself of the task, that increased the horror of his narrative.

He spoke of the mode of his escape, which was extremely ingenious, but of which the details, long in themselves, did not interest me, and I understood them too imperfectly to repeat. He had encountered a sea-faring traveller on the road, whom he had knocked down with a stone, and robbed of his glazed hat and pea-jacket, as well as of a small sum in coin, which last enabled him to pay his fare in a railway that conveyed him eighty miles away from the asylum. Some trifling remnant of this money still in his pocket, he then travelled on foot along the high road till he came to a town about twenty miles distant from L——; there he had stayed a day or two, and there he said "that the Devil had told him to buy a case-knife, which he did." "He knew by that order that the Devil meant him to do something great." "His Master," as he called the fiend, then directed him the road he should take.

He came to L——, put up, as he had correctly stated before, at a small inn, wandered at night about the town, was surprised by the sudden storm, took shelter under the convent arch, overheard somewhat more of my conversation with Sir Philip than he had previously deposed—heard enough to excite his curiosity as to the casket: "While he listened his Master told him that he must get possession of that casket." Sir Philip had quitted the archway almost immediately after I had done so, and he would then have attacked him if he had not caught sight of a policeman going his rounds. He had followed Sir Philip to a house (Mr. Jeeve's). "His Master told him to wait and watch." He did so. When Sir Philip came forth, towards the dawn, he followed him, saw him enter a narrow street, came up to him, seized him by the arm, demanded all he had about him. Sir Philip tried to shake him off —struck at him. What follows, I spare the reader. The deed was done. He robbed the dead man, both of the casket and of the purse that he found in the pockets; had scarcely done so when he heard footsteps.

He had just time to get behind the portico of a detached house at angles with the street, when I came up. He witnessed, from his hiding-place, the brief conference between myself and the policemen, and when they moved on, bearing the body, stole unobserved away. He was going back towards the inn, when it occurred to him that it would be safer if the casket and purse were not about his person; that he asked his Master to direct him how to dispose of them: that his Master guided him to an open yard (a stone-mason's) at a very little distance from the inn; that in this yard there stood an old wych-elm tree, from the gnarled roots of which the earth was worn away, leaving chinks and hollows, in one of which he placed the casket and purse, taking from the latter only two sovereigns and some silver, and then heaping loose mould over the hiding-place. That he then repaired to his inn, and left it late in the morning, on the pretence of seeking for his relations—persons, indeed, who really had been related to him, but of whose death years ago he was aware. He returned to L—— a few days afterwards, and, in the dead of the night, went to take up the casket and money. He found the purse with its contents undisturbed; but the lid of the casket was unclosed.

From the hasty glance he had taken of it before burying it, it had seemed to him firmly locked—he was alarmed lest some one had been to the spot. But his Master whispered to him not to mind, told him that he might now take the casket, and would be guided what to do with it; that he did so, and opening the lid, found the casket empty; that he took the rest of the money out of the purse, but that he did not take the purse itself, for it had a crest and initials on it, which might lead to the discovery of what had been done; that he therefore left it in the hollow amongst the roots, heaping the mould over it as before; that, in the course of the day, he heard the people at the inn talk of the murder, and that his own first impulse was to get out of the town immediately, but that his Master "made him too wise for that," and bade him stay; that passing through the streets, he saw me come out of the sash-window door, go to a stable yard on the other side of the house, mount on horseback and ride away; that he observed the sash-door was left partially open; that he walked by it and saw the room empty; there was only a dead wall opposite; the place was solitary, unobserved; that his Master directed him to lift up the sash gently, enter the room, and deposit the knife and the casket in a large walnut-tree bureau which stood unlooked near the window. All that followed—his visit to Mr. Vigors, his accusation against myself, his whole tale—was, he said, dictated by his Master, who was highly pleased with him, and promised to bring him safely through. And here he turned round with a hideous smile, as if for approbation of his notable cleverness and respect for his high employ.

Mr. Jeeves had the curiosity to request the keeper to inquire how, in what form, or in what manner, the Fiend appeared to the narrator, or conveyed his infernal dictates. The man at first refused to say; but it was gradually drawn from him that the Demon had no certain and invariable form; sometimes it appeared to him in the form of a rat: sometimes even of a leaf, or a fragment of wood, or a rusty nail; but, that his Master's voice always came to him distinctly, whatever shape he appeared in; only, he said, with an air of great importance, his Master, this time, had graciously condescended, ever since he left the asylum, to communicate with him in a much more pleasing and imposing aspect than he had ever done before—in the form of a beautiful youth, or, rather, like a bright rose-colored shadow, in which the features of a young man were visible, and that he had heard the voice more distinctly than usual, though in a milder tone, and seeming to come to him from a great distance.

After these revelations the man became suddenly disturbed. He shook from limb to limb, he seemed convulsed with terror; he cried out that he had betrayed the secret of his Master, who had warned him not to describe his appearance and mode of communication, or he would surrender his servant to the tormentors. Then the maniac's terror gave way to fury; his more direful propensity made itself declared; he sprang into the midst of his frightened listeners, seized Mr. Vigors by the throat, and would have strangled him but for the prompt rush of the superintendent and his satellites. Foaming at the mouth, and horribly raving, he was then manacled, a strait-waistcoat thrust upon him, and the group so left him in charge of his captors. Inquiries were immediately directed towards such circumstantial evidence as might corroborate the details he had so minutely set forth. The purse, recognized as Sir Philip's, by the valet of the deceased, was found buried under the wych-elm. A policeman despatched, express, to the town in which the maniac declared the knife to have been purchased, brought back word that a cutler in the place remembered perfectly to have sold such a knife to a seafaring man, and identified the instrument when it was shown to him.

From the chink of a door ajar, in the wall opposite my sash-window, a maid-servant, watching for her sweetheart (a journeyman carpenter, who habitually passed that way on going home to dine), had, though unobserved by the murder, seen him come out of my window at a time that corresponded with the dates of his own story, though she had thought nothing of it at the moment. He might be a patient, or have called on business; she did not know that I was from home. The only point of importance not cleared up was that which related to the opening of the casket—the disappearance of the contents; the lock had been unquestionably forced. No one, however, could suppose that some third person had discovered the hiding-place and forced open the casket to abstract its contents and then rebury it. The only probable supposition was, that the man himself had forced it open, and, deeming the contents of no value, had thrown them away before he had hidden the casket and purse, and, in the chaos of his reason, and forgotten that he had so done. Who could expect that every link in a madman's tale would be found integral and perfect?

In short, little importance was attached to this solitary doubt. Crowds accompanied me to my door, when I was set free, in open court, stainless;—it was a triumphal procession. The popularity I had previously enjoyed, superseded for a moment by so horrible a charge, came back to me tenfold, as with the reaction of generous repentance for a momentary doubt. One man shared the public favor—the young man whose acuteness had delivered me from the peril, and cleared the truth from so awful a mystery; but Margrave had escaped from congratulation and compliment; he had gone on a visit to Strahnn, at Derval Court.

Alone, at last, in the welcome sanctuaary of my own home, what were my thoughts? Prominent amongst them all was that assertion of the madman; which had made me shudder when repeated to me; he had been guided to the murder and to all the subsequent proceedings by the luminous shadow of the beautiful youth—the Scin-Læa to which I had pledged myself. If Sir Philip Derval could be believed, Margrave was possessed of powers, derived from fragmentary recollections of a knowledge acquired in a former state of being, which wonld render his remorseless intelligence infinitely dire, and frustrate the endeavors of a reason, unassisted by similar powers, to thwart his designs or bring the law against his crimes. Had he then the arts that could thus influence the minds of others to serve his fell purposes, and achieve securely his own evil ends through agencies that could not be traced home to himself?

But for what conceivable purpose had I been subjected as a victim to influences as much beyond my control as the Fate or Demoniac Necessity of a Greek Myth? In the legends of the classic world some august sufferer is oppressed by powers more than mortal, but with an ethical if gloomy vindication of his chastisement—he pays the penalty of crime committed by his ancestors or himself, or he has braved, by arrogating equality with the gods, the mysterious calamity which the gods alone can inflict.

But I, no descendant of Pelops, no Œdipus boastful of a wisdom whom could interpret the enigmas of the Sphynx, while ignorant even of his own birth—what had I done to be singled out from the herd of men for trials and visitations from the Shadowland of ghosts and sorcerers? It would be ludicrously absurd to suppose that Dr. Lloyd's dying imprecation could have had a prophetic effect upon my destiny; to believe that the pretences of mesmerizers were specially favored by Providence, and that to question their assumptions was an offence of profanation to be punished by exposure to preternatural agencies. There was not even that congruity between cause and effect which fable seeks in excuse for its inventions. Of all men living, I, unimaginative disciple of austere science, should be the last to become the sport of that witchcraft which even imagination reluctantly allows to the machinery of poets, and science casts aside into the mouldy lumber-room of obsolete superstition.

Rousing my mind from enigmas impossible to solve—it was with intense and yet most melancholy satisfaction that I turned to the image of Lilian, rejoicing, though with a thrill of awe, that the promise so mysteriously conveyed to my senses had, here too, been already fulfilled—Margrave had left the town; Lilian was no longer subjected to his evil fascination. But an instinct told me that that fascination had already produced an effect adverse to all hope of happiness for me. Lilian's love for myself was gone. Impossible otherwise that she —in whose nature I had always admired that generous devotion which is more or less inseparable from the romance of youth—should have never conveyed to me one word of consolation in the hour of my agony and trial: that she who, till the last evening we had met, had ever been so docile, in the sweetness of a nature femininely submissive to my slightest wish, should have disregarded my solemn injunction, and admitted Margrave to acquaintance, nay, to familiar intimacy; at the very time, too, when to disobey my injunctions was to embitter my ordeal, and add her own contempt to the degradation imposed upon my honor! No, her heart must be wholly gone from me; her very nature wholly warped. An union between us had become impossible. My love for her remained unshattered; the more tender, perhaps, for a sentiment of compassion. But my pride was shocked, my heart was wounded. My love was not mean and servile. Enough for me to think that she would be at least saved from Margrave. *Her* life associated with his!—contemplation, horrible and ghastly!—from that fate she was saved. Later, she would recover the effect of an influence happily so brief. She might form some new attachment—some new tie. But love once withdrawn is never to be restored—and her love was withdrawn from me. I had but to release her, with my own lips, from our engagement—she would welcome that release. Mournful but firm in these thoughts and these resolutions, I sought Mrs. Ashleigh's house.

CHAPTER XLII.

It was twilight when I entered, unannounced (as had been my wont in our familiar intercourse), the quiet sitting-room in which I expected to find mother and child. But Lilian was there alone, seated by the open window, her hands crossed and drooping on her knee, her eye fixed upon the darkening summer skies, in which the evening star had just stolen forth, bright and steadfast, near the pale sickle of a half-moon that was dimly visible, but gave as yet no light.

Let any lover imagine the reception he would expect to meet from his betrothed, coming into her presence after he had passed triumphant through a terrible peril to life and fame—and conceive what ice froze my blood, what anguish weighed down my heart, when Lilian, turning towards me, rose not, spoke not—gazed at me heedlessly as if at some indifferent stranger—and—and —— But no matter. I cannot bear to recall it even now, at the distance of years! I sat down beside her, and took her hand, without pressing it; it rested languidly, passively in mine—one moment;—I dropped it then, with a bitter sigh.

"Lilian," I said quietly, you love me no longer. Is it not so?"

She raised her eyes to mine, looked at me wistfully, and pressed her hand on her forehead, then said, in a strange voice, "Did I ever love you? What do you mean?"

"Lilian, Lilian, rouse yourself; are you not, while you speak, under some spell, some influence which you cannot describe nor account for?"

She paused a moment before she answered, calmly, "No! Again I ask what do you mean?"

"What do I mean? Do you forget that we are betrothed? Do you forget how often, and how recently, our vows of affection and constancy have been exchanged?"

"No, I do not forget; but I must have deceived you and myself—"

"It is true, then, that you love me no more?"

"I suppose so."

"But, oh, Lilian, is it that your heart is only closed to me? or is it—oh, answer truthfully—is it given to another?—to him—to him—against whom I warned you, whom I implored you not to receive? Tell me, at least, that your love is not gone to Margrave—"

"To him—love to him. Oh no—no—"

"What, then, is your feeling towards him?"

Lilian's face grew visibly paler—even in that dim light." "I know not," she said, almost in a whisper; "but it is partly awe—partly—"

"What!"

"Abhorrence!" she said, almost fiercely, and rose to her feet, with a wild defying start.

"If that be so," I said gently, "you would not grieve were you never again to see him—"

"But I shall see him again," she murmured in a tone of weary sadness, and sank back once more into her chair.

"I think not," said I, "and I hope not. And now hear me and heed me, Lilian. It is enough for me, no matter what your feelings towards another, to learn from yourself that the affection you once professed for me is gone. I release you from your troth. If folks ask why we two henceforth separate the lives we had agreed to join, you may say, if you please, that you could not give your hand to a man who had known the taint of a felon's prison, even on a false charge. If that seems to you an ungenerous reason, we will leave it to your mother to find a better. Farewell! For your own sake I can yet feel happiness—happiness to hear that you do not love the man against whom I warn you still more solemnly than before! Will you not give me your hand in parting—and have I not spoken your own wish?"

She turned away her face, and resigned her hand to me in silence. Silently I held it in mine, and my emotions nearly stifled me. One symptom of regret, of reluctance, on her part, and I should have fallen at her feet, and cried, "Do not let us break a tie which our vows should have made indissoluble; heed not my offers—wrung from a tortured heart! You cannot have ceased to love me!" But no such symptom of relenting showed in her, and with a groan I left the room.

CHAPTER XLIII.

I WAS just outside the garden-door, when I felt an arm thrown round me, my cheek kissed and wetted with tears. Could it be Lilian? Alas, no! It was her mother's voice, that, between laughing and crying, exclaimed hysterically: "This is joy, to see you again, and on these thresholds. I have just come from your house; I went there on purpose to congratulate you, and to talk to you about Lilian. But you have seen her?"

"Yes; I have but this moment left her. Come this way." I drew Mrs. Ashleigh back into the garden, along the old winding walk, which the shrubs concealed from view of the house. We sat down on a rustic seat where I had often sat with Lilian, midway between the house and the Monk's Well. I told the mother what had passed between me and her daughter; I made no complaint of Lilian's coldness and change; I did not hint at its cause. "Girls of her age will change," said I, "and all that now remains is for us two to agree on such a tale to our curious neighbors, as may rest the whole blame on me. Man's Name is of robust fibre; it could not push its way to a place in the world, if it could not bear, without sinking, the load idle tongues may lay on it. Not so Woman's Name—what is but gossip against Man, is scandal against Woman."

"Do not be rash, my dear Allen," said Mrs Ashleigh, in great distress. "I feel for you, I understand you; in your case I might act as you do. I cannot blame you. Lilian is changed—changed unaccountably. Yet sure I am that the change is only on the surface, that her heart is really yours, as entirely and as faithfully as ever it was; and that later, when she recovers from the strange, dreamy kind of torpor which appears to have come over all her faculties and all her affections, she would awake with a despair which you cannot conjecture, to the knowledge that you had renounced her."

"I have not renounced her," said I, impatiently; "I did but restore her freedom of choice. But pass by this now, and explain to me more fully the change in your daughter, which I gather from your words is not confined to me.

"I wished to speak of it before you saw her, and for that reason came to your house. It was on the morning in which we left her aunt's to return hither that I first noticed something peculiar in her look and manner. She seemed absorbed and absent, so much so that I asked her several times to tell me what made her so grave, but I could only get from her that she had a confused dream which she could not recall distinctly enough to relate, but that she was sure it boded evil. During the journey she became gradually more herself, and began to look forward with delight to the idea of seeing you again. Well, you came that evening. What passed between you and her you know best. You complained that she slighted your request to shun all acquaintance with Mr. Margrave. I was surprised that, whether your wish were reasonable or not, she could have hesitated to comply with it. I spoke to her about it after you had gone, and she wept bitterly at thinking that she had displeased you."

"She wept! You amaze me. Yet the next day what a note she returned to mine!"

"The next day the change in her became very visible to me. She told me, in an excited manner, that she was convinced that she ought not to marry you. Then came, the following day, the news of your committal. I heard of it, but dared not break it to her. I went to our friend the mayor, to consult with him what to say, what do; and to learn more distinctly than I had done from terrified, incoherent servants, the rights of so dreadful a story. When I returned, I found, to my amazement, a young stranger in the drawing-room; it was Mr. Margrave—Miss Brabazon had brought him at his request. Lilian was in the room, too, and my astonishment was increased, when she said to me with a singular smile, vague but tranquil: 'I know all about Allen Fenwick; Mr. Margrave has told me all. He is a friend of Allen's. He says there is no cause for fear.' Mr. Margrave then apologized to me for his intrusion in a caressing, kindly manner, as if one of the family. He said he was so intimate with you that he felt that he could best break to Miss Ashleigh an information she might receive elsewhere, for that he was the only man in the town who treated the charge with ridicule.

"You know the wonderful charm of this young man's manner. I cannot explain to you how it was, but in a few moments I was as much at home with him as if he had been your brother. To be brief, having once come, he came constantly. He had moved, two days before you went to Derval Court, from his hotel to apartments in Mr. ——'s house, just opposite. We could see him on his balcony from our terrace; he would smile to us and come across. I did wrong in slighting your injunction, and suffering Lilian to do so. I could not help it, he was such a comfort to me—to her, too—in her tribulation. He alone had no doleful words, wore no long face; he alone was invariably cheerful. 'Everything,' he said, 'would come right in a day or two.'"

"And Lilian could not but admire this young man, he is so beautiful."

"Beautiful? Well, perhaps. But if you have a jealous feeling, you were never more mistaken. Lilian, I am convinced, does more than dislike him; he has inspired her with repugnance, with terror. And much as I own I like him, in his wild, joyous, careless, harmless way, do not think I flatter you if I say that Mr. Margrave is not the man to make any girl untrue to you—untrue to a lover with infinitely less advantages than you may pretend to. He would be an universal favorite, I grant; but there is something in him, or a something wanting in him, which makes liking and admiration stop short of love. I know not why; perhaps, because, with all his good humor, he is so absorbed in himself, so intensely egotistical — so light; were he less clever, I should say so frivolous. He could not make love, he could not say in the serious tone of a man in earnest, 'I love you.' He owned as much to me, and owned, too, that he knew not even what love was. As to myself—Mr. Margrave appears rich; no whisper against his character or his honor ever reached me. Yet were you out of the question, and were there no stain on his birth, nay, were he as high in rank and wealth as he is favored by Nature in personal advantages, I confess I could never consent to trust him with my daughter's fate. A voice at my heart would cry, 'No!' It may be an unreasonable prejudice, but I could not bear to see him touch Lilian's hand!"

"Did she never, then—never suffer him even to take her hand?"

"Never. Do not think so meanly of her as to suppose that she could be caught by a fair face, a graceful manner. Reflect; just before, she had refused, for your sake, Ashleigh Sumner, whom Lady Haughton said 'no girl in her senses could refuse;' and this change in Lilian really began before we returned to L——; before she had even seen Mr. Margrave. I am convinced it is something in the reach of your skill as physician—it is on the nerves, the system. I will give you a proof of what I say, only do not betray me to her. It was during your imprisonment, the night before your release, that I was awakened by her coming to my bedside. She was sobbing as if her heart would break. 'O mother, mother!' she cried, 'pity me, help me — I am so wretched.' 'What is the matter, darling?' 'I have been so cruel to Allen, and I know I shall be so again. I cannot help it. Do not question me; only if we are separated, if he cast me off, or I reject him, tell him some day—perhaps when I am in my grave—not to believe appearances; and that I, in my heart of hearts, never ceased to love him!'"

"She said that! You are not deceiving me?"

"Oh no! how can you think so?"

"There is hope still," I murmured; and I bowed my head upon my hands, hot tears forcing their way through the clasped fingers.

"One word more," said I; "you tell me that Lilian has a repugnance to this Margrave, and yet that she found comfort in his visits—a comfort that could not be wholly ascribed to cheering words he might say about myself, since it is all but certain that I was not, at that time, uppermost in her mind. Can you explain this apparent contradiction?"

"I cannot, otherwise than by a conjecture which you would ridicule."

"I can ridicule nothing now. What is your conjecture?"

I know how much you disbelieve in the stories one hears of animal magnetism and electro biology, otherwise—"

"You think that Margrave exercises some power of that kind over Lilian? Has he spoken of such a power?"

"Not exactly; but he said that he was sure Lilian possessed a faculty that he called by some hard name, not clairvoyance, but a faculty, which he said, when I asked him to explain, was akin to prevision—to second sight. Then he talked of the Priestesses who had administered the ancient oracles. Lilian, he said, reminded him of them, with her deep eyes and mysterious smile."

"And Lilian heard him? What said she?"

"Nothing; she seemed in fear while she listened."

"He did not offer to try any of those arts practised by professional mesmerists and other charlatans?"

"I thought he was about to do so, but I forestalled him; saying I never would consent to any experiment of that kind, either on myself or my daughter."

"And he replied—?"

"With his gay laugh, 'that I was very foolish; that a person possessed of such a faculty as he attributed to Lilian, would, if the faculty were developed, be an invaluable adviser.' He would have said more, but I begged him to desist. Still I fancy at times—do not be angry—that he does somehow or other bewitch her, unconsciously to herself; for she always knows when he is coming. Indeed, I am not sure that he does not bewitch myself, for I by no means justify my conduct in admitting him to an intimacy so familiar, and in spite of your wish; I have reproached myself, resolved to shut my door on him, or to show by my manner that his visits were unwelcome; yet when Lilian has said, in the drowsy lethargic tone which has come into her voice (her voice naturally earnest and impressive, though always low), 'Mother, he will be here in two minutes—I wish to leave the room and cannot'—I, too, have felt as if something constrained me against my will; as if, in short, I were under that influence which Mr. Vigors—whom I will never forgive for his conduct to you—would ascribe to mesmerism. But will you not come in and see Lilian again?"

"No, not to-night; but watch and heed her, and if you see aught to make you honestly believe that she regrets the rupture of the old tie from which I have released her—why, you know, Mrs. Ashleigh, that—that—" My voice failed—I wrung the good woman s hand, and went my way.

I had always till then considered Mrs. Ashleigh—if not as Mrs. Poyntz described her—"commonplace weak"—still of an intelligence somewhat below medocrity. I now regarded her with respect as well as grateful tenderness; her plain sense had divined what all my boasted knowledge had failed to detect in my earlier intimacy with Margrave—viz. that in him there was a something present, or a something wanting, which forbade love and excited fear. Young, beautiful, wealthy, seemingly blameless in life as he was, she would not have given her daughter's hand to him!

CHAPTER XLIV.

THE next day my house was filled with visitors. I had no notion that I had so many friends. Mr. Vigors wrote me a generous and handsome letter, owning his prejudices against me on account of his sympathy with poor Dr. Lloyd, and begging my pardon for what he now felt to have been harshness, if not distorted justice. But what most moved me, was the entrance of Strahan, who rushed up to me with the heartiness of old college days. "Oh, my dear Allen can you ever forgive me; that I should have bisbelieved your word—should have suspected you of abstracting my poor cousin's memoir?"

"Is it found, then?"

"Oh, yes; you must thank Margrave. He, clever fellow, you know, came to me on a visit yesterday. He put me at once on the right scent. Only guess; but you never can! It was that wretched old housekeeper who purloined the manuscript. You remember she came into the room while you were looking at the memoir. She heard us talk about it; her curiosity was roused; she longed to know the history of her old master, under his own hand; she could not sleep; she heard me go up to bed; she thought you might leave the book on the table when you, too, went to rest. She stole down stairs, peeped through the keyhole of the library, saw you asleep, the book lying before you, entered, took away the book softly, meant to glance at its contents and to return it. You were sleeping so soundly she thought you would not wake for an hour; she carried it into the library, leaving the door open, and there began to pour over it; she stumbled first on one of the passages in Latin; she hoped to find some part in plain English, turned over the leaves, putting her candle close to them, for the old woman's eyes were dim, when she heard you make some sound in your sleep. Alarmed, she looked round; you were moving uneasily in your seat, and muttering to yourself.

"From watching you she was soon diverted by the consequence of her own confounded curiosity and folly. In moving, she had unconsciously brought the poor manuscript close to the candle; the leaves caught the flame; her own cap and hand burning first made her aware of the mischief done. She threw down the book; her sleeve was in flames; she had first to tear off the sleeve, which was, luckily for her, not sewn to her dress. By the time she recovered presence of mind to attend to the book, half its leaves were reduced to tinder. She did not dare then to replace what was left of the manuscript on your table; returned, with it, to her room, hid it, and resolved to keep her own secret. I should never have guessed it; I had never even spoken to her of the occurrence; but when I talked over the disappearance of the book to Margrave last night, and expressed my disbelief of your story, he said in his merry way: 'But do you think that Fenwick is the only person curious about your cousin's odd ways and strange history? Why, every servant in the household would have been equally curious. You have examined your servants, of course?' 'No, I never thought of it.' 'Examine them now, then. Examine especially that old housekeeper. I observe a great change in her manner since I came her, weeks ago, to look over the house. She has something on her mind—I see it in her eyes.' Then it occurred to me, too, that the woman's manner had altered, and that she seemed always in a tremble and a fidget. I went at once to her room, and charged her with stealing the book. She fell on her knees, and told the whole story as I have told it you, and as I shall take care to tell it to all to whom I have so foolishly blabbed my yet more foolish suspicions of yourself. But can you forgive me, old friend?"

"Heartily, heartily! And the book is burned?"

"See;" and he produced a mutilated manuscript. Strange, the part burned—reduced, indeed, to tinder—was the concluding part that related to Haroun—to Grayle: no vestige of that part was left; the earlier portions were scorched and mutilated, though in some places still decipherable; but as my eye hastily run over those places, I saw only mangled sentences of the experimental problems which the writer had so minutely elaborated.

"Will you keep the manuscript as it is, and as long as you like?" said Strahan.

"No, no; I will have nothing more to do with it. Consult some other man of science. And so this is the old woman's whole story? No accomplice—none? No one else shared her curiosity and her task?"

"No. Oddly enough, though, she made much the same excuse for her pitiful folly that the madman made for his terrible crime; she said, 'the Devil put it into her head.' Of course he did, as he puts everything wrong into any one's head. That does not mend the matter."

"How! did she, too, say she saw a Shadow and heard a voice?"

"No; not such a liar as that, and not mad enough for such a lie. But she said that when she was in bed, thinking over the book, something irresistible urged her to get up and go down into the study; swore she felt something lead her by the hand; swore, too, that when she first discovered the manuscript was not in English, something whispered in her ear to turn over the leaves and approach them to the candle. But I had no patience to listen to all this rubbish. I sent her out of the house, bag and baggage. But, alas! is this to be the end of all my wise cousin's grand discoveries?"

True, of labors that aspired to bring into the chart of science new worlds, of which even the traditionary rumor was but a voice from the land of fable—nought left but broken vestiges of a daring foot-step! The hope of a name imperishable amidst the loftiest hierarchy of Nature's secret temple, with all the pomp of recorded experiment, that applied to the mysteries of Egypt and Chaldæa the inductions of Bacon, the tests of Liebig—was there nothing left of this but what, here and there, some puzzled student might extract, garbled, mutilated, perhaps unintelligible, from shreds of sentences, wrecks of problems! O mind of man, can the works, on which thou wouldst found immortality below, be annulled into smoke and tinder by an inch of candle in the hand of an old woman!

When Strahan left me, I went out, but not yet to visit patients. I stole through by-paths into the fields; I needed solitude to bring my thoughts into shape and order. What was delusion, and what not?—Was I right or the Public? Was Margrave really the most innocent and serviceable of human beings, kindly affectionate, employing a wonderful acuteness for benignant ends? Was I, in truth, indebted to him for the greatest boon one man can bestow on another? For life rescued, for fair name justified? Or had he, by some demoniac sorcery, guided the hand of the murderer against the life of the person who alone could imperil his own? had he, by the same dark spells, urged the woman to the act that had destroyed the only record of his monstrous being—the only evidence that I was not the sport of an illusion in the horror with which he inspired me?

But if the latter supposition could be admissible, did he use his agents only to betray them afterwards to exposure, and that, without any possible clue to his own detection as the instigator? Then, there came over me confused recollections of tales of mediæval withcraft, which I had read in boyhood. Were there not on judical record, attestation and evidence solemn and circumstantial, of powers analogous to those now exercised by Margrave? Of sorcerers instigating to sin through influences ascribed to Demons—making their apparitions glide through guarded walls, their voices heard from afar in the solitude of dungeons or monastic cells? subjugating victims to their will, by means which no vigilance could have detected, if the victims themselves had not confessed the witchcraft that had ensnared—courting a sure and infamous death in that confession—preferring such death to a life so haunted? Were stories so gravely set forth in the pomp of judicial evidence, and in the history of times comparatively recent, indeed, to be massed—pell-mell together, as a *moles indigesta* of senseless superstition,—all the witnesses to be deemed liars? all the victims and tools of the sorcerers lunatics? all the examiners or judges, with their solemn gradations—lay and clerical—from Commissions of Inquiry to Courts of Appeal,—to be despised for credulity, loathed for cruelity; or, amidst records so numerous, so imposingly attested,—were there the fragments of a terrible truth? And had our ancestors been so unwise in those laws we now deem so savage, by which the world was rid of scourges more awful and more potent than the felon with his candid dagger? Fell instigators of the evil in men's secret hearts—shaping into action the vague, half-formed desire, and guiding with agencies, impalpable, unseen, their spell-bound instruments of calamity and death.

Such were the gloomy questions that I—by repute, the sternest advocate of common sense against fantastic errors;—by profession, the searcher into flesh and blood, and tissue, and nerve, and sinew, for the causes of all that disease the mechanism of the universal human frame;—I, self-boasting physician, sceptic, philosopher, materialist — revolved, not amidst gloomy pines, under grim winter skies, but as I paced slow through laughing meadows, and by the banks of merry streams, in the ripeness of the golden August: the hum of insects in the fragrant grass, the flutter of birds amid the delicate green of boughs chequered by playful sunbeams and gentle shadows, and ever in sight of the resorts of busy word-day man. Walls, roof-tops church-spires rising high. There, white and modern, the handwriting of our race, in this practical nineteenth century, on its square plain masonry and Doric shafts, the Town-Hall, central in the animated market-place. And I—I—prying into long-neglected corners and dust-holes of memory for what my reason had flung there as worthless rubbish; reviving the jargon of French law, in the *procès verbal*, against a Gille de Retz, or an Urbain Grandier, and sifting the equity of sentences on witchcraft!

Bursting the links of this ghastly soliloquy with a laugh at my own folly, I struck into a narrow path that led back towards the city, by a quiet and rural suburb: the path wound on through a wide and solitary churchyard, at the base of the Abbey-hill. Many of the former dwellers on that eminence now slept in the lowly burial-ground at its foot. And the place, mournfully decorated with the tombs which still jealously mark distinctions of rank amidst the levelling democracy of the grave, was kept trim with the care which comes half from piety, half from pride.

I seated myself on a bench, placed between the clipped yew-trees that bordered the path from the entrance to the church porch; deeming vaguely that my own perplexing thoughts might imbibe a quiet from the quiet of the place.

"And oh," I murmured to myself, "oh that I had one bosom friend to whom I might freely confide all these torturing riddles which I cannot solve—one who could read my heart; light up its darkness; exorcise its spectres; one in whose wisdom I could welcome a guide through the Nature which now suddenly changes her aspect, opening out from the walls with which I had fenced and enclosed her as mine own formal garden —all her pathways, therein, trimmed to my footstep; all her blooms grouped and harmonized to my own taste in color; all her groves, all her caverns, but the soothing retreats of a Muse or a Science; opening out—opening out, desert on desert, into clueless and measureless space! Gone is the garden? Were its confines too narrow for Nature? Be it so! The Desert replaces the garden, but where ends the Desert? Reft from my senses are the laws which gave order and place to their old questionless realm. I stand lost and appalled amidst Chaos. Did my Mind misconstrue the laws it deemed fixed and immutable? Be it so! But still Nature cannot be lawless; Creation is not a Chaos. If my senses deceive me in some things, they are still unerring in others; if thus, in some things, fallacious, still, in other things, truthful. Are there within me senses finer than those I have cultured, or without me vistas of knowledge which instincts, apart from my senses, divine? So long as I deal with the Finite alone, my senses suffice me; but when the Infinite is obtruded upon me, there, are my senses faithless deserters? If so, is there aught else in my royal resources of Man—whose ambition it is, from the first dawn of his glory as Thinker, to invade, and to subjugate Nature,—is there aught else to supply the place of those traitors the senses, who report to my Reason, their judge and their sovereign, as truths, seen and heard, tales which my Reason forfeits her sceptre if she does not disdain as lies? Oh, for a friend! oh, for a guide!

And as I so murmured, my eye fell upon the form of a kneeling child;—at the farther end of the burial-ground, beside a grave with its new headstone gleaming white amidst the older moss-grown tombs, a female child, her head bowed, her hands clasped. I could see but the outline of her small form in its sable dress—an infant beside the dead.

My eye and my thoughts were turned from that silent figure, too absorbed in my own restless tumult of doubt and dread, for sympathy with the grief or the consolation of a kneeling child. And yet I should have remembered that tomb! Again I murmured with a fierce impatience, "Oh, for a friend! oh, for a guide!"

I heard steps on the walk under the yews. And an old man came in sight, slightly bent, with long gray hair, but still with enough of vigor for years to come—in his tread, firm though slow—in the unshrunken muscle of his limbs and the steady light of his clear blue eye. I started. Was it possible? That countenance, marked, indeed, with the lines of laborious thought, but sweet in the mildness of humanity, and serene in the peace of conscience! I could not be mistaken. Julius Faber was before me. The profound pathologist, to whom my own proud self-esteem acknowledged inferiority, without humiliation; the generous benefactor to whom I owed my own smoothed entrance into the arduous road of fame and fortune. I had longed for a friend, a guide; what I sought stood suddenly at my side.

CHAPTER XLV.

Explanation, on Faber's part, was short and simple. The nephew whom he designed as the heir to his wealth, had largely outstripped the liberal allowance made to him—had incurred heavy debts; and in order to extricate himself from the debts, had plunged into ruinous speculations. Faber had come back to England to save his heir from prison or outlawry, at the expense of more than three-fourths of the destined inheritance. To add to all, the young man had married a young lady without fortune; the uncle only heard of this marriage on arriving in England. The spendthrift was hiding from his creditors in the house of his father-in-law, in one of the western counties. Faber there sought him; and, on becoming acquainted with his wife, grew reconciled to the marriage, and formed hopes of his nephew's future redemption. He spoke, indeed, of the young wife with great affection. She was good and sensible; willing and anxious to encounter any privation by which her husband might retrieve the effects of his folly. "So," said Faber, "on consultation with this excellent creature—for my poor nephew is so broken down by repentance, that others must think for him how to exalt repentance into reform—my plans were determined. I shall remove my prodigal from all scenes of temptation. He has youth, strength, plenty of energy, hitherto misdirected. I shall take him from the Old World into the New. I have decided on Australia. The fortune still left to me, small here, will be ample capital there. It is not enough to maintain us separately, so we must all live together. Besides, I feel that, though I have neither the strength nor the experience which could best serve a young settler on a strange soil, still, under my eye, my poor boy will be at once more prudent and more persevering. We sail next week."

Faber spoke so cheerfully that I knew not how to express compassion; yet, at his age, after a career of such prolonged and distinguished labor, to resign the ease and comforts of the civilized state for the hardships and rudeness of an infant colony, seemed to me a dreary prospect; and, as delicately, as tenderly as I could to one whom I loved and honored as a father, I placed at his disposal the fortune which, in great part, I owed to him,—pressing him at least to take from it enough to secure to himself in his own country, a home suited to his years and worthy of his station. He rejected all my offers, however earnestly urged on him, with his usual modest and gentle dignity; and assuring me that he looked forward with great interest to a residence in lands new to his experience, and affording ample scope for the hardy enjoyments which had always most allured his tastes, he hastened to change the subject.

"And who, think you, is the admirable helpmate my scapegrace has had the saving good luck to find? A daughter of the worthy man who undertook the care of poor Dr. Lloyd's orphans—the orphans who owed so much to your generous exertions to secure a provision for them—and that child, now just risen from her father's grave, is my pet companion, my darling ewe-lamb—Dr. Lloyd's daughter Amy."

Here the child joined us, quickening her pace as she recognized the old man, and nestling to his side as she glanced wisfully towards myself. A winning, candid, lovable child's face, somewhat melancholy, somewhat more thoughtful than is common to the face of childhood, but calm, intelligent, and ineffably mild. Presently she stole from the old man, and put her hand in mine:

"Are you not the kind gentleman who came to see Him that night when he passed away from us, and who, they all say at home, was so good to my brothers and me? Yes, I recollect you now." And she put her pure face to mine, wooing me to kiss it.

I kind! I good! I—I! Alas! she little knew, little guessed, the wrathful imprecation her father had bequeathed to me that fatal night!

I did not dare to kiss Dr. Lloyd's orphan daughter, but my tears fell over her hand. She took them as signs of pity, and, in her infant thankfulness, silently kissed me.

"Oh, my friend!" I murmured to Faber, "I have much that I yearn to say to you—alone—alone—come to my house with me, be at least my guest as long as you stay in this town."

"Willingly," said Faber, looking at me more intently than he had done before, and, with the true eye of the practised Healer, at once soft and penetrating.

He rose, took my arm, and whispering a word in the ear of the little girl, she went on before us, turning her head, as she gained the gate, for another look at her father's grave. As we walked to my house, Julius Faber spoke to me much of this child. Her brothers were all at school; she was greatly attached to his nephew's wife; she had become yet more attached to Faber himself, though on so short an acquaintance; it had been settled that she was to accompany the emigrants to Australia.

"There," said he, "the sum, that some munificent but unknown, friend of her father has settled on her, will provide her no mean dower for a colonist's wife, when the time comes for her to bring a blessing to some other hearth than ours." He went on to say that she had wished to accompany him to L——, in order to visit her father's grave before crossing the wide seas; "and she has taken such fond care of me all the way, that you might fancy I were the child of the two. I come back to this town, partly to dispose of a few poor houses in it which still belong to me, principally to bid you farewell before quitting the Old World, no doubt for ever. So, on arriving to-day, I left Amy by herself in the churchyard while I went to your house, but you were from home. And now I must congratulate you on the reputation you have so rapidly acquired, which has even surpassed my predictions."

"You are aware," said I falteringly, "of the extraordinary charge from which that part of my reputation dearest to all men has just emerged?"

He had but seen a short account in a weekly journal, written after my release. He asked details, which I postponed.

Reaching my home, I hastened to provide for the comfort of my two unexpected guests; strove to rally myself—to be cheerful. Not till night, when Julius Faber and I were alone together, did I touch on what was weighing at my heart. Then, drawing to his side, I told him all;—all of which the substance is herein written, from the death-scene in Dr. Lloyd's chamber to the hour in which I had seen Dr. Lloyd's child at her father's grave. Some of the incidents and conversations which had most impressed me, I had already committed to writing, in the fear that, otherwise, my fancy might forge for its own thraldom the links of reminiscence which my memory might let fall from its chain. Faber listened with a silence only interrupted by short pertinent questions; and when I had done, he remained thoughtful for some moments; then the great physician replied thus:

"I take for granted your conviction of the reality of all you tell me, even of the Luminous Shadow, of the bodiless Voice; but, before admitting the reality itself, we must abide by the old maxim, not to accept as cause to effect those agencies which belong to the Marvellous, when causes less improbable for the effect can be rationally conjectured. In this case are there not such causes? Certainly there are—"

"There are?"

"Listen: you are one of those men who attempt to stifle their own imagination. But in all completed intellect, imagination exists, and will force its way; deny it healthful vents, and it may stray into morbid channels. The death-room of Dr. Lloyd deeply impressed your heart, far more than your pride would own. This is clear, from the pains you took to exonerate your conscience, in your generosity to the orphans. As the heart was moved, so was the imagination stirred; and, unaware to yourself, prepared for much that subsequently appealed to it. Your sudden love, conceived in the very grounds of the house so associated with recollections in themselves strange and romantic; the peculiar temperament and nature of the girl to whom your love was attracted; her own visionary beliefs, and the keen anxiety which infused into your love a deeper poetry of sentiment,—all insensibly tended to induce the imagination to dwell on the Wonderful; and, in overstriving to reconcile each rarer phenomenon to the most positive laws of Nature, your very intellect could discover no solution but in the Preternatural.

"You visit a man who tells you he has seen Sir Philip Derval's ghost: on that very evening, you hear a strange story, in which Sir Philip's name is mixed up with a tale of murder, implicating two mysterious pretenders to magic—Louis Grayle, and the Sage of Aleppo. The tale so interests your fancy that even the glaring impossibility of a not unimportant part of it escapes your notice—viz., the account of a criminal trial in which the circumstantial evidence was more easily attainable than in all the rest of the narrative, but which could not legally have taken place as told. Thus it is whenever the mind begins, unconsciously, to admit the shadow of the Supernatural; the Obvious is lost to the eye that plunges its gaze into the Obscure. Almost immediately afterwards you become acquainted with a young stranger, whose traits of character interest and perplex, attract yet revolt you. All this time you are engaged in a physiological work which severely tasks the brain, and in which you examine the intricate question of soul distinct from mind.

"And here, I can conceive a cause deep hid amongst what metaphysicians would call latent associations, for a train of thought which disposed you to accept the fantastic impressions afterwards made on you by the scene in the Museum and visionary talk of Sir Philip Derval. Doubtless, when, at college, you first studied metaphysical speculation, you would have glanced over Beattie's Essay on Truth as one of the works written in opposition to your favorite David Hume."

"Yes, I read the book, but I have long since forgotten its arguments."

"Well, in that essay, Beattie * cites the extraordinary instance of Simon Browne, a learned and pious clergyman, who seriously disbelieved the existence of his own soul; and imagined that, by interposition of Divine power, his soul was annulled, and nothing left but a principle of animal life, which he held in common with the brutes! When, years ago, a thoughtful imaginative student, you came on that story, probably enough you would have paused, revolved in your own mind and fancy what kind of a creature a man might be, if, retaining human life and merely human understanding, he was deprived of the powers and properties which reasoners have ascribed to the existence of soul. Something in this young man, unconsciously to yourself, revives that forgotten train of meditative ideas. His dread of death as the final cessation of being, his brute-like want of sympathy with his kind, his incapacity to comprehend the motives which carry men on to scheme and to build for a future that extends beyond his grave, all start up before you at the very moment your reason is overtasked, your imagination fevered, in seeking the solution of problems which, to a philosophy based upon your system, must always remain insoluble. The young man's conversation not only thus excites your fancies, it disturbs your affections. He speaks not only of drugs that renew youth, but of charms that secure love. You tremble for your Lilian while you hear him! And the brain thus tasked, the imagination thus inflamed, the heart thus agitated, you are pre-

* Beattie's Essay on Truth, part i. c. ii. 3. The story of Simon Browne is to be found in The Adventurer.

sented to Sir Philip Derval, whose ghost your patient had supposed he saw a week ago.

"This person, a seeker after an occult philosophy, which had possibly acquainted him with some secrets in nature beyond the pale of our conventional experience, though, when analyzed, they might prove to be quite reconcilable with sober science, startles you with an undefined mysterious charge against the young man who had previously seemed to you different from ordinary mortals. In a room stored with the dead things of the brute soulless world, your brain becomes intoxicated with the fumes of some vapor which produces effects not uncommon in the superstitious practices of the East; your brain, thus excited, brings distinctly before you the vague impressions it had before received. Margrave becomes identified with the Louis Grayle of whom you had previously heard an obscure legendary tale, and all the anomalies in his character are explained by his being that which you had contended, in your physiological work, it was quite possible for man to be—viz. mind and body without soul! You were startled by the monster which man would be were your own theory possible; and in order to reconcile the contradictions in this very monster, you account for knowledge and for powers that mind without soul could not have attained, by ascribing to this prodigy broken memories of a former existence, demon attributes from former proficiency in evil magic. My friend, there is nothing here which your own study of morbid idiosyncrasies should not suffice to solve."

"So then," said I, "you would reduce all that have affected my senses as realities into the deceit of illusions? But," I added, in a whisper, terrified by my own question, "do not physiologists agree in this: viz., that though illusory phantasms may haunt the sane as well as the insane, the sane know that they are only illusions, and the insane do not?"

"Such a distinction," answered Faber, "is far too arbitrary and rigid for more than a very general and qualified acceptance. Müller, indeed, who is, perhaps, the highest authority on such a subject, says, with prudent reserve, 'When a person who is not insane sees spectres and believes them to be real, his intellect must be imperfectly exercised.'* He would, indeed, be a bold physician who maintained that every man who believed he had really seen a ghost was of unsound mind. In Dr. Abercrombie's interesting account of spectral illusions, he tells us of a servant-girl who believed she saw, at the foot of her bed, the apparition of Curran, in a sailor's jacket and an immense pair of whiskers.* No doubt the spectre was an illusion, and Dr. Abercrombie very ingeniously suggests the association of ideas by which the apparition was conjured up with the grotesque adjuncts of the jacket and the whiskers; but the servant-girl, in believing the reality of the apparition, was certainly not insane.

When I read in the American public journals† of 'spirit manifestations,' in which large numbers of persons of at least the average degree of education, declares that they have actually witnessed various phantasms, much more extraordinary than all which you have confided to me, and arrive, at once, at the conclusion that they are thus put into direct communication with departed souls, I must assume that they are under an illusion, but I should be utterly unwarranted in supposing that, because they credited that illusion, they were insane. I should only say with Müller, that in their reasoning on the phenomena presented to them, 'their intellect was imperfectly exercised.' And an impression made on the senses, being in itself sufficiently rare to excite our wonder, may be strengthened till it takes the form of a positive fact, by various coincidences which are accepted as corroborative testimony, yet which are, nevertheless, nothing more than coincidences found in every-day matters of business, but only emphatically noticed when we can exclaim, 'How astonishing!' In your case such coincidences have been, indeed, very signal, and might well aggravate the perplexities into which your reason was thrown. Sir Philip Derval's murder, the missing casket, the exciting nature of the manuscript, in which a snperstitious interest is already enlisted by your expectation to find in it the key to the narrator's boasted

* Müller's Physiology of the Senses, p. 394.

* Abercrombie on the Intellectual Powers, p. 281. (15th edition.)

† At the date of Faber's conversation with Allen Fenwick, the (so-called) spirit manifestations had not spread from America over Europe. But if they had, Faber's views would, no doubt, have remained the same.

powers, and his reasons for the astounding denunciation of the man whom you suspect to be his murderer; in all this there is much to confirm, nay, to cause, an illusion, and for that very reason, when examined by strict laws of evidence, in all this there is but additional proof that the illusion was—only illusion. Your affections contribute to strengthen your fancy in its war on your reason.

"The girl you so passionately love develops, to your disquietude and terror, the visionary temperament which, at her age, is ever liable to fantastic caprices. She hears Margrave's song, which, you say, has a wildness of charm that affects and thrills even you. Who does not know the power of music? and of all music, there is none so potential as that of the human voice. Thus, in some languages, charm and song are identical expressions; and even when a critic, in our own sober newspapers, extols a Malibran or a Grisi, you may be sure that he will call her 'enchantress.' Well, this lady, your betrothed, in whom the nervous system is extremely impressionable, hears a voice which, even to your ear, is strangely melodious, and sees a form and face which, even to your eye, are endowed with a singular character of beauty. Her fancy is impressed by what she thus hears and sees; and impressed the more because, by a coincidence not very uncommon, a face like that which she beholds has before been presented to her in a dream or a reverie. In the nobleness of genuine, confiding, reverential love, rather than impute to your beloved a levity of sentiment that would seem to you a treason, you accept the chimera of 'magical fascination.' In this frame of mind you sit down to read the memoir of a mystical enthusiast. Do you begin now to account for the Luminous Shadow? A dream! And a dream no less because your eyes were open and you believed yourself awake. The diseased imagination resembles those mirrors which, being themselves distorted, represent distorted pictures as correct.

"And even this Memoir of Sir Philip Derval's;—can you be quite sure that you actually read the part which relates to Haroun and Louis Grayle? You say that, while perusing the manuscript, you saw the Luminous Shadow and became insensible. The old woman says you were fast asleep. May you not really have fallen into a slumber, and in that slumber have dreamed the parts of the tale that relate to Grayle? dreamed that you beheld the Shadow? Do you remember what is said so well by Dr. Abercrombie, to authorize the explanation I suggest to you: 'A person under the influence of some strong mental impression falls asleep for a few seconds, perhaps without being sensible of it: some scene or person appears in a dream, and he starts up under the conviction that it was a spectral appearance.'" *

"But," said I, "the apparition was seen by me again, and when, certainly, I was not sleeping."

"True; and who should know better than a physician so well read as yourself that a spectral illusion once beheld is *alwoys apt to return again in the same form?* Thus, Goethe was long haunted by one image; the phantom of a flower unfolding itself, and developing new flowers.† Thus, one of our most distinguished philosophers tells us of a lady known to himself, who would see her husband, hear him move and speak, when he was not even in the house.‡ But instances of the facility with which phantasms, once admitted, repeat themselves to the senses, are numberless. Many are recorded by Hibbert and Abercrombie,

* Abercrombie on the Intellectual Powers, p. 278. 15th edition.) This author, not more to be admired for his intelligence than his candor, and who is entitled to praise for a higher degree of original thought than that to which he modestly pretends, relates a curious anecdote illustrating "the anology between dreaming and spectral illusion, which he received from the gentleman to which it occurred—an eminent medical friend:"—"Having sat up late one evening, under considerable anxiety for one of his children, who was ill, he fell asleep in his chair, and had a frightful dream, in which the prominent figure was an immense baboon. He awoke with the fright, got up instantly, and walked to a table which was in the middle of the room. He was then quite awake, and quite conscious of the articles around him; but close to the wall in the end of the apartment he distinctly saw the baboon making the same grimaces which he had seen in his dream; and this spectre continued visible for about half a minute." Now, a man who saw only a baboon would be quite ready to admit that it was but an optical illusion; but if, instead of a baboon, he had seen an intimate friend, and that friend, by some coincidence of time, had died about that date, he would be a very strong-minded man if he admitted for the mystery of seeing his friend, the same natural solution which he would readily admit for seeing a baboon.

† See Müller's observation on this phenomenon, Physiology on the Senses, Baley's translation, p. 1395.

‡ Sir David Brewster's Letters on Natural Magic, p. 39.

and every physician in extensive practice can add largely, from his own experience, to the list. Intense self-concentration is, in itself, a mighty magician. The magicians of the East inculcate the necessity of fast, solitude, and meditation for the due development of their imaginary powers. And I have no doubt with effect; because fast, solitude, and meditation —in other words, thought or fancy intensely concentred, will both raise apparitions and produce the invoker's belief in them. Spinello, striving to conceive the image of Lucifer for his picture of the Fallen Angels, was at last actually haunted by the Shadow of the Fiend. Newton himself has been subjected to a phantom, though to him, Son of Light, the spectre presented was that of the sun! You remember the account that Newton gives to Locke of this visionary appearance. He says that 'though he had looked at the sun with his right eye only, and *not* with the left, yet his fancy began to make an impression upon his left eye as well as his right, for if he shut his right and looked upon the clouds, or a book, or any bright object with his left eye, he could see the sun almost as plain as with the right, if he did but *intend* his fancy a little while on it;' nay, 'for some months after, as often as he began to meditate on the phenomena, the spectrum of the sun began to return, even though he lay in bed at midnight, with his curtains drawn!'

"Seeing, then, how any vivid impression once made will recur, what wonder that you should behold in your prison the Shining Shadow that had first startled you in a wizard's chamber when poring over the records of a murdered visionary? The more minutely you analyze your own hallucinations—pardon me the word—the more they assume the usual characteristics of a dream; contradictory, illogical, even in the marvels they represent. Can any two persons be more totally unlike each other, not merely as to form and years, but as to all the elements of character, than the Grayle of whom you read, or believe you read, and the Margrave in whom you evidently think that Grayle is existent still! The one represented, you say, as gloomy, saturnine, with vehement passions, but with an original grandeur of thought and will, consumed by an internal remorse; the other you paint to me as a joyous and wayward darling of Nature, acute yet frivolous, free from even the ordinary passions of youth, taking delight in innocent amusements incapable of continuous study, without a single pang of repentance for the crimes you so fancifully impute to him. And now when your suspicions. so romantically conceived, are dispelled by positive facts, now, when it is clear that Margrave neither murdered Sir Philip Derval nor abstracted the memoir, you still, unconsciously to yourself, draw on your imagination in order to excuse the suspicion your pride of intellect declines to banish, and suppose that this youthful sorcerer tempted the madman to the murder, the woman to the theft—"

"But you forget the madman said 'that he was led on by the Luminous Shadow of a beautiful youth,' that the woman said also that she was impelled by some mysterious agency."

"I do not forget those coincidences; but how your learning would dismiss them as nugatory were your imagination not disposed to exaggerate them! When you read the authentic histories of any popular illusion, such as the spurious inspirations of the Jansenist Convulsionaries, the apparitions that invaded convents, as deposed in the trial of Urbain Grandier, the confessions of witches and wizards in places the most remote from each other, or, at this day, the tales of 'spirit-manisfestation' recorded in half the towns and villages of America—do not all the superstitious impressions of a particular time have a common family likeness? What one sees another sees, though there has been no communication between the two. I cannot tell you why these phantasms thus partake of the nature of an atmospheric epidemic; the fact remains incontestable. And strange as may be the coincidence between your impressions of a mystic agency and those of some other brains not cognizant of the chimeras of your own, still, is it not simpler philosophy to say, 'They are coincidences of the same nature which made witches in the same epoch all tell much the same story of the broomsticks they rode and the *sabbats* at which they danced to the fiend's piping,' and there leave the matter, as in science we must leave many of the most elementary and familar phenomena inexplicable as to their causes—is not this I say, more philosophical than to insist upon an explanation which accepts the supernatural rather than leave the extraordinary unaccounted for?"

"As you speak," said I, resting my downcast face upon my hand, "I should speak to any patient who had confided in me the tale I have told to you."

"And yet the explanation does not wholly satisfy you? Very likely to some phenomena there is, as yet, no explanation. Perhaps Newton himself could not explain quite to his own satisfaction why he was haunted at midnight by the spectrum of a sun; though I have no doubt that some later philosopher, whose ingenuity has been stimulated by Newton's account, has, by this time, suggested a rational solution of that enigma.* To return to your own case. I have offered such interpretations of the mysteries that confound you, as appeared to me authorized by physiological science. Should you adduce other facts which physiological science wants the data to resolve into phenomena always natural, however rare, still hold fast to that simple saying of Goethe's,—'Mysteries are not necessarily miracles.' And, if all which physiological science comprehends in its experience wholly fails us, I may then hazard certain conjectures which, by acknowledging ignorance, is compelled to recognize the Marvellous—(for as where knowledge enters the Marvellous recedes, so where knowledge falters the Marvellous advances)—yet still, even in these conjectures, I will distinguish the Marvellous from the Supernatural. But, for the present, I advise you to accept the guess that may best quiet the fevered imagination which any bolder guess would only more excite."

"You are right," said I, rising proudly to the full height of my stature, my head erect and my heart defying. "And so let this subject be renewed no more between us. I will brood over it no more myself. I regain the unclouded realm of my human intelligence;

* Newton's explanation is as follows:—"This story I tell you to let you understand, that in the observation related by Mr. Boyle, the man's fancy probably concurred with the impression made by the sun's light to produce that phantasm of the sun which he constantly saw in bright objects, and so your question about the cause of this phantasm *involves another about the power of the fancy, which I must confess is too hard a knot for me to untie.* To place this effect in a constant motion is hard, because the sun ought then to appear perpetually. It seems rather to consist in a disposition of the sensorium to move the imagination strongly, and to be easily moved both by the imagination and by the light as often as bright objects are looked upon."—*Letter from Sir I. Newton to Locke, Lord King's Life of Locke*, vol. i. pp. 405—8.

Dr. Roget (Animal and Vegetable Physiology considered with reference to Natural Theology, Bridgewater treatise, pp. 524, 525) thus refers to this phenomenon, which he states "all of us may experience:"—"When the impressions are very vivid" (Dr. Roget is speaking of visual impressions), "another phenomenon often takes place, namely, *their subsequent recurrence after a certain interval, during which they are not felt, and quite independently of any renewed application of the cause which had originally excited them.*" (I mark by italics the words which more precisely coincide with Julius Faber's explanations.) "If, for example, we look steadfastly at the sun for a second or two, and then immediately close our eyes, the image or spectrum of the sun remains for a long time present to the mind as if the light were still acting on the retina. It then gradually fades and disappears; but if we continue to keep the eyes shut, the *same impression will, after a certain time, recur and again vanish:* and this phenomenon will be repeated at intervals, the sensation becoming fainter at each renewal. It is probable that these reappearances of the image, after the light which produced the original impression has been withdrawn, are occasioned by spontaneous affections of the retina itself which are conveyed to the sensorium. In other cases, where the impressions are less strong, the physical changes producing these changes are perhaps confined to the censorium."

It may be said that there is this difference between the spectrum of the sun and such a phantom as that which perplexed Allen Fenwick—viz., that the sun has been actually beheld before its visionary appearance can be reproduced, and that Allen Fenwick only imagines he has seen the apparition which repeats itself to his fancy. "But there are grounds for the suspicion" (says Dr. Hibbert, Philosophy of Apparitions, p. 250), "*that when ideas of vision are vivified to the height of sensation, a corresponding affection of the optic nerve accompanies the illusion.*" Müller (Physiology of the Senses, p. 1392, Baley's translation) states the same opinion still more strongly, and Sir David Brewster, quoted by Dr. Hibbert (p. 251), says: "In examining these mental impressions, I have found that they follow the motions of the eyeball exactly like the spectral impressions of luminous objects, and that they resemble them also in their apparent immobility when the eye is displaced by an external force. If this result (which I state with much diffidence, from having only my own experience in its favor) shall be found generally true by others, it will follow that the objects of mental contemplation may be seen as distinctly as external objects, and will occupy the same local position in the axis of vision, as if they had been formed by the agency of light." Hence the impression of an image once conveyed to the senses, no matter how, whether by actual or illusory vision, is liable to renewal, "independently of any renewed application of the cause which had originally excited it," and the image can be seen in that renewal "as distinctly as external objects," for indeed "the revival of the fantastic figure really does affect those points of the retina which had been previously impressed."

and, in that intelligence, I mock the sorcerer and disdain the spectre."

CHAPTER XLVI.

JULIUS FABER and Amy Lloyd stayed in my house three days, and in their presence I felt a healthful sense of security and peace. Amy wished to visit her father's house, and I asked Faber, in taking her there, to seize the occasion to see Lilian, that he might communicate to me his impression of a case so peculiar. I prepared Mrs. Ashleigh for this visit by a previous note. When the old man and the child came back, both brought me comfort. Amy was charmed with Lilian, who had received her with the sweetness natural to her real character, and I loved to hear Lilian's praise from those innocent lips.

Faber's report was still more calculated to console me:

"I have seen, I have conversed with her long and familiarly. You were quite right, there is no tendency to consumption in that exquisite, if delicate, organization; nor do I see cause for the fear to which your statement had preinclined me. That head is too nobly formed for any constitutional cerebral infirmity. In its organization, ideality, wonder, veneration are large, it is true, but they are balanced by other organs, now perhaps almost dormant, but which will come into play as life passes from romance into duty. Something at this moment evidently oppresses her mind. In conversing with her, I observe abstraction —listlessness; but I am so convinced of her truthfulness, that if she has once told you she returned your affection, and pledged to you her faith, I should, in your place, rest perfectly satisfied that whatever be the cloud that now rests on her imagination, and for the time obscures the idea of yourself, it will pass away."

Faber was a believer in the main divisions of phrenology, though he did not accept all the dogmas of Gall and Spurzheim; while, to my mind, the refutation of phrenology in its fundamental propositions had been triumphantly established by the lucid arguments of Sir W. Hamilton.* But when Faber rested on phrenological observations, assurances in honor of Lilian, I forgot Sir W. Hamilton, and believed in phrenology. As iron girders and pillars expand and contract with the mere variations of temperature, so will the strongest conviction on which the human intellect rests its judgment, vary with the changes of the human heart; and the building is only safe where these variations are foreseen and allowed for by a wisdom intent on self-knowledge." *

There was much in the affection that had sprung up between Julius Faber and Amy Lloyd which touched my heart and softened all its emotions. This man, unblessed, like myself, by conjugal and parental ties, had, in his solitary age, turned for solace to the love of a child, as I, in the pride of manhood, had turned to the love of woman. But his love was without fear, without jealousy, without trouble. My sunshine came to me, in a fitful ray, through clouds that had gathered over my noon; his sunshine covered all his landscape, hallowed, and hallowing, by the calm of declining day.

And Amy was no common child. She had no exuberant imagination; she was haunted by no whispers from afar; she was a creature fitted for the earth—to accept its duties and to gladden its cares. Her tender observation, fine and tranquil, was alive to all the important household trifles by which, at the earliest age, man's allotted soother asserts her privilege to tend and to comfort. It was pleasant to see her moving so noiselessly through the rooms I had devoted to her venerable protector, knowing all his simple wants, and providing for them as if by the mechanism of a heart exquisitely moulded to the loving uses of life. Sometimes when I saw her setting his chair by the window (knowing as I did, how much he habitually loved to be near the light) and smoothing his papers (in which he was apt to be unmethodical), placing the mark in his

* The summary of this distinguished lecturer's objections to phrenology is to be found in the Appendix to vol. i. of Lectures on Metaphysics, p. 404, et seq. Edition 1859.

* The change of length in iron girders caused by variation of temperature, has not unfrequently brought down the whole edifice into which they were admitted. Good engineers and architects allow for such changes produced by temperature. In the tubular bridge across the Menai Straits, a self-acting record of the daily amount of its contraction and expansion is ingeniously contrived.

book when he ceased to read, divining, almost without his glance, some wish passing through his mind, and then seating herself at his feet, often with her work—which was always destined for him or for one of her absent brothers --now and then, with the one small book that she had carried with her, a selection of Bible stories complied for children;— sometimes when I saw her thus, how I wished that Lilian, too, could have seen her, and have compared her own ideal phantasies with those young developments of the natural heavenly Woman!

But was there nothing in that sight from which I, proud of my arid reason even in its perplexities, might have taken lessons for myself?

On the second evening of Faber's visit I brought to him the draft of deeds for the sale of his property. He had never been a man of business out of his profession; he was impatient to sell his property, and disposed to accept an offer at half its value. I insisted on taking on myself the task of negotiator; perhaps, too, in this office I was egotistically anxious to prove to the great physician that that which he believed to be my "hallucination" had in no way obscured my common sense in the daily affairs of life. So I concluded, and in a few hours, terms for his property that were only just, but were infinitely more advantageous than had appeared to himself to be possible. But, as I approached him with the papers, he put his finger to his lips. Amy was standing by him with her little book in her hand, and his own Bible lay open on the table. He was reading to her from the Sacred Volume itself, and impressing on her the force and beauty of one of the Parables, the adaptation of which had perplexed her; when he had done, she kissed him, bade him good night, and went away to rest. Then said Faber thoughtfully, and as if to himself more than me—

"What a lovely bridge between old age and childhood is religion! How intuitively the child begins with prayer and worship on entering life, and how intuitively on quitting life the old man turns back to prayer and worship, putting himself again side by side with the infant!"

I made no answer, but, after a pause, spoke of fines and freeholds, title-deeds and money; and when the business on hand was concluded, asked my learned guest if, before he departed, he would deign to look over the pages of my ambitious Physiological Work. There were parts of it on which I much desired his opinion, touching on subjects in which his special studies made him an authority as high as our land possessed.

He made me bring him the manuscript, and devoted much of that night and the next day to its persual.

When he gave it me back, which was not till the morning of his departure, he commenced with eulogies on the scope of its design, and the manner of its execution, which flattered my vanity so much that I could not help exclaiming, "Then, at least, there is no trace of 'hallucination' here!"

Alas, my poor Allen! here, perhaps, hallucination, or self-deception, is more apparent than in all the strange tales you confided to me. For here is the hallucination of the man seated on the shores of Nature, and who would say to its measureless sea, 'So far shalt thou go and no farther;'—here is the hallucination of the creature, who, not content with exploring the laws of the Creator, ends with submitting to his interpretation of some three or four laws, in the midst of a code of which all the rest are in a language unknown to him—the powers and free-will of the Law-giver Himself; here is the hallucination by which Nature is left Godless—because man is left soulless. What would matter all our speculations on a Deity who would cease to exist for us when we are in the grave? Why mete out, like Archytas, the earth and the sea, and number the sands on the shore that divides them, if the end of this wisdom be a handful of dust sprinkled over a skull!

'Nec quidquam tibi prodest
Aerias tentasse domos, *animoque* rotundum
Percurrisse polum *morituro*.'

Your book is a proof of the soul that you fail to discover. Without a soul, no man would work for a Future that begins for his fame when the breath is gone from his body. Do you remember how you saw that little child praying at the grave of her father? Shall I tell you that in her simple orisons she prayed for the benefactor—who had cared for the orphan; who had reared over dust that tomb which, in a Christian burial-ground, is a mute but perceptible memorial of Christian hopes;

that the child prayed, haughty man, for you? And you sat by, knowing nought of this; sat by, amongst the graves, troubled and tortured with ghastly doubts—vain of a reason that was sceptical of eternity, and yet shaken like a reed by a moment's marvel. Shall I tell the child to pray for you no more?—that you disbelieve in a soul? If you do so, what is the efficacy of prayer? Speak—shall I tell her this? Shall the infant pray for you never more?"

I was silent—I was thrilled.

"Has it never occurred to you, who, in denying all innate perceptions as well as ideas, have passed on to deductions from which poor Locke, humble Christian that he was, would have shrunk in dismay; has it never occurred to you as a wonderful fact, that the easiest thing in the world to teach a child is that which seems to metaphysical school-men the abstrusest of all problems? Read all those philosophers wrangling about a First Cause, deciding on what *are* miracles, and then again deciding that such miracles cannot be; and when one has answered another, and left in the crucible of wisdom a *caput mortuum* of ignorance, then turn your eyes, and look at the infant praying to the invisible God at his mother's knees. This idea, so miraculously abstract, of a Power that the infant has never seen, that cannot be symbolled forth and explained to him by the most erudite sage,—a Power, nevertheless, that watches over him, that hears him, that sees him, that will carry him across the grave, that will enable him to live on for ever;—this double mystery of a Divinity and of a Soul the infant learns with the most facile readiness, at the first glimpse of his reasoning faculty. Before you can teach him a rule in addition, before you can venture to drill him into his horn-book, he leaps, with one intuitive spring of all his ideas, to the comprehension of the truths which are only incomprehensible to blundering sages! And you, as you stand before me, *dare* not say, 'Let the child pray for me no more!' But will the Creator accept the child's prayer for the man who refuses prayer for himself? Take my advice—pray! And in this counsel I do not overstep my province. I speak not as a preacher, but as a physician. For health is a word that comprehends our whole organization, and a just equilibrium of all faculties and functions is the condition of health.

"As in your Lilian, the equilibrium is deranged by the over-indulgence of a spiritual mysticism which withdraws from the nutriment of duty the essential pabulum of sober sense, so in you, the resolute negation of disciplined spiritual communion between Thought and Divinity robs imagination of its noblest and safest vent. Thus, from opposite extremes, you and your Lilian meet in the same region of mist and cloud, losing sight of each other and of the true ends of life, as her eyes only gaze on the stars and yours only bend to the earth. Were I advising *her*, I should say: 'Your Creator has placed the scene of your trial below, and not in the stars.' Advising *you*, I say: 'But in the trial below, man should recognize education for heaven.' In a word, I would draw somewhat more downward her fancy, raise somewhat more upward your reason. Take my advice then—Pray. Your mental system needs the support of prayer in order to preserve its balance. In the embarrassment and confusion of your senses, clearness of perception will come with habitual and tranquil confidence in Him who alike rules the universe and reads the heart. I only say here what has been said much better before by a reasoner in whom all students of Nature recognize a guide. I see on your table the very volume of Bacon which contains the passage I commend to your reflections. Here it is. Listen:

"'Take an example of a dog, and mark what a generosity and courage he will put on when he finds himself maintained by a man who, to him, is instead of a God, or *melior natura*, which courage is manifestly such as that creature without that confidence of a better nature than his own, could never attain. So man, when he resteth and assureth himself upon Divine protection and favor, gathereth a force and faith which human nature could not obtain.' * You are silent, but your gesture tells me your doubt—a doubt which your heart, so femininely tender, will not speak aloud lest you should rob the old man of a hope with which your strength of manhood dispenses—you doubt the efficacy of prayer! Pause

---

* Bacon's Essay on Atheism. This quotation is made with admirable felicity and force by Dr. Whewell, page 378 of Bridgewater Treatise on Astronomy and General Physics considered with reference to Natural Theology.

and reflect, bold but candid inquirer into the laws of that guide you call Nature. If there were no efficacy in prayer—if prayer were as mere an illusion of superstitious phantasy as aught against which your reason now struggles—do you think that Nature herself would have made it amongst the most common and facile of all her dictates? Do you believe that if there really did not exist that tie between Man and his Maker—that link between life here and life hereafter which is found in what we call Soul, alone—that wherever you look through the universe, you would behold a child at prayer? Nature inculcates nothing that is superfluous.

"Nature does not impel the leviathan or the lion, the eagle or the moth, to pray; she impels only man. Why? Because man only has soul, and Soul seeks to commune with the Everlasting, as a fountain struggles up to its source. Burn your book. It would found you a reputation for learning and intellect and courage, I allow; but learning and intellect and courage wasted against a truth—like spray against a rock! A truth valuable to the world, the world will never part with. You will not injure the truth, but you will mislead and may destroy many, whose best security is in the truth which you so eruditely insinuate to be a fable. Soul and Hereafter are the heritage of all men; the humblest journeyman in those streets, the pettiest trader behind those counters, have in those beliefs their prerogatives of royalty. You would dethrone and embrute the lords of the earth by your theories. For my part, having given the greater part of my life to the study and analysis of facts, I would rather be the author of the tritest homily, or the baldest poem, that inculcated that imperishable essence of the soul to which I have neither scalpel nor probe, than be the founder of the subtlest school, or the framer of the loftiest verse, that robbed my fellow-men of their faith in a spirit that eludes the dissecting-knife—in a being that escapes the grave-digger. Burn your book—Accept this Book instead; Read and Pray."

He placed his Bible in my hand, embraced me, and, an hour afterwards, the old man and the child left my hearth solitary once more.

CHAPTER XLVII.

That night, as I sat in my study, very thoughtful and very mournful, I revolved all that Julius Faber had said; and the impression his words had produced became gradually weaker and weaker, as my reason, naturally combative, rose up with all the replies which my philosophy suggested. No; if my imagination had really seduced and betrayed me into monstrous credulities, it was clear that the best remedy to such morbid tendencies towards the Superstitious was in the severe exercise of the faculties most opposed to Superstition—in the culture of pure reasoning—in the science of absolute fact. Accordingly, I placed before me the very book which Julius Faber had advised me to burn; I forced all my powers of mind to go again over the passages which contained the doctrines that his admonition had censured; and before daybreak, I had stated the substance of his argument, and the logical reply to it, in an elaborate addition to my chapter on "Sentimental Philosophers." While thus rejecting the purport of his parting counsels, I embodied in another portion of my work his views on my own "illusions," and as here my common sense was in concord with his, I disposed of all my own previous doubts in an addition to my favorite chapter "On the Cheats of the Imagination." And when the pen dropped from my hand, and the day-star gleamed through the window, my heart escaped from the labor of my mind, and flew back to the image of Lilian. The pride of the philosopher died out of me, the sorrow of the man reigned supreme, and I shrank from the coming of the sun, despondent.

CHAPTER XLVIII.

Not till the law had completed its proceedings, and satisfied the public mind as to the murder of Sir Philip Derval, were the remains of the deceased consigned to the family mausoleum. The funeral was, as may be supposed, strictly private, and when it was over, the excitement caused by an event so tragical and singular, subsided. New topics engaged the public talk, and—in my presence, at least—the delicate consideration due to one whose name had been so painfully mixed up in the dismal story, forebore a topic which I could not be expected to hear without distressful emotion. Mrs. Ashleigh I saw frequently at my own house; she honestly confessed that Lilian had not shown that grief at the concelling of our engagement which would alone justify Mrs. Ashleigh in asking me again to see her daughter, and retract my conclusions against our union. She said that Lilian was quiet, not uncheerful, never spoke of me nor of Margrave, but seemed absent and pre-occupied as before, taking pleasure in nothing that had been wont to please her; not in music, nor books, nor that tranquil pastime which women call work, and in which they find excuse to meditate, in idleness, their own fancies. She rarely stirred out—even in the garden; when she did, her eyes seemed to avoid the house in which Margrave had lodged, and her steps the old favorite haunt by the Monks' Well. She would remain silent for long hours together, but the silence did not appear melancholy. For the rest, her health was more than usually good. Still, Mrs. Ashleigh persisted in her belief that, sooner or later, Lilian would return to her former self, her former sentiments for me; and she entreated me not, as yet, to let the world know that our engagement was broken off. "For if," said she, with good sense, "if it should prove not to be broken off, only suspended, and afterwards happily renewed, there will be two stories to tell when no story be needed. Besides, I should dread the effect on Lilian, if offensive gossips babbled to her on a matter that would excite so much curiosity as the rupture of a union in which onr neighbors have taken so general an interest."

I had no reason to refuse acquiescence in Mrs. Ashleigh's request, but I did not share in her hopes; I felt that the fair prospects of my life were blasted; I could never love another, never wed another; I resigned myself to a solitary hearth, rejoiced, at least, that Margrave had not revisted at Mrs. Ashleigh's—had not, indeed, reappeared in the town. He was still staying with Strahan, who told me that his guest had ensconced himself in Forman's old study, and amused himself with reading—though not for long at a time—the curious old books and manuscripts found in the library, or climbing trees like a schoolboy, and familiarizing himself with the deer and the cattle, which would group round him quite tame, and feed from his hand. Was this the description of a criminal? But if Sir Philip's assertion were really true; if the criminal were man without soul; if without soul, man would have no conscience, never be troubled by repentance, and the vague dread of a future world, —why, then, should not the criminal be gay despite his crimes, as the white bear gambols as friskly after his meal on human flesh? These questions would haunt me, despite my determination to accept as the right solution of all marvels the construction put on my narrative by Julius Faber.

Days passed; I saw and heard nothing of Margrave. I began half to hope that, in the desultory and rapid changes of mood and mind which characterized his restless nature, he had forgotten my existence.

One morning I went out early on my rounds, when I met Strahan unexpectedly.

"I was in search of you," he said, "for more than one person has told me that you are looking ill and jaded. So you are! And the town now is hot and unhealthy. You must come to Derval Court for a week or so. You can ride into town every day to see your patients. Don't refuse. Margrave, who is still with me, sends all kind messages, and bade me say that *he* entreats you to come to the house at which he also is a guest!"

I started. What, had the Scin-Læca required of me, and obtained to that condition my promise? "If you are asked to the house at which I also am a guest, you will come; you will meet and converse with me as guest speaks to guest in the house of a host!" Was this one of the coincidences which my reason was bound to accept as coincidences, and nothing more? Tut, tut! Was I returning again to my "hallucinations?" Granting that Faber and common sense were in the right, what was this Margrave? A man to whose friendship, acuteness, and energy I was under the deepest obligations—to whom I was indebted for active services that had saved my life from a serious danger, acquitted my honor of a horrible suspicion. "I thank you," I said to Strahan, "I will come: not, indeed, for a week, but, at all events, for a day or two."

"That's right; I will call for you in the carriage at six o'clock. You will have done your day's work by then?"

"Yes; I will so arrange."

On our way to Derval Court that evening, Strahan talked much about Margrave, of whom, nevertheless, he seemed to be growing weary.

"His high spirits are too much for one," said he; "and then so restless—so incapable of sustained quiet conversation. And, clever though he is, he can't help me in the least about the new house I shall build. He has no notion of construction. I don't think he could build a barn."

"I thought you did not like to demolish the old house, and would content yourself with pulling down the more ancient part of it?"

"True. At first it seemed a pity to destroy so handsome a mansion; but you see, since poor Sir Philip's manuscript, on which he set such store, has been too mutilated, I fear, to allow me to effect his wish with regard to it, I think I ought, at least, scrupulously to obey his other whims. And, besides, I don't know, there are odd noises about the old house. I don't believe in haunted houses, still there is something dreary in strange sounds at the dead of night, even if made by rats, or winds through decaying rafters. You, I remember at college, had a taste for architecture, and can draw plans. I wish to follow out Sir Philip's design, but on a smaller scale, and with more attention to comfort."

Thus he continued to run on, satisfied to find me a silent and attentive listener. We arrived at the mansion an hour before sunset, the westering light shining full against the many windows cased in mouldering pilasters, and making the general dilapidation of the old place yet more mournfully evident.

It was but a few minutes to the dinner-hour. I went up at once to the room appropriated to me—not the one I had before occupied. Strahan had already got together a new establishment. I was glad to find in the servant who attended me an old acquaintance. He had been in my own employ when I first settled at L——, and left me to get married. He and his wife were both now in Strahan's service. He spoke warmly of his new master and his contentment with his situation, while he unpacked my carpet-bag and assisted me to change my dress. But the chief object of his talk and his praise was Mr. Margrave.

"Such a bright young gentleman, like the first fine day in May!"

When I entered the drawing-room, Margrave and Strahan were both there. The former was blithe and genial as usual, in his welcome. At dinner, and during the whole evening till we retired severally to our own rooms, he was the principal talker; recounting incidents of travel, always very loosely strung together, jesting, good-humoredly enough, at Strahan's sudden hobby for building, then putting questions to me about mutual acquaintances, but never waiting for an answer; and every now and then, as if at random, startling us with some brilliant aphorism, or some suggestion drawn from abstract science or unfamiliar erudition. The whole effect was sparkling, but I could well understand that, if long continued, it would become oppressive. The soul has need of pauses of repose—intervals of escape, not only from the flesh, but even from the mind. A man of the loftiest intellect will experience times when mere intellect not only fatigues him, but amidst its most original conceptions, amidst its proudest triumphs, has a something trite and commonplace compared with one of those vague intimations of a spiritual destiny which are not within the ordinary domain of reason; and, gazing abstractedly into space, will leave suspended some problem of severest thought, or uncompleted some golden palace of imperial poetry, to indulge in hazy reveries, that do not differ from those of an innocent quiet child! The soul has a long road to travel—from time through eternity. It demands its halting hours of contemplation. Contemplation is serene. But with such wants of an immortal immaterial spirit, Margrave had no fellowship, no sympathy; and for myself, I need scarcely add that the lines I have just traced I should not have written at the date at which my narrative has now arrived.

CHAPTER XLIX.

I HAD no case that necessitated my return to L—— the following day. The earlier hours of the forenoon I devoted to Strahan and his building plans. Margrave flitted in and out of the room, fitfully as an April sunbeam, sometimes flinging himself on a sofa, and reading for a few mintues one of the volumes of the ancient mystics, in which Sir Philip's library was so rich. I remember it was a volume of Proclus. He read that crabbed and difficult Greek with a fluency that surprised me. "I picked up the ancient Greek," said he, "years ago, in learning the modern." But the book soon tired him; then he would come and disturb us, archly enjoying Strahan's peevishness at interruption; then he would throw open the window and leap down, chanting one of his wild savage airs; and in another moment he was half hid under the drooping boughs of a broad lime-tree, amidst the antlers of deer that gathered fondly round him. In the afternoon my host was called away to attend some visitors of importance, and I found myself on the sward before the house, right in view of the mausoleum and alone with Margrave.

I turned my eyes from that dumb House of Death wherein rested the corpse of the last lord of the soil, so strangely murdered, with a strong desire to speak out to Margrave the doubts respecting himself that tortured me. But—setting aside the promise to the contrary, which I had given, or dreamed I had given—to the Luminous Shadow, to fulfil that desire would have been impossible—impossible to any one gazing on that radiant youthful face! I think I see him now as I saw him then: a white doe, that even my presence could not scare away from him, clung lovingly to his side, looking up at him with her soft eyes. He stood there like the incarnate principle of mythological senuous life. I have before applied to him that illustration; let the repetition be pardoned. Impossible, I repeat it, to say to that creature, face to face, "Art thou the master of demoniac arts, and the instigator of secret murder?" As if from redundant happiness within himself, he was humming, or rather cooing, a strain of music, so sweet, and so wildly sweet, and so unlike the music, one hears from tutored lips in crowded rooms! I passed my hand over my forehead in bewilderment and awe.

"Are there," I said, unconsciously—"are there, indeed, such prodigies in Nature?"

"Nature!" he cried, cratching up the word; "talk to me of Nature! Talk of her, the wondrous blissful mother! Mother I may well call her. I am her spoiled child, her darling—. But oh, to die, ever to die, ever to lose sight of Nature!—to rot, senseless, whether under these turfs or within those dead walls—"

I could not resist the answer.

"Like yon murdered man! murdered, and by whom?"

"By whom? I thought that was clearly proved."

"The hand was proved; what influence moved the hand?"

"Tush! the poor wretch spoke of a Demon. Who can tell? Nature herself is a grand destroyer. See that pretty bird, in its beak a writhing worm! All Nature's children live to take life; none, indeed, so lavishly as a man. What hecatombs slaughtered, not to satisfy the irresistible sting of hunger, but for the wanton ostentation of a feast, which he may scarcely taste, or for the mere sport that he finds in destroying. We speak with dread of the beasts of prey: what beast of prey is so dire a ravager as man?—so cruel and so treacherous? Look at yon flock of sheep, bred and fattened for the shambles; and this hind that I caress,—if I were the park-keeper, and her time for my bullet had come, would you think her life was the safer because, in my own idle whim, I had tamed her to trust to the hand raised to slay her?"

"It is true," said I—"a grim truth. Nature, on the surface so loving and so gentle, is full of terror in her deeps when our thought descends into their abyss!"

Strahan now joined us with a party of country visitors.

"Margrave is the man to show you the beauties of this park," said he. "Margrave knows every bosk and dingle, twisted old thorn-tree, or opening glade, in its intricate, undulating ground."

Margrave seemed delighted at this proposition; and as he led us through the park, though the way was long, though the sun was fierce, no one seemed fatigued. For the pleasure he felt in pointing out detached beauties which escaped an ordinary eye was contagious. He did not talk as talks the poet or the painter: but at some lovely effect of light amongst the tremulous leaves, some sudden glimpse of a sportive rivulet below, he would halt, point it out to us in silence, and with a kind of childlike ecstacy in his own bright face, that seemed to reflect the life and the bliss of the blithe summer-day itself.

Thus seen, all my doubts in his dark secret nature faded away—all my horror, all my hate; it was imposible to resist the charm that breathed round him, not to feel a tender, affectionate yearning towards him as to some fair happy child. Well might he call himself the Darling of Nature. Was he not the mysterious likeness of that awful Mother, beautiful as Apollo in one aspect, direful as Typhon in another.

CHAPTER L.

"WHAT a strange-looking cane you have, sir!" said a little girl, who was one of the party, and who had entwined her arm round Margrave's. "Let me look at it."

"Yes," said Strahan; "that cane, or rather walking-staff, is worth looking at. Margrave bought it in Egypt, and declares that it is very ancient."

This staff seemed constructed from a reed: looked at, it seemed light, in the hand it felt heavy; it was of a pale, faded yellow, wrought with black rings at equal distances, and graven with half-obliterated characters that seemed hieroglyphic. I remembered to have seen Margrave with it before, but I had never noticed it with any attention until now, when it was passed from hand to hand. At the head of the cane there was a large unpolished stone of a dark blue.

"Is this a pebble or a jewel?" asked one of the party.

"I cannot tell you its name or nature," said Margrave; "but it is said to cure the bite of serpents,* and has other supposed virtues—a talisman in short."

He here placed the staff in my hands, and bade me look at it with care. Then he changed the conversation and renewed the way, leaving the staff with me, till suddenly, I forced it back on him. I could not have explaimed why, but its touch, as it warmed in my clasp, seemed to send through my whole frame a singular thrill, and a sensation as if I no longer felt my own weight—as if I walked on air.

Our rambles came to a close; the visitors went away; I re-entered the house through the sash-window of Forman's study. Margrave threw his hat and staff on the table, and amused himself with examining minutely the tracery on the mantel-piece. Strahan and myself left him thus occupied, and, going into the adjoining library, resumed our task of examining the plans for the new house. I continued to draw outlines and sketches of various alterations, tending to simplify and contract Sir Philip's general design. Margrave soon joined us, and, this time, took his seat patiently beside our table, watching me use ruler and compass with unwonted attention.

"I wish I could draw," he said "but I can do nothing useful."

"Rich men like you," said Strahan, peevishly, "can engage others, and are better em-

---

* The following description of a stone at Corfu, celebrated as an antidote to the venom of the serpent's bite, was given to me by an eminent scholar and legal functionary in that island:—

"DESCRIPTION OF THE BLUE STONE.—This stone is of an oval shape one and two-tenths inch long, seventenths broad, three-tenths thick, and, having been broken formerly, is now set in gold.

"When a person is bitten by a poisonous snake, the bite must be opened by a cut of a lancet or razor longways. and the stone applied within twenty-four hours. The stone then attaches itself firmly on the wound, adn when it has done its office falls off; the cure is then complete. The stone must then be thrown into milk, whereupon it vomits the poison it has absorbed, which remains green on top of the milk, and the stone is then again fit for use.

"This stone has been from time immemorial in the family of Ventura, of Corfu, a house of Italian origin, and is notorious, so that peasants immediately apply for its aid. Its virtue has not been impaired by the fracture. Its nature or composition is unknown.

"In a case where two were stung at the same time by serpents, the stone was applied to one, who recovered; but the other, for whom it could not be used, died.

"It never failed but once, and then it was applied *after* the twenty-four hours.

"Its color is so dark as not to be distingnished from black. "P. M. COLQUHOUN.

"Corfu, 7th Nov., 1860."

Sir Emerson Tennent, in his popular and excellent work on Ceylon, gives an account of "snake stones" apparently similar to the one at Corfu, except that they are "intensely black and highly polished," and which are applied, in much the same manner, to the wounds inflicted by the cobra-capella.

Query.—Might it not be worth while to ascertain the chemical properties of these stones, and, if they be efficacious in the extraction of venom conveyed by a bite, might they not be as successful if applied to the bite ot a mad dog as to that of a cobra-capella?

ployed in rewarding good artists than in making bad drawings themselves."

"Yes, I can employ others; and—Fenwick when you have finished with Strahan, I will ask permission to employ you, though without reward; the task I would impose will not take you a minute."

He then threw himself back in his chair, and seemed to fall into a doze.

The dressing-bell rang; Strahan put away the plans—indeed, they were now pretty well finished and decided on.

Margrave woke up as our host left the room to dress, and drawing me towards another table in the room, placed before me one of his favorite mystic books, and, pointing to an old woodcut, said:

"I will ask you to copy this for me; it pretends to be a fac-simile of Solomon's famous seal. I have a whimsical desire to have a copy of it. You observe two triangles interlaced and inserted in a circle?—the pentacle, in short. Yes, just so. You need not add the astrological characters: they are the senseless superfluous accessories of the dreamer who wrote the book. But the pentacle itself has an intelligible meaning; it belongs to the only universal language, the language of symbol, in which all races that think—around, and above, and below us—can establish communion of thought. If in the external universe any one constructive principle can be detected, it is the geometrical; and in every part of the world in which magic pretends to a written character, I find that its hieroglyphics are geometrical figures. Is it not laughable that the most positive of all the sciences should thus lend its angles and circles to the use of—what shall I call it?—the ignorance?—ay, that is the word—the ignorance of dealers in magic?"

He took up the paper, on which I had hastily described the triangles and the circle, and left the room chanting the serpent-charmer's song.

CHAPTER LI.

When we separated for the night, which we did at eleven o'clock, Margrave said:

"Good night and good-bye. I must leave you to-morrow, Strahan, and before your usual hour for rising. I took the liberty of requesting one of your men to order me a chaise from L——. Pardon my seeming abruptness, but I always avoid long leave-takings, and I had fixed the date of my departure almost as soon as I accepted your invitation."

"I have no right to complain. The place must be dull, indeed, to a gay young fellow like you. It is dull even to me. I am meditating flight already. Are you going back to L——?"

"Not even for such things as I left at my lodgings. When I settle somewhere and can give an address, I shall direct them to be sent to me. There are, I hear, beautiful patches of scenery towards the north, only known to pedestrian tourists. I am a good walker; and you know, Fenwick, that I am also a child of Nature. Adieu to you both; and many thanks to you Strahan, for your hospitality."

He left the room.

"I am not sorry he is going," said Strahan, after a pause, and with a quick breath as if of relief. "Do you not feel that he exhausts one? An excess of oxygen, as you would say in a lecture."

I was alone in my own chamber; I felt indisposed for bed and for sleep; the curious conversation I had held with Margrave weighed on me. In that conversation, we had indirectly touched upon the prodigies which I had not brought myself to speak of with frank courage, and certainly nothing in Margrave's manner had betrayed consciousness of my suspicions; on the contrary, the open frankness with which he evinced his predilection for mystic speculation, or uttered his more unamiable sentiments, rather tended to disarm than encourage belief in gloomy secrets or sinister powers. And as he was about to quit the neighborhood, he would not again see Lilian, not even enter the town of L——. Was I to ascribe this relief from his presence to the promise of the Shadow, or was I not rather right in battling firmly against any grotesque illusion, and accepting his departure as a simple proof that my jealous fears had been amongst my other chimeras, and that as he had really only visited Lilian out of friendship to me, in my peril, so he might, with his characteristic acuteness, have guessed my jealousy, and ceased his visits from a kindly motive delicately concealed? And might not the same motive now have dictated the words which were intended to assure me that L—— contained no attractions to tempt him to return to it? Thus, gradually soothed and cheered by the course to which my reflections led me, I continued to muse for hours. At length, looking at my watch, I was surprised to find it was the second hour after midnight. I was just about to rise from my chair to undress, and secure some hours of sleep, when the well-remembered cold wind passed through the room, stirring the roots of my hair; and before me stood, against the wall, the Luminous Shadow.

"Rise and follow me," said the voice, sounding much nearer than it had ever done before.

At those words I rose mechanically, and like a sleep-walker.

"Take up the light."

I took it.

The Scin-Læca glded along the wall towards the threshold, and motioned me to open the door. I did so. The Shadow flitted on through the corridor. I followed, with hushed footsteps, down a small stair into Forman's study. In all my subsequent proceedings, about to be narrated, the Shadow guided me, sometimes, by voice, sometimes by sign. I obeyed the guidance not only unresistingly, but without a desire to resist. I was unconscious either or curiosity or of awe—only of a calm and passive indifference, neither pleasurable nor painful. In this obedience, from which all will seemed extracted, I took into my hands the staff which I had examined the day before, and which lay on the table, just where Margrave had cast it on re-entering the house. I unclosed the shutter to the casement, lifted the sash, and, with the light in my left hand, the staff in my right, stepped forth into the garden. The night was the flame of the candle scarcely trembled in the air; the Shadow moved on before towards the old pavilion described in an earlier part of this narrative, and of which th mouldering doors stood wide open. I followed the Shadow into the pavilion, up the crazy stair to the room above, with its four great blank unglazed windows, or rather arcades, north, south, east, and west.

I halted on the middle of the floor: right before my eyes, through the vista made by breathless boughs, stood out from the moonlit air the dreary mausoleum. Then, at the command conveyed to me, I placed the candle on a wooden settle, touched a spring in the handle of the staff, a lid flew back, and I drew from the hollow, first a lump of some dark bituminous substance, next a smaller slender wand of polished steel, of which the point was tipped with a translucent material, which appeared to me like crystal. Bending down, still obedient to the direction conveyed to me, I described on the floor with the lump of bitumen (if I may so call it) the figure of the pentacle with the interlaced triangles, in a circle nine feet in diameter, just as I had drawn it for Margrave the evening before. The material used made the figure perceptible, in a dark color of mingled black and red. I applied the flame of the candle to the circle, and immediately it became lambent with a low steady splendor that rose about an inch from the floor, and gradually from this light there emanted a soft gray transparent mist and a faint but exquisite odor. I stood in the midst of the circle, and within the circle also, close by my side, stood the Scin-Læca; no longer reflected on the wall, but apart from it, erect, rounded into more integral and distinct form, yet impalpable, and from it there breathed an icy air.

Then lifting the wand, the broader end of which rested in the palm of my hand, the two forefingers closing lightly over it in a line parallel with the point, I directed it towards the wide aperture before me, fronting the mausoleum. I repeated aloud some words whispered to me in a language I knew not: those words I would not trace on this paper, could I remember them. As they came to a close, I heard a howl from the watch-dog in the yard—a dismal, lugubrious howl. Other dogs in the distant village caught up the sound, and bayed in a dirge-like chorus; and the howling went on louder and louder. Again strange words were whispered to me, and I repeated them in mechanical submission; and when they, too, were ended, I felt the ground tremble beneath me, and as my eyes looked straight forward down the vista, that, stretching from the casement, was bounded by the solitary mausoleum, vague formless shadows seemed to pass cross the moonlight—below, along the sward—above, in the air; and then suddenly a terror, not before conceived, came upon me.

And a third time words were whispered; but, though I knew no more of their meaning than I did of those that had preceded them, I felt a repugnance to utter them aloud. Mutely I turned towards the Scin-Læca, and the expression of its face was menacing and terrible; my will became yet more compelled to the control imposed upon it, and my lips commenced the formula again whispered into my ear, when I heard distinctly a voice of warning and of anguish, that murmured "Hold!" I knew the voice; it was Lilian's. I paused—I turned towards the quarter from which the voice had come, and in the space afar I saw the features, the form of Lilian. Her arms were stretched towards me in supplication, her countenance was deadly pale and anxious with unutterable distress. The whole image seemed in unison with the voice;—the look, the attitude, the gesture of one who sees another in deadly peril, and cries, "Beware!"

This apparition vanished in a moment; but that moment sufficed to free my mind from the constraint which had before enslaved it. I dashed the wand to the ground, sprang from the circle, rushed from the place. How I got into my own room I can remember not—I know not; I have a vague reminiscence of some intervening wanderings, of giant trees, of shroud-like moonlight, of the Shining Shadow and its angry aspect, of the blind walls and the iron door of the House of the Dead, of spectral images—a confused and dreary phantasmagoria. But all I can recall with distinctness is the sight of my own hueless face in the mirror in my own still room, by the light of the white moon through the window; and sinking down, I said to myself, "This, at least, is an hallucination or a dream!"

CHAPTER LII

A Heavy sleep came over me at daybreak, but I did not undress nor go to bed. The sun was high in the heavens when, on waking, I saw the servant who had attended me bustling about the room.

"I beg your pardon, sir, I am afraid I disturbed you; but I have been three times to see if you were not coming down, and I found you so soundly asleep I did not like to wake you. Mr. Strahan has finished breakfast, and gone out riding; Mr. Margrave has left—left before six o'clock."

"Ah, he said he was going early."

"Yes, sir; and he seemed so cross when he went. I could never have supposed so pleasant a gentleman could put himself into such a passion!"

"What was the matter?"

"Why, his walking-stick could not be found; it was not in the hall. He said he had left it in the study; we could not find it there. At last he found it himself in the old summer-house, and said—I beg pardon, he said—'he was sure you had taken it there: that some one, at all events, had been meddling with it.' However, I am very glad it was found, since he seems to set such store on it."

Did Mr. Margrave go himself into the summer-house to look for it?"

"Yes, sir; no one else would have thought of such a place: no one likes to go there, even in the day-time."

"Why?"

"Why, sir, they say it is haunted since poor Sir Philip's death; and, indeed, there are strange noises in every part of the house. I am afraid you had a bad night, sir," continued the servant, with evident curiosity glancing towards the bed, which I had not pressed, and towards the evening-dress, which, while he spoke, I was rapidly changing for that which I habitually wore in the morning. "I hope you did not feel yourself ill?"

"No! but it seems I fell asleep in my chair."

"Did you hear, sir, how the dogs howled about two o'clock in the morning? They woke me. Very frightful!"

"The moon was at her full. Dogs will bay the moon."

I felt relieved to think that I should not find Strahan in the breakfast-room, and hastening through the ceremony of a meal which I scarcely touched, I went out into the park, unobserved, and creeping round the copses and into the neglected gardens, made my way to the pavilion. I mounted the stairs—I looked on the floor of the upper room; yes, there still was the black figure of the pentacle—the circle. So, then, it was not a dream! Till then I had doubted. Or might it not still be so far a dream, that I had walked in my sleep, and with an imagination preoccupied by my conversations with Margrave—by the hieroglyphics on the staff I had handled—by the very figure associated with superstitious practices which I had copied from some weird book at his request—by all the strange impressions previously stamped on my mind;—might I not, in truth, have carried thither in sleep the staff, described the circle and all tha rest been but visionary delusion? Surely—surely, so common sense and so Julius Faber would interpret the riddles that perplexed me! But that as it may, my first thought was to efface the marks on the floor. I found this easier than I had ventured to hope. I rubbed the circle and the pentacle away from the boards with the sole of my foot, leaving but an undistinguishable smudge behind. I know not why, but I felt the more nervously anxious to remove all such evidences of my nocturnal visit to that room, because Margrave had so openly gone thither to seek for the staff, and had so rudely named me to the servant as having meddled with it. Might he not awake some suspicion against me? Suspicion, what of? I knew not, but I feared!

The healthful air of day gradually nerved my spirits and relieved my thoughts. But the place had become hateful to me. I resolved not to wait for Strahan's return, but to walk back to L——, and leave a message for my host. It was sufficient excuse that I could not longer absent myself from my patients; accordingly, I gave directions to have the few things which I had brought with me sent to my house by any servant who might be going to L——, and was soon pleased to find myself outside the park-gates and on the high-road.

I had not gone a mile before I met Strahan on horseback. He received my apologies for not waiting his return to bid him farewell, without observation, and, dismounting, led his horse and walked beside me on my road. I saw that there was something on his mind; at last he said, looking down:

"Did you hear the dogs howl last night?"

"Yes! the full moon!"

"You were awake, then, at the time. Did you hear any other sound? Did you see anything?"

"What should I hear or see?"

Strahan was silent for some moments; then he said, with great seriousness:

"I could not sleep when I went to bed last night; I felt feverish and restless. Somehow or other, Margrave got into my head, mixed up in some strange way with Sir Philip Derval. I heard the dogs howl, and at the same time, or rather a few minutes later, I felt the whole house tremble, as a frail corner-house in London seems to tremble at night when a carriage is driven past it. The howling had then ceased, and ceased as suddenly as it had begun. I felt a vague superstitious alarm; I got up, and went to my window, which was unclosed (it is my habit to sleep with my windows open)—the moon was very bright—and I saw, I declare I saw, along the green alley that leads from the old part of the house to the mausoleum—No, I will not say what I saw or believed I saw—you would ridicule me, and justly. But, whatever it might be, on the earth without or in the fancy within my brain, I was so terrified, that I rushed back to my bed, and buried my face in my pillow. I I would have come to you; but I did not dare to stir. I have been riding hard all the morning in order to recover my nerves. But I dread sleeping again under that roof, and now that you and Margrave leave me, I shall go this very day to London. I hope all that I have told you is no bad sign of any coming disease; blood to the head, eh?"

"No; but imagination overstrained can produce wondrous effects. You do right to change the scene. Go to London at once amuse yourself, and—"

"Not return, till the old house is razed to the ground. That is my resolve. You approve? That's well. All success to you Fenwick. I will canter back and get my portmanteau ready and the carriage out, in time for the five o'clock train."

So then he, too, had seen—what? I did not dare and I did not desire to ask him. But he, at least, was not walking in his sleep! Did we both dream, or neither?

CHAPTER LIII.

There is an instance of the absorbing tyranny of every-day life which must have struck all such of my readers as have ever experienced one of those portents which are so at variance with every-day life, that the ordinary epithet bestowed on them is "supernatural."

And be my readers few or many, there will be no small proportion of them to whom, once, at least in the course of their existence, a something strange and *eirie* has occurred—a something which perplexed and baffled rational conjecture, and struck on those chords which vibrate to superstition. It may have been only a dream unaccountably verified—an undefinable presentiment or forewarning; but up from such slighter and vaguer tokens of the realm of marvel—up to the portents of ghostly apparitions or haunted chambers, I believe that the greater number of persons arrived at middle age, however instructed the class, however civilized the land, however sceptical the period, to which they belong, have either in themselves experienced, or heard recorded by intimate associates whose veracity they accept as indisputable in all ordinary transactions of life—phenomena which are not to be solved by the wit that mocks them, nor, perhaps, always and entirely, to the contentment of the reason or the philosophy that explains them away.

Such phenomena, I say, are infinitely more numerous than would appear from the instances currently quoted and dismissed with a jest; for few of those who have witnessed them are disposed to own it, and they who only hear of them through others, however trustworthy, would not impugn their character for common sense by professing a belief to which common sense is a merciless persecutor. But he who reads my assertion in the quiet of his own room will, perhaps, pause, ransack his memory, and find there, in some dark corner which he excludes from "the babbling and remorseless day," a pale recollection that proves the assertion not untrue.

And it is, I say, an instance of the absorbing tyranny of every-day life, that whenever some such startling incident disturbs its regular tenor of thought and occupation, that same every-day-life hastens to bury in its sands the object which has troubled its surface; the more unaccountable, the more prodigious has been the phenomenon which has scared and astounded us; the more, with involuntary effort, the mind seeks to rid itself of an enigma which might disease the reason that tries to solve it. We go about our mundane business with renewed avidity; we feel the necessity of proving to ourselves that we are still sober practical men, and refuse to be unfitted for the world which we know, by unsolicited visitations from worlds into which every glimpse is soon lost amid shadows. And it amazes us to think how soon such incidents, though not actually forgotten, though they can be recalled—and recalled too vividly for health—at our will, are, nevertheless, thrust, as it were, out of the mind's sight as we cast into lumber-rooms the crutches and splints that remind us of a broken limb which has recovered its strength and tone. It is a felicitous peculiarity in our organization, which all members of my profession will have noticed, how soon, when a bodily pain is once past, it becomes erased from the recollection—how soon and how invariably the mind refuses to linger over and recall it.

No man freed an hour before from a raging tooth-ache, the rack of a neuralgia, seats himself in his armchair to recollect and ponder upon the anguish he has undergone. It is the same with certain afflictions of the mind—not with those that strike on our affections, or blast our fortunes, overshadowing our whole future with a sense of loss; but where a trouble or calamity has been an accident, an episode in our wonted life, where it affects ourselves alone, where it is attended with a sense of shame and humiliation, where the pain of recalling it seems idle, and if indulged would almost madden us—agonies of that kind we do not brood over as we do over the death or falsehood of beloved friends, or the train of events by which we are reduced from wealth to penury. No one, for instance, who has escaped from a shipwreck, from the brink of a precipice, from the jaws of a tiger, spends his days and nights in reviving his terrors past, re-imagining dangers not to occur again, or, if they do occur, from which the experience undergone can suggest no additional safeguards. The current of our life, indeed, like that of the rivers, is most rapid in the midmost channel, where all streams are alike comparatively slow in the depth and along the shores in which each life, as each river, has a character peculiar to itself. And hence, those who would sail *with* the tide of the world, as those who sail with the tide of a river, hasten to take the middle of the stream, as those who sail *against* the tide are found clinging to the shore. I returned to my habitual duties and avocations with renewed energy; I did not suffer my thoughts to dwell on the dreary wonders that had haunted me, from the evening I first met Sir Philip Derval to the morning on which I had quitted the house of his heir: whether realities or hallucinations, no guess of mine could unravel such marvels, and no prudence of mine guard me against their repetition. But I had no fear that they would be repeated, any more than the man who had gone through shipwreck, or the hairbreath escape from a fall down a glacier, fears again to be found in a similar peril. Margrave had departed, whither I knew not, and, with his departure, ceased all sense of his influence. A certain calm within me, a tranquillizing feeling of relief, seemed to me like a pledge of permanent delivery.

But that which did accompany and haunt me, through all my occupations and pursuits, was the melancholy remembrance of the love I had lost in Lilian. I heard from Mrs. Ashleigh, who still frequently visited me, that her daughter seemed much in the same quiet state of mind—perfectly reconciled to our separation—seldom mentioning my name—if mentioning it, with indifference; the only thing remarkable in her state was her aversion to all society, and a kind of lethargy that would come over her, often in the daytime. She would suddenly fall into sleep and so remain for hours, but a sleep that seemed very serene and tranquil, and from which she woke of herself. She kept much within her own room, and always retired to it when visitors were announced.

Mrs. Ashleigh began reluctantly to relinquish the persuasion she had so long and so obstinately maintained, that this state of feeling towards myself—and, indeed, this general change in Lilian—was but temporary and abnormal; she began to allow that it was best to drop all thoughts of a renewed engagement—a future union. I proposed to see Lilian in her presence and in my professional capacity; perhaps some physical cause, especially for this lethargy, might be detected and removed. Mrs. Ashleigh owned to me that the idea had occurred to herself; she had sounded Lilian upon it; but her daughter had so resolutely opposed it—had said with so quiet a firmness "that all being over between us, a visit from me would be unwelcome and painful;" that Mrs. Ashleigh felt that an interview thus deprecated would only confirm estrangement. One day, in calling, she aaked my advice whether it would not be better to try the effect of change of air and scene, and, in some other place, some other medical opinion might be taken! I approved of this suggestion with unspeakable sadness.

"And," said Mrs. Ashleigh, shedding tears, "if that experiment prove unsuccesful, I will write and let you know; and we must then consider what to say to the world as a reason why the marriage is broken off. I can render this more easy by staying away. I will not return to L—— till the matter has ceased to be the topic of talk, and at a distance any excuse will be less questioned, and seem more natural. But still—still—let us hope still."

"Have you one ground for hope?"

"Perhaps so; but you will think it very frail and fallacious."

"Name it, and let me judge."

"One night—in which you were on a visit to Derval Court——"

"Ay, that night."

"Lilian woke me by a loud cry (she sleeps in the next room to me, and the door was left open); I hastened to her bedside in alarm; she was asleep, but appeared extremely agitated and convulsed. She kept calling on your name in a tone of passionate fondness, but as if in great terror. She cried, 'Do not go, Allen!—do not go!—you know not what you brave!—what you do!' Then she rose in her bed, clasping her hands. Her face was set and rigid: I tried to awake her, but could not. After a little time, she breathed a deep sigh, and murmured, 'Allen, dear love! did you not hear?—did you not see me? What could thus baffle matter and traverse space but love and soul? Can you still doubt me, Allen?—doubt that I love you now, shall love you ever more?—yonder, yonder, as here below?' She then sank back on her pillow, weeping, and then I woke her."

"And what did she say on waking?"

"She did not remember what she had dreamed, except that she had passed through some great terror; but added, with a vague smile, 'It is over, and I feel happy now. Then she turned round and fell asleep again, but quietly as a child, the tears dried, the smile resting."

"Go, my dear friend, go; take Lilian away from this place as soon as you can; divert her mind with fresh scenes. I hope!—I do hope! Let me know where you fix yourself. I will seize a holiday—I need one; I will arrange as to my patients—I will come to the same place; she need not know of it—but I must be by to watch, to hear your news of her. Heaven bless you for what you have said! I hope!—I do hope!"

CHAPTER LIV.

Some days after, I received a few lines from Mrs. Ashleigh. Her arrangements for departure were made. They were to start the next morning. She had fixed on going into the north of Devonshire, and staying some weeks either at Ilfracombe or Lynton, whichever place Lilian preferred. She would write as soon as they were settled.

I was up at my usual early hour the next morning. I resolved to go out towards Mrs. Ashleigh's house, and watch, unnoticed, where I might, perhaps, catch a glimpse of Lilian as the carriage that would convey her to the railway passed my hiding-place.

I was looking impatiently at the clock; it was yet two hours before the train by which Mrs. Ashleigh proposed to leave. A loud ring at my bell! I opened the door. Mrs. Ashleigh rushed in, falling on my breast.

"Lilian! Lilian!"

"Heavens! What has happened?"

"She has left—she is gone—gone away! Oh, Allen! how?—whither? Advise me. What is to be done?"

"Come in—compose yourself—tell me all—clearly, quickly. Lilian gone?—gone away? Impossible! She must be hid somewhere in the house—the garden; she, perhaps, did not like the journey. She may have crept away to some young friend's house. But *I* talk when you should talk: tell me all."

Little enough to tell! Lilian had seemed unusually cheerful the night before, and pleased at the thought of the excursion. Mother and daughter retired to rest early. Mrs. Ashleigh saw Lilian sleeping quietly before she herself went to bed. She woke betimes in the morning, dressed herself, went into the next room to call Lilian—Lilian was not there. No suspicion of flight occurred to her. Perhaps her daughter might be up already, and gone downstairs, remembering something she might wish to pack and take with her on the journey. Mrs. Ashleigh was confirmed in this idea when she noticed that her own room door was left open. She went downstairs, met a maid-servant in the hall, who told her, with alarm and surprise, that both the street and garden doors were found unclosed. No one had seen Lilian. Mrs. Ashleigh now became seriously uneasy. On remounting to her daughter's room, she missed Lilian's bonnet and mantle. The house and garden were both searched in vain. There could be no doubt that Lilian had gone—must have stolen noiselessly at night through her mother's room, and let herself out of the house and through the garden.

"Do you think she could have received any letter, any message, any visitor unknown to you?"

"I cannot think it. Why do you ask? Oh, Allen, you do not believe there is any accomplice in this disappearance! No, you do not believe it. But my child's honor! What will the world think?"

Not for the world cared I at that moment. I could think only of Lilian, and without one suspicion that imputed blame to her.

"Be quiet, be silent; perhaps she has gone on some visit, and will return. Meanwhile, leave inquiry to me."

CHAPTER LV.

It seemed incredible that Lilian could wander far without being observed. I soon ascertained that she had not gone away by the railway—by any public conveyance—had hired no carriage; she must therefore be still in the town, or have left it on foot. The greater part of the day was consumed in unsuccessful inquiries, and faint hopes that she would return; meanwhile, the news of her disappearance had spread: how could such news fail to do so?

An acquaintance of mine met me under the archway of Monks' Gate. He wrung my hand, and looked at me with great compassion.

"I fear," said he, "that we were all deceived in that young Margrave. He seemed so well conducted, in spite of his lively manners, But—"

"But what?"

"Mrs. Ashleigh was, perhaps, imprudent to admit him into her house so familiarly. He was certainly very handsome. Young ladies will be romantic."

"How dare you, sir!" I cried, choked with rage. "And without any coloring to so calumnious a suggestion! Margrave has not been in the town for many days. No one knows even where he is."

"Oh, yes, it is known where he is. He wrote to order the effects which he had left here to be sent to Penrith."

"When?"

"The letter arrived the day before yesterday. I happened to be calling at the house where he last lodged, when at L——, the house opposite Mrs. Ashleigh's garden. No doubt the servants in both houses gossip with each other. Miss Ashleigh could scarcely fail to hear of Mr. Margrave's address from her maid; and since servants will exchange gossip, they may also convey letters. Pardon me, you know I am your friend."

"Not from the moment you breathe a word against my betrothed wife," said I, fiercely.

I wrenched myself from the clasp of the man's hand, but his words still rang in my ears. I mounted my horse; I rode into the adjoining suburbs, the neighboring villages; there, however, I learned nothing till, just at nightfall, in a hamlet about ten miles from L——, a laborer declared he had seen a young lady dressed as I described, who passed by him in a path through the fields a little before noon; that he was surprised to see one so young, so well dressed, and a stranger to the neighborhood (for he knew by sight the ladies of the few families scattered round), walking alone; that as he stepped out of the path to make way for her, he looked hard into her face, and she did not heed him—seemed to gaze right before her, into space. If her expression had been less quiet and gentle, he should have thought, he could scarcely say why, that she was not quite right in her mind—there was a strange unconscious stare in her eyes, as if she were walking in her sleep. Her pace was very steady— neither quick nor slow. He had watched her till she passed out of sight, amidst a wood through which the path wound its way to a village at some dstauce.

I followed up this clue. I arrived at the village to which my informant directed me, but night had set in. Most of the houses were closed, so I could glean no further information from the cottages or the inn. But the police superintendent of the district lived in the village, and to him I gave instructions which I had not given, and, indeed, would have been disinclined to give, to the police at L——. He was intelligent and kindly: he promised to communicate at once with the different police-stations for miles round, and with all delicacy and privacy. It was not probable that Lilian could have wandered in one day much farther than the place at which I then was; it was scarcely to be conceived that she could baffle my pursuit and the practised skill of the police. I rested but a few hours, at a small public-house, and was on horseback again at dawn. A little after sunrise I again heard of the wanderer. At a lonely cottage, by a brick-kiln, in the midst of a wide common, she had stopped the previous evening, and asked for a draught of milk. The woman who gave it to her inquired if she had lost her way? She said "No;" and, only tarrying a few minutes, had gone across the common; and the woman supposed she was a visitor at a gentleman's house which was at the farther end of waste, for the path she took led to no town, no village. It occurred to me, then, that Lilian oided all high-roads, all places, even the humblest, where men congregated together.

But where could she have passed the night? Not to fatigue the reader with the fruitless result of frequent inquiries, I wil but say that at the end of the second day I had succeeded in ascertaining that I was stil on her track; and though I had ridden to and fro nearly double the distance—coming back again to places I had left behind—it was at the distance of forty miles from L—— that I last heard of her that second day. She had been seen sitting alone by a little brook only an hour before. I was led to the very spot by a woodman—it was at the hour of twilight when he beheld her—she was leaning her face on her hand, and seemed weary. He spoke to her; she did not answer, but rose, and resumed her way along the banks of the streamlet. That night I put up at no inn; I followed the course of the brook for miles, then struck into every path that I could conceive her to have taken—in vain. Thus I consumed the night on foot, tying my horse to a tree, for he was tired out, and returning to him at sunrise. At noon, the third day, I again heard of her, and in a remote, savage part of the country. The features of the landscape were changed; there was little foliage and little culture, but the ground was broken into mounds and hollows, and covered with patches of heath and stunted brushwood. She had been seen by a shepherd, and he made the same observation as the first who had guided me on her track—she looked to him "like some one walking in her sleep." An hour or two later, in a dell, amongst the furze-bushes, I chanced on a knot of ribbon. I recognized the color Lilian habitually wore; I felt certain that the ribbon was hers. Calculating the utmost speed I could ascribe to her, she could not be far off, yet still I failed to discover. The scene now was as solitary as a desert; I met no one on my way. At length, a little after sunset, I found myself in view of the sea. A small town nestled below the cliffs, on which I was guiding my weary horse. I entered the town, and while my horse was baiting went in search of the resident policeman. The information I had directed to be sent round the country had reached him; he had acted on it, but without result. I was surprised to hear him address me by name, and looking at him more narrowly, I recognized him for the policeman Waby. This young man had always expressed so grateful a sense of my attendance on his sister, and had, indeed, so notably evinced his gratitude in prosecuting with Margrave the inquiries which terminated in the discovery of Sir Philip Derval's murderer, that I confided to him the name of the wanderer, of which he had not been previously informed; but which it would be, indeed, impossible to conceal from him should the search in which his aid was asked proved successful,—as he knew Miss Ashleigh by sight. His face immediately became thoughtful. He paused a minute or two, and then said:

"I think I have it, but I do not like to say; I may pain you, sir."

"Not by confidence; you pain me by concealmant."

The man hesitated still; I encouraged him, and then he spoke out frankly.

"Sir, did you never think it strange that Mr. Margrave should move from his handsome rooms in the hotel to a somewhat uncomfortable lodging, from the window of which he could look down on Mrs. Ashleigh's garden? I have seen him at night in the balcony of that window, aud when I noticed him going so frequently into Mrs. Ashleigh's house during your unjust detention, I own, sir, I felt for you—"

"Nonsense! Mr. Margrave went to Mrs. Ashleigh's house as my friend. He has left L—— weeks ago. What has all this to do with—?"

"Patience, sir; hear me out. I was sent from L—— to this station (on promotion, sir) a fortnight since last Friday, for there has been a good deal of crime hereabouts; it is a bad neighborhood, and full of smugglers;—some days ago, in watching quietly near a lonely house, of which the owner is a suspicious character down in my books, I saw, to my amazement, Mr. Margrave come out of that house—come out of a private door in it, which belongs to a part of the building not inhabited by the owner, but which used formerly, when the house was a sort of inn, to be let to night lodgers of the humblest description. I followed him; he went down to the sea-shore, walked about, singing to himself; then returned to the house, and re-entered by the same door. I soon learned that he lodged in the house—had lodged there for several days. The next morning, a fine yacht arrived at a tolerably convenient creek about a mile from the house, and there anchored. Sailors came ashore, rambling down to this town. The yacht belonged to Mr. Margrave; he had purchased it by commission in London. It is stored for a long voyage. He had directed it to come to him in this out-of-the-way place, where no gentleman's yacht ever put in before, though the creek, or bay, is handy enough for such craft. Well, sir, is it not strange that a rich young gentleman should come to this unfrequented sea-shore, put up with accommodation that must be of the rudest kind, in the house of a man known as a desperate smuggler, suspected to be worse?—order a yacht to meet him here; is not all this strange? But would it be strange if he were waiting for a young lady? And if a young lady has fled at night from her home, and has come secretly along by-paths, which must have been very fully explained to her beforehand, and is now near that young gentleman's lodging, if not actually in it—if this be so, why, the affair is not so very strange after all. And now do you forgive me, sir?"

"Where is the house? Lead me to it."

"You can hardly get to it on foot; rough walking, sir, and about seven miles off by the shortest cut."

"Come, and at once; come quickly. We must be there before—before—"

"Before the young lady can get to the place. Well, from what you say of the spot in which she was last seen, I think, on reflection, we may easily do that. I am at your service, sir. But I should warn you that the owners of the house, man and wife, are both of villanous character—would do anything for money. Mr. Margrave, no doubt, has money enough; and if the young lady chooses to go away with Mr. Margrave, you know I have no power to help it."

"Leave all that to me; all I ask of you is to show me the house."

We were soon out of the town; the night had closed in; it was very dark, in spite of a few stars; the path was rugged and preciptous, sometimes skirting the very brink of perilous cliffs; sometimes delving down to the sea-shore —there stopped by rock or wave—and painfully re-winding up the ascent.

"It is an ugly path, sir, but it saves four miles; and anyhow the road is a bad one."

We came, at last, to a few wretched fishermen's huts. The moon had now risen, and revealed the squalor of poverty-stricken ruinous hovels; a couple of boats moored to the shore; a moaning, fretful sea; and at a distance, a vessel, with lights on board, lying perfectly still at anchor in a sheltered curve of the bold rude shore. The policeman pointed to the vessel.

"The yacht, sir; the wind will be in her favor if she sails to-night."

We quickened our pace as well as the nature of the path would permit, left the huts behind us, and, about a mile farther on, came to a solitary house, larger than, from the policeman's description of Margrave's lodgment, I should have presupposed: a house that in the wilder parts of Scotland might be almost a laird's; but even in the moonlight it looked very dilapidated and desolate. Most of the windows were closed, some with panes broken, stuffed with wisps of straw; there were the remains of a wall round the house; it was broken in some parts (only its foundation left). On approaching the house, I observed two doors—one on the side fronting the sea, one on the other side facing a patch of broken ground that might once have been a garden, and lay waste within the enclosure of the ruined wall, encumbered with various litter—heaps of rubbish, a ruined shed, the carcase of a worn-out boat. This latter door stood wide open—the other was closed. The house was still and dark, as if either deserted, or all within it retired to rest.

"I think that open door leads at once to the rooms Mr. Margrave hires; he can go in and out without disturbing the other inmates. They used to keep, on the side which they inhabit, a beer-house, but the magistrates shut it up; still, it is a resort for bad characters. Now, sir, what shall we do?"

"Watch separately. You wait within the enclosure of the wall, hid by those heaps of rubbish, near the door; none can enter but what you will observe them. If you see her, you will accost and stop her, and call aloud for me; I shall be in hearing. I will go back to the high part of the ground yonder—it seems to me that she must pass that way; and I would desire, if possible, to save her from the humiliation, the—the shame of coming within the precincts of that man's abode. I feel I may trust you now and hereafter. It is a great thing for the happiness and honor of the poor young lady and her mother, that I may be able to declare that I did not take her from that man, from any man—from that house, from any house. You comprehend me, and will obey? I speak to you as a confidant—a friend."

"I thank you with my whole heart, sir, for so doing. You saved my sister's life, and the least I can do is to keep secret all that would pain your life if blabbed abroad. I know what mischief folk's tongues can make. I will wait by the door, never fear, and will rather lose my place than not strain all the legal power I possess to keep the young lady back from sorrow."

This dialogue was interchanged in close hurried whisper behind the broken wall, and out of all hearing. Waby now crept through a wide gap into the enclosure, and nestled himself silently amidst the wrecks of the broken boat, not six feet from the open door, and close to the wall of the house itself. I went back some thirty yards up the road, to the rising ground which I had pointed out to him. According to the best calculation I could make—considering the pace at which I had cleared the precipitous pathway, and reckoning from the place and time at which Lilian had been last seen—she could not possibly have yet entered that house. I might presume it would be more than half an hour before she could arrive; I was in hopes that, during the interval, Margrave might show himself, perhaps at the door, or from the windows, or I might even by some light from the latter be guided to the room in which to find him.

If, after waiting a reasonable time, Lilian should fail to appear, I had formed my plan of action; but it was important for the success of that plan that I should not lose myself in the strange house, nor bring its owner's to Margrave's aid—that I should surprise him alone and unawares. Half an hour, three quarters, a whole hour thus passed—no sign of my poor wanderer; but signs there were of the enemy, from whom I resolved, at whatever risk, to free and to save her. A window on the ground-floor to the left of the door, which had long fixed my attention because I had seen light through the chinks of the shutters, slowly unclosed, the shutters fell back, the casement opened, and I beheld Margrave distinctly; he held something in his hand that gleamed in the moonlight, directed not towards the mound on which I stood, nor towards the path I had taken, but towards an open space beyond the ruined wall, to the right. Hid by a cluster of stunted shrubs, I watched him with a heart that beat with rage, not with terror. He seemed so intent in his own gaze, as to be unheeding or unconscious of all else. I stole from my post, and, still under cover, sometimes of the broken wall, sometimes of the shaggy ridges that skirted the path, crept on, on till I reached the side of the house itself; then, there secure from his eyes, should he turn them, I stepped over the ruined wall, scarcely two feet high in that place, on—on towards the door. I passed the spot on which the policeman had shrouded himself; he was seated, his back against the ribs of the broken boat. I put my hand to his mouth that he might not cry out in surprise, and whispered in his ear; he stirred not. I shook him by the arm: still he stirred not. A ray of the moon fell on his face. I saw that he was in a profound slumber. Persuaded that it was no natural sleep, and that he had become useless to me, I passed him by. I was at the threshold of the open door; the light from the window close by falling on the ground; I was in the passage; a glimmer came through the chinks of a door to the left; I turned the handle noiselessly, and, the next moment, Margrave was locked in my grasp.

"Call out," I hissed in his ear, "and I strangle you before any one can come to your help!"

He did not call out; his eye, fixed on mine as he writhed round, saw, perhaps, his peril if he did. His countenance betrayed fear, but as I tightened my grasp that expression gave way to one of wrath and fierceness; and as, in turn, I felt the grip of his hand, I knew that the struggle between us would be that of two strong men, each equally bent on the mastery of the other.

I was, as I have said before, endowed with an unusual degree of physical power, disciplined in early youth by athletic exercise and contest. In height and in muscle I had greatly the advantage over my antagonist, but such was the nervous vigor, the elastic energy of his incomparable frame, in which sinews seemed springs of steel, that had our encounter been one in which my strength was less heightened by rage, I believe that I could no more haved coped with him than the bison can cope with the boa; but I was animated by that passion which trebles for a time all our forces—which makes even the weak man a match for the strong. I felt that if I were worsted, disabled, stricken down, Lilian might be lost in losing her sole protector; and on the other hand, Margrave had been taken at the disadvantange of that surprise which will half unnerve the fiercest of the wild beasts; while as we grappled, reeling and rocking to and fro in our struggle, I soon observed that his attention was distracted—that his eye was turned towards an object which he had dropped involuntarily when I first seized him.

He sought to drag me towards that object, and when near it stooped to seize. It was a bright, slender, short wand of steel. I remembered when and where I seen it, whether in my waking state or in vision; and as his hand stole down to take it from the floor, I set on the wand my strong foot. I cannot tell by what rapid process, of thought and association I came to the belief that the possession of a little piece of blunted steel would decide the conflict in favor of the possessor, but the struggle now was concentred on the attainment of that seemingly idle weapon. I was becoming breathless and exhausted, while Margrave seemed every moment to gather up new force, when, collecting all my strength for one final effort, I lifted him suddenly high in the air, and hurled him to the farthest end of the cramped arena to which our contest was confined. He fell, and with a force by which most men would have been stunned; but he recovered himself with a quick rebound, and, as he stood facing me, there was something grand as well as terrible in his aspect. His eyes literally flamed, as those of a tiger; his rich hair, flung back from his knitted forehead, seemed to erect itself as an angry mane; his lips, slightly parted, showed the glitter of his set teeth: his whole frame seemed larger in the tension of the muscles, and as, gradually relaxing his first defying and haughty attitude, he crouched as the panther crouches for its deadly spring, I felt as if it were a wild beast whose rush was coming upon me—wild beast, but still Man, the king of the animals, fashioned forth from no mixture of humbler races by the slow revolutions of time, but his royalty stamped on his form when the earth became fit for his coming.*

At that moment I snatched up the wand, directed it towards him, and advancing with a fearless stride, cried—

"Down to my feet, miserable sorcerer!"

To my own amaze, the effect was instantaneous. My terrible antagonist dropped to the floor as a dog drops at the word of his master. The muscles of his frowning countenance relaxed, the glare of his wrathful eyes grew dull and rayless; his limbs lay prostrate and unnerved, his head rested against the wall, his arms limp and drooping by his side. I approached him slowly and cautiously; he seemed cast into a profound slumber.

"You are at my mercy now!" said I.

He moved his head as in sign of deprecating submission.

"You hear and understand me? Speak!"

His lips faintly muttered, "Yes."

"I command you to answer truly the questions I shall address to you."

"I must while yet sensible of the power that has passed to your hand."

"Is it by some occult magnetic property in this wand that you have exercised so demoniac an influence over a creature so pure as Lilian Ashleigh?"

"By that wand and by other arts which you could not comprehend."

"And for what infamous object?—her seduction, her dishonor?"

"No! I sought in her the aid of a gift which would cease, did she cease to be pure. At first I but cast my influence upon her that through her I might influence yourself. I needed your help to discover a secret. Circumstances steeled your mind against me. I could no longer hope that you would voluntarily lend yourself to my will. Meanwhile, I had found in her the light of a loftier knowledge than that of your science; through that knowledge, duly heeded and cultivated, I hoped to divine what I cannot of myself discover. Therefore I deepened over her mind the spells I command—therefore I have drawn her hither as the load-stone draws the steel, and therefore I would have borne her with me to the shores to which I was about this night to sail. I had cast the inmates of the house and all around it, into slumber, in order that none might witness her departure; had I not done so, I should have summoned others to my aid, in spite of your threat."

"And would Lilian Ashleigh have passively accompanied you, to her own irretrievable disgrace?"

"She could not have helped it; she would

* "And yet, even if we entirely omit the consideration of the soul, that immaterial and immortal principle which is for a time united to his body, and view him only in his merely animal character, man is still the most excellent of animals."—Dr. Kidd on the Adaptation of External Nature to the Physical Condition of Man (Sect. iii., p. 18).

have been unconscious of her acts; she was, and is, in a trance; nor, had she gone with me, would she have waked from that state while she lived; that would not have been long."

"Wretch! and for what object of unhallowed curiosity do you exert an influence which whithers away the life of its victim?"

"Not curiosity, but the instinct of self-preservation. I count on no life beyond the grave. I would defy the grave, and live on."

"And was it to learn, through some ghastly agencies, the secret of renewing existence, that you lured me by the shadow of your own image on the night when we met last?"

The voice of Margrave here became very faint as he answered me, and his countenance began to exhibit the signs of an exhaustion almost mortal.

"Be quick," he murmured, "or I die. The fluid which emanates from that wand, in the hand of one who envenoms the fluid with his own hatred and rage, will prove fatal to my life. Lower the wand from my forehead; low—low;—lower still!"

"What was the nature of that rite in which you constrained me to share?"

"I cannot say. You are killing me. Enough that you were saved from a great danger by the apparition of the protecting image vouchsafed to your eye; otherwise you would—you would—Oh, release me! Away! away!"

The foam gathered to his lips; his limbs became fearfully convulsed.

"One question more: where is Lilian at this moment? Answer that question, and I depart."

He raised his head, made a visible effort to rally his strength, and gasped out—

"Yonder. Pass through the open space up the cliff, beside a thorn-tree—you will find her there, where she halted when the wand dropped from my hand. But—but—beware! Ha! you will serve me yet, and through her! They said so that night, though you heard them not. THEY said it!" Here his face became deathlike; he pressed his hand on his heart, and shrieked out, "Away—away! for you are my murderer!"

I retreated to the other end of the room, turning the wand from him, and when I gained the door, looked back; his convulsions had ceased, but he seemed locked in a profound swoon. I left the room—the house—paused by Waby; he was still sleeping "Awake!" I said, and touched him with the wand. He started up at once, rubbed his eyes, began stammering out excuses. I checked them, and bade him follow me. I took the way up the open ground towards which Margrave had pointed the wand, and there, motionless, beside a gnarled fantastic thorn-tree, stood Lilian. Her arms were folded across her breast; her face, seen by the moonlight, looked so innocent and so infantine, that I needed no other evidence to tell me how unconscious she was of the peril to which her steps had been drawn. I took her gently by the hand. "Come with me," I said in a whisper, and she obeyed me silently, and with a placid smile.

Rough though the way, she seemed unconscious of fatigue. I placed her arm in mine, but she did not lean on it. We got back to the town. I obtained there an old chaise and a pair of horses. At morning Lilian was under her mother's roof. About the noon of that day fever seized her; she became rapidly worse, and, to all appearance, in imminent danger. Dilirium set in; I watched beside her night and day, supported by an inward conviction of her recovery, but tortured by the sight of her sufferings. On the third day a change for the better became visible; her sleep was calm, her breathing regular.

Shortly afterwards she woke out of danger. Her eyes fell at once on me, with all their old ineffable tender sweetness.

"Oh, Allen, beloved, have I not been very ill? But I am almost well now. Do not weep; I shall live for you—for your sake." And she bent forward, drawing my hand from my streaming eyes, and kissing me with a child's guileless kiss on my burning forehead.

CHAPTER LVI.

LILIAN recovered, but the strange thing was this: all memory of the weeks that had elapsed since her return from visiting her aunt was completely obliterated; she seemed in profound ignorance of the charge on which I had been confined—perfectly ignorant even of the existence of Margrave. She had, indeed, a very vague reminiscence of her conversation with me in the garden—the first conversation which had ever been embittered by a disagreement—but that disagreement itself she did not recollect. Her belief was that she had been ill and light-headed since that evening. From that evening to the hour of her waking, conscious and revived, all was a blank. Her love for me was restored, as if its thread had never been broken. Some such instances of oblivion after bodily illness or mental shock are familiar enough to the practice of all medical men; * and I was therefore enabled to appease the anxiety and wonder of Mrs. Ashleigh, by quoting various examples of loss, or suspension, of memory. We agreed that it would be necessary to break to Lilian, though very cautiously, the story of Sir Philip Derval's murder, and the charge to which I had been subjected. She could not fail to hear of those events from other. How shall I express her womanly terror, her loving, sympathizing pity, on hearing the tale, which I softened as well as I could?

"And to think that I knew nothing of this!" she cried, clasping my hand; "to think that you were in peril, and that I was not by your side!"

Her mother spoke of Margrave as a visitor—an agreeable, lively stranger; Lilian could not even recollect his name, but she seemed shocked to think that any visitor had been admitted while I was in circumstances so awful! Need I say that our engagement was renewed? Renewed! To *her* knowledge and to her heart it had never been interrupted for a moment. But oh! the malignity of the wrong world! Oh! that strange lust of mangling reputations, which seizes on hearts the least wantonly cruel! Let two idle tongues utter a tale against some third person, who never offended the babblers, and how the tale spreads, like fire, lighted none know how, in the herbage of an American prairie! Who shall put it out?

What right have we to pry into the secrets of other men's hearths? True or false, the tale that is gabbled to us, what concern of ours can it be? I speak not of cases to which the law has been summoned, which law has sifted, on which law has pronounced. But how, when the law is silent, can we assume its verdicts? How be all judges, where there has been no witness-box, no cross-examination, no jury? Yet, every day we put on our ermine, and make ourselves judges—judges sure to condemn, and on what evidence? That which no court of law will receive. Somebody has said something to somebody, which somebody repeats to everybody!

The gossip of L—— had set in full current against Lilian's fair name. No ladies called on or sent to congratulate Mrs. Ashleigh on her return, or to inquire after Lilian herself during her struggle between life and death.

How I missed the Queen of the Hill at this critical moment! How I longed for aid to crush the slander, with which I knew not how to grapple—aid in her knowledge of the world, and her ascendency over its judgments! I had heard from her once since her absence, briefly but kindly expressing her amazement at the ineffable stupidity which could for a moment have subjected me to a suspicion of of Sir Philip Dervol's strange murder, and congratulating me heartily on my complete vindication from so monstrous a charge. To this letter no address was given. I supposed the omission to be accidental, but on calling at her house to inquire her direction, I found that her servants did not know it.

What, then, was my joy when, just at this juncture, I received a note from Mrs. Poyntz, stating that she had returned the night before, and would be glad to see me.

I hastened to her house. "Ah," thought I, as I sprang lightly up the ascent to the Hill, "how the tattlers will be silenced by a word

* Such instances of suspense of memory are recorded in most physiological and in some metaphysieal works. Dr. Abercrombie notices some, more or less similar to that related in the text:—"A young lady who was present at a catastrophe in Scotland, in which many people lost their lives by the fall of the gallery of a church, escaped without any injury, but with the complete loss of the recollection of any of the circumstances; and this extended not only to the accident, but to everything that had occurred to her for a certain time before going to church. A lady whom I attended some years ago in a protracted illness, in which her memory became much impaired, lost the recollection of a period of about ten or twelve years, but spoke with perfect consistency of things as they stood before that time." Dr. Abercrombie adds:—"As far as I have been able to trace it, the principle in such cases seems to be, that when the memory is impaired to a certain degree, the loss of it extends backward to some event or some period by which a particularly deep impression had been made upon the mind."—Abercrombie on the Intellectual Powers, pages 118, 119 (15th edition).

from her imperial lips!" And only just as I approached her door did it strike me how difficult—nay, how impossible to explain to her—the hard positive woman, her who had, less ostensibly but more ruthlessly than myself, destroyed Dr. Lloyd for his belief in the comparatively rational pretensions of clairvoyance—all the mystical excuses for Lilian's flight from her home? How speak to her—or, indeed, to any one—about an occult fascination and a magic wand? No matter; surely it would be enough to say that, at the time, Lilien had been light-headed, under the influence of the fever which had afterwards nearly proved fatal. The early friend of Anne Ashleigh would nor be a severe critic on any tale that might right the good name of Anne Ashleigh's daughter. So assured, with a light heart and cheerful face, I followed the servant into the great lady's pleasant but decorous presence-chamber.

CHAPTER LVII.

Mrs. Poyntz was on her favorite seat by the window, and, for a wonder, not knitting—that classic task seemed done; but she was smoothing and folding the completed work with her white comely hand, and smiling over it, as if in complacent approval, when I entered the room. At the fireside sat the he-colonel, inspecting a newly-invented barometer; at another window, in the farthest recess of the room, stood Miss Jane Poyntz with a young gentlemen whom I had never before seen, but who turned his eyes full upon me with a haughty look as the servant announced my name. He was tall, well-proportioned, decidedly handsome, but with that expression of cold and concentred self-esteem in his very attitude, as well as his countenance, which makes a man of merit unpopular, a man without merit ridiculous.

The he-colonel, always punctiliously civil, rose from his seat, shook hands with me cordially, and said, "Coldish weather to-day; but we shall have rain to-morrow. Rainy seasons come in cycles. We are about to commence a cycle of them with heavy showers." He sighed and returned to his barometer.

Miss Jane bowed to me graciously enough, but was evidently a little confused, a circumstance which might well attract my notice, for I had never before seen that high-bred young lady deviate a hair's breadth from the even tenor of a manner admirable for a cheerful and courteous ease, which, one felt convinced, would be unaltered to those around her, if an earthquake swallowed one up an inch before her feet.

The young gentleman continued to eye me loftily, as the heir-apparent to some celestial planet might eye an inferior creature from a half-formed nebula suddenly dropped upon his sublime and perfected star.

Mrs. Poyntz extended to me two fingers, and said, frigidly, "Delighted to see you again! How kind to attend so soon to my note!" Motioning me to a seat beside her, she here turned to her husband, and said, "Poyntz, since a cycle of rain begins to-morrow, better secure your ride to-day. Take these young people with you. I want to talk with Dr. Fenwick."

The colonel carefully put away his barometer, and saying to his daughter "Come!" went forth. Jane followed her father; the young gentleman followed Jane.

The reception I had met chilled and disappointed me. I felt that Mrs. Poyntz was changed, and in her change the whole house seemed changed. The very chairs looked civilly unfriendly, as if preparing to turn their backs on me. However, I was not in the false position of an intruder; I had been summoned; it was for Mrs. Poyntz to speak first, and I waited quietly for her to do so.

She finished the careful folding of her work, and then laid it at rest in the drawer of the table at which she sat. Having so done, she turned to me, and said,—

"By the way, I ought to have introduced to you my young guest, Mr. Ashleigh Sumner. You would like him. He has talents—not showy, but solid. He will succeed in public life."

"So that young man is Mr. Ashleigh Sumner? I do not wonder that Miss Ashleigh rejected him."

I said this, for I was nettled, as well as surprised, at the coolness with which a lady who had professed a friendship for me, mentioned that fortunate young gentleman, with so complete an oblivion of all the antecedents that had once made his name painful to my ear.

In turn, my answer seemed to nettle Mrs. Poyntz.

"I am not so sure that she did reject; perhaps she rather misunderstood him; gallant compliments are not always proposals of marriage. However that be, his spirits were not much damped by Miss Ashleigh's disdain, nor his heart deeply smitten by her charms; for he is now very happy, very much attached to another young lady, to whom he proposed, three days ago, at Lady Delafield's, and not to make a mystery of what all our little world will know before to-morrow, that young lady is my daughter Jane."

"Were I acquainted with Mr. Sumner, I should offer to *him* my sincere congratulations."

Mrs. Poyntz resumed, without heeding a reply more complimentary to Miss Jane than to the object of her choice:

"I told you that I meant Jane to marry a rich country gentleman, and Ashleigh Sumner is the very country gentleman I had then in my thoughts. He is cleverer and more ambitious than I could have hoped: he will he a minister some day, in right of his talents, and a peer, if he wishes it, in right of his lands. So that matter is settled."

There was a pause, during which my mind passed rapidly through links of reminiscence and reasoning, which led me to a mingled sentiment of admiration for Mrs. Poyntz as a diplomatist and of distrust for Mrs. Poyntz as a friend. It was now clear why Mrs. Poyntz, before so little disposed to approve my love, had urged me at once to offer my hand to Lilian, in order that she might depart affianced and engaged to the house in which she would meet Mr. Ashleigh Sumner. Hence, Mrs. Poyntz's anxiety to obtain all the information I could afford her of the sayings and doings at Lady Haughton's; hence, the publicity she had so suddenly given to my engagement; hence, when Mr. Sumner had gone away a rejected suitor, her own departure from L——; she had seized the very moment when a vain and proud man, piqued by the mortification received from one lady, falls the easier prey to the arts which allure his suit to another. All was so far clear to me. And I—was my self-conceit less egregious and less readily duped than that of yon gilded popinjay's! How skilfully this woman had knitted me into her work with the noiseless turn of her white hands! and yet, forsooth, I must vaunt the superior scope of my intellect, and plumb all the fountains of Nature—I, who could not fathom the little pool of this female schemer's mind!

But that was no time for resentment to her or rebuke to myself. She was now the woman who could best protect and save from slander my innocent, beloved Lilian. But how approach that perplexing subject?

Mrs. Poyntz approached it, and with her usual decision of purpose, which bore so deceitful a likeness to candor of mind.

"But it was not to talk of my affairs that I asked you to call, Allen Fenwick." As she uttered my name, her voice softened, and her manner took that maternal, caressing tenderness which had sometimes amused and sometimes misled me. "No, I do not forget that you asked me to be your friend, and I take, without scruple, the licence of friendship. What are these stories that I have heard already about Lilian Ashleigh, to whom you were once engaged?"

"To whom I am still engaged."

"Is it possible? Oh, then, of course the stories I have heard are all false. Very likely; no fiction in scandal ever surprises me. Poor dear Lilian, then, never ran away from her mother's house?"

I smothered the angry pain which this mode of questioning caused me; I knew how important it was to Lilian to secure to her the countenance and support of this absolute autocrat; I spoke of Lilian's long previous distemper of mind; I accounted for it as any intelligent physician, unacquainted with all that I could not reveal, would account. Heaven forgive me for the venial falsehood, but I spoke of the terrible charge against myself as enough to unhinge, for a time, the intellect of a girl so acutely sensitive as Lilian; I sought to create that impression as to the origin of all that might otherwise seem strange; and in this state of cerebral excitement she had wandered from home—but alone. I had tracked every step of her way; I had found and restored her to her home. A critical delirium had followed, from which she now rose, cured in health, unsuspicious that there could be a whisper against her name. And then, with all the eloquence I could command, and in words as adapted as I could frame them to soften the heart of a woman, herself a mother, I implored Mrs. Poyntz's aid to silence all the cruelties of calumny, and extend her shield over the child of her own early friend.

When I came to an end, I had taken, with caressing force, Mrs. Poyntz's reluctant hands in mine. There were tears in my voice, tears in my eyes. And the sound of her voice in reply gave me hope, for it was unusually gentle. She was evidently moved. The hope was soon quelled.

"Allen Fenwick," she said, "you have a noble heart; I grieve to see how it abuses your reason. I cannot aid Lilian Ashleigh in the way you ask. Do not start back so indignantly. Listen to me as patiently as I have listened to you. That when you brought back the unfortunate young woman to her poor mother, her mind was disordered, and became yet more dangerously so, I can well believe: that she is now recovered and thinks with shame, or refuses to think at all, of her imprudent flight, I can believe also; but I do not believe, the World cannot believe, that she did not, knowingly and purposely, quit her mother's roof, and in quest of that young stranger so incautiously, so unfeelingly admitted to her mother's house during the very time you were detained on the most awful of human accusations. Every one in the town knows that Mr. Margrave visited daily at Mrs. Ashleigh's during that painful period; every one in the town knows in what strange out-of-the-way place this youug man had niched himself; and that a yacht was bought, and lying in wait there. What for? It is said that the chaise in which you brought Miss Ashleigh back to her home was hired in a village within an easy reach of Mr. Margrave's lodging—of Mr. Margrave's yacht. I rejoice that you saved the poor girl from ruin; but her good name is tarnished, and if Anne Ashleigh, whom I sincerely pity, asks me my advice, I can but give her this: 'Leave L——, take your daughter abroad; and if she is not to marry Mr. Margrave, marry her as quietly and as quickly as possible to some foreigner.'"

"Madam! madam! this, then, is your friendship to her—to me! Oh, shame on you to insult thus an affianced husband! Shame on me ever to have thought you had a heart!"

"A heart, man!" she exclaimed, almost fiercely, springing up, and startling me with the change in her countenance and voice. "And little you would have valued, and pitilessly have crushed this heart, if I had suffered myself to show it to you! What right have you to reproach me? I felt a warm interest in your career, an unusual attraction in your conversation and society. Do you blame me for that, or should I blame myself? Condemned to live amongst brainless puppets, my dull occupation to pull the strings that moved them, it was a new charm to my life to establish friendship and intercourse with intellect and spirit, and courage. Ah! I understand that look, half incredulous, half inquisitive."

"Inquisitive, no! incredulous, yes! You desired my friendship, and how does your harsh judgment of my betrothed wife prove either to me or to her mother, whom you have known from your girlhood, the first duty of a friend—which is surely not that of leaving a friend's side the moment that he needs countenance in calumny, succor in trouble!"

"It is a better duty to prevent the calumny and avert the trouble. Leave aside Anne Ashleigh, a cipher that I can add or abstract from my sum of life as I please. What is my duty to yourself? It is plain. It is to tell you that your honor commands you to abandon all thoughts of Lilian Ashleigh as your wife. Ungrateful that you are! Do you suppose it was no mortification to my pride of woman and friend, that you never approached me in confidence except to ask my good offices in promoting your courtship to another?—no shock to the quiet plans I had formed as to our familiar though harmless intimacy, to hear that you were bent on a marriage in which my friend would be lost to me?"

"Not lost!—not lost! On the contrary, the regard I must suppose you had for Lilian would have been a new link between our homes."

"Pooh! Between me and that dreamy girl there could have been no sympathy, there could have grown up no regard. You would have been chained to your fireside, and—and—but no matter. I stifled my disappointment as soon as I felt it—stifled it, as all my life I have stifled that which either destiny or duty—duty to myself as to others—forbids me to indulge. Ah! do not fancy me one of the weak criminals who can suffer a worthy liking to grow into a debasing love! I was not in love with you, Allen Fenwick."

"Do you think I was ever so presumptuous a coxcomb as to fancy it?"

"No," she said, more softly; I was not so false to my household ties and to my own nature. But there are some friendships which are as jealous as love. I could have cheerfully aided you in any choice which my sense could have approved for you as wise; I should have been pleased to have found in such a wife my most intimate companion. But that silly child!—absurd! Nevertheless, the freshness and enthusiasm of your love touched me; you asked my aid and I gave it—perhaps I did believe that when you saw more of Lilian Ashleigh you would be cured of a fancy conceived by the eye—I should have known better what dupes the wisest men can be to the witcheries of a fair face and eighteen! When I found your illusion obstinate I wrenched myself away from a vain regret, turned to my own schemes, and my own ambition, and smiled bitterly to think that, in pressing you to propose so hastily to Lilian, I made your blind passion an agent in my own plans. Enough of this. I speak thus openly and boldly to you now, because now I have not a sentiment that can interfere with the dispassionate soundness of my counsels. I repeat, you cannot now marry Lilian Ashleigh; I cannot take my daughter to visit her; I cannot destroy the social laws that I myself have set in my petty kingdom."

"Be it as you will. I have pleaded for her while she is still Lilian Ashleigh. I plead for no one to whom I have once given my name. Before the woman whom I have taken from the altar, I can place, as a shield sufficient, my strong breast of man. Who has so deep an interest in Lilian's purity as I have? Who is so fitted to know the exact truth of every whisper against her? Yet when I, whom you admit to have some reputation for shrewd intelligence,—I, who tracked her way,—I, who restored her to her home,—when I, Allen Fenwick, am so assured of her inviolable innocence in thought as in deed, that I trust my honor to her keeping,—surely, surely, I confute the scandal which you yourself do not believe, though you refuse to reject and to annul it?"

"Do not deceive yourself, Allen Fenwick," said she, still standing beside me, her countenance now hard and stern "Look, where I stand, I am the WORLD! The World, not as satirists depreciate or as optimists extol its immutable properties, its all-persuasive authority. I am the World! And my voice is the World's voice when it thus warns you. Should you make this marriage, your dignity of character and position would be gone!—if you look only to lucre and professional success, possibly *they* may not ultimately suffer. You have skill, which men need; their need may still draw patients to your door and pour guineas into your purse. But you have the pride, as well as the birth, of a gentleman, and the wounds to that pride will be hourly chafed and never healed. Your strong breast of man has no shelter to the frail name of woman. The World, in its health, will look down on your wife, though its sick may look up to you. This is not all. The World, in its gentlest mood of indulgence, will say, compassionately, 'Poor man! how weak, and how deceived! What an unfortunate marriage!' But the World is not often indulgent—it looks most to the motives most seen on the surface. And the World will more frequently say, 'No, much too clever a a man to be duped! Miss Ashleigh had money. A good match to the man who liked gold better than honor.'"

I sprang to my feet, with difficulty suppressing my rage; and, remembering it was a woman who spoke to me, "Farewell, madam," said I, through my grinded teeth. "Were you, indeed, the Personation of The World, whose mean notions you mouth so calmly, I could not disdain you more." I turned to the door, and left her still standing erect and menacing, the hard sneer on her resoulute lip, the red glitter in her remorseless eye.

CHAPTER LVIII.

If ever my heart vowed itself to Lilian, the vow was now the most trustful and the most sacred. I had relinquished our engagement before, but then her affection seemed, no matter from what cause, so estranged from me, that though I might be miserable to lose her, I deemed that she would be unhappy in our union. Then, too, she was the gem and darling of the little world in which she lived: no whisper assailed her: now, I knew that she loved me; I knew that her estrangement had been involuntary; I knew that appearances wronged her, and that they never could be explained. I was in the true position of man to woman: I was the shield, the bulwark, the fearless confiding protector! Resign her now because the world babbled, because my career might be impeded, because my good name might be impeached—resign her, and, in that resignation, confirm all that was said against her! Could I do so, I should be the most craven of gentlemen, the meanest of men?

I went to Mrs. Ashleigh, and entreated her to hasten my union with her daughter, and fix the marriage-day.

I found the poor lady dejected and distressed. She was now sufficiently relieved from the absorbing anxiety for Lilian to be aware of the change on the face of that World which the woman I had just quitted personified and concentred; she had learned the cause from the bloodless lips of Miss Brabazon.

"My child—my poor child!" murmured the mother. "And she so guileless—so sensitive! Could she know what is said, it would kill her. She would never marry you, Allen—she would never bring shame to you!"

"She never need learn the barbarous calumny. Give her to me, and at once; patients, fortune, fame, are not found only at L——. Give her to me at once. But let me name a condition: I have a patrimonial independence — I have amassed large savings -- I have my profession and my repute. I cannot touch her fortune—I cannot—never can! Take it while you live; when you die, leave it to accumulate for her children, if children she have; not to me; not to her—unless I am dead or ruined!"

"Oh, Allen, what a heart!—what a heart! No, not heart, Allen—that bird in its cage has a heart: *soul*—what a soul!"

CHAPTER LIX.

How innocent was Lilian's virgin blush when I knelt to her, and prayed that she would forestall the date that had been fixed for our union, and be my bride before the breath of the autumn had withered the pomp of the woodland and silenced the song of the birds! Meanwhile, I was so fearfully anxious that she should risk no danger of hearing, even of surmising, the cruel slander against her—should meet no cold contemptuous looks—above all, should be safe from the barbed talk of Mrs. Poyntz—that I insisted on the necessity of immediate change of air and scene. I proposed that we should all three depart, the next day, for the banks of my own beloved and native Windermere. By that pure mountain air, Lilian's health would be soon re-established: in the church hallowed to me by the graves of my fathers our vows could be plighted. No calumny had ever cast a shadow over those graves. I felt as if my bride would be safer in the neighborhood of my mother's tomb.

I carried my point: it was so arranged. Mrs. Ashleigh, however, was reluctant to leave before she had seen her dear friend, Margaret Poyntz. I had not the courage to tell her what she might expect to hear from that dear friend, but, as delicately as I could, I informed her that I had already seen the Queen of the Hill, and contradicted the gossip that had reached her; but that as yet, like other absolute sovereigns, the Queen of the Hill thought it politic to go with the popular stream, reserving all check on its direction till the rush of its torrent might slacken; and that it would be infinitely wiser in Mrs. Ashleigh to postpone conversation with Mrs. Poyntz until Lilian's return to L—— as my wife. Slander by that time would have wearied itself out, and Mrs. Poyntz (assuming her friendship to Mrs. Ashleigh to be sincere) would then be enabled to say with authority to her subjects, "Dr. Fenwich alone knows the facts of the story, and his marriage with Miss Ashleigh refutes all the gossip to her prejudice."

I made that evening arrangements with a young and rising practitioner to secure attendance on my patients during my absence. I passed the greater part of the night in drawing up memoranda to guide my proxy in each case.

however humble the sufferer. This task finished, I chanced, in searching for a small microscope, the wonders of which I thought might interest and amuse Lilian, to open a drawer in which I kept the manuscript of my cherished Physiological Work, and, in so doing, my eye fell upon the wand which I had taken from Margrave. I had thrown it into that drawer on my return home, after restoring Lilian to her mother's house, and, in the anxiety which had subsequently preyed upon my mind, had almost forgotten the strange possession I had as strangely acquired. There it now lay, the instrument of agencies over the mechanism of nature which no doctrine admitted by my philosophy could accept, side by side with the presumptuous work which had analyzed the springs by which nature is moved, and decided the principles by which reason metes out, from the inch of its knowledge, the plan of the Infinite Unknown.

I took up the wand and examined it curiously. It was evidently the work of an age far remote from our own, scored over with half-obliterated characters in some Eastern tongue, perhaps no longer extant. I found that it was hollow within. A more accurate observation showed, in the centre of this hollow, an exceedingly fine thread-like wire, the unattached end of which would slightly touch the palm when the wand was taken into the hand. Was it possible that there might be a natural and even a simple cause for the effects which this instrument produced? Could it serve to collect, from that great focus of animal heat and nervous energy which is placed in the palm of the human hand, some such latent fluid as that which Reichenbach calls the "odic," and which, according to him, "rushes through and pervades universal Nature?" After all, why not? For how many centuries lay unknown all the virtues of the loadstone and the amber? It is but as yesterday that the forces of vapor have become to men genii more powerful than those conjured up by Aladdin; that light, at a touch, springs forth from invisible air; that thought finds a messenger swifter than the wings of the fabled Afrite. As, thus musing, my hand closed over the wand, I felt a wild thrill through my frame. I recoiled; I was alarmed lest (according to the plain commonsense theory of Julius Faber) I might be preparing my imagination to form and to credit its own illusions.

Hastily I laid down the wand. But then it occurred to me, that whatever its properties, it had so served the purposes of the dread Fascinator from whom it had been taken, that he might probably seek to repossess himself of it; he might contrive to enter my house in my absence; more prudent to guard in my own watchful keeping the incomprehensible instrument of incomprehensible arts. I resolved, therefore, to take the wand with me, and placed it in my travelling-trunk, with such effects as I selected for use in the excursion that was to commence with the morrow. I now lay down to rest, but I could not sleep. The recollections of the painful interview with Mrs. Poyntz became vivid and haunting. It was clear that the sentiment she had conceived for me was that of no simple friendship—something more or something less—but certainly something else; and this conviction brought before me that proud hard face, disturbed by a pang wrestled against but not subdued, and that clear metallic voice, troubled by the quiver of an emotion which, perhaps, she had never analyzed to herself. I did not need her own assurance to know that this sentiment was not to be confounded with a love which she would have despised as a weakness and repelled as a crime; it was an inclination of the intellect, not a passion of the heart. But still it admitted a jealousy little less keen than that which has love for its cause—so true it is that jealousy is never absent where self-love is always present. Certainly, it was no susceptibility of sober friendship which had made the stern arbitress of a coterie ascribe to her interest in me her pitiless judgment of Lilian. Strangely enough, with the image of this archetype of conventional usages and the trite social life, came that of the mysterious Margrave, surrounded by all the attributes with which superstition clothes the being of the shadowy border-land that lies beyond the chart of our visual world itself. By what link were creatures so dissimiliar rivited together in the metaphysical chain of association? Both had entered into the record of my life when my life admitted its own first romance of love. Through the aid of this cynical schemer I had been made known to Lilian.

At her house I had heard the dark story of

that Louis Grayle, with whom, in mocking spite of my reason, conjectures, which that very reason must despose itself before it could resolve into distempered fancies, identified the enigmatical Margrave. And now both she, the representative of the formal world most oppressed to visionary creeds, and he, who gatered around him all the terrors which haunt the realm of fable, stood united against me—foes with whom the intellect I had so haughtily cultured knew not how to cope. Whatever assault I might expect from either, I was unable to assail again. Alike, then, in this, are the Slander and and the Phantom; that which appals us most in their power over us is our impotence against them.

But up rose the sun, chasing the shadows from the earth, and brightening insensibly the thoughts of man. After all, Margrave had been baffled and defeated, whatever the arts he had practised and the secrets he possessed. It was, at least, doubtful whether his evil machinations would be renewed. He had seemed so incapable of long-sustained fixity of purpose, that it was probable he was in the pursuit of some new agent or victim; and as to this commonplace and conventional spectre, the so-called World, if it is everywhere to him whom it awes, it is nowhere to him who despises it. What was the good or bad word of a Mrs. Poyntz to me? Ay, but to Lilian? There, indeed, I trembled; but still, even in trembling, it was sweet to think that my home would be her shelter—my choice her vindication. Ah! how unutterably tender and reverential Love becomes when it assmes the duties of the guardian, and hallows its own heart into a sanctuary of refuge for the beloved!

CHAPTER LX.

THE beautiful lake! We two are on its grassy margin—twilight melting into night; the stars stealing forth, one after one. What a wonderful change is made within us when we come from our callings amongst men, chafed, wearied, wounded; gnawed by our cares, perplexed by the doubts of our very wisdom, stung by the adder that dwells in cities—Slander; nay, even if renowned, fatigued with the burden of the very names that we have won! What a change is made within us when suddenly we find ourselves transported into the calm solitudes of Nature;—into scenes familiar to our happy dreaming childhood; back, back from the dusty thoroughfares of our toil-worn manhood to the golden fountain of our youth! Blessed is the change, even when we have no companion beside us to whom the heart can whisper its sense of relief and joy. But if the one, in whom all our future is garnered up, be with us there, instead of that weary World which has so magically varnished away from the eye and the thought, then does the change make one of those rare epochs of life in which the charm is the stillness. In the pause from all by which our own turbulent struggles for happiness trouble existence, we feel with a rapt amazement, how calm a thing it is to be happy. And so as the night, in deepening, brightened, Lilian and I wandered by the starry lake. Conscious of no evil in ourselves, how secure we felt from evil! A few days more—a few days more, and we two should be as one! And that thought we uttered in many forms of words, brooding over it in the long intervals of enamoured silence.

And when he turned back to the quiet inn at which we had taken up our abode, and her mother, with her soft face, advanced to meet us, I said to Lilian:

"Would that in these scenes we could fix our home for life, away and afar from the dull town we have left behind us, with the fret of its wearying cares and the jar of its idle babble!"

"And why not, Allen? Why not? But no, you would not be happy."

"Not be happy, and with you? Sceptic, by what reasonings do you arrive at that ungracious conclusion?"

"The heart loves repose and the soul contemplation, but the mind needs action. Is it not so?"

"Where learned you that aphorism, out of place on such rosy lips?"

"I learned it in studying you," murmured Lilian, tenderly.

Here Mrs. Ashleigh joined us. For the first time I slept under the same roof as Lilian. And I forgot that the universe contained an enigma to solve or an enemy to fear.

CHAPTER LXI.

TWENTY days—the happiest my life had ever known—thus glided on. Apart from the charm which love bestows on the beloved, there was that in Lilian's conversation which made her a delightful companion. Whether it was that, in this pause from the toils of my career, my mind could more pliantly supple itself to her graceful imagination, or that her imagination was less vague and dreamy amidst those rural scenes, which realized in their loveliness and grandeur its long-conceived ideals, than it had been in the petty garden-ground neighbored by the stir and hubbub of the busy town,—in much that I had once slighted or contemned, as the vagaries of undisciplined fancy, I now recognized the sparkle and play of an intuitive genius, lighting up many a depth obscure to instructed thought. It is with some characters as with the subtler and more ethereal order of poets. To appreciate them we must suspend the course of artificial life. In the city we call them dreamers, on the mountain-top we find them interpreters.

In Lilian, the sympathy with Nature was not, as in Margrave, from the joyous sense of Nature's lavish vitality; it was refined into exquisite preception of the diviner spirit by which that vitality is informed. Thus, like the artist, from outward forms of beauty she drew forth the covert types, lending to things the most familiar exquisite meanings unconceived before. For it is truly said by a wise critic of old, that "the attribute of Art is to suggest infinitely more than it expresses;" and such suggestions, passing from the Artist's innermost thought into the mind that receives them, open on and on into the Infinite of Ideas, as a moonlit wave struck by a passing oar impels wave upon wave along one track of light.

So the days glided by, and brought the eve of our bridal morn. It had been settled, that after the ceremony (which was to be performed by licence in the village church, at no great distance, which adjoined my paternal home, now passed away to strangers), we should make a short excursion into Scotland, leaving Mrs. Ashleigh to await our return at the little inn.

I had retired to my own room to answer some letters from anxious patients, and having finished these, I looked into my trunk for a Guide-Book to the North, which I had brought with me. My hand came upon Margrave's wand, and, remembering that strange thrill which had passed through me when I last handled it, I drew it forth, resolved to examine calmly if I could detect the cause of the sensation. It was not now the time of night in which the imagination is most liable to credulous impressions, nor was I now in the anxious and jaded state of mind in which such impressions may be the more readily conceived. The sun was slowly setting over the delicious landscape; the air cool and serene; my thoughts collected—heart and conscience alike at peace. I took, then, the wand, and adjusted it to the palm of the hand as I had done before. I felt the slight touch of the delicale wire within, and again the thrill!

I did not this time recoil; I continued to grasp the wand, and sought deliberately to analyze my own sensations in the contact. There came over me an increased consciousness of vital power: a certain exhilaration, elasticity, vigor, such as a strong cordial may produce on a fainting man. All the forces of my frame seemed refreshed, redoubled; and as such effects on the physical system are ordinarily accompanied by correspondent effects on the mind, so I was sensible of a proud elation of spirits—a kind of defying, superb self-glorying. All fear seemed blotted out from my thought, as a weakness impossible to the grandeur and might which belong to Intellectual Man; I felt as if it were a royal delight to scorn Earth and its opinions, brave Hades and its spectres. Rapidly this new-born arrogance enlarged itself into desires vague but daring. My mind reverting to the wild phenomena associated with its memories of Margrave, I said, half-aloud, "If a creature so beneath myself in constancy of will and completion of thought can wrest from Nature favors so marvellous, what could not be won from her by me, her patient persevering seeker? What if there be spirits around and about, invisible to the common eye, but whom we can submit to our control; and what if this rod be charged with some occult fluid, that runs through all creation, and can be so disciplined as to establish communication wherever life and thought can reach to beings that live and think? So would the mystics of old explain what perplexes me. Am I sure that the mystics of old duped themselves or their pupils?

This, then, this slight wand, light as a reed in my grasp, this, then, was the instrument by which Margrave sent his irresistible will through air and space, and by which I smote himself, in the midst of his tiger-like wrath, into the helplessness of a sick man's swoon! Can the instrument at this distance still control him; if now meditating evil, disarm and disable his purpose?" Involuntarily, as I revolved these ideas, I stretched forth the wand, with a concentred energy of desire that its influence should reach Margrave and command him. And since I knew not his whereabout, yet was vaguely aware that, according to any conceivable theory by which the wand could be supposed to carry its imagined virtues to definite goals in distant space, it should be pointed in the direction of the object it was intended to affect, so I slowly moved the wand as if describing a circle, and thus, in some point of the circle—east, west, north, or south—the direction could not fail to be true. Before I had performed half the circle, the wand of itself stopped, resisting palpably the movement of my hand to impel it onward. Had it, then, found the point to which my will was guiding it, obeying my will by some magnetic sympathy never yet comprehended by any recognized science? I know not; but I had not held it thus fixed for many seconds, before a cold air, well remembered, passed by me, stirring the roots of my hair; and, reflected against the opposite wall, stood the hateful Scin-Læca. The Shadow was dimmer it its light than when before beheld, and the outline of the features was less distinct—still it was the unmistakable *lemur*, or image, of Margrave.

And a voice was conveyed to my senses, saying, as from a great distance, and in weary yet angry accents—

"You have summoned me? Wherefore?"

I overcame the startled shudder with which, at first, I beheld the Shadow and heard the Voice.

"I summoned you not," said I; "I sought but to impose upon you my will, that you should persecute, with your ghastly influences, me and mine no more. And now, by whatever authority this wand bestows on me, I so adjure and command you!"

I thought there was a sneer of disdain on the lip through which the answer seemed to come:

"Vain and ignorant; it is but a shadow you command. My body you have cast into a sleep, and it knows not that the shadow is here; nor, when it wakes, will the brain be aware of one reminiscence of the words that you utter or the words that you hear."

"What, then, is this shadow that simulates the body? Is it that which in popular language is called the soul?"

"It is not: soul is no shadow."

"What then?"

"Ask not me. Use the wand to invoke Intelligences higher than mine."

"And how?"

"I will tell you not. Of yourself you may learn, if you guide the wand by your own pride of will and desire; but in the hands of him who has learned not the art, the wand has its dangers. Again, I say you have summoned me! Wherefore?"

"Lying shade, I summoned thee not."

"So wouldst thou say to the demons, did they come in their terrible wrath, when the bungler, who knows not the springs that he moves, calls them up unawares, and can neither control nor dispel. Less revengeful than they, I leave thee unharmed, and depart."

"Stay. If, as thou sayest, no command I address to thee—to thee, who art only the image or shadow—can have effect on the body and mind of the being whose likeness thou art, still thou canst tell me what passes now in his brain. Does it now harbor schemes against me through the woman I love? Answer truly."

"I reply for the sleeper, of whom I am more than a likeness, though only the shadow. His thought speaks thus: 'I know, Allen Fenwick, that in thee is the agent I need for achieving the end that I seek. Through the woman thou lovest I hope to subject thee. A grief that will harrow thy heart is at hand; when the grief shall befall, thou wilt welcome my coming. In me alone thy hope will be placed—through me alone wilt thou seek a path out of thy sorrow. I shall ask my conditions: they will make thee my tool and my slave!"

The shadow waned—it was gone. I did not seek to detain it, nor, had I sought, could

I have known by what process. But a new idea now possessed me. This Shadow, then, that had once so appalled and controlled me, was, by its own confession, nothing more than a shadow! It had spoken of higher Intelligences; from them I might learn what the Shadow could not reveal. As I still held the wand firmer and firmer in my grasp, my thoughts grew haughtier and bolder. Could the wand, then, bring those loftier beings thus darkly referred to before me? With that thought, intense and engrossing, I guided the wand towards the space, opening boundless and blue from the casement that let in the skies. The wand no longer resisted my hand.

In a few moments I felt the floors of the room vibrate; the air was darkened: a vaporous, hazy cloud seemed to rise from the ground without the casement; an awe, infinitely more deep and solemn than that which the Scin-Læca had caused in his earliest apparition curdled through my veins, and stilled the very beat of my heart.

At that moment I heard, without, the voice of Lilian, singing a simple, sacred song which I had learned at my mother's knees, and taught to her the day before: singing low, and as with a warning angel's voice. By an irresistible impulse I dashed the wand to the ground, and bowed my head as I had bowed it when my infant mind comprehended, without an effort, mysteries more solemn than those which perplexed me now. Slowly I raised my eyes, and looked round: the vaporous, hazy cloud had passed away, or melted into the ambient rose-tints amidst which the sun had sunk.

Then, by one of those common reactions from a period of over-strained excitement, there succeeded to that sentiment of arrogance and daring with which these wild, half-conscious invocations had been fostered and sustained, a profound humility, a warning fear.

"What!" said I, inly, "have all those sound resolutions, which my reason founded on the wise talk of Julius Faber, melted away in the wrack of haggard, dissolving fancies! Is this my boasted intellect, my vaunted science! I—I, Allen Fenwick, not only the credulous believer, but the blundering practitioner, of an evil magic! Grant what may be possible, however uncomprehended—grant that in this accursed instrument of antique superstition there be some real powers—chemical, magnetic, no matter what—by which the imagination can be aroused, inflamed, deluded, so that it shapes the things I have seen, speaks in the tones I have heard—grant this, shall I keep ever ready, at the caprice of will, a constant temper to steal away my reason and fool my senses? Or if, on the other hand, I force my sense to admit what all sober men must reject—if I unschool myself to believe that in what I have just experienced there is no mental illusion, that sorcery is a fact, and a demon world has gates which open to a key that a mortal can forge—who but a saint would not shrink from the practice of powers by which each passing thought of ill might find in a fiend its abettor? In either case—in any case—while I keep this direful relic of obsolete arts, I am haunted—cheated out of my senses—unfitted for the uses of life. If, as my ear or my fancy informs me, grief—human grief—is about to befall me, shall I, in the sting of impatient sorrow, have recourse to an aid which, the same voice declares, will reduce me to a tool and a slave?—tool and slave to a being I dread as a foe! Out on these nightmares! and away with the thing that bewitches the brain to conceive them!"

I rose; I took up the wand, holding it so that its hollow should not rest on the palm of the hand. I stole from the house by the back way, in order to avoid Lilian, whose voice I still heard, singing low, on the lawn in front. I came to a creek, to the bank of which a boat was moored, undid its chain, rowed on to a deep part of the lake, and dropped the wand into its waves. It sank at once; scarcely a ripple furrowed the surface, not a bubble arose from the deep And, as the boat glided on, the star mirrored itself on the spot where the placid waters had closed over the tempter to evil.

Light at heart I sprang again on the shore, and hastening to Lilian, where she stood on the silvered shining sward, clasped her to my breast.

"Spirit of my life!" I murmured, "no enchantments for me but thine! Thine are the spells by which creation is beautified, and, in that beauty, hallowed. What though we can see not into the measureless future from the verge of the moment—what though sorrow may smite us while we are dreaming of bliss, let the future not rob me of thee, and a balm will be found for each wound! Love me ever as now, oh my Lilian; troth to troth, side by side, till the grave!"

"And beyond the grave," answered Lilian, softly.

CHAPTER LXII

OUR vows are exchanged at the altar—the rite which made Lilian my wife is performed—we are returned from the church, amongst the hills, in which my fathers had worshipped; the joy-bells that had pealed for my birth, had rung for my marriage. Lilian has gone to her room to prepare for our bridal excursion; while the carriage we have hired is waiting at the door. I am detaining her mother on the lawn, seeking to cheer and compose her spirits, painfully affected by that sense of change in the relations of child and parent which makes itself suddenly felt by the parent's heart on the day that secures to the child another heart on which to lean.

But Mrs. Ashleigh's was one of those gentle womanly natures which, if easily afflicted, are easily consoled. And, already smiling through her tears, she was about to quit me and join her daughter, when one of the inn-servants came to me with some letters, which had just been delivered by the postman. As I took them from the servant, Mrs. Ashleigh asked if there were any for her? She expected one from her housekeeper at L——, who had been taken ill in her absence, and about whom the kind mistress felt anxious. The servant replied that there was no letter for her, but one directed to Miss Ashleigh, which he had just sent up to the young lady.

Mrs. Ashleigh did not doubt that her housekeeper had written to Lilian, whom she had known from the cradle, and to whom she was tenderly attached, instead of to her mistress; and, saying something to me to that effect, quickened her steps towards the house.

I was glancing over my own letters, chiefly from patients, with a rapid eye, when a cry of agony, a cry as it of one suddenly stricken to the heart, pierced my ear—a cry from within the house. "Heavens! was not that Lilian's voice?" The same doubt struck Mrs. Ashleigh, who had already gained the door. She rushed on, disappearing within the threshold, and calling to me follow. I bounded forward—passed her on the stairs—was in Lilian's room before her.

My bride was on the floor, prostrate, insensible: so still, so colorless! that my first dreadful thought was that life had gone. In her hand was a letter, crushed, as with a convulsive sudden grasp.

It was long before the color came back to her cheek, before the breath was perceptible on her lip. She woke, but not to health, not to sense. Hours were passed in violent convulsions, in which I momently feared her death. To these succeeded stupor, lethargy, not benignant sleep. That night, my bridal night, I passed as in some chamber to which I had been summoned to save youth from the grave. At length—at length, life was rescued, was assured! Life came back, but the mind was gone. She knew me not, nor her mother. She spoke little and faintly; iu the words she uttered there was no reason.

I pass hurriedly on; my experience here was in fault, my skill ineffectual. Day followed day, and no ray came back to the darkened brain. We bore her, by gentle stages, to London. I was sanguine of good result from skill more consummate than mine, and more specially devoted to diseases of the mind. I summoned the first advisers. In vain!—in vain!

CHAPTER LXIII.

AND the cause of this direful shock? Not this time could it be traced to some evil spell, some phantasmal influence. The cause was clear, and might have produced effects as sinister on nerves of stronger fibre if accompanied by a heart as delicately sensitive, an honor as exquisitely pure.

The letter found in her hand was without name; it was dated from L——, and bore the postmark of that town. It conveyed to Lilian, in the biting words which female malice can make so sharp, the tale we had sought sedulously to guard from her ear—her flight, the construction that scandal put upon it. It affected for my blind infatuation a contemptuous pity; it asked her to pause before she brought on the name I offered to her an indelible disgrace. If she was so decided, she was warned not to return to L——, or to prepare there for the sentence that would exclude her from the society of her own sex. I cannot repeat more, I cannot minute down all that the letter expressed or implied, to wither the orange blossoms in a bride's wreath. The heart that took in the venom cast its poison on the brain, and the mind fled before the presence of a thought so deadly to all the ideas which its innocence had heretofore conceived.

I knew not whom to suspect of the malignity of this mean and miserable outrage, nor did I much care to know. The handwriting, though evidently disguised, was that of a woman, and, therefore, had I discovered the author, my manhood would have forbidden me the idle solace of revenge. Mrs. Poyntz, however resolute and pitiless her hostility when once aroused, was not without a certain largeness of nature irreconcilable with the most dastardly of all the weapons that envy or hatred can supply to the vile. She had too lofty a self-esteem and too decorous a regard for the moral sentiment of the world that she typified, to do, or connive at, an act which degrades the gentlewoman. Putting her aside, what other female enemy had Lilian provoked? No matter! What other woman at L—— was worth the condescension of a conjecture!

After listening to all that the ablest of my professional brethren in the metropolis could suggest to guide me, and trying in vain their remedies, I brought back my charge to L——. Retaining my former residence for the visits of patients, I engaged, for the privacy of my home, a house two miles from the town, secluded in its own grounds, and guarded by high walls.

Lilian's mother removed to my mournful dwelling-place. Abbots' House, in the centre of that tattling coterie, had become distasteful to her, and to me it was associated with thoughts of anguish and of terror. I could not, without a shudder, have entered its grounds—could not, without a stab at the heart, have seen again the old fairy-land round the Monks' Well, nor the dark cedar-tree under which Lilian's hand had been placed in mine: and a superstitious remembrance, banished while Lilian's angel face had brightened the fatal precincts, now revived in full force. The dying man's curse—had is not been fulfilled! A new occupant for the old house was found within a week after Mrs. Ashleigh had written from London to a house-agent at L———, intimating her desire to dispose of the lease. Shortly before we had gone to Windermere, Miss Brabazon had become enriched by a liberal life-annuity bequeathed to her by her uncle, Sir Phelim. Her means thus enabled her to move, from the comparatively humble lodging she had hitherto occupied, to Abbots' House; but just as she had there commenced a series of ostentatious entertainments, implying an ambitious desire to dispute with Mrs. Poyntz the sovereignty of the Hill, she was attacked by some severe malady which appeared complicated with spinal disease, and after my return to L——— I sometimes met her, on the spacious platform of the Hill, drawn along slowly in a Bath chair, her livid face peering forth from piles of Indian shawls and Siberian furs, and the gaunt figure of Dr. Jones stalking by her side, taciturn and gloomy as some sincere mourner who conducts to the grave the patron on whose life he himself had conveniently lived. It was in the dismal month of February that I returned to L———, and I took possession of my blighted nuptial home on the anniversary of the very day in which I had passed through the dead dumb world from the naturalist's gloomy death-room.

CHAPTER LXIV.

Lilian's wondrous gentleness of nature did not desert her in the suspension of her reason. She was habitually calm—very silent; when she spoke it was rarely on earthly things—on things familiar to her past—things one could comprehend. Her thought seemed to have quitted the earth, seeking refuge in some imaginary heaven. She spoke of wanderings with her father as if he were living still; she did not seem to understand the meaning we attach to the word Death. She would sit for hours murmuring to herself: when one sought to catch the words, they seemed in converse with invisible spirits. We found it cruel to disturb her at such times, for it left unmolested, her face was serene—more serenely beautiful than I had seen it even in our happiest hours; but when we called her back to the wrecks of her real life, her eye became troubled, restless, anxious, and she would sigh —oh, so heavily! At times, if we did not seem to observe her, she would quietly resume her once favorite accomplishments—drawing, music. And in these her young excellence was still apparent, only the drawings were strange and fantastic: they had a resemblance to those with which the painter Blake, himself a visionary, illustrated the Poems of the "Night Thoughts" and "The Grave." Faces of exquisite loveliness, forms of aërial grace, coming forth from the bells of flowers, or floating upwards amidst the spray of fountains, their outlines melting away in fountain or in flower. So with her music: her mother could not recognize the airs she played, for a while so sweetly and with so ineffable a pathos, that one could scarcely hear her without weeping; and then would come, as if involuntarily an abrupt discord, and, starting, she would cease and look around, disquieted, aghast.

And still she did not recognize Mrs. Ashleigh nor myself as her mother, her husband; but she had by degrees learned to distinguish us both from others. To her mother she gave no name, seemed pleased to see her, but not sensibly to miss her when away; me she called her brother: if longer absent than usual, me she missed. When, after the toils of the day, I came to join her, even if she spoke not, her sweet face brightened. When she sang, she beckoned me to come near to her, and looked at me fixedly, with eyes ever tender, often tearful; when she drew, she would pause and glance over her shoulder to see that I was watching her, and point to the drawings with a smile of strange insignificance, as if they conveyed, in some covert allegory, messages meant for me; so, at least, I interpreted her smile, and taught myself to say, "Yes, Lilian, I understand!"

And more than once, when I had so answered, she rose and kissed my forehead. I thought my heart would have broken when I felt that spirit-like melancholy kiss.

And yet how marvellously the human mind teaches itself to extract consolations from its sorrows. The least wretched of my hours were those that I passed in that saddened room, seeking how to establish fragments of intercourse, invent signs, by which each might interpret each, between the intellect I had so laboriously cultured, so arrogantly vaunted, and the fancies wandering through the dark, deprived of their guide in reason. It was something even of joy to feel myself needed for her guardianship, endeared and yearned for still by some unshattered instinct of her heart; and when parting from her for the night, I stole the moment in which on her soft face seemed resting least of shadow, to ask, in a trembling whisper, "Lilian, are the angels watching over you?" and she would answer "Yes," sometimes in words, sometimes with a mysterious happy smile—then—then I went to my lonely room, comforted and thankful.

CHAPTER LXV.

THE blow that had fallen on my hearth effectually, inevitably killed all the slander that might have troubled me in joy. Before the awe of a great calamity the small passions of a mean malignity slink abashed. I had requested Mrs. Ashleigh not to mention the vile letter which Lilian had received. I would not give a triumph to the unknown calumniator, nor wring forth her vain remorse, by the pain of acknowledging an indignity to my darling's honor; yet, somehow or other, the true cause of Lilian's affliction had crept out —perhaps through the talk of servants—and the Public shock was universal. By one of those instincts of justice that lie deep in human hearts, though in ordinary movements overlaid by many a worldly layer, all felt (all mothers felt, especially) that innocence alone could have been so unprepared for reproach. The explanation I had previously given, discredited then, was now accepted without a question. Lilian's present state accounted for all that ill nature had before misconstrued. Her good name was restored to its maiden whiteness by the fate that had severed the ties of the bride. The formal dwellers on the Hill vied with the franker, warmer-hearted household of Low Town in the nameless attentions by which sympathy and respect are rather delicately indicated than noisily proclaimed. Could Lilian have then recovered and been sensible of its repentant homage, how reverently that petty world would have thronged around her!

And, ah! could fortune and man's esteem have atoned for the blight of hopes that had been planted and cherished on ground beyond their reach, ambition and pride might have been well contented with the largeness of the exchange that courted their acceptance. Patients on patients crowded on me. Sympathy with my sorrow seemed to create and endear a more trustful belief in my skill. But the profession I had once so enthusiastically loved became to me wearisome, insipid, distasteful; the kindness heaped on me gave no comfort, it but brought before me more vividly the conviction that it came too late to avail me: it could not restore to me the mind, the love, the life of my life, which lay dark and shattered in the brain of my guileless Lilian. Secretly I felt a sullen resentment. I knew that to the crowd the resentment was unjust. The world itself is but an appearance; who can blame it if appearances guide its laws? But to those who had been detached from the crowd by the professions of friendship—those who, when the slander was yet new, and might have been awed into silence had they stood by my side,—to the pressure of *their* hands, *now*, I had no response.

Against Mrs. Poyntz, above all others, I bore a remembrance of unrelaxed, unmitigable indignation. Her schemes for her daughter's marriage had triumphed: Jane was Mrs. Ashleigh Sumner. Her mind was, perhaps, softened now that the object which had sharpened its worldly faculties was accomplished; but in vain, on first hearing of my affliction, had this she-Machiavel owned a humane remorse, and, with all her keen comprehension of each facility that circumstance gave to her will, availed herself of the general compassion to strengthen the popular reaction in favor of Lilian's assaulted honor—in vain had she written to me with a gentleness of sympathy foreign to her habitual characteristics—in vain besought me to call on her—in vain waylaid and accosted me with a humility that almost implored forgiveness; I vouchsafed no reproach, but I could imply no pardon. I put between her and my great sorrow the impenetrable wall of my freezing silence.

One word of hers at the time that I had so pathetically besought her aid, and the parrot-flock that repeated her very whisper in noisy shrillness, would have been as loud to defend as it had been to defame; that vile letter might never have been written. Whoever its writer, it surely was one of the babblers who took their malice itself from the jest or the nod of their female despot; and the writer might have justified herself in saying she did but coarsely proclaim what the oracle of worldly opinion, and the early friend of Lilian's own mother, hed authorized her to believe.

By degrees, the bitterness at my heart diffused itself to the circumference of the circle in which my life went its cheerless mechanical round. That cordial brotherhood with his patients, which is the true physician's happiest gift and humanest duty, forsook my breast. The warning words of Mrs. Poyntz had come true. A patient that monopolized my thoughts awaited me at my own hearth! My conscience became troubled; I felt that my skill was lessened. I said to myself, "The physician who, on entering the sick room, feels, while there, something that distracts the finest powers of his intellect from the sufferer's case, is unfit for his calling." A year had scarcely passed since my fatal wedding-day, before I had formed a resolution to quit L—— and abandon my profession: and my resolution was confirmed, and my goal determined, by a letter I received from Julius Faber.

I had written at length to him, not many days after the blow that had fallen on me, stating all circumstances as calmly and clearly as my grief would allow, for I held his skill at a higher estimate than that of any living brother of my art, and I was not without hope in the efficacy of his advice. The letter I now received from him had been begun, and continued at some length, before my communication reached him. And this earlier portion contained animated and cheerful descriptions of his Australian life and home which contrasted with the sorrowful tone of the supplement written in reply to the tidings with which I had wrung his friendly and tender heart. In this, the latter part of his letter, he suggested that if time had wrought no material change for the better, it might be advisable to try the effect of foreign travel. Scenes entirely new might stimulate observation, and the observation of things external withdraw the sense from that brooding over images delusively formed within, which characterized the kind of mental alienation I had described. "Let any intellect create for itself a visionary world, and all reasonings built on it are fallacious: the visionary world vanishes in proportion as we can arouse a predominant interest in the actual."

This grand authority, who owed half his consummate skill as a practitioner to the scope of his knowledge as a philosopher, then proceded to give me a hope which I had not dared, of myself, to form. He said, "I distinguish the case you so minutely detail from that insanity which is reason lost; here it seems rather to be reason held in suspense. Where there is hereditary predisposition, where there is organic change of structure in the brain—nay, where there is that kind of insanity which takes the epithet of moral, whereby the whole character becomes so transformed that the prime element of sound understanding, conscience itself, is either erased or warped into the sanction of what, in a healthful state, it would most disapprove, it is only charlatans who promise effectual cure. But here I assume that there is no hereditary taint; here I am convinced, from my own observation, that the nobility of the organs, all fresh as yet in the vigor of youth, would rather submit to death than to the permament overthrow of their equilibrium in reason; here, where you tell me the character preserves all its moral attributes of gentleness and purity, and but over-indulges its own early habit of estranged contemplation; here, without deceiving you in false kindness, I give you the guarantee of my experience when I bid you 'hope!' I am persuaded that, sooner or later, the mind, thus for a time affected, will right itself; because here, in the cause of the malady, we do but deal with the nervous system. And *that*, once righted, and the mind once disciplined in those practical duties which conjugal life necessitates, the malady itself will never return; never be transmitted to the children on whom your wife's restoration to health may permit you to count hereafter. If the course of travel I recommend and the prescriptions I conjoin with that course fail you, let me know; and though I would fain close my days in this land, I will come to you. I love you as my son. I will tend your wife as my daughter."

Foreign travel! The idea smiled on me. Julius Faber's companionship, sympathy, matchless skill! The very thought seemed as a raft to a drowning mariner. I now read more attentively the earlier portions of his letter. They described, in glowing colors, the wondrous country in which he had fixed his home; the joyous elasticity of its atmostphere; the freshness of its primitive, pastoral life; the strangeness of its scenery, with a Flora and a Fauna which have no similitudes in the ransacked quarters of the Old World. And the strong impulse seized me to transfer to the solitudes of that blithesome and hardy Nature a spirit no longer at home in the civilized haunts of men, and household gods that shrunk from all social eyes, and would fain have found a wilderness for the desolate hearth, on which they had ceased to be sacred if unveiled. As if to give practical excuse and reason for the idea that seized me, Julius Faber mentioned, incidentally, that the house and property of a wealthy speculator in his immediate neighborhood were on sale at a price which seemed to me alluringly trivial, aud, according to his judgment, far below the value they would soon reach in the hands of a more patient capitalist. He wrote at the period of the agricultural panic in the colony which preceded the discovery of its earliest gold-fields. But his geological science had convinced him that strata within and around the property now for sale were auriferous, and his intelligence enabled him to predict how inevitably man would be attracted towards the gold, and how surely the gold would fertilize the soil and enrich its owners. He described the house thus to be sold—in case I might know of a purchaser. It had been built at a cost unusual in those early times, and by one who clung to English tastes amidst Australian wilds, so that in this purchase a settler would escape the hardships he had then ordinarily to encounter: it was, in short, a home to which a man, more luxurious than I, might bear a bride with wants less simple than those which now sufficed for my darling Lilian.

This communication dwelt on my mind through the avocations of the day on which I received it, and in the evening I read all, except the supplement, aloud to Mrs. Ashleigh in her daughter's presence. I desired to see if Faber's descriptions of the country and its life, which in themselves were extremely spirited and striking, would arouse Lilian's interest. At first she did not seem to heed me while I read, but when I came to Faber's loving account of little Amy, Lilian turned her eyes towards me, and evidently listened with attention. He wrote how the Child had already become the most useful person in the simple household. How watchful the quickness of the heart had made the service of the eye; all their associations of comfort had grown round her active, noiseless movements; it was she who had contrived to monopolize the management, or supervision of all that added to Home the nameless, interior charm. Under her eyes the rude furniture of the log-house grew inviting with English neatness; she took charge of the dairy; she had made the garden gay with flowers selected from the wild, and suggested the trellised walk, already covered with hardy vine. She was their confidant in every plan of improvement, their comforter in every anxious doubt, their nurse in every passing ailment, her very smile a refreshment in the weariness of daily toil. "How all that is best in womanhood," wrote the old man, with the enthusiasm which no time had reft from his hearty, healthful genius,—"how all that is best in womanhood is here opening fast into flower from the bud of the infant's soul! The atmosphere seems to suit it—the child-woman in the child-world!"

I heard Lilian sigh; I looked towards her furtively; tears stood in her softened eyes; her lip was quivering. Presently, she began to rub her right hand over the left—over the wedding-ring—at first, slowly; then with quicker movement.

"It is not here," she said, impatiently; "it is *not* here!"

"What is not here?" asked Mrs. Ashleigh, hanging over her.

Lilian lent back her head on her mother's bosom, and answered faintly:

"The stain! some one said there was a stain on this hand. I do not see it—do you?"

"There is no stain, never was," said I; "the hand is white as your own innocence, or the lily from which you take your name."

"Hush! you do not know my name. I will whisper it. Soft!—my name is Nightshade! Do you want to know where the lily is now, brother? I will tell you. There, in that letter—you call her Amy—she is the lily—take her to your breast—hide her. Hist! what are those bells? Marriage-bells. Do not let her hear them. For there is a cruel wind that whispers the bells, and the bells ring out what it whispers, louder and louder,

'Stain on lily,
Shame on lily,
Wither lily.'

If she hears what the wind whispers to the bells, she will creep away into the dark, and then she, too, will turn to Nightshade."

"Lilian, look up, awake! You have been in a long, long dream: it is passing away. Lilian, my beloved, my blessed Lilian!"

Never till then had I heard from her even so vague an illusion to the fatal calumny, and its dreadful effect, and while her words now pierced my heart, it beat, amongst its pangs, with a thrilling hope.

But, alas! the idea that had gleamed upon her had vanished already. She murmured something about Circles of Fire, and a Veiled Woman in black garments; became restless, agitated, and unconscious of our presence, and finally sank into a heavy sleep.

That night (my room was next to hers with the intervening door open), I heard her cry out. I hastened to her side. She was still asleep, but there was an anxious laboring expression on her young face, and yet not an expression wholly of pain—for her lips were parted with a smile—that glad yet troubled smile with which one who has been revolving some subject of perplexity or fear, greets a sudden thought that seems to solve the riddle, or prompt the escape from danger; and as I softly took, her hand she returned my gentle pressure, and inclining towards me, said, still in sleep:

"Let us go."

"Whither?" I answered, under my breath, so as not to awake her; "is it to see the child of whom I read, and the land that is blooming out of the earth's childhood?"

"Out of the dark into the light; where the leaves do not change; where the night is our day, and the winter our summer. Let us go—let us go!"

"We will go. Dream on undisturbed, my bride. Oh, that the dream could tell you that my love has not changed in our sorrow, holier and deeper than on the day in which our vows were exchanged! In you still all my hopes fold their wings: where you are, there still I myself have my dreamland!"

The sweet face grew bright as I spoke; all trouble left the smile; softly she drew her hand from my clasp, and rested it for a moment on my bended head, as if in blessing.

I rose; stole back to my own room, closing the door, lest the sob I could not stifle should mar her sleep.

CHAPTER LXVI.

I UNFOLDED my new prospects to Mrs. Ashleigh. She was more easily reconciled to them than I could have supposed, judging by her habits, which were naturally indolent, and averse to all that disturbed their even tenor. But the great grief which had befallen her had roused up that strength of devotion which lies dormant in all hearts that are capable of loving another more than self. With her full consent I wrote to Faber, communicating my intentions, instructing him to purchase the property he had so commended, and inclosing my banker's order for the amount, on an Australian firm. I now announced my intention to retire from my profession; made prompt arrangements with a successor to my practice; disposed of my two houses at L——; fixed the day of my departure. Vanity was dead within me, or I might have been gratified by the sensation which the news of my design created. My faults became at once forgotten: such good qualities as I might possess were exaggerated. The public regret vented and consoled itself in a costly testimonial, to which even the poorest of my patients insisted on the privilege to contribute, graced with an inscription flattering enough to have served for the epitaph on some great man's tomb. No one who has served an art and striven for a name, is a stoic to the esteem of others, and sweet indeed would such honors have been to me had not publicity itself seemed a wrong to the sanctity of that affliction which set Lilian apart from the movement and the glories of the world.

The two persons most active in "getting up" this testimonial were, nominally, Colonel Poyntz—in truth, his wife—and my old disparager, Mr. Vigors! It is long since my narrative has referred to Mr. Vigors. It is due to him now to state that, in his capacity of magistrate, and in his own way, he had been both active and delicate in the inquiries set on foot for Lilian during the unhappy time in which she had wandered, spellbound, from her home. He, alone, of all the more influential magnates of the town, had upheld her innocence against the gossip that aspersed it; and during the last trying year of my residence at L——, he had sought me, with frank and manly confessions of his regret for his former prejudice against me, and assurance of the respect in which he had held me ever since my marriage—marriage but in rite—with Lilian. He had then, strong in his ruling passion, besought me to consult his clairvoyants as to her case. I declined this invitation, so as not to affront him—declined it, not as I should once have done, but with no word nor look of incredulous disdain. The fact was, that I had conceived a solemn terror of all practices and theories out of the beaten track of sense and science. Perhaps in my refusal I did wrong. I know not. I was afraid of my own imagination. He continued not less friendly in spite of my refusal. And, such are the vicissitudes in human feeling, I parted from him whom I had regarded as my most bigoted foe with a warmer sentiment of kindness than for any of those on whom I had counted on friendship. *He* had not deserted Lilian. It was not so with Mrs. Poyntz. I would have paid tenfold the value of the testimonial to have erased, from the list of those who subscribed to it, her husband's name.

The day before I quitted L——, and some weeks after I had, in fact, renounced my practice, I received an urgent entreaty from Miss Brabazon to call on her. She wrote in lines so blurred that I could with difficulty decipher them, that she was very ill, given over by Dr. Jones, who had been attending her. She implored my opinion.

CHAPTER LXVII.

ON reaching the house, a formal man-servant, with indifferent face, transferred me to the guidance of a hired nurse, who led me up the stairs, and, before I was well aware of it, into the room in which Dr. Lloyd had died. Widely different, indeed, the aspect of the walls, the character of the furniture. The dingy paper-hangings were replaced by airy muslins, showing a rose-colored ground through their fanciful open-work; luxurious fauteuils, gilded wardrobes, full-length mirrors, a toilet-table tricked out with lace and ribbons, and glittering with an array of silver gewgaws and jewelled trinkets,—all transformed the sick chamber of the simple man of science to a boudoir of death for the vain coquette. But the room itself, in its high lattice and heavy ceiling, was the same—as the coffin itself has the same confines whether it be rich in velvets and bright with blazoning, or rude as a pauper's shell.

And the bed, with its silken coverlid, and its pillows edged with the thread-work of Louvain, stood in the same sharp angle as that over which had flickered the frowning smoke-reek above the dying resentful foe. As I approached, a man, who was seated beside the sufferer, turned round his face, and gave me a silent kindly nod of recognition. He was Mr. C., one of the clergy of the town, the one with whom I had the most frequently come into contact wherever the physician resigns to the priest the language that bids man hope. Mr. C., as a preacher, was renowned for his touching eloquence; as a pastor, revered for his benignant piety; as friend and neighbor, beloved for a sweetness of nature which seemed to regulate all the movements of a mind eminently masculine by the beat of a heart tender as the gentlest woman's.

This good man, then whispering something to the sufferer which I did not overhear, stole towards me, took me by the hand, and said, also in a whisper, "Be merciful as Christians are." He led me to the bedside, there left me, went out, and closed the door.

"Do you think I am really dying Dr. Fenwick?" said a feeble voice "I fear Dr. Jones has misunderstood my case. I wish I had called you in at the first,—but—but I could not—I could not! Will you feel my pulse? Don't you think you could do me good?"

I had no need to feel the pulse in that skeleton wrist; the aspect of the face sufficed to tell me that death was drawing near.

Mechanically, however, I went through the hackneyed formulæ of professional questions. This vain ceremony done; as gently and delicately as I could I implied the expediency of concluding, if not yet settled, those affairs which relate to this world.

"This duty," I said, "in relieving the mind from care for others to whom we owe the forethought of affection, often relieves the body also of many a gnawing pain, and sometimes, to the surprise of the most experienced physician, prolongs life itself."

"Ah," said the old maid, peevishly, "I understand! But it is not my will that troubles me. I should not be left to a nurse from a hospital if my relations did not know that my annuity dies with me; and I forestalled it in furnishing this house, Dr. Fenwick, and all these pretty things will be sold to pay those horrid tradesmen!—very hard! so hard!—just as I had got things about me in the way I always said I would have them if I could ever afford it! I always said I would have my bed-room hung with muslin, like dear Lady L's;—and the drawing-room in geranium-colored silk: so pretty. You have not seen it: you would not know the house, Dr. Fenwick. And just when all is finished, to be taken away and thrust into the grave. It is so cruel!" And she began to weep. Her emotion brought on a violent paroxysm, which, when she recovered from it, had produced one of those startling changes of mind that are sometimes witnessed before death: changes whereby the whole character of a life seems to undergo solemn transformation. The hard will become gentle, the proud meek, the frivilous earnest. That awful moment when the things of earth pass away like dissolving scenes, leaving death visible on the background by the glare that shoots up in the last flicker of life's lamp.

And when she lifted her haggard face from my shoulder, and heard my pitying, soothing voice, it was not the grief of a trifler at the loss of fondled toys that spoke in the fallen lines of her lip, in the woe of her pleading eyes.

"So this is death," she said. "I feel it hurrying on. I must speak. I promised Mr. C. that I would. Forgive me, can you—can you? That letter—that letter to Lilian Ashleigh, I wrote it! Oh, do not look at me so terribly; I never thought it could do such evil! And am I not punished enough? I trully believed when I wrote that Miss Ashleigh was deceiving you, and once I was silly enough to fancy that you might have liked me. But I had another motive; I had been so poor all my life—I had become rich unexpectedly; I set my heart on this house—I had always fancied it—and I thought if I could prevent Miss Ashleigh marrying you, and scare her and her mother from coming back to L——, I could get the house. And I did get it. What for?—to die. I had not been here a week before I got the hurt that is killing me—a fall down the stairs—coming out of this very room; the stairs had been polished. If I had stayed in my old lodging, it would not have happened. Oh, say you forgive me! Say it, even if you do not feel you can! Say it!" And the miserable woman grasped me by the arm as Dr. Lloyd had grasped me.

I shaded my averted face with hands; my heart heaved with the agony of my suppress passion. A wrong, however deep, only to myself, I could have pardoned without effort; *such* a wrong to Lilian,—no! I could not say, "I forgive."

The dying wretch was perhaps more appalled by my silence than she would have been by my reproach. Her voice grew shrill in her despair.

"You will not pardon me! I shall die with your curse on my head. Mercy! mercy! That good man, Mr. C., assured me you would be merciful. Have *you* never wronged another? Has the Evil One never tempted *you?*"

Then I spoke in broken accents: "Me! Oh, had it been I whom you defamed—but a young creature so harmless, so unoffending, and for so miserable a motive!"

"But I tell you, I swear to you. I never dreamed I could cause such sorrow; and that young man, that Margrave, put it into my head!"

"Margrave! He had left L—— long before that letter was written."

"But he came back for a day just before I wrote: it was the very day. I met him in the lane yonder. He asked after you—after Miss Ashleigh; and when he spoke he laughed, and I said, "Miss Ashleigh had been ill, and was gone away;" and he laughed again. And I thought he knew more than he would tell me, so I asked him if he supposed Mrs. Ashleigh would come back, and said how much I should like to take this house if she did not; and again he laughed, and said, 'Birds never stay in the nest after the young ones are hurt,' and went away singing. When I got home, his laugh and his song haunted me. I thought I saw him still in my room, prompting me to write, and I sat down and wrote. Oh, pardon, pardon me! I have been a foolish poor creature, but never meant to do such harm. The Evil One tempted me! There he is, near me now! I see him yonder! there, at the doorway, He comes to claim me! As you hope for mercy yourself, free me from him! Forgive me!"

I made an effort over myself. In naming Margrave as her tempter, the woman had suggested an excuse, echoed from that innermost cell of my mind, which I recoiled from gazing into, for there I should behold his image. Inexpiable though the injury she had wrought against me and mine, still the woman was human—fellow-creature—like myself;—but HE?

I took the pale hand that still pressed my arm, and said, with firm voice,

"Be comforted. In the name of Lilian, my wife, I forgive you for her and for me as freely and as fully as we are enjoined by Him against whose precepts the best of us daily sin, to forgive—we children of wrath—to forgive one another!"

"Heaven bless you!—oh, bless you!" she murmured, sinking back upon her pillow.

"Ah!" thought I, "what if the pardon I grant for a wrong far deeper than I inflicted on him whose imprecation smote me in this chamber, should indeed be received as atonement, and this blessing on the lips of the dying annul the dark curse that the dead has left on my path through the Valley of the Shadow!"

I left my patient sleepiug quietly—the sleep that precedes the last. As I went down the stairs into the hall, I saw Mrs. Poyntz standing at the threshold, speaking to the man-servant and the nurse.

I would have passed her with a formal bow but she stopped me.

"I came to inquire after poor Miss Brabazon," said she. "You can tell me more than the servants can: is there no hope?"

"Let the nurse go up and watch beside her

She may pass away in the sleep into which she has fallen."

"Allen Fenwick, I must speak with you—nay, but for a few minutes. I hear that you leave L—— to-morrow. It is scarcely among the chances of life that we should meet again." While thus saying, she drew me along the lawn down the path that led towards her own home. "I wish," said she, earnestly "that you could part with a kindlier feeling towards me; but I can scarcely expect it. Could I put myself in your place, and be moved by your feelings, I know that I should be implacable; but I—"

"But you, madam, are The World! and the World governs itself, and dictates to others, by laws which seem harsh to those who ask from its favor the services which the World cannot tender, for the World admits favorites but ignores friends. You did but act to me as the World ever acts to those who mistake its favor for its friendship."

"It is true," said Mrs Poyntz, with blunt candor: and we continued to walk on silently. At length, she said, abrptly, "But do you not rashly deprive yourself of your only consolation in sorrow? When the heart suffers, does your skill admit any remedy like occupation to the mind? Yet you abandon that occupation to which your mind is most accustomed; you desert your career; you turn aside, in the midst of the race, from the fame which awaits at the goal; you go back from civilization itself, and dream that all your intellectual cravings can find content in the life of a herdsman, amidst the monotony of a wild! No, you will repent, for you are untrue to your mind!"

"I am sick of the word 'mind!'" said I, bitterly. And therewith I relapsed into musing.

The emigmas which had foiled my intelligence in the unravelled Sibyl Book of Nature were mysteries strange to every man's normal practice of thought, even if reducible to the fraudulent impressions of outward sense; for illusions in a brain otherwise healthy, suggest problems of our human organization which the colleges that record them rather guess at than solve. But the blow which had shattered my life had been dealt by the hand of a fool. Here, there were no mystic enchantments. Motives the most commonplace and paltry, suggested to a brain as trivial and shallow as ever made the frivolity of woman a theme for the satire of poets, had sufficed, in devastating the field of my affections, to blast the uses for which I had cultured my mind; and had my intellect been as great as heaven ever gave to man, it would have been as vain a shield as mine against the shaft that had lodged in my heart. While I had, indeed, been preparing my reason and my fortitude to meet such perils, weird and marvellous, as those by which tales round the winter fire-side scare the credulous child—a contrivance so vulgar and hackneyed that not a day passes but what some hearth is vexed by an anonymous libel—had wrought a calamity more dread than aught which my dark guess into the Shadow-Land unpierced by Philosophy, could trace to the prompting of malignant witchcraft. So, ever this truth runs through all legends of ghost and demon—through the uniform records of what wonder accredits and science rejects as the supernatural—lo! the dread machinery whose wheels roll through Hades! What need such awful engines for such mean results? The first blockhead we meet in our walk to our grocer's can tell us more than the ghost tells us; the poorest envy we ever aroused hurts us more than the demon.

How true an interpreter is Genius to Hell as to Earth! The Fiend comes to Faust, the tired seeker of knowledge; Heaven and Hell stake their cause in the Mortal's temptation. And what does the Fiend to astonish the Mortal? Turn wine into fire, turn love into crime. We need no Mephistopheles to accomplish these marvels every day!

Thus silently thinking, I walked by the side of the world-wise woman; and when she next spoke, I looked up, and saw that we were at the Monks' Well, where I had first seen Lilian gazing into heaven!

Mrs. Poyntz had, as we walked, placed her hand on my arm, and, turning abruptly from the path into the glade, I found myself standing by her side in the scene where a new sense of being had first disclosed to my sight the hues with which Love, the passionate beautifier, turns into purple and gold the grey of the common air. Thus, when romance has ended in sorrow, and the Beautiful fades from the landscape, the trite and positive forms of life banished for a time, reappear, and deepen our mournful remembrance of the glories they replace. And the Woman of the World, finding how little I was induced to respond to her when she had talked of myself, began to speak, in her habitual, clear, ringing accents, of her own social schemes and devices:

"I shall miss you when you are gone, Allen Fenwick, for though, during the last year or so, all actual intercourse between us has ceased, yet my interest in you gave some occupation to my thoughts when I sat alone—having lost my main object of ambition in settling my daughter, and having no longer any one in the house with whom I could talk of the future, or for whom I could form a project. It is so wearisome to count the changes which pass within us, that we take interest in the changes that pass without. Poyntz still has his weather-glass; I have no longer my Jane."

"I cannot linger with you on this spot," said I, impatiently turning back into the path; she followed, treading over fallen leaves. And unheeding my interruption, she thus continued her hard talk:

"But I am not sick of my mind as you seem to be of yours; I am only somewhat tired of the little cage in which, since it has been alone, it ruffles its plumes against the flimsy wires that confine it from wider space. I shall take up my home for a time with the new-married couple: they want me. Ashleigh Sumner has come into Parliament. He means to attend regularly and work hard, but he does not like Jane to go into the world by herself, and he wishes her to go into the world, because he wants a wife to display his wealth for the improvement of his position. In Ashleigh Sumner's house, I shall have ample scope for my energies, such as they are. I have a curiosity to see the few that perch on the wheels of the State, and say, 'It is we who move the wheels!' It will amuse me to learn if I can maintain in a capital the authority I have won in a country town; if not, I can but return to my small principality. Wherever I live, I must sway, not serve. If I succeed—as I ought, for in Jane's beauty and Ashleigh's fortune I have materials for the woof of ambition, wanting which here, I fall asleep over my knitting—if I succeed, there will be enough to occupy the rest of my life. Ashleigh Sumner must be a power; the power will be represented and enjoyed by my child, and created and maintained by me! Allen Fenwick, do as I do. Be world with the world, and it will be only in moments of spleen and chagrin that you will sigh to think that the heart may be void when the mind is full. Confess you envy me while you listen."

"Not so; all that you seems so great, appears to me so small! Nature alone is always grand, in her terrors as well as her charms. The World for you, Nature for me. Farewell!"

"Nature," said Mrs. Poyntz, compassionately. "Poor Allen Fenwick! Nature, indeed—intellectual suicide! Nay, shake hands, then, if for the last time."

So we shook hands and parted, where the wicket-gate and the stone stairs separated my blighted fairy-land from the common thoroughfare.

CHAPTER LXVIII.

That night as I was employed in collecting the books and manuscripts which I proposed to take with me, including my long-suspended physiological work, and such standard authorities as I might want to consult or refer to in the portions yet incompleted, my servant entered to inform me, in answer to the inquiries I had set him to make, that Miss Brabazon had peacefully breathed her last an hour before. Well! my pardon had perhaps soothed her last moments: but how unavailing her death-bed repentance to undo the wrong she had done!

I turned from that thought, and, glancing at the work into which I had thrown all my learning, methodized into system with all my art, I recalled the pity which Mrs. Poyntz had expressed for my meditated waste of mind. The tone of superiority which this incarnation of common sense, accompanied by uncommon will, assumed over all that was too deep or too high for her comprehension, had sometimes amused me; thinking over it now, it piqued. I said to myself, "After all, I shall bear with me such solace as intellectual occupation can afford. I shall have leisure to complete this labor, and a record that I have lived and thought may outlast all the honors which worldly ambition may bestow upon an Ashleigh Summer!" And, as I so murmured, my hand, mechanically, selecting the books I needed, fell on the Bible that Julius Faber had given to me.

It opened at the Second Book of Esdras, which our Church places amongst the Apocrypha, and is generally considered by scholars to have been written in the first or second century of the Christian era.* But in which, the questions raised by man in the remotest ages, to which we can trace back his desire "to comprehend the ways of the Most High," are invested with a grandeur of thought and sublimity of word to which I know of no parallel in writers we call profane.

My eye fell on this passage in the lofty argument between the Angel whose name was Uriel, and the Prophet, perplexed by his own cravings for knowledge:

"He (the Angel) answered me, and said, I went into a forest, into a plain, and the trees took counsel.

"And said, Come, let us go and make war against the sea, that it may depart away before us, and that we may make us more woods.

"The floods of the sea also in like manner took counsel, and said, Come, let us go up and subdue the woods of the plain, that there also we may make us another country.

"The thought of the wood was in vain, for the fire came and consumed it.

"The thought of the floods of the sea came likewise to nought, for the sand stood up and stopped them.

"If thou wert judge now betwixt these two, whom woundest thou begin to justify? or whom wouldest thou condemn?

"I answered and said, Verily it is a foolish thought that they both have devised; for the ground is given unto the wood, and the sea also hath his place to bear his floods.

"Then answered he me, and said, Thou hast given a right judgment; but why judgest thou not thyself also?

"For like as the ground is given unto the wood, and the sea to his floods: even so they that dwell upon the earth may understand nothing but that which is upon the earth: and He that dwelleth above the heavens may only understand the things that are above the height of the heavens."

I paused at those words, and closing the Sacred Volume fell into deep unquiet thought.

* Such is the supposition of Jahn. Dr. Lee, however, is of opinion that the author was contemporary, and, indeed, identical, with the author of the Book of Enoch.

CHAPTER LXIX.

I HAD hoped that the voyage would produce some beneficial effect upon Lilian; but no effect, good or bad, was perceptible, except, perhaps, a deeper silence, a gentler calm. She loved to sit on the deck when the nights were fair, and the stars mirrored on the deep. And, once thus, as I stood beside her, bending over the rail of the vessel, and gazing on the long wake of light which the moon made amidst the darkness of an ocean to which no shore could be seen, I said to myself, "Where is my track of light through the measureless future? Would that I could believe as I did when a child! Woe is me, that all the reasonings I take from my knowledge should lead me away from the comfort which the peasant who mourns finds in faith! Why should riddles so dark have been thrust upon me?—me, no fond child of fancy; me, sober pupil of schools the severest. Yet what marvel—the strangest my senses have witnessed or feigned in the fraud they have palmed on me—is greater than that by which a simple affection, that all men profess to have known, has changed the courses of life pre-arranged by my hopes and confirmed by my judgment? How calmly before I knew love I have anatomized its mechanism, as the tyro who dissects the webwork of tissues and nerves in the dead! Lo! it lives, lives in me; and, in living, escapes from my scalpel and mocks all my knowledge. Can love be reduced to the realm of the senses? No; what nun is more barred by her grate from the realm of the senses than my bride by her solemn affliction? Is love, then, the union of kindred, harmonious minds? No, my beloved one sits by my side, and I guess not her thoughts, and my mind is to her a sealed fountain. Yet I love her more —oh ineffably more! for the doom which destroys the two causes philosophy assigns to love—in the form, in the mind! How can I now, in my vain physiology, say what is love —what is not? Is it love which must tell me that man has a soul, and that in soul will be found the solution of problems, never to be solved in body or mind alone?"

My self-questionings halted here as Lilian's hand touched my shoulder. She had risen from her seat, and had come to me.

"Are not the stars very far from earth?" she said.

"Very far."

"Are they seen for the first time to-night?"

"They were seen, I presume, as we see them, by the father's of all human races!"

"Yet close below us they shine reflected in the waters; and yet, see, wave flows on wave before we can count it!"

"Lilian, by what sympathy do you read and answer my thought?"

Her reply was incoherent and meaningless. If a gleam of intelligence had mysteriously lighted my heart to her view, it was gone. But drawing her nearer towards me, my eye long followed wistfully the path of light, dividing the darkness on either hand, till it closed in the sloping horizon.

CHAPTER LXX.

THE voyage is over. At the seaport at which we landed I found a letter from Faber. My instructions had reached him in time to effect the purchase on which his descriptions had fixed my desire. The stock, the implements of husbandry, the furniture of the house, were included in the purchase. All was prepared for my arrival, and I hastened from the then miserable village, which may some day rise into one of the mightiest capitals of the world, to my lodge in the wilderness.

It was the burst of the Australian spring, which commences in our autumn month of October. The air was loaded with the perfume of the acacias. Amidst the glades of the open forest land, or climbing the craggy banks of winding silvery creeks,* creepers and flowers of dazzling hue contrasted the olive-green of the surrounding foliage. The exhilarating effect of the climate in that season heightens the charm of the strange scenery. In the brilliancy of the sky, in the lightness of the atmosphere, the sense of life is wondrously quickened. With the very breath the Adventurer draws in from the racy air, he feels as if inhaling hope.

We have reached our home—we are settled in it; the early unfamiliar impressions are worn away. We have learned to dispense with much that we at first missed, and are reconciled to much that at first disappointed or displeased.

The house is built but of logs—the late proprietor had commenced, upon a rising ground, a mile distant, a more imposing edifice of stone; but it is not half finished.

This log-house is commodious, and much has been done, within and without, to conceal or adorn its primitive rudeness. It is of irregular, picturesque form, with verandahs round three sides of it, to which the grape-vine has been trained, with glossy leaves that clamber up to the gable roof. There is a large garden in front, in which many English fruit-trees have been set, and grow fast amongst the plants of the tropics and the orange-trees of Southern Europe. Beyond, stretch undulous pastures, studded not only with sheep, but with herds of cattle, which my speculative predecessor had bred from parents of famous stock, and imported from England at mighty cost; but as yet the herds had been of little profit, and they range their luxuriant expanse of pasture with as little heed. To the left, soar up, in long range, the many-colored hills; to the right meanders a creek, belted by feathery trees; and on its opposite bank a forest opens, through frequent breaks into park-like glades and alleys. The territory, of which I so suddenly find myself the lord, is vast, even for a colonial capitalist.

It had been originally purchased as "a special survey," comprising twenty thousand acres, with the privilege of pasture over forty thousand more. In very little of this land, though it includes some of the most fertile districts in the known world, has cultivation been even commenced. At the time I entered into possession even sheep were barely profitable; labor was scarce and costly. Regarded as a speculation, I could not wonder that my predecessor fled in fear from his domain. Had I invested the bulk of my capital in this lordly purchase, I should have deemed myself a ruined man; but a villa near London, with a hundred acres, would have cost me as much to

* Creek is the name given by Australian colonists to precarious watercourses and tributary streams.

buy, and thrice as much to keep up. I could afford the investment I had made. I found a Scotch bailiff already on the estate, and I was contented to escape from rural occupations, to which I brought no experience by making it worth his while to serve me with zeal. Two domestics of my own, and two who had been for many years with Mrs. Ashleigh, had accompanied us: they reminded faithful and seemed contented. So the clockwork of our mere household arrangements went on much the same as in our native home. Lilian was not subjected to the ordinary privations and discomforts that await the wife even of the wealthy emigrant. Alas! would she have heeded them if she had been?

The change of scene brought a decided change for the better in her health and spirits, but not such as implied a dawn of reviving reason. But her countenance was now more rarely overcast. Its usual aspect was glad with a soft mysterious smile. She would murmur snatches of songs, that were partly borrowed from English poets, and partly glided away into what seemed additions of her own—wanting intelligible meaning, but never melody nor rhyme. Strange, that memory and imitation—the two earliest parents of all inventive knowledge—should still be so active, and judgment—the after faculty, that combines the rest into purpose and method—be annulled!

Julius Faber I see continually, though his residence is a few miles distant. He is sanguine as to Lilian's ultimate recovery: and, to my amazement and to my envy, he has contrived, by some art which I cannot attain, to establish between her and himself intelligible communion. She comprehends his questions, when mine, though the simplest, seem to her in unknown language; and he construes into sense her words, that to me are meaningless riddles.

"I was right," he said to me one day, leaving her seated in the garden beside her quiet, patient mother, and joining me where I lay—listless yet fretful—under the shadeless gum-trees, gazing not on the flocks and fields that I could call my own, but on the far mountain range, from which the arch of the horizon seemed to spring;—"I was right," said the great physician; "this is reason suspended, not reason lost. Your wife will recover; but—"

"But what?"

"Give me your arm as I walk homeward, and I will tell you the conclusion to which I have come."

I rose, the old man leant on me, and we went down the valley, along the craggy ridges of the winding creek. The woodland on the opposite bank was vocal with the chirp, and croak, and chatter of Australian birds—all mirthful, all songless, save that sweetest of warblers, which some early irreverent emigrant degraded to the name of magpie, but whose note is sweeter that the nightingale's, and trills through the lucent air with a distinct ecstatic melody of joy that dominates all the discords;—so ravishing the sense, that, while it sings, the ear scarcely heeds the scream of the parrots.

CHAPTER LXXI.

"You may remember," said Julius Faber, "Sir Humphry Davy's eloquent description of the effect produced on him by the inhalation of nitrous oxide. He states that he began to lose the perception of external things; trains of vivid visible images rapidly passed through his mind, and were connected with words in such a manner as to produce perceptions perfectly novel. 'I existed,' he says, 'in a world of newly-connected and newly-modified ideas.' When he recovered, he exclaimed: 'Nothing exists but thoughts; the universe is composed of impressions, ideas, pleasures, and pains!'

"Now observe, that thus, a cultivator of positive science, endowed with one of the healthiest of human brains, is, by the inhalation of a gas, abstracted from all eternal life—enters into a new world, which consists of images he himself creates, and animates so vividly—that, on waking, he resolves the universe itself into thoughts."

"Well," said I, "but what inference do you draw from that voluntary experiment, applicable to the malady of which you bid me hope the cure?"

"Simply this: that the effect produced on a healthful brain by the nitrous oxide may be produced also by moral causes operating on the blood, or on the nerves. There is a degree of mental excitement in which ideas are more vivid than sensations, and then the world of external things gives way to the world within the brain.* But this, though a suspension of that reason which comprehends accuracy of judgment, is no more a permanent aberration of reason than were Sir Humphry Davy's visonary ecstasies under the influence of the gas. The difference between the two states of suspension is that of time, and it is but an affair of time with our beloved patient. Yet prepare yourself. I fear that the mind will not recover without some critical malady of the body!"

"Critical! but not dangerous?—say not dangerous. I can endure the pause of her reason; I could not endure the void in the universe if her life were to fade from the earth."

"Poor friend! would not you yourself rather lose life than reason?"

"I—yes! But we men are taught to set cheap value on our own lives; we do not estimate at the same rate the lives of those we love. Did we do so, Humanity would lose its virtues."

"What, then! Love teaches that there is something of nobler value than mere mind? yet surely it cannot be the mere body? What is it, if not that continuance of being which your philosophy declines to acknowledge—viz., SOUL? If you fear so painfully that your Lilian should die, is it not that you fear to lose her for ever?"

"Oh, cease, cease!" I cried impatiently. "I cannot now argue on metaphysics. What is it that you anticipate of harm to her life? Her health has been stronger ever since her affliction. She never seems to know ailment now. Do you not perceive that her cheek has a more hardy bloom, her frame a more rounded symmetry, than when you saw her in England?"

"Unquestionably. Her physical forces have been silently recruiting themselves in the dreams which half lull, half amuse her imagination. IMAGINATION! that faculty, the most glorious which is bestowed on the human mind, because it is the faculty which enables thought to create, is of all others the most exhausting to life when unduly stimulated, and consciously reasoning on its own creations. I think it probable that, had this sorrow not befallen you, you would have known a sorrow yet graver—you would have long survived your Lilian. As it is now, when she recovers, her whole organization, phyisical and mental, will have undergone a beneficient change. But, I repeat my prediction—some severe malady of the body will precede the restoration of the mind; and it is my hope that the present suspense or aberration of the more wearing powers of the mind may fit the body to endure and surmount the physical crisis. I remember a case, within my own professional experience, in many respects similar to this, but in other respects it was less hopeful. I was consulted by a young student of a very delicate physical frame, of great mental energies, and consumed by an intense ambition. He was reading for university honors. He would not listen to me when I entreated him to rest his mind. I thought that he was certain to obtain the distinction for which he toiled, and equally certain to die a few months after obtaining it.

"He falsified both my prognostics. He so overworked himself that, on the day of examination, his nerves were agitated, his memory failed him; he passed, not without a certain credit, but fell far short of the rank amongst his fellow-competitors to which he aspired. Here, then, the irritated mind acted on the disappointed heart, and raised a new train of emotions. He was first visited by spectral illusions; then he sank into a state in which the external world seemed quite blotted out. He heeded nothing that was said to him; seemed to see nothing that was placed before his eyes; in a word, sensations became dormant, ideas preconceived usurped their place and those ideas gave him pleasure. He believed that his genius was recognized, and lived amongst its supposed creations enjoying an imaginary fame. So it went on for two years; during which suspense of his reason, his frail form became robust and vigorous. At the end of that time he was siezed with a fever, which would have swept him in three days to the grave, had it occurred when I was first called in to attend him. He conquered the fever, and, in recovering, acquired the full possession of the intellectual faculties so long suspended.

"When I last saw him, many years after-

* See, on the theory elaborated from this principle, Dr. Hibbert's interesting and valuable work on the Philosophy of Apparitions.

wards, he was in perfect health, and the object of his young ambition was realized; the body had supported the mind—he had achieved distinction. Now what had so, for a time, laid this strong intellect into visionary sleep? the most agonizing of human emotions in a noble spirit—shame! What has so stricken down your Lilian? You have told me the story: shame!—the shame of a nature pre-eminently pure. But observe that, in his case as in hers, the shock inflicted does not produce a succession of painful illusions: on the contrary, in both, the illusions are generally pleasing. Had the illusions been painful, the body would have suffered—the patient died. Why did a painful shock produce pleasing illusions? because, no matter how a shock on the nerves may originate, if it affects the reason, it does but make more vivid, than impressions from actual external objects, the ideas previously most cherished. Such ideas in the young student were ideas of earthly fame; such ideas in the young maiden are ideas of angel comforters and heavenly Edens. You miss her mind on the earth, and, while we speak, it is in paradise."

"Much that you say, my friend, is authorized by the speculations of great writers, with whom I am not unfamiliar; but in none of those writers, nor in your encouraging words, do I find a solution for much that has no precedents in my experience—much, indeed, that has analogies in my reading, but analogies which I have hitherto despised as old wives' fables. I have bared to your searching eye the weird mysteries of my life. How do you account for facts which you cannot resolve into illusions? for the influence which that strange being, Margrave, exercised over Lilian's mind or fancy, so that for a time her love for me was as dormant as is her reason now: so that he could draw her—her whose nature you admit to be singularly pure and modest—from her mother's home. The magic wand! the trance into which that wand threw Margrave himself; the apparition which it conjured up in my own quiet chamber, when my mind was without a care and my health without a flaw. How account for all this—as you endeavored, and perhaps successfully, to account for all my impressions of the Vision in the Museum, of the luminous, haunting shadow in its earlier apparitions, when my fancy was heated, my heart tormented, and, it might be, even the physical forces of this strong frame disordered?"

"Allen," said the old pathologist, "here we approach a ground which few physicians have dared to examine. Honor to those who, like our bold contemporary, Elliotson, have braved scoff and sacrificed dross in seeking to extract what is practical in uses, what can be tested by experiment, from those exceptional phenomena on which magic sought to found a philosophy, and to which philosophy tracks the origin of magic."

"What! Do I understand you? Is it you, Julius Faber, who attach faith to the wonders attributed to animal magnetism and electro-biology, or subscribe to the doctrines which their practitioners teach?"

"I have not examined into those doctrines, nor seen with my own eyes the wonders recorded, upon evidence too respectable, nevertheless, to permit me peremptorily to deny what I have not witnessed.* But wherever I

* What Faber here says is expressed with more authority by one of the most accomplished metaphysicians of our time (Sir W. Hamilton):—

"Somnambulism is a phenomenon still more astonishing (than dreaming). In this singular state a person performs a regular series of rational actions, and those frequently of the most difficult and delicate nature; and what is still more marvellous, with a talent to which he could make no pretension when awake. (Cr. Ancillon, Essais Philos. ii. 161.) His memory and reminiscence supply him with recollections of words and things which, perhaps, never were at his disposal in the ordinary state—he speaks more fluently a more refined language. And if we are to credit what the evidence on which it rests hardly allows us to disbelieve, he has not only perception of things through other channels than the common organs of sense, but the sphere of his cognition is amplified to an extent far beyond the limits to which sensible perception is confined. This subject is one of the most perplexing in the whole compass of philosophy; for, on the one hand, the phenomena are so remarkable that they cannot be believed, and yet, on the other, they are of so unambiguous and palpable a character, and the witnesses to their reality are so numerous, so intelligent, and so high above every suspicion of deceit, that it is equally impossible to deny credit to what is attested by such ample and unexceptionable evidence."—Sir W. Hamilton's Lectures on Metaphysics and Logic, vol. ii. p. 274.

This perplexity, in which the distinguished philosopher leaves the judgment so equally balanced that it finds it impossible to believe, and yet impossible to disbelieve, forms the right state of mind in which a candid thinker should come to the examination of those more extraordinary phenomena which he has not himself yet witnessed, but the fair inquiry into which may be tendered to him by persons above the look through the History of Mankind in all ages and all races, I find a concurrence in certain beliefs which seems to countenance the theory that there is in some peculiar and rare temperaments a power over forms of animated organization, with which they establish some unaccountable affinity; and even, though much more rarely, a power over inanimate matter. You are familiar with the theory of Descartes, 'that those particles of the blood which penetrate to the brain do not only serve to nourish and sustain its substance, but to produce there a certain very subtle Aura, or rather a flame very vivid and pure that obtains the name of the Animal Spirits;' * and at the close of his great fragment upon Man, he asserts that 'this flame is of no other nature than all the fires which are in inanimate bodies.'† This notion does but forestall the more recent doctrine that electricity is more or less in all, or nearly all, known matter. Now, whether in the electric fluid or some other fluid akin to it of which we know still less, thus equally pervading all matter, there may be a certain magnetic property more active, more operative upon sympathy in some human constitutions than in others, and which can account for the mysterious power I have spoken of, is a query I might suggest, but not an opinion I would hazard. For an opinion I must have that basis of experience or authority which I do not need when I submit a query to the experience and authority of others. Still the supposition conveyed in the query is so far worthy of notice, that the ecstatic temperament (in which phrase I comprehend all constitutional mystics) is peculiarly sensitive to electric atmostpheric influences. This is a fact which most medical observers will have remarked in the range of their practice. Accordingly, I was prepared to find Mr. Hare Townshend, in his interesting work, * state that he himself was of 'the electric temperament,' sparks flying from his hair when combed in the dark, etc.

"That accomplished writer, whose veracity no one would impugn, affirms that 'between this electrical endowment and whatever mesmeric properties he might possess, there is a remarkable relationship and parallelism. Whatever state of the atmosphere tends to accumulate and insulate electricity in the body, promotes equally' (says Mr. Townshend), 'the power and facility with which I influence others mesmerically. What Mr. Townshend thus observes in himself, American physicians and professors of chemistry depose to have observed in those modern magicians, the mediums of (so-called) 'spirit manifestation.' They state that all such mediums are of the electric temperament, thus everywhere found allied with the ecstatic, and their power varies in proportion as the state of the atmosphere serves to depress or augment the electricity stored in themselves. Here, then, in the midst of vagrant phenomena, either too hastily dismissed as altogether the tricks of fraudful imposture, or too credulously accepted as supernatural portents—here, at least, in one generalized fact, we may, perhaps, find a starting-point, from which inductive experiment may arrive soon, or late, at a rational theory. But however the power of which we are speaking (a power accorded to special physical temperament) may or may not be accounted for by some patient student of nature, I am persuaded that it is in that power we are to seek for whatever is not wholly imposture, in the attributes assigned to magic or witchcraft.

"It is well said, by a writer who has gone into the depth of these subjects with the research of a scholar and the science of a pathologist, 'that if magic had exclusively reposed on credulity and falsehood, its reign would never have endured so long. But that its art took its origin in singular phenomena, proper

imputation of quackery and fraud. Müller, who is not the least determined. as he is certainly one of the most distinguished disbelievers of mesmeric phenomena, does not appear to have witnessed, or at least to have carefully examined, them, or he would, perhaps, have seen that even the more extraordinary of those phenomena confirm, rather than contradict, his own general theories, and may be explained by the sympathies one sense has with another—"the laws of reflection through the medium of the brain." (Physiology of Senses, p. 1311.) And again by the maxim "that the mental principle, or cause of the mental phenomena, cannot be confined to the brain, but that it exists in a latent state in every part of the organism." (Ib. p. 1355.) The "nerve power," contended for by Mr. Bein, also may suggest a rational solution of much that has seemed incredible to those physiologists who have not condescended to sift the genuine phenomena of mesmerism from the imposture to which, in all ages, the phenomena exhibited by what may be called the ecstatic temperament, have been applied.

* Descartes, L'Homme, vol. iv. p. 345. Cousin's Edition.

† Ibid., p. 428.

* Facts in Mesmerism.

to certain affections of the nerves, or manifested in the conditions of sleep. These phenomena, the principle of which was at first unknown, served to root faith in magic, and often abused even enlightened minds. The enchanters and magicians arrived, by divers practices, at the faculty of provoking in other brains a determined order of dreams, of engendering hallucinations of all kinds, of inducing fits of hypnotism, trance, mania, during which the persons so affected imagined that they saw, heard, touched supernatural beings, conversed with them, proved their influences, assisted at prodigies of which magic proclaimed itself to possess the secret. The public, the enchanters, and the enchanted were equally dupes.' * Accepting this explanation, unintelligible to no physician of a practice so lengthened as mine has been, I draw from it the corollary, that as these phenomena are exhibited only by certain special affections, to which only certain special constitutions are susceptible, so not in any superior faculties of intellect, or of spiritual endowment, but in peculiar physical temperaments, often strangely disordered, the power of the sorcerer in affecting the imagination of others is to be sought.

"In the native tribes of Australasia the elders are instructed in the arts of this so-called sorcery, but only in a very few constitutions does instruction avail to produce effects in which the savages recognize the powers of a sorcerer: it is so with the Obi of the negroes. The fascination of Obi is an unquestionable fact, but the Obi man cannot be trained by formal lessons; he is born a fascinator, as a poet is born a poet. It is so with the Laplanders, of whom Tornæus reports that of those instructed in the magical art 'only a few are capable of it.' 'Some,' he says, 'are naturally magicians.' And this fact is emphatically insisted upon by the mystics of our own middle ages, who state that a man must be *born* a magician; in other words, that the gift is constitutional, though developed by practice and art. Now, that this gift and its practice should principally obtain in imperfect states of civilization, and fade into insignificance in the busy social enlightenment of cities, may be accounted for by reference to the known influences of imagination.

"In the cruder states of social life not only is imagination more frequently predominant over all other faculties, but it has not the healthful vents which the intellectual competition of cities and civilization affords. The man who in a savage tribe, or in the dark feudal ages, would be a magician, is in our country a poet, an orator, a daring speculator, an inventive philosopher. In other words, his imagination is drawn to pursuits congenial to those amongst whom it works. It is the tendency of all intellect to follow the directions of the public opinion amidst which it is trained. Where a magician is held in reverence or awe, there will be more practitioners of magic than where a magician is despised as an impostor or shut up as a lunatic. In Scandinavia, before the introduction of Christianity, all tradition records the wonderful powers of the Vala, or witch, who was then held in reverence and honor. Christianity was introduced, and the early Church denounced the Vala as the instrument of Satan, and from that moment down dropped the majestic prophetess into a miserable and execrated old hag!"

"The ideas you broach," said I musingly, "have at moments crossed me, though I have shrunk from reducing them to a theory which is but one of pure hypothesis. But this magic, after all, then, you would place in the imagination of the operator, acting on the imagination of those whom it affects? Here, at least, I can follow you, to a certain extent, for here we get back into the legitimate realm of physiology."

"And possibly," said Faber, "we may find hints to guide us to useful examination, if not to complete solution, of problems that, once demonstrated, may lead to discoveries of infinite value—hints, I say, in two writers of widely opposite genius—Van Helmont and Bacon. Van Helmont of all the mediæval mystics, is, in spite of his many extravagant whims, the one whose intellect is the most suggestive to the disciplined reasoners of our day. He supposed that the faculty which he calls Phantasy, and which we familiarly call Imagination, is invested with the power of creating for itself ideas independent of the senses, each idea clothed in a form fabricated by the imagination, and becoming an operative entity. This notion is so far favored by

* La Magie et l'Astrologie dans l'Antiquité et au Moyen-Age. Par. L. F. Alfred Maury, Membre de l'Institut. P. 225.

modern physiologists, that Lincke reports a case where the eye itself was extirpated; yet the extirpation was followed by the appearance of luminons figures before the orbit. And again, a woman, stone-blind, complained of 'luminous images, with pale colors, before her eyes.' Abercrombie mentions the case 'of a lady quite blind, her eyes being also disorganized and sunk, who never walked out without seeing a little old woman in a red cloak who seemed to walk before her.' *

"Your favorite authority, the illustrious Müller, who was himself in the habit of 'seeing different images in the field of vision when he lay quietly down to sleep, asserts that these images are not merely presented to the fancy, but that even the images of dreams *are really seen*,' and that 'any one may satisfy himself of this by accustoming himself regularly to open his eyes when waking after a dream—the images seen in the dream are then sometimes visible, and can be observed to disappear gradually.' He confirms this statement, not only by the result of his own experience, but by the observations made by Spinoza, and the yet higher authority of Aristotle, who accounts for spectral appearance as *the internal action of the sense of vision*.† And this opinion is favored by Sir David Brewster, whose experience leads him to suggest 'that the objects of mental contemplation may be seen as distinctly as external objects, and will occupy the same local position in the axis of vision as if they had been formed by the agency of light.' Be this as it may, one fact remains, that images can be seen even by the blind as distinctly and vividly as you and I now see the stream below our feet and the opossums at play upon yonder boughs.

"Let us come next to some remarkable suggestions of Lord Bacon. In his Natural History, treating of the force of the imagination, and the help it receives 'by one man working by another,' he cites an instance he had witnessed of a kind of juggler, who could tell a person what card he thought of. He mentioned this 'to a pretended learned man, curious in such things,' and this sage said to him, "It is not the knowledge of the man's thought, for that is proper to God, but the enforcing of a thought upon him, and binding his imagination by a stronger, so that he could think of no other card.' You see this sage anticipated our modern electro-biologists! And the learned man then shrewdly asked Lord Bacon, 'Did the juggler tell the card to the man himself who had thought of it, or bid another tell it?' He bade another tell it,' answered Lord Bacon. 'I thought so,' returned his learned acquaintance, 'for the juggler himself could not have put on so strong an imagination; but by telling the card to the other, who believed the juggler was some strange man who could do strange things, that other man caught a strong imagination.'* The whole story is worth reading, because Lord Bacon evidently thinks it conveys a guess worth examining. And Lord Bacon, were he now living, would be the man to solve the mysteries that branch out of mesmerism or (so-called) spiritual manifestation, for he would not pretend to despise their phenomena for fear of hurting his reputation for good sense.

"Bacon then goes on to state that there are three ways to fortify the imagination: 'First, authority derived from belief in an art and in the man who exercises it; secondly, means to quicken and corroborate the imagination; thirdly, means to repeat and refresh it.' For the second and the third he refers to the practices of magic, and proceeds afterwards to state on what things imagination has most force: 'upon things that have the lightest and easiest motions, and, therefore, above all, upon the spirits of men, and, in them, on such affections as move lightest—in love, in fear, in

* She had no illusions when within doors.—Abercrombie on the Intellectual Powers, p. 277. (15th edition.

† Müller, Physiology of the Senses, Baley's translation, pp. 1068—1395, and elsewhere. Mr. Bain, in his thoughtful and suggestive work on the Senses and Intellect, makes very powerful use of these statements in support of his proposition, which Faber advances in other words, viz., "the return of the nervous currents exactly on their old track in revived sensations."

* Perhaps it is for the reason suggested in the text, viz., that the magician requires the interposition of a third imagination between his own and that of the consulting believer, and that any learned adept in (so-called) magic will invariably refuse to exhibit without the presence of a third person. Hence the author of Dogme et Rituel de la Haute Magie, printed at Paris, 1852-53—a book less remarkable for its learning than for the earnest belief of a scholar of our own day in the reality of the art of which he records the history—insists much on the necessity of rigidly observing Le Ternaire, in the number of persons who assist in an enchanter's experiments.

irresolution. And,' adds Bacon, earnestly, in a very different spirit from that which dictates to the sages of our time the philosophy of rejecting without trial that which belongs to the Marvellous, 'and whatsoever is of this kind, should be *thoroughly inquired into.'* And this great founder or renovator of the sober inductive system of investigation, even so far leaves it a matter of speculative inquiry, whether imagination may not be so powerful that it can actually operate upon a plant, that he says,—'This likewise should be made upon plants, and that diligently, as if you should tell a man that such a tree would die this year, and *will* him, at these and these times, to go unto it and see how it thriveth.' I presume that no philosopher has followed such recommendations: had some great philosopher done so, possibly we should by this time know all the secrets of what is popularly called witchcraft."

And as Faber here paused there came a strange laugh from the fantastic she-oak-tree overhanging the stream—a wild, impish laugh.

"Pooh! it is but the great king-fisher, the laughing-bird of the Australian bush," said Julius Faber, amused at my start of superstitious alarm.

We walked on for some minutes in musing silence, and the rude log-hut in which my wise companion had his home came in view—the flocks grazing on undulous pastures, the kine drinking at a watercourse fringed by the slender gum-trees, and a few fields, laboriously won from the luxuriant grass-land, rippling with the wave of corn.

I halted, and said, "Rest here for a few moments, till I gather up the conclusions to which your speculative reasoning seems to invite me."

We sat down on a rocky crag, half mantled by luxuriant creepers with vermillion buds.

"From the guesses," said I, "which you have drawn from the erudition of others and your own ingenious and reflective inductions, I collect this solution of the mysteries, by which the experience I gain from my senses confounds all the dogmas approved by my judgment. To the rational conjectures by which, when we first conversed on the marvels that perplexed me, you ascribe to my imagination, predisposed by mental excitement, physical fatigue or derangement, and a concurrence of singular events tending to strengthen such predisposition, the phantasmal impressions produced on my senses; to these conjectures you now add a new one, more startling and less admitted by sober physiologists. You conceive it possible that persons endowed with a rare and peculiar temperament can so operate on the imagination, and, through the imagination, on the senses of others, as to exceed even the powers ascribed to the practitioners of mesmerism and electrobiology, and give a certain foundation of truth to the old tales of magic and witchcraft. You imply that Margrave may be a person thus gifted, and hence the influence he unquestionably exercised over Lilian, and over, perhaps, less innocent agents, charmed or impelled by his will. And not discarding, as I own I should have been originally induced to do, the queries of suggestions adventured by Bacon in his discursive speculations on Nature, to wit 'that there be many things, some of them inanimate, that operate upon the spirits of men by secret sympathy and antipathy,' and to which Bacon gave the quaint name of 'imaginants;' so even that wand, of which I have described to you the magic-like effects, may have had properties communicated to it by which it performs the work of the magician, as mesmerists pretend that some substance mesmerised by them can act on the patient as sensibly as if it were the mesmerizer himself. Do I state your suppositions correctly?"

"Yes; always remembering that they are only suppositions, and volunteered with the utmost diffidence. But since, thus seated in the early wilderness, we permit ourselves the indulgence of childlike guess, may it not be possible, apart from the doubtful question whether a man can communicate to an inanimate material substance a power to act upon the mind or imagination of another man—may it not, I say, be possible that such a substance may contain in itself such a virtue or property potent over certain constitutions, though not over all? For instance, it is in my experience that the common hazel-wood will strongly affect some nervous temperaments, though wholly without effect on others. I remember a young girl who, having taken up a hazel-stick freshly cut, could not relax her hold of it; and when it was wrenched away from her by force was irresistibly attracted towards it, repossessed herself of it, and, after holding it a few minutes, was cast into a kind of trance, in which she beheld phantasmal visions. Mentioning this curious case, which I supposed unique, to a learned brother of our profession, he told me that he had known other instances of the effect of the hazel upon nervous temperaments in persons of both sexes. Possibly it was some such peculiar property in the hazel that made it the wood selected for the old divining-rod.

"Again, we know that the bay-tree, or laurel, was dedicated to the oracular Pythian Apollo. Now wherever, in the old world, we find that the learning of the priests enabled them to exhibit exceptional phenomena, which imposed upon popular credulity, there was a something or other which it is worth a philosopher's while to explore. And, accordingly, I always suspected that there was in the laurel some property favorable to ecstatic vision in highly impressionable temperaments. My suspicion, a few years ago, was justified by the experience of a German physician, who had under his care a cataleptic or ecstatic patient, and who assured me that he found nothing in this patient so stimulated the state of 'sleep-waking,' or so disposed that state to indulge in the hallucinations of prevision, as the berry of the laurel.* Well, we do not know what this wand that produced a seemingly magical effect upon you was really composed of. You did not notice the metal employed in the wire which you say communicated a thrill to the sensitive nerves in the palm of the hand. You cannot tell how far it might have been the vehicle of some fluid force in nature. Or still more probably, whether the pores of your hand insensibly imbibed, and communicated to the brain, some of those powerful narcotics from which the Boudhists and the Arabs make unguents that induce visionary hallucinations, and in which substances undetected in the hollow of the wand, or the handle of the wand itself might be steeped.†

"One thing we do know, viz., that amongst the ancients, and especially in the East, the construction of wands for magical purposes was no commonplace mechanical craft—but a special and secret art appropriated to men who cultivated with assiduity all that was then known of natural science in order to extract from it agencies that might appear supernatural. Possibly, then, the rods or wands of the East, of which Scripture makes mention, were framed upon some principles of which we in our day are very naturally ignorant, since we do not ransack science for the same secrets. And thus, in the selection or preparation of the material employed, mainly consisted, whatever may be referable to natural philosophical causes, in the antique science of Rhabdomancy, or divination and enchantment by wands. The staff or wand of which you tell me, was, you say, made of iron or steel and tipped with crystal. Possibly, iron and crystal do really contain some properties not hitherto scientifically analyzed, and only, indeed, potential over exceptional temperaments, which may account for the fact that iron and crystal have been favorites with all professed mystics, ancient and modern. The Delphic Pythoness had her iron tripod, Mesmer his iron bed; and many persons, indisputably honest, cannot gaze long upon a ball of crystal but what they begin to see visions. I suspect that a philosophical cause for such seemingly preternatural effects of crystal and iron will be found in connectien with the extreme impressionability to changes in temperatures which is the characteristic both of crystal and iron. But if these materials do contain certain powers over exceptional constitutions, we do not arrive at a supernatural, but at a natural phenomenon."

"Still," said I, "even granting that your explanatory hypotheses hit or approach the truth —still what a terrible power you would assign to man's will over men's reason and deeds!"

"Man's will," answered Faber, "has over men's deeds and reason, habitual and daily, power infinitely greater, and, when uncounterbalanced, infinitely more dangerous than that which superstition exaggerates in magic. Man's will moves a war that decimates a race, and leaves behind it calamities little less dire than slaughter. Man's will frames, but it also corrupts laws; exalts, but also demoralizes opinion; sets the world mad with fanaticism, as often as it curbs the heart's fierce instincts by the wisdom of brother-like mercy. You

* I may add that Dr. Kerner instances the effect of laurel-berries on the Seeress of Prevorst, corresponding with that asserted by Julius Faber in the text.

† See for these unguents the work of M. Maury, before quoted, La Magie et l'Astrologie, etc., p. 417.

revolt at the exceptional, limited sway over some two or three individuals which the arts of a sorcerer (if sorcerer there be) can effect; and yet, at the very moment in which you were perplexed and appalled by such sway, or by your reluctant belief in it, your will was devising an engine to unsettle the reason and wither the hopes of millions!"

"My will! What engine?"

"A book conceived by your intellect, adorned by your learning, and directed by your will, to steal from the minds of other men their persuasion of the soul's everlasting Hereafter."

I bowed my head, and felt myself grow pale.

"And if we accept Bacon's theory of 'secret sympathy,' or the plainer physiological maxim that there must be in the imagination, morbidly impressed by the will of another, some trains of idea in affinity with such influence and preinclined to receive it, no magician could warp you to evil, except through thoughts that themselves went astray. Grant that the Margrave who still haunts your mind did really, by some occult, sinister magnetism, guide the madman to murder—did influence the servant-woman's vulgar desire to pry into the secrets of her ill-fated master—or the old maid's covetous wish and envious malignity—what could this awful magican do more than any commonplace guilty adviser, to a mind predisposd to accept the advice?"

"You forgot one example which destroys your argument—the spell which this mysterious fascinator could cast upon a creature so pure from all guilt as Lilian!"

"Will you forgive me if I answer frankly?"

"Speak."

"Your Lilian is spotless and pure as you deem her, and the fascination, therefore, attempts no lure through a sinful desire; it blends with its attraction no sentiment of affection untrue to yourself. Nay, it is justice to your Lilian, and may be a melancholy comfort to you, to state my conviction, based on the answers my questions have drawn from her, that you were never more cherished by her love than when that love seemed to forsake you. Her imagination impressed her with the illusion that through your love for her you were threatened with a great peril. What seemed the levity of her desertion was the devotion of self-sacrifice. And, in her strange, dream-led wanderings, do not think that she was conscious of the fascination you impute to this mysterious Margrave: in her belief it was your own guardian angel that guided her steps, and her pilgrimage was ordained to disarm the foe that menaced you, and dissolve the spell that divided her life from yours! But had she not, long before this, wilfully prepared herself to be so deceived? Had not her fancies been deliberately encouraged to dwell remote from the duties we are placed on the earth to perform? The loftiest faculties in our nature are those that demand the finest poise, not to fall from their height and crush all the walls that they crown. With this exquisite beauty of illustration, Hume says of the dreamers of 'bright fancies,' 'that they may be compared to those angels whom the Scriptures represent as covering their eyes with their wings.'

"Had you been, like my nephew, a wrestler for bread with the wilderness, what helpmate would your Lilian have been to you? How often would you have cried out in justifitable anger, 'I, son of Adam, am on earth, not in paradise? Oh, that my Eve were at home on my hearth, and not in the skies with the seraphs!' No Margrave, I venture to say, could have suspended the healthful affections, or charmed into danger, the wide-awake soul of my Amy. When she rocks in its cradle the babe the young parents intrust to her heed—when she calls the kine to the milking, the chicks to their corn—when she but flits through my room to renew the flowers on the stand, or range in neat order the books that I read—no spell on her fancy could lead her a step from the range of her provident cares! At day she is contented to be on the commonplace earth; at evening she and I knock together at the one door of heaven, which opes to thanksgiving and prayer; and thanksgiving and prayer send us back, calm and hopeful, to the task that each morrow renews."

I looked up as the old man paused, and in the limpid clearness of the Australian atmosphere, I saw the child he thus praised standing by the garden-gate, looking towards us, and, though still distant, she seemed near. I felt wroth with her. My heart so cherished my harmless, defenceless Lilian, that I was jealous of the praise taken from her to be bestowed on another.

"Each of us," said I coldly, "has his or her own nature, and the uses harmonious to that nature's idiosyncrasy. The world, I grant, would get on very ill if women were not, more or less, actively useful and quietly good, like your Amy. But the world would lose standards that exalt and refine, if no woman were permitted to gain, through the indulgence of fancy, thoughts exquisite as those which my Lilian conceived, while thought, alas! flowed out of fancy. I do not wound you by citing your Amy as a type of the mediocre. I do not claim for Lilian the rank we accord to the type of genius. But both are alike to such types in this: viz., that the uses of mediocrity are for every-day life, and the uses of genuis, amidst a thousand mistakes which mediocrity never commits, are to suggest and perpetuate ideas which raise the standard of the mediocre to a nobler level. There would be fewer Amys in life if there were no Lilian! as there would be far fewer good men of sense if there were no erring dreamer of genius!"

"You say well, Allen Fenwick. And who should be so indulgent to the vagaries of the imagination as the philosophers who taught your youth to doubt everything in the Maker's plan of creation which could not be mathematically proved? 'The human mind,' said Luther, 'is like a drunkard on horseback; prop it in on one side, and it falls on the other.' So the man who is much too enlightened to believe in a peasant's religion, is always sure to set up some inane superstition of his own. Open biographical volumes wherever you please, and the man who has no faith in religion, is a man who has faith in a nightmare. See that type of the elegant sceptics—Lord Herbert of Cherbury. He is writing a book against Revelation; he asks a sign from heaven to tell him if his book is approved by his Maker, and the man who cannot believe in the miracles performed by his Saviour, gravely tells us of a miracle vouchsafed to himself. Take the hardest and strongest intellect which the hardest and strongest race of mankind ever schooled and accomplished. See the greatest of great men, the great Julius Cæsar! Publicly he asserts in the Senate that the immortality of the soul is a vain chimera.

"He professes the creed which Roman voluptuaries deduced from Epicurus, and denies all interference in the affairs of the earth. A great authority for the Materialists—they have none greater! They can show on their side no intellect equal to Cæsar's! and yet this magnificent free-thinker, rejecting a soul and a Deity, habitually entered his chariot in muttering a charm; crawled on his knees up the steps of a temple to propitiate the abstraction called 'Nemesis;' and did not cross the Rubicon till he had consulted the omens. What does all this prove?—a very simple truth. Man has some instinct with the brutes; for instance, hunger and sexual love. Man has one instinct peculiar to himself, found universally (or with alleged exceptions in savage states so rare, that they do not affect the general law *)—an instinct of an invisible power without this earth, and of a life beyond the grave, which that power vouchsafes to his spirit. But the best of us cannot violate an instinct with impunity. Resist hunger as long as you can, and, rather than die of starvation, your instinct will make you a cannibal; resist love when youth and nature impel to it, and what pathologist does not track one broad path into madness or crime? So with the noblest instinct of all. Reject the internal conviction by which the grandest thinkers have sanctioned the hope of the humblest Christian, and you are servile at once to some faith inconceivably more hard to believe.

"The imagination will not be withheld from its yearnings for vistas beyond the walls of the flesh and the span of the present hour. Philosophy itself, in rejecting the healthful creeds by which man finds his safeguards in sober prayer, and his guide through the wilderness of visionary doubt, invents systems compared to which the mysteries of theology are simple Suppose any man of strong, plain understand-

* It seems extremely doubtful whether the very few instances in which it has been asserted that a savage race has been found without recognition of a Deity and a future state would bear searching examination. It is set forth, for example, in most of the popular works on Australia, that the Australian savages have no notion of a Deity or a Hereafter, that they only worship a devil, or evil spirit. This assumption, though made more peremptorily, and by a greater number of writers than any similar one regarding other savages, is altogether erroneous, and has no other foundation than the ignorance of the writers. The Australian Savages recognize a Deity, but He is too august tor a name in their own language; in English they call Him The Great Master—an expression synonymous with "The Great Lord." They believe in a hereafter of eternal joy, and place it amongst the stars.—See Strzelecki's Physical Description of New South Wales.

ing had never heard of a Deity like Him whom we Christians adore, then ask this man which he can the better comprehend in his mind, and accept as a natural faith—viz. the simple Christianity of his shepherd or the Pantheism of Spinoza? Place before an accomplished critic (who comes with a perfectly unprejudiced mind to either inquiry), first, the arguments of David Hume against the Gospel miracles, and then the metaphysical crotchets of David Hume himself. This subtle philosopher, not content, with Berkeley, to get rid of matter—not content, with Condillac, to get rid of spirit or mind—proceeds to a miracle greater than any his Maker has yet vouchsafed to reveal. He, being then alive and in the act of writing, gets rid of himself altogether. Nay, he confesses he cannot reason with any one who is stupid enough to think he has a self.

"His words are: 'What we call a mind is nothing but a heap or collection of different perceptions or objects united together by certain relations, and supposed, though falsely, to be endowed with perfect simplicity and identity. If any one, upon serious and candid reflection, thinks he has a different notion of himself, I must confess I can reason with him no longer.' Certainly I would rather believe all the ghost stories upon record, than believe that I am not even a ghost, distinct and apart from the perceptions conveyed to me, no matter how—just as I am distinct and apart from the furniture in my room, no matter whether I found it there or whether I bought it. If some old cosmogonist asked you to believe that the primitive cause of the solar system was not to be traced to a Divine Intelligence, but to a nebulosity, originally so diffused that its existence can with difficulty be conceived, and that the origin of the present system of organized beings equally dispensed with the agency of a creative mind, and could be referred to molecules formed in the water by the power of attraction, till by modifications of cellular tissue in the gradual lapse of ages, one monad became an oyster and another a Man—would you not say this cosmogony could scarcely have misled the human understanding even in the earliest dawn of speculative inquiry?

Yet such are the hypotheses to which the desire to philosophize away that simple proposition of a Divine First Cause, which every child can comprehend, led two of the greatest geniuses and profoundest reasoners of modern times—La Place and La Marck.* Certainly, the more you examine those arch phantasmagorists, the philosophers who would leave nothing in the universe but their own delusions, the more your intellectual pride may be humbled. The wildest phenomena which have startled you, are not more extravagant than the grave explanations which intellectual presumption adventures on the elements of our own organism and the relations between the world of matter and the world of ideas."

Here our conversation stopped, for Amy had now joined us, and, looking up to reply, I saw the child's innocent face between me and the furrowed brow of the old man.

CHAPTER LXXII.

I TURNED back alone. The sun was reddening the summits of the distant mountain-range, but dark clouds, that portended rain, were gathering behind my way and deepening the shadows in many a chasm and hollow which volcanic fires had wrought on the surface of uplands undulating like diluvian billows fixed into stone in the midst of their stormy swell. I wandered on and away from the beaten track, absorbed in thought. Could I acknowledge in Julius Faber's conjectures any basis for logical ratiocination? or were they not the ingenious fancies of that empirical Philosophy of Sentiment by which the aged, in the decline of severer faculties, sometimes, assimilate their theories to the hazy romance of youth? I can well conceive that the story I tell will be regarded by most as a wild and fantastic fable; that by some it may be considered a vehicle for guesses at various riddles of Nature, without or within us, which are free to the licence of romance, though forbidden to the caution of science. But, I—I—know unmistakeably my own identity, my own positive place in a substantial universe. And beyond that knowledge, what do I know? Yet had Faber no ground for his startling parallels

---

* See the observation on La Place and La Marck in the Introduction to Kirby's Bridgewater Treatise.

between the chimeras of superstition and the alternatives to faith volunteered by the metaphysical speculations of knowledge? On the theorems of Condillac, I, in common with numberless contemporaneous students (for, in my youth, Condillac held sway in the schools, as now, driven forth from the schools, his opinions float loose through the talk and the scribble of men of the world, who perhaps never opened his page)—on the theorems of Condillac I had built up a system of thought designed to immure the swathed form of material philosophy from all rays and all sounds of a world not material, as the walls of some blind mausoleum shut out, from the mummy within, the whisper of winds, and the gleaming of stars.

And did not those very theorems, when carried out to their strict and completing results by the close reasonings of Hume, resolve my own living idenity, the one conscious indivisible ME, into a bundle of memories derived from the senses which had bubbled and duped my experience, and reduce into a phantom, as spectral as that of the Luminous Shadow, the whole solid frame of creation?

While pondering these questions, the storm whose forewarnings I had neglected to heed, burst forth with all the suddenness peculiar to the Australian climes. The rains descended like the rushing of floods. In the beds of the watercourses, which, at noon, seemed dried up and exhausted, the torrents began to swell and to rave; the grey crags around them were animated into living waterfalls. I looked round and the landscape was as changed as a scene that replaces a scene on a player's stage. I was aware that I had wandered far from my home, and I knew not what direction I should take to regain it. Close at hand, and raised above the torrents that now rushed in many a gulley and tributary creek, around and before me, the mouth of a deep cave, overgrown with bushes and creeping flowers tossed wildly to and fro, between the rain from above and the spray of cascades below, offered a shelter from the storm. I entered; scaring innumerable flocks of bats striking against me, blinded by the glare of lightning that followed me into the cavern; and hastening to re-settle themselves on the pendants of stalactites, or the jagged buttresses of primæval wall.

From time to time the lightning darted into the gloom and lingered amongst its shadows; and I saw, by the flash, that the floors on which I stood were strewed with strange bones, some amongst them the fossilized relics of races destroyed by the Deluge. The rain continued for more than two hours with unabated violence; then it ceased almost as suddenly as it had come on. And the lustrous moon of Australia burst from the clouds, shining, bright as an English dawn, into the hollows of the cave. And then simultaneously arose all the choral songs of the wilderness—creatures whose voices are heard at night—the loud whirr of the locusts, the musical boom of the bullfrog, the cuckoo note of the morepork, and, mournful amidst all those merrier sounds, the hoot of the owl, through the wizard she-oaks and the pale green of the gum-trees.

I stepped forth into the open air and gazed, first instinctively on the heavens, next, with more heedful eye, upon the earth. The nature of the soil bore the evidence of volcanic fires long since extinguished. Just before my feet, the rays fell full upon a bright yellow streak in the block of quartz half embedded in the soft moist soil. In the midst of all the solemn thoughts and the intense sorrows which weighed upon heart and mind, that yellow gleam startled the mind into a direction remote from philosophy, quickened the heart to a beat that chimed with no household affections. Involuntarily I stooped; impulsively I struck the block with the hatchet, or tomahawk, I carried habitually about me, for the purpose of marking the trees that I wished to clear from the waste of my broad domain. The quartz was shattered by the stroke, and left disburied its glittering treasure. My first glance had not deceived me. I, vain seeker after knowledge, had, at least, discovered gold. I took up the bright metal—gold! I paused; I looked round; the land that just before had seemed to me so worthless, took the value of Ophir. Its features had before been as unknown to me as the Mountains of the Moon, and now my memory became wonderfully quickened. I recalled the rough map of my possessions, the first careless ride round their boundaries. Yes, the land on which I stood—for miles, to the spur of those father mountains—the land was mine, and, beneath its surface, there was gold! I closed my eyes; for some moments, visions of boundless wealth, and of the royal power which such wealth could command, swept athwart my brain. But my heart rapidly settled back to its real treasure. "What matters," I sighed, "all this dross? Could Ophir itself buy back to my Lilian's smile one ray of the light which gave 'glory to the grass and splendor to the flower?'"

So muttering, I flung the gold into the torrent that raged below, and went on through the moonlight, sorrowing silently—only thankful for the discovery that had quickened my reminiscence of the landmarks by which to steer my way through the wilderness.

The night was half gone, for even when I had gained the familiar track through the pastures, the swell of the many winding creeks that now intersected the way obliged me often to retrace my steps; to find, sometimes, the bridge of a felled tree which had been providently left unremoved over the now foaming torrent, and, more than once, to swim across the current, in which swimmers less strong or less practical would have been dashed down the falls, where loose logs and torn trees went clattering and whirled: for I was in danger of life. A band of the savage natives were stealthily creeping on my track—the natives in those parts were not then so much awed by the white man as now. A boomerang* had whirred by me, burying itself amongst the herbage close before my feet. I had turned, sought to find and to face these distardly foes; they contrived to elude me. But when I moved on, my ear, sharpened by danger, heard them moving, too, in my rear. Once only three hideous forms suddenly faced me, springing up from a thicket, all tangled with honey-suckles and creepers of blue and vermilion. I walked steadily up to them; they halted a moment or so in suspense, but perhaps they were scared by my stature or awed by my aspect; and the Unfamiliar, though Human, had terror for them, as the Unfamiliar, although but a Shadow, had had terror for me. They vanished, and as quickly as if they had crept into the earth.

At length the air brought me the soft perfume of my well-known acacias, and my house stood before me, and amidst English flowers and English fruit-trees, under the effulgent Australian moon. Just as I was opening the little gate which gave access from the pasture-land into the garden, a figure in white rose up from under light, feathery boughs, and a hand was laid on my arm. I started; but my surprise was changed into fear when I saw the pale face and sweet eyes of Lilian.

"Heavens! you here! you! at this hour! Lilian, what is this?"

"Hush!" she whispered, clinging to me; "hush! do not tell: no one knows. I missed you when the storm came on; I have missed you ever since. Others went in search of you and came back. I could not sleep, but the rest are sleeping, so I stole down to watch for you. Brother, brother, if any harm chanced to you, even the angels could not comfort me; all would be dark, dark! But you are safe, safe, safe!" And she clung to me yet closer.

"Ah! Lilian, Lilian, your vision in the hour I first beheld you was indeed prophetic —'Each has need of the other.' Do you remember?"

"Softly, softly," she said, "let me think!" She stood quietly by my side, looking up into the sky, with all its numberless stars, and its solitary moon now sinking slow behind the verge of the forest. "It comes back to me," she murmured softly—"the Long ago—the sweet Long ago!"

I held my breath to listen.

"There—there!" she resumed, pointing to the heavens; "do you see? You are there, and my father, and—and—Oh! that terrible face—those serpent eyes—the dead man's skull! Save me—save me!"

She bowed her head upon my bosom, and I led her gently back towards the house. As we gained the door which she had left open, the starlight shining across the shadowy gloom within, she lifted her face from my breast, and cast a hurried fearful look round the shining garden, then into the dim recess beyond the threshold.

"It is there—there!—the Shadow that lured me on, whispering that if I followed it I should join my beloved. False dreadful Shadow! it will fade soon—fade into the grinning horrible skull. Brother, brother, where is my Allen? Is he dead—dead—or is it I who am dead to him?"

* A missile weapon peculiar to the Australian savages.

I could but clasp her again to my breast, and seek to mantle her shivering form with my dripping garments, all the while my eyes—following the direction which hers had taken—dwelt on the walls of the nook within the threshold, half lost in darkness, half white in starlight. And there I, too, beheld the haunting Luminous Shadow, the spectral effigies of the mysterious being, whose very existence in the flesh was a riddle unsolved by my reason. Distinctly I saw the Shadow, but its light was far paler, its outline far more vague, than when I had beheld it before. I took courage, as I felt Lilian's heart beating against my own. I advanced, I crossed the threshold—the Shadow was gone.

"There is no Shadow here—no phantom to daunt thee, my life's life," said I, bending over Lilian.

"It has touched me in passing; I feel it—cold, cold, cold!" she answered, faintly.

I bore her to her room, placed her on her bed, struck a light, watched over her. At dawn there was a change in her face, and from that time health gradually left her; strength slowly, slowly, yet to me perceptibly, ebbed from her life away.

CHAPTER LXXIII.

MONTHS upon months have rolled on since the night in which Lilian had watched for my coming amidst the chilling airs under the haunting moon. I have said that from the date of that night her health began gradually to fail, but in her mind there was evidently at work some slow revolution. Her visionary abstractions were less frequent; when they occurred, less prolonged. There was no longer in her soft face that celestial serenity which spoke her content in her dreams, but often a look of anxiety and trouble. She was even more silent than before; but when she did speak, there were now evident some struggling gleams of memory. She startled us, at times, by a distinct allusion to the events and scenes of her early childhood. More than once she spoke of commonplace incidents and mere acquaintances at L——. At last she seemed to recognize Mrs. Ashleigh as her mother; but me, as Allen Fenwick, her betrothed, her bridegroom, no! Once or twice she spoke to me of her beloved as of a stranger to myself, and asked me not to deceive her—should she ever see him again? There was one change in this new phase of her state that wounded me to the quick. She had always previously seemed to welcome my presence; now there were hours, sometimes days together, in which my presence was evidently painful to her. She would become agitated when I stole into her room—make signs to me to leave her—grow yet more disturbed if I did not immediately obey, and become calm again when I was gone.

Faber sought constantly to sustain my courage and administer to my hopes by reminding me of the prediction he had hazarded—viz., that through some malady to the frame the reason would be ultimately restored.

He said, "Observe! her mind was first roused from its slumber by the affectionate, unconquered impulse of her heart. You were absent—the storm alarmed her—she missed you—feared for you. The love within her, not alienated, though latent, drew her thoughts into definite human tracks. And thus, the words that you tell me she uttered when you appeared before her were words of love, stricken, though as yet irregularly, as the winds strike the harp-strings, from chords of awakened memory. The same unwonted excitement, together with lengthened exposure to the cold night-air, will account for the shock to her physical system, and the languor and waste of strength by which it has been succeeded.

"Ay, and the Shadow that we *both* saw within the threshold. What of that?"

"Are there no records on evidence, which most physicians of very extended practice will perhaps allow that their experience more or less tends to confirm—no records of the singular coincidences between individual impressions which are produced by sympathy? Now, whether you or your Lilian were first haunted by this Shadow I know not. Perhaps before it appeared to you in the wizard's chamber, it had appeared to her by the Monks' Well. Perhaps, as it came to you in the prison, so it lured her through the solitudes, associating its illusory guidance with dreams of you. And again, when she saw it within your threshold, your phantasy, so abruptly invoked, made you see with the eyes of your Lilian! Does this doctrine of sympathy, though by that very mystery you two loved each other at first—though, without it, love at first sight were in itself an incredible miracle,—does, I say, this doctrine of sympathy seem to you inadmissible? Then nothing is left for us but to revolve the conjecture I before threw out. Have certain organizations like that of Margrave the power to impress, through space, the imaginations of those over whom they have forced a control? I know not. But if they have, it is not supernatural; it is but one of those operations in Nature so rare and exceptional, and of which testimony and evidence are so imperfect and so liable to superstitious illusions, that they have not yet been traced—as, if truthful, no doubt they can be, by the patient genius of science—to one of those secondary causes by which the Creator ordains that Nature shall act on Man."

By degrees I became dissatisfied with my conversations with Faber. I yearned for explanations; all guesses but bewildered me more. In his family, with one exception, I found no congenial association. His nephew seemed to me an ordinary specimen of a very trite human nature—a young man of limited ideas, fair moral tendencies, going mechanically right where not tempted to wrong. The same desire of gain which had urged him to gamble and speculate when thrown in societies rife with such example, led him, now in the Bush, to healthful, industrious, persevering labor. *Spes fovet agricolas*, says the poet; the same Hope which entices the fish to the hook, impels the plough of the husbandman. The young farmer's young wife was somewhat superior to him; she had more refinement of taste, more culture of mind, but, living in his life, she was inevitably levelled to his ends and pursuits. And, next to the babe in the cradle, no object seemed to her so important as that of guarding the sheep from the scab and the dingoes. I was amazed to see how quietly a man whose mind was so stored by life and by books as that of Julius Faber—a man who had loved the clash of conflicting intellects, and acquired the rewards of fame—could accommodate himself to the cabined range of his kinsfolks' half-civilized existence, take interest in their trivial talk, find varying excitement in the monotonous household of a peasant-like farmer. I could not help saying as much to him once. "My friend," replied the old man, "believe me that the happiest art of intellect, however lofty, is that which enables it to be cheerfully at home with the Real!"

The only one of the family in which Faber was domesticated in whom I found an interest, to whose talk I could listen without fatigue, was the child Amy. Simple though she was in language, patient of labor as the most laborious, I recognized in her a quiet nobleness of sentiment, which exalted above the commonplace the acts of her commonplace life. She had no precocious intellect, no enthusiastic fancies, but she had an exquiste activity of heart. It was her heart that animated her sense of duty, and made duty a sweetness and a joy. She felt to the core the kindness of those around her; exaggerated with the warmth of her gratitude, the claims which that kindness imposed. Even for the blessing of life, which she shared with all creation, she felt as if singled out by the undeserved favor of the Creator, and thus was filled with religion because she was filled with love.

My interest in this child was increased and deepened by my saddened and not wholly unremorseful remembrance of the night on which her sobs had pierced my ear—the night from which I secretly dated the mysterious agencies that had wrenched from their proper field and career both my mind and my life. But a gentler interest endeared her to my thoughts in the pleasure that Lilian felt in her visits, in the affectionate intercoruse that sprang up between the afflicted sufferer and the harmless infant. Often when we failed to comprehend some meaning which Lilian evidently wished to convey to us—*we*, her mother and her husband—she was understood with as much ease by Amy, the unlettered child, as by Faber, the gray-haired thinker.

"How is it—how is it?" I asked, impatently and jealously, of Faber. "Love is said to interpret where wisdom fails, and you, yourself, talk of the marvels which sympathy may effect between lover and beloved; yet when, for days together, I cannot succeed in unravelling Lilian's wish or her thought—and her own mother is eqally in fault—you or Amy, closeted alone with her for five minutes, comprehend and are comprehended."

"Allen," answered Faber, "Amy and I believe in spirit, and she, in whom mind is dormant but spirit awake, feels in such belief a sympathy which she has not, in that respect, with yourself nor even with her mother. You seek only through your mind to conjecture hers. Her mother has sense clear enough where habitual experience can guide it, but that sense is confused, and forsakes her when forced from the regular pathway in which it has been accustomed to tread. Amy and I, through soul guess at soul, and though mostly contented with earth, we can both rise at times into heaven. We pray."

"Alas!" I, said, half mournfully, half angrily: "when you thus speak of Mind as distinct from Soul, it was only in that Vision which you bid me regard as the illusion of a fancy stimulated by chemical vapors, producing on the brain an effect similar to that of opium or the inhalation of the oxide gas, that I have ever seen the silver spark of the Soul, distinct from the light of the Mind. And holding, as I do, that all intellectual ideas are derived from the experiences of the body, whether I accept the theory of Locke, or that of Condillac, or that into which their propositions reach their final development in the wonderful subtlety of Hume, I cannot detect the immaterial spirit in the material substance—much less follow its escape from the organic matter in which the principle of thought ceases with the principle of life. When the metaphysician, contending for the immortality of the thinking faculty, analyzes Mind, his analysis comprehends the mind of the brute, nay, of the insect, as well as that of man. Take Reid's definition of Mind, as the most comprehensive which I can at the moment remember: 'By the mind of a man, we understand that in him which thinks, remembers, reasons, and wills.' But this definition only distinguishes the mind of man from that of the brute by superiority in the same attributes, and not by attributes denied to the brute. An animal, even an insect thinks, remembers, reasons, and wills.*

"Few naturalists will now support the doctrine that all the mental operations of brute or insect are to be exclusively referred to instincts; and, even if they do, the word instinct is a very vague word—loose and large enough to cover an abyss which our knowledge has not sounded. And, indeed, in proportion as an animal, like the dog, becomes cultivated by intercourse, his instincts grow weaker, and his ideas, formed by experience (viz. his mind), more developed, often to the conquest of the instincts themselves. Hence, with his usual candor, Dr. Abercrombie—in contending 'that everything mental ceases to exist after death, when we know that everything corporeal continues to exist, is a gratuitous assumption contrary to every rule of philosophical inquiry,'—feels compelled, by his reasoning, to admit the probability of a future life even to the lower animals. His words are: 'To this mode of reasoning it has been objected that it would go to establish an immaterial principle in the lower animals, which in them exhibits many of the phenomena of mind. I have only to answer, Be it so. There are in the lower animals many of the phenomena of mind, and with regard to these, we also contend that they are entirely distinct from anything we know of the properties of matter, which is all that we mean, or can mean, by being immaterial.'* Am I then driven to admit that if man's mind is immaterial and imperishable, so also is that of the ape and the ant?"

"I own," said Faber, with his peculiar smile, arch and genial, "that if I were compelled to make that admission, it would not shock my pride. I do not presume to set any limit to the goodness of the Creator; and

* "Are intelligence and instinct, thus differing in their relative proportion in man as compared with all other animals, yet the same in kind and manner of operation in both? To this question we must give at once an affirmative answer. The expression of Cuvier, regarding the faculty of reasoning in lower animals, 'Leur intelligence exécute des opérations du même genre,' is true in its full sense. We can in no manner define reason so as to exclude acts which are at every moment present to our observation, and which we find in many instances to contravene the natural instincts of the species. The demeanor and acts of the dog in reference to his master, or the various uses to which he is put by man, are as strictly logical as those we witness in the ordinary transactions of life."—(Sir Henry Holland, chapters on Mental Physiolooy, p. 220.) The whole of the chapter on Instincts and Habits in this work should be read in connection with the passage just quoted. The work itself, at once cautious and suggestive, is not one of the least obligations which philosophy and religion alike owe to the lucubrations of English medical men.

* Abercrombie's Intellectual Powers, p. 26. 15th Edition.

should be as humbly pleased as the Indian, if in

> '——yonder sky,
> My faithful dog should bear me company.'

You are too familiar with the works of that Titan in wisdom and error, Descartes, not to recollect the interesting correspondence between the urbane philosopher and our combative countryman, Henry More,* on this very subject; in which certainly More has the best of it when Descartes insists on reducing what he calls the soul (l'âme) of brutes into the same kind of machines as man constructs from inorganized matter. The learning, indeed, lavished on the insoluble question involved in the psychology of the inferior animals, is a proof at least of the all-inquisitive, redundant spirit of man.† We have almost a literature in itself devoted to endeavors to interpret the language of brutes.‡ Dupont de Nemours has discovered that dogs talk in vowels, using only two consonants, G, Z, when they are angry. He asserts that cats employ the same vowels as dogs; but their language is more affluent in consonants, including M, N, B, R, V, F. How many laborious efforts have been made to define and to construe the song of the nightingale! One version of that song by Beckstein, the naturalist, published in 1840, I remember to have seen. And I heard a lady, gifted with a singularly charming voice, chant the mysterious vowels with so exquisite a pathos, that one could not refuse to believe her when she declared that she fully comprehended the bird's meaning, and gave to the nightingale's warble the tender interpretation of her own woman's heart.

"But leaving all such discussions to their proper place amongst the Curiosities of Literature, I come in earnest to the question you have so earnestly raised; and to me the distinction between man and the lower animals in reference to a spiritual nature designed for a future existence, and the mental operations whose uses are bounded to an existence on earth, seems ineffaceably clear. Whether ideas or even perceptions be innate or all formed by experience is a speculation for methaphysicians, which, so far as it affects the question of an immaterial principle, I am quite willing to lay aside. I can well understand that a materiallst may admit innate ideas in Man, as he must admit them in the instinct of brutes, tracing them to hereditary predispositions. On the other hand, we know that the most devout believers in our spiritual nature have insisted, with Locke, in denying any idea, even of the Deity, to be innate.

"But here comes my argument. I care not how ideas are formed—the material point is, how are the *capacities to receive ideas formed?* The ideas may all come from experience, but the capacity to receive the ideas must be inherent. I take the word capacity as a good plain English word, rather than the more technical word 'receptivity,' employed by Kant. And by capacity I mean the passive power * to receive ideas, whether in man or in any living thing by which ideas are received. A man and an elephant is each formed with capacities to receive ideas suited to the several place in the universe held by each.

"The more I look through nature the more I find that on all varieties of organized life is carefully bestowed the *capacity* to receive the impressions, be they called perceptions or ideas, which are adapted to the uses each creature is intended to derive from them. I find, then, that Man alone is endowed with the capacity to receive the ideas of a God, of Soul, of Worship, of a Hereafter. I see no trace of such a capacity in the inferior races; nor, however their intelligence may be refined by culture, is such capacity ever apparent in them.

"But wherever capacities to receive impressions are sufficiently general in any given species of creature to be called universal to that species, and yet not given to another species, then, from all analogy throughout Nature, those capacities are surely designed by Providence for the distinct use and con-

* Œuvres de Descartes, vol. x. p. 178, et seq. (Cousin's Edition.)

† M. Tissot, the distinguished Professor of Philosophy at Dijon, in his recent work, La Vie dans l'Homme, p. 255, gives a long and illustrious list of philosophers who assign a rational soul (l'âme) to the inferior animals, though he truly adds, "that they have not always the courage of their opinion."

‡ Some idea of the extent of research and imagination bestowed on this subject may be gleaned from the sprightly work of Pierquin de Gemblouz, Idiomologie des Animaux, published at Paris, 1844.

* "Faculty is active power; capacity is passive power."—Sir W. Hamilton, Lectures on Metaphysics and Logic, vol. i. p. 178.

servation of the species to which they are given.

"It is no answer to me to say that the inherent capacities thus bestowed on Man do not suffice in themselves to make him form right notions of a Deity or a Hereafter; because it is plainly the design of Providence that Man must learn to correct and improve all his notions by his own study and observation. He must build a hut before he can build a Parthenon; he must believe with the savage or the heathen before he can believe with the philosopher or Christian. In a word, in all his capacities, Man has only given to him, not the immediate knowledge of the Perfect, but the means to strive towards the Perfect. And thus one of the most accomplished of modern reasoners, to whose lectures you must have listened with delight in your college days, says well: 'Accordingly, the sciences always studied with keenest interest are those in a state of progress and uncertainty; absolute certainty and absolute completion would be the paralysis of any study, and the last worst calamity that could befall Man, as he is at present constituted, would be that full and final possession of speculative truth which he now vainly anticipates as the consummation of his intellectual happiness.' *

"Well, then, in all those capacities for the reception of impressions from external Nature which are given to Man and not to the brutes, I see the evidence of Man's soul. I can understand why the inferior animal has no capacity to receive the idea of a Deity and of Worship—simply because the inferior animal, even if graciously admited to a future life, may not therein preserve the sense of its identity. I can understand even why that sympathy with each other which we men possess, and which constitutes the great virtue we emphatically call humanity, is not possessed by the lesser animals (or, at least, in a very rare and exceptional degree) even where they live in communities, like beavers, or bees, or ants; because men are destined to meet, to know, and to love each other in the life to come, and the bond between the brutes ceases here.

"Now the more, then, we examine the inherent capacities bestowed distinctly and solely on Man, the more they seem to distinguish him from the other races by their comprehension of objects beyond his life upon this earth. 'Man alone,' says Müller, 'can conceive abstract notions:' and it is in abstract notions—such as time, space, matter, spirit, light, form, quantity, essence—that man grounds, not only all philosophy, all science, but all that practically improves one generation for the benefit of the next. And why? Because all these abstract notions unconsciously lead the mind away from the material into the immaterial—from the present into the future. But if man ceases to exist when he disappears in the grave, you must be compelled to affirm that he is the only creature in existence whom Nature or Providence has condescended to deceive and cheat by capacities for which there are no available objects. How nobly and how truly has Chalmers said: 'What inference shall we draw from this remarkable law in Nature that there is nothing waste and nothing meaningless in the feelings and faculties wherewith living creatures are endowed? For each desire there is a counterpart object; for each faculty there is room and opportunity for exercise, either in the present or the coming futurity. Now, but for the doctrine of immortality, Man would be an exception to this law—he would stand forth as an anomaly in Nature, with aspirations in his heart for which the universe had no antitype to offer, with capacities of understanding and thought that never were to be followed by objects of corresponding greatness through the whole history of his being!

* * * * *

"'With the inferior animals there is a certain squareness of adjustment, if we may so term it, between each desire and its correspondent gratification. The one is evenly met by the other, and there is a fuluess and definiteness of enjoyment up to the capacity of enjoyment. Not so with Man who, both from the vastness of his propensities and the vastness of his powers, feels himself chained and beset in a field too narrow for him. He alone labors under the discomfort of an incongruity between his circumstances and his powers; and unless there be new circumstances awaiting him in a more advanced state of being, he, the noblest of Nature's products here, would turn out to be the greatest of her failures.' *

* Sir W. Hamilton's Lectures, vol. i. p. 10.

* Chalmers, Bridgewater Treatise, vol. ii. pp. 28, 30. Perhaps I should observe, that here and elsewhere in

"This, then, I take to be the proof of Soul in Man, not that he has a mind—because, as you justly say, inferior animals have that, though in a lesser degree—but because he has the capacities to comprehend, as soon as he is capable of any abstract ideas whatsoever, the very truths not needed for self-conservation on earth, and therefore not given to yonder ox and opossum—viz. the nature of Deity—Soul—Hereafter. And in the recognition of these truths, the Human society, that excels the society of beavers, bees, and ants, by perpetual and progressive improvement on the notions inherited from its progenitors, rests its basis. Thus, in fact, this world is benefited for men hy their belief in the next, while the society of brutes remains age after age the same. Neither the bee nor the beaver has, in all probability, improved since the Deluge.

"But, inseparable from the conviction of these truths is the impulse of prayer and worship. It does not touch my argument when a philosopher of the school of Bolingbroke or Lucretius says, 'that the origin of prayer is in Man's ignorance of the phenomena of Nature.' That it is fear or ignorance which, 'when rocked the mountains or when groaned the ground, taught the weak to bend, the proud to pray,' my answer is—the brutes are much more forcibly impressed by natural phenomena than Man is; the bird and the beast know before you and I do when the mountain will rock and the ground groan, and their instinct leads them to shelter; but it does not lead them to prayer. If my theory be right that Soul is to be sought not in the question whether mental ideas be innate or formed by experience, by that sense, by association or habit, but in the *inherent capacity* to receive ideas,—then, the capacity bestowed on Man alone, to be impressed by Nature herself with the idea of a Power superior to Nature, with which Power he can establish commune, is a proof that to Man alone the Maker has made Nature itself proclaim His existence—that to Man alone the Deity vouchsafes the communion with Himself which comes from prayer.

"Even were this so," said I, "is not the Creator omniscient? if all-wise, all-foreseeing? If all-foreseeing, all-preordaining? Can the prayer of His creature alter the ways of His will?"

"For the answer to a question," returned Faber, "which is not unfrequently asked by the clever men of the world, I ought to refer you to the skilled theologians who have so triumphantly carried the reasoner over that ford of doubt which is crossed every day by the infant. But as we have not their books in the wilderness, I am contented to draw my reply as a necessary and logical sequence from the propositions I have sought to ground on the plain observation of Nature. I can only guess at the Deity's Omniscience, or His modes of enforcing His power, by the observation of His general laws; and of all His laws, I know of none more general than the impulse which bids men pray—which makes Nature so act, that all the phenomena of Nature, we can conceive, however startling and inexperienced, do not make the brute pray; but there is not a trouble that can happen to Man, but what his impulse is to pray,—always provided, indeed, that he is not a philosopher. I can say this in scorn of the philosopher, to whose wildest guess our obligations are infinite, but simply because for all which is impulsive to Man, there is a reason in Nature which no philosophy can explain away. I do not, then bewilder myself by seeking to bind and limit the Omniscience of the Deity to my finite ideas. I content myself with supposing that, somehow or other, He has made it quite compatible with His Omniscience that Man should obey the impulse which leads him to believe that, in addressing a Deity, he is addressing a tender, compassionate, benignant Father, and in that obedience shall obtain beneficial results. If that impulse be an illusion, then we must say that Heaven governs the earth by a lie; and that is impossible, because, reasoning by analogy, all Nature is truthful—that is, Nature gives to no species instincts or impulses which are not of service to it. Should I not be a shallow physician if, where I find in the human organization a principle or a property so general that I must believe it normal to the healthful conditions of that organization, I should refuse to admit that Nature intended it for use?

"Reasoning by all analogy, must I not say the habitual neglect of its use must more or

the dialogues between Faber and Fenwick, it has generally been thought better to substitute the words of the author quoted for the mere outline or purport of the quotation which memory afforded to the interlocutor.

less injure the harmonious wellbeing of the whole human system? I could have much to add upon the point in dispute by which the creed implied in your question would enthral the Divine mercy by the necessities of its Divine wisdom, and substitute for a benignant Deity a relentless Fate. But here I should exceed my province. I am no theologian. Enough for me that in all my afflctions, all my perplexities, an impulse, that I obey as an instinct, moves me at once to prayer. Do I find by experience that the prayer is heard, that the affliction is removed, the doubt is solved? That, indeed, would be presumptuous to say. But it is not presumptuous to think that by the efficacy of prayer my heart becomes more fortified against the sorrow, and my reason more serene amidst the doubt."

I listened, and ceased to argue. I felt as if in that solitude, and in the pause of my wonted mental occupations, my intellect was growing languid, and its old weapons rusting in disuse. My pride took alarm. I had so from my boyhood cherished the idea of fame, and so glorified the search after knowledge, that I recoiled in dismay from the thought that I had relinquished knowledge, and cut myself off from fame. I resolved to resume my once favorite philosophical pursuits, re-examine and complete the Work to which I had once committed my hopes of renown; and, simultaneously, a restless desire seized me to communicate, though but at brief intervals, with other minds than those immediately within my reach—minds fresh from the old world, and reviving the memories its vivid civilization. Emigrants frequently passed my doors, but I had hitherto shrunk from tendering the hospitalities so universally accorded in the colony. I could not endure to expose to such rough strangers my Lilian's mournful affliction, and that thought was not less intolerable to Mrs. Ashleigh.

I now hastily constructed a log-building a few hundred yards from the house, and near the main track taken by travellers through the spacious pastures. I transported to this building my books and scientific instruments. In an upper storey I placed my telescopes and lenses, my crucibles and retorts. I renewed my chemical experiments—I sought to invigorate my mind by other branches of science which I had hitherto less cultured—meditated new theories on Light and Color—collected specimens in Natural History — subjected animalcules to my microscope—geological fossils to my hammer. With all these quickened occupations of thought, I strove to distract myself from sorrow, and strengthen my reason against the illusions of my fantasy. The Luminous Shadow was not seen again on my wall, and the thought of Margrave himself was banished.

In this building I passed many hours of each day; more and more earnestly plunging my thoughts into the depths of abstract study, as Lilian's unaccountable dislike to my presence became more and more decided. When I thus ceased to think that my life cheered and comforted hers, my heart's occupation was gone. I had annexed to the apartment reserved for myself in this log-hut a couple of spare rooms, in which I could accommodate passing strangers. I learned to look forward to their coming with interest, and to see them depart with regret; yet, for the most part, they were of the ordinary class of colonial adventurers: bankrupt tradesmen, unlucky farmers, forlorn mechanics, hordes of unskilled laborers, now and then a briefless barrister, or a sporting collegian who had lost his all on the Derby. One day, however, a young man of education and manners that unmistakably proclaimed the cultured gentleman of Europe, stopped at my door. He was a cadet of a noble Prussian family, which for some political reasons had settled itself in Paris; there he had become intimate with young French nobles, and, living the life of a young French noble, had soon scandalized his German parents, forstalled his slender inheritance, and been compelled to fly his father's frown and his tailor's bills. All this he told me with a lively frankness which proved how much the wit of a German can be quickened in the atmosphere of Paris.

An old college friend, of birth inferior to his own, had been as unfortunate in seeking to make money as this young prodigal had been an adept in spending it. The friend, a few years previously, had accompanied other Germans in a migration to Australia, and was already thriving; the spendthrift noble was on his way to join the bankrupt trader, at a German settlement fifty miles distant from my house. This young man was unlike any German I ever met. He had all the exquisite levity by which the well-bred Frenchman gives to the doctrines of the Cynic the grace of the Epicurean. He owned himself to be good for nothing with an elegance of candor which not only disarmed censure, but seemed to challenge admiration; and, withal, the happy spendthrift was so inebriate with hope —sure that he should be rich before he was thirty, How and wherefore rich?—he could have no more explained than I can square a circle. When the grand serious German nature does Frenchify itself, it can become so extravagantly French!

I listened, almost enviously, to this light-hearted profligate's babble, as we sat by my rude fireside—I, sombre man of science and sorrow, he, smiling child of idleness and pleasure, so much one of Nature's courtier-like nobles, that there, as he smoked his villanous pipe, in his dust-soiled shabby garments, and with his ruffianly revolver stuck into his belt, I would defy the daintiest Aristarch who ever presided as critic over the holiday world not to have said, "There smiles the genius beyond my laws, the born darling of the Graces, who in every circumstance, in every age, like Aristippus, would have socially charmed—would have been welcome to the orgies of a Cæsar or a Clodius, to the boudoirs of a Montespan or a Pompadour—have lounged through the Mulberry Gardens with a Rochester and a Buckingham, or smiled from the death-cart, with a Richelieu and a Lauzun, a gentleman's disdain of a mob!"

I was so thinking as we sat, his light talk frothing up from his careless lips, when suddenly from the spray and the sparkle of that light talk was flung forth the name of Margrave.

"Margrave!" I exclaimed. "Pardon me. What of him?"

"What of him! I asked if, by chance, you knew the only Englishman I ever had the meanness to envy?"

"Perhaps you speak of one person, and I thought of another."

"*Pardieu*, my dear host, there can scarcely be two Margrave's! The one of whom I speak flashed like a metoer upon Paris, bought from a prince of the Bourse a palace that might have lodged a prince of the blood-royal, eclipsed our Jew bankers in splendor, our *jeunesse dorée* in good looks and hair-brain adventures, and, strangest of all, filled his *salons* with philosophers and charlatans, chemists and spirit-rappers; insulting the gravest dons of the schools by bringing them face to face with the most impudent quacks, the most ridiculous dreamers—and yet, withal, himself so racy and charming, so *bon prince*, so *bon enfant!* For six months he was the rage at Paris: perhaps he might have continued to be the rage there for six years, but all at once the metoer vanished as suddenly as it had flashed. Is this the Margrave whom you know!"

"I should not have thought the Margrave whom I knew could have reconciled his tastes to the life of cities."

"Nor could this man: cities were too tame for him. He has gone to some far-remote wilds in the East—some say in search of the Philosopher's Stone; for he actually maintained in his house a Sicilian adventurer, who, when at work on that famous discovery, was stifled by the fumes of his own crucible. After that misfortune, Margrave took Paris in disgust, and we lost him."

"So this is the only Englishman whom you envy! Envy him? Why?"

"Because he is the only Englishman I ever met who contrived to be rich and yet free from the spleen; I envied him because one had only to look at his face and see how thoroughly he enjoyed the life of which your countrymen seem to be so heartily tired! But now that I have satisfied your curiosity, pray satisfy mine. Who and what is this Englishman?"

"Who and what was he supposed at Paris to be?"

"Conjecures were numberless. One of your countrymen suggested that which was most generally favored. This gentleman, whose name I forget, bnt who was one of those old *roués* who fancy themselves young because they live with the young, no sooner set eyes upon Margrave, than he exclaimed, 'Louis Grayle come to life again, as I saw him forty-four years ago! But no—still younger, still handsomer—it must be his son!'"

"Louis Grayle, who was said to be murdered at Aleppo?"

"The same. That strange old man was enormously rich; but it seems that he hated his lawful heirs, and left behind him a fortune so far below that which he was known to possess, that he must certainly have disposed of it secretly before his death. Why so dispose, if not to enrich some natural son, whom, for private reasons, he might not have wished to acknowledge, or point out to the world by the signal bequest of his will? All that Margrave ever said of himself and the source of his wealth confirmed this belief. He frankly proclaimed himself a natural son, enriched by a father whose name he knew not nor cared to know."

"It is true. And Margrave quitted Paris for the East. When?"

"I can tell you the date within a day or two, for his flight preceded mine by a week; and, happily, all Paris was so busy in talking of it, that I slipped away without notice."

And the Prussian then named a date which it thrilled me to hear, for it was in that very month, and about that very day, that the Luminous Shadow and stood within my threshold.

The young Count now struck off into other subjects of talk; nothing more was said of Margrave. An hour or two afterwards he went on his way, and I remained long gazing musingly on the embers of the fire dying low on my hearth.

CHAPTER LXXIV.

My Work, my Philosophical Work—the ambitious hope of my intellectual life—how eagerly I returned to it again! Far away from my household grief, far away from my haggard perplexities—neither a Lilian nor a Margrave there!

As I went over what I had before written, each link in its chain of reasoning seemed so serried, that to alter one were to derange all: and the whole reasoning was so opposed to the possibility of the wonders I myself had experienced, so hostile to the subtle hypotheses of a Faber, or the childlike belief of an Amy, that I must have destroyed the entire work if I had admitted such contradictions to its design!

But the Work was I myself!—I, in my solid, sober, healthful mind, before the brain had been perplexed by a phantom. Were phantoms to be allowed as testimonies against science? No; in returning to my Book, I returned to my former Me!

How strange is that contradiction between our being as man and our being as Author! Take any writer enamoured of a system—a thousand things may happen to him every day which might shake his faith in that syetem; and while he moves about as mere man, his faith *is* shaken. But when he settles himself back into the phase of his being as author, the mere act of taking pen in hand and smoothing the paper before him, restores his speculations to their ancient mechanical train. The system, the beloved system, re-asserts its tyrannic sway, and he either ignores, or moulds into fresh proofs of his theory as author, all which, an hour before, had given his theory the lie in his living perceptions as man.

I adhered to my system;—I continued my work. Here, in the barbarous desert, was a link between me and the Cities of Europe. All else might break down under me. The love I had dreamed of was blotted out from the world and might never be restored; my heart might be lonely, my life be an exile's. My reason might, at last, give way before the spectres which awed my senses, or the sorrows which stormed my heart. But here, at least, was a monument of my rational thoughtful Me—of my individualized identity in multiform creation. And my mind, in the noon of its force, would shed its light on the earth when my form was resolved to its elements. Alas! in this very yearning for the Hereafter, though but the Hereafter of a Name, could I see only the craving of Mind, and hear not the whisper of Soul!

The avocation of a colonist, usually so active, had little interest for me. This vast territorial lordship, in which, could I have endeared its possession by the hopes that animate a Founder, I should have felt all the zest and the pride of ownership, was but the run of a common to the passing emigrant, who would leave no son to inherit the tardy products of his labor. I was not goaded to industry by the stimulus of need. I could only be ruined if I risked all my capital in the attempt to improve. I lived, therefore, amongst my fertile pastures, as careless of culture as the English occupant of the Highland moor, which he rents for the range of its solitudes.

I knew, indeed, that if ever I became avaricious, I might swell my modest affluence into absolute wealth. I had revisited the spot in which I had discovered the nugget of gold, and had found the precious metal in rich abundance just under the first coverings of the alluvial soil. I concealed my discovery from all. I knew that, did I proclaim it, the charm of my bushlife would be gone. My fields would be infested by all the wild adventurers who gather to gold as the vultures of prey round a carcase; my servants would desert me, my very flocks would be shepherdless!

Months again rolled on months. I had just approached the close of my beloved Work, when it was again suspended, and by an anguish keener than all which I had previously known.

Lilian became alarmingly ill. Her state of health, long gradually declining, had hitherto admitted chequered intervals of improvement, and exhibited no symptoms of actual danger. But now she was seized with a kind of chronic fever, attended with absolute privation of sleep, an aversion to even the lightest nourishment, and an acute nervous susceptibility to all the outward impressions of which she had long seemed so unconscious; morbidly alive to the faintest sound, shrinking from the light as from a torture. Her previous impatience at my entrance into her room became aggravated into vehement emotions, convulsive paroxysms of distress; so that Faber banished me from her chamber, and, with a heart bleeding at every fibre, I submitted to the cruel sentence.

Faber had taken up his abode in my house and brought Amy with him; one or the other never left Lilian, night or day. The great physician spoke doubtfully of the case, but not despairingly.

"Remember," he said, "that in spite of the want of sleep, the abstinence from food, the form has not wasted as it would do were this fever inevitably mortal. It is upon that phenomenon I build a hope that I have not been mistaken in the opinion I hazarded from the first. We are now in the midst of the critical struggle between life and reason; if she preserve the one, my conviction is that she will regain the other. The seeming antipathy to yourself is a good omen. You are inseparably associated with her intellectual world; in proportion as she revives to it, must become vivid and powerful the reminiscences of the shock that annulled, for a time, that world to her. So I welcome, rather than fear, the over-susceptibility of the awakening senses to external sights and sounds. A few days will decide if I am right. In this climate the progress of acute maladies is swift, but the recovery from them is yet more startlingly rapid. Wait—endure—be prepared to submit to the will of Heaven; but do not despond of its mercy."

I rushed away from the consoler—away into the thick of the forests, the heart of solitude. All around me, there, was joyous with life; the locust sang amidst the herbage; the cranes gamboled on the banks of the creek; the squirrel-like opposums frolicked on the feathery boughs. "And what," said I to myself—"what if that which seems so fabulous in the distant being whose existence has bewitched my own, be substantially true? What if to some potent medicament Margrave owes his glorious vitality, his radiant youth? Oh! that I had not so disdainfully turned away from his hinted solicitations—to what?—to nothing guiltier than lawful experiment. Had I been less devoted a bigot to this vain schoolcraft, which we call the Medical Art, and which, alone in this age of science, has made no perceptible progress since the days of its earliest teachers—had I said, in the true humility of genuine knowledge, 'these alchemists were men of genius and thought; we owe to them nearly all the grand hints of our chemical science—it is likely that they would have been wholly drivellers and idiots in the one faith they clung to the most?'—had I said that, I might now have no fear of losing my Lilian. Why, after all, should there not be in Nature one primary essence, one master substance, in which is stored the specific nutriment of life?"

Thus incoherently muttering to the woods what my pride of reason would not have suffered me gravely to say to my fellow-men, I fatigued my tormented spirits into a gloomy calm, and mechanically retraced my steps at the decline of day. I seated myself at the door of my solitary log-hut, leaning my cheek upon my hand, and musing. Wearily I looked up, roused by a discord of clattering hoofs and lumbering wheels on the hollow-sounding grass-track. A crazy groaning vehicle, drawn by four horses, emerged from the copse of gum-trees—fast, fast along the road, which no such pompous vehicle had traversed since that which had borne me—luxurious satrap for an early colonist—to my lodge in the wilderness. What emigrant, rich enough to squander in the hire of such an equipage more than its cost in England, could thus be entering on my waste domain? An ominous thrill shot through me.

The driver—perhaps some broken-down son of luxury in the Old World, fit for nothing in the New World but to ply, for hire, the task that might have led to his ruin when plied in sport—stopped at the door of my hut, and called out, "Friend, is not this the great Fenwick Section, and is not yonder long pile of building the Master's house?"

Before I could answer I heard a faint voice, within the vehicle, speaking to the driver; the last nodded, descended from his seat, opened the carriage-door, and offered his arm to a man, who, waving aside the proffered aid, descended slowly and feebly; paused a moment as if for breath, and then, leaning on his staff, walked from the road across the sward rank with luxuriant herbage, through the little gate in the new-set fragrant wattle-fence, wearily, languidly, halting often, till he stood facing me, leaning both wan and emaciated hands upon his staff, and his meagre form shrinking deep within the folds of a cloak lined thick with costly sables. His face was sharp, his complexion of a livid yellow, his eyes shone out from their hollow orbits, unnaturally enlarged and fatally bright. Thus, in ghastly contrast to his former splendor of youth and opulence of life, Margrave stood before me.

"I come to you," said Margrave, in accents hoarse and broken, "from the shores of the East. Give me shelter and rest. I have that to say which will more than repay you."

Whatever, till that moment, my hate and my fear of this unexpected visitant, hate would have been inhumanity, fear a meanness—conceived for a creature so awfully stricken down.

Silently, involuntarily, I led him into the house. There he rested a few minutes, with closed eyes and painful gasps for breath. Meanwhile, the driver brought from the carriage a travelltng-bag and a small wooden chest or coffer, strongly banded with iron clamps. Margrave, looking up as the man drew near, exclaimed fiercely, "Who told you to touch that chest? How dare you? Take it from that man, Fenwick! Place it here—here by my side!"

I took the chest from the driver, whose rising anger, at being so imperiously rated in the land of democratic equality, was appeased by the gold which Margrave lavishly flung to him.

"Take care of the poor gentleman, squire," he whispered to me, in the spontaneous impulse of gratitude—"I fear he will not trouble you long. He must be monstrous rich. Arrived in a vessel hired all to himself, and a train of outlandish attendants, whom he has left behind in the town yonder! May I bait my horses in your stables? They have come a long way."

I pointed to the neighboring stables, and the man nodded his thanks, remounted his box, and drove off.

I returned to Margrave. A faint smile came to his lips as I placed the chest beside him.

"Ay, ay," he muttured. "Safe! safe! I shall soon be well again—very soon! And now I can sleep in peace!"

I led him into an inner room, in which there was a bed. He threw himself on it with a loud sigh of relief. Soon, after raising himself on his elbow, he exclaimed, "The chest—bring it hither! I need it always beside me? There, there! Now for a few hours of sleep; and then, if I can take food, or some such restoring cordial as your skill may suggest, I shall be strong enough to talk. We will talk!—we will talk!"

His eyes closed heavily as his voice fell into a drowsy mutter: a moment more and he was asleep.

I watched beside him, in mingled wonder and compassion. Looking into that face, so altered yet still so young, I could not sternly question what had been the evil of that mystic life, which seemed now oozing away through the last sands in the hour-glass. I placed my hand softly on his pulse: it scarcely beat. I put my ear to his breast, and involuntarily sighed, as I distinguished in its fluttering heave that dull, dumb sound, in which the heart seems knelling inself to the greedy grave!

Was this, indeed, the potent magician whom

I had so feared!—this the guide to the Rosicrucian's secret of life's renewal, in whom, but an hour or two ago, my fancies gulled my credulous trust!

But suddenly, even while thus chiding my wild superstitions, a fear, that to most will seem scarcely less superstitious, shot across me. Could Lilian be affected by the near neighborhood of one to whose magnetic influence she had once been so strangely subjected? I left Margrave still sleeping, closed and locked the door of the hut, went back to my dwelling, and met Amy at the threshold. Her smile was so cheering that I felt at once relieved.

"Hush!" said the child, putting her finger to her lips, "she is so quiet! I was coming in search of you, with a message from her."

"From Lilian to me—what! to me?"

"Hush! About an hour ago, she beckoned me to draw near to her, and then said, very softly; 'Tell Allen, that light is coming back to me, and it all settles on him—on him. Tell him that I pray to be spared to walk by his side on earth, hand-in-hand to that heaven which is no dream, Amy. Tell him that;—no dream!'"

While the child spoke my tears gushed, and the strong hands in which I veiled my face quivered like the leaf of the aspen. And when I could command my voice, I said, plaintively,—

"May I not, then, see hee her?—only for a moment, and answer her message, though but by a look?"

"No, no!"

"No! Where is Faber?"

"Gone into the forest, in search of some herbs, but he gave me this note for you."

I wiped the blinding tears from my eyes, and read these lines:

"I have, though with hesitation, permitted Amy to tell you the cheering words, by which our beloved patient confirms my belief that reason is coming back to her—slowly, laboringly, but if she survive, for permanent restoration. On no account, attempt to precipitate or disturb the work of Nature. As dangerous as a sudden glare of light to eyes long blind and newly regaining vision in the friendly and soothing dark, would be the agitation that your presence at this crisis would cause. Confide in me."

I remained brooding over these lines and over Lilian's message, long and silently, while Amy's soothing whispers stole into my ear, soft as the murmurs of a rill heard in the gloom of forests. Rousing myself at length, my thoughts returned to Margrave. Doubtless he would soon awake. I bade Amy bring me such slight nutriment as I thought best suited to his enfeebled state, telling her it was for a sick traveller, resting himself in my hut. When Amy returned, I took from her the little basket, with which she was charged, and having, meanwhile, made a careful selection from the contents of my medicine-chest, went back to the hut, I had not long resumed my place beside Margrave's pillow before he awoke.

"What o'clock is it?" he asked, with an anxious voice.

"About seven."

"Not later? That is well; my time is precious."

"Compose yourself, and eat."

I placed the food before him, aud he partook of it, though sparingly, and as if with effort. He then dozed for a short time, again woke up and impatiently demanded the cordial, which I had prepared in the meanwhile. Its effect was greater and more immediate than I could have anticipated, proving, perhaps, how much of youth there was still left in his system, however undermined and ravaged by disease. Color came back to his cheek, his voice grew perceptibly stronger. And as I lighted the lamp on the table near us—for it was growing dark—he gathered himself up, and spoke thus:

"You remember that I once pressed on you certain experiments. My object then was to discover the materials from which is extracted the specific that enables the organs of life to expel disease and regain vigor. In that hope, I sought your intimacy. An intimacy you gave, but withdrew."

"Dare you complain? Who and what was the being from whose intimacy I shrunk appalled?"

"Ask what questions you please," cried Margrave, impatiently, "later — if I have strength left to answer them. But do not interrupt me, while I husband my force to say what alone is important to me and to you. Disappointed in the hopes I had placed in you, I resolved to repair to Paris,—that great furnace of all bold ideas. I questioned learned formalists; I listened to audacious empirics. The first, with all their boasted knowledge, were too timid to concede my premises; the second, with all their speculative daring, too knavish to let me trust to their conclusions. I found but one man, a Sicilian, who comprehended the secrets that are called occult, and had the courage to meet Nature and all her agencies face to face. He believed, and sincerely that he was approaching the grand result, at the very moment when he perished from want of the common precautions which a tyro in chemistry would have taken. At his death the gaudy city became hateful; all its pretended pleasures only served to exhaust life the faster. The true joys of youth are those of the wild bird and wild brute, in the healthful enjoyment of Nature. In cities, youth is but old age with a varnish. I fled to the East; I passed through the tents of the Arabs; I was guided—no matter by whom or by what—to the house of a Dervish, who had had for his teacher the most erudite master of secrets occult, whom I knew years ago at Aleppo—why that exclamation?"

"Proceed. What I have to say will come—later."

"From this Dervish I half forced and half purchased the secret I sought to obtain. I now know from what peculiar substance the so-called elixir of life is extracted; I know also the steps of the process through which that task is accomplished. You smile incredulously. What is your doubt? State it while I rest for a moment. My breath labors; give me more of the cordial."

"Need I tell you my doubt? You have, you say, at your command the elixir of life of which Cagliostro did not leave his disciples the recipe; and you stretch out your hand for a vulgar cordial which any village chemist could give you!"

"I can explain this apparent contradiction. The process by which the elixir is extracted from the material which hoards its essence, is one that requires a hardihood of courage which few possess. This Dervish, who had passed through that process once, was deaf to all prayer, and unmoved by all bribes, to attempt it again. He was poor; for the secret by which metals may be transmuted is not, as the old alchemists seem to imply identical with that by which the elixir of life is extracted. He had only been enabled to discover, in the niggard strata of the lands within range of his travel, a few scanty morsels of the glorious substance. From these he had extracted scarcely enough of the elixir to fill a third of that little glass which I have just drained. He guarded every drop for himself. Who that holds healthful life as the one boon above all price to the living, would waste upon others what prolongs and recruits his own being? Therefore, though he sold me his secret, he would not sell me his treasure."

"Any quack may sell you the information how to make not only an elixir, but a sun and a moon, and then scare you from the experiment by tales of the danger of trying it! How do you know that this essence which the Dervish possessed was the elixir of life, since, it seems, you have not tried on yourself what effect its precious drops could produce? Poor wretch! who once seemed to me so awfully potent, do you come to the Antipodes in search of a drug that only exists in the fables by which a child is amused?"

"The elixir of life is no fable," cried Margrave, with a kindling of eye, a power of voice, a dilation of form, that startled me in one just before so feeble. "That elixir was bright in my veins when we last met. From that golden draught of the life-spring of joy I took all that can gladden creation. What sage would not have exchanged his wearisome knowledge for my lusty revels with Nature? What monarch would not have bartered his crown, with its brain-ache of care, for the radiance that circled my brows, flashing out from the light that was in me? Oh again, oh again! to enjoy the freedom of air with the bird, and the glow of the sun with the lizard; to sport through the blooms of the earth, Nature's playmate and darling; to face, in the forest and desert, the pard and the lion,—Nature's bravest and fiercest,—her first-born, the heir of her realm, with the rest of her children for slaves!"

As these words burst from his lips, there was a wild grandeur in the aspect of this enigmatical being which I had never beheld in the former time of his affluent, dazzling youth. And, indeed, in his language, and in the thoughts it clothed, there was an earnestness, a concentration, a directness, a purpose, which had seemed wanting to his desultory talk in the earlier days. I expected that reaction of languor and exhaustion would follow his vehement outbreak of passion; but, after a short pause, he went on with steady accents. His will was sustaining his strength. He was determined to force his convictions on me, and the vitality, once so rich, rallied all its lingering forces to the aid of his intense desire.

"I tell you, then," he resumed, with deliberate calmness, "that, years ago, I tested in my own person that essence which is the sovereign medicament. In me, as you saw me at L——, you beheld the proof of its virtues. Feeble and ill as I am now, my state was incalculably more hopeless when formerly restored by the elixir. He from whom I then took the sublime restorative, died without revealing the secret of its composition. What I obtained was only just sufficient to recruit the lamp of my life, then dying down—and no drop was left for renewing the light which wastes its own rays in the air that it gilds. Though the Dervish would not sell me his treasure, he permitted me to see it. The appearance and odor of this essence are strangely peculiar—unmistakeable by one who has once beheld and partaken of it. In short, I recognized in the hands of the Dervish the bright life-renewer, as I had borne it away from the corpse of the Sage of Aleppo."

"Hold! Are you then, in truth, the murderer of Haroun, and is your true name Louis Grayle?"

"I am no murderer, and Louis Grayle did not leave me his name. I again adjure you to postpone for this night, at least, the questions you wish to address to me.

"Seeing that this obstinate pauper possessed that for which the pale owners of millions, at the first touch of palsy or gout, would consent to be paupers, of course I coveted the possession of the essence even more than the knowledge of the substance from which it is extracted. I had no coward fear of the experiment, which this timid driveller had not the nerve to renew. But still the experiment might fail. I must traverse land and sea to find the fit place for it. While, in the rags of the Dervish, the unfailing result of the experiment was at hand. The Dervish suspected my design—he dreaded my power. He fled on the very night in which I had meant to seize what he refused to sell me. After all, I should have done him no great wrong; for I should have left him wealth enough to transport himself to any soil in which the material for the elixir may be most abundant; and the desire of life would have given his shrinking nerves the courage to replenish its ravished store. I had Arabs in my pay, who obeyed me as hounds their master. I chased the fugitive. I came on his track, reached a house in a miserable village, in which, I was told, he had entered but an hour before. The day was declining—the light in the room imperfect. I saw in a corner what seemed to me the form of the Dervish—stooped to seize it, and my hand closed on an asp. The artful Dervish had so piled his rags that they took the shape of the form they had clothed, and he had left, as a substitute for the giver of life, the venomous reptile of death.

"The strength of my system enabled me to survive the effect of the poison; but during the torpor that numbed me, my Arabs, alarmed, gave no chase to my quarry. At last, though enfeebled and languid, I was again on my horse:—again the pursuit—again the track! I learned—but by this time by a knowledge surer than man's—that the Dervish had taken his refuge in a hamlet that had sprung up over the site of a city once famed through Assyria. The same voice that informed me of his whereabouts warned me not to pursue. I rejected the warning. In my eager impatience I sprang on to the chase; in my fearless resolve I felt sure of the prey. I arrived at the hamlet wearied out, for my forces were no longer the same since the bite of the asp. The Dervish eluded me still; he had left the floors, on which I sank exhausted, but a few minutes before my horse stopped at the door. The carpet, on which he had rested, still lay on the ground. I dismissed the youngest and keenest of my troop in search of the fugitive. Sure that this time he would not escape, my eyes closed in sleep.

"How long I slept I know not—a long dream of solitude, fever, and anguish. Was it the curse of the Dervish's carpet? Was it a taint in the walls of the house, or of the air, which broods sickly and rank over places where cities lie buried? I know not; but the

Pest of the East had seized me in slumber. When my senses recovered I found myself alone, plundered of my arms, dispoiled of such gold as I had carried about me. All had deserted and left me, as the living leave the dead whom the Plague has claimed for its own. As soon as I could stand I crawled from the threshold. The moment my voice was heard, my face seen, the whole squalid populace rose as on a wild beast—a mad dog. I was driven from the place with imprecations and stones, as a miscreant whom the Plague had overtaken while plotting the death of a holy man. Bruised and bleeding, but still defying, I turned in wrath on that dastardly rabble; they slunk away from my path. I knew the land for miles around. I had been in that land years, long years, ago. I came at last to the road which the caravans take on their way to Damascus. There I was found, speechless and seemingly lifeless, by some European travellers. Conveyed to Damascus, I languished for weeks between life and death.

"But for the virtue of that essence, which lingered yet in my veins, I could not have survived—even thus feeble and shattered. I need not say that I now abandoned all thought of discovering the Dervish. I had at least, his secret, if I had failed of the paltry supply he had drawn from its uses. Such appliances as he had told me were needful, are procured in the East with more ease than in Europe. To sum up, I am here, instructed in all the knowledge, and supplied with all the aids, which warrant me in saying, 'Do you care for new life in its richest enjoyments, if not for yourself, for one whom you love and would reprieve from the grave? Then, share with me in a task that a single night will accomplish, and ravish a prize by which the light that you value the most will be saved from the dust and the worm, to live on, ever young, ever blooming, when each infant, new-born while I speak, shall have passed to the grave. Nay, where is the limit to life while the earth hides the substance by which life is renewed?'"

I give as faithfully as I can recall them the words in which Margrave addressed me. But who can guess by cold words transcribed, even were they artfully ranged by a master of language, the effect words produce when warm from the breath of the speaker? Ask one of an audience which some orator held enthralled, why his words do not quicken a beat in the reader's pulse, and the answer of one who had listened will be, "The words took their charm, from the voice and the eye, the aspect, the manner, the man!" So it was with the incomprehensible being before me. Though his youth was faded, though his beauty was dimmed, though my fancies clothed him with memories of abhorrent dread, though my reason opposed his audacious beliefs and assumptions, still he charmed and spell-bound me—still he was the mystical fascinator—still, if the legends of magic had truth for their basis, he was the *born magician;* as genius, in what calling soever, *is* born with the gift to enchant and subdue us.

Constraining myself to answer calmly, I said, "You have told me your story; you have defined the object of the experiment in which you ask me to aid. You do right to bid me postpone my replies or my questions. Seek to recruit by sleep the strength you have so sorely tasked. To-morrow—"

"To-morrow, ere night, you will decide whether the man whom out of all earth I have selected to aid me, shall be the foe to condemn me to perish! I tell you plainly I need your aid, and your prompt aid. Three days from this, and all aid will be too late!"

I had already gained the door of the room, when he called to me to come back.

"You do not live in this hut, but with your family yonder. Do not tell them that I am here; let no one but yourself see me as I now am. Lock the door of the hut when you quit it. I should not close my eyes if I were not secure from intruders."

"There is but one in my house, or in these parts, whom I would except from the interdict you impose. You are aware of your own imminent danger; the life, which you believe the discovery of a Dervish will indefinitely prolong, seems to my eye of physician to hang on a thread. I have already formed my own conjecture as to the nature of the disease that enfeebles you. But I would fain compare that conjecture with the weightier opinion of one whose experience and skill are superior to mine. Permit me, then, when I return to you to-morrow, to bring with me the great physician to whom I refer. His name will not, perhaps, be unknown to you: I speak of Julius Faber."

"A physician of the schools! I can guess well enough how learnedly he would prate, and how little he could do. But I will not object to his visit, if it satisfies you that, since I should die under the hands of the doctors, I may be permitted to indulge my own whim in placing my hopes in a Dervish. Yet stay. You have, doubtless, spoken of me to this Julius Faber, your fellow-physician and friend? Promise me, if you bring him here, that you will not name me—that you will not repeat to him the tale I have told you, or the hope which has led me to these shores. What I have told to you, no matter whether, at this moment, you consider me the dupe of a chimera, is still under the seal of the confidence which a patient reposes in the physician he himself selects for his confidant. I select you, and not Julius Faber!"

"Be it as you will," said I, after a moment's reflection. "The moment you make yourself my patient I am bound to consider what is best for you. And you may more respect, and profit by, an opinion based upon your purely physical condition than by one in which you might suppose the advice was directed rather to the disease of the mind than to that of the body."

"How amazed and indignant your brother-physician will be if he ever see me a second time! How learnedly he will prove that, according to all correct principles of science and nature, I ought to be dead!"

He uttered this jest with a faint dreary echo of his old merry, melodious laugh, then turned his face to the wall; and so I left him to repose.

CHAPTER LXXV.

I FOUND Mrs. Ashleigh waiting for me in our usual sitting-room. She was in tears. She had begun to despond of Lilian's recovery, and she infected me with her own alarm. However, I disguised my participation in her fears, soothed and sustained her as I best could, and persuaded her to retire to rest. I saw Faber for a few minutes before I sought my own chamber. He assured me that there was no perceptible change for the worse in Lilian's physical state since he had last seen me, and that her mind, even within the last few hours, had become decidedly more clear. He thought that, within the next twenty-four hours, the reason would make a strong and successful effort for complete recovery; but he declined to hazard more than a hope that the effort would not exhaust the enfeebled powers of the frame. He himself was so in need of a few hours of rest that I ceased to harass him with questions which he could not answer, and fears which he could not appease. Before leaving him for the night, I told him briefly that there was a traveller in my hut smitten by a disease which seemed to me so grave that I would ask his opinion of the case, if he could accompany me to the hut the next morning.

My own thoughts that night were not such as would suffer me to sleep.

Before Margrave's melancholy state much of my former fear and abhorrence faded away. This being, so exceptional that fancy might well invest him with preternatural attributes, was now reduced by human suffering to human sympathy and comprehension; yet his utter want of conscience was still as apparent as in his day of joyous animal spirits. With what hideous candor he had related his perfidy and ingratitude to the man to whom, in his belief, he owed an inestimable obligation, and with what insensibility to the signal retribution which in most natures would have awakened remorse!

And by what dark hints and confessions did he seem to confirm the incredible memoir of Sir Philip Derval! He owned that he had borne from the corpse of Haroun the medicament to which he ascribed his recovery from a state yet more hopeless than that under which he now labored! He had alluded, rapidly, obscurely, to some knowledge at his command "surer than man's!" And now, even now the mere wreck of his former existence—by what strange charm did he still control and confuse my reason? And how was it that I felt myself murmuring, again and again, "But what, after all, if his hope be no chimera, and if Nuture do hide a secret by which I could save the life of my beloved Lilian?"

And again and again, as that thought would force itself on me, I rose and crept to Lilian's threshold, listening to catch the faintest sound of her breathing. All still, all dark! In that sufferer recognized science detects no mortal disease, yet dares not bid me rely on its amplest resources of skill to turn aside from her slumber the stealthy advance of death; while in yon log-hut one whose malady recognized science could not doubt to be mortal has composed himself to sleep confident of life! Recognized science! recognized ignorance! The science of to-day is the ignorance of to-morrow! Every year some bold guess lights up a truth to which, but the year before, the schoolmen of science were as blinded as moles.

"What then," my lips kept repeating—"what if Nature do hide a secret by which the life of my life can be saved! What do we know of the secrets of Nature? What said Newton himself of his knowledge? 'I am like a child picking up pebbles and shells on the sand, while the great ocean of Truth lies all undiscovered around me!' And did Newton himself, in the ripest growth of his matchless intellect, hold the creed of the alchemists in scorn? Had he not given to one object of their research, in the transmutation of metals, his days and his nights? Is there proof that he ever convinced himself that the research was the dream, which we, who are not Newtons, call it? * And that other great sage, inferior only to Newton—the calculating doubt-weigher, Descartes—had he not believed in the yet nobler hope of the alchemists—believed in some occult nostrum or process by which human life could attain to the age of the Patriarchs?" *

* "Besides the three great subjects of Newton's labors—the fluxional calculus, physical astronomy, and optics—a very large portion of his time, while resident in his college, was devoted to researches of which scarcely a trace remains. Alchemy, which had fascinated so many eager and ambitious minds, seems to have tempted Newton with an overwhelming force. What theories he formed, what experiments he tried, in that laboratory where, it is said, the fire was scarcely extinguished for weeks together, will never be known. It is certain that no success attended his labors; and Newton was not a man—like Kepler—to detail to the world all the hopes and disappointments, all the crude and mystical fancies, which mixed themselves up with his career of philosophy. . . . Many years later we find Newton in correspondence with Locke, with reference to a mysterious red earth by which Boyle, who was then recently dead, had asserted that he could effect the grand desideratum of multiplying gold. By this time, however, Newton's faith had become somewhat shaken by the unsatisfactory communications which he had himself received from Boyle on the subject of the golden recipe, though he did not abandon the idea of giving the experiment a further trial as soon as the weather should become suitable for furnace experiments."—Quarterly Review, No. 220, pp. 125-6.

* Southey, in his Doctor, vol. vi. p. 2, reports the conversation of Sir Kenelm Digby with Descartes, in which the great geometrician said, "That as for rendering man immortal, it was what he could not venture to promise, but that he was very sure he could prolong his life to the standard of the patriarchs." And Southey adds, "that St. Evremond, to whom Digby repeated this, says that this opinion of Descartes was well known both to his friends in Holland and in France." By the stress Southey lays on this hearsay evidence, it is clear that he was not acquainted with the works and biography of Descartes, or he would have gone to the fountain-head for authority on Descartes' opinions—viz., Descartes himself. It is to be wished that Southey had done so, for no one more than he would have appreciated the exquisitely candid and loveable nature of the illustrious Frenchman, and the sincerity with which he cherished in his heart whatever doctrine he conceived in his understanding. Descartes, whose knowledge of anatomy was considerable, had that passion for the art of medicine which is almost inseparable from the pursuit of natural philosophy. At the age of twenty-four he had sought (in Germany) to obtain initiation into the brotherhood of the Rosicrucians, but unluckily could not discover any member of the society to introduce him. "He desired," says Cousin, "to assure the health of man, diminish his ills, extend his existence. He was terrified by the rapid and almost momentary passage of man upon earth. He believed it was not, perhaps, impossible to prolong its duration." There is a hidden recess of grandeur in this idea, and the means proposed by Descartes for the execution of his project were not less grand. In his Discourse on Method, Descartes says, "If it is possible to find some means to render generally men more wise and more able than they have been till now, it is, I believe, in medicine that those means must be sought. * * * I am sure that there is no one, even in the medical profession, who will now avow that all which one knows of the medical art is almost nothing in comparison to that which remains to learn, and that one could be exempted from an infinity of maladies, both of body and mind, and even, perhaps, from the decrepitude of old age, if one had sufficient lore of their causes and of all the remedies which nature provides for them. Therefore, having *design to employ all my life in the research of a science so necessary, and having discovered a path which appears to me such that one ought infallibly, in following to find it*, if one is not hindered prematurely by the brevity of life or by the defects of experience, I consider that there is no better remedy against those two hindrances than to communicate faithfully to the public the little I have found," etc. (Discourse de la Méthode, vol. i. Œuvres de Descartes, Cousin's Edition.) And again, in his Correspondence (vol. ix. p. 341), he says: "The conservation of health has been always the principal object of my studies, and I have no doubt that there is a means of acquiring much knowledge touching medicine which, up to this time, is ignored." He then refers to his meditated Treatise on Animals as only an entrance upon that knowledge. But whatever secrets Descartes may have thought to discover, they are not made known to the public ac-

In thoughts like these the night wore away, the moonbeams that streamed through my window lighting up the spacious solitudes beyond—mead and creek, forest-land, mountain-top—and the silence without broken by the wild cry of the night-hawk and the sibilant melancholy dirge of the shining chrysococyx; * —bird that never sings but at night, and obstinately haunts the roofs of the sick and dying, ominous of woe and death.

But up sprang the sun, and, chasing these gloomy sounds, out burst the wonderful chorus of Australian groves, the great kingfisher opening the jocund melodious babble with the glee of his social laugh.

And now I heard Faber's step in Lilian's room—heard through the door, her soft voice, though I could not distinguish the words. It was not long before I saw the kind physician standing at the threshold of my chamber. He pressed his finger to his lip, and made me a sign to follow him. I obeyed, with noiseless tread and stifled breathing. He awaited me in the garden under the flowering acacias, passed his arm in mine, and drew me into the open pasture-land.

"Compose yourself," he then said; "I bring you tidings both of gladness and of fear. Your Lilian's mind is restored: even the memories which had been swept away by the fever that followed her return to her home in L—— are returning, though as yet indistinct. She yearns to see you, to bless you for all your noble devotion, your generous, great-hearted love; but I forbid such interview now. If, in a few hours, she becomes either decidedly stronger or decidedly more enfeebled, you shall be summoned to her side. Even if you are condemned to a loss for which the sole consolation must be placed in the life hereafter, you shall have, at least, the last mortal commune of soul with soul. Courage —courage! You are man! Bear as man what you have so often bid other men submit to endure."

I had flung myself on the ground—writhing worm that had no home but on earth! Man, indeed! Man! All, at that moment, I took from manhood was its acute sensibility to love and to anguish!

But after all such paroxysms of mortal pain, there comes a strange lull. Thought itself halts, like the still hush of water between two descending torrents. I rose in a calm, which Faber might well mistake for fortitude.

"Well," I said, quietly, "fulfil your promise. If Lilian is to pass away from me, I shall see her, at least, again; no wall, you tell me, between our minds; mind to mind once more—once more!"

"Allen," said Faber, mournfully and softly, "why do you shun to repeat my words—soul to soul?"

"Ay, ay—I understand. Those words mean that you have resigned all hope that Lilian's life will linger here, when her mind comes back in full consciousness; I know well that last lightning flash and the darkness which swallows it up!"

"You exaggerate my fears. I have not resigned the hope that Lilian will survive the struggle through which she is passing, but it will be cruel to deceive you—my hope is weaker than it was."

"Ay, ay. Again, I understand! Your science is in fault—it desponds. Its last trust is in the wonderful resources of Nature—the vitality stored in the young!"

"You have said: Those resources of Nature *are* wondrous. The vitality of youth is a fountain springing up from the deeps out of sight, when, a moment before, we had measured the drops oozing out from the sands, and thought that the well was exhausted."

"Come with me—come. I told you of another sufferer yonder. I want your opinion

cording to the promise. And in a letter to M. Chanut, written 1646 (four years before he died), he says ingenuously: "I will tell you in confidence that the notion, such as it is, which I have endeavored to acquire in physical philosophy, had greatly assisted me to establish certain foundations for moral philosophy; and that I am more easily satisfied upon this point than I am on many others touching medicine, to which I have, nevertheless, devoted much more time. So that" (adds the grand thinker with a pathetic nobleness)—"so that, *instead of finding the means to preserve life, I have found another good, more easy and more sure, which is—not to fear death.*"

* Chrysococyx lucidus—viz., the bird popularly called the shining or bronzed cuckoo. "Its note is an exceedingly melancholy whistle, heard at night, when it is very annoying to any sick or nervous person who may be inclined to sleep. I have known many instances where the bird has been perched on a tree in the vicinity of the room of an invalid uttering its mournful notes, and it was only with the greatest difficulty that it could be dislodged from its position." —Dr. Bennett's Gatherings of a Naturalist in Australasia.

of his case. But can you be spared a few minutes from Lilian's side?"

"Yes; I left her asleep. What is the case that perplexes your eye of physician, which is usually keener than mine, despite all the length of my practice?"

"The sufferer is young—his organization rare in its vigor. He has gone through and survived assaults upon life that are commonly fatal. His system has been poisoned by the fangs of a venomous asp, and shattered by the blast of the plague. These alone, I believe, would not suffice to destroy him. But he is one who has a strong dread of death. And while the heart was thus languid and feeble, it has been gnawed by emotions of hope or of fear. I suspect that he is dying, not from the bite of the reptile, not from the taint of the pestilence, but from the hope and the fear that have overtasked the heart's functions. Judge for yourself."

We were now at the door of the hut. I unlocked it: we entered. Margrave had quitted his bed, and was pacing the room slowly. His step was less feeble, his countenance less haggard than on the previous evening.

He submitted himself to Faber's questioning with a quiet indifference, and evidently cared nothing for any opinion which the great physician might found on his replies.

When Faber had learned all he could, he said, with a grave smile: "I see that my advice will have little weight with you; such as it is, at least reflect on it. The conclusions to which your host arrived in his view of your case, and which he confided to me, are, in my humble judgment, correct. I have no doubt that the great organ of the heart is involved in the cause of your sufferings; but the heart is a noble and much-enduring organ. I have known men in whom it has been more severely and unequivocally affected with disease than it is in you, live on for many years, and ultimately die of some other disorder. But then life was held, as yours must be held, upon one condition—repose. I enjoin you to abstain from all violent action—to shun all excitements that cause moral disturbance. You are young: would you live on, you must live as the old. More than this—it is my duty to warn you that your tenure on earth is very precarious; you may attain to many years; you may be suddenly called hence to-morrow. The best mode to regard this uncertainty with the calm in which is your only chance of long life, is so to arrange all your worldly affairs, and so to discipline all your human anxieties, as to feel always prepared for the summons that may come without warning. For the rest, quit this climate as soon as you can—it is the climate in which the blood courses too quickly for one who should shun all excitement. Seek the most equable atmosphere—choose the most tranquil pursuits—and Fenwick himself, in his magnificent pride of stature and strength, may be nearer the grave than you are."

"Your opinion coincides with that I have just heard?" asked Margrave, turning to me.

"In much—yes."

"It is more favorable than I should have supposed. I am far from disdaining the advice so kindly offered. Permit me, in turn, two or three questions, Dr. Faber. Do you prescribe to me no drugs from your pharmacopœia?"

"Drugs may palliate many sufferings incidental to organic disease, but drugs cannot reach organic disease itself."

"Do you believe that, even where disease is plainly organic, Nature herself has no alterative and reparative powers, by which the organ assailed may recover itself?"

"A few exceptional instances of such forces in nature are upon record; but we must go by general laws, and not by exceptions."

"Have you never known instances—do you not at this moment know one—in which a patient whose malady baffles the doctor's skill, imagines or dreams of a remedy? Call it a whim if you please, learned sir; do you not listen to the whim, and, in despair of your own prescriptions, comply with those of the patient?"

Faber changed countenance, and even started. Margrave watched him and laughed.

"You grant that there are such cases, in which the patient gives the law to the physician. Now, apply your experience to my case. Suppose some strange fancy had seized upon my imagination—that is the doctor's cant word for all phenomena which we call exceptional—some strange fancy that I had thought of a cure for this disease for which you have no drugs; and suppose this fancy of mine to be so strong, so vivid, that to deny me its gratification would produce the very emotion from which you warn me as fatal—storm the heart, that you would soothe to repose, by the passions of rage and despair—would you, as my trusted physician concede or deny me my whim?"

"Can you ask? I should grant it at once, if I had no reason to know that the thing that you fancied was harmful."

"Good man and wise doctor! I have no other question to ask. I thank you."

Faber looked hard on the young, wan face, over which played a smile of triumph and irony; then turned away with an expression of doubt and trouble on his own noble countenance. I followed him silently into the open air.

"Who and what is this visitor of yours?" he asked, abruptly.

"Who and what! I cannot tell you."

Faber reminded some moments musing, and muttering slowly to himself, "Tut! but a chance coincidence—a haphazard allusion to a fact which he could not have known!"

"Faber," said I, abruptly, "can it be that Lilian is the patient in whose self-suggested remedies you confide more than in the various learning at command of your practised skill?"

"I cannot deny it," replied Faber, reluctantly. "In the intervals of that suspense from waking sense, which in her is not sleep, nor yet altogether catalepsy, she has, for the last few days, stated accurately the precise moment in which the trance—if I may so call it—would pass away, and prescribed for herself the remedies that should be then administered. In every instance, the remedies so self-prescribed, though certainly not those which would have occurred to my mind, have proved efficacious. Her rapid progress to reason I ascribe to the treatment she herself ordained in her trance, without remembrance of her own suggestions when she awoke. I had meant to defer communicating these phenomena in the idiosyncrasy of her case until our minds could more calmly inquire into the process by which ideas—not apparently derived, as your metaphysical school would derive all ideas, from preconceived experiences—will thus sometimes act like an instinct on the human sufferer for self-preservation, as the bird is directed to the herb or the berry which heals or assuages its ailments.

"We know how the mesmerists would account for this phenomenon of hygienic introvision and clairvoyance. But here, there is no mesmerizer, unless the patient can be supposed to mesmerize herself. Long, however, before mesmerism was heard of, medical history attests examples in which patients who baffled the skill of the ablest physicians have fixed their fancies on some remedy that physicians would call inoperative for good or for harm, and have recovered by the remedies thus singularly self-suggested. And Hippocrates himself, if I construe his meaning rightly, recognizes the powers for self-cure which the condition of trance will sometimes bestow on the sufferer, 'where' (says the father of our art) 'the sight being closed to the external, the soul more truthfully perceives the affections of the body.' In short—I own it—in this instance, the skill of the physician has been a compliant obedience to the instinct called forth in the patient. And the hopes I have hitherto permitted myself to give you, were founded on my experience that her own hopes, conceived in trance, had never been fallacious or exaggerated. The simples that I gathered for her yesterday she had described; they are not in our herbal. But as they are sometimes used by the natives, I had the curiosity to analyze their chemical properties shortly after I came to the colony, and they seemed to me as innocent as line-blossoms. They are rare in this part of Australia, but she told me where I should find them—a remote spot, which she has certainly never visited.

"Last night, when you saw me disturbed, dejected, it was because, for the first time, the docility with which she had hitherto, in her waking state, obeyed her own injunctions in the state of trance, forsook me. She could not be induced to taste the decoction I had made from the herbs; and if you found me this morning with weaker hopes than before, this is the real cause—viz., that when I visited her at sunrise, she was not in sleep but in trance, and in that trance she told me that she had nothing more to suggest or reveal; that on the complete restoration of her senses, which was at hand, the abnormal faculties vouchsafed to trance would be withdrawn. 'As for my life,' she said quietly, as if unconscious of our temporary joy or woe in the term of its tenure here—'as for my life, your aid is now idle; my own vision obscure; on my life a dark and cold shadow is resting. I cannot foresee if it will pass away. When I strive to look around, I see but my Allen—'"

"And so," said I, mastering my emotions, "in bidding me hope, you did not rely on your own resources of science, but on the whisper of nature in the brain of your patient?"

"It is so."

We both remained silent some moments, and then, as he disappeared within my house, I murmured:

"And when she strives to look beyond the shadow, she sees only me! Is there some prophet-hint of Nature there also, directing me not to scorn the secret which a wanderer, so suddenly dropt on my solitude, assures me that Nature will sometimes reveal to her seeker? And oh! that dark wanderer—has Nature a marvel more weird than himself?"

CHAPTER LXXVI.

I STRAYED through the forest till noon, in debate with myself, and strove to shape my wild doubts into purpose, before I could nerve and compose myself again to face Margrave alone.

I re-entered the hut. To my surprise, Margrave was not in the room in which I had left him, nor in that which adjoined it. I ascended the stairs to the kind of loft in which I had been accustomed to pursue my studies, but in which I had not set foot since my alarm for Lilian had suspended my labors. There I saw Margrave quietly seated before the manuscript of my Ambitious Work, which lay open on the rude table just as I had left it, in the midst of its concluding summary.

"I have taken the licence of former days, you see," said Margrave, smiling, "and have hit by chance on a passage I can understand without effort. But why such a waste of argument to prove a fact so simple? In man, as in brute, life once lost is lost for ever; and that is why life is so precious to man."

I took the book from his hand, and flung it aside in wrath. His approval revolted me more with my own theories than all the argumentative rebukes of Faber.

"And now," I said, sternly, "the time has come for the explanation you promised. Before I can aid you in any experiment that may serve to prolong your life, I must know how far that life has been a baleful and destroying influence?"

"I have some faint recollection of having saved *your* life from an imminent danger, and if gratitude were the attribute of man, as it is of the dog, I should claim your aid to serve mine as a right. Ask me what you will. You must have seen enough of me to know that I do not affect either the virtues or vices of others. I regard both with so supreme an indifference, that I believe I am vicious or virtuous unawares. I know not if I can explain what seems to have perplexed you, but if I cannot explain I have no intention to lie. Speak—I listen! We have time enough now before us."

So saying, he reclined back in the chair, stretching out his limbs wearily. All round this spoilt darling of Material Nature the aids and appliances of Intellectual Science! Books, and telescopes, and crucibles, with the light of day coming through a small circular aperture in the boarded casement, as I had constructed the opening for my experimental observation of the prismal rays.

While I write, his image is as visible before my remembrance as if before the actual eye—beautiful even in its decay, awful even in its weakness, mysterious as is Nature herself amidst all the mechanism by which our fancied knowledge attempts to measure her laws and analyze her light.

But at that moment no such subtle reflections delayed my inquisitive eager mind from its immediate purpose—who and what was this creature boasting of a secret through which I might rescue from death the life of her who was my all upon the earth?

I gathered rapidly and succinctly together all that I knew and all that I guessed of Margrave's existence and arts. I commenced from my Vision in that mimic Golgotha of creatures inferior to man, close by the scene of man's most trivial and meaningless pastime. I went on—Derval's murder; the missing contents of the casket; the apparition seen by the maniac assassin guiding him to the horrid deed; the luminous haunting Shadow; the positive charge in the murdered man's memoir connecting Margrave with Louis Grayle, and accusing him of the murder of Haroun; the night in the moonlit pavilion at Derval Court; the baneful influence on Lilian; the struggle between me and himself in the house by the seashore;—The strange All that is told in this Strange Story.

But, warming as I spoke, and in a kind of fierce joy to be thus enabled to free my own heart of the doubts that had burdened it, now that I was fairly face to face with the being by whom my reason had been so perplexed and my life so tortured, I was restrained by none of the fears lest my own fancy deceive me, with which in his absence I had striven to reduce to natural causes the portents of terror and wonder. I stated plainly, directly, the beliefs, the impressions which I had never dared even to myself to own without seeking to explain them away. And coming at to a close, I said: "Such are the evidences that seem to me to justify abhorrence of the life that you ask me to aid in prolonging. Your own tale of last night but confirms them. And why to me—to me—do you come with wild entreaties to lengthen the life that has blighted my own? How did you even learn the home in which I sought unavailing refuge? How—as your hint to Faber clearly revealed—were you aware, that in yon house, where the sorrow is veiled, where the groan is surpressed, where the foot-tread falls ghostlike, there struggles now between life and death my heart's twin, my world's sunshine? Ah! through my terror for her, is it a demon that tells you how to bribe my abhorrence into submission, and supple my reason into use to your ends?"

Margrave had listened to me throughout with a fixed attention, at times with a bewildered stare, at times with exclamations of surprise, but not of denial. And when I had doue, he remained for some moments silent, seemingly stupefied, passing his hand repeatedly over his brow, in the gesture so familiar to him in former days.

At length he said, quietly, without evincing any sign either of resentment or humiliation: "In much that you tell me I recognize myself: in much I am as lost in amazement as you in wild doubt or fierce wrath. Of the effect that you say Philip Derval produced on me I have no recollection. Of himself I have only this—that he was my foe, that he came to England intent on schemes to shorten my life or destroy its enjoyments. All my faculties tend to self-preservation; there, they converge as rays in a focus; in that focus they illumine and—they burn. I willed to destroy my intended destroyer. Did my will enforce itself on the agent to which it was guided? Likely enough. Be it so. Would you blame me for slaying the tiger or serpent—not by the naked hand, but by weapons that arm it? But what could tiger and serpent do more against me than the man who would rob me of life? He had his arts for assault—I had mine for self-defence. He was to me as the tiger that creeps through the jungle, or the serpent uncoiling his folds for the spring. Death to those whose whose life is destruction to mine, be they serpent, or tiger, or man! Derval perished. Yes! the spot in which the maniac had buried the casket *was* revealed to me—no matter how; the contents of the casket passed into my hands. I coveted that possession because I believed that Dervale had learned from Haroun of Aleppo the secret by which the elixir of life is prepared, and I suppose that some stores of the essence would be found in his casket. I was deceived!—not a drop! What I there found I knew not how to use or apply, nor did I care to learn. What I sought was not there. You see a luminous shadow of myself; it haunts, it accosts, it compels you. Of this I know nothing. Was it the emanation of my intense will really producing the spectre of myself? or was it the thing of your own imagination—an imagination which my will impressed and subjugated? I know not. At the hours when my shadow, real or supposed, was with you, my senses would have been locked in sleep.

"It is true, however, that I intensely desire to learn from races always near to man, but concealed from his every-day vision, the secret that I believed Philip Derval had carried with him to the tomb; and from some cause or another I cannot now of myself alone, as I could years ago, subject those races to my command—I must, in that, act through or with the mind of another. It is true that I sought to impress upon your waking thoughts the images of the circle, the powers of the wand, which, in your trance or sleep-waking, made you the involuntary agent of my will. I knew by a dream—for by dreams, more or less vivid, are the results of my waking will sometimes divulged to myself—that the spell had been broken, the discovery I sought not affected. All my hopes were then transferred from yourself, the dull votary of science, to the girl whom I charmed to my thraldom through her love for you and through her dreams of a realm which the science of schools never enters. In her, imagination was all pure and all potent; and tell me, O practical reasoner, if reason has ever advanced one step into knowledge except through that imaginative faculty which is strongest in the wisdom of ignorance, and weakest in the ignorance of the wise. Ponder this, and those marvels that perplex you will cease to be marvellous. I pass on to the riddle that puzzles you most. By Philip Derval's account I am, in truth, Louis Grayle restored to youth by the elixir, and while yet infirm, decrepit, murdered Haroun—a man of a frame as athletic as yours! By accepting this notion you seem to yourself alone to unravel the mysteries you ascribe to my life and my powers. Oh, wise philosopher! oh, profound logician! you accept that notion, yet hold my belief in the Dervish's tale a chimera! I am Grayle made young by the elixir, and yet the elixir itself is a fable!"

He paused and laughed, but the laugh was no longer even an echo of its former merriment or playfulness—a sinister and terrible laugh, mocking, threatening, malignant.

Again he swept his hand over his brows and resumed:

"Is it not easier to so accomplished a sage as you to believe that the idlers of Paris have guessed the true solution of that problem—my place on this earth? May I not be the loveson of Louis Grayle? And when Haroun refused the elixir to him, or he found that his frame was too far exhausted for even the elixir to repair organic lesions of structure in the worn frame of old age, may he not have indulged the common illusion of fathers, and soothed his death-pangs with the thought that he should live again in his son? Haroun is found dead on his carpet—rumor said strangled. What proof of the truth of that rumor? Might he not have passed away in a fit? Will it lessen your perplexity if I state recollections? They are vague—they often perplex myself; but so far from a wish to deceive you, my desire is to relate them so truthfully that you may aid me to reduce them into more definite form."

His face now became very troubled, the tone of his voice very irresolute: the face and the voice of a man who is either blundering his way through an intricate falsehood, or through obscure reminiscences.

"This Louis Grayle! this Louis Grayle! I remember him well, as one remembers a nightmare, Whenever I look back, before the illness of which I will presently speak, the image of Louis Grayle returns to me. I see myself with him in African wilds, commanding the fierce Abyssinians. I see myself with him in the fair Persian valley—lofty, snow-covered mountains encircling the garden of roses. I see myself with him in the hush of the golden noon, reclined by the spray of cool fountains; now listening to cymbals and lutes—now arguing with greybeards on secrets bequeathed by the Chaldees. With him, with him in moonlit nights, stealing into the sepulchres of mythical kings. I see myself with him in the aisles of dark caverns, surrounded by awful shapes, which have no likeness amongst the creatures of earth. Louis Grayle! Louis Grayle! all my earlier memories go back to Louis Grayle! All my arts and powers, all that I have learned of the languages spoken in Europe, of the sciences taught in her schools, I owe to Louis Grayle. But am I one and the same with him? No—I am but a pale reflection of his giant intellect. I have not even a reflection of his childlike agonies of sorrow. Louis Grayle! He stands apart from me, as a rock from the tree that grows out from its chasms. Yes, the gossip was right; I must be his son."

He leant his face on both hands, rocking himself to and fro. At length, with a sigh, he resumed:

"I remember, too, a long and oppressive illness, attended with racking pains—a dismal journey in a wearisome litter—the light hand of the woman Ayesha, so sad and so stately, smoothing my pillow or fanning my brows. I remember the evening on which my nurse drew the folds of the litter aside, and said, 'See Aleppo! and the star of thy birth shining over its walls!'

"I remember a face inexpressibly solemn and mournful. I remember the chill that the calm of its ominous eye sent through my veins

—the face of Haroun, the Sage of Aleppo. I remember the vessel of crystal he bore in his hand, and the blessed relief from my pains that a drop from the essence which flashed through the crystal bestowed! And then—and then—I remember no more till the night on which Ayesha came to my couch and said, 'Rise.'

"And I rose, leaning on her, supported by her. We went through dim narrow streets, faintly lit by wan stars, disturbing the prowl of the dogs, that slunk from the look of that woman. We came to a solitary house, small, and low, and my nurse said, 'Wait.'

"She opened the door and went in; I seated myself on the threshold. And after a time she came out from the house, and led me, still leaning on her, into a chamber.

"A man lay, as in sleep, on the carpet, and beside him stood another man, whom I recognized as Ayesha's special attendant—an Indian. 'Haroun is dead,' said Ayesha. 'Search for that which will give thee new life. Thou hast seen, and wilt know it, not I.'

"And I put my hand on the breast of Haroun—for the dead man was he—and drew from it the vessel of crystal.

"Having done so, the frown on his marble brow appalled me. I staggered back, and swooned away.

"I came to my senses, recovered and rejoicing, miles afar from the city, the dawn red on its distant walls. Ayesha had tended me; the elixir had already restored me.

"My first thought, when full consciousness came back to me, rested on Louis Grayle, for he, also, had been at Aleppo. I was but one of his numerous train. He, too, was enfeebled and suffering; he had sought the known skill of Haroun for himself as for me; and this woman loved and had tended him as she had loved and tended me. And my nurse told me that he was dead, and forbade me henceforth to breathe his name.

"We travelled on—she and I, and the Indian, her servant—my strength still renewed by the wondrous elixir. No longer supported by her, what gazelle ever roved through its pasture with a bound more elastic than mine?

"We came to a town, and my nurse placed before me a mirror. I did not recognize myself. In this town we rested, obscure, till the letter there reached me by which I learned that I was the offspring of love, and enriched by the care of a father recently dead. Is it not clear that Louis Grayle was this father?"

"If so, was the woman, Ayesha, your mother?"

"The letter said that 'my mother had died in my infancy.' Nevertheless, the care with which Ayesha had tended me induced a suspicion that made me ask her the very question you put. She wept when I asked her, and said. 'No, only my nurse. And now I needed a nurse no more.' The day after I received the letter which announced an inheritance that allowed me to vie with the nobles of Europe, this woman left me, and went back to her tribe."

"Have you never seen her since?"

Margrave hesitated a moment, and then answered, though with seeming reluctance, "Yes, at Damascus. Not many days after I was borne to that city by the strangers, who found me half-dead on their road, I woke one morning to find her by my side. And she said, 'In joy and in health you did not need me. I am needed now.'"

"Did you then deprive yourself of one so devoted? You have not made this long voyage—from Egypt to Australia—alone; you, to whom wealth gave no excuse for privation?"

"The woman came with me; and some chosen attendants. I engaged to ourselves the vessel we sailed in."

"Where have you left your companions?"

"By this hour," answered Margrave, "they are in reach of my summons; and when you and I have achieved the discovery—in the results of which we shall share—I will exact no more from your aid. I trust all that rests for my cure to my nurse and her swarthy attendants. You will aid me now, as a matter of course; the physician whose counsel you needed to guide your own skill enjoins you to obey my whim—if whim you still call it; you will obey it, for on that whim rests your own sole hope of happiness;—you, who can love—I love nothing but life. Has my frank narrative solved all the doubts that stood between you and me, in the great meeting-ground of an interest in common?"

"Solved all the doubts! Your wild story but makes some the darker, leaving others untouched: the occult powers of which you boast, and some of which I have witnessed—your very insight into my own household sorrows, into the interest I have, with yourself, in the truth of a faith so repugnant to reason—"

"Pardon me," interrupted Margrave, with that slight curve of the lip which is half smile and half sneer, "if, in my account of myself, I omitted what I cannot explain, and you cannot conceive: let me first ask how many of the commonest actions of the commonest men are purely involuntary and wholly inexplicable? When, for instance, you open your lips and utter a sentence, you have not the faintest idea beforehand what word will follow another; when you move a muscle, can you tell me the thought that prompts to the movement? And, wholly unable thus to account for your own simple sympathies between impulse and act, do you believe that there exists a man upon earth who can read all the riddles in the heart and brain of another? Is it not true that not one drop of water, one atom of matter, ever really touches another? Between each and each there is always a space, however infinitesimally small. How, then, could the world go on, if every man asked another to make his whole history and being as lucid as daylight before he would buy and sell with him? All the interchange and alliance rest but on this—an interest in common. You and I have established that interest, all else, all you ask more, is superfluous. Could I answer each doubt you would raise, still, whether the answer should please or revolt you, your reason would come back to the same starting-point, viz., In one definite proposal have we two an interest in common?"

And again Margrave laughed, not in mirth, but in mockery. The laugh and the words that preceded it were not the laugh and the words of the young. Could it be possible that Louis Grayle had indeed revived to false youth in the person of Margrave, such might have been his laugh and such his words. The whole mind of Margrave seemed to have undergone change since I last saw him; more rich in idea, more crafty even in candor, more powerful, more concentred. As we see in our ordinary experience, that some infirmity, threatening dissolution, brings forth more vividly the reminiscences of early years, when impressions were vigorously stamped, so I might have thought, that as Margrave neared the tomb, the memories he had retained from his former existence, in a being more amply endowed, more formidably potent, struggled back to the brain; and the mind that had lived in Louis Grayle moved the lips of the dying Margrave.

"For the powers and the arts that it equally puzzles your reason to assign or deny to me," resumed my terrible guest, "I will say briefly but this: they come from faculties stored within myself, and doubtless conduce to my self-preservation—faculties more or less, perhaps (so Van Helmont asserts), given to all men, though dormant in most;—vivid and active in me because in me self-preservation has been and yet is the strong master-passion, or instinct; and because I have been taught how to use and direct such faculties by disciplined teachers—Some by Louis Grayle, the enchanter; some by my nurse, the singer of charmed songs. But in much that I will to have done, I know no more than yourself how the agency acts. Enough for me to will what I wish, and sink calmly into slumber, sure that the will would work somehow its way. But when I have willed to know what, when known, should shape my own courses, I could see, without aid from your pitiful telescopes, all objects howsoever far. What wonder in that? Have you no learned puzzle-brained metaphysicians, who tell you that space is but an idea, all this palpable universe an idea in the mind, and no more! Why am I an engima as dark as the Sibyls, and your metaphysicians as plain as a hornbook?" Again the sardonic laugh. "Enough: let what I have said obscure or enlighten your guesses, we come back to the same link of union, which binds man to man, bids states arise from the desert, and foemen embrace as brothers. I need you and you need me: without your aid my life is doomed; without my secret the breath will have gone from the lips of your Lilian before the sun of to-morrow is red on yon hill-tops."

"Fiend or juggler," I cried in rage, "you shall not so enslave and enthrall me by this mystic farrago and jargon. Make your fantastic experiment on yourself if you will: trust to your arts and your powers. My Lilian's life shall not hang on your fiat. I trust it—to—"

"To what—to man's skill? Hear what the sage of the college shall tell you before I ask you again for your aid. Do you trust to

God's saving mercy? Ah! of course you believe in a God? Who, except a philosopher, can reason a Maker away? But that the Maker will alter His courses to hear you; that, whether or not you trust in Him, or in your doctor, it will change by a hairbreadth the thing that must be—do you believe *this*, Allen Fenwick?"

And there sat this reader of hearts! a boy in his aspect, mocking me and the greybeards of schools.

I could listen no more; I turned to the door and fled down the stairs, and heard, as I fled, a low chant; feeble and faint, it was still the old barbaric chant, by which the serpent is drawn from its hole by the charmer.

CHAPTER LXXVII.

To those of my readers who may seek with Julius Faber to explore, through intelligible causes, solutions of the marvels I narrate, Margrave's confession may serve to explain away much that my own superstitious beliefs had obscured. To them Margrave is evidently the son of Louis Grayle. The elixir of life is reduced to some simple restorative, owing much of its effect to the faith of a credulous patient: youth is so soon restored to its joy in the sun, with or without an elixir. To them Margrave's arts of enchantment are reduced to those idiosyncrasies of temperament on which the disciples of Mesmer build up their theories; exaggerated, in much, by my own superstitions; aided, in part, by such natural, purely physical magic as, explored by the ancient priestcrafts, is despised by the modern philosophies, and only remains occult because Science delights no more in the slides of the lantern which fascinated her childhood with simulated phantoms. To them Margrave is, perhaps, an enthusiast, but, because an enthusiast, not less an impostor. "*L'Homme se pique*," says Charron. Man cogs the dice for himself ere he rattles the box for his dupes. Was there ever successful impostor who did not commence by a fraud on his own understanding? Cradled in Orient Fable-land, what though Margrave believes in its legends; in a wand, an elixir; in sorcerers or Afrites? That belief in itself makes him keen to detect, and skilful to profit by, the latent but kindred credulities of others. In all illustrations of Duper and Duped through the records of superstition — from the guile of a Cromwell, a Mahomet, down to the cheats of a gipsy—professional visionaries are amongst the astutest observers. The knowledge that Margrave had gained of my abode, of my affliction, or of the innermost thoughts in my mind, it surely demanded no preternatural aids to acquire. An Old Bailey attorney could have got at the one, and any quick student of human hearts have readily mastered the other. In fine, Margrave, thus rationally criticised, is no other prodigy (save in degree and concurrence of attributes simple, though not very common) than may be found in each alley that harbors a fortune-teller who has just faith enough in the stars or the cards to bubble himself while he swindles his victims; earnest, indeed, in the self-conviction that he is really a seer, but reading the looks of his listeners, divining the thoughts that induce them to listen, and acquiring by practice a startling ability to judge what the listeners will deem it most seer-like to read in the cards or divine from the stars.

I leave this interpretation unassailed. It is that which is the most probable, it is clearly that which, in a case not my own, I should have accepted; and yet I revolved and dismissed it. The moment we deal with things beyond our comprehension, and in which our own senses are appealed to and baffled, we revolt from the Probable, as it seems to the senses of those who have not experienced what we have. And the same principle of Wonder that led our philosophy up from inert ignorance into restless knowledge, now winding back into Shadow-land, reverses its rule by the way, and, at last, leaves us lost in the maze, our knowledge inert, and our ignorance restless.

And putting aside all other reasons for hesitating to believe that Margrave was the son of Louis Grayle—reasons which his own narrative, might suggest—was it not strange that Sir Philip Derval, who had instituted inquiries so minute, and reported them in his memoir with so faithful a care, should not have discovered that a youth, attended by the same woman who had attended Grayle, had disappeared from the town on the same night as Grayle himself disappeared? But Derval had related truthfully, according to Margrave's account, the flight of Ayesha and her Indian servant, yet not alluded to the flight, not even to the existence of the boy, who must have been of no mean importance in the suite of Louis Grayle, if he were, indeed, the son whom Grayle had made his constant companion, and constituted his principal heir.

Not many minutes did I give myself up to the cloud of reflections through which no sunbeam of light forced its way, One thought overmastered all; Margrave had threatened death to my Lilian, and warned me of what I should learn from the lips of Faber, "the sage of the college." I stood, shuddering, at the door of my home; I did not dare to enter.

"Allen," said a voice, in which my ear detected an unwonted tremulous faltering, "be firm—be calm. I keep my promise. The hour is come in which you may again see the Lilian of old—mind to mind, soul to soul."

Faber's hand took mine, and led me into the house.

"You do, then, fear that this interview will be too much for her strength?" said I, whisperingly.

"I cannot say; but she demands the interview, and I dare not refuse it."

CHAPTER LXXVIII.

I LEFT Faber on the stairs, and paused at the door of Lilian's room. The door opened suddenly, noiselessly, and her mother came out with one hand before her face, and the other locked in Amy's, who was leading her as a child leads the blind. Mrs. Ashleigh looked up, as I touched her, with a vacant, dreary stare. She was not weeping, as was her womanly wont in every pettier grief, but Amy was. No word was exchanged between us. I entered, and closed the door; my eyes turned mechanically to the corner in which was placed the small virgin bed, with its curtains white as a shroud. Lilian was not there. I looked around, and saw her half reclined on a couch near the window. She was dressed, and with care. Was not that her bridal robe?

"Allen—Allen," she murmured.

"Again, again my Allen—again, again your Lilian!" And, striving in vain to rise, she stretched out her arms in the yearning of reunited love. And as I knelt beside her those arns closed round me for the first time in the frank, chaste, holy tenderness of a wife's embrace.

"Ah!" she said, in her low voice (her voice, like Cordelia's, was ever low), "all has come back to me—all that I owe to your protecting, noble, trustful, guardian love!"

"Hush! hush! the gratitude rests with me—it is so sweet to love, to trust, to guard! my own, my beautiful—still my beautiful! Suffering has not dimmed the light of those dear eyes to me! Put your lips to my ear. Whisper but these words: 'I love you, and for your sake I wish to live!'"

"For your sake, I pray—with my whole weak human heart—I pray to live! Listen. Some day hereafter, if I am spared, under the purple blossoms of yonder waving trees I shall tell you all, as I see it now; all that darkened or shone on me in my long dream, and before that dream closed around me, like a night in which cloud and star chase each other! Some day hereafter, some quiet, sunlit, happy, happy day. But now, all I would say is this: Before that dreadful morning." Here she paused, shuddered, and passionately burst forth—"Allen, Allen! you did not believe that slanderous letter! God bless you! God bless you! Great-hearted, high-souled—God bless you, my darling! my husband! And He will! Pray to Him humbly as I do, and He will bless you." She stooped and kissed away my tears—then she resumed, feebly, meekly, sorrowfully:

"Before that morning I was not worthy of such a heart, such a love as yours. No, no; hear me. Not that a thought of love for another ever crossed me! Never, while conscious and reasoning, was I untrue to you—even in fancy? But I was a child—wayward as the child who pines for what earth cannot give, and covets the moon for a toy. Heaven had been so kind to my lot on earth, and yet with my lot on earth I was secretly discontented. When I felt that you loved me, and my heart told me that I loved again, I said to myself, 'Now the void that my soul finds on earth will be filled.' I longed for your coming, and yet when you went I murmured, 'But is this the ideal of which I had dreamed?' I asked for an impossible sympathy. Sympathy with what? Nay, smile on me, dearest!

—sympathy with what? I could not have said. Ah! Allen, then, then, I was not worthy of you: Infant that I was, I asked you to understand me: now I know that I am a woman, and my task is to study you! Do I make myself clear? Do you forgive me? I was not untrue to you; I was untrue to my own duties in life. I believed, in my vain conceit, that a mortal's dim vision of heaven raised me above the earth; I did not perceive the truth that earth is a part of the same universe as heaven! Now, perhaps, in the awful affliction that darkened my reason, my soul has been made more clear. As if to chastise but to teach me, my soul has been permitted to indulge its own presumptuous desire; it has wandered forth from the trammels of mortal duties and destinies; it comes back, alarmed by the dangers of its own rash and presumptuous escape from the tasks which it should desire upon earth to perform. Allen, Allen, I am less unworthy of you now! Perhaps in my darkness one rapid glimpse of the true world of spirit has been vouchsafed to me. If so, how unlike to the visions my childhood indulged as divine! Now, while I know still more deeply that there is a world for the angels, I know, also, that the mortal must pass through probation in the world of mortals. Oh! may I may pass through it with you:—grieving in your griefs, rejoicing in your joys!"

Here language failed her. Again the dear arms embraced me, and the dear face, eloquent with love, hid itself on my human breast.

CHAPTER LXXIX.

THAT interview is over! Again I am banished from Lilian's room; the agitation, the joy of that meeting has overstrained her enfeebled nerves. Convulsive tremblings of the whole frame, accompanied with vehement sobs, succeeded our brief interchange of sweet and bitter thoughts. Faber, in tearing me from her side, imperiously and sternly warned me that the sole chance yet left of preserving her life was in the merciful suspense of the emotions that my presence excited. He and Amy resumed their place in her chamber. Even her mother shared my sentence of banishment. So Mrs. Ashleigh and I sat facing each other in the room below; over me a leaden stupor had fallen, and I heard as a voice from afar or in a dream, the mother's murmured wailings:

"She will die—she will die! Her eyes have the same heavenly look as my Gilbert's on the day on which his closed for ever. Her very words are his last words—'Forgive me all my faults to you.' She will die—she will die!"

Hours thus passed away. At length, Faber entered the room; he spoke first to Mrs. Ashleigh—meaningless soothings, familiar to the lips of all who pass from the chamber of the dying to the presence of mourners, and know that it is a falsehood to say "hope," and a mockery as yet, to say, "endure."

But he led her away to her own room docile as a wearied child led to sleep, stayed with her some time, and then returned to me, pressing me to his breast father-like.

"No hope—no hope!" said I, recoiling from his embrace. "You are silent. Speak! speak! Let me know the worst."

"I have a hope, yet I scarcely dare to bid you share it; for it grows rather out of my heart as man, than my experience as physician. I cannot think that her soul would be now so reconciled to earth, so fondly, so earnestly cling to this mortal life, if it were about to be summoned away. You know how commonly even the sufferers who have dreaded death the most become calmly resigned to its coming, when death visibly reveals itself out from the shadows in which its shape has been guessed and not seen. As it is a bad sign for life when the patient has lost all will to live on, so there is hope while the patient, yet young and with no perceptible breach in the great centres of life (however violently their forts may be stormed), has still intense faith in recovery, perhaps drawn (who can say?) from the whispers conveyed from above to the soul.

"I cannot bring myself to think that all the uses for which a reason, always so lovely even in its errors, has been restored, are yet fulfilled. It seems to me as if your union, as yet so imperfect, has still for its end that holy life on earth by which two mortal beings strengthen each other for a sphere of existence to which this is the spiritual ladder. Through yourself I have hope yet for her. Gifted with powers that rank you high in the manifold orders of man; thoughtful, laborious, and brave; with a heart that makes intellect vibrate to every fine touch of humanity; in error itself, conscientious; in delusion, still eager for truth; in anger, forgiving; in wrong, seeking how to repair; and, best of all, strong in a love which the mean would have shrunk to defend from the fangs of the slanderer—a love, raising passion itself out of the realm of the senses, made sublime by the sorrows that tried its devotion:—with all these noble proofs in yourself, of a being not meant to end here, your life has stopped short in its uses, your mind itself has been drifted, a bark without rudder or pilot, over seas without shore, under skies without stars. And wherefore? Because the Mind you so haughtily vaunted has refused its companion and teacher in Soul.

"And therefore, through you, I hope that she will be spared yet to live on;—she, in whom soul has been led dimly astray, by unheeding the checks and the definite goals which the mind is ordained to prescribe to its wanderings while here; the mind taking thoughts from the actual and visible world, and the soul but vague glimpses and hints from the instinct of its ultimate heritage. Each of you two seems to me as yet incomplete, and your destinies yet uncompleted. Through the bonds of the heart, through the trials of time, ye have both to consummate your marriage. I do not—believe me—I do not say this in the fanciful wisdom of allegory and type, save that, wherever deeply examined, allegory and type run through all the most commonplace phases of outward and material life. I hope, then, that she may yet be spared to you; hope it, not from my skill as physician, but my inward belief as a Christian. To perfect your own being and end, '*Ye will need one another!*'"

I started—the very words that Lilian had heard in her vision!

"But," resumed Faber, "how can I presume to trace the numberless links of effect up to the First Cause, far off—oh; far off—out of the scope of my reason. I leave that to philosophers, who would laugh my meek hope to scorn. Possibly, probably, where I, whose calling has been but to save flesh from the worm, deem that the life of your Lilian is needed yet, to develop and train your own convictions of soul, Heaven in its wisdom may see that her death would instruct you far more than her life. I have said: Be prepared for either; wisdom through joy, or wisdom through grief. Enough that, looking only through the mechanism by which this moral world is impelled and improved, you know that cruelty is impossible to wisdom. Even a man, or man's law, is never wise but when merciful. But mercy has general conditions; and that which is mercy to the myriads may seem hard to the one, and that which seems hard to the one in the pang of a moment may be mercy when viewed by the eye that looks on through eternity."

And from all this discourse—of which I now, at calm distance of time, recall every word—my human, loving heart bore away for the moment but this sentence, "Ye will need one another;" so that I cried out, "Life, life, life! Is there no hope for her life? Have you no hope as physician? I am physician, too; I will see her. I will judge. I will not be banished from my post."

"Judge, then, as physician, and let the responsibility rest with you. At this moment, all convulsion, all struggle, has ceased—the frame is at rest. Look on her, and perhaps only the physician's eye could distinguish her state from death. It is not sleep, it is not trance, it is not the dooming coma from which there is no awaking. Shall I call it by the name received in our schools? Is it the catalepsy in which life is suspended, but consciousness acute? She is motionless, rigid; it is but with a strain of my own sense that I know that the breath still breathes, and the heart still beats. But I am convinced that though she can neither speak, nor stir, nor give sign, she is fully, sensitively conscious of all that passes around her. She is like those who have seen the very coffin carried into their chamber, and been unable to cry out, 'Do not bury me alive!' Judge then for yourself, with this intense consciousness and this impotence to evince it, what might be the effect of your presence—first an agony of despair, and then the complete extinction of life!"

"I have known but one such case—a mother whose heart was wrapped up in a suffering infant. She had lain for two days and two nights, still, as if in her shroud. All, save myself, said, 'Life is gone.' I said, 'Life still is there.' They brought in the infant, to try what effect its presence would produce; then her lips moved, and the hands crossed upon her bosom trembled."

"And the result?" exclaimed Faber, eagerly. "If the result of your experience sanction your presence, come; the sight of the babe rekindled life?"

"No; extinguished its last spark! I will not enter Lilian's room. I will go away—away from the house itself. That acute consciousness! I know it well! She may even hear me move in the room below, hear me speak at this moment. Go back to her, go back! But if hers be the state which I have known in another, which may be yet more familiar to persons of far ampler experience than mine, there is no immediate danger of death. The state will last through to-day, through to-night, perhaps for days to come. Is it so?"

"I believe that for at least twelve hours there will be no change in her state. I believe also that if she recover from it, calm and refreshed, as from a sleep, the danger of death will have passed away."

"And for twelve hours my presence would be hurtful?"

"Rather say fatal, if my diagnosis be right."

I wrung my friend's hand, and we parted.

Oh! to lose her now! now that her love and her reason had both returned, each more vivid than before! Futile, indeed, might be Margrave's boasted secret; but at least in that secret was hope. In recognized science I saw only despair.

And, at that thought, all dread of this mysterious visitor vanished—all anxiety to question more of his attributes or his history. His life itself became to me dear and precious. What if it should fail me in the steps of the process, whatever that was, by which the life of my Lilian might be saved!

The shades of evening were now closing in. I remembered that I had left Margrave without even food for many hours. I stole round to the back of the house, filled a basket with aliments more generous than those of the former day; extracted fresh drugs from my stores, and, thus laden, hurried back to the hut. I found Margrave in the room below, seated on his mysterious coffer, leaning his face on his hand. When I entered, he looked up, and said:

"You have neglected me. My strength is waning. Give me more of the cordial, for we have work before us to-night, and I need support."

He took for granted my assent to his wild experiment; and he was right.

I administered the cordial. I placed food before him, and this time he did not eat with repugnance. I poured out wine, and he drank it sparingly, but with ready compliance, saying, "In perfect health, I looked upon wine as poison; now it is like a foretaste of the glorious elixir."

After he had thus recruited himself, he seemed to acquire an energy that startlingly contrasted his languor the day before; the effort of breathing was scarcely perceptible; the color came back to his cheeks; his bended frame rose elastic and erect.

"If I understand you rightly," said I, "the experiment you ask me to aid can be accomplished in a single night?"

"In a single night—this night."

"Command me. Why not begin at once? What apparatus or chemical agencies do you need?"

"Ah!" said Margrave. "Formerly, how I was misled! Formerly, how my conjectures blundered! I thought, when I asked you to give a month to the experiment I wish to make, that I should need the subtlest skill of the chemist. I then believed, with Van Helmont, that the principle of life is a gas, and that the secret was but in the mode by which the gas might be rightly administered. But now, all that I need is contained in this coffer, save one very simple material—fuel sufficient for a steady fire for six hours. I see even that is at hand, piled up in your outhouse. And now for the substance itself—to that you must guide me."

"Explain."

"Near this very spot is there not gold—in mines yet undiscovered?—and gold of the purest metal?"

"There is. What then? Do you, with the alchemists, blend in one discovery—gold and life?"

"No. But it is only where the chemistry of earth or of man produces gold, that the substance from which the great pabulum of life is extracted by ferment can be found.

Possibly, in the attempts at that transmutation of metals, which I think your own great chemist, Sir Humphry Davy, allowed might be possible, but held not to be worth the cost of the process,—possibly, in those attempts, some scanty grains of this substance were found by the alchemists, in the crucible, with grains of the metal as niggardly yielded by pitiful mimicry of Natures stupendous laboratory; and from such grains enough of the essence might, perhaps, have been drawn forth, to add a few years of existence to some feeble gray-beard,—granting, what rests on no proofs, that some of the alchemists reached at age rarely given to man. But it is not in the miserly crucible, it is in the matrix of Nature herself, that we must seek in prolific abundance Nature's grand principle—life. As the loadstone is rife with the magnetic virtue, as amber contains the electric, so in the substance, to which we yet want a name, is found the bright life-giving fluid. In the old gold-mines of Asia and Europe the substance exists, but can rarely be met with. The soil for its nutriment may there be wellnigh exhausted. It is here, where Nature herself is all vital with youth, that the nutriment of youth must be sought. Near this spot is gold—guide me to it."

"You cannot come with me. The place which I know as auriferous is some miles distant—the way rugged. Yau cannot walk to it. It is true, I have horses, but—"

"Do you think I have come this distance, and not foreseen and forestalled all that I want for my object? Trouble yourself not with conjectures how I can arrive at the place. I have provided the means to arrive at and leave it. My litter and its bearers are in reach of my call. Give me your arm to the rising ground, fifty yards from your door."

I obeyed mechanically, stifling all surprise. I had made my resolve, and admitted no thought that could shake it.

When we reached the summit of the grassy hillock, which sloped from the road that led to the seaport, Margrave, after pausing to recover breath, lifted up his voice in a key, not loud, but shrill, and slow, and prolonged, half cry and half chant, like the night-hawk's. Through that air—so limpid and still, bringing near far objects, far sounds—the voice pierced its way, artfully pausing, till wave after wave of the atmosphere bore and transmitted it on.

In a few minutes the call seemed re-echoed, so exactly, so cheerily, that for the moment I thought that the note was the mimicry of the sly mocking Lyre-Bird, which mimics so merrily all that it hears in its coverts, from the whirr of the locust to the howl of the wild dog.

"What king," said the mystical charmer, and as he spoke he carelessly rested his hand on my shoulder, so that I trembled to feel that this dread son of Nature, Godless and soulless, who had been—and, my heart whispered, who still could be—my bane and mind-darkener, leant upon me for support, as the spoilt younger-born on his brother—"what king," said this cynical mocker, with his beautiful boyish face—"what king in your civilized Europe has the sway of a chief of the East? What link is so strong between mortal and mortal, as that between lord and slave? I transport yon poor fools from the land of their birth; they preserve here their old habits—obedience and awe. They would wait till they starved in the solitude—wait to hearken and answer my call. And I, who thus rule them, or charm them—I use and despise them. They know that, and yet serve me! Between you and me, my philosopher, there is but one thing worth living for—life for oneself."

Is it age, is it youth, that thus shocks all my sense, in my solemn completeness of man? Perhaps, in great capitals, young men of pleasure will answer, "It is youth; and we think what he says!" Young friends, I do not believe you.

CHAPTER LXXX.

ALONG the grass-track I saw now, under the moon, just risen, a strange procession—never seen before in Australian pastures. It moved on, noiselessly but quickly. We descended the hillock, and met it on the way; a sable litter, borne by four men, in unfamiliar Eastern garments; two other swarthy servitors, more bravely dressed, with yataghans and silver-hilted pistols in their belts, preceding this sombre equipage. Perhaps Margrave divined the disdainful thought that passed through my mind, vaguely and half-consciously; for he said, with the hollow, bitter laugh that had replaced the lively peal of his once melodious mirth:

" A little leisure and a little gold, and your raw colonist, too, will have the tastes of a pacha."

I made no answer. I had ceased to care who and what was my tempter. To me his whole being was resolved into one problem: Had he a secret by which Death could be turned from Lilian ?

But now, as the litter halted, from the long dark shadow which it cast upon the turf, the figure of a woman emerged and stood before us. The outlines of her shape were lost in the lose folds of a black mantle, and the features of her face were hidden by a black veil, except only the dark-bright, solemn eyes. Her stature was lofty, her bearing majestic, whether in movement or repose.

Margrave accosted her in some language unknown to me. She replied in what seemed to my ear the same tongue. The tones of her voice were sweet, but inexpressibly mournful. The words that they uttered appeared intended to warn, or deprecate, or dissuade; for they called to Margrave's brow a lowering frown, and drew from his lips a burst of unmistakable anger. The woman rejoined, in the same melancholy music of voice. And Margrave then, leaning his arm upon her shoulder, as he had leant it on mine, drew her away from the group into a neighboring copse of the flowering eucalypti—mystic trees, never changing the hues of their pale-green leaves, ever shifting the tints of their ash-gray, shedding, bark. For some moments, I gazed on the two human forms, dimly seen by the glinting moonlight through the gaps in the foliage. Then, turning away my eyes, I saw, standing close at my side, a man whom I had not noticed before. His footstep, as it stole to me, had fallen on the sward without sound. His dress, though Oriental, differed from that of his companions, both in shape and color; fitting close to the breast, leaving the arms bare to the elbow, and of an uniform ghastly white, as are the cerements of the grave. His visage was even darker than those of the Syrians or Arabs behind him, and his features were those of a bird of prey—the beak of the eagle, but the eye of the vulture. His cheeks were hollow—the arms, crossed on his breast, were long and fleshless. Yet in that skeleton form there was a something which conveyed the idea of a serpent's suppleness and strength; and as the hungry, watchful eyes met my own startled gaze, I recoiled impulsively, with that inward warning of danger which is conveyed to man, as to inferior animals, in the very aspect of the creatures that sting or devour. At my movement the man inclined his head in the submissive Eastern salutation, and spoke in his foreign tongue, softly, humbly, fawningly, to judge by his tone and his gesture.

I moved yet farther away from him with loathing, and now the human thought flashed upon me: was I, in truth, exposed to no danger in trusting myself to the mercy of the weird and remorseless master of those hirelings from the East:—seven men in number, two at least of them formidably armed, and docile as bloodhounds to the hunter, who has only to show them their prey ? But fear of man like myself is not my weakness; where fear found its way to my heart, it was through the doubts or the fancies in which man like myself disappeared in the attributes, dark and unknown, which we give to a fiend or a spectre. And, perhaps, if I could have paused to analyze my own sensations, the very presence of this escort—creatures of flesh and blood—lessened the dread of my incomprehensible tempter. Rather, a hundred times, front and defy those seven Eastern slaves—I, haughty son of the Anglo-Saxon who conquers all races because he fears no odds—than have seen again on the walls of my threshold, the luminous, bodiless Shadow! Besides: Lilian—Lilian ! for one chance of saving her life, however wild and chimercial that chance might be, I would have shrunk not a foot from the march of an army.

Thus reassured and thus resolved, I advanced with a smile of disdain, to meet Margrave and his veiled companion, as they now came from the moonlit copse.

" Well," I said to him, with an irony that unconsciously mimicked his own, " have you taken advice with your nurse ? I assume that the dark form by your side is that of Ayesha !"

The woman looked at me from her sable veil, with her steadfast solemn eyes, and said, in English, though with a foreign accent: " The nurse born in Asia is but wise through her love; the pale son of Europe is wise through his art. The nurse says, 'Forbear!' Do you say, 'Adventure ?' "

"Peace !" exclaimed Margrave, stamping his foot on the ground. "I take no counse from either; it is for me to resolve, for you to obey, and for him to aid. Night is come, and we waste it; move on."

The woman made no reply, nor did I. He took my arm and walked back to the hut. The barbaric escort followed. When we reached the door of the building Margrave said a few words to the woman and to the litter bearers. They entered the hut with us. Margrave pointed out to the woman his coffer—to the men the fuel stowed in the out-house. Both were borne away and placed within the litter. Meanwhile, I took from the table, on which it was carelessly thrown, the light hatchet that I habitually carried with me in my rambles.

"Do you think that you need that idle weapon?" said Margrave. "Do you fear the good faith of my swarthy attendants?"

"Nay, take the hatchet yourself; its use is to sever the gold from the quartz in which we may find it imbedded, or to clear, as this shovel, which will also be needed, from the slight soil above it, the ore that the mine in the mountain flings forth, as the sea casts its waifs on the sands."

"Give me your hand, fellow-laborer!" said Margrave, joyfully. "Ah, there is no faltering terror in his pulse! I was not mistaken in the Man. What rests, but the Place and the Hour?—I shall live—I shall live!"

CHAPTER LXXXI.

MARGRAVE now entered the litter, and the Veiled Woman drew the black curtains round him. I walked on, as the guide, some yards in advance. The air was still, heavy, and parched with the breath of the Australasian sirocco.

We passed through the meadow-lands, studded with slumbering flocks; we followed the branch of the creek, which was linked to its source in the mountains by many a trickling waterfall; we threaded the gloom of stunted, misshapen trees, gnarled with the stringy bark which makes one of the signs of the strata that nourish gold; and at length the moon, now in all her pomp of light, mid-heaven amongst her subject stars, gleamed through the fissures of the cave, on whose floor lay the relics of antediluvian races, and rested in one flood of silvery splendor upon the hollows of the extinct volcano, with tufts of dank herbage, and wide spaces of paler sward, covering the gold below—Gold, the dumb symbol of organized Matter's great mystery, storing in itself, according as Mind, the informer of Matter, can distinguish its uses, evil and good, bane and blessing.

Hitherto the Veiled Woman had remained in the rear, with the white-robed skeleton-like image that had crept to my side unawares with its noiseless step. Thus, in each winding turn of the difficult path at which the convoy following behind me came into sight, I had seen, first, the two gaily-dressed armed men, next the black bier-like litter, and last the Black-veiled Woman and the White-robed Skeleton.

But now, as I halted on the table-land, backed by the mountain and fronting the valley, the woman left her companion, passed by the litter and the armed men, and paused by my side, at the mouth of the moonlit cavern.

There for a moment she stood, silent, the procession below mounting upward laboriously and slow; then she turned to me, and her veil was withdrawn.

The face on which I gazed was wondrously beautiful, and severely awful. There, was neither youth nor age, but beauty, mature and majestic as that of a marble Demeter.

"Do you believe in that which you seek?" she asked, in her foreign, melodious, melancholy accents.

"I have no belief," was my answer. "True science has none. True science questions all things, takes nothing upon credit. It knows but three states of the mind—Denial, Conviction, and that vast interval between the two, which is not belief, but suspense of judgment."

The woman let fall her veil, moved from me, and seated herself on a crag above that cleft between mountain and creek, to which, when I had first discovered the gold that the land nourished, the rain from the clouds had given the rushing life of the cataract; but which now, in the drought and the hush of the skies, was but a dead pile of stones.

The litter now ascended the height: its bearers halted; a lean hand tore the curtains aside, and Margrave descended, leaning, this time, not on the Black-veiled Woman, but on the White-robed Skeleton.

There, as he stood, the moon shone full on his wasted form; on his face, resolute, cheerful, and proud, despite its hollowed outlines and sicklied hues. He raised his head, spoke in the language unknown to me, and the armed men and the litter-bearers grouped round him, bending low, their eyes fixed on the ground. The Veiled Woman rose slowly and came to his side, motioning away, with a mute sign, the ghastly form on which he leant, and passing round him silently, instead, her own sustaining arm. Margrave spoke again a few sentences, of which I could not even guess the meaning. When he had concluded, the armed men and the litter-bearers came nearer to his feet, knelt down, and kissed his hand. They then rose, and took from the bier-like vehicle the coffer and the fuel. This done, they lifted again the litter, and, again preceded by the armed men, the procession descended down the sloping hillside, down into the valley below.

Margrave now whispered, for some moments, into the ear of the hideous creature who had made way for the Veiled Woman. The grim skeleton bowed his head submissively, and stole noiselessly away through the long grasses; the slender stems, trampled under his stealthy feet, relifting themselves, as a passing wind. And thus he, too, sank out of sight down into the valley below. On the table-land of the hill remained only we three—Margrave, myself, and the Veiled Woman.

She had reseated herself apart, on the grey crag above the dried torrent. He stood at the entrance of the cavern, round the sides of which clustered parasital plants, with flowers of all colors, some amongst them opening their petals and exhaling their fragrance only in the hours of night; so that, as his form filled up the jaws of the dull arch, obscuring the moonbeam that strove to pierce the shadows that slept within, it stood now—wan and blighted—as I had seen it first, radiant and joyous, literally "framed in blooms."

CHAPTER LXXXII.

"So," said Margrave, turning to me, "under the soil that spreads around us, lies the gold which to you and to me is at this moment of no value, except as a guide to its twin-born—the regenerator of life!"

"You have not yet described to me the nature of the substance which we are to explore, nor of the process by which the virtues you impute to it are to be extracted."

"Let us first find the gold, and instead of describing the life-amber, so let me call it, I will point it out to your own eyes. As to the process, your share in it is so simple, that you will ask me why I seek aid from a chemist. The life-amber, when found, has but to be subjected to heat and fermentation for six hours; it will be placed, in a small cauldron which that coffer contains, over the fire which that fuel will feed. To give effect to the process, certain alkalies and other ingredients are required. But these are prepared, and mine is the task to commingle them. From your science as chemist I need and ask nought. In you I have sought only the aid of a man."

"If that be so, why, indeed, seek me at all? Why not confide in those swarthy attendants, who doubtless are slaves to your orders?"

"Confide in slaves! when the first task enjoined to them would be to discover, and refrain from purloining, gold. Seven such unscrupulous knaves, or even one such, and I, thus defenceless and feeble! Such is not the work that wise masters confide to fierce slaves. But that is the least of the reasons which exclude them from my choice, and fix my choice of assistant on you. Do you forget what I told you of the danger which the Dervish declared no bribe I could offer could tempt him a second time to brave?"

"I remember now; those words had passed away from my mind."

"And because they had passed away from your mind, I chose you for my comrade. I need a man by whom danger is scorned."

"But in the process of which you tell me I see no possible danger, unless the ingredients you mix in your cauldron have poisonous fumes."

"It is not that. The ingredients I use are not poisons."

"What other danger, except you dread your own Eastern slaves? But, if so, why lead them to these solitudes?—and if so, why not bid me be armed?"

"The Eastern slaves, fulfilling my commands, wait for my summons, where their eyes cannot see what we do. The danger is of a kind in which the boldest son of the East would be more craven, perhaps, than the daintiest Sybarite of Europe, who would shrink from a panther and laugh at a ghost. In the creed of the Dervish, and of all who adventure into that realm of nature which is closed to philosophy and open to magic, there are races in the magnitude of space unseen as animalcules in the world of a drop. For the tribes of the drop, science has its microscope. Of the hosts of yon azure Infinite magic gains sight, and through them gains command over fluid conductors that link all the parts of creation. Of these races, some are wholly indifferent to man, some benign to him, and some dreadly hostile. In all the regular and prescribed conditions of mortal being, this magic realm seems as blank and tenantless as yon vacant air. But when a seeker of powers beyond the rude functions by which man plies the clockwork, that measures his hours, and stops when its chain reaches the end of its coil, strives to pass over those boundaries at which philosophy says, 'Knowledge ends,' then, he is like all other travellers in regions unknown; he must propitiate or brave the tribes that are hostile—must depend for his life on the tribes that are friendly.

"Though your science discredits the alchemist's dogmas, your learning informs you that all alchemists were not ignorant impostors; yet those whose discoveries prove them to have been the nearest allies to your practical knowledge, ever hint in their mystical works at the reality of that realm which is open to magic—ever hint that some means less familiar than furnace and bellows, are essential to him who explores the elixir of life. He who once quaffs that elixir, obtains in his very veins the bright fluid by which he transmits the force of his will to agencies dormant in nature, to giants unseen in the space. And here, as he passes the boundary which divides his allotted and normal mortality from the regions and races that magic alone can explore, so, here, he breaks down the safeguard between himself and the tribes that are hostile. Is it not ever thus between man and man? Let a race the most gentle and timid and civilized dwell on one side a river or mountain, and another have home in the region beyond, each, if it pass not the intervening barrier, may with each live in peace. But if ambitious adventurers scale the mountain, or cross the river, with design to subdue and enslave the populations they boldly invade, then all the invaded arise in wrath and defiance—the neighbors are changed into foes.

"And therefore this process—by which a simple though rare material of nature is made to yield to a mortal the boon of a life which brings, with its glorious resistance to Time, desires and faculties to subject to its service beings that dwell in the earth, and the air, and the deep—has ever been one of the same peril which an invader must brave when he crosses the bounds of his nation. By this key alone you unlock all the cells of the alchemist's lore; by this alone understand how a labor, which a chemist's crudest apprentice could perform, has baffled the giant fathers of all your dwarfed children of science. Nature, that stores this priceless boon, seems to shrink from conceding it to man—the invisible tribes that abhor him, oppose themselves to the gain that might give them a master. The duller of those who were the life-seekers of old, would have told you how some chance, trivial, unlooked-for, foiled their grand hope at the very point of fruition; some doltish mistake, some improvident oversight, a defect in the sulphur, a wild overflow in the quicksilver, or a flaw in the bellows, or a pupil who failed to replenish the fuel, by falling asleep by the furnace. The invisible foes seldom vouchsafe to make themselves visible where they can frustrate the bungler, as they mock at his toils from their ambush.

But the mightier adventurers, equally foiled in despite of their patience and skill, would have said, 'Not with us rests the fault; we neglected no caution, we failed from no oversight. But out from the cauldron dread faces arose, and the spectres or demons dismayed and baffled us.' Such, then, is the danger which seems so appalling to a son of the East, as it seemed to a seer in the dark age of Europe. But we can deride all its threats, you and I. For myself, I own frankly I take all the safety that the charms and resources of magic bestow. You, for your safety, have the cultured and disciplined reason which reduces all phantasies to nervous impressions; and I rely on the courage of one who has questioned, unquailing, the Luminous Shadow, and wrested from the hand of the magican himself the wand which concentred the wonders of will!"

To this strange and long discourse I listened without interruption, and now quietly answered—

"I do not merit the trust you affect in my courage; but I am now on my guard against the cheats of the fancy, and the fumes of a vapor can scarcely bewilder the brain in the open air of this mountain-land. I believe in no races like those which you tell me lie viewless in space, as do gases. I believe not in magic; I ask not its aids, and I dread not its terrors. For the rest, I am confident of one mournful courage—the courage that comes from despair. I submit to your guidance whatever it be, as a sufferer whom colleges doom to the grave submits to the quack who says, 'Take my specific and live!' My life is nought in itself; my life lives in another. You and I are both brave from despair; you would turn death from yourself—I would turn death from one I love more than myself. Both know how little aid we can win from the colleges, and both, therefore, turn to the promises most audaciously cheering: Dervish or magician, alchemist or phantom, what care you and I? And if they fail us, what then? They cannot fail us more than the colleges do!"

———

CHAPTER LXXXIII.

THE gold has been gained with an easy labor. I knew where to seek for it, whether under the turf or in the bed of the creek. But Margrave's eyes, hungrily gazing round every spot from which the ore was disburied, could not detect the substance of which he alone knew the outward appearance. I had begun to believe that, even in the description given to him of this material, he had been credulously duped, and that no such material existed; when, coming back from the bed of the watercourse, I saw a faint yellow gleam amidst the roots of a giant parasite plant, the leaves and blossoms of which climbed up the sides of the cave with its antediluvian relics. The gleam was the gleam of gold, and on removing the loose earth round the roots of the plant, we came on—No, I will not—I dare not, describe it. The gold-digger would cast it aside, the naturalist would pause not to heed it; and did I describe it, and chemistry deign to subject it to analysis, could chemistry alone detach or discover its boasted virtues?

Its particles, indeed, are very minute, not seeming readily to crystallize with each other; each in itself of uniform shape and size, spherical as the egg which contains the germ of life, and small as the egg from which the life of aninsect may quicken.

But Margrave's keen eye caught sight of the atoms upcast by the light of the moon. He exclaimed to me, "Found! I shall live!" And then, as he gathered up the grains with tremulous hands, he called out to the Veiled Woman, hitherto still seated motionless on the crag. At his word she rose and went to the place hard by, where the fuel was piled, busying herself there. I had no leisure to heed her. I continued my search in the soft and yielding soil that time and the decay of vegetable life had accumulated over the Pre-Adamite strata on which the arch of the cave rested its mighty keystone.

When we had collected of these particles about thrice as much as a man might hold in his hand, we seemed to have exhausted their bed. We continued still to find gold, but no more of the delicate substance, to which, in our sight, gold was as dross.

"Enough," then said Margrave, reluctantly desisting. "What we have gained already will suffice for a life thrice as long as legend attributes to Haroun. I shall live—I shall live through the centuries."

"Forget not that I claim my share."

"Your share—yours! True—your half of my life! It is true." He paused with a low, ironical, malignant laugh; and then added, as he rose and turned away, "But the work is yet to be done."

———

CHAPTER LXXXIV.

WHILE we had thus labored and found, Ayesha had placed the fuel where the moonlight fell fullest on the sward of the table-land —a part of it already piled up as for a fire, the rest of it heaped confusedly close at hand; and by the pile she had placed the coffer. And there she stood, her arms folded under her mantle, her dark image seeming darker still as the moonlight whitened all the ground from which the image rose motionless. Margrave opened his coffer, the Veiled Woman did not aid him, and I watched in silence, while he as silently made his weird and wizard-like preparations.

CHAPTER LXXXV.

ON the ground a wide circle was traced by a small rod, tipped apparently with sponge saturated with some combustible naphtha-like fluid, so that a pale lambent flame followed the course of the rod as Margrave guided it, burning up the herbage over which it played, and leaving a distinct ring, like that which, in our lovely native fable-talk we call the "Fairy's Ring," but yet more visible because marked in phosphorescent light. On the ring thus formed were placed twelve small lamps, fed with the fluid from the same vessel, and lighted by the same rod. The light emitted by the lamps was more vivid and brilliant than that which circled round the ring.

Within the circumference, and immediately round the wood-pile, Margrave traced certain geometrical figures, in which—not without a shudder, that I overcame at once by a strong effort of will in murmuring to myself the name of "Lilian"—I recognized the interlaced triangles which by my own hand, in the spell enforced on a sleep-walker, had described on the floor of the wizard's pavilion. The figures were traced, like the circle, in flame, and at the point of each triangle (four in number) was placed a lamp, brilliant as those on the ring. This task performed, the cauldron, based on an iron tripod, was placed on the wood-pile. And then the woman, before inactive and unheeding, slowly advanced, knelt by the pile, and lighted it. The dry wood crackled and the flame burst forth, licking the rims of the cauldron with tongues of fire.

Margrave flung into the cauldron the particles we had collected, poured over them first a liquid, colorless as water, from the largest of the vessels drawn from his coffer, and then, more sparingly, drops from small crystal phials, like the phials I had seen in the hand of Philip Derval.

Having surmounted my first impulse of awe, I watched these proceedings, curious yet disdainful, as one who watches the mummeries of an enchanter on the stage.

"If," thought I, "these are but artful devices to inebriate and fool my own imagination, my imagination is on its guard, and reason shall not, this time, sleep at her post!"

"And now," said Margrave, "I consign to you the easy task by which you are to merit your share of the elixir. It is my task to feed and replenish the cauldron; it is Ayesha's to heed the fire, which must not for a moment relax in its measured and steady heat. Your task is the lightest of all: it is but to renew from this vessel the fluid that burns in the lamps, and on the ring. Observe, the contents of the vessel must be thriftily husbanded; there is enough, but not more than enough, to sustain the light in the lamps, on the lines traced round the cauldron, and on the farther ring, for six hours. The compounds dissolved in this fluid are scarce—only obtainable in the East, and even in the East months might have passed before I could have increased my supply. I had no months to waste. Replenish, then, the light only when it begins to flicker or fade. Take heed, above all, that no part of the outer ring—no, not an inch—and no lamp of the twelve, that are to its zodiac like stars, fade for one moment in darkness."

I took the crystal vessel from his hand.

"The vessel is small," said I, "and what is yet left of its contents is but scanty; whether its drops suffice to replenish the lights I cannot guess—I can but obey your instructions. But, more important by far than the light to the lamps and the circle, which in Asia or Africa might scare away the wild beasts unknown to this land—more important than light to a lamp, is the strength to your frame, weak magician! What will support you through six weary hours of night-watch?"

"Hope," answered Margrave, with a ray of his old dazzling style. "Hope! I shall live —I shall live through the centuries."

CHAPTER LXXXVI.

ONE hour passed away, the fagots under the cauldron burned clear in the sullen sultry air. The materials within began to seethe, and their color, at first dull and turbid, changed into a pale-rose hue; from time to time the Veiled Woman replenished the fire, after she had done so reseating herself close by the pyre, with her head bowed over her knees, and her face hid under her veil.

The lights in the lamps and along the ring and the triangles now began to pale. I resupplied their nutriment from the crystal vessel. As yet nothing strange startled my eye or my ear beyond the rim of the circle. Nothing audible, save, at a distance, the musical wheel-like click of the locusts, and, farther still in the forest, the howl of the wild dogs that never bark. Nothing visible, but the trees and the mountain-range girding the plains silvered by the moon, and the arch of the cavern, the flush of wild blooms on its sides, and the gleam of dry bones on its floor, where the moonlight shot into the gloom.

The second hour passed like the first. I had taken my stand by the side of Margrave, watching with him the process at work in the cauldron, when I felt the ground slightly vibrate beneath my feet, and, looking up, it seemed as if all the plains beyond the circle were heaving like the swell of the sea, and as if in the air itself there was a perceptible tremor.

I placed my hand on Margrave's shoulder and whispered, "To me earth and air seem to vibrate. Do they seem to vibrate to you?"

"I know not, I care not," he answered impetuously. "The essence is bursting the shell that confined it. Here are my air and my earth! Trouble me not. Look to the circle—feed the lamps if they fail."

I passed by the Veiled Woman as I walked towards a place in the ring in which the flame was waning dim. And I whispered to her the same question which I had whispered to Margrave. She looked slowly around and answered, "So is it before the Invisible make themselves visible! Did I not bid him forbear?" Her head again drooped on her breast, and her watch was again fixed on the fire.

I advanced to the circle and stopped to replenish the light where it waned. As I did so, on my arm, which stretched somewhat beyond the line of the ring, I felt a shock like that of electricity. The arm fell to my side numbed and nerveless, and from my hand dropped, but within the ring, the vessel that contained the fluid. Recovering my surprise or my stun, hastily with the other hand I caught up the vessel, but some of the scanty liquid was already spilled on the sward; and I saw with a thrill of dismay, that contrasted indeed the tranquil indifference with which I had first undertaken my charge, how small a supply was now left.

I went back to Margrave, and told him of the shock, and of its consequence in the waste of the liquid.

"Beware," said he, "that not a motion of the arm, not an inch of the foot, pass the verge of the ring; and if the fluid be thus unhappily stinted, reserve all that is left for the protecting circle and the twelve outer lamps! See how the Grand Work advances! how the hues in the cauldron are glowing blood-red through the film on the surface!"

And now four hours of the six were gone; my arm had gradually recovered its strength. Neither the ring nor the lamps had again required replenishing; perhaps their light was exhausted less quickly, as it was no longer to be exposed to the rays of the intense Australian moon. Clouds had gathered over the sky, and though the moon gleamed at times in the gaps that they left in blue air, her beam was more hazy and dulled. The locusts no longer were heard in the grass, nor the howl of the dogs in the forest. Out of the circle, the stillness was profound.

And about this time I saw distinctly in the distance a vast Eye! It drew nearer and nearer, seeming to move from the ground at the height of some lofty giant. Its gaze riveted mine; my blood curdled in the blaze from its angry ball; and now as it advanced larger and larger, other Eyes, as if of giants in its train, grew out from the space in its rear; numbers on numbers, like the spear-heads of some Eastern army, seen afar by pale warders of battlements doomed to the dust. My voice long refused an utterance to my awe; at length it burst forth shrill and loud:

"Look—look! Those terrible Eyes! Legions on legions. And hark! that tramp of numberless feet; *they* are not seen, but the hollows of earth echo the sound of their march!"

Margrave, more than ever intent on the

cauldron, in which, from time to time, he kept dropping powders or essences drawn forth from his coffer, looked up, defyingly, fiercely:

"Ye come," he said in a low mutter, his once mighty voice sounding hollow and laboring, but fearless and firm—"ye come,—not to conquer, vain rebels!—ye whose dark chief I struck down at my feet in the tomb where my spell had raised up the ghost of your first human master, the Chaldee! Earth and air have their armies still faithful to me, and still I remember the war-song that summons them up to confront you! Ayesha—Ayesha! recall the wild troth that we pledged amongst roses; recall the dread bond by which we united our sway over hosts that yet own thee as queen, though my sceptre is broken, my diadem reft from my brows!"

The Veiled Woman rose at this adjuration. Her veil now was withdrawn, and the blaze of the fire between Margrave and herself flushed, as with the rosy bloom of youth, the grand beauty of her softened face. It was seen, detached as it were, from her dark-mantled form; seen through the mist of the vapors which rose from the cauldron, framing it round like the clouds that are yieldingly pierced by the light of the evening star.

Through the haze of the vapor came her voice, more musical, more plaintive than I heard it before, but far softer, more tender; still in her foreign tongue; the words unknown to me, and yet their sense, perhaps, made intelligible by the love, which has one common language and one common look to all who have loved—the love unmistakeably heard in the loving tone, unmistakeably seen in the loving face.

A moment or so more, and she had come round from the opposite side of the fire-pile, and bending over Margrave's upturned brow, kissed it quietly, solemnly: and then her countenance grew fierce, her crest rose erect; it was the lioness protecting her young. She stretched forth her arm from the black mantle, athwart the pale front that now again bent over the cauldron; stretched it towards the haunted and hollow-sounding space beyond, in the gesture of one whose right hand has the sway of the sceptre. And then her voice stole on the air in the music of a chant, not loud yet far-reaching; so thrilling, so sweet, and yet so solemn, that I could at once comprehend how legend united of old the spell of enchantment with the power of song. All that I recalled of the effects which, in the former time, Margrave's strange chants had produced on the ear that they ravished and the thoughts they confused, was but as the wild bird's imitative carol, compared to the depth, and the art, and the soul of the singer, whose voice seemed endowed with a charm to enthral all the tribes of creation, though the language it used for that charm might to them, as to me, be unknown. As the song ceased, I heard, from behind, sounds like those I had heard in the spaces before me; the tramp of invisible feet, the whirr of invisible wings, as if armies were marching to aid against armies in march to destroy.

"Look not in front nor around," said Ayesha, "Look, like him, on the cauldron below. The circle and the lamps are yet bright; I will tell thee when the light again fails."

I dropped my eyes on the cauldron.

"See," whispered Margrave, "the sparkles at last begin to arise, and the rose-hues to deepen—signs that we near the last process."

CHAPTER LXXXVII.

THE fifth hour had passed away, when Ayesha said to me, "Lo! the circle is fading; the lamps grow dim. Look now without fear on the space beyond; the eyes that appalled thee are again lost in air, as lightnings that fleet back into cloud."

I looked up, and the spectres had vanished. The sky was tinged with sulphurous hues, the red and the black intermixed. I replenished the lamps and the ring in front, thriftily, heedfully; but when I came to the sixth lamp, not a drop in the vessel that fed them was left. In a vague dismay, I now looked round the half of the wide circle in rear of the two bended figures intent on the cauldron. All along that disc the light was already broken, here and there flickering up, here and there dying down; the six lamps in that half of the circle still twinkled, but faintly, as stars shrinking fast from the dawn of day. But it was not the fading shine in that half of the magical ring which daunted my eye and quickened with terror the pulse of my heart; the Bush-land beyond was on fire. From the background of the forest rose the flame and the smoke—the smoke, there, still half smothering the flame. But along the width of the grasses and herbage, between the verge of the forest and the bed of the water-creek just below the raised platform from which I beheld the dread conflagration, the fire was advancing; wave upon wave, clear and red against the columns of rock behind; as the rush of a flood through the mists of some Alp crowned with lightnings.

Roused from my stun at the first sight of a danger not foreseen by the mind I had steeled against for rarer portents of nature, I cared no more for the lamps and the circle. Hurrying back to Ayesha, I exclaimed: "The phantoms have gone from the spaces in front; but what incantation or spell can arrest the red march of the foe, speeding on in the rear! While we gazed on the cauldron of life, behind us, unheeded, behold the Destroyer!"

Ayesha looked and made no reply; but, as by involuntary instinct, bowed her majestic head, then rearing it erect, placed herself yet more immediately before the wasted form of the young magician (he still bending over the cauldron, and hearing me not in the absorption and hope of his watch): placed herself before him, as the bird whose first care is her fledgling.

As we two there stood, fronting the deluge of fire we heard Margrave behind us, murmuring low, "See the bubbles of light, how they sparkle and dance—I shall live, I shall live!" And his words scarcely died in our ears before crash upon crash, came the fall of the age-long trees in the forest; and nearer, all near us, through the blazing grasses, the hiss of the serpents, the scream of the birds, and the bellow and the tramp of the herds plunging wild through the billowy red of their pastures. Ayesha now wound her arms around Margrave, and wrenched him reluctant and struggling, from his watch over the seething cauldron. In rebubke of his angry exclamations, she pointed to the march of the fire, spoke in sorrowful tones a few words in her own language, and then appealing to me in English, said:

"I tell him that, here, the Spirits who oppose us have summoned a foe that is deaf to my voice, and—"

"And," exclaimed Margrave, no longer with gasp and effort, but with the swell of a voice which drowned all the discords of terror and of agony sent forth from the Phlegethon burning below—"and this witch, whom I trusted, is a vile slave and impostor, more desiring my death than my life. She thinks that in life I should scorn and forsake her, that in death I should die in her arms! Sorceress, avaunt! Art thou useless and powerless now when I need thee most? Go! Let the world be one funeral pyre! What to *me* is the world? My world is my life! Thou knowest that my last hope is here—that all the strength left me this night will die down, like the lamps in the circle, unless the elixir restore it. Bold friend, spurn that sorceress away. Hours yet ere those flames can assail us! A few minutes more, and life to your Lilian and me!"

Thus having said, Margrave turned from us, and cast into the cauldron the last essence yet left in his emptied coffer.

Ayesha silently drew her black veil over her face; and turned, with the being she loved, from the terror he scorned, to share in the hope that he cherished.

Thus left alone, with my reason disenthralled, disenchanted, I surveyed more calmly the extent of the actual peril with which we were threatened, and the peril seemed less, so surveyed.

It is true, all the Bush-land behind, almost up to the bed of the creek, was on fire; but the grasses, through which the flame spread so rapidly, ceased at the opposite marge of the creek. Watery pools were still, at intervals, left in the bed of the creek, shining tremulous, like waves of fire, in the glare reflected from the burning land; and even, where the water failed, the stony course of the exhausted rivulet was a barrier against the march of the conflagration. Thus, unless the wind, now still, should rise, and waft some sparks to the parched combustible herbage immediately around us, we were saved from the fire, and our work might yet be achieved.

I whispered to Ayesha the conclusion to which I came.

"Thinkest thou," she answered, without raising her mournful head, "that the Agencies of Nature are the movements of chance? The Spirits I invoked to his aid are leagued with the hosts that assail. A mightier than I am has doomed him!"

Scarcely had she uttered these words before Margrave exclaimed, "Behold how the Rose of the alchemist's dream enlarges its blooms from the folds of its petals! I shall live, I shall live!"

I looked, and the liquid which glowed in the cauldron had now taken a splendor that mocked all comparisons borrowed from the lustre of gems. In its prevelant color it had, indeed, the dazzle and flash of the ruby; but, out from the mass of the molten red, broke coruscations of all prismal hues. shooting, shifting, in a play that made the wavelets themselves seem living things, sensible of their joy. No longer was there scum or film upon the surface; only ever and anon a light rosy vapor floating up, and quick lost in the haggard, heavy, sulphurous air, hot with the conflagation rushing towards us from hehind. And these coruscations formed, on the surface of the molten ruby, literally the shape of a Rose, its leaves made distinct in their outlines by sparks of emerald, and diamond, and sapphire.

Even while gazing on this animate liquid lustre, a buoyant delight seemed infused into my senses; all terrors conceived before, were annulled; the phantoms, whose armies had filled the wide spaces in front, were forgotten; the crash of the forest behind was unheard. In the reflection of that glory, Margrave's wan cheek seemed already restored to the radiance it wore when I saw it first in the framework of blooms.

As I gazed, thus enchanted, a cold hand touched my own.

"Hush!" whispered Ayesha, from the black veil, against which the rays from the cauldron fell blunt, and absorbed into Dark. "Behind us, the light of the circle is extinct, but, there, we are guarded from all save the brutal and soulless destroyers. But, before!—but, before!—see, two of the lamps have died out!—see the blank of the gap in the ring! Guard that breach—there, the demons will enter."

"Not a drop is there left in this vessel by which to replenish the lamps on the ring."

"Advance, then; thou hast still the light of the soul, and the demons may recoil before a soul that is dauntless and guiltless. If not, Three are lost!—as it is, One is doomed."

Thus adjured, silently, involuntarily, I passed from the Veiled Woman's side, over the sere lines on the turf which had been traced by the triangles of light long since extinguished, and towards the verge of the circle. As I advanced, overhead rushed a dark cloud of wings—birds dislodged from the forest on fire, and screaming, in dissonant terror, as they flew towards the farthermost mountains; close by my feet hissed and glided the snakes, driven forth from their blazing coverts, and glancing through the ring, unscared by its waning lamps; all undulating by me, bright-eyed and hissing—all made innocuous by fear: even the terrible Death-adder, which I trampled on as I halted at the verge of the verge of the circle, did not turn to bite, but crept harmless away. I halted at the gap between the two dead lamps, and bowed my head to look again into the crystal vessel. Were there, indeed, no lingering drops yet left, if but to recruit the lamps for some priceless minutes more? As I thus stood, right into the gap between the two dead lamps, strode a gigantic Foot. All the rest of the form was unseen; only, as volume after volume of smoke poured on from the burning land behind, it seemed as if one great column of vapor, eddying round, settled itself aloft from the circle, and that out from that column strode the giant Foot. And, as strode the Foot, so with it came, like the sound of its tread, a roll of muttered thunder.

"I recoiled, with a cry that rang loud through the lurid air

"Courage!" said the voice of Ayesha. "Trembling soul, yield not an inch to the demon!"

At the charm, the wonderful charm, in the tone of the Veiled Woman's voice, my will seemed to take a force more sublime than its own. I folded my arms on my breast, and stood as if rooted to the spot, confronting the column of smoke and the stride of the giant Foot. And the foot halted, mute.

Again, in the momentary hush of that suspense, I heard a voice—it was Margrave's.

"The last hour expires—the work is accomplished! Come! come!—aid me to take the cauldron from the fire; and, quick!—or a drop may be wasted in vapor—the Elixir of Life from the cauldron!"

At that cry I receded, and the Foot advanced.

And at that moment, suddenly unawares; from behind, I was stricken down. Over me.

as I lay, swept a whirlwind of trampling hoofs and glancing horns. The herds, in their flight from the burning pastures, had rushed over the bed of the watercourse—scaled the slopes of the banks. Snorting and bellowing, they plunged their blind way to the mountains. One cry alone, more wild than their own savage blare, pierced the reek through which the Brute Hurricane swept. At that cry of wrath and despair I struggled to rise, again dashed to earth by the hoofs and the horns. But was it the dream-like deceit of my reeling senses, or did I see that giant Foot stride past through the close-serried ranks of the maddening herds? Did I hear, distinct through all the huge uproar of animal terror, the roll of low thunder which followed the stride of that Foot?

CHAPTER LXXXVIII.

When my senses had recovered its shock, and my eyes looked dizzily round, the charge of the beasts had swept by; and of all the wild tribes which had invaded the magical circle, the only lingerer was the brown Death-adder, coiled close by the spot where my head had rested. Beside the extinguished lamps which the hoofs had confusedly scattered, the fire, arrested by the watercourse, had consumed the grasses that fed it, and there the plains stretched, black and deserted as the Phlegræan Field of the Poet's Hell. But the fire still raged in the forest beyond: white flames, soaring up from the trunks of the tallest tress, and forming, through the sullen dark of the smoke-reek, innumerable pillars of fire, like the halls in the City af Fiends.

Gathering myself up, I turned my eyes from the terrible pomp of the lurid forest, and looked fearfully down on the hoof-trampled sward for my two companions.

I saw the dark image of Ayesha still seated, still bending, as I had seen it last. I saw a pale hand feebly grasping the rim of the magical cauldron, which lay, hurled down from its tripod by the rush of the beasts, yards away from the dim fading embers of the scattered wood-pyre. I saw the faint writhings of a frail wasted frame, over which the Veiled Woman was bending. I saw, as I moved with bruised limbs to the place, close by the lips of the dying magician, the flash of the ruby-like essence spilt on the sward, and, meteor-like, sparkling up from the torn tufts of herbage.

I now reached Margrave's side. Bending over him as the Veiled Woman bent, and as I sought gently to raise him, he turned his face, fiercely faltering out, "Touch me not, rob me not! *You* share with me! Never—never! These glorious drops are all mine! Die all else! I will live—I will live!" Writhing himself from my pitying arms, he plunged his face amidst the beautiful, playful flame of the essence, as if to lap the elixir with lips scorched away from its intolerable burning. Suddenly, with a low shriek, he fell back, his face upturned to mine, and on that face unmistakeably reigned Death!

Then Ayesha tenderly, silently, drew the young hend to her lap, and it vanished from my sight behind her black veil.

I knelt beside her, murmuring some trite words of comfort; but she heeded me not, rocking herself to and fro as the mother who cradles a child to sleep. Soon, the fast-flickering sparkles of the lost elixir died out on the grass; and with their last sportive diamond-like tremble of light, up, in all the suddenness of Australian day, rose the sun, lifting himself royally above the mountain-tops, and fronting the meaner blaze of the forest as a young king fronts his rebels. And as there, where the bush-fires had ravaged, all was a desert; so there, where their fury had not spread, all was a garden. Afar, at the foot of the mountains, the fugitive herds were grazing; the cranes, flocking back to the pools, renewed the strange grace of their gambols; and the great kingfisher, whose laugh, half in mirth, half in mockery, leads the choir that welcome the morn—which in Europe is night—alighted bold on the roof of the cavern, whose floors were still white with the bones of races, extinct before—so helpless through instincts, so royal through Soul—rose Man!

But there, on the ground where the dazzling elixir had wasted its virtues—there the herbage already had a freshness of verdure which, amid the duller sward round it, was like an oasis of green in a desert. And, there, wild flowers, whose chill hues the eye would have scarcely distinguished the day before, now glittered forth in blooms of unfamiliar beauty. Towards that spot were attracted myriads of happy insects, whose hum of intense joy was musically loud. But the form of the life-seeking sorcerer lay rigid and stark;—blind to the bloom of the wild flowers, deaf to the glee of the insects—one hand still resting heavily on the rim of the emptied cauldron, and the face still hid behind the Black Veil. What! the wondrous elixir sought with such hope and well-nigh achieved through such dread, fleeting back to the earth from which its material was drawn, to give bloom, indeed,—but to herbs; joy indeed,—but to insects!

And now in the flash of the sun, slowly wound up the slopes that led to the circle, the same barbaric procession which had sunk into the valley under the ray of the moon. The armed men came first, stalwart and tall, their vests brave with crimson and golden lace—their weapons gaily gleaming with holiday silver. After them, the Black Litter. As they came to the place, Ayesha, not raising her head, spoke to them in her own Eastern tongue. A wail was her answer. The armed men bounded forward, and the bearers left the litter.

All gathered round the dead form with the face concealed under the black veil—all knelt, and all wept. Far in the distance, at the foot of the blue mountains, a crowd of the savage natives had risen up as if from the earth; they stood motionless, leaning on their clubs and spears, and looking towards the spot on which we were; strangely thus brought into the landscape, as if they too, the wild dwellers on the verge which Humanity guards from the Brute, were among the mourners for the mysterious Child of mysterious Nature! And still, in the herbage, hummed the small insects, and still, from the cavern, laughed the great kingfisher. I said to Ayesha, "Farewell! your love mourns the dead, mine calls me to the living. You are now with your own people, they may console you—say if I can assist."

"There is no consolation for me! What mourner can be consoled if the dead die for ever? Nothing for him is left but a grave; that grave shall be in the land where the song of Ayesha first lulled him to sleep. Thou assist ME—thou, the wise man of Europe! From me ask assistance. What road wilt thou take to thy home?"

"There is but one road known to me through the maze of the solitude—that which we took to this upland."

"On that road Death lurks, and awaits thee! Blind dupe, couldst thou think that if the grand secret of life had been won, he whose head rests on my lap would have yielded thee one petty drop of the essence which had filched from his store of life but a moment? Me, who so loved and so cherished him—me he would have doomed to the pitiless cord of my servant, the Strangler, if my death could have lengthened a hairbreadth the span of his being. But what matters to me his crime or his madness? I loved him—I loved him!"

She bowed her veiled head lower and lower; perhaps under the veil, her lips kissed the lips of the dead. Then she said whisperingly:

"Juma, the Strangler, whose word never failed to his master, whose prey never slipped from his snare, waits thy step on the road to thy home! But thy death cannot now profit the dead, the beloved. And thou hast had pity for him who took but thine aid to design thy destruction. His life is lost, thine is saved!"

She spoke no more in the tongue that I could interpret. She spoke, in the language unknown, a few murmured words to her swarthy attendants; then the armed men, still weeping, rose, and made a dumb sign to me to go with them. I understood by the sign that Ayesha had told them to guard me on my way; but she gave no reply to my parting thanks.

CHAPTER LXXXIX.

I DESCENDED into the valley; the armed men followed. The path, on that side of the watercourse not reached by the flames, wound through meadows still green, or amidst groves unscathed. As a turning in the way brought in front of my sight the place I had left behind, I beheld the black litter creeping down the descent, with its curtains closed, and the Veiled Woman walking by its side. But soon the funeral procession was lost to my eyes, and the thoughts that it roused were erased. The waves in man's brain are like those of the sea, rushing on, rushing over the wrecks of the vessels that rode on their surface, to sink, after storm, in their deeps. One thought cast forth into the future now mastered all in the past: "Was Lilian living still?" Absorbed in the gloom of that thought, hurried on by the goad that my heart, in its tortured impatience, gave to my footstep, I outstripped the slow stride of the armed men, and, midway between the place I had left and the home which I sped to, came, far iu advance of my guards, into the thicket in which the bushmen had started up in my path on the night that Lilian had watched for my coming. The earth at my feet was rife with creeping plants and many colored flowers, the sky overhead was half hid by motionless pines. Suddenly, whether crawling out from the herbage or dropping down from the trees, by my side stood the white-robed and skeleton form—Ayesha's attendant, the Strangler.

I sprang from him in shuddering, then halted and faced him. The hideous creature crept towards me, cringing and fawning, making signs of humble goodwill and servile obeisance. Again I recoiled—wrathfully, loathingly; turned my face homeward, and fled on. I thought I had baffled his chase, when, just at the mouth of the thicket, he dropped from a bough in my path close behind me. Before I could turn, some dark muffling substance fell between my sight and the sun, and I felt a fierce strain at my throat. But the words of Ayesha had warned me; with one rapid hand I seized the noose before it could tighten too closely, with the other I tore the bandage away from my eyes, and, wheeling round on the dastardly foe, struck him down with one spurn of my foot. His hand, as he fell, relaxed its hold on the noose; I freed my throat from the knot, and sprang from the copse into the broad sunlit plain. I saw no more of the armed men or the Strangler. Panting and breathless, I paused at last before the fence, fragrant with blossoms, that divided my home from the solitude.

The windows of Lilian's room were darkened—all within the house seemed still.

Darkened and silenced Home! with the light and sounds of the jocund day all around it. Was there yet Hope in the Universe for me? All to which I had trusted Hope, had broken down; the anchors I had forged for her hold in the beds of the ocean, her stay from the drifts of the storm, had snapped like the reeds which pierce the side that leans on the barb of their points, and confides in the strength of their stems. No hope in the baffled resources of recognized knowledge! No hope in the daring adventures of Mind into regions unknown; vain alike the calm lore of the practised physician, and the magical arts of the fated Enchanter! I had fled from the commonplace teachings of Nature, to explore in her Shadow-land marvels at variance with reason. Made brave by the grandeur of love, I had opposed without quailing the stride of the Demon, and my hope, when fruition seemed nearest, had been trodden into dust by the hoofs of the beast! And yet, all the while, I had scorned, as a dream more wild than the word of a sorcerer, the hope that the old man and child, the wise and the ignorant, took from their souls as inborn. Man and fiend had alike failed a mind, not ignoble, not skilless, not abjectly craven; alike failed a heart not feeble and selfish, not dead to the hero's devotion, willing to shed every drop of its blood for a something more dear than an animal's life for itself! What remained—what remained for man's hope?—man's mind and man's heart thus exhausting their all with no other result but despair? What remained but the mystery of mysteries, so clear to the sunrise of childhood, the sunset of age, only dimmed by the clouds which collect round the noon of our manhood? Where yet was Hope found? In the soul; in its every-day impulse to supplicate comfort and light, from the Giver of soul, wherever the heart is afflicted, the mind is obscured.

Then the words of Ayesha rushed over me: "What mourner can be consoled, if the Dead die for ever?" Through every pulse of my frame throbbed that dread question. All Nature around seemed to murmur it. And suddenly, as by a flash from Heaven, the grand truth in Faber's grand reasoning shone on me, and lighted up all, within and without. Man alone, of all earthly creatures, asks, "Can the Dead die for ever?" and the instinct that urges the question is God's answer to man! No instinct is given in vain.

And, born with the instinct of soul is the instinct that leads the soul from the seen to the unseen, from time to eternity, from the torrent that foams towards the Ocean of Death, to the source of its stream, far aloft from the Ocean.

"Know thyself," said the Pythian of old. "That precept descended from Heaven." Know thyself! is that maxim wise? If so, know thy soul. But never yet did man come to the thorough conviction of soul, but what he acknowledged the sovereign necessity of prayer. In my awe, in my rapture, all my thoughts seemed enlarged and illumed and exalted. I prayed—all my soul seemed one prayer. All my past, with its pride and presumption and folly, grew distinct as the form of a penitent, kneeling for pardon before setting forth on the pilgrimage vowed to a shrine. And, sure now, in the deeps of a soul first revealed to myself, that the Dead do not die for ever, my human love soared beyond its brief trial of terror and sorrow. Daring not to ask from Heaven's wisdom that Lilian, for my sake, might not yet pass away from the earth, I prayed that my soul might be fitted to bear with submission whatever my Maker might ordain. And, if surviving her—without whom no beam from yon material sun could ever warm into joy a morrow in human life—so to guide my steps that they might rejoin her at last, and, in rejoining, regain for ever!

How trivial now became the weird riddles that, a little while before, had been clothed in so solemn an awe? What mattered it to the vast interests involved in the clear recognition or Soul and Herafter,—whether or not my bodily sense, for a moment, obscured the face of the Nature I should one day behold as a spirit? Doubtless the sights and the sounds which had haunted the last gloomy night, the calm reason of Faber would strip of their magical seemings;—the Eyes in the space and the Foot in the circle might be those of no terrible Demons, but of the wild's savage children whom I had seen, halting, curious and mute, in the light of the morning. The tremor of the ground (if not, as heretofore, explicable by the illusory impression of my own treacherous senses) might be but the natural effect of elements struggling yet under a soil unmistakably charred by volcanoes. The luminous atoms dissolved in the cauldron might as little be fraught with a vital elixir as are the splendors of naphtha or phosphor. As it was, the weird rite had no magic result. The magician was not rent limb from limb by the fiends. By causes as natural as ever extinguished life's spark in the frail lamp of clay, he had died out of sight—under the black veil.

What mattered henceforth to Faith, in its far grander questions and answers, whether Reason, in Faber, or Fancy, in me, supplied the more probable guess at a hieroglyph which, if construed aright, was but a word of small mark in the mystical language of Nature? If all the arts of enchantment recorded by Fable were attested by facts which Sages were forced to acknowledge, Sages would sooner or later find some cause for such portents—not supernatural. But what Sage, without cause supernatural, both without and within him, can guess at the wonders he views in the growth of a blade of grass, or the tints on an insect's wing? Whatever art Man can achieve in his progress through time, Man's reason, in time, can suffice to explain. But the wonders of God? These belong to the Infinite; and these, O Immortal! will but develop new wonder on wonder, though thy sight be a spirit's, and thy leisure to track and to solve, an eternity.

As I raised my face from my clasped hands, my eyes fell full upon a form standing in the open door-way, There, where on the night in which Lilian's long struggle for reason and life had begun, the Luminous Shadow had been beheld in the doubtful light of a dying moon and a yet hazy dawn; there, on the threshold, gathering round her bright locks the auriole of the glorious sun, stood Amy, the blessed child! And as I gazed, drawing nearer and nearer to the silenced house, and that Image of Peace on its threshold, I felt that Hope met me at the door—Hope in the child's steadfast eyes—Hope in the child's welcoming smile!

"I was at watch for you," whispered Amy. "All is well."

"She still lives—she will recover!" said another voice, as my head sunk on Faber's shoulder. "For some hours in the night her sleep was disturbed—convulsed. I feared, then, the worst. Suddenly, just before the dawn, she called out aloud, still in sleep—

"'The cold and dark shadow has passed away from me, and from Allen—passed away from us both for ever!'

"And from that moment the fever left her; the breathing became soft, the pulse steady, and the color stole gradually back to her cheek. The crisis is past. Nature's benign Disposer has permitted Nature to restore your life's gentle partner, heart to heart, mind to mind——"

"And soul to soul," I cried, in my solemn joy. "Above as below, soul to soul!" Then, at a sign from Faber, the child took me by the hand and led me up the stairs into Lilian's room.

Again those dear arms closed round me in wife-like and holy love, and those true lips kissed away my tears;—even as now, at the distance of years from that happy morn, while I write the last words of this Strange Story, the same faithful arms close around me, the same tender lips kiss away my tears.

END OF "A STRANGE STORY."

THE HAUNTED AND THE HAUNTERS:

OR,

THE HOUSE AND THE BRAIN.

A FRIEND of mine, who is a man of letters and a philosopher, said to me one day, as if between jest and earnest,—"Fancy! since we last met, I have discovered a haunted house in the midst of London."

"Really haunted?—and by what? ghosts?"

"Well I can't answer that question: all I know is this—six weeks ago my wife and I were in search of a furnished apartment. Passing a quiet street, we saw on the window of one of the houses a bill, 'Apartments Furnished.' The situation suited us: we entered the house—liked the rooms—engaged them by the week—and left them the third day. No power on earth could have reconciled my wife to stay longer; and I don't wonder at it."

"What did you see?"

"Excuse me—I have no desire to be ridiculed as a superstitious dreamer—nor, on the other hand, could I ask you to accept on my affirmation what you would hold to be incredible without the evidence of your own senses. Let me only say this, it was not so much what we saw or heard (in which you might fairly suppose that we were the dupes of our own excited fancy, or the victims of imposture in others) that drove us away, as it was an undefinable terror which seized both of us whenever we passed by the door of a certain unfurnished room, in which we neither saw nor heard anything. And the strangest marvel of all was, that for once in my life I agreed with my wife, silly woman though she be—and allowed, after the third night, that it was impossible to stay a fourth in that house. Accordingly, on the fourth morning I summoned the woman who kept the house and attended on us, and told her that the rooms did not quite suit us, and we would not stay out our week. She said, dryly, 'I know why: you have stayed longer than any other lodger. Few ever stayed a second night; none before you a third. But I take it they have been very kind to you.'

"'They—who?' I asked, affecting to smile.

"'Why, they who haunt the house, whoever they are. I don't mind them; I remember them many years ago, when I lived in this house, not as a servant; but I know they will be the death of me some day. I don't care—I'm old, and must die soon anyhow; and then I shall be with them, and in this house still.' The woman spoke with so dreary a calmness, that really it was a sort of awe that prevented my conversing with her further. I paid for my week, and too happy were my wife and I to get off so cheaply."

"You excite my cusiosity," said I; "nothing I should like better than to sleep in a haunted house. Pray give me the address of the one which you left so ignominiously."

My friend gave me the address; and when we parted, I walked straight towards the house thus indicated.

It is situated on the North side of Oxford Street, in a dull but respectable thoroughfare. I found the house shut up—no bill at the window, and no response to my knock. As I was turning away, a beer-boy, collecting pewter pots at the neighboring areas, said to me, "Do you want any one at that house, sir?"

"Yes, I heard it was to be let."

"Let!—why, the woman who kept it is dead—has been dead these three weeks, and no one can be found to stay there, though Mr. J——

offered ever so much. He offered mother, who chars for him, £1 a week just to open and shut the windows, and she would not."

"Would not!—and why?"

"The house is haunted: and the old woman who kept it was found dead in her bed, with her eyes wide open. They say the devil strangled her."

"Pooh!—you speak of Mr. J——. Is he the owner of the house?"

"Yes."

"Where does he live?"

"In G—— Street, No. —.

"What is he?—in any business?"

"No, sir—nothing particular; a single gentleman."

I gave the pot-boy the gratuity earned by his liberal information, and proceeded to Mr. J——, in G—— Street, which was close by the street that boasted the haunted house. I was lucky enough to find Mr. J—— at home—an elderly man, with intelligent countenance and prepossessing manners.

I communicated my name and my business frankly. I said I heard the house was considered to be haunted—that I had a strong desire to examine a house with so equivocal a reputation—that I should be greatly obliged if he would allow me to hire it, though only for a night. I was willing to pay for that privilege whatever he might be inclined to ask. "Sir," said Mr. J——, with great courtesy, "the house is at your service, for as short or as long a time as you please. Rent is out of the question—the obligation will be on my side should you be able to discover the cause of the strange phenomena which at present deprive it of all value. I cannot let it, for I cannot even get a servant to keep it in order or answer the door. Unluckily the house is haunted, if I may use that expression, not only by night, but by day; though at night the disturbances are of a more unpleasant and sometimes of a more alarming character. The poor old woman who died in it three weeks ago was a pauper whom I took out of a workhouse, for in her childhood she had been known to some of my family, and had once been in such good circumstances that she had rented that house of my uncle. She was a woman of superior education and strong mind, and was the only person I could ever induce to remain in the house. Indeed, since her death, which was sudden, and the coroner's inquest, which gave it a notoriety in the neighborhood, I have so despaired of finding any person to take charge of the house, much more a tenant, that I would willingly let it rent-free for a year to any one who would pay its rates and taxes."

"How long is it since the house acquired this sinister character?"

"That I can scarcely tell you, but very many years since. The old woman I spoke of said it was haunted when she rented it between thirty and forty years ago. The fact is, that my life has been spent in the East Indies, and in the civil service of the Company. I returned to England last year, on inheriting the fortune of an uncle, among whose possessions was the house in question. I found it shut up and uninhabited. I was told that it was haunted, that no one would inhabit it. I smiled at what seemed to me so idle a story. I spent some money in repairing it—added to its old-fashioned furniture a few modern articles—advertised it, and obtained a lodger for a year. He was a colonel retired on half-pay. He came in with his family, a son and a daughter, and four or five servants: they all left the house the next day; and, although each of them declared that he had seen something different from that which had scared the others, a something still was equally terrible to all. I really could not in conscience sue, nor even blame, the colonel for breach of agreement. Then I put in the old woman I have spoken of, and she was empowered to let the house in apartments. I never had one lodger who stayed more than three days. I do not tell you their stories—to no two lodgers have there been exactly the same phenomena repeated. It is better that you should judge for yourself, than enter the house with an imagination influenced by previous narratives; only be prepared to see and to hear something or other, and take whatever precautions you yourself please."

"Have you never had a curiosity yourself to pass a night in that house?"

"Yes. I passed not a night, but three hours in broad daylight alone in that house. My curiosity is not satisfied but it is quenched. I have no desire to renew the experiment. You cannot complain, you see, sir, that I am not sufficiently candid; and unless your interest be exceedingly eager and your nerves unusually strong, I honestly add, that I advise you not to pass a night in that house."

"My interest *is* exceedingly keen," said I, "and though only a coward will boast of his nerves in situations wholly unfamiliar to him, yet my nerves have been seasoned in such variety of danger that I have the right to rely on them—even in a haunted house."

Mr. J—— said very little more; he took the keys of the house out of his bureau, gave them to me,—and, thanking him cordially for his frankness, and his urbane concession to my wish, I carried off my prize.

Impatient for the experiment, as soon as I reached home, I summoned my confidential servant—a young man of gay spirits, fearless temper, and as free from superstitious prejudice as any one I could think of.

"F——," said I, "you remember in Germany how disappointed we were at not finding a ghost in that old castle, which was said to be haunted by a headless apparition? Well, I have heard of a house in London which, I have reason to hope, is decidedly haunted. I mean to sleep there to-night. From what I hear, there is no doubt that something will allow itself to be seen or to be heard—something, perhaps, excessively horrible. Do you think if I take you with me, I may rely on your presence of mind, whatever may happen?"

"Oh, sir! pray trust me," answered F——, grinning with delight.

"Very well; then here are the keys of the house—this is the address. Go now,—select for me any bedroom you please; and since the house has not been inhabited for weeks, make up a good fire—air the bed well—see, of course, that there are candles as well as fuel. Take with you my revolver and my dagger—so much for my weapons—arm yourself equally well; and if we are not a match for a dozen ghosts, we shall be but a sorry couple of Englishmen."

I was engaged for the rest of the day on business so urgent that I had not leisure to think much on the nocturnal adventure to which I had plighted my honor. I dined alone, and very late, and while dining, read, as is my habit. I selected one of the volumes of Macaulay's Essays. I thought to myself that I would take the book with me; there was so much of healthfulness in the style, and practical life in the subjects, that it would serve as an antidote against the influence of superstitious fancy.

Accordingly, about half-past nine, I put the book into my pocket, and strolled leisurely towards the haunted house. I took with me a favorite dog—an exceedingly sharp, bold and vigilant bull-terrier,—a dog fond of prowling about strange ghostly corners and passages at night in search of rats—a dog of dogs for a ghost.

It was a summer night, but chilly, the sky somewhat gloomy and overcast. Still there was a moon—faint and sickly, but still a moon—and if the clouds permitted, after midnight it would be brighter.

I reached the house, knocked, and my servant opened with a cheerful smile.

"All right, sir, and very comfortable."

"Oh!" said I, rather disappointed; "have you not seen nor heard anything remarkable?"

"Well, sir, I must own I have heard something queer."

"What?—what?"

"The sound of feet pattering behind me; and once or twice small noises like whispers close at my ear—nothing more."

"You are not at all frightened?"

"I! not a bit of it, sir;" and the man's bold look reassured me on one point—viz., that happen what might, he would not desert me.

We were in the hall, the street-door closed, and my attention was now drawn to my dog. He had at first run in eagerly enough, but had sneaked back to the door, and was scratching and whining to get out. After patting him on the head, and encouraging him gently, the dog seemed to reconcile himself to the situation, and followed me and F—— through the house, but keeping close at my heels instead of hurrying inquisitively in advance, which was his usual and normal habit in all strange places. We first visited the subterranean apartments, the kitchen and other offices, and especially the cellars, in which last there were two or three bottles of wine still left in a bin, covered with cobwebs, and evidently, by their appearance, undisturbed for many years. It was clear that the ghosts were not wine-bibbers. For the rest we discovered nothing of interest. There was a gloomy little backyard, with very high walls. The stones of this yard were very damp; and what with the damp, and what with the dust and smoke-grime on the pavement, our feet left a slight impression where we passed.

And now appeared the first strange phenomenon witnessed by myself in this strange abode. I saw, just before me, the print of a foot suddenly form itself, as it were. I stopped, caught hold of my servant, and pointed to it. In advance of that footprint as suddenly dropped another. We both saw it. I advanced quickly to the place; the footprint kept advancing before me, a small footprint—the foot of a child; the impression was too faint thoroughly to distinguish the shape, but it seemed to us both that it was the print of a naked foot. This phenomenon ceased when we arrived at the opposite wall, nor did it repeat itself on returning. We remounted the stairs, and entered the rooms on the ground floor, a dining-parlor, a small back parlor, and a still smaller third room that had been probably appropriated to a footman—all still as death. We then visited the drawing-rooms, which seemed fresh and new. In the front room I seated myself in an armchair. F—— placed on the table the candlestick with which he had lighted us. I told him to shut the door. As he turned to do so, a chair opposite to me moved from the wall quickly and noiselessly, and dropped itself about a yard from my own chair, immediately fronting it.

"Why, this is better than the turning tables," said I, with a half-laugh; and as I laughed, my dog put back his head and howled.

F——, coming back, had not observed the movement of the chair. He employed himself now in stilling the dog. I continued to gaze on the chair, and fancied I saw on it a pale blue misty outline of a human figure, but an outline so indistinct that I could only distrust my own vision. The dog now was quiet.

"Put back that chair opposite to me," said I to F——; "put it back to the wall."

F—— obeyed. "Was that you, sir?" said he, turning abruptly.

"I!—what?"

"Why, something struck me. I felt it sharply on the shoulder—just here."

"No," said I. "But we have jugglers present, and though we may not discover their tricks, we shall catch *them* before they frighten *us*."

We did not stay long in the drawing-rooms—in fact, they felt so damp and so chilly that I was glad to get to the fire upstairs. We locked the doors of the drawing-rooms—a precaution which, I should observe, we had taken with all the rooms we had searched below. The bedroom my servant had selected for me was the best on the floor—a large one, with two windows fronting the street. The four-posted bed, which took up no inconsiderable space, was opposite to the fire, which burnt clear and bright; a door in the wall to the left, between the bed and the window communicated with the room which my servant appropriated to himself. This last was a small room with a sofa-bed, and had no communication with the landing-place—no other door but that which conducted to the bedroom I was to occupy. On either side of my fireplace was a cupboard, without locks, flush with the wall and covered with the same dull-brown paper. We examined these cupboards—only hooks to suspend female dresses — nothing else; we sounded the walls—evidently solid—the outer walls of the building. Having finished the survey of these apartments, warmed myself a few moments, and lighted my cigar, I then, still accompanied by F——, went forth to complete my reconnoitre. In the landing-place there was another door; it was closed firmly. "Sir," said my servant, in surprise, "I unlocked this door with all the others when I first came; it cannot have got locked from the inside, for——"

Before he had finished his sentence, the door, which neither of us then was touching, opened quetly of itself. We looked at each other a single instant. The same thought seized both—some human agency might be detected here. I rushed in first, my servant followed. A small blank dreary room without furniture—few empty boxes and hampers in a corner—a small window—the shutters closed—not even a fire-place—no other door than that by which we had entered—no carpet on the floor, and the floor seemed very old, uneven, worm-eaten mended here and there, as was shown by the whiter patches on the wood; but no living being, and no visible place in which a living being could have hidden. As we stood gazing round, the door by which we had entered closed as quietly as it had before opened: we were imprisoned.

For the first time I felt a creep of undefinable horror. Not so my servant. "Why, they don't think to trap us, sir; I could break the trumpery door with a kick of my foot."

"Try first if it will open to your hand," said I, shaking off the vague apprehension that had seized me, "while I unclose the shutters and see what is without."

I unbarred the shutters—the window looked on the little back yard I have before described; there was no ledge without—nothing to break the sheer descent of the wall. No man getting out of that window would have found any footing till he had fallen on the stones below.

F——, meanwhile, was vainly attempting to open the door. He now turned round to me and asked my permission to use force. And I should here state, in justice to the servant, that, far from evincing any superstitious terrors, his nerve, composure, and even gaiety amidst circumstances so extraordinary, compelled my admiration, and made me congratulate myself on having secured a companion in every way fitted to the occasion. I willingly gave him the permission he required. But though he was a remarkably strong man, his force was as idle as his milder efforts; the door did not even shake to his stoutest kick. Breathless and panting, he desisted. I then tried the door myself, equally in vain. As I ceased from the effort, again that creep of horror came over me; but this time it was more cold and stubborn. I felt as if some strange and ghastly exhalation were rising up from the chinks of that rugged floor, and filling the atmosphere with a venomous influence hostile to human life. The door now very slowly and quietly opened as of its own accord. We precipitated ourselves into the landing-place. We both saw a large pale light—as large as the human figure but shapeless and unsubstantial—move before us, and ascend the stairs that led from the landing into the attics. I followed the light, and my servant followed me. It entered, to the right of the landing, a small garret, of which the door stood open. I entered in the same instant. The light then collapsed into a small globule, exceedingly brilliant and vivid; rested a moment on a bed in the corner, quivered, and vanished.

We approached the bed and examined it—a half-tester, such as is commonly found in attics devoted to servants. On the drawers that stood near it we perceived an old faded silk kerchief, with the needle still left in a rent half repaired. The kerchief was covered with dust; probably it had belonged to the old woman who had last died in that house, and this might have been her sleeping room. I had sufficient curiosity to open the drawers: there were a few odds and end of female dress, and two letters tied round with a narrow ribbon of faded yellow. I took the liberty to possess myself of the letters. We found nothing else in the room worth noticing—nor did the light reappear; but we distinctly heard, as we turned to go, a pattering footfall on the floor—just before us. We went through the other attics (in all four), the footfall still preceding us. Nothing to be seen—nothing but the footfall heard. I had the letters in my hand: jast as I was descending the stairs I distinctly felt my wrist seized, and a faint soft effort made to draw the letters from my clasp. I only held them the more tightly, and the effort ceased.

We regained the bedchamber appropriated to myself, and I then remarked that my dog had not followed us when we had left it. He was thrusting himself close to the fire, and trembling. I was impatient to examine the letters; and while I read them, my servant opened a little box in which he had deposited the weapons I had ordered him to bring; took them out, placed them on a table close at my bed-head, and then occupied himself in soothing the dog, who, however, seemed to heed him very little.

The letters were short—they were dated; the dates exactly thirty-five years ago. They were evidently from a lover to his mistress, or a husband to some young wife. Not only the terms of expression, but a distinct reference to a former voyage, indicated the writer to have been a seafarer. The spelling and handwriting were those of a man imperfectly educated, but still the language itself was forcible. In the expressions of endearment there was a kind of rough wild love; but here and there were dark and unintelligible hints at some secret not of love—some secret that seemed of crime. "We ought to love each other," was one of the sentences I remember, "for how every one else would execrate us if all was known." Again: "Don't let any one be in the same room with you at night—you talk in your sleep." And again: "What's done can't be undone; and I tell you there's nothing against us unless the dead could come to life." Here there was underlined in a better handwriting (a female's), "They do!" At the end of the letter latest in date the same female hand had written these words: "Lost at sea the 4th of June, the same day as ——."

I put down the letters, and began to muse over their contents.

Fearing, however, that the train of thought into which I fell might unsteady my nerves, I fully determined to keep my mind in a fit state to cope with whatever of marvellous the advancing night might bring forth. I roused myself—laid the letters on the table—stirred up the fire, which was still bright and cheering—and opened my volume of Macaulay. I read quietly enough till about half-past eleven. I then threw myself dressed upon the bed, and told my servant he might retire to his own room, but must keep himself awake. I bade him leave open the door between the two rooms. Thus alone, I kept two candles burning on the table by my bed-head. I placed my watch beside the weapons, and calmly resumed my Macaulay. Opposite to me the fire burned clear; and on the hearthrug, seemingly asleep, lay the dog. In about twenty minutes I felt an exceedingly cold air pass by my cheek, like a sudden draught. I fancied the door to my right, communicating with the landing-place, must have got open; but no—it was closed. I then turned my glance to my left, and saw the flame of the candles violently swayed as by a wind. At the same moment the watch beside the revolver softly slid from the table—softly, softly—no visible hand—it was gone. I sprang up, seizing the revolver with the one hand, the dagger with other: I was not willing that my weapons should share the fate of the watch. Thus armed, I looked round the floor—no sign of the watch. Three slow, loud, distinct knocks were now heard at the bed-head; my servant called out, "Is that you, sir?"

"No; be on your guard."

The dog now roused himself and sat on his haunches, his ears moving quickly backwards and forwards. He kept his eyes fixed on me with a look so strange that he concentred all my attention on himself. Slowly he rose up, all his hair bristling, and stood perfectly rigid, and with the same wild stare. I had no time, however, to examine the dog. Presently my servant emerged from his room; and if ever I saw horror in the human face, it was then. I should not have recognized him had we met in the street, so altered was every lineament. He passed by me quickly, saying in a whisper that seemed scarcely to come from his lips, "Run—run! it is after me!" He gained the door to the landing, pulled it open, and rushed forth. I followed him into the the landing involuntarily, calling him to stop; but, without heeding me, he bounded down the stairs, clinging to the balusters, and taking several steps at a time. I heard, where I stood, the street-door open—heard it again clap to. I was left alone in the haunted house.

It was but for a moment that I remained undecided whether or not to follow my servant; pride and curiosity alike forbade so dastardly a flight. I re-entered my room, closing the door after me, and proceeded cautiously into the interior chamber. I encountered nothing to justify my servant's terror. I again carefully examined the walls, to see if there were any concealed door. I could find no trace of one—not even a seam in the dull-brawn paper with which the room was hung. How, then, had the THING, whatever it was, which had so scared him, obtained ingress except through my own chamber?

I returned to my room, shut and locked the door that opened upon the interior one, and stood on the hearth, expectant and prepared. I now perceived that the dog had slunk into an angle of the wall, and was pressing himself close against it, as if literally striving to force his way into it. I approached the animal and spoke to it; the poor brute was evidently beside itself with terror. It showed all its teeth, the slaver dropping from its jaws, and would certainly have bitten me if I had touched it. It did not seem to recognize me. Whoever has seen at the Zoological Gardens a rabbit fascinated by a serpent, cowering in a corner, may form some idea of the anguish which the dog exhibited. Finding all efforts to soothe the animal in vain, and fearing that his bite might be as venomous in that state as in the madness of hydrophobia, I left him alone, placed my weapons on the table beside the fire, seated myself, and recommenced my Macaulay.

Perhaps, in order not to appear seeking credit for a courage, or rather a coolness, which the reader may conceive I exaggerate, I may be pardoned if I pause to indulge in one or two egotistical remarks.

As I hold presence of mind, or what is called courage, to be precisely proportioned to familiarity with the circumstances that lead to it, so I should say that I had been long sufficiently familiar with all experiments that appertain to the Marvellous. I had witnessed many very extraordinary phenomena in various parts of the world—phenomena that would be either totally disbelieved if I stated them, or ascribed to supernatural agencies. Now, my theory is that the Supernatural is the Impossible, and that what is called supernatural is only a something in the laws of nature of which we have been hitherto ignorant. Therefore, if a ghost rise before me, I have not the right to say, "So, then, the supernatural is possible," but rather, "So, then, the apparition of a ghost is, contrary to received opinion, within the laws of nature—*i.e.*, not supernatural."

Now, in all that I had hitherto witnessed, and indeed in all the wonders which the amateurs of mystery in our age record as facts, a material living agency is always required. On the continent you will find still magicians who assert that they can raise spirits. Assume for the moment that they assert truly, still the living material form of the magician is present; and he is the material agency by which, from some constitutional peculiarities, certain strange phenomena are represented to your natural senses.

Accept, again, as truthful, the tales of spirit Manifestation in America—musical or other sounds—writings on paper, produced by no discernible hand—articles of furniture moved without apparent human agency—or the actual sight and touch of hands, to which no bodies seem to belong—still there must be found the MEDIUM or living being, with constitutional peculiarities capable of obtaining these signs. In fine, in all such marvels, supposing even that there is no imposture, there must be a human being like ourselves by whom, or through whom, the effects presented to human beings are produced. It is so with the now familiar phenomena of mesmerism or electro-biology; the mind of the person operated on is affected through a material living agent. Nor, supposing it true that a mesmerised patient can repond to to the will or passes of a mesmeriser a hundred miles distant, is the response less occasioned by a material fluid—call it Electric, call it Odic, call it what you will—which has the power of traversing space and passing obstacles, that the material effect is communicated from one to the other. Hence all that I had hitherto witnessed, or expected to witness, in this strange house, I believed to be occasioned through some agency or medium as mortal as myself: and this idea necessarily prevented the awe with which those who regard as supernatural, things that are not within the ordinary operations of nature, might have been impressed by the adventures of that memorable night.

As, then, it was my conjecture that all that was presented, or would be presented to my senses, must originate in some human being gifted by constitution with the power so to present them, and having some motive so to do, I felt an interest in my theory which, in its way, was rather philosophical than superstitious. And I can sincerely say that I was in as tranquil a temper for observation as any practical experimentalist could be in awaiting the effect of some rare, though perhaps perilous, chemical combination. Of course, the more I kept my mind detached from fancy, the more the temper fitted for observation would be obtained; and I therefore riveted eye and thought on the strong daylight sense in the page of my Macaulay.

I now became aware that something interposed between the page and the light—the page was over-shadowed: I looked up, and I saw what I shall find it very difficult, perhaps impossible, to describe.

It was a Darkness shaping itself forth from the air in very undefined outline. I cannot say it was of a human form, and yet it had more resemblance to a human form, or rather shadow, than to anything else. As it stood, wholly apart and distinct from the air and the light around it, its dimensions seemed gigantic, the summit nearly touching the ceiling. While I gazed, a feeling of intense cold seized me. An iceberg before me could not more have chilled me; nor could the cold of an iceberg have been more purely physical. I feel convinced that it was not the cold caused by fear. As I continued to gaze, I thought—but this I cannot say with precision—that I distinguished two eyes looking down on me from the height. One moment I fancied that I distinguished them clearly, the next they seemed gone; but still two rays of a pale-blue light frequently shot through the darkness, as from the height on which I half believed, half doubted, that I had encountered the eyes.

I strove to speak—my voice utterly failed me; I could only think to myself, "Is this fear? it is *not* fear!" I strove to rise—in vain; I felt as if weighed down by an irresistible force. Indeed, my impressions was that of an immense and overwhelming Power opposed to any volition;—that sense of utter inadequacy to cope with a force beyond man's, which one may feel *physically* in a storm at sea, in a conflagration, or when confronting some terrible wild beast, or rather, perhaps, the shark of the ocean, I felt *morally*. Opposed to my will was another will, as far superior to its strength as storm, fire, and shark are superior in material force to the force of man.

And now, as this impression grew on me—now came, at last, horror—horror to a degree that no words can convey. Still I retained pride, if not courage; and in my own mind I said, "This is horror, but it is not fear; unless I fear I cannot be harmed; my reason rejects this thing; it is an illusion—I do not fear." With a violent effort I succeeded at last in stretching out my hand towards the weapon on the table: as I did so, on the arm and shoulder I received a strange shock, and my arm fell to my side powerless. And now, to add to my horror, the light began slowly to wane from the candles—they were not, as it were, extinguished, but their flame seemed very gradually withdrawn: it was the same with the fire—the light was extracted from the fuel; in a few minutes the room was in utter darkness.

The dread that came over me, to be thus in the dark with that dark Thing, whose power was so intensely felt, brought a reaction of nerve. In fact, terror had reached that climax, that either my senses must have deserted me, or I must have burst through the spell. I did burst through it. I found voice, though the voice was a shriek. I remember that I broke forth with words like these—"I do not fear, my soul does not fear;" and at the same time I found the strength to rise. Still in that profound gloom I rushed to one of the windows—tore aside the curtain—flung open the shutters; my first thought was—LIGHT.—And when I saw the moon high, clear, and calm, I felt a joy that almost compensated for the previous terror. There, was the moon, there, was also the light from the gas-lamps in the deserted slumberous street. I turned to look back into the room; the moon penetrated its shadow very palely and partially—but still there was light. The dark Thing, whatever it might be, was gone—except that I could yet see a dim shadow, which seemed the shadow of that shade, against the opposite wall.

My eye now rested on the table, and from under the table (which was without cloth or cover—an old mahogany round table) there rose a hand, visible as far as the wrist. It was a hand, seemingly, as much of flesh and blood as my own, but the hand of an aged person—lean, wrinkled, small, too—a woman's hand. That hand very softly closed on the two letters that lay on the table: hand and letters both vanished. There then came the same three loud measured knocks I heard at the bed-head before this extaordinary drama had commenced.

As those sounds slowly ceased, I felt the whole room vibrate sensibly; and at the far end there rose, as from the floor, sparks or globules like bubbles of light, many-colored—green, yellow, fire-red, azure. Up and down, to and fro, hither, thither, as tiny Will-o'-the-Wisps, the sparks moved, slow or swift, each at his own caprice. A chair (as in the drawing-room below) was now advanced from the wall without apparent agency, and placed at the opposite side of the table. Suddenly, as forth from the chair, there grew a shape—a woman's shape. It was distinct as a shape of life—ghastly as a shape of death. The face was that of youth, with a strange mournful beauty; the throat and shoulders were bare, the rest of the form in a loose robe of cloudy white. It began sleeking its long yellow hair, which fell over its shoulders; its eyes were not turned towards me, but to the door; it seemed listening, watching, waiting. The shadow of the shade in the background grew darker; and again I thought I beheld the eyes gleaming out from the summit of the shadow—eyes fixed upon that shape.

As if from the door, though it did not open,

there grew out another shape, equally distinct, equally ghastly—a man's shape—a young man's. It was in the dress of the last century, or rather in a likeness of such dress (for both the male shape and the female, though defined, were evidently unsubstantial, impalpable —simulacra — phantasms); and there was something incogruous, gtotesque, yet fearful, in the contrast between the elaborate finery, the courtly precision of that old-fashioned garb, with its ruffles and lace and buckles, and the corpse-like aspect and ghost-like stillness of the flitting wearer. Just as the male shape approached the female, the dark Shadow started from the wall, all three for a moment wrapped in darkness. When the pale light returned, the two phantoms were as in the grasp of the shadow that towered between them; and there was a bloodstain on the breast of the female; and the phantom male was leaning on its phantom sword, and blood seemed trickling fast from the ruffles, from the lace; and the darkness of the intermediate Shadow swallowed them up —they were gone. And again the bubbles of light shot, and sailed, and undulated, growing thicker and thicker and more wildly confused in their movements.

The closet door to the right of the fireplace now opened, and from the aperture there came the form of an aged woman. In her hand she held letters,—the very letters over which I had seen *the* Hand close; and behind her I heard a footstep. She turned round as if to listen, and then she opened the letters and seemed to read; and over her shoulder I saw a livid face, the face as of a man long drowned—bloated, bleached—seaweed tangled in its dripping hair; and at her feet lay a form as of a corpse, and beside the corpse there cowered a child, a miserable squalid child, with famine in its cheeks and fear in its eyes. And as I looked in the old woman's face, the wrinkles and lines vanished and it became a face of youth—hard-eyed, stony, but still youth; and the Shadow darted forth, and darkened over these phantoms as it had darkened over the last.

Nothing now was left but the Shadow, and on that my eyes were intently fixed, till again eyes grew out of the Shadow — malignant, serpent eyes. And the bubbles of light again rose and fell, and in their disorder, irregular, turbulent maze, mingled with the wan moonlight. And now from these globules themselves, as from the shell of an egg, monstrous things burst out; the air grew filled with them: larvæ so bloodless and so hideous that I can in no way describe them except to remind the reader of the swarming life which the solar microscope brings before his eyes in a drop of water—things transparent, supple, agile, chasing each other, devouring each other—forms like nought ever beheld by the naked eye. As the shapes were without symmetry, so their movements were without order. In their very vagrancies their was no sport; they came round me and round, thicker and faster and swifter, swarming over my head, crawling over my right arm, which was outstretched in involuntary command against all evil beings. Sometimes I felt myself touched, but not by them; invisible hands touched me. Once I felt the clutch as of cold soft fingers at my throat. I was still equally conscious that if I gave way to fear I should be in bodily peril; and I concentrated all my faculties in the single focus of resisting, stubborn will. And I turned my sight from the Shadow—above all, from those strange serpent eyes—eyes that had now become distinctly visible. For there, though in nought else around me. I was aware that there was a WILL, and a will of intense, creative, working evil, which might crush down my own.

The pale atmosphere in the room began now to redden as if in the air of some near conflagration. The larvæ grew lurid as things that live in fire. Again the room vibrated; again were heard the three measured knocks; and again all things were swallowed up in the darkness of the dark Shadow, as if out of that darkness all had come, into that darkness all returned.

As the gloom receded, the Shadow was wholly gone. Slowly as it had been withdrawn, the flame grew again into the candles on the table, again into the fuel in the grate. The whole room came once more calmly, healthfully into sight.

The two doors were still closed, the door communicating with the servant's room still locked. In the corner of the wall into which he had so convulsively niched himself, lay the dog. I called to him—no movement; I approached—the animal was dead; his eyes protruded; his tongue out of his mouth; the froth gathered round his jaws. I took him in my arms; I brought him to the fire; I felt acute grief for the loss of my poor favorite—acute self-reproach; I accused myself of his death; I imagined he had died of fright. But what was my surprise on finding that his neck was actually broken. Had this been done in the dark?—must it not have been by a hand human as mine?—must there not have been a human agency all the while in that room? Good cause to suspect it. I cannot tell. I cannot do more than state the fact fairly; the reader may draw his own inference.

Another surprising circumstance—my watch was restored to the table from which it had been so mysteriously withdrawn; but it had stopped at the very moment it was so withdrawn; nor, despite all the skill of the watchmaker, has it ever gone slnce—that is, it will go in a strange erratic way for a few hours, and then come to a dead stop—it is worthless.

Nothing more chanced for the rest of the night. Nor, indeed, had I long to wait before the dawn broke. Nor till it was broad daylight did I quit the haunted house. Before I did so, I revisited the little blind room in which my servant and myself had been for a time imprisoned. I had a strong impression—for which I could not account—that from that room had originated the mechanism of the phenomena—if I may use the term—which had been experienced in my chamber. And though I entered it now in the clear day, with the sun peering through the filmy window, I still felt, as I stood on its floor, the creep of the horror which I had first there experienced the night before, and which had been so aggravated by what had passed in my own chamber. I could not, indeed, bear to stay more than half a minute within those walls. I descended the stairs, and again I heard the footfall before me; and when I opened the street door, I thought I could distinguish a very low laugh. I gained my own home, expecting to find my runaway servant there. But he had not presented himself; nor did I hear more of him for three days, when I received a letter from him, dated from Liverpool to this effect:—

"Honored Sir,—I humbly entreat your pardon, though I can scarcely hope that you will think I deserve it, unless—which Heaven forbid—you saw what I did. I feel that it will be years before I can recover myself· and as to being fit for service, it is out of the question. I am therefore going to my brother-in-law at Melbourne. The ship sails to-morrow. Perhaps the long voyage may set me up. I do nothing now but start and tremble, and fancy IT is behind me. I humbly beg you, honored sir, to order my clothes, and whatever wages are due to me, to be sent to my mother's, at Walworth.—John knows her address."

The letter ended with additional apologies, somewhat incoherent, and explanatory details as to effects that had been under the writer's charge.

This flight may perhaps warrant a suspicion that the man wished to go to Australia, and had been somehow or other fraudulently mixed up with the events of the night. I say nothing in refutation of that conjecture; rather, I suggest it as one that would seem to many persons the most probable solution of improbable occurrences. My belief in my own theory remained unshaken. I returned in the evening to the house, to bring away in a hack cab the things I had left there, with my poor dog's body. In this task I was not disturbed, nor did any incident worth note befall me, except that still, on ascending and descending the stairs, I heard the same footfall in advance. On leaving the house, I went to Mr. J.'s. He was at home. I returned him the keys, told him that my curiosity was sufficiently gratified, and was about to relate quickly what had passed, when he stopped me, and said, though with much politeness, that he had no longer any interest in a mystery which none had ever solved.

I determined at least to tell him of the two letters I had read, as well as of the extraordinary manner in which they had disappeared, and I then inquired if he thought they had been addressed to the woman who had died in the house, and if there were anything in her early history which could possibly confirm the dark suspicions to which the letters gave rise. Mr. J—— seemed startled, and, after musing a few moments, answered, "I am but little acquainted with the woman's earlier history, except, as I before told you, that her family were known to mine. But you revive some vague reminiscences to her prejudice. I will make inquiries, and inform you of their result. Still. even if we could admit the popular superstition that a person who had been either the perpetrator or the victim of dark crimes in life could revisit, as a restless spirit, the scene in which those crimes had been committed, I should observe that the house was infested by strange sights and sounds before the old woman died—you smile—what would you say?"

"I would say this, that I am convinced, if we could get to the bottom of these mysteries, we should find a living human agency."

"What! you believe it is all an imposture? for what object?"

"Not an imposture in the ordinary sense of the word. If suddenly I were to sink into a deep sleep, from which you could not awake me, but in that sleep could answer questions with an accuracy which I could not pretend to when awake—tell you what money you had in your pocket—nay, describe your very thoughts—it is not necessarily an imposture, any more than it is necessarily supernatural. I should be, unconsciously to myself, under a mesmeric influence, conveyed to me from a distance by a human being who had acquired power over me by previous *rapport*."

"But if a mesmeriser could so affect another living being, can you suppose that a mesmeriser could also affect inanimate objects: move chairs—open and shut doors?"

"Or impress our senses with the belief in such effects—we never having been *en rapport* with the person acting on us? No. What is commonly called mesmerism could not do this; but there may be a power akin to mesmerism, and superior to it—the power that in the old days was called Magic. That such a power may extend to all inanimate objects of matter, I do not say; but if so, it would not be against nature—it would be only a rare power in nature which might be given to constitutions with certain peculiarities, and cultivated by practice to an extraordinary degree. That such a power might extend over the dead—that is over certain thoughts and memories that the dead may still retain—and compel, not that which ought properly to be called the Soul, and which is far beyond human reach, but rather a phantom of what has been most earth-stained on earth, to make itself apparent to our senses—is a very ancient though obsolete theory, upon which I will hazard no opinion. But I do not conceive the power would be supernatural. Let me illustrate what I mean from an experiment which Paracelsus describes as not difficult, and which the author of the *Curiosities of Literature* cites as credible:—A flower perishes; you burn it. Whatever were the elements of that flower while it lived are gone, dispersed, you know not whither; you can never discover nor re-collect them. But you can, by chemistry, out of the burnt dust of that flower, raise a spectrum of the flower, just as it seemed in life. It may be the same with the human being. The soul has as much escaped you as the essence or elements of the flower. Still you may make a spectrum of it.

"And this phantom, though in the popular superstition it is held to be the soul of the departed, must not be confounded with the true soul; it is but the eidolon of the dead form. Hence, like the best attested stories of ghosts or spirits, the thing that most strikes us is the absence of what we hold to be soul; that is, of superior emancipated intelligence. These apparitions come for little or no object—they seldom speak when they do come; if they speak, they utter no ideas above those of an ordinary person on earth. American spirit-seers have published volumes of communications in prose and verse, which they assert to be given in the names of the most illustrious dead—Shakespeare, Bacon—heaven knows whom. Those communications, taking the best, are certainly not a whit of higher order than would be communications from living persons of fair talent and education; they are wondrously inferior to what Bacon, Shakespeare, and Plato said and wrote when on earth. Nor, what is more noticeable, do they ever contain an idea that was not on the earth before. Wonderful, therefore, as such phenomena may be (granting them to be truthful), I see much that philosophy may question, nothing that it is incumbent on philosophy to deny viz., nothing supernatural. They are but ideas conveyed somehow or other (we have not yet discovered the means) from one mortal brain to another. Whether, in so doing, tables walk of their own accord, or fiend-like shapes appear in a magic circle, or bodyless hands rise and remove material objects, or a Thing of Darkness, such as presented itself to me, freeze our blood—still am I persuaded that these are but agencies conveyed, as fiby electric wires, to my own brain from the brain of another. In some constitutions there is a natural chemistry, and these constitutions may produce chemic wonders—in others a natural fluid, call it electricity, and these may produce electric wonders.

"But the wonders differ from Normal Science in this—they are alike objectless, purposeless, puerile, frivolous. They lead on to no grand results; and therefore the world does not heed, and true sages have not cultivated them. But sure I am, that of all I saw or heard, a man, human as myself, was the remote originator; and I believe unconsciously to himself as to the exact effects produced, for this reason: no two persons, you say, have ever told you that they experienced exactly the same thing. Well, observe, no two persons ever experience exactly the same dream. If this were an ordinary imposture, the machinery would be arranged for results that would but little vary; if it were a supernatural agency permitted by the Almighty, it would surely be for some definite end. These phenomena belong to neither class; my persuasion is, that they originate in some brain now far distant; that that brain had no distinct volition in anything that occurred; that what does occur reflects but its devious, motley, ever-shifting, half-formed thoughts; in short, that it has been but the dreams of such a brain put into action and invested with a semi-substance. That this brain is of immense power, that it can set matter into movement, that it is malignant and destructive, I believe; some material force must have killed my dog; the same force might, for aught I know, have sufficed to kill myself, had I been as subjugated by terror as the dog—had my intellect or my spirit given me no counter-vailing resistance in my will."

"It killed your dog! that is fearful! indeed it is strange that no animal can be induced to stay in that house; not even a cat. Rats and mice are never found in it."

"The instincts of the brute creation detect influences deadly to their existence. Man's reason has a sense less subtle, because it has a resisting power more supreme. But enough; do you comprehend my theory?"

"Yes, though imperfectly—and I accept any crotchet (pardon the word), however odd, rather than embrace at once the notion of ghosts and hob-goblins we imbibed in our nurseries. Still, to my unfortunate house the evil is the same. What on earth can I do with the house?"

"I will tell you what I would do. I am convinced from my own internal feelings that the small unfurnished room at right angles to the door of the bedroom which I occupied, forms a starting-point or receptacle for the influences which haunt the house; and I strongly advise you to have the walls opened, the floor removed—nay, the whole room pulled down. I observe that it is detached from the body of the house, built over the small back-yard, and could be removed without injury to the rest of the building."

"And you think, if I did that——'

"You would cut off the telegraph wires. Try it. I am so persuaded that I am right, that I will pay half the expense if you will allow me to direct the operations."

"Nay, I am well able to afford the cost; for the rest, allow me to write to you."

About ten days afterwards I received a letter from Mr. J——, telling me that he had visited the house since I had seen him; that he had fonnd the two letters I had described replaced in the drawer from which I had taken them; that he had read them with misgivings like my own; that he had instituted a cautious inquiry about the woman to whom I rightly conjectured they had been written. It seemed that thirty six years ago (a year before the date of the letters) she had married, against the wish of her relations, an American of very suspicious character, in fact, he was generally believed to have been a pirate. She herself was the daughter of very respectable tradespeople, and had served in the capacity of a nursery governess before her marriage. She had a brother, a widower, who was considered wealthy, and who had one child of about six years old. A month after the marriage, the body of this brother was found in the Thames, near London Bridge; there seemed some marks of violence about his throat, but they were not deemed sufficient to warrant the inquest in any other verdict than that of "found drowned."

The American and his wife took charge of the little boy, the deceased brother having by his will left his sister the guardian of his only child—and in the event of the child's death, the sister inherited. The child died about six months afterwards—it was supposed to have been neglected and ill-treated. The neighbors deposed to have heard it shriek at night. The surgeon who had examined it after death, said that it was emaciated as if from want of nourishment, and the body was covered with livid bruises. It seemed that one winter night the child had sought to escape—crept out into the back-yard—tried to scale the wall—fallen back exhausted, and been found at morning on the stones in a dying state. But though there was some evidence of cruelty, there was none of murder; and the aunt and her husband had sought to palliate cruelty by alleging the exceeding stubbornness and perversity of the child, who was declared to be half-witted. Be that as it may, at the orphan's death the aunt inherited her brother's fortune. Before the first wedded year was out the American quitted England abruptly, and never returned to it. He obtained a cruising vessel, which was lost in the Atlantic two years afterwards. The widow was left in affluence: but reverses of various kinds had befallen her; a bank broke—an investment failed—she went into a small business and became insolvent—then she entered into service, sinking lower and lower, from housekeeper down to maid-of-all-work—never long retaining a place, though nothing decided agáinst her character was ever alleged. She was considered sober, honest, and peculiarly quiet in her ways; still nothing prospered with her. And so she had dropped into the workhouse, from which Mr. J—— had taken her, to be placed in charge of the very house which she had rented as mistress in the first year of her wedded life.

Mr. J—— added that he had passed an hour alone in the unfurnished room which I had urged him to destroy, and that his impressions of dread while there were so great, though he had neither heard nor seen anything, that he was eager to have the walls bared and the floors removed as I had suggested. He had engaged persons for the work, and would commence any day I would name.

The day was accordingly fixed. I repaired to the haunted house—we went into the blind dreary room, took up the skirting, and then the floors. Under the rafters, covered with rubbish, was found a trap-door, quite large enough to admit a man. It was closely nailed down, with clamps and rivets of iron. On removing these we descended into a room below, the existence of which had never been suspected. In this room there had been a window and a flue, but they had been bricked over, evidently for many years. By the help of candles we examined this place; it still retained some mouldering furniture — three chairs, an oak settle, a table—all of the fashion of about eighty years ago. There was a chest of drawers against the wall, in which we found, half-rotted away, old-fashioned articles of a man's dress, such as might have been worn eighty or a hundred years ago by a gentleman of some rank—costly steel buckles and buttons, like those yet worn in court-dresses, a handsome court sword—in a waistcoat which had once been rich with gold-lace, but which was now blackened and foul with damp, we found five guineas, a few silver coins, and an ivory ticket, probably for some place of entertainment long since passed away. But our main discovery was in a kind of iron safe fixed to the wall, the lock of which it cost us much trouble to get picked.

In this safe were three shelves, and two small drawers. Ranged on the shelves were several small bottles of crystal, hermetically stopped. They contained colorless volatile essences, of the nature of which I shall only say that they were not poisons—phosphor and ammonia entered into some of them. There were also some very curious glass tubes, and a small pointed rod of iron, with a large lump of rock-crystal, and another of amber—also a loadstone of great power.

In one of the drawers we found a miniature portrait set in gold, and retaining the freshness of its colors most remarkably, considering the length of time it had probably been there. The portrait was that of a man who might be somewhat advanced in middle life, perhaps forty-seven or forty-eight.

It was a remarkable face—a most impressive face. If you could fancy some mighty serpent transformed into a man, preserving in the human lineaments the old serpent type, you would have a better idea of that countenance than long descriptions can convey: the width and flatness of frontal—the tapering elegance of contour disguising the strength of the deadly jaw—the long, large, terrible eye, glittering and green as the emerald—and withal a certain ruthless calm, as if from the consciousness of an immense power.

Mechanilly I turned round the miniature to examine the back of it, and on the back was engraved a pentacle; in the middle of the pentacle a ladder, and the third step of the ladder was formed by the date 1765. Examining still more minutely, I detected a spring; this, on being pressed, opened the back of the miniature as a lid. Withinside the lid were engraved, 'Marianna to thee—be faithful in life and in death to ——.' Here follows a name that I will not mention, but it was not unfamiliar to me. I had heard it spoken of by old men in my childhood as the name borne by a dazzling charlatan who had made a great sensation in London for a year or so, and had fled the country on the charge of a double murder within his own house—that of his mistress and his rival. I said nothing of this to Mr. J——, to whom reluctantly I resigned the miniature.

We had found no difficulty in opening the first drawer within the iron safe; we found great difficulty in opening the second: it was not locked, but it resisted all efforts, till we inserted in the clinks the edge of a chisel. When we had thus drawn it forth, we found a very singular apparatus in the nicest order. upon a small thin book, or rather tablet, was placed a saucer of crystal: this saucer was filled with a clear liquid—on that liquid floated a kind of compass, with a needle shifting rapidly round; but instead of the usual points of a compass were seven strange characters, not very unlike those used by astrologers to denote the planets.

"A peculiar, but not strong nor displeasing odor came from this drawer, which was lined with a wood that we afterwards discovered to be hazel. Whatever the cause of this odor, it produced a material effect on the nerves. We all felt it, even the two workmen who were in the room—a creeping tingling sensation from the tips of the fingers to the roots of the hair. Impatient to examine the tablet, I removed the saucer. As I did so the needle of the compass went round and round with exceeding swiftness, and I felt a shock that ran through my whole frame, so that I dropped the saucer on the floor. The liquid was spilt—the saucer was broken—the compass rolled to the end of the room—and at that instant the walls shook to and fro, as if a giant had swayed and rocked them.

The two workmen were so frightened that they ran up the ladder by which we had descended from the trap-door; but seeing that nothing more happened, they were easily induced to return.

Meanwhile I had opened the tablet: it was bound in plain red leather, with a silver clasp; it contained but one sheet of thick vellum, and on that sheet were inscribed, within a double pentacle, words in old monkish Latin, which are literally to be translated thus: "On all that it can reach within these walls—sentient or inanimate, living or dead—as moves the needle, so work my will! Accursed be the house, and restless be the dwellers therein."

We found no more. Mr. J—— burnt the tablet and its anathema. He razed to the foundations the part of the building containing the secret room with the chamber over it. He had then the courage to inhabit the house himself for a month, and a quieter, better-conditional house could not be found in all London. Subsequently he let it to advantage, and his tenant has made no complaints.

END OF "THE HAUNTED AND THE HAUNTERS."

LAST OF THE BARONS.

THE LAST OF THE BARONS.

DEDICATORY EPISTLE.

I DEDICATE to you, my indulgent Critic and long-tired Friend, the work which owes its origin to your suggestion. Long since, you urged me to attempt a fiction which might borrow its characters from our own Records, and serve to illustrate some of those truths which History is too often compelled to leave to the Tale-teller, the Dramatist, and the Poet. Unquestionably, Fiction, when aspiring to something higher than mere romance, does not pervert, but elucidate Facts. He who employs it worthily must, like a biographer, study the time and the characters he selects, with a minute and earnest diligence which the general historian, whose range extends over centuries, can scarcely be expected to bestow upon the things and the men of a single epoch; his descriptions should fill up with color and detail the cold outlines of the rapid chronicler; and, in spite of all that has been argued by pseudo-critics, the very fancy which urged and animated his theme should necessarily tend to increase the reader's practical and familiar acquaintance with the habits, the motives, and the modes of thought, which constitute the true idiosyncrasy of an age. More than all, to Fiction is permitted that liberal use of Analogical Hoypothesis which is denied to History, and which, if sobered by research, and enlightened by that knowledge of mankind (without which Fiction can neither harm nor profit, for it becomes unreadable), tends to clear up much that were otherwise obscure, and to solve the disputes and difficulties of contradictory evidence by the philosophy of the human heart.

My own impression of the greatness of the labor to which you invited me, made me the more diffident of success, inasmuch as the field of English historical fiction had been so amply cultivated not only by the most brilliant of our many glorious Novelists, but by later writers of high and merited reputation. But however the annals of our History have been exhausted by the industry of Romance, the subject you finally pressed on my choice is unquestionably one which, whether in the delineation of character, the expression of passion, or the suggestion of historical truths, can hardly fail to direct the Novelist to paths wholly untrodden by his predecessors in the Land of Fiction.

Encouraged by you, I commenced my task —encouraged by you, I venture, on concluding it, to believe that, despite the partial adoption of that established compromise between the modern and the elder diction, which Sir Walter Scott so artistically improved from the more rugged phraseology employed by Strutt, and which later writers have perhaps somewhat over-hacknied, I may yet have avoided all material trespass upon ground which others have already redeemed from the waste.—Whatever the produce of the soil I have selected, I claim, at least, to have cleared it with my own labor, and ploughed it with my own heifer.

The reign of Edward IV. is in itself suggestive of new considerations and unexhausted interest to those who accurately regard it. Then commenced the policy consummated by Henry VII.; then were broken up the great elements of the old feudal order; a new Nobility was called into power, to aid the growing Middle Class in its struggles with the ancient; and in the fate of the hero of the age, Richard Nevile, Earl of Warwick, popularly called the King-maker, "the greatest as well as the last of those mighty Barons who formerly overawed the Crown," * was involved the very principle of our existing civilization. It adds to the wide scope of Fiction, which ever loves to explore the twilight, that, as Hume has truly observed—"No part of English history since the Conqust, is so obscure, so uncertain, so little authentic or consistent, as that of the Wars between the two roses."† It adds also to the importance of that conjectural research in which Fiction may be made so interesting and so useful, that—"this profound darkness falls upon us just on the eve of the restoration of letters;"‡ while, amidst the gloom, we perceive the movement of those great and heroic passions in which Fiction finds delineations everlastingly new, and are brought in contact with characters sufficiently familiar for interest, sufficiently remote for adaptation to romance, and, above all, so frequently obscured by contradictory evidence, that we lend ourselves willingly to any one who seeks to help our judgment of the individual by tests taken from the general knowledge of mankind.

Round the great image of the Last of the Barons group Edward the Fourth, at once frank and false; the brilliant but ominous boyhood of Richard the Third; the accomplished Hastings, "a good knight and gentle, but somewhat dissolute of living;" § the vehement and fiery Margaret of Anjou, the meek image of her "holy Henry," and the pale shadow of their son: there, may we see, also, the gorgeous Prelate, refining in policy and wile, as the enthusiasm and energy which had formerly upheld the Ancient Church pass into the stern and persecuted votaries of the New: We behold, in that social transition, the sober Trader—outgrowing the prejudices of the rude retainer or rustic franklin, from he is sprung—recognizing sagaciously, and supporting sturdily, the sectarian interests of his order, and preparing the way for the mighty Middle Class in which our modern Civilization, with its faults and its merits, has established its strong hold; while, in contrast to the measured and thoughtful notions of liberty which prudent Commerce entertains, we are reminded of the political fanaticism of the secret Lollard—of the *jacquire* of the turbulent mobleader; and perceive, amidst the various tyrannies of the time, and often partially allied with the warlike seignorie*—ever jealous against all kingly despotism,—the restless and ignorant movement of a democratic principle, ultimately suppressed, though not destroyed, under the Tudors, by the strong union of a Middle Class, anxious for security and order, with an Executive Authority determined upon absolute sway.

Nor should we obtain a complete and comprehensive view of that most interesting Period of Transition, unless we saw something of the influence which the sombre and sinister wisdom of Italian policy began to exercise over the councils of the great—a policy of refined stratagem—of complicated intrigue—of systematic falsehood—of ruthless, but secret violence: a policy which actuated the fell statecraft of Louis XI., which darkened, whenever he paused to think and to scheme, the gaudy and jovial character of Edward IV.; which appeared in its fullest combination of profound guile and resolute will in Richard III., and,—softened down into more plausible and specious purpose by the unimpassioned sagacity of Henry VII.—finally attained the object which justified all its villanies to the princes of its native land—namely, the tranquillity of a settled state, and the establishment of a civilized but imperious despotism.

Again, in that twilight time, upon which was dawning the great Invention that gave to Letters and to Science the precision and durability of the printed page; it is interesting to conjecture what would have been the fate of any scientific achievement for which the world was less prepared. The reception of printing into England, chanced just at the happy period when Scholarship and Literature were favored by the great. The princes of York, with the exception of Edward IV. himself, who had, however, the grace to lament his own want of

* Hume adds, "and rendered the people incapable of divil government;" a sentence, which, perhaps, judges too hastily the whole question at issue in our earlier history, between the jealousy of the Barons and the authority of the King.

† HUME. ‡ Ibid.

§ Chronicle of Edward V. in Stowe.

* For it is noticeable that in nearly all the popular risings—that of Cade, of Robin of Fedesdale, and afterwards of that which Perkin Warbeck made subservient to his extraordinary enterprise, the proclamations of the rebels always announced, among their popular grievances, the depression of the ancient nobles and the elevation of new men.

learning, and the taste to appreciate it in others, were highly educated. The Lords Rivers and Hastings * were accomplished in all the "witte and lere" of their age. Princes and peers vied with each other in their patronage of Caxton, and Richard III., during his brief reign, spared no pains to circulate to the utmost the invention destined to transmit his own memory to the hatred and the horror of all succeeding time. But when we look around us, we see, in contrast to the gracious and fostering reception of the mere mechanism by which science is made manifest, the utmost intolerance to science itself. The mathematics in especial are deemed the very cabala of the black art—accusations of witchcraft were never more abundant, and yet, strange to say, those who openly professed to practise the unhallowed science,† and contrived to make their deceptions profitable to some unworthy political purpose, appear to have enjoyed safety, and sometimes even honor, while those who, occupied with some practical, useful, and noble pursuits, uncomprehended by prince or people, denied their sorcery, were dispatched without mercy. The Mathematician and Astronomer, Bolingbroke (the greatest clerk of his age), is hanged and quartered as a wizard, while not only impunity but reverence seems to have awaited a certain Friar Bungey, for having raised mists and vapors, which greatly befriended Edward IV. at the battle of Barnet.

Our knowledge of the intellectual spirit of the age, therefore, only becomes perfect when we contrast the success of the Impostor with the fate of the true Genius. And as the prejudices of the populace ran high against all mechanical contrivances for altering the settled conditions of labor, ‡ so, probably, in the very instinct and destiny of Genius, which ever drive it to a war with popular prejudice, it would be towards such contrivances that a man of great ingenuity and intellect, if studying the physical sciences, would direct his ambition.

Whether the author, in the invention he has assigned to his Philosopher (Adam Warner), has too boldly assumed the possibility of a conception so much in advance of the time, they who have examined such of the works of Roger Bacon as are yet given to the world, can best decide; but the assumption in itself belongs strictly to the most acknowledged prerogatives of Fiction; and the true and important question will obviously be, not whether Adam Warner could have constructed his model, but whether, having so constructed it, the fate that befel him was probable and natural.

Such characters as I have here alluded to seemed, then, to me, in meditating the treatment of the high and brilliant subject which your eloquence animated me to attempt, the proper Representatives of the multiform Truths which the time of Warwick, the Kingmaker, affords to our interests and suggests for our instruction; and I can only wish that the powers of the author were worthier of the theme.

It is necessary that I now state briefly the foundation of the Historical portions of this narrative. The charming and popular History, of Hume, which, however, in its treatment of the reign of Edward IV. is more than ordinarily incorrect, has probably left upon the minds of many of my readers, who may not have directed their attention to more recent and accurate researches into that obscure period, an erroneous impression of the causes which led to the breach between Edward IV. and his great kinsman and subject, the Earl of Warwick. The general notion is probably still strong, that it was the marriage of the young king to Elizabeth Gray, during Warwick's negotiations in France for the alliance of Bona of Savoy, (sister-in-law to Louis XI.,) which exasperated the fiery earl, and induced his union with the House of Lancaster. All our more recent historians have justly rejected this groundless fable, which even Hume (his extreme penetration supplying the defects of

* The erudite Lord Worcester had been one of Caxton's warmest patrons, but that nobleman was no more, at the time in which Printing is said to have been actually introduced into England.

† Nigromancy or Sorcery even took its place amongst the regular callings. Thus, "Thomas Vandyke late of Cambridge," is styled (Rolls Parl. 6, p. 273) Nigromancer, as his profession. SHARON TURNER, *Hist. of Eng.*, vol. iv. p. 6. BUCKE, *History of Richard III.*

‡ Even in the article of bonnets and hats, it appears that certain wicked Fulling Mills were deemed worthy of a special anathema in the reign of Edward IV. These engines are accused of having sought, "by subtle imagination," the destruction of the original makers of hats and bonnets, "by man's strength—that is, with hands and feet." And an act of parliament was passed (22nd of Edward IV.) to put down the fabrication of the said hats and bonnets by *Mechanical* contrivance.

nis superficial research) admits with reserve.* A short summary of the reasons for this rejection is given by Dr. Lingard, and annexed below.† And, indeed, it is a matter of wonder that so many of our chroniclers could have gravely admitted a legend contradicted by all the suubsequent conduct of Warwick himself. For we find the earl specially doing honor to the publication of Edward's marriage, standing godfather to his first-born, (the Princess Elizabeth), employed as ambassador, or acting as minister, and fighting *for* Edward, and *against* the Lancastrians during the five years that elapsed between the coronation of Elizabeth and Warwick's rebellion.

The real causes of this memorable quarrel, in which Warwick acquired his title of Kingmaker, appear to have been these.

It is probable enough, as Sharon Turner suggests,‡ that Warwick was dissappointed that, since Edward chose a subject for his wife, he neglected the more suitable marriage he might have formed with the earl's eldest daughter: and it is impossible but that the earl should have been greatly chafed in common with all his order, by the promotion of the queen's relations,§ new men, and apostate Lancastrians. But it is clear that these causes for discontent never weakened his zeal for Edward till the year 1467, when we chance upon the true origin of the romance concerning Bona of Savoy, and the first open dissension between Edward and the earl.

In that year Warwick went to France, to conclude an alliance with Louis XI., and to secure the hand of one of the French princes * for Margaret, sister to Edward IV.; during this period, Edward received the bastard brother of Charles, Count of Charolis, afterwards Duke of Burgundy, and arranged a marriage between Margaret and the count.

Warwick's embassy was thus dishonored, and the dishonor was aggravated by personal enmity to the bridegroom Edward had preferred † The earl retired in disgust to his castle. But Warwick's nature, which Hume has happily described as one of "undesigning frankness and openness,"‡ does not seem to have long harbored this resentment. By the intercession of the Archbishop of York and others, a reconciliation was effected, and the next year, 1468, we find Warwick again in favor, and even so far forgetting his own former cause of complaint as to accompany the procession in honor of Margaret's nuptials with his private foe.§ In the following year, however, arose the second dissension between the king and his minister—viz., in the king's refusal to sanction the marriage of his brother Clarence with the earl's daughter Isabel, a refusal which was attended with a resolute oppo-

* "There may even some doubt arise with regard to the proposal of marriage made to Bona of Savoy," etc.—HUME, note to p. 222, vol. iii., edit. 1825.

† "Many writers tell us that the enmity of Warwick arose from his disappointment, caused by Edward's clandestine marriage with Elizabeth. If we may believe them, the earl was at the very time in France negotiating on the part of the king a marriage with Bona of Savoy, sister to the Queen of France; and having succeeded in his mission, brought back with him the Count of Dampmartin as ambassador from Louis. To me the whole story appears a fiction. 1. It is not to be found in the more ancient historians. 2. Warwick was not at the time in France. On the 20th of April, ten days before the marriage, he was employed in negotiating a truce with the French envoys in London (Rym. xi. 521), and on the 26th of May, about three weeks after it, was appointed to treat of another truce with the King of Scots (Rym. xi. 424). 3. Nor could he bring Dampmartin with him to England. For that nobleman was committed a prisoner to the Bastile in September, 1463, and remained there till May, 1465. (Monstrel. iii. 97, 109.) Three contemporary and well-informed writers, the two continuators of the history of Croyland, and Wyrcester, attribute his discontent to the marriages and honors granted to the Wydeviles, and the marriage of the Princess Margaret with the Duke of Burgundy." LINGARD, vol. iii. c. 24, p. 5, 19, 4to edition.

‡ SHARON TURNER, *Hist. England*, vol. iii. p. 269.

§ W. WYR. 506, 7. CROYL. 542.

* Which of the princes this was, does not appear, and can scarcely be conjectured. The Pictorial History of England, (Book v. 102,) in a tone of easy decision, says "it was one of the sons of Louis XI." But Louis had no living sons at all at the time. The Dauphin was not born till three years afterwards. The most probable person was the Duke of Guienne, Louis's brother.

† The Croyland Historian, who, as far as his brief and meagre record extends, is the best authority for the time of Edward IV., very decidedly states the Burgundian alliance to be the original cause of Warwick's displeasure, rather than the king's marriage with Elizabeth:—"Upon which (the marriage of Margaret with Charolois), Richard Nevile, Earl of Warwick, who had for so many years taken party with the French against the Burgundians, conceived great indignation; and I hold this to be the truer cause of his resentment, than the king's marriage with Elizabeth, for he had rather have procured a husband for the aforesaid Princess Margaret in the kingdom of France." The Croyland Historian also speaks emphatically of the strong animosity existing between Charolois and Warwick.—CONT. CROYL. 551.

‡ HUME, Henry VI., vol. iii. p. 172, edit. 1825.

§ LINGARD.

sition that must greatly have galled the pride of the earl, since Edward even went so far as * to solicit the Pope to refuse his sanction, on the ground of relationship. The Pope, nevertheless, grants the dispensation, and the marriage takes place at Calais. A popular rebellion then breaks out in England. Some of Warwick's kinsmen—those, however, belonging to the branch of the Nevile family, that had always been Lancastrians, and at variance with the earl's party—are found at its head. The king, who is in imminent danger, writes a supplicating letter to Warwick to come to his aid.† The earl again forgets former causes for resentment, hastens from Calais, rescues the king, and quells the rebellion, by the influence of his popular name.

We next find Edward at Warwick's castle of Middleham, where, according to some historians, he is forcibly detained, an assertion, treated by others as a contemptible invention; this question will be examined in the course of this work; ‡ but, whatever the true construction of the story, we find that Warwick and the king are still on such friendly terms, that the earl marches in person against a rebellion on the borders—obtains a signal victory—and that the rebel leader (the earl's own kinsman) is beheaded by Edward at York. We find that, immediately after this supposed detention, Edward speaks of Warwick and his brothers "as his best friends" §—that he betroths his eldest daughter to Warwick's nephew, the male heir of the family. And then suddenly, only three months afterwards (in Feb. 1470), and without any clear and apparent cause, we find Warwick in open rebellion, animated by a deadly hatred to the king, refusing, from first to last, all overtures of conciliation; and so determined is his vengeance that he bows a pride, hitherto morbidly susceptible, to the vehement insolence of Margaret of Anjou, and forms the closest alliance with the Lancastrian party, in the destruction of which his whole life had previously been employed!

Here, then, where History leaves us in the dark—where our ouriosity is the most excited, Fiction gropes amidst the ancient chronicles, and seeks to detect and to guess the truth. And then, Fiction, accustomed to deal with the human heart, seizes upon the paramount importance of a Fact which the modern historian has been contented to place amongst dubious and collateral causes of dissension. We find it broadly and strongly stated, by Hall and others, that Edward had coarsely attempted the virtue of one of the earl's female relations. "And farther it erreth not from the truth," says Hall, "that the king did attempt a thing once in the earl's house, which was much against the earl's honesty;—but whether it was the daughter or the neice," adds the chronicler, "was not, for both their honors, openly known; but *surely* such a thing WAS attempted by King Edward," etc.

Any one at all familiar with Hall, (and, indeed, with all our principal chroniclers, except Fabyan), will not expect any accurate precision as to the date he assigns for the outrage. He awards to it, therefore, the same date he erroneously gives to Warwick's other grudges, (viz., a period brought some years lower by all judicious historians),—a date at which Warwick was still Edward's fastest friend.

Once grant the probability of this insult to the earl (the probability is conceded at once by the more recent historians, and received without scruple as a fact by Rapin, Habington, and Carte), and the whole obscurity which involves this memorable quarrel vanishes at once. Here was, indeed a wrong never to be forgiven, and yet never to be proclaimed. As Hall implies, the honor of the earl was implicated in hushing the scandal, and the honor of Edward in concealing the offence.—That, if ever the insult were attempted, it must have

---

* CARTE. WM. WYRE.

† Paston Letters, cxcviii. vol. ii., Knight's edition. See Lingard, c. 24, for the true date of Edward's letters to Warwick, Clarence, and the Archbishop of York.

‡ See Note II.

§ Paston Letters, cciv. vol. ii., Knight's edition. The date of this letter, which puzzled the worthy annotator, is clearly to be referred to Edward's return from York, after his visit to Middleham in 1469. No mention is therein made by the gossiping contemporary of any rumor that Edward had suffered imprisonment. He enters the city in state, as having returned safe and victorious from a formidable rebellion. The letter goes on to say—"The king himself hath (that is, *holds*) good language of the Lords Clarence, of Warwick, etc., saying, 'they be his best friends.'" Would he say this if just escaped from a prison? Sir John Paston, the writer of the letter, adds, it is true, "But his household men have (hold) other language." Very probably, for the household men were the court creatures always at variance with Warwick, and held, no doubt, the same language they had been in the habit of holding before.

been *just* previous to the earl's declared hostility, is clear. Offences of that kind hurry men to immediate action at the first, or else, if they stoop to dissimulation, the more effectually to avenge afterwards, the outbreak bides its seasonable time. But the time selected by the earl for *his* outbreak was the very worst he could have chosen, and attests the influence of a sudden passion—a new and uncalculated cause of resentment. He had no forces collected—he had not even sounded his own brother-in-law, Lord Stanley, (since he was uncertain of his intentions), while, but a few months before, had he felt any desire to dethrone the king, he could either have suffered him to be crushed by the popular rebellion the earl himself had quelled, or have disposed of his person as he pleased, when a guest at his own castle of Middleham. His evident want of all preparation and forethought—a want which drove into rapid and compulsory flight from England the baron to whose banner, a few months afterwards, flocked sixty thousand men—proves that the cause of his alienation was fresh and recent.

If, then, the cause we have referred to, as mentioned by Hall and others, seems the most probable we can find, (*no other* cause for such *abrupt* hostility being discernible), the date for it must be placed where it is in this work—viz., just prior to the earl's revolt. The next question is, who could have been the lady thus offended, whether a niece or daughter; scarcely a niece. For Warwick had one married brother, Lord Montagu, and several sisters, but the sisters were married to lords who remained friendly to Edward,* and Montagu seems to have had no daughter out of childhood,† while that nobleman himself did not share Warwick's rebellion at the first, but continued to enjoy the confidence of Edward. We cannot reasonably, then, conceive the uncle to have been so much more revengeful than the parents—the legitimate guardians of the honor of a daughter. It is, therefore, more probable that the insulted maiden should have been one of Lord Warwick's daughters, and this is the general belief. Carte plainly declares it was Isabel. But Isabel it could hardly have been; she was then married to Edward's brother, the Duke of Clarence, and within a month of her confinement. The earl had only one other daughter, Anne, then in the flower of her youth; and though Isabel appears to have possessed a more striking character of beauty, Anne must have had no inconsiderable charms to have won the love of the Lancastrian Prince Edward, and to have inspired a tender and human affection in Richard Duke of Gloucester.* It is also noticeable, that when, not as Shakspeare represents, but after long solicitation, and apparently by positive coercion, Anne formed her second marriage, she seems to have been kept carefully by Richard from his gay brother's court, and rarely, if ever, to have appeared in London till Edward was no more.

That considerable obscurity should always rest upon the facts connected with Edward's meditated crime—that they should never be published amongst the grievances of the

* Except the sisters married to Lord Fitzhugh and Lord Oxford. But though Fitzhugh, or rather his son, broke into rebellion, it was for some cause in which Warwick did not sympathize, for by Warwick himself was that rebellion put down; nor could the aggrieved lady have been a daughter of Lord Oxford's, for he was a stanch, though not avowed, Lancastrian, and seems to have carefully kept aloof from the court.

† Montagu's wife could have been little more than thirty at the time of his death. She married again, and had a family by her second husband.

* Not only does Majerus, the Flemish Annalist, speak of Richard's early affection to Anne, but Richard's pertinacity in marrying her, at a time when her family was crushed and fallen, seems to sanction the assertion. True, that Richard received with her a considerable portion of the estates of her parents. But both Anne herself and her parents were attainted, and the whole property at the disposal of the crown. Richard at that time had conferred the most important services on Edward. He had remained faithful to him during the rebellion of Clarence—he had been the hero of the day both at Barnet and Tewksbury. His reputation was then exceedingly high, and if he had demanded, as a legitimate reward, the lands of Middleham, without the bride, Edward could not well have refused them. He certainly had a much better claim than the only other competitor for the confiscated estates—viz., the perjured and despicable Clarence. For Anne's reluctance to marry Richard, and the disguise she assumed, see Miss Strickland's Life of Anne of Warwick. For the honor of Anne, rather than of Richard, to whose memory, one crime more or less, matters but little, it may here be observed that so far from there being any ground to suppose that Gloucester was an accomplice in the assassination of the young Prince Edward of Lancaster, there is some ground to believe that that prince was not assassinated at all, but died (as we would fain hope the grandson of Henry V. did die) fighting manfully in the field.—HARLEIAN MSS.; STOWE, *Chronicle of Tewksbury*; SHARON TURNER, vol. iii. p. 335.

haughty rebel, is natural from the very dignity of the parties, and the character of the offence—that in such obscurity, sober History should not venture too far on the hypothesis suggested by the chronicler, is right and laudable. But probably it will be conceded by all, that here Fiction finds its lawful province, and that it may reasonably help, by no improbable nor groundless conjecture, to render connected and clear the most broken and the darkest fragments of our annals.

I have judged it better partially to forestall the interest of the reader in my narrative, by stating thus openly what he may expect, than to encounter the far less favorable impression, (if he had been hitherto a believer in the old romance of Bona of Savoy,*) that the author was taking an unwarrantable liberty with the real facts, when, in truth, it is upon the real facts, as far as they can be ascertained, that the author has built his tale, and his boldest inventions are but deductions from the amplest evidence he could collect. Nay, he even ventures to believe, that whoever, hereafter, shall write the history of Edward IV., will not disdain to avail himself of some suggestions scattered throughout these volumes, and tending to throw new light upon the events of that intricate but important period.

It is probable that this work will prove more popular in its nature than my last fiction of "Zanoni," which could only be relished by those interested in the examination of the various problems in human life which it attempts to solve. But both fictions, however different and distinct their treatment, are constructed on those principles of art to which, in all my later works, however imperfect my success, I have sought at least steadily to adhere.

To my mind, a writer should sit down to compose a fiction as a painter prepares to compose a picture. His first care should be the conception of a whole as lofty as his intellect can grasp—as harmonious and complete as his art can accomplish; his second care, the *character* of the interest which the details are intended to sustain.

It is when we compare works of imagination in writing, with works of imagination on the canvas, that we can best form a critical idea of the different schools which exist in each; for common both to the author and the painter are those styles which we call the Familiar, the Picturesque, and the Intellectual. By recurring to this comparison we can without much difficulty classify works of Fiction in their proper order, and estimate the rank they should severally hold. The Intellectual will probably never be the most widely popular for the moment. He who prefers to study in this school must be prepared for much depreciation, for its greatest excellences, even if he achieve them, are not the most obvious to the many. In discussing, for instance, a modern work, we hear it praised, perhaps, for some striking passage, some prominent character; but when do we ever hear any comment on its harmony of construction, on its fulness of design, on its ideal character,—on its essentials, in short, as a work of art? What we hear most valued in the picture, we often find the most neglected in the book—viz., *the composition;* and this, simply, because in England painting is recognized as an art, and estimated according to definite theories. But in literature, we judge from a taste never formed—from a thousand prejudices and ignorant predilections. We do not yet comprehend that the author is an artist, and that the true rules of art by which he should be tested are precise and immutable. Hence the singular and fantastic caprices of the popular opinion—its exaggerations of praise or censure—its passion and re-action. At one while, its solemn contempt for Wordsworth—at another, its absurd idolatry. At one while we are stunned by the noisy celebrity of Byron—at another, we are calmly told that he can scarcely be called a poet. Each of these variations in the public is implicitly followed by the vulgar criticism; and as a few years back our journals vied with each other in ridiculing Wordsworth for the faults which he did not possess, they vie now with each other in eulogiums upon the merits which he has never displayed.

These violent fluctuations betray both a public and a criticism utterly unschooled in the elementary principles of literary art, and en-

* I say, the old romance of Bona of Savoy—so far as Edward's rejection of her hand for that of Elizabeth Gray, is stated to have made the cause of his quarrel with Warwick. But I do not deny the possibility that such a marriage had been contemplated and advised by Warwick, though he neither sought to negotiate it, nor was wronged by Edward's preference of his fair subject.

title the humblest author to dispute the censure of the hour, while they ought to render the greatest suspicious of its praise.

It is, then, in conformity, not with any presumptuous conviction of his own superiority, but with his common experience and common sense, that every author who addresses an English audience in serious earnest is permitted to feel that his final sentence rests not with the jury before which he is first heard. The literary history of the day consists of a a series of judgments set aside.

But this uncertainty must more essentially betide every student, however lowly, in the school I have called the Intellectual, which must ever be more or less at variance with the popular canons; it is its hard necessity to vex and disturb the lazy quietude of vulgar taste, for unless it did so, it could neither elevate nor move. He who resigns the Dutch art for the Italian must continue through the dark to explore the principles upon which he founds his design—to which he adapts his execution; in hope or in despondence, still faithful to the theory which cares less for the amount of interest created, than for the sources from which the interest is to be drawn—seeking in action the movement of the grander passions, or the subtler springs of conduct—seeking in repose the coloring of intellectual beauty.

The Low and the High of Art are not very readily comprehended; they depend not upon the worldly degree or the physical condition of the characters delineated; they depend entirely upon the quality of the emotion which the characters are intended to excite—viz., whether of sympathy for something low, or of admiration for something high. There is nothing high in a boor's head by Teniers—there is nothing low in a boor's head by Guido. What makes the difference between the two?—The absence or presence of the Ideal! But every one can judge of the merit of the first—for it is of the Familiar school—it requires a connoisseur to see the merit of the last, for it is of the Intellectual.

I have the less scrupled to leave these remarks to cavil or to sarcasm, because this fiction probaby the last with which I shall trespass upon the Public, and I am desirous that it shall contain, at least, my avowel of the principles upon which it and its later predecessors have been composed; you know well, however others may dispute the fact, the earnestness with which those principles have been meditated and pursued,—with high desire, if but with poor results.

It is a pleasure to feel that the aim, which I value more than the success, is comprehended by one, whose exquisite taste as a critic is only impaired by that far rarer quality—the disposition to *over*-estimate the person you *profess* to esteem! Adieu, my sincere and valued friend; and accept as a mute token of gratitude and regard, these flowers gathered in the Garden where we have so often roved together.

E. L. B.

LONDON, *January*, 1843.

PREFACE.

THIS was the first attempt of the Author in Historical Romance upon English ground. Nor would he have risked the disadvantage of comparison with the genius of Sir Walter Scott, had he not believed that that great writer and his numerous imitators had left altogether unoccupied the peculiar field in Historical Romance which the Author has here sought to bring into cultivation. In "The Last of the Barons," as in "Harold," the aim has been to illustrate the actual history of the period; and to bring into fuller display than general History itself has done, the characters of the principal personages of the time,—the motives by which they were probably actuated, —the state of parties,—the condition of the people,—and the great social interests which were involved in what, regarded imperfectly, appear but the feuds of rival factions.

"The Last of the Barons" has been by many esteemed the best of the Author's romances; and perhaps in the portraiture of actual character, and the grouping of the various interests and agencies of the time, it may have produced effects which render it more vigorous and life-like than any of the other attempts in romance by the same hand.

It will be observed that the purely imaginary characters introduced are very few; and, however prominent they may appear, still, in order not to interefere with the genuine passions and events of history, they are represented as the passive sufferers, not the active agents, of the real events. Of these imaginary characters, the most successful is Adam Warner, the philosopher in advance of his age; indeed, as an ideal portrait, I look upon it as the most original in conception, and the most finished in execution, of any to be found in my numerous prose works. "Zanoni" alone excepted.

For the rest, I venture to think that the general reader will obtain from these pages a better notion of the important age, characterized by the decline of the feudal system, and immediately preceding that great change in society which we usually date from the accession of Henry VII., than he could otherwise gather without wading through a vast mass of neglected chronicles and antiquarian dissertations.

BOOK FIRST.

THE ADVENTURES OF MASTER MARMADUKE NEVILE.

CHAPTER I.

The Pastime Ground of Old Cockaigne.

WESTWARD, beyond the still pleasant, but, even then, no longer solitary, hamlet of Charing, a broad space broken, here and there, by scattered houses and venerable pollards, in the early spring of 1467, presented the rural scene for the sports and pastimes of the inhabitants of Westminster and London. Scarcely need we say that open spaces for the popular games and diversions were then numerous in the suburbs of the metropolis. Grateful to some, the fresh pools of Islington; to others, the grass-bare fields of Finsbury; to all, the hedgeless plains of vast Mile-end. But the site to which we are now summoned, was a new and maiden holiday ground, lately bestowed upon the townsfolk of Westminster, by the powerful Earl of Warwick.

Raised by a verdant slope above the low marsh-grown soil of Westminster, the ground communicated to the left with the Brook-fields, through which stole the peaceful Ty-bourne, and commanded prospects, on all sides fair, and on each side varied. Behind, rose the twin green hills of Hampstead and Highgate, with the upland park and chase of Marybone—its stately manor-house half hid in woods. In front, might be seen the Convent of the Lepers, dedicated to St. James—now a palace; then, to the left, York House,* now Whitehall; farther on, the spires of Westminster Abbey and the gloomy tower of the Sanctuary; next, the Palace, with its bulwark and vawmure, soaring from the river; while, eastward, and nearer to the scene, stretched the long bush-grown passage of the Strand, picturesquely varied with bridges, and flanked to the right by the embattled halls of feudal nobles, or the inns of the no less powerful prelates,—while sombre and huge, amidst hall and inn, loomed the gigantic ruins of the Savoy, demolished in the insurrection of Wat Tyler. Farther on, and farther yet, the eye wandered over tower, and gate, and arch, and spire, with frequent glimpses of the broad sunlit river, and the opposite shore crowned by the palace of Lambeth, and the Church of St. Mary Overies, till the indistinct cluster of battlements around the Fortress-Palatine bounded the curious gaze. As whatever is new is for a while popular, so to this pastime-ground, on the day we treat of, flocked, not only the idlers of Westminster, but the lordly dwellers of Ludgate and the Flete, and the wealthy citizens of tumultuous Chepe.

The ground was well suited to the purpose to which it was devoted. About the outskirts, indeed, there were swamps and fish-pools; but a considerable plot towards the centre presented a level sward, already worn bare and brown by the feet of the multitude. From this, towards the left, extended alleys, some recently planted, intended to afford, in summer, cool and shady places for the favorite game of bowels; while scattered, clumps chiefly of old pollards, to the right, broke the space agreeably enough into detached portions, each of which afforded its separate pastime or diversion. Around were ranged many carts, or wagons—horses of all sorts and value were led to and fro, while their owners were at sport. Tents, awnings, hostelries—temporary

* The residence of the Archbishops of York.

buildings—stages for showmen and jugglers—abounded, and gave the scene the appearance of a fair. But what particularly now demands our attention was a broad plot in the ground, dedicated to the noble diversion of archery. The reigning House of York owed much of its military success to the superiority of the bowmen under its banners, and the Londoners themselves were jealous of their reputation in this martial accomplishment. For the last fifty years, notwithstanding the warlike nature of the times, the practice of the bow, in the intervals of peace, had been more neglected than seemed wise to the rulers. Both the king and his loyal city had of late taken much pains to enforce the due exercise of "Goddes instrumente,"* upon which an edict had declared that "the liberties and honor of England principally rested!"

And numerous now was the attendance, not only of the citizens, the burghers, and the idle populace, but of the gallant nobles who surrounded the court of Edward IV., then in the prime of his youth; the handsomest, the gayest, and the bravest prince in Christendom.

The royal tournaments, (which were, however, waning from their ancient lustre to kindle afresh, and to expire in the reigns of the succeeding Tudors), restricted to the amusements of knight and noble, no doubt presented more of pomp and splendor than the motley and mixed assembly of all ranks that now grouped around the competitors for the silver arrow, or listened to the itinerant jongleur, dissour, or minstrel;—or, seated under the stunted shade of the old trees, indulged with eager looks, and hands often wandering in their dagger hilts, in the absorbing passion of the dice; but no later and earlier scenes of revelry ever, perhaps, exhibited that heartiness of enjoyment, that universal holiday, which attended this mixture of every class, and established a rude equality for the hour—between the knight and the retainer, the burgess and the courtier.

The Revolution that placed Edward IV. upon the throne, had, in fact, been a popular one. Not only had the valor and moderation of his father Richard, Duke of York, bequeathed a heritage of affection to his brave and accomplished son—not only were the most beloved of the great barons, the leaders of his party—but the King himself, partly from inclination, partly from policy, spared no pains to win the good graces of that slowly rising, but even then important part of the population—the Middle Class. He was the first king who descended, without loss of dignity and respect, from the society of his peers and princes, to join familiarly in the feasts and diversions of the merchant and the trader. The lord mayor and council of London were admitted, on more than one solemn occasion, into the deliberations of the Court; and Edward had not long since, on the coronation of his queen, much to the discontent of certain of his barons, conferred the Knighthood of the Bath upon four of the citizens. On the other hand, though Edward's gallantries—the only vice which tended to diminish his popularity with the sober burgesses—were little worthy of his station, his frank, joyous familiarity with his inferiors, was not debased by the buffooneries that had led to the reverses and the awful fate of two of his royal predecessors.

There must have been a popular principle, indeed, as well as a popular fancy, involved in the steady and ardent adherence which the population of London, in particular, and most of the great cities, exhibited to the person and the cause of Edward IV. There was a feeling that his reign was an advance, in civilization, upon the monastic virtues of Henry VI., and the stern ferocity which accompanied the great qualities of "The Foreign Woman," as the people styled and regarded Henry's consort, Margaret of Anjou. While thus the gifts, the courtesy, and the policy of the young sovereign made him popular with the middle classes, he owed the allegiance of the more powerful barons and the favor of the rural population to a man who stood colossal amidst the iron images of the Age—the greatest and the last of the old Norman Chivalry—kinglier in pride, in state, in possessions, and in renown, than the king himself—Richard Nevile, Earl of Salisbury and Warwick.

This princely personage, in the full vigor of his age, possessed all the attributes that endear the noble to the commons. His valor in the field was accompanied with a generosity rare in the captains of the time. He valued himself on sharing the perils and the hardships of his meanest soldier. His haughtiness to

* So called emphatically by Bishop Latimer, in his celebrated Sixth Sermon.

the great was not incompatible with frank affability to the lowly. His wealth was enormous, but it was equalled by his magnificence, and rendered popular by his lavish hospitality. No less than thirty thousand persons are said to have feasted daily at the open tables with which he allured to his countless castles the strong hands and grateful hearts of a martial and unsettled population. More haughty than ambitious, he was feared because he avenged all affront; and yet not envied because he seemed above all favor.

The holiday on the archery-ground was more than usually gay, for the rumor had spread from the court to the city, that Edward was about to increase his power abroad, and to repair what he had lost in the eyes of Europe, through his marriage with Elizabeth Gray—by allying his sister Margaret with the brother of Louis XI., and that no less a person than the Earl of Warwick had been the day before selected as ambassador on the important occasion.

Various opinions were entertained upon the preference given to France in this alliance, over the rival candidate for the hand of the princess—viz., the Count de Charolois, afterwards Charles the Bold, Duke of Burgundy.

"By'r Lady," said a stout citizen, about the age of fifty, "but I am not over pleased with this French marriage-making! I would liefer the stout earl were going to France with bows and bills, than sarcenets and satins. What will become of our trade with Flanders—answer me that, Master Stokton? The House of York is a good house, and the king is a good king, but trade is trade. Every man must draw water to his own mill."

"Hush, Master Heyford!" said a small lean man in a light-gray surcoat. "The king loves not talk about what the king does. 'Tis ill jesting with lions. Remember William Walker, hanged for saying his son should be heir to the Crown."

"Troth," answered Master Heyford, nothing daunted, for he belonged to one of the most powerful corporations of London—"it was but a scurvy Pepperer* who made that joke. But a joke from a worshipful goldsmith, who has monies and influence, and a fair wife of his own, whom the king himself has been pleased to commend, is another guess sort of matter. But here's my grave-visaged headman, who always contrives to pick up the last gossip astir, and has a deep eye into millstones. Why, ho, there! Alwyn—I say, Nicholas Alwyn!—who would have thought to see thee with that bow, a good half ell taller than thyself? Methought thou wert too sober and studious for such man-at-arms sort of devilry."

"An' it please you, Master Heyford," answered the person thus addressed—a young man, pale and lean, though sinewy and large-boned, with a countenance of great intelligence, but a slow and somewhat formal manner of speech, and a strong provincial accent—"An' it please you, King Edward's edict ordains every Englishman to have a bow of his own height; and he who neglects the shaft on a holiday, forfeiteth one halfpenny and some honor. For the rest, methinks that the citizens of London will become of more worth and potency every year; and it shall not be my fault if I do not, though but a humble headman to your worshipful mastership, help to make them so."

"Why, that's well said, lad; but if the Londoners prosper, it is because they have nobles in their gipsires,* not bows in their hands."

"Thinkest thou, then, Master Heyford, that any king at a pinch would leave them the gipsire, if they could not protect it with the bow? That Age may have gold, let not Youth despise iron."

"Body o' me!" cried Master Heyford, "but thou hadst better curb in thy tongue. Though I have my jest—as a rich man and a corpulent—a lad who has his way to make good should be silent and—but he's gone."

"Where hooked you up that young jack-fish?" said Master Stokton—the thin mercer, who had reminded the goldsmith of the fate of the grocer.

"Why he was meant for the cowl, but his mother, a widow, at his own wish, let him make choice of the flat cap. He was the best 'prentice ever I had. By the blood of St. Thomas, he will push his way in good time; he has a head, Master Stokton—a head—and an ear; and a great big pair of eyes always looking out for something to his proper advantage."

In the meanwhile, the goldsmith's headman had walked leisurely up to the Archery-Ground, and even in his gait and walk, as he thus re-

* Old name for Grocer.

* Gipsire, a kind of pouch worn at the girdle.

paired to a pastime, there was something steady, staid, and business-like.

The youths of his class and calling were at that day very different from their equal in this. Many of them the sons of provincial retainers, some even of franklins and gentlemen, their childhood had made them familiar with the splendor and the sports of knighthood; they had learned to wrestle, to cudgel, to pitch the bar or the quoit, to draw the bow, and to practise the sword and buckler, before transplanted from the village green to the city stall. And, even then, the constrant broils and wars of the time—the example of their betters—the holiday spectacle of mimic strife—and, above all, the powerful and corporate association they formed amongst themselves—tended to make them as wild, as jovial, and as dissolute a set of young fellows as their posterity are now sober, careful, and discreet. And as Nicholas Alwyn, with a slight inclination of his head, passed by, two or three loud, swaggering, bold-looking groups of apprentices—their shaggy hair streaming over their shoulders—their caps on one side—their short cloaks of blue, torn or patched, though still passably new—their bludgeons under their arms—and their whole appearance and manner not very dissimiliar from the German collegians in the last century—notably contrasted Alwyn's prim dress, his precise walk, and the feline care with which he stepped aside from any patches of mire that might sully the soles of his square-toed shoes.

The idle apprentices winked and whispered, and lolled out their tongues at him as he passed. "Oh! but that must be as good as a May-Fair day—sober Nick Alwyn's maiden flight of the shaft. Hollo, puissant archer, take care of the goslings yonder! Look this way when thou pull'st, and then woe to the other side!" Venting these and many similar specimens of the humor of Cockaigne, the apprentices, however, followed their quondam colleague, and elbowed their way into the crowd gathered around the competitors at the butts; and it was at this spot, commanding a view of the whole space, that the spectator might well have formed some notion of the vast following of the House of Nevile. For everywhere along the front lines—everywhere in the scattered groups—might be seen, glistening in the sunlight, the armorial badges of that mighty family. The Pied Bull, which was the proper cognizance * of the Neviles, was principally borne by the numerous kinsmen of Earl Warwick, who rejoiced in the Nevile name. The Lord Montagu, Warwick's brother, to whom the King had granted the forfeit title and estates of the Earls of Northumberland, distinguished his own retainers, however, by the special crest of the ancient Montagus—a Gryphon issuant from a ducal crown.

But far more numerous than Bull or Gryphon (numerous as either seemed) were the badges borne by those who ranked themselves among the peculiar followers of the great Earl of Warwick:—The cognizance of the Bear and Ragged Staff, which he assumed in right of the Beauchamps, whom he represented through his wife, the heiress of the Lords of Warwick, was worn in the hats of the more gentle and well-born clansmen and followers, while the Ragged Staff alone was worked, front and back, on the scarlet jackets of his more humble and personal retainers. It was a matter of popular notice and admiration, that in those who bore those badges, as in the wearers of the hat and staff of the ancient Spartans, might be traced a grave loftiness of bearing, as if they belonged to another caste—another race than the herd of men. Near the place where the rivals for the silver arrow were collected, a lordly party had reined in their palfreys, and conversed with each other, as the judges of the field were marshalling the competitors.

"Who," said one of these gallants, "who is that comely young fellow just below us, with the Neville cognizance of the Bull on his hat? He has the air of one I should know."

"I never saw him before, my Lord of Northumberland," answered one of the gentlemen thus addressed, "but, pardieu, he who knows all the Neviles by eye, must know half England." The Lord Montagu, for though at that moment invested with the titles of the Percy, by that name Earl Warwick's brother is known to history, and by that, his rightful name, he shall therefore be designated in these pages; —the Lord Montagu smiled graciously at this remark, and a murmur through the crowd announced that the competition for the silver arrow was about to commence. The butts, formed of turf, with a small white mark fast-

* **The Pied Bull the cognizance—the Dun Bull's head the crest.**

ened to the centre by a very minute peg, were placed apart, one at each end, at the distance of eleven score yards. At the extremity, where the shooting commenced, the crowd assembled, taking care to keep clear from the opposite butt, as the warning word of "Fast" was thundered forth; but eager was the general murmur, and many were the wagers given and accepted, as some well-known archer-tried his chance. Near the butt, that now formed the target, stood the marker with his white wand; and the rapidity with which archer after archer discharged his shaft, and then, if it missed, hurried across the ground to pick it up, (for arrows were dear enough not to be lightly lost), amidst the jeers and laughter of the bystanders, was highly animated and diverting. As yet, however, no marksman had hit the white, though many had gone close to it, when Nicholas Alwyn stepped forward; and there was something so un-warlike in his whole air, so prim in his gait, so careful in his deliberate survey of the shaft, and his precise adjustment of the leathern gauntlet that protected the arm from the painful twang of the string, that a general burst of laughter from the bystanders attested their anticipation of a signal failure.

"'Fore heaven!" said Montagu, "he handles his bow an' it were a yard measure. One would think he were about to bargain for the bow-string, he eyes it so closely."

"And now," said Nicholas, slowly adjusting the arrow, "a shot for the honor of old Westmoreland!" And as he spoke, the arrow sprang gallanty forth, and quivered in the very heart of the white. There was a general movement of surprise among the spectators, as the marker thrice shook his wand over his head. But Alwyn, as indifferent to their respect as he had been to their ridicule, turned round and said, with a significant glance at the silent, nobles, "We springals of London can take care of our own, if need be."

"These fellows wax insolent. Our good king spoils them," said Montagu with a curl of his lip. "I wish some young squire of gentle blood would not disdain a shot for the Nevile against the craftsman. How say you, fair sir?" And, with a princely courtesy of mien and smile, Lord Montagu turned to the young man he had noticed, as wearing the cognizance of the First House in England. The bow was not the customary weapon of the well-born; but still, in youth, its exercise formed one of the accomplishments of the future knight, and even princes did not disdain, on a popular holiday, to match a shaft against the yeoman's cloth-yard.* The young man thus addressed, and whose honest, open, handsome, hardy face augured a frank and fearless nature, bowed his head in silence, and then slowly advancing to the umpires, craved permission to essay his skill, and to borrow the loan of a shaft and bow. Leave given and the weapons lent—as the young gentleman took his stand, his comely person, his dress, of a better quality than that of the competitors hitherto, and above all, the Nevile badge worked in silver on his hat, diverted the general attention from Nicholas Alwyn. A mob is usually inclined to aristocratic predilections, and a murmur of goodwill and expectation greeted him, when he put aside the gauntlet offered to him, and said, "In my youth I was taught so to brace the bow that the string should not touch the arm; and though eleven score yards be but a boy's distance, a good archer will lay his body into his bow † as much as if he were to hit the *blanc* four hundred yards away."

"A tall fellow this!" said Montagu; "and one, I wot, from the North," as the young gallant fitted the shaft to the bow. And graceful and artistic was the attitude he assumed, the head slightly inclined, the feet firmly planted, the left a little in advance, and the stretched sinews of the bow-hand alone evincing that into that grasp was pressed the whole strength of the easy and careless frame. The public expectation was not disappointed—the youth performed the feat considered of all the most dexterous, his arrow disdaining the white mark, struck the small peg which fastened it to the butts, and which seemed literally invisible to the bystanders.

"Holy St. Dunstan! there's but one man who can beat me in that sort that I know of," muttered Nicholas, "and I little expected to

* At a later period, Henry VIII. was a match for the best bowman in his kingdom. His accomplishment was hereditary, and distinguished alike his wise father and his pious son.

† "My father taught me to lay my body in my bow," etc., said Latimer, in his well-known sermon before Edward VI.—1549. The Bishop also herein observes, that "it is best to give the bow so much bending that the string need never touch the arm. This," he adds, "is practised by many good archers with whom I am acquainted."

see him take a bite out of his own hip." With that he approached his successful rival.

"Well, Master Marmaduke," said he, "it is many a year since you showed me that trick at your father, Sir Guy's—God rest him! But I scarce take it kind in you to beat your own countryman!"

"Beshrew me!" cried the youth, and his cheerful features brightened into hearty and cordial pleasure; "but if I see in thee, as it seems to me, my old friend and foster-brother, Nick Alwyn, this is the happiest hour I have known for many a day. But stand back and let me look at thee, man! Thou! thou a tame London trader! Ha! ha!—is it possible?"

"Hout, Master Marmaduke," answered Nicholas, "Every crow thinks his own baird bonniest, as they say in the North. We will talk of this anon, an' thou wilt honor me. I suspect the archery is over now. Few will think to mend that shot."

And here, indeed, the umpires advanced, and their chief—an old mercer, who had once borne arms, and indeed been a volunteer at the battle of Touton—declared that the contest was over, "Unless," he added, in the spirit of a lingering fellow-feeling with the Londoner, "this young fellow, whom I hope to see an alderman one of these days, will demand another shot, for as yet there hath been but one prick each at the butts."

"Nay, master," returned Alwyn, "I have met with my betters—and, after all," he added, indifferently, "the silver arrow, though a pretty bauble enough, is over light in its weight."

"Worshipful sir," said the young Nevile, with equal generosity, "I cannot accept the prize for a mere trick of the craft—the blanc was already disposed of by Master Alyn's arrow. Moreover, the contest was intended for the Londoners, and I am but an interloper—beholden to their courtesy for a practice of skill—and even the loan of a bow—wherefore the silver arrow be given to Nicholas Alwyn."

"That may not be, gentle sir," said the umpire, extending the prize. "Sith Alwyn vails of himself, it is thine, by might and by right."

The Lord Montagu had not been inattentive to this dialogue, and he now said, in a loud tone that silenced the crowd, "Young Badgeman, thy gallantry pleases me no less than thy skill. Take the arrow, for thou hast won it; but, as thou seemest a new comer, it is right thou shouldst pay thy tax upon entry—this be my task. Come hither, I pray thee, good sir," and the nobleman graciously beckoned to the mercer; "be these five nobles the prize of whatever Londoner shall acquit himself best in the bold English combat of quarter-staff, and the prize be given in this young archer's name. Thy name, youth?"

"Marmaduke Nevile, good my lord."

Montagu smiled, and the umpire withdrew to make the announcement to the bystanders. The proclamation was received with a shout that traversed from group to group, and line to line, more hearty from the love and honor attached to the name of Nevile, than even from a sense of the gracious generosity of Earl Warwick's brother. One man alone, a sturdy, well-knit fellow, in a franklin's Lincoln broadcloth, and with a hood half-drawn over his features, did not join the popular applause. "These Yorkists," he muttered, "know well how to fool the people."

Meanwhile, the young Nevile still stood by the gilded stirrup of the great noble who had thus honored him, and contemplated him with that respect and interest which a youth's ambition ever feels for those who have won a name.

The Lord Montagu bore a very different character from his puissant brother. Though so skilful a captain, that he had never been known to lose a battle, his fame as a warrior was, strange to say, below that of the great Earl, whose prodigious strength had accomplished those personal feats that dazzled the populace, and revived the legendary renown of the earlier Norman knighthood. The caution and wariness indeed which Montagu displayed in battle, probably caused his success as a general, and the injustice done to him, (at least by the vulgar), as a soldier. Rarely had Lord Montagu, though his courage was indisputable, been known to mix personally in the affray. Like the captains of modern times, he contented himself with directing the manœuvres of his men, and hence preserved that inestimable advantage of coldness and calculation, which was not always characteristic of the eager hardihood of his brother. The character of Montagu differed yet more from that of the

Earl in peace than in war. He was supposed to excel in all those supple arts of the courtier, which Warwick neglected or despised; and if the last was, on great occasions, the adviser, the other, in ordinary life, was the companion of his sovereign.

Warwick owed his popularity to his own large, open, daring, and lavish nature. The subtle Montagu sought to win, by care and pains, what the other obtained without an effort. He attended the various holiday meetings of the citizens, where Warwick was rarely seen. He was smooth-spoken and courteous to his equals, and generally affable, though with constraint, to his inferiors. He was a close observer, and not without that genins for intrigue, which in rude ages passes for the talent of a statesman. And yet in that thorough knowledge of the habits and tastes of the great mass, which gives wisdom to a ruler, he was far inferior to the Earl. In common with his brother, he was gifted with the majesty of mien which imposes on the eye, and his port and countenance were such as became the prodigal expense of velvet, minever, gold, and jewels, by which the gorgeous magnates of the day communicated to their appearance the arrogant splendor of their power.

"Young gentleman," said the earl, after eyeing with some attention the comely archer, "I am pleased that you bear the name of Nevile. Vouchsafe to inform me to what scion of our house we are this day indebted for the credit with which you have upborne its cognizance?"

"I fear," answered the youth with a slight but not ungraceful hesitation, "that my Lord of Montagu and Northumberland will hardly forgive the presumption with which I have intruded upon this assembly a name borne by nobles so illustrious, especially if it belong to those less fortunate branches of his family which have taken a different side from himself in the late unhappy commotions. My father was Sir Guy Nevile, of Arsdale, Westmoreland."

Lord Montagu's lip lost its gracious smile —he glanced quickly at the courtiers round him, and said, gravely,—"I grieve to hear it. Had I known this, certes my gipsire had still been five nobles the richer. It becomes not one, fresh from the favor of King Edward IV., to show countenance to the son of a man, kinsman though he was, who bore arms for the usurpers of Lancaster. I pray thee, sir, to doff, henceforth, a badge dedicated only to the service of Royal York. No more, young man: we may not listen to the son of Sir Guy Nevile.——Sirs, shall we ride to see how the Londoners thrive at quarter-staff?"

With that, Montagu, deigning no farther regard at Nevile, wheeled his palfrey towards a distant part of the ground, to which the multitude was already pressing its turbulent and noisy way.

"Thou art hard on thy namesake, fair my lord," said a young noble, in whose dark-auburn hair, aquiline haughty features, spare but powerful frame, and inexpressible air of authority and command, were found all the attributes of the purest and eldest Norman race—the Patricians of the World.

"Dear Raoul de Fulke," returned Montagu, coldly, "when thou hast reached my age of thirty and four, thou wilt learn that no man's fortune casts so broad a shadow as to shelter from the storm the victims of a fallen cause."

"Not so would say thy bold brother," answered Raoul de Fulke, with a slight curl of his proud lip. "And I hold, with him, that no king is so sacred that we should render to his resentments our own kith and kin. God's wot, whosoever wears the badge, and springs from the stem, of Raoul de Fulke, shall never find me question overmuch whether his father fought for York or Lancaster.

"Hush, rash babbler!" said Montagu, laughing gently; "what would King Edward say if this speech reached his ears? Our friend," added the courtier, turning to the rest, "in vain would bar the tide of change; and in this our New England, begirt with new men and new fashions, affect the feudal baronage of the worn-out Norman. But thou art a gallant knight, De Fulke, though a poor courtier."

"The saints keep me so!" returned De Fulke. "From over-gluttony, from over wine-bibbing, from cringing to a king's leman, from quaking at a king's frown, from unbonnetting to a greasy mob, from marrying an old crone for vile gold, may the saints ever keep Raoul de Fulke and his sons! Amen!"

This speech, in which every sentence struck its stinging satire into one or other of the listeners, was succeeded by an awkward silence, which Montagu was the first to break.

"Pardieu!" he said, "when did Lord Hastings leave us? and what fair face can have lured the truant?"

"He left us suddenly on the archery ground," answered the young Lovell. "But as well might we track the breeze to the rose, as Lord William's sigh to maid or matron."

While thus conversed the cavaliers, and their plumes waved, aud their mantles glittered along the broken ground, Marmaduke Nevile's eye pursued the horsemen with all that bitter feeling of wounded pride and impotent reesntment with which Youth regards the first insult it receives from Power.

CHAPTER II.

The broken Gittern.

ROUSING himself from his indignant reverie, Marmaduke Nevile followed one of the smaller streams into which the crowd divided itself on dispersing from the archery-ground, and soon found himself in a part of the holiday scene appropriated to diversions less manly, but no less characteristic of the period, than those of the staff and arrow. Beneath an awning, under which an itinerant landlord dispensed cakes and ale, the humorous Bourdour (the most vulgar degree of minstrel, or rather tale-teller), collected his clownish audience, while seated by themselves--apart, but within hearing—two harpers, in the king's livery, consoled each other for the popularity of their ribald rival, by wise reflections on the base nature of common folk. Farther on, Marmaduke started to behold what seemed to him the heads of giants at least six yards high; but on a nearer approach these formidable apparitions resolved themselves to a company of dances upon stilts. There, one *joculator* exhibited the antics of his well-tutored ape—there, another eclipsed the attractions of the baboon by a marvellous horse, that beat a tabor with his fore feet—there the more sombre *Tregetour*, before a table raised upon a lofty-stage, promised to cut off and refix the head of a sad-faced little boy, who, in the meantime, was preparing his mortal frame for the operation by apparently larding himself with sharp knives and bodkins. Each of these wonder-dealers found his separate group of admirers, and great was the delight and loud the laughter in the pastime-ground of old Cockaigne.

While Marmaduke, bewildered by this various bustle, stared around him, his eye was caught by a young maiden, in evident distress, struggling in vain to extricate herself from a troop of timbrel girls, or *tymbesteres*, (as they were popularly called), who surrounded her with mocking gestures, striking their instruments to drown her remonstrances, and dancing about her in a ring at every effort towards escape. The girl was modestly attired, as one of the humbler ranks, and her wimple in much concealed her countenance, but there was, despite her strange and undignified situation and evident alarm, a sort of quiet, earnest self-possession—an effort to hide her terror, and to appeal to the better and more womanly feelings of her persecutors. In the intervals of silence from their clamor, her voice, though low, clear, well-tuned, and impressive, forcibly arrested the attention of young Nevile; for at that day, even more than this, (sufficiently apparent, as it now is,) there was a marked distinction in the intonation, the accent, the modulation of voice between the better bred and better educated, and the inferior classes. But this difference, so ill according with her dress and position, only served to heighten more the bold insolence of the musical Bacchantes, who, indeed, in the eyes of the sober, formed the most immoral nuisance attendant on the sports of the time, and whose hardy license and peculiar sisterhood might tempt the antiquarian to search for their origin amongst the relics of ancient Paganism. And now, to increase the girl's distress, some half score of dissolute apprentices and journeymen suddenly broke into the ring of the Mænads, and were accosting her with yet more alarming insults, when Marmaduke, pushing them aside, strode to her assistance. "How now, ye lewd varlets!—ye make me blush for my countrymen in the face of day? Are these the sports of merry England—these your manly contests —to strive which can best affront a poor maid? Out on ye, cullions and bezonians! Cling to me, gentle donzell, and fear not. Whither shall I lead thee?"

The apprentices were not, however, so easily daunted. Two of them approached to the rescue, flourishing their bludgeons about their heads with formidable gestures—"Ho, ho!"

cried one, "what right hast thou to step between the hunters and the doe? The young quean is too much honored by a kiss from a bold 'prencice of London."

Marmaduke stepped back, and drew the small dagger which then formed the only habitual weapon of a gentleman.* This movement, discomposing his mantle, brought the silver arrow he had won, (which was placed in his girdle), in full view of the assailants. At the same time they caught sight of the badge on his hat. These intimidated their ardor more than drawn poniard.

"A Nevile!" said one retreating. "And the jolly marksman who beat Nick Alwyn," said the other, lowering his bludgeon, and doffing his cap. "Gentle sir, forgive us, we knew not your quality. But as for the girl—your gallantry misleads you."

"The Wizard's daughter! ha! ha!—the Imp of Darkness!" screeched the timbrel girls, tossing up their instruments, and catching them again on the points of their fingers. "She has enchanted him with her glamour. Foul is fair! Foul fair thee, young springal, if thou go to the nets. Shadow and goblin to goblin and shadow! Flesh and blood to blood and flesh!—and dancing round him, with wanton looks and bare arms, and gossamer robes that brushed him as they circled, they chanted—

"Come kiss me, my darling,
Warm kisses I trade for;
Wine, music, and kisses—
What else was life made for!"

With some difficulty, and with a disgust which was not altogether without a superstitious fear of the strange words and the outlandish appearance of these loathsome Dalilahs, Marmaduke broke from the ring with his new charge; and in a few moments the Nevile and the maiden found themselves, unmolested and unpursued, in a deserted quarter of the ground; but still the scream of the timbrel girls, as they hurried, wheeling and dancing, into the distance, was borne ominously to the young man's ear,—"Ha, ha! the witch and her lover! Foul is fair!—foul is fair! Shadow to goblin, goblin to shadow—and the Devil will have his own!"

"And what mischance, my poor girl," asked the Nevile, soothingly, "brought thee into such evil company?"

"I know not, fair sir," said the girl, slowly recovering herself, "but my father is poor, and I had heard that on these holiday occasions one who had some slight skill on the gittern might win a few groats from the courtesy of the bystanders. So I stole out with my serving-woman, and had already got more than I dared hope, when those wicked timbrel players came round me, and accused me of taking the money from them. And then they called an officer of the ground, who asked me my name and holding; so when I answered, they called my father a wizard, and the man broke my poor gittern—see!"—and she held it up, with innocent sorrow in her eyes, yet a half smile on her lips—"and they soon drove poor old Madge from my side, and I knew no more till you, worshipful sir, took pity on me."

"But why," asked the Nevile, "did they give to your father so unholy a name?"

"Alas, sir! he is a great scholar, who has spent his means in studying what he says will one day be of good to the people."

"Humph!" said Marmaduke, who had all the superstitions of his time, who looked upon a scholar, unless in the Church, with mingled awe and abhorence, and who, therefore, was but ill satisfied with the girl's artless answer,—"Humph! your father—but"—checking what was he about, perhaps harshly, to say, as he caught the bright eyes and arch intelligent face lifted to his own—"but it is hard to punish the child for the father's errors."

"Errors, sir!" repeated the damsel, proudly, and with a slight disdain in her face and voice. "But yes, wisdom is ever, perhaps, the saddest error!"

This remark was of an order superior in intellect to those which had preceded it; it contrasted with the sternness of experience the simplicity of the child; and of such contrasts, indeed, was that character made up. For with a sweet, an infantine change of tone and countenance, she added, after a short pause—"They took the money!—the gittern,—see, they left that, when they had made it useless."

"I cannot mend the gittern, but I can refill the gipsire," said Marmaduke.

The girl colored deeply. "Nay, sir, to earn is not to beg."

Marmaduke did not heed this answer, for as they were now passing by the stunted trees,

* Swords were not worn, in peace, at that period.

under which sate several revellers, who looked up at him from their cups and tankards, come with sneering, some with grave looks, he began, more seriously than in his kindly impulse he had hitherto done, to consider the appearance it must have, to be thus seen walking, in public, with a girl of inferior degree, and perhaps doubtful repute. Even in our own day, such an exhibition would be, to say the least, suspicious, and in that day, when ranks and classes were divided with iron demarcations, a young gallant, whose dress bespoke him of gentle quality, with one of opposite sex, and belonging to the humbler orders, in broad day too, was far more open to censure. The blood mounted to his brow, and halting abruptly, he said, in a dry and altered voice—"My good damsel, you are now, I think, out of danger; it would ill beseem you, so young and so comely, to go further with one not old enough to be your protector, so, in God's name, depart quickly, and remember me when you buy your new gittern—poor child!" So saying, he attempted to place a piece of money in her hand. She put it back, and the coin fell on the ground.

"Nay, this is foolish," said he.

"Alas, sir!" said the girl, gravely. "I see well that you are ashamed of your goodness. But my father begs not. And once—but that matters not."

"Once what?" persisted Marmaduke, interested in her manner, in spite of himself.

"Once," said the girl, drawing herself up, and with an expression that altered the whole character of her face—"the beggar ate at my father's gate. He is a born gentleman and a knight's son."

"And what reduced him thus?"

"I have said," answered the girl, simply, yet with the same half scorn on her lip that it had before betrayed—"he is a scholar, and thought more of others than himself."

"I never saw any good come to a gentleman from those accursed books," said the Nevile; "fit only for monks and shavelings. But still, for your father's sake, though I am ashamed of the poorness of the gift——"

"No—God be with you, sir, and reward you." She stopped short, drew her wimple round her face, and was gone. Nevile felt an uncomfortable sensation of remorse and disapproval at having suffered her to quit him while there was yet any chance of molestation or annoyance, and his eye followed her till a group of trees veiled her from his view.

The young maiden slackened her pace as she found herself alone under the leafless boughs of the dreary pollards;—a desolate spot, made melancholy by dull swamps, half overgrown with rank verdure, through which forced its clogged way the shallow Brook that now gives its name (though its waves are seen no more) to one of the main streets in the most polished quarter of the metropolis. Upon a mound formed by the gnarled roots of the dwarfed and gnome-like oak, she sat down, and wept. In our earlier years, most of us may remember, that there was one day which made an epoch in life—the day that separated Childhood from Youth; for that day seems not to come gradually, but to be a sudden crisis, an abrupt revelation. The buds of the heart open to close no more. Such a day was this in that girl's fate.

But the day was not yet gone! That morning, when she dressed for her enterprise of filial love, perhaps for the first time Sibyll Warner felt that she was fair—who shall say, whether some innocent, natural vanity had not blended with the deep, devoted earnestness, which saw no shame in the act by which the child could aid the father? Perhaps she might have smiled to listen to old Madge's praises of her winsome face—old Madge's predictions that the face and the gittern would not lack admirers on the gay ground. Perhaps some indistinct, vague forethoughts of the Future to which the sex will deem itself to be born, might have caused the cheek—no, not to blush, but to take a roiser hue, and the pulse to beat quicker, she knew not why. At all events, to that ground went the young Sibyll, cheerful and most happy, in her inexperience of actual life, and sure, at least, that youth and innocence sufficed to protect from insult. And now, she sat down under the leafless tree, to weep; and in those bitter tears, childhood itself was laved from her soul for ever.

"What ailest thou, maiden?" asked a deep voice; and she felt a hand laid lightly on her shoulder. She looked up in terror and confusion, but it was no form or face to inspire alarm that met her eye. It was a cavalier, holding by the rein a horse richly caparisoned, and though his dress was plainer and less exaggerated than that usually worn by men of rank, its materials were those which the sumptuary laws (constantly broken, indeed, as such laws ever must be), confined to nobles. Though his surcoat was but of cloth, and the color dark and sober, it was woven in foreign looms—an unpatriotic luxury, above the degree of knight—and edged deep with the costliest sables. The hilt of the dagger, suspended round his breast, was but of ivory, curiously wrought, but the scabbard was sown with large pearls. For the rest, the stranger was of ordinary stature, well knit, and active rather than powerful, and of that age (about thirty-five) which may be called the second prime of man. His face was far less handsome than Marmaduke Nevile's, but infinitely more expressive, both of intelligence and command, the features straight and sharp, the complexion clear and pale, and under the bright grey eyes a dark shade spoke either of disipation or of thought.

"What ailest thou, maiden?—weepest thou some faithless lover? Tush! love renews itself in youth, as flower succeeds flower in spring."

Sibyll made no reply; she rose, and moved a few paces, then arrested her steps, and looked around her. She had lost all clue to her way homeward, and she saw with horror, in the distance, the hateful trimbel girls, followed by the rabble, and weaving their strange dances towards the spot.

"Dost thou fear me, child? there is no cause," said the stranger, following her. "Again, I say, 'What ailest thou?'"

This time his voice was that of command, and the poor girl involuntarily obeyed it. She related her misfortunes, her persecution by the tymbesteres, her escape—thanks to the Nevile's courtesy—her separation from her attendant, and her uncertainty as to the way she should pursue.

The nobleman listened with interest; he was a man sated and wearied by pleasure and the world, and the evident innocence of Sibyll was a novelty to his experience, while the contrast between her language and her dress moved his curiosity. "And," said he, "thy protector, left thee, his work half done;—fie on his chivalry! But I, donzell, wear the spurs of knighthood, and to succor the distressed is a duty my oath will not let me swerve from. I will guide thee home, for I know well all the purlieus of this evil den of London. Thou hast but to name the suburb in which thy father dwells."

Sibyll involuntarily raised her wimple, lifted her beautiful eyes to the stranger, in bewildered gratitude and surprise.—Her childhood had passed in a court—her eye, accustomed to rank, at once perceived the high degree of the speaker; the contrast between this unexpected and delicate gallantry, and the condescending tone and abrupt desertion of Marmaduke, affected her again to tears.

"Ah, worshipful sir!" she said, falteringly, "what can reward thee for this unlooked for goodness?"

"One innocent smile, sweet virgin!—for such, I'll be sworn, thou art."

He did not offer her his hand, but hanging the gold-enamelled rein over his arm, walked by her side; and a few words sufficing for his guidance, led her across the ground, through the very midst of the throng. He felt none of the young shame, the ingenuous scruples of Marmakuke, at the gaze he encountered, thus companioned. But Sibyll noted that ever and anon bonnet and cap were raised as they passed along, and the respectful murmur of the vulgar, who had so lately jeered her anguish, taught her the immeasurable distance in men's esteem, between poverty shielded but by virtue, and poverty protected by power.

But suddenly a gaudy tinsel group broke through the crowd, and wheeling round their path, the foremost of them daringly approached the nobleman, and looking full into his disdainful face, exclaimed—"Tradest thou, too, for kisses? Ha! ha!—life is short—the witch is outwitched by thee! But witchcraft and death go together, as, peradventure, thou mayest learn at the last, sleek wooer." Then darting off, and heading her painted, tawdry throng, the timbrel girl sprung into the crowd, and vanished.

This incident produced no effect upon the strong and cynical intellect of the stranger. Without allusion to it, he continued to converse with his young companion, and artfully to draw out her own singular but energetic and gifted mind. He grew more than interested, he was both touched and surprised. His manner became yet more respectful, his voice more subdued and soft.

On what hazards turns our fate! On that day—a little, and Sibyll's pure, but sensitive heart had, perhaps, been given to the young Nevile. He had defended and saved her; he was fairer than the stranger, he was more of her own years, and nearer to her in station; but in showing himself *ashamed* to be seen with her, he had galled her heart, and moved the bitter tears of her pride. What had the stranger done? Nothing, but reconciled the wounded delicacy to itself; and suddenly he became to her one ever to be remembered—wondered at—perhaps more. They reached an obscure suburb, and parted at the threshold of a large, gloomy, ruinous house, which Sibyll indicated as her father's home.

The girl lingered before the porch; and the stranger gazed, with the passionless admiration which some fair object of art produces on one who has refined his taste, but who has survived enthusiasm, upon the downcast cheek that blushed beneath his gaze—"Farewell!" he said; and the girl looked up wistfully. He might, without vanity, have supposed that look to imply what the lip did not dare to say—"And shall we meet no more?"

But he turned away, with formal though courteous salutation; and as he remounted his steed, and rode slowly towards the interior of the city, he muttered to himself, with a melancholy smile upon his lips—"Now might the grown infant make to himself a new toy; but an innocent heart is a brittle thing, and one false vow can break it. Pretty maiden, I like thee well eno' not to love thee. So, as my young Scotch minstrel sings and prays,

"Christ keep these birdis bright in bowers,
Sic peril lies in paramours!" *

We must now return to Marmaduke. On leaving Sibyll, and retracing his steps towards the more crowded quarter of the space, he was agreeably surprised by encountering Nicholas Alwyn, escorted in triumph by a legion of roaring apprentices from the victory he had just obtained over six competitors at the quarter-staff.

* A Scotch poet, in Lord Hailes's Collection, has the following lines in the very pretty poem called "Peril in Paramours:"—

"Wherefore I pray, in termys short,
Christ keep these birdis bright in bowers,
Fra false lovers and their disport,
Sic peril lies in paramours."

When the cortège came up to Marmaduke, Nicholas halted, and fronting his attendants, said, with the same cold and formal stiffness that had characterized him from the beginning—"I thank you, lads, for your kindness. It is your own triumph. All I cared for was to show that you London boys are able to keep up your credit in these days, when there's little luck in a yard measure, if the same hand cannot bend a bow, or handle cold steel. But the less we think of the strife when we are in the stall, the better for our pouches. And so I hope we shall hear no more about it, until I get a ware of my own, when the more of ye that like to talk of such matters the better ye will be welcome,—always provided ye be civil customers, who pay on the nail, for, as the saw saith, 'Ell and tell makes the crypt swell.' For the rest, thanks are due to this brave gentleman, Marmaduke Nevile, who, though the son of a knight-banneret, who never furnished less to the battle-field than fifty men-at-arms, has condescended to take part and parcel in the sports of us peaceful London traders; and if ever you can do him a kind turn—for turn and turn is fair play—why you will, I answer for it. And so one cheer for old London, and another for Marmaduke Nevile. Here goes! Hurrah, my lads!" And with this pithy address Nicholas Alwyn took off his cap and gave the signal for the shouts, which, being duly performed, he bowed stiffly to his companions, who departed with a hearty laugh, and coming to the side of Nevile, the two walked on to a neighboring booth, where, under a rude awning, and over a flagon of clary, they were soon immersed in the confidential communications each had to give and receive.

CHAPTER III.

The Trader and the Gentile; or, the Changing Generation.

"No, my dear foster-brother," said the Nevile, "I do not yet comprehend the choice you have made. You were reared and brought up with such careful book-lere, not only to read and to write—the which, save the mark! I hold to be labor eno'—but chop Latin and logic and theology with St. Aristotle (is not that his hard name?) into the bargain, and all because you had an uncle of high note in Holy Church. I cannot say I would be a shaveling myself; but surely a monk, with the hope of preferment, is a nobler calling to a lad of spirit and ambition than to stand out at a door and cry, 'Buy, buy'—'What d'ye lack' —to spend youth as a Flatcap, and drone out manhood in measuring cloth, hamering metals, or weighing out spices?"

"Fair and softly, Master Marmaduke," said Alwyn, "you will understand me better anon. My uncle, the sub-prior, died—some say of austerities, others of ale—that matters not; he was a learned man and a cunning. 'Nephew Nicholas,' said he on his death-bed, 'think twice before you tie yourself up to the cloister; it's ill leaping nowadays in a sackcloth bag. If a pious man be moved to the cowl by holy devotion, there is nothing to be said on the subject; but if he take to the Church as a calling, and wish to march a-head like his fellows, these times show him a prettier path to distinction. The nobles begin to get the best things for themselves: and a learned monk, if he is the son of a yeoman, cannot hope, without a speciality of grace, to become abbot or bishop. The king, whoever he be, must be so drained by his wars, that he has little land or gold to bestow on his favorites; but his gentry turn an eye to the temporalities of the Church, and the Church and the King wish to strengthen themselves by the gentry. This is not all; there are free opinions afloat. The House of Lancaster has lost ground, by its persecutions and burnings. Men dare not openly resist, but they treasure up recollections of a fried grandfather, or a roasted cousin; recollections which have done much damage to the Henries, and will shake Holy Church itself one of these days. The Lollards lie hid, but Lollardism will never die. There is a new class rising amain, where a little learning goes a great way, if mixed with spirit and sense. Thou likest broad pieces, and a creditable name—go to London, and be a trader. London begins to decide who shall wear the crown, and the traders to decide what king London shall befriend. Wherefore, cut thy trace from the cloister, and take thy road to the shop.' The next day my uncle gave up the ghost.—They had better clary than this at the convent, I must own. But every stone has its flaw!"

"Yet," said Marmaduke, "if you took dis taste to the cowl, from reasons that I pretend not to judge of, but which seem to my poor head very bad ones, seeing that the Church is as mighty as ever, and King Edward is no friend of the Lollards, and that your uncle himself was at least a sub-prior——"

"Had he been son to a baron, he had been a cardinal," interrupted Nicholas, "for his head was the longest that ever came out of the north country. But go on; you would say my father was a sturdy yeoman, and I might have followed his calling?"

"You hit the mark, Master Nicholas."

"Hout,—man. I crave pardon of your rank, Master Nevile. But a yeoman is born a yeoman, and he dies a yeoman—I think it better to die Lord Mayor of London; and so I craved my mother's blessing and leave, and a part of the old hyde has been sold to pay for the first step to the red gown, which I need not say must be that of the Flat-cap. I have already taken my degrees, and no longer wear blue. I am headman to my master, and my master will be sheriff of London."

"It is a pity," said the Nevile, shaking his head; "you were ever a tall, brave lad, and would have made a very pretty soldier."

"Thank you, Master Marmaduke, but I leave cut and thrust to the gentles. I have seen eno' of the life of a retainer. He goes out on foot with his shield and his sword, or his bow and his quiver, while sir knight sits on horseback, armed from the crown to the toe, and the arrow slants off from rider and horse, as a stone from a tree. If the retainer is not sliced and carved into mincemeat, he comes home to a heap of ashes, and a handful of acres; harried and rivelled into a common; sir knight thanks him for his valor, but he does not build up his house; sir knight gets a grant from the king, or an heiress for his son, and Hob Yeoman turns gisarme and bill into ploughshares. Tut, tut, there's no liberty, no safety, no getting on, for a man who has no right to the gold spurs, but in the guild of his fellows; and London is the place for a born Saxon, like Nicholas Alywn."

As the young aspirant thus uttered the sentiments, which, though others might not so plainly avow and shrewdly enforce them, tended towards the slow revolution, which, under all the stormy events that the superficial record we call HISTORY alone deigns to enumerate, was working that great change in the thoughts and habits of the people—that impulsion of the provincials citywards—that gradual formation of a class between knight and vassal—which became first *constitutionally* visible and distinct in the reign of Henry VII., Marmaduke Nevile, only half-regretting and half-despising the reasonings of his foster-brother, was playing with his dagger, and glancing at his silver arrow.

"Yet you could still have eno' of the tall yeoman and the stout retainer about you to try for this bauble, and to break half-a-dozen thick heads with your quarter-staff!"

"True," said Nicholas; "you must recollect we are only, as yet, between the skin and the selle—half trader, half retainer. The old leaven will out:—'Eith to learn the cat to the kirn,'—as they say in the north. But that's not all; a man, to get on, must win respect from those who are to jostle him hereafter, and it's good policy to show those roystering youngsters that Nick Alwyn, stiff and steady though he be, has the old English metal in him, if it comes to a pinch; it's a lesson to yon lords too, save your quality, if they ever wish to ride roughshod over our guilds and companies. But eno' of me—Drawer, another stoup of the clary. Now, gentle sir, may I make bold to ask news of yourself? I saw, though I spake not before of it, that my Lord Montagu showed a cold face to his kinsman. I know something of these great men, though I be but a small one—a dog is no bad guide in the city he trots through.

"My dear foster-brother," said the Nevile; "you had ever more brains than myself, as is meet that you should have, since you lay by the steel casque, which, I take it, is meant as a substitute for us gentlemen and soldiers who have not so many brains to spare; and I will willingly profit by your counsels. You must know," he said, drawing nearer to the table, and his frank, hardy face assuming a more earnest expresssion, "that though my father, Sir Guy, at the instigation of his chief, the Earl of Westmoreland, and of the Lord Nevile, bore arms, at the first, for King Henry—"

"Hush! hush! for Henry of Windsor!"

"Henry of Windsor!—so be it! yet being connected, like the nobles I have spoken of, with the blood of Warwick and Salisbury, it was ever with doubt and misgiving, and rather in the hope of ultimate compromise, between both parties, (which the Duke of York's moderation rendered probable), than of the extermination of either. But when, at the battle of York, Margaret of Anjou and her generals stained their victory by cruelties which could not fail to close the door on all cconciliation; when the infant son of the duke himself was murdered, though a prisoner, in cold blood; when my father's kinsman, the Earl of Salisbury, was beheaded without trial; when the head of the brave and good duke, who had fallen in the field, was, against all knightly and kinglike generosity, mockingly exposed, like a dishonored robber, on the gates of York, my father, shocked and revolted, withdrew at once from the army, and slacked not, bit or spur, till he found himself in his hall at Arsdale. His death, caused partly by his travail and vexation of spirit, together with his timely withdrawal from the enemy, preserved his name from the attainder passed on the Lords Westmoreland and Nevile; and my eldest brother, Sir John, accepted the king's proffer of pardon, took the oaths of allegiance to Edward, and live's safe, if obsure, in his father's halls.

"Thou knowest, my friend, that a younger brother has but small honor at home. Peradventure, in calmer times, I might have bowed my pride to my calling, hunted my brother's dogs, flown his hawks, rented his keeper's lodge, and gone to my grave contented. But to a young man, who, from his childhood, had heard the stirring talk of knights and captains, who had seen valor and fortune make the way to distinction, and whose ears, of late, had been filled by the tales of wandering minstrels and dissours, with all the gay wonders of Edward's court, such a life soon grew distasteful. My father, on his death-bed, (like thy uncle, the sub-prior), encouraged me little to follow his own footsteps. 'I see,' said he, 'that King Henry is too soft to rule his barons, and Margaret too fierce to conciliate the commons—the only hope of peace is in the settlement of the House of York. Wherefore let not thy father's errors stand in the way of thy advancement;'—and therewith he made his confessor—for he was no penman himself, the worthy old knight!—indite a letter to his great kinsman, the Earl of Warwick, commending me to his protection. He signed his mark, and set his seal to this missive, which I now have at mine hostelrie, and died the same day. My brother judged me too young then to quit his roof, and condemned me to bear his humors till, at the age of twenty-three, I could bear no more ! So, having sold him my scant share in the heritage, and turned, like thee, bad land into good nobles,—I joined a party of horse in their journey to London, and arrived yesterday at Master Sackbut's hostelry, in Eastchepe. I went this morning to my Lord of Warwick, but he was gone to the king's, and hearing of the merry-makings here, I came hither for kill-time. A chance word of my Lord of Montagu, whom St. Dunstan confound, made me conceit that a feat of skill with the cloth-yard, might not ill preface my letter to the great earl. But, pardie ! it seems I reckoned without my host, and in seeking to make my fortunes too rashly, I have helped to mar them." Wherewith he related the particulars of his interview with Montagu.

Nicholas Alwyn listened to him with friendly and thoughtful interest, and, when he had done, spoke thus:—

" The Earl of Warwick is a generous man, and, though hot, bears little malice, except against those whom he deems misthink or insult him; he is proud of being looked up to as a protector, especially by those of his own kith and name. Your father's letter will touch the right string, and you cannot do better than deliver it with a plain story. A young partisan like thee is not to be despised. Thou must trust to Lord Warwick to set matters right with his brother; and now, before I say further, let me ask thee plainly, and without offence, Dost thou so love the House of York, that no chance could ever make thee turn sword against it ? Answer as I ask—under thy breath; those drawers are parlous spies ! "

And here, in justice to Marmaduke Nevile and to his betters, it is necessary to preface his reply, by some brief remarks, to which we must crave the earnest attention of the reader. What we eall PATRIOTISM, in the high and Catholic acceptation of the word, was little if at all understood in days when passion, pride, and interest were motives little softened by reflection and education, and softened still less by the fusion of classes that characterized the small states of old, and marks the civilization of a modern age. Though the right by descent of the House of York, if genealogy alone were consulted, was indisputably prior to that of Lancaster, yet the long exercise of power in the latter house, the genius of the Fourth Henry and the victories of the Fifth would, no doubt, have completely superseded the obsolete claims of the Yorkists, had Henry VI, possessed any of the qualities necessary for the time. As it was, men had got puzzled by genealogies and cavils; the sanctity attached to the king's name was weakened by his doubtful right to his throne, and the Wars of the rival Roses were at last (with two exceptions, presently to be noted), the mere contests of exasperated factions, in which public considerations were scarcely even made the blind to individual interest, prejudice, or passion.

Thus instances of desertion, from the one to the other party, even by the highest nobles, and on the very eve of battle, had grown so common, that little if any disgrace was attached to them: and any knight or captain held an affront to himself an amply sufficient cause for the transfer of his allegiance. It would be obviously absurd to expect in any of the actors of that age the more elevated doctrines of party faith and public honor, which clearer notions of national morality, and the salutary exercise of a large general opinion, free from the passions of single individuals, have brought into practice in our more enlightened days. The individual feelings of the individual MAN, strong in himself became his guide, and he was free in much from the regular and thoughtful virtues, as well as from the mean and plausible vices of those who act only in bodies and corporations. The two exceptions to this idiosyncrasy of motive and conduct, were, first, in the general disposition of the rising middle class, especially in London, to connect great political interests with the more popular House of York. The commons in parliament had acted in opposition to Henry the Sixth, as the laws they wrung from him tended to show, and it was a popular and trading party that came, as it were, into power under King Edward. It is true that Edward was sufficiently arbitrary in himself, but a popular party will stretch as much as its antagonists in favor of despotism—*exercised on its enemies.*

And Edward did his best to consult the interests of commerce, though the prejudices of the merchants interpreted those interests in a way opposite to that in which political economy now understands them. The second exception to the mere hostilities of individual chiefs, and feudal factions has, not less than the former, being too much overlooked by historians.

But this was a still more powerful element in the success of of the House of York. The hostility against the Roman Church, and the tenets of the Lollards, were shared by an immense part of the population. In the Previous century an ancient writer computes that one-half the population were Lollards; and though the sect were diminished and silenced by fear, they still ceased not to exist, and their doctrines not only shook the Church under Henry VIII., but destroyed the throne by the strong arm of their children, the Puritans, under Charles I. It was impossible that these men should not have felt the deepest resentment at the fierce and steadfast persecution they endured under the House of Lancaster; and without pausing to consider how far they would benefit under the dynasty of York, they had all those motives of revenge which are mistaken so often for the counsels of policy, to rally round any standard raised against their oppressors. These two great exceptions to merely selfish policy, which it remains for the historian clearly and at length to enforce, these and these alone will always, to a sagacious observer, elevate the Wars of the Roses above those bloody contests for badges which we are, at first sight, tempted to regard them. But these deeper motives animated very little the nobles and the knightly gentry,* and with them the governing principles were, as we have just said, interest, ambition, and the zeal for the honor and advancement of houses and chiefs.

"Truly," said Marmaduke, after a short and rather embarrassed pause, "I am little beholden as yet to the House of York. There, where I see a noble benefactor, or a brave and wise leader, shall I think my sword and heart may best proffer allegiance."

"Wisely said," returned Alwyn, with a slight, but half sarcastic smile; "I asked thee the question because—(draw closer)—there are wise men in our city who think the ties between Warwick and the king less strong than a ship's cable. And if thou attachest thyself to Warwick, he will be better pleased, it may be, with talk of devotion to himself than professions of exclusive loyalty to King Edward. He who has little silver in his pouch must have the more silk on his tongue. A word to a Westmoreland or a Yorkshire-man is as good as a sermon to men not born so far north. One word more, and I have done. Thou art kind, and affable, and gentle, my dear foster-brother, but it will not do for thee to be seen again with the goldsmith's headman. If thou wantest me, send for me at nightfall; I shall be found at Master Heyford's, in the Chepe. And if," added Nicholas, with a prudent reminiscence, "thou succeedest at court, and canst recommend my master—there is no better goldsmith—it may serve me when I set up for myself, which I look to do shortly."

"But, to send for thee, my own foster-brother, at nightfall, as if I were ashamed!"—

"Hout, Master Marmaduke, if thou wert not ashamed of me I should be ashamed to be seen with a gay springal like thee. Why, they would say in the Chepe that Nick Alwyn was going to ruin. No, no. Birds of a feather must keep shy of those that moult other colors; and so, my dear young master, this is my last shake of the hand. But hold. Dost thou know thy way back?"

"Oh, yes—never fear!" answered Marmaduke; "though I see not why so far, at least, we may not be companions."

"No, better as it is; after this day's work, they will gossip about both of us, and we shall meet many who know my long visage on the way back. God keep thee; avise me how thou prosperest."

So saying, Nicholas Alwyn walked off, too delicate to propose to pay his share of the reckoning with a superior. But when he had gone a few paces, he turned back, and accosting the Nevile, as the latter was rebuckling his mantle, said—

---

* Amongst many instances of the self seeking of the time, not the least striking is the subservience of John Mowbray, the great Duke of Norfolk, to his old political enemy, the Earl of Oxford, the moment the last comes into power, during the brief restoration of Henry VI. John Paston, whose family had been sufficiently harassed by this great Duke, says, with some glee, "The Duke and Duchess (of Norfolk) sue to him (Lord Oxford) as humbly as ever I did to them."—Paston Letters, cccii.

"I have been thinking, Master Nevile, that these gold nobles, which it has been my luck to bear off, would be more useful in thy gipsire than mine. I have sure gains and small expenses—but a gentleman gains nothing, and his hand must be ever in his pouch—so——"

"Foster-brother!" said Marmaduke, haughtily, "a gentleman never borrows—except of the Jews, and with due interest. Moreover, I too have my calling; and as thy stall to thee, so to me my good sword. Saints keep thee! Be sure I will serve thee when I can."

"The devil's in these young strips of the herald's tree," muttered Alwyn, as he strode off; "as if it were dishonest to borrow a broad piece without cutting a throat for it! Howbeit, money is a prolific mother: and here is eno' to buy me a gold chain against I am alderman of London. Hout, thus goes the world—the knight's baubles become the alderman's badges—so much the better."

CHAPTER IV.

Ill fares the Country Mouse in the Traps of Town.

WE trust we shall not be deemed discourteous, either, on the one hand, to those who value themselves on their powers of reflection, or, on the other, to those who lay claim to what, in modern phrenological jargon, is called the Organ of Locality, when we venture to surmise that the two are rarely found in combination; nay, that it seems to us a very evident truism, that in proportion to the general activity of the intellect upon subjects of pith and weight, the mind will be indifferent to those minute external objects by which a less contemplative understanding will note, and map out, and impress upon the memory, the chart of the road its owner has once taken. Master Marmaduke Nevile, a hardy and acute forester from childhood, possessed to perfection the useful faculty of looking well and closely before him as he walked the earth, and ordinarily, therefore, the path he had once taken, however intricate and obscure, he was tolerably sure to retrace with accuracy, even at no inconsiderable distance of time—the outward senses of men are usually thus alert and attentive in the savage or the semi-civilized state. He had not, therefore, overvalued his general acuteness in the note and memory of localities, when he boasted of his power to refind his way to his hostelrie without the guidance of Alwyn. But it so happened that the events of this day, so memorable to him, withdrew his attention from external objects, to concentrate it within. And in marvelling and musing over the new course upon which his destiny had entered, he forgot to take heed of that which his feet should pursue, so that after wandering unconsciously onward for some time, he suddenly halted in perplexity and amaze to find himself entangled in a labyrinth of scattered suburbs, presenting features wholly different from the road that had conducted him to the archery ground in the forenoon.

The darkness of the night had set in, but it was relieved by a somewhat faint and mist-clad moon, and some few and scattered stars, over which rolled, fleetly, thick clouds, portending rain. No lamps at that time cheered the steps of the belated wanderer; the houses were shut up, and their inmates, for the most part, already retired to rest, and the suburbs did not rejoice, as the city, in the round of the watchman with his drowsy call to the inhabitants, "Hang out your lights!" The passengers, who at first, in various small groups and parties, had enlivened the stranger's way, seemed to him, unconscious as he was of the lapse of time, to have suddenly vanished from the thoroughfares; and he found himself alone in places thoroughly unknown to him, waking to the displeasing recollection that the approaches to the city were said to be beset by brawlers and ruffians of desperate characters, whom the cessation of the civil wars had flung loose upon the skirts of society, to maintain themselves by deeds of rapine and plunder. As might naturally be expected, most of these had belonged to the defeated party, who had no claim to the good offices or charity of those in power. And although some of the Neviles had sided with the Lancastrians, yet the badge worn by Marmaduke was considered a pledge of devotion to the reigning House, and added a new danger to those which beset his path. Conscious of this—for he now called to mind the admonitions of his host in parting from the hostelrie—he deemed it but discreet to draw the hood of his mantle over the silver ornament; and while thus occupied, he heard not a step emerging from a lane at his rear, when suddenly a heavy hand was placed on his shoulder; he started, turned, and before him stood a man, whose aspect and dress betokened little to lessen the alarm of the uncourteous salutation. Marmaduke's dagger was bare on the instant.

"And what would'st thou with me?" he asked.

"Thy purse and thy dagger!" answered the stranger.

"Come and take them," said the Nevile, unconscious that he uttered a reply famous in classic history, as he sprang backward a step or so, and threw himself into an attitude of defence. The stranger slowly raised a rude kind of mace, or rather club, with a ball of iron at the end, garnished with long spikes, as he replied, "Art thou mad eno' to fight for such trifles?"

"Art thou in the habit of meeting one Englishman who yields his goods, without a blow, to another?" retorted Marmaduke. "Go to —thy club does not daunt me." The stranger warily drew back a step, and applied a whistle to his mouth. The Nevile sprang at him, but the stranger warded off the thrust of the poniard with a light flourish of his heavy weapon; and had not the youth drawn back on the instant, it had been good night and a long day to Marmaduke Nevile. Even as it was, his heart beat, quick, as the whirl of the huge weapon sent the air like a strong wind against his face. Ere he had time to renew his attack, he was suddenly seized from behind, and found himself struggling in the arms of two men. From these he broke, and his dagger glanced harmless against the tough jerkin of his first assailant. The next moment his right arm fell to his side, useless and deeply gashed. A heavy blow on the head,—the moon, the stars reeled in his eyes—and then darkness;—he knew no more. His assailants very deliberately proceeded to rifle the inanimate body, when one of them, perceiving the silver badge, exclaimed, with an oath, "One of the rampant Neviles! This cock at least shall crow no more?" And laying the young man's head across his lap, while he stretched back the throat with one hand, with the other he drew forth a long sharp knife, like those used by huntsmen in dispatching the hart. Suddenly, and in the very moment when the blade was about to inflict the fatal gash, his hand was forcibly arrested, and a man who had silently and unnoticed joined the ruffians, said, in a stern whisher, "Rise, and depart from thy brotherhood for ever. We admit no murderer."

The ruffian looked up in bewilderment. "Robin—captain—thou here!" he said falteringly.

"I must needs be everywhere, I see, if I would keep such fellows as thou and these from the gallows. What is this?—a silver arrow—the young archer.—Um."

"A Nevile!" growled the would-be murderer.

"And for that very reason his life should be safe. Knowest thou not that Richard of Warwick, the great Nevile, ever spares the commons. Begone! I say." The captain's low voice grew terrible as he uttered the last words. The savage rose, and without a word stalked away.

"Look you, my masters," said Robin, turning to the rest, "soldiers must plunder a hostile country. While York is on the throne, England is a hostile country to us Lancastrians. Rob, then, rifle, if ye will. But he who takes life shall lose it. Ye know me!" The robbers looked down, silent and abashed. Robin bent a moment over the youth. "He will live," he muttered. "So! he already begins to awaken. One of these houses will give him shelter. Off, fellows, and take care of your necks!"

When Marmaduke, a few minutes after this colloquy, began to revive, it was with a sensation of dizziness, pain, and extreme cold. He strove to lift himself from the ground, and at length succeeded. He was alone; the place where he had lain was damp and red with stiffening blood. He tottered on for several paces, and perceived from a lattice, at a little distance, a light still burning. Now reeling—now falling, he still dragged on his limbs as the instinct attracted him to that sign of refuge. He gained the doorway of a detached and gloomy house, and sank on the stone before it to cry aloud. But his voice soon sank into deep groans, and once more, as his efforts increased the rapid gush of the blood, became insensible. The man styled Robin, who had so opportunely saved his life, now approached from the shadow of a wall, beneath which he had watched Marmaduke's movements. He neared the door of the house, and cried, in a sharp, clear voice—"Open, for the love of Christ!"

A head was now thrust from the lattice—the light vanished—a minute more, the door opened; and Robin, as if satisfied, drew hastily back, and vanished—saying to himself. as he strode along, "A young man's life must needs be dear to him; yet, had the lad been a lord, methinks I should have cared little to have saved for the people one tyrant more."

After a long interval, Marmaduke again recovered, and his eyes turned with pain from the glare of a light held to his face.

"He wakes, father!—he will live!" cried a sweet voice.

"Ay, he will live, child!" answered a deeper tone; and the young man muttered to himself, half audibly, as in a dream, "Holy Mother be blessed! it is sweet to live!"

The room, in which the sufferer lay, rather exhibited the remains of better fortunes than testified to the solid means of the present possessor. The ceiling was high and groined, and some tints of faded, but once gaudy painting, blazoned its compartments and hanging pendants. The walls had been rudely painted, (for arras* then was rare, even among the wealthiest,) but the colors were half obliterated by time and damp. The bedstead on which the wounded man reclined was curiously carved, with a figure of the Virgin at the head, and adorned with draperies, in which were wrought huge figures from scriptural subjects, but in the dress of the date of Richard II.—Solomon in pointed upturned shoes, and Goliath, in the armor of a crusader,—frowning grimly upon the sufferer. By the bedside stood a personage, who, in reality, was but little past the middle age, but whose pale visage intersected with deep furrows, whose long beard and hair, partially gray, gave him the appearance of advanced age: nevertheless there was something peculiarly striking in the aspect of the man. His forehead was singularly high and massive, but the back of the head was disproportionately small as if the intellect too much preponderated over all the animal qualities for strength in character and success in life. The eyes were soft, dark, and brilliant but dreamlike and vague; the features in youth must have been regular and beautiful, but their contour was now sharpened by the hollowness of the cheeks and temples. The form, in the upper part, was nobly shaped, sufficiently muscular, if not powerful, and with the long throat aud falling shoulders, which always give something of grace and dignity to the carriage; but it was prematurely bent, and the lower limbs were thin and weak, as is common with men who have sparely used them; they seem disproportioned to that broad chest, and still more to that magnificent and spacious brow. The dress of this personage corresponded with the aspect of his abode. The materials were those worn by the gentry, but they were old, threadbare, and discolored with innumerable spots and stains. His hands were small and delicate with large blue veins, that spoke of relaxed fibres, but their natural whiteness was smudged with smoke-stains, and his beard—a masculine ornament utterly out of fashion among the younger race in King Edward's reign, but when worn by the elder gentry, carefully trimmed and perfumed—was dishevelled into all the spiral and tangled curls, pisplayed in the sculptured head of some old Grecian sage or poet.

On the other side of the bed knelt a young girl, of about sixteen, with a face exquisitely lovely in its delicacy and expression. She seemed about the middle stature, and her arms and neck, as displayed by the close-fitting vest, had already the smooth and rounded contour of dawning womanhood, while the face had still the softness, innocence, and inexpressible bloom of the child. There was a strong likeness between her and her father, (for such the relationship), despite the differ-

* Mr. Hallam (History of the Middle Ages, chap. ix. part 2), implies a doubt whether great houses were furnished with hangings so soon as the reign of Edward IV. But there is abundant evidence to satisfy our learned historian upon that head. The Narrative of the "Lord of Grauthuse," edited by Sir F. Madden, specifies the hangings of cloth of gold in the apartments in which that lord was received by Edward IV.; also the hangings of white silk and linen in the chamber appropriated to himself at Windsor. But long before this period (to say nothing of the Bayeux Tapestry)—viz., in the reign of Edward III. (in 1344), a writ was issued to inquire into the mystery of working tapestry; and In 1398, Mr. Britton observes that the celebrated arras hangings at Warwick's Castle are mentioned. (See Britton's Dictionary of Architecture and Archæology—art. Tapestry.)

ence of sex and years—the same beautiful form of lip and brow—the same rare color of the eyes, dark-blue, with black fringing lashes —and perhaps the common expression, at that moment, of gentle pity and benevolent anxiety contributed to render the resemblance stronger.

"Father, he sinks again!" said the girl.

"Sibyll," answered the man, putting his finger upon a line in a manuscript book that he held, "the authority saith, that a patient so contused should lose blood, and then the arm must be tightly bandaged. Verily, we lack the wherewithal."

"Not so, father!" said the girl, and blushing, she turned aside, and took off the partelet of lawn, upon which holiday finery her young eyes perhaps that morning had turned with pleasure, and white as snow was the neck which was thus displayed—"this will suffice to bind his arm."

"But the book," said the father, in great perplexity—"the book telleth us not how the lancet should be applied. It is easy to say, 'Do this and do that'—but to do it once, it should have been done before! This is not among my experiments."

Luckily, perhaps, for Marmaduke, at this moment there entered an old woman, the solitary servant of the house, whose life, in those warlike times, had made her pretty well acquainted with the simpler modes of dealing with a wounded arm and a broken head. She treated with great disdain the learned authority referred to by her master, she bound the arm, plaistered the head, and taking upon herself the responsibility to promise a rapid cure, insisted upon the retirement of father and child, and took her solitary watch beside the bed.

"If it had been any other mechanism than that of the vile human body!" muttered the philosopher, as if apologizing to himself;—and with that he recovered his self-complacency, and looked round him proudly.

CHAPTER V.

Weal to the Idler—Woe to the Workman.

As Providence tempers the wind to the shorn lamb, so it possibly might conform the heads of that day to a thickness suitable for the blows and knocks to which they were variously subjected;—yet it was not without considerable effort, and much struggling, that Marmaduke's senses recovered the shock received, less by his flesh wound, and the loss of blood, than a blow on the seat of reason, that might have dispatched a passable ox of these degenerate days. Nature, to say nothing of Madge's leechcraft, ultimately triumphed, and Marmaduke woke one morning in full possession of such understanding as Nature had endowed him with. He was then alone, and it was with much simple surprise that he turned his large hazel eyes from corner to corner of the unfamiliar room. He began to retrace and weave together sundry disordered and vague reminiscences: he commenced with the commencement, and clearly satisfied himself that he had been grievously wounded and sorely bruised; he then recalled the solitary light at the high lattice, and his memory found itself at the porch of the large, lonely, ruinous old house; then all became a bewildered and feverish dream. He caught at the vision of an old man with a long beard, whom he associated, displeasingly, with recollections of pain; he glanced off to a fair young face, with eyes that looked tender pity whenever he writhed or groaned under the tortures, that, no doubt, that old accursed carle had inflicted upon him. But even this face did not dwell with pleasure in his memory—it woke up confused and laboring associations of something weird and witchlike—of sorceresses and tymbesteres—of wild warning screeched in his ear—of incantations and devilries, and doom. Impatient of these musings, he sought to leap from his bed, and was amazed that the leap subsided into a tottering crawl. He found an ewer and basin, and his ablutions refreshed and invigorated him. He searched for his rainment, and discovered it all except the mantle, dagger, hat, and girdle; and, while looking for these, his eye fell on an old tarnished steel mirror. He started as if he had seen his ghost; was it possible that his hardy face could have waned into that pale, and almost femininely delicate visage. With the pride (call it not coxcombry) that then made the care of person the distinction of gentle birth, he strove to reduce into order the tangled locks of the long hair, of which a considerable portion above a part that seemed peculiarly sensitive to the touch, had been mercilessly clipped; and as he had just completed this task, with little satisfaction and much inward chafing at the lack of all befitting essences and perfumes, the door gently opened, and the fair face he had dreamed of appeared at the aperture.

The girl uttered a cry of astonishment and alarm at seeing the patient thus arrayed and convalescent, and would sddenly have retreated, but the Nevile advanced and courteously taking her hand—

"Fair maiden," said he, "if, as I trow, I owe to thy cares my tending and cure—nay, it may be a life hitherto of little worth, save to myself—do not fly from my thanks. May our Lady of Walsingham bless and reward thee!"

"Sir," answered Sibyll, gently withdrawing her hands from his clasp, "our poor cares have been a slight return for thy generous protection to myself."

"To thee! ah, forgive me,—how could I be so dull? I remember thy face now; and, perchance, I deserved the disaster I met with in leaving you so discourteously. My heart smote me for it as thy light footfall passed from my side."

A slight blush, succeeded by a thoughtful smile—the smile of one who recalls and caresses some not displeasing remembrance, passed over Sibyll's charming countenance, as the sufferer said this with something of the grace of a well-born man, whose boyhood had been taught to serve God and the Ladies.

There was a short pause before she answered, looking down, "Nay, sir, I was sufficiently beholden to you;—and for the rest, all molestation was over. But I will now call your nurse—for it is to our servant, not us, that your thanks are due—to see to your state, and administer the proper medicaments."

"Truly, fair damsel, it is not precisely medicaments that I hunger and thirst for; and if your hospitality could spare me from the larder a manchet, or a corner of a pasty, and from the cellar a stoup of wine or a cup of ale, methinks it would tend more to restore me, than those potions which are so strange to my taste that they rather offend than tempt it; and, pardie, it seemeth to my poor senses as if I had not broken bread for a week!"

"I am glad to hear you of such good cheer," answered Sibyll; "wait but a moment or so, till I consult your physician."

And, so saying, she closed the door, slowly descended the steps, and pursued her way into what seemed more like a vault than a habitable room, where she found the single servant of the household. Time, which makes changes so fantastic in the dress of the better classes, has a greater respect for the costume of the humblier; and, though the garments were of a very coarse sort of serge, there was not so great a difference, in point of comfort and sufficiency, as might be supposed, between the dress of old Madge and that of some primitive servant in the north during the last century. The old woman's face was thin and pinched, but its sharp expression brightened into a smile as she caught sight, through the damps and darkness, of the gracious form of her young mistress. "Ah, Madge," said Sibyll, with a sigh, "it is a sad thing to be poor!"

"For such as thou, Mistress Sibyll, it is indeed. It does not matter for the like of us. But it goes to my old heart when I see you shut up here, or worse, going out in that old courtpin and wimple—you a knight's grandchild—you, who have played round a queen's knees, and who might have been so well to do, an' my master had thought a little more of the gear of this world. But patience is a good palfrey, and will carry us a long day. And when the master has done what he looks for, why the king—sith we must call the new man on the throne—will be sure to reward him; but, sweetheart, tarry not here; it's an ill air for your young lips to drink in. What brings you to old Madge?"

"The stranger is recovered, and—"

"Ay, I warrant me, I have cured worse than he. He must have a spoonful of broth—I have not forgot it. You see I wanted no dinner myself—what is dinner to old folks!—so I e'en put it all in the pot for him. The broth will be brave and strong."

"My poor Madge, God requite you for what you suffer for us! But he has asked"—here was another sigh and a downcast look that did not dare to face the consternation of Madge, as she repeated, with a half smile—"he has asked—for meat, and a stoup of wine, Madge!"

"Eh, sirs! And where is he to get them! Not that it will be bad for the lad, either.

Wine! There's Master Sancroft, of the Oak, will not trust us a penny, the seely hilding, and——"

"Oh, Madge, I forgot!—we can still sell the gittern for something. Get on your wimple, Madge—quick—while I go for it."

"Why, Mistress Sibyll, that's your only pleasure, when you sit all alone, the long summer days."

"It will be more pleasure to remember that it supplied the wants of my father's guest," said Sibyll; and retracing the way up the stairs, she returned with the broken instrument, and dispatched Madge with it, laden with instructions that the wine should be of the best. She then once more mounted the rugged steps, and halting a moment at Marmaduke's door, as she heard his feeble step walking impatiently to and fro, she ascended higher, where the flight, winding up a square dilapidated turret, became rougher, narrower, and darker, and opened the door of her father's retreat.

It was a room so bare of ornament and furniture that it seemed merely wrought out of the mingled rubble and rough stones which composed the walls of the mansion, and was lighted towards the street by a narrow slit, glazed it is true,—which all the windows of the house were not,—but the sun scarcely apierced the dull panes and the deep walls in which they were sunk. The room contained a strong furnace, and a rude laboratory. There were several strange-looking mechanical contrivances scattered about, several manuscripts upon some oaken shelves, and a large panier of wood and charcoal in the corner. In that poverty-stricken house, the money spent on fuel alone, in the height of summer, would have comfortably maintained the inmates; but neither Sibyll nor Madge ever thought to murmur at this waste, dedicated to what had become the vital want of a man who drew air in a world of his own. This was the first thing to be provided for; and Science was of more imperative necessity than even Hunger.

Adam Warner was indeed a creature of remarkable genius—and genius in an age where it is not appreciated, is the greatest curse the iron Fates can inflict on man. If not wholly without the fond fancies which led the wisdom of the darker ages to the philosopher's stone and the elixir, he had been deterred from the chase of a chimera by want of means to pursue it; for it required the resources or the patronage of a prince or noble to obtain the costly ingredients consumed in the alchemist's crucible. In early life, therefore, and while yet in possession of a competence, derived from a line of distinguished and knightly ancestors, Adam Warner had devoted himself to the surer, and less costly, study of the mathematics, which then had begun to attract the attention of the learned, but which was still looked upon by the vulgar as a branch of the black art. This pursuit had opened to him the insight into discoveries equally useful and sublime. They necessitated a still more various knowledge; and in an age when there was no division of labor, and rare and precarious communication among students, it became necessary for each discoverer to acquire sufficient science for his own collateral experiments.

In applying mathematics to the practical purposes of life, in recognizing its mighty utilities to commerce and civilization, Adam Warner was driven to conjoin with it, not only an extensive knowledge of languages, but many of the rudest tasks of the mechanist's art; and chemistry was, in some of his researches, summoned to his aid. By degrees, the tyranny that a man's genius exercises over his life, abstracted him from all external objects. He had loved his wife tenderly, but his rapid waste of his fortune in the purchase of instruments and books, then enormously dear, and the neglect of all things not centred in the hope to be the benefactor of the world, had ruined her health and broken her heart. Happily Warner perceived not her decay till just before her death; happily he never conceived its cause; for her soul was wrapped in his. She revered, and loved, and never upbraided him. Her heart was the martyr to his mind. Had she foreseen the future destinies of her daughter it might have been otherwise. She could have remonstrated with the father, though not with the husband. But, fortunately, as it seemed to her, she (a Frenchwoman by birth) had passed her youth in the service of Margaret of Anjou, and that haughty queen, who was equally warm to friends and inexorable to enemies, had, on her attendant's marriage, promised to ensure the fortunes of her offspring. Sibyll, at the age of nine,—between seven and eight years before the date the story enters on, and two years prior to the fatal field of Touton, which gave to Edward the throne of England, had been admitted among the young girls whom the custom of the day ranked amidst the attendants of the queen; and in the interval that elapsed before Margaret was obliged to dismiss her to her home, her mother died.

She died without foreseeing the reverses that were to ensue, in the hope that her child, at least, was nobly provided for, and not without the belief (for there is so much faith in love!) that her husband's researches, which, in his youth had won favor of the Protector-duke of Gloucester, the most enlightened prince of his time, would be crowned at last with the rewards and favors of his king. That precise period was, indeed, the fairest that had yet dawned upon the philosopher. Henry VI., slowly recovering from one of those attacks which passed for imbecility, had condescended to amuse himself with various conversations with Warner, urged to it first by representations of the unholy nature of the student's pursuits; and, having satisfied his mind of his learned subject's orthodoxy, the poor monarch had taken a sort of interest, not so much, perhaps, in the objects of Warner's occupations, as in that complete absorption from actual life which characterized the subject, and gave him in this, a melancholy resemblance to the king. While the House of Lancaster was on the throne, the wife felt that her husband's pursuits would be respected, and his harmless life safe from the fierce prejudices of the people; and the good queen would not suffer him to starve, when the last mark was expanded in devices how to benefit his country:—and in these hopes the woman died!

A year afterwards, all at court was in disorder—armed men supplied the service of young girls, and Sibyll, with a purse of broad pieces, soon converted into manuscripts, was sent back to her father's desolate home. There had she grown a flower amidst ruins—with no companion of her own age, and left to bear, as her sweet and affectionate nature well did, the contrast between the luxuries of a court and the penury of a hearth, which, year after year, hunger and want came more and more sensibly to invade.

Sibyll had been taught, even as a child, some accomplishments little vouchsafed, then, to either sex—she could read and write; and Margaret had not so wholly lost, in the sterner north, all reminiscence of the accomplishments that graced her father's court, as to neglect the education of those brought up in her household. Much attention was given to music, for it soothed the dark hours of king Henry; the blazoning of missals or the lives of saints, with the labors of the loom, were also among the resources of Sibyll's girlhood, and by these last she had, from time to time, served to assist the maintenance of the little family of which, child though she was, she became the actual head. But latterly—that is, for the last few weeks, even these sources failed her; for as more peaceful times allowed her neighbors to interest themselves in the affairs of others, the dark reports against Warner had revived. His name became a by-ward of horror—the lonely light at the lattice burning till midnight—against all the early usages and habits of the day—the dark smoke of the furnace, constant in summer as in winter, scandalized the religion of the place far and near, and finding, to their great dissatisfaction, that the King's government and the Church interfered not for their protection, and unable themselves to volunteer any charges against the recluse, (for the cows in the neighborhood remained provokingly healthy,) they came suddenly, and, as it were, by one of those common sympathies which in all times the huge persecutor we call the PUBLIC manifests, when a victim is to be crushed, —to the pious resolution of starving where they could not burn. Why buy the quaint devilries of the wizard's 'daughter?—no luck could come of it. A missal blazoned by such hands—an embroidery worked at such a loom, was like the Lord's Prayer read backwards. And one morning when poor Sibyll stole out as usual to vend a month's labor, she was driven from door to door with oaths and curses.

Though Sybill's heart was gentle, she was not without a certain strength of mind. She had much of the patient devotion of her mother, much of the quiet fortitude of her father's nature. If not comprehending to the full the loftiness of Warner's pursuits, she still anticipated from them an ultimate success which reconciled her to all temporary sacrifices. The violent prejudices—the ignorant cruelty, thus brought to bear against existence itself, filled her with sadness, it is true, but not unmixed with that contempt for her persecutors, which, even in the meekest tempers, takes the sting from despair. But hunger pressed. Her father was nearing the goal of his discoveries, and in a moment of that pride which in its very contempt for appearances braves them all, Sibyll had stolen out to the pastime-ground,—with what result has been seen already. Having thus accounted for the penury of the mansion, we return to its owner.

Warner was contemplating with evident complacency and delight the model of a machine which had occupied him for many years, and which he imagined he was now rapidly bringing to perfection. His hands and face were grimed with the smoke of his forge, and his hair and beard, neglected as usual, looked parched and dried up, as if with the constant fever that burned within.

"Yes—yes," he muttered—"How they will bless me for this! What Roger Bacon only suggested I shall accomplish! How it will change the face of the globe! What wealth it will bestow on ages yet unborn!"

"My father," said the gentle voice of Sibyll—"my poor father, thou hast not tasted bread to-day."

Warner turned, and his face relaxed into a tender expression as he saw his daughter.

"My child," he said, pointing to his model, "the time comes when *it will live!* Patience—patience!"

"And who would not have patience with thee, and *for* thee, father?" said Sibyll, with enthusiasm speaking on every feature.—"What is the valor of knight and soldier—dull statues of steel—to thine? Thou, with thy naked breast, confronting all dangers—sharper than the lance and glaive, and all——"

"All to make England great!"

"Alas! what hath England merited from men like thee! The people more savage than their rulers, clamor for the stake, the gibbet and the dungeon, for all who strive to make them wiser. Remember the death of Bolingbroke: *—a wizard, because, O father!—because his pursuits were thine!"

Adam, startled by this burst, looked at his daughter with more attention than he usually evinced to any living thing: "Child," he said, at length, shaking his head in grave reproof, "Let me not say to thee, 'O thou of little faith!' There were no heroes were there no martyrs!"

"Do not frown on me, father," said Sibyll, sadly; "let the world frown—not thou! Yes, thou art right. Thou must triumph at last." And suddenly her whole countenance, changing into a soft and caressing endearment, she added—"But now come, father. Thou hast labored well for this morning. We shall have a little feast for thee in a few minutes. And the stranger is recovered, thanks to our leechcraft. He is impatient to see and thank thee."

"Well—well, I come, Sibyll," said the student, with a regretful, lingering look at his model, and a sigh to be disturbed from its contemplation; and he slowly quitted the room with Sibyll.

"But not, dear sir and father, not thus—not quite thus—will you go to the stranger, well-born like yourself. Oh, no!—your Sibyll is proud, you know—proud of her father." So saying, she clung to him fondly, and drew him mechanically, for he had sunk into a reverie, and heeded her not, into an adjoining chamber in which he slept. The comforts even of the gentry, of men with the acres that Adam had sold, were then few and scanty. The nobles and the wealthy merchants, indeed, boasted many luxuries that excelled in gaud and pomp those of their equals now. But the class of the *gentry* who had very little money at command, were contented with hardships from which a menial of this day would revolt. What they could spend in luxury was usually consumed in dress and the table they were obliged to keep. These were the essentials of dignity. Of furniture there was a woeful stint. In many houses, even of knights, an edifice large enough to occupy a quadrangle, was composed more of offices than chambers inhabited by the owners; rarely boasting more than three beds, which were bequeathed in wills as articles of great value. The reader must, therefore, not be surprised that Warner's abode contained but one bed, properly so called, and that was now devoted to Nevile. The couch

* A mathematician accused as an accomplice, in sorcery, of Eleanor Cobham, wife of Humphrey Duke of Gloucester, and hanged upon that charge. His contemporary (William Wyrcestre) highly extols his learning.

which served the philosopher for bed was a wretched pallet, stretched on the floor, stuffed with straw,—with rough say or serge, and an old cloak for the coverings. His daughter's, in a room below, was little better. The walls were bare; the whole house boasted but one chair, which was in Marmaduke's chamber—stools, or settles, of rude oak, elsewhere supplied their place. There was no chimney, except in Nevile's room, and in that appropriated to the forge.

To this chamber, then, resembling a dungeon in appearance, Sibyll drew the student, and here, from an old worm-eaten chest, she carefully extracted a gown of brown velvet, which his father, Sir Armine, had bequeathed to him by will, faded, it is true, but still such as the low-born wore not,* trimmed with fur, and clasped with a brooch of gold. And then she held the ewer and basin to him, while with the docility of a child, he washed the smoke-soil from his hands and face. It was touching to see in this, as in all else, the reverse of their natural position—the child tending and heeding, and protecting, as it were, the father; and that not from his deficiency, but his greatness; not because he was below the vulgar intelligences of life, but above them. And certainly, when, his patriarchal hair and beard smoothed into order, and his velvet gown flowing in majestic folds, around a figure tall and commanding, Sibyll followed her father into Marmaduke's chamber,—she might well have been proud of his appearance. And she felt the innocent vanity of her sex and age, in noticing the half-start of surprise with which Marmaduke regarded his host, and the tone of respect in which he proffered him salutations and thanks. Even his manner altered to Sibyll; it grew less frank and affable, more courtly and reserved; and when Madge came to announce that the refection was served, it was with a blush of shame, perhaps, at his treatment of the poor gittern-player on the pastime ground, that the Nevile extended his left hand, for his right was still not at his command, to lead the damsel to the hall.

This room, which was divided from the entrance by a screen, and, except a small closet that adjoined it, was the only sitting-room in a day, when, as now on the Continent, no shame was attached to receiving visitors in sleeping apartments, was long and low; an old and very narrow table, that might have feasted thirty persons, stretched across a dais raised upon a stone floor; there was no rere-dosse, or fire-place, which does not seem at that day to have been an absolute necessity in the houses of the metropolis, and its suburbs; its place being supplied by a moveable brazier; three oak stools were placed in state at the board, and to one of these Marmaduke, in a silence unusual to him, conducted the fair Sibyll.

"You will forgive our lack of provisions," said Warner, relapsing into the courteous fashions of his elder days, which the unwonted spectacle of a cold capon, a pasty, and a flask of wine, brought to his mind by a train of ideas that actively glided by the intervening circumstances which ought to have filled him with astonishment at the sight, "for my Sibyll is but a young housewife, and I am a simple scholar, of few wants."

"Verily," answered Marmaduke, finding his tongue as he attacked the pasty, "I see nothing that the most dainty need complain of; fair mistress Sibyll, your dainty lips will not, I trow, refuse me the waisall.* To you also, worshipful sir! Gramercy! it seems that there is nothing which better stirs a man's appetite than a sick bed. And, speaking thereof, deign to inform me, kind sir, how long I have been indebted to your hospitality. Of a surety, this pasty hath an excellent flavor, and if not vension, is something better. But to return, it mazes me much to think what time hath passed since my encounter with the robbers."

"They were robbers, then, who so cruelly assailed thee?" observed Sibyll.

"Have I not said so—surely, who else? and, as I was remarking to your worshipful father, whether this mischance happened hours, days, months, or years ago, beshrew me if I can venture the smallest guess."

Master Warner smiled, and observing that some reply was expected from him, said, "Why, indeed, young sir, I fear I am almost as oblivious as yourself. It was not yesterday

* By the sumptuary laws only a knight was entitled to wear velvet.

* *i. e.* Waissail or wassal; the spelling of the time is adopted in the text.

that you arrived, nor the day before, nor—Sibyll, my child, how long is it since this gentleman hath been our guest?"

"This is the fifth day," answered Sibyll.

"So long! and I like a senseless log by the way-side, when others are pushing on bit and spur, to the great road. I pray you, sir, tell me the news of the morning. The Lord Warwick is still in London—the Court still at the Tower?"

Poor Adam, whose heart was with his model, and who had now satisfied his temperate wants, looked somewhat bewildered and perplexed by this question: "The king, save his honored head," said he, inclining his own, "is, I fear me, always at the Tower since his unhappy detention, but he minds it not, sir—he heeds it not; his soul is not on this side Paradise."

Sibyll uttered a faint exclamation of fear at this dangerous indiscretion of her father's absence of mind; and, drawing closer to Nevile, she put her hand with touching confidence on his arm, and whispered—"You will not repeat this, sir! my father lives only in his studies, and he has never known but one king!"

Marmaduke turned his bold face to the maid, and pointed to the salt-celler, as he answered in the same tone—"Does the brave man betray his host?"

There was a moment's silence. Marmaduke rose. "I fear," said he, "that I must now leave you; and, while it is yet broad noon, I must indeed be blind if I again miss my way."

This speech suddenly recalled Adam from his meditations, for whenever his kindly and simple benevolence was touched, even his mathematics and his model were forgotten. "No, young sir," said he, "you must not quit us yet; your danger is not over. Exercise may bring fever. Celsus recommends quiet. You must consent to tarry with us a day or two more."

"Can you tell me," said the Nevile, hesitatingly, "what distance it is to the Temple Gate, or the nearest wharf on the river?"

"Two miles, at the least," answered Sibyll.

"Two miles!—and now I mind me, I have not the accoutrements that beseem me. Those hildings have stolen my mantle, (which I perceive, by the way, is but a rustic garment, now laid aside for the super-tunic), and my hat and dague, nor have they left even a half groat to supply their place. Verily, therefore, since ye permit me to burden your hospitality longer, I will not say ye nay, provided you, worshipful sir, will suffer one of your people to step to the house of one Master Heyfort, goldsmith, in the Chepe, and crave one Nicholas Alwyn, his freedman, to visit me. I can commission him, touching my goods left at mine hostelrie, and learn some other things which it behoves me to know."

"Assuredly. Sibyll, tell Simon or Jonas to put himself under our guest's order."

Simon or Jonas! The poor Adam absolutely forgot that Simon and Jonas had quitted the house these six years! How could he look on the capon, the wine, and the velvet gown trimmed with fur, and not fancy himself back in the heyday of his wealth?

Sibyll half smiled and half sighed, as she withdrew to consult with her sole counsellor, Madge, how the guest's orders were to be obeyed, and how, alas, the board was to be replenished for the evening meal. But in both these troubles she was more fortunate than she anticipated. Madge had sold the broken gittern, for musical instruments were then, comparatively speaking, dear, (and this had been a queen's gift), for sufficient to provide decently for some days, and elated herself with the prospect of so much good cheer, she readily consented to be the messenger to Nicholas Alwyn.

When, with a light step, and a lighter heart, Sibyll tripped back to the hall, she was scarcely surprised to find the guest alone. Her father, after her departure, had begun to evince much restless perturbation. He answered Marmaduke's queries, but by abstracted and desultory monosyllables, and seeing his guest at length engaged in contemplating some old pieces of armor hung upon the walls, he stole stealthily and furtively away, and halted not till once more before his beloved model.

Unaware of his departure, Marmaduke, whose back was turned to him, was, as he fondly imagined, enlightening his host with much soldier-like learning as to the old helmets and weapons that graced the hall. "Certes, my host," said he, musingly, "that sort of casque, which has not, I opine, been worn this century has its merits; the vizor is less open to the arrows. But, as for these chain suits, they suited only—I venture, with due deference, to declare—the Wars of the Crusades, where the enemy fought chiefly with dart and scymetar. They would be but a sorry defence against the mace and battle-axe; nevertheless they were light for man and horse, and, in some service, especially against foot, might be revived with advantage. Think you not so?"

He turned, and saw the arch face of Sibyll.

"I crave pardon for my blindness, gentle damsel," said he, in some confusion, "but your father was here anon."

"His mornings are so devoted to labor," answered Sibyll, "that he entreats you to pardon his discourtesy. Meanwhile, if you would wish to breathe the air, we have a small garden in the rear;" and so saying, she led the way into the small with-drawing-room, or rather closet, which was her own favorite chamber, and which communicated, by another door, with a broad, neglected grass-plot, surrounded by high walls, having a raised terrace in front, divided by a low stone gothic palisade from the green sward.

On the palisade sate droopingly, and half asleep, a solitary peacock; but when Sibyll and the stranger appeared at the door, he woke up suddenly, descended from his height, and, with a vanity not wholly unlike his young mistress's wish to make the best possible display in the eyes of a guest—spread his plumes broadly in the sun. Sibyll threw him some bread, which she had taken from the table for that purpose: but the proud bird, however hungry, disdained to eat, till he had thoroughly satisfied himself that his glories had been sufficiently observed.

"Poor proud one," said Sibyll, half to herself, "thy plumage lasts with thee through all changes."

"Like the name of a brave knight," said Marmaduke, who overheard her.

"Thou thinkest of the career of arms."

"Surely—I am a Nevile!"

"Is there no fame to be won but that of a warrior?"

"Not that I weet of, or heed for, Mistress Sibyll."

"Thinkest thou it were nothing to be a minstrel, who gave delight?—a scholar, who dispelled darkness?"

"For the scholar? certes, I respect holy Mother Church, which they tell me alone produces that kind of wonder with full safety to the soul, and that only in the higher prelates and dignitaries. For the minstrel, I love him—I would fight for him—I would give him at need the last penny in my gipsire. But it is better to do deeds than to sing them."

Sibyll smiled, and the smile perplexed, and half displeased the young adventurer. But the fire of the young man had its charm.

By degrees, as they walked to and fro the neglected terrace, their talk flowed free and familiar; for Marmaduke, like most young men, full of himself, was joyous with the happy egotism of a frank and careless nature. He told his young confidante of a day his birth, his history, his hopes, and fears; and in return he learned, in answer to the questions he addressed to her, so much, at least, of her past and present life—as the reverses of her father, occasioned by costly studies—her own brief sojourn at the court of Margaret—and the solitude, if not the struggles, in which her youth was consumed. It would have been a sweet and grateful sight to some kindly bystander to hear these pleasant communications between two young persons so unfriended, and to imagine that hearts thus opened to each other might unite in one. But Sibyll, though she listened to him with interest, and found a certain sympathy in his aspirations, was ever and anon secretly comparing him to one, the charm of whose voice still lingered in her ears; and her intellect, cultivated and acute, detected in Marmaduke deficient education—and that limited experience which is the folly and the happiness of the young.

On the other hand, whatever admiration Nevile might conceive, was strangely mixed with surprise, and, it might almost be said, with fear. This girl, with her wise converse and her child's face, was a character so thoroughly new to him. Her language was superior to what he had ever heard, the words more choice, the current more flowing—was that to be attributed to her court-training, or her learned parentage?

"Your father, fair mistress," said he, rousing himself in one of the pauses of their conversation—"your father, then, is a mighty scholar, and I suppose knows Latin like English?"

"Why a hedge priest pretends to know Latin," said Sibyll, smiling; "my father is one of the six men living who have learned the Greek and the Hebrew."

"Gramercy!" cried Marmaduke, crossing himself. "That is awsome indeed! He has taught you his lere in the tongues?"

"Nay, I know but my own and the French; my mother was a native of France."

"The Holy Mother be praised!" said Marmaduke, breathing more freely; "for French I have heard my father and uncle say is a language fit for gentles and knights, specially those who come, like the Neviles from Norman stock. This Margaret of Anjou—didst thou love her well, Mistress Sibyll?"

"Nay," answered Sybill, "Margaret commanded awe, but she scarcely permitted love from an inferior; and though gracious and well-governed when she so pleased, it was but to those whom she wished to win. She cared not for the heart, if the hand or the brain could not assist her. But, poor queen, who could blame her for this?—her nature was turned from its milk; and, when, more lately, I have heard how many she trusted most have turned against her, I rebuked myself that——"

"Thou wert not by her side!" added the Nevile, observing her pause, and with the generous thought of a gentleman and a soldier.

"Nay, I meant not that so expressly. Master Nevile, but rather that I had ever murmured at her haste and shrewdness of mood. By her side, said you?—alas! I have a nearer duty at home; my father is all in this world to me! Thou knowest not, Master Nevile, how it flatters the weak to think there is some one they can protect. But eno' of myself. Thou wilt go to the stout earl, thou wilt pass to the court, thou wilt win the gold spurs, and thou wilt fight with the strong hand, and leave others so cozen with the keen head."

"She is telling my fortune!" muttered Marmaduke, crossing himself again. "The gold spurs—I thank thee, Mistress Sibyll!—will it be on the battle-field that I shall be knighted, and by whose hand?"

Sibyll glanced her bright eye at the questioner, and seeing his wistful face, laughed outright.

"What, thinkest thou, Master Nevile, I can read thee all riddles without my sieve and my shears?"

"They are essentials, then, Mistress Sibyll?" said the Nevile, with blunt simplicity. "I thought ye more learned damozels might tell by the palm, or the—why dost thou laugh at me?"

"Nay," answered Sibyll, composing herself. "It is my right to be angered. Sith thou wouldst take me to be a witch, all that I can tell thee of thy future (she added touchingly) is from that which I have seen of thy past. Thou hast a brave heart, and a gentle; thou hast a frank tongue, and a courteous; and these qualities make men honored and loved—except they have the gifts which turn all into gall, and bring oppression for honor, and hate for love."

"And those gifts, gentle Sibyll?"

"Are my father's," answered the girl, with another and a sadder change in her expressive countenance. And the conversation flagged till Marmaduke, feeling more weakened by his loss of blood than he had conceived it possible, retired to his chamber to repose himself.

CHAPTER VI.

Master Marmaduke Nevile fears for the Spiritual Weal of his Host and Hostess.

Before the hour of supper, which was served at six o'clock, Nicholas Alwyn arrived at the house indicated to him by Madge. Marmaduke, after a sound sleep, which was little flattering to Sibyll's attractions, had descended to the hall in search of the maiden and his host, and finding no one, had sauntered in extreme weariness and impatience into the little withdrawing closet, where, as it was now dusk, burned a single candle in a melancholy and rusted sconce; standing by the door that opened on the garden he amused himself with watching the peacock, when his friend, following Madge into the chamber, tapped him on the shoulder.

"Well, Master Nevile. Ha! by St. Thomas, what has chanced to thee? Thine arm swathed up, thy locks shorn, thy face blanched! My honored foster-brother, thy Westmoreland blood seems over-hot for Cockaigne!"

"If so, there are plenty in this city of cut-throats, to let out the surplusage," returned Marmaduke; and he briefly related his adventure to Nicholas.

When he had done, the kind trader reproached himself for having suffered Marmaduke to find his way alone. "The suburbs abound with these miscreants," said he; "and there is more danger in a night-walk near London, than in the loneliest glens of green Sherwood—more shame to the city! An' I be Lord Mayor, one of these days, I will look to it better. But our civil wars make men hold human life very cheap, and there's parlous little care from the great, of the blood and limbs of the wayfarers. But war makes thieves—and peace hangs them! Only wait till I manage affairs!"

"Many thanks to thee, Nicholas," returned the Nevile; "but foul befall me if ever I seek protection from sheriff or mayor! A man who cannot keep his own life with his own right hand, merits well to hap-lose it; and I, for one, shall think ill of the day when an Englishman looks more to the laws than his good arm for his safety; but, letting this pass, I beseech thee to avise me if my Lord Warwick be still in the city?"

"Yes, marry, I know that by the hostelries, which swarm with his badges, and the oxen, that go in scores to the shambles! It is a shame to the Estate to see one subject so great, and it bodes no good to our peace. The earl is preparing the most magnificent embassage that ever crossed the salt seas—I would it were not to the French, for our interests lie contrary; but thou hast some days yet to rest here and grow stout, for I would not have thee present thyself with a visage of chalk to a man who values his kind mainly by their thews and their sinews. Moreover, thou shouldst send for the tailor, and get thee trimmed to the mark. It would be a long step in thy path to promotion, an' the earl would take thee in his train; and the gaudier thy plumes, why the better chance for thy flight. Wherefore, since thou sayest they are thus friendly to thee under this roof, bide yet awhile peacefully—I will send thee the mercer and the clothier and the tailor to divert thy impatience. And, as these fellows are greedy, my gentle and dear Master Nevile, may I ask, without offence, how thou art provided?"

"Nay, nay, I have monies at the hostelrie, an' thou wilt send me my mails. For the rest I like thy advice, and will take it."

"Good!" answered Nicholas. "Hem! thou seemest to have got into a poor house—a decayed gentleman, I wot, by the slovenly ruin!"

"I would that were the worst," replied Marmaduke, solemnly, and under his breath, and therewith he repeated to Nicholas the adventure on the pastime ground, the warnings of the timbrel-girls, and the "awsome" learning and strange pursuits of his host. As for Sibyll, he was evidently inclined to attribute to glamour the reluctant admiration with which she had inspired him. "For," said he, "though I deny not that the maid is passing fair—there be many with rosier cheeks, and taller by this hand!"

Nicholas listened, at first, with the peculiar expression of shrewd sarcasm which mainly characterized his intelligent face, but his attention grew more earnest before Marmaduke had concluded.

"In regard to the maiden," said he, smiling and shaking his head, "it is not always the handsomest that win us the most—while fair Meg went a maying, black Mog got to church—and I give thee more reasonable warning than thy timbrel-girls, when, in spite of thy cold language, I bid thee take care of thyself against her attractions; for, verily, my dear foster-brother, thou must mend, and not mar thy fortune, by thy love matters; and keep thy heart whole for some fair one with marks in her gipsire, whom the earl may find out for thee. Love and raw pease are two ill things in the porridge-pot. But, the father!—I mind me now that I have heard of his name, through my friend Master Caxton, the mercer, as one of prodigious skill in the mathematics. I should like much to see him, and, with thy leave (an' he ask me), will tarry to supper. But what are these!"—and Nicholas took up one of the illuminated MSS. which Sibyll had prepared for sale. "By the blood! this is couthly and marvellously blazoned."

The book was still in his hand when Sibyll entered. Nicholas stared at her, as he bowed with a stiff and ungraceful embarrassment, which often at first did injustice to his bold, clear intellect, and perfect self-possession in matters of trade or importance.

"The first woman face," muttered Nicholas to himself, "I ever saw that had the sense of a man's. And by the rood, what a smile!"

"Is this thy friend, Master Nevile?" said

Sibyll, with a glance at the goldsmith. "He is welcome. But is it fair and courteous, Master Nelwyn—"

"Alwyn, an' it please you, fair mistress. A humble name, but good Saxon—which, I take it, Nelwyn is not," interrupted Nicholas.

"Master Alwyn, forgive me; but can I forgive thee so readily for thy espial of my handiwork, without licence or leave?"

"Yours, comely mistress!" exclaimed Nicholas, opening his eyes, and unheeding the gay rebuke—"why, this is a master-hand. My Lord Scales—nay, the Earl of Worcester himself, hath scarce a finer in all his amassment."

"Well, I forgive thy fault for thy flattery; and I pray thee, in my father's name, to stay and sup with thy friend."

Nicholas bowed low, and still riveted his eyes on the book with such open admiration, that Marmaduke thought it right to excuse his abstraction; but there was something in that admiration which raised the spirits of Sibyll, which gave her hope when hope was well nigh gone, and she became so vivacious, so debonnair, so charming, in the flow of a gaiety natural to her, and very uncommon with English maidens, but which she took partly, perhaps, from her French blood, and partly from the example of girls and maidens of French extraction in Margaret's court, that Nicholas Alwyn thought he never seen any one so irresistible. Madge having now served the evening meal, put in her head to announce it, and Sibyll withdrew to summon her father.

"I trust he will not tarry too long, for I am sharp set!" muttered Marmaduke. "What thinkest thou of the damozel?"

"Marry," answered Alwyn, thoughtfully, "I pity and marvel at her. There is eno' in her to furnish forth twenty court beauties. But what good can so much wit and cunning do to an honest maiden?"

"That is exactly my own thought," said Marmaduke; and both the young men sunk into silence, till Sibyll re-entered with her father.

To the surprise of Marmaduke, Nicholas Alwyn, whose less gallant manner he was inclined to ridicule, soon contrived to rouse their host from his lethargy, and to absorb all the notice of Sibyll; and the surprise was increased, when he saw that his friend appeared not unfamiliar with those abstruse and mystical sciences in which Adam was engaged.

"What!" said Adam. "You know, then, my deft and worthy friend, Master Caxton! He hath seen notable things abroad——"

"Which he more than hints," said Nicholas, "will lower the value of those manuscripts this fair damozel has so couthly enriched: and that he hopes, ere long, to show the Englishers how to make fifty, a hundred,—nay, even five hundred exemplars of the choicest book, in a much shorter time than a scribe would take in writing out two or three score pages in a single copy."

"Verily," said Marmaduke, with a smile of compassion, "the poor man must be somewhat demented; for I opine that the value of such curiosities must be in their rarity—and who would care for a book, if five hundred others had precisely the same?—allowing always, good Nicholas, for thy friend's vaunting and over-crowing. Five hundred! By'r lady, there would be scarcely five hundred fools in merry England to waste good nobles on spoilt rags, especially while bows and mail are so dear."

"Young gentleman," said Adam, rebukingly, "meseemeth that thou wrongest our age and country, to the which, if we have but peace and freedom, I trust the birth of great discoveries is ordained. Certes, Master Alwyn," he added, turning to the goldsmith, "this achievement may be readily performed, and hath existed, I heard an ingenious Fleming say, years ago, for many ages amongst a strange people* known to the Venetians! But dost thou think there is much appetite among those who govern the state to lend encouragement to such matters?"

"My master serves my Lord Hastings, the King's Chamberlain, and my lord has often been pleased to converse with me, so that I venture to say, from my knowledge of his affection to all excellent craft and lere, that whatever will tend to make men wiser will have his countenance and favor with the king."

"That is it—that is it!" exclaimed Adam, rubbing his hands. "My invention shall not die!"

"And that invention——"

'Is one that will multiply exemplars of

* Query, the Chinese?

books without hands; works of craft without 'prentice or journeyman; will give more wagons and litters without horses; will direct ships without sails; will—but alack! it is not yet complete, and, for want of means, it never may be.'

Sibyll still kept her animated countenance fixed on Alwyn, whose intelligence she had already detected, and was charmed with the profound attention with which he listened. But her eye glancing from his sharp features to the handsome, honest face of the Nevile, the contrast was so forcible, that she could not restrain her laughter, though, the moment after, a keen pang shot through her heart. The worthy Marmaduke had been in the act of conveying his cup to his lips—the cup stood arrested midway, his jaws dropped, his eyes opened to their widest extent, an expression of the most evident consternation and dismay spoke in every feature, and, when he heard the merry laugh of Sibyll, he pushed his stool from her as far as he well could, and surveyed her with a look of mingled fear and pity.

"Alas! thou art sure my poor father is a wizard now?"

"Pardie!" answered the Nevile. "Hath he not said so? Hath he not spoken of wagons without horses—ships without sails? And is not all this what every dissour and jongleur tells us of in his stories of Merlin? Gentle maiden," he added, earnestly drawing nearer to her, and whispering in a voice of much simple pathos—"thou art young, and I owe thee much. Take care of thyself. Such wonders and derring-do are too solemn for laughter."

"Ah!" answered Sibyll, rising, "I fear they are. How can I expect the people to be wiser than thou, or their hard natures kinder in their judgment than thy kind heart?" Her low and melancholy voice went to the heart thus appealed to. Marmaduke also rose, and followed her into the parlor, or withdrawing-closet, while Adam and the goldsmith continued to converse (though Alwyn's eye followed the young hostess), the former appearing perfectly unconscious of the secession of his other listeners. But Alwyn's attention occasionally wandered, and he soon contrived to draw his host into the parlor.

When Nicholas rose, at last, to depart, he beckoned Sibyll aside: "Fair mistress," said he, with some awkward hesitation, "forgive a plain, blunt tongue; but ye of the better birth are not always above aid, even from such as I am. If you would sell these blazoned manuscripts, I cannot only obtain you a noble purchaser, in my Lord Scales, or in my Lord Hastings, an equally ripe scholar, but it may be the means of my procuring a suitable patron for your father; and, in these times, the scholar must creep under the knight's manteline."

"Master Alwyn," said Sibyll, suppressing her tears, "it was for my father's sake that these labors were wrought. We are poor and friendless. Take the manuscripts, and sell them as thou wilt, and God and St. Mary requite thee!"

"Your father is a great man," said Alwyn, after a pause.

"But, were he to walk the streets, they would stone him," replied Sibyll, with a quiet bitterness.

Here the Nevile, carefully shunning the magican, who, in the nervous excitement produced by the conversation of a mind less uncongenial than he had encountered for many years, seemed about to address him—here, I say, the Nevile chimed in—"Hast thou no weapon but thy bludgeon? Dear foster-brother, I fear for thy safety."

"Nay, robbers rarely attack us mechanical folk; and I know my way better than thou. I shall find a boat near York House, so pleasant night and quick cure to thee, honored foster-brother; I will send the tailor and other craftsmen to-morrow."

"And at the same time," whispered Marmaduke, accompanying his friend to the door, "send me a breviary, just to patter an ave or so. This gray-haired carle puts my heart in a tremble. Moreover, buy me a gittern—a brave one—for the damozel. She is too proud to take money, and, 'fore heaven, I have small doubts the old wizard could turn my hose into nobles an' he had a mind for such gear. Wagons without horses—ships without sails, quotha!"

As soon as Alwyn had departed, Madge appeared with the final refreshment called "the Wines," consisting of spiced hippocras and confections, of the former of which the Nevile partook in solemn silence.

———

CHAPTER VII.

There is a Rod for the Back of every Fool who would be wiser than his Generation.

THE next morning, when Marmaduke descended to the hall, Madge, accosting him on the threshold, informed him that Mistress Sibyll was unwell, and kept her chamber, and that Master Warner was never visible much before noon. He was, therefore, prayed to take his meal alone. "Alone" was a word peculiarly unwelcome to Marmaduke Nevile, who was an animal thoroughly social and gregarious. He managed, therefore, to detain the old servant, who, besides the liking a skilful leech naturally takes to a thriving patient, had enough of her sex about her to be pleased with a comely face, and a frank, good-humored voice. Moreover, Marmaduke, wishing to satisfy his curiosity, turned the conversation upon Warner and Sibyll, a theme upon which the old woman was well disposed to be garrulous. He soon learned the poverty of the mansion, and the sacrifice of the gittern; and his generosity and compassion were busily engaged in devising some means to requite the hospitality he had received, without wounding the pride of his host, when the arrival of his mails, together with the visits of the tailor and mercer, sent to him by Alwyn, diverted his thoughts into a new channel.

Between the comparative merits of gowns and surcoats, broad-toed shoes, and pointed, some time was disposed of with much cheerfulness and edification; but when his visitors had retired, the benevolent mind of the young guest again recurred to the penury of his host. Placing his marks before him on the table in the little withdrawing parlor, he began counting them over, and putting aside the sum he meditated devoting to Warner's relief. "But how," he muttered, "how to get him to take the gold. I know, by myself, what a gentleman and a knight's son must feel at the proffer of alms—pardie! I would as lief Alwyn had struck me as offered me his gipsire—the ill-mannered affectionate fellow! I must think—I must think——"

And while still thinking, the door softly opened, and Warner himself, in a high state of abstraction and reverie, stalked noiselessly into the room, on his way to the garden, in which, when musing over some new spring for his invention, he was wont to peripatise. The sight of the gold on the table struck full on the philosopher's eyes, and waked him at once from his reverie. That gold—oh, what precious instruments, what learned manuscripts it could purchase! That gold, it was the breath of life to his model! He walked deliberately up to the table, and laid his hand upon one of the little heaps. Marmaduke drew back his stool, and stared at him with open mouth.

"Young man, what wantest thou with all this gold?" said Adam, in a petulent, reproachful tone. "Put it up—put it up! Never let the poor see gold; it tempts them, sir—it tempts them." And so saying, the student abruptly turned away his eyes, and moved towards the garden.

Marmaduke rose and put himself in Adam's way—

"Honored sir," said the young man, "you say justly—what want I with all this gold? The only gold a young man should covet is eno' to suffice for the knight's spurs to his heels. If, without offence, you would—that is—ehem!—I mean, Gramercy! I shall never say it, but I believe my father owed your father four marks, and he bade me repay them. Here, sir!" He held out the glittering coins—the philosopher's hand closed on them as the fish's maw closes on the bait. Adam burst into a laugh, that sounded strangely weird and unearthly upon Marmaduke's startled ear.

"All this for me!" he exclaimed. "For me! No—no! not for *me*, for IT—I take it—I take it, sir! I will pay it back with large usury. Come to me this day year, when this world will be a new world, and Adam Warner will be—ha! ha! Kind Heaven, I thank thee!" Suddenly turning away, the philosopher strode through the hall, opened the front door, and escaped into the street.

"By'r Lady!" said Marmaduke, slowly recovering his surprise, "I need not have been so much at a loss; the old gentleman takes to my gold as kindly as if it were mother's milk. 'Fore heaven, mine host's laugh is a ghastly thing!" So soliloquising, he prudently put up the rest of his money, and locked his mails.

As time went on, the young man became exceedingly weary of his own company

Sibyll still withheld her appearance: the gloom of the old hall, the uncultivated sadness of the lonely garden, preyed upon his spirits. At length, impatient to get a view of the world without, he mounted a high stool in the hall, and so contrived to enjoy the prospect, which the unglazed wicker lattice, deep set in the wall, afforded. But the scene without was little more animated than that within—all was so deserted in the neighborhood!—the shops mean and scattered—the thoroughfare almost desolate. At last, he he heard a shout, or rather hoot, at a distance; and, turning his attention whence it proceeded, he beheld a figure emerge from an alley opposite the casement, with a sack under one arm, and several books heaped under the other. At his heels followed a train of ragged boys, shouting and hallooing, "The wizard! the wizard!—Ah!—Bah!—The old devil's-kin!" At this cry the dull neighborhood seemed suddenly to burst forth into life. From the casements and thresholds of every house, curious faces emerged, and many voices of men and women joined, in deeper bass, with the shrill tenor of the coral urchins, "The wizard! the wizard!—out at day-light!" The person thus stigmatized, as he approached the house, turned his face, with an expression of wistful perplexity, from side to side. His lips moved convulsively, and his face was very pale, but he spoke not. And now, the children seeing him near his refuge, became more outrageous. They placed themselves menacingly before him—they pulled his robe—they even struck at him—and one, bolder than the rest, jumped up, and plucked his beard. At this last insult, Adam Warner, for it was he, broke silence; but such was the sweetness of his disposition, that it was rather with pity than reproof in his voice, that he said—

"Fie, little one!—I fear me thine own age will have small honor if thou thus mockest mature years in me."

This gentleness only served to increase the audacity of his persecutors, who now, momently augmenting, presented a formidable obstacle to his further progress. Perceiving that he could not advance, without offensive measures on his own part, the poor scholar halted; and looking at the crowd with mild dignity, he asked, "What means this, my children? How have I injured you?"

"The wizard—the wizard!" was the only answer he received.

Adam shrugged his shoulders, and strode on with so sudden a step, that one of the smaller children, a curly-headed laughing rogue, of about eight years old, was thrown down at his feet, and the rest gave way. But the poor man, seeing one of his foes thus fallen, instead of pursuing his victory, again paused, and, forgetful of the precious burdens he carried, let drop the sack and books, and took up the child in his arms. On seeing their companion in the embrace of the wizard, a simultaneous cry of horror broke from the assemblage.—"He is going to curse poor Tim!"

"My child!—my boy!" shrieked a woman, from one of the casements—"let go my child!"

On his part, the boy kicked and shrieked lustily, as Adam, bending his noble face tenderly over him, said, "Thou art not hurt, child. Poor boy! thinkest thou I would harm thee?" While he spoke, a storm of missiles—mud, dirt, sticks, bricks, stones,—from the enemy, that had now fallen back in the rear, burst upon him. A stone struck him on the shoulder. Then his face changed—an angry gleam shot from his deep, calm eyes—he put down the child—and, turning steadily to the grown people at the windows, said, "Ye train your children ill"—picked up his sack and books—sighed, as he saw the latter stained by the mire, which he wiped with his long sleeve, and too proud to show fear, slowly made for his door. Fortunately Sibyll had heard the clamor, and was ready to admit her father, and close the door upon the rush which instantaneously followed his escape. The baffled rout set up a yell of wrath, and the boys were now joined by several foes more formidable from the adjacent houses: Assured in their own minds that some terrible execration had been pronounced upon the limbs and body of Master Tim, who still continued bellowing and howling, probably from the excitement of finding himself raised to the dignity of a martyr,—the pious neighbors poured forth, with oaths, and curses, and such weapons as they could seize in haste, to storm the wizard's fortress.

From his casement Marmaduke Nevile had espied all that had hitherto passed, and though indignant at the brutality of the persecutors, he had thought it by no means unnatural. "If men, gentlemen born, will read uncanny books, and resolve to be wizards, why they must reap what they sow," was the logical reflection that passed through the mind of that ingenuous youth; but when he now perceived the arrival of more important allies—when stones began to fly through the wicker lattices—when threats of setting fire to the house and burning the sorcerer, who muttered spells over innocent little boys, were heard, seriously increasing in depth and loudness—Marmaduke felt his chivalry called forth, and, with some difficulty, opening the rusty wicket in the casement, he exclaimed, "Shame on you, my countrymen, for thus disturbing, in broad day, a peaceful habitation! Ye call mine host a wizard. Thus much say I on his behalf: I was robbed and wounded a few nights since in your neighborhood, and in this house alone I found shelter and healing."

The unexpected sight of the fair young face of Marmaduke Nevile, and the healthful sound of his clear ringing voicc, produced a momentary effect on the besiegers when one of them, a sturdy baker, cried out, "Heed him not—he is a goblin! Those devil-mongers can bake ye a dozen such every moment, as deftly as I can draw loaves from the oven!"

This speech turned the tide, and at that instant a savage-looking man, the father of the aggrieved boy, followed by his wife, gesticulating and weeping, ran from his house, waving a torch in his right hand, his arm bare to the shoulder, and the cry of "Fire the door!" was universal.

In fact, the danger now grew imminent: several of the party were already piling straw and fagots against the threshold, and Marmaduke began to think the only chance of life to his host and Sibyll was in flight by some back way, when he beheld a man, clad somewhat in the fashion of a country yeoman, a formidable knotted club in his hand, pushing his way, with Herculean shoulders, through the crowd, and stationing himself before the threshold and brandishing aloft his formidable weapon, he exclaimed, "What! In the devil's name, do you mean to get yourselves all hanged for riot? Do you think that King Edward is as soft a man as King Henry was, and that he will suffer any one but himself to set fire to people's houses in this way? I dare say you are all right enough on the main, but by the blood of St. Thomas, I will brain the first man who advances a step,—by way of preserving the necks of the rest!"

"A Robin! a Robin!" cried several of the mob. "It is our good friend Robin. Hearken to Robin. He is always right!"

"Ay that I am!" quoth the defender; "you know that well enough. If I had my way, the world should be turned upside down, but what the poor folk should get nearer to the sun! But what I say is this, never go against law, while the law is too strong. And it were a sad thing to see fifty fine fellows trussed up for burning an old wizard. So, be off with you, and let us, at least all that can afford it, make for Master Sancroft's hostelrie, and talk soberly over our ale. For little, I trow, will ye work now your blood's up."

This address was received with a shout of approbation. The father of the injured child set his broad foot on his torch, the baker chucked up his white cap, the ragged boys yelled out, "A Robin! a Robin!" and in less than two minutes the place was as empty as it had been before the appearance of the scholar. Marmaduke, who, though so ignorant, of books, was acute and penetrating in all matters of action, could not help admiring the address and dexterity of the club-bearer; and the danger being now over, withdrew from the casement, in search of the inmates of the house. Ascending the stairs, he found on the landing-place, near his room, and by the embrasure of a huge casement which jutted from the wall, Adam and his daughter. Adam was leaning against the wall, with his arms folded, and Sibyll, hanging upon him, was uttering the softest and most soothing words of comfort her tenderness could suggest.

"My child," said the old man, shaking his head sadly. "I shall never again have heart for these studies—never. A king's anger I could brave, a priest's malice I could pity—but to find the very children, the young race, for whose sake I have made thee and myself paupers, to find them thus—thus——" He stopped, for his voice failed him, and the tears rolled down his cheeks.

"Come and speak comfort to my father,

Master Nevile!" exclaimed Sibyll, "come and tell him that whoever is above the herd, whether knight or scholar, must learn to despise the hootings that follow Merit. Father, father, they threw mud and stones at thy king as he passed threw the streets of London. Thou art not the only one whom this base world misjudges."

"Worthy mine host!" said Marmaduke, thus appealed to: "Algates, it were not speaking truth to tell thee that I think a gentleman of birth and quality should walk the thoroughfares with a bundle of books under his arm, yet as for the raptril vulgar, the hildings and cullions who hiss one day what they applaud the next, I hold it the duty of every Christian and well-born man to regard them as the dirt on the crossings. Brave soldies term it no disgrace to receive a blow from a base hind. An' it had been knights and gentles who had insulted thee, thou mightest have cause for shame. But a mob of lewd rascallions and squalling infants—bah! verily, it is mere matter for scorn and laughter."

These philosophical propositions and distinctions did not seem to have their due effect upon Adam. He smiled, however, gently upon his guest, and with a blush over his pale face, said, "I am rightly chastised, good young man; mean was I, methinks, and sordid, to take from thee thy good gold. But thou knowest not what fever burns in the brain of a man who feels that, had he wealth, his knowledge could do great things,—such things!—I thought to repay thee well. Now the frenzy is gone, and I, who an hour agone esteemed myself a puissant sage, sink in mine own conceit to a miserable blinded fool. Child, I am very weak; I will lay me down and rest."

So saying, the poor philosopher went his way to his chamber, leaning on his daughter's arm.

In a few minutes Sibyll rejoined Marmaduke, who had returned to the hall, and informed him, that her father had lain down awhile to compose himself.

"It is a hard fate, sir," said the girl, with a faint smile; "a hard fate, to be banned and accursed by the world, only because one has sought to be wiser than the world is."

"Douce maiden," returned the Nevile; "it is happy for thee that thy sex forbids thee to follow thy father's footsteps, or I should say his hard fate were thy fair warning."

Sibyll smiled faintly, and after a pause, said, with a deep blush:—

"You have been generous to my father; do not misjudge him. He would give his last groat to a starving beggar. But when his passion of scholar and inventor masters him—thou mightest think him worse than miser. It is an over-noble yearning that ofttimes makes him mean."

"Nay," answered Marmaduke, touched by the heavy sigh and swimming eyes with which the last words were spoken; "I have heard Nick Alwyn's uncle, who was a learned monk, declare that he could not constrain himself to pray to be delivered from temptation—seeing that he might thereby lose an occasion for filching some notable book! For the rest," he added, "you forget how much I owe to Master Warner's hospitality."

He took her hand with a frank and brotherly gallantry as he spoke; but the touch of that small, soft hand, freely and innocently resigned to him, sent a thrill to his heart—and again the face of Sibyll seemed to him wondrous fair.

There was a long silence, which Sibyll was the first to break. She turned the conversation once more upon Marmaduke's views in life. It had been easy for a deeper observer than he was, to see, that under all that young girl's simplicity and sweetness, there lurked something of dangerous ambition. She loved to recall the court-life her childhood had known, though her youth had resigned it with apparent cheerfulness. Like many who are poor and fallen, Sibyll built herself a sad consolation out of her pride; she never forgot that she was well-born. But Marmaduke, in what was ambition, saw but interest in himself, and his heart beat more quickly as he bent his eyes upon that downcast, thoughtful, earnest countenance.

After an hour thus passed, Sibyll left the guest, and remounted to her father's chamber. She found Adam pacing the narrow floor, and and muttering to himself. He turned abruptly as she entered, and said, "Come hither, child—I took four marks from that young man, for I wanted books and instruments, and there are two left;—see—take them back to him."

"My father, he will not receive them. Fear not, thou shalt repay him some day."

"Take them, I say, and if the young man

says thee nay, why, buy thyself gauds and gear, or let us eat, and drink, and laugh. What else is life made for? Ha! ha! Laugh, child, laugh!"

There was something strangely pathetic in this outburst, this terrible mirth, born of profound dejection. Alas for this guileless, simple creature, who had clutched at gold with a huckster's eagerness — who, forgetting the wants of his own child, had employed it upon the service of an Abstract Thought, and whom the scorn of his kind now pierced through all the folds of his close-webbed philosophy and self-forgetful genius. Awful is the duel between MAN and THE AGE in which he lives! For the gain of posterity Adam Warner had martyrised existence,—and the children pelted him as he passed the streets! Sibyll burst into tears

"No, my father, no," she sobbed, pushing back the money into his hands. "Let us both starve, rather than you should despond. God and man will bring you justice yet."

"Ah!" said the baffled enthusiast, "my whole mind is one sore now. I feel as if I could love man no more. Go, and leave me. Go, I say!" and the poor student, usually so mild and gall-less, stamped his foot in impotent rage. Sibyll, weeping as if her heart would break, left him.

Then Adam Warner again paced to and fro restlessly, and again muttered to himself for several minutes. At last he approached his Model—the model of a mighty and stupendous invention — the fruit of no chimerical and visionary science—a great Promethean THING, that, once matured, would divide the Old World from the New, enter into all operations of Labor, animate all the future affairs, color all the practical doctrines, of active men. He paused before it, and addressed it as if it heard and understood him—"My hair was dark, and my tread was firm, when one night, A THOUGHT passed into my soul—a thought to make Matter the gigantic slave of Mind. Out of this thought, thou, not yet born after five-and-twenty years of travail, wert conceived. My coffers were then full, and my name was honored; and the rich respected, and the poor loved me. Art thou a devil, that has tempted me to ruin; or a god, that has lifted me above the earth? I am old before my time, my hair is blanched, my frame is bowed, my wealth is gone, my name is sullied. And all, dumb Idol of Iron and the Element, all for thee! I had a wife whom I adored—she died—I forgot her loss in the hope of *thy* life. I have a child still—God and our Lady forgive me—she is less dear to me than thou hast been. And now—" the old man ceased abruptly, and folding his arms, looked at the deaf iron sternly, as on a human foe. By his side was a huge hammer, employed in the toils of his forge; suddenly he seized and swung it aloft. One blow, and the labor of years was shattered into pieces! One blow! —But the heart failed him, and the hammer fell heavily to the ground.

"Ay!" he muttered, "true—true: if thou, who hast destroyed all else, wert destroyed too, what were left me? Is it a crime to murder Man?—a greater crime to murder Thought, which is the life of all men. Come—I forgive thee!"

And all that day, and all that night, the Enthusiast labored in his chamber, and the next day the remembrance of the hootings, the pelting, the mob, was gone—clean gone from his breast. The Model began to move—life hovered over its wheels, and the Martyr of Science had forgotten the very world for which he, groaning and rejoicing, toiled!

CHAPTER VIII.

Master Marmaduke Nevile makes love and is frightened.

FOR two or three days, Marmaduke and Sibyll were necessarily brought much together. Such familiarity of intercourse was peculiarly rare in that time, when, except perhaps in the dissolute court of Edward IV., the virgins of gentle birth mixed sparingly, and with great reserve, amongst those of opposite sex. Marmaduke, rapidly recovering from the effect of his wounds, and without other resource than Sibyll's society, in the solitude of his confinement, was not proof against the temptation which one so young and so sweetly winning brought to his fancy or his senses. The poor Sibyll—she was no faultless paragon —she was a rare and singular mixture of many opposite qualities in heart and in intellect! She was one moment infantine in simplicity and gay playfulness—the next, a shade passed over her bright face, and she uttered some sentence of that bitter and chilling wisdom, which the sense of persecution, the cruelty of the world, had already taught her. She was, indeed, at that age when the Child and the Woman are struggling against each other. Her character was not yet formed—a little happiness would have ripened it at once into the richest bloom of goodness. But sorrow, that ever sharpens the intellect, might only serve to sour the heart. Her mind was so innately chaste and pure, that she knew not the nature of the admiration she excited. But the admiration pleased her as it pleases some young child—she was vain then, but it was an infant's vanity, not a woman's. And thus, from innocence itself, there was a fearlessness, a freedom, a something endearing and familiar in her manner, which might have turned a wiser head than Marmaduke Nevile's And this the more, because, while liking her young guest, confiding in him, raised in her own esteem by his gallantry, enjoying that intercourse of youth with youth, so familiar to her, and surrendering herself the more to its charm from the joy that animated her spirits, in seeing that her father had forgotten his humiliation, and returned to his wonted labors—she yet knew not for the handsome Nevile one sentiment that approached to love. Her mind was so superior to his own, that she felt almost as if older in years, and in their talk, her rosy lips preached to him in grave advice.

On the landing, by Marmaduke's chamber, there was a large oriel casement jutting from the wall. It was only glazed at the upper part, and that most imperfectly, the lower part being closed at night, or in inclement weather, with rude shutters. The recess formed by this comfortless casement answered, therefore, the purpose of a balcony; it commanded a full view of the vicinity without, and gave to those who might be passing by, the power also of indulging their own curiosity by a view of the interior.

Whenever he lost sight of Sibyll, and had grown weary of the peacock, this spot was Marmaduke's favorite haunt. It diverted him, poor youth, to look out of the window upon the livelier world beyond. The place, it is true, was ordinarily deserted, but still the spires and turrets of London were always discernible—and they were something.

Accordingly, in this embrasure stood Marmaduke, when one morning, Sibyll, coming from her father's room, joined him.

"And what, Master Nevile," said Sybill, with a malicious yet charming smile, "what claimed thy meditations? Some misgiving as to the trimming of thy tunic, or the length of thy shoon?"

"Nay," returned Marmaduke, gravely, "such thoughts, though not without their importance in the mind of a gentleman, who would not that his ignorance of court delicacies should commit him to the japes of his equals, were not at that moment uppermost. I was thinking——"

"Of those mastiffs, quarrelling for a bone. Avow it."

"By our Lady I saw them not, but now I look, they are brave dogs. Ha!—seest thou how gallantly each fronts the other, the hair bristling, the eyes fixed, the tail on end, the fangs glistening. Now the lesser one moves slowly round and round the bigger, who, mind you, Mistress Sibyll, is no dullard, but moves, too, quick as thought, not to be taken unawares. Ha! that is a brave spring! Heigh, dogs, heigh! a good sight—it makes the blood warm!—the little one hath him by the throat!"

"Alack," said Sibyll, turning away her eyes, "can you find pleasure in seeing two poor brutes mangle each other for a bone!"

"By St. Dunstan! doth it matter what be the cause of quarrel, so long as dog or man bears himself bravely, with a due sense of honor and derring-do. See! the big one is up again. Ah! foul fall the butcher, who drives them away. Those seely mechanics know not the joyaunce of fair fighting to gentle and to hound. For a hound, mark you, hath nothing mechanical in his nature. He is a gentleman all over—brave against equal and stranger, forbearing to the small and defenceless, true in poverty and need where he loveth, stern and ruthless where he hateth, and despising theives, hildings, and the vulgar, as e'er a gold spur in King Edward's court! Oh! certes, your best gentleman is the best hound!"

"You moralize to-day. And I know not how to gainsay you,'" returned Sibyll, as the dogs, reluctantly beaten off, retired each from each, snarling and reluctant, while a small black cur, that had hitherto sat unobserved at the door of a small hostelrie, now cooly approached and dragged off the bone of contention. "But what say'st thou now? See! see! the patient mongrel carries off the bone from the gentlemen-hounds. Is that the way of the world?"

"Pardie! it is a naught world, if so, and much changed from the time of our fathers, the Normans. But these Saxons are getting uppermost again, and the yard-measure, I fear, me, is more potent in these holiday times than the mace or the battle-axe." The Nevile paused, sighed, and changed the subject: "This house of thine must have been a stately pile in its day. I see but one side of the quadrangle is left, thongh it be easy to trace where the other three have stood."

"And you may see their stones and their fittings in the butcher's and baker's stalls over the way," replied Sibyll.

"Ay!" said the Nevile, "the parings of the gentry begin to be the wealth of the varlets."

"Little ought we pine at that," returned Sibyll, "if the varlets were but gentle with our poverty; but they loathe the humbled fortunes on which they rise, and while slaves to the rich, are tyrants to the poor."

This was said so sadly, that the Nevile felt his eyes overflow; andthe humble dress of the girl, the melancholy ridges which evinced the site of a noble house, now shrunk into a dismal ruin, the remembrance of the pastime-ground, the insults of the crowd, and the broken gittern, all conspired to move his compassion, and to give force to yet more tender emotions.

"Ah!" he said, suddenly, and with a quick, faint blush over his handsome and manly countenance—"ah, fair maid—fair Sibyll!—God grant that I may win something of gold and fortune amidst yonder towers, on which the sun shines so cheerly. God grant it, not for my sake—not for mine; but that I may have something besides a true heart and a stainless name to lay at thy feet. Oh, Sibyll! By this hand—by my father's soul—I love thee, Sibyll! Have I not said it before? Well, hear me now—I love thee!"

As he spoke, he clasped her hand in his own, and she suffered it for one instant to rest in his. Then withdrawing it, and meeting his enamoured eyes, with a strange sadness in her own darker, deeper and more intelligent orbs, she said—

"I thank thee—thank thee for the honor of such kind thoughts; and frankly, I answer as thou hast frankly spoken. It was sweet to me, who have known little in life not hard and bitter—sweet to wish I had a brother like thee, and, as a brother, I can love and pray for thee. But ask not more, Marmaduke. I have aims in my life which forbid all other love!"

"Art thou too aspiring for one who has his spurs to win?"

"Not so; but listen. My mother's lessons and my own heart have made my poor father the first end and object of all things on earth to me. I live to protect him, work for him, honor him, and for the rest—I have thoughts thou canst not know—and ambition thou canst not feel. Nay," she added, with that delightful smile which chased away the graver thought which had before saddened her aspect, "what would thy sober friend Master Alwyn say to thee, if he heard thou hadst courted the wizard's daughter?"

"By my faith," exclaimed Marmaduke, "thou art a very April—smiles and clouds in a breath! If what thou despisest in me be my want of bookcraft, and such like, by my halidame I will turn scholar for thy sake; and—"

Here, as he had again taken Sibyll's hand, with the passionate ardor of his bold nature, not to be lightly daunted by a maiden's first "No," a sudden shrill, wild burst of laughter, accompanied with a gusty fit of unmelodious music from the street below, made both maiden and youth start, and turn their eyes: there, weaving their immodest dance, tawdry in their tinsel attire, their naked arms glancing above their heads, as they waved on high their instruments, went the timbrel-girls.

"Ha! ha!" cried their leader, "see the gallant and the witch-leman! The glamor has done its work! Foul is fair!—foul is fair! and the devil will have his own!"

But these creatures, whose bold license the ancient chronicler records, were rarely seen alone. They haunted parties of pomp and pleasure; they linked together the extremes of life—the grotesque Chorus that introduced the terrible truth of foul vice, and abandoned wretchedness in the midst of the world's holiday and pageant. So now, as they wheeled into the silent, squalid street, they heralded a goodly company of dames and cavaliers, on horseback, who were passing through the neighboring plains into the park of Marybone, to enjoy the sport of falconry. The splendid dresses of this procession, and the grave and measured dignity with which it swept along, contrasted forcibly with the wild movements, and disorderly mirth of the timbrel players. These last darted round and round the riders, holding out their instruments for largess, and retorting, with laugh and gibe, the disdainful look or sharp rebuke with which their salutations were mostly received.

Suddenly, as the company, two by two, paced up the street, Sibyll uttered a faint exclamation, and strove to snatch her hand from the Nevile's grasp. Her eye rested upon one of the horseman who rode last, and who seemed in earnest conversation with a dame, who, though scarcely in her first youth, excelled all her fair companions in beauty of face, and grace of horsemanship, as well as in the costly equipments of the white barb that caracolled beneath her easy hand. At the same moment the horseman looked up and gazed steadily at Sibyll, whose countenance grew pale, and flushed in a breath. His eye then glanced rapidly at Marmaduke—a half-smile passed his pale firm lips; he slightly raised the plume cap from his brow—inclined gravely to Sibyll—and, turning once more to his companion, appeared to answer some question she addressd to him, as to the object of his salutation, for her look, which was proud, keen, and lofty, was raised to Sibyll, and then dropped somewhat disdainfully, as she listened to the words addressed her by the cavalier.

The lynx eyes of the tymbesteres had seen the recognition; and their leader, laying her bold hand on the embossed bridle of the horseman, exclaimed, in a voice shrill and loud ehough to be heard in the balcony above, "Largess! noble lord, largess! for the sake of the lady thou lovest best!"

The fair equestrian turned away her head at these words, the nobleman watched her, a moment, and dropped some coins into the timbrel.

"Ha! ha!" cried the tymbestere, pointing her long arm to Sibyll, and springing towards the balcony—

"The cushat would mate
Above her state,
And she flutters her wings round the falcon's beak;
But death to the dove
Is the falcon's love—
Oh, sharp is the kiss of the falcon's beak!"

Before this rude song was ended, Sibyll had vanished from the place; the cavalcade had disappeared. The timbrel-players, without deigning to notice Marmaduke, darted elsewhere to ply their discordant trade, and the Nevile, crossing himself devoutly, muttered, "Jesu defend us! Those she Will-o'-the-wisps are eno' to scare all the blood out of one's body. What—a murrain on them!—do they portend, flitting round and round, and skirting off, as if the devil's broom-stick was behind them? By the mass! they have frightened away the damozel, and I am not sorry for it. They have left me small heart for the part of Sir Launval."

His meditations were broken off by the sudden sight of Nicholas Alwyn, mounted on a small palfrey, and followed by a sturdy groom on horse-back, leading a steed handsomely caparisoned. In another moment, Marmaduke had descended—opened the door—and drawn Alwyn into the hall.

CHAPTER IX.

Master Marmaduke Nevile leaves the Wizard's House for the Great World.

"RIGHT glad am I," said Nicholas, "to see you so stout and hearty, for I am the bearer of good news. Though I have been away, I have not forgotten you; and it so chanced that I went yesterday to attend my Lord of Warwick with some nowches * and knackeries, that he takes out as gifts and exemplars of English work. They were indifferently well wrought, specially a chevesail, of which the——"

"Spare me the fashion of thy mechanicals, and come to the point," interrupted Marmaduke, impatiently.

"Pardon me, Master Nevile. I interrupt thee not when thou talkest of bassinets and hauberks—every cobbler to his last. But, as thou sayest, to the point; the stout earl, while scanning my workmanship, for in much the

* Nowches—buckles and other ornaments.

chevesail was mine, was pleased to speak graciously of my skill with the bow, of which he had heard; and he then turned to thyself, of whom my Lord Montagu had already made disparaging mention: when I told the earl somewhat more about thy qualities and disposings; and when I spoke of thy desire to serve him, and the letter of which thou art the bearer, his black brows smoothed mighty graciously, and he bade me tell thee to come to him this afternoon, and he would judge of thee with his own eyes and ears. Wherefore I have ordered the craftsmen to have all thy gauds and gear ready at thine hostelrie, and I have engaged thee henchmen and horses for thy fitting appearance. Be quick: time and the great wait for no man. So take whatever thou needest for present want, from thy mails, and I will send a porter for the rest ere sunset.

"But the gittern for the damozel?"

"I have provided that for thee, as is meet." And Nicholas, stepping back, eased the groom of a case which contained a gittern, whose workmanship and ornaments delighted the Nevile.

"It is of my lord the young Duke of Gloucester's own musical-vender; and the duke, though a lad yet, is a notable judge of all appertaining to the gentle craft.* So dispatch, and away!"

Marmaduke retired to his chamber, and Nicholas, after a moment spent in silent thought, searched the room for the hand-bell, which then made the mode of communication between the master and domestics. Not finding this necessary luxury, he contrived at last to make Madge hear his voice from her subterranean retreat; and, on her arrival, sent her in quest of Sibyll.

The answer he received was, that Mistress Sibyll was ill, and unable to see him. Alwyn looked disconcerted at this intelligence, but, drawing from his girdle a small gipsire, richly broidered, he prayed Madge to deliver it to her young mistress, and inform her that it was the fruit of the commission with which she had honored him.

"It is passing strange," said he, pacing the hall alone—"passing strange, that the poor child should have taken such hold on me. After all, she would be a bad wife for a plain man like me. Tush! that is the trader's thought all over. Have I brought no fresher feeling out of my fair village-green? Would it not be sweet to work for her, and rise in life, with her by my side? And these girls of the city—so prim and so brainless!—as well marry a painted puppet. Sibyll! Am I dement? Stark wode? What have I to do with girls and marriage? Humph! I marvel what Marmaduke still thinks of her—and she of him."

"While Alwyn thus soliloquized, the Nevile, having hastily arranged his dress, and laden himself with the monies his mails contained, summoned old Madge to receive his largess, and to conduct him to Warner's chamber, in order to proffer his farewell.

"With somewhat of a timid step he followed the old woman (who kept muttering thanks and benedicites, as she eyed the coin in her palm), up the rugged stairs,—and for the first time knocked at the door of the student's sanctuary. No answer came. "Eh, sir! you must enter," said Madge; "an' you fired a bombard under his ear he would not heed you." So, suiting the action to the word, she threw open the door, and closed it behind him, as Marmaduke entered.

The room was filled with smoke, through which mirky atmostphere the clear red light of the burning charcoal peered out steadily like a Cyclop's eye. A small, but heaving, regular, laboring, continuous sound, as of a fairy hammer, smote the young man's ear. But, as his gaze accustoming itself to the atmosphere, searched around, he could not perceive what was its cause. Adam Warner was standing in the middle of the room, his arms folded, and contemplating something at a little distance, which Marmaduke could not accurately distinguish. The youth took courage, and approached. "Honored mine host," said he, "I thank thee for hospitality and kindness, I crave pardon for disturbing thee in thy incanta—ehem!—thy—thy studies, and I come to bid thee farewell."

Adam turned round with a puzzled, absent air, as if scarcely recognizing his guest; at length, as his recollection slowly came back to him, he smiled graciously, and said; "Good youth, thou art richly welcome to what little

* For Richard III.'s love of music, and patronage of musicians and minstrels, see the discriminating character of that Prince in Sharon Turner's History of England, vol. iv. p. 66.

it was in my power to do for thee. Peradventure, a time may come when they who seek the roof of Adam Warner may find less homely cheer—a less rugged habitation — for look you!" he exclaimed, suddenly, with a burst of irrepressible enthusiasm—and laying his hand on Nevile's arm, as, through all the smoke and grime that obscured his face, flashed the ardent soul of the triumphant Inventor,—" look you! since you have been in this house, one of my great objects is well-nigh matured—achieved. Come hither," and he dragged the wondering Marmaduke to his model, or Eureka, as Adam had fondly named his contrivance. The Nevile then perceived that it was from the interior of this machine that the sound which had startled him, arose; to his eye the THING was uncouth and hideous; from the jaws of an iron serpent, that, wreathing round it, rose on high with erect crest, gushed a rapid volume of black smoke, and a damp spray fell around. A column of iron in the centre kept in perpetual and regular motion, rising and sinking successively, as the whole mechanism within seemed alive with noise and action.

"The Syracusan asked an inch of earth beyond the earth, to move the earth," said Adam; "I stand *in* the world, and lo! with this engine the world shall one day be moved."

"Holy Mother!" faltered Marmaduke; "I pray thee, dread sir, to ponder well ere thou attemptest any such sports with the habitation in which every woman's son is so concerned. Bethink thee, that if in moving the world thou shouldst make any mistake, it would——"

"Now stand there and attend," interrupted Adam, who had not heard one word of this juducious exhortation.

"Pardon me, terrible sir!" exclaimed Marmaduke, in great trepidation, and retreating, rapidly to the door; "but I have heard that the fiends are mighty malignant to all lookers on, not initiated."

While he spoke, fast gushed the smoke, heavily heaved the fairy hammers, up and down, down and up, sunk or rose the column, with its sullen sound. The young man's heart sank to the soles of his feet.

"In deed and in truth," he stammered out, "I am but a dolt in these matters; I wish thee all success compatible with the weal of a Christian, and bid thee, in sad humility, good day;" and he added, in a whisper—"the Lord's forgiveness! Amen!"

Marmaduke, then, fairly rushed through the open door, and hurried out of the chamber as fast as possible.

He breathed more freely as he descended the stairs. Before I would call that grey carle my father, or his child my wife, may I feel all the hammers of the elves and sprites he keeps tortured within that ugly little prison-house, playing a death's march on my body. Holy St. Dunstan, the timbrel-girls came in time! They say these wizards always have fair daughters, and their love can be no blessing!"

As he thus muttered, the door of Sibyll's chamber opened, and she stood before him at the threshold. Her countenance was very pale, and bore evidence of weeping. There was a silence on both sides, which the girl was the first to break.

"So, Madge tells me, thou art about to leave us?"

"Yes, gentle maiden! I—I—that is my Lord of Warwick has summoned me. I wish and pray for all blessings on thee! and—and —if ever it be mine to serve or aid thee, it will be—that is—verily, my tongue falters, but my heart—that is—fare thee well, maiden! Would thou hadst a less wise father; and so may the saints (St. Anthony especially) whom the Evil One was parlous afraid of—guard and keep thee!"

With this strange and incoherent address, Marmaduke left the maiden standing by the threshold of her miserable chamber. Hurrying into the hall, he summoned Alwyn from his meditations, and, giving the gittern to Madge, with an injunction to render it to her mistress, with his greeting and service, he vaulted lightly on his steed; the steady and more sober Alwyn mounted his palfry with slow care and due caution. As the air of spring waved the fair locks of the young cavalier, as the good horse caracolled under his lithesome weight, his natural temper of mind, hardy, healthful, joyous, and world-awake, returned to him. The image of Sibyll and her strange father fled from his thoughts like sickly dreams.

BOOK SECOND.

THE KING'S COURT.

CHAPTER I.

Earl Warwick the King-Maker.

THE young men entered the Strand, which, thanks to the profits of a toll-bar, was a passable road for equestrians, studded towards the river, as we have before observed, with stately and half-fortified mansions; while on the opposite side, here and there, were straggling houses of a humbler kind—the medieval villas of merchant and trader—(for from the earliest period since the Conquest, the Londoners had delighted in such retreats), surrounded with blossoming orchards,* and adorned in front with the fleur-de-lis, emblem of the vain victories of renowned Agincourt. But by far the greater portion of the road northward, stretched, unbuilt upon, towards a fair chain of fields and meadows, refreshed by many brooks, "turning water-mills with a pleasant noise." High rose, on the thoroughfare, the famous Cross, at which "the Judges Itinerant whilome sate, without London."† There hallowed and solitary, stood the inn for the penitent pilgrims, who sought "the murmuring runnels" of St. Clement's healing well; for in this neighborhood, even from the age of the Roman, springs of crystal wave and salubrious virtue received the homage of credulous disease. Through the gloomy arches of the Temple Gate and Lud, our horsemen wound their way, and finally arrived in safety at Marmaduke's hostelrie in the East Chepe. Here Marmaduke found the decorators of his comely person already assembled.

* Fitzstephen.—"On all sides, without the suburbs are the citizens gardens' and orchards," etc.

† Stowe.

The simpler, yet more manly fashions he had taken from provinces, were now exchanged for an attire worthy the kinsman of the great minister of a court, unparalled, since the reign of William, the Red King, for extravagant gorgeousness of dress. His corset was of the finest cloth, sown with seed pearls; above it, the lawn shirt, worn without collar, partially appeared, fringed with gold; over this was loosely hung a supertunic of crimson sarcenet, slashed and pounced with a profusion of fringes. His velvet cap, turned up at the sides, extended in a point far over the forehead. His hose—under which appellation is to be understood what serves us of the modern day both for stockings and pantaloons—were of white cloth, and his shoes, very narrow, were curiously carved into chequer work at the instep, and tied with bobbins of gold thread, turning up, like skates at the extremity, three inches in length. His dagger was suspended by a slight silver-gilt chain, and his girdle contained a large gipsire, or pouch, of embossed leather, richly gilt.

And this dress, marvellous as it seemed to the Nevile, the tailor gravely assured him was far under the mark of the highest fashion, and that an' the noble youth had been a knight, the shoes would have stretched at least three inches farther over the natural length of the feet, the placard have shone with jewels, and the tunic luxuriated in flowers of damascene. Even as it was, however, Marmaduke felt a natural diffidence of his habiliments, which cost him a round third of his whole capital. And no bride ever unveiled herself with more shamefaced bashfulness than did Marmaduke Nevile experience when he remounted his horse, and taking leave of his foster-brother, bent his way to Warwick Lane, where the earl lodged.

The narrow streets were, however, crowded with equestrians, whose dress eclipsed his own, some bending their way to the Tower, some to the palaces of the Flete. Carriages there were none, and only twice he encountered the huge litters, in which some aged prelate or some high-born dame, veiled greatness from the day. But the frequent vistas to the river gave glimpses of the gay boats and barges that crowded the Thames, which was then the principal thoroughfare for every class, but more especially the noble. The ways were fortunately dry and clean for London; though occasionally deep holes and furrows in the road menaced perils to the unwary horseman. The streets themselves might well disappoint in splendor the stranger's eye; for although viewed at a distance, ancient London was incalculably more picturesque and stately than the modern; yet, when fairly in its tortuous labyrinths, it seemed to those who had improved the taste by travel, the meanest and the mirkiest capital of Christendom. The streets were marvellously narrow, the upper stories, chiefly of wood, projecting far over the lower, which were formed of mud and plaster. The shops were pitiful booths, and the 'prentices standing at the entrance bareheaded and cap in hand, and lining the passages, as the old French writer avers *comme idoles*,* kept up an eternal dim with their clamorous invitations, often varied by pert witticisms on some churlish passenger, or loud vituperations of each other. The whole ancient family of the London criers were in full bay. Scarcely had Marmaduke's ears recovered the shock of "Hot peascods—all hot," than they were saluted with "mackeral," "sheep's feet—hot sheep's feet." At the smaller taverns stood the inviting vociferators of "cock-pie," "ribs of beef—hot beef," while, blended with these multitioned discords, whined the vielle or primitive hurdy-gurdy, screamed the pipe, twanged the harp, from every quarter where the thirsty paused to drink, or the idler stood to gape.†

Through this Babel, Marmaduke at last slowly wound his way, and arrived before the mighty mansion in which the chief baron of England held his state.

As he dismounted and resigned his steed to the servitor hired for him by Alywn, Marmaduke paused a moment, struck by the disparity, common as it was to eyes more accustomed to the metropolis, between the stately edifice and the sordid neighborhood. He had not noticed this so much, when he had repaired to the earl's house on his first arrival in London—for his thoughts then had been too much bewildered by the general bustle and novelty of the scene,—but now it seemed to him, that he better comprehended the homage accorded to a great noble in surveying, at a glance, the immeasurable eminence to which he was elevated above his fellow-men by wealth and rank.

Far on either side of the wings of the earl's abode stretched, in numerous deformity, sheds rather than houses, of broken plaster and crazy timbers. But, here and there, were open places of public reception, crowded with the lower followers of the puissant chief; and the eye rested on many idle groups of sturdy swash-bucklers, some half-clad in armor, some in rude jerkins of leather, before the doors of these resorts,—as others, like bees about a hive, swarmed in and out with a perpetual hum.

The exterior of Warwick House was of a grey, but dingy stone, and presented a half-fortified and formidable appearance. The windows, or rather loop-holes, towards the street, were few, and strongly barred. The black and massive arch of the gateway yawned between two huge square towers; and from a yet higher, but slender tower on the inner side, the flag gave the "White Bear and Ragged Staff" to the smoky air. Still, under the portal as he entered, hung the grate of the portcullis, and the square court which he saw before him swarmed with the more immediate retainers of the earl, in scarlet jackets, wrought with their chieftain's cognizance. A man of gigantic girth and stature, who officiated as porter, leaning against the wall under the arch, now emerged from the shadow, and with sufficient civility demanded the young visitor's name and business. On hearing the former, he bowed low as he doffed his cap, and conducted Marmaduke through the first quadrangle. The two sides to the right and left were devoted to the offices and rooms of re-

* Perlin.

† See Lydgate's "London Lyckpenny."

tainers, of whom no less than six hundred, not to speak of the domestic and more orderly retinue, attested the state of the Last of the English Barons on his visits to the capital. Far from being then, as now, the object of the great to thrust all that belongs to the service of the house out of sight, it was their pride to strike awe into the visitor by the extent of accommodation afforded to their followers: some seated on benches of stone ranged along the walls—some grouped in the centre of the court—some lying at length upon the two oblong patches of what had been turf, till worn away by frequent feet—this domestic army filled the young Nevile with an admiration far greater than the gay satins of the knights and nobles who had gathered round the Lord of Montagu and Northumberland at the pastime-ground.

This assemblage, however, were evidently under a rude discipline of their own. They were neither noisy nor drunk. They made way with surly obeisance as the cavalier passed, and closing on his track like some horde of wild cattle, gazed after him with earnest silence, and then turned once more to their indolent whispers with each other.

And now, Nevile entering the last side of the quadrangle, the huge hall, divided from the passage by a screen of stone fret-work, so fine as to attest the hand of some architect in the reign of Henry III., stretched to his right; and so vast, in truth, it was, that though more than fifty persons were variously engaged therein, their number was lost in the immense space; of these, at one end of the longer and lower table beneath the dais, some squires of good dress and mien were engaged at chess or dice; others were conferring in the gloomy embrasures of the casements; some walking to and fro; others gathered round the shovel-board. At the entrance of this hall, the porter left Marmaduke, after exhanging a whisper with a gentleman whose dress eclipsed the Nevile's in splendor; and this latter personage, who, though of high birth, did not disdain to perform the office of chamberlain, or usher, to the king-like earl, advanced to Marmaduke with a smile, and said—

"My lord expects you, sir, and has appointed this time to receive you, that you may not be held back from his presence by the crowds that crave audience in the forenoon. Please to follow me!" This said, the gentleman slowly preceded the visitor, now and then stopping to exchange a friendly word with the various parties he passed in his progress; for the urbanity which Warwick possessed himself, his policy inculcated as a duty on all who served him. A small door at the other extremity of the hall admitted into an ante-room, in which some half-score pages, the sons of knights and barons, were gathered round an old warrior, placed at their head as a sort of tutor, to instruct them in all knightly accomplishments; and beckoning forth one of these youths from the ring, the earl's chamberlain said, with a profound reverence—"Will you be pleased, my young lord, to conduct your cousin, master Marmaduke Nevile, to the earl's presence." The young gentleman eyed Marmaduke with a supercilious glance.

"Marry!" said he, pertly, "if a man born in the north were to feed all his cousins, he would sound have a tail as long as my uncle, the stout earl's. Come, Sir Cousin, this way."

And without tarrying even to give Nevile information of the name and quality of his new-found ralation—who was no less than Lord Montagu's son, the sole male heir to the honors of that mighty family, though now learning the apprenticeship of chivalry amongst his uncle's pages—the boy passed before Marmaduke with a saunter, that, had they been in plain Westmoreland, might have cost him a cuff from the stout hand of the indignant elder cousin. He raised the tapestry at one end of the room, and ascending a short flight of broad stairs, knocked gently on the panels of an arched door, sunk deep in the walls.

"Enter!" said a clear, loud voice, and the next moment Marmaduke was in the presence of the king-maker.

He heard his guide pronounce his name, and saw him smile maliciously at the momentary embarrassment the young man displayed, as the boy passed by Marmaduke, and vanished. The Earl of Warwick was seated near a door that opened upon an inner court, or rather garden, which gave communication to the river. The chamber was painted in the style of Henry III., with huge figures representing the battle of Hastings, or rather, for there were many separate pieces, the conquest of Saxon England. Over each head, to enlighten the ignorant, the artist had taken the precaution to insert a label, which told the name and the subject. The ceiling was groined, vaulted, and emblazoned with the richest gilding and colors. The chimney-piece (a modern ornament) rose to the roof, and represented in bold reliefs, gilt and decorated, the signing of Magna Charta. The floor was strewn thick with dried rushes, and odorous herbs; the furniture was scanty, but rich. The low-backed chairs, of which there were but four, carved in ebony, had cushions of velvet with fringes of massive gold. A small cupboard, or beaufet, covered with *carpetz de cuir*, (carpets of gilt and painted leather), of great price, held various quaint and curious ornaments of plate inwrought with precious stones; and beside this—a singular contrast—on a plain Gothic table lay the helmet, the gauntlets, and the battle-axe of the master. Warwick himself, seated before a large cumbrous desk, was writing—but slowly and with pain—and he lifted his finger as the Nevile approached, in token of his wish to conclude a task, probably little congenial to his tastes. But Marmaduke was grateful for the moments afforded him to recover his self-possession, and to examine his kinsman.

The earl was in the lusty vigor of his age. His hair, of the deepest black, was worn short, as if in disdain of the effeminate fashions of the day, and fretted bare from the temples, by the constant and early friction of his helmet, gave to a forehead naturally lofty yet more majestic appearance of expanse and height. His complexion, though dark and sunburnt, glowed with rich health. The beard was closely shaven, and left in all its remarkable beauty the contour of the oval face and strong jaw—strong as if clasped in iron. The features were marked and aquiline, as was common to those of Norman blood. The form spare, but of prodigious width and depth of chest, the more apparent from the fashion of the short surcoat which was thrown back, and left in broad expanse a placard, not of holiday velvet and satins, but of steel polished as a mirror, and inlaid with gold. And now, as concluding his task, the earl rose and motioned Marmaduke to a stool by his side, his great stature, which, from the length of his limbs, was not so observable when he sate, actually startled his guest. Tall as Marmaduke was himself the earl towered * above, him,—with his high, majestic, smooth, unwrinkled forehead,—like some Paladin of the rhyme of poet or romancer; and, perhaps, not only in this masculine advantage, but in the rare and harmonious combination of colossai strength with graceful lightness, a more splendid union of all the outward qualities we are inclined to give to the heroes of old, never dazzled the eye, or impressed the fancy. But even this effect of mere person was subordinate to that which this eminent nobleman created —upon his *inferiors*, at least,—by a manner so void of all arrogance, yet of all condescension, so simple, open, cordial, and herolike, that Marmaduke Nevile, peculiarly alive to external impressions, and subdued and fascinated by the earl's first word, and that word was "Welcome!" dropped on his knee, and kissing the hand extended to him, said—"Noble kinsman, in thy service, and for thy sake let me live and die!" Had the young man been prepared by the sublest master of court-craft for this interview, so important to his fortunes, he could not have advanced a hundreth part so far with the great earl, as he did by that sudden, frank burst of genuine emotion; for Warwick was extremely sensitive to the admiration he excited—vain or proud of it, it matters not which—grateful as a child for love, and inexorable as a woman for slight or insult; in rude ages, one sex has often the qualities of the other.

"Thou hast thy father's warm heart, and hasty thought, Marmaduke," said Warwick, raising him, "and now he is gone where, we trust, brave men shrived of their sins, look down upon us, who should be thy friend but Richard Nevile? So—so—yes—let me look at thee. Ha! stout Guy's honest face, every line of it; but to the girls, perhaps, comelier, for wanting a scar or two. Never blush—thou shalt win the scars yet. So thou hast a letter from thy father?"

"It is here, noble lord."

"And why," said the earl, cutting the silk with his dagger—"why hast thou so long hung back from presenting it? But I need not ask

* The faded portrait of Richard Nevile, Earl of Warwick, in the Rous Roll, preserved at the Herald's College, does justice, at least, to the height and majesty of his stature. The portrait of Edward IV. is the only one in that long series which at all rivals the stately proportions of the king-maker.

thee. These uncivil times have made kith and kin doubt worse of each other than thy delay did of me. Sir Guy's mark, sure eno'! Brave old man! I loved him the better, for that, like me, the sword was more meet than the pen for his hold hand." Here Warwick scanned, with some slowness, the lines dictated by the dead to the priest; and when he had done, he laid the letter respectfully on his desk, and bowing his head over it, muttered to himself—it might be an Ave for the deceased. "Well," he said, reseating himself and again motioning Marmaduke to follow his example—"thy father was, in sooth, to blame for the side he took in the Wars. What son of the Norman could bow knee or vale plume to that shadow of a king—Henry of Windsor?—and, for his bloody wife, she knew no more of an Englishman's pith and pride than I know of the rhymes and roundels of old Renè, her father. Guy Nevile—good Guy—many a day in my boyhood did he teach me how to bare my lance at the crest, and direct my sword at the mail-joints. He was cunning at fence—thy worshipful father—but I was ever a bad scholar; and my dull arm, to this day, hopes more from its strength than its craft."

"I have heard it said, noble earl, that the stoutest hand can scarcely lift your battle-axe."

"Fables! romaunt!" answered the earl, smiling; "there it lies—go and lift it."

Marmaduke went to the table, and, though with some difficulty, raised and swung this formidable weapon.

"By my halidame, well swung, cousin mine! Its use depends not on the strength, but the practice. Why look you now,—there is the boy Richard of Gloucester, who comes not up to thy shoulder, and by dint of custom each day can wield mace or axe with as much ease as a jester doth his lathe-sword. Ah! trust me, Marmaduke—the York House is a princely one; and if we must have a king, we barons, by stout St. George, let no meaner race ever furnish our lieges. But to thyself, Marmaduke—what are thy views and thy wishes?"

"To be one of thy following, noble Warwick."

"I thank and accept thee, young Nevile; but thou hast heard that I am about to leave England, and in the mean time thy youth would run danger without a guide." The earl paused a moment, and resumed. "My brother of Montagu showed thee cold countenance; but a word from me will win thee his grace and favor. What sayest thou—wilt thou be one of his gentlemen? If so, I will tell thee the qualities a man must have:—a discreet tongue, a quick eye, the last fashion in hood and shoe-bobbins, a perfect seat on thy horse, a light touch for the gittern, a voice for a love-song, and—"

"I have none of these, save the horsemanship, gracious my lord; and if thou wilt not receive me thyself, I will not burden my Lord of Montagu and Northumberland."

"Hot and quick! No!—John of Montagu could not suit thee, nor thou him. But how to provide for thee till my return, I know not."

"Dare I not hope, then, to make one of your embassage, noble earl?"

Warwick bent his brows, and looked at him in surprise.

"Of our embassage! Why, thou art haughty, indeed! Nay, and so a soldier's son and a Nevile should be! I blame thee not; but I could not make thee one of my train, without creating a hundred enemies—to me (but that's nothing),—and to thee, which were much. Knowest thou not that there is scarce a gentleman of my train below the state of a peer's son, and that I have made, by refusals, malcontents eno' as it is—yet, hold! there is my learned brother, the Archbishop of York. Knowest thou Latin and the schools?"

"'Fore Heaven, my lord," said the Nevile, bluntly, "I see already I had best go back to green Westmoreland, for I am as unfit for his Grace the Ardhbishop, as I am for my Lord Montagu."

"Well, then," said the earl, drily, "since thou hast not yet station enough for my train, nor glosing for Northumberland, nor wit and lere for the archbishop, I suppose, my poor youth, I must e'en make you only a gentleman about the king! It is not a post so sure of quick rising and full gipsires as one about myself, or my brethren, but it will be less envied, and is good for thy first essay. How goes the clock? Oh! here is Nick Alwyn's new horolge. He tells me that the English will soon rival the Dutch * in these baubles

* Clockwork appears to have been introduced into England in the reign of Edward III., when three

The more the pity!—our red-faced yeomen, alas, are fast sinking into lank-jawed mechanics! We shall find the king in his garden within the next half-hour. Thou shalt attend me."

Marmaduke expressed, with more feeling than eloquence, the thanks he owed for an offer that, he was about to say, exceeded his hopes, but he had already, since his departure from Westmoreland, acquired sufficient wit to think twice of his words. And so eagerly, at that time, did the youth of the nobility contend for the honor of posts about the person of Warwick, and even of his brothers, and so strong was the belief that the Earl's power to make or to mar fortune was all paramount in England, that even a place in the king's household was considered an inferior appointment to that which made Warwick the immediate patron and protector. This was more expecially the case amongst the more haughty and ancient gentry, since the favor shown by Edward to the relations of his wife, and his own indifference to the rank and birth of his associates. Warwick had therefore spoken with truth when he expressed a comparative pity for the youth, whom he could not better provide for than by a place about the Court of his Sovereign!

The earl then drew from Marmaduke some account of his early training, his dependence on his brother, his adventures at the archery ground, his misadventure with the robbers, and even his sojourn with Warner—though Marmaduke was discreetly silent as to the very existence of Sibyll. The earl, in the meanwhile, walked to and fro the chamber, with a light, careless stride, every moment pausing to laugh at the frank simplicity of his kinsman, or to throw in some shrewd remark, which he cast purposely in the rough Westmoreland dialect; for no man ever attains to the popularity that rejoiced or accursed the Earl of Warwick, without a tendency to broad and familiar humor, without a certain common-place of character in its shallower and more every-day properties. This charm—always great *in* the the great—Warwick possessed to perfection; and in him—such was his native and unaffected majesty of bearing, and such the splendor that surrounded his name—it never seemed coarse or unfamiliar, but "everything he did became him best." Marmaduke had just brought his narrative to a conclusion, when, after a slight tap at the door, which Warwick did not hear, two fair young forms bounded joyously in, and, not seeing the stranger, threw themselves upon Warwick's breast with the caressing familiarity of infancy.

"Ah, father," said the elder of these two girls, as Warwick's hand smoothed her hair fondly, "you promised you would take us in your barge to see the sports on the river, and now it will be too late."

"Make your peace with your young cousins here," said the earl, turning to Marmaduke; you will cost them an hour's joyaunce. This is my eldest daughter, Isabel; and this soft-eyed, pale-cheeked damozel—too loyal for a leaf of the red rose—is the Lady Anne."

The two girls had started from their father's arms at the first address to Marmaduke, and their countenances had relapsed from their caressing and childlike expression, into all the stately demureness with which they had been brought up to regard a stranger. Howbeit, this reserve, to which he was accustomed, awed Marmaduke less than the alternate gaiety and sadness of the wilder Sibyll, and he addressed them with all the galantry to the exercise of which he had been reared; concluding his compliments with a declaration that he would rather forego the advantage proffered him by the earl's favor with the king than foster one obnoxious and ungracious memory in damozels so fair and honored.

A haughty smile flited for a moment over the proud, young face of Isabel Nevile; but the softer Anne blushed, and drew bashfully behind her sister.

As yet these girls, born for the highest and fated to the most wretched fortunes, were in all the bloom of earliest youth; but the difference between their characters might be already observable in their mien and countenance. Isabel, of tall and commanding stature, had some resemblance to her father, in her aquiline features, rich, dark hair, and the lustrous brilliancy of her eyes; while Anne, less striking, yet not less lovely, of smaller size and slighter proportions, bore in her pale

---

Dutch horologers were invited over from Delft. They must soon have passed into common use, for Chaucer thus familiarly speaks of them:—

"Full sickerer was his crowning in his loge,
Than is a clock or any abbey orloge."

clear face, her dove-like eyes, and her gentle brow, an expression of yielding meekness not unmixed with melancholy, which, cojoined with an exquisite symmetry of features, could not fail of exciting interest where her sister commanded admiration. Not a word, however, from either did Marmaduke abstract in return for his courtesies, nor did either he or the earl seem to expect it; for the latter, seating himself and drawing Anne on his knee, while Isabella walked with stately grace towards the table that bore her father's warlike accoutrements, and played, as it were, unconsciously with the black plume on his black burgonot, said to Nevile—

"Well, thou hast seen enough of the Lancastrian raptrils to make thee true to the Yorkists. I would I could say as much for the king himself, who is already crowding the court with that venomous faction, in honor of Dame Elizabeth Gray—born Mistress Woodville, and now Queen of England. Ha! my proud Isabel, thou wouldst have better filled the throne that thy father built!"

And at these words a proud flash broke from the earl's dark eyes, betraying even to Marmaduke the secret of perhaps his earliest alienation from Edward IV.

Isabella pouted her rich lip, but said nothing. "As for thee, Anne, continued the earl, "it is a pity that monks cannot marry—thou wouldst have suited some sober priest better than a mailed knight. 'Fore George, I would not ask thee to buckle my baldrick when the war-steeds were snorting, but I would trust Isabel with the links of my hauberk."

"Nay, father," said the low timid voice of Anne, "if thou wert going to danger, I could be brave in all that could guard thee!"

"Why, that's my girl—kiss me! Thou hast a look of thy mother now—so thou hast! and I will not chide thee the next time I hear thee muttering soft treason, in pity of Henry of Windsor."

"Is he not to be pitied?—Crown, wife, son, and Earl Warwick's stout arm—lost—lost!"

"No!" said Isabel, suddenly; "no, sweet sister Anne, and fie on thee for the words! He lost all, because he had neither the hand of a knight nor the heart of a man! For the rest—Margaret of Anjou, or her butchers, beheaded our father's father!"

"And may God and St. George forget me, when I forget those grey and gory hairs!" exclaimed the earl; and, putting away the Lady Anne somewhat roughly, he made a stride across the room, and stood by his hearth. "And yet Edward, the son of Richard of York, who fell by my father's side—he forgets—he forgives! And the minions of Rivers the Lancastrian, tread the heals of Richard of Warwick!"

At this unexpected turn in the conversation, peculiarly unwelcome, as it may be supposed, to the son of one who had fought on the Lancastrian side, in the very battle referred to, Marmaduke felt somewhat uneasy, and, turning to the Lady Anne, he said, with the gravity of wounded pride, "I owe more to my lord, your father, than I even wist of—how much he must have overlooked to——"

"Not so!" interrupted Warwick, who overheard him—"not so; thou wrongest me! Thy farher was shocked at those butcheries—thy father recoiled from that accursed standard—thy father was of a stock ancient and noble as my own! But, these Woodvilles!—tush! my passion overmasters me. We will go to the king—it is time."

Warwick here rung the hand-bell on his table, and on the entrance of his attendant gentleman, bade him see that the barge was in readiness; then, beckoning to his kinsman, and with a nod to his daughters, he caught up his plumed cap, and passed at once into the garden.

"Anne," said Isabel, when the two girls were alone, "thou hast vexed my father, and what marvel? If the Lancastrians can be pitied, the Earl of Warwick must be condemned!'

"Unkind!" said Anne, shedding tears; I can pity woe and mischance, without blaming those whose hard duty it might be to achieve them."

"In good sooth, cannot I! Thou wouldst pity and pardon till thou left'st no distinction between foeman and friend—liefe and loathing. Be it mine, like my great father, to love and to hate!"

"Yet why art thou so attached to the White Rose?" said Anne, stung, if not to malice, at least to archness. "Thou knowest my father's nearest wish was that his eldest daughter might be betrothed to King Edward. Dost thou not pay good for evil when thou seest no excellence out of the House of York?"

"Saucy Anne," answered Isabel, with a half smile, "I am not raught by thy shafts, for I was a child for the nurses, when King Edward sought a wife for his love. But were I chafed —as I may be vain enough to know myself— whom should I blame?—Not the king, but the Lancastrian who witched him!"

She paused a moment, and, looking away, added in a low tone—"Didst thou hear, sister Anne, if the Duke of Clarence visited my father the forenoon?"

"Ah! Isabel—Isabel!"

"Ah! sister Anne—sister Anne! Wilt thou know all my secrets ere I know them myself?"—and Isabel, with something of her father's playfulness, put her hand to Anne's laughing lips.

Meanwhile Warwick, after walking musingly a few moments along the garden, which was formed by plots of sward, bordered with fruit trees, and white rose trees not yet in blossom, turned to his silent kinsman, and said—"Forgive me, cousin mine, my mannerless burst against thy brave father's faction; but when thou hast been a short while at court, thou wilt see where the sore is. Certes, I love this king!" Here his dark face lighted up. "Love him as a king,—ay, and as a son! And who would not love him; brave as his sword, gallant, and winning, and gracious as the noon-day in summer? Besides, I placed him on his throne—I honor myself in him!"

The earl's stature dilated as he spoke the last sentence, and his hand rested on his dagger hilt. He resumed, with the same daring and incautious candor that stamped his dauntless soldier-like nature, "God hath given me no son. Isabel of Warwick had been a mate for William the Norman; and my grandson, if heir to his grandsire's, soul, should have ruled from the throne of England over the realms of Charlemagne! But it hath pleased Him, whom the Christian knight alone bows to without shame, to order otherwise. So be it. I forgot my just pretensions—forgot my blood, and counselled the king to strengthen his throne with the alliance of Louis XI. He rejected the Princess Bona of Savoy, to marry widow Elizabeth Gray—I sorrowed for his sake, and forgave the slight to my counsels. At his prayer I followed the train of his queen, and hushed the proud hearts of our barons to obeisance. But since then, this Dame Woodville, whom I queened, if her husband mated, must dispute this roiaulme with mine and me —a Nevile, now-a-days, must vail his plume to a Woodville! And not the great barons whom it will suit Edward's policy to win from the Lancastrians—not the Exeters and the Somersets—but the craven varlets, and lackeys, and dross of the camp—false alike to Henry and to Edward—are to be fondled into lordships and dandled into power. Young man, I am speaking hotly—Richard Nevile never lies nor conceals. But I am speaking to a kinsman, am I not? Thou hearest—thou wilt not repeat?"

"Sooner would I pluck forth my tongue by the roots."

"Enough!" returned the earl, with a pleased smile. "When I come from France, I will speak more to thee. Meanwhile be courteous to all men—servile to none. Now to the king."

So speaking, he shook back his surcoat, drew his cap over his brow, and passed to the broad stairs, at the foot of which fifty rowers, with their badges on their shoulders, waited in the huge barge, gilt richly at prow and stern, and with an awning of silk, wrought with the earl's arms and cognizance. As they pushed off, six musicians, placed towards the helm, began a slow and half eastern march, which, doubtless, some crusader of the Temple had brought from the cymbals and trumps of Palestine.

CHAPTER II.

King Edward the Fourth.

THE tower of London, more consecrated to associations of gloom and blood than those of gaiety and splendor, was, nevertheless, during the reign of Edward IV., the seat of a gallant and gorgeous court. That king, from the first to the last so dear to the people of London, made it his principal residence when in his metropolis; and its ancient halls and towers were then the scene of many a brawl and galliard. As Warwick's barge now approached its huge walls, rising from the river, there was much that might either animate or awe, according to the mood of the spectator. The king's barge, with many lesser craft, reserved for the use of the courtiers, gay, with awnings and streamers, and painting and gilding, lay below the wharfs, not far from the gate of St. Thomas, now called the Traitor's Gate. On the walk raised above the battlemented wall of the inner ward, not only paced the sentries, but there, dames and knights were inhaling the noon-day breezes, and the gleam of their rich dresses of cloth of gold glanced upon the eye at frequent intervals from tower to tower.

Over the vast round turret, behind the Traitor's Gate, now called "The Bloody Tower," floated cheerily in the light wind, the royal banner. Near the Lion's Tower, two or three of the keepers of the menagerie, in the king's livery, were leading forth, by a strong chain, the huge white bear that made one of the boasts of the collection, and was an especial favorite with the king and his brother Richard. The sheriffs of London were bound to find this grizzly minion his chain and his cord, when he deigned to amuse himself with bathing or "fishing" in the river; and several boats, filled with gape-mouthed passengers, lay near the wharf, to witness the diversions of Bruin. These folk set up a loud shout of—"A Warwick!—a Warwick!" "The stout earl, and God bless him!" as the gorgeous barge shot towards the fortress. The earl acknowledged their greeting by vailing his plumed cap, and passing the keepers with a merry allusion to their care of his own badge, and a friendly compliment to the grunting bear, he stepped ashore, followed by his kinsman. Now, however, he paused a moment, and a more thoughtful shade passed over his countenance, as, glancing his eye carelessly aloft towards the standard of King Edward, he caught sight of the casement, in the neighboring tower, of the very room in which the sovereign of his youth, Henry the Sixth, was a prisoner, almost within hearing of the revels of his successor; then, with a quick stride, he hurried on through the vast court, and, passing the White Tower, gained the royal lodge. Here, in the great hall, he left his companion, amidst a group of squires and gentlemen, to whom he formally presented the Nevile as his friend and kinsman, and was ushered by the deputy chamberlain, (with an apology for the absence of his chief, the Lord Hastings, who had gone abroad to fly his falcon), into the small garden, where Edward was idling away the interval between the noon and evening meals—repasts to which already the young king inclined with that intemperate zest and ardor which he carried into all his pleasures, and which finally destroyed the handsomest person, and embruted one of the most vigorous intellects of the age.

The garden, if bare of flowers, supplied their place by the various and brilliant-colored garbs of the living beauties assembled on its straight walks and smooth sward. Under one of those graceful cloisters, which were the taste of the day, and had been recently built, and gaily decorated, the earl was stopped in his path by a group of ladies playing at closheys (ninepins) of ivory;* and one of these fair dames, who excelled the rest in her skill, had just bowled down the central or crowned pin—the king of the closheys. This lady, no less a person than Elizabeth, the Queen of England, was then in her thirty-sixth year—ten years older than her lord—but the peculiar fairness and delicacy of her complexion, still preserved to her beauty the aspect and bloom of youth. From a lofty head-gear, embroidered with fleur-de-lis, round which wreathed a light diadem of pearls, her hair of the pale yellow, considered then the perfection of beauty, flowed so straight and so shining down her shoulders, almost to the knees, that it seemed like a mantle of gold. The baudekin stripes, (blue and gold), of her tunic, attested her royalty. The blue court-pie of satin was bordered with ermine, and the sleeves, fitting close to an arm of exquisite contour, shone with seed-pearls. Her features were straight and regular, yet would have been insipid, but for an expression rather of cunning than intellect;—and the high arch of her eyebrows, with a slight curve downward of a mouth otherwise beautiful, did not improve the expression, by an addition of something supercilious and contemptuous, rather than haughty or majestic.

"My lord of Warwick," said Elizabeth, pointing to the fallen closhey, "what would my enemies say if they heard I had toppled down the king?"

"They would content themselves with asking which of your grace's brothers you would

* Narrative of Louis of Bruges, Lord Grauthuse. Edited by Sir F. Madden. Archæologia, 1836.

place in his stead," answered the hardy earl, unable to restrain the sarcasm.

The queen blushed, and glanced round her ladies with an eye which never looked direct or straight upon its object, but wandered sidelong with a furtive and stealthy expression, that did much to obtain for her the popular character of falseness and self-seeking. Her displeasure was yet more increased by observing the ill-concealed smile which the taunt had called forth.

"Nay, my lord," she said, after a short pause, "we value the peace of our roiaulme too much for so high an ambition. Were we to make a brother even the prince of the closheys, we should disappoint the hopes of a Nevile."

The earl disdained pursuing the war of words, and answering, coldly—"The Neviles are more famous for making ingrates than asking favors. I leave your highness to the closheys"—turned away, and strode towards the king, who, at the opposite end of the garden, was reclining on a bench beside a lady, in whose ear, to judge by her downcast and blushing cheek, he was breathing no unwelcome whispers.

"Mort-Dieu!" muttered the earl, who was singularly exempt, himself, from the amorous follies of the day, and eyed them with so much contempt that it often obscured his natural downright penetration into character, and never more than when it led him afterwards to underrate the talents of Edward IV.—"Mort-Dieu! if, an hour before the battle of Touton, some wizard had shown me, in his glass, this glimpse of the gardens of the Tower, that giglet for a queen, and that squire of dames for a king, I had not slain my black destrier, (poor Malech!) that I might conquer or die for Edward Earl of March!"

"But see!" said the lady, looking up from the enamoured and conquering eyes of the king; "art thou not ashamed, my lord?—the grim earl comes to chide thee for thy faithlessness to thy queen, whom he loves so well."

"Pasque-Dieu! as my cousin Louis of France says or swears," answered the king, with an evident petulance in his altered voice —"I would that Warwick could be only worn with one's armor! I would as lief try to kiss through my visor as hear him talk of glory and Touton, and King John and poor Edward II., because I am not always in mail. Go! leave us, sweet bonnibel!—we must brave the bear alone!"

The lady inclined her head, drew her hood round her face, and striking into the contrary path from that in which Warwick was slowly striding, gained the group round the queen, whose apparent freedom from jealousy, the consequence of cold affections and prudent calculation, made one principal cause of the empire she held over the powerful mind, but the indolent temper, of the gay and facile Edward.

The king rose as Warwick now approached him; and the appearance of these two eminent persons was in singular contrast. Warwick, though richly and even gorgeously attired—nay, with all the care which in that age was considered the imperative duty a man of station and birth owed to himself, held in lofty disdain whatever vagary of custom tended to cripple the movements or womanize the man. No loose flowing robes—no shoon half a yard long—no flaunting tawdiness of fringe and aiglet, characterized the appearance of the baron, who, even in peace, gave his dress a half-martial fashion.

But Edward, who in common with all the princes of the House of York carried dress to a passion, had not only re-introduced many of the most effeminate modes in vogue under William the Red King, but added to them whatever could tend to impart an almost oriental character to the old Norman garb. His gown (a womanly garment which had greatly superseded, with men of the highest rank, not only the mantle but the surcoat) flowed to his heels, trimmed with ermine, and broidered with large flowers of crimson wrought upon cloth of gold. Over this he wore a tippet of ermine, and a collar or necklace of uncut jewels set in filagree gold; the nether limbs were, it is true, clad in the more manly fashion of tight-fitting hosen, but the folds of the gown, as the day was somewhat fresh, were drawn around so as to conceal the only part of the dress which really betokened the male sex. To add to this unwarlike attire, Edward's locks, of a rich golden color, and perfuming the whole air with odors, flowed, not in curls, but straight to his shoulders, and the cheek of the fairest lady in his court might have seemed less fair beside the dazzling clearness of a complexion, at once radiant with health and delicate with youth. Yet, in spite of all this effeminacy, the appearance of Edward IV. was *not* effeminate. From this it was preserved, not only by a stature little less commanding than that of Warwick himself, and of great strength and breadth of shoulder, but also by features, beautiful indeed, but preeminently masculine,—large and bold in their outline, and evincing by their expression all the gallantry and daring characteristic of the hottest soldier, next to Warwick, and, without any exception, the ablest captain, of the age.

"And welcome—a merry welcome, dear Warwick, and cousin mine," said Edward, as Warwick slightly bent his proud knee to his king; "your brother, Lord Montagu, has but left us. Would that our court had the same joyaunce for you as for him."

"Dear and honored my liege," answered Warwick, his brow smoothing at once—for his affectionate though hasty and irritable nature was rarely proof against the kind voice and winning smile of his young sovereign—"could I ever serve you at the court as I can with the people, you would not complain that John of Montagu was a better courtier than Richard of Warwick. But each to his calling. I depart to-morrow for Calais, and thence to King Louis. And, surely, never envoy nor delegate had better chance to be welcome than one empowered to treat of an alliance that will bestow on a prince, deserving, I trust, his fortunes, the sister of the bravest sovereign in Christian Europe."

"Now, out on thy flattery, my cousin; though I must needs own I provoked it by my complaint of thy courtiership. But thou hast learned only half thy business, good Warwick; and it is well Margaret did not hear thee. Is not the Prince of France more to be envied for winning a fair lady than having a fortunate soldier for his brother-in-law?"

"My liege," replied Warwick, smiling, "thou knowest I am a poor judge of a lady's fair cheek, though indifferently well skilled as to the valor of a warrior's stout arm. Algates, the Lady Margaret is indeed worthy in her excellent beauties to become the mother of brave men?"

"And that is all we can wring from thy stern lip, man of iron. Well, that must content us. But to more serious matters." And the king, leaning his hand on the earl's arm, and walking with him slowly to and fro the terrace, continued—"Knowest thou not, Warwick, that this French alliance, to which thou hast induced us, displeases sorely our good traders of London?"

"Mort-Dieu!" returned Warwick, bluntly; "and what business have the flat-caps with the marriage of a king's sister? Is it for them to breathe garlick on the alliances of Bourbons and Plantagenets? Faugh! You have spoiled them, good my lord king—you have spoiled them by your condescensions. Henry IV. staled not his majesty to consultations with the mayor of his city. Henry V. gave the knighthood of the Bath to the heroes of Agincourt, not to the venders of cloth and spices."

"Ah, my poor Knights of the Bath!" said Edward, good humoredly, "wilt thou never let that sore scar quietly over? Ownest thou not that the men had their merits?"

"What the merits were, I weet not," answered the earl;—"unless, peradventure, their wives were comely and young!"

"Thou wrongest me, Warwick," said the king, carelessly; "Dame Cook was awry, Dame Philips a grandmother, Dame Jocelyn had lost her front teeth, and Dame Waer saw seven ways at once! But thou forgettest, man, the occasion of those honors—the eve before Elizabeth was crowned—and it was policy to make the city of London have a share in her honors. As to the rest," pursued the king, earnestly and with dignity, "I and my house have owed much to London. When the Peers of England, save thee and thy friends, stood aloof from my cause, London was ever loyal and true. Thou seest not, my poor Warwick, that these burgesses are growing up into power by the decline of the orders above them. And if the sword is the monarch's appeal for his right, he must look to contented and honored industry for his buckler in peace. This is policy—policy, Warwick; and Louis XI. will tell thee the same truths, harsh though they grate in a warriors's ear."

The earl bowed his haughty head, and answered, shortly, but with a touching grace—"Be it ever thine, noble king, to rule as it likes thee; and mine to defend with my blood even what I approve not with my brain. But if thou doubtest the wisdom of this alliance, it is not too late yet. Let me dismiss my following, and cross not the seas. Unless thy heart is with the marriage, the ties I would form are threads and cobwebs."

"Nay," returned Edward, irresolutely; "in these great state matters, thy wit is elder than mine; but men do say the Count of Charolois is a mighty lord, and the alliance with Burgundy will be more profitable to staple and mart."

"Then, in God's name, so conclude it!" said the earl hastily, but with so dark a fire in his eyes, that Edward, who was observing him, changed countenance;—"only ask me not, my liege, to advance such a marriage. The Count of Charolois knows me as his foe—shame were mine, did I shun to say where I love, where I hate. That proud dullard once slighted me when we met at his father's court—and the wish next to my heart, is to pay back my affront with my battle-axe. Give thy sister to the heir of Burgundy, and forgive me if I depart to my Castle at Middleham."

Edward, stung by the sharpness of this reply, was about to answer as became his majesty of king, when Warwick more deliberately resumed—"Yet think well, Henry of Windsor is thy prisoner, but his cause lives in Margaret and his son. There is but one power in Europe that can threaten thee with aid to the Lancastrians, that power is France. Make Louis thy friend and ally, and thou givest peace to thy life and thy lineage—make Louis thy foe, and count on plots, and stratagems, and treason—uneasy days and sleepless nights. Already thou hast lost one occasion to secure that wiliest and most restless of princes, in rejecting the hand of the Princess Bona. Happily, this loss now can be retrieved. But alliance with Burgundy is war with France—war more deadly because Louis is a man who declares it not—a war carried on by intrigue and bribe, by spies and minions, till some disaffection ripens the hour when young Edward of Lancaster shall land on thy coasts, with the Oriflamme and the Red Rose,—with French soldiers and English malcontents. Wouldst thou look to Burgundy for help?—Burgundy will have enough to guard its own frontiers from the gripe of Louis the Sleepless. Edward, my king, my pupil in arms—Edward, my loved, my honored liege, forgive Richard Nevile his bluntness, and let not his faults stand in bar of his counsels."

"You are right, as you are ever—safeguard of England, and pillar of my state," said the king frankly, and pressing the arm he still held "Go to France and settle all as thou wilt."

Warwick bent low and kissed the hand of his sovereign. "And," said he, with a slight, but a sad smile—"when I am gone, my liege will not repent, will not misthink me, will not listen to my foes, nor suffer merchant and mayor to sigh him back to the mechanics of Flanders?"

"Warwick, thou deemest ill of thy king's kingliness."

"Not of thy kingliness, but that same gracious quality of yielding to counsel which bows this proud nature to submission—often makes me fear for thy firmness, when thy will is won through thy heart. And now, good my liege, forgive me one sentence more. Heaven forefend that I should stand in the way of thy princely favors. A king's countenance is a sun that should shine on all. But bethink thee well, the barons of England are a stubborn and haughty race; chafe not thy most puissant peers by too cold a neglect of their past services, and too lavish a largess to new men."

"Thou aimest at Elizabeth's kin," interrupted Edward, withdrawing his hand from his minister's arm—"and I tell thee, once for all times, that I would rather sink again to mine Earldom of March, with a subject's right to honor where he loves, than wear crown and wield sceptre without a king's unquestioned prerogative to ennoble the line and blood of one he has deemed worthy of his throne. As for the barons, with whose wrath thou threatenest me, I banish them not—if they go in gloom from my court—why let them chafe themselves sleek again!"

"King Edward," said Warwick, moodily,—"tried services merit not this contempt. It is not as the kith of the queen that I regret to see lands and honors lavished upon men, rooted so nearly to the soil that the first blast of the war-trump will scatter their greenness to the winds. But what sorrows me is to mark those who have fought against thee, preferred to the stout loyalty that braved block and field for thy cause. Look round thy court; where are the men of bloody York and victorious Touton?—unrequited, sullen in their strongholds—begirt with their yeomen and retainers. Thou standest—thou, the heir of York—almost alone, (save where the Neviles—whom one day thy court will seek also to disgrace and discard—vex their old comrades in arms by their defection)—thou standest almost alone among the favorites and minions of Lancaster. Is there no danger in proving to men that to have served thee is discredit—to have warred against thee is guerdon and grace?"

"Enough of this, cousin," replied the king, with an effort which preserved his firmness. "On this head we cannot agree. Take what else thou wilt of royalty—make treaties and contract marriages—establish peace or proclaim war; but trench not on my sweetest prerogative to give and to forgive. And now, wilt thou tarry and sup with us? The ladies grow impatient of a commune that detains from their eyes the stateliest knight since the Round Table was chopped into fire-wood."

"No, my liege," said Warwick, whom flattery of this sort rather angered than soothed—"I have much yet to prepare. I leave your highness to fairer homage and more witching counsels than mine." So saying, he kissed the king's hand, and was retiring, when he remembered his kinsman, whose humble interests, in the midst of more exciting topics, he had hitherto forgotten, and added, "May I crave, since you are so merciful to the Lancastrians, one grace for my namesake—a Nevile, whose father repented the side he espoused—a son of Sir Guy of Arsdale."

"Ah," said the king, smiling maliciously, "it pleaseth us much to find that it is easier to the warm heart of our cousin Warwick to preach sententiaries of sternness to his king, than to enforce the same by his own practice!"

"You misthink me, sire. I ask not that Marmaduke Nevile should supplant his superiors and elders—I ask not that he should be made baron and peer—I ask only that, as a young gentleman, who hath taken no part himself in the wars, and whose father repented his error, your grace should strengthen your following by an ancient name and a faithful servant. But I should have remembered me that his name of Nevile would have procured him a taunt in the place of advancement."

"Saw man ever so froward a temper?" cried Edward, not without reason. "Why, Warwick, thou art as shrewish to a jest as a woman to advice. Thy kinsman's fortunes shall be my care. Thou sayest thou hast enemies—I weet not who they be. But to show what I think of them, I make thy namesake and client a gentleman of my chamber. When Warwick is false to Edward, let him think that Warwick's kinsman wears a dagger within reach of the king's heart day and night."

This speech was made with so noble and touching a kindness of voice and manner, that the earl, thoroughly subdued, looked at his sovereign with moistened eyes, and only trusting himself to say,—"Edward, thou art king, knight, gentleman, and soldier, and I verily trow that I love thee best when my petulent zeal makes me anger thee most,"—turned away with evident emotion, and passing the queen and her ladies with a lowlier homage than that with which he had before greeted them, left the garden. Edward's eye followed him, musingly. The frank expression of his face vanished, and, with the deep breath of a man who is throwing a weight from his heart, he muttered—

"He loves me—yes,—but will suffer no one else to love me! This must end some day. I am weary of the bondage." And sauntering towards the ladies, he listened in silence, but not apparently in displeasure, to his queen's sharp sayings on the imperious mood and irritable temper of the iron-handed builder of his throne.

CHAPTER III.

The Ante-Chamber.

As Warwick passed the door that led from the garden, he brushed by a young man, the baudekin stripes of whose vest announced his relationship to the king, and who, though far less majestic than Edward, possessed sufficient of family likeness to pass for a very handsome and comely person. But his countenance wanted the open and fearless expression which gave that of the king so masculine and heroic a character. The features were smaller, and less clearly cut, and to a physiognomical observer there was much that was weak and irresolute in the light blue eyes and the smiling lips, which never closed firmly over the teeth. He did not wear the long gown then so much in vogue, but his light figure was displayed to advantage by a vest, fitting it exactly, descending half-way down the thigh, and trimmed at the border and the collar with ermine. The sleeves of the doublet were slit, so as to show the white lawn beneath, and adorned with aiglets and knots of gold. Over the left arm hung a rich jacket of furs and velvet, something like that adopted by the modern hussar. His hat or cap was high and tiara-like, with a single white plume, and the ribbon of the garter bound his knee. Though the dress of this personage was thus far less effeminate than Edward's, the effect of his appearance was infinitely more so—partly, perhaps, from a less muscular frame, and partly from his extreme youth. For George Duke of Clarance was then, though initiated not only in the gaieties, but all the intrigues of the court, only in his eighteenth year. Laying his hand, every finger of which sparkled with jewels, on the earl's shoulder—"Hold!" said the young prince, in a whisper, "a word in thy ear, noble Warwick."

The earl, who, next to Edward, loved Clarence the most of his princely house, and who always found the latter as docile as the other (when humor or affection seized him) was intractable, relaxed into a familiar smile at the duke's greeting, and suffered the young prince to draw him aside from the groups of courtiers, with whom the chamber was filled, to the leaning places (as they were called) of a large mullion window. In the meanwhile, as they thus conferred, the courtiers interchanged looks, and many an eye of fear and hate was directed towards the stately form of the earl. For these courtiers were composed principally of the kindred or friends of the queen, and though they dared not openly evince the malice with which they retorted Warwick's lofty scorn, and undisguised resentment at their new fortunes, they ceased not to hope for his speedy humiliation and disgrace, recking little what storm might rend the empire, so that it uprooted the giant oak, which still, in some measure, shaded their sunlight, and checked their growth. True, however, that amongst these were mingled, though rarely, men of a hardier stamp and nobler birth—some few of the veterans friends of the king's great father—and these, keeping sternly and loftily aloof from the herd, regarded Warwick with the same almost reverential, and yet affectionate admiration which he inspired amongst the yeomen, peasants, and mechanics; for in that growing, but quiet struggle of the burgesses, as it will often happen, in more civilized times, the great Aristocracy and the Populace were much united in affection, though with very different objects; and the Middle and Trading Class, with whom the earl's desire for French alliances and disdain of commerce had much weakened his popularity, alone shared not the enthusiasm of their countrymen for the lion-hearted minister.

Nevertheless, it must here be owned, that the rise of Elizabeth's kindred introduced a far more intellectual, accomplished, and literary race into court favor, than had for many generations flourished in so uncongenial a soil: and in this ante-chamber feud, the pride of education and mind retaliated with juster sarcasm, the pride of birth and sinews.

Amongst those opposed to the earl, and fit in all qualities to be the head of the new movement—if the expressive modern word be allowed us—stood at that moment in the very centre of the chamber, Anthony Woodville—in right of the rich heiress he had married, the Lord Scales. As when some hostile and formidable foe enters the meads where the flock grazes, the gazing herd gather slowly round their leader,—so grouped the queen's faction slowly, and by degrees, round this accomplished nobleman, at the prolonged sojourn of Warwick.

"Gramercy!" said the Lord Scales, in a somewhat affected intonation of voice, "the conjunction of the bear and the young lion is a parlous omen, for the which I could much desire we had a wise astrologer's reading."

"It is said," observed one of the courtiers, that the Duke of Clarence much affects either the lands or the person of Lady Isabel."

"A passably fair damozel," returned Anthony, "though a thought or so too marked and high in her lineaments, and wholly unlettered, no doubt: which were a pity, for George of Clarence hath some pretty taste in the arts and poesies. But as Occleve hath it—

> "Gold, silver, jewel, cloth, beddying, array,"

would make gentle George amorous of a worse-race than high-nosed Isabel; 'strange to spell or rede,' as I would wager my best destrier to a tailor's hobby, the damozel surely is."

"Notest thou yon gaudy popinjay?" whispered the Lord of St. John to one of his Touton comrades, as, leaning against the wall, they overheard the sarcasms of Anthony, and the laugh of the courtiers, who glassed their faces and moods to his; "Is the time so out of joint that Master Anthony Woodville can vent his scurrile japes on the heiress of Salisbury and Warwick, in the king's chamber?"

"And prate of spelling and reading, as if they were the cardinal virtues," returned his sullen companion. "By my halidame, I have two fair daughters, at home, who will lack husbands, I trow, for they can only spin and be chaste—two maidenly gifts out of bloom with the White Rose."

In the meanwhile, unwitting, or contemptuous of the attention they excited, Warwick and Clarence continued yet more earnestly to confer.

"No, George, no," said the earl, who, as the descendant of John of Gaunt, and of kin to the king's blood, maintained in private, a father's familiarity with the princes of York, though on state occasions, and when in the hearing of others, he sedulously marked his deference for their rank—"no, George, calm and steady thy hot mettle, for thy brother's and England's sake. I grieve as much as thou to hear that the queen does not spare even thee in her froward and unwomanly peevishness. But there is a glamour in this, believe me, that must melt away, soon or late, and our kingly Edward recover his senses."

"Glamour!" said Clarence, "thinkest thou indeed, that her mother, Jacquetta, has bewitched the king? One word of thy belief in such spells, spread abroad amongst the people, would soon raise the same storm that blew Eleanor Cobham from Duke Humphrey's bed, along London streets in her penance shift."

"Troth," said the earl, indifferently, "I leave such grave questions as these to prelate and priest; the glamour I spoke of, is that of a fair face over a wanton heart; and Edward is not so steady a lover, that this should never wear out!"

"It amates me much, noble cousin, that thou leavest the court in this juncture. The queen's heart is with Burgundy—the city's hate is with France—and when once thou art gone, I fear that the king will be teased into mating my sister with the Count of Charolois."

"Ho!" exclaimed Warwick, with an oath so loud that it rung through the chamber, and startled every ear that heard it. Then, perceiving his indiscretion, he lowered his tone into a deep and hollow whisper, and griped the prince's arm, almost fiercely, as he spoke.

"Could Edward so dishonor my embassy—so palter and juggle with my faith—so flout me in the eyes of Chistendom, I would—I would—" he paused, and relaxed his hold of the duke, and added, with an altered voice—"I would leave his wife and his lemans, and yon things of silk, whom he makes peers (*that* is easy), but cannot make men—to guard his throne from the grandson of Henry V. But thy fears, thy zeal, thy love for me, dearest prince and cousin, make, thee misthink Edward's kingly honor and knightly faith. I go, with the sure knowledge that by alliance with France I shut the house of Lancaster from all hope of this roiaulme."

"Had'st thou not better at least, see my sister Margaret—she has a high spirit, and she thinks thou mightst, at least, woo her assent, and tell her of the good gifts of her lord to be!"

"Are the daughters of York spoilt to this by the manners and guise of a court, in which beshrew me if I well know which the woman and whom the man? Is it not enough to give peace to broad England—root to her brother's stem? Is it not enough to wed the son of a king—the descendant of Charlemagne and St. Louis? Must I go bonnet in hand and simper forth, the sleek personals of the choice of her kith and house; swear the bridegroom's side-locks are as long King Edward's, and that he bows with the grace of Master Anthony Woodville? Tell her this thyself, genle Clarence, if thou wilt: all Warwick could say would but anger her ear, if she be the maid thou bespeakest her."

The Duke of Clarence hesitated a moment, and then, coloring slightly, said—"If, then, the daughter's hand be the gift of her kith alone, shall I have thy favor when the Lady Isabel—"

"George," interrupted Warwick, with a fond and paternal smile, "when we have made England safe, there is nothing the son of

Richard of York can ask of Warwick in vain. Alas!" he added, mournfully, "thy father and mine were united in the same murtherous death, and I think they will smile down on us from their seats in heaven, when a happier generation cements that bloody union with a marriage bond!"

Without waiting for further parlance, the earl turned suddenly away, threw his cap on his towering head, and strode right through the centre of the whispering courtiers, who shrunk, louting low, from his haughty path, to break into a hubbub of angry exclamations, or sarcastic jests, at his unmannerly bearing, as his black plume disappeared in the arch of the vaulted door.

While such the scene in the interior chambers of the palace, Marmaduke, with the frank simpleness which belonged to his youth and training, had already won much favor and popularity, and he was laughing loud with a knot of young men by the shovel-board, when Warwick re-entered. The earl, though so disliked by the courtiers more immediately about the person of the king, was still the favorite of the less elevated knights and gentry who formed the subordinate household and retainers; and with these, indeed, his manner, so proud and arrogant to his foes and rivals, relapsed at once into the ease of the manly and idolized chief.

He was pleased to see the way made by his young namesake, and lifting his cap, as he nodded to the group, and leant his arm upon Marmaduke's shoulder, he said—"Thanks, and hearty thanks, to you, knights and gentles, for the courteous reception of an old friend's young son. I have our king's most gracious permission to see him enrolled one of the court ye grace. Ah! Master Falconer, and how does thy worthy uncle?—braver knight never trod.—What young gentleman is yonder?—a new face and a manly one; by your favor present him!—the son of a Savile! Sir, on my return, be not the only Savile who shuns our table of Warwick-court. Master Dacres, commend me to the lady, your mother; she and I have danced many a measure together in the old time—we all live again in our children. Good den to you, sirs. Marmaduke, follow me to the office—you lodge in the palace. You are gentleman to the most gracious, and if Warwick lives, to the most puissant of Europe's sovereigns. I shall see Montagu at home; he shall instruct thee in thy duties, and requite thee for all discourtesies on the archery ground."

BOOK THIRD.

IN WHICH THE HISTORY PASSES FROM THE KING'S COURT TO THE STUDENT'S CELL, AND RELATES THE PERILS THAT BEFEL A PHILOSOPHER FOR MEDDLING WITH THE AFFAIRS OF THE WORLD.

CHAPTER I.

The Solitary Sage and the Solitary Maid.

WHILE such the entrance of Marmaduke Nevile into a court, that if far less intellectual and refined than those of later days, was yet more calculated to dazzle the fancy, to sharpen the wit, and to charm the senses; for round the throne of Edward IV. chivalry was magnificent, intrigue restless, and pleasure ever on the wing—Sibyll had ample leisure, in her solitary home, to muse over the incidents that had preceded the departure of the young guest. Though she had rejected Marmaduke's proffered love, his tone, so suddenly altered—his abrupt, broken words and confusion—his farewell, so soon succeeding his passionate declaration—could not fail to wound that pride of woman which never sleeps till modesty is gone. But this made the least cause of the profound humiliation which bowed down her spirit. The meaning taunt, conveyed in the rhyme of the tymbesteres, pierced her to the quick; the calm indifferent smile of the stranger, as he regarded her; the beauty of the dame he attended, woke mingled and contrary feelings, but those of jealousy were, perhaps, the keenest: and in the midst of all she started to ask herself—if indeed she had suffered her vain thoughs to dwell too tenderly upon one from whom the vast inequalities of human life must divide her ever more—What to her was his indifference? Nothing—yet had she given worlds to banish that careless smile from her remembrance.

Shrinking, at last, from the tyranny of thoughts till of late unknown, her eye rested upon the gipsire which Alwyn had sent her by the old servant. The sight restored to her the holy recollection of her father, the sweet joy of having ministered to his wants. She put up the little treasure, intending to devote it all to Warner; and, after bathing her heavy eyes, that no sorrow of hers might afflict the student, she passed, with a listless step into her father's chamber.

There is, to the quick and mercurial spirits of the young, something of marvellous and preternatural in that life within life, which the strong passion of science and genius forms and feeds—that passion so much stronger than love, and so much more self-dependent—which asks no sympathy, leans on no kindred heart—which lives alone in its works and fancies like a god amidst his creations.

The philosopher, too, had experienced a great affliction since they met last. In the pride of his heart, he had designed to show Marmaduke the mystic operations of his model, which had seemed that morning to open into life; and when the young man was gone, and he made the experiment alone, alas ! he found that new progress but involved him in new difficulties He had gained the first steps in the gigantic creation of modern days, and he was met by the obstacle that baffled so long the great modern sage. There was the cylinder—there the boiler; yet, work as he would, the steam failed to keep the cylinder at work. And now, patiently as the spider re-weaves the broken web, his untiring ardor was bent upon constructing a new cylinder of other materials

"Strange," he said to himself, "that the heat of the mover aids not the movement;" and so, blundering near the truth, he labored on.

Sibyll, meanwhile, seated herself abstractedly on a heap of fagots, piled in the corner, and seemed busy in framing characters on the dusty floor with the point of her tiny slipper. So fresh and fair and young she seemed, in that murky atmosphere, that strange scene, and beside that worn man, that it might have seemed to a poet as if the youngest of the Graces were come to visit Mulciber at his forge.

The man pursued his work—the girl renewed her dreams—the dark evening hour gradually stealing over both. The silence was unbroken, for the forge and the model were now at rest, save by the grating of Adam's file upon the metal, or by some ejaculation of complacency now and then vented by the enthusiast. So, apart from the many-noised, gaudy, babbling world without, even in the midst of that bloody, turbulent, and semi-barbarous time, went on (the one neglected and unknown, the other loathed and hated), the two movers of the ALL that continues the airy life of the Beautiful from age to age—the Woman's dreaming Fancy, and the Man's active Genius.

CHAPTER II.

Master Adam Warner grows a miser, and behaves shamefully.

FOR two or three days nothing disturbed the outward monotony of the recluse's household. Apparently all had settled back as before the advent of the young cavalier. But Sibyll's voice was not heard singing, as of old, when she passed the stairs to her father's room. She sate with him in his work, no less frequently and and regularly than before; but her childish spirits no longer broke forth in idle talk or petulant movement, vexing the good man from his absorption and his toils. The little cares and anxieties, which had formerly made up so much of Sibyll's day, by forethought of provision for the morrow, were suspended; for the money transmitted to her by Alwyn, in return for the emblazoned MSS., was sufficient to supply their modest wants for months to come. Adam, more and more engrossed in his labors, did not appear to perceive the daintier plenty of his board, nor the purchase of some small comforts unknown for years. He only said, one morning—"It is strange, girl, that as *that* gathers in life, and he pointed to the model), it seems already to provide, to my phantasy, the luxuries it will one day give to us all in truth. Methought my very bed last night seemed wondrous easy, and the coverings were warmer, for I woke not with the cold!"

"Ah!" thought the sweet daughter, smiling through moist eyes—"while my cares can smooth thy barren path through life, why should I cark and pine?"

Their solitude was now occasionally broken in the evenings by the visits of Nicholas Alwyn. The young goldsmith was himself not ignorant of the simpler mathematics; he had some talent for invention, and took pleasure in the construction of horologes, though, properly speaking, not a part of his trade. His excuse for his visits was the wish to profit by Warner's mechanical knowledge; but the student was so wrapped in his own pursuits, that he gave but little instruction to his visitor. Nevertheless, Alwyn was satisfied, for he saw Sibyll. He saw her in the most attractive phase of her character—the loving, patient, devoted daughter; and the view of her household virtues affected more and more his honest English heart. But, ever awkward and embarrassed, he gave no vent to his feelings. To Sibyll he spoke little, and with formal constraint; and the girl, unconscious of her conquest, was little less indifferent to his visits than her abstracted father.

But all at once Adam woke to a sense of the change that had taken place—all at once he caught scent of gold, for his works were brought to a pause for want of some finer and more costly materials than the coins in his own possession (the remnant of Marmaduke's gift) enabled him to purchase. He had stolen out at dusk unknown to Sibyll, and lavished the whole upon the model, but in vain! The model in itself was, indeed, completed; his invention had mastered the difficulty that it had encountered. But Adam had complicated the contrivance by adding to it experimental proofs of the Agency it was intended to exercise. It was necessary in that age, if he were to convince others, to show more than the principle of his engine, he must show also something of its effects; turn a mill without wind or water, or set in motion some mimic vehicle without other force than that the contrivance itself supplied. And here, at every step, new obstacles arose. It was the misfortune to science in those days, not only that all books and mathematical instruments were enormously dear, but that the students, still struggling into light, through the glorious delusions of alchemy and mysticism—imagined that, even in simple practical operations, there were peculiar virtues in virgin gold and certain precious stones.

A link in the process upon which Adam was engaged failed him: his ingenuity was baffled, his work stood still; and in poring again and again over the learned MSS.—alas! now lost, in which certain German doctors had sought to explain the pregnant hints of Roger Bacon, he found it inculcated that the axle of a certain wheel must be composed of a diamond. Now in truth, it so happened that Adam's contrivance, which (even without the appliances which were added in illustration of the theory) was infinitely more complicated than modern research has found necessary, did not even require the wheel in question, much less the absent diamond: it happened, also, that his understanding, which, though so obtuse in common life, was in these matters astonishingly clear, could not trace any mathematical operatious by which the diamond axle would in the least correct the difficulty that had suddenly started up; and yet the accursed diamond began to haunt him—the German authority was so positive on the point, and that authority had in many respects been accurate. Nor was this all—the diamond was to be no vulgar diamond: it was to be endowed, by talismaniac skill, with certain properties and virtues; it was to be for a certain number of hours exposed to the rays of the full moon; it was to be washed in a primitive and wondrous elixir, the making of which consumed no little of the finest gold. This diamond was to be to the machine what the soul is to the body—a glorious, all-pervading, mysterious principle of activity and life. Such were the dreams that obscured the cradle of infant science!

And Adam, with all his reasoning powers, his lore in the hard truths of mathematics, was but one of the giant children of the dawn. The magnificent phrases and solemn promises of the mystic Germans got firm hold of his fancy. Night and day, waking or sleeping, the diamond, basking in the silence of the full moon, sparkled before his eyes—meanwhile all was at a stand. In the very last steps of his discovery he was arrested. Then suddenly looking round for vulgar moneys to purchase the precious gem, and the materials for the soluble elixir, he saw that MONEY had been at work around him—that he had been sleeping softly and faring sumptuously. He was seized with a divine rage. How had Sibyll dared to secrete from him this hoard? how presumed to *waste* upon the base body what might have so profited the eternal mind? In his relentless ardor, in his sublime devotion and loyalty to his abstract idea, there was a devouring cruelty, of which this meek and gentle scholar was wholly unconscious. The grim iron model, like a Moloch, eat up all things—health, life, love; and its jaws now opened for his child. He rose from his bed—it was daybreak—he threw on his dressing robe—he strode into his daughter's room—the grey twilight came through the comfortless, curtainless casement, deep sunk into the wall. Adam did not pause to notice that the poor child, though she had provoked his anger, by refitting his dismal chamber, had spent nothing in giving a less rugged frown to her own.

The scanty worm-worn furniture, the wretched pallet, the poor attire folded decently beside—nothing, save that inexpressible purity and cleanliness which, in the lowliest hovel, a pure and maiden mind gathers round it—nothing to distinguish the room of her whose childhood had passed in courts from the hut of the meanest daughter of drudgery and toil! No—he who had lavished the fortunes of his father and his child into the grave of his idea—no—he saw nothing of this self-forgetful penury—the diamond danced before him! He approached the bed—and oh! the contrast of that dreary room and peasant pallet, to the delicate, pure, enchanting loveliness of the sleeping inmate. The scanty covering left partially exposed the snow-white neck and rounded shoulder; the face was pillowed upon the arm, in an infantine grace; the face was slightly flushed, and the fresh red lips parted into a smile—for in her sleep the virgin dreamed—a happy dream? It was a sight to have touched a father's heart, to have stopped his footstep, and hushed his breath into prayer. And call not Adam hard, unnatural, that he was not then, as men far more harsh than he—for the father at that moment was not in his breast—the human man was gone—he himself, like his model, was a machine of iron!—his life was his one idea!"

"Wake, child, wake!" he said, in a loud but hollow voice. "Where is the gold thou hast hidden from me? Wake—confess!"

Roused from her gracious dreams thus savagely, Sibyll started, and saw the eager, darkened face of her father. Its expression was peculiar and undefinable, for it was not threatening, angry, stern; there was a vacancy in the eyes, a strain in the features, and yet a wild, intense animation lighting and pervading all—it was as the face of one walking in his sleep; and, at the confusion of waking, Sibyll thought indeed that such was her father's state. But the impatience with which he shook the arm he grasped, and repeated, as he opened convulsively his other hand, "The gold, Sibyll—the gold! Why did'st thou hide it from me?" speedily convinced her that her father's mind was under the influence of the prevailing malady that made all its weakness and all its strength.

"My poor father!" she said, pityingly, "wilt thou not leave thyself the means whereby to keep strength and health for thine high hopes. Ah! father thy Sibyll only hoarded her poor gains for thee!"

"The gold!" said Adam, mechanically, but in a softer voice—"all—all thou hast? How didst thou get it—how?"

"By the labors of these hands. Ah! do not frown on me!"

"Thou—the child of knightly fathers—*thou* labor!" said Adam, an instinct of his former state of gentle-born and high-hearted youth flashing from his eyes. "It was wrong in thee!"

"Dost thou not labor too?"

"Ay, but for the world. Well—the gold!"

Sibyll rose, and modestly throwing over her form the old mantle which lay on the pallet, passed to a corner of the room, and opening a chest, took from it the gipsire, and held it out to her father.

"If it please thee, dear and honored sir, so be it; and Heaven prosper it in thy hands!"

Before Adam's clutch could close on the gipsire, a rude hand was laid on his shoulder, the gipsire was snatched from Sibyll, and the gaunt, half-clad form of Old Madge interposed between the two.

"Eh, sir!" she said, in her shrill, cracked tone, "I thought, when I heard your door open, and your step hurrying down, you were after no good deeds. Fie, master, fie! I have clung to you when all reviled, and when starvation within and foul words without made all my hire; for I ever thought you a good and mild man, though little better than stark wode. But, augh! to rob your poor child thus—to leave her to starve and pine! We old folks are used to it. Look round—look round; I remember this chamber, when ye first came to your father's hall. Saints of heaven! There stood the brave bed all rustling with damask of silk; on those stone walls once hung fine arras of the Flemings—a marriage gift to my lady from Queen Margaret, and a mighty show to see, and good for the soul's comforts, with Bible stories wrought on it. Eh, sir! don't you call to mind your namesake, Master Adam, in his brave scarlet hosen, and Madam Eve, in her bonny blue kirtle and laced courtpie; and now—now look round, I say, and see what you have brought your child to!"

"Hush! hush! Madge, hush!" cried Siybll, while Adam gazed in evident perturbation and awakening shame at the intruder, turning his eyes round the room as she spoke, and heaving from time to time short deep sighs.

"But I will not hush," pursued the old woman; "I will say my say, for I love ye both, and I loved my poor mistress, who is dead and gone. Ah, sir, groan! it does you good. And now when this sweet damsel is growing up, now when you should think of saving a marriage dower for her (for no marriage where no pot boils), do you rend from her the little that she has drudged to gain!—She!—Oh, out on your heart? and for what—for what, sir? For the neighbors to set fire to your father's house, and the little ones to ——"

"Forbear, woman!" cried Adam, in a voice of thunder, "forbear! Leave us!" And he waved his hand as he spoke, with so unexpected a majesty that Madge was awed into sudden silence, and, darting a look of compassion at Sibyll, she hobbed from the room. Adam stood motionless an instant; but when he felt his child's soft arms round his neck—when he heard her voice struggling against tears, praying him not to heed the foolish words of the old servant—to take—to take all—that it would be easy to gain more—the ice of his philosophy melted at once—the man broke forth, and, clasping Sibyll to his heart, and kissing her cheek, her lips, her hands, he faltered out—"No! no!—forgive me!—forgive thy cruel father! Much thought has maddened me, I think—it has indeed! Poor child, poor Sibyll," and he stroked her cheek gently, and with a movement of pathetic pity—"poor child, thou art pale—and so slight and delicate! And this chamber—and thy loneliness—and—ah! my life hath been a curse to thee, yet I meant to bequeath it a boon to all!"

"Father, dear father, speak not thus. You break my heart. Here, here—take the gold—or rather, for thou must not venture out to insult again, let me purchase with it what thou needest. Tell me, trust me——"

"No!" exclaimed Adam, with that hollow energy by which a man resolves to impose restraint on himself; "I will not, for all that science ever achieved—I will not lay this shame on my soul;—spend this gold on thyself—trim this room—buy thee raiment—all that thou needest—I order—I command it! And hark thee, if thou gettest more, hide it from me—hide it well—men's desires are foul tempters! I never knew, in following wisdom, that I had a vice. I wake and find myself a miser and a robber!"

And with these words he fled from the girl's chamber, gained his own and locked the door.

CHAPTER III.

A Strange Visitor—All Ages of the World breed World-Betters.

Sibyll, whose soft heart bled for her father, and who now reproached herself for having concealed from him her little hoard, began hastily to dress that she might seek him out, and soothe the painful feelings which the honest rudeness of Madge had aroused. But before her task was concluded, there pealed a loud knock at the outer door. She heard the old housekeeper's quivering voice responding to a loud clear tone; and presently Madge herself ascended the stairs to Warner's room, followed by a man whom Sibyll instantly recognized, for he was not one easily to be forgotten,—as their protector from the assault of the mob. She drew back hastily as he passed her door, and in some wonder and alarm awaited the descent of Madge. That venerable personage having with some difficulty induced her master to open his door and admit the stranger, came straight into her young lady's chamber. "Cheer up—cheer up, sweetheart," said the old woman, "I think better days will shine soon; for the honest man I have admitted says he is but come to tell Master Warner something that will redound much to his profit. Oh! he is a wonderful fellow, this same Robin! You saw how he turned the cullions from burning the old-house!"

"What! you know this man, Madge! What is he, and who?"

Madge looked puzzled. "That is more than I can say, sweet mistress. But though he has been but some weeks in the neighborhood, they all hold him in high count and esteem. For why—it is said he is a rich man and a kind one. He does a world of good to the poor."

While Sibyll listened to such expalnations as Madge could give her, the stranger, who had carefully closed the door of the student's chamber, after regarding Adam for a moment, while silent but keen scrutiny, thus began:—

"When last we met, Adam Warner, it was with satchells on our backs. Look well at me!"

"Troth," answered Adam, languidly, for he saw still under the deep dejection that had followed the scene with Sibyll, "I cannot call you to mind, nor seems it veritable that our school-days passed together, seeing that my hair is grey and men call me old; but thou art in all the lustihood of this human life."

"Nathless," returned the stranger, "there are but two years or so between thine age and mine. When thou wert poring over the crabbed text, and pattering Latin by the ell, dost thou not remember a lack-grace, good-for-nought, Robert Hilyard, who was always setting the school in an uproar, and was finally outlawed from that boy-world as he hath been since from the man's world, for inciting the weak to resist the strong?"

"Ah!" exclaimed Adam, with a gleam of something like joy on his face; "art thou, indeed, that riotous, brawling, fighting, frank-hearted, bold fellow, Robert Hilyard? Ha! ha!—those were merry days! I have known none like them ——"

The old schoolfellows shook hands heartily.

"The world has not fared well with thee in person or pouch, I fear me, poor Adam," said Hilyard; "thou canst scarcely have passed thy fiftieth year, and yet thy learned studies have given thee the weight of sixty; while I, though ever in toil and bustle, often wanting a meal, and even fearing the halter, am strong and hearty as when I shot my first fellow buck in the king's forest, and kissed the forester's pretty daughter. Yet, methinks, Adam, if what I hear of thy tasks be true, thou and I have each been working for one end; thou to make the world other than it is, and I to ——"

"What! hast thou, too, taken nourishment from the bitter milk of Philosophy,—thou, fighting Rob?"

"I know not whether it be called philosophy—but marry, Edward of York would call it rebellion; they are much the same, for both war against rules established!" returned Hilyard, with more depth of thought than his careless manner seemed to promise. He paused, and laying his broad brown hand on Warner's shoulder, resumed—"Thou art poor, Adam!"

"Very poor—very—very!"

"Does thy philosophy disdain gold?"

"What can philosophy achieve without it? She is a hungry dragon, and her very food is gold!"

"Wilt thou brave some danger—thou wert ever a fearless boy when thy blood was up, though so meek and gentle—wilt thou brave some danger for large reward?"

"My life braves the scorn of men, the pinchings of famine, and, it may be, the stake and the fagot. Soldiers brave not the dangers that are braved by a wise man in an unwise age!"

"Gramercy! thou hast a hero's calm aspect while thou speakest, and thy words move me! Listen! Thou were wont, when Henry of Windsor was King of England, to visit and confer with him on learned matters. He is now a captive in the Tower; but his jailers permit him still to receive the visits of pious monks and harmless scholars. I ask thee to pay him such a visit, and for this office I am empowered by richer men than myself to award thee the guerdon of twenty broad pieces of gold."

"Twenty!—A mine!—A Tmolus!" exclaimed Adam, in uncontrollable glee. "Twenty!—O true friend!—then my work will be born at last!"

"But hear me further, Adam, for I will not deceive thee; the visit hath its peril! Thou must first see if the mind of King Henry, for king he is, though the ursuper wear his holy crown, be clear and healthful. Thou knowest he is subject to dark moods—suspension of man's reason; and if he be, as his friends hope, sane and right-judging, thou wilt give him certain papers, which, after his hand has signed them, thou wilt bring back to me. If in this thou succeedest, know that thou mayest restore the royalty of Lancaster to the purple and the throne; that thou wilt have princes and earl's for favorers and protectors to thy learned life; that thy fortunes and fame are made! Fail, be discovered—and Edward of York never spares!—Thy guerdon will be the nearest tree and the strongest rope!"

"Robert," said Adam, who had listened to this address with unusual attention, "thou dealest with me plainly, and as man should deal with man I know little of stratagem and polity, wars and kings; and save that King Henry, though passing ignorant in the mathematics, and more given to alchemists than to solid seekers after truth, was once or twice gracious to me, I could have no choice, in these four walls, between an Edward and a Henry on the throne. But I have a king whose throne is in mine own breast, and, alack, it taxeth me heavily, and with sore burdens."

"I comprehend," said the visitor, glancing round the room—"I comprehend—thou wantest money for thy books and instruments, and thy melancholic passion is thy sovereign. Thou wilt incur the risk?"

"I will," said Adam. "I would rather seek in the lion's den for what I lack, than do what I well nigh did this day."

" What crime was that, poor scholar ? " said Robin, smiling.

" My child worked for *her* bread, and *my* luxuries—I would have robbed her, old school-fellow. Ha !—ha !—what is cord and gibbet to one so tempted ? "

A tear stood in the bright grey eyes of the bluff visitor.

" Ah ! Adam," he said, sadly, " only by the candle held in the skeleton hand of Poverty can man read his own dark heart. But thou, Workman of Knowledge, hast the same interest as the poor, who dig and delve. Though strange circumstance hath made me the servant and emissary of Margaret, think not that I am but the varlet of the great."

Hilyard paused a moment and resumed—

" Thou knowest, peradventure, that my race dates from an elder date than these Norman nobles, who boast their robber-fathers. From the renowned Saxon Thane, who, free of hand and of cheer, won the name of Hildegardis,* our family took its rise. But under these Norman barons, we sank with the nation to which we belonged. Still were we called gentlemen, and still were dubbed knights. But, as I grew up to man's estate, I felt myself more Saxon than gentleman, and, as one of a subject and vassal race, I was a son of the Saxon people. My father, like thee, was a man of thought and bookcraft. I dare own to thee, that he was a Lollard, and with the religion of those bold foes to priest-vice, goes a spirit that asks why the people should be evermore the spoil and prey of lords and kings. Early in my youth, my father, fearing rack and fagot in England, sought refuge in the Hans Town of Lubeck. There I learned grave truths—how liberty can be won and guarded. Later in life I saw the republics of Italy, and I asked why they were so glorious in all the arts and craft of civil life, while the braver men of France and England seemed as savages by the side of the Florentine burgess, nay, of the Lombard vine-dresser. I saw that, even when those republics fell a victim to some tyrant or podesta, their men still preserved rights and uttered thoughts which left them more free and more great than the Commons of England, after all their boasted wars. I came back to my native land and settled in the North, as my franklin ancestry before me. The broad lands of my forefathers had devolved on the elder line, and gave a knight's fee to Sir Robert Hilyard, who fell afterwards at Touton for the Lancastrians.

" But I had won gold in the far countree, and I took farm and homestead near Lord Warwick's tower of Middleham. The feud between Lancaster and York broke forth; Earl Warwick summoned his retainers, myself amongst them, since I lived upon his land; I sought the great earl, and I told him boldly—him whom the Commons deemed a friend and a foe to all malfaisance and abuse—I told him that the war he asked me to join seemed to me but a war of ambitious lords, and that I saw not how the Commons were to be bettered, let who would be king. The earl listened and deigned to reason; and when he saw I was not convinced, he left me to my will; for he is a noble chief, and I admired even his angry pride, when he said, 'Let no man fight for Warwick whose heart beats not in his cause.' I lived afterwards to discharge my debt to the proud earl, and show him how even the lion may be meshed, and how even the mouse may gnaw the net. But to my own tragedy. So I quitted those parts, for I feared my own resolution near so great a man: I made a new home not far from the city of York. So, Adam, when all the land around bristled with pike and gisarme, and while my own cousin and namesake, the head of my house, was winning laurels and wasting blood—I, thy quarrelsome, fighting friend—lived at home in peace with my wife and child—(for I was now married, and wife and child were dear to me) —and tilled my lands. But in peace I was active and astir, for my words inflamed the bosoms of laborers and peasants, and many of them, benighted as they were, thought with me.

" One day—I was absent from home, selling my grain in the marts of York—one day there entered the village a young captain, a boy-chief, Edward Earl of March, beating for recruits. Dost thou heed me, Adam ? Well, man—well, the peasants stood aloof from tromp and banner, and they answered, to all the talk of hire and fame, 'Robin Hilyard tells us we have nothing to gain but blows—leave us to hew and to delve.' Oh ! Adam,

* Hildegardis, viz., old German, a person of noble or generous disposition. Watton's Baronetage. Art. Hilyard, or Hildyard, of Pattrington.

this boy—this chief—the Earl of March, now crowned King Edward, made but one reply—'This Robin Hilyard must be a wise man—show me his house.' They pointed out the ricks, the barns, the homestead, and in five minutes all—all were in flames. 'Tell the hilding, when he returns, that thus Edward of March, fair to friends and terrible to foes, rewards the coward who disaffects the men of Yorkshire to their chief.' And by the blazing rafters, and the pale faces of the silent crowd, he rode on his way to battle and the throne!"

Hilyard paused, and the anguish of his countenance was terrible to behold.

"I returned to find a heap of ashes—I returned to find my wife a maniac—I returned to find my child—my boy—great God!—he had run to hide himself, in terror at the torches and the grim men—they had failed to discover him, till, too late, his shrieks, amidst the crashing walls, burst on his mother's ear;—and the scorched, mangled, lifeless corpse, lay on that mother's bosom!"

Adam rose; his figure was transformed—not the stooping student, but the knight descended man, seemed to tower in the murky chamber; his hands felt at his side, as for a sword; he stifled a curse, and Hilyard, in that suppressed low voice which evinces a strong mind in deep emotion, continued his tale.

"Blessed be the divine Intercessor, the mother of the dead died too! Behold me, a lonely, ruined, wifeless, childless wretch! I made all the world my foe! The old love of liberty (alone left me) became a crime; I plunged into the gloom of the forest, a robber-chief, sparing—no, never—never—never!—one York captain—one spurred knight—one belted lord! But the poor, my Saxon countrymen, *they* had suffered, and were safe!

"One dark twilight—thou hast heard the tale—every village minstrel sets it to his viol—a majestic woman—a hunted fugitive—crossed my path; she led a boy in her hand, a year or so younger than my murdered child. 'Friend!' said the woman fearlessly, 'save the son of your king: I am Margaret, Queen of England!' I saved them both. From that hour, the robber-chief, the Lollard's son, became a queen's friend. Here opened, at least, vengeance against the fell destroyer. Now see you why I seek you—why tempt you into danger? Pause if you will, for my passion heats my blood;—and all the kings since Saul, it may be, are not worth one scholar's life! And yet," continued Hilyard, regaining his ordinary calm tone, "and yet, it seemeth to me, as I said at first, that all who labor have, in this a common cause and interest with the poor. This woman-king, though bloody man, with his wine-cups and his harlots—this usurping York—his very existence flaunts the life of the sons of toil. In civil war and in broil, in strife that needs the arms of the people, the people shall get their own."

"I will go," said Adam, and he advanced to the door.

Hilyard caught his arm. "Why, friend, thou hast not even the documents, and how wouldst thou get access to the prison? Listen to me; or," added the conspirator, observing poor Adam's abstracted air, "or let me rather speak a word to thy fair daughter; women have ready wit, and are the pioneers to the advance of men! Adam! Adam! thou art dreaming!"—He shook the philosopher's arm roughly.

"I heed you," said Warner, meekly.

"The first thing required," renewed Hilyard, "is a permit to see King Henry. This is obtained either from the Lord Worcester, governor of the Tower, a cruel man, who may deny it—or the Lord Hastings, Edward's chamberlain, a humane and gentle one, who will readily grant it. Let not thy daughter know why thou wouldst visit Henry; let her suppose it is solely to make report of his health to Margaret; let her not know there is scheming or danger; so, at least, her ignorance will secure her safety. But let her go to the lord chamberlain, and obtain the order for a learned clerk to visit the learned prisoner—to—ha! well thought of—this strange machine is doubtless, the invention of which thy neighbors speak; this shall make thy excuse; thou wouldst divert the prisoner with thy mechanical—comprehendest thou Adam?"

"Ah! King Henry will see the model, and when he is on the throne—

"He will protect the scholar!" interrupted Hilyard, "Good! good! Wait here—I will confer with thy daughter."

He gently pushed aside Adam, opened the door, and on descending the stairs, found Sibyll by the large casement where she had stood with Marmaduke, and heard the rude stave of the tymbesteres.

The anxiety the visit of Hilyard had occasoned her was at once allayed, when he informed her that he had been her father's schoolmate, and desired to become his friend. And when he drew a moving picture of the exiled condition of Margaret and the young prince, and their natural desire to learn tidings of the health of the deposed king, her gentle heart, forgetting the haughty insolence with which her royal mistress had often wounded and chilled her childhood, felt all the generous and compassionate sympathy the conspirator desired to awaken. "The occasion," added Hilyard, "for learning the poor captive's state now offers! He hath heard of your father's labors; he desires to learn their nature from his own lips. He is allowed to receive, by an order from King Edward's chamberlain, the visits of those scholars in whose converse he was ever wont to delight. Wilt thou so far aid the charitable work as to seek the Lord Hastings, and crave the necessary license? Thou seest that thy father has wayward and abstract moods; he might forget that Henry of Windsor is no longer king, and might give him that title in speaking to Lord Hastings—a slip of the tongue which the law styles treason."

"Certes," said Sibyll, quickly, "if my father would seek the poor captive, I will be his messenger to my Lord Hastings. But, oh, sir! as thou hast known my father's boyhood, and as thou hopest for mercy in the last day, tempt to no danger one so guileless?"

Hilyard winced as he interrupted her hastily—

"There is no danger if thou wilt obtain the license. I will say more—a reward awaits him, that will not only banish his poverty but save his life."

"His life!"

"Ay! seest thou not, fair mistress, that Adam Warner is dying, not of the body's hunger, but of the soul's? He craveth gold, that his toils may reap their guerdon. If that gold be denied, his toils will fret him to the grave!"

"Alas! alas!—it is true.

"That gold he shall honorably win! Nor is this all. Thou wilt see the Lord Hastings: he is less learned, perhaps, than Worcester—less dainty in accomplishments and gifts than Anthony Woodville, but his mind is profound and vast; all men praise him, save the queen's kin. He loves scholars; he is mild to distress; he laughs at the superstitions of the vulgar. Thou wilt see the Lord Hastings, and thou mayst interest him in thy father's genius and his fate!"

"There is frankness in thy voice, and I will trust thee," answered Sibyll. When shall I seek this lord?"

"This day, if thou wilt. He lodges at the Tower, and gives access, it is said, to all who need his offices, or seek succor from his power."

"This day, then, be it!" answered Sibyll, calmly.

Hilyard gazed at her countenance, rendered so noble in its youthful resignation—in its soft firmness of expression, and muttering, "Heaven prosper thee, maiden; we shall meet to-morrow," descended the stairs, and quitted the house.

His heart smote him when he was in the street. "If evil should come to this meek scholar—to that poor child's father, it would be a sore sin to my soul. But no; I will not think it. The saints will not suffer this bloody Edward to triumph long; and in this vast chess-board of vengeance and great ends, we must move men to and fro, and harden our natures to the hazard of the game."

Sibyll sought her father; his mind had flown back to the model. He was already living in the life that the promised gold would give to the dumb thought. True that all the ingenious additions to the engine—additions that were to co convince the reason and startle the fancy, were not yet complete, (for want, of course, of the diamond bathed in moonbeams)—but still there was enough in the inventions already achieved to excite curiosity and obtain encouragement. So, with care and diligence and sanguine hope, the philosopher prepared the grim model for exhibition to a man who had worn a crown, and might wear again. But with that innocent and sad cunning which is so common with enthusiasts of one idea, the sublime dwellers of the narrow border between madness and inspiration, Adam, amidst his excitement, contrived to conceal from his daughter all glimpse of the danger he run, of the correspondence of which he was to be the medium,—or rather, may we think that he had forgotten both! Not the stout Warwick himself, in the roar of battle, thought so little of peril to life and limb of that gentle student, in the reveries of his lonely closet; and therefore, all unsuspicious, and seeing but diversion to Adam's recent gloom of despair, an opening to all his bright prospects, Sibyll attired herself in her holiday garments, drew her wimple closely round her face, and summoning Madge to attend her, bent her way to the Tower. Near York House, within view of the Sanctuary and the palace of Westminster, they took a boat, and arrived at the stairs of the Tower.

CHAPTER IV.

Lord Hastings.

WILLIAM Lord Hastings was one of the most remarkable men of the age. Philip de Comines bears testimony to his high repute for wisdom and virtue. Born the son of a knight of ancient lineage but scanty lands, he had risen, while yet in the prime of life, to a rank and an influence second, perhaps, only, to the house of Nevile. Like Lord Montagu, he united in happy combination the talents of a soldier and a courtier. But as a statesman, —a schemer—a thinker—Montagu, with all his craft, was inferior to Hastings. In this, the latter had but two equals—viz., George, the youngest of the Nevile brothers, Archbishop of York; and a boy, whose intellect was not yet fully developed, but in whom was already apparent to the observant, the dawn of a restless, fearless, calculating and subtle genius—that boy, whom the philosophers of Utrecht had taught to reason, whom the lessons of Warwick had trained to arms, was Richard, Duke of Gloucester, famous even now for his skill in the tilt-yard, and his ingenuity is the rhetoric of the schools.

The manners of Lord Hastings had contributed to his fortunes. Despite the newness of his honors, even the haughtiest of the ancient nobles bore him no grudge, for his demeanor was at once modest and manly. He was peculiarly simple and unostentatious in his habits, and possessed that nameless charm which makes men popular with the lowly, and welcome to the great.* But in that day a certain mixture of vice was necessary to success; and Hastings wounded no self-love by the assumption of unfashionable purism. He was regarded with small favor by the queen, who knew him as the companion of Edward in his pleasures, and at a latter period accused him of enticing her faithless lord into unworthy affections. And certain it is, that he was foremost amongst the courtiers in those adventures which we call the excesses of gaiety and folly, though too often leading to Solomon's wisdom and his sadness. But profligacy, with Hastings, had the excuse of ardent passions: he had loved deeply, and unhappily, in his earlier youth, and he gave into the dissipation of the time with the restless eagerness common to strong and active natures when the heart is not at ease; and under all the light fascination of his converse, or the dissipation of his life lurked the melancholic temperament of a man worthy of nobler things. Nor was the courtly vice of the libertine the only drawback to the virtuous character assigned to Hastings by Comines. His experience of men had taught him something of the disdain of the cynic, and he scrupled not at serving his pleasures or his ambition by means which his loftier nature could not excuse to his clear sense.*

Still, however, the world, which had deteriorated, could not harden, him. Few persons so able acted so frequently from impulse; the impulses were, for the most part, affectionate and generous, but then came the regrets of caution and experience; and Hastings summoned his intellect to correct the movement of his heart—in other words, reflection sought to undo what impulse had suggested. Though so successful a gallant, he had not acquired the ruthless egotism of the sensualist; and his conduct to women often evinced the weakness of giddy youth, rather than the cold deliberation of profligate manhood. Thus in his veriest

* On Edward's accession, so highly were the services of Hastings appreciated by the party, that not only the king, but many of the nobility, contributed to render his wealth equal to his new station, by grants of lands and moneys. Several years afterwards, when he went with Edward into France, no less than two lords, nine knights, fifty-eight squires, and twenty gentlemen, joined his train.—Dugdale's Baronage, p. 583. Sharon Turner's History of England, vol. iii. p. 380.

* See Comines, b. vi. for a curious anecdote of what Mr. Sharon Turner happily calls "the moral coquetry" of Hastings;—an anecdote which reveals much of his character.

vices there was a spurious amiability—a seductive charm; while in the graver affairs of life, the intellectual susceptibility of his nature served but to quicken his penetration and stimulate his energies, and Hastings might have said, with one of his Italian contemporaries,—"That in subjection to the influences of women he had learned the government of men." In a word, his powers to attract, and his capacities to command, may be guessed by this,—that Lord Hastings was the only man Richard III. seems to have loved, when Duke of Gloucester,* and the only man he seems to have feared, when resolved to be King of England. Hastings was alone in the apartments assigned to him in the Tower, when his page, with a peculiar smile, announced to him the visit of a young donzell, who would not impart her business to his attendants.

The accomplished chamberlain looked up somewhat impatiently from the beautiful MS., enriched with the silver verse of Petrarch, which lay open on his table, and, after muttering to himself—"It is only Edward, to whom the face of a woman never is unwelcome," bade the page admit the visitor.

The damsel entered, and the door closed upon her.

"Be not alarmed, maiden," said Hastings, touched by the downcast bend of her hooded countenance, and the unmistakable and timid modesty of his visitor's bearing. "What hast thou to say to me?"

At the sound of his voice, Sibyll Warner started, and uttered a faint exclamation. The stranger of the pastime-ground was before her. Instinctively the drew the wimple yet more closely round her face, and laid her hand upon the bolt of the door as if in the impulse of retreat.

The nobleman's curiosity was roused. He looked again and earnestly on the form that seemed to shrink from his gaze; then rising slowly, he advanced, and laid his hand on her arm;—"Donzell, I recognize thee," he said, in a voice that sounded cold and stern—"what service wouldst thou ask me to render thee! Speak! Nay! I pray thee, speak."

"Indeed, good my lord," said Sibyll, conquering her confusion; and, lifting her wimple, her dark blue eyes met those bent on her, with fearless truth and innocence, "I knew not, and you will believe me—I knew not till this moment that I had such cause for gratitude to the Lord Hastings. I sought you but on the behalf of my father, Master Adam Warner, wbo would fain have the permission accorded to other scholars, to see the Lord Henry of Windsor, who was gracious to him in other days, and to while the duress of that princely captive with the show of a quaint instrument he has invented."

"Doubtless," answered Hastings, who deserved his character (rare in that day) for humanity and mildness—"doubtless it will pleasure me, nor offend his grace the king, to show all courtesy and indulgence to the unhappy gentleman and lord, whom the weal of England condemns us to hold incarcerate. I have heard of thy father, maiden, an honest and simple man, in whom we need not fear a conspirator; and of the young mistress, I have heard also, since we parted."

"Of me, noble sir?'

"Of thee," said Hastings, with a smile; and, placing a seat for her, he took from the table an illuminated MS. "I have to thank thy friend, Master Alwyn, for procuring me this treasure!"

"What, my lord!" said Sibyll, and her eyes glistened, "were you—you the—the——"

"The fortunate person whom Alwyn has enriched at so slight a cost. Yes. Do not grudge me my good fortune in this. Thou hast nobler treasures, methinks, to bestow on another!"

"My good lord!"

"Nay, I must not distress thee. And the young gentleman has a fair face: may it bespeak a true heart!"

These words gave Sibyll an emotion of strange delight. They seemed spoken sadly—they seemed to betoken a jealous sorrow—they awoke the strange, wayward, woman-feeling, which is pleased at the pain that betrays the woman's influence: the girl's rosy lips smiled maliciously. Hastings watched her, and her face was so radiant with that rare gleam of secret happiness—so fresh, so young, so pure, and withal so arch and captivating, that hackneyed and jaded as he was in the vulgar pursuit of pleasure, the sight moved better and tenderer feelings than those of the sensualist. "Yes," he muttered to himself,

* Sir Thomas More, Life of Edward V., speaks of "the great love" Richard bore to Hastings.

"there *are* some toys it were a sin to sport with and cast away amidst the broken rubbish of gone passions!"

He turned to the table, and wrote the order of admission to Henry's prison, and as he gave it to Sibyll, he said, "Thy young gallant, I see, is at the court now. It is a perilous ordeal, and especially to one for whom the name of Nevile opens the road to advancement and honor. Men learn betimes in courts to forsake Love for Plutus, and many a wealthy lord would give his heiress to the poorest gentleman who claims kindred to the Earl of Salisbury and Warwick."

"May my father's guest so prosper," answered Sibyll, "for he seems of loyal heart and gentle nature!"

"Thou art unselfish, sweet mistress," said Hastings; and, surprised by her careless tone, he paused a moment, "or art thou, in truth, indifferent? Saw I not thy hand in his, when even those loathly tymbesteres chanted warning to thee for loving, not above thy merits, but, alas, it may be, above thy fortunes?"

Sibyll's delight increased. Oh, then, he had not applied that hateful warning to himself. He guessed not her secret. She blushed, and the blush was so chaste and maidenly, while the smile that went with it was so ineffably animated and joyous, that Hastings exclaimed, with unaffected admiration, "Surely, fair donzell, Petarch dreamed of thee, when he spoke of the woman-blush and the angel smile of Laura. Woe to the man who would injure thee. Farewell! I would not see thee too often, unless I saw thee ever."

He lifted her hand to his lips, with a chivalrous respect, as he spoke; opened the door, and called his page to attend her to the gates.

Sibyll was more flattered by the abrupt dismissal, than if he had knelt to detain her. How different seemed the world as her light step wended homeward!

CHAPTER V.

Master Adam Warner and King Henry the Sixth.

THE next morning Hilyard revisited Warner, with the letters for Henry. The conspirator made Adam reveal to him the interior mechanism of the Eureka to which Adam, who had toiled all night, had appended one of the most ingenious contrivances he as yet been enambled (*sans* the diamond) to accomplish, for the better display of the agencies which the engine was designed to achieve. This contrivance was full of strange cells and recesses, in one of which the documents were placed. And there they lay, so well concealed as to puzzle the minutest search, if not aided by the inventor, or one to whom he had communicated the secrets of the contrivance.

After repeated warnings and exhortations to discretion, Hilyard then, whose busy active mind had made all the necessary arrangements, summoned a stout-looking fellow, whom he had left below, and, with his aid, conveyed the heavy machine across the garden, to a back lane, where a mule stood ready to receive the burden.

"Suffer this trusty fellow to guide thee, dear Adam; he will take thee through ways where thy brutal neighbors are not likely to meet and molest thee. Call all thy wits to the surface. Speed and prosper!"

"Fear not," said Adam, disdainfully. "In the neighborhood of kings, science is ever safe. Bless thee, child," and he laid his hand upon Sibyll's head, for she had accompanied them thus far in silence—"now go in."

"I go with thee, father," said Sibyll, firmly. "Master Hilyard, it is best so," she whispered; "what if my father fall into one of his reveries!"

"You are right: go with him, at least, to the Tower-gate. Hard by, is the house of a noble dame, and a worthy, known to our friend Hugh, where thou mayest wait Master Warner's return. It will not suit thy modesty and sex to loiter amongst the pages and soldiery in the yard. Adam, thy daughter must wend with thee."

Adam had not attended to this colloquy, and mechanically bowing his head, he set off, and was greatly surprised, on gaining the river side (where a boat was found large enough to accommodate not only the human passengers, but the mule and its burden), to see Sibyll by his side.

The imprisonment of the unfortunate Henry, though guarded with sufficient rigor against all chances of escape, was not, as the reader has perceived, at this period embittered by unnecessary harshness. His attendants treated him with respect, his table was supplied more abundantly and daintily than his habitual abstinence required, and the monks and learned men whom he had favored, were, we need not repeat, permitted to enliven his solitude with their grave converse.

On the other hand, all attempts at correspondence between Margaret, or the exiled Lancastrians and himself, had been jealously watched, and when detected, the emissaries had been punished with relentless severity. A man named Hawkins had been racked for attempting to borrow money for the queen from the great London merchant, Sir Thomas Cook. A shoemaker had been tortured to death, with red-hot pincers, for abetting her correspondence with her allies. Various persons had been racked for similar offences, but the energy of Margaret, and the zeal of her adherents, were still unexhausted and unconquered.

Either unconscious or contemptuous of the perils to which he was subjected, the student, with his silent companions, performed the voyage, and landed in sight of the Fortress-Palatine. And now Hugh stopped before a house of good fashion, knocked at the door, which opened by an old servitor, disappeared for a few moments, and returning, informed Sibyll, in a meaning whisper, that the gentlewoman within was a good Lancastrian, and prayed the donzell to rest in her company, till Master Warner's return.

Sibyll, accordingly, after pressing her father's hand without fear, for she had deemed the sole danger Adam risked was from the rabble by the way, followed Hugh into a fair chamber, strewed with rushes, where an aged dame, of noble air and aspect, was employed at her broidery frame. This gentlewoman, the widow of a nobleman who had fallen in the service of Henry, received her graciously, and Hugh then retired to complete his commission. The student, the mule, the model, and the porter, pursued their way to the entrance of that part of the gloomy palace inhabited by Henry. Here they were stopped, and Adam, after rummaging long in vain, for the chamberlain's passport, at last happily discovered it, pinned to his sleeve, by Sibyll's forethought. On this a gentleman was summoned to inspect the order, and in a few moments Adam was conducted to the presence of the illustrious prisoner.

"And what," said a subaltern officer, lolling by the archway of the (now styled) "Bloody Tower," hard by the turret devoted to the prisoner,* and speaking to Adam's guide, who still mounted guard by the model,—'what may be the precious burden of which thou art the convoy?"

"Marry, sir," said Hugh, who spoke in the strong Yorkshire dialect, which we are obliged to render into intelligible English—"marry, I weet not,—it is some curious puppet-box, or queint contrivance, that Master Warner, whom they say is a very deft and ingenious personage, is permitted to bring hither for the Lord Henry's diversion."

"A puppet-box!" said the officer, with much animated curiosity. "'Fore the mass! that must be a pleasant sight. Lift the lid, fellow!"

"Please your honor, I do not dare," returned Hugh—"I but obey orders."

"Obey mine, then. Out of the way!" and the officer lifted the lid of the pannier wite the point of his dagger, and peered within. He drew back, much disappointed—"Holy mother!" said he, "this seemeth more like an instrument of torture, than a juggler's merry device. It looks parlous ugly!"

"Hush!" said one of the lazy bystanders, with whom the various gate-ways and courts of the palace-fortress were crowded, "hush!—thy cap and thy knee, sir!"

The officer started; and, looking round, perceived a young man of low stature, followed by three or four knights and nobles, slowly approaching towards the arch, and every cap in the vicinity was off, and every knee bowed.

The eye of this young man was already bent with a searching and keen gaze upon the motionless mule, standing patiently by the Wakefield Tower; and turning from the mule to the porter, the latter shrunk, and grew pale, at that dark, steady, penetrating eye, which seemed to pierce at once into the secrets and hearts of men.

"Who may this young lord be?" he whispered to the officer.

* The Wakefield Tower.

"Prince Richard, Duke of Gloucester, man," was the answer. "Uncover, varlet!"

"Surely," said the prince, pausing by the gate, "surely this is no sumpter-mule, bearing provisions to the Lord Henry of Windsor. It would be but poor respect to that noble person, whom, alas the day! his grace the king is unwillingly compelled to guard from the malicious designs of rebels and mischief-seekers, that one not bearing the king's livery should attend to any of the needful wants of so worshipful a lord and guest!"

"My lord," said the officer at the gate, "one Master Adam Warner hath just, by permission, been conducted to the Lord Henry's presence, and the beast beareth some strange and grim-look device for my lord's diversion."

"The singular softness and urbanity which generally characterized the Duke of Gloucester's tone and bearing at that time,—which, in a court so full of factions and intrigues, made him the enemy of none, and seemingly the friend of all, and, conjoined with abilities already universally acknowledged, had given to his very boyhood a pre-eminence of grave repute and good opinion, which, indeed, he retained, till the terrible circumstances connected with his accession to the throne, under the bloody name of Richard the Third, roused all men's hearts and reasons into the persuasion that what before had seemed virtue was but dissimulation;—this singular sweetness, we say, of manner and voice, had in it, nevertheless, something that imposed, and thrilled, and awed. And, in truth, in our common and more vulgar intercourse with life, we must have observed, that where external gentleness of hearing is accompanied by a repute for iron will, determined resolution, and a serious, profound, and all-inquiring intellect, it carries with it a majesty wholly distinct from that charm which is exercised by one whose mildness of nature corresponds with the outward humility; and, if it does not convey the notion of falseness, bears the appearance of that perfect self-possession, that calm repose of power, which intimidates those it influences far more than the imperious port and the loud voice.

And they who best knew the duke, knew also that, despite this general smoothness of mien, his temperament was naturally irritable, quick, and subject to stormy gusts of passion, the which defects his admirers praised him for laboring hard and sedulously to keep in due control. Still, to a keen observer, the constitutional tendencies of that nervous teperament were often visible, even in his blandest moments—even when his voice was most musical, his smile most gracious. If something stung, or excited him, an uneasy gnawing of the nether lip, a fretful playing with his dagger drawing it up and down from its sheath,* a slight twiching of the muscles of the face, and a quiver of the eyelid, betokened the efforts he made at self command; and now, as his dark eyes rested upon Hugh's pale countenance, and then glanced upon the impassive mule, dozing quietly under the weight of poor Adam's model, his hand mechanically sought his dagger-hilt, and his face took a sinister and sombre expression.

"Thy name, friend?"

"Hugh Withers—please you, my lord duke."

"Um! North country, by thine accent. Dost thou serve this Master Warner?"

"No, my lord, I was only hired with my mule to carry——"

"Ah! true! to carry what thy pannier contains; open it. Holy Paul! a strange jonglerie indeed! This master Adam Warner.—methinks, I have heard his name—a learned man—um—let me see his safe conduct. Right—it is Lord Hastings's signature." But still the prince held the passport, and still suspiciously eyed the Eureka and its appliances, which, in complicated and native ugliness of doors, wheels, pipes, and chimney, were exposed to his view. At this moment one of the attendants of Henry descended the stairs of the Wakefield Tower, with a request that the model might be carried up to divert the prisoner.

Richard paused a moment, as the officer hesitatingly watched his countenance before giving the desired permission. But the prince, turning to him, and smoothing his brow, said mildly—"Certes! all that can divert the Lord Henry must be innocent pastime. And I am well pleased that he hath this cheerful mood for recreation. It gainsayeth those who would accuse us of rigor in his durance. Yes, this warrant is complete and formal;" and the prince returned the passport to the officer, and walked slowly on through that gloomy arch evermore

---

* Pol. Virg. 565.

associated with Richard of Gloucester's memory, and beneath the very room in which our belief yet holds that the infant sons of Edward IV. breathed their last; still as Gloucester moved, he turned and turned, and kept his eye furtively fixed upon the porter.

"Lovell," he said, to one of the gentlemen who attended him, and who was among the few admitted to his more peculiar intimacy—"that man is of the north."

"Well, my lord?"

"The north was always well affected to the Lancastrians. Master Warner hath been accused of witchcraft. Marry, I should like to see his device—um, Master Catesby, come hither—approach, sir. Go back, and the instant Adam Warner and his contrivance are dismissed—bring them both to me in the king's chamber. Thou understandest? We too would see his device—and let neither man nor mechanical, when once they re-appear, out of thine eye's reach. For divers and subtle are the contrivances of treasonable men!"

Catesby bowed, and Richard, without speaking further, took his way to the royal apartments, which lay beyond the White Tower, towards the river, and are long since demolished.

Meanwhile the porter, with the aid of one of the attendants, had carried the model into the chamber of the august captive. Henry, attired in a loose robe, was pacing the room with a slow step, and his head sunk on his bosom,—while Adam, with much animation, was enlarging on the wonders of the contrivance he was about to show him. The chamber was commodious, and furnished with sufficient attention to the state and dignity of the prisoner; for Edward, though savage and relentless when his blood was up, never descended into the cool and continuous cruelty of detail.

The chamber may yet be seen; its shape a spacious octagon; but the walls, now rude and bare, were then painted and blazoned with scenes from the Old Testament. The door opened beneath the pointed arch in the central side, (not where it now does), giving entrance from a small ante-room, in which the visitor now beholds the receptacle for old rolls and papers. At the right, on entering, where now, if our memory mistake not, is placed a press, stood the bed, quaintly carved, and with hangings of damascene. At the farther end, the deep recess which faced the ancient door was fitted up as a kind of oratory, And there, were to be seen, besides the crucifix and the mass-book, a profusion of small vessels of gold and crystal, containing the relics, supposed or real, of Saint and Martyr, treasures which the deposed king had collected in his palmier days, at a sum that, in the minds of his followers, had been better bestowed on arms and war-steeds. A young man named Allerton one of the three gentlemen personally attached to Henry, to whom Edward had permitted general access, and who in fact lodged in other apartments of the Wakefield Tower, and might be said to share his captivity—was seated before a table, and following the steps of his musing master, with earnest and watchful eyes.

One of the small spaniels employed in springing game—for Henry, despite his mildness, had been fond of all the sports of the field—lay curled round on the floor, but started up, with a shrill bark, at the entrance of the bearer of the model, while a starling, in a cage, by the window, seemingly delighted at the disturbance, flapped his wings, and screamed out, "Bad men!—Bad world!—Poor Henry!"

The captive paused at that cry, and a sad and patient smile of inexpressible melancholy and sweetness hovered over his lips. Henry still retained much of the personal comeliness he possessed at the time when Margaret of Anjou, the theme of minstrel and minne-singer, left her native court of poets, for the fatal throne of England. But beauty, usually so popular and precious a gift to kings, was not in him of that order which commanded the eye and moved the admiration of a turbulent people and a haughty chivalry. The features, if regular, were small; their expression meek and timid; the form, though tall, was not firm-knit and muscular; the lower limbs were too thin, the body had too much flesh, the delicate hands betrayed the sickly paleness of feeble health; there was a dreamy vagueness in the clear soft blue eyes, and a listless absence of all energy in the habitual bend, the slow, heavy sauntering tread—all about that benevolent aspect, that soft voice, that resigned mien, and gentle manner, spoke the exquisite unresisting goodness, which provoked the lewd to taunt, the hardy to despise, the insolent to rebel:—for the foes of a king in stormy times are often less his vices than his virtues.

"And now, good my lord," said Adam, hastening, with eager hands, to assist the bearer in depositing the model on the table—"now will I explain to you the contrivance, which it hath cost me long years of patient toil to shape from thought into this iron form."

"But first, said Allerton, "were it not well that these good people withdrew? A contriver likes not others to learn his secret ere the time hath come to reap its profits."

"Surely—surely!" said Adam, and alarmed at the idea thus suggested, he threw the folds of his gown over the model.

The attendant bowed and retired: Hugh followed him, but not till he had exchanged a significant look with Allerton.

As soon as the room was left clear to Adam, the captive, and Master Allerton,—the last rose, and looking hastily round the chamber, approached the mechanician. "Quick, sir!" said he, in a whisper, "we are not often left without witnesses."

"Verily," said Adam, who had now forgotten kings and stratagems, plots and counterplots, and was all-absorbed in his invention, "verily, young man, hurry not in this fashion—I am about to begin. Know, my lord," and he turned to Henry, who, with an indolent, dreamy gaze, stood contemplating the Eureka,—"know that, more than a hundred years before the Christian era, one Hero, an Alexandrian, discovered the force produced by the vapor begot by heat on water. That this power was not unknown to the ancient sages—witness the contrivances, not otherwise to be accounted for, of the heathen oracles; but to our great countryman and predecessor, Roger Bacon, who first suggested that vehicles might be drawn without steeds or steers, and ships might——"

"Marry, sir," interrupted Allerton, with great impatience, "it is not to prate to us of such trivial fables of Man, or such wanton sports of the Foul Fiend, that thou hast risked limb and life. Time is precious. I have been prevised that thou hast letters for King Henry; produce them—quick!"

A deep glow of indignation had overspread the Enthusiast's face at the commencement of this address; but the close reminded him, in truth, of his errand.

"Hot youth," said he, with dignity, "a future age may judge differently of what thou deemest trivial fables, and may rate high this poor invention when the brawls of York and Lancaster are forgotten."

"Hear him," said Henry, with a soft smile, and laying his hand on the shoulder of the young man, who was about to utter a passionate and scornful retort—"Hear him, sir. Have I not often and ever said this same thing to thee? We children of a day imagine our contests are the sole things that move the world. Alack! our fathers thought the same; and they and their turmoils sleep forgotten! Nay, Master Warner"—for here Adam, poor man, awed by Henry's mildness into shame at his discourteous vaunting, began to apologize,—"nay, sir, nay—thou art right to contemn our bloody and futile struggles for a crown of thorns; for

'Kingdoms are but cares,
State is devoid of stay;
Riches are ready snares,
And hasten to decay.' *

And yet, sir, believe me, thou hast no cause for vain glory in thine own craft and labors; for to wit and to lere there are the same vanity and vexation of spirit as to war and empire. Only, O would-be wise man, only when we muse on Heaven do our souls ascend from the Fowler's snare!"

"My saint-like liege," said Allerton, bowing low, and with tears in his eyes, "thinkest thou not that thy very disdain of thy rights make thee more worthy of them? If not for thine, for thy son's sake—remember that the usurper sits on the throne of the conqueror of Agincourt!—Sir Clerk, the letters."

Adam, already anxious to retrieve the error of his first forgetfulness, here, after a moment's struggle for the necessary remembrance, drew the papers from the labrinthine receptacle which concealed them; and Henry uttered an exclamation of joy, as, after cutting the silk, his eye glanced over the writing—"My Margaret! my wife!" Presently, he

* Lines ascribed to Hernry VI., with commendation "as a prettie verse," by Sir John Harrington, in the Nugæ Antiquæ. They are also given, with little alteration, to the unhappy king by Baldwin, in his tragedy of King Henry VI.

grew pale, and his hands trembled! "Saints defend her!—Saints defend her! She is here, disguised, in London!"

"Margaret! our heroe-queen! the manlike woman!" exclaimed Allerton, clasping his hands—"Then be sure that——" He stopped, and abruptly taking Adam's arm, drew him aside, while Henry continued to read—"Master Warner, we may trust thee—thou art one of us—thou art sent here, I know, by Robin of Redesdale—we may trust thee?"

"Young sir," replied the philosopher, gravely, "the fears and hopes of power are not amidst the uneasier passions of the student's mind. I pledge myself but to bear these papers hither, and to return with what may be sent back."

"But thou didst this for love of the cause, the truth, and the right?"

"I did it partly from Hilyard's tale of wrong—but partly, also, for the gold," answered Adam, simply; and his noble air, his high brow, the serene calm of his features, so contrasted the meanness implied in the latter words of his confession, that Allerton stared at him amazed, and without reply.

Meanwhile Henry had concluded the letter, and with a heavy sigh glanced over the papers that accompanied it.

"Alack! alack! more turbulance, more danger, and disquiet—more of my people's blood!" He motioned to the young man, and drawing him to the window, while Adam returned to his model, put the papers in his hand. "Allerton," he said, "thou lovest me, but thou art one of the few in this distraught land who love also God. Thou art not one of the warriors, the men of steel. Counsel me. See—Margaret demands my signature to these papers; the one, empowering and craving the levy of men and arms in the northern counties; the other, promising free pardon to all who will desert Edward; the third,—it seemeth to me more strange and less kinglike than the others,—undertaking to abolish all the imposts and all the laws that press upon the commons, and (is this a holy and pious stipulation)? to inquire into the exactions and prosecutions of the priesthood of our Holy Church!"

"Sire!" said the young man, after he had hastily perused the papers, "my Lady Liege showeth good argument for your assent to two, at least, of these undertakings. See the names of fifty gentlemen ready to take arms in your cause if authorized by your royal warrant. The men of the North are malcontent with the usurper, but they will not yet stir, unless at your own command. Such documents will, of course, be used with discretion, and not imperil your grace's safety,"

"My safety!" said Henry, with a flash of his father's hero-soul in his eyes—"of *that* I think not! If I have small courage to attack, I have some fortitude to bear! But, three months after these be signed, how many brave hearts will be still!—how many stout hands be dust! O Margaret! Margaret! why temptest thou? Wert thou so happy when a queen?'

The prisoner broke from Allerton's arm, and walked, in great disorder and irresolution, to and fro the chamber; and strange it was to see the contrast between himself and Warner—both, in so much alike—both so purely creatures out of the common world, so gentle—abstract—so utterly living in the life apart: and now, the student so calm, the prince so disturbed? The contrast struck Henry himself! He paused abruptly, and, folding his arms, contemplated the philosopher, as with an affectionate complacency, Adam played and toyed, as it were, with his beloved model, now opening and shutting again its doors—now brushing away with his sleeve some particles of dust that had settled on it—now retiring a few paces to gaze the better on its stern symmetry.

"Oh, my Allerton!" cried Henry, "behold! the kingdom a man makes out of his own mind is the only one that delighteth man to govern! Behold, he is lord over its springs and movements, its wheels revolve and stop at his bidding. Here, here, alone, God never asketh the ruler—'Why was the blood of thousands poured forth like water, that a worm might wear a crown?'"

"Sire," said Allerton, solemnly, "when our Heavenly King appoints his anointed representative on earth, he gives to that human delegate no power to resign the ambassade and trust. What suicide is to a man, abdication is to a king! How canst thou dispose of thy son's rights! And what become of those rights, if thou wilt prefer for him the exile—for thyself, the prison,—when one effort may restore a throne!"

Henry seemed struck by a tone of argument, that suited both his own mind and the reasoning of the age. He gazed a moment on the face of the young man, muttered to himself, and suddenly moving to the table, signed the papers, and restored them to Adam, who mechanically replaced them in their iron hiding-place:—

"Now begone, sir!" whispered Allerton, afraid that Henry's mind might again change.

"Will not my lord examine the engine?" asked Warner hulf-beseechingly.

"Not to-day! See, he has already retired to his oratory—he is in prayer!" and, going to the door, Allerton summoned the attendants in waiting to carry down the model.

"Well, well—patience, patience—thou shalt have thine audience at last," muttered Adam, as he retired from the room, his eyes fixed upon the neglected infant of his brain.

CHAPTER VI.

How on leaving King Log, foolish Wisdom runs a-muck on King Stork.

At the outer door of the Tower by which he had entered, the philosopher was accosted by Catesby—a man who, in imitation of his young patron, exhibited the soft and oily manner which concealed intense ambition and innate ferocity.

"Worshipful, my master," said he, bowing low, but with a half sneer on his lips, "the king and his Highness the Duke of Gloucester have heard much of your strange skill, and command me to lead you to their presence. Follow, sir, and you, my men, convey this quaint contrivance to the king's apartments."

With this, not waiting for any reply, Catesby strode on. Hugh's face fell—he turned very pale, and, imagining himself unobserved, turned round to slink away. But Catesby, who seemed to have eyes at the back of his head, called out, in a mild tone,

"Good fellow, help to bear the mechanical—you too may be needed."

"Cog's wounds!" muttered Hugh, "an' I had but known what it was to set my foot in a king's palace! Such walking may do for the silken shoon, but the hobnail always gets into a hobble." With that, affecting a cheerful mien, he helped to replace the model on the mule.

Meanwhile, Adam, elated, poor man! at the flattery of the royal mandate, persuaded that his fame had reached Edward's ears, and chafed at the little heed paid by the pious Henry to his great work, stalked on, his head in the air. "Verily," mused the student, "King Edward may have been a cruel youth, and over hasty; it is horrible to think of Robin Hilyard's calamities! But men do say he hath an acute and masterly comprehension. Doubtless, he will perceive at a glance how much I can advantage his kingdom." With this, we grieve to say, selfish reflection, which if the thought of his model could have slept awhile, Adam would have blushed to recall, as an affront to Hilyard's wrongs, the philosopher followed Catesby across the spacious yard, along a narrow passage, and up a winding turret-stair, to a room in the third story, which opened at one door into the king's closet, at the other into the spacious gallery, which was already a feature in the plan of the more princely houses. In another minute Adam and his model were in the presence of the king. The part of the room in which Edward sate was distinguished from the rest by a small eastern carpet on the floor (a luxury more in use in the palaces of that day, than it appears to have been a century later); * a table was set before him, on which the model was placed. At his right hand sat Jacquetta Duchess of Bedford, the queen's mother; at his left, Prince Richard. The duchess, though not without the remains of beauty, had a stern, haughty, scornful expression, in her sharp aquiline features, compressed lips, and imperious eye. The paleness of her complexion, and the care-worn anxious lines of her countenance, were ascribed by the vulgar to studies of no holy cast. Her reputation for sorcery and witchcraft was daily increasing, and served well the purpose of the discontented barons, whom the rise of her children mortified and enraged.

"Approach, Master——What say you his name is, Richard?"

"Adam Warner," replied the sweet voice of the Duke of Gloucester, "of excellent skill in the mathematics."

"Approach, sir, and show us the nature of this notable invention."

* See the Narrative of the Lord Grauthuse, before referred to.

"I desire nothing better, my lord king," said Adam, boldly. "But first, let me crave a small modicum of fuel. Fire, which is the life of the world, as the wise of old held it, is also the soul of this—my mechanical."

"Peradventure," whispered the duchess, "the wizard desireth to consume us!"

"More likely," replied Richard, in the same under tone, "to consume whatever of treasonable nature may lurk concealed in his engine."

"True," said Edward, and then, speaking aloud, "Master Warner," he added, "put thy puppet to its purpose — without fire;—we will it."

"It is impossible, my lord," said Adam, with a lofty smile. "Science and nature are more powerful than a king's word."

"Do not say that in public, my friend," said Edward, drily, "or we must hang thee! I would not my subjects were told anything so treasonable. Howbeit, to give thee no excuse in failure, thou shalt have what thou needest."

"But surely not in our presence," exclaimed the duchess. "This may be a device of the Lancastrians for our perdition."

"As you please, belle mère," said Edward, and he motioned to a gentleman, who stood a few paces behind his chair, and who, from the entrance of the mechanician, had seemed to observe him with intense interest. "Master Nevile, attend this wise man; supply his wants, and hark, in thy ear, watch well that he abstract nothing from the womb of his engine —observe what he doeth—be all eyes." Marmaduke bowed low to conceal his change of countenance, and, stepping forward, made a sign to Adam to follow him.

"Go also, Catesby," said Richard to his follower, who had taken his post near him, "and clear the chamber."

As soon as the three members of the royal family were left alone, the king, stretching himself, with a slight yawn, observed, "This man looks not like a conspirator, brother Richard, though his sententiary as to nature and science lacked loyalty and respect."

"Sire and brother," answered Richard, "great leaders often dupe their own tools; at least, meseemeth that they would reason well so to do. Remember, I have told thee, that there is strong cause to suppose Margaret to be in London. In the suburbs of the city has also appeared, within the last few weeks, that strange and dangerous person, whose very objects are a mystery, save that he is our foe,—Robin of Redesdale. The men of the North have exhibited a spirit of insurrection; a man of that country attends this reputed wizard, and he himself was favored in past times by Henry of Windsor. These are ominous signs when the conjunctions be considered!"

"It is well said; but a fair day for breathing our palfreys is half spent!" returned the indolent Prince. "By'r lady! I like the fashion of thy supertunic well, Richard; but thou hast it too much puffed over the shoulders."

Richard's dark eye shot fire, and he gnawed his lip as he answered—"God hath not given to me the fair shape of my kinsman!"

"Thy pardon, dear boy," said Edward, kindly; "yet little needest thou our broad backs and strong sinews, for thou hast a tongue to charm women, and a wit to command men."

Richard bowed his face, little less beautiful than his brother's, though wholly different from it in feature, for Edward had the long oval countenance, the fair hair, the rich coloring, and the large outline of his mother, the Rose of Raby. Richard, on the contrary, had the short face, the dark brown locks, and the pale olive complexion of his father, whom he alone of the royal brothers strikingly resembled.* The cheeks, too, were somewhat sunken, and already, though scarcely past childhood, about his lips were seen the lines of thoughtful manhood. But then those small features, delicately aquiline, were so regular —that dark eye was so deep, so fathomless in its bright musing intelligence—that quivering lip was at once so beautifully formed and so expressive of intellectual subtlety and haughty will—and that pale forehead was so massive, high, and majestic, that when, at a later period, the Scottish prelate † commended Richard's

* Pol. Virge. 544.

† Archibald Quhitlaw.—"Faciem tuam summo imperio principatu dignam inspicit, quam moralis et heroica, virtus illustrat," etc.—We need scarcely observe that even a Scotchman would not have risked a public compliment to Richard's face, if so inappropriate as to seem a sarcasm, especially as the orator immediately proceeds to notice the shortness of Richard's stature—a comment not likely to have been peculiarly acceptable. In the Rous Roll, the portrait of Richard

'princely *countenance*,' the compliment was not one to be disputed, much less contemned. But now as he rose, obedient to a whisper from the duchess, and followed her to the window, while Edward appeared engaged in admiring the shape of his own long upturned shoes, those defects in his shape which the popular hatred and the rise of the House of Tudor exaggerated into the absolute deformity, that the unexamining ignorance of modern days, and Shakspere's fiery tragedy, have fixed into established caricature, were sufficiently apparent.

Deformed or hunchbacked we need scarcely say he was not, for no man so disfigured could have possessed that great personal strength which he invariably exhibited in battle, despite the comparative slightness of his frame. He was considerably below the ordinary height, which the great stature of his brother rendered yet more disadvantageous by contrast, but his lower limbs were strong-jointed and muscular. Though the back was not curved, yet one shoulder was slightly higher than the other, which was the more observable from the evident pains that he took to disguise it, and the gorgeous splendor, savoring of personal coxcombry,—from which no Plantagenet was ever free,—that he exhibited in his dress. And as, in a warlike age, the physical conformation of men is always critically regarded, so this defect, and that of his low stature, were not so much redeemed as they would be in our day by the beauty and intelligence of his face. Added to this, his neck was short, and a habit of bending his head on his bosom, (arising either from thought or the affectation of humility, which was a part of his character), made it seem shorter still. But this peculiarity, while taking from the grace, added to the strength of his frame, which, spare, sinewy, and compact, showed to an observer that power of endurance — that combination of solid stubbornness and active energy, which, at the battle of Barnet, made him no less formidable to encounter than the ruthless sword of the mighty Edward.

"So, prince," said the duchess, "this new gentleman of the king's is, it seems, a Nevile. When will Edward's high spirit cast off that hateful yoke?"

Richard sighed and shook his head. The duchess, encouraged by these signs of sympathy, continued—

"Your brother Clarence, Prince Richard, despises us, to cringe to the proud earl. But you——"

"I am not suitor to the Lady Isabel; Clarence is over-lavish, and Isabel has a fair face and a queenly dowry."

"May I perish," said the duchess, "ere Warwick's daughter wears the baudekin of royalty, and sits in as high a state as the queen's mother! Prince, I would fain confer with thee; we have a project to abase and banish this hateful lord. If you but join us, success is sure. The Count of Charolois ——"

"Dear lady," interrupted Richard, with an air of profound humility, "tell me nothing of plot or project; my years are too few for such high and subtle policy; and the Lord Warwick hath been a leal friend to our House of York."

The duchess bit her lip—"Yet I have heard you tell Edward that a subject can be too powerful?"

"Never, lady! *you* have never heard me."

"Then Edward has told Elizabeth that you so spoke."

"Ah!" said Richard, turning away with a smile; "I see that the king's conscience hath a discreet keeper. Pardon me. Edward, now that he hath sufficiently surveyed his shoon, must marvel at this prolonged colloquy. And see, the door opens."

With this, the duke slowly moved to the table, and resumed his seat.

Marmaduke, full of fear for his ancient host, had in vain sought an opportunity to address a few words of exortation to him to forbear all necromancy, and to abstain from all perilous distinctions between the power of Edward IV. and that of his damnable Nature and Science; but Catesby watched him with so feline a vigilance, that he was unable to slip in more than—"Ah, Master Warner, for our blessed Lord's sake, recollect that rack and cord are more than mere words here!" To the which pleasant remark, Adam, then busy in filling his miniature boiler, only replied by a wistful stare, not in the least recognizing the Nevile in his fine attire, and the new-fashioned mode of dressing his long hair.

---

represents him as undersized, but compactly and strongly built, and without any sign of deformity, unless the inelegant defect of a short neck can be so called.

But Catesby watched in vain for the abstraction of any treasonable contents in the engine, which the Duke of Gloucester had so shrewdly suspected. The truth must be told. Adam had entirely forgotten that in the intricacies of his mechanical lurked the papers that might overthrow a throne! Magnificent Incarnation was he (in that oblivion) of Science itself, which cares not a jot for men and natons, in their ephemeral existences; which only remembers THINGS—things that endure for ages; and in its stupendous calculations loses sight of the unit of a generation! No—he had thoroughly forgotten Henry, Edward, his own limbs and life—not only York and Lancaster, but Adam Warner and the rack. Grand in his forgetfulness, he stood before the tiger and the tiger-cat—Edward and Richard—A Pure thought—a Man's Soul; Science fearless in the presence of Cruelty, Tyranny, Craft, and Power.

In truth, now that Adam was thoroughly in his own sphere—was in the domain of which *he* was king, and those beings in velvet and ermine were but as ignorant savages admitted to the frontier of his realm, his form seemed to dilate into a majesty the beholders had not before recognized. And even the lazy Edward muttered, involuntarily—"By my halidame, the man has a noble presence!"

"I am prepared now, sire," said Adam, loftily, "to show to my king and to his court, that unnoticed and obscure, in study and retreat, often live those men whom kings may be proud to call their subjects. Will it please you, my lords, this way!" and he motioned so commandingly to the room in which he had left the Eureka, that his audience rose by a common impulse, and in another minute stood grouped round the model in the adjoining chamber. This really wonderful invention—so wonderful, indeed, that it will surpass the faith of those who do not pause to consider what vast forestalments of modern science have been made and lost in the darkness of ages not fitted to receive them,—was, doubtless, in many important details, not yet adapted for the practical uses to which Adam designed its application. But as a mere model, as a marvellous essay, for the suggestion of gigantic results, it was, perhaps, to the full as effective as the ingenuity of a mechanic of our own day could construct. It is true that it was crowded with unnecessary cylinders, slides, cocks, and wheels—hideous and clumsy to the eye—but through this intricacy the great simple design accomplished its main object. It contrived to show what force and skill man can obtain from the alliance of nature; the more clearly, inasmuch as the mechanism affixed to it, still more ingenious than itself, was well calculated to illustrate practically one of the many uses to wnich the principle was destined to be applied.

Adam had not yet fathomed the secret by which to supply the miniature cylinder with sufficient steam for any prolonged effect, the great truth of latent heat was unknown to him; but he had contrived to regulate the supply of water so as to make the engine discharge its duties sufficiently for the satisfaction of curiosity, and the explanation of its objects. And now the strange thing of iron was in full life. From its serpent-chimney issued the thick rapid smoke, and the groan of its travail was heard within.

"And what propose you to yourself and to the kingdom, in all this, Master Adam?" asked Edward, curiously, bending his tall person over the tortured iron.

"I propose to make Nature the laborer of man," answered Warner. "When I was a child of some eight years old, I observed that water swelleth into vapor when fire is applied to it. Twelve years afterwards, at the age of twenty, I observed that while undergoing this change, it exerts a mighty mechanical force. At twenty-five, constantly musing, I said, 'Why should not that force become subject to man's art?' I then began the first rude model, of which this is the descendant. I noticed that the vapor so produced is elastic—that is, that as it expands, it presses against what opposes it; it has a force applicable everywhere a force is needed by man's labor. Behold a second agency of gigantic resources. And then, still studying this, I perceived that the vapor thus produced can be re-converted into water, shrinking necessarily, while so retransformed, from the space it filled as vapor, and leaving that space a vacuum. But Nature abhors a vacuum—produce a vacuum, and the bodies that surround rush into it. Thus the vapor again, while changing back into water, becomes also a force—our agent. And all the while these truths were shaping themselves to my mind, I was devising and improving also the material form by which I might render them useful to man,—so at last, out of these truths, arose this invention ! "

"Pardie," said Edward, with the haste natural to royalty, "what in common there can be between thy jargon of smoke and water and this hudge ugliness of iron, passeth all understanding. But spare us thy speeches, and on to thy puppet-show."

Adam stared a moment at the king in the surprise, that one full of his subject feels when he sees it impossible to make another understand it, sighed, shook his head, and prepared to begin.

"Observe," he said, "that there is no juggling, no deceit. I will place in this deposit this small lump of brass—would the size of this toy would admit of larger experiment ! I will then pray ye to note, as I open the door after door, how the metal passes through various changes, all operated by this one agency of vapor. Heed and attend. And if the crowning work please thee, think, great king, what such an agency upon the large scale would be to thee: think how it would multiply all arts, and lessen all labor; think that thou hast, in this, achieved for a whole people the true philosopher's stone. Now, note ! "

He placed the rough ore in its receptacle, and suddenly it seemed seized by a vice within, and vanished. He proceeded, then, while dexterously attending to the complex movements, to open door after door, to show the astonished spectators the rapid transitious the metal underwent, and suddenly, in the midst of his pride, he stopped short, for, like a lightning flash, came across his mind the remembrance of the fatal papers. Within the next door he was to open, they lay concealed. His change of countenance did not escape Richard, and he noted the door which Adam forbore to open, as the student hurriedly, and with some presence of mind, passed to the next, in which the metal was shortly to appear.

"Open *this* door," said the prince, pointing to the handle.

"No !—forbear ! There is danger !—forbear ! " exclaimed the mechanician.

"Danger to thine own neck, varlet and impostor !" exclaimed the duke; and he was about himself to open the door, when suddenly a loud roar—a terrific explosion was heard. Alas ! Adam Warner had not yet discovered for his engine what we now call the safety-valve. The steam contained in the miniature boiler had acquired an undue pressure; Adam's attention had been too much engrossed to notice the signs of the growing increase, and the rest may be easily conceived. Nothing could equal the stupor and horror of the spectators at this explosion, save only the boy-duke, who remained immovable, and still frowning. All rushed to the door, huddling one on the other, scarcely knowing what next was to befall them; but certain that the wizard was bent upon their destruction. Edward was the first to recover himself; and seeing that no lives were lost, his first impulse was that of ungovernable rage.

"Foul traitor !" he exclaimed, "was it for this that thou hast pretended to beguile us with thy damnable sorceries ! Seize him ! Away to the Tower Hill ! and let the priest patter an ave, while the doomsman knots the rope."

Not a hand stirred; even Catesby would as lief have touched the king's lion before meals, as that poor mechanician, standing aghast, and unheeding all, beside his mutilated engine.

"Master Nevile," said the king, sternly, "dost thou hear us ?"

"Verily," muttered the Nevile, approaching very slowly, "I knew what would happen; but to lay hands on my host, an' he were fifty times a wizard—No ! My liege," he said, in a firm tone, but falling on his knee, and his gallant countenance pale with generous terror —"My liege, forgive me. This man succored me when struck down and wounded by a Lancastrian ruffian—this man gave me shelter, food, and healing. Command me not, O gracious my lord, to aid in taking the life of one to whom I owe my own."

"His life !" exclaimed the Duchess of Bedford—"the life of this most illustrious person ! Sire, you do not dream it ! "

"Heh ! by the saints, what now ? " cried the king, whose choler, though fierce and ruthless, was as short-lived as the passions of the indolent usually are, and whom the earnest interposition of his mother-in-law much surprised and diverted. "If, fair belle mère, thou thinkest it so illustrious a deed to frighten us out of our mortal senses, and narrowly to 'scape sending us across the river like a bevy of balls from a bombard, there is no disputing of tastes. Rise up, Master Nevile, we esteem thee not less for thy boldness; ever be the host and the benefactor revered by English gentleman and Christian youth. Master Warner may go free."

Here Warner uttered so deep and hollow a groan, that it startled all present."

"Twenty-five years of labor, and not to have seen this!" he ejaculated. "Twenty and five years, and all wasted! How repair this disaster—O fatal day!"

"What says he?—what means he?" said Jacquetta.

"Come home!—home!" said Marmaduke, approaching the philosopher, in great alarm lest he should once more jeopardize his life. But Adam, shaking him off, began eagerly, and with tremulous hands, to examine the machine, and not perceiving any mode by which to guard in future against a danger that he saw at once would, if not removed, render his invention useless, tottered to a chair and covered his face with his hands.

"He seemeth mightily grieved that our bones are still whole!" muttered Edward. "And why, belle mère mine, wouldst thou protect this pleasant *tregetour?*"

"What!" said the duchess—"see you not that a man capable of such devises must be of doughty service against our foes?"

"Not I—how?"

"Why, if merely to signify displeasure at our young Richard's over-curious meddling, he can cause this strange engine to shake the walls—nay, to destroy itself, think what he might do were his power and malice at our disposing. I know something of these nigromancers."

"And would you knew less! for already the Commons murmur at your favor to them. But be it as you will. And now—ho, there! —let our steeds be caparisoned."

"You forget, sire," said Richard, who had hitherto silently watched the various parties, "the object for which we summoned this worthy man. Please you now, sir, to open that door."

"No—no!" excaimed the king, hastily, "I will have no more provoking the foul fiend—conspirator or not, I have had enough of Master Warner. Pah! My poor placard is turned lampblack. Sweet mother-in-law, take him under thy protection, and Richard, come with me."

So saying, the king linked his arm in that of the reluctant Gloucester, and quitted the room. The duchess then ordered the rest also to depart, and was left alone with the crest-fallen philosopher.

CHAPTER VII.

My Lady Duchess's Opinion of the Utility of Master Warner's invention, and her esteem for its—explosion.

ADAM, utterly unheeding, or rather deaf to, the discussion that had taken place, and his narrow escape from cord and gibbet, lifted his head peevishly from his bosom, as the duchess rested her hand almost caressingly on his shoulder, and thus addressed him:—

"Most puissant sir, think not that I am one of those, who, in their ignorance and folly, slight the mysteries of which thou art clearly so great a master. When I heard thee speak of subjecting Nature to Man, I at once comprehended thee, and blushed for the dulness of my kindred."

"Ah! lady, thou hast studied, then, the mathematics. Alack! this is a grievous blow; but it is no inherent fault in the device. I am clearly of mind that it can be remedied. But oh! what time—what thought—what sleepless nights—what gold will be needed!"

"Give me thy sleepless nights and thy grand thoughts, and thou shalt not want gold."

"Lady," cried Adam, starting to his feet, "do I hear aright? Art thou, in truth, the patron I have so long dreamed of? Hast thou the brain and the heart to aid the pursuits of science?"

"Ay! and the power to protect the students! Sage, I am the Duchess of Bedford, whom men accuse of witchcraft—as thee of wizardry. From the wife of a private gentleman, I have become the mother of a queen. I stand amidst a court full of foes; I desire gold to corrupt, and wisdom to guard against, and means to destroy, them. And I seek all these in men like thee!"

Adam turned on her his bewildered eyes, and made no answer.

"They tell me," said the duchess, "that

Henry of Windsor employed learned men to transmute the baser metals into gold. Wert thou one of them?"

"No."

"Thou knowest that art?"

"I studied it in my youth, but the ingredients of the crucible were too costly."

"Thou shalt not lack them with me—thou knowest the lore of the stars, and canst foretell the designs of enemies—the hour whether to act or to forbear?"

"Astrology I have studied, but that also was in youth, for there dwelleth in the pure mathematics that have led me to this invention ——"

"Truce with that invention, whatever it be—think of it no more, it has served its end in the explosion, which proved thy power of mischief—high objects are now before thee. Wilt thou be of my household, one of my alchemists and astrologers? Thou shalt have leisure, honor, and all the moneys thou canst need."

"Moneys!" said Adam eagerly, and casting his eyes upon the mangled model—"well, I agree—what you will—alchemist, astrologist, wizard—what you will. This shall all be repaired—all—I begin to see now—ah! I begin to see—yes, if a pipe by which the too excessive vapor could—ay, ay!—right, right," and he rubbed his hands.

Jacquetta was struck with his enthusiasm—"But surely, Master Warner, this has some virtue you have not vouchsafed to explain;—confide in me—can it change iron into gold?"

"No—but ——"

"Can it predict the future?"

"No—but ——"

"Can it prolong life?"

"No—but ——"

"Then in God's name let us waste no more time about it!" said the duchess, impatiently—"your art is mine now. Ho, there!—I will send my page to conduct thee to thy apartments, and thou shalt lodge next to Friar Bungey, a man of wondrous lere, Master Warner, and a worthy confrere in thy researches. Hast thou any one of kith and kin at home, to whom thou wilt announce thy advancement?"

"Ah, lady! Heaven forgive me, I have a daughter—an only child—my Sibyll, I cannot leave her alone, and ——"

"Well, nothing should distract thy cares from thine art—she shall be sent for. I will rank her amongst my maidens. Fare-thee-well, Master Warner! At night I will send for thee, and appoint the tasks I would have thee accomplish."

So saying, the duchess quitted the room, and left Adam alone, bending over his model in deep reverie.

From this absorption it was the poor man's fate to be again aroused.

The peculiar character of the boy-prince of Gloucester was that of one who having once seized upon an object, never willingly relinquished it. First he crept and slid, and coiled around it as the snake. But if craft failed, his passion, roused by resistance, sprang at his prey with a lion's leap: and whoever examines the career of this extroardinary personage, will perceive, that whatever might be his habitual hypocrisy, he seemed to lose sight of it wholly, when once resolved upon force. When the naked ferocity with which the destructive propensity swept away the objects in his path becomes fearfully and startlingly apparent, and offers a strange contrast to the wily duplicity with which, in calmer moments, he seems to have sought to coax the victim into his folds.

Firmly convinced that Adam's engine had been made the medium of dangerous and treasonable correspondence with the royal prisoner, and, of that suspicious, restless, feverish temperament, which never slept when a fear was wakened, a doubt conceived, he had broke from his brother, whose more open valor and less unquiet intellect were ever willing to leave the crown defended but by the gibbet for the detected traitor—the sword for the declared foe; and obtaining Edward's permission "to inquire further into these strange matters," he sent at once for the porter who had conveyed the model to the Tower; but that suspicious accomplice was gone. The sound of the explosion of the engine had no less startled the guard below than the spectators above. Releasing their hold of their prisoner, they had, some taken fairly to their heels, others rushed into the palace to learn what mischief had ensued; and Hugh, with the quick discretion of his north country, had not lost so favorable an opportunity for escape. There, stood the dozing mule at the door below, but the guide was vanished. More confirmed in his suspicions by this disappearance of Adam's companion, Richard, giving some preparatory orders to Catesby, turned at once to the room which still held the philosopher and his device. He closed the door on entering, and his brow was dark and sinister as he approached the musing inmate. But here we must return to Sibyll.

CHAPTER VIII.

The Old Woman talks of sorrows—The Young Woman dreams of Love—The Courtier flies from Present Power to Remembrances of Past Hopes—And the World-Betterer opens Utopia, with a View of the Gibbet for the silly Sage he has seduced into his Schemes—So, ever and evermore, runs the World away!

The old lady looked up from her embroidery-frame, as Sibyll sate musing on a stool before her; she scanned the maiden with a wistful and somewhat melancholy eye.

"Fair girl," she said, breaking a silence that had lasted for some moments, "it seems to me that I have seen thy face before. Wert thou never in Queen Margaret's court?"

"In childhood, yes, lady."

"Do you not remember me, the Dame of Longueville?"

Sibyll started in surprise, and gazed long before she recognized the features of her hostess; for the Dame of Longueville had been still, when Sibyll was a child at the court, renowned for matronly beauty, and the change was greater than the lapse of years could account for. The lady smiled sadly: "Yes, you marvel to see me thus bent and faded. Maiden, I lost my husband at the battle of St. Alban's, and my three sons in the field of Touton. My lands and my wealth have been confiscated to enrich new men; and to one of them—one of the enemies of the only king whom Alice de Longueville will acknowledge, I owe the food for my board, and the roof for my head. Do you marvel now that I am so changed?"

Sibyll rose and kissed the lady's hand, and the tear that sparkled on its surface was her only answer.

"I learn," said the Dame of Longueville, "that your father has an order from the Lord Hastings to see King Henry. I trust that he will rest here as he returns, to tell me how the monarch-saint bears his afflictions. But I know: his example should console us all." She paused a moment, and resumed, "Sees your father much of the Lord Hastings?"

"He never saw him that I weet of," answered Sibyll, blushing; "the order was given, but as of usual form to a learned scholar."

"But given to whom?" persisted the lady.

"To—to me," replied Sibyll, falteringly.

The Dame of Longueville smiled.

"Ah! Hastings could scarcely say no to a prayer from such rosy lips. But let me not imply aught to disparage his humane and gracious heart. To Lord Hastings, next to God and His saints, I owe all that is left to me on earth. Strange, that he is not yet here. This is the usual day and hour on which he comes, from pomp and pleasurement, to visit the lonely widow." And, pleased to find an attentive listener to her grateful loquacity, the dame then proceeded, with warm eulogies upon her protector, to inform Sibyll that her husband had, in the first outbreak of the Civil War chanced to capture Hastings, and, moved by his valor and youth, and some old connections with his father, Sir Leonard had favored his escape from the certain death that awaited him from the wrath of the relentless Margaret. After the field of Touton, Hastings had accepted one of the manors confiscated from the attainted House of Longueville, solely that he might restore it to the widow of the fallen lord; and, with a chivalrous consideration, not contented with beneficence, he omitted no occasion to show to the noblewoman whatever homage and respect might soothe the pride, which, in the poverty of those who have been great, becomes disease. The loyalty of the Lady Longueville was carried to a sentiment most rare in that day, and rather resembling the devotion inspired by the later Stuarts. She made her home within the precincts of the Tower, that, morning and eve, when Henry opened his lattice to greet the rising and the setting sun, she might catch a dim and distant glance of the captive king, or animate, by that sad sight, the hopes and courage of the Lancastrian emissaries, to whom, fearless of danger, she scrupled not to give counsel, and, at need, asylum.

While Sibyll, with enchanted sense, was listening to the praise of Hastings, a low knock at the door was succeeded by the entrance of that nobleman himself. Not to Elizabeth, in the alcoves of Shene, or on the dais of the palace hall, did the graceful courtier bend with more respectful reverence than to the powerless widow, whose very bread was his alms, for the true high-breeding of chivalry exists not without delicacy of feeling, formed originally by warmth of heart; and though the warmth may lose its glow, the delicacy endures, as the steel, that acquires through heat its polish, retains its lustre, even when the shine but betrays the hardness.

"And how fares my noble lady of Longueville? But need I ask? for her cheek still wears the rose of Lancaster. A companion? Ha! Mistress Warner, I learn now how much pleasure exists in surprise!"

"My young visitor," said the dame, "is but an old friend; she was one of the child-maidens reared at the court of Queen Margaret."

"In sooth!" exclaimed Hastings, and then, in an altered tone, he added, "but I should have guessed so much grace had not come all from nature. And your father has gone to see the Lord Henry, and you rest, here, his return? Ah, noble lady! may you harbor always such innocent Lancastrians."

The fascinations of this eminent person's voice and manner was such, that it soon restored Sibyll to the ease she had lost at his sudden entrance. He conversed gaily with the old dame upon such matters of court anecdote as in all the changes of state were still welcome to one so long accustomed to court air; but from time to time he addressed himself to Sibyll, and provoked replies which startled herself—for she was not yet well aware of her own gifts—by their spirit and intelligence.

"You do not tell us," said the Lady Longueville, sarcastically, "of the happy spousailles of Elizabeth's brother with the Duchess of Norfolk—a bachelor of twenty, a bride of some eighty-two.* Verily, these alliances are new things in the history of English royalty. But when Edward, who, even if not a rightful king, is at least a born Plantagenet, condescended to marry Mistress Elizabeth, a born Woodville, scarce of good gentleman's blood, nought else seems strange enough to provoke marvel."

"As to the last matter," returned Hastings, gravely, "though her grace the queen be no warm friend to me, I must needs become her champion and the king's. The lady who refused the dishonoring suit of the fairest prince and the boldest knight in the Christian world, thereby made herself worthy of the suit that honored her; it was not Elizabeth Woodville alone that won the purple. On the day she mounted a throne, the chastity of woman herself was crowned."

"What!" said the Lady Longueville angrily, "mean you to say that there is no disgrace in the mal-alliance of kite and falcon—of Plantagenet and Woodville—of high-born and mud-descended?"

"You forget, lady, that the widow of Henry the Fifth, Katharine of Valois, a king's daughter, married the Welch soldier, Owen Tudor—that all England teems with brave men born from similar spousailles, where love has levelled all distinctions, and made a purer hearth, and raised a bolder offspring, than the lukewarm likings of hearts that beat but for lands and gold. Wherefore, lady, appeal not to me, a squire of dames, a believer in the old Parliament of Love;—whoever is fair and chaste, gentle and loving, is, in the eyes of William De Hastings, the mate and equal of a king!"

Sibyll turned involuntarily as the courtier spoke thus, with animation in his voice, and fire in his eyes; she turned, and her breath came quick; as she turned, and her look met his, and those words and that look sank deep into her heart; they called forth brilliant and ambitious dreams; they rooted the growing love, but they aided to make it holy; they gave to the delicious fancy what before it had not paused, on its wing, to sigh for; they gave it that without which all fancy, sooner or later, dies; they gave it that which, once received in a noble heart, is the excuse for untiring faith; they gave it—Hope!

"And thou wouldst say," replied the lady of Longueville, with a meaning smile, still more emphatically—"thou wouldst say that a youth, brave and well nurtured, ambitious and loving, ought, in the eyes of rank and pride, to be the mate and equal of——"

"Ah, noble dame," interrupted Hastings, quickly; "I must not prolong encounter with

* The old chronicler justly calls this a "diabolical marriage." It greatly roused the wrath of the nobles, and indeed of all honorable men, as a proof of the shameless avarice of the queen's family.

so sharp a wit. Let me leave that answer to this fair maiden, for, by rights, it is a challenge to her sex, not to mine."

"How say you, then, Mistress Warner?" said the dame. "Suppose a young heiress, of the loftiest birth, of the broadest lands, of the comeliest form—suppose her wooed by a gentleman, poor and stationless, but with a mighty soul, born to achieve greatness, would she lower herself by hearkening to his suit?"

"A maiden, methinks," answered Sibyll, with reluctant but charming hesitation, "cannot love truly, if she love unworthily; and if she love worthily, it is not rank nor wealth she loves."

"But her parents, sweet mistress, may deem differently; and should not her love refuse submission to their tyranny?" asked Hastings.

"Nay, good my lord, nay," returned Sibyll, shaking her head with thoughtful demureness. "Surely the wooer, if *he* love worthily, will not press her to the curse of a child's disobedience and a parent's wrath!"

"Shrewdly answered," said the dame of Longueville.

"Then she would renounce the poor gentleman if the parent ordain her to marry a rich lord. Ah, you hesitate, for a woman's ambition is pleased with the excuse of a child's obedience."

Hastings said this so bitterly, that Sibyll could not but perceive that some personal feeling gave significance to his words. Yet how could they be applied to him,—to one now in rank and repute equal to the highest below the throne?

"If the demoiselle should so choose," said the dame of Longueville, "it seemeth to me that the rejected suitor might find it facile to disdain and to forget."

Hastings made no reply; but that remarkable and deep shade of melancholy which sometimes in his gayest hours startled those who beheld it, and which had perhaps induced many of the prophecies that circulated, as to the untimely and violent death that should close his bright career, gathered like a cloud over his brow. At this moment the door opened gently, and Robert Hilyard stood at the aperture. He was clad in the dress of a friar, but the raised cowl showed his features to the lady of Longueville, to whom alone he was visible; and those bold features were literally haggard with agitation and alarm. He lifted his finger to his lips, and motioning the lady to follow him, closed the door.

The dame of Longueville rose, and praying her visitors to excuse her absence for a few moments, she left Hastings and Sibyll to themselves.

"Lady," said Hilyard, in a hollow whisper as soon as the dame appeared in the low hall, communicating on one hand with the room just left, on the other with the street,—"I fear all will be detected. Hush! Adam and the iron coffer that contains the precious papers have been conducted to Edward's presence. A terrible explosion, possibly connected with the contrivance, caused such confusion among the guards, that Hugh escaped to scare me with his news. Stationed near the gate in this disguise, I ventured to enter the court-yard, and saw—saw—the TORMENTOR!—the torturer—the hideous, masked, minister of agony, led towards the chambers in which our hapless messenger is examined by the ruthless tyrants. Gloucester, the lynx-eyed mannikin, is there!"

"O Margaret, my queen!" exclaimed the lady of Longueville, "the papers will reveal her whereabout."

"No—she is safe," returned Hilyard; "but thy poor scholar, I tremble for him, and for the heads of all whom the papers name."

"What can be done! Ha! Lord Hastings is here—he is ever humane and pitiful. Dare we confide in him?"

A bright gleam shot over Hilyard's face. "Yes—yes; let me confer with him alone. I wait him here—quick!"

The lady hastened back. Hastings was conversing in a low voice with Sibyll. The dame of Longueville whispered in the courtier's ear, drew him into the hall, and left him alone with the false friar, who had drawn the cowl over his face.

"Lord Hastings," said Hilyard, speaking rapidly, "you are in danger, if not of loss of life, of loss of favor. You gave a passport to one Warner to see the ex-king Henry. Warner's simplicity (for he is innocent) hath been duped—he is made the bearer of secret intelligence from the unhappy gentlemen who still cling to the Lancaster cause. He is suspected,—he is examined—he may be questioned by the torture. If the treason be discovered, it was thy hand that signed the passport—the queen, thou knowest, hates thee—the Woodvilles thirst for thy downfall. What handle may this give them! Fly, my lord—fly to the Tower—thou mayest yet be in time—thy wit can screen all that may otherwise be bare. Save this poor scholar—conceal this correspondence.—Hark ye, lord! frown not so haughtily—that correspondence names thee as one who has taken the gold of Count Charolois, and whom, therefore, King Louis may outbuy. Look to thyself!"

A slight blush passed over the pale brow of the great statesman, but he answered with a steady voice, "Friar or layman, I care not which; the gold of the heir of Burgundy was a gift, not a bribe. But I need no threats to save, if not too late, from rack and gibbet, the life of a guiltless man. I am gone. Hold! bid the maiden, the scholar's daughter, follow me to the Tower."

CHAPTER IX.

How the destructive Organ of Prince Richard promises goodly Development.

THE Duke of Gloucester approached Adam as he stood gazing on his model. "Old man," said the prince, touching him with the point of his sheathed dagger, "look up and answer. What converse hast thou held with Henry of Windsor, and who commissioned thee to visit him in his confinement? Speak, and the truth! for by Holy Paul, I am one who can detect a lie, and without that door stands—the Tormentor!"

Upon a pleasing and joyous dream broke these harsh words; for Adam then was full of the contrivance by which to repair the defect of the engine; and with this suggestion was blent confusedly the thought, that he was now protected by royalty, that he should have means and leisure to accomplish his great design, that he should have friends whose power could obtain its adoption by the king. He raised his eyes, and that young dark face frowned upon him—the child menacing the sage—brute force in a pigmy shape, having authority of life and death over the giant strength of genius. But these words, which recalled Warner from his existence as a philosopher, woke that of the gentle, but brave and honorable man which he was, when reduced to earth.

"Sir," he said, gravely, "If I have consented to hold converse with the unhappy, it was not as the tell-tale and the espier. I had formal warrant for my visit, and I was solicited to render it by an early friend and comrade who sought to be my benefactor in aiding with gold my poor studies for the king's people.

"Tut!" said Richard, impatiently, and playing with his dagger hilt, "thy words, stealthy and evasive, prove thy guilt! Sure am I that this iron traitor, with its intricate hollows and recesses, holds what, unless confessed, will give thee to the hangman! Confess all, and thou art spared."

"If, said Adam, mildly, "your Highness—for though I know not your quality, I opine that no one less than royal could so menace; if your highness imagines that I have been entrusted by a fallen man, wrong me not by supposing that I could fear death more than dishonor; for certes!" (continued Adam, with innocent pedantry), "to put the case scholastically, and in the logic familiar, doubtless, to your Highness, either I have something to confess, or I have not—if I have——"

"Hound!" interrupted the prince, stamping his foot, "thinkest thou to banter me—see!" As his foot shook the floor, the door opened, and a man with his arms bare, covered from head to foot in a black gown of serge, with his features concealed by a hideous mask, stood ominously at the aperture.

The prince motioned to the torturer (or tormentor, as he was technically styled), to approach, which he did noiselessly, till he stood, tall, grim, and lowering, beside Adam, like some silent and devouring monster by its prey.

"Dost thou repent thy contumacy?—A moment, and I render my questioning to another!"

"Sir," said Adam, drawing himself up, and with so sudden a change of mien, that his loftiness almost awed even the dauntless Richard—"Sir, my fathers feared not death when they did battle for the throne of England; and why?—because in their loyal valor they placed not the interests of a mortal man, but the cause of imperishable honor! And though their son be a poor scholar, and wears not the spurs of gold—though his frame be weak and his hairs grey, he loveth honor also well eno' to look without dread on death!"

"Fierce and ruthless, when irritated and opposed, as the prince was, he was still in his first youth—ambition had here no motive to harden him into stone. He was naturally so brave himself that bravery could not fail to win from something of respect and sympathy, and he was taken wholly by surprise in hearing the language of a knight and hero from one whom he had regarded but as the artful impostor or the despicable intriguer.

He changed countenance as Warner spoke, and remained a moment silent. Then as a thought occurred to him, at which his features relaxed into a half smile—he beckoned to the tormentor—said a word in his ear—and the horrible intruder nodded and withdrew.

"Master Warner," then said the prince, in his customary sweet and gliding tones—"it were a pity that so gallant a gentleman should be exposed to peril for adhesion to a cause that can never prosper, and that would be fatal, could it prosper, to our common country. For look you, this Margaret, who is now, we believe, in London," (here he examined Adam's countenance, which evinced surprise), "this Margaret, who is seeking to rekindle the brand and brennen of civil war, has already sold for base gold, to the enemy of the realm, to Louis XI., that very Calais which your fathers, doubtless, lavished their blood to annex to our possessions. Shame on the lewd harlot! What woman so bloody and so dissolute? What man so feeble and craven as her Lord?"

"Alas! sir," said Adam—"I am unfitted for these high considerations of state. I live but for my art, and in it. And now, behold how *my* kingdom is shaken and rent!" he pointed wlth so touching a smile, and so simple a sadness, to the broken engine, that Richard was moved.

"Thou lovest this, thy toy? I can comprehend that love for some dumb thing that we have toiled for. Ay!" continued the prince, thoughtfully—"ay! I have noted myself in life, that there are objects, senseless as that mould of iron, which if we labor at them, wind round our hearts as if they were flesh and blood. So some men love learning, others glory, others power. Well, man, thou lovest that mechanical? How many years hast thou been about it?"

"From the first to the last, twenty-five years, and it is still incomplete."

"Um!" said the prince, smiling—"Master Warner, thou hast read of the judgment of Solomon—how the wise king discovered the truth by ordering the child's death."

"It was indeed," said Adam, unsuspectingly—"a most shrewd suggestion of native wit and clerkly wisdom."

"Glad am I thou approvest it, Master Warner," said Richard. And as he spoke the tormentor re-appeared with a smith, armed with the implements of his trade.

"Good smith, break into pieces this stubborn iron; bare all its receptacles: leave not one fragment standing on the other! *Delenda est tua Carthago*, Master Warner. There is Latin in answer to thy logic."

It is impossible to convey any notion of the terror, the rage, the despair, which seized upon the unhappy sage when these words smote his ear, and he saw the smith's brawny arms swing on high the ponderous hammer. He flung himself between the murderous stroke and his beloved model. He embraced the grim iron tighty. "Kill *me!*" he exclaimed, sublimely, "kill *me!*—not my THOUGHT!"

"Solomon was verily and indeed a wise king," said the duke, with a low, inward laugh. "And now, man, I have thee! To save thy infant—thine art's hideous infant—confess the whole!"

It was then that a fierce struggle evidently took place in Adam's bosom. It was, perhaps—O reader! thou, whom pleasure, love, ambition, hatred, avarice, in thine and our ordinary existence, tempt—it was, perhaps, to him the one arch-temptation of a life. In the changing countenance, the heaving breast, the trembling lip, the eyes that closed and opened to close again, as if to shut out the unworthy weakness—yea, in the whole physical man—was seen the crisis of the moral struggle. And what, in truth, to him, an Edward or a Henry, a Lancaster or a York? Nothing. But still that instinct, that principle, that conscience, ever strongest in those whose eyes are accustomed to the search of truth, prevailed. So he rose suddenly and quietly, drew himself apart, left his work to the Destroyer, and said—

"Prince, thou art a boy! Let a boy's voice annihilate that which should have served all time. Strike!"

Richard motioned—the hammer descended—the engine and its appurtenances reeled, and crashed—the doors flew open—the wheels rattled—the sparks flew. And Adam Warner fell to the ground, as if the blow had broken his own heart. Little heeding the insensible victim of his hard and cunning policy, Richard advanced to the inspection of the interior recesses of the machinery. But that which promised Adam's destruction, saved him. The heavy stroke had battered in the receptacle of the documents—had buried them in the layers of iron. The faithful Eureka, even amidst its injuries and wrecks, preserved the secret of its master.

The prince, with impatient hands explored all the apertures yet revealed, and after wasting many minutes in a fruitless search, was about to bid the smith complete the work of destruction, when the door suddenly opened and Lord Hastings entered. His quick eye took in the whole scene—he arrested the lifted arm of the smith, and passing deliberately to Gloucester, said with a profound reverence, but a half reproachful smile, "My lord! my lord! your highness is indeed severe upon my poor scholar."

"Canst thou answer for thy scholar's loyalty?" said the duke, gloomily.

Hastings drew the prince aside, and said, in a low tone, "His loyalty! poor man, I know not; but his guilelessness. surely, yes. Look you, sweet prince, I know the interest thou hast in keeping well with the Earl of Warwick, whom I, in sooth, have slight cause to love. Thou hast trusted me with thy young hopes of the Lady Anne; this new Nevile placed about the King, and whose fortunes Warwick hath made his care, hath, I have reason to think, some love passages with the scholar's daughter—the daughter came to me for the passport. Shall this Marmaduke Nevile have it to say to his fair kinswoman, with the unforgiving malice of a lover's memory, that the princely Gloucester stooped to be the torturer of yon poor old man? If there be treason in the scholar, or in yon battered craft-work, leave the search to me."

The duke raised his dark, penetrating eyes to those of Hastings, which did not quail. For here world-genins encountered world-genius, and art, art.

"Thine argument hath more subtlety and circumlocution than suit with simple truth," said the prince, smiling. "But it is enough to Richard that Hastings wills protection even to a spy!"

Hastings kissed the duke's hand in silence, and going to the door, he disappeared a moment and returned with Sibyll. As she entered, pale and trembling, Adam rose, and the girl with a wild cry flew to his bosom.

"It is a winsome face, Hastings," said the duke, drily. "I pity Master Nevile the lover, and envy my Lord Chamberlain the protector."

Hastings laughed, for he was well pleased that Richard's suspicion took that turn.

"And now," he said, "I suppose Master Nevile and the Duchess of Bedford's page, may enter. Your guard stopped then hitherto. They come for this gentleman from her Highness the Queen's Mother."

"Enter, Master Nevile, and you, Sir Page. What is your errand?"

"My lady, the duchess," said the page, "has sent me to conduct Master Warner to the apartments prepared for him as her special multiplier and alchemist."

"What!" said the prince, who, unlike the irritable Clarence, made it his policy to show all decorous homage to the queen's kin; "hath that illustrious lady taken this gentleman into her service? Why announced you not Master Warner, what at once had saved you from further questioning? Lord Hastings, I thank you *now* for your intercession."

Hastings, in answer, pointed archly at Marmaduke, who was aiding Sibyll to support her father. "Do you suspect me still, prince?" he whispered.

The duke shrugged his shoulders, and Adam, breaking from Marmaduke and Sibyll, passed with tottering steps to the shattered labor of his solitary life. He looked at the ruin with mourful despondence, with quivering lips. "Have you done with me?" then he said, bowing his head lowlily, for his pride was gone—"may we—that is, I and this, my poor device, withdraw from your palace? I see we are not fit for kings!"

"Say not so," said the young duke, gently, "we have now convinced ourselves of our error, and I crave thy pardon, Master Warner, for my harsh dealings. As for this, thy toy, the king's workman shall set it right for thee. Smith, call the fellows yonder, to help bear this to——" He paused, and glanced at Hastings.

"To my apartments," said the Chamberlain. "Your highness may be sure that I will there inspect it. Fear not, Master Warner; no further harm shall chance to thy contrivance."

"Come, sir, forgive me," said the duke. With gracious affability the young prince held out his hand, the fingers of which sparkled with costly gems, to the old man. The old man bowed as if his beard would have swept the earth, but he did not touch the hand. He seemed still in a state between dream and reason, life and death: he moved not, spoke not, till the men came to bear the model; and he then followed it, his arms folded in his gown, till, on entering the court, it was borne in a contrary direction from his own, to the Chamberlain's apartment; then wistfully pursuing it with his eyes, he uttered such a sigh as might have come from a resigned father losing the last glimpse of a beloved son.

Richard hesitated a moment, loth to relinquish his research, and doubtful whether to follow the Eureka for renewed investigation; but, partly unwilling to compromise his dignity in the eyes of Hastings, should his suspicions prove unfounded, and partly indisposed to risk the displeasure of the vindictive Duchess of Bedford by further molestation of one now under her protection, he reluctantly trusted all further inquiry to the well-known loyalty of Hastings.

"If Margaret be in London," he muttered to himself as he turned slowly away, "now is the time to seize and chain the lioness! Ho, Catesby,—hither (a valuable man that Catesby—a lawyer's nurturing with a bloodhound's nature!)—Catesby, while King Edward rides for pleasure, let thou and I track the scent of his foes. If the she-wolf of Anjou hath ventured hither, she hides in some convent or monastery, be sure. See to our palfreys, Catesby! Strange," (added the prince, muttering to himself), "that I am more restless to guard the crown than he who wears it! Nay, a crown is a goodly heirloom in a man's family, and a fair sight to see near—and near—and near——"

The prince abruptly paused, opened and shut his right hand convulsively, and drew a long sigh.

BOOK FOURTH.

INTRIGUES OF THE COURT OF EDWARD IV.

CHAPTER I.

Margaret of Anjou.

THE day after the events recorded in the last section of this narrative, and about the hour of noon, Robert Hilyard (still in the reverend disguise in which he had accosted Hastings) bent his way through the labyrinth of alleys that wound in dingy confusion from the Chepe towards the River.

The purlieus of the Thames, in that day of ineffective police, sheltered many who either lived upon plunder, or sought abodes that proffered, at alarm, the facility of flight. Here, sauntering in twos or threes, or lazily reclined by the thresholds of plaster huts, might be seen that refuse population which is the unholy offspring of Civil War—disbanded soldiers of either Rose, too inured to violence and strife for peaceful employment, and ready for any enterprise, by which keen steel wins bright gold. At length, our friend stopped before the gate of a small house, on the very marge of the river, which belonged to one of the many religious Orders then existing; but from its site and aspect, denoted the poverty seldom their characteristic. Here he knocked; the door was opened by a lay-brother; a sign and a smile were interchanged, and the visitor was ushered into a room belonging to the superior, but given up for the last few days to a foreign priest, to whom the whole community appeared to consider the reverence of a saint was due. And yet this priest, who, seated alone, by a casement which commanded a partial view of the distant Tower of London, received the conspirator, was clad in the humblest serge. His face was smooth and delicate; and the animation of the aspect, the vehement impatience of the gesture, evinced little of the holy calm that should belong to those who have relinquished the affairs of earth for meditation on the things of heaven. To this person the sturdy Hilyard bowed his manly knees; and casting himself at the priest's feet, his eyes, his countenance, changed from their customary hardihood and recklessness, into an expression at once of reverence and of pity.

"Well, man—well friend—good friend, tried and leal friend—speak! speak!" exclaimed the priest, in an accent that plainly revealed a foreign birth.

"Oh! gracious lady! all hope is over: I come but to bid you fly. Adam Warner was brought before the usurper; he escaped, indeed, the torture, and was faithful to the trust. But the papers—the secret of the rising,—are in the hands of Hastings."

"How long, O Lord," said Margaret of Anjou, for she it was, under that reverend disguise; "how long wilt thou delay the hour of triumph and revenge?"

The princess, as she spoke, had suffered her hood to fall back, and her pale commanding countenance, so well fitted to express fiery and terrible emotion, wore that aspect in which many a sentenced man had read his doom; an aspect the more fearful inasmuch as the passion that pervaded it did not distort the features, but left them locked, rigid, and marble-like in beauty, as the head of the Medusa.

"The day will dawn at last," said Hilyard, "but the judgments of Heaven are slow. We are favored, at the least, that our secret is confined to a man more merciful than his tribe." He then related to Margaret his interview with Hastings, at the house of the Lady Longueville, and continued:—"This morning, not an hour since, I sought him (for last evening he did not leave Edward—a council met at the Tower), and learned that he had detected the documents in the recesses of Warner's engine. Knowing, from your highness and your spies, that he had been open to the gifts of Charolois, I spoke to him plainly of the guerdon that should await his silence. Friar," he answered, "if in this court and this world I have found that it were a fool's virtue to be more pure than others, and if I know that I should but provoke the wrath of those who profit by Burgundian gold, were I alone to disdain its glitter; I have still eno' of my younger conscience left me not to make barter of human flesh. Did I give these papers to King Edward, the heads of fifty gallant men, whose error is but loyalty to their ancient sovereign, would glut the doomsman. But," he continued, "I am yet true to my king and his cause; I shall know how to advise Edward to the frustrating all your schemes. The districts where you hoped a rising, will be guarded, the men ye count upon will be watched; the Duke of Gloucester, whose vigilance never sleeps, has learned that the Lady Margaret is in England, disguised as a priest. To-morrow, all the Religious Houses will be searched; if thou knowest where she lies concealed, bid her lose not an hour to fly."

"I will NOT fly!" exclaimed Margaret; "let Edward, if he dare, proclaim to my people that their Queen is in her city of London. Let him send his hirelings to seize her. Not in this dress shall she be found. In robes of state, the sceptre in her hand, shall they drag the consort of their king, to the prison-house of her palace."

"On my knees, great queen, I implore you to be calm; with the loss of your liberty ends indeed all hope of victory, all chance even of struggle. Think not Edward's fears would leave to Margaret the life that his disdain has spared to your royal spouse. Between your prison and your grave, but one secret and bloody step! Be ruled, no time to lose! My trusty Hugh, even now, waits with his boat below. Relays of horses are ready, night and day, to bear you to the coast: while seeking your restoration, I have never neglected the facilities for flight. Pause not, O gracious lady; let not your son say—'My mother's passion has lost me the hope of my grandsire's crown.'"

"My boy, my princely boy, my Edward!" exclaimed Margaret, bursting into tears, all the warrior-queen merged in the remembrance of the fond mother. "Ah! faithful friend! he is so gallant and so beautiful! Oh, he shall reward thee well hereafter!"

"May he live to crush these barons, and raise this people!" said the demagogue of Redesdale. "But now, save thyself."

"But what!—is it not possible yet to strike the blow! Rather let us spur to the north—rather let us hasten the hour of action, and raise the Red Rose through the length and breadth of England!"

"Ah, lady, if without warrant from your lord—if without foreign subsidies—if without having yet ripened the time—if without gold, without arms, and without one great baron on our side, we forestall a rising, all that we have gained is lost; and instead of war, you can scarcely provoke a riot. But for this accursed alliance of Edward's daughter with the brother of the icy-hearted Louis, our triumph had been secure. The French king's gold would have manned a camp, bribed the discontented lords, and his support have sustained the hopes of the more leal Lancastrians. But it is in vain to deny, that if Lord Warwick win Louis——"

"He will not!—he shall not!—Louis, mine own kinsman!" exclaimed Margaret, in a voice in which the anguish pierced through the louder tone of resentment and disdain.

"Let us hope that he will not," replied Hilyard, soothingly; "some chance may yet break off these nuptials, and once more give us France as our firm ally. But now we must be patient. Already Edward is fast wearing away the gloss of his crown—already the great lords desert his court—already, in the rural provinces, peasant and franklin complain of the exactions of his minions—already the mighty House of Nevile frowns sullen on the throne it built. Another year, and who knows but the Earl of Warwick—the beloved and the fearless—whose statesman-art alone hath severed from you the arms and aid of France—at whose lifted finger all England would bristle with armed men—may ride by the side of Margaret through the gates of London?

"Evil-omened consoler, never!" exclaimed the princess, starting to her feet, with eyes that literally shot fire. "Thinkest thou that the spirit of a queen lies in me so low and crushed, that I, the descendant of Charlemagne, could forgive the wrongs endured from Warwick and his father. But thou, though wise and loyal, art of the Commons; thou knowest not how they feel through whose veins rolls the blood of kings!"

A dark and cold shade fell over the bold face of Robin of Redesdale at these words.

"Ah, lady," he said, with bitterness, "if no misfortune can curb thy pride, in vain would we rebuild thy throne. It is these Commons, Margaret of Anjou—these English Commons—this Saxon People, that can alone secure to thee the holding of the realm, which the right arm wins. And, beshrew me, much as I love thy cause—much as thou hast, with thy sorrows and thy princely beauty, glamoured and spelled my heart and my hand—ay, so that I, the son of a Lollard, forget the wrongs the Lollards sustained from the House of Lancaster—so that I, who have seen the glorious fruitage of a Republic, yet labor for thee, to overshadow the land with the throne of ONE—yet—yet, lady—yet, if I thought thou wert to be the same Margaret as of old, looking back to thy dead kings, and contemptuous of thy living people, I would not bid one mother's son lift lance or bill on thy behalf."

So resolutely did Robin of Redesdale utter these words, that the Queen's haughty eye fell abashed as he spoke; and her craft, or her intellect, which was keen and prompt where her passions did not deafen and blind her judgment, instantly returned to her. Few women equalled this once idol of knight and minstrel, in the subduing fascination that she could exert in her happier moments. Her affability was as gracious as her wrath was savage; and with a dignified and winniug frankness, she extended her hand to her ally, as she answered, in a sweet, humble, womanly, and almost penitent voice—

"O, bravest and lealest of friends, forgive thy wretched queen. Her troubles distract her brain, chide her not if they sour her speech. Saints above! will ye not pardon Margaret, if at times her nature be turned from the mother's milk into streams of gall and bloody purpose—when ye see, from your homes serene, in what a world of strife and falsehood, her very womanhood hath grown unsexed!" she paused a moment, and her uplifted eyes shed tears fast and large. Then, with a sigh, she turned to Hilyard, and resumed more calmly—"Yes, thou art right—adversity hath taught me much. And though adversity will too often but feed and not starve our pride; yet thou—thou hast made me know, that there is more of true nobility in the blunt Children of the People, than in many a breast over which flows the kingly robe. Forgive me, and the daughter of Charlemagne shall yet be a mother to the Commons, who claim thee as their brother!"

Thoroughly melted, Robin of Redesdale bowed over the hand held to his lips, and his rough voice trembled as he answered—though that answer took but the shape of prayer.

"And now," said the princess, smiling, "to make peace lasting between us;—I conquer myself—I yield to thy counsels. Once more the fugitive, I abandon the city that contains Henry's unheeded prison. See, I am ready. Who will know Margaret in this attire? Lead on!"

Rejoiced to seize advantage of this altered and submissive mood, Robin instantly took the way through a narrow passage, to a small door communicating with the river. There Hugh was waiting in a small boat, moored to the damp and discolored stairs.

Robin, by a gesture, checked the man's impulse to throw himself at the feet of the pretended priest, and bade him put forth his best speed. The princess seated herself by the helm, and the little boat cut rapidly through the noble stream. Galleys, gay and gilded, with armorial streamers, and filled with nobles and gallants, passed them, noisy with mirth or music, on their way. These the fallen sovereign heeded not; but, with all her faults, the woman's heart beating in her bosom—she who, in prosperity, had so often wrought ruin, and shame, and woe to her gentle lord; she who had been reckless of her trust as queen, and incurred grave—but, let us charitably hope, unjust—suspicion, of her faith as wife, still fixed her eyes on the gloomy tower that contained her captive husband, and felt that she could have forgotten awhile even the loss of power if but permitted to fall on that plighted heart, and weep over the past with the woe worn bridegroom of her youth.

CHAPTER II.

In which are laid open to the Reader the Character of Edward the Fourth and that of his Court, with the Machinations of the Woodvilles against the Earl of Warwick.

SCARCELY need it be said to those who have looked with some philosophy upon human life, that the young existence of Master Marmaduke Nevile, once fairly merged in the great common sea, will rarely reappear before us individualized and distinct. The type of the provincial cadet of the day, hastening courtwards to seek his fortune, he becomes lost amidst the gigantic characters and fervid passions that alone stand forth in history. And as, in reading biography, we first take interest in the individual who narrates, but if his career shall pass into that broader and more stirring life, in which he mingles with men who have left a more dazzling memory than his own, we find the interest change from the narrator to those by whom he is surrounded and eclipsed, —so, in this record of a time, we scarce follow our young adventurer into the Court of the brilliant Edward, ere the scene itself allures and separates us from our guide; his mission is, as it were, well nigh done. We leave, then, for awhile, this bold, frank nature—fresh from the health of the rural life—gradually to improve, or deprave itself, in the companionship it finds.

The example of the Lords Hastings, Scales, and Worcester, and the accomplishments of the two younger Princes of York, especially the Duke of Gloucester, had diffused among the younger and gayer part of the court that growing taste for letters which had somewhat slept during the dynasty of the House of Lancaster; and Marmaduke's mind became aware that learning was no longer the peculiar distinction of the Church, and that Warwick was behind his age, when he boasted "that the sword was more familiar to him than the pen." He had the sagacity to perceive that the alliance with the great earl did not conduce to his popularity at court; and, even in the king's presence, the courtiers permitted themselves many taunts and jests at the fiery Warwick, which they would have bitten out their tongues ere they would have vented before the earl himself. But, though the Nevile sufficiently controlled his native candor not to incur unprofitable quarrel, by ill-mannered and unseasonable defence of the hero-baron, when sneered at or assailed, he had enough of the soldier and the man in him, not to be tainted by the envy of the time and place—not to lose his gratitude to his patron, nor his respect for the bulwark of the country. Rather, it may be said, that Warwick gained in his estimation whenever compared with the gay and silken personages who avenged themselves by words for his superiority in deeds.

Not only as a soldier, but as a statesman—the great and peculiar merits of the earl were visible in all those measures which emanated solely from himself. Though so indifferently educated, his busy, practical career, his affable mixing with all classes, and his hearty, national sympathies, made him so well acquainted with the interests of his country and the habits of his countrymen, that he was far more fitted to rule than the scientific Worcester or the learned Scales. The young Duke of Gloucester presented a marked contrast to the general levity of the court, in speaking of this powerful nobleman. He never named him but with respect, and was pointedly courteous to even the humblest member of the earl's family. In this he appeared to advantage by the side of Clarence, whose weakness of disposition made him take the tone of the society in which he was thrown, and who, while really loving Warwick, often smiled at the jests against him—not, indeed, if uttered by the queen or her family, of whom he ill concealed his jealousy and hatred.

The whole court was animated and pregnant with a spirit of intrigue, which the artful cunning of the queen, the astute policy of Jacquetta, and the animosity of the different factions had fomented, to a degree quite unknown under former reigns. It was a place in which the wit of young men grew old rapidly: amidst stratagem, and plot, and ambitious design, and stealthy overreaching, the boyhood of Richard III. passed to its relentles manhood; such is the inevitable fruit of that era in civilization when a martial aristocracy first begins to merge into a voluptuous court.

Through this moving and shifting web of ambition and intrigue the royal Edward moved with a careless grace: simple himself, because his object was won, and pleasure had supplanted ambition. His indolent, joyous temper, served to deaden his powerful intellect; or, rather, his intellect was now lost in the sensual stream through which it flowed. Ever in pursuit of some new face, his schemes and counter-schemes were limited to cheat a husband or deceive a wife; and dexterous and successful, no doubt they were. But a vice always more destructive than the love of women began also to reign over him,—viz., the intemperance of the table. The fastidious and graceful epicurism of the early Normans, inclined to dainties but abhorring excess, and regarding with astonished disdain the heavy meals and deep draughts of the Saxon, had long ceased to charactcrize the offspring of that noblest of all noble races. Warwick, whose stately manliness was disgusted with whatever savored of effeminacy or debauch, used to declare that he would rather fight fifty battles for Edward IV. than once sup with him! Feats were prolonged for hours, and the banquets of this king of the Middle Ages almost resembled those of the later Roman emperors. The Lord Montagu did not share the abstemiousness of his brother of Warwick. He was, next to Hastings, the king's chosen and most favorite companion. He ate almost as much as the king, and drank very little less.

Of few courtiers could the same be said! Over the lavish profligacy and excess of the court, however, a veil, dazzling to the young and high-spirited, was thrown. Edward was thoroughly the cavalier, deeply imbued with the romance of chivalry, and, while making the absolute woman his plaything, always treated the ideal woman as a goddess. A refined gallantry—a deferential courtesy to dame and demoiselle—united the language of an Amadis with the licentiousness of a Gaolor; and a far more alluring contrast than the court of Charles II. presented to the grim Commonwealth, seduced the vulgar in that of this most brave and most beautiful prince, when compared with the mournful and lugubrious circles in which Henry VI. had reigned and prayed. Edward himself, too, it was so impossible to judge with severe justice, that his extraordinary popularity in London, where he was daily seen, was never diminished by his faults; he was so bold in the field, yet so mild in the chamber; when his passions slept, he was so thoroughly good-natured and social—so kind to all about his person—so hearty and gladsome in his talk and in his vices—so magnificent and so generous withal; and, despite his indolence, his capacities for business were marvellous:—and these last commanded the reverence of the good Londoners: he often administered justice himself, like the Caliphs of the East, and with great acuteness and address, Like most extravagant men, he had a wholesome touch of avarice. That contempt for commerce which characterizes a modern aristocracy was little felt by the nobles of that day, with the exception of such blunt patricians as Lord Warwick or Raoul de Fulke. The great house of De la Pole (Duke of Suffolk), the heir of which married Edward's sister, Elizabeth, had been founded by a merchant of Hull.

Earls and archbishops scrupled not to derive revenues from what we should now esteem the literal resources of trade.* No

* The Abbot of St. Albans (temp. Henry III.) was a vender of Yarmouth bloaters. The Cistercian Monks were wool-merchants; and Macpherson tells us of a couple of Iceland bishops who got a license from Henry VI. for smuggling. (Matthew Paris. Macpherson's Annals of Commerce, 10.) As the Whig historians generally have thought fit to consider the Lancastrian cause the more "*liberal*" of the two, because Henry IV. was the popular choice, and, in fact, an elected, not an hereditary king, so it cannot be too emphatically repeated, that the accession of Edward IV. was the success of two new and two highly popular principles—the one, that of church reform, the other, that of commercial calculation. All that immense section, almost a majority of the people, who had been persecuted by the Lancastrian kings as Lollards, revenged on Henry the aggrieved rights of religious toleration. On the other hand, though Henry IV., who was immeasurably superior to his warlike son in intellect and statesmanship, had favored the growing commercial spirit, it had received nothing but injury under Henry V., and little better than contempt under Henry VI. The accession of the Yorkists was, then, on two grounds, a great popular movement; and it was followed by a third advantage to the popular cause—viz., in the determined desire both of Edward and Richard III. to destroy the dangerous influence of the old feudal aristocracy. To this end Edward labored in the creation of a court noblesse; and Richard, with the more dogged resolution that belonged to him, went at once to the root of the feudal power, in

house had ever shown itself on this point more liberal in its policy, more free from feudal prejudices, than that of the Plantagenets. Even Edward II. was tenacious of the commerce with Genoa, and an intercourse with the merchant princes of that republic probably served to associate the pursuits of commerce with the notion of rank and power. Edward III. is still called the Father of English Commerce; but Edward IV. carried the theories of his ancestors into far more extensive practice, for his own personal profit. This king, so indolent in the palace, was literally the most active merchant in the mart. He traded largely in ships of his own, freighted with his own goods; and though, according to sound modern œconomics, this was anything but an aid to commerce, seeing that no private merchant could compete with a royal trader, who went out and came in duty-free, yet certainly the mere companionship and association in risk and gain, and the common conversation that it made between the affable monarch and the homeliest trader, served to increase his popularity, and to couple it with respect for practical sense. Edward IV. was in all this pre-eminently THE MAN OF HIS AGE—not an inch behind it or before! And, in addition to this happy position, he was one of those darlings of Nature, so affluent and blest in gifts of person, mind, and outward show, that it is only at the distance of posterity we ask why men of his own age admired the false, the licentious, and the cruel, where those contemporaries, over-dazzled, saw but the heroic and the joyous, the young, the beautiful,—the affable to friend, and the terrible to foe!

It was necessary to say thus much on the commercial tendencies of Edward, because, at this epoch, they operated greatly, besides other motives shortly to be made clear, in favor of the plot laid by the enemies of the Earl of Warwick, to dishonor that powerful minister, and drive him from the councils of the king.

One morning Hastings received a summons to attend Edward, and, on entering the royal chamber, he found already assembled, Lord Rivers, the queen's father, Anthony Woodville, and the Earl of Worcester.

The king seemed thoughtful; he beckoned Hastings to approach, and placed in his hand a letter, dated from Rouen. "Read and judge, Hastings," said Edward.

The letter was from a gentleman in Warwick's train. It gave a glowing account of the honors accorded to the earl by Louis XI., greater than those ever before manifested to a subject, and proceeded thus:—"but it is just I should apprise you that there be strange rumors as to the marvellous love that King Louis shows my lord the earl. He lodgeth in the next house to him, and hath even had an opening made in the partition-wall between his own chamber and the earl's. Men do say that the king visits him nightly, and there be those who think that so much stealthy intercourse between an English ambassador and the kinsman of Margaret of Anjou bodeth small profit to our grace the king."

"I observe," said Hastings, glancing to the superscription, "that this letter is addressed to my Lord Rivers. Can he avouch the fidelity of his correspondent?"

"Surely, yes," answered Rivers; "it is a gentleman of my own blood."

"Were he not so accredited," returned Hastings, "I should question the truth of a man who can thus consent to play the spy upon his lord and superior."

"The public weal justifies all things," said the Earl of Worcester, (who, though by marriage nearly connected to Warwick, eyed his power with the jealous scorn which the man of book-lore often feels for one whose talent lies in action,)—"so held our masters in all statecraft, the Greek and Roman."

"Certes," said Sir Anthony Woodville, "it grieveth the pride of an English knight, that we should be beholden for courtesies to the born foe of England, which I take the Frenchman naturally to be."

"Ah," said Edward, smiling sternly, "I would rather be myself, with banner and trump, before the walls of Paris, than sending my cousin, the earl, to beg the French king's

forbidding the nobles to give badges and liveries;* in other words, to appropriate armies under the name of retainers. Henry VII., in short, did not originate the policy for which he has monopolized the credit; he did but steadily follow out the theory of raising the middle class and humbling the baronial, which the House of York first put into practice.

* This also was forbidden, it is true, by the edict of Edward IV., as well as by his predecessors from the reign of Richard II., but no king seems to have had the courage to enforce the prohibition before Richard III.

brother to accept my sister as a bride. And what is to become of my good merchant-ships, if Burgundy take umbrage, and close its ports?"

"Beau sire," said Hastings, "thou knowest how little cause I have to love the Earl of Warwick. We all here, save your gracious self, bear the memory of some affront rendered to us by his pride and heat of mood; but in this counsel I must cease to be William de Hastings, and be all and wholly the king's servant. I say first, then with reference to these noble peers, that Warwick's faith to the House of York is too well proven to become suspected because of the courtesies of King Louis—an artful craft, as it clearly seems to me of the wily Frenchman, to weaken your throne, by provoking your distrust of its great supporter. Fall we not into such a snare! Moreover, we may be sure that Warwick cannot be false, if he achieve the object of his embassy—viz., detach Louis from the side of Margaret and Lancaster, by close alliance with Edward and York. Secondly, sire, with regard to that alliance which it seems you would repent—I hold now, as I have held ever, that it is a master-stroke in policy, and the earl in this proves his sharp brain worthy his strong arm; for as his highness the Duke of Gloucester hath now clearly discovered that Margaret of Anjou has been of late in London, and that treasonable designs were meditated, though now frustrated, so we may ask why the friends of Lancaster really stood aloof? why all conspiracy was, and is in vain?—Because, sire, of this very alliance with France; because the gold and subsidies of Louis are not forthcoming; because the Lancastrians see that if once Lord Warwick win France from the Red Rose, nothing short of such a miracle as their gaining Warwick instead can give a hope to their treason. Your highness fears the anger of Burgundy, and the suspension of your trade with the Flemings; but forgive me—this is not reasonable. Burgundy dare not offend England, matched, as its arms are, with France; the Flemings gain more by you than you gain by the Flemings, and those interested burghers will not suffer any prince's quarrel to damage their commerce. Charolois may bluster and threat, but the storm will pass; and Burgundy will be contented, if England remain neutral in the feud with France. All these reasons, sire, urge me to support my private foe, the Lord Warwick, and to pray you to give no ear to the discrediting his honor and his embassy."

The profound sagacity of these remarks, the repute of the speaker, and the well-known grudge between him and Warwick, for reasons herafter to be explained, produced a strong effect upon the intellect of Edward, always vigorous, save when clouded with passion. But Rivers, whose malice to the earl was indomitable, coldly recommenced.

"With submission to the Lord Hastings, sire, whom we know that love sometimes blinds, and whose allegiance to the earl's fair sister, the Lady of Bonville, perchance somewhat moves him to forget the day when Lord Warwick——"

"Cease, my lord," said Hastings, white with suppressed anger; "these references beseem not the councils of grave men."

"Tut, Hastings," said Edward, laughing merrily—"women mix themselves up in all things: board or council, bed or battle—wherever there is mischief astir, there, be sure, peeps a woman's sly face from her wimple. Go on, Rivers."

"Your pardon, my Lord Hastings," said Rivers—"I knew not my thrust went so home, there is another letter I have not yet laid before the king." He drew forth a scroll from his bosom, and read as follows:—

"Yesterday the earl feasted the king, and as, in discharge of mine office, I carved for my lord, I heard King Louis say—'Pasque Dieu, my Lord Warwick; our couriers bring us word that Count Charolois declares he shall yet wed the Lady Margaret, and that he laughs at your ambassage. What if our brother, King Edward, fall back from the treaty?' 'He durst not!' said the earl."

"Durst not!" exclaimed Edward, starting to his feet, and striking the table with his clenched hand, "Durst not! Hastings, hear you that?"

Hastings bowed his head, in assent. "Is that all, Lord Rivers?"

"All! and methinks enough."

"Enough, by my halidame!" said Edward, laughing bitterly; "he shall see what a king dares, when a subject threatens. Admit the worshipful the deputies from our city of London—lord chamberlain, it is thine office—they await in the ante-room."

Hastings gravely obeyed, and in crimson gowns, with purple hoods, and gold chains, marshalled into the king's presence a goodly deputation from the various corporate companies of London.

These personages advanced within a few paces of the dais, and there halted and knelt, while their spokesman read, on his knees, a long petition, praying the king to take into his gracious consideration the state of the trade with the Flemings; and though not absolutely venturing to name or to deprecate the meditated alliance with France, beseeching his grace to satisfy them as to certain rumors, already very prejudicial to their commerce, of the possibility of a breach with the Duke of Burgundy. The merchant-king listened with great attention and affability to this petition; and replied, shortly, that he thanked the deputation for their zeal for the public weal—that a king would have enough to do, if he contravened every gossip's tale; but that it was his firm purpose to protect, in all ways, the London traders, and to maintain the most amicable understanding with the Duke of Burgundy.

The supplicators then withdrew from the royal presence.

"Note you how gracious the king was to me?" whispered Master Heyford to one of his brethren; "he looked at me while he answered."

"Coxcomb!" muttered the confidant, "as if I did not catch his eye, when he said, 'Ye are the pillars of the public weal.' But because Master Heyford has a handsome wife, he thinks he tosseth all London on his own horns!"

As the citizens were quitting the palace, Lord Rivers joined them. "You will thank me for suggesting this deputation, worthy sirs," said he, smiling significantly; "you have timed it well!"—and passing by them, without further comment, he took the way to the queen's chamber.

Elizabeth was playing with her infant daughter, tossing the child in the air, and laughing at its riotous laughter. The stern old Duchess of Bedford, leaning over the back of the state-chair, looked on with all a grandmother's pride, and half-chanted a nursery rhyme. It was a sight fair to see! Elizabeth never seemed more lovely: her artificial, dissimulating smile, changed into hearty, maternal glee; her smooth cheek flushed with exercise, a stray ringlet escaping from the stiff coif!—And, alas, the moment the two ladies caught sight of Rivers, all the charm was dissolved—the child was hastily put on the floor—the queen, half ashamed of being natural, even before her father, smoothed back the rebel lock, and the duchess, breaking off in the midst of her grandam song, exclaimed—

"Well, well!—how thrives our policy?"

"The king," answered Rivers, "is in the very mood we could desire. At the words, 'He durst not!' the Platagenet sprung up in his breast; and now, lest he ask to see the rest of the letter, thus I destroy it;"—and flinging the scroll in the blazing hearth, he watched it consume.

"Why this, sir?" said the queen.

"Because, my Elizabeth, the bold words glided off into a decent gloss—'*He durst not,*' said Warwick, '*because what a noble heart dares least, is to belie the plighted word, and what the kind heart shuns most is to wrong the confiding friend.*'"

"It was fortunate," said the duchess, "that Edward took heat at the first words, nor stopped, it seems, for the rest!"

"I was prepared, Jacquetta;—had he asked to see the rest, I should have dropped the scroll into the brazier, as containing what I would not presume to read. Courage! Edward has seen the merchants; he has flouted Hastings—who would gainsay us. For the rest, Elizabeth, be it yours to speak of affronts paid by the earl to your highness; be it yours, Jacquetta, to rouse Edward's pride, by dwelling on Warwick's overweening power. Be it mine, to enlist his interest on behalf of his merchandise; be it Margaret's, to move his heart by soft tears for the bold Charolois; and ere a month be told, Warwick shall find his embassy a thriftless laughing-stock, and no shade pass between the house of Woodville and the sun of England."

"I am scarce queen, while Warwick is minister," said Elizabeth, vindictively. "How he taunted me in the garden, when we met last!"

"But hark you, daughter and lady liege, hark you! Edward is not prepared for the decisive stroke. I have arranged with Anthony, whose chivalrous follies fit him not for full comprehension of our objects, how upon fair excuse the heir of Burgundy's brother—the Count de la Roche—shall visit London, and the count once here, all is ours! Hush! take up the little one—Edward comes!"

CHAPTER III.

Wherein Master Nicholas Alwyn visits the Court, and there learns matter of which the acute Reader will judge for himself.

It was a morning towards the end of May, (some little time after Edward's gracious reception of the London deputies,) when Nicholas Alwyn, accompanied by two servitors armed to the teeth—for they carried with them goods of much value, and even in the broad daylight, and amidst the most frequented parts of the city, men still confided little in the security of the law—arrived at the Tower, and was conducted to the presence of the queen.

Elizabeth and her mother were engaged in animated but whispered conversation, when the goldsmith entered; and there was an unusual gaiety in the queen's countenance as she turned to Alwyn and bade him show her his newest gauds.

While, with a curiosity and eagerness that seemed almost childlike, Elizabeth turned over rings, chains, and brooches, scarcely listening to Alwyn's comments on the lustre of the gems or the quaintness of the fashion, the duchess disappeared for a moment, and returned with the Princess Margaret.

This young princess had much of the majestic beauty of her royal brother, but, instead of the frank, careless expression, so fascinating in Edward, there was, in her full and curved lip, and bright, large eyes, something at once of haughtiness and passion, which spoke a decision and vivacity of character beyond her years.

"Choose for thyself, sweetheart and daughter mine, said the duchess, affectionately placing her hand on Margaret's luxuriant hair, "and let the noble visitor we await confess that our rose of England outblooms the world."

The princess colored with complacent vanity at these words, and, drawing near the queen, looked silently at a collar of pearls, which Elizabeth held.

"If I may adventure so to say," observed Alwyn, "pearls will mightily beseem her highness's youthful bloom; and lo! here be some adornments for the bodice or partelet, to sort with the collar; not," added the goldsmith, bowing low, and looking down, "not perchance, displeasing to her highness, in that they are wrought in the guise of the fleur-de lis——"

An impatient gesture in the queen, and a sudden cloud over the fair brow of Margaret, instantly betokened to the shrewd trader that he had committed some most unwelcome error in this last allusion to the alliance with King Louis of France, which, according to rumor, the Earl of Warwick had well nigh brought to a successful negotiation; and to convince him yet more of his mistake, the duchess said, haughtily—"Good fellow, be contented to display thy goods, and spare us thy comments. As for thy hideous fleur-de-lis, an' thy master had no better device, he would not long rest the king's jeweller!"

"I have no heart for the pearls," said Margaret, abuptly; "they are at best pale and sicklied. What hast thou of bolder ornament, and more dazzling lustrousness?"

These emeralds, it is said, were once among the jewels of the great House of Burgundy," observed Nicholas, slowly, and fixing his keen, sagacious look on the royal purchasers.

"Of Burgundy!" exclaimed the queen.

"It is true," said the Duchess of Bedford, looking at the ornament with care, and slightly coloring—for, in fact, the jewels had been a present from Philip the Good to the Duke of Bedford, and the exigencies of the civil wars had led, some time since, first, to their mortgage, or rather pawn, and then to their sale.

The princess passed her arm affectionately round Jacquetta's neck, and said, "If you leave me my choice, I will have none but these emeralds."

The two elder ladies exchanged looks and smiles.

"Hast thou travelled, young man?" asked the duchess,

"Not in foreign parts, gracious lady, but I have lived much with those who have been great wanderers."

"Ah! and what say they of the ancient friends of mine house, the Princess of Burgundy?"

"Lady, all men agree that a nobler prince and a juster than Duke Philip never reigned over brave men; and those who have seen the wisdom of his rule, grieve sorely to think so excellent and mighty a lord should have trouble brought to his old age by the turbulence of his son, the Count of Charolois."

Again Margaret's fair brow lowered, and the duchess hastened to answer—"The disputes between princes, young man, can never be rightly understood by such as thou and thy friends. The Count of Charolois is a noble gentleman; and fire in youth will break out. Richard the Lion-Hearted of England, was not less puissant a king for the troubles he occasioned to his sire when prince."

Alwyn bit his lip, to restrain a reply that might not have been well received; and the queen, putting aside the emeralds and a few other trinkets, said, smilingly, to the duchess, "Shall the king pay for these, or have thy learned men yet discovered the great secret?"

"Nay, wicked child" said the duchess, "thou lovest to banton me; and truth to say, more gold has been melted in the crucible than as yet promises ever to come out of it; but my new alchemist, Master Warner, seems to have gone nearer to the result than any I have yet known. Meanwhile the king's treasurer must perforce, supply the gear to the king's sister."

The queen wrote an order on the officer thus referred to, who was no other than her own father, Lord Rivers; and Alwyn, putting up his goods, was about to withdraw, when the duchess said, carelessly, "Good youth, the dealings of our merchants are more with Flanders than with France—is it not so?"

"Surely," said Alwyn, "the Flemings are good traders and honest folk."

"It is well known, I trust, in the city of London, that this new alliance with France is the work of their favorite, the Lord Warwick," said the duchess, scornfully; "but whatever the earl does is right with ye of the hood and cap, even though he were to leave yon river without one merchant-mast."

"Whatever be our thoughts, puissant lady," said Alwyn, cautiously, "we give them not vent to the meddling with state affairs."

"Ay," persisted Jacquetta, "thine answer is loyal and discreet. But an' the Lord Warwick had sought alliance with the Count of Charolois, would there have been brighter bonfires than ye will see in Smithfield, when ye hear that business with the Flemings is surrendered for fine words from King Louis the Cunning?"

"We trust too much to our king's love for the citizens of London, to fear that surrender, please your highness," answered Alwyn; "our king himself is the first of our merchants, and he hath given a gracious answer to the deputation from our city."

"You speak wisely, sir," said the queen; "and your king will yet defend you from the plots of your enemies. You may retire."

Alwyn, glad to be released from questionings but little to his taste, hastened to depart. At the gate of the royal lodge, he gave his caskets to the servitors who attended him, and passing slowly along the courtyard, thus soliloquized:—

"Our neighbors the Scotch say, 'It is good fishing in muddy waters;' but he who fishes into the secrets of courts must bait with his head. What mischief doth that crafty queen—the proud duchess—devise? Um! They are thinking still to match the young princess with the hot Count of Charolois. Better for trade, it is true, to be hand in hand with the Flemings; but they are two sides to a loaf. If they play such a trick on the stout earl, he is not a man to sit down and do nothing. More food for the ravens, I fear—more brown bills and bright lances in the green fields of poor England!—and King Louis is an awful carle, to sow flax in his neighbor's house, when the torches are burning. Um! Here is fair Marmaduke. He looks brave in his gay super-tunic. Well, sir, and foster-brother, how fare you at court?"

"My dear Nicholas, a merry welcome and hearty to your sharp, thoughtful face. Ah, man! we shall have a gay time for you venders of gewgaws. There are to be revels and jousts—revels in the Tower, and jousts in Smithfield. We gentles are already hard at practice in the tilt-yard."

"Sham battles are better than real ones, Master Nevile! But what is in the wind?"

"A sail, Nicholas! a sail, bound to England! Know that the Count of Charolois has permitted Sir Anthony Count de la Roche, his bastard brother, to come over to London, to cross lances with our own Sir Anthony Lord

Scales. It is an old challenge, and right royally will the encounter be held."

"Um!" muttered Alwyn—"this bastard, then, is the carrier pigeon. "And," said he, aloud—"is it only to exchange hard blows that Sir Anthony of Burgundy comes over to confer with Sir Anthony of England? Is there no court rumor of other matters between them?"

"Nay. What else? Plague on you craftsmen! Ye cannot even comprehend the pleasure and pastime two knights take in the storm of the lists!"

"I humbly avow it, Master Nevile. But it seemeth, indeed, strange to me that the Count of Charolois should take this very moment to send envoys of courtesy, when so sharp a slight has been put on his pride, and so dangerous a blow struck at his interests, as the alliance between the French prince and the Lady Margaret. Bold Charles has some cunning, I trow, which your kinsman of Warwick is not here to detect."

"Tush, man! Trade, I see, teaches ye all so to cheat and overreach, that ye suppose a knight's burgonot is as full of tricks and traps as a citizen's flat-cap. Would, though, that my kinsman of Warwick *were* here," added Marmaduke in a low whisper, "for the women and the courtiers are doing their best to belie him."

"Keep thyself clear of them all, Marmaduke," said Alwyn; "for, by the Lord, I see that the evil days are coming once more, fast and dark, and men like thee will again have to choose between friend and friend, kinsman and king. For my part, I say nothing; for I love not fighting, unless compelled to it. But if ever I do fight, it will not be by thy side, under Warwick's broad flag."

"Eh, man?" interrupted the Nevile.

"Nay, nay," continued Nicholas, shaking his head, "I admire the great earl, and were I lord or gentle, the great earl should be my chief. But each to his order; and the trader's tree grows not out of a baron's walking-staff. King Edward may be a stern ruler, but he is a friend to the goldsmiths, and has just confirmed our charter. Let every man praise the bridge he goes over, as the saw saith. Truce to this talk, Master Nevile. I hear that your young hostess — ehem — Mistress Sibyll, is greatly marvelled at among the court gallants —is it so?"

Marmaduke's frank face grew gloomy. "Alas! dear foster-brother, he said, dropping the somewhat affected tone in which he had before spoken,—"I must confess, to my shame, that I cannot yet get the damsel out of my thoughts, which is, what I consider it a point of manhood and spirit to achieve."

"How so?"

"Because, when a maiden chooseth steadily to say nay to your wooing—to follow her heels, and whine and beg, is a dog's duty, not a man's."

"What!" exclaimed Alwyn, in a voice of great eagerness—"mean you to say that you have wooed Sibyll Warner as your wife?"

"Verily, yes!"

"And failed?"

"And failed!"

"Poor Marmaduke!"

"There is no 'poor' in the matter, Nick Alwyn," returned Marmaduke, sturdily; "if a girl likes me, well;—if not, there are too many others in the wide world, for a young fellow to break his heart about one. Yet," he added, after a short pause, and with a sigh,—"yet, if thou hast not seen her since she came to the court, thou will find her wonderously changed."

"More's the pity!" said Alwyn, reciprocating his friend's sigh.

"I mean that she seems all the comelier for the court air, And beshrew me, I think the Lord Hastings, with his dulcet flatteries, hath made it a sort of frenzy for all the gallants to flock round her."

"I should like to see Master Warner again," said Alwyn;—"where lodges he?"

"Yonder—by the little postern, on the third flight of the turret that flanks the corridor,* next to Friar Bungey, the magician; but it is broad daylight, and therefore not so dangerous —not but thou mayest as well patter an Ave in going up-stairs.

"Farewell, Master Nevile," said Alwyn, smiling; "I will seek the mechanician, and if I find there Mistress Sibyll, what shall I say from thee?"

"That young bachelors in the reign of Edward IV. will never want fair feres," answered the Nevile, debonnairly smoothing his lawn partelet.

*** This description refers to that part of the Tower called the King's or Queen's Lodge, and long since destroyed.**

CHAPTER IV.

Exhibiting the Benefits which Royal Patronage confers on Genius. Also the early Loves of the Lord Hastings; with other Matters edifying and delectable.

THE furnace was still at work, the flame glowed, the bellows heaved, but these were no longer ministering to the service of a mighty and practical invention. The mathematician—the philosopher—had descended to the alchemist. The nature of the TIME had conquered the nature of a GENIUS meant to subdue time. Those studies that had gone so far to forestall the master-triumph of far later ages were exchanged for occupations that played with the toys of infant wisdom. O! true Tartarus of Genius—when its energies are misapplied, when the labor but rolls the stone up the mountain, but pours water upon water, through the sieve!

There is a sanguineness in men of great intellect, which often leads them into follies avoided by the dull. When Adam Warner saw the ruin of his contrivance; when he felt that time, and toil, and money was necessary to its restoration; and when the gold he lacked was placed before him as a reward for alchemical labors—he at first turned to alchemy, as he would have turned to the plough—as he had turned to conspiracy—simply as a means to his darling end. But by rapid degrees, the fascination which all the elder sages experienced in the grand secret, exercised its witchery over his mind. If Roger Bacon, though catching the notion of the steam-engine, devoted himself to the philosopher's stone—if even in so much more enlightend an age, Newton has wasted some precious hours in the transmutation of metals, it was natural that the solitary sage of the reign of Edward IV. should grow, for a while at least, wedded to a pursuit which promised results so august. And the worst of alchemy is, that it always allures on its victims: one gets so near, and so near the object—it seems that so small an addition will complete the sum! So there he was—this great practical genius, hard at work on turning the copper into gold!

"Well, Master Warner," said the young goldsmith, entering the student's chamber—"methinks you scarcely remember your friend and visitor, Nicholas Alwyn?"

"Remember, oh, certes! doubtless one of the gentlemen present when they proposed to put me to the brake *—please to stand a little on this side—what is your will?"

"I am not a gentleman, and I should have been loth to stand idly by when the torture was talked of, for a free-born Englishman, let alone a scholar. And where is your fair daughter, Master Warner? I suppose you see but little of her now she is the great dame's waiting-damsel?"

"And why so, Master Alwyn?" asked a charming voice; and Alwyn, for the first time, perceived the young form of Sibyll, by the embrasure of a window, from which might be seen in the court below, a gay group of lords and courtiers, with the plain, dark dress of Hastings, contrasting their gaudy surcoats, glittering with cloth of gold. Alwyn's tongue clove to his mouth; all he had to say was forgotten in a certain bashful and indescribable emotion.

The alchemist had returned to his furnace, and the young man and the girl were as much alone as if Adam Warner had been in heaven.

"And why should the daughter forsake the sire more in a court where love is rare than in the humbler home, where they may need each other less?"

"I thank thee for the rebuke, mistress," said Alwyn, delighted with her speech; "for I should have been sorry to see thy heart spoiled by the vanities that kill most natures." Scarcely had he uttered these words, than they seemed to him overbold and presuming; for his eye now took in the great change of which Marmaduke had spoken. Sibyll's dress beseemed the new rank which she held: the corset, fringed with gold, and made of the finest thread, showed the exquisite contour of the throat and neck, whose ivory it concealed. The kirtle of rich blue became the fair complexion and dark chestnut hair; and over all she wore that most graceful robe called the sasquenice, of which the old French poet sang:—

> "Car nulle robe n'est si belle,
> A dame ne à demoiselle."

This garment, worn over the rest of the dress, had perhaps a classical origin, and with slight variations, may be seen on the Etruscan vases; it was long and loose—of the whitest

* Brake, the old work for rack.

and finest linen—with hanging sleeves, and open at the sides. But it was not the mere dress that had embellished the young maiden's form and aspect—it was rather an indefinable alteration in the expression and the bearing. She looked as if born to the air of courts; still modest, indeed, and simple—but with a consciousness of dignity, and almost of power; and in fact the woman had been taught the power that womanhood possesses. She had been admired, followed, flattered; she had learned the authority of beauty. Her accomplishments, uncommon in that age among her sex, had aided her charm of person: her natural pride, which though hitherto latent, was high and ardent, fed her heart with sweet hopes—a bright career seemed to extend before her; and, at peace as to her father's safety—relieved from the drudging cares of poverty—her fancy was free to follow the phantasms of sanguine youth through the airy land of dreams. And therefore it was that the maid was changed !

At the sight of the delicate beauty—the self possessed expression—the courtly dress—the noble air of Sibyll—Nicholas Alwyn recoiled, and turned pale—he no longer marvelled at her rejection of Marmaduke, and he started at the remembrance of the bold thoughts which he had dared himself to indulge.

The girl smiled at the young man's confusion.

"It is not prosperity that spoils the heart," she said, touchingly, "unless it be mean, indeed. Thou rememberest, Master Alwyn, that when God tried his saint, it was by adversity and affliction."

"May thy trial in these last be over," answered Alwyn; "but the humble must console their state by thinking that the great have their trials too; and as our homely adage hath it, 'That is not always good in the maw which is sweet in the mouth.' Thou seest much of my gentle foster-brother, Mistress Sibyll?"

"But in the court dances, Master Alwyn; for most of the hours in which my lady duchess needs me not are spent here. Oh, my father hopes great things! and now at last fame dawns upon him."

"I rejoice to hear it, mistress; and so, having paid ye both my homage, I take my leave, praying that I may visit you from time to time, if it be only to consult this worshipful master, touching certain improvements in the horologe, in which his mathematics can doubtless instruct me—Farewell. I have some jewels to show to the Lady of Bonville."

"The Lady of Bonville!" repeated Sibyll, changing color; "she is a dame of notable loveliness."

"So men say—and mated to a foolish lord; but scandal, which spares few breathes not on her—rare praise for a court dame. Few houses can have the boast of Lord Warwick's—'that all the men are without fear, and all the women without stain.'"

"It is said," observed Sibyll, looking down, "that my Lord Hastings once much affectioned the Lady Bonville. Hast thou heard such gossip?"

"Surely, yes: in the city we hear all the tales of the court; for many a courtier, following King Edward's exemplar, dines with the citizen to-day, that he may borrow gold from the citizen to-morrow. Surely, yes; and hence, they say, the small love the wise Hastings bears to the stout earl."

"How runs the tale? Be seated, Master Alwyn."

"Marry, thus: when William Hastings was but a squire, and much favored by Richard, Duke of York, he lifted his eyes to the Lady Katherine Nevile, sister to the Earl of Warwick; and in beauty and in dower, as in birth, a mate for a king's son."

"And, doubtless, the Lady Katherine returned his love?"

"So it is said, maiden; and the Earl of Salisbury, her father, and Lord Warwick, her brother, discovered the secret, and swore that no new man (the stout earl's favorite word of contempt) though he were made a duke, should give to an upstart posterity the quarterings of Montagu and Nevile. Marry, Mistress Sibyll, there is a north country and pithy proverb, 'Happy is the man whose father went to the devil.' Had some old Hastings been a robber and extortioner, and left to brave William the heirship of his wickedness in lordships and lands, Lord Warwick had not called him 'a new man.' Master Hastings was dragged, like a serf's son, before the earl on his dais, and be sure he was rated soundly, for his bold blood was up, and he defied the earl, as a gentleman born, to single battle. Then the earl's followers would have fallen on him; and in those days, under King Henry, he who bearded a baron in his hall must have a troop at his back, or was like to have a rope round his neck; but the earl (for the lion is not as fierce as they paint him) came down from his dais, and said, 'Man, I like thy spirit, and I myself will dub thee knight, that I may pick up thy glove and give thee battle.'"

"And they fought? Brave Hastings!"

"No. For, whether the Duke of York forbade it, or whether the Lady Katherine would would not hear of such strife between fere and frere, I know not; but Duke Richard sent Hastings to Ireland, and, a month after, the Lady Katherine married Lord Bonville's son and heir—so, at least, tell the gossips and sing the ballad-mongers. Men add, that Lord Hastings still loves the dame, though, certes, he knows how to console himself."

"Loves her! Nay, nay,—I trow not," answered Sibyll, in a low voice, and with a curl of her dewy lip.

At this moment the door opened gently, and Lord Hastings himself entered. He came in with the familiarity of one accustomed to the place.

"And how fares the grand secret, Master Warner? Sweet mistress! thou seemest lovelier to me in this dark chamber than outshining all in the galliard. Ha! Master Alwyn, I owe thee many thanks for making me know first the rare arts of this fair emblazoner. Move me yon stool, good Alwyn."

As the goldsmith obeyed, he glanced from Hastings to the blushing face and heaving bosom of Sibyll, and a deep and exquisite pang shot through his heart. It was not jealousy alone; it was anxiety, compassion, terror. The powerful Hastings—the ambitious lord—the accomplished libertine—what a fate for poor Sibyll, if for such a man the cheek blushed, and the bosom heaved!

"Well, Master Warner," resumed Hastings, "thou art still silent as to thy progress."

The philosopher uttered an impatient groan.

"Ah, I comprehend. The gold-maker must not speak of his craft before the goldsmith. Good Alwyn, thou mayst retire. All arts have their mysteries."

Alwyn, with a sombre brow, moved to the door.

"In sooth," he said, "I have over-tarried, good my lord. The lady Bonville will chide me; for she is of no patient temper."

"Bridle thy tongue, artisan, and begone!" said Hastings, with unusual haughtiness and petulance.

"I stung him there," muttered Alwyn, as he withdrew—"oh! fool that I was to—nay, I *thought* it never, I did but *dream* it. What wonder we traders hate these silken lords. They reap, we sow—they trifle, we toil—they steal wlth soft words into the hearts which—Oh! Marmaduke, thou art right—right!—Stout men sit not down to weep beneath the willow. But she—the poor maiden!—she looked so haughty and so happy. This is early May; will she wear that look when the autumn leaves are strewn?"

CHAPTER V.

The Woodville Intrigue prospers—Montagu confers with Hastings—Visits the Archbishop of York, and is met on the Road by a strange personage.

And now the one topic at the court of King Edward IV. was the expected arrival of Anthony of Burgundy, Count da la Roche, bastard brother of Charolois, afterwards, as Duke of Burgundy, so famous as Charles the Bold. Few indeed, out of the immediate circle of the Duchess of Bedford's confidants, regarded the visit of this illustrious foreigner as connected with any object beyond the avowed one of chivalrous encounter with Anthony Woodville; the fulfilment of a challenge given by the latter two years before, at the time of the queen's coronation. The origin of this challenge, Anthony Woodville Lord Scales has himself explained in a letter to the bastard, still extant, and of which an extract may be seen in the popular and delightful biographies of Miss Strickland.*

It seems that, on the Wednesday before Easter-day, 1465, as Sir Anthony was speaking to his royal sister, "on his knees," all the ladies of the court gathered round him, and bound to his left knee a band of gold, adorned with stones fashioned into the letters S. S., (souvenance or remembrance,) and to this band was suspended an enamelled "Forget-me-not." "And one

* Queens of England, vol. iii. p. 380.

to day! We Neviles must hold fast to each other. Not a stick should be lost if the faggot is to remain unbroken. What say you?" and the earl's keen eye turned sharply on the young man.

"I say, my lord, that the Earl of Warwick was to me, patron, lord, and father, when I entered yon city a friendless orphan; and that, though I covet honors, and love pleasure, and would be loth to lift finger or speak word against King Edward, yet were that princely lord—the head of mine house—an outcast and a beggar, by his side I would wander, for his bread I would beg!"

"Young man," exclaimed Montagu, "from this hour I admit thee to my heart! Give me thy hand. Beggar and outcast?—No!—If the storm come, the meaner birds take to shelter, the eagle remains solitary in heaven!" So saying, he relapsed into silence, and put spurs to his steed.

Towards the decline of day they drew near to the favorite palace of the Archbishop of York. There, the features of the country presented a more cultivated aspect that it had hitherto worn. For at that period the lands of the churchmen were infinitely in advance of those of the laity, in the clementary arts of husbandry, partly because the ecclesiastic proprietors had greater capital at their command, partly because their superior learning had taught them to avail themselves, in some measure, of the instructions of the Latin writers. Still the prevailing characteristic of the scenery was pasture land—immense tracts of common supported flocks of sheep; the fragrance of new-mown hay breathed sweet from many a sunny field. In the rear, stretched woods of Druid growth; and in the narrow lanes, that led to unfrequent farms and homesteads, built almost entirely either of wood or (more primitive still) of mud and clay, profuse weeds, brambles, and wild flowers, almost concealed the narrow pathway, never intended for cart or wagon, and arrested the slow path of the ragged horse bearing the scanty produce of acres to yard or mill. But, though to the eye of an economist or philanthropist, broad England now, with its variegated agriculture, its wide roads, its whitewalled villas, and numerous towns, may present a more smiling countenance,—to the early lover of Nature, fresh from the child-like age of poetry and romance, the rich and lovely verdure which gave to our mother-country the name of "Green England;" its wild woods and covert alleys, proffering adventure to fancy; its tranquil heaths, studded with peaceful flocks, and vocal, from time to time, with the rude scrannel of the shepherd—had a charm which we can understand alone by the luxurious reading of our elder writers. For the country itself ministered to that mingled fancy and contemplation which the stirring and ambitious life of towns and civilization has in much banished from our later literature.

Even the thoughtful Montagu relaxed his brow as he gazed around, and he said to Marmaduke, in a gentle and suddued voice—

"Methinks, young cousin, that in such scenes, those silly rhymes, taught us in our childhood, of the green woods and the summer cuckoos, of bold Robin and Maid Marian, ring back in our ears. Alas, that this fair land should be so often dyed in the blood of her own children! Here how the thought shrinks from broils and war—civil war—war between brother and brother, son and father! In the city and the court, we forget others overmuch, from the too keen memory of ourselves."

Scarcely had Mantagu said these words, before there suddenly emerged from a bosky lane to the right a man mounted upon a powerful roan horse. His dress was that of a substantial franklin; a green surtout of broad cloth, over a tight vest of the same color, left, to the admiration of a soldierly eye, an expanse of chest that might have vied with the mighty strength of Warwick himself. A cap, somewhat like a turban, fell in two ends over the left cheek, till they touched the shoulder, and the upper part of the visage was concealed by a half vizard, not unfrequently worn out of doors with such head-gear, as a shade from the sun. Behind this person rode, on a horse equally powerful, a man of shorter stature, but scarcely less muscular a frame, clad in a leathern jerkin, curiously fastened with thongs, and wearing a steel bonnet, projecting far over the face.

The foremost of these strangers, coming thus unawares upon the courtiers, reined in his steed, and said, in a clear, full voice—"Good evening to you, my masters. It is not often that these roads witness riders in silk and pile."

"Friend," quoth the Montagu, "may the peace we enjoy under the White Rose increase the number of all travellers through our land, whether in pile or russet!"

"Peace, sir!" retuned the horseman, roughly—"peace is no blessing to poor men, unless it bring something more than life—the means to live in security and ease. Peace hath done nothing for the poor of England. Why, look you towards yon grey tower,—the owner is, forsooth, gentleman and knight; but yesterday, he and his men broke open a yoeman's house, carried off his wife and daughters to his tower, and refuseth to surrender them till ransomed by half the year's produce on the yoeman's farm."

"A caitiff, and illegal act," said Montagu.

"Illegal! But the law will notice it not—why should it? Unjust, if it punish the knight, and dare not touch the king's brother!"

"How, sir?"

"I say the king's brother. Scarcely a month since, twenty-four persons, under George, Duke of Clarence, entered by force a lady's house, and seized her jewels and her money, upon some charge, God wot, of contriving mischief to the boy-duke.* Are not the Commons ground by imposts for the queen's kindred? Are not the king's officers and purveyors licensed spoilers and rapiners? Are not the old chivalry banished for new upstarts? And in all this, is peace better than war?"

"Knowest thou not that these words are death, man?"

"Ay, in the city! but in the fields and waste, thought is free. Frown not, my lord. Ah! I know you; and the time may come when the baron will act what the franklin speaks. What! think you I see not the signs of the storm? Are Warwick and Montagu more safe with Edward than they were with Henry? Look to thyself! Charolois will outwit King Louis, and ere the year be out, the young Margaret of England will be lady of your brave brother's sternest foe!"

"And who art thou, knave?" cried Montagu, aghast, and laying his gloved hand on the bold prophet's bridle.

* See for this and other instances of the prevalent contempt of law in the reign of Edward IV., and, indeed, during the 15th century, the extracts from the Parliamentary Rolls, quoted by Sharon Turner, History of England, vol. iii. p. 399.

"One who has sworn the fall of the house of York, and may live to fight side by side, in that cause with Warwick; for Warwick, whatever be his faults, has an English heart, and loves the Commons."

Montagu, uttering an exclamation of astonishment, relaxed hold of the franklin's bridle; and the latter waived his hand, and spurring his steed across the wild chain of commons, disappeared with his follower.

"A sturdy traitor!" muttered the earl, following him with his eye. "One of the exiled Lancastrian lords, perchance. Strange how they pierce into our secrets! heardst thou that fellow, Marmaduke?"

"Only in a few sentences, and those brought my hand to my dagger. But as thou madest no sign, I thought his grace the king could not be much injured by empty words."

"True! and misfortune has ever a shrewish tongue."

"An' it please you, my lord," quoth Marmaduke, "I have seen the man before, and it seemeth to me that he holds much power over the rascal rabble." And here Marmaduke narrated the attack upon Warner's house and how it was frustrated by the intercession of Robin of Redesdale.

"Art thou sure it is the same man, for his face was masked?"—

"My lord, in the north, as thou knowest, we recognize men by their forms, not faces, as, in truth, we ought, seeing that it is the sinews and bulk not the lips and nose, that make a man a useful friend or dangerous foe."

Montagu smiled at this soldierly simplicity.

"And heard you the name the raptrils shouted?"

"Robin?" lord. They cried out 'Robin,' as if it had been a 'Montagu' or a 'Warwick.'"

"Robin! ah, then, I guess the man—a most perilous and staunch Lancastrian. He has more weight with the poor than had Cade the rebel, and they say Margaret trusts him as much as she doth an Exeter or Somerset. I marvel that he should show himself so near the gates of London. It must be looked to. But come, cousin. Our steeds are breathed—let us on!"

"On arriving at the More, its stately architecture, embellished by the prelate with a facade of double arches, painted aud blazoned somewhat in the fashion of certain old Italian houses, much dazzled Marmaduke. And the splendor of the archbishop's retinue—less martial, indeed, than Warwick's—was yet more imposing to the common eye. Every office that pomp could devise for a king's court was to be found in the household of this magnificent prelate:—master of the horse and the hounds, chamberlain, treasurer, pursuivant, herald, seneschal, captain of the body guard, etc.—and all emulously sought for and proudly held by gentlemen of the first blood and birth. His mansion was at once a court for middle life, a school for youth, an asylum for age; and thither, as to a Medici, fled the letters and the arts.

Through corridor and hall, lined with pages and squires, passed Montagu and Marmaduke, till they gained a quaint garden, the wonder and envy of the time, planned by an Italian of Mantua, and perhaps the stateliest one of the kind existent in England. Straight walks, terraces, and fountains, clipped trees, green alleys and smooth bowling-greens abounded, but the flowers were few and common; and if here and there a statue might be found, it possessed none of the art so admirable in our earliest ecclesiastical architecture, but its clumsy proportions were made more uncouth by a profusion of barbaric painting and gilding. The fountains, however, were especially curious, diversified, and elaborate: some shot up as pyramids, others coiled in undulating streams, each jet chasing the other as serpents; some, again, branched off in the form of trees, while mimic birds, perched upon leaden boughs, poured water from their bills. Marmaduke, much astounded and bewildered, muttered a pater-noster in great haste; and even the clerical rank of the prelate did not preserve him from the suspicion of magical practices in the youth's mind.

Remote from all his train, in a little arbor overgrown with the honey-suckle and white rose, a small table before him bearing fruits, confectionary, and spiced wines, (for the prelate was a celebrated epicure, though still in the glow of youth,) they found George Nevile, reading lazily a Latin MS.

"Well, my dear lord and brother," said Montagu, laying his arm on the prelate's shoulder—"first let me present to thy favor a gallant youth, Marmaduke Nevile, worthy his name, and thy love."

"He is welcome, Montagu, to our poor house," said the archbishop, rising, and complacently glancing at his palace, splendidly gleaming through the trellis-work. "'*Puer ingenui vultûs.*' Thou art acquainted, doubtless, young sir, with the Humaner Letters?"

"Well-a-day, my lord, my nurturing was somewhat neglected in the province," said Marmaduke, disconcerted, and deeply blushing, "and only of late have I deemed the languages fit study for those not reared for our Mother Church."

"Fie, sir, fie! Correct that error, I pray thee. Latin teaches the courtier how to thrive, the soldier how to manœuvre, the husbandman how to sow; and if we churchmen are more cunning, as the profane call us (and the prelate smiled), than ye of the laity, the Latin must answer for the sins of our learning."

With this, the archbishop passed his arm affectionately through his brother's, and said, "Beshrew me, Montagu, thou lookest worn and weary. Surely thou lackest food, and supper shall be hastened. Even I, who have but slender appetite, grow hungered in these cool gloaming hours."

"Dismiss my comrade, George—I would speak to thee," whispered Montagu.

"Thou knowest not Latin?" said the archbishop, turning with a compassionate eye to Nevile, whose own eye was amorously fixed on the delicate confectionaries—"never too late to learn. Hold, here is a grammar of the verbs, that, with mine own hand, I have drawn up for youth. Study thine *amo* and thy *moneo*, while I confer on church matters with giddy Montagu. I shall expect, ere we sup, that thou wilt have mastered the first tenses."

"But——"

"Oh, nay, nay; but me no buts. Thou art too tough, I fear me, for flagellation, a wondrous improver of tender youth"—and the prelate forced his grammar into the reluctant hands of Marmaduke, and sauntered down one of the solitary alleys with his brother.

Long and earnest was their conference, and at one time keen were their disputes.

The archbishop had very little of the energy of Montagu or the impetuosity of Warwick, but he had far more of what we now call *mind*, as distinct from *talent*, than either; that is, he had not their capacities for action, but he had a judgment and sagacity that made him considered a wise and sound adviser: this he owed principally to the churchman's love of ease, and to his freedom from the wear and tear of the passions which gnawed the great minister and the aspiring courtier; his natural intellect was also fostered by much learning. George Nevile had been reared, by an Italian ecclesiastic, in all the subtle diplomacy of the church; and his ambition, despising lay objects (though he consented to hold the office of chancellor), was concentrated in that kingdom over kings, which had animated the august dominators of religious Rome.

Though, as we have said, still in that age when the affections are usually vivid,* George Nevile loved no human creature—not even his brothers—not even King Edward, who, with all his vices, possessed so eminently the secret that wins men's hearts. His early and entire absorption in the great religious community, which stood apart from the laymen in order to control them, alienated him from his kind; and his superior instruction only served to feed him with a calm and icy contempt for all that prejudice, as he termed it, held dear and precious, He despised the knight's wayward honor—the burger's crafty honesty. For him no such thing as principle existed; and conscience itself lay dead in the folds of a fancied exemption from all responsibility to the dull herd, that were but as wool and meat to the Churchman-Shepherd. But withal, if somewhat pedantic, he had in his manner a suavity and elegance aad polish, which suited well his high station, and gave persuasion to his counsels. In all externals, he was as little like a priest as the high-born prelates of that day usually were. In dress, he rivalled the fopperies of the Plantagenet brothers. In the chase, he was more ardent than Warwick had been in his earlier youth; and a dry sarcastic humor, sometimes elevated into wit, gave liveliness to his sagacious converse.

Montagu desired that the archbishop and himself should demand solemn audience of Edward, and gravely remonstrate with the king on the impropriety of receiving the brother of a rival suitor, while Warwick was negotiating the marriage of Margaret with a prince of France.

"Nay," said the Archbishop, with a bland smile, that fretted Montagu to the quick—"surely, even a baron, a knight, a franklin—a poor priest like myself, would rise against the man who dictated to his hospitality. Is a king less irritable than baron, knight, franklin, and priest?—or rather, being, as it were, *per legem*, lord of all, hath he not irritability eno' for all four? Ay—tut and tush as thou wilt, John—but thy sense must do justice to my counsel at the last. I know Edward well; he hath something of mine own idlesse and ease of temper, but with more of the dozing lion than priests, who have only, look you, the mildness of the dove. Prick up his higher spirit, not by sharp, remonstrance, but by seeming trust. Observe to him, with thy gay, careless laugh—which, methinks, thou hast somewhat lost of late—that with any other prince Warwick might suspect some snare—some humiliating overthrow of his embassage—but that all men know how steadfast in faith and honor is Edward IV."

"Truly," said Montagu, with a forced smile, "you understand mankind; but yet, bethink you—suppose this fail, and Warwick return to England to hear that he hath been cajoled and fooled; that the Margaret he hath crossed the seas to affiance to the brother of Louis is betrothed to Charolois—bethink you, I say, what manner of heart beats under our brother's mail."

"Impiger, iracundus!" said the archbishop; "a very Achilles, to whom our English Agamemnon, if he cross him, is a baby. All this is sad truth; our parents spoilt him in his childhood, and glory in his youth, and wealth, power, success, in his manhood. Ay! if Warwick be chafed, it will be as the stir of the sea-serpent, which, according to the Icelanders, moves a world. Still the best way to prevent the danger is to enlist the honor of the king in his behalf—to show that our eyes are open, but that we disdain to doubt—and are frank to confide. Meanwhile send messages and warnings privately to Warwick."

These reasonings finally prevailed with Montagu, and the brothers returned with one mind to the house. Here, as after their ablutions, they sate down to the evening meal, the archbishop remembered poor Marmaduke,

* He was consecrated Bishop of Exeter at the age of twenty, at twenty-six he became Archbishop of York, and was under thirty at the time referred to in the text.

and despatched to him one of his thirty household chaplains. Marmaduke was found fast asleep over the second tense of the verb *amo*.

CHAPTER VI.

The Arrival of the Count de la Roche, and the various Excitement produced on many Personages by that Event.

The prudence of the archbishop's counsel was so far made manifest, that on the next day Montagu found all remonstrance would have been too late. The Count de la Roche had already landed, and was on his way to London. The citizens, led by Rivers partially to suspect the object of the visit, were delighted not only by the prospect of a brilliant pageant, but by the promise such a visit conveyed of a continued peace with their commercial ally; and the preparations made by the wealthy merchants increased the bitterness and discontent of Montagu. At length, at the head of a gallant and princely retinue, the Count de la Roche entered London. Though Hastings made no secret of his distate to the Count de la Roche's visit, it became his office as Lord Chamberlain to meet the count at Blackwall, and escort him and his train, in gilded barges, to the palace.

In the great hall of the Tower, in which the story of Antiochus was painted, by the great artists employed under Henry III., and on the elevation of the dais, behind which, across Gothic columns, stretched draperies of cloth of gold, was placed Edward's chair of state. Around him were grouped the Dukes of Clarence and Gloucester, the Lords Worcester, Montagu, Rivers, D'Eyncourt, St. John, Raoul de Fulke, and others. But at the threshold of the chamber stood Anthony Woodville, the knightly challenger, his knee bound by the ladye-badge of the S. S., and his fine person clad in white-flowered velvet of Genoa, adorned with pearls. Stepping forward, as the count appeared, the gallant Englishman bent his knee half-way to the ground, and raising the count's hand to his lips, said in French—"Deign, noble sir, to accept the gratitude of one who were not worthy of encounter from so peerless a hand, save by the favor of the ladies of England, and your own courtesy, which ennobles him whom it stoops to." So saying, he led the count towards the king.

De la Roche, an experienced and profound courtier, and justly deserving Hall's praise as a man of "great witte, courage, valiantness, and liberalitie," did not affect to conceal the admiration which the remarkable presence of Edward never failed to excite; lifting his hand to his eyes, as if to shade them from a sudden blaze of light, he would have fallen on both knees, but Edward with quick condescension raised him, and, rising himself, said gaily—

"Nay, Count de la Roche, brave and puissant chevalier, who hath crossed the seas in honor of knighthood and the ladies—we would, indeed, that our roiaulme boasted a lord like thee, from whom we might ask such homage. But since thou art not our subject, it consoles us at least that thou art our guest. By our halidame, Lord Scales, thou must look well to thy lance and thy steeds' girths, for never, I trow, hast thou met a champion of goodlier strength and knightlier metal."

"My lord king," answered the count, "I fear me, indeed, that a knight like the Sieur Anthony, who fights under the eyes of such a king, will prove invincible. Did kings enter the lists with kings, where, through broad Christendom, find a compeer for your highness?"

"Your brother, Sir Count, if fame lies not," returned Edward, slightly laughing, and lightly touching the bastard's shoulder, "were a fearful lance to encounter, even thou Charlemagne himself were to revive, with his twelve paladins at his back. Tell us, Sir Count," added the king, drawing himself up—"tell us, for we soldiers are curious in such matters, hath not the Count of Charolois the advantage of all here in sinews and stature?"

"Sire," returned De la Roche, "my princely brothet is indeed mighty with the brand and battle-axe, but your grace is taller by half the head,—and, peradventure, of even a more stalwart build, but that mere strength in your highness is not that gift of God which strikes the heholder most."

Edward smiled good-humoredly at a compliment, the truth of which was too obvious to move much vanity, and said, with a royal and knightly grace—"Our House of York hath been taught, Sir Count, to estimate men's beauty by men's deeds, and therefore the

Count of Charolois hath long been known to us —who, alas, have seen him not !—as the fairest gentleman of Europe. My Lord Scales, we must here publicly crave your pardon. Our brother-in-law, Sir Count, would fain have claimed his right to hold you his guest, and have graced himself by exclusive service to your person. We have taken from him his lawful office, for we kings are jealous, and would not have our subjects more honored than ourselves." Edward turned round to his courtiers as he spoke, and saw that his last words had called a haughty and angry look to the watchful countenance of Montagu. "Lord Hastings," he continued, "to your keeping, as our representative, we intrust this gentleman. He must need refreshment, ere we present him to our queen."

The count bowed to the ground, and reverently withdrew from the royal presence, accompanied by Hastings. Edward then, singling Anthony Woodville and Lord Rivers from the group, broke up the audience, and followed by those two nobleman, quitted the hall.

Montagu, whose countenance had recovered the dignified and high-born calm habitual to it, turned to the duke of Clarence, and observed, indifferently—"The Count de la Roche hath a goodly mien, and a fair tongue."

"Pest on these Bungundians !" answered Clarence, in an undertone, and drawing Montagu aside—"I would wager my best greyhound to a scullion's cur, that our English knights will lower their burgonots."

"Nay, sir, an idle holiday show. What matters whose lance breaks, or whose destrier stumbles?"

"Will you not, yourself, cousin Montagu—you who are so peerless in the joust—take part in the fray?"

"I, your highness—I, the brother of the Earl of Warwick, whom this pageant hath been devised by the Woodvilles to mortify and disparage in his solemn embassy to Burgundy's mightiest foe !—I !"

"Sooth to say," said the young prince, much embarrassed, "it grieves me sorely to hear thee speak as if Warwick would be angered at this pastime. For look you, Montagu—I, thinking only of my hate to Burgundy, and my zeal for our English honor, have consented, as high constable, and despite my grudge to the Woodvilles, to bear the bassinet of our own champion—and——"

"Saints in heaven !" exclaimed Montagu, with a burst of his fierce brother's temper, which he immediately checked, and changed into a tone that concealed, beneath outward respect, the keenest irony, "I crave your pardon, humbly, for my vehemence, Prince of Clarence. I suddenly remember me, that humility is the proper virtue of knighthood. Your grace does indeed set a notable example of that virtue to the peers of England; and my poor brother's infirmity of pride will stand rebuked for aye, when he hears that George Plantagenet bore the bassinet of Anthony Woodville."

"But it is for the honor of the ladies," said Clarence, falteringly, "in honor of the fairest maid of all—the flower of English beauty—the Lady Isabel—that I——"

"Your highness will pardon me," interrupted Montagu, "but I do trust to your esteem for our poor and insulted house of Nevile, so far as to be assured that the name of my niece, Isabel, will not be submitted to the ribald comments of a base-born Burgundian."

"Then I will break no lance in the lists !"

"As it likes you, prince," replied Montagu, shortly; and, with a low bow, he quitted the chamber, and was striding to the outer gate of the Tower, when a sweet, clear voice behind him called him by his name. He turned abruptly, to meet the dark eye and all subduing smile of the boy-Duke of Gloucester.

"A word with you, Montagu—noblest and most prized, with your princely brothers, of the champions of our house,—I read your generous indignation with our poor Clarence. Ay, sir !—ay !—it was a weakness in him that moved even me. But you have not now to learn that his nature, how excellent soever, is somewhat unsteady. His judgment alone lacks weight and substance,—ever persuaded against his better reason by those who approach his infirmer side. But if it be true that our cousin Warwick intends for him the hand of the peerless Isabel, wiser heads will guide his course."

"My brother," said Montagu, greatly softened, "is much beholden to your highness for a steady countenance and friendship, for which I also, believe me—and the families of

Beauchamp, Montagu, and Nevile—are duly grateful. But to speak plainly (which your grace's youthful candor, so all-acknowledged, will permit), the kinsmen of the queen do now so aspire to rule this land, to marry or forbid to marry, not only our own children, but your illustrious father's, that I foresee, in this visit of the Bastard Anthony, the most signal disgrace to Warwick that ever king passed upon ambassador, or gentleman. And this moves me more!—yea, I vow to St. George, my patron, it moves me more—by the thought of danger to your royal house, than by the grief of slight to mine; for Warwick—but you know him."

"Montagu, you must soothe and calm your brother if chafed. I impose that task on your love for us. Alack, would that Edward listened more to me and less to the queen's kith:—These Woodvilles!—and yet they may live to move not wrath but pity. If aught snapped the thread of Edward's life, (Holy Paul forbid!) what would chance to Elizabeth—her brothers—her children?"

"Her children would mount the throne that our right hands built," said Montagu sullenly.

"Ah! think you so?—you rejoice me! I had feared that the Barons might, that the Commons would, that the Church *must*, pronounce the unhappy truth, that—but you look amazed, my lord! Alas, my boyish years are too garrulous!"

"I catch not your highness's meaning."

"Pooh, pooh! By St. Paul, your seeming dulness proves your loyalty; but, with me, the king's brother, frankness were safe. Thou knowest well that the king was betrothed before to the lady Eleanor Talbot; that such betrothal, not set aside by the pope, renders his marriage with Elizabeth against law; that his children may (would to Heaven it were not so!) be set aside as bastards, when Edward's life no longer shields them from the sharp eyes of men."

"Ah!" said Montagu, thoughtfully; "and in that case, George of Clarence would wear the crown, and his children reign in England."

"Our Lord forefend," said Richard, "that I should say that Warwick thought of this when he deemed George worthy of the hand of Isabel. Nay, it could not be so; for, however clear the claim, strong and powerful would be those who would resist it, and Clarence is not, as you will see, the man who can wrestle boldly—even for a throne. Moreover, he is too addicted to wine and pleasure to bid fair to outlive the king."

Montagu fixed his penetrating eyes on Richard, but dropped them, abashed, before that steady, deep unrevealing gaze, which seemed to pierce into other hearts, and show nothing of the heart within.

"Happy Clarence!" resumed the prince, with a heavy sigh, and after a brief pause—"a Nevile's husband and a Warwick's son!—what can the saints do more for men? You must excuse his errors—all our errors—to your brother. You may not know, peradventure, sweet Montagu, how deep an interest I have in maintaining all amity between Lord Warwick and the king. For methinks there is one face fairer than fair Isabel's, and one man more to be envied than even Clarence. Fairest face to me in the wide world is the Lady Anne's—happiest man, between the cradle and the grave, is he whom the Lady Anne shall call her lord! and if I—oh, look you, Montagu, let there be no breach between Warwick and the king! Fare-you-well, dear lord and cousin—I go to Baynard's Castle till these feasts are over."

"Does not your grace," said Montagu, recovering from the surprise into which one part of Gloucester's address had thrown him—"does not your grace—so skilled in lance and horsemanship—preside at the lists?"

"Montagu, I love your brother well enough to displease my king. The great earl shall not say, at least, that Richard Plantagenet, in his absence, forgot the reverence due to loyalty and merit. Tell him that; and if I seem (unlike Clarence) to forbear to confront the queen and her kindred, it is because youth should make no enemies—not the less for that, should princes forget no friends."

Richard said this with a tone of deep feeling, and, folding his arms within his furred surcoat, walked slowly on to a small postern admitting to the river; but there, pausing by a buttress which concealed him till Montagu had left the yard, instead of descending to his barge, he turned back into the royal garden. Here several of the court, of both sexes, were assembled, conferring on the event of the day. Richard halted at a distance, and contemplated their gay dresses and animated coun tenances with something between melancholy and scorn upon his young brow. One of the most remarkable social characteristics of the middle ages is the prematurity at which the great arrived at manhood, shared in its passions, and indulged its ambitions.

Among the numerous instances in our own and other countries that might be selected from history, few are more striking than that of this Duke of Gloucester—great in camp and in council, at an age when nowadays a youth is scarcely trusted to the discipline of a college. The whole of his portentous career was closed, indeed, before the public life of modern ambition usually commences. Little could those accustomed to see, on our stage, "the elderly ruffian" * our actors represent, imagine that at the opening of Shakspeare's play of "Richard the Third," the hero was but in his nineteenth year; but at the still more juvenile age in which he appears in this our record, Richard of Gloucester was older in intellect, and almost in experience, than many a wise man at the date of thirty-three—the fatal age when his sun set for ever on the field of Bosworth!"

The young prince, then, eyed the gaudy, fluttering, babbling assemblage before him with mingled melancholy and scorn. Not that he felt, with the acuteness which belongs to modern sentiment, his bodily defects amidst that circle of the stately and the fair, for they were not of a nature to weaken his arm in war or lessen his persuasive influences in peace. But it was rather that sadness which so oftens comes over an active and ambitious intellect in early youth, when it pauses to ask, in sorrow and disdain, what its plots and counterplots, its restlessness and strife, are really worth. The scene before him was of pleasure—but in pleasure, neither the youth nor the manhood of Richard III. was ever pleased; though not absolutely of the rigid austerity of Amadis, or our Saxon Edward, he was comparatively free from the licentiousness of his times. His passions were too large for frivolous excitements. Already the Italian, or, as it is falsely called, the Machiavelian policy, was pervading the intellect of Europe, and the effects of its ruthless, grand, and deliberate state-craft, are visible from the accession of Edward IV. till the close of Elizabeth's reign. With this policy, which reconciled itself to crime as a necessity of wisdom, was often blended a refinement of character which disdained vulgar vices. Not skilled alone in those knightly accomplishments which induced Caxton, with propriety, to dedicate to Richard "The Book of the Order of Chivalry," the Duke of Gloucester's more peaceful amusements were borrowed from severer Graces than those which presided over the tastes of his royal brothers. He loved, even to passion, the Arts, Music—especially of the more Doric and warlike kind—Painting, and Architecture; he was a reader of books, as of men—the books that become princes—and hence that superior knowledge of the principles of law and of commerce, which his brief reign evinced. More like an Italian in all things than the careless Norman or the simple Saxon, Machiavel might have made of his character a companion, though a contrast, to that of Castruccio Castrucani.

The crowd murmured and rustled at the distance, and still, with folded arms, Richard gazed aloof, when a lady, entering the garden from the palace, passed by him so hastily, that she brushed his surcoat, and, turning round in surprise, made a low reverence, as she exclaimed—"Prince Richard! and alone amidst so many!"

"Lady," said the duke, "it was a sudden hope that brought me into this garden,—and that was the hope to see your fair face shining above the rest."

"Your highness jests," returned the lady, though her superb countenance and haughty carriage evinced no opinion of herself so humble as her words would imply.

"My lady of Bonville," said the young duke, laying his hand on her arm; "mirth is not in my thoughts at this hour."

"I believe your highness; for the Lord Richard Plantagenet is not one of the Woodvilles. The mirth is theirs to-day."

"Let who will have mirth—it is the breath of a moment. Mirth cannot tarnish Glory—the mirror in which the gods are glassed."

"I understand you, my lord," said the proud lady; and her face, before stern and high, brightend into so lovely a change, so soft and winning a smile, that Gloucester no longer marvelled that that smile had raised so large an influence on the fate and heart of his favorite Hastings. The beauty of this noble woman

* Sharon Turner.

was indeed remarkable in its degree, and peculiar in its character. She bore a stronger likeness in feature to the archbishop, than to either of her other brothers; for the prelate had the straight and smooth outline of the Greeks—not, like Montagu and Warwick, the lordlier and manlier aquiline of the Norman race—and his complexion was feminine in its pale clearness. But though in this resembling the subtlest of the brethren, the fair sister shared with Warwick an expression, if haughty, singularly frank and candid in its imperious majesty; she had the same splendid and steady brilliancy of eye—the same quick quiver of the lip, speaking of nervous susceptibility and haste of mood. The hateful fashion of that day, which pervaded all ranks, from the highest to the lowest, was the prodigal use of paints and cosmetics, and all imaginable artificial adjuncts of a spurious beauty. This extended often even to the men, and the sturdiest warrior deemed it no shame to recur to such arts of the toilet as the vainest wanton in our day would never venture to acknowledge.

But the Lady Bonville, proudly confident of her beauty, and possessing a purity of mind that revolted from the littleness of courting admiration, contrasted forcibly in this the ladies of the court. Her cheek was of a marble whiteness, thongh occasionally a rising flush through the clear, rich, transparent skin, showed that in earlier youth the virgin bloom had not been absent from the surface. There was in her features, when they reposed, somewhat of the trace of suffering,—of a struggle, past it may be, but still remembered. But when she spoke, those features lighted up and undulated in such various and kindling life as to dazzle, to bewitch, or to awe the beholder, according as the impulse moulded the expression. Her dress suited her lofty and spotless character. Henry VI. might have contemplated, with holy pleasure, its matronly decorum; the jewelled gorget ascended to the rounded and dimpled chin; the arms were bare only at the wrists, where the blue veins were seen through a skin of snow: the dark glossy locks, which her tire-woman boasted, when released, swept the ground, were gathered into a modest and simple braid, surmounted by the beseeming coronet that proclaimed her rank. The Lady Bonville might have stood by the side of Cornelia, the model of a young and high-born matron, in whose virtue the honor of man might securely dwell.

"I understand you, my lord," she said, with her bright, thankful smile; "and as Lord Warwick's sister, I am grateful."

"Your love for the great earl proves you are noble enough to forgive," said Richard, meaningly. "Nay, chide me not with that lofty look: you know that there are no secrets between Hastings and Gloucester."

"My lord duke, the head of a noble house hath the right to dispose of the hands of the daughters; I know nothing in Lord Warwick to forgive."

But she turned her head as she spoke, and a tear for a moment trembled in that haughty eye.

"Lady," said Richard, moved to admiration, "to you let me confide my secret. I would be your nephew. Boy though I be in years, my heart beats as loudly as a man's; and that heart beats for Anne."

"The love of Richard Plantagenet honors even Warwick's daughter!"

"Think you so. Then stand my friend; and, being thus my friend, intercede with Warwick, if he angers at the silly holiday of this Woodville pageant."

"Alas, sir! you know that Warwick listens to no interceders between himself and his passions. But what then? Grant him wronged, aggrieved, trifled with,—what then? Can he injure the House of York?"

Richard looked in some surprise at the fair speaker.

"Can he injure the House of York?—Marry, yes," he replied, bluntly.

"But for what end? Whom else should he put upon the throne?"

"What if he forgive the Lancastrians? What if——"

"Utter not the thought, Prince, breathe it not," exclaimed the Lady Bonville, almost fiercely. "I love and honor my brave brother, despite—despite——." She paused a moment, blushed, and proceeded rapidly, without concluding the sentence, "I love him as a woman of his house must love the hero who forms its proudest boast. But if for any personal grudge, any low ambition, any rash humor, the son of my father, Salisbury, could forget that Margaret of Anjou placed the gory head of that old man upon the gates of York, could by word or deed abet the cause of usurping and bloody Lancaster,—I would—I would; —Out upon my sex! I *could* do nought but weep the glory of Nevile and Monthermer gone for ever."

Before Richard could reply, the sound of musical instruments, and a procession of heralds and pages proceeding from the palace, announced the approach of Edward. He caught the hand of the Dame of Bonville, lifted it to his lips, and saying, "May fortune one day permit me to face as the earl's son the earl's foes," made his graceful reverence, glided from the garden, gained his barge, and was rowed to the huge pile of Baynard's Castle, lately reconstructed, but in a gloomy and barbaric taste, and in which, at that time, he principally resided with his mother, the once peerless Rose of Raby.

The Lady of Bonville paused a moment, and in that pause her countenance recovered its composure. She, then, passed on with a stately step towards a group of the ladies of the court, and her eye noted with proud pleasure that the hightest names of the English knighthood and nobility, comprising the numerous connections of her family, formed a sullen circle apart from the rest, betokening, by their grave countenances and moody whispers, how sensitively they felt the slight to Lord Warwick's embassy in the visit of the Count de la Roche, and how little they were disposed to cringe to the rising sun of the Woodvilles. There, collected into a puissance whose discontent had sufficed to shake a firmer throne, (the young Raoul de Fulke, the idolater of Warwick, the personation in himself of the old Norman seignorie, in their centre), with folded arms and lowering brows, stood the earl's kinsmen, the Lords Fitzhugh and Fauconberg; with them, Thomas Lord Stanley, a prudent noble, who rarely sided with a malcontent, and the Lord St. John, and the heir of the ancient Bergavennies. and many another chief, under whose banner marched an army! Richard of Gloucester had shown his wit in refusing to mingle in intrigues which provoked the ire of that martial phalanx. As the Lady of Bonville swept by these gentlemen, their murmur of respectful homage, their profound salutation, and unbonneted heads, contrasted forcibly with the slight and grave, if not scornful, obeisance they had just rendered to one of the queen's sisters, who had passed, a moment before, in the same direction. The lady still moved on, and came suddenly across the path of Hastings, as in his robes of state he issued from the palace. Their eyes met, and both changed color.

"So, my lord chamberlain," said the dame, sarcastically, "the Count de la Roche is, I hear, consigned to your especial charge."

"A charge the chamberlain cannot refuse, and which William Hastings does not covet."

"A king had never asked Montagu and Warwick to consider amongst their duties any charge they had deemed dishonoring."

"Dishonoring, Lady Bonville!" exclaimed Hastings, with a bent brow and a flushed cheek,—"neither Montagu nor Warwick had, with safety, applied to me the word that has just passed your lips."

"I crave your pardon," answered Katharine, bitterly. "Mine articles of faith in men's honor are obsolete or heretical. I had deemed it dishonoring in a noble nature to countenance insult to a noble enemy in his absence. I had deemed it dishonoring in a brave soldier, a well-born gentleman, (now from his valiantness, merit, and wisdom, become a puissant and dreaded lord), to sink into that lackeydom and varletaille which falsehood and cringing have stablished in these walls, and baptized under the name of 'courtiers.' Better had Katharine de Bonville esteemed Lord Hastings had he rather fallen under a king's displeasure than debased his better self to a Woodville's dastard schemings."

"Lady, you are cruel and unjust, like all your haughty race. And idle were reply to one who, of all persons, should have judged me better. For the rest, if this mummery humbles Lord Warwick, Gramercy! there is nothing in my memory that should make my share in it a gall to my conscience; nor do I owe the Neviles so large a gratitude, that rather than fret the pile of their pride, I should throw down the scaffolding on which my fearless step hath clombe to as fair a height, and one perhaps that may overlook as long a posterity, as the best baron that ever quartered the Raven Eagle and the Dun Bull. But, (resumed Hastings, with a withering sarcasm,) doubtless the Lady de Bonville more admires the happy lord who holds himself, by right of pedigree, superior to all things that make the statesman wise, the scholar learned, and the soldier famous. Way there—back, gentles,"—and Hastings turned to the crowd behind,—"Way there for my lord of Harrington and Bonville!"

The bystanders smiled at each other as they obeyed; and a heavy, shambling, graceless man, dressed in the most exaggerated fopperies of the day, but with a face which even sickliness, that refines most faces, could not divest of the most vacant dulness, and a mien and gait to which no attire could give dignity, passed through the group, bowing awkwardly to the right and left, and saying in a thick husky voice—"You are too good, sirs—too good: I must not presume so overmuch on my seignorie. The king would keep me—he would indeed, sirs; um—um—why, Katherine—dame—thy stiff gorget makes me ashamed of thee. Thou wouldst not think, Lord Hastings, that Katherine had a white skin—a parlous white skin. La, you now—fie on these mufflers!"

The courtiers sneered. Hastings, with a look of malignant and pitiless triumph, eyed the Lady of Bonville. For a moment the color went and came across her transparent cheek, but the confusion passed, and returning the insulting gaze of her ancient lover with an eye of unspeakable majesty, she placed her arm upon her lord's, and saying calmly:—"An English matron cares but to be fair in her husband's eyes,"—drew him away; and the words and manner of the lady were so dignified and simple, that the courtiers hushed their laughter, and for the moment the lord of such a woman was not only envied but respected.

While this scene had passed, the procession, preceding Edward, had filed into the garden in long and stately order. From another entrance, Elizabeth, the Princess Margaret, and the Duchess of Bedford, with their trains, had already issued, and were now ranged upon a flight of marble steps, backed by columned alcove, hung with velvets striped into the royal baudekin, while the stairs themselves were covered with leathern carpets, powdered with the white rose and the fleur de lis; either side lined by the bearers of the many banners of Edward, displaying the white lion of March, the black bull of Clare, the cross of Jerusalem, the dragon of Arragon, and the rising sun, which he had assumed as his peculiar warbadge since the battle of Mortimer's Cross. Again, and louder, came the flourish of music; and a murmur through the crowd, succeeded by deep silence, announced the entrance of the king. He appeared, leading by the hand the Count de la Roche, and followed by the Lords Scales, Rivers, Dorset, and the Duke of Clarence. All eyes were bent upon the count, and though seen to disadvantage by the side of the comeliest and stateliest and most gorgeously attired prince in Christendom, his high forehead, bright sagacious eye, and powerful frame, did not diappoint the expectations founded upon the fame of one equally subtle in council and redoubted in war.

The royal host and the princely guest made their way, where Elizabeth, blazing in jewels and cloth of gold, shone royally, begirt by the ladies of her brilliant court. At her right hand stood her mother, at her left, the Princess Margaret.

"I present to you, my Elizabeth," said Edward, "a princely gentleman, to whom we nevertheless wish all ill-fortune,—for we can not desire that he may subdue our knights, and we would fain hope that he may be conquered by our ladies."

"The last hope is already fulfilled," said the count, gallantly, as on his knee he kissed the fair hand extended to him. Then rising, and gazing full and even boldly upon the young Princess Margaret, he added—"I have seen too often the picture of the lady Margaret not to be aware that I stand in that illustrious presence."

"Her picture! Sir Count," said the queen; we knew not that it had ever been limned."

"Pardon me, it was done by stealth."

"And where have you seen it?"

"Worn at the heart of my brother the Count of Charolois!" answered De la Roche, in a whispered tone.

Margaret blushed with evident pride and delight; and the wily envoy, leaving the impression his words, had made to take their due effect, addressed himself, with all the gay vivacity he possessed, to the fair queen and her haughty mother.

After a brief time spent in this complimentary converse, the count then adjourned to inspect the menagerie, of which the king was very proud. Edward, offering his hand to his queen, led the way, and the Duchess of Bedford, directing the count to Margaret by a shrewd and silent glance of her eye, so far smothered her dislike to Clarence as to ask his highness to attend herself.

"Ah! lady," whispered the Count, as the procession moved along, "what thrones would not Charolois resign for the hand that his unworthy envoy is allowed to touch!"

"Sir," said Margaret, demurely looking down, "the count of Charolois is a lord, who, if report be true, makes war his only mistress."

"Because the only living mistress his great heart could serve is denied to his love! Ah, poor lord and brother, what new reasons for eternal war to Burgundy, when France, not only his foe, becomes his rival!"

Margaret sighed, and the count continued, till by degress he warmed the royal maiden from her reserve; and his eye grew brighter, and a triumphant smile played about his lips, when, after the visit to the menagerie, the procession re-entered the palace, and the Lord Hastings conducted the count to the bath prepared for him, previous to the crowning banquet of the night. And far more luxurious and more splendid than might be deemed by those who read but the general histories of that sanguinary time, or the inventories of furniture in the houses even of the great barons, was the accomodation which Edward afforded to his guest. His apartments and chambers were hung with white silk and linen, the floors covered with richly woven carpets; the counterpane of his bed was cloth of gold, trimmed with ermine; the cupboard shone with vessels of silver and gold; and over two baths were pitched tents of white cloth of Rennes, fringed with silver.*

Agreeably to the manners of the time, Lord Hastings assisted to disrobe the count; and the more to bear him company, afterwards undressed himself and bathed in the one bath, while the count refreshed his limbs in the other.

"Pri'thee," said De la Roche, drawing aside the curtain of his tent, and putting forth his head—"pri'thee, my Lord Hastings, deign to instruct my ignorance of a court which I would fain know well, and let me weet, whether the splendor of your king, far exceeding what I was taught to look for, is derived from his revenue, as sovereign of England, or chief of the House of York?"

"Sir," returned Hastings, gravely, putting out his own head—"it is Edward's happy fortune to be the wealthiest proprietor in England, except the Earl of Warwick, and thus he is enabled to indulge a state which yet oppresses not his people."

"Except the Earl of Warwick," repeated the count, musingly, as the fumes of the odors, with which the bath was filled, rose in a cloud over his long hair—"ill would fare that subject, in most lands, who was as wealthy as his king! You have heard that Warwick has met King Louis at Rouen, and that they are inseparable?"

"It becomes an ambassador to win grace of him he is sent to please."

"But none win grace of Louis whom Louis does not dupe."

"You know not Lord Warwick, Sir Count. His mind is so strong and so frank, that it is as hard to deceive him, as it is for him to be deceived."

"Time will show," said the count, pettishly, and he withdrew his head into the tent.

And now there appeared the attendants, with hippocras, syrups, and comfits, by way of giving appetite for the supper, so that no farther opportunity for private conversation was left to the two lords. While the count was dressing, the Lord Scales entered with a superb gown, clasped with jewels, and lined with minever, with which Edward had commissioned him to present the Bastard. In this robe the Lord Scales insisted upon enduing his antagonist with his own hands, and the three knights then repaired to the banquet. At the king's table no male personage out of the royal family sate, except Lord Rivers—as Elizabeth's father—and the Count De la Roche, placed between Margaret and the Duchess of Bedford.

At another table, the great peers of the realm feasted under the presidence of Anthony Woodville, while, entirely filling one side of the hall, the ladies of the court held their "mess," (so called,) apart, and "great and mighty was the eating thereof!"

The banquet ended, the dance begun. The admirable "featliness" of the Count de la Roche, in the pavon, with the Lady Margaret, was rivalled only by the more majestic grace

* See Madden's Narrative of the Lord Grauthuse: *Archæologia*, 183c.

of Edward and the dainty steps of Anthony Woodville. But the lightest and happiest heart which beat in that revel was one in which no scheme and no ambition but those of love nursed the hope and dreamed the triumph.

Stung by the coldness, even more than by the disdain of the Lady Bonville, and enraged to find that no taunt of his own, however galling, could ruffle a dignity which was an insult both to memory and to self-love, Hastings had exerted more than usual, both at the banquet and in the revel, those general powers of pleasing, which, even in an age when personal qualifications ranked so high, had yet made him no less renowned for successes in gallantry than the beautiful and youthful king. All about this man witnessed to the triumph of mind over the obstacles that beset it;—his rise without envy, his safety amidst foes, the happy ease with which he moved through the snares and pits of everlasting stratagem and universal wile! Him alone the arts of the Woodvilles could not supplant in Edward's confidence and love; to him alone dark Gloucester bent his haughty soul; him alone, Warwick, who had rejected his alliance, and knew the private grudge the rejection bequeathed;—him alone, among the "new men," Warwick always treated with generous respect, as a wise patriot, and a fearless soldier; and in the more frivolous scenes of courtly life, the same mind raised one no longer in the bloom of youth, with no striking advantages of person, and studiously disdainful of all the fopperies of the time, to an equality with the youngest, the fairest, the gaudiest courtier, in that rivalship, which has pleasure for its object and love for its reward.

Many a heart beat quicker as the graceful courtier, with that careless wit which veiled his profound mournfulness of character, or with that delicate flattery which his very contempt for human nature had taught him, moved from dame to donzell;—till at length, in the sight and hearing of the Lady Bonville, as she sate, seemingly heedless of his revenge, amidst a group of matrons elder than herself, a murmur of admiration made him turn quickly, and his eye following the gaze of the bystanders, rested upon the sweet, animated face of Sibyll, flushed into rich bloom at the notice it excited. Then as he approached the maiden, his quick glance darting to the woman he had first loved, told him that he had at last discovered the secret how to wound. An involuntary compression of Katherine's proud lips, a hasty rise and fall of the stately neck, a restless, indescribable flutter, as it were, of the whole frame, told the experienced woman-reader of the signs of jealousy and fear. And he passed at once to the young maiden's side. Alas! what wonder that Sibyll that night surrendered her heart to the happiest dreams; and finding herself on the floors of a court—intoxicated by its perfumed air,—hearing on all sides the murmured eulogies which approved and justified the seeming preference of the powerful noble,—what wonder that she thought the humble maiden, with her dower of radaint youth and exquisite beauty, and the fresh and countless treasures of virgin love, might be no unworthy mate of the "new lord."

It was morning * before the revel ended; and, when dismissed by the Duchess of Bedford, Sibyll was left to herself, not even amidst her happy visions did the daughter forget her office. She stole into her father's chamber. He, too, was astir and up—at work at the untiring furnace, the damps on his brow, but all hope's vigor at his heart. So while Pleasure feasts, and Youth reveals, and Love deludes itself, and Ambition chases its shadows—(chased itself by Death)—so works the world-changing and world-despised SCIENCE, the life within life, for all living—and to all dead!

CHAPTER VII.

The renowned Combat between Sir Anthony Woodville and the Bastard of Burgundy.

AND now the day came for the memorable joust between the queen's brother and the Count de la Roche. By a chapter solemnly convoked at St. Paul's, the preliminaries were settled;—upon the very timber used in decking the lists, King Edward expended half the yearly revenue derived from all the forests of his duchy of York. In the wide space of Smithfield, destined at a later day to blaze with the fires of intolerant bigotry, crowded

* The hours of our ancestors, on great occasions, were not always more seasonable than our own. Froissart speaks of Court Balls, in the reign of Richard II., kept up till day.

London's holiday population; and yet, though all the form and parade of chivalry were there —though, in the open balconies, never presided a braver king or a comelier queen—though never a more accomplished chevalier than Sir Anthony Lord of Scales, nor a more redoubted knight than the brother of Charles the Bold, met lance to lance,—it was obvious to the elder and more observant spectators, that the true spirit of the lists was already fast wearing out from the influences of the age; that the *gentleman* was succeeding to the *knight*, that a more silken, and scheming race had become the heirs of the iron men, who, under Edward III., had realized the fabled Paladins of Charlemagne and Arthur. But the actors were less changed than the spectators,—the Well-born than the People. Instead of that hearty sympathy in the contest, that awful respect for the champions, that eager anxiety for the honor of the national lance, which, a century or more ago, would have moved the throng as one breast, the comments of the bystanders, evinced rather the cynicism of ridicule, the feeling that the contest was unreal, and that chivalry was out of place in the practical temper of the times. On the great chessboard, the pawns were now so marshalled, that the knights' moves were no longer able to scour the board and hold in check both castle and king.

"Gramercy!" said Master Stokton, who sate in high state as Sheriff,* "this is a sad waste of moneys; and where, after all, is the glory in two tall fellows, walled a yard thick in armor, poking at each other with poles of painted wood?"

"Give me a good bull-bait!" said a sturdy butcher, in the crowd below—"that's more English, I take it, than these fooleries."

Amongst the ring, the bold 'prentices of London, up and away betimes, had pushed their path into a foremost place, much to the discontent of the gentry, and with their flat caps, long hair, thick bludgeons, loud exclamations, and turbulent demeanor, greatly scandalized the formal heralds. That, too, was a sign of the times. Nor less did it show the growth of commerce, that, on seats very little below the regal balconies, and far more conspicuous than the places of earls and barons, sate in state the mayor (that mayor a grocer *) and aldermen of the city.

A murmur, rising gradually into a general shout, evinced the admiration into which the spectators were surprised, when Anthony Woodville Lord Scales—his head bare—appeared at the entrance of the lists—so bold and so fair was his countenance, so radiant his armor, and so richly caparisoned his gray steed, in the gorgeous housings that almost swept the ground; and around him grouped such an attendance of knights and peers as seldom graced the train of any subject, with the Duke of Clarence at his right hand, bearing his bassinet.

But Anthony's pages, supporting his banner, shared at least the popular admiration with their gallant lord: they were, according to the old custom, which probably fell into disuse under the Tudors, disguised in imitation of the heraldic beasts that typified his armorial cognizance:† and horrible and laidley looked they in the guise of griffins, with artful scales of thin steel painted green, red forked tongues, and griping the banner in one hugh claw, while, much to the marvel of the bystanders, they contrived to walk very statelily on the other. "Oh, the brave monsters!" exclaimed the butcher, "Cogs bones, this beats all the rest!"

But when the trumpets of the heralds had ceased, when the words "*Laissez aller!*" were pronounced, when the lances were set and the charge began, this momentary admiration was converted into a cry of derision, by the sudden restiveness of the Burgundian's horse. This animal, of the pure race of Flanders, of a bulk approaching to clumsiness, of a rich bay, where, indeed, amidst the barding and the housings, its color could be discerned, had borne the valiant Bastard through many a sanguine field, and in the last had received a wound which had greatly impaired its sight. And now, whether scared by the shouting, or terrified by its obscure vision, and the reccollection of its wound when last bestrode by its lord, it halted midway, reared on end, and, fairly turning round, despite spur and bit, carried back the Bastard, swearing strange oaths, that grumbled hoarsely through his vizor, to the very place whence he had started.

* Fabyan.

* Sir John Yonge—Fabyan.

† Hence the origin of *Supporters*.

The uncourteous mob yelled and shouted and laughed, and wholly disregarding the lifted wands, and drowning the solemn rebukes of the heralds, they heaped upon the furious Burgundian all the expressions of ridicule in which the wit of Cockaigne is so immemorially rich. But the courteous Anthony of England, seeing the strange and involuntary flight of his redoubted foe, incontinently reigned-in, lowered his lance, and made his horse, without turning round, back to the end of the lists in a series of graceful gambadas and caracols. Again the signal was given, and this time the gallant bay did not fail his rider;—ashamed, doubtless, of its late misdemeanor,—arching its head till it almost touched the breast, laying its ears level on the neck, and with a snort of anger and disdain, the steed of Flanders rushed to the encounter. The Bastard's lance shivered fairly against the small shield of the Englishman, but the Woodville's weapon more deftly aimed, struck full on the count's bassinet, and at the same time the pike projecting from the gray charger's chaffron pierced the nostrils of the unhappy bay, whom rage and shame had blinded more than ever. The noble animal, stung by the unexpected pain, and bitted sharply by the rider, whose seat was sorely shaken by the stroke on his helmet, reared again, stood an instant perfectly erect, and then fell backwards, rolling over and over the illustrious burden it had borne. Then the debonnair Sir Anthony of England, casting down his lance, drew his sword, and dexterously caused his distrier to curvet in a close circle round the fallen Bastard, courteously shaking at him the brandished weapon, but without attempt to strike.

"Ho, marshal!" cried King Edward, "assist to his legs the brave count."

The marshal hastened to obey. "*Ventrebleu!*" quoth the Bastard, when extricated from the weight of his steed, "I cannot hold by the clouds, but though my horse failed me, surely I will not fail my companions"—and as he spoke, he placed himself in so gallant and superb a posture, that he silenced the inhospitable yell which had rejoiced in the foreigner's discomfiture. Then, observing that the gentle Anthony had dismounted, and was leaning gracefully against his destrier, the Burgundian called forth—

"Sir Knight, thou hast conquered the steed, not the rider. We are now foot to foot. The pole-axe, or the sword—which? Speak?"

"I pray thee, noble sieur," quoth the Woodville, mildly, "to let the strife close for this day, and when rest hath ——"

"Talk of rest to striplings—I demand my rights!"

"Heaven forefend," said Anthony Woodville, lifting his hand on high, "that I, favored so highly by the fair dames of England, should demand repose on their behalf. But bear witness—" he said, (with the generosity of the last true chevalier of his age, and lifting his vizor, so as to be heard by the king, and even through the foremost ranks of the crowd)—"bear witness, that in this encounter, my cause hath befriended me, not mine arm. The Count de la Roche speaketh truly; and his steed alone be blamed for his mischance."

"It is but a blind beast!" muttered the Burgundian.

"And," added Anthony, bowing towards the tiers rich with the beauty of the court—"and the count himself assureth me that the blaze of yonder eyes blinded his goodly steed." Having delivered himself of this gallant conceit, so much in accordauce with the taste of the day, the Englishman, approaching the king's balcony, craved permission to finish the encounter with the axe or brand.

"The former, rather, please you, my liege; for the warriors of Burgundy have ever been deemed unconquered in that martial weapon."

Edward, whose brave blood was up and warm at the clash of steel, bowed his gracious assent, and two pole-axes were brought into the ring.

The crowd now evinced a more earnest and respectful attention than they had hitherto shown, for the pole-axe, in such stalwart hands, was no child's toy. "Hum," quoth Master Stokton, "there may be some merriment now—not like those silly poles! Your axe lops off a limb mighty cleanly."

The knights themselves seemed aware of the greater gravity of the present encounter. Each looked well to the bracing of his vizor;—and poising their weapons with method and care, they stood apart some moments, eyeing each other steadfastly,—as adriot fencers with the small sword do in our schools at this day.

At length, the Burgundian, darting forward,

launched a mighty stroke at the Lord Scales, which, though rapidly parried, broke down the guard, and descended with such weight on the shoulder, that but for the thrice-proven steel of Milan, the benevolent expectation of Master Stokton had been happily fulfilled. Even as it was, the Lord Scales uttered a slight cry—which might be either of anger or of pain—and lifting his axe with both hands, levelled a blow on the Burgundian's helmet that well nigh brought him to his knee. And now, for the space of some ten minutes, the crowd, with charmed suspense, beheld the almost breathless rapidity with which stroke on stroke was given and parried; the axe shifted to and fro—wielded now with both hands—now the left, now the right—and the combat reeling, as it were, to and fro, so that one moment it raged at one extreme of the lists—the next at the other; and so well inured, from their very infancy, to the weight of mail were these redoubted champions, that the very wrestlers on the village green, nay, the naked gladiators of old, might have envied their lithe agility and supple quickness.

At last, by a most dexterous stroke, Anthony Woodville forced the point of his axe into the vizor of the Burgundian, and there so firmly did it stick, that he was enabled to pull his antagonist to and fro at his will, while the Bastard, rendered as blind as his horse by the stoppage of the eye-hole, dealt his own blows about at random, and was placed completely at the mercy of the Englishman. And gracious as the gentle Sir Anthony was, he was still so smarting under many a bruise felt through his dinted mail, that small mercy, perchance, would the Bastard have found, for the gripe of the Woodville's left hand was on his foe's throat, and the right seemed about to force the point deliberately forward into the brain, when Edward, roused from his delight at that pleasing spectacle by a loud shriek from his sister Margaret, echoed by the Duchess of Bedford, who was by no means anxious that her son's axe should be laid at the root of all her schemes, rose, and crying, "Hold!" with that loud voice which had so often thrilled a mightier field, cast down his warderer.

Instantly the lists opened—the marshals advanced—severed the champions—and unbraced the count's helmet. But the Bastard's martial spirit, exceedingly dissatisfied at the unfriendiy interruption, rewarded the attention of the marshals by an oath, worthy his relationship to Charles the Bold; and hurrying straight to the king, his face flushed with wrath, and his eyes sparkling with fire—

"Noble sire and king," he cried, "do me not this wrong! I am not overthrown, nor scathed, nor subdued—I yield not. By every knightly law, till one champion yields, he can call upon the other to lay on and do his worst."

Edward paused, much perplexed and surprised at finding his intercession so displeasing. He glanced first at the Lord Rivers, who sate a little below him, and whose cheek grew pale at the prospect of his son's renewed encounter with one so determined—then at the immovable aspect of the gentle apathetic Elizabeth—then at the agitated countenance of the duchess—then at the imploring eyes of Margaret, who, with an effort, preserved herself from swooning; and, finally, beckoning to him the Duke of Clarence, as high constable, and the Duke of Norfork, as earl marshal, he said, "Tarry a moment, Sir Count, till we take the counsel in this grave affair." The count bowed sullenly—the spectators maintained an anxious silence—the curtain before the king's gallery was closed while the council conferred. At the end of some three minutes however, the drapery was drawn aside by the Duke of Norfolk; and Edward, fixing his bright blue eye upon the fiery Burgundian, said gravely, "Count de la Roche, your demand is just. According to the laws of the list, you may fairly claim that the encounter go on."

"Oh! knightly prince, well said. My thanks! We lose time—squires, my bassinet!"

"Yea," renewed Edward, "bring hither the count's bassinet. By the laws, the combat may go on at thine asking—I retract my warderer. But, Count de la Roche, by those laws you appeal to, the said combat must go on precisely at the point at which it was broken off. Wherefore brace on thy bassinet, Count de la Roche—and thou, Anthony Lord Scales, fix the pike of thine axe, which I now perceive was inserted exactly where the right eye giveth easy access to the brain, precisely in the same place. So renew the contest, and the Lord have mercy on thy soul, Count de la Roche!"

At this startling sentence, wholly unexpected, and yet wholly according to those laws of which Edward was so learned a judge, the Bastard's visage fell. With open mouth and astounded eyes, he stood gazing at the king, who, majestically reseating himself, motioned to the heralds.

"Is that the law, sire?" at length faltered forth the Bastard.

"Can you dispute it? Can any knight or gentleman gainsay it?"

"Then," quoth the Bastard, gruffly, and throwing his axe to the ground, "by all the saints in the calendar! I have had enough. I came hither to dare all that beseems a chevalier, but to stand still while Sir Anthonr Woodville deliberately pokes out my right eye, were a feat to show that very few brains would follow. And so, my Lord Scales, I give thee my right hand, and wish thee joy of thy triumph, and the golden collar." *

"No triumph," replied the Woodville, modestly, "for thou art only, as brave knights should be, subdued by the charms of the ladies, which no breast however valiant, can with impunity dispute."

So saying, the Lord Scales led the count to a seat of honor near the Lord Rivers. And the actor was contented, perforce, to become a spectator of the ensuing contests. These were carried on till late at noon between the Burgundians and the English, the last maintainiug the superiority of their principal champion; and among those in the melée, to which squires were admitted, not the least distinguished and conspicious was our youthful friend, Master Marmaduke Nevile.

CHAPTER VIII.

How the Bastard of Burgundy prospered more in his Policy than with the Pole-Axe—And how King Edward holds his Summer Chase in the fair Groves of Shene.

It was some days after the celebrated encounter Between the Bastard and Lord Scales; and the court had removed to the Palace of Shene. The Count de la Roche's favor with the Duchess of Bedford and the young princess had not rested upon his reputation for skill with the pole-axe, and it had now increased to a height that might well recompense the diplomatist for his discomfiture in the lists.

In the meanwhile, the arts of Warwick's enemies had been attended with signal success. The final preparations for the alliance, now virtually concluded, with Louis's brother, still detained the earl at Rouen, and fresh accounts of the French king's intimacy with the ambassador were carefully forwarded to Rivers, and transmitted to Edward. Now, we have Edward's own authority for stating that his first grudge against Warwick originated in this displeasing intimacy, but the English king was too clear-sighted to interpret such courtesies into the gloss given them by Rivers. He did not for a moment conceive that Lord Warwick was led into any absolute connection with Louis which could link him to the Lancastrians, for this was against common sense; but Edward, with all his good-humor, was implacable and vindictive, and he could not endure the thought that Warwick should gain the friendship of the man he deemed his foe. Putting aside his causes of hatred to Louis, in the encouragement which that king had formerly given to the Lancastrian exiles, Edward's pride as sovereign felt acutely the slighting disdain with which the French king had hitherto treated his royalty and his birth.

The customary nickname with which he was maligned in Paris was "the Son of the Archer." a taunt upon the fair fame of his mother, whom scandal accused of no rigid fidelity to the Duke of York. Besides this, Edward felt somewhat of the jealousy natural to a king, himself so spirited and able, of the reputation for profound policy and state-craft, which Louis XI. was rapidly widening and increasing throughout the courts of Europe. And, what with the resentment, and what with the jealousy, there had sprung up in his warlike heart a secret desire to advance the claims of England to the throne of France, and retrieve the conquest won by the Fifth Henry, to be lost under the Sixth. Possessing these feelings and these views, Edward necessarily saw, in the alliance with Burgundy, all that could gratify both his hate and his ambition. The Count of Chorolois had sworn to Louis the most deadly enmity, and would have every

* The prize was a collar of gold, enamelled with the flower of the souvenance.

motive, whether of vengeance or of interest, to associate himself heart in hand with the arms of England in any invasion of France; and to these warlike objects Edward added, as we have so often had cause to remark, the more peaceful aims and interests of commerce. And, therefore, although he could not so far emancipate himself from that influence, which both awe and gratitude invested in the Earl of Warwick, as to resist his great minister's embassy to Louis; and though, despite all these reasons in favor of connection with Burgundy, he could not but reluctantly allow that Warwick urged those of a still larger and wiser policy, when showing that the infant dynasty of York could only be made secure by effectually depriving Margaret of the sole ally that could venture to assist her cause, yet no sooner had Warwick fairly departed, than he inly chafed at the concession he had made, and his mind was open to all the impressions which the earl's enemies sought to stamp upon it.

As the wisdom of every man, however able, can but run through those channels which are formed by the soil of the character, so Edward, with all his talents, never possessed the prudence which fear of consequences inspires. He was so eminently fearless—so scornful of danger—that he absolutely forgot the arguments on which the affectionate zeal of Warwick had based the alliance with Louis—argu ments as to the unceasing peril, whether to his person or his throne, so long as the unprincipled and plotting genius of the French king had an interest against both—and thus he became only alive to the representations of his passions, his pride, and his mercantile interests. The Duchess of Bedford, the queen, and all the family of Woodville, who had but one object at heart—the downfall of Warwick and his house—knew enough of the earl's haughty nature to be aware that he would throw up the reins of government the moment he knew that Edward had discredited and dishonored his embassy; and, despite the suspicions they sought to instil into their king's mind, they calculated upon the earl's love and near relationship to Edward—upon his utter, and seemingly irreconcilable breach with the house of Lancaster—to render his wrath impotent—and to leave him only the fallen minister, not the mighty rebel.

Edward had been thus easily induced to permit the visit of the Count de la Roche, although he had by no means then resolved upon the course he should pursue. At all events, even if the alliance with Louis was to take place, the friendship of Burgundy was worth much to maintain. But De la Roche, soon made aware, by the Duchess of Bedford, of the ground on which he stood, and instructed by his brother to spare no pains and to scruple no promise that might serve to alienate Edward from Louis, and win the hand and dower of Margaret, found it a more facile matter than his most sanguine hopes had deemed, to work upon the passions and the motives which inclined the king to the pretensions of the heir of Burgundy. And what more than all else favored the envoy's mission was the very circumstance that should most have defeated it—viz., the recollection of the Earl of Warwick. For in the absence of that powerful baron, and master-minister, the king had seemed to breathe more freely. In his absence, he forgot his power. The machine of government, to his own surprise, seemed to go on as well, the Commons were as submissive, the mobs as noisy in their shouts, as if the earl was by. There was no longer any one to share with Edward the joys of popularity, the sweets of power. Though Edward was not Diogenes, he loved the popular sunshine, and no Alexander now stood between him and its beams. Deceived by the representations of his courtiers, hearing nothing but abuse of Warwick, and sneers at his greatness, he begin to think the hour had come when he might reign alone, and he entered, though tacitly, and not acknowledging it even to himself, into the very object of the womankind about him—viz., the dismissal of his minister.

The natural carelessness and luxurious indolence of Edward's temper did not, however, permit him to see all the ingratitude of the course he was about to adopt. The egotism a king too often acquires, and no king so easily as one, like Edward IV., not born to a throne, made him consider that he alone was entitled to the prerogatives of pride. As sovereign and as brother, might he not give the hand of Margaret as he listed? If Warwick was offended, pest on his disloyalty and presumption! And so saying to himself, he dismissed the very thought of the absent earl, and glided unconsciously down the current of the hour. And yet, notwithstanding all these prepossessions and dispositions, Edward might no doubt have deferred, at least, the meditated breach with his great miniser until the return of the latter, and then have acted with the delicacy and precaution that became a king bound by ties of gratitude and blood to the statesman he desired to discard, but for a habit,—which, while history mentions, it seems to forget, in the consequences it ever engenders—the habit of intemperance. Unquestionably, to that habit many of the imprudences and levities of a king possessed of so much ability, are to be ascribed; and over his cups with the wary and watchful De la Roche, Edward had contrived to entangle himself far more than in his cooler moments he would have been disposed to do.

Having thus admitted our readers into those recesses of that *cor inscrutabile*—the heart of kings—we summon them to a scene peculiar to the pastimes of the magnificent Edward. Amidst the shades of the vast park or chase which then appertained to the Palace of Shene, the noonday sun shone upon such a spot as Armida might have dressed for the subdued Rinaldo. A space had been cleared of trees and underwood, and made level as a howling green. Around this space the huge oak and the broad beech were hung with trellis-work, wreathed with jasmine, honeysuckle, and the white rose, trained in arches. Ever and anon through these arches extended long alleys, or vistas, gradually lost in the cool depth of foliage; amidst these alleys and around this space, numberless arbors, quaint with all the flowers then known in England, were constructed. In the centre of the sward was a small artificial lake, long since dried up, and adorned then with a profusion of fountains, that seemed to scatter coolness around the glowing air. Pitched in various and appropriate sites, were tents of silk and the white cloth of Rennes, each tent so placed as to command one of the alleys; and at the opening of each stood cavalier or dame, with the bow or cross-bow, as it pleased the fancy or suited best the skill, looking for the quarry, which horn and hound drove fast and frequent across the alleys.

Such was the luxurious "summer-chase" of the Sardanapalus of the North. Nor could any spectacle more thoroughly represent that poetical yet effeminate taste, which, borrowed from the Italians, made a short interval between the chivalric and the modern age! The exceeding beauty of the day—the richness of the foliage in the first suns of bright July—the bay of the dogs—the sound of the mellow horn—the fragrance of the air, heavy with noontide flowers—the gay tents—the rich dresses and fair faces and merry laughter of dame and donzell—combined to take captive every sense, and to reconcile ambition itself, that eternal traveller through the future, to the enjoyment of the voluptuous hour. But there were illustrious exceptions to the contentment of the general company.

A courier had arrived that morning to apprise Edward of the unexpected debarkation of the Earl of Warwick, with the Archbishop of Narbonne and the Bastard of Bourbon,—the ambassadors commissioned by Louis to settle the preliminaries of the marriage between Margaret and his brother.

This unwelcome intelligence reached Edward at the very moment he was sallying from his palace gates to his pleasant pastime. He took aside Lord Hastings, and communicated the news to his able favorite.—"Put spurs to thy horse, Hastings, and hie thee fast to Raynard's Castle. Bring back Gloucester. In these difficult matters, that boy's head is better than a council."

"Your highness," said Hastings, tightening his girdle with one hand, while with the other he shortened his stirrups, "shall be obeyed. I foresaw, sire that this coming would occasion much that my Lords Rivers and Worcester have overlooked. I rejoice that you summon the Prince Richard, who hath wisely forborne all countenance to the Burgundian envoy. But is this all, sire? Is it not well to assemble also your trustiest lords and most learned prelates, if not to over-awe Lord Warwick's anger, at least to confer on the fitting excuses to be made to King Louis's ambassadors?"

"And so lose the fairest day this summer hath bestowed upon us? Tush!—the more need for pleasaunce to-day, since business must come to-morrow. Away with you, dear Will!"

Hastings looked grave, but he saw all further remonstrance would be in vain, and hoping much from the intercession of Gloucester, put spurs to his steed and vanished. Edward mused a moment; and Elizabeth, who knew every expression and change of his countenance, rode from the circle of her ladies, and approached him timidly. Casting down her eyes, which she always affected in speaking to her lord, the queen said, softly,

"Something hath disturbed my liege and my life's life."

"Marry, yes, sweet Bessee. Last night, to pleasure thee and thy kin (and sooth to say, small gratitude ye owe me, for it also pleased myself), I promised Margaret's hand, through De la Roche, to the heir of Burgundy."

"O princely heart!" exclaimed Elizabeth, her whole face lighted up with triumph—"ever seeking to make happy those it cherishes. But is it that which disturbs thee—that which thou repentest?"

"No, sweetheart—no. Yet had it not been for the strength of the clary, I should have kept the Bastard longer in suspense. But what is done is done. Let not thy roses wither when thou hearest Warwick is in England—nay, nay, child, look not so appalled—thine Edward is no infant, whom ogre and goblin scare; and"—glancing his eye proudly round as he spoke, and saw the goodly cavalcade of his peers and knights, with his bodyguard—tall and chosen veterans—filling up the palace-yard, with the show of casque and pike,—"and if the struggle is to come between Edward of England and his subject, never an hour more ripe than this;—my throne assured—the new nobility I have raised, around it—London true, marrow and heart, true—the provinces at peace—the ships and the steel of Burgundy mine allies! Let the White Bear growl as he list, the Lion of March is lord of the forest. And now, my Bessee," added the king, changing his haughty tone into a gay, careless laugh, "now let the lion enjoy his chase."

He kissed the gloved hand of his queen, gallantly bending over his saddle-bow, and the next moment he was by the side of a younger, if not a fairer lady, to whom he was devoting the momentary worship of his inconstant heart. Elizabeth's eye shot an angry gleam as she beheld her faithless lord thus engaged; but so accustomed to conceal and control the natural jealousy, that it never betrayed itself to the court or to her husband, she soon composed her countenance to its ordinary smooth and artificial smile, and rejoining her mother, she revealed what had passed. The proud and masculine spirit of the duchess felt only joy at the intelligence. In the anticipated humiliation of Warwick, she forgot all cause for fear—not so her husband and son, the Lords Rivers and Scales, to whom the news soon travelled.

"Anthony," whispered the father, "in this game we have staked our heads."

"But our right hands can guard them well, sir," answered Anthony; "and so God and the ladies for our rights!"

Yet this bold reply did not satisfy the more thoughtful judgment of the Lord Treasurer, and even the brave Anthony's arrows that day wandered wide of their quarry.

Amidst this gay scene, then, there were anxious and thoughtful bosoms. Lord Rivers was silent and abstracted; his son's laugh was hollow and constrained; the queen, from her pavilion, cast, ever and anon, down the green alleys more restless and prying looks than the hare or the deer could call forth; her mother's brow was knit and flushed—and keenly were those illustrious persons watched by one deeply interested in the coming events. Affecting to discharge the pleasant duty assigned him by the king, the Lord Montague glided from tent to tent, inquiring courteously into the accommodation of each group, lingering, smiling, complimenting, watching, heeding, studying, those whom he addressed. For the first time since the Bastard's visit, he had joined in the dirversions in its honor, and yet, so well had Mortagu played his part at the court, that he did not excite amongst the queen's relatives any of the hostile feelings entertained toward his brother. No man, except Hastings, was so "entirely loved" by Edward; and Montagu, worldly as he was, and indignant against the king, as he could not fail to be, so far repaid the affection, that his chief fear at that moment sincerely was, not for Warwick, but for Edward. He alone of those present was aware of the cause of Warwick's hasty return, for he had privately dispatched to him the news of the Bastard's visit, its real object, and the inevitable success of the intrigues afloat, unless the earl could return at once, his mission accomplished, and the ambassadors of France in his train; and even before the courier dispatched to the king had arrived at

Shene, a private hand had conveyed to Montagu the information that Warwick, justly roused and alarmed, had left the state procession behind at Dover, and was hurrying, fast as relays of steeds and his own fiery spirit could bear him, to the presence of the ungrateful king.

Meanwhile the noon had now declined, the sport relaxed, and the sound of the trumpet from the king's pavilion proclaimed that the lazy pastime was to give place to the luxurious banquet.

At this moment, Montagu approached a tent remote from the royal pavilions, and, as his noiseless footstep crushed the grass, he heard the sound of voices, in which there was little in unison with the worldly thoughts that filled his breast.

"Nay, sweet mistress, nay," said a young man's voice, earnest with emotion—"do not misthink me—do not deem me bold and overweening. I have sought to smother my love, and to rate it, and bring pride to my aid, but in vain; and, now, whether you will scorn my suit or not, I remember, Sibyll—O Sibyll! I remember the days when we conversed together, and as a brother, if nothing else—nothing dearer—I pray you to pause well, and consider what manner of man this Lord Hastings is said to be!"

"Master Nevile, is this generous?—why afflict me thus?—why couple my name with so great a lord's?"

"Because—beware—the young gallants already so couple it, and their prophecies are not to thine honor, Sibyll. Nay, do not frown on me. I know thou art fair and winsome, and deftly gifted, and thy father may, for aught I know, be able to coin thee a queen's dower out of his awsome engines. But Hastings will not wed thee, and his wooing, therefore, but stains thy fair repute; while I——"

"You!" said Montagu, entering suddenly—"you, kinsman, may look to higher fortunes than the Duchess of Bedford's waiting-damsel can bring to thy honest love. How now, mistress, say—wilt thou take this young gentleman for loving fere and plighted spouse? If so, he shall give thee a manor for jointure, and thou shalt wear velvet robe and gold chain, as a knight's wife."

This unexpected interference, which was perfectly in character with the great lords, who frequently wooed in very peremptory tones for their clients and kinsmen,* completed the displeasure which the blunt Marmaduke had already called forth in Sibyll's gentle but proud nature. "Speak, maiden, ay or no?" continued Montagu, surprised and angered at the haughty silence of one whom he just knew by sight and name, though he had never before addressed her.

"No, my lord," answered Sibyll, keeping down her indignation at this tone, though it burned in her cheek, flashed in her eye, and swelled in the heave of her breast. "No! and your kinsman might have spared this affront to one whom—but it matters not." She swept from the tent as she said this, and passed up the alley, into that of the queen's mother.

"Best so; then art too young for marriage, Marmaduke," said Montagu, coldly. "We will find thee a richer bride ere long. There is Mary of Winstown—the archbishop's ward—with two castles, and seven knight's fees."

"But so marvellously ill-featured, my lord," said poor Marmaduke, sighing.

Montagu looked at him in surprise. "Wives, sir," he said, "are not made to look at,—unless, indeed, they be the wives of other men. But dismiss these follies for the nonce. Back to thy post by the king's pavilion; and by the way, ask Lord Fauconberg and Aymer Nevile, whom thou wilt pass by yonder arbor—ask them in my name, to be near the pavilion while the king banquets. A word in thine ear—ere yon sun gilds the tops of those green oaks, the Earl of Warwick will be with Edward IV.; and come what may, some brave hearts should be by to welcome him. Go!"

Without tarrying for an answer, Montagu turned into one of the tents, wherein Raoul de Fulke and the Lord St. John, heedless of hind and hart, conferred, and Marmaduke, much bewildered, and bitterly wroth with Sibyll, went his way.

* See, in Miss Strickland's "Life of Elizabeth Woodville," the curious letters which the Duke of York and the Earl of Warwick addressed to her, then a simple maiden, in favor of their *protege*, Sir R. Johnes.

CHAPTER IX.

The Great Actor returns to fill the Stage.

AND now, in various groups, these summer foresters were at rest in their afternoon banquet; some lying on the smooth sward around the lake—some in the tents—some again in the arbors; here and there the forms of dame and cavalier might be seen, stealing apart from the rest, and gliding down the alleys till lost in the shade—for under that reign, gallantry was universal. Before the king's pavilion a a band of those merry jongleurs, into whom the ancient and honored minstrels were fast degenerating, stood waiting for the signal to commence their sports, and listening to the laughter that came in frequent peals from the royal tent. Within feasted Edward, the Count de la Roche, the Lord Rivers; while in a larger and more splendid pavilion, at some little distance, the queen, her mother, and the great dames of the court, held their own slighter and less noisy repast.

"And here, then," said Edward, as he put his lips to a gold goblet, wrought with gems, and passed it to Anthony the Bastard—"here, count, we take the first waissall to the loves of Charolois and Margaret!"

The count drained the goblet, and the wine gave him new fire.

"And with those loves, king," said he, "we bind for ever Burgundy and England. Woe to France!"

"Ay, woe to France!" exclaimed Edward, his face lighting up with that martial joy which it ever took at the thoughts of war—"for we will wrench her lands from this huckster, Louis. By Heaven! I shall not rest in peace till York hath regained what Lancaster hath lost; and out of the parings of the realm which I will add to England, thy brother of Burgundy shall have eno' to change his duke's diadem for a king's. How now, Rivers? Thou gloomest, father mine."

"My liege," said Rivers wakening himself, "I did but think that if the Earl of Warwick——"

"Ah! I had forgotten," interrupted Edward; "and, sooth to say, Count Anthony, I think if the earl were by, he would not much mend our boon-fellowship!"

"Yet a good subject," said De la Roche, sneeringly, "usually dresses his face by that of his king."

"A subject! Ay, but Warwick is much such a subject to England as William of Normandy or Duke Rollo was to France. Howbeit, let him come—our realm is at peace—we want no more his battle-axe; and in our new designs on France, thy brother, old count, is an ally that might compensate for a greater loss than a sullen minister. Let him come!"

As the king spoke, there was heard gently upon the smooth turf the sound of the hoofs of steeds. A moment more and from the outskirts of the scene of revel, where the king's guards were stationed, there arose a long, loud shout. Nearer and nearer came the hoofs of the steeds—they paused. "Doubtless Richard of Gloucester, by that shout! The soldiers love that brave boy," said the king.

Marmaduke Nevile, as gentleman in waiting, drew aside the curtain of the pavilion; and as he uttered a name that paled the cheeks of all who heard, the Earl of Warwick entered the royal presence.

The earl's dress was disordered and soiled by travel; the black plume on his cap was broken, and hung darkly over his face; his horseman's boots coming half way up the thigh, were sullied with the dust of the journey; and yet as he entered, before the majesty of his mien, the grandeur of his stature, suddenly De la Roche, Rivers, even the gorgeous Edward himself, seemed dwarfed into common men! About the man—his air, his eye, his form, his attitude—there was THAT which, in the earlier times, made kings, by the acclamation of the crowd,—an unmistakable sovereignty, as of one whom Nature herself had shaped and stamped for power and for rule. All three had risen as he entered; and to a deep silence succeeded an exclamation from Edward, and then again all was still.

The earl stood a second or two calmly gazing on the effect he had produced; and turning his dark eye from one to the other, till it rested full upon De la Roche, who, after vainly trying not to quail beneath the gaze, finally smiled with affected disdain, and, resting his hand on his dagger, sunk back into his seat.

"My liege," then said Warwick doffing his cap, and approaching the king with slow and grave respect, "I crave pardon for presenting myself to your highness thus travel-worn and disordered, but I announce that news which ensures my welcome. The solemn embassy of trust committed to me by your grace has prospered with God's blessing; and the Fils de Bourbon and the Archbishop of Narbonne are on their way to your metropolis. Alliance between the two great monarchies of Europe is concluded on terms that insure the weal of England, and augment the lustre of your crown. Your claims on Normandy and Guienne, King Louis consents to submit to the arbitrement of the Roman Pontiff,* and to pay to your treasury annual tribute; these advantages, greater than your highness even empowered me to demand, thus obtained, the royal brother of your new ally joyfully awaits the hand of the Lady Margaret."

"Cousin," said Edward, who had thoroughly recovered himself,—motioning the earl to a seat, "you are ever welcome, no matter what your news; but I marvel much that so deft a statesman should broach these matters of council in the unseasonable hour, and before the gay comrades, of a revel."

"I speak, sire," said Warwick, calmly, though the veins in his forehead swelled, and his dark countenance was much flushed—"I speak openly of that which hath been done nobly; and this truth has ceased to be matter of council, since the meanest citizen who hath ears and eyes, ere this, must know for what purpose the ambassadors of King Louis arrive in England with your highness's representative."

Edward, more embarassed at this tone than he could have foreseen, remained silent; but De la Roche, impatient to humble his brother's foe, and judging it also discreet to arouse the king, said carelessly—

"It were a pity, sir earl, that the citizens, whom you thus deem privy to the thoughts of kings, had not prevised the Archhishop of Narbonne, that, if he desire to see a fairer show than even the palaces of Westminster and the Tower, he will hasten back to behold the banners of Burgundy and England waving from the spires of Nôtre Dame."

Ere the Bastard had concluded, Rivers, leaning back, whispered the king—"For Christ's sake, sire, select some fitter scene for what must follow! Silence your guest!"

But Edward, on the contrary, pleased to think that De la Roche was breaking the ice, and hopeful that some burst from Warwick would give him more excuse than he felt at present for a rupture, said sternly, "Hush, my lord, and meddle not!"

"Unless I mistake," said Warwick, coldly, "he who now accosts me is Count de la Roche—a foreigner."

"And the brother of the heir of Burgundy," interrupted De la Roche—"brother to the betrothed and princely spouse of Margaret of England."

"Doth this man lie, sire?" said Warwick, who had seated himself a moment, and who now rose again.

The Bastard sprung also to his feet, but Edward, waiving him back, and reassuming the external dignity which rarely forsook him, replied,—"Cousin, thy question lacketh courtesy to our noble guest: since thy departure, reasons of state, which we will impart to thee at a meeter season, have changed our purpose, and we will now that our sister Margaret shall wed with the Count of Charolois."

"And this to me, king!" exclaimed the earl, all his passions at once released—"this to me!—Nay, frown not, Edward—I am of the race of those who, greater than kings, have built thrones and toppled them! I tell thee, thou hast misused mine honor, and belied thine own—thou hast debased thyself in juggling me, delegated as the representative of thy royalty!—Lord Rivers, stand back—there are barriers eno' between truth and a king!"

"By St. George and my father's head!" cried Edward, with a rage no less fierce than Warwick's—"thou abusest, false lord, my mercy and our kindred blood. Another word, and thou leavest this pavilion for the Tower!"

"King!" replied Warwick, scornfully, and folding his arms on his broad breast—"there is not a hair on this head which thy whole house, thy guards, and thine armies could dare to touch. ME to the Tower! Send me—and when the third sun reddens the roof of prison-house and palace,—look round broad England, and miss a throne!"

"What ho there!" exclaimed Edward,

* The Pope, moreover, was to be engaged to decide the question within four years. A more brilliant treaty for England, Edward's ambassador could not have effected.

stamping his foot; and at that instant the curtain of the pavilion was hastily torn aside, and Richard of Gloucester entered, followed by Lord Hastings, the Duke of Clarence, and Anthony Woodville.

"Ah!" continued the king, "ye come in time. George of Clarence, Lord High Constable of England—arrest yon haughty man, who dares to menace his liege and suzerain!"

Gilding between Clarence, who stood dumb and thunderstricken, and the earl of Warwick, —Prince Richard said, in a voice which, though even softer than usual, had in it more command over those who heard than when it rolled in thunder along the ranks of Barnet or of Bosworth,—"Edward, my brother, remember Touton, and forbear—Warwick, my cousin, forget not thy king nor his dead father!"

At these last words the earl's face fell; for to that father he had sworn to succor and defend the sons: his sense recovering from his pride, showed him how much his intemperate anger had thrown away his advantages in the foul wrong he had sustained from Edward. Meanwhile the king himself, with flashing eyes, and a crest as high as Warwick's, was about, perhaps, to overthrow his throne, by the attempt to enforce his threat, when Anthony Woodville, who followed Clarence, whispered to him—"Beware, sire! a countless crowd that seem to have followed the earl's steps, have already pierced the chase, and can scarcely be kept from the spot, so great is their desire to behold him. Beware!"—and Richard's quick ear catching these whispered words, the duke suddenly backed them by again drawing aside the curtain of the tent.

Along the sward, the guard of the king summoned from their unseen but neighboring post within the wood, were drawn up as if to keep back an immense multitude—men, women, children, who swayed, and rustled, and murmured in the rear. But no sooner was the curtain drawn aside, and the guards themselves caught sight of the royal princes, and the great earl towering amidst them, than supposing, in their ignorance, the scene thus given to them was intended for their gratification, from that old soldierly of Touton rose a loud and long "Hurrah—Warwick and the king" —"The king and the stout earl." The multitude behind caught the cry; they rushed forward, mingling with the soldiery, who no longer sought to keep them back.

"A Warwick! a Warwick!" they shouted.

"God bless the people's friend!"

"Edward, startled and aghast, drew sullenly into the rear of the tent.

De la Roche grew pale, but with the promptness of a practised statesman, he hastily advanced, and he drew the curtain.

"Shall varlets," he said to Richard, in French "gloat over the quarrels of their lords?"

"You are right, Sir Count," murmured Richard, meekly; his purpose was effected, and leaning on his riding staff, he awaited what was to ensue.

A softer shade had fallen over the earl's face, at the proof of the love in which his name was held; it almost seemed to his noble, though haughty and impatient nature, as if the affection of the people had reconciled him to the ingratitude of the king. A tear started to his proud eye, but he twinkled it away, and approaching Edward, (who remained erect, and with all a sovereign's wrath, though silent on his lip, lowering on his brow), he said, in a tone of suppressed emotion:—

"Sire, it is not for me to crave pardon of living man, but the grievous affront put upon my state and mine honor, hath led my words to an excess which my heart repents. I grieve that your grace's highness hath chosen this alliance; hereafter you may find at need what faith is to be placed in Burgundy."

"Darest thou gainsay it?" exclaimed De la Roche.

"Interrupt me not, sir!" continued Warwick, with a disdainful gesture. "My liege, I lay down mine offices, and I leave it to your grace to account as it lists you to the ambassadors of France—I shall vindicate myself to their king. And now, ere I depart for my hall of Middleham, I alone here, unarmed, and unattended, save, at least, by a single squire, I Richard Nevile, say that if any man, peer or knight, can be found to execute your grace's threat, and arrest me, I will obey your royal pleasure, and attend him to the Tower." Haughtily he bowed his head as he spoke, and raising it again, gazed around—"I await your grace's pleasure."

"Begone where thou wilt, earl. From this day Edward IV. reigns alone," said the king. Warwick turned.

"My Lord Scales," said he, "lift the curtain; nay, sir, it misdememeans you not. You are still the son of the Woodville, I still the descendant of John of Gaunt."

"Not for the dead ancestor, but for the living warrior," said the Lord Scales, lifting the curtain, and bowing with knightly grace as the earl passed. And scarcely was Warwick in the open space, than the crowd fairly broke through all restraint, and the clamor of their joy filled with its hateful thunders the royal tent.

"Edward," said Richard, whisperingly, and laying his finger on his brother's arm—"forgive me if I offended, but had you, at such a time, resolved on violence ——"

"I see it all—you were right. But is this to be endured for ever?"

"Sire," returned Richard, with his dark smile, "rest calm; for the age is your best ally, and the age is out-growing the steel and hauberk. A little while and ——"

"And what ——"

"And—ah, sire, I will answer that question when our brother George (mark him)! either refrains from listening, or is married to Isabel Nevile, and hath quarrel with her father about the dowry.—What, ho, there!—let the jongleurs perform."

"The jongleurs!" exclaimed the king; "why, Richard, thou hast more levity than myself!"

"Pardon me! Let the jongleurs perform, and bid the crowd stay. It is by laughing at the mountebanks that your grace can best lead the people to forget their Warwick!"

CHAPTER X.

How the great Lords come to the King-maker, and with what Proffers.

MASTERING the emotions that swelled within him, Lord Warwick returned, with his wonted cheerful courtesy, the welcome of the crowd, and the enthusiastic salutations of the king's guard; but as, at length, he mounted his steed, and attended but by the squire who had followed him from Dover, penetrated into the solitudes of the chase, the recollection of the indignity he had suffered smote his proud heart so sorely, that he groaned aloud. His squire, fearing the fatigue he had undergone might have affected even that iron health, rode up at the sound of the groan, and Warwick's face was hueless as he said, with a forced smile—"it is nothing, Walter. But these heats are oppressive, and we have forgotten our morning draught, friend. Hark! I hear the brawl of a rivulet, and a drink of fresh water were more grateful now than the daintiest hippocras." So saying, he flung himself from his steed; following the sound of the rivulet, he gained its banks, and after quenching his thirst in the hollow of his hand, laid himself down upon the long grass, waving cooly over the margin, and fell into profound thought. From this reverie he was roused by a quick footstep, and as he lifted his gloomy gaze, he beheld Marmaduke Nevile by his side.

"Well, young man," said he sternly, "with what messages art thou charged?"

"With none, my lord earl. I await now no commands but thine."

"Thou knowest not, poor youth, that I can serve thee no more. Go back to the court."

"Oh, Warwick," said Marmaduke, with simple eloquence, "send me not from thy side! This day I have been rejected by the maid I loved. I loved her well, and my heart chafed sorely, and bled within; but now, methinks, it consoles me to have been so cast off—to have no faith, no love, but that which is best of all, to a brave man,—love and faith for a hero-chief! Where thy fortunes, there be my humble fate—to rise or fall with thee!"

Warwick looked intently upon his young kinsman's face, and said, as to himself, "Why this is strange! I gave no throne to this man, and he deserts me not! My friend," he added, aloud, "have they told thee already that I am disgraced?"

"I heard the Lord Scales say to the young Lovell, that thou wert dismissed from all thine offices; and I came hither; for I will serve no more the king who forgets the arm and heart to which he owes a kingdom."

"Man, I accept thy loyalty!" exclaimed Warwick, starting to his feet; "and know that thou hast done more to melt, and yet to nerve my spirit than—but complaints in me are idle, and praise were no reward to thee."

"But see, my lord, if the first to join thee, I am not the sole one. See, brave Raoul de Fulke, the Lords of St. John, Bergavenny, and

Fitzhugh, ay, and fifty others of the best blood of England, are on thy track."

And as he spoke, plumes and tunics were seen gleaming up the forest path, and in another moment a troop of knights and gentlemen, comprising the flower of such of the ancient nobility as yet lingered round the court, came up to Warwick, bare-headed.

"Is it possible," cried Raoul de Fulke, "that we have heard aright, noble earl? And has Edward IV. suffered the base Woodvilles to triumph over the bulwark of his realm?"

"Knights and gentles!" said Warwick, with a bitter smile, "is it so uncommon a thing that men in peace should leave the battle-axe and brand to rust? I am but an useless weapon, to be suspended at rest amongst the trophies of Touton in my hall of Middleham."

"Return with us," said the Lord of St. John, "and we will make Edward do thee justice, or, one and all, we will abandon a court where knaves and varlets have become mightier than English valor, and nobler than Norman birth."

"My friends," said the earl, laying his hand on St. John's shoulder, "not even in my just wrath will I wrong my king. He is punished eno' in the choice he hath made. Poor Edward and poor England! What woes and wars await ye both, from the gold, and the craft, and the unsparing hate of Louis XI.! No; if I leave Edward, he hath more need of you. Of mine own free will, I have resigned mine offices."

"Warwick," interrupted Raoul de Fulke, "this deceives us not; and in disgrace to you, the ancient barons of England behold the first blow at their own state. We have wrongs we endured in silence, while thou wert the shield and sword of yon merchant-king. We have seen the ancient peers of England set aside for men of yesterday; we have seen our daughters, sisters,—nay, our very mothers—if widowed and dowered—forced into disreputable and base wedlock, with creatures dressed in titles, and gilded with wealth stolen from ourselves. Merchants and artificers thread upon our knightly heels, and the avarice of trade eats up our chivalry as a rust. We nobles, in our greater day, have had the crown at our disposal, and William the Norman dared not *think* what Edward Earl of March hath been permitted with impunity to *do*. We, sir earl—we knights and barons—*would* a king simple in his manhood, and princely in his truth. Richard Earl of Warwick, thou art of royal blood—the descendant of old John of Gaunt. In thee we behold the true, the living likeness of the Third Edward, and the Hero-Prince of Cressy. Speak but the word, and we make thee king!"

The descendant of the Norman, the representative of the might faction that no English monach had ever braved in vain looked round as he said these last words, and a choral murmur was heard through the whole of that august nobility—"We make thee king!"

"Richard, descendant of the Plantagenet,* speak the word," repeated Raoul de Fulke.

"I speak it not," interrupted Warwick; "nor shalt thou continue, brave Raoul de Fulke. What, my lords and gentlemen," he added, drawing himself up, and with his countenance animated with feelings it is scarcely possible in our times to sympathize with or make clear—"what! think you that Ambition limits itself to the narrow circlet of a Crown?—Greater, and more in the spirit of our mighty fathers, is the condition of men like us THE BARONS who make and unmake kings. What! who of us would not rather descend from the Chiefs of Runnymede than from the royal craven whom they controlled and chid! By Heaven, my lords, Richard Nevile has too proud a soul to be a king! A king—a puppet of state and form! A king—a holiday show for the crowd, to hiss or hurrah, as the humor seizes! A king—a beggar to the nation, wrangling with his parliament for gold! A king!—Richard II. was a king, and Lancaster dethroned him. Ye would debase me to a Henry of Lancaster. Mort Dieu! I thank ye. The Commons and the Lords raised *him*, forsooth,—for what? To hold him as the creature they had made, to rate him, to chafe him, to pry into his very household, and quarrel with his wife's chamberlains and lavourers.† What! dear Raoul de Fulke, is

* By the female side, through Joan Beaufort, or Plantagnet, Warwick was third in descent from John of Gaunt, as Henry VII., through the male line, was *fourth* in descent.

† Laundresses. The Parliamentary Rolls in the reign of Henry IV. abound in curious specimens of the interference of the Commons with the household of Henry's wife, Queen Joan.

thy friend fallen now so low, that he—Earl of Salisbury and of Warwick, chief of the threefold race of Montagu, Monthermer, and Nevile, lord of a hundred baronies, leader of sixty thousand followers—is not greater than Edward of March, to whom we will deign still, with your permission, to vouchsafe the name and pageant of a king?"

This extraordinary address, strange to say, so thoroughly expressed the peculiar pride of the old barons, that when it ceased a sound of admiration and applause circled though that haughty audience, and Raoul de Fulke, kneeling suddenly, kissed the earl's hand: "Oh, noble earl," he said, "ever live as one of US, to maintain our Order, and teach kings and nations what WE are."

"Fear it not, Raoul! fear it not—we will have our rights yet. Return, I beseech ye. Let me feel I have such friends about the king. Even at Middleham my eye shall watch over our common cause; and till seven feet of earth suffice him, your brother baron, Richard Nevile, is not a man whom kings and courts can forget, much less dishonor. Sirs, our honor is in our bosoms,—and there, is the only throne armies cannot shake, nor cozeners undermine."

With these words he gently waved his hand, motioned to his squire, who stood out of hearing with the steeds, to approach, and mounting, gravely rode on. Ere he had got many paces, he called to Marmaduke, who was on foot, and bade him follow him to London that night. "I have strange tidings to tell the French envoys, and for England's sake I must soothe their anger if I can,—then to Middleham."

The nobles returned slowly to the pavilions. And as they gained the open space, where the gaudy tents still shone against the setting sun, they beheld the mob of that day, whom Shakespeare hath painted with such contempt, gathering, laughing and loud, around the mountebank and the conjurer, who had already replaced in their thoughts (as Gloucester had foreseen) the hero-idol of their worship.

———

BOOK FIFTH.

THE LAST OF THE BARONS IN HIS FATHER'S HALLS.

CHAPTER I.

Rural England in the Middle Ages—Noble Visitors seek the Castle of Middleham.

AUTUMN had succeeded to summer—winter to autumn—and the spring of 1468 was green in England, when a gallant cavalcade were seen slowly winding the ascent of a long and gradual hill, towards the decline of day. Different, indeed from the aspect which that part of the country now presents was the landscape that lay around them, bathed in the smiles of the westering sun. In a valley to the left, a full view of which the steep road commanded, (where now roars the din of trade through a thousand factories,) lay a long secluded village. The houses, if so they might be called, were constructed entirely of wood, and that of the more perishable kind—willow, sallow, elm, and plumtree. Not one could boast a chimney; but the smoke from the single fire in each, after duly darkening the atmosphere within, sent its surplusage, lazily and fitfully, through a circular aperture in the roof. In fact, there was long in the provinces a prejudice against chimneys! The smoke was considered good both for house and owner; the first it was supposed to season, and the last to guard "from rheums, catarrhs, and poses." * Neither did one of these habitations boast the comfort of a glazed window, the substitute being lattice, or chequer-work—even in the house of the franklin, which rose statelily above the rest, encompassed with barns and out-sheds. And yet greatly should we err, did we conceive that these deficiencies were an index to the general condition of the working-class. Far better off was the laborer, *when employed*, than now. Wages were enormously high, meat extremely low; * and our mother land bountifully maintained her children.

On that greensward, before the village (now foul and reeking with the squalid population, whom commerce rears up—the victims, as the movers of the modern world) were assembled youth and age; for it was a holiday evening, and the stern Puritan had not yet risen to sour the face of Mirth. Well clad in leathern jerkin, or even broadcloth, the young peasants vied with each other in quoits, and wrestling; while the merry laughter of the girls, in their gay-colored kirtles, and ribboned hair, rose oft and cheerily to the ears of the cavalcade. From a gentle eminence beyond the village, and half veiled by trees, on which the first verdure of spring was budding, (where now, around the gin-shop, gather the fierce and sickly children of toil and of discontent), rose the venerable walls of a monastery, and the chime of its heavy bell swung far and sweet over the pastoral landscape. To the right of the road (where now stands the sober meeting-house) was one of those small shrines, so fre-

* So worthy HOLLINSHED (Book II., c. 22)—"Then had we none but reredosses, and our heads did never ache. For as the smoke, in those days, was supposed to be a sufficient hardening for the timber of the house, so it was reputed a far better medicine to keep the goodman and his familie from the quacke, or pose, wherewith as then very few were oft acquainted.

* See HALLAM'S "*Middle Ages*," chap. xx., Part II. So also HOLLINSHED, Book XI., c. 12, comments on the amazement of the Spaniards, in Queen Mary's time, when they saw "what large diet was used in these so homlie cottages," and reports one of the Spaniards to have said, "These English have their houses of sticks and dirt, but they fare commonlie so good as the king!"

quent in Italy, with an image of the Virgin gaudily painted, and before it each cavalier in the procession halted an instant to cross himself, and mutter an ave. Beyond still, to the right, extended vast chains of woodland, interspersed with strips of pasture, upon which numerous flocks were grazing, with horses, as yet unbroken to bit and selle, that neighed and snorted as they caught scent of their more civilized brethern pacing up the road.

In front of the cavalcade rode two, evidently of superior rank to the rest. The one small and slight, with his long hair flowing over his shoulders; and the other, though still young, many years older, and indicating his clerical profession by the absence of all love-locks, compensated by a curled and glossy beard, trimmed with the greatest care. But the dress of the ecclesiastic was so little according to our modern notions of what beseems the church as can well be conceived: his tunic and surcoat, of a rich amber, contrasted well with the clear darkness of his complexion; his piked shoes, or beakers, as they were called, turned up half-way to the knee; the buckles of his dress were of gold, inlaid with gems; and the housings of his horse, which was of great power, were edged with gold fringe. By the side of his steed walked a tall greyhound, upon which he ever and anon glanced with affection. Behind these, rode two gentlemen, whose golden spurs announced knighthood; and then followed a long train of squires and pages, richly clad and accoutred, bearing generally the Nevile badge of the bull; though interspersed amongst the retinue might be seen the grim boar's head, which Richard of Gloucester, in right of his duchy, had assumed as his cognizance.

"Nay, sweet prince," said the ecclesiastic, "I pray thee to consider that a greyhound is far more of a gentleman than any other of the canine species. Mark his stately, yet delicate length of limb—his sleek coat—his keen eye—his haughty neck."

"These are but the externals, my noble friend. Will the greyhound attack the lion, as our mastiff doth? The true character of the gentleman is to know no fear, and to rush through all danger at the throat of his foe; wherefore I uphold the dignity of the mastiff above all his tribe, though others have a daintier hide, and a statelier crest. Enough of such matters, archbishop—we are nearing Middleham."

"The Saints be praised! for I am hungered," observed the archbishop, piously; "but, sooth to say, my cook at the More far excelleth what we can hope to find at the board of my brother. He hath some faults, our Warwick! Hasty and careless, he hath not thought eno' of the blessings he might enjoy, and many a poor abbot hath daintier fare on his humble table."

"Oh, George Nevile! who that heard thee, when thou talkest of hounds and interments,* would recognize the Lord Chancellor of England—the most learned dignitary—the most subtle statesman?"

"And oh, Richard Plantagenet!" retorted the archbishop, dropping the mincing and affected tone, which he in common with the coxcombs of that day, usually assumed, "who that heard thee, when thou talkest of humility and devotion, would recognize the sternest heart and the most daring ambition God ever gave to prince?"

Richard started at these words, and his eye shot fire as it met the keen, calm gaze of the prelate.

"Nay, your grace wrongs me," he said, gnawing his lip—"or I should not say wrongs, but flatters; for sternness and ambition are no vices in a Nevile's eyes."

"Fairly answered, royal son," said the archbishop, laughing; "but let us be frank.—Thou hast persuaded me to accompany thee to Lord Warwick as a mediator: the provinces in the north are disturbed; the intrigues of Margaret of Anjou are restless; the king reaps what he has sown in the Court of France, and, as Warwick foretold, the emissaries and gold of Louis are ever at work against his throne; the great barons are moody and discontented; and our liege King Edward is at last aware that, if the Earl of Warwick do not return to his councils, the first blast of a hostile trumpet may drive him from his throne. Well, I attend thee: my fortunes are woven with those of York, and my interest and my loyalty go hand in hand. Be equally frank with me. Hast thou, Lord Richard, no interest to serve in this mission save that of the public weal?"

"Thou forgettest that the Lady Isabel is dearly loved by Clarence, and that I would fain see removed all barrier to his nuptial

* Interments, *Entremets* (side dishes).

biiss. But yonder rise the towers of Middleham. Beloved walls, which sheltered my childhood! and, by holy Paul, a noble pile, which would resist an army, or hold one."

While thus conversed the prince and the archbishop, the Earl of Warwick, musing and alone, slowly paced the lofty terrace that crested the battlements of his outer fortifications.

In vain had that restless and powerful spirit sought content in retirement. Trained from his childhood to active life—to move mankind to and fro at his beck—this single and sudden interval of repose in the prime of his existence, at the height of his fame, served but to swell the turbulent and dangerous passions to which all vent was forbidden.

The statesman of modern days has at least food for intellect, in letters, when deprived of action; but with all his talents, and thoroughly cultivated as his mind was in the camp the council, and the state, the great earl cared for nothing in book-lore, except some rude ballad that told of Charlemagne or Rollo. The sports that had pleased the leisure of his earlier youth were tedious and flat to one snatched from so mighty a career. His hound lay idle at his feet, his falcon took holiday on the perch, his jester was banished to the page's table.—Behold the repose of this great unlettered spirit?

But while his mind was thus debarred from its native sphere, all tended to pamper Lord Warwick's infirmity of pride. The ungrateful Edward might forget him; but the king seemed to stand alone in that oblivion. The mightiest peers, the most renowned knights gathered to his hall. Middleham, not Windsor, nor Shene, nor Westminster, nor the Tower, seemed the COURT OF ENGLAND. As the Last of the Barons paced his terrace, far as his eye could reach his broad domains extended, studded with villages, and towns, and castles, swarming with his retainers. The whole country seemed in mourning for his absence. The name of Warwick was in all men's mouths, and not a group gathered in market-place or hostel, but what the minstrel who had some ballad in praise of the stout earl found a rapt and thrilling audience.

"And is the river of my life," muttered Warwick, "shrunk into this stagnant pool! Happy the man who hath never known what it is to taste of Fame—to have it is a purgatory, to want it is a hell!"

Wrapped in this gloomy self-commune, he heard not the light step that sought his side, till a tender arm was thrown around him, and a face, in which sweet temper and pure thought had preserved to matronly beauty all the bloom of youth, looked up smilingly to his own.

"My Lord—my Richard," said the countess, "why didst thou steal so churlishly from me? Hath there, alas! come a time when thou deemest me unworthy to share thy thoughts, or soothe thy troubles?"

"Fond one! no," said Warwick, drawing her form still light, though rounded, nearer to his bosom. "For nineteen years hast thou been to me a leal and loving wife. Thou wert a child on our wedding-day, *m'amie*, and I but a beardless youth; yet wise enough was I then to see, at the first glance of thy blue eye, that there was more treasure in thy heart than in all the lordships thy hand bestowed."

"My Richard!" murmured the countess, and her tears of grateful delight fell on the hand she kissed.

"Yes, let us recall those early and sweet days," continued Warwick, with a tenderness of voice and manner that strangers might have marvelled at, forgetting how tenderness is almost ever a part of such peculiar manliness of character—"yes, sit we here under this spacious elm, and think that our youth has come back to us once more. For verily, *m'amie*, nothing in life has ever been so fair to me, as those days when we stood hand in hand on its threshold, and talked, boy-bridegroom and child-bride as we were, of the morrow that lay beyond."

"Ah, Richard, even in those days thy ambition sometimes vexed my woman vanity, and showed me that I could never be all in all to so large a heart!"

"Ambition! No, thou mistakest—Montagu is ambitious, I but proud. Montagu ever seeks to be higher than he is, I but assert the right to be what I am and have been; and my pride, sweet wife, is a part of my love for thee. It is thy title, Heiress of Warwick, and not my father's, that I bear; thy badge, and not the Nevile's, which I have made the symbol of my power. Shame, indeed, on my knighthood, if the fairest dame in England could not justify my pride! Ah! *belle amie*, why have we not a son?"

"Peradventure, fair lord," said the countess, with an arch, yet half-melancholy smile, "because that pride or ambition, name it as thou wilt, which thou excusest so gallantly, would become to insatiate and limitless, if thou sawest a male heir to thy greatness; and God, perhaps, warns thee that, spread and increase as thou wilt,—yea, until half our native country becometh as the manor of one man—all must pass from the Beauchamp and the Nevile into new houses; thy glory, indeed, an eternal heirloom, but only to thy land—thy lordships and thy wealth melting into the dowry of a daughter."

"At least, no king hath daughters so dowried," answered Warwick; "and though I disdain for myself the hard vassalage of a throne, yet, if the channel of our blood must pass into other streams—into nothing meaner than the veins of royalty should it merge." He paused a moment, and added, with a sigh—"Would that Clarence were more worthy Isabel!"

"Nay," said the countess, gently, "he loveth her as she merits. He is is comely, brave, gracious, and learned."

"A pest upon that learning—it sicklies and womanizes men's minds!" exclaimed Warwick, bluntly. "Perhaps it is his learning that I am to thank for George of Clarence's fears, and doubts, and calculations, and scruples. His brother forbids his marriage with any English donzell, for Edward dares not specialize what alone he dreads. His letters burn with love, and his actions freeze with doubts. It was not thus I loved thee, sweetheart. By all the saints in the calendar, had Henry V., or the Lion Richard started from the tomb to forbid me thy hand, it would but have made me a hotter lover! Howbeit Clarence shall decide ere the moon wanes, and but for Isabel's tears and thy entreaties, my father's grandchild should not have waited thus long the coming of so hesitating a wooer. But lo, our darlings! Anne hath thine eyes, *m'amie;* and she groweth more into my heart every day, since daily she more favors thee."

While he thus spoke, the fair sisters came lightly and gaily up the terrace: the arm of the statelier Isabel was twined round Anne's slender waist; as they came forward in that gentle link, with their lithesome and bounding step, a happier blending of contrasted beauty was never seen. The months that had passed since the sisters were presented first to the reader had little changed the superb and radiant loveliness of Isabel, but had added surprisingly to the attractions of Anne. Her form was more rounded, her bloom more ripened, and though something of timidity and bashfulness still lingered about the grace of her movements and the glance of her dove-like eye, the more earnest thoughts of the awakening woman gave sweet intelligence to her countenance, and that divinest of all attractions—the touching and conscious modesty to the shy, but tender smile—and the blush that so came and went, so went and came, that it stirred the heart with a sort of delighted pity for one so evidently susceptible to every emotion of pleasure and of pain. Life seemed too rough a thing for so soft a nature, and gazing on her, one sighed to guess her future.

"And what brings ye hither, young truants?" said the earl, as Anne, leaving her sister, clung lovingly to his side, (for it was ever her habit to cling to some one), while Isabel kissed her mother's hand, and then stood before her parents, coloring deeply, and with downcast eyes. "What brings ye hither, whom I left so lately deeply engaged in the loom, upon the helmet of Goliath, with my burgonot before you as a sample? Wife, you are to blame—our room of state will be arrasless for the next three generations, if these rosy fingers are suffered thus to play the idlers."

"My father," whispered Anne, "guests are on their way hither,—a noble cavalcade; you note them not from this part of the battlements, but from our turret it was fair to see how their plumes, and banners shone in the setting sun."

"Guests!" echoed the earl; "well, is that so rare an honor, that your hearts should beat like village girls at a holiday? Ah, Isabel! look at her blushes. Is it George of Clarence at last? Is it?"

"We see the Duke of Gloucester's cognizance, whispered Anne, "and our own Nevile Bull. Perchance our cousin George, also, may——"

Here she was interrupted by the sound of the warder's horn, followed a moment after by the roar of one of the bombards on the keep.

"At least," said Warwick, his face lighting up, "that signal announces the coming of king's blood. We must honor it,—for it is our own. We will go forth and meet our guests—your hand, countess."

And gravely and silently, and in deep, but no longer gloomy thought, Warwick descended from the terrace, followed by the fair sisters; and who that could have looked upon that princely pair, and those lovely and radiant children, could have forseen, that in that hour, Fate, in tempting the earl once more to action, was busy on their doom!

CHAPTER II.

Councils and Musings.

THE lamp shone through the lattice of Warwick's chamber at the unwonted hour of midnight, and the earl was still in deep commune with his guests. The archbishop, whom Edward, alarmed by the state of the country, and the disaffection of his barons, had reluctantly commissioned to mediate with Warwick, was, as we have before said, one of those men peculiar to the early Church. There was nothing more in the title of Archbishop of York than in that of the Bishop of Osnaburg, (borne by the royal son of George III).,* to prevent him who enjoyed it from leading armies, guiding states, or indulging pleasure. But beneath the coxcombry of George Nevile, which was what he shared most in common with the courtiers of the laity, there lurked a true ecclesiastic's mind. He would have made, in later times, an admirable Jesuit, and no doubt, in his own time, a very brilliant pope. His objects in his present mission were clear and perspicuous, any breach between Warwick and the king must necessarily weaken his own position, and the power of his house was essential to all his views. The object of Gloucester in his intercession, was less defined, but not less personal: in smoothing the way to his brother's marriage with Isabel, he removed all apparent obstacle to his own with Anne. And it is probable that Richard, who, whatever his crimes, was far from inaccessible to affection, might have really loved his early playmate, even while his ambition calculated the wealth of the baronies that would swell the dower of the heiress, and gild the barren coronet of his duchy.*

"God's truth!" said, Warwick as he lifted his eyes from the scroll in the king's writing, "ye know well, princely cousin, and thou, my brother, ye know well how dearly I have loved King Edward; and the mother's milk overflows my heart, when I read these gentle and tender words, which he deigns to bestow upon his servant. My blood is hasty and over hot, but a kind thought from those I love puts out much fire. Sith he thus beseeches me to return to his councils, I will not be sullen enough to hold back; but, oh, Prince Richard! is it indeed a matter past all consideration that your sister, the Lady Margaret, must wed with the Duke of Burgundy?"

"Warwick," replied the prince, "thou mayst know that I never looked with favor on that alliance; that when Clarence bore the Bastard's helmet, I withheld my countenance from the Bastard's presence, I incurred Edward's anger by refusing to attend his court while the Count de la Roche was his guest. And therefore you may trust me when I say now that Edward, after promises, however rash, most solemn and binding, is dishonored for ever if he break off the contract. New circumstances, too, have arisen, to make what were dishonor, danger also. By the death of his father, Charolois has succeeded to the Duke of Burgundy's diadem. Thou knowest his warlike temper, and though in a contest popular in England we need fear no foe, yet thou knowest also that no subsidies could be raised for strife with our most profitable commercial ally. Wherefore, we earnestly implore thee magnanimously to forgive the past, accept Edward's assurance of repentance, and be thy thought—as it has been ever—the weal of our common country."

"I may add, also," said the archbishop, observing how much Warwick was touched and softened—"that in returning to the helm of state, our gracious king permits me to say, that, save only in the alliance with Burgundy. which toucheth his plighted word, you have full liberty to name conditions, and to ask

---

* The late Duke of York.

* Majerus, the Flemish Chronicler, quoted by Bucke (Life of Richard III.), mentions the early attachment of Richard to Anne. They were much together, as children, at Middleham.

whatever grace or power a monarch can bestow."

"I name none but my prince's confidence," said Warwick, generously, "in that, all else is given, and in return for that, I will make the greatest sacrifice that my nature knoweth, or can conceive—I will mortify my familiar demon—I will subdue my PRIDE. If Edward can convince me that it is for the good of England that his sister should wed with mine antient and bitter foe, I will myself do honor to his choice. But of this hereafter. Enough, now that I forget past wrongs in present favor; and that for peace or war, I return to the side of that man whom I loved as my son, before I served him as my king."

Neither Richard nor the archbishop was prepared for a conciliation so facile, for neither quite understood that peculiar magnanimity which often belongs to a vehement and hasty temper, and which is as eager to forgive as prompt to take offence—which, ever in extremes, is not contented with anything short of fiery aggression, or trustful generosity—and where it once passes over an offence, seeks to oblige the offender. So, when after some further conversation on the state of the country, the earl lighted Gloucester to his chamber, the young prince said to himself, musingly:—

"Does ambition besot and blind men?—or can Warwick think that Edward can ever view him but as one to be destroyed when the hour is ripe?"

Catesby, who was the duke's chamberlain, was in attendance, as the prince unrobed—"A noble castle this," said the duke, "and one in the midst of a warlike population—our own countrymen of York."

"It would be no mean addition to the dowry of the Lady Isabel," said Catesby, with his bland, false smile.

"Methinks rather that the lordships of Salisbury, (and this is the chief,) pass to the Lady Anne," said Richard, musingly. "No, Edward were imprudent to suffer this stronghold to fall to the next heir to his throne. Marked you the Lady Anne—her beauty is most excellent."

"Truly your highness," answered Catesby, unsuspiciously, "the Lady Isabel seems to me the taller and the statelier."

"When man's merit and woman's beauty are measured by the ell, Catesby, Anne will certainly be less fair than Isabel, and Richard a dolt compared to Clarence. Open the casement—my dressing robe—good night to you!"

CHAPTER III.

The Sisters.

THE next morning at an hour when modern beauty falls into its first sickly sleep, Isabel and Anne conversed on the same terrace, and near the same spot which had witnessed their father's meditations the day before. They were seated on a rude bench in an angle of the wall, flanked by a low heavy bastion. And from the parapet their gaze might have wandered over a goodly sight, for on a broad space, covered with sand and sawdust, within the vast limits of the castle range, the numerous knights, and youths who sought apprenticeship in arms and gallantry under the earl, were engaged in those martial sports which falling elsewhere into the disuse, the Last of the Baron's kinglily maintained. There, boys of fourteen, on their small horses, ran against each other with blunted lances. There, those of more advanced adolescence, each following the other in a circle, rode at the ring; sometimes (at the word of command from an old knight who had fought at Agincourt, and was the preceptor in those valiant studies), leaping from their horses at full speed, and again vaulting into the saddle.

A few grim old warriors sate by to censure or applaud. Most skilled among the younger was the son of the Lord Montagu, among the maturer, the name of Marmaduke Nevile was the most often shouted. If the eye turned to the left, through the Babrican might be seen flocks of beeves entering to supply the mighty larder; and at a smaller postern, a dark crowd of mendicant friars, and the more destitute poor waited for their daily crumbs from the rich man's table. What need of a poor law then! the baron and the abbot made the parish! But not on these evidences of wealth and state turned the eyes—so familiar to them, that they woke no vanity, and roused no pride.

With downcast looks and a pouting lip, Isabel listened to the silver voice of Anne.

"Dear sister, be just to Clarence. He cannot openly defy his king and brother. Believe that he would have accompanied our uncle and cousin had he not deemed that their mediation would be more welcome, at least to King Edward, without his presence."

"But not a letter—not a line!"

"Yet when I think of it, Isabel, are we sure that he even knew of the visit of the archbishop and his brother?"

"How could he fail to know?"

"The Duke of Gloucester, last evening, told me that the king had sent him southward."

"Was it about Clarence that the duke whispered to thee so softly by the oriel window?"

'Surely, yes!" said Anne, simply. "Was not Richard as a brother to us when we played as children on yon greensward?"

"Never as a brother to me—never was Richard of Gloucester one whom I could think of without fear, and even loathing," answered Isabel, quickly.

It was at this turn in the conversation that the noiseless step of Richard himself neared the spot, and hearing his own name thus discourteously treated, he paused, screened from their eyes by the bastion, in the angle.

"Nay, nay, sister," said Anne; "what is there in Richard that misbeseems his princely birth?"

"I know not, but there is no youth in his eye and in his heart. Even as a child he had the hard will and the cold craft of gray hairs. Pray St. Mary you give me not Gloucester for a brother!"

Anne sighed and smiled—"Ah no," she said, after a short pause—"when thou art Princess of Clarence, may I——"

"May thou, what?"

"Pray for thee and thine in the house of God! Ah! thou knowest not, sweet Isabel, how often at morn and eve mine eyes and heart turn to the spires of yonder convent!" she rose as she said this, her lip quivered, and she moved on in the opposite direction to that in which Richard stood, still unseen, and no longer within his hearing. Isabel rose also, and hastening after her, threw her arms round Anne's neck, and kissed away the tears that stood in those meek eyes.

"My sister—my Anne! Ah! trust in me, thou hast some secret, I know it well—I have long seen it. Is it possible that thou canst have placed thy heart, thy pure love—thou blushest! Ah! Anne, Anne! thou canst not have loved beneath thee."

"Nay," said Anne, with a spark of her ancestral fire lighting her meek eyes through its tears, "not beneath me, but above. What do I say! Isabel, ask me no more. Enough that it is a folly—a dream—and that I could smile with pity at myself, to think from what light causes love and grief can spring."

"Above thee!" repeated Isabel, in amaze, "and who in England is above the daughter of Earl Warwick? Not Richard of Gloucester? if so, pardon my foolish tongue."

"No, not Richard—though I feel kindly towards him, and his sweet voice soothes me when I listen—not Richard. Ask no more."

"Oh, Anne—speak—speak!—we are not both so wretched. Thou lovest not Clarence? It is—it must be!"

"Canst thou think me so false and treacherous—a heart pledged to thee? Clarence! Oh no!"

"But who then—who then?" said Isabel, still suspiciously; "nay, if thou wilt not speak, blame thyself if I must still wrong thee."

Thus appealed to, and wounded to the quick by Isabel's tone and eye, Anne at last, with a strong effort, suppressed her tears, and, taking her sister's hand, said in a voice of touching solemnity—"Promise, then, that the secret shall be ever holy; aud, since I know that it will move thine anger—perhaps thy scorn—strive to forget what I will confess to thee."

Isabel for answer pressed her lips on the hand she held; and the sisters, turning under the shadow of a long row of venerable oaks, placed themselves on a little mound, fragrant with the violets of spring. A different part of the landscape beyond was now brought in view;—calmly slept in the valley the roofs of the subject town of Middleham — calmly flowed through the pastures the noiseless waves of Ure. Leaning on Isabel's bosom, Anne thus spake, "Call to mind, sweet sister, that short breathing-time in the horrors of the Civil War, when a brief peace was made between our father and Queen Margaret. We were left in the palace—mere children that we were—to play with the young prince, and the children in Margaret's train."

"I remember."

"And I was unwell, and timid, and kept aloof from the sports with a girl of my own years, whom I think—see how faithful my memory!—they called Sibyll; and Prince Edward, Henry's son, stealing from the rest, sought me out; and we sate together, or walked together alone, apart from all, that day and the few days we were his mother's guests. Oh! if you could have seen him and heard him then—so beautiful, so gentle, so wise beyond his years, and yet so sweetly sad; and when we parted, he bade me ever love him, and placed his ring on my finger, and wept,—as we kissed each other, as children will."

"Children!—ye were infants!" exclaimed Isabel, whose wonder seemed increased by this simple tale.

"Infant though I was, I felt as if my heart would break when I left him; and then the wars ensued; and do you not remember how ill I was, and like to die, when our house triumphed, and the prince and heir of Lancaster was driven into friendless exile? From that hour my fate was fixed. Smile if you please at such infant folly, but children often feel more deeply than later years can weet of."

"My sister, this is indeed a wilful invention of sorrow for thine own scourge. Why, ere this, believe me, the boy-prince hath forgotten thy very name."

"Not so, Isabel," said Anne, coloring, and quickly, "and perchance, did all rest here, I might have outgrown my weakness. But last year, when we were at Rouen with my father—"

"Well?"

"One evening, on entering my chamber, I found a packet—how left I know not, but the French king and his suite, thou rememberest, made our house almost their home—and in this packet was a picture, and on its back these words, '*Forget not the exile, who remembers thee!*'"

"And that picture was Prince Edward's?"

Anne blushed, and her bosom heaved beneath the slender and high-laced gorget. After a pause, looking round her, she drew forth a small miniature, which lay on the heart that beat thus sadly, and placed it in her sister's hands.

"You see I deceive you not, Isabel. And is not this a fair excuse for—"

She stopped short, her modest nature shrinking from comment upon the mere beauty that might have won the heart.

And fair indeed was the face upon which Isabel gazed admiringly, in spite of the stiff and rude art of the limner; full of the fire and energy which characterized the countenance of the mother, but with a tinge of the same profound and inexpressible melancholy that gave its charm to the pensive features of Henry VI.—a face, indeed, to fascinate a young eye, even if not associated with such remembrances of romance and pity.

Without saying a word, Isabel gave back the picture, but she pressed the hand that took it, and Anne was contented to interpret the silence into sympathy.

"And now you know why I have so often incurred your anger—by compassion for the adherents of Lancaster; and for this, also, Richard of Gloucester hath been endeared to me;—for fierce and stern as he may be called, he hath ever been gentle in his mediation for that unhappy House."

"Because it is his policy to be well with all parties. My poor Anne, I cannot bid you hope; and yet, should I ever wed with Clarence, it may be possible—that—that—but you in turn will chide me for ambition."

"How?"

"Clarence is heir to the throne of England, for King Edward has no male children; and the hour may arrive when the son of Henry of Windsor may return to his native land, not as sovereign, but as Dukc of Lancaster, and thy hand may reconcile him to the loss of a crown."

"Would love reconcile thee to such a loss, proud Isabel?" said Annie, shaking her head and smiling mournfully.

"No," answered Isabel, emphatically.

"And are men less haught than we?" said Anne. "Ah! I know not f I could love him so well could he resign his rights, or even could he regain them. It is his position that gives him a holiness in my eyes. And this love, that must be hopeless, is half pity and half respect."

At this moment a loud shout arose from the youths in the yard, or sporting ground, below, and the sisters, startled, and looking up, saw that the sound was occasioned by the sight of the young Duke of Gloucester, who was standing on the parapet near the bench the demoiselles had quitted, and who acknowledged the greeting by a wave of his plumed cap and a lowly bend of his head; at the same time the figures of Warwick and the archbishop, seemingly in earnest conversation, appeared at the end of the terrace. The sisters rose hastily, and would have stolen away, but the archbishop caught a glimpse of their robes, and called aloud to them. The reverent obedience, at that day, of youth to relations, left the sisters no option but to advance towards their uncle, which they did with demure reluctance.

"Fair brother," said the archbishop, "I would that Gloucester were to have my stately niece instead of the gaudy Clarence."

"Wherefore?"

"Because he can protect those he loves, and Clarence will ever need a protector."

"I like George not the less for that," said Warwick, "for I would not have my son-in-law my master."

"Master!" echoed the archbishop, laughing, "the soldan of Babylon himself, were he your son-in-law, would find Lord Warwick a tolerably stubborn servant!"

"And yet," said Warwick, also laughing, but with a franker tone, "beshrew me, but much as I approve young Gloucester, and deem him the hope of the House of York, I never feel sure, when we are of the same mind, whether I agree with him, or whether he leadeth me. Ah, George! Isabel should have wedded the king, and then Edward and I would have had a sweet mediator in all our quarrels. But not so hath it been decreed."

There was a pause.

"Note how Gloucester steals to the side of Anne. Thou mayst have him for a son-in-law, though no rival to Clarence. Montagu hath hinted that the duke so aspires."

"He has his father's face—well," said the earl, softly. "But yet," he added, in an altered and reflective tone, "the boy is to me a riddle. That he will be bold in battle and wise in council I foresee; but would he had more of a young man's honest follies! There is a medium between Edward's wantonness and Richard's sanctimony; and he who in the hey-day of youth's blood scowls alike upon sparkling wine and smiling woman, may hide in his heart darker and more sinful fancies. But fie on me! I will not wrongfully mistrust his father's son. Thou spokest of Montagu; he seems to have been mighty cold to his brother's wrongs—ever at the the court—ever sleek with Villein and Woodville."

"But the better to watch thy interests;—I so counselled him."

"A priest's counsel! Hate frankly or love freely is a knight's and soldier's motto. A murrain on all double-dealing!"

The archbishop shrugged his shoulders, and applied to his nostril a small pouncet-box of dainty essences.

"Come hither, my haughty Isabel," said the prelate, as the demoiselles now drew near. He placed his niece's arm within his own, and took her aside to talk of Clarence. Richard remained with Anne, and the young cousins were joined by Warwick. The earl noted in silence the soft address of the eloquent prince, and his evident desire to please Anne. And, strange as it may seem, although he had hitherto regarded Richard with admiration and affection, and although his pride for both daughters coveted alliances not less than royal, yet, in contemplating Gloucester for the first time as a probable suitor to his daughter, (and his favorite daughter,) the anxiety of a father sharpened his penetration, and placed the character of Richard before him in a different point from that in which he had hitherto looked only on the fearless heart and accomplished wit of his royal godson.

CHAPTER IV.

The Destrier.

It was three days afterwards that the earl, as, according to custom, Anne knelt to him for his morning blessing in the oratory, where the Christian baron at matins and vespers offered up his simple worship, drew her forth into the air, and said, abruptly—

"Wouldst thou be happy if Richard of Gloucester were thy betrothed?"

Anne started, and with more vivacity than

usually belonged to her, exclaimed, "O no, my father!"

"This is no maiden's silly coyness, Anne? It is a plain yea or nay that I ask from thee!"

"Nay, then," answered Anne, encouraged by her father's tone—"nay, if it so please you."

"It doth please me," said the earl, shortly; and after a pause, he added, "Yes, I am well pleased. Richard gives promise of an illustrious manhood; but Anne, thou growest so like thy mother, that, whenever my pride seeks to see thee great, my heart steps in, and only prays that it may see thee happy!—so much so, that I would not have given thee to Clarence, whom it likes me well to view as Isabel's betrothed, for, to her, greatness and bliss are one; and she is of firm nature, and can rule in her own house; but thou,—where out of romaunt can I find a lord loving enough for thee, soft child?"—

Inexpressibly affected, Anne threw herself on her father's breast and wept. He caressed and soothed her fondly; and, before her emotion was well over, Gloucester and Isabel joined them.

"My fair cousin," said the duke, "hath promised to show me thy renowned steed, Saladin; and since, on quitting thy halls, I go to my apprenticeship in war on the turbulent Scottish frontier, I would fain ask thee for a destrier of the same race as that which bears the thunderbolt of Warwick's wrath through the storm of battle."

"A steed of the race of Saladin," answered the earl, leading the way to the destrier's stall, apart from all other horses, and rather a chamber of the castle than a stable, "were indeed a boon worthy a soldier's gift and a prince's asking. But, alas! Saladin, like myself, is sonless—the last of a long line."

"His father, methinks, fell for us on the field of Touton. Was it not so? I have heard Edward say, that when the archers gave way, and the victory more than wavered, thou, dismounting, didst slay thy steed with thine own hand, and kissing the cross on thy sword, swore, on that spot, to stem the rush of the foe, and win Edward's crown or Warwick's grave." *

"It was so; and the shout of my merry men, when they saw me amongst their ranks on foot—all flight forbid—was Malech's death-dirge! It is a wondrous race that of Malech and his son Saladin, (continued the earl, smiling). When my ancestor, Aymer de Nevile, led his troops to the Holy Land, under Cœur de Lion, it was his fate to capture a lady beloved by the mighty Saladin. Need I say that Aymer, under a flag of truce, escorted her ransomless, her veil never raised from her face, to the tent of the Saracen king. Saladin, too gracious for an infidel, made him tarry awhile, an honored guest; and Aymer's chivalry became sorely tried, for the lady he had delivered loved and tempted him; but the good knight prayed and fasted, and defied satan and all his works. The lady (so runs the legend) grew wroth at the pious crusader's disdainful coldness; and when Aymer returned to his comrades, she sent, amidst the gifts of the soldan, two coal black steeds, male and mare, over which some foul and weird spells had been duly muttered. Their beauty, speed, art, and fierceness were a marvel. And Aymer, unsuspecting, prized the boon, and selected the male destrier for his war-horse. Great were the feats, in many a field, which my forefather wrought, bestriding his black charger.

But one fatal day, on which the sudden war-trump made him forget his morning ave, the beast had power over the Christian, and bore him, against bit and spur, into the thickest of the foe. He did all a knight can do against many—(pardon his descendant's vaunting,—so runs the tale)—and the Christians for awhile beheld him solitary in the melée, mowing down moon and turban. Then the crowd closed, and the good knight was lost to sight. 'To the rescue!' cried bold King Richard, and on rushed the crusaders to Aymer's help; when lo! and suddenly, the ranks severed, and the black steed emerged! Aymer still on the selle, but motionless, and his helm battered and plumeless—his brand broken—his arm drooping. On came man and horse, on—charging on, not against Infidel, but Christian. On dashed the steed, I say, with fire bursting from eyes and nostrils,

* "Every Palm Sunday, the day on which the Battle of Touton was fought, a rough figure, called the Red Horse, on the side of a hill in Warwickshire, is scoured out. This is suggested to be done in commemoration of the horse which the Earl of Warwick slew on that day, determined to vanquish or die."—ROBERT'S "*York and Lancaster*," vol. i., p. 429.

and the pike of his chaffron bent lance-like against the crusaders' van.

"The foul fiend seemed in the destrier's rage and puissance. He bore right against Richard's standard-bearer, and down went the lion and the cross. He charged the king himself; and Richard, unwilling to harm his own dear soldier Aymer, halted wondering, till the pike of the destrier pierced his own charger through the barding, and the king lay rolling in the dust. A panic seized the cross-men—they fled—the Saracens pursued—and still with the Saracens came the black steed and the powerless rider. At last, when the crusaders reached the camp, and the flight ceased, there, halted also Aymer. Nor a man dared near him. He spoke not—none spoke to him—till a holy priest and palmer approached and sprinkled the good knight and the black barb with holy water, and exorcised both—the spell broke, and Aymer dropped to the earth. They unbraced his helm—he was cold and stark. The fierce steed had but borne a dead man."

"Holy Paul!" cried Gloucester, with seeming sanctimony, though a covet sneer played round the firm beauty of his pale lips—"a notable tale, and one that proveth much of Sacred Truth, now lightly heeded. But, verily, Lord Earl, I should have little loved a steed with such a pedigree!"

"Hear the rest," said Isabel—"King Richard ordered the destrier to be slain forthwith; but the holy palmer who had exorcised it, forbade the sacrifice. 'Mighty shall be the service,' said the reverend man, 'which the posterity of this steed shall render to thy royal race, and great glory shall they give to the sons of Nevile. Let the war-horse, now duly exorcised from infidel spells, live long to bear a Christian warrior!'"

"And so," quoth the earl, taking up the tale—"so mare and horse were brought by Aymer's squires to his English hall; and Aymer's son, Sir Reginald, bore the cross, and bestrode the fatal steed, without fear and without scathe. From that hour the House of Nevile rose amain, in fame and in puissance, and the legend further saith, that the same palmer encountered Sir Reginald at Joppa, bade him treasure that race of war-steeds as his dearest heritage, for with that race his own should flourish and depart; and the sole one of the Infidel's spells which could not be broken, was that which united the gift—generation after generation, for weal or for woe, for honor or for doom—to the fate of Aymer and his house. 'And,' added the palmer, 'as with woman's love and woman's craft was woven the indissoluble charm, so shall woman, whether in craft or in love, ever shape the fortunes of thee and thine.'"

"As yet," said the prince, "the prophecy is fulfilled in a golden sense, for nearly all thy wide baronies, I trow, have come to thee through the female side. A woman's hand brought to the Nevile this castle and its lands.* From a woman came the heritage of Monthermer and Montagu, and Salisbury's famous earldom;—and the dower of thy peerless countess was the broad domains of Beauchamp."

"And a woman's craft, young prince, wrought my king's displeasure! But enough of these dissour's tales: behold the son of poor Malech, whom, forgetting all such legends, I slew at Touton. Ho! Saladin—greet thy master!"

They stood now in the black steeds stall—an ample and high-vaulted space, for halter never insulted the fierce destrier's mighty neck, which the God of Battles had clothed in thunder. A marble cistern contained his limpid drink, and in a gilded manger the finest wheaton bread was mingled with the oats of Flanders. On entering, they found young George, Montagu's son, with two or three boys, playing familiarly with the noble animal, who had all the affectionate docility inherited from an Arab origin. But at the sound of Warwick's voice, its ears rose, its mane dressed itself, and with a short neigh it came to his feet, and kneeling down, in slow and stately grace, licked its master's hand. So perfect and so matchless a steed never had knight bestrode! Its hide without one white hair, and glossy as the sheenest satin; a lady's tresses were scarcely finer than the hair of its noble mane; the exceeding smallness of its head, its broad frontal, the remarkable and almost human intelligence of its

* Middleham Castle was built by Robert Fitz Ranulph, grandson of Ribald, younger brother of the Earl of Bretagne and Richmond, nephew to the Conqueror. The founder's line failed in male heirs, and the heiress married Robert Neville, son of Lord Raby. Warwick's father held the earldom of Salisbury in right of his wife, the heiress of Thomas de Montacute.

eye, seemed actually to elevate its conformation above that of its species. Though the race had increased, generation after generation, in size and strength, Prince Richard still marvelled (when, obedient to a sign from Warwick, the destrier rose, and leant its head, with a sort of melancholy and quiet tenderness, upon the earl's shoulder) that a horse, less in height and bulk than the ordinary battle steed, could bear the vast weight of the giant earl in his ponderous mail. But his surprise ceased when the earl pointed out to him the immense strength of the steed's ample loins, the sinewy cleanness, the iron muscle, of the stag-like legs, the bull-like breadth of chest, and the swelling power of the shining neck.

"And after all," added the earl, "both in man and beast, the spirit and the race, not the stature and the bulk, bring the prize. Mort Dieu, Richard! it often shames me of mine own thews and broad breast—I had been more vain of laurels had I been shorter by the head!"

"Nevertheless," said young George of Montagu, with a page's pertness, "I had rather have thine inches than Prince Richard's, and thy broad breast than his grace's short neck."

The Duke of Gloucester turned as if a snake had stung him. He gave but one glance to the speaker, but that glance lived for ever in the boy's remembrance, and the young Montagu turned pale and trembled, even before he heard the earl's stern rebuke.

"Young magpies chatter, boy—young eagles in silence measure the space between the eyrie and the sun!"

The boy hung his head, and would have slunk off, but Richard detained him with a gentle hand—"My fair young cousin," said he, "thy words gall no sore, and if ever thou and I charge side by side into the foeman's ranks, thou shalt comprehend what thy uncle designed to say,—how in the hour of strait and need, we measure men's stature not by the body but the soul!"

"A noble answer," whispered Anne, with something like sisterly admiration.

"Too noble," said the more ambitious Isabel, in the same voice, "for Clarence's future wife not to fear Clarence's dauntless brother."

"And so," said the prince, quitting the stall with Warwick, while the girls still lingered behind, "so Saladin hath no son! Wherefore? Can you mate him with no bride?"

"Faith," answered the earl, "the females of his race sleep in yonder dell, their burial place, and the proud beast disdains all meaner loves. Nay, were it not so, to continue the breed if adulterated, were but to mar it."

"You care little for the legend, meseems."

"Pardieu! at times, yes, overmuch; but in sober moments, I think that the brave man who does his duty lacks no wizard prophecy to fulfil his doom; and whether in prayer or in death, in fortune or defeat, his soul goes straight to God!"

"Umph," said Richard, musingly, and there was a pause.

"Warwick," resumed the Prince, "doubtless even on your return to London, the queen's enmity and her mother's will not cease. Clarence loves Isabel, but Clarence knows not how to persuade the king and rule the king's womankind. Thou knowest how I have stood aloof from all the factions of the court. Unhappily I go to the borders, and can but slightly serve thee. But ——" (he stopped short, and sighed heavily.)

"Speak on, prince."

"In a word, then, if I were thy son, Anne's husband—I see—I see—I see—" (thrice repeated the prince, with a vague dreaminess in his eye, and stretching forth his hand)—"a future that might defy all foes, opening to me and thee!"

Warwick hesitated in some embarrassment.

"My gracious and princely cousin," he said, at length, "this proffer is indeed sweet incense to a father's pride. But pardon me, as yet, noble Richard, thou art so young that the king and the world would blame me did I suffer my ambition to listen to such temptation. Enough at present, if all disputes between our house and the king can be smoothed and laid at rest, without provoking new ones. Nay, pardon me, prince, let this matter cease,—at least, till thy return from the borders."

"May I take with me hope?"

"Nay," said Warwick, "thou knowest that I am a plain man; to bid thee hope, were to plight my word. And," he added, seriously, "there be reasons grave, and well to be considered, why both the daughters of a subject should not wed with their king's brothers. Let this cease now, I pray thee, sweet lord."

Here the demoiselles joined their father, and the conference was over; but when Richard, an hour after, stood musing alone on the battlements, he muttered to himself—"Thou art a fool, stout earl, not to have welcomed the union between thy power and my wit. Thou goest to a court where, without wit, power is nought. Who may foresee the future? Marry, that was a wise ancient fable, that he who seized and bound Proteus, could extract from the changeful god, the prophecy of the days to come. Yea! the man who can seize fate, can hear its voice predict to him. And by my own heart and brain, which never yet relinquished what affection yearned for or thought aspired to, I read, as in a book, Anne, that thou shalt be mine; and that where wave on yon battlements the ensigns of Beauchamp, Monthermer, and Nevile, the Boar of Gloucester shall liege it over their broad baronies and hardy vassals."

BOOK SIXTH.

WHEREIN ARE OPENED SOME GLIMPSES OF THE FATE, BELOW, THAT ATTENDS THOSE WHO ARE BETTER THAN OTHERS, AND THOSE WHO DESIRE TO MAKE OTHERS BETTER. LOVE, DEMAGOGUY, AND SCIENCE EQUALLY OFFSPRING OF THE SAME PROLIFIC DELUSION—VIZ., THAT MEAN SOULS (THE EARTH'S MAJORITY) ARE WORTH THE HOPE AND THE AGONY OF NOBLE SOULS, THE EVERLASTINGLY SUFFERING AND ASPIRING FEW.

CHAPTER I.

New Dissensions.

WE must pass over some months. Warwick and his family had returned to London, and the meeting between Edward and the earl, had been cordial and affectionate. Warwick was reinstated in the offices which gave him apparently the supreme rule in England. The Princess Margaret had left England, as the bride of Charles the Bold; and the earl had attended the procession, in honor of her nuptials. The king, agreeably with the martial objects he had had long at heart, had then declared war on Louis XI., and parliament was addressed, and troops were raised for that impolitic purpose.* To this war, however, Warwick was inflexibly opposed. He pointed out the madness of withdrawing from England all her best affected chivalry, at a time when the adherents of Lancaster, still powerful, would require no happier occasion to raise the Red Rose banner. He showed how hollow was the hope of steady aid from the hot, but reckless and unprincipled Duke of Burgundy, and how different now was the condition of France under a king of consummate sagacity, and with an overflowing treasury, to its distracted state in the former conquests of the English. This opposition to the king's will gave every opportunity for Warwick's enemies to renew their old accusation of secret and treasonable amity with Louis. Although the proud and hasty earl had not only forgiven the affront put upon him by Edward, but had sought to make amends for his own intemperate resentment, by public attendance on the ceremonials that accompanied the betrothal of the princess, it was impossible for Edward ever again to love the minister who had defied his power, and menaced his crown. His humor and his suspicions broke forth despite the restraint that policy dictated to him; and in the disputes upon the invasion of France, a second and more deadly breach between Edward and his minister must have yawned, had not events suddenly and unexpectedly proved the wisdom of Warwick's distrust of Burgundy. Louis XI. bought off the Duke of Bretagne, patched up a peace with Charles the Bold, and thus frustrated all the schemes, and broke all the alliances of Edward at the very moment his military preparations were ripe.*

Still the angry feelings that the dispute had occasioned between Edward and the earl were not removed with the cause; and, under pretence of guarding against hostilities from Louis, the king requested Warwick to depart to his government of Calais, the most important and honorable post, it is true, which a subject could then hold; but Warwick considered the request as a pretext for his removal from the Court. A yet more irritating and insulting cause of offence was found in Edward's withholding his consent to Clarence's often-urged demand for permission to wed with the Lady

* Parliamentary Rolls, 623. The fact in the text has been neglected by most historians.

* W. Wyr, 518.

Isabel. It is true that this refusal was accompanied with the most courteous protestations of repect for the earl, and placed only upon the general ground of state policy.

"My dear George," Edward would say, "the heiress of Lord Warwick is certainly no mal-alliance for a king's brother; but the safety of the throne imperitively demands, that my brothers should strengthen my rule, by connections with foreign potentates. I, it is true, married a subjeet, and see all the troubles that have sprung from my boyish passion! No, no Go to Bretagne. The duke hath a fair daughter, and we will make up for any scantiness in the dower. Weary me no more, George. *Fiat voluntas mea!*"

But the motives assigned were not those which influenced the king's refusal. Reasonably enough, he dreaded that the next male heir to his crown should wed the daughter of the subject who had given that crown, and might at any time take it away. He knew Clarence to be giddy, unprincipled, and vain. Edward's faith in Warwick was shaken by the continual and artful representations of the queen and her family. He felt that the alliance between Clarence and the earl would be the union of two interests, almost irresistible, if once arrayed against his own.

But Warwick, who penetrated into the true reasons for Edward's obstinacy, was yet more resentful against the reasons than the obstinacy itself. The one galled him through his affections, the other through his pride; and the first were as keen as the last was morbid. He was the more chafed, inasmuch as his anxiety of father became aroused. Isabel was really attached to Clarence, who, with all his errors, possessed every superficial attraction that graced his house; gallant and handsome, gay and joyous, and with manners that made him no less popular than Edward himself.

And if Isabel's affections were not deep, disinterested, and tender, like those of Anne, they were strengthened by a pride which she inherited from her father, and a vanity which she took from her sex. It was galling in the extreme to feel that the loves between her and Clarence were the court gossip, and the king's refusal the court jest. Her health gave way, and pride and love both gnawed at her heart.

It happened, unfortunately for the king and for Warwick, that Gloucester, whose premature acuteness and sagacity would have the more served both, inasmuch as the views he had formed in regard to Anne, would have blended his interest, in some degree, with that of the Duke of Clarence, and certainly with the object of conciliation between Edward and his minister,—it happened, we say, unfortunately, that Gloucester was still absent with the forces employed on the Scottish frontier, whither he had repaired on quitting Middleham, and where his extraordinary military talents found their first brilliant opening,—and he was therefore absent from London during all the disgusts he might have removed, and the intrigues he might have frustrated.

But the interests of the house of Warwick, during the earl's sullen and indignant sojourn at his government of Calais, were not committed to unskilful hands; and Montagu and the archbishop were well fitted to cope with Lord Rivers and the Duchess of Bedford.

Between these able brothers, one day, at the More, an important conference took place.

"I have sought you," said Montagu, with more than usual care upon his brow—"I have sought you in consequence of an event that may lead to issues of no small moment, whether for good or evil. Clarence has suddenly left England for Calais."

"I know it, Montagu; the Duke confided to me his resolution to proclaim himself old enough to marry—and discreet enough to choose for himself."

"And you approved?"

"Certes; and, sooth to say, I brought him to that modest opinion of his own capacities. What is more still I propose to join him at Calais!"

"George!"

"Look not so scared, O valiant captain, who never lost a battle—where the Church meddles all prospers. Listen!" And the young prelate gathered himself up from his listless posture, and spoke with earnest unction—"Thou knowest that I do not much busy myself in lay schemes—when I do, the object must be great. Now, Montagu, I have of late narrowly and keenly watched that spidery web which ye call a court, and I see that the spider will devour the wasp, unless the wasp boldly break the web—for womancraft I call the spider, and soldier-pride I style the wasp. To speak plainly, these

Woodvilles must be bravely breasted and determinately abashed. I do not mean that we can deal with the king's wife and her family as with any other foes; but we must convince them that they cannot cope with us, and that their interest will best consist in acquiescing to that condition of things which places the rule of England in the hands of the Neviles."

"My own thought, if I saw the way!"

"I see the way in this alliance; the Houses of York and Warwick must become so indissolubly united, that an attempt to injure the one, must destroy both. The queen and the Woodvilles plot against us; we must raise in the king's family a counterpoise to their machinations. It brings no scandal on the queen to conspire against Warwick, but it would ruin her in the eyes of England to conspire against the king's brother; and Clarence and Warwick must be as one. This is not all! If our sole aid was in giddy George, we should but buttress our house with a weathercock. This connection is but as a part of the grand scheme on which I have set my heart—Clarence shall wed Isabel, Gloucester wed Anne, and (let thy ambitious heart beat high, Montagu) the king's eldest daughter shall wed thy son—the male representative of our triple honors. Ah, thine eyes sparkle now! Thus the whole royalty of England shall centre in the Houses of Nevile and York; and the Woodvilles will be caught and hampered in their own meshes—their resentment impotent; for how can Elizabeth stir against us, if her daughter be betrothed to the son of Montagu, the nephew of Warwick. Clarence, beloved by the shallow commons;* Gloucester, adored both by the army and the church; and Montagu and Warwick, the two great captains of the age—is not this a combination of power, that may defy Fate?"

"Oh, George!" said Montague, admiringly, "what pity that the church should spoil such a statesman!"

"Thou art profane, Montagu; the church spoils no man—the church leads and guides ye all; and, mark, I look farther still. I would have intimate league with France; I would strengthen ourselves with Spain and the German Emperor; I would buy, or seduce the votes of the sacred college; I would have thy poor brother, whom thou so pitiest because he has no son to marry a king's daughter—no daughter to wed with a king's son—I would have thy unworthy brother, Montagu, the father of the whole Christian world, and, from the chair of the Vatican, watch over the weal of kingdoms. And now, seest thou why with to-morrow's sun I depart for Calais, and lend my voice in aid of Clarence's, for the first knot in this complicated bond?"

"But, will Warwick consent while the king opposes? Will his pride—"

"His pride serves us here; for, so long as Clarence did not dare to gain-say the king, Warwick, in truth, might well disdain to press his daughter's hand upon living man. The king opposes, but with what right? Warwick's pride will but lead him, if well addressed, to defy affront, and to resist dictation. Besides, our brother has a woman's heart for his children; and Isabel's face is pale, and that will plead more than all my eloquence."

"But can the king forgive your intercession, and Warwick's contumacy?"

"Forgive!—the marriage once over, what is left for him to do? He is then one with us, and when Gloucester returns all will be smooth again—smooth for the second and more important nuptials—and the second shall preface the third; meanwhile, you return to the court. To these ceremonials you need be no party: keep but thy handsome son from breaking his neck in over-riding his hobby, and 'bide thy time!'"

Agreeably with the selfish, but sagacious policy, thus detailed, the prelate departed the next day for Calais, where Clarence was already urging his suit with the ardent impatience of amorous youth. The archbishop found, however, that Warwick was more reluctant than he had anticipated to suffer his daughter to enter any house without the consent of its chief, nor would the earl, in all probability, have acceded to the prayers of the princely suitor, had not Edward, enraged at the flight of Clarence, and worked upon by the artful queen, committed the imprudence of writing an intemperate and menacing letter to the earl, which called up all the passions of the haughty Warwick.

"What!" he exclaimed, "thinks this un-

* Singular as it may seem to those who know not that popularity is given to the vulgar qualities of men, and that where a noble nature becomes popular (a rare occurrence), it is despite the nobleness—not because of it, Clarence was a popular idol even to the time of his death.—*Croyl.*, 562.

grateful man not only to dishonor me, by his method of marrying his sisters, but will he also play the tyrant with me in the disposal of mine own daughter! He threats! he!—enough. It is due to me to show that there lives no man whose threats I have not the heart to defy!" And the prelate, finding him in this mood, had no longer any difficulty in winning his consent. The ill-omened marriage was, accordingly, celebrated with great and regal pomp at Calais, and the first object of the archbishop was attained.

While thus stood affairs between the two great factions of the state, those discontents which Warwick's presence at the court had awhile laid at rest, again spread, broad and far, throughout the land. The luxury and indolence of Edward's disposition, in ordinary times, always surrendered him to the guidance of others. In the commencement of his reign he was eminently popular, and his government, though stern, suited to the times; for then the presiding influence was that of Lord Warwick. As the queen's counsels pervailed over the consummate experience and masculine vigor of the earl, the king's government lost both popularity and respect, except only in the metropolis; and if at the close of his reign, it regained all its earlier favor with the people, it must be principally ascribed to the genius of Hastings, then England's most powerful subject, and whose intellect calmly moved all the springs of action. But now everywhere the royal authority was weakened; and while Edward was feasting at Shene, and Warwick absent at Calais, the provinces were exposed to all the abuses which most gall a population.

The poor complained that undue exactions were made on them by the hospitals, abbeys, and barons; the Church complained that the queen's relations had seized and spent church moneys; the men of birth and merit, complained of the advancement of new men who had done no service; and all these several discontents fastened themselves upon the odious Woodvilles, as the cause of all. The second breach now, notorious, between the king and the all-beloved Warwick, was a new aggravation of the popular hatred to the queen's family, and seemed to give occasion for the malcontents to appear with impunity, at least so far as the earl was concerned: it was, then, at this critical time that the circumstances we are about to relate occurred.

CHAPTER II.

The would-be improvers of Jove's Foot-ball, Earth—The sad Father and the sad Child—The fair Rivals.

Adam Warner was at work on his crucible when the servitor commissioned to attend him opened the chamber door, and a man dressed in the black gown of a student entered.

He approached the alchemist, and after surveying him for a moment in a silence that seemed not without contempt, said, "What, Master Warner, are you so wedded to your new studies, that you have not a word to bestow on an old friend?"

Adam turned, and after peevishly gazing at the intruder a few moments, his face brightened up into recognition.

"*En iterum!*" he said. "Again, bold Robin Hilyard, and in a scholar's garb. Ha! doubtless thou hast learned ere this, that peaceful studies do best ensure man's weal below, and art come to labor with me in the high craft of mind-work!"

"Adam," quoth Hilyard, "ere I answer, tell me this—Thou, with thy science wouldst change the world,—art thou a jot nearer to thy end?"

"Well-a-day," said poor Adam, "you know little what I have undergone; for danger to myself by rack and gibbet, I say nought. Man's body is fair prey to cruelty, and what a king spares to-day the worm shall gnaw tomorrow. But mine invention—my Eureka—look!" and stepping aside, he lifted a cloth, and exhibited the mangled remains of the unhappy model.

"I am forbid to restore it," continued Adam, dolefully. "I must work day and night to make gold, and the gold comes not: and my only change of toil is when the queen bids me construct little puppet-boxes for her children! How, then, can I change the world? And thou," he added, doubtingly and eagerly—"thou, with thy plots and stratagem, and active demagoguy, thinkest thou that *thou* hast changed the world, or extracted one drop of evil out of the mixture of gall and hyssop which man is born to drink?"

Hilyard was silent, and the two world-betterers—the philosopher and the demagogue—gazed on each other, half in sympathy, half contempt. At last Robin said—

"Mine old friend, hope sustains us both; and in the wilderness we yet behold the Pisgah! But to my business. Doubtless thou art permitted to visit Henry in his prison."

"Not so," replied Adam; "and for the rest, since I now eat King Edward's bread, and enjoy what they call his protection, ill would it beseem me to lend myself to plots against his throne."

"Ah! man—man—man," exclaimed Hilyard, bitterly, "thou art like all the rest—scholar or serf, the same slave; a king's smile bribes thee from a people's service!"

Before Adam could reply, a panel in the wainscot slid back, and the bald head of a friar peered into the room. "Son Adam," said the holy man, "I crave your company an instant, *oro vestrum aurem;*" and with thi sabominable piece of Latinity the friar vanished.

With a resigned and mournful shrug of the shoulders, Adam walked across the room, when Hilyard, arresting his progress, said crossing himself, and in a subdued and in fearful whisper, "Is not that Friar Bungey, the notable magician?"

"Magician or not," answered Warner, with a lip of inexpressible contempt and a heavy sigh, "God pardon his mother for giving birth to such a numbskull!" and with this pious and charitable ejaculation Adam disappeared in the adjoining chamber, appropriated to the friar.

"Hum," soliloquized Hilyard, "they say that Friar Bungey is employed by the witch duchess in everlasting diabolisms against her foes. A peep into his den might suffice me for a stirring tale to the people."

No sooner did this daring desire arise, than the hardy Robin resolved to gratify it; and stealing on tiptoe along the wall, he peered cautiusly through the aperture made by the sliding panel. An enormous stuffed lizard hung from the ceiling, and various strange reptiles, dried into mummy, were ranged around, and glared at the spy with green glass eyes. A huge book lay open on a tripod stand, and a caldron seethed over a slow and dull fire. A sight yet more terrible.presently awaited the rash beholder.

"Adam," said the friar, laying his broad palm on the student's reluctant shoulders, "*inter sapentes.*"

"*Sapientes*, brother," groaned Adam.

"That's the old form Adam," quoth the friar, superciliously—"*sapentes* is the last improvement. I say, between wise men there is no envy. Our noble and puissant patroness, the Duchess of Bedford, hath committed to me a task that promiseth much profit. I have worked at it night and day *stotis filibus.*"

"O, man, what lingo speakest thou!—*stotis filibus!*"

"Tush, if it is not good Latin it does as well, son Adam. I say I have worked at it night and day, and it is now advanced eno' for experiment. But thou art going to sleep."

"Dispatch—speak out—speak on!" said Adam, desperately—"what is thy achievement?"

"See!" answered the friar, majestically; and drawing aside a black pall, he exhibited to the eyes of Adam, and to the more startled gaze of Robin Hilyard, a pale, cadaverous, corpse-like image, of pigmy proportions, but with features moulded into a coarse caricature of the lordly countenance of the Earl of Warwick.

"There," said the friar, complacently, and rubbing his hands; "that is no piece of bungling, eh! As like the stout earl as one pea to another."

"And for what hast thou kneaded up all this waste of wax?" asked Adam. "Forsooth I knew not you had so much of ingenious art; algates, the toy is somewhat ghastly."

"Ho, ho!" quoth the friar, laughing so as to show a set of jagged, discolored fangs from ear to ear, "surely thou, who art so notable a wizard and scholar, knowest for what purpose we image forth our enemies. Whatever the duchess inflicts upon this figure, the Earl of Warwick, whom it representeth, will feel through his bones and marrow—waste wax, waste man!"

"Thou art a devil to do this thing, and a blockhead to think it, O miserable friar!" exclaimed Adam, roused from all his gentleness.

"Ha!" cried the friar, no less vehemently, and his burly face purple with passion, "dost thou think to bandy words with me? Wretch! I will set goblins to pinch thee black and blue.

I will drag thee at night over all the jags of Mount Pepanon, at the tail of a mad nightmare. I will put aches in all thy bones, and the blood in thy veins shall run into sores and blotches. Am I not Friar Bungey? and what art thou?"

At these terrible denunciations, the sturdy Robin, though far less superstitious than most of his contemporaries, was seized with a trembling from head to foot; and expecting to see goblins and imps start forth from the walls, he retired hastily from his hiding-place, and, without waiting for further commune with Warner, softly opened the chamber door, and stole down the stairs. Adam, however, bore the storm unquailingly, and when the holy man paused to take breath, he said, calmly—

"Verily, if thou canst do these things, there must be secrets in Nature, which I have not yet discovered. Howbeit, though thou art free to try all thou canst against me, thy threats make it necessary that this communication between us should be nailed up, and I shall so order."

The friar, who was ever in want of Adam's aid, either to construe a bit of Latin, or to help him in some chemical illusion, by no means relished this quiet retort; and, holding out his huge hand to Adam, said, with affected cordiality—

"Pooh! we are brothers, and must not quarrel. I was over hot, and thou too provoking; but I honor and love thee, man—let it pass. As for this figure, doubtless we might pink it all over, and the earl be never the worse. But if our employers order these things, and pay for them, we cunning men make profit by fools!"

"It is men like thee that brings shame on science," answered Adam, sternly; "and I will not listen to thee longer."

"Nay, but you must," said the friar clutching Adam's robe, and concealing his resentment by an affected grin. "Thou thinkest me a mere ignoramus—ha! ha!—I think the same of thee. Why, man, thou hast never studied the parts of the human body, I'll swear."

"I'm no leech," said Adam. "Let me go."

"No—not yet. I will convict thee of ignorance. Thou dost not even know where the liver is placed."

"I do," answered Adam, shortly; "but what then?"

"Thou dost!—I deny it. Here is a pin; stick it into this wax, man, where thou sayest the liver lies in the human frame."

Adam unsuspiciously obeyed.

"Well!—the liver is there, eh. Ah! but where are the lungs?"

"Why, here."

"And the midriff?"

"Here, certes."

"Right!—thou mayst go now," said the friar, drily. Adam disappeared through the aperture, and closed the panel.

"Now I know where the lungs, midriff, and liver are," said the friar to himself. "I shall get on famously. 'Tis an useful fellow, that, or I should have him hanged long ago!"

Adam did not remark, on his re-entrance, that his visitor, Hilyard, had disappeared, and the philosopher was soon re-immersed in the fiery interest of his thankless labors.

It might be an hour afterwards, when, wearied and exhausted by perpetual hope and perpetual disappointment, he flung himself on his seat; and that deep sadness, which they who devote themselves in this noisy world to wisdom and to truth alone can know—suffused his thoughts, and murmured from his feverish lips.

"Oh, hard condition of my life!" groaned the sage—"ever to strive, and never to accomplish. The sun sets and the sun rises upon my eternal toils, and my age stands as distant from the goal, as stood my youth! Fast, fast the mind is wearing out the frame, and my schemes have but woven the ropes of sand, and my name shall be writ in water. Golden dreams of my young hope, where are ye? Methought once, that could I obtain the grace of royalty, the ear of power, the command of wealth, my path to glory was made smooth and sure—I should become the grand inventor of my time and land; I should leave my lore a heritage and blessing wherever labor works to civilize the round globe. And now my lodging is a palace—royalty my patron—they give me gold at my desire—my wants no longer mar my leisure. Well! and for what? On condition that I forego the sole task for which patronage, wealth, and leisure were desired! There, stands the broken iron, and there, simmers the ore I am to turn to gold—the iron worth more than all the gold, and the gold, never to be won! Poor, I was an inventor, a creator, the true magician—protected, patronized, enriched, I am but the alchemist, the bubble, the dupe or duper, the fool's fool. God, brace up my limbs! Let me escape—give me back my old dream, and die, at least, if accomplishing nothing, hoping all!"

He rose as he spoke, he strode across the chamber with majestic step, with resolve upon his brow. He stopped short, for a sharp pain shot across his heart. Premature age, and the disease that labor brings, were at their work of decay within: the mind's excitement gave way to the body's weakness, and he sank again upon his seat, breathing hard, gasping, pale, the icy damps upon his brow. Bubblingly seethed the molten metals, redly glowed the poisonous charcoal, the air of death was hot within the chamber where the victim of royal will pandered to the desire of gold:—Terrible and eternal moral for Wisdom and for Avarice, for sages and for kings—ever shall he who would be the maker of gold, breathe the air of death!

"Father," said the low and touching voice of one who had entered unperceived, and who now threw her arms round Adam's neck, "father, thou art ill, and sorely suffering—"

"At heart—yes, Sibyll. Give me thine arm; let us forth and taste the fresher air."

It was so seldom that Warner could be induced to quit his chamber, that these words almost startled Sibyll, and she looked anxiously in his face, as she wiped the dews from his forehead.

"Yes—air—air!" repeated Adam, rising.

Sibyll placed his bonnet over his silvered locks, drew his gown more closely round him, and slowly, and in silence, they left the chamber, and took their way across the court to the ramparts of the fortress-palace.

The day was calm and genial, with a low but fresh breeze stirring gently through the warmth of noon. The father and child seated themselves on the parapet, and saw, below, the gay and numerous vessels that glided over the sparkling river, while the dark walls of Baynard's Castle, the adjoining bulwark and battlements of Montfichet, and the tall watch-tower of Warwick's mighty mansion, frowned in the distance, against the soft blue sky. "There," said Adam, quietly, and pointing to the feudal roofs, "there seems to rise power—and yonder, (glancing to the river),—yonder seems to flow Genius! A century or so hence, the walls shall vanish, but the river shall roll on. Man makes the castle, and founds the power—God forms the river, and creates the genius. And yet, Sibyll, there may be streams as broad and stately as yonder Thames, that flow afar in the waste, never seen, never heard by man. What profits the river unmarked?—what the genius never to be known?"

It was not a common thing with Adam Warner to be thus eloquent. Usually silent and absorbed, it was not his gift to moralize or declaim. His soul must be deeply moved before the profound and buried sentiment within it could escape into words.

Sibyll pressed her father's hand, and, though her own heart was very heavy, she forced her lips to smile, and her voice to soothe. Adam interrupted her.

"Child, child, ye women know not what presses darkest and most bitterly on the minds of men. You know not what it is to form out of immaterial things some abstract but glorious object—to worship—to serve it—to sacrifice to it, as on an altar, youth, health, hope, life—and suddenly, in old age, to see that the idol was a phantom, a mockery, a shadow laughing us to scorn because we have sought to clasp it."

"Oh, yes, father, woman have known that illusion."

"What! Do they study?"

"No, father, but they feel!"

"Feel! I comprehend thee not."

"As man's genius to him, is woman's heart to her," answered Sibyll, her dark and deep eyes suffused with tears. "Doth not the heart create—invent? Doth it not dream? Doth it not form its idol out of air? Goeth it not forth into the future, to prophesy to itself? And, sooner or later, in age or youth, doth it not wake at last, and see how it hath wasted its all on follies? Yes, father, my heart can answer, when thy genius would complain."

"Sibyll," said Warner, roused and surprised, and gazing on her wistfully, "time flies apace. Till this hour I have thought of thee but as a child—an infant. Thy words disturb me now."

"Think not of them, then. Let me never add one grief to thine."

"Thou art brave and gay in thy silken sheen," said Adam, curiously stroking down the rich, smooth stuff of Sibyll's tunic; "her grace the duchess is generous to us. Thou art surely happy here!"

"Happy!"

"Not happy!" exclaimed Adam, almost joyfully, "wouldst thou that we were back once more in our desolate ruined home?"

"Yes, oh, yes!—but rather away, far away, in some quiet village, some green nook; for the desolate ruined home was not safe for thine old age."

"I would we could escape, Sibyll," said Adam, earnestly, in a whisper, and with a kind of innocent cunning in his eye, "we and the poor Eureka! The palace is a prison-house to me. I will speak to the Lord Hastings, a man of great excellence, and gentle too. He is ever kind to us."

"No, no, father, not to him," cried Sibyll, turning pale,—"let him not know a word of what we would propose, nor whither we would fly."

"Child, he loves me, or why does he seek me so often, and sit and talk not?"

Sibyll pressed her clasped hands tightly to her bosom, but made no answer; and, while she was summoning courage to say something that seemed to oppress her thoughts with intolerable weight, a footstep sounded gently near, and the Lady of Bonville, (then on a visit to the queen), unseen, and unheard by the two, approached the spot. She paused, and gazed at Sibyll, at first haugtily; and then, as the deep sadness of that young face struck her softer feelings, and the pathetic picture of father and child, thus alone in their commune, made its pious and sweet effect, the gaze changed from pride to compassion, and the lady said, courteously—

"Fair mistress, canst thou prefer this solitary scene to the gay company about to take the air in her Grace's gilded barge?"

Sibyll looked up in surprise, not unmixed with fear. Never before had the great lady spoken to her thus gently. Adam, who seemed for awhile restored to the actual life, saluted Katherine with simple dignity, and took up the word—

"Noble lady, whoever thou art, in thine old age, and thine hour of care, may thy child, like this poor girl, forsake all gayer comrades for a parent's side!"

The answer touched the Lady of Bonville, and involuntarily she extended her hand to Sibyll. With a swelling heart, Sibyll, as proud as herself, bent silently over that rival's hand. Katherine's marble cheek colored, as she interpreted the girl's silence.

"Gentle sir," she said, after a short pause, "wilt thou permit me a few words with thy fair daughter? and if in aught, since thou speakest of care, Lord Warwick's sister can serve thee, prithee bid thy young maiden impart it, as to a friend."

"Tell her, then, my Sibyll—tell Lord Warwick's sister, to ask the king to give back to Adam Warner his poverty, his labor, and his hope," said the scholar, and his noble head sank gloomily on his bosom.

The lady of Bonville, still holding Sibyll's hand, drew her a few paces up the walk, and then she said suddenly, and with some of that blunt frankness which belonged to her great brother, "Maiden, can there be confidence between thee and me?"

"Of what nature, lady?"

Again Katherine blushed, but she felt the small hand she held tremble in her clasp, and was emboldened—

"Maiden, thou mayest resent and marvel at my words; but, when I had fewer years than thou, my father said, 'There are many carks in life which a little truth could end.' So would I heed his lesson. William de Hastings has followed thee with a homage that has broken, perchance, many as pure a heart—nay, nay, fair child, hear me on. Thou hast heard that in youth he wooed Katherine Nevile—that we loved, and were severed. They who see us now marvel whether we hate or love,—no, *not* love—that question were an insult to Lord Bonville's wife.—Ofttimes we seem pitiless to each other,—why? Lord Hastings would have wooed me, an English matron, to forget mine honor and my house's. *He* chafes that he moves me not. *I* behold him debasing a great nature, to unworthy triflings with man's conscience and a knight's bright faith. But mark me!—the heart of Hastings is everlastingly mine, and mine alone! What seek I in this confidence? To warn thee. Wherefore? Because for months, amidst all the vices of this foul court air—amidst the flatteries of the softest voice that ever fell upon woman's ear—amidst, peradventure, the pleadings of thine own young and guileless love—thine innocence is unscathed. And therefore Katherine of Bonville may be the friend of Sibyll Warner."

However generous might be the true spirit of these words, it was impossible that they should not gall and humiliate the young and flattered beauty to whom they were addressed. They so wholly discarded all belief in the affection of Hastings for Sibyll; they so haughtily arrogated the mastery over his heart; they so plainly implied that his suit to the poor maiden was but a mockery or dishonor, that they made even the praise for virtue an affront to the delicate and chaste ear on which they fell. And, therefore, the reader will not be astonished, though the Lady of Bonville certainly was, when Sibyll, drawing her hand from Katherine's clasp, stopping short, and calmly folding her arms upon her bosom, said,—

"To what this tends, lady, I know not. The Lord Hastings is free to carry his homage where he will. He has sought me—not I Lord Hastings. And if to-morrow he offered me his hand, I would reject it, if I were not convinced that the heart——"

"Damsel," interrupted the Lady Bonville, in amazed contempt, "the hand of Lord Hastings! Look ye indeed so high, or has he so far paltered with your credulous youth as to speak to you, the daughter of the alchemist, of marriage? If so, poor child, beware!"

"I knew not," replied Sibyll, bitterly, "that Sibyll Warner was more below the state of Lord Hastings, than Master Hastings was once below the state of Lady Katherine Nevile."

"Thou art distraught with thy self-conceit," answered the dame, scornfully; and, losing all the compassion and friendly interest she had before felt, "my rede is spoken—reject it, if thou wilt, in pride. Rue thy folly thou wilt in shame."

She drew her wimple round her face as she said these words, and, gathering up her long robe, swept slowly on.

CHAPTER III.

Wherein the Demagogue seeks the Courtier.

On quitting Adam's chamber, Hilyard paused not till he reached a stately house, not far from Warwick Lane, which was the residence of the Lord Montagu.

The nobleman was employed in reading, or rather, in pondering over, two letters, with which a courier from Calais had just arrived—the one from the archbishop, the other from Warwick. In these epistles were two passages, strangely contradictory in their counsel. A sentence in Warwick's letter ran thus: "It hath reached me, that certain disaffected men meditate a rising against the king, under pretext of wrongs from the queen's kin. It is even said that our kinsmen, Coniers and Fitzhugh, are engaged therein. Need I caution thee to watch well that they bring our name into no disgrace or attaint. We want no aid to right our own wrongs; and if the misguided men rebel, Warwick will best punish Edward, by proving that he is yet of use."

On the other hand, thus wrote the prelate:—

"The king, wroth with my visit to Calais, has taken from me the Chancellor's seal. I humbly thank him, and shall sleep the lighter for the fardel's loss. Now, mark me, Montagu: our kinsman, Lord Fitzhugh's son, and young Henry Nevile, aided by old Sir John Coniers, meditate a fierce and well-timed assault upon the Woodvilles. Do thou keep neuter—neither help nor frustrate it. Howsoever it end, it will answer our views, and shake our enemies."

Montagu was yet musing over these tidings, and marvelling that he in England should know less than his brethren in Calais of events so important, when his page informed him that a stranger, with urgent messages from the north country, craved an audience. Imagining that these messages would tend to illustrate the communications just received, he ordered the visitor to be admitted.

He scarcely noticed Hilyard on his entrance, and said, abruptly, "Speak shortly, friend—I have but little leisure."

"And yet, Lord Montagu, my business may touch thee home!"

Montagu, surprised, gazed more attentively on his visitor: "Surely, I know thy face, friend—we have met before."

"True; thou wert then on thy way to the More."

"I remember me: and thou then seem'dst,

from thy bold words, on a still shorter road to the gallows."

"The tree is not planted," said Robin, carelessly, "that will serve for my gibbet. But were there no words uttered by me that thou couldst not disapprove? I spoke of lawless disorders—of shameful malfaisance throughout the land—which the Woodvilles govern under a lewd tyrant——"

"Traitor, hold!"

"A tyrant," continued Robin (heeding not the interruption nor the angry gesture of Montagu), "a tyrant who, at this moment, meditates the destruction of the house of Nevile. And not contented with this world's weapons, palters with the Evil One for the snares and devilries of witchcraft."

"Hush, man! Not so loud," said Montagu, in an altered voice. "Approach nearer—nearer yet. They who talk of a crowned king—whose right hand raises armies, and whose left hand reposes on the block—should beware how they speak above their breath. Witchcraft, sayest thou? Make thy meaning clear."

Here Robin detailed, with but little exaggeration, the scene he had witnessed in Friar Bungey's chamber—the waxen image, the menaces against the Earl of Warwick, and the words of the friar, naming the Duchess of Bedford as his employer. Montagu listened in attentive silence. Though not perfectly free from the credulities of the time, shared even by the courageous heart of Edward, and the piercing intellect of Gloucester, he was yet more alarmed by such proofs of determined earthly hostility in one so plotting and so near to the throne as the Duchess of Bedford, than by all the pins and needles that could be planted into the earl's waxen counterpart——

"A devilish malice, indeed," said he, when Hilyard had concluded; "and yet this story, if thou wilt adhere to it, may serve us well at need. I thank thee, trusty friend, for thy confidence, and beseech thee to come at once with me to the king. There will I denounce our foe, and, with thine evidence, he will demand her banishment."

"By your leave, not a step will I budge, my Lord Montagu," quoth Robin, bluntly—"I know how these matters are managed at court. The king will patch up a peace between the duchess and you, and chop off my ears and nose as a liar and common scandal-maker. No, no; denounce the duchess and all the Woodvilles, I will;—but it shall not be in the halls of the Tower, but on the broad plains of Yorkshire, with twenty thousand men at my back."

"Ha! thou a leader of armies—and for what end?—to dethrone the king?"

"That as it may be—but first for justice to the people; it is the people's rising, that I will head, and not a faction's. Neither White Rose nor Red shall be on my banner, but our standard shall be the gory head of the first oppressor we can place upon a pole."

"What is it, the people, as you word it, would demand?"

"I scarce know what we demand as yet—that must depend upon how we prosper," returned Hilyard, with a bitter laugh; "but the rising will have some good, if it shows only to you lords and Normans, that a Saxon people does exist, and will turn when the iron heel is upon its neck. We are taxed, ground, pillaged, plundered—sheep, maintained to be sheared for your peace, or butchered for your war. And now will we have a petition and a charter of our own, Lord Montagu. I speak frankly—I am in thy power—thou canst arrest me—thou canst strike off the head of this revolt. Thou art the king's friend—wilt thou do so? No, thou and thy house have wrongs as well as we, the people. And a part at least of our demands and our purpose is your own."

"What part, bold man?"

"This: we shall make our first complaint the baneful domination of the queen's family; and demand the banishment of the Woodvilles, root and stem."

"Hem!" said Montagu, involuntarily glancing over the archbishop's letter,—"hem, but without outrage to the king's state and person?"

"Oh, trust me, my lord, the franklin's head contains as much north-country cunning as the noble's. They who would speed well, must feel their way cautiously."

"Twenty thousand men—impossible! Who art thou, to collect and head them?"

"Plain Robin of Redesdale."

"Ha!" exclaimed Montagu, "is it indeed, as I was taught to suspect! Art thou that bold, strange, mad fellow, whom, by pike and brand—a soldier's oath—I a soldier, have often longed to see. Let me look at thee.

'Fore St. George, a tall man, and well knit with dariment in thy brow. Why, there are as many tales of thee in the north, as of my brother the earl. Some say thou art a lord of degree and birth, others that thou art the robber of Hexham, to whom Margaret of Anjou trusted her own life and her son's."

"Whatever they say of me," returned Robin, "they all agree in this, that I am a man of honest word, and bold deed—that I can stir up the hearts of men, as the wind stirreth fire—that I came an unknown stranger into the parts where I abide, and that no peer in this roiaulme, save Warwick himself, can do more to raise an army, or shake a throne."

"But by what spell?"

"By men's wrongs, lord," answered Robin, in a deep voice;—"and now, ere this moon wanes, Redesdale is a camp!"

"What the immediate cause of complaint?"

"The hospital of St. Leonard's has compelled us unjustly to render them a thrave of corn."

"Thou art a cunning knave! Pinch the belly if you would make Englishmen rise."

"True," said Robin, smiling grimly—"and now—what say you—will you head us?"

"Head you! No!"

"Will you betray us?"

"It is not easy to betray twenty thousand men; if ye rise merely to free yourselves from a corn-tax, and England from the Woodvilles, I see no treason in your revolt."

"I understand you, Lord Montagu," said Robin, with a stern and half-scornful smile—"you are not above thriving by our danger; but we need now no lord and baron—we will suffice for ourselves. And the hour will come, believe me, when Lord Warwick, pursued by the king, must fly to the commons. Think well of these things and this prophecy, when the news from the north startles Edward of March in the lap of his harlots."

Without saying another word, he turned and quitted the chamber as abruptly as he had entered.

Lord Montagu was not, for his age, a bad man; though worldly, subtle, and designing; with some of the craft of his prelate brother, he united something of the high soul of his brother soldier. But that age had not the virtue of later times, and cannot be judged by its standard. He heard this bold dare-devil menace his country with civil war upon grounds not plainly stated, nor clearly understood—he aided not, but he connived: "Twenty thousand men in arms," he muttered to himself—"say half—well, ten thousand—not against Edward, but the Woodvilles! It must bring the king to his senses—must prove to him how odious the mushroom race of the Woodvilles, and drive him for safety and for refuge to Montagu and Warwick. If the knaves presume too far," (and Montagu smiled),—"what are undisciplined multitudes to the eye of a skilful captain? Let the storm blow, we will guide the blast. In this world man must make use of man."

CHAPTER IV.

Sibyll.

WHILE Montagu, in anxious forethought, awaited the revolt that Robin of Redesdale had predicted—while Edward feasted and laughed, merry-made with his courtiers, and aided the conjugal duties of his good citizens in London—while the queen and her father, Lord Rivers, more and more in the absence of Warwick, encroached on all the good things power can bestow and avarice seize—while the Duchess of Bedford and Friar Bungey toiled hard at the waxen effigies of the great earl, who still held his royal son-in-law in his court at Calais—the stream of our narrative winds from its noiser channels, and lingers, with a quiet wave, around the temple of a virgin's heart. Wherefore is Sibyll sad? Some short months since, and we beheld her gay with hope, and basking in the sunny atmosphere of pleasure and of love. The mind of this girl was a singular combination of tenderness and pride—the first wholly natural, the last the result of circumstance and position.

She was keenly conscious of her gentle birth, and her earlier prospects in the court of Margaret; and the poverty and distress and solitude in which she had grown up from the child into the woman, had only served to strengthen what, in her nature, was already strong, and to heighten whatever was already proud. Ever in her youngest dreams of the future, ambition had visibly blent itself with the vague ideas of love. The imagined wooer was less to be young and fair, than renowned and stately. She viewed him through the mists of the future, as the protector of her persecuted father — as the rebuilder of a fallen house — as the ennobler of a humbled name. And from the moment in which her girl's heart beat at the voice of Hastings, the ideal of her soul seemed found. And when transplanted to the court, she learned to judge of her native grace and loveliness, by the common admiration they excited, her hopes grew justified to her inexperienced reason. Often and ever the words of Hastings, at the house of the Lady Longueville, rang in her ear, and thrilled through the solitude of night—"Whoever is fair and chaste, gentle and loving, is in the eyes of William de Hastings, the mate and equal of a king."

In visits that she found opportunity to make to the Lady Longueville, these hopes were duly fed; for the old Lancastrian detested the Lady Bonville, as Lord Warwick's sister, and she would have reconciled her pride to view with complacency his alliance with the alchemist's daughter, if it led to his estrangement from the memory of his first love; and, therefore, when her quick eye penetrated the secret of Sibyll's heart, and when she witnessed—for Hastings often encountered (and seemed to seek the encounter) the young maid at Lady Longueville's house—the unconcealed admiration which justified Sibyll in her high-placed affection, she scrupled not to encourage the blushing girl, by predictions in which she forced her own better judgment to believe. Nor, when she learned Sibyll's descent from a family that had once ranked as high as that of Hastings, would she allow that there was any disparity in the alliance she foretold. But more, far more than Lady Longueville's assurances, did the delicate and unceasing gallantries of Hastings himself flatter the fond faith of Sibyll. True, that he spoke not actually of love, but every look implied, every whisper seemed to betray it.

And to her he spoke as to an equal, not in birth alone, but in mind; so superior was she in culture, in natural gifts, and, above all, in that train of high thought, and elevated sentiment, in which genius ever finds a sympathy, to the court-flutterers of her sex, that Hastings, whether or not he cherished a warmer feeling, might well take pleasure in her converse, and feel the lovely infant worthy the wise man's trust. He spoke to her without reserve of the Lady Bonville, and he spoke with bitterness. "I loved her," he said, "as woman is rarely loved. She deserted me for another—rather should she have gone to the convent than the altar; and now, forsooth, she deems she hath the right to taunt and to rate me, to dictate to me the way I should walk, and to flaunt the honors I have won."

"May that be no sign of a yet tender interest?" said Sibyll, timidly.

The eyes of Hastings sparkled for a moment, but the gleam vanished. "Nay, you know her not. Her heart is marble, as hard and as cold. Her very virtue but the absence of emotion—I would say, of gentler emotion—for, pardieu, such emotions as come from ire and pride and scorn, are the daily growth of that stern soil. Oh, happy was my escape!—happy the desertion, which my young folly deemed a curse. No!" he added, with a sarcastic quiver of his lip—"No; what stings and galls the Lady of Harrington and Bonville—what makes her countenance change in my presence, and her voice sharpen at my accost, is plainly this: in wedding her dull lord, and rejecting me, Katherine Nevile deemed she wedded power and rank, and station; and now, while we are both young, how proves her choice? The Lord of Harrington and Bonville is so noted a dolt, that even the Neviles cannot help him to rise—the meanest office is above his mind's level; and, dragged down by the heavy clay to which her wings are yoked, Katherine, Lady of Harrington and Bonville—oh, give her her due titles!—is but a pageant figure in the court. If the war-trump blew, his very vassals would laugh at a Bonville's banner, and beneath the flag of poor William Hastings would gladly march the best chivalry of the land. And this it is, I say, that galls her. For evermore she is driven to compare the state she holds, as the dame of the accepted Bonville, with that she lost as the wife of the disdained Hastings."

And if, in the heat and passion that such words betrayed, Sibyll sighed to think that something of the old remembrance yet swelled and burned, they but impressed her more with the value of a heart, in which the characters once writ endured so long,—and roused her to a tender ambition to heal and to console.

Then looking into her own deep soul, Sibyll beheld there a fund of such generous, pure, and noble affection—such reverence as to the fame—such love as to the man, that she proudly felt herself worthier of Hastings than the haughty Katherine. She entered then, as it were, the lists with this rival—a memory rather, so the thought, than a corporeal being; and her eye grew brighter, her step statelier, in the excitement of the contest—the anticipation of the triumph. For what diamond without its flaw? what rose without its canker? And bedded deep in that exquisite and charming nature, lay the dangerous and fatal weakness which has cursed so many victims, broken so many hearts—the vanity of the sex. We may now readily conceive how little predisposed was Sibyll to the blunt advances and displeasing warnings of the Lady Bonville, and the more so from the time in which they chanced. For here comes the answer to the question—"Why was Sibyll sad?"

The reader may determine for himself what were the ruling motives of Lord Hastings in the court he paid to Sibyll. Whether to pique the Lady Bonville, and force upon her the jealous pain he restlessly sought to inflict—whether, from the habit of his careless life, seeking the pleasure of the moment, with little forethought of the future, and reconciling itself to much cruelty, by that profound contempt for human beings, man, and still more for woman, which sad experience often brings to acute intellect—or whether, from the purer and holier complacency with which one, whose youth has fed upon nobler aspirations than manhood cares to pursue, suns itself back to something of its earlier lustre in the presence and the converse of a young bright soul:—Whatever, in brief, the earlier motives of gallantries to Sibyll, once begun, constantly renewed,—by degrees wilder, and warmer, and guiltier emotions, roused up in the universal and all-conquering lover the vice of his softer nature. When calm and unimpassioned, his conscience had said to him,—"Thou shalt spare that flower." But when once the passion was roused within him, the purity of the flower was forgotten in the breath of its voluptuous sweetness.

And but three days before the scene we have described with Katherine, Sibyll's fabric of hope fell to the dust. For Hastings spoke for the first time of love—for the first time knelt at her feet—for the first time, clasping to his heart that virgin hand, poured forth the protestation and the vow. And oh! woe—woe! for the first time she learned how cheaply the great man held the poor maiden's love, how little he deemed that purity and genius and affection equalled the possessor of fame and wealth and power; for plainly visible, boldly shown and spoken, the love that she had foreseen as a glory from the Heaven, sought but to humble her to the dust.

The anguish of that moment was unspeakable—and she spoke it not. But as she broke from the profaning clasp, as escaping to the threshold, she cast on the unworthy wooer one look of such reproachful sorrow, as told at once all her love and all her horror,—the first act in the eternal tragedy of man's wrong and woman's grief was closed. And therefore was Sibyll sad!

CHAPTER V.

Katherine.

For several days Hastings avoided Sibyll; in truth, he felt remorse for his design, and in his various, active, and brilliant life, he had not the leisure for obstinate and systematic siege to a single virtue, nor was he, perhaps, any longer capable of deep and enduring passion; his heart, like that of many a chevalier in the earlier day, had lavished itself upon one object, and sullenly, upon regrets and dreams, and vain anger and idle scorn, it had exhausted those sentiments which make the sum of true love. And so, like Petrarch, whom his taste and fancy worshipped, and many another votary of the *gentil Dieu*, while his imagination devoted itself to the chaste and distant ideal—the spiritual Laura—his senses, ever vagrant and disengaged, settled, without scruple, upon the thousand Cynthias of the minute. But then, those Cynthias were, for the most part, and especially of late years, easy and light-won nymphs: their coyest were of another clay from the tender but lofty Sibyll. And Hastings shrunk from the cold-blooded and deliberate seduction of one so pure, while he could not reconcile his mind to contemplate marriage with a girl who could give nothing to his ambition; and yet it was not, in this last reluctance, only his ambition that startled and recoiled. In that strange tyranny over his whole soul, which Katherine Bonville secretly exercised, he did not dare to place a new barrier evermore between her and himself. The Lord Bonville was of infirm health; he had been more than once near to death's door, and Hastings, in every succeding fancy that beguiled his path, recalled the thrill of his heart, when it had whispered, "Katherine, the loved of thy youth, may yet be thine!" And then that Katherine rose before him, not as she now swept the earth, with haughty step, and frigid eye, and disdainful lip, but as—in all her bloom of maiden beauty, before the temper was soured, or the pride aroused,—she had met him in the summer twilight, by the trysting-tree;—broken with him the golden ring of faith, and wept upon his bosom.

And yet, during his brief and self-inflicted absence from Sibyll, this wayward and singular personage, who was never weak but to women, and ever weak to them, felt that she had made herself far dearer to him than he had at first supposed it possible. He missed that face, ever, till the last interview, so confiding in the unconsciously betrayed affection. He felt how superior in sweetness, and yet in intellect, Sibyll was to Katherine; there was more in common between her mind and his in all things, save one. But oh, *that one exception!*—what a world lies within it—*the memory of the spring of life!* In fact, though Hastings knew it not, he was in love with two objects at once; the one, a chimera, a fancy, an ideal, an Eidolon, under the name of Katherine; the other, youth, and freshness, and mind, and heart, and a living shape of beauty, under the name of Sibyll. Often does this double love happen to men; but when it does, alas for the human object! for the shadowy and the spiritual one is immortal,—until, indeed, it be possessed!

It might be, perhaps, with a resolute desire to conquer the new love and confirm the old, that Hastings, one morning, repaired to the house of the Lady Bonville, for her visit to the court had expired. It was a large mansion, without the Lud Gate.

He found the dame in a comely chamber, seated in the sole chair the room contained, to which was attached a foot-board, that served as a dais, while around her, on low stools, sate—some spinning, others broidering—some ten or twelve young maidens of good family, sent to receive their nurturing under the high-born Katherine,* while two other and somewhat elder virgins sate a little apart, but close under the eye of the lady, practising the courtly game of "prime;" for the diversion of cards was in its zenith of fashion under Edward IV., and even half a century later was considered one of the essential accomplishments of a well-educated young lady.† The exceeding stiffness, the solemn silence of this female circle, but little accorded with the mood of the graceful visitor. The demoiselles stirred not at his entrance, and Katherine quietly motioned him to a seat at some distance.

"By your leave, fair lady," said Hastings, "I rebel against so distant an exile from such sweet company;" and he moved the tabouret close to the formidable chair of the presiding chieftainess.

Katherine smiled faintly, but not in displeasure.

"So gay a presence," she said, "must, I fear me, a little disturb these learners."

Hastings glanced at the prim demureness written on each blooming visage and replied—

"You wrong their ardor in such noble studies. I would wager that nothing less than my entering your bower on horseback, with helm on head and lance in rest, could provoke even a smile from one pair of the twenty rosy lips round which, methinks, I behold Cupido hovering in vain!"

The Baroness bent her stately brows, and the twenty rosy lips were all tightly pursed up, to prevent the indecorous exhibition which the wicked courtier had provoked. But it would not do: one and all the twenty lips broke into a smile—but a smile so tortured, constrained,

* And strange as it may seem to modern notions, the highest lady who received such pensioners accepted a befitting salary for their board and education.

† So the Princess Margaret, daughter of Henry VII., at the age of fourteen, exhibits her skill, in prime or trump, to her betrothed husband, James IV. of Scotland; so, among the womanly arts of the unhappy Katherine of Arragon, it is mentioned that she could play at "cardis and dyce." (See STRUTT'S *Games and Pastimes*, Hone's edition, p. 327.) The legislature was very anxious to keep these games sacred to the aristocracy, and very wroth with 'prentices and the vulgar for imitating the ruinous amusements of their betters.

and nipped in the bud, that it only gave an expression of pain to the features it was forbidden to enliven.

"And what brings the Lord Hastings hither?" asked the baroness, in a formal tone.

"Can you never allow, for motive, the desire of pleasure, fair dame?"

That peculiar and exquisite blush, which at moments changed the whole physiognomy of Katherine, flitted across her smooth cheek, and vanished. She said, gravely—

"So much do I allow it in you, my lord, that hence my question."

"Katherine!" exclaimed Hastings, in a voice of tender reproach, and attempting to seize her hand, forgetful of all other presence save that to which the blush, that spoke of old, gave back the ancient charm.

Katherine cast a hurried and startled glance over the maiden group, and her eye detected on the automaton faces one common expression of surprise. Humbled and deeply displeased, she rose from the awful chair, and then, as suddenly reseating herself, she said, with a voice and lip of the most cutting irony, "My lord chamberlain is it seems, so habituated to lackey his king amidst the goldsmiths and grocers, that he forgets the form of language and respect of bearing which a noblewoman of repute is accustomed to consider seemly."

Hastings bit his lip, and his falcon eye shot indignant fire. "Pardon, my Lady of Bonville and Harrington, I did indeed forget what reasons the dame of so wise and so renowned a lord hath to feel pride in the titles she hath won. But I see that my visit hath chanced out of season. My business, in truth, was rather with my lord, whose counsel in peace is as famous as his truncheon in war!"

"It is enough," replied Katherine, with a dignity that rebuked the taunt, "that Lord Bonville has the name of an honest man,—who never rose at court."

"Woman, without one soft woman-feeling!" muttered Hastings, between his ground teeth, as he approached the lady and made his profound obeisance. The words were intended only for Katherine's ear, and they reached it. Her bosom swelled beneath the brocaded gorget, and when the door closed on Hastings, she pressed her hands convulsively together, and her dark eyes were raised upward.

"My child, thou art entangling thy skein," said the Lady of Bonville, as she passed one of the maidens, towards the casement, which she opened,—"The air to-day weighs heavily!"

CHAPTER VI.

Joy for Adam, and Hope for Sibyll—And popular Friar Bungey!

Leaping on his palfrey, Hastings rode back to the Tower—dismounted at the gate—passed on to the little postern in the inner court,—and paused not till he was in Warner's room.

"How now, friend Adam? Thou art idle."

"Lord Hastings, I am ill."

"And thy child not with thee?"

"She is gone to her grace the duchess, to pray her to grant me leave to go home, and waste no more life on making gold."

"Home! Go hence! We cannot hear it! The duchess must not grant it. I will not suffer the king to lose so learned a philosopher."

"Then pray the king to let the philosopher achieve that which is in the power of labor." He pointed to the Eureka. "Let me be heard in the king's council, and prove to sufficing judges what this iron can do for England."

"Is that all? So be it. I will speak to his highness forthwith. But promise that thou wilt think no more of leaving the king's palace."

"Oh, no, no! If I may enter again into mine own palace—mine own royalty of craft and hope—the court or the dungeon all one to me!"

"Father," said Sibyll, entering, "be comforted. The duchess forbids thy departure, but we will yet flee——"

She stopped short as she saw Hastings. He approached her timidly, and with so repentant, so earnest a respect in his mien and gesture, that she had not the heart to draw back the fair hand he lifted to his lips.

"No, flee not, sweet donzell; leave not the desert court, without the flower and the laurel, the beauty and the wisdom, that scent the hour, and foretype eternity. I have conferred with thy father—I will obtain his prayer from the king. His mind shall be free to follow its own impulse, and thou—(he whispered)—pardon—pardon an offence of too much love. Never shall it wound again."

Her eyes, swimming with delicious tears, were fixed upon the floor. Poor child! with so much love, how could she cherish anger? With so much purity, how distrust herself? And while, at least, he spoke, the dangerous lover was sincere. So from that hour peace was renewed between Sibyll and Lord Hastings.—Fatal peace! alas for the girl who loves—and has no mother!

True to his word, the courtier braved the displeasure of the Duchess of Bedford, in inducing the king to consider the expediency of permitting Adam to relinquish alchemy, and repair his model. Edward summoned a deputation from the London merchants and traders, before whom Adam appeared, and explained his device. But these practical men at first ridiculed the notion as a madman's fancy, and it required all the art of Hastings to overcome their contempt, and appeal to the native acuteness of the king. Edward, however, was only caught by Adam's incidental allusions to the application of his principle to ships. The merchant-king suddenly roused himself to attention, when it was promised to him that his galleys could cross the seas without sail, and against wind and tide.

"By St. George!" said he then, "let the honest man have his whim. Mend thy model, and every saint in the calendar speed thee! Master Heyford, tell thy comely wife that I and Hastings will sup with her to-morrow, for her hippocras is a rare dainty. Good day to you, worshipful my masters. Hastings, come hither—enough of these trifles—I must confer with thee on matters really pressing—this damnable marriage of gentle Georgie's!"

And now Adam Warner was restored to his native element of thought; now the crucible was at rest, and the Eureka began to rise from its ruins. He knew not the hate that he had acquired, in the permission he had gained; for the London deputies, on their return home, talked of nothing else for a whole week, but the favor the king had shown to a strange man, half-maniac, half conjuror, who had undertaken to devise a something which would throw all the artisans and journeymen out of work! From merchant to mechanic travelled the news, and many an honest man cursed the great scholar, as he looked at his young children, and wished to have one good blow at the head that was hatching such devilish malice against the poor! The name of Adam Warner became a byword of scorn and horror. Nothing less than the deep ditch and strong walls of the Tower could have saved him from the popular indignation; and these prejudices were skilfully fed by the jealous enmity of his fellow-student, the terrible Friar Bungey. This man, though in all matters of true learning and science, worthy the utmost contempt Adam could heap upon him, was by no means of despicable abilities in the arts of imposing upon men. In his youth he had been an itinerant mountebank, or, as it was called, *tregetour*.

He knew well all the curious tricks of juggling that, then, amazed the vulgar, and, we fear, are lost to the craft of our modern necromancers. He could clothe a wall with seeming vines, that vanished as you approached; he could conjure up in his quiet cell the likeness of a castle manned with soldiers, or a forest tenanted by deer.* Besides these illusions, probably produced by more powerful magic lanterns than are now used, the friar had stumbled upon the wondrous effects of animal magnetism, which was then unconsciously practiced by the alchemists and cultivators of white or sacred magic. He was an adept in the craft of fortune-telling; and his intimate acquaintance with all noted characters in the metropolis, their previous history, and present circumstances, enabled his natural shrewdness to hit the mark, at least, now and then, in his oracular predictions. He had taken for safety and for bread, the friar's robes, and had long enjoyed the confidence of the Duchess of Bedford, the traditional descendant of the serpent-witch, Melusina. Moreover, and in this the friar especially valued himself, Bungey had, in the course of his hardy, vagrant, early life, studied, as shepherds and mariners do now, the signs of the weather, and as weather-glasses were then unkown, nothing could be more convenient to

---

* See CHAUCER, *House of Time*, Book iii.; also the account given by BAPTISTA PORTA, of his own magical Delusions, of which an extract may be seen in the CURIOSITIES OF LITERATURE—Art. "*Dreams at the Dawn of Philosophy*."

the royal planners of a summer chase or a hawking company, than the neighborhood of a skilful predictor of storm and shunshine. In fact, there was no part in the lore of magic which the popular seers found so useful and studied so much as that which enabled them to prognosticate the humors of the sky, at a period when the lives of all men were principally spent in the open air.

The fame of Friar Bungey had travelled much farther than the repute of Adam Warner: it was known in the distant provinces; and many a northern peasant grew pale as he related to his gaping listeners the tales he had heard of the Duchess Jacquetta's dread magician.

And yet, though the friar was an atrocious knave, and a ludicrous impostor, on the whole he was by no means unpopular, especially in the metropolis, for he was naturally a jolly, social fellow: he often ventured boldly forth into the different hostelries and reunions of the populace, and enjoyed the admiration he there excited, and pocketed the groats he there collected. He had no pride—none in the least, this Friar Bungey!—and was as affable, as a magician could be, to the meanest mechanic who crossed his broad horn palm. A vulgar man is never unpopular with the vulgar. Moreover, the friar, who was a very cunning person, wished to keep well with the mob: he was fond of his own impudent, cheating, burly carcase, and had the prudence to foresee that a time might come when his royal patrons might forsake him, and a mob might be a terrible monster to meet in his path; therefore he always affected to love the poor, often told their fortunes gratis, now and then gave them something to drink, and was esteemed a man exceedingly good-natured, because he did not always have the devil at his back.

Now Friar Bungey had, naturally enough, evinced, from the first, a great distaste and jealousy of Adam Warner; but occasionally profiting by the science of the latter, he suffered his resentment to sleep latent till it was roused into fury by learning the express favor shown to Adam by the king, and the marvellous results expected from his contrivance. His envy, then, forbad all tolerance and mercy; the world was not large enough to contain two such giants—Bungey and Warner—the genius and the quack. To the best of our experience, the quacks have the same creed to our own day. He vowed deep vengeance upon his associate, and spared no arts to foment the popular hatred agaist him.—Friar Bungey would have been a great critic in our day!

But besides his jealousy, the fat friar had another motive for desiring poor Adam's destruction; he coveted his model! True, he despised the model, he jeered the model, he abhorred the model; but, nevertheless, for the model, every string in his bowels fondly yearned. He believed that if that model were once repaired, and in his possession, he could do—what he knew not—but certainly all that was wanting to complete his glory, and to bubble the public.

Unconscious of all that was at work against him, Adam threw his whole heart and soul into his labor, and, happy in his happiness, Sibyll once more smiled gratefully upon Hastings, from whom the rapure came.

CHAPTER VII.

A Love Scene.

MORE than ever chafed against Katherine, Hastings surrendered himself, without reserve, to the charm he found in the society of Sibyll. Her confidence being again restored, again her mind showed itself to advantage, and the more because her pride was farther roused, to assert the equality with rank and gold which she took from nature and from God.

It so often happens that the first love of woman is accompanied with a bashful timidity, which overcomes the effort, while it increases the desire, to shine, that the union of love and timidity has been called inseparable, in the hackneyed language of every love-tale. But this is no invariable rule, as Shakspeare has shown us in the artless Miranda, in the eloquent Juliet, in the frank and healthful Rosalind;—and the love of Sibyll was no common girl's spring-fever of sighs and blushes. It lay in the mind, the imagination, the intelligence, as well as in the heart and fancy. It was a breeze that stirred from the modest leaves of the rose all their diviner odor. It was impossible but what this strong, fresh, young nature, with its free gaiety when happy

—its earnest pathos when sad—its various faculties of judgment and sentiment, and covert play of innocent wit—should not contrast forcibly, in the mind of a man who had the want to be amused and interested,—with the cold pride of Katherine, the dull atmosphere in which her stiff, unbending virtue, breathed unintellectual air, and still more with the dressed puppets, with painted cheeks and barren talk, who filled u p the common world, under the name of women.

His feelings for Sibyll, therefore, took a more grave and respectful color, and his attentions, if gallant ever, were those of a man wooing one whom he would make his wife, and studying the qualities in which he was disposed to intrust his happiness; and so pure was Sibyll's affection, that she could have been contented to have lived for ever thus—have seen and heard him daily—have talked but the words of friendship, though with the thoughts of love; for some passions refine themselves through the very fire of the imagination into which the senses are absorbed, and by the ideal purification elevated up to spirit. Wrapped in the exquisite happiness she now enjoyed, Sibyll perceived not, or, if perceiving, scarcely heeded that the admirers, who had before fluttered round her, gradually dropped off—that the ladies of the court, the damsels who shared her light duties, grew distant and silent at her approach—that strange looks were bent on her—that sometimes, when she and Hastings were seen together, the stern frowned and the godly crossed themselves.

The popular prejudices had reacted on the court. The wizard's daughter was held to share the gifts of her sire, and the fascination of beauty was imputed to evil spells. Lord Hastings was regarded,—especially by all the ladies he had once courted and forsaken,—as a man egregiously bewitched!

One day, it chanced that Sibyll encountered Hastings in the walk that girded the ramparts of the Tower. He was pacing musingly, with folded arms, when he raised his eyes and beheld her.

"And whither go you thus alone fair mistress?"

"The Duchess bade me seek the queen, who is taking the air yonder. My lady has received some tidings she would impart to her highness."

"I was thinking of thee, fair damsel, when thy face brightened on my musings, and I was comparing thee to others, who dwell in the world's high places;—and marvelling at the whims of fortune."

Sibyll smiled faintly, and answered, "Provoke not too much the aspiring folly of my nature. Content is better than ambition."

"Thou ownest thy ambition?" asked Hastings, curiously.

"Ah, sir, who hath it not?"

"But for thy sweet sex, ambition has so narrow and cribbed a field."

"Not so, for it lives in others. I would say," continued Sibyll, coloring, fearful that she had betrayed herself, "for example, that so long as my father toils for fame, I breathe in his hope, and am ambitious for his honor."

"And so, if thou wert wedded to one worthy of thee, in his ambition thou wouldst soar and dare?"

"Perhaps," answered Sibyll, coyly.

"But, if thou wert wedded to sorrow, and poverty, and troublous care, thine ambition, thus struck dead, would, of consequence, strike dead thy love?"

"Nay, noble lord, nay—canst thou so wrong womanhood in me unworthy? for surely true ambition lives not only in the goods of fortune. Is there no nobler ambition than that of the vanity? Is there no ambition of the heart?—an ambition to console, to cheer the griefs of those who love and trust us?—an ambition to build a happiness out of the reach of fate?—an ambition to soothe some high soul, in its strife with a mean world—to lull to sleep its pain, to smile to serenity its cares? Oh, methinks a woman's true ambition would rise the bravest when, in the very sight of death itself, the voice of him in whom her glory had dwelt through life should say, 'Thou fearest not to walk to the grave, and to heaven, by my side!'"

Sweet and thrilling were the tones in which these words were said said—lofty and solemn the upward and tearful look with which they closed.

And the answer struck home to the native and original heroism of the listener's nature, before debased into the cynic sourness of worldly wisdom. Never had Katherine herself more forcibly recalled to Hastings the pure and virgin glory of his youth.

"Oh, Sibyll!" he exclaimed, passionately, and yielding to the impulse of the moment—"oh, that *for* me, as *to* me, such high words were said! Oh that all the triumphs of a life men call prosperous were excelled by the one triumph of waking such an ambition in such a heart!"

Sibyll stood before him transformed—pale, trembling, mute—and Hastings, clasping her hand and covering it with kisses, said—

"Dare I aread thy silence? Sibyll, thou lovest me!—Oh, Sibyll, speak!"

With a convulsive effort, the girl's lips moved, then closed, then moved again, into low and broken words.

"Why this—why this? Thou hadst promised not to—not to——"

"Not to insult thee by unworthy vows! Nor do I! But *as my wife*"—he paused abruptly, alarmed at his own impetuous words, and scared by the phantom of the world, that rose like a bodily thing before the generous impulse, and grinned in scorn of his folly.

But Sibyll heard only that one holy word of WIFE, and so sudden and so great was the transport it called forth, that her senses grew faint and dizzy, and she would have fallen to the earth but for the arms that circled her, and the breast upon which, now, the virgin might veil the blush that did not speak of shame.

With various feelings, both were a moment silent. But, oh, that moment! what centuries of bliss were crowded into it for the nobler and fairre nature!

At last, gently releasing herself, she put her hands before her eyes, as if to convince herself she was awake, and then, turning her lovely face full upon the wooer, Sibyll said, ingenuously—

"Oh, my lord—oh, Hastings! if thy calmer reason repent not these words—if thou canst approve in me what thou didst admire in Elizabeth the queen—if thou canst raise one who has no dower but her heart, to the state of thy wife and partner—by this hand, which I place fearlessly in thine, I pledge to thee such a love as minstrel hath never sung. No!" she continued, drawing loftily up her light stature,—"no, thou shalt not find me unworthy of thy name—mighty though it is, mightier though it shall be! I have a mind that can share thine objects, I have pride that can exult in thy power, courage to partake thy dangers, and devotion—" she hesitated, with the most charming blush—"but of *that*, sweet lord, thou shalt judge hereafter! This is my dowry!—it is all!"

"And all I ask or covet," said Hastings. But his cheek had lost its first passionate glow. Lord of many a broad land and barony, victorious captain in many a foughten field, wise statesman in many a thoughtful stratagem, high in his king's favor, and linked with a nation's history—William de Hastings at that hour was as far below, as earth is to heaven, the poor maiden whom he already repented to have so honored, and whose sublime answer woke no echo from his heart.

Fortunately, as he deemed it, at that very instant he heard many steps rapidly approaching, and his own name called aloud by the voice of the king's body squire.

"Hark, Edward summons me," he said, with a feeling of repreive. "Farewell, dear Sibyll, farewell for a brief while—we shall meet anon."

At this time, they were standing in that part of the rampart walk which is now backed by the barracks of a modern soldiery, and before which, on the other side of the moat, lay a space that had seemed solitary and deserted; but, as Hastings, in speaking his adieu, hurriedly pressed his lips on Sibyll's forehead—from a tavarn without the fortress, and opposite the spot on which they stood, suddenly sallied a disorderly troop of half-drunken soldiers, with a gang of the wretched women that always continue the clastic association of a false Venus with a brutal Mars; and the last words of Hastings were scarcely spoken, before a loud laugh startled both himself and Sibyll, and a shudder came over her when she beheld the tinsel robes of the tymbesteres glittering in the sun, and heard their leader sing, as she darted from the arms of a reeling soldier:—

"Ha! death to the dove
Is the falcon's love—
Oh sharp is the kiss of the falcon's beak:"

BOOK SEVENTH.

THE POPULAR REBELLION.

CHAPTER I.

The White Lion of March shakes his Mane.

"And what news?" asked Hastings, as he found himself amidst the king's squires; while yet was heard the laugh of the tymbesteres, and yet, gliding through the trees, might be seen the retreating form of Sibyll.

"My lord, the king needs you instantly. A courier has just arrived from the North. The Lords St. John, Rivers, De Fulke, and Scales, are already with his highness."

"Where?"

"In the great council chamber."

To that memorable room,* in the White Tower, in which the visitor, on entrance, is first reminded of the name and fate of Hastings, strode the unprophetic lord.

He found Edward not reclining on cushions and carpets—not womanlike in loose robes—not with his lazy smile upon his sleek beauty. The king had doffed his gown, and stood erect in the tight tunic, which gave in full perfection the splendid proportions of a frame unsurpassed in activity and strength. Before him, on the long table, lay two or three open letters —beside the dagger with which Edward had cut the silk that bound them. Around him gravely sate Lord Rivers, Anthony Woodville, Lord St. John, Raoul de Fulke, the young and valiant D'Eyncourt, and many other of the principal lords. Hastings saw at once that something of pith and moment had occurred; and by the fire in the king's eye, the dilation of his nostril, the cheerful and almost joyous pride of his mien and brow, the experienced courtier read the signs of War.

"Welcome, brave Hastings," said Edward, in a voice wholly changed from its wonted soft affectation—loud, clear, and thrilling as it went through the marrow and heart of all who heard its stirring and trumpet accent—"Welcome now to the field, as ever to the banquet! We have news from the North, that bid us brace on the burgonot, and buckle-to the brand—a revolt that requires a king's arm to quell. In Yorkshire, fifteen thousand men are in arms, under a leader they call Robin of Redesdale—the pretext, a thrave of corn demanded by the Hospital of St. Leonard's—the true design that of treason to our realm. At the same time, we hear from our brother of Gloucester, now on the border, that the Scotch have lifted the Lancaster Rose. There is peril if these two armies meet;—no time to lose—they are saddling our war-steeds—we hasten to the van of our royal force. We shall have warm work, my lords. But who is worthy of a throne that cannot guard it!"

"This is sad tidings indeed, sire," said Hastings, gravely.

"Sad! Say it not, Hastings! War is the chase of kings! Sir Raoul de Fulke!—why lookest thou brooding and sorrowful?"

"Sire, I but thought that had Earl Warwick been in England, this ——"

"Ha!" interrupted Edward, haughtily and hastily—"and is Warwick the sun of heaven that no cloud can darken where his face may shine? The rebels shall need no foe, my realm no regent, while I, the heir of the Plantaganets, have the sword for one, the sceptre for the

* In was from this room that Hastings was hurried to execution, June 13, 1483.

other. We depart this evening ere the sun be set."

"My liege," said the Lord St. John, gravely—"on what forces do you count to meet so formidable an array?"

"All England, Lord of St. John!"

"Alack! my liege, may you not deceive yourself! But in this crisis, it is right that your leal and trusty subjects should speak out and plainly. It seems that these insurgents clamor not against yourself, but against the queen's relations—yes, my Lord Rivers, against you and your house, and I fear me that the hearts of England are with them here."

"It is true, sire," put in Raoul de Fulke, boldly—"and if these new men are to head your armies, the warriors of Touton will stand aloof—Raoul de Fulke serves no Woodville's banner. Frown not, Lord de Scales! it is the griping avarice of you and yours that has brought this evil on the king. For you the commons have been pillaged—for you the daughters of our peers have been forced into monstrous marriages, at war with birth and with nature herself. For you, the princely Warwick, near to the throne in blood, and front and pillar of our time-honored order of seigneur and of knight, has been thrust from our suzerain's favor. And if now ye are to march at the van of war—*you* to be avengers of the strife of which *ye* are the cause—I say that the soldiers will lack heart, and the provinces ye pass through, will be the country of a foe!"

"Vain man!" began Anthony Woodville, when Hastings laid his hand on his arm, while Edward, amazed at this outburst from two of the supporters on whom he principally counted, had the prudence to suppress his resentment—and remained silent, but with the aspect of one resolved to command obedience, when he once deemed it right to interfere.

"Hold, Sir Anthony!" said Hastings, who, the moment he found himself with men, woke to all the manly spirit and profound wisdom that had rendered his name illustrious—"hold, and let me have the word; my lords St. John and De Fulke, your charges are more against me than against these gentlemen, for *I* am a new man—a squire by birth—and proud to derive mine honors from the same origin as all true nobility—I mean the grace of a noble liege, and the happy fortune of a soldier's sword. It may be," (and here the artful favorite, the most beloved of the whole court, inclined himself meekly)—"it may be that I have not borne those honors so mildly as to disarm blame. In the war to be, let me atone. My liege, hear your servant: give me no command—let me be a simple soldier, fighting by your side. My example who will not follow?—proud to ride but as a man of arms along the track which the sword of his sovereign shall cut through the ranks of battle? Not you, Lord de Scales, redoubtable and invincible with lance and axe; let us new men soothe envy by our deeds; and you, Lords St. John and De Fulke—you shall teach us how your fathers led warriors who did not fight more gallantly than we will. And when rebellion is at rest—when we meet again in our suzerain's hall—accuse us new men, if you can find us faulty, and we will answer you as we best may!"

This address, which could have come from no man with such effect as from Hastings, touched all present. And though the Woodvilles, father and son, saw in it much to gall their pride, and half believed it a snare for their humiliation, they made no opposition. Raoul de Fulke, ever generous as fiery, stretched forth his hand, and said—

"Lord Hastings, you have spoken well. Be it as the king wills."

"My lords," returned Edward, gaily, "my will is that ye be friends while a foe is in the field. Hasten, then, I beseech you, one and all, to raise your vassals, and join our standard at Fotheringay. I will find ye posts that shall content the bravest."

The king made a sign to break up the conference, and, dismissing even the Woodvilles, was left alone with Hastings.

"Thou hast served me at need, Will," said the king. "But I shall remember" (and his eye flashed a tiger's fire) "the mouthing of those mock-pieces of the lords at Runnymede. I am no John, to be bearded by my vassals. Enough of them now. Think you Warwick can have abetted this revolt?"

"A revolt of peasants and yeomen! No, sire. If he did so, farewell for ever to the love the barons bear him."

"Um! and yet Montagu, whom I dismissed ten days since to the Borders, hearing of disaffection, hath done nought to check it. But come what may, his must be a bold lance that shivers against a king's mail. And now one kiss of my Lady Bessee, one cup of the bright canary, and then God and St. George for the White Rose!"

CHAPTER II.

The Camp at Olney.

IT was some weeks after the citizens of London had seen their gallant king, at the head of such forces as were collected in haste in the metropolis, depart from their walls to the encounter of the rebels. Surprising and disastrous had been the tidings in the interim.

At first, indeed, there were hopes that the insurrection had been put down by Montagu, who had defeated the troops of Robin of Redesdale, near the city of York, and was said to have beheaded their leader. But the spirit of discontent was only fanned by an adverse wind. The popular hatred to the Woodvilles was so great, that in proportion as Edward advanced to the scene of action, the country rose in arms as Raoul de Fulke had predicted. Leaders of lordly birth now headed the rebellion; the sons of the Lords Latimer and Fitzhugh, (near kinsmen of the House of Nevile), lent their names to the cause; and Sir John Coniers, an experienced soldier, whose claims had been disregarded by Edward, gave to the insurgents the aid of a formidable capacity for war. In every mouth was the story of the Duchess of Bedford's witchcraft; and the waxen figure of the earl did more to rouse the people, than perhaps the earl himself could have done in person.* As yet, however, the language of the insurgents was tempered with all personal respect to the king; they declared in their manifestoes that they desired only the banishment of the Woodvilles, and the recall of Warwick, whose name they used unscrupulously, and whom they declared they were on their way to meet. As soon as it was known that the kinsmen of the beloved earl were in the revolt, and naturally supposed that the earl himself must countenance the enterprise, the tumultuous camp swelled every hour, while knight after knight, veteran after veteran, abandoned the royal standard.

The Lord d'Eyncourt, (one of the few lords of the highest birth and greatest following, over whom the Neviles had no influence, and who bore the Woodvilles no grudge), had, in his way to Lincolnshire, where his personal aid was necessary to rouse his vassals, infected by the common sedition,—been attacked and wounded by a body of marauders, and thus Edward's camp lost one of its greatest leaders. Fierce dispute broke out in the king's councils; and, when the witch Jacquette's practices against the earl travelled from the hostile into the royal camp, Raoul de Fulke, St. John, and others, seized with pious horror, positively declared they would throw down their arms and retire to their castles, unless the Woodvilles were dismissed from the camp, and the Earl of Warwick was recalled to England. To the first demand the king was constrained to yield; with the second he temporized. He marched from Fotheringay to Newark; but the signs of disaffection, though they could not dismay him as a soldier, altered his plans as a captain of singular military acuteness; he fell back on Nottingham, and dispatched, with his own hands, letters to Clarence, the Archbishop of York, and Warwick. To the last he wrote touchingly. "We do do not believe" (said the letter) "that ye should be of any such disposition towards us, as the rumor here runneth, considering the trust and affection we bear you—and cousin, ne think ye shall be to us welcome." * But ere these letters reached the destination, the crown seemed well nigh lost. At Edgecote, the Earl of Pembroke was defeated and slain, and five thousand royalists were left on the field. Earl Rivers, and his son, Sir John Woodville,† who, in obedience

* See *Parliamentary Rolls*, vi. 232, for the accusations of witchcraft, and the fabrication of a necromantic image of Lord Warwick, circulated against the Duchess of Bedford. She herself quotes, and complains of, them.

* *Paston Letters*, ccxcviii., (Knight's edition) vol. ii., p. 59. See also *Lingard*, vol. iii., p. 522, (4to edition,) *note* 43, for the proper date to be assigned to Edward's letter to Warwick, etc.

† This Sir John Woodville was the most obnoxious of the queen's brothers, and infamous for the avarice which had led him to marry the old Duchess of Norfolk, an act which, according to the old laws of chivalry, would have disabled him from entering the lists of knighthood, for the ancient code disqualified and degraded any knight who should marry an old woman for her money! Lord Rivers was the more odious to the people at the time of the insurrection, because, in his capacity of treasurer, he had lately tampered with the coin and circulation.

to the royal order, had retired to the earl's country seat of Grafton, were taken prisoners, and beheaded by the vengeance of the insurgents. The same lamentable fate befell the Lord Stafford, on whom Edward relied as one of his most puissant leaders; and London heard with dismay, that the king, with but a handful of troops, and those lukewarm and disaffected, was begirt on all sides by hostile and marching thousands.

From Nottingham, however, Edward made good his retreat to a village called Olney, which chanced at that time to be partially fortified with a wall and a strong gate. Here the rebels pursued him; and Edward, hearing that Sir Anthony Woodville, who conceived that the fate of his father and brother cancelled all motive for longer absence from the contest, was busy in collecting a force in the neighborhood of Coventry, while other assistance might be daily expected from London, strengthened the fortifications as well as the time would permit, and awaited the assult of the insurgents.

It was at this crisis, and while throughout all England reigned terror and commotion—that one day, towards the end of July, a small troop of horsemen were seen riding rapidly towards the neighborhood of Olney. As the village came in view of the cavalcade, with the spire of its church, and its gray stone gateway, so, also, they beheld, on the pastures that stretched around wide and far a moving forest of pikes and plumes.

"Holy Mother!" said one of the foremost riders, "Good knight and strong man though Edward be, it were sharp work to cut his way from that hamlet through yonder fields! Brother, we were more welcome, had we brought more bills and bows at our backs!"

"Archbishop," answered the stately personage thus addressed, "we bring what alone raises armies and disbands them—a NAME that a People honors! From the moment the White Bear is seen on yonder archway, side by side with the king's banner—that army will vanish as smoke before the wind."

"Heaven grant it, Warwick!" said the Duke of Clarence, "for, though Edward hath used us sorely, it chafes me as Plantagenet and as prince, to see how peasants and varlets can hem round a king."

"Peasants and varlets are pawns in the chess board, cousin George," said the prelate, "and knight and bishop find them mighty useful, when pushing forward to an attack. Now knight and bishop appear themselves and take up the game—Warkwick," added the prelate, in a whisper, unheard by Clarence, "forget not, while appeasing rebellion, that the king is in your power."

"For shame, George! I think not now of the unkind king; I think only of the brave boy I dandled on my knee, and whose sword I girded on at Touton. How his lion heart must chafe, condemned to see a foe whom his skill as captain tells him it were madness to confront!"

"Ay, Richard Nevile!—ay," said the prelate, with a slight sneer, "play the Paladin, and become the dupe—release the prince, and betray the people!"

"No! I can be true to both. Tush! brother, your craft is slight to the plain wisdom of bold honesty. You slacken your steeds, sirs, on—on—see the march of the rebels! On, for an Edward and a Warwick!" and spurring to full speed, the little company arrived at the gates. The loud bugle of the new comers was answered by the cheerful note of the joyous warder,—while dark, slow, and solemn, over the meadows, crept on the mighty cloud of the rebel army.

"We have forestalled the insurgents! said the earl, throwing himself from his black steed. "Marmaduke Nevile, advance our banner; heralds, announce the Duke of Clarence, the Archbishop of York, and the Earl of Salisbury and Warwick."

Through the anxious town, along the crowded walls and housetops, into the hall of an old mansion (that then adjoined the church), where the king, in complete armor, stood at bay, with stubborn and disaffected officers, rolled the thunder cry—"A Warwick—a Warwick! all saved! a Warwick!"

Sharply, as he heard the clamor, the king turned upon his startled council. "Lords and captains!" said he, with that inexpressible majesty which he could command in his happier hours, "God and our Patron Saint have sent us at least one man who has the heart to fight fifty times the odds of yon miscreant rabble, by his king's side, and for the honor of loyalty and knighthood!"

"And who says, sire," answered Raoul de

Fulke, "that we your lords and captains would not risk blood and life for our king and our knighthood in a just cause? But we will not butcher our countrymen for echoing our own complaint, and praying your grace that a grasping and ambitious family which you have raised to power may no longer degrade your nobles and oppress your commons. We shall see if the Earl of Warwick blame us or approve."

"And I answer," said Edward, loftily, "that whether Warwick approve or blame, come as friend or foe, I will sooner ride alone through yonder archway, and carve out a soldier's grave amongst the ranks of rebellious war, than be the puppet of my subjects, and serve their will by compulsion. Free am I—free ever will I be, while the crown of the Plantagenet is mine, to raise those whom I love, to defy the threats of those sworn to obey me. And were I but Earl of March, instead of king of England, this hall should have swam with the blood of those who have insulted the friends of my youth—the wife of my bosom. Off, Hastings!—I need no mediator with my servants. Nor here, nor anywhere in broad England, have I my equal, and the king forgives or scorns—construe it as ye will, my lords—what the simple gentleman would avenge."

It were in vain to describe the sensation that this speech produced. There is ever something in courage and in will that awes numbers, though brave themselves. And what with the unquestioned valor of Edward—what with the effect of his splendid person, towering above all present by the head, and moving lightly, with each impulse, through the mass of a mail that few there could have borne unsinking, this assertion of absolute power in the midst of mutiny—an army marching to the gates—imposed an unwilling reverence and sullen silence, mixed with anger, that, while it chafed, admired. They who, in peace, had despised the voluptuous monarch, feasting in his palace, and reclining on the lap of harlot-beauty, felt that in war, all Mars seemed living in his person. Then, indeed, he was a king; and had the foe, now darkening the landscape, been the noblest chivalry of France, not a man there but had died for a smile from that haughty lip. But the barons were knit heart in heart with the popular outbreak, and to put down the revolt seemed to them but to raise the Woodvilles. The silence was still unbroken, save where the persuasive whisper of Lord Hastings might be faintly heard in remonstrance with the more powerful or the more stubborn of the chiefs—when the tread of steps resounded without, and, unarmed, bareheaded, the only form in Christendom grander and statelier than the king's, strode into the Hall.

Edward, as yet unaware what course Warwick would pursue, and half doubtful whether a revolt that had borrowed his name, and was led by his kinsmen, might not originate in his consent, surrounded by those to whom the earl was especially dear, and aware that if Warwick were against him all was lost, still relaxed not the dignity of his mien; and leaning on his large two-handed sword, with such inward resolves as brave kings and gallant gentleman form, if the worst should befall, he watched the majestic strides of his great kinsman, and said, as the earl approached, and the mutinous captains louted low—

"Cousin, you are welcome! for truly do I know that when *you* have aught whereof to complain, you take not the moment of danger and disaster. And whatever has chanced to alienate your heart from me, the sound of the rebel's trumpet chases all difference, and marries your faith to mine."

"Oh, Edward, my king, why did you so misjudge me in the prosperous hour!" said Warwick, simply, but with affecting earnestness; "since in the adverse hour you aread me well?"

As he spoke, he bowed his head, and bending his knee, kissed the hand held out to him.

Edward's face grew radiant, and raising the earl, he glanced proudly at the barons who stood round, surprised and mute.

"Yes, my lords and sirs, see—it is not the earl of Warwick, next to our royal brethren, the nearest subject to the throne, who would desert me in the day of peril!"

"Nor do *we*, sire," retorted Raoul de Fulke, "you wrong us before our mighty comrade if you so misthink us. We will fight for the king, but not for the queen's kindred; and this alone brings on us your anger."

"The gates shall be opened to ye. Go! Warwick and I are men enough for the rabble yonder."

The earl's quick eye, and profound experience of his time, saw at once the dissension and its causes. Nor, however generous, was he willing to forego the present occasion for permanently destroying an influence which he knew hostile to himself and hurtful to the realm. His was not the generosity of a boy, but of a statesman. Accordingly, as Raoul de Fulke ceased, he took up the word.

"My liege, we have yet an hour good ere the foe can reach the gates. Your brother and mine accompany me. See, they enter! Please you, a few minutes to confer with them; and suffer me, meanwhile, to reason with these noble captains."

"Edward paused; but before the open brow of the earl fled whatever suspicion might have crossed the king's mind.

"Be it so, cousin: but remember this:—to councillors who can menace me with desertion in such an hour, I concede nothing."

Turning hastily away, he met Clarence and the prelate, midway in the hall, threw his arm caressingly over his brother's shoulder, and, taking the archbishop by the hand, walked with them towards the battlements.

"Well, my friends," said Warwick, "and what would you of the king?"

"The dismissal of all the Woodvilles, except the queen—the revocation of the grants and land accorded to them, to the despoiling the ancient noble—and, but for your presence, we had demanded your recall."

"And, failing these, what your resolve!"

"To depart, and leave Edward to his fate. These granted, we doubt little but that the insurgents will disband. These not granted, we but waste our lives against a multitude whose cause we must approve."

"The cause! But ye know not the real cause," answered Warwick. "I know it; for the sons of the North are familiar to me, and their rising hath deeper meaning than ye deem. What! have they not decoyed to their head my kinsmen, the heirs of Latimer and Fitzhugh, and bold Coniers, whose steel casque should have circled a wiser brain? Have they not taken my name as their battle-cry? And do ye think this falsehood veils nothing but the simple truth of just complaint?"

"Was their rising, then," asked St. John, in evident surprise, "wholly unauthorized by you."

"So help me Heaven! If I would resort to arms to redress a wrong, think not that I myself would be absent from the field? No, my lords, friends, and captains—time presses; a few words must suffice to explain what, as yet, may be dark to you. I have letters from Montagu and others, which reached me the same day as the king's, and which clear up the purpose of our misguided countrymen. Ye know well that ever in England, but especially since the reign of Edward III., strange, wild notions of some kind of liberty other than that we enjoy, have floated loose through the land. Among the commons, a half conscious recollection that the nobles are a different race from themselves, feeds a secret rancor and mislike, which at any fair occasion for riot, shows itself bitter and ruthless—as in the outbreak of Cade and others. And if the harvest fail, or a tax gall, there are never wanting men to turn the popular distress to the ends of private ambition or state design. Such a man has been the true head and front of this commotion."

"Speak you of Robin Redesdale, now dead?" asked one of the captains.

"He is not dead.* Montagu informs me that the report was false. He was defeated off York, and retired for some days into the woods; but it is he who has enticed the sons of Latimer and Fitzhugh into the revolt, and resigned his own command to the martial cunning of Sir John Coniers. This Robin of Redesdale is no common man. He hath had a clerkly education—he hath travelled among the Free Towns of Italy—he hath deep purpose in all he doth; and among his projects is the destruction of the nobles here, as it was whilome effected in Florence, the depriving us of all offices and posts, with other changes, wild to think of, and long to name."

* The fate of Robin of Redesdale has been as obscure as most of the incidents in this most perplexed part of English history. While some of the chroniclers finish his career according to the report mentioned in the text, Fabyan not only more charitably prolongs his life, but rewards him with the king's pardon: and according to the annals of his ancient and distinguished family (who will pardon, we trust, a licence with one of their ancestry equally allowed by history and romance), as referred to in WOTTON'S *English Baronetage* (Art., *Hilyard*), and which probably rests upon the authority of the life of Richard III., in STOWE'S *Annals*, he is represented as still living in the reign of that king. But the whole account of this famous demagogue in WOTTON is, it must be owned full of historical mistakes.

"And we would have suffered this man to triumph!" exclaimed De Fulke: "we have been to blame."

"Under fair pretence he has gathered numbers, and now wields an army. I have reason to know that, had he succeeded in estranging ye from Edward, and had the king fallen, dead or alive, into his hands, his object would have been to restore Henry of Windsor, but on conditions that would have left king and baron little more than pageants in the state. I knew this man years ago. I have watched him since; and, strange though it may seem to you, he hath much in him that I admire as a subject and should fear were I a king. Brief, thus runs my counsel:—For our sake and the realm's safety we must see this armed multitude disbanded—that done, we must see the grievances they with truth complain of fairly redressed. Think, not, my lords, I avenge my own wrongs alone, when I go with you in your resolve to banish from the king's councils the baleful influence of the queen's kin. Till that be compassed, no peace for England. As a leprosy, their avarice crawls over the nobler parts of the state, and devours while it sullies. Leave this to me: and, though we will redress ourselves, let us now assist our king!"

With one voice, the unruly officers clamored their assent to all the earl urged, and expressed their readiness to sally at once from the gates, and attack the rebels.

"But," observed an old veteran, "what are we amongst so many?—Here a handful—there an army!"

"Fear not, reverend sir," answered Warwick, with an assured smile; "is it not this army in part gathered from my own province of Yorkshire? Is it not formed of men who have eaten of my bread and drank of my cup? Let me see the man who will discharge one arrow at the walls which contain Richard Nevile of Warwick. Now each to your posts—I to the king.

Like the pouring of new blood into a decrepit body seemed the arrival, at that feeble garrison, of the Earl of Warwick. From despair into the certainty of triumph leaped every heart. Already, at the sight of his banner floating by the side of Edward's, the gunner had repaired to his bombard—the archer had taken up his bow—the village itself, before disaffected, poured all its scanty population—women, and age, and children—to the walls. And when the earl joined the king upon the ramparts, he found that able general sanguine and elated, and pointing out to Clarence the natural defences of the place. Meanwhile the rebels, no doubt apprized by their scouts of the new aid, had already halted in their march, and the dark swarm might be seen indistinctly undulating, as bees ere they settle, amidst the verdure of the plain.

"Well, cousin," said the king, "have ye brought these Hotspurs to their allegiance?"

"Sire, yes;" said Warwick, gravely, "but we have here no force to resist yon army."

"Bring you not succours?" said the king, astonished. "You must have passed through London. Have you left no troops upon the road?"

"I had no time, sire; and London is well nigh palsied with dismay. Had I waited to collect troops, I might have found a king's head blackening over those gates."

"Well," returned Edward, carelessly, "few or many, one gentleman is more worth than a hundred varlets. 'We are eno' for glory,' as Henry said, at Agincourt."

"No, sire; you are too skilful and too wise to believe your boast. These men we cannot conquer—we may disperse them."

"By what spell?"

"By their king's word to redress their complaints."

"And banish my queen?"

"Heaven forbid that man should part those whom God has joined," returned Warwick. "Not my lady, your queen, but my lady's kindred."

"Rivers is dead, and gallant John," said Edward, sadly—"is not that enough for revenge?"

"It is not revenge that we require, but pledges for the land's safety," answered Warwick. "And to be plain, without such a promise these walls may be your tomb."

Edward walked apart, strongly debating within himself. In his character were great contrasts; no man was more frank in common—no man more false when it suited—no man had more levity in wanton love, or more firm affection for those he once thoroughly took to his heart. He was the reverse of grateful for service yielded, yet he was warm in protecting those on whom service was conferred. He was resolved not to give up the Woodvilles, and, after a short self-commune, he equally determined not to risk his crown and life by persevering in resistance in the demand for their downfall. Inly obstinate, outwardly yielding, he concealed his falsehood with his usual soldierly grace.

"Warwick," he said, returning to the earl's side, "you cannot advise me to what is misbeseeming, and therefore, in this strait, I resign my conduct to your hands. I will not unsay to yon mutinous gentlemen what I have already said; but what you judge it right to promise in my name to them, or to the insurgents, I will not suppose that mine honor will refuse to concede. But go not hence, O noblest friend that ever stood by a king's throne!—go not hence till the grasp of your hand assures me that all past unkindness is gone and buried; yea, and by this hand, and while its pressure is warm in mine, bear not too hard on thy king's affection for his lady's kindred."

"Sire," said Warwick, though his generous nature well nigh melted into weakness, and it was with an effort that he adhered to his purpose—"Sire," if dismissed for awhile, they shall not be degraded. And if it be, on consideration, wise to recall from the family of Woodvile your grants of lands and lordships, take from your Warwick—who, rich in his king's love, hath eno' to spare—take the double of what you would recall. O, be frank with me—be true—be steadfast, Edward, and dispose of my lands whenever you would content a favorite."

"Not to impoverish thee, my Warwick," answered Edward, smiling, "did I call thee to my aid; for the rest, my revenues as Duke of York are at least mine to bestow. Go now to the hostile camp—go as sole minister and captain-general of this realm—go with all powers and honors a king can give; and when these districts are at peace, depart to our Welch provincess, as chief justiciary of that principality. Pembroke's mournful death leaves that high post in my gift. It cannot add to your greatness, but it proves to England your sovereign's trust."

"And while that trust is given," said Warwick, with tears in his eyes, "may Heaven strengthen my arm in battle, and sharpen my brain in council. But I play the laggard. The sun wanes westward; it should not go down while a hostile army menaces the son of Richard of York."

The earl strode rapidly away, reached the broad space where his followers still stood, dismounted, but beside their steeds—

"Trumpets advance—pursuivants and heralds go before—Marmaduke, mount! The rest I need not. We ride to the insurgent camp."

CHAPTER III.

The Camp of the Rebels.

THE rebels had halted about a mile from the town, and were already pitching their tents for the night. It was a tumultuous, clamorous, but not altogether undisciplined array: for Coniers was a leader of singular practice in reducing men into the machinery of war, and where his skill might have failed, the prodigious influence and energy of Robin of Redesdale ruled the passions and united the discordant elements. This last was, indeed, in much worthy the respect in which Warwick held his name. In times more ripe for him, he would have been a mighty demagogue and a successful regenerator. His birth was known but to few; his education and imperious temper made him vulgarly supposed of noble origin; but had he descended from a king's loins, Robert Hilyard had still been the son of the Saxon people. Warwick overrated, perhaps, Hilyard's wisdom; for, despite his Italian experience, his ideas was far from embracing any clear and definite system of democracy. He had much of the frantic levelism and *jacquerie* of his age and land, and could probably not have explained to himself all the changes he desired to effect; but, coupled with his hatred to the nobles, his deep and passionate sympathy with the poor, his heated and fanatical chimeras of a republic, half-political and half religious,—he had, with no uncommon inconsistency, linked the cause of a dethroned king. For as the Covenanters linked with the Stuarts against the succeeding and more tolerant dynasty never relinquishing their own anti-monarchic theories; as in our time, the extreme party on the popular side has leagued with the extreme of the aristocratic, in order to crush the medium policy, as a common foe; so the bold leveller united with his zeal for Margaret the very cause which the House of Lancaster might be supposed the least to favor.

He expected to obtain from a sovereign, dependent upon a popular reaction for restoration, great popular privileges. And as the church had deserted the Red Rose for the White, he sought to persuade many of the Lollards, ever ready to show their discontent, that Margaret (in revenge on the hierarchy) would extend the protection they had never found in the previous sway of her husband and Henry V. Possessed of extraordinary craft, and even cunning in secular intrigues—energetic, versatile, bold, indefatigable, and, above all, marvellously gifted with the arts that inflame, stir up, and guide the physical force of masses, Robert Hilyard had been, indeed, the soul and life of the present revolt; and his prudent moderation in resigning the nominal command to those whose military skill and high birth raised a riot into the dignity of rebellion, had given that consistency and method to the rising which popular movements never attain without aristocratic aid.

In the principal tent of the encampment the leaders of the insurrection were assembled.

There was Sir John Coniers, who had married one of the Neviles, the daughter of Fauconberg, Lord High Admiral, but who had profited little by this remote connection with Warwick; for with all his merit, he was a greedy, grasping man, and he had angered the hot earl in pressing his claims too imperiously. This renowned knight was a tall, gaunt man, whose iron frame sixty winters had not bowed; there, were the young heirs of Latimer and Fitzhugh, in gay gilded armor and scarlet mantelines; and there, in a plain cuirass, trebly welded, and of immense weight, but the lower limbs left free and unincumbered, in thick leathern hose, stood Robin of Redesdale. Other captains there were, whom different motives had led to the common confederacy. There, might be seen the secret Lollard, hating either Rose, stern and sour, and acknowledging no leader but Hilyard, whom he knew as a Lollard's son; there might be seen the ruined spendthrift, discontented with fortune, and regarding civil war as the cast of a die—death for the forfeiture, lordships for the gain; there, the sturdy Saxon squire, oppressed by the little baron of his province, and rather hopeful to abase a neighbor than dethrone a king, of whom he knew little, and for whom he cared still less; and there, chiefly distinguished from the rest by grizzled beard, and upturned moustache, erect mien, and grave, not thoughtful aspect, were the men of a former period—the soldiers who had fought against the Maid of Arc—now without place, station, or hope, in peaceful times, already half robbers by profession, and decoyed to any standard that promised action, pay, or plunder.

The conclave were in high and warm debate.

"If this be true," said Coniers, who stood at the head of the table, his helmet, axe, truncheon, and a rough map of the walls of Olney before him—"if this be true—if our scouts are not deceived—if the Earl of Warwick is in the village, and if his banner float beside King Edward's—I say bluntly, as soldiers should speak, that I have been deceived and juggled!"

"And by whom, Sir Knight and cousin!" said the heir of Fitzhugh, reddening.

"By you, young-kinsman, and this hot-mouthed dare-devil, Robin of Redesdale! Ye assured me, both, thal the earl approved the rising—that he permitted the levying yon troops in his name—that he knew well the time was come to declare against the Woodvilles, and that no sooner was an army mustered than he would place himself at its head; and, I say, if this be not true, you have brought these grey hairs into dishonor!"

"And what, Sir John Coniers," exclaimed Robin, rudely, "what honor had your grey hairs till the steel cap covered them? What honor, I say under lewd Edward and his lusty revellers? You were thrown aside, like a broken scythe, Sir John Coniers! You were forsaken in you rust! Warwick himself, your wife's great kinsman, could do nought in your favor! You stand now, leader of thousands, lord of life and death, master of Edward and the throne! We have done this for you, and you reproach us!"

"And," began the heir of Fitzhugh, encouraged by the boldness of Hilyard, "we had all reason to believe my noble, uncle, the Earl of Warwick, approved our emprise. When this brave fellow (pointing to Robin) came to inform me that, with his own eyes, he had seen the waxen effigies of my great kinsman, the hellish misdeed of the queen's witch-dam, I repaired to my Lord Montagu; and, though that prudent courtier refused to declare openly, he let me see that war with the Woodvilles was not unwelcome to him."

"Yet this same Montagu," observed one of the ringleaders, "when Hilyard was well-nigh at the gates of York, sallied out and defeated him, sans ruth, sans ceremony."

"Yes, but he spared my life, and beheaded the dead body of poor Hugh Withers in my stead; for John Nevile is cunning, and he picks nuts from the brennen without lesing his own paw. It was not the hour for him to join us, so he beat us civilly and with discretion. But what hath he done since?—He stands aloof while our army swells—while the bull of the Neviles, and the ragged staff of the earl, are the ensigns of our war—and while Edward gnaws out his fierce heart in yon walls of Olney. How say ye, then, that Warwick, even if now in person with the king, is in heart against us? Nay, he may have entered Olney but to capture the tyrant."

"If so," said Coniers, "all is as it should be; but if Earl Warwick, who, though he hath treated me ill, is a stout carle, and to be feared if not loved, join the king, I break this wand, and ye will seek out another captain."

"And a captain shall be found!" cried Robin. "Are we so poor in valor that when one man leaves us we are headless and undone? What if Warwick so betray us and himself—he brings no forces. And never, by God's blessing, should we separate, till we have redressed the wrongs of our countrymen!"

"Good!" said the Saxon squire, winking and looking wise—"not till we have burned to the ground the Baron of Bullstock's castle."

"Not," said a Lollard, sternly—"till we have shortened the purple gown of the churchman—not till abbot and bishop have felt on their backs the whips wherewith they have scourged the godly believer and the humble saint."

"Not," added Robin, "till we have assured bread to the poor man, and the filling of the flesh-pot, and the law to the weak, and the scaffold to the evil-doer."

"All this is mighty well," said, bluntly, Sir Geoffrey Gates, the leader of the mercenaries, a skilful soldier, but a predatory and lawless bravo—"but who is to pay me and my tall fellows?"

At this pertinent question, there was a general hush of displeasure and disgust.

"For look you, my masters," continued Sir Geoffrey—"as long as I and my comrades here believed that the rich earl, who hath half England for his provant, was at the head or the tail of this matter, we were contented to wait awhile; but devil a groat hath yet gone into my gipsire, and as for pillage, what is a farm or a homestead! an' it were a church or a castle, there might be pickings."

"There is much plate of silver, and a sack or so of marks and royals in the stronghold of the Baron of Bullstock," quoth the Saxon squire, doggedly hounding on to his revenge.

"You see, my friends," said Coniers, with a smile, and shrugging his shoulders—"that men cannot gird-kingdom with ropes of sand. Suppose we conquer and take captive—nay, or slay King Edward—what then?"

"The Duke of Clarence, male heir to the throne," said the heir of Latimer, "is Lord Warwick's son-in-law, and therefore akin to you, Sir John."

"That is true," observed Coniers, musingly.

"Not ill thought of, sir," said Sir Geoffrey Gates—and my advice is to proclaim Clarence king, and Warwick lord protector. We have some chance of the angels then."

"Besides," said the heir of Fitzhugh, "our purpose once made clear, it will be hard either for Warwick or Clarence to go against us—harder still for the country not to believe them with us. Bold measures are our wisest councillors."

"Um!" said the Lollard—"Lord Warwick is a good man, and hath never, though his brother be a bishop, abetted the church tyrannies. But as for George of Clarence——"

"As for Clarence," said Hilyard, who saw, with dismay and alarm, that the rebellion he designed to turn at the fitting hour to the service of Lancaster, might now only help to shift, from one shoulder to the other, the hated dynasty of York—"as for Clarence, he hath Edward's vices without his manhood." He paused, and seeing that the crisis had ripened the hour for declaring himself, his bold temper pushed at once to its object. "No!" he continued, folding his arms, raising his head, and comprehending the whole council in his keen and steady gaze—"no! lords and gentlemen—since speak I must, in this emergency, hear me calmly. Nothing has prospered in England since we abandoned our lawful king. If we rid ourselves of Edward, let it not be to sink from a harlot-monger to a drunkard. In the Tower pines our true lord, already honored as a saint. Hear me, I say—hear me out! On the frontiers, an army that keeps Gloucester at bay, hath declared for Henry and Margaret. Let us, after seizing Olney, march thither at once, and unite forces. Margaret is already prepared to embark for England. I have friends in London who will attack the Tower, and deliver Henry. To you, Sir John Coniers, in the queen's name, I promise an earldom and the garter. To you, the heirs of Latimer and Fitzhugh, the high posts that beseem your birth; to all of you knights and captains, just share and allotment in the confiscated lands of the Woodvilles and the Yorkists. To you, brethren," and addressing the Lollards, his voice softened into a meaning accent, that, compelled to worship in secret, they yet understood—"shelter from your foes, and mild laws; and to you, brave soldiers. that pay which a king's coffers alone can supply. Wherefore I say, down with all subject banners! up with the Red Rose and the Antelope, and long live Henry the Sixth!"

This address, however subtle in its adaptation to the various passions of those assembled, however aided by the voice, spirit, and energy of the speaker, took too much by surprise those present to produce at once its effect. The Lollards remembered the fires lighted for their martyrs by the House of Lancaster; and though blindly confident in Hilyard, were not yet prepared to respond to his call. The young heir of Fitzhugh, who had, in truth, but taken arms to avenge the supposed wrongs of Warwick, whom he idolized, saw no object gained in the rise of Warwick's enemy—Queen Margaret. The mercenaries called to mind the woful state of Henry's exchequer in the former time. The Saxon squire muttered to himself—'And what the devil is to become of the castle of Bullstock?" But Sir Henry Nevile (Lord Latimer's son) who belonged to that branch of his house which had espoused the Lancaster cause, and who was in the secret councils of Hilyard, caught up the cry, and said—"Hilyard doth not exceed his powers; and he who strikes for the Red Rose, shall carve out his own lordship from the manors of every Yorkist that he slays!" Sir John Coniers hesitated: poor, long neglected, ever enterprising and ambitious, he was dazzled by the proffered bribe—but age is slow to act, and he expressed himself with the measured caution of grey hairs.

"A king's name," said he, "is a tower of strength, especially when marching against a king; but this is a matter for general assent and grave forethought."

Before any other (for ideas did not rush at once to words in those days) found his tongue, a mighty uproar was heard without. It did not syllable itself into distinct sound; it uttered no name—it was such a shout as numbers alone could raise, and to such a shout would some martial leader have rejoiced to charge to battle, so full of depth and fervor, and enthusiasm, and good heart, it seemed, leaping from rank to rank, from breast to breast, from earth to heaven. With one accord the startled captains made to the entrance of the tent, and there they saw, in the broad space before them, enclosed by the tents which were grouped in a wide semicircle,—for the mass of the hardy rebel army slept in the open air, and the tents were but for leaders,—they saw, we say, in that broad space, a multitude kneeling, and in the midst, upon his good steed Saladin, bending graciously down, the martial countenance, the lofty stature, of the Earl of Warwick. Those among the captains, who knew him not personally, recognized him by the popular description—by the black war-horse, whose legendary fame had been hymned by every minstrel; by the sensation his appearance had created; by the armorial insignia of his heralds, grouped behind him, and whose gorgeous tabards blazed with his cognizance and quarterings in azure, or, and argent. The sun was slowly setting, and poured its rays upon the bare head of the mighty noble, gathering round it in the hazy atmosphere like a halo. The homage of the crowd to that single form, unarmed, and scarce attended, struck a deathknell to the hopes of Hilyard—struck awe into all his comrades! The presence of that one man seemed to ravish from them, as by magic, a vast army; power and state, and command, left them suddenly to be absorbed in HIM! Captains, they were troopless—the wielder of men's hearts was amongst them, and from his barb assumed reign, as from his throne!

"Gads, my life!" said Coniers, turning to his comrades, "we have now, with a truth, the earl amongst us; but, unless he come to lead us on to Olney, I would as lief see the king's provost at my shoulder."

"The crowd separates—he rides this way!" said the heir of Fitzhugh. "Shall we go forth to meet him?"

"Not so!" exclaimed Hilyard, "we are still the leaders of this army; let him find us deliberating on the siege of Olney!"

"Right!" said Coniers; "and if there come dispute, let not the rabble hear it."

The captains re-entered the tent, and in grave silence awaited the earl's coming; nor was this suspense long. Warwick, leaving the multitude in the rear, and taking only one of the subaltern officers in the rebel camp as his guide and usher, arrived at the tent, and was admitted into the council.

The captains, Hilyard alone excepted, bowed with great reverence as the earl entered.

"Welcome, puissant sir, and illstrious kinsman!" said Coniers, who had decided on the line to be adopted—"you are come at last to take the command of the troops raised in your name, and into your hands I resign this truncheon."

"I accept it, Sir John Coniers," answered Warwick, taking the place of dignity; "and since you thus constitute me your commander, I proceed at once to my stern duties. How happens it, knights and gentlemen, that in my absence ye have dared to make my name the pretext of rebellion? Speak thou, my sister's son!"

"Cousin and lord," said the heir of Fitzhugh, reddening but not abashed, "we could not believe but what you would smile on those who have risen to assert your wrongs and defend your life." And he then briefly related the tale of the Duchess of Bedford's waxen effigies, and pointed to Hilyard as the eye-witness.

"And," began Sir Henry Nevile, "you, meanwhile, were banished, seemingly, from the king's court; the dissensions between you and Edward sufficiently the land's talk—the king's vices, the land's shame!"

"Nor did we act without at least revealing our intentions to my uncle and your brother, the Lord Montagu," added the heir of Fitzhugh.

"Meanwhile," said Robin of Redesdale "the commons were oppressed, the people discontented, the Woodvilles plundering us, and the king wasting our substance on concubines and minions. We have had cause eno' for our rising!"

The earl listened to each speaker in stern silence!"

"For all this," he said at last, "you have, without my leave or sanction, levied armed men in my name, and would have made Richard Nevile seem to Europe a traitor, without the courage to be a rebel! Your lives are in my power, and those lives are forfeit to the laws.

"If we have incurred your disfavor from our over-zeal for you," said the son of Lord Fitzhugh, touchingly, "take our lives, for they are of little worth." And the young nobleman unbuckled his sword, and laid it on the table.

"But," resumed Warwick, not seeming to heed his nephew's humility, "I, who have ever loved the people of England, and before king and parliament have ever pleaded their cause—I, as captain-general and first officer of these realms, here declare, that whatever motives of ambition or interest may have misled men of mark and birth, I believe that the commons at least never rise in arms without some excuse for their error. Speak out then, you, their leaders; and putting aside all that relates to me as the one man, say what are the grievances of which the many would complain."

And now there was silence, for the knights and gentlemen knew little of the complaints of the populace; the Lollards did not dare to expose their oppressed faith, and the squires and franklins were too uneducated to detail the grievances they had felt. But then, the immense superiority of the man of the people at once asserted itself; and Hilyard, whose eye the earl had hitherto shunned, lifted his deep voice. With clear precision, in indignant, but not declamatory eloquence, he painted the disorders of the time—the insolent exactions of the hospitals and abbeys—the lawless violence of each petty baron—the weakness of the royal authority in restraining oppression—its terrible power in aiding the oppressor.

He accumulated instance on instance of misrule; he showed the insecurity of property; the adulteration of the coin; the burden of the imposts; he bespoke of wives and maidens violated—of industry defrauded—of houses forcibly entered—of barns and granaries despoiled—of the impunity of all offenders, if high-born—of the punishment of all complaints, if poor and lowly. "Tell us not," he said, "that this is the necessary evil of the times, the hard condition of mankind. It was otherwise, Lord Warwick, when Edward first swayed; for *you* then made yourself dear to the people by your justice. Still men talk, hereabouts, of the golden rule of Earl Warwick; but since you have been, though great in office, powerless in deed, absent in Calais or idle at Midleham, England hath been but the plaything of the Woodvilles, and the king's ears have been stuffed with flattery as with wool. And," continued Hilyard, warming with his subject, and, to the surprise of the Lollard's, entering boldly on their master-grievance—"and this is not all. When Edward ascended the throne, there was, if not justice, at least repose, for the persecuted believers who hold that God's word was given to man to read, study and digest into godly deeds. I speak plainly. I speak of that faith which your great father, Salisbury, and many of the house of York, were believed to favor—that faith which is called the Lollard, and the oppression of which, more than aught else, lost to Lancaster the hearts of England. But of late, the church, assuming the power it ever grasps the most under the most licentious kings (for the sinner prince hath ever the tyrant priest!) hath put in vigor old laws, for the wronging man's thought and conscience; * and we sit at our doors under the shade, not of the vine-tree, but the gibbet. For all these things we have drawn the sword; and if now, you, taking advantage of the love borne to you by the sons of England, push that sword back into the sheath, you, generous, great, and princely though you be, well deserve the fate that I foresee and can foretell. Yes!" cried the speaker, extending his arms, and gazing fixedly on the proud face of the earl, which was not inexpressive of emotion—"yes! I see you, having deserted the people, deserted by them also, in your need—I see you, the dupe of an ungrateful king, stripped of power and honor, an exile and an outlaw; and when you call in vain upon the people, in whose hearts you now reign, remember, O fallen star, son of the morning! that in the hour of their might you struck down the people's right arm, and paralyzed their power. And now, if you will, let your friends and England's champions glut the scaffolds of your woman-king!"

He ceased—a murmur went round the conclave; every breast breathed hard—every eye turned to Warwick. That mighty statesman mastered the effect which the thrilling voice or the popular pleader produced on him; but at that moment he had need of all his frank and honorable loyalty to remind him that he was there but to fulfil a promise and discharge a trust—that he was the king's delegate, not the king's judge.

"You have spoken, bold men," said he, "as, in an hour when the rights of princes are weighed in one scale, the subject's swords in the other, I, were I king, would wish free men to speak. And now you, Robert Hilyard, and you, gentlemen, hear me, as envoy to King Edward IV. To all of you I promise complete amnesty and entire pardon. His highness believes you misled, not criminal, and your late deeds will not be remembered in your future services. So much for the leaders. Now for the commons. My liege the king is pleased to recall me to the high powers I once exercised, and to increase rather than to lessen them. In his name, I pledge myself to full and strict inquiry into all the grievances Robin of Redesdale hath set forth, with a view to speedy and complete redress. Nor is this all. His highness, laying aside his purpose of war with France, will have less need of imposts on his subjects, and the burdens and taxes will be reduced. Lastly—his grace, ever anxious to content his people, hath most benignly empowered me to promise that, whether or not ye rightly judge the queen's kindred, they will no longer have part or weight in the king's councils. The Duchess of Bedford, as beseems a lady so sorrowfully widowed, will retire to her

* The Lollards had greatly contributed to seat Edward on the throne; and much of the subsequent discontent, no doubt, arose from their disappointment, when, as Sharon Turner well expresses it, "his indolence allied him to the Church," and he became "*hereticorum severissimus hostis*."—CROYL, p. 564.

own home; and the Lord Scales will fulfil a mission to the Court of Spain. Thus, then, assenting to all reasonable demands—promising to heal all true grievances—proffering you gracious pardon—I discharge my duty to king and to people. I pray that these unhappy sores may be healed evermore, under the blessing of God and our patron saint; and in the name of Edward IV., Lord Suzerain of England and of France, I break up this truncheon and disband this army!"

Among those present, this moderate and wise address produced a general sensation of relief; for the earl's disavowel of the revolt took away all hope of its success. But the common approbation was not shared by Hilyard. He sprang upon the table, and seizing the broken fragments of the truncheon which the earl had snapped as a willow twig, exclaimed—"And thus, in the name of the people, I seize the command that ye unworthily resign! Oh, yes, what fools were yonder drudges of the hard hand and the grimed brow, and the leather jerkin, to expect succor from knight and noble!"

So saying, he bounded from the tent, and rushed towards the multitude at the distance.

"Ye, knights and lords, men of blood and birth, were but the tools of a manlier and wiser Cade!" said Warwick, calmly. "Follow me!"

The earl strode from the tent, sprang on his steed, and was in the midst of the troops with his heralds by his side, ere Hilyard had been enabled to begin the harangue he had intended. Warwick's trumpets sounded to silence; and the earl himself, in his loud clear voice, briefly addressed the immense audience. Master, scarcely less than Hilyard, of the popular kind of eloquence which—short, plain, generous and simple—cuts its way at once through the feelings to the policy, Warwick briefly but forcibly recapitulated to the commons the promises he had made to the captains; and as soon as they heard of taxes removed, the coinage reformed, the corn thrave abolished, the Woodvilles dismissed, and the earl recalled to power, the rebellion was at an end. They answered with a joyous shout his order to disperse and retire to their homes forthwith. But the indomitable Hilyard, ascending a small eminence, began his counter agitation. The earl saw his robust form and waving hand—he saw the crowd sway towards him; and too well acquainted with mankind to suffer his address, he spurred to the spot, and turning to Marmaduke, said, in a loud voice, "Marmaduke Nevile, arrest that man in the king's name!"

Marmaduke sprang from his steed, and laid his hand on Hilyard's shoulder. Not one of the multitude stirred on behalf of their demagogue. As before the sun recede the stars, all lesser lights had died in the blaze of Warwick's beloved name. Hilyard griped his dagger, and struggled an instant; but when he saw the awe and apathy of the armed mob a withering expression of disdain passed over his hardy face.

"Do ye suffer this?" he said. "Do ye suffer me, who have placed swords in your hands, to go forth in bonds and to the death?"

"The stout earl wrongs no man," said a single voice, and the populace echoed the word.

"Sir, then, I care not for life, since liberty is gone. I yield myself your prisoner."

"A horse for my captive!" said Warwick, laughing—"and hear me promise you, that he shall go unscathed in goods and in limbs. God wot, when Warwick and the people meet, no victim should be sacrificed! Hurrah for King Edward and fair England!"

He waved his plumed cap as he spoke, and within the walls of Olney was heard the shout that answered.

Slowly the earl and his scanty troop turned the rein: as he receded, the multitude broke up rapidly and when the moon rose, that camp was a solitude!" *

Such, for our nature is ever grander in the individual than the mass,—such is the power of man above mankind!

* The dispersion of the rebels at Olney is forcibly narrated by a few sentences, graphic from their brief simplicity, in the *Pictorial History of England*, Book v., p. 104. "They (Warwick, etc.) repaired in a very friendly manner to Olney, where they found Edward in a most unhappy condition; his friends were dead or scattered, flying for their lives, or hiding themselves in remote places: the insurgents were almost upon him. *A word from Warwick sent the insurgents quietly back to the North.*"

CHAPTER IV.

The Norman Earl and the Saxon Demagogue confer.

On leaving the camp, Warwick rode in advance of his train, and his countenance was serious and full of thought. At length, as a turn in the road hid the little band from the view of the rebels, the earl motioned to Marmaduke to advance with his prisoner. The young Nevile then fell back, and Robin and Warwick rode breast to breast, out of hearing of the rest.

"Master Hilyard, I am well content that my brother, when you fell into his hands, spared your life, out of gratitude for the favor you once showed to mine."

"Your noble brother, my lord," answered Robin, drily—"is, perhaps, not aware of the service I once rendered you. Methinks he spared me rather, because, without me, an enterprise which has shaken the Woodvilles from their roots around the throne, and given back England to the Neviles, had been nipped in the bud!—Your brother is a deep thinker!"

"I grieve to hear thee speak thus of the Lord Montagu. I know that he hath wilier devices than become, in my eyes, a well-born knight and a sincere man; but he loves his king, and his ends are juster than his means. Master Hilyard, enough of the past evil. Some months after the field of Hexham, I chanced to fall, when alone, amongst a band of roving and fierce Lancastrian outlaws. Thou, their leader, recognizing the crest on my helm, and mindful of some slight indulgence once shown to thy strange notions of republican liberty, didst save me from the swords of thy followers. from that time I have sought in vain to mend thy fortunes. Thou hast rejected all mine offers, and I know well that thou hast lent thy service to the fatal cause of Lancaster. Many a time I might have given thee to the law, but gratitude for thy aid in the needful strait, and to speak sooth, my disdain of all individual efforts to restore a fallen house, made me turn my eyes from transgressions, which once made known to the king, had placed thee beyond pardon. I see now that thou art a man of head and arm to bring great danger upon nations; and though this time Warwick bids thee escape and live,—if once more thon offend, know me only as the king's minister. The debt between us is now cancelled. Yonder lies the path that conducts to the forest. Farewell. Yet stay!—poverty may have led thee into treason."

"Poverty," interrupted Hilyard—"poverty Lord Warwick, leads men to sympathize with the poor, and therefore I have done with riches." He paused, and his breast heaved 'Yet," he added, sadly, "now that I have seen the cowardice and ingratitude of men, my calling seems over, and my spirit crushed."

"Alas!" said Warwick, "whether man be rich or poor, ingratitude is the vice of men; and you, who have felt it from the mob, menace me with it from a king. But each must carve out his own way through this earth, without over care for applause or blame; and the tomb is the sole judge of mortal memory!"

Robin looked hard at the earl's face, which was dark and gloomy, as he thus spoke, and approaching nearer, he said—"Lord Warwick, I take from you liberty and life the more willingly, because a voice I cannot mistake tells me, and hath long told, that, sooner or later, time will bind us to each other. Unlike other nobles, you have owed your power not so much to lordship, land, and birth, and a king's smile, as to the love you have nobly won; you alone, true knight and princely Christian—you alone, in war, have spared the humble—you alone, stalwart and resistless champion, have directed your lance against your equals, and your order hath gone forth to the fierce of heart—'Never smite the commons!' In peace, you alone have stood up in your haughty parliament for just law or for gentle mercy; your castle hath had a board for the hungry, and a shelter for the houseless; your pride, which hath bearded kings and humbled upstarts, hath never had a taunt for the lowly; and therefore I—son of the people—in the people's name, bless you living, and sigh to ask whether a people's gratitude will mourn you dead! Beware Edward's false smile—beware Clarence's fickle faith—beware Gloucester's inscrutable wile. Mark, the sun set! and while we speak, yon dark cloud gathers over your plumed head."

He pointed to the heavens as he ceased, and a low roll of gathering thunder seemed to answer his ominous warning. Without tarrying for the earl's answer, Hilyard shook the reins of his steed, and disappeared in the winding of the lane through which he took his way.

CHAPTER V.

What Faith Edward IV. purposeth to keep with Earl and People.

EDWARD received his triumphant envoy with open arms and profuse expressions of gratitude. He exerted himself to the utmost in the banquet that crowned the day, not only to conciliate the illustrious new comers, but to remove from the minds of Raoul de Fulke and his officers all memory of their past disaffection. No gift is rarer or more suceessful in the intrigues of life than that which Edward eminently possessed—viz., the *hypocrisy of frankness*. Dissimulation is often humble—often polished—often grave, sleek, smooth, decorous; but it is rarely gay and jovial, a hearty laugher, a merry, cordial, boon companion. Such, however, was the felicitous craft of Edward IV.; and, indeed, his spirits were naturally so high—his good humor so flowing—that this joyous hypocrisy cost him no effort. Elated at the dispersion of his foes—at the prospect of his return to his ordinary life of pleasure—there wss something so kindly and so winning in his mirth, that he subjugated entirely the fiery temper of Raoul de Fulke and the steadier suspicions of the more thoughtful St. John. Clarence, wholly reconciled to Edward, gazed on him with eyes swimming with affection, and soon drank himself into uproarious joviality. Ths archbishop, more reserved, still animated the society by the dry and epigrammatic wit not uncommon to his learned and subtle mind; but Warwick, in vain, endeavored to shake off an uneasy, ominous gloom. He was not satisfied with Edward's avoidance of discussion upon the grave matters involved in the earl's promise to the insurgents, and his masculine spirit regarded with some disdain, and more suspicion, a levity that he considered ill-suited to the emergence.

The banquet was over, and Edward, having dismissed his other attendants, was in his chamber with Lord Hastings, whose office always admitted him to the wardrobe of the king.

Edward's smile had now left his lip; he paced the room with a hasty stride, and then suddenly opening the casement, pointed to the landscape without, which lay calm and suffused in moonlight.

"Hastings, said he, abruptly, "a few hours since, and the earth grew spears! Behold the landscape now!"

"So vanish all the king's enemies!"

"Ay, man, ay—if at the king's word, or before the king's battle-axe; but at a subject's command ——. No, I am not a king, while another scatters armies in my realm, at his bare will. 'Fore Heaven, this shall not last!"

Hastings regarded the countenance of Edward, changed from affable beauty into terrible fierceness, with reflections suggested by his profound and mournful wisdom. "How little a man's virtues profit him in the eyes of men!" thought he. "The subject saves the crown, and the crown's wearer never pardons the presumption!"

"You do not speak, sir!" exclaimed Edward, irritated and impatient. "Why gaze you thus on me?"

"*Beau sire*," returned the favorite, calmly, "I was seeking to discover if your pride spoke, or your nobler nature."

"Tush!" said the king, petulantly—"the noblest part of a king's nature is his pride as king!" Again he strode the chamber, and again halted. "But the earl hath fallen into his own snare—he hath promised in my name what I will not perform. Let the people learn that their idol hath deceived them. He asks me to dismiss from the court the queen's mother and kindred!"

Hastings, who in this went thoroughly with the earl and the popular feeling, and whose only enemies in England were the Woodvilles, replied simply—

"These are cheap terms, sire, for a king's life, and the crown of England."

Edward started, and his eyes flashed that cold, cruel fire, which makes eyes of a light coloring so far more expressive of terrible passions than the quicker and warmer heat of dark orbs. "Think you so, sir? By God's blood, he who proffered them shall repent it in every vein of his body! Harkye, William Hastings de Hastings, I know you to be a deep and ambitious man; but better for you, had you covered that learned brain under the cowl of a mendicant friar, than lent one thought to the councils of the Earl of Warwick."

Hastings, who felt even to fondness the affection which Edward generally inspired in those about his person, and who, far from sympathizing, except in hate of the Woodvilles, with the earl, saw that beneath that mighty tree no new plants could push into their fullest foliage, reddened with anger at this imperious menace.

"My liege," said he, with becoming dignity and spirit, "if you can thus address your most tried confidant and your lealest friend, your most dangerous enemy is yourself."

"Stay, man," said the king, softening, "I was over warm, but the wild beast within me is chafed. Would Gloucester were here!"

"I can tell you what would be the counsels of that wise young prince, for I know his mind," answered Hastings.

"Ay, he and you love each other well. Speak out."

"Prince Richard is a great reader of Italian lere. He saith that those small states are treasuries of all experience. From that lere Prince Richard would say to you—'where a subject is so great as to be feared, and too much beloved to be destroyed, the king must remember how Tarpeia was crushed.'"

"I remember nought of Tarpeia, and I detest parables."

"Tarpeia, sire, (it is a story of old Rome), was crushed under the weight of presents. Oh, my liege," continued Hastings, warming with that interest which an able man feels in his own superior art, "were I king for a year, by the end of it Warwick should be the most unpopular (and therefore the weakest) lord in England!"

"And how, O wise in thine own conceit?"

"*Beau sire,*" resumed Hastings, not heeding the rebuke—and strangely enough he proceeded to point out, as the means of destroying the earl's influence, the very method that the archbishop had detailed to Montagu, as that which would make the influence irresistible and permanent,—"*Beau sire,*" resumed Hastings, "Lord Warwick is beloved by the people, because they consider him maltreated; he is esteemed by the people, because they consider him above all bribe; he is venerated by the people, because they believe that in all their complaints and struggles he is independent (he alone) of the king. Instead of love, I would raise envy; for instead of cold countenance I would heap him with grace. Instead of esteem and veneration I would raise suspicion, for I would so knit him to your house, that he could not stir hand or foot against you; I would make his heirs your brothers. The Duke of Clarence hath married one daughter—wed the other to Lord Richard. Betroth your young princess to Montagu's son, the representative of all the Neviles. The earl's immense possessions must thus ultimately pass to your own kindred. The earl himself will be no longer a power apart from the throne, but a part of it. The barons will chafe against one who half ceases to be of their order, and yet monopolizes their dignities; the people will no longer see in the earl their champion, but a king's favorite and deputy. Neither barons nor people will flock to his banner."

"All this is well and wise," said Edward, musing; "but meanwhile my queen's blood—am I to reign in a solitude?—for look you, Hastings, you know well that, uxorious as fools have deemed me, I had purpose and design in the elevation of new families, I wished to raise a fresh nobility to counteract the pride of the old, and only upon new nobles can a new dynasty rely."

"My lord, I will not anger you again; but still, for awhile, the queen's relations will do well to retire."

"Good night, Hastings," interrupted Edward, abruptly, "my pillow in this shall be my counsellor."

Whatever the purpose solitude and reflection might ripen in the king's mind, he was saved from immediate decision by news, the next morning, of fresh outbreaks. The commons had risen in Lincolnshire and the county of Warwick; and Anthony Woodville wrote word that, if the king would but show himself among the forces he had raised near Coventry, all the gentry around would rise against the rebellious rabble. Seizing advantage of these tidings, borne to him by his own couriers, and eager to escape from the uncertain soldiery quartered at Olney, Edward, without waiting to consult even with the earl, sprang to horse, and his trumpets were the first signal of departure that he deigned to any one.

This want of ceremony displeased the pride of Warwick; but he made no complaint, and took his place by the king's side, when Edward said, shortly,

"Dear cousin, this is a time that needs all our energies. I ride towards Coventry, to give head and heart to the raw recruits I shall find there; but I pray you and the archbishop to use all means, in this immediate district, to raise fresh troops; for at your name armed men spring up from pasture and glebe, dyke and hedge. Join what troops you can collect in three days with mine at Coventry, and, ere the sickle is in the harvest, England shall be at peace. God speed you! Ho! there, gentlemen, away!—*à franc étrier!*"

Without pausing for reply—for he wished to avoid all questioning, lest Warwick might discover that it was to a Woodville that he was bound—the king put spurs to his horse, and, while his men were yet hurrying to and fro, rode on almost alone, and was a good mile out of the town before the force led by St. John and Roul de Fulke, and followed by Hastings, who held no command, overtook him.

"I misthink the king," said Warwick, gloomily, "but my word is pledged to the people, and it shall be kept!"

"A man's word is best kept, when his arm is the strongest," said the sententious archbishop; "yesterday you dispersed an army; to-day, raise one!"

Warwick answered not, but, after a moment's thought, beckoned to Marmaduke.

"Kinsman," said he, "spur on, with ten of my little company, to join the king. Report to me if any of the Woodvilles be in his camp near Coventry."

Whither shall I send the report?

"To my castle of Warwick!"

Marmaduke bowed his head, and accustomed to the brevity of the earl's speech, proceeded to the task enjoined him. Warwick next summoned his second squire.

"My lady and her children," said he, "are on their way to Middleham. This paper will instruct you of their progress. Join them with all the rest of my troop, except my heralds and trumpeters; and say that I shall meet them ere long at Middleham."

"It is a strange way to raise an army," said the archbishop, drily, "to begin by getting rid of all the force one possesses!"

"Brother," answered the earl. "I would fain show my son-in-law, who may be the father of a line of kings, that a general may be helpless at the head of thousands, but that a man may stand alone who has the love of a nation."

"May Clarence profit by the lesson! Where is he all this while?"

"Abed," said the stout earl, with a slight accent of disdain; and then, in a softer voice, he added—"youth is ever luxurious. Better the slow man than the false one."

Leaving Warwick to discharge the duty enjoined him, we follow the dissimulating king.

CHAPTER VI.

What befalls King Edward on his Escape from Olney.

As soon as Edward was out of sight of the spire of Olney he slackened his speed, and beckoned Hastings to his side.

"Dear Will," said the king, "I have thought over thy counsel, and will find the occasion to make experiment thereof. But, methinks, thou wilt agree with me, that concessions come best from a king who has an army of his own. 'Fore Heaven! in the camp of a Warwick I have less power than a lieutenant! Now mark me. I go to head some recruits raised in haste near Coventry. The scene of contest must be in the northern counties. Wilt thou, for love of me, ride night and day, thorough brake, thorough brier, to Gloucester on the borders? Bid him march, if the Scot will let him, back to York; and if he cannot himself quit the borders, let him send what men can be spared, under thy banner. Failing this, raise through Yorkshire all the men-at-arms thou canst collect. But, above all, see Montagu. Him and his army secure at all hazards. If he demur, tell him his son shall marry his king's daughter, and wear the coronal of a duke. Ha! ha! a large bait for so large a fish! I see this is no casual outbreak, but a general convulsion of the realm; and the Earl of Warwick must not be the only man to smile or to frown back the angry elements."

"In this, *beau sire*," answered Hastings, "you speak as a king and a warrior should, and I will do my best to assert your royal motto—'*Modus et ordo.*' If I can but promise that your highness has for awhile dismissed the Woodville lords, rely upon it, that ere two months I will place under your truncheon an army worthy of the liege lord of hardy England."

"Go, dear Hastings, I trust all to thee!" answered the king.

The nobleman kissed his sovereign's extended hand, closed his visor, and motioning to his body squire to follow him, disappeared down a green lane, avoiding such broader thoroughfares as might bring him in contact with the officers left at Olney.

In a small village near Coventry, Sir Anthony Woodville had collected about two thousand men; chiefly composed of the tenants and vassals of the new nobility, who regarded the brilliant Anthony as their head. The leaders were gallant and ambitious gentlemen, as they who arrive at fortunes above their birth mostly are—but their vassals were little to be trusted. For in that day clanship was still strong, and these followers had been bred in allegiance to Lancastrian lords, whose confiscated estates were granted to the Yorkist favorites. The shout that welcomed the arrival of the king was therefore feeble and lukewarm—and, disconcerted by so chilling a reception, he dismounted, in less elevated spirits than those in which he had left Olney, at the pavilion of his brother-in-law.

The mourning dress of Anthony, his countenance saddened by the barbarous execution of his father and brother, did not tend to cheer the king.

But Woodville's account of the queen's grief and horror at the afflictions of her house, and of Jacquetta's indignation at the foul language which the report of her practices put into the popular mouth, served to endear to the king's mind the family that he considered unduly persecuted. Even in the coldest breasts affection is fanned by opposition, and the more the queen's kindred were assailed, the more obstinately Edward clung to them. By suiting his humor, by winking at his gallantries, by a submissive sweetness of temper, which soothed his own hasty moods and contrasted with the rough pride of Warwick and the peevish fickleness of Clarence, Elizabeth had completely wound herself iuto the king's heart. And the charming graces, the elegant accomplishments, of Anthony Woodville, were too harmonious with the character of Edward, who in all—except truth and honor—was the perfect model of the gay *gentilhomme* of the time, not to have become almost a necessary companionship. Indolent natures may be easily ruled—but they grow stubborn when their comforts and habits are interfered with. And the whole current of Edward's merry, easy life, seemed to him to lose flow and and sparkle, if the faces he loved best were banished or even clouded.

He was yet conversing with Woodville, and yet assuring him, that however he might temporize, he would never abandon the interests of his queen's kindred—when a gentleman entered aghast, to report that the Lords St. John and de Fulke, on hearing that Sir Anthony Woodville was in command of the forces, had, without even dismounting, left the camp, and carried with them their retainers, amounting to more than half of the little troop that rode from Olney.

"Let them go," said Edward, frowning; "a day shall dawn upon their headless trunks!"

"Oh, my king," said Anthony, now Earl of Rivers,—who, by far the least selfish of his house, was struck with remorse at the penalty Edward paid for his love marriage,—"now that your highness can relieve me of my command, let me retire from the camp. I would fain go, a pilgrim to the shrine of Compostella, to pray for my father's sins and my sovereign's weal."

"Let us first see what forces arrive from London," answered the king. "Richard ere long will be on the march from the frontiers, and whatever Warwick's resolves, Montagu, whose heart I hold in my hand, will bring his army to my side. Let us wait.

But the next day brought no reinforcements, nor the next; and the king retired betimes to his tent, in much irritation and perplexity; when at the dead of the night, he was startled from slumber by the tramp of horses, the sound of horns, the challenge of the sentinels—and, as he sprang from his couch, and hurried on his armor in alarm,—the Earl of Warwick abruptly entered. The earl's face was stern, but calm and sad; and Edward's brave heart beat loud as he gazed on his formidable subject.

"King Edward," said Warwick, slowly and mournfully, "you have deceived me! I promised to the commons the banishment of the Woodvilles, and to a Woodville you have flown."

"Your promise was given to rebels, with whom no faith can be held; and I passed from a den of mutiny to the camp of a loyal soldier."

"We will not now waste words, king," answered Warwick. "Please you to mount, and ride northward. The Scotch have gained great advantages on the marches. The Duke of Gloucester is driven backwards. All the Lancastrians in the North have risen. Margaret of Anjou is on the coast of Normandy,* ready to set sail at the first decisive victory of her adherents."

"I am with you," answered Edward; "and I rejoice to think that at last I may *meet* a foe. Hitherto it seems as if I had been chased by shadows. Now may I hope to grasp the form and substance of danger and of battle."

"A steed prepared for your grace awaits you."

"Whither ride we first?"

"To my castle of Warwick, hard by. At noon to-morrow all will be ready for our northward march."

Edward, by this time, having armed himself, strode from the tent into the open air. The scene was striking—the moon was extremely bright and the sky serene, but around the tent stood a troop of torch-bearers, and the red glare shone luridly upon the steel of the serried horsemen and the banners of the earl, in which the grim white bear was wrought upon an ebon ground, quartered with the dun bull, and crested in gold, with the eagle of the Monthermers. Far as the king's eye could reach, he saw but the spears of Warwick; while a confused hum in his own encampment told that the troops Anthony Woodville had collected were not yet marshalled into order—Edward drew back.

"And the Lord Anthony of Scales and Rivers," said he, hesitatingly.

"Choose, king, between the Lord Anthony of Scales and Rivers, and Richard Nevile!" answered Warwick, in a stern whisper.

Edward paused, and at that moment Anthony himself emerged from his tent (which adjoined the king's) in company with the Archbishop of York, who had rode thither in Warwick's train."

"My liege," said that gallant knight, putting his knee to the ground, "I have heard from the archbishop the new perils that await your highness, and I grieve sorely that, in this strait, your counsellors deem it meet to forbid me the glory of fighting or falling by your side! I know too well the unhappy odium attached to my house and name in the northern parts, to dispute the policy which ordains my absence from your armies. Till these feuds are over, I crave your royal leave to quit England, and perform my pilgrimage to the sainted shrine of Compostella."

A burning flush passed over the king's face, as he raised his brother-in-law, and clasped him to his bosom.

"Go or stay, as you will, Anthony!" said he, "but let these proud men know that neither time nor absence can tear you from your king's heart. But envy must have its hour! Lord Warwick, I attend you, but, it seems, rather as your prisoner than your liege."

Warwick made no answer: the king mounted, and waved his hand to Anthony. The torches tossed to and fro, the horns sounded, and in a silence, moody and resentful on either part, Edward and his terrible subject rode on to the towers of Warwick.

The next day the king beheld with astonishment, the immense force that, in a time so brief, the earl had collected round his standard.

From his casement, which commanded that lovely slope on which so many a tourist now gazes with an eye that seeks to call back the stormy and chivalric past, Edward beheld the earl on his renowned black charger, reviewing the thousands that, file on file, and rank on rank, lifted pike and lance in the cloudless sun.

"After all," muttered the king, "I can never make a new noble a great baron! And if in peace a great baron overshadows the throne, in time of war a great baron is a throne's bulwark! Gramercy, I had been mad to cast away such an army—an army fit for a king to lead! They serve Warwick now—but Warwick is less skilful in the martial art than I—and soldiers, like hounds, love best the most dexterous huntsman!"

CHAPTER VII.

How King Edward arrives at the Castle of Middleham.

On the ramparts of feudal Middleham, in

* At this time, Margaret was at Horfleurs.—Will. Wyre.

the same place where Anne had confessed to Isabel the romance of her childish love, again the sisters stood, awaiting the coming of their father and the king. They had only, with their mother reached Middleham two days before, and the preceding night an advanced guard had arrived at the castle to announce the approach of the earl with his royal comrade and visitor. From the heights, already, they beheld the long array winding in glorious order towards the mighty pile.

"Look!" exclaimed Isabel, "look! already methinks I see the white steed of Clarence. Yes! it is he! it is my George—my husband! The banner borne before, shows his device."

"Ah! happy Isabel!" said Anne, sighing, "what rapture to await the coming of him one loves!"

"My sweet Anne," returned Isabel, passing her arm tenderly round her sister's slender waist, "when thou hast conquered the vain folly of thy childhood, thou wilt find a Clarence of thine own. And yet," added the young duchess, smiling, "it must be the opposite of a Clarence, to be to thy heart what a Clarence is to mine. I love George's gay humor—thou lovest a melancholy brow. I love that charming weakness which supples to my woman will—thou lovest a proud nature that may command thine own. I do not respect George less, because I know my mind stronger than his own; but thou (like my gentle mother) wouldst have thy mate lord and chief in all things, and live from his life as the shadow from the sun. But where left you our mother?"

"In the oratory, at prayer!"

"She has been sad of late."

"The dark times darken her; and she ever fears the king's falseness or caprice will stir the earl up to some rash emprise. My father's letter, brought last night to her, contains something that made her couch sleepless."

"Ha!" exclaimed the duchess, eagerly, "my mother confides in thee more than me. Saw you the letter?"

"No."

"Edward will make himself unfit to reign," said Isabel, abruptly. "The barons will call on him to resign; and then—and *then*, Anne—sister Anne,—Warwick's daughters cannot be born to be simple subjects!"

"Isabel, God temper your ambition! Oh! curb it—crush it down! Abuse not your influence with Clarence. Let not the brother aspire to the brother's crown."

"Sister, a king's diadem covers all the sins schemed in the head that wins it!"

As the duchess spoke, her eyes flashed and her form dilated. Her beauty seemed almost terrible.

The gentle Anne gazed and shuddered; but ere she found words to rebuke, the lovely shape of the countess-mother was seen moving slowly towards them. She was dressed in her robes of state to receive her kingly guest; the vest fitting high to the throat, where it joined the ermine tippet, and thickly sown with jewels; the sleeves tight, with the second or over sleeves, that, loose and large, hung pendent and sweeping even to the ground; and the gown, velvet of cramousin, trimmed with ermine, made a costume not less graceful than magnificent, and which, when compressed, set off the exquisite symmetry of a form still youthful, and where flowing, added majesty to a beauty naturally rather soft and feminine than proud and stately. As she approached her children, she looked rather like their sister than their mother, as if Time, at least, shrunk from visiting harshly one for whom such sorrows were reserved!

The face of the countess was so sad in its aspect of calm and sweet resignation, that even the proud Isabel was touched; and kissing her mother's hand, she asked, "If any ill tidings preceded her father's coming?"

"Alas, my Isabel, the times themselves are bad tidings! Your youth scarcely remembers the days when brother fought against brother, and the son's sword rose against the father's breast. But I, recalling them, tremble to hear the faintest murmur that threatens a civil war." She paused, and forcing a smile to her lips, added, "Our woman fears must not, however, sadden our lords with an unwelcome countenance; for men, returning to their hearths, have a right to a wife's smile; and so, Isabel, thou and I, wives both, must forget the morrow in to-day. Hark! the trumpets sound near and nearer—let us to the hall."

Before, however, they had reached the castle, a shrill blast rang at the outer gate. The portcullis was raised; the young Duke of Clarence, with a bridegroom's impatience, spurred alone through the gloomy arch, and Isabel, catching sight of his countenance, lifted towards the ramparts, uttered a cry and waved her hand. Clarence heard and saw, leapt from his steed, and had clasped Isabel to his breast, almost before Anne or the countess had recognized the new comer.

Isabel, however, always stately, recovered in an instant from the joy she felt at her lord's return, and gently escaping his embrace, she glanced with a blush towards the battlements crowded with retainers; Clarence caught and interpreted the look.

"Well, *belle mère*," he said, turning to the countess—"and if yon faithful followers *do* witness with what glee a fair bride inspires a returning bridegroom—is there cause for shame in this cheek of damascene?"

"Is the king still with my father?" asked Isabel hastily, and interrupting the countess's reply.

"Surely, yes; and hard at hand. And pardon me that I forgot, dear lady, to say that my royal brother has announced his intention of addressing the principal officers of the army in Middleham Hall. This news gave me fair excuse for hastening to you and Isabel."

"All is prepared for his highness," said the countess, "save our own homage. We must quicken our steps—come Anne—

The countess took the arm of the younger sister, while the duchess made a sign to Clarence,—he lingered behind, and Isabel drawing him aside, asked—

"Is my father reconciled to Edward!"

"No—nor Edward to him."

"Good! The king has no soldiers of his own amidst yon armed train?"

"Save a few of Anthony Woodville's recruits—none. Raoul de Fulke and St. John have retired to their towers in sullen dudgeon. But have you no softer questions for my return, *bella mia?*"

"Pardon me—many—my *king*."

"*King!*"

"What other name should the successor of Edward IV. bear?"

"Isabel," said Clarence, in great emotion, "What is it you would tempt me to? Edward IV. spares the life of Henry VI., and shall Edward IV.'s brother conspire against his own?"

"Saints forefend!" exclaimed Isabel—"can you so wrong my honest meaning? O George! can you conceive that your wife—Warwick's daughter—harbors the thought of murder? No! surely the career before you seems plain and spotless! Can Edward reign? Deserted by the barons, and wearing away even my father's long credulous love; odious! except in luxurious and unwarlike London, to all the commons—how reign? What other choice left? none—save Henry of Lancaster or George of York."

"Were it so," said the weak duke, and yet he added, falteringly—"believe me, Warwick meditates no such changes in my favor."

"Time is a rapid ripener," answered Isabel—"but hark, they are lowering the drawbridge for our guests."

CHAPTER VIII.

The Ancients rightly gave to the Goddess of Eloquence—a Crown.

THE lady of Warwick stood at the threshold of the porch, which in the inner side of the broad quadrangle, admitted to the apartments used by the family; and, heading the mighty train that, line after line, emerged through the grim jaws of the arch, came the earl on his black destrier, and the young king.

Even where she stood, the anxious *Châtelaine* beheld the moody and gloomy air with which Edward glanced around the strong walls of the fortress, and up to the battlements that bristled with the pikes and sallets of armed men, who looked on the pomp below, in the silence of military discipline.

"Oh, Anne!" she whispered to her youngest daughter, who stood beside her—"what are women worth in the strife of men? Would that our smiles could heal the wounds which a taunt can make in a proud man's heart!"

Anne, affected and interested by her mother's words, and with a secret curiosity to gaze upon the man who ruled on the throne of the prince she loved, came nearer and more in front, and suddenly, as he turned his head, the king's regard rested upon her intent eyes and blooming face.

"Who is that fair donzell, cousin of Warwick?" he asked.

"My daughter, sire."

"Ah! your youngest!—I have not seen her since she was a child."

Edward reined in his charger, and the earl threw himself from his selle, and held the king's stirrup to dismount. But he did so with a haughty and unsmiling visage. "I would be the first, sire," said he, with a slight emphasis, and as if excusing to himself his condescension—"to welcome to Middleham the son of Duke Richard."

"And your suzerain, my lord earl," added Edward, with no less proud a meaning, and leaning his hand lightly on Warwick's shoulder, he dismounted slowly. "Rise, lady," he said, raising the countess, who knelt at the porch—"and you too, fair demoiselle. Pardieu,—we envy the knee that hath knelt to *you.*" So saying, with royal graciousness, he took the countess's hand, and they entered the hall as the musicians, in the gallery raised above, rolled forth their stormy welcome.

The archbishop, who had followed close to Warwick and the king, whispered now to his brother—

"Why would Edward address the captains?"

"I know not."

"He hath made himself familiar with many in the march."

"Familiarity with a steel casque better becomes a king than waisall with a greasy flat-cap."

"You do not fear lest he seduce from the White Bear its retainers?"

"As well fear that he can call the stars from their courses around the sun."

While these words were interchanged, the countess conducted the king to a throne-chair, raised upon the dais, by the side of which were placed two seats of state, and, from the dais at the same time, advanced the Duke and Duchess of Clarence. The king prevented their kneeling, and kissed Isabel slightly and gravely on the forehead. "Thus, noble lady, I greet the entrance of the Duchess of Clarence into the royalty of England."

Without pausing for reply, he passed on and seated himself on the throne, while Isabel and her husband took possession of the state chairs on either hand. At a gesture of the king's, the countess and Anne placed themselves on seats less raised, but still upon the dais. But now as Edward sate, the hall grew gradually full of lords and knights who commanded in Warwick's train, while the earl and the archbishop stood mute in the centre, the one armed *cap-à-pie,* leaning on his sword, the other with his arms folded in his long robes.

The king's eye, clear, steady, and majestic, roved round that martial audience, worthy to be a monarch's war-council, and not one of whom marched under a monarch's banner! Their silence, their discipline, the splendor of their arms, the greater splendor of their noble names, contrasted painfully with the little mutinous camp of Olney, and the surly untried recruits of Anthony Woodville. But Edward, whose step, whose form, whose aspect, proclaimed the man conscious of his rights to be lord of all, betrayed not to those around him the kingly pride, the lofty grief that swelled within his heart. Still seated, he raised his left hand to command silence; with the right he replaced his plumed cap upon his brow.

"Lords and gentlemen," he said (arrogating to himself at once, as a thing of course, that gorgeous following), "we have craved leave of our host to address to you some words—words which it pleases a king to utter, and which may not be harsh to the ears of a loyal subject. Nor will we, at this great current of unsteady fortune, make excuse, noble ladies, to you, that we speak of war to knighthood, which is ever the sworn defender of the daughter and the wife:—the daughters and the wife of our cousin, Warwick, have too much of hero-blood in their blue veins to grow pale at the sight of heroes. Comrades in arms! thus far towards our foe upon the frontiers we have marched, without a sword drawn or an arrow launched from an archer's bow. We believe that a blessing settles on the head of a true king, and that the trumpet of a good angel goes before his path, announcing the victory which awaits him. Here, in the hall of the Earl of Warwick, our captain-general, we thank you for your cheerful countenance, and your loyal service; and here, as befits a king, we promise to you those honors *a king alone* worthily can bestow." He paused, and his keen eye glanced from chief to chief as he resumed: "We are informed that certain misguided and traitor lords have joined the Rose of Lancaster. Whoever so doth is attainted, life and line, evermore! His lands and dignities are forfeit to enrich and to ennoble the men who strike for me. Heaven grant I may have foes eno' to reward all my friends! To every baron who owns Edward IV. king, (ay, and not king in name—king in banquet and in bower—but leader and captain in the war,) I trust to give a new barony—to every knight a new knight's fee—to every yeoman a hyde of land—to every soldier a year's pay. What more I can do, let it be free for any one to suggest—for my domains of York are broad, and my heart is larger still!"

A murmur of applause and reverence went round. Vowed, as those warriors were, to the earl, they felt that A MONARCH was amongst them.

"What say you, then? We are ripe for glory. Three days will we halt at Middleham, guest to our noble subject."

"Three days, sire!" repeated Warwick, in a voice of surprise.

"Yes; and this, fair cousin, and ye, lords and gentlemen, is my reason for the delay. I have dispatched Sir William, Lord de Hastings, to the Duke of Gloucester, with command to join us here—(the archbishop started, but instantly resumed his earnest, placid, aspect) to the Lord Montagu, Earl of Northumberland, to muster all the vassals of our shire of York. As three streams that dash into the ocean, shall our triple army meet and rush to the war. Not even, gentlemen, not even to the great Earl of Warwick will Edward IV. be so beholden for roiaulme and renown, as to march but a companion to the conquest. If ye were raised in Warwick's name, not mine—why, be it so! I envy him such friends; but I will have an army of mine own, to show mine English soldiery how a Plantagenet battles for his crown. Gentlemen, ye are dismissed to your repose. In three days we march! and if any of you know in these fair realms the man, be he of York or Lancaster, more fit to command brave subjects than he who now addressss you, I say to that man—turn rein, and leave us! Let tyrants and cowards enforce reluctant service, *my* crown was won by the hearts of my people! Girded by those hearts, let me reign—or, mourned by them, let me fall! So God and St. George favor me as I speak the truth!"

And as the king ceased, he uncovered his head, and kissed the cross of his sword. A thrill went through the audience. Many were there, disaffected to his person, and whom Warwick's influence alone could have roused to arms; but, at the close of an address, spirited and royal in itself, and borrowing thousand-fold effect by the voice and mien of the speaker, no feeling but that of enthusiastic loyalty, of almost tearful admiration, was left in those steed-clad breasts.

As the king lifted on high the cross of his sword, every blade leapt from its scabbard, and glittered in the air; and the dusty banners in the hall waved, as to a mighty blast, when, amidst the rattle of armor, burst forth the universal cry—"Long live Edward IV.! Long live the king!"

The sweet countess, even amidst the excitement, kept her eyes anxiously fixed on Warwick, whose countenance, however, shaded by the black plumes of his casque, though the visor was raised, revealed nothing of his mind. Her daughters were more powerfully affected; for Isabel's intellect was not so blinded by her ambition, but that the kingliness of Edward forced itself upon her with a might and solemn weight, which crushed, for the moment, her aspiring hopes—Was *this* the man unfit to reign? *This* the man voluntarily to resign a crown? *This* the man whom George of Clarence, without fratricide, could succeed? No!—*there*, spoke the soul of the First and the Third Edward! There, shook the mane, and there, glowed the eye, of the indomitable lion of the august Plantagenets! And the same conviction, rousing softer and holier sorrow, sate on the heart of Anne: she saw, as for the first time, clearly before her, the awful foe with whom her ill-omened and beloved prince had to struggle for his throne. In contrast beside that form, iu the prime of manly youth—a giant in its strength, a god in its beauty—rose the delicate shape of the melancholy boy who, afar in exile, coupled in his dreams the sceptre and the bride! By one of those mysteries which magnetism seeks to explain, in the strong intensity of her emotions, in the tremor of her shaken nerves, fear seemed to grow prophetic. A stream as of blood rose up from the dizzy floors. The image of her young prince, bound and friendless, stood before the throne of that warrior-king. In the waving glitter of the countless swords raised on high, she saw the murderous blade against the boy-heir of Lancaster descend—descend! Her passion, her terror, at the spectre which fancy thus evoked, seized and overcame her; and ere the last hurrah sent its hollow echo to the raftered roof, she sank from her chair to the ground, hueless and insensible as the dead.

The king had not without design permitted the unwonted presence of the woman in this warlike audience. Partly because he was not unaware of the ambitious spirit of Isabel, partly because he counted on the affection shown to his boyhood by the countess, who was said to have singular influence over her lord, but principally because in such a presence he trusted to avoid all discussion and all questioning, and to leave the effect of his eloquence, in which he excelled all his contemporaries, Gloucester alone excepted, single and unimpaired; and, therefore, as he rose, and returned with a majestic bend the acclamation of the warriors, his eye now turned towards the chairs, where the ladies sat, and he was the first to perceive the swoon of the fair Anne.

With the tender grace that always characterized his service to women, he descended promptly from his throne, and raised the lifeless form in his stalwart arms; and Anne, as he bent over her, looked so strangely lovely, in her marble stillness, that even in that hour a sudden thrill shot through a heart always susceptible to beauty, as the harp string to the breeze.

"It is but the heat, lady," said he to the alarmed countess, "and let me hope that interest which my fair kinswoman may take in the fortunes of Warwick and of York, *hitherto* linked together——"

"May they ever be so!" said Warwick, who, on seeing his daughter's state had advanced hastily to the dais; and, moved by the king's words, his late speech, the evils that surrounded his throne, the gentleness shown to the beloved Anne, forgetting resentment and ceremony alike, he held out his mailed hand. The king, as he resigned Anne to her mother's arms, grasped with soldierly frankness, and with the ready wit of the cold intellect which reigned beneath the warm manner, the hand thus extended, and holding still that iron gauntlet in his own ungloved and jewelled fingers, he advanced to the verge of the dias, of which, in the confusion occasioned by Anne's swoon, the principal officers had crowded, and cried aloud—

"Behold! Warwick and Edward, thus hand in hand, as they stood when the clarions sounded the charge at Touton! and that link, what swords, forged on a mortal's anvil, can rend or sever?"

In an instant, every knee, there, knelt; and Edward exultingly beheld, that what before had been allegiance to the earl was now only homage to the king."

CHAPTER IX.

Wedded Confidence and Love—The Earl and the Prelate—The Prelate and the King—Schemes—Wiles—And the Birth of a dark thought destined to eclipse a Sun.

WHILE, preparatory to the banquet, Edward, as was then the daily classic custom, relaxed his fatigues, mental or bodily, in the hospitable bath, the archbishop sought the closet of the earl.

"Brother," said he, throwing himself with some petulance into the only chair the room, otherwise splendid, contained—"when you left me, to seek Edward in the camp of Anthony Woodville, what was the understanding between us?"

"I know of none," answered the earl, who, having doffed his armor, and dismissed his squires, leaned thoughtfully against the wall, dressed for the banquet, with the exception of the short surcoat, which lay glittering on the tabouret.

"You know of none? Reflect! Have you brought hither Edward as a guest or as a prisoner?"

The earl knit his brows—"A prisoner, archbishop!"

The prelate regarded him with a cold smile.

"Warwick, you who would deceive no other man, now seek to deceive yourself." The earl drew back, and his hardy countenance grew a shade paler. The prelate resumed—"You have carried Edward from his camp, and severed him from his troops; you have placed him in the midst of your own followers—you have led him, chafing and resentful all the way, to this impregnable keep; and you now pause, amazed by the grandeur of your captive; a man who leads to his home a tiger—a spider who has entangled a hornet in its web!"—

"Nay, reverend brother," said the earl, calmly, "ye churchmen never know what passes in the hearts of those who feel and do not scheme. When I learned that the king had fled to the Woodvilles—that he was bent upon violating the pledge given in his name to the insurgent commons; I vowed that he should redeem my honor and his own, or that for ever, I would quit his service. And here, within these walls which sheltered his childhood I trusted, and trust still, to make one last appeal to his better reason."

"For all that, men now, and history hereafter, will consider Edward as your captive."

"To living men, my words and deeds can clear themselves; and as for history, let clerks and scholars fool themselves in the lies of parchment. He who has *acted* history, despises the gownsmen who sit in cloistered ease, and write about what they know not." The earl paused, and then continued—"I confess, however, that I have had a scheme. I have wished to convince the king how little his mush-room lords can bestead him in the storm; and that he holds his crown only from his barons and his people."

"That is, from the Lord Warwick!"

"Perhaps I *am* the personation of both seignorie and people; But I design this solely for his welfare. Ah, the gallant prince—how well he bore himself to-day!"

"Ay, when stealing all hearts from thee to him."

"And, *Vive Dieu*, I never loved him so well as when he did! Methinks it was for a day like this that I reared his youth and achieved his crown. Oh, priest—priest, thou mistakest me. I am rash, hot, haughty, hasty; and I love not to bow my knees to a man because they call him king, if his life be vicious and his word be false. But, could Edward be ever as to-day, then, indeed should I hail a sovereign whom a baron may reverence and a soldier serve!"

Before the archbishop could reply, the door gently opened, and the countess appeared. Warwick seemed glad of the interruption; he turned quickly—"And how fares my child?"

"Recovered from her strange swoon, and ready to smile at thy return. Oh, Warwick, thou art reconciled to the king!"

"That glads thee, sister?" said the archbishop.

"Surely. Is it not for my lord's honor?"

"May he find it so!" said the prelate, and he left the room.

"My priest-brother is chafed," said the earl, smiling. "Pity he was not born a trader he would have made a shrewd hard bargain.—Verily our priests burn the Jews out of envy! Ah, *m'amie*, how fair thou art to-day. Methinks even Isabel's cheek less blooming." And the warrior drew the lady towards him and smoothed her hair, and tenderly kissed her brow. "My letter vexed thee, I know, for thou lovest Edward, and blamest me not for my love to him. It is true that he hath paltered with me, and that I had stern resolves, not against the crown, but to leave him to his fate, and in these halls to resign my charge. But while he spoke, and while he looked, methought I saw his mother's face, and heard his dear father's tones, and the past rushed over me, and all wrath was gone. Sonless myself, why would he not be my son?" The earl's voice trembled, and the tears stood in his dark eyes.

"Speak thus, dear lord, to Isabel, for I fear her over-vaulting spirit——"

"Ah—had Isabel been his wife!" he paused and moved away. Then, as if impatient to escape the thoughts that tended to an ungracious recollection, he added—"and now, sweetheart—these slight fingers have ofttimes buckled on my mail, let them place on my breast this badge of St. George's chivalry; and, if angry thoughts return, it shall remind me that the day on which I wore it first, Richard of York said to his young Edward, 'Look to that star, boy, if ever, in cloud and trouble, thou wouldst learn what safety dwells in the heart which never knew deceit!'"

During the banquet, the king, at whose table sate only the Duke of Clarence and the earl's family, was gracious as day to all, but especially to the Lady Anne; attributing her sudden illness to some cause not unflattering to himself, her beauty, which somewhat resembled that of the queen, save that it had more advantage of expression and of youth, was precisely of the character he most admired. Even her timidity, and the reserve with which she answered him, had their charm; for like many men, themselves of imperious nature and fiery will, he preferred even imbecility in a woman to whatever was energetic or determined; and hence, perhaps, his indifference to the more dazzling beauty of Isabel. After the feast, the numerous demoiselles, highborn and fair, who swelled the more than regal train of the countess, were assembled in the long gallery, which was placed in the third story of the castle, and served for the principal state apartment. The dance began; but Isabel excused herself from the Pavon, and the king led out the reluctant and melancholy Anne.

The proud Isabel, who had never forgiven Edward's slight to herself, resented deeply his evident admiration of her sister, and conversed apart with the archbishop, whose subtle craft easily drew from her lips confessions of an ambition higher even than his own. He neither encouraged nor dissuaded; he thought there were things more impossible than the accession of Clarence to the throne, but he was one who never plotted,—save for himself and for the church.

As the revel waned, the prelate approached the earl, who, with that remarkable courtesy which charmed those below his rank, and contrasted with his haughtiness to his peers, had well played amongst his knights the part of host, and said, in a whisper, "Edward is in a happy mood—let us lose it not. Will you trust me to settle all differences, ere he sleep? Two proud men can never agree without a third of a gentler temper."

"You are right," said Warwick, smiling, "yet the danger is, that I should rather concede too much, than be too stubborn. But look you; all I demand is, satisfaction to mine own honor, and faith to the army I disbanded in the king's name."

"*All!*" muttered the archbishop, as he turned away, "but that *all* is everything to provoke quarrel for you, and nothing to bring power to *me!*"

The earl and the archbishop attended the king to his cnamber, and after Edward was served with the parting refection, or livery, the earl said, with his most open smile—"Sire, there are yet affairs between us; whom will you confer with—me or the archbishop?"

"Oh! the archbishop, by all means fair cousin," cried Edward, no less frankly, "for if you and I are left alone, the Saints help both of us!—when flint and steel meet, fire flies and the house may burn."

The earl half smiled at the candor—half sighed at the levity—of the royal answer, and silently left the room. The king, drawing round him his loose dressing robe, threw himself upon the gorgeous coverlid of the bed, and lying at lazy length, motioned to the prelate to seat himself at the foot. The archbishop obeyed. Edward raised himself on his elbow, and, by the light of seven gigantic tapers, set in sconces of massive silver, the priest and the king gravely gazed on each other, without speaking.

At last, Edward bursting into his hale, clear, silvery laugh, said, "Confess, dear sir and cousin—confess that we are like two skilful masters of Italian fence, each fearing to lay himself open by commencing the attack."

"Certes," quoth the archbishop, "your grace over-estimates my vanity, in opining that I deemed myself equal to so grand a duello. If there were dispute between us, I should only win by baring my bosom."

The king's bow-like lip curved with a slight sneer, quickly replaced by a serious and earnest expression—"Let us leave word-making, and to the point, George. Warwick is displeased because I will not abandon my wife's kindred; you, with more reason, because I have taken from your hands the chancellor's great seal—"

"For myself, I humbly answer that your grace errs. I never coveted other honors than those of the church."

"Ay," said Edward, keenly examining the young prelate's smooth face, "is it so? Yes, now I begin to comprehend thee. What offence have I given to the church? Have I suffered the law too much to sleep against the Lollards? If so, blame Warwick."

"On the contrary, sire, unlike other priests, I have ever deemed that persecution heals no schism. Blow not dying embers. Rather do I think of late that too much severity hath helped to aid, by Lollard bows and pikes, the late rising. My lady, the queen's mother, unjustly accused of witchcraft, hath sought to clear herself, and perhaps too zealously, in exciting your grace against that invisible giant—ycleped heresy."

"Pass on," said Edward. "It is not then

indifference to the ecclesia that you complain of. Is it neglect of the ecclesiastic? Ha! ha! you and I, though young, know the colors that make up the patchwork world. Archbishop, I love an easy life, if your brother and his friends will but give me *that*, let them take all else. Again, I say, to the point,—I cannot banish my lady's kindred, but I will bind your house still more to mine. I have a daughter, failing male issue, the heiress to my crown. I will betroth her to your nephew, my beloved Montagu's son. They are children yet, but their ages not unsuited. And when I return to London, young Nevile shall be Duke of Bedford, a title hitherto reserved to the royal race.* Let that be a pledge of peace between the queen's mother, bearing the same honors, and the house of Nevile, to which they pass."

The cheek of the archbishop flushed with proud pleasure; he bowed his head, and Edward, ere he could answer, went on,—"Warwick is already so high that, *pardie*, I have no other step to give him save my throne itself, and God's truth, I would rather be Lord Warwick than King of England! But for you—listen—our only English cardinal is old and sickly—whenever he pass to Abraham's bosom, who but you should have the suffrage of the holy college? Thou knowest that I am somewhat in the good favor of the sovereign pontiff. Command me to the utmost. Now, George, are we friends?"

The archbishop kissed the gracious hand extended to him, and, surprised to find, as by magic, all his schemes frustrated by sudden acquiescence in the objects of them all, his voice faltered with real emotion as he gave vent to his gratitude. But abruptly he checked himself, his brow lowered, and with a bitter remembrance of his brother's plain, blunt sense of honor, he said, "Yet, alas, my liege, in all this there is nought to satisfy our stubborn host."

"By dear Saint George and my father's head!" exclaimed Edward, reddening, and starting to his feet, "what would the man have?"

"You know," answered the archbishop, "that Warwick's pride is only roused when he deems his honor harmed. Unhappily, as he thinks, by your grace's full consent, he pledged himself to the insurgents of Olney to the honorable dismissal of the lords of the Woodville race. And unless this be conceded, I fear me that all else he will reject, and the love between ye can be but hollow!"

Edward took but three strides across the chamber, and then halted opposite the archbishop, and laid both hands on his shoulders, as, looking him full in the face, he said, "Answer me frankly, am I a prisoner in these towers, or not?"

"Not, sire."

"You palter with me, priest. I have been led hither against my will. I am almost without an armed retinue. I am at the earl's mercy. This chamber might be my grave, and this couch my bed of death."

"Holy mother! Can you think so of Warwick? Sire, you freeze my blood."

"Well, then, if I refuse to satisfy Warwick's pride, and disdain to give up loyal servants to rebel insolence, what will Warwick do? Speak out, archbishop."

"I fear me, sire, that he will resign all office, whether of peace or war. I fear me that the goodly army now at sleep within and around these walls will vanish into air, and that your highness will stand alone amidst new men, and against the disaffection of the whole land!"

Edward's firm hand trembled. The prelate continued, with a dry, caustic smile—

"Sire, Sir Anthony Woodville, now Lord Rivers, has relieved you of all embarrassment; no doubt, my Lord Dorset and his kinsmen will be chevaliers enough to do the same. The Duchess of Bedford will but suit the decorous usage to retire awhile into privacy, to mourn her widowhood. And when a year is told, if these noble persons re-appear at court, your word and the earl's will at least have been kept."

"I understand thee," said the king, half laughing; "but I have my pride as well as Warwick. To concede this point is to humble the conceder."

"I have thought how to soothe all things, and without humbling either party. Your grace's mother is dearly beloved by Warwick, and revered by all. Since your marriage she hath lived secluded from all state affairs. As

* And indeed there was but one Yorkist duke then in England out of the royal family—viz., the young boy, Buckingham, who afterwards vainly sought to bend the Ulysses bow of Warwick against Richard III.

so nearly akin to Warwick—so deeply interested in your grace—she is a fitting mediator in all disputes. Be they left to her to arbitrate."

"Ah! cunning prelate, thou knowest how my proud mother hates the Woodvilles—thou knowest how her judgment will decide."

"Perhaps so; but at least your grace will be spared all pain and all abasement."

"Will Warwick consent to this?"

"I trust so."

"Learn, and report to me. Enough for to-night's conference."

Edward was left alone, and his mind ran rapidly over the field of action open to him."

"I have half won the earl's army," he thought; "but it would be to lose all hold in their hearts again, if they knew that these unhappy Woodvilles were the cause of a second breach between us. Certes, the Lancastrians are making strong head! Certes, the times must be played with and appeased! And yet these poor gentlemen love me after my own fashion, and not with the bear's hug of that intolerable earl. How came the grim man by so fair a daughter? Sweet Anne! I caught her eye often fixed on me, and with a soft fear which my heart beat loud to read aright. Verily, this is the fourth week I have passed without hearing a woman's sigh! What marvel that so fair a face enamours me! Would that Warwick made her his ambassador; and yet it were all over with the Woodvilles if he did! These men know not how to manage me, and well-a-day, that task is easy eno' to women!"

He laughed gaily to himself as he thus concluded his soliloquy, and extinguished the tapers. But rest did not come to his pillow; and after tossing to and fro for some time in vain search for sleep, he rose and opened his casement to cool the air which the tapers had overheated. In a single casement, in a broad turret, projecting from an angle in the building, below the tower in which his chamber was placed, the king saw a solitary light burning steadily. A sight so unusual at such an hour, surprised him. "Peradventure, the wily prelate," thought he. "Cunning never sleeps." But a second look showed him the very form that chased his slumbers. Beside the casement, which was partially open, he saw the soft profile of the Lady Anne; it was bent downwards; and what with the clear moonlight, and the lamp within her chamber, he could see distinctly that she was weeping. "Ah! Anne," muttered the amorous king, "would that I were by to kiss away those tears!" While yet the unholy wish murmured on his lips, the lady rose. The fair hand, that seemed almost transparent in the moonlight, closed the casement; and though the light lingered for some minutes ere it left the dark walls of the castle without other sign of life than the step of the sentry, Anne was visible no more.

"Madness—madness—madness!" again murmured the king. "These Neviles are fatal to me in all ways—in hatred or in love!"

BOOK EIGHTH.

WHICH THE LAST LINK BETWEEN KING-MAKER AND KING SNAPS ASUNDER.

CHAPTER I.

The Lady Anne visits the Court.

IT was some weeks after the date of the events last recorded. The storm that hung over the destinies of King Edward was dispersed for the hour, though the scattered clouds still darkened the horizon: the Earl of Warwick had defeated the Lascastrians on the frontier,* and their leader had perished on the scaffold, but Edward's mighty sword had not shone in the battle. Chained by an attraction yet more powerful than slaughter, he had lingered at Middleham, while Warwick led his army to York; and when the earl arrived at the capital of Edward's ancestral duchy, he found that the able and active Hastings—having heard, even before he reached the Duke of Gloucester's camp, of Edward's apparent seizure by the earl and the march to Middleham—had deemed it best to halt at York, and to summon in all haste a council of such of the knights and barons, as either love to the king or envy to Warwick could collect. The report was general that Edward was detained against his will at Middleham, and this rumor Hastings gravely demanded Warwick, on the arrival of the latter at York, to disprove. The earl, to clear himself from a suspicion that impeded all his military movements, dispatched Lord Montagu to Middleham, who returned not only with the king, but the countess and her daughters, whom Edward, under pretence of proving the complete amity that existed between Warwick and himself, carried in his train. The king's appearance at York reconciled all differences. But he suffered Warwick to march alone against the enemy, and not till after the decisive victory, which left his reign for awhile without an open foe, did he return to London.

Thither the earl, by the advice of his friends, also repaired, and in a council of peers, summoned for the purpose, deigned to refute the rumors still commonly circulated by his foes, and not disbelieved by the vulgar, whether of his connivance at the popular rising, or his forcible detention of the king at Middleham. To this, agreeably to the council of the archbishop, succeeded a solemn interview of the heads of the houses of York and Warwick, in which the once fair Rose of Raby (the king's mother) acted as mediator and arbiter. The earl's word to the commons at Onley was ratified. Edward consented to the temporary retirement of the Woodvilles, though the gallant Anthony yet delayed his pilgrimage to Compostella. The vanity of Clarence was contented by the government of Ireland, but, under various pretenses, Edward deferred his brother's departure to that important post. A general amnesty was proclaimed, a parliament summoned, for the redress of popular grievances, and the betrothal of the king's daughter to Montagu's heir was proclaimed: the latter received the title of Duke of Bedford; and the whole land rejoiced in the recovered peace of the realm, the retirement of the Woodvilles and the reconciliation of the young king with his all-beloved subject. Never had the power of the Neviles seemed so secure—never did the throne of Edward appear so stable.

* Croyle, 552.

It was at this time that the king prevailed upon the earl and his countess to permit the Lady Anne to accompany the Duchess of Clarence in a visit to the palace of the Tower. The queen had submitted so graciously to the humiliation of her family, that even the haughty Warwick was touched and softened; and the visit of his daughter at such a time became a homage to Elizabeth, which it suited his chivalry to render. The public saw in this visit, which was made with great state and ceremony, the probability of a new and popular alliance. The archbishop had suffered the rumor of Gloucester's attachment to the Lady Anne to get abroad, and the young prince's return from the north was anxiously expected by the gossips of the day.

It was on this occasion that Warwick showed his gratitude for Marmaduke Nevile's devotion. "My dear and gallant kinsman," he said, "I forget not that when thou didst leave the king and the court for the discredited minister and his gloomy hall—I forget not that thou didst tell me of love to some fair maiden, which had not prospered according to thy merits. At least it shall not be from lack of lands, or of the gold spur, which allows the wearer to ride by the side of king or kaisar, that thou canst not choose thy bride as the heart bids thee. I pray thee, sweet cousin, to attend my child Anne to the court, where the king will show thee no ungracious countenance; but it is just to recompense thee for the loss of thy post in his highness's chamber. I hold the king's commission to make knights of such as can pay the fee, and thy lands shall suffice for the dignity. Kneel down, and rise up, Sir Marmaduke Nevile, Lord of the Manor of Borrodaile, with its woodlands and it farms, and may God and our lady render thee puissant in battle and prosperous in love!"

Accordingly, in his new rank, and entitled to ruffle it with the bravest, Sir Marmaduke Nevile accompanied the earl and the lady Anne to the palace of the tower.

As Warwick, leaving his daughter amidst the brilliant circle that surrounded Elizabeth, turned to address the king, he said, with simple and affected nobleness—

"Ah, my liege, if you needed a hostage of my faith, think that my heart is here, for verily its best blood were less dear to me than that slight girl,—the likeness of her mother, when her lips first felt the touch of mine!"

Edward's bold brow fell, and he blushed as he answered, "My Elizabeth will hold her as a sister. But, cousin, part you not now for the north?"

"By your leave, I go first to Warwick."

"Ah! you do not wish to approve of my seeming preparations against France?"

"Nay, your highness is not in earnest. I promised the commons that you would need no supplies for so thriftless a war."

"Thou knowest I mean to fulfil all thy pledges. But the country so swarms with disbanded soldiers, that it is politic to hold out to them a hope of service, and so let the clouds gradually pass away."

"Alack my liege!" said Warwick, gravely, "I suppose that a crown teaches the brow to scheme; but hearty peace or open war seems ever the best to me."

Edward smiled, and turned aside. Warwick glanced at his daughter, whom Elizabeth flatteringly caressed, stifled a sigh, and the air seemed lighter to the insects of the court as his proud crest bowed beneath the doorway, and, with the pomp of his long retinue, he vanished from the scene.

"And choose, fair Anne," said the queen, "choose from my ladies, whom you will have for your special train. We would not that your attendance should be less than royal."

The gentle Anne in vain sought to excuse herself from an honor at once arrogant and invidious, though too innocent to perceive the cunning so characteristic of the queen; for under the guise of a special compliment, Anne had received the royal request to have her female attendants chosen from the court, and Elizabeth now desired to force upon her a selection which could not fail to mortify those not preferred. But glancing timidly round the circle, the noble damsel's eye rested on one fair face, and in that face there was so much that awoke her own interest, and stirred up a fond and sad remembrance, that she passed involuntarily to the stranger's side, and artlessly took her hand. The high-born maidens, grouped around, glanced at each other with a sneer, and slunk back. Even the queen looked surprised, but recovering herself, inclined her head graciously, and said, "Do we read your meaning aright, Lady Anne, and would you this gentlewoman, Mistress Sibyll Warner, as one of your chamber?"

"Sibyll, ah, I knew that my memory failed me not," murmured Anne; and, after bowing assent to the queen, she said, "Do you not also recall, fair demoiselle, our meeting, when children, long years ago?"

"Well, noble dame,"* answered Sibyll. And as Anne turned, with her air of modest gentleness, yet of lofty birth and breeding, to explain to the queen that she had met Sibyll in earlier years, the king approached to monopolize his guest's voice and ear. It seemed natural to all present that Edward should devote peculiar attention to the daughter of Warwick and the sister of the Duchess of Clarence; and even Elizabeth suspected no guiltier gallantry in the subdued voice, the caressing manner, which her handsome lord adopted throughout that day, even to the close of the nightly revel,—towards a demoiselle too high (it might well appear) for licentious homage.

But Anne herself, though too guileless to suspect the nature of Edward's courtesy, yet shrunk from it in vague terror. All his beauty, all his fascination, could not root from her mind the remembrance of the exiled prince—nay, the brilliancy of his qualities made her the more averse to him. It darkened the prospects of Edward of Lancaster that Edward of York should wear so gracious and so popular a form. She hailed with delight the hour when she was conducted to her chamber, and dismissing gently the pompous retinue allotted to her, found herself alone with the young maiden whom she had elected to her special service.

"And you remember me, too, fair Sibyll?" said Anne, with her dulcet and endearing voice.

"Truly, who would not? for as you, then, noble lady, glided apart from the other children, hand in hand with the young prince, in whom all dreamed to see their future king—I heard the universal murmur of—a false prophecy!"

"Ah! and of what?" asked Anne.

"That in the hand the prince clasped, with his small rosy fingers—the hand of great Warwick's daughter—lay the best defence of his father's throne."

Anne's breast heaved, and her small foot began to mark strange characters on the floor.

"So," she said, musingly, "so, even here, amidst a new court, you forget not Prince Edward of Lancaster. Oh, we shall find hours to talk of the past days. But how, if your childhood was spent in Margaret's court, does your youth find a welcome in Elizabeth's?"

"Avarice and power had need of my father's science. He is a scholar of good birth, but fallen fortunes—even now, and even while night lasts, he is at work. I belonged to the train of her grace of Bedford, but when the duchess quitted the court, and the king retained my father in his own royal service, her highness the queen was pleased to receive me among her maidens. Happy that my father's home is mine—who else could tend him!"

"Thou art his only child?—He must love thee dearly?"

"Yet not as I love him—he lives in a life apart from all else that live. But, after all, preadventure it is sweeter to love than to be loved."

Anne, whose nature was singularly tender and womanlike, was greatly affected by this answer; she drew nearer to Sibyll; she twined her arm round her slight form, and kissed her forehead.

"Shall *I* love thee, Sibyll?" she said, with a girl's candid simplicity, "and wilt thou love me?"

"Ah, lady! there are so many to love thee; father, mother, sister—all the world;—the very sun shines more kindly upon the great!"

"Nay!" said Anne, with that jealousy of a claim to suffering, to which the gentler natures are prone, "I may have sorrows from which thou art free. I confess to thee, Sibyll, that something, I know not how to explain, draws me strangely towards thy sweet face. Marriage has lost me my only sister--for since Isabel is wed, she is changed to me—would that her place were supplied by thee! Shall I steal thee from the queen, when I depart? Ah! my mother—at least thou wilt love her! for, verily, to love my mother you have but to breathe the same air. Kiss me Sibyll."

Kindness, of late, had been strange to Sibyll, especially from her own sex, one of her own age; it came like morning upon the folded

* The title of Dame was at that time applied indiscriminately to ladies, whether married or single, if of high birth.

blossom. She threw her arms round the new friend that seemed sent to her from heaven; she kissed Anne's face and hands with grateful tears.

"Ah!" she said, at last, when she could command a voice still broken with emotion—"if I could ever serve—ever repay thee—though those gracious words were the last thy lips should ever deign to address to me!"

Anne was delighted; she had never yet found one to protect; she had never yet found one in whom thoroughly to confide. Gentle as her mother was, the distinction between child and parent was, even in the fond family she belonged to, so great in that day, that she could never have betrayed to the countess the wild weakness of her young heart.

The wish to communicate—to reveal—is so natural to extreme youth, and in Anne that disposition was so increased by a nature at once open and inclined to lean on others, that she had, as we have seen, sought a confidant in Isabel; but with her, even at the first, she found but the half contemptuous pity of a strong and hard mind; and lately, since Edward's visit to Middleham, the Duchess of Clarence had been so wrapt in her own imperious egotism and discontented ambition, that the timid Anne had not even dared to touch, with her, upon those secrets which it flushed her own bashful cheek to recall. And this visit to the court—this new, unfamiliar scene—this estrangement from all the old accustomed affections, had produced in her that sense of loneliness which is so irksome, till grave experience of real life accustoms us to the common lot. So with the exaggerated and somewhat morbid sensibility that belonged to her, she turned at once, and by impulse, to this sudden, yet graceful friendship. Here was one of her own age, one who had known sorrow, one whose voice and eyes charmed her; one who would not chide even folly; one, above all, who had seen her beloved prince, one associated with her fondest memories, one who might have a thousand tales to tell of the day when the outlaw-boy was a monarch's heir. In the childishness of her soft years, she almost wept at another channel for so much natural tenderness. It was half the woman gaining a woman-friend—half the child clinging to a new playmate.

"Ah, Sibyll!" she whispered, "do not leave me to-night—this strange place daunts me, and the figures on the arras seem so tall and spectre-like—and they say, the old tower is haunted.—Stay, dear Sibyll!"

And Sibyll stayed.

CHAPTER II.

The sleeping Innocence—The wakeful crime.

WHILE these charming girls thus innocently conferred; while, Anne's sweet voice running on in her artless fancies, they helped each other to undress; while hand in hand they knelt in prayer by the crucifix in the dim recess; while timidly they extinguished the light, and stole to rest; while, conversing in whispers, growing gradually more faint and low, they sank into guileless sleep;—the unholy king paced his solitary chamber, parched with the fever of the sudden and frantic passion, that swept away from a heart, in which every impulse was a giant, all the memories of honor, gratitude, and law.

The mechanism of this strong man's nature was that almost unknown to the modern time; it belonged to those earlier days which furnish to Greece the terrible legends Ovid has clothed in gloomy fire, which a similar civilization produced no less in the Middle Ages, whether of Italy or the North—that period when crime took a grandeur from its excess—when power was so great and absolute, that its girth burst the ligaments of conscience—when a despot was but the incarnation of WILL—when honor was indeed a religion, but its faith was valor, and it wrote its decalogue with the point of a fearless sword.

The youth of Edward IV. was as the youth of an ancient Titan—of an Italian Borgia; through its veins the hasty blood rolled as a devouring flame. This impetuous and fiery temperament was rendered yet more fearful by the indulgence of every intemperance; it fed on wine and lust: its very virtues strengthened its vices—its courage stifled every whisper of prudence—its intellect uninured to all discipline, taught it to disdain every obstacle to its desires. Edward could, indeed, as we have seen, be false and crafty—a temporizer—a dissimulator—but it was only as the tiger creeps, the better to spring, undetected on its prey. If detected, the cunning ceased, the daring rose, and the mighty savage had fronted ten thousand foes, secure in its fangs and talons, its bold heart, and its deadly spring. Hence, with all Edward's abilities, the astonishing levities and indiscretions of his younger years. It almost seemed, as we have seen him play fast and loose with the might of Warwick, and with that power, whether of barons or of people, which any other prince of half his talents would have trembled to arouse against an unrooted throne;—it almost seemed as if he loved to provoke a danger, for the pleasure it gave the brain to baffle, or the hand to crush it. His whole nature coveting excitement, nothing was left to the beautiful, the luxurious Edward, already wearied with pomp and pleasure, but what was unholy and forbidden. In his court were a hundred ladies, perhaps not less fair than Anne, at least of a beauty more commanding the common homage, but these he had only to smile on, with ease to win. No awful danger, no inexpiable guilt, attended those vulgar frailties, and therefore they ceased to tempt. But here the virgin guest, the daughter of his mightiest subject, the beloved treasure of the man whose hand had built a throne, whose word had dispersed an army,—here, the more the reason warned, the conscience started, the more the hell-born passion was aroused!

Like men of his peculiar constitution, Edward was wholly incapable of pure and steady love. His affection for his queen the most resembled that diviner affection; but when analyzed, it was composed of feelings widely distinct. From a sudden passion, not otherwise to be gratified, he had made the rashest sacrifices for an unequal marriage. His vanity, and something of original magnanimity, despite his vices, urged him to protect what he himself had raised,—to secure the honor of the subject who was honored by the king. In common with most rude and powerful natures, he was strongly alive to the affections of a father, and the faces of his children helped to maintain the influence of the mother. But in all this, we need scarcely say, that that true love, which is at once a passion and a devotion, existed not. Love with him cared not for the person loved, but solely for its own gratification; it was desire for possession—nothing more. But that desire was the will of a king who never knew fear or scruple; and, pampered by eternal indulgence, it was to the feeble lusts of common men what the storm is to the west wind. Yet still, as in the solitude of night he paced his chamber, the shadow of the great crime advancing upon his soul appalled even that dauntless conscience. He gasped for breath—his cheek flushed crimson, and the next moment grew deady pale. He heard the loud beating of his heart. He stopped still.

He flung himself on a seat, and covered his face with his hands, then starting up he exclaimed—"No—no! I cannot shut out that sweet face, those blue eyes, from my gaze. They haunt me to my destruction and her own. Yet why say destruction? If she love me, who shall know the deed; if she love me not, will she dare to reveal her shame? Shame!—nay, a king's embrace never dishonors. A king's bastard is a house's pride. All is still—the very moon vanishes from heaven. The noiseless rushes in the gallery give no echo to the footstep. Fie on me! Can a Plantagenet know fear?" He allowed himself no further time to pause; he opened the poor gently, and stole along the gallery. He knew well the chamber, for it was appointed by his command; and, besides the usual door from the corridor, a small closet conducted to a secret panel behind the arras. It was the apartment occupied, in her visits to the court, by the queen's rival, the Lady Elizabeth Lucy. He passed into the closet—he lifted the arras—he stood in that chamber which gratitude, and chivalry, and hospitable faith, should have made sacred as a shrine. And suddenly, as he entered, the moon, before hid beneath a melancholy cloud, broke forth in awful splendor, and her light rushed through the casement opposite his eye, and bathed the room with the beams of a ghostlier day.

The abruptness of the solemn and mournful glory scared him as the rebuking face of a living thing; a presence as if not of earth seemed to interpose between the victim and the guilt. It was, however, but for a moment that his step halted. He advanced: he drew aside the folds of the curtain heavy with tissue of gold, and the sleeping face of Anne lay hushed before him. It looked pale in the moonlight, but ineffably serene, and the smile on its lips seemed still sweeter than that which it wore awake. So fixed was his gaze—so ardently did his whole heart and being feed through his eyes upon that exquisite picture of innocence and youth, that he did not see for some moments that the sleeper was not alone. Suddenly an exclamation rose to his lips—he clenched his hand in jealous agony—he approached—he bent over—he heard the regular breathing which the dreams of guilt never know, and then, when he saw that pure and interlaced embrace—the serene yet somewhat melancholy face of Sibyll, which seemed hueless as marble in the moonlight—bending partially over that of Anne, as if, even in sleep, watchful,—both charming forms so linked and woven that the two seemed as one life, the very breath in each rising and ebbing with the other, the dark ringlets of Sibyll mingling with the auburn gold of Anne's luxuriant hair, and the darkness and the gold, tress with in tress, falling impartially over either neck, that gleamed like ivory beneath that common veil,—when he saw this twofold loveliness, the sentiment—the conviction of that mysterious defence which exisits in purity—thrilled like ice through his burning veins. In all his might of monarch and of man, he felt the awe of that unlooked-for protection—maidenhood sheltering maidenhood—innocence guarding innocence. The double virtue appalled and baffled him; and that slight arm which encircled the neck he would have perilled his realm to clasp, shielded his victim more effectually than the bucklers of all the warriors that ever gathered round the banner of the lofty Warwick. Night and the occasion be-friended him; but in vain. While Sibyll was there, Anne was saved. He ground his teeth, and muttered to himself. At that moment Anne turned restlessly. This movement disturbed the light sleep of her companion. She spoke half inaudibly, but the sound was as the hoot of shame in the ear of the guilty king. He let fall the curtain, and was gone. And if one who lived afterwards to hear, and to credit, the murderous doom which, unless history lies, closed the male line of Edward, had beheld the king stealing, felon-like, from the chamber, his step reeling to and fro the gallery floors—his face distorted by stormy passion—his lips white and murmuring—his beauty and his glory dimmed and humbled—the spectator might have half believed that while Edward gazed upon those harmless sleepers, A VISION OF THE TRAGEDY TO COME had stricken down his thought of guilt, and filled up its place with horror,—a vision of a sleep as pure—of two forms wrapped in an embrace as fond—of intruders meditating a crime scarce fouler than his own; and the sins of the father starting into grim corporeal shapes, to become the deathsmen of the sons!

CHAPTER III.

New Dangers to the House of York—And the King's Heart allies itself with Rebellion against the King's Throne.

OH! beautiful is the love of youth to youth, and touching the tenderness of womanhood to woman; and fair in the eyes of the happy sun is the waking of holy sleep, and the virgin kiss upon virgin lips smiling and murmuring the sweet "Good morrow!"

Anne was the first to wake; and as the bright winter morn, robust with frosty sunbeams, shone cheerily upon Sibyll's face, she was struck with a beauty she had not sufficiently observed the day before; for in the sleep of the young the traces of thought and care vanish, the aching heart is lulled in the body's rest, the hard lines relax into flexile ease, a softer, warmer bloom steals over the cheek, and, relieved from the stiff restraints of dress, the rounded limbs repose in a more alluring grace! Youth seems younger in its slumber, and beauty more beautiful, and purity more pure. Long and dark, the fringe of the eyelash rested upon the white lids, and the freshness of the parting pouted lips invited the sister kiss that wakened up the sleeper.

"Ah! lady," said Sibyll, parting her tresses from her dark blue eyes, "you are here—you are safe!—blessed be the saints and Our Lady—for I had a dream in the night that startled and appalled me."

"And my dreams were all blithe and golden," said Anne. "What was thine?"

"Methought you were asleep and in this chamber, and I not by your side, but watching you, at a little distance; and, lo! a horrible serpent glided from yon recess, and, crawling to your pillow, I heard its hiss, and strove to come to your aid, but in vain; a spell seemed in her own promotion to the queen's service, Sibyll could not but recognize the influence of her powerful lover. His tones now were tender, though grave and earnest. Surely, in the meeting he asked, all not comprehended would be explained. And so, with a light heart, she passed on.

Hastings sighed as his eye followed her from the room, and thus said he to himself—

"Were I the obscure gentlemen I once was, how sweet a lot would that girl's love choose to me from the urn of fate! But, oh! when we taste of power and greatness, and master the world's dark wisdom, what doth love shrink to?—an hour's bliss, and a life's folly." His delicate lip curled, and breaking from his soliloquy, he entered the king's closet. Edward was resting his face upon the palms of his hands, and his bright eyes dwelt upon vacant space, till they kindled into animation as they lighted on his favorite.

"Dear Will," said the king, "knowest thou that men say thou art bewitched?"

"*Beau sire*, often have men, when a sweet face hath captured thy great heart, said the same of thee!"

"It may be so, with truth, for, verily, love is the arch-devil's birth."

The king rose, and strode his chamber with a quick step; at last, pausing—

"Hastings," he said, "so thou lovest the multiplier's pretty daughter. She hath just left me. Art thou jealous?"

"Happily, your highness sees no beauty in locks that have the gloss of the raven, and eyes that have the hue of the violet."

"No, I am a constant man—constant to one idea of beauty in a thousand forms—eyes like the summer's light-blue sky, and locks like its golden sunbeams! But to set thy mind at rest, Will, know that I have but compassionated the sickly state of the scholar, whom thou prizest so highly; and I have placed thy fair Sibyll's chamber near her father's. Young Lovell says thou art bent on wedding the wizard's daughter."

"And if I were, *beau sire?*"

Edward looked grave.

"If thou wert, my poor Will, thou wouldst lose all the fame for shrewd wisdom which justifies thy sudden fortunes. No—no—thou art the flower and prince of my new seignorie—thou must mate thyself with a name and a barony that shall be worthy thy fame and thy prospects. Love beauty, but marry power, Will. In vain would thy king draw thee up, if a despised wife draw thee down!"

Hastings listened with profound attention to these words. The king did not wait for his answer, but added, laughingly—

"It is thine own fault, crafty gallant, if thou dost not end all her spells."

"What ends the spells of youth and beauty, *beau sire?*"

"Possession!" replied the king, in a hollow and muttered voice.

Hastings was about to answer, when the door opened, and the officer in waiting announced the Duke of Clarence.

"Ha!" said Edward, "George comes, to importune me for leave to depart to the government of Ireland, and I have to make him weet that I think my Lord Worcester a safer viceroy of the two!"

"Your highness will pardon me; but, though I deemed you too generous in the appointment, it were dangerous now to annul it."

"More dangerous to confirm it. Elizabeth has caused me to see the folly of a grant made over the malmsey—a wine, by the way, in which poor George swears he would be content to drown himself. Viceroy of Ireland! My father had that government, and once tasting the sweets of royalty, ceased to be a subject! No, no, Clarence ——"

"Can never meditate treason against a brother's crown. Has he the wit, or the energy, or the genius, for so desperate an ambition?"

"No; but he hath the vanity. And I will wager thee a thousand marks to a silver penny that my jester shall talk giddy Georgie into advancing a claim to be soldan of Egypt, or pope of Rome!"

CHAPTER IV.

The Foster Brothers.

SIR MARMADUKE NEVILE was sunning his bravery in the Tower Green, amidst the other idlers of the court, proud of the gold chain and the gold spurs which attested his new rank, and not grieved to have exchanged the solemn walls of Middleham for the gay delights, of the voluptuous palace, when, to his pleasure and surprise he perceived his foster-brother enter the gateway; and no sooner had Nicholas entered, than a bevy of the younger courtiers hastened eagerly towards him.

"Gramercy!" quoth Sir Marmaduke, to one of the bystanders, "what hath chanced to make Nick Alwyn a man of such note, that so many wings of satin and pile should flutter round him, like sparrows round an owl, which, by the Holy Rood, his wise face somewhat resembleth."

"Know you not that Master Alwyn, since he hath commenced trade for himself, hath acquired already the repute of the couthliest goldsmith in London? No dague-hilts—no buckles are to be worn, save those that he fashions; and—an' he live, and the House of York prosper—verily, Master Alwyn, the goldsmith, will, ere long, be the richest and best man from Mile-end to the Sanctuary."

"Right glad am I to hear it," said honest Marmaduke, heartily; and approaching Alwyn, he startled the precise trader by a friendly slap on the shoulder.

"What, man, art thou too proud to remember Marmaduke Nevile! Come to my lodgement, yonder, and talk of old days over the king's canary."

"I crave your pardon, dear Master Nevile."

"Master — avaunt! *Sir* Marmaduke — knighted by the hand of Lord Warwick, Sir Marmaduke Nevile, lord of a manor he hath never yet seen—sober Alwyn."

Then drawing his foster-brother's arm in his, Marmaduke led him to the chamber in which he lodged.

The young men spent some minutes in congratulating each other on their respective advances in life: — the gentleman, who had attained competence and station, simply by devotion to a powerful patron—the trader, who had already won repute and the prospect of wealth, by ingenuity, application, and toil; and yet, to do justice, as much virtue went to Marmaduke's loyalty to Warwick, as to Alwyn's capacities for making a fortune. Mutual compliments over, Alwyn said—hesitatingly—

"And dost thou find Mistress Sibyll more gently disposed to thee than when thou didst complain to me of her cruelty?"

"Marry, good Nicholas, I will be frank with thee. When I left the court to follow Lord Warwick, there were rumors of the gallantries of Lord Hastings to the girl, which grieved me to the heart. I spoke to her thereof bluntly and honorably, and got but high looks and scornful words in return. Good fellow, I thank thee for that squeeze of the hand and that doleful sigh. In my absence at Middleham, I strove hard to forget one who cared so little for me. My dear Alwyn, those Yorkshire lasses are parlously comely, and mighty douce and debonnair. So I stormed cruel Sibyll out of my heart, perforce of numbers."

"And thou lovest her no more?"

"Not I, by this goblet! On coming back, it is true, I felt pleased to clank my gold spurs in her presence, and curious to see if my new fortunes would bring out a smile of approval; and verily, to speak sooth, the donzell was kind and friendly, and spoke to me so cheerfully of the pleasure she felt in my advancement, that I adventured again a few words of the old folly. But my lassie drew up like a princess, and I am a cured man."

"By your troth?"

"By my troth!"

Alwyn's head sank on his bosom, in silent thought. Sir Marmaduke emptied his goblet; and really the young knight looked so fair and so gallant, in his new surcoat of velvet, that it was no marvel if he should find enough food for consolation in a court where men spent six hours a day in making love—nor in vain.

"And what say they still of the lord Hastings?" asked Alwyn, breaking silence. "Nothing, I trow and trust, that arraigns the poor lady's honor—though much that may scoff at her simple faith, in a nature so vain and fickle. 'The tongue's not steel, yet it cuts,' as the proverb saith of the slanderer."

"No! scandal spares her virtue as woman—to run down her cunning as witch! They say that Hastings hath not prevailed, nor sought to prevail—that he is spell-bound. By St. Thomas, from a maid of such character, Marmaduke Nevile is happily rescued!"

"Sir Marmaduke," then said Alwyn, in a grave and earnest voice—"it behoves me, as true friend, though humble, and as honest man, to give thee my secret, in return for thine own. I love this girl. Ay, ay! thou thinkest that love is a strange word in a craftsman's lips, but 'cold flint hides hot fire.' I would not have been thy rival, Heaven forefend! hadst thou still cherished a hope—or if thou now will forbid my aspiring, but if thou wilt not say me nay, I will try my chance in delivering a pure soul from a crafty wooer."

Marmaduke stared in great surprise at his foster-brother; and though, no doubt, he spoke truth, when he said he was cured of his love for Sibyll, he yet felt a sort of jealousy at Alwyn's unexpected confession, and his vanity was hurt at the notion that the plain-visaged trader should attempt where the handsome gentleman had failed. However, his blunt, generous manly nature, after a brief struggle, got the better of these sore feelings, and holding out his hand to Alwyn, he said, "My dear foster-brother, try the hazard and cast thy dice, if thou wilt. Heaven prosper thee, if success be for thine own good! But if she be really given to witchcraft—(plague on thee, man, sneer not at the word)—small comfort to bed and hearth can such practices bring!"

"Alas!" said Alwyn, "the witchcraft is on the side of Hastings—the witchcraft of fame and rank, and a glozing tongue and experienced art. But she shall not fall, if a true arm can save her; and 'though Hope be a small child, she can carry a great anchor?'"

These words were said so earnestly that they opened new light into Marmaduke's mind, and his native generosity standing in lieu of intellect, he comprehended sympathetically the noble motives which actuated the son of commerce.

"My poor Alwyn," he said, "if thou canst save this young maid—whom by my troth I loved well, and who tells me yet, that she loveth me as a sister loves—right glad shall I be. But thou stakest thy peace of mind against hers:—fair luck to thee, say I again—and if thou wilt risk thy chance at once, (for suspense is love's purgatory), seize the moment. I saw Sibyll, just ere we met, pass to the Ramparts, alone; at this sharp season, the place is deserted—go."

"I will, this moment!" said Alwyn, rising and turning very pale; but as he gained the door, he halted—"I had forgot, Master Nevile, that I bring the king his signet ring, new set, of the falcon and fetter-lock."

"They will keep thee three hours in the ante-room. The Duke of Clarence is now with the king. Trust the ring to me, I shall see his highness ere he dines."

Even in his love, Alwyn had the Saxon's considerations of business; he hesitated—"May I not endanger thereby the king's favor and loss of custom?" said the trader.

"Tush, man! little thou knowest King Edward; he cares nought for the ceremonies, moreover, the Neviles are now all-puissant in favor. I am here in attendance on sweet Lady Anne, whom the king loves as a daughter, though too young for sire to so well-grown a donzell; and a word from her lip, if need be, will set all as smooth as this gorget of lawn!"

Thus assured, Alwyn gave the ring to his friend, and took his way at once to the Ramparts. Marmaduke remained behind to finish the canary, and marvel how so sober a man should form so ardent a passion. Nor was he much less surprised to remark that his friend, though still speaking with a strong provincial accent, and still sowing his discourse with rustic saws and proverbs, had risen in language and in manner with the rise of his fortunes. "An' he go on so, and become lord mayor," muttered Marmaduke, "verily he will half look like a gentleman!"

To these meditations the young knight was not long left in peace. A messenger from Warwick House sought and found him, with the news that the earl was on his road to London, and wished to see Sir Marmaduke the moment of his arrival, which was hourly expected. The young knight's hardy brain, somewhat flustered by the canary, Alwyn's secret, and this sudden tidings, he hastened to obey his chief's summons, and forgot, till he gained the earl's mansion, the signet ring entrusted to him by Alwyn. "What matters it?" said he then, philosophically—"the king hath rings eno' on his fingers not to miss one for an hour or so, and I dare not send any one else with it. Marry, I must plunge my head in cold water, to get rid of the fumes of the wine."

CHAPTER V.

The Lover and the Gallant—Woman's Choice.

ALWYN bent his way to the Ramparts, a part of which, then, resembled the boulevards of a

French town, having rows of trees, green sward, a winding walk, and seats placed at frequent intervals, for the repose of the loungers. During the summer evenings, the place was a favorite resort of the court idlers; but now, in winter, it was usually deserted, save by the sentries, placed at distant intervals. The trader had not gone far in his quest when he perceived, a few paces before him, the very man he had most cause to dread; and Lord Hastings, hearing the sound of a foot-ball amongst the crisp, faded leaves, that stewed the path, turned abruptly as Alwyn approached his side.

At the sight of his formidable rival, Alwyn had formed one of those resolutions which occur only to men of his decided, plain-spoken, energetic character. His distinguishing shrewdness and penetration had given him considerable insight into the nobler as well as the weaker qualities of Hastings; and his hope in the former influenced the determination to which he came. The reflections of Hastings at that moment were of a nature to augur favorably to the views of the humbler lover; for, during the stirring scenes in which his late absence from Sibyll had been passed, Hastings had somewhat recovered from her influence; and feeling the difficulties of reconciling his honor and his worldly prospects to further prosecution of the love, rashly expressed but not deeply felt, he had determined frankly to cut the Gordian knot he could not solve, and inform Sibyll that marriage between them was impossible. With that view he had appointed this meeting, and his conference with the king but confirmed his intention.

It was in this state of mind that he was thus accosted by Alwyn:—

"My lord, may I make bold to ask, for a few moments, your charitable indulgence to words you may deem presumptuous."

"Be brief, then, Master Alwyn—I am waited for."

"Alas, my lord! I can guess by whom—by the one whom I seek myself — by Sibyll Warner?"

"How, Sir Goldsmith!" said Hastings, haughtily—"what knowest thou of my movements, and what care I for thine?"

"Hearken, my Lord Hastings—hearken!" said Alwyn, repressing his resentment, and in a voice so earnest that it riveted the entire attention of the listener—"hearken and judge not as noble judges craftsman, but as man should judge man. As the saw saith, 'We all lie alike in our graves.' From the first moment I saw this Sibyll Warner I loved her. Yes; smile disdainfully, but listen still. She was obscure and in distress. I loved her not for her fair looks alone—I loved her for her good gifts, for her patient industry, for her filial duty, for her struggles to give bread to her father's board. I did not say to myself, 'This girl will make a comely fere—a delicate paramour!' I said, 'This good daughter will make a wife whom an honest man may take to his heart and cherish.'" Poor Alwyn stopped, with tears in his voice, struggled with his emotions, and pursued: "My fortunes were more promising than hers; there was no cause why I might not hope. True, I had a rival then; young as myself—better born—comelier; but she loved him not. I foresaw that his love for her—if love it were—would cease. Methought that her mind would understand mine; as mine—verily I say it—*yearned* for hers! I could not look on the maidens of mine own rank, and who had lived around me, but what --Oh, no, my lord, again I say, *not* the beauty, but the gifts, the mind, the heart of Sibyll, threw them all into the shade.

"You may think it strange that I—a plain, steadfast, trading, working, careful man--should have all these feelings; but I will tell you wherefore such as I sometimes have them, nurse them, brood on them, more than you lords and gentlemen, with all your graceful arts in pleasing. We know no light loves! no brief distractions to the one arch passion! We sober sons of the stall and the ware are no general gallants we love plainly, we love but once, and we love heartily. But who knows not the proverb, 'What's a gentleman but his pleasure?'—and what's pleasure but change? When Sibyll came to the palace, I soon heard her name linked with yours; I saw her cheek blush when you spoke. Well—well—well! after all, as the old wives tell us, 'blushing is virtue's livery.' I said, 'She is a chaste and high-hearted girl.' This will pass, and the time will come when she can compare your love and mine. Now, my lord, the time has come—I know that you seek her. Yea, at this moment, I know that her heart beats for your footstep.

Say but one word—say that you love Sibyll Warner with the thought of wedding her—say *that*, on your honor, noble Hastings, as gentleman and peer, and I will kneel at your feet, and beg your pardon for my vain follies, and go back to my ware, and work, and not repine. Say it! You are silent! Then I implore you, still as peer and gentleman, to let the honest love save the maiden from the wooing that will blight her peace and blast her name! And now, Lord Hastings, I wait your gracious answer."

The sensations experienced by Hastings, as Alwyn thus concluded, were maniform and complicated; but at the first, admiration and pity were the strongest.

"My poor friend," said he, kindly, "if you thus love a demoiselle deserving all my reverence, your words and your thoughts bespeak you no unworthy pretender; but take my counsel, good Alwyn. Come not—thou from the Chepe—come not to the court for a wife. Forget this fantasy."

"My lord, it is impossible! Forget I can not—regret I may."

"Thou canst not succeed man," resumed the nobleman more coldly, "nor couldst if William Hastings had never lived. The eyes of women accustomed to gaze on the gorgeous externals of the world, are blinded to plain worth like thine. It might have been different had the donzell never abided in a palace; but, as it is, brave fellow, learn how these wounds of the heart scar over, and the spot becomes hard and callous evermore. What art thou, Master Nicholas Alwyn, (continued Hastings, gloomily, and with a withering smile), what art thou to ask for a bliss denied to me—to all of us—the bliss of carrying poetry into life—youth into manhood, by winning—the FIRST LOVED? But think not, sir lover, that I say this in jealousy or disparagement. Look yonder, by the leafless elm, the white robe of Sibyll Warner. Go, and plead thy suit."

"Do I understand you, my lord?" said Alwyn, somewhat confused and perplexed by the tone and the manner Hastings adopted. "Does report err, and you do not love this maiden?"

"Fair master," returned Hastings, scornfully, "thou hast no right that I trow of, to pry into my thoughts and secrets; I cannot acknowledge my judge in thee, good jeweller and goldsmith—enough, surely, in all courtesy, that I yield thee the precedence. Tell thy tale, as movingly, if thou wilt, as thou hast told it to me; say of me all thou fanciest thou hast reason to suspect; and if, Master Alwyn, thou woo and win the lady fail not to ask me to thy wedding!"

There was in this speech, and the bearing of the speaker, that superb levity, that inexpressible and conscious superiority,—that cold ironical tranquillity—which awe and humble men more than grave disdain or imperious passion. Alwyn ground his teeth as he listened, and gazed in silent despair and rage upon the calm lord. Neither of these men could strictly be called handsome. Of the two, Alwyn had the advantage of more youthful prime, of a taller stature, of a more powerful, though less supple and graceful, frame. In their very dress, there was little of that marked distinction between classes which then usually prevailed, for the dark cloth tunic and surcoat of Hastings, made a costume even simpler than the bright-colored garb of the trader with its broad trimmings of fur, and its aiglettes of elaborate lace. Between man and man, then, where was the visible, the mighty, the insurmountable difference in all that can charm the fancy and captivate the eye, which, as he gazed, Alwyn confessed to himself there existed between the two? Alas! how the distinctions least to be analized are ever the sternest! What lofty ease in that high-bred air—what histories of triumph seemed to speak in that quiet eye, sleeping in its own imperious lustre—what magic of command in that pale brow—what spells of persuasion in that artful lip! Alwyn muttered to himself, bowed his head involuntarily, and passed on at once from Hastings to Sibyll, who now, at the distance of some yards, had arrested her steps, in surprise to see the conference between the nobleman and the burgher.

But as he approached Sibyll, poor Alwyn felt all the firmness and courage he had exhibited with Hastings, melt away. And the trepidation with a fearful but deep affection ever occasions in men of his character, made his movements more than usually constrained and awkward, as he cowered beneath the looks of the maid he so truly loved.

"Seekest thou me, Master Alwyn?" asked

Sibyll, gently, seeing that, though he paused by her side, he spoke not.

"I do," returned Alwyn, abruptly, and again he was silent.

At length, lifting his eyes, and looking round him,—he saw Hastings at the distance, leaning against the rampart, with folded arms, and the contrast of his rival's cold and arrogant indifference, and his own burning veins and bleeding heart, roused up his manly spirit, and gave to his tongue the eloquence which emotion gains when it once breaks the fetters it forges for itself.

"Look—look, Sibyll!" he said, pointing to Hastings—"look! that man you believe loves you!—if so—if he loved thee, would he stand yonder—mark him—aloof, contemptuous, careless—while he knew that I was by your side?"

Sibyll turned upon the goldsmith eyes full of innocent surprise—eyes that asked, plainly as eyes could speak—"And wherefore not, Master Alwyn?"

Alwyn so interpreted the look, and replied, as if she had spoken—"Because he must know how poor and tame is that feeble fantasy, which alone can come from a soul, worn bare with pleasure, to that which I feel and now own for thee—the love of youth, born of the heart's first vigor,—because he ought to fear that that love should prevail with thee,—because that love *ought* to prevail. Sibyll, between us, there are not imparity and obstacle. Oh, listen to me—listen still! Frown not, turn not away." And, stung and animated by the sight of his rival, fired by the excitement of a contest on which the bliss of his own life and the weal of Sibyll's might depend, his voice was as the cry of a mortal agony, and affected the girl to the inmost recess of her soul.

"Oh, Alwyn, I frown not!" she said, sweeetly—"oh, Alwyn, I turn not away! Woe is me to give pain to so kind and brave a heart; but——"

"No, speak not yet. I have studied thee—I have read thee as a scholar would read a book. I know thee proud—I know thee aspiring—I know thou art vain of thy gentle blood, and distasteful of my yeoman's birth. There, I am not bllnd to thy faults, but I love thee despite them; and to please those faults, I have toiled, schemed, dreamed, risen—I offer to thee the future with the certainty of a man who can command it. Wouldst thou wealth?—be patient (as ambition ever is): in a few years thou shalt have more gold than the wife of Lord Hastings can command; thou shalt lodge more statelier, fare more sumptuously;* thou shalt walk on cloth of gold if thou wilt! Wouldst thou titles?—I will win them. Richard de la Pole who founded the greatest duchy in the realm, was poorer than I, when he first served in a merchant's ware. Gold buys all things now. Oh, would to Heaven it could but buy me *thee!*"

"Master Alwyn, it is not gold that buys love. Be soothed. What can I say to thee to soften the harsh word 'Nay.'"

"You reject me, then, and at once. I ask not your hand now. I will wait, tarry, hope—I care not if for years;—wait till I can fulfil all I promise thee!"

Sibyll, affected to tears, shook her head mournfully; and there was a long and painful silence. Never was wooing more strangely circumstanced than this—the one lover pleading while the other was in view—the one, ardent, impassioned, the other, calm and passive—and the silence of the last, alas! having all the success which the words of the other lacked. It might be said that the choice before Sybill was a type of the choice ever given, but in vain, to the child of genius. I ere a secure and peaceful life—an honored home—a tranquil lot, free from ideal visions, it is true, but free also from the doubt and the terror—the storms of passion;—there, the fatal influence of an affection, born of imagination, sinister, equivocal, ominous, but irresistible. And the child of genius fulfilled her destiny!

"Master Alwyn," said Sibyll, rousing herself to the necessary exertion, "I shall never cease gratefully to recall thy generous friendship—never cease to pray fervently for thy weal below. But for ever and for ever let this content thee—I can no more."

Impressed by the grave and solemn tone of Sibyll, Alwyn hushed the groan that struggled to his lips, and gloomily replied—"I obey you, fair mistress, and I return to my work-day

* This was no vain promise of Master Alwyn. At that time, a successful trader made a fortune with signal rapidity, and enjoyed greater luxuries than most of the barons. All the gold in the country flowed into the coffers of the London merchants.

life; but ere I go, I pray you misthink me not if I say this much;—not alone for the bliss of hoping for a day in which I might call thee mine have I thus importuned—but, not less—I swear not less—from the soul's desire to save thee from what I fear will but lead to woe and wayment, to peril and pain, to weary days and sleepless nights. 'Better a little fire that warms than a grate that burns.' Dost thou think that Lord Hastings, the vain, the dissolute——"

"Cease, sir!" said Sibyll, proudly; "me reprove if thou wilt, but lower not my esteem for thee by slander against another!"

"What!" said Alwyn, bitterly; "doth even one word of counsel chafe thee? I tell thee that if thou dreamest that Lord Hastings loves Sibyll Warner as man loves the maiden he would wed,—thou deceivest thyself to thine own misery. If thou wouldst prove it, go to him now—go and say, 'Wilt thou give me that home of peace and honor—that shelter for my father's old age under a son's roof which the trader I despise proffers me in vain?"

"If it were already proffered me—by *him?*" said Sibyll, in a low voice, and blushing deeply.

Alwyn started. "Then I wronged him: and—and——" he added, generously, though with a faint sickness at his heart, "I can yet be happy in thinking *thou* art so. Farewell, maiden, the saints guard thee from one memory of regret at what hath passed between us!"

He pulled his bonnet hastily over his brows, and departed with unequal and rapid strides. As he passed the spot where Hastings stood leaning his arm upon the wall, and his face upon his hand, the nobleman looked up, and said—

"Well, Sir Goldsmith, own at least that thy trial hath been a fair one!" Then, struck with the anguish written upon Alwyn's face, he walked up to him, and, with a frank, compassionate impulse, laid his hand on his shoulder: "Alwyn," he said, "I have felt what you feel now—I have survived it, and the world hath not prospered with me less! Take with you a compassion that respects, and does not degrade you."

"Do not deceive her, my lord—she trusts and loves you! You never deceived man—the wide world says it—do not deceive woman! Deeds kill men—words women!" Speaking thus simply, Alwyn strode on, and vanished.

Hastings slowly and silently advanced to Sibyll. Her rejection of Alwyn had by no means tended to reconcile him to the marriage he himself had proffered. He might well suppose that the girl, even if unguided by affection, would not hesitate between a mighty nobleman and an obscure goldsmith. His pride was sorely wounded that the latter should have even thought himself the equal of one whom *he* had proposed, though but in a passionate impulse, to raise to his own state. And yet, as he neared Sibyll, and, with a light footstep, she sprang forward to meet him, her eyes full of sweet joy and confidence, he shrank from an avowal which must wither up a heart opening thus all its bloom of youth and love to greet him.

"Ah, fair lord," said the maiden, "was it kindly in thee to permit poor Alwyn to inflict on me so sharp a pain, and thou to stand calmly distant? Sure, alas! that had thy humble rival proffered a crown, it had been the same to Sibyll! Oh, how the grief it was mine to cause grieved me; and yet, through all, I had one selfish, guilty gleam of pleasure—to think that I had not been loved so well, if I were all unworthy the sole love I desire or covet!"

"And yet, Sibyll, this young man can in all, save wealth and a sounding name, give thee more than I can,—a heart undarkened by moody memories—a temper unsoured by the world's dread and bitter lore of man's frailty and earth's sorrow. Ye are not far separated by ungenial years, and might glide to a common grave hand in hand; but I, older in heart than in age, am yet so far thine elder in the last, that these hairs will be grey, and this form bent, while thy beauty is in its prime, and—but thou weepest!"

"I weep that thou shouldst bring one thought of time to sadden my thoughts, which are of eternity. Love knows no age—it foresees no grave! its happiness and its trust behold on the earth but one glory, melting into the hues of heaven, where they who love lastingly pass calmly on to live for ever! See, I weep not now!"

"And did not this honest burgher," pursued Hastings, softened and embarrassed, but striving to retain his cruel purpose, "tell thee to distrust me?—tell thee that my vows were false?"

"Methinks, if an angel told me so, I should disbelieve!"

"Why, look thee, Sibyll, suppose his warning true—suppose that at this hour I sought thee with intent to say that that destiny which ambition weaves for itself forbade me to fulfil a word hotly spoken?—that I could not wed thee?—should I not seem to thee a false wooer—a poor trifler with thy earnest heart—and so, couldst thou not recall the love of him whose truer and worthier homage yet lingers in thine ear, and with him be happy?"

Sibyll lifted her dark eyes, yet humid, upon the unrevealing face of the speaker, and gazed on him with wistful and inquiring sadness, then, shrinking from his side, she crossed her arms meekly on her bosom, and thus said—

"If ever, since we parted, one such thought hath glanced across thee—one thought of repentance at the sacrifice of pride, or the lessening of power—which—(she faltered, broke off the sentence, and resumed)—in one word, if thou wouldst retract, say it now, and I will not accuse thy falsehood, but bless thy truth."

"Thou couldst be consoled, then, by thy pride of woman, for the loss of an unworthy lover?"

"My lord, are these questions fair?"

Hastings was silent. The gentler part of his nature struggled severely with the harder. The pride of Sibyll moved him no less than her trusts, and her love in both was so evident—so deep—so exquisitely contrasting the cold and frivolous natures amidst which his lot had fallen—that he recoiled from casting away for ever a heart never to be replaced. Standing on that bridge of life, with age before and youth behind, he felt that never again could he be so loved, or, if so loved, by one so worthy of whatever of pure affection, of young romance, was yet left to his melancholy and lonely soul.

He took her hand, and, as she felt its touch, her firmness forsook her, her head drooped upon her bosom, and she burst into an agony of tears.

"Oh, Sibyll, forgive me! Smile on me again, Sibyll!" exclaimed Hastings, subdued and melted. But, alas! the heart once bruised and galled recovers itself but slowly and it was many minutes before the softest words the eloquent lover could shape to sound sufficed to dry those burning tears, and bring back the enchanting smile,—nay, even then the smile was forced and joyless. They walked on for some moments, both in thought, till Hastings said—"Thou lovest me Sibyll, and art worthy of all the love that man can feel for maid; and yet, canst thou solve me this question, nor chide me that I ask it—Dost thou not love the world and the world's judgment more than me? What is that which women call honor? What makes them shrink from all love that takes not the form and circumstance of the world's hollow rites? Does love cease to be love, unless over its wealth of trust and emotion the priest mouths his empty blessing? Thou in thy graceful pride art angered if I, in wedding thee, should remember the sacrfice which men like me—I own it fairly—deem as great as man can make; and yet thou wouldst fly my love, if it wooed thee to a sacrifice of thine own?"

Artfully was the question put, and Hastings smiled to himself in imagining the reply it must bring; and then Sibyll answered with the blush which the very subject called forth.

"Alas, my lord, I am but a poor casuist, but I feel that if I asked thee to forfeit whatever men respect,—honor, and repute for valor, to be traitor and dastard, thou couldst love me no more; and marvel you, if when man woes woman to forfeit all that her sex holds highest—to be in woman what dastard and traitor is in man—she hears her conscience and her God speak in a louder voice than can come from a human lip? The goods and pomps of the world we are free to sacrifice, and true love needs and counts them not; but true love cannot sacrifice that which makes up love—it cannot sacrifice the right to be loved below, the hope to love on in the realm above, the power to pray with a pure soul for the happiness it yearns to make, the blessing to seem ever good and honored in the eyes of the one by whom alone it would be judged—and therefore, sweet and true love never contemplates this sacrifice; and if once it believe itself truly loved, it trusts with a fearless faith in the love on which it leans."

"Sibyll, would to Heaven I had seen thee in my youth! Would to Heaven I were more worthy of thee!" And in that interview Hastings had no heart to utter what he had resolved—"Sibyll, I sought thee but to say farewell."

CHAPTER VI.

Warwick returns—Appeases a discontented Prince—And confers with a revengeful Conspirator.

IT was not till late in the evening that Warwick arrived at his vast residence in London, where he found not only Marmaduke Nevile ready to receive him, but a more august expectant, in George Duke of Clarence. Scarcely had the earl crossed the threshold, when the duke seized his arm, and leading him into the room that adjoined the hall, said—

"Verily Edward is besotted no less than ever by his wife's leech-like family. Thou knowest my appointment to the government of Ireland; Isabel, like myself, cannot endure the subordinate vassalage we must brook at the court, with the queen's cold looks and sour words. Thou knowest, also, with what vain pretexts Edward hath put me off; and now, this very day, he tells me that he hath changed his humor—that I am not stern enough for the Irish kernes—that he loves me too well to banish me, forsooth, and that Worcester, the people's butcher, but the queen's favorite, must have the post so sacredly pledged to me. I see, in this, Elizabeth's crafty malice. Is this struggle between king's blood and queen's kith to go for ever?"

"Calm thyself, George; I will confer with the king to-morrow, and hope to compass thy not too arrogant desire. Certes, a king's brother is the fittest vice-king for the turbulent kernes of Ireland, who are ever flattered into obeisance by ceremony and show. The government was pledged to thee—Edward can scarcely be serious. Moreover, Worcester, though forsooth a learned man—(Mort Dieu! methinks that same learning fills the head to drain the heart!)—is so abhorred for his cruelties that his very landing in Ireland will bring a new rebellion to add to our already festering broils and sores. Calm thyself, I say. Where didst thou leave Isabel?"

"With my mother."

"And Anne?—the queen chills not her young heart with cold grace?"

"Nay—the queen dare not unleash her malice against Edward's will and, to do him justice, he hath shown all honor to Lord Warwick's daughter."

"He is a gallant prince, with all his faults," said the father, heartily, "and we must bear with him, George; for verily he hath bound men by a charm to love him. Stay, thou, and share my hasty repast, and over the wine we will talk of thy views. Spare me now for a moment; I have to prepare work eno' for a sleepless night. This Lincolnshire rebellion promises much trouble. Lord Willoughby has joined it—more than twenty thousand men are in arms. I have already sent to convene the knights and barons on whom the king can best depend, and must urge their instant departure for their halls, to raise men and meet the foe. While Edward feasts, his minister must toil. Tarry awhile, till I return."

The earl re-entered the hall, and beckoned to Marmaduke, who stood amongst a group of squires.

"Follow me, I may have work for thee." Warwick took a taper from one the survitors, and led the way to his own more private apartment. On the landing of the staircase, by a small door, stood his body squire—"Is the prisoner within?"

"Yes, my Lord."

"Good!"—The earl opened the door by which the squire had mounted guard, and bade Marmaduke wait without.

The inmate of the chamher, whose dress bore the stains of fresh travel and hard riding, lifted his face hastily as the earl entered.

"Robin Hilyard," said Warwick, "I have mused much how to reconcile my service to the king with the gratitude I owe to a man who saved me from great danger. In the midst of thy unhappy and rebellious designs, thou wert captured and brought to me; the papers found on thee attest a Lancastrian revolt; so ripening towards a mighty gathering—and so formidable from the adherents whom the gold and intrigues of King Louis have persuaded to risk land and life for the Red Rose, that all the king's friends can do to save his throne is now needed. In this revolt thou hast been the scheming brain, the master hand, the match to the bombard, the firebrand to the flax. Thou smilest, man! Alas! seest thou not that it is my stern duty to send thee bound hand and foot before the king's council—for the brake to wring from thee thy guilty secrets, and the gibbet to close thy days?"

"I am prepared," said Hilyard; "when the bombard explodes, the match has become useless—when the flame smites the welkin, the firebrand is consumed!"

"Bold man! what seest thou in this rebellion that can profit thee?"

"I see, looming through the chasms and rents made in the feudal order by civil war—the giant image of a free people."

"And thou wouldst be a martyr for the multitude, who deserted thee at Olney?"

"As thou for the king, who dishonored thee at Shene!"

Warwick frowned, and there was a moments' pause; at last, said the earl—"Look you, Robin, I would fain not have on my hands the blood of a man who saved my life. I believe thee, though a fanatic and half madman I believe thee true in word, as rash of deed. swear to me on the cross of this dagger, that thou wilt lay aside all scheme and plot for this rebellion, all aid and share in civil broil and dissension, and thy life and liberty are restored to thee. In that intent, I have summoned my own kinsman, Marmaduke Nevile. He waits without the door—he shall conduct thee safely to the sea-shore—thou shalt gain in peace my government Calais, and my seneschal there shall find thee all thou canst need—meat for thy hunger, and monies for thy pastime. Accept my mercy—take the oath, and begone."

"My Lord," answered Hilyard, much touched and affected—"blame not thyself if this carcase feed the crows—my blood be on mine own head! I cannot take this oath; I cannot live in peace; strife and broil are grown to me food and drink. Oh, my lord! thou knowest not what dark and baleful memories made me an agent in God's hand against this ruthless Edward;" and then passionately, with whitening lips and convulsive features, Hilyard recounted to the startled Warwick the same tale which had roused the sympathy of Adam Warner.

The earl, whose affections were so essentially homely and domestic, was even more shocked than the scholar by the fearful narrative.

"Unhappy man!" he said, with moistened eyes—"from the core of my heart, I pity thee. But thou, the scathed sufferer from civil war, wilt *thou* be now its dread reviver?"

"If Edward had wronged thee, great earl, as me, poor franklin, what would be thine answer? In vain moralize to him whom the spectre of a murdered child and the shriek of a maniac wife haunt and hound on to vengeance! So send me to rack and halter. Be there one curse more on the soul of Edward!"

"Thou shalt not die through my witness," said the earl, abruptly, and he quitted the chamber.

Securing the door by a heavy bolt on the outside, he gave orders to his squire to attend to the comforts of the prisoner; and then turning into his closet with Marmaduke, said —"I sent for thee, young cousin, with design to commit to thy charge one whose absence from England I deemed needful—that design I must abandon. Go back to the palace, and see, if thou canst, the king, before he sleeps—say that this rising in Lincolnshire is more than a riot; it is the first burst of a revolution! that I hold council here to-night, and every shire, ere the morrow, shall have its appointed captain. I will see the king at morning. Yet stay—gain sight of my child Anne; she will leave the court to-morrow. I will come for her—bid her train be prepared; she and the countess must away to Calais—England again hath ceased to be a home for women! What to do with this poor rebel?" muttered the earl, when alone—"release him I cannot, slay him I will not. Hum—there is space enough in these walls to enclose a captive."

CHAPTER VII.

The Fear and the Flight.

King Edward feasted high, and Sibyll sate in her father's chamber—she silent with thought of love, Adam silent in the toils of science. The Eureka was well-nigh finished —rising from its ruins, more perfect, more elaborate, than before. Maiden and scholar, each seeming near to the cherished goal—one to love's genial altar, the other to fame's lonely shrine.

Evening advanced — night began — night deepened. King Edward's feast was over, but still in his perfumed chamber the wine sparkled in the golden cup. It was announced to him that Sir Marmaduke Nevile, just arrived from the earl's house, craved an audience. The king, preoccupied in deep reverie, impatiently postponed it till the morrow.

"To-morrow!" said the gentleman in attendance. "Sir Marmaduke bids me say, fearful that the late hour would forbid his audience, that Lord Warwick himself will visit your grace. I fear, sire, that the disturbances are great indeed, for the squires and gentlemen in Lady Anne's train have orders to accompany her to Calais to-morrow."

"To-morrow, to-morrow!" repeated the king—"well, sir, you are dismissed."

The Lady Anne, (to whom Sibyll had previously communicated the king's kindly consideration for Master Warner), had just seen Marmaduke, and learned the new dangers that awaited the throne and the realm. The Lancastrians were then openly in arms for the prince of her love, and against her mighty father.

The Lady Anne, sate awhile, sorrowful and musing, and then, before yon crucifix, the Lady Anne knelt in prayer.

Sir Marmaduke Nevile descends to the court below, and some three or four busy, curious gentlemen, not yet a-bed, seize him by the arm, and pray him to say what storm is in the wind.

The night deepened still—the wine is drained in King Edward's goblet—King Edward has left his chamber—and Sibyll, entreating her father, but in vain, to suspend his toil, has kissed the damps from his brow, and is about to retire to her neighboring room. She has turned to the threshold, when, hark!—a faint, a distant cry, a woman's shriek, the noise of a clapping door! The voice—it is the voice of Anne! Sibyll passed the threshold—she is in the corridor—the winter moon shines through the open arches—the air is white and cold with frost. Suddenly the door at the farther end is thrown wide open, a form rushes into the corridor, it passes Sibyll, halts, turns round—"Oh, Sibyll!" cried the Lady Anne, in a voice wild with horror, "save me — aid — help! Merciful Heaven, the king!"

Instinctively, wonderingly, tremblingly, Sibyll drew Anne into the chamber she had just quitted, and as they gained its shelter—as Anne sunk upon the floor, the gleam of cloth of gold flashed through the dim atmosphere, and Edward, yet in the royal robe in which he had dazzled all the eyes at his kingly feast, stood within the chamber. His countenance was agitated with passion, and its clear hues flushed red with wine. At his entrance, Anne sprang from the floor, and rushed to Warner, who, in dumb bewilderment, had suspended his task, and stood before the Eureka, from which steamed and rushed the dark rapid smoke, while round, and round, laboring and groaning, rolled its fairy wheels.*

"Sir," cried Anne, clinging to him convulsively, "You are a father—by your child's soul, protect Lord Warwick's daughter!"

Roused from his abstraction by this appeal, the poor scholar wound his arm round the form thus clinging to him, and raising his head with dignity, replied, "Thy name, youth, and sex protect thee!"

"Unhand that lady, vile sorcerer," exclaimed the king—"*I* am her protector. Come, Anne, sweet Anne, fair lady—thou mistakest—come!" he whispered. "Give not to these low natures matter for guesses that do but shame thee. Let thy king and cousin lead thee back to thy sweet rest."

He sought, though gently, to loosen the arms that wound themselves round the old man; but Anne, not heeding, not listening, distracted by a terror that seemed to shake her whole frame, and to threaten her very reason, continued to cry out loudly upon her father's name—her great father, wakeful, then, for the baffled ravisher's tottering throne!

Edward had still sufficient possession of his reason to be alarmed lest some loiterer or sentry in the outer court might hear the cries which his attempts to soothe but the more provoked. Grinding his teeth, and losing patience, he said to Adam, "Thou knowest me, friend—I am thy king. Since the Lady Anne, in her

* The gentle reader will doubtless bear in mind that Master Warner's complicated model had but little resemblance to the models of the steam engine in our own day, and that it was usually connected with other contrivances, for the better display of the principle it was intended to illustrate.

bewilderment, prefers thine aid to mine, help to bear her back to her apartment; and thou, young mistress, lend thine arm. This wizard's den is no fit chamber for our high-born guest."

"No, no; drive me not hence, Master Warner. That man—that king—give me not up to his—his——"

"Beware!" exclaimed the king.

It was not till now that Adam's simple mind comprehended the true cause of Anne's alarm, which Sibyll still conjectured not, but stood trembling by her friend's side, and close to her father.

"Do not fear, maiden," said Adam Warner, laying his hand upon the loosened locks that swept over his bosom, "for though I am old and feeble, God and his angels are in every spot where virtue trembles and resists. My lord king, thy sceptre extends not over a human soul!"

"Dotard, prate not to me!" said Edward, laying his hand on his dagger.

Sibyll saw the movement, and instinctively placed herself between her father and the king. That slight form, those pure steadfast eyes, those features, noble at once and delicate, recalled to Edward the awe which had seized him in his first dark design; and again that awe came over him. He retreated.

"I mean harm to none," said he, almost submissively; "and if I am so unhappy as to scare with my presence the Lady Anne, I will retire, praying you, donzell, to see to her state, and lead her back to her chamber when it so pleases herself. Saying this much I command you, old man, and you, maiden, to stand back while I but address one sentence to the Lady Anne."

With these words he gently advanced to Anne, and took her hand; but, snatching it from him, the poor lady broke from Adam, rushed to the casement, opened it, and seeing some figures indistinct and distant in the court below, she called out in a voice of such sharp agony, that it struck remorse and even terror into Edward's soul.

"Alas!" he muttered, "she will not listen to me, her mind is distraught! What frenzy has been mine! Pardon—pardon, Anne—oh, pardon!"

Adam Warner laid his hand on the king's arm, and he drew the imperious despot away as easily as a nurse leads a docile child.

"King!" said the brave old man, "may God pardon thee! for if the last evil hath been wrought upon this noble lady, David sinned not more heavily than thou."

"She is pure—inviolate—I swear it!" said the king, humbly. "Anne, only say that I am forgiven."

But Anne spoke not: her eyes were fixed—her lips had fallen—she was insensible as a corpse—dumb and frozen with her ineffable dread. Suddenly steps were heard upon the stairs; the door opened, and Marmaduke Nevile entered abruptly.

"Surely I heard my lady's voice—surely! What marvel this?—the king! Pardon, my liege?"—and he bent his knee.

The sight of Marmaduke dissolved the spell of awe and repentant humiliation, which had chained a king's dauntless heart. His wonted guile returned to him with his self-possession.

"Our wise craftsman's strange and weird invention—" (and Edward pointed to the Eureka)—"has scared our fair cousins senses, as, by sweet St. George, it well might! Go back, Sir Marmaduke, we will leave Lady Anne for the moment to the care of Mistress Sibyll. Donzell, remember my command. Come, sir—" (and he drew the wondering Marmaduke from the chamber)—but as soon as he had seen the knight descend the stairs and regain the court, he returned to the room, and in a low stern voice, said—"Look you, Master Warner, and you, damsel, if either of ye breathe one word of what has been your dangerous fate to hear and witness, kings have but one way to punish slanderers, and silence but one safe-guard;—trifle not with death!"

He then closed the door, and resought his own chamber. The eastern spices, which were burned in the sleeping-rooms of the great, still made the air heavy with their feverish fragrance. The king seated himself, and strove to recollect his thoughts, and examine the peril he had provoked. The resistance and the terror of Anne had effectually banished from his heart the guilty passion it had before harbored; for emotions like his, and in such a nature, are quick of change. His prevailing feeling was one of sharp repentance, and reproachful shame. But, as he roused himself from a state of mind which light characters ever seek to escape, the image of the dark-browed earl rose before him, and fear succeeded to mortification; but even this, however well-founded, could not endure long in a disposition so essentially scornful of all danger. Before morning, the senses of Anne must return to her. So gentle a bosom could be surely reasoned out of resentment, or daunted, at least, from betraying to her stern father a secret that, if told, would smear the sward of England with the gore of thousands. What woman will provoke war and bloodshed? And for an evil not wrought—for a purpose not fulfilled? The king was grateful that his victim had escaped him. He would see Anne before the earl could—and appease her anger —obtain her silence! For Warner, and for Sibyll, they would not dare to reveal; and, if they did, the lips that accuse a king soon belie themselves, while a rack can torture truth, and the doomsman be the only judge between the subject and the head that wears a crown!

Thus reasoning with himself, his soul faced the solitude. Meanwhile Marmaduke regained the court-yard, where, as we have said, he had been detained in conferring with some of the gentlemen in the king's service, who, hearing that he brought important tidings from the earl, had abstained from rest till they could learn if the progress of the new rebellion would bring their swords into immediate service. Marmaduke, pleased to be of importance, had willingly satisfied their curiosity, as far as he was able, and was just about to retire to his own chamber, when the cry of Anne had made him enter the postern door which led up the stairs to Adam's apartment, and which was fortunately not locked; and now, on returning, he had again a new curiosity to allay. Having briefly said that Master Warner had taken that untoward hour to frighten the women with a machine that vomited smoke and howled piteously, Marmaduke dismissed the group to their beds, and was about to seek his own, when, looking once more towards the casement, he saw a white hand gleaming in the frosty moonlight, and beckoning to him.

Thd knight crossed himself, and reluctantly ascended the stairs, and re-entered the wizard's den.

The Lady Anne had so far recovered herself, that a kind of unnatural calm had taken possession of her mind, and changed her ordinary sweet and tractable nature into one stern, obstinate resolution,—to escape, if possible, that unholy palace. And as soon as Marmaduke re-entered, Anne met him at the threshold, and laying her hand convulsively on his arm, said—

"By the name you bear—by your love to my father, aid me to quit these walls."

"In great astonishment, Marmaduke stared, without reply.

"Do you deny me, sir?" said Anne, almost sternly.

"Lady and mistress mine," answered Marmaduke, "I am your servant in all things. Quit these walls—the palace!—How?—the gates are closed. Nay, and what would my lord say, if at night ——"

"*If at night!*" repeated Anne, in a hollow voice; and then pausing, burst into a terrible laugh. Recovering herself abruptly, she moved to the door—"I will go forth alone, and trust in God and our Lady."

Sibyll sprang forward to arrest her steps, and Marmaduke hastened to Adam, and whispered—"Poor lady, is her mind unsettled? Hast thou, in truth, distracted her with thy spells and glamour?"

"Hush!" answered the old man; and he whispered in the Nevile's ear.

Scarcely had the knight caught the words, than his cheek paled—his eyes flashed fire. "The great earl's daughter!" he exclaimed—"infamy!—horror—she is right!" He broke from the student, approached Anne, who still struggled with Sibyll, and kneeling before her, said, in a voice choked with passions at once fierce and tender—

"Lady, you are right. Unseemly it may be for one of your quality and sex to quit this place with me, and alone; but at least I have a man's heart—a knight's honor. Trust to me your safety, noble maiden, and I will cut your way, even through yon foul king's heart, to your great father's side!"

Anne did not seem quite to understand his words, but she smiled on him as he knelt, and gave him her hand. The responsibility he had assumed quickened all the intellect of the young knight. As he took and kissed the hand extended to him, he felt the ring upon his finger—the ring entrusted to him by Alwyn—the king's signet-ring, before which would fly open every gate. He uttered a joyous exclamation, loosened his long night-cloak, and praying Anne to envelop her form in its folds, drew the hood over her head;—he was about to lead her forth, when he halted suddenly.

"Alack," said he, turning to Sibyll, even though we may escape the Tower, no boatman now can be found on the river. The way through the streets is dark and perilous, and beset with midnight ruffians."

"Verily," said Warner, "the danger is past now. Let the noble demoiselle rest here till morning. The king dare not again——"

"Dare not!" interrupted Marmaduke. "Alas! you little know King Edward."

At that name Anne shuddered, opened the door, and hurried down the stairs; Sibyll and Marmaduke followed her.

"Listen, Sir Marmaduke," said Sibyll. "Close without the Tower is the house of a noble lady, the dame of Longueville, where Anne may rest in safety, while you seek Lord Warwick. I will go with you if you can obtain egress for us both."

"Brave damsel!" said Marmaduke, with emotion—"But your own safety—the king's anger—no—besides, a third, your dress not concealed, would create the warder's suspicion. Describe the house."

"The third to the left, by the river's side, with an arched porch, and the fleur-de-lis embossed on the walls."

"It is not so dark but we shall find it. Fare you well, gentle mistress."

While they yet spoke, they had both reached the side of Anne. Sibyll still persisted in the wish to accompany her friend; but Marmaduke's representation of the peril to life itself, that might befall her father, if Edward learned she had abetted Anne's escape, finally prevailed. The knight and his charge gained the outer gate.

"Haste—haste, Master Warder!" he cried, beating at the door with his dagger till it opened jealously—"messages of importance to the Lord Warwick. We have the king's signet.—Open!"

The sleepy warder glance at the ring—the gates were opened: They were without the fortress—they hurried on.

"Cheer up, noble lady; you are safe—you shall be avenged!" said Marmaduke, as he felt the steps of his companion falter.

But the reaction had come. The effort Anne had hitherto made was for escape—for liberty; the strength ceased, the object gained;—her head drooped—she muttered a few incoherent words, and then sense and life left her. Marmaduke paused in great perplexity and alarm. But lo, a light in a house before him!—that house the third to the river—the only one with the arched porch described by Sibyll. He lifted the light and holy burthen in his strong arms—he gained the door: to his astonishment, it was open—a light burned on the stairs—he heard, in the upper room, the sound of whispered voices, and quick, soft footsteps, hurrying to and fro. Still bearing the insensible form of his companion, he ascended the staircase, and entered at once upon a chamber, in which, by a dim lamp, he saw some two or three persons assembled round a bed in the recess. A grave man advanced to him, as he paused at the threshold—

"Whom seek you?"

"The Lady Longueville."

"Hush!"

"Who needs me?" said a faint voice, from the curtained recess.

"My name is Nevile," answered Marmaduke, with straightforward brevity. "Mistress Sibyll Warner told me of this house, where I come for an hour's shelter to my companion, the Lady Anne, daughter of the Earl of Warwick."

Marmaduke resigned his charge to an old woman, who was the nurse in that sick chamber, and who lifted the hood, and chafed the pale, cold hands of the young maiden;—the knight then strode to the recess. The Lady of Longueville was on the bed of death—an illness of two days had brought her to the brink of the grave—but there was in her eye and countenance a restless and preternatural animation, and her voice was clear and shrill, as she said—

"Why does the daughter of Warwick, the Yorkist, seek refuge in the house of the fallen and childless Lancastrian?"

"Swear, by thy hopes in Christ, that thou wilt tend and guard her while I seek the earl, and I reply."

"Stranger, my name is Longueville—my birth noble—those pledges of hospitality and trust are stronger than hollow oaths. Say on!"

"Because, then," whispered the knight, after waiving the bystanders from the spot—"because the earl's daughter flies dishonor in a king's palace, and her insulter is the king!"

Before the dying woman could reply, Anne, recovered by the cares of the experienced nurse, suddenly sprung to the recess, and kneeling by the bedside, exclaimed, wildly—

"Save me!—hide me!—save me!"

"Go and seek the earl, whose right hand destroyed my house and his lawful sovereign's throne—go! I will live till he arrives!" said the childless widow, and a wild gleam of triumph shot over her haggard features.

CHAPTER VIII.

The Group round the Death-bed of the Lancastrian Widow.

THE dawning sun gleamed through grey clouds upon a small troop of men, armed in haste, who were grouped round a covered litter by the outer door of the Lady Longuville's house; while in the death-chamber, the Earl of Warwick, with a face as pale as the dying woman's stood beside the bed—Anne calmly leaning on his breast, her eyes closed, and tears yet moist on their long fringes.

"Ay—ay—ay!" said the Lancastrian noblewoman, "ye men of wrath and turbulence, should reap what ye have sown! *This* is the king for whom ye dethroned the sainted Henry! *this* the man for whom ye poured forth the blood of England's best! Ha—ha!—Look down from Heaven my husband, my martyr-sons! The daughter of your mightiest foe—flies to this lonely hearth—flies to the death-bed of the powerless woman for refuge from the foul usurper whom that foe placed upon the throne!"

"Spare me," muttered Warwick, in a low voice, and between his grinded teeth. The room had been cleared, and Doctor Godard (the grave man who had first accosted Marmaduke, and who was the priest summoned to the dying), alone—save the scarce conscious Anne herself—witnessed the ghastly and awful conference.

"Hush, daughter," said the man of peace, lifting the solemn crucifix—"calm thyself to holier thoughts."

The lady impatiently turned from the priest, and grasping the strong right arm of Warwick with her shrivelled and trembling fingers, resumed, in a voice that struggled to repress the gasps which broke its breath—

"But thou—oh, thou, wilt bear this indignity! thou, the chief of England's Barons, wilt see no dishonor in the rank love of the vilest of England's kings! Oh, yes, ye Yorkists have the hearts of varlets—not of men and fathers!"

"By the symbol from which thou turnest, woman!" exclaimed the earl, giving vent to the fury which the presence of death had before suppressed—"by Him, to whom morning and night I have knelt in grateful blessing for the virtuous life of this beloved child, I will have such revenge on the recreant whom I kinged, as shall live in the Rolls of England till the trump of the Judgment Angel!"

"Father," said Anne, startled by her father's vehemence, from her half-swoon, half-sleep—"Father, think no more of the past—take me to my mother! I want the clasp of my mother's arms!"

"Leave us—leave the dying, Sir Earl and son," said Godard. "I, too, am Lancastrian—I too would lay down my life for the holy Henry; but I shudder, in the hour of death, to hear yon pale lips, that should pray for pardon, preach to thee of revenge."

"Revenge!" shrieked out the Dame of Longueville, as, sinking fast and fast, she caught the word—"Revenge! Thou hast sworn revenge on Edward of York, Lord Warwick—sworn it, in the chamber of death—in the ear of one who will carry that word to the hero-dead of a hundred battle-fields! Ha—the sun has risen! Priest—Godard—thine arms—support—raise—bear me to the casement! Quick—quick! I would see my king once more! Quick—quick! and then—*then*—I will hear thee pray!"

The priest, half chiding, yet half in pity, bore the dying woman to the casement. She motioned to him to open it: he obeyed. The sun, just above the welkin, shone over the lordly Thames, gilded the gloomy fortress of the Tower, and glittered upon the window of Henry's prison.

"There—there! It is he—it is my king! Hither,—lord, rebel earl—hither. Behold your sovereign! Repent, revenge!"

With her livid and outstretched hand, the Lancastrian pointed to the huge Wakefield Tower. The earl's dark eye beheld, in the dim distance, a pale and reverend countenance, recognized even from afar. The dying woman fixed her glazing eyes upon the wronged and mighty baron, and suddenly her arm fell to her side, the face became set as into stone, the last breath of life gurgled within, and fled,—and still those glazing eyes were fixed on the earl's hueless face; and still in his ear, and echoed by a thousand passions in his heart—thrilled the word which had superseded prayer, and in which the sinner's soul had flown—REVENGE!

BOOK NINTH.

THE WANDERERS AND THE EXILES.

CHAPTER I.

How the great Baron becomes as great a Rebel.

HILYARD was yet asleep in the chamber assigned to him as his prison, when a rough grasp shook off his slumbers, and he saw the earl before him, with a countenance so changed from its usual open majesty—so dark and sombre, that he said, involuntarily, "You send me to the doomsman—I am ready!"

"Hist, man! Thou hatest Edward of York?"

"An' it were my last word—yes!"

"Give me thy hand—we are friends! Stare not at me with those eyes of wonder—ask not the why nor wherefore! This last night gave Edward a rebel more in Richard Nevile. A steed waits thee at my gates—ride fast to young Sir Robert Welles with this letter. Bid him not be dismayed; bid him hold out—for ere many days are past, Lord Warwick and it may be, also, the Duke of Clarence will join their force with his. Mark, I say not that I am for Henry of Lancaster—I say only that I am again Edward of York. Farewell, and when we meet again, blessed be the arm that first cuts its way to a tyrant's heart!"

Without another word, Warwick left the chamber. Hilyard, at first, could not believe his senses; but as he dressed himself in haste, he pondered over all those causes of dissension which had long notoriously subsisted between Edward and the earl, and rejoiced that the prophecy he had long so shrewdly hazarded was at last fulfilled. Descending the stairs, he gained the gate, where Marmaduke awaited him, while a groom held a stout *haquenée*, (as the common riding-horse was then called), whose points and breeding promised speed and endurance.

"Mount, Master Robin," said Marmaduke; "I little thought we should ever ride as friends together! Mount—our way for some miles out of London is the same. You go into Lincolnshire—I into the shire of Hertford."

"And for the same purpose?" asked Hilyard, as he sprung on his horse, and the two men rode briskly on.

"Yes!"

"Lord Warwick is changed at last."

"At last!"

"For long?"

"Till death!"

"Good—I ask no more!"

A sound of hoofs behind made the franklin turn his head, and he saw a goodly troop, armed to the teeth, emerge from the earl's house and follow the lead of Marmaduke.

Meanwhile Warwick was closeted with Montagu.

Worldly as the latter was, and personally attached to Edward, he was still keenly alive to all that touched the honor of his house; and his indignation at the deadly insult offered to his niece was even more loudly expressed than that of the fiery earl.

"To deem," he exclaimed, "to deem Elizabeth Woodville worthy of his throne, and to see in Anne Nevile one only worthy to be his leman!"

"Ay!" said the earl, with a calmness perfectly terrible, from its unnatural contrast to his ordinary heat, when but slightly chafed, "Ay! thou sayest it! But be tranquil—cold—cold as iron, and as hard! We must *scheme* now, not storm and threaten—I never schemed before! You are right—honesty is a fool's policy! Would I had known this but an hour before the news reached me! I have already dismissed our friends to their different districts, to support King Edward's cause—he is still king—a little while longer king! Last night, I dismissed them—last night, at the very hour when—O God give me patience!" He paused, and added, in a low voice, "Yet—yet—how long the moments are—how long! Ere the sun sets, Edward, I trust, will be in my power!"

"How?"

"He goes, to-day, to the More—he will not go the less for what hath chanced; he will trust to the archbishop to make his peace with me—churchmen are not fathers! Marmaduke Nevile, hath my orders—a hundred armed men, who would march against the fiend himself, if I said the word, will surround the More, and seize the guest!"

"But what then? Who, *if* Edward—I dare not say the word;—*who is to succeed him?*"

"Clarence is the male heir!"

"But with what face to the people—proclaim——"

"There—there it is!" interrupted Warwick. "I have thought of that—I have thought of all things; my mind seems to have traversed worlds since daybreak! True! all commotion to be successful must have a cause that men can understand. Nevertheless, you, Montagu—you have a smoother tongue than I; go to our friends—to those who hate Edward—seek them, sound them!"

"And name to them Edward's infamy!"

"'Sdeath, dost thou think it! Thou, a Monthermer and Montagu! proclaim to England the foul insult to the hearth of an English gentleman and peer! feed every ribald Bourdour with song and roundel of Anne's virgin shame! how King Edward stole to her room at the dead of night, and wooed and pressed, and swore, and—God of Heaven, that this hand were on his throat! No, brother, no! there are some wrongs we may not tell—tumours and swellings of the heart, which are eased not till blood can flow!"

During this conference between the brothers, Edward, in his palace, was seized with consternation and dismay on hearing that the Lady Anne could not be found in her chamber. He sent forthwith to summon Adam Warner to his presence, and learned from the simple sage, who concealed nothing, the mode in which Anne had fled from the Tower. The king abruptly dismissed Adam, after a few hearty curses and vague threats; and awaking to the necessity of inventing some plausible story, to account to the wonder of the court for the abrupt disappearance of his guest, he saw that the person who could best originate and circulate such a tale was the queen; and he sought her at once, with the resolution to choose his confidant in the connection most rarely honored by marital trust, in similar offences. He, however, so softened his narrative as to leave it but a venial error. He had been indulging over-freely in the wine-cup—he had walked into the corridor, for the refreshing coolness of the air—he had seen the figure of a female whom he did not recognize; and a few gallant words, he scarce remembered what, had been misconstrued. On perceiving whom he had thus addressed, he had sought to soothe the anger or alarm of the Lady Anne; but still mistaking his intention, she had hurried into Warner's chamber—he had followed her thither—and now she had fled the palace. Such was his story, told lightly and laughingly, but ending with a grave enumeration of the dangers his imprudence had incurred.

Whatever Elizabeth felt, or however she might interpret the confession, she acted with her customary discretion; affected, after a few tender reproaches, to place implicit credit in her lord's account, and volunteered to prevent all scandal by the probable story, that the earl, being prevented from coming in person for his daughter, as he had purposed, by fresh news of there bellion which might call him from London with the early day, had commissioned his kinsman Marmaduke to escort her home. The quick perception of her sex told her that, whatever licence might have terrified Anne into so abrupt a flight, the haughty earl would shrink no less than Edward himself from making public an insult which slander could well distort into the dishonor of his daughter: and that whatever pretext might be invented, Warwick would not deign to contradict it. And as, despite Elizabeth's hatred to the earl, and desire of permanent breach between Edward and his minister, she could not, as queen, wife, and woman, but be anxious that some cause more honorable in Edward, and less odious to the people, should be assigned for quarrel,—she earnestly recommended the king to repair at once to the More, as had been before arranged, and to spare no pains, disdain no expressions of penitence and humiliation, to secure the mediation of the archbishop. His mind somewhat relieved by this interview and counsel, the king kissed Elizabeth with affectionate gratitude, and returned to his chamber to prepare for his departure to the archbishop's palace. But then, remembering that Adam and Sibyll possessed his secret, he resolved at once to banish them from the Tower. For a moment he thought of the dungeons of his fortress—of the rope of his doomsman; but his conscience at that hour was sore and vexed.

His fierceness humbled by the sense of shame, he shrunk from a new crime; and, moreover, his strong common sense assured him that the testimony of a shunned and abhorred wizard ceased to be of weight the moment it was deprived of the influence it took from the protection of a king. He gave orders for a boat to be in readiness by the gate of St. Thomas, again summoned Adam into his presence, and said, briefly, "Master Warner, the London mechanics cry so loudly against thine invention for lessening labor and starving the poor, the sailors on the wharfs are so mutinous, at the thought of vessels without rowers, that, as a good king is bound, I yield to the voice of my people. Go home, then at once; the queen dispenses with thy fair daughter's service—the damsel accompanies thee. A boat awaits ye at the stairs; a guard shall attend ye to your house. Think what has passed within these walls has been a dream; a dream that, if told, is deathful—if concealed and forgotten, hath no portent!"

Without waiting a reply, the king called from the ante-room one of his gentlemen, and gave him special directions as to the departure and conduct of the worthy scholar and his gentle daughter. Edward next summoned before him the warder of the gate, learned that he alone was privy to the mode of his guest's flight, and deeming it best to leave at large no commentator on the tale he had invented, sentenced the astonished warder to three months' solitary imprisonment—for appearing before him with soiled hosen! An hour afterwards, the king, with a small though gorgeous retinue, was on his way to the More.

The archbishop had, according to his engagement, assembled in his palace the more powerful of the discontented seigneurs; and his eloquence had so worked upon them, that Edward beheld, on entering the hall, only countenances of cheerful loyalty and respectful welcome. After the first greetings, the prelate, according to the custom of the day, conducted Edward into a chamber, that he might refresh himself with a brief rest and the bath, previous to the banquet.

Edward seized the occasion, and told his tale; but, however, softened, enough was left to create the liveliest dismay in his listener. The lofty scaffolding of hope, upon which the ambitious prelate was to mount to the papal throne seemed to crumble into the dust. The king and the earl were equally necessary to the schemes of George Nevile. He chid the royal layman with more than priestly unction for his offence; but Edward so humbly confessed his fault, that the prelate at length relaxed his brow, and promised to convey his penitent assurances to the earl.

"Not an hour should be lost," he said; "the only one who can soothe his wrath is your highness's mother, our noble kinswoman. Permit me to despatch to her Grace a letter, praying her to seek the earl, while I write by the same courier to himself."

"Be it all as you will," said Edward doffing his surcoat, and dipping his hands in a perfumed ewer, "I shall not know rest till I have knelt to the Lady Anne, and won her pardon."

The prelate retired, and scarcely had he left the room when Sir John Ratcliffe,* one of the king's retinue, and in waiting on his person, entered the chamber, pale and trembling.

"My liege," he said, in a whisper, "I fear some deadly treason awaits you. I have seen,

* Afterwards Lord Fitzwalter. See Lingard, note, vol. iii., p. 507, quarto edition, for the proper date to be assigned to this royal visit to the More;—a date we have here adopted—not as Sharon Turner and others place,—viz., (upon the authority of Hearne's Fragm., 302, which subsequent events disprove,) *after* the open rebellion of Warwick, but just *before* it—that is, not after Easter, but before Lent.

amongst the trees below this tower, the gleam of steel; I have crept through the foliage, and counted no less than a hundred armed men—their leader is Sir Marmaduke Nevile, Earl Warwick's kinsman!"

"Ha!" muttered the king, and his bold face fell—"comes the Earl's revenge so soon?"

"And, continued Ratcliffe, "I overheard Sir Marmaduke say, 'The door of the Garden Tower is unguarded—wait the signal!' Fly, my liege! Hark! even now, I hear the rattling of arms!"

The king stole to the casement—the day was closing; the foliage grew thick and dark around the wall; he saw an armed man emerge from the shade—a second, and a third.

"You are right, Ratcliffe! Flight—but how?"

"This way, my liege. By the passage I entered, a stair winds to a door on the inner court; there, I have already a steed in waiting. Deign, for precaution, to use my hat and manteline."

The king hastily adopted the suggestion, followed the noiseless steps of Ratcliffe, gained the door, sprung on his steed, and dashing right through a crowd assembled by the gate, galloped alone and fast, untracked by human enemy, but goaded by the foe that mounts the rider's steed—over field, over fell, ever dyke, through hedge, and in the dead of night, reined in, at last, before the royal towers of Windsor.

CHAPTER II.

Many Things briefly told.

THE events that followed the king's escape were rapid and startling. The barons assembled at the More, enraged at Edward's seeming distrust of them, separated in loud anger. The archbishop learned the cause from one of his servitors, who detected Marmaduke's ambush, but he was too wary to make known a circumstance suspicious to himself. He flew to London, and engaged the mediation of the Duchess of York to assist his own.*

The earl received their joint overtures with stern and ominous coldness, and abruptly repaired to Warwick, taking with him the Lady Anne. There he was joined, the same day, by the Duke and Duchess of Clarence.

The Lincolnshire rebellion gained head: Edward made a dexterous feint in calling, by public commission, upon Clarence and Warwick to aid in dispersing it, if they refused, the odium of first aggression would seemingly rest with them. Clarence, more induced by personal ambition than sympathy with Warwick's wrong, incensed by his brother's recent slights, looking to Edward's resignation and his own consequent accession to the throne, and inflamed by the ambition and pride of a wife whom he at once feared and idolized, went hand in heart with earl; but not one lord and captain whom Montagu had sounded lent favor to the deposition of one brother for the advancement of the next. Clarence, though popular, was too young to be respected; many there were who would rather have supported the earl, if an aspirant to the throne; but that choice, forbidden by the earl himself, there could be but two parties in England—the one for Edward IV.. the other for Henry VI.

Lord Montagu had repaired to Warwick Castle, to communicate in person this result of his diplomacy. The earl, whose manner was completely changed, no longer frank and hearty, but close and sinister, listened in gloomy silence.

"And now," said Montagu, with the generous emotion of a man whose nobler nature was stirred deeply, "if you resolve on war with Edward, I am willing to renounce my own ambition, the hand of a king's daughter for my son—so that I may avenge the honor of our common name. I confess that I have so loved Edward that I would fain pray you to pause, did I not distrust myself, lest in such delay, his craft should charm me back to the old affection. Nathless, to your arm, and your great soul, I have owed all, and if you are resolved to strike the blow, I am ready to share the hazard."

The earl turned away his face, and wrung his brother's hand.

"Our father, methinks, hears thee from the grave!" said he, solemnly, and there was a long pause. At length Warwick resumed: "Return to London; seem to take no share in my actions, whatever they be; if I fail, why drag thee into my ruin?—and yet, trust me, I

* Lingard. See for the dates, Fabyan, 657.

am rash and fierce no more. He who sets his heart on a great object suddenly becomes wise. When a throne is in the dust—when from St. Paul's Cross a voice goes forth, to Carlisle and the Land's End, proclaiming that the reign of Edward the Fourth is past and gone—then, Montagu, I claim thy promise of aid and fellowship—not before!"

Meanwhile, the king, eager to dispel thought in action, rushed in person against the rebellious forces. Stung by fear into cruelty, he beheaded, against all kingly faith, his hostages, Lord Welles and Sir Thomas Dymoke, summoned Sir Robert Welles, the leader of the revolt, to surrender; received for answer, that Sir Robert Welles would not trust the perfidy of the man who had murdered his father!"—pushed on to Erpingham, defeated the rebels in a signal battle, and crowned his victory by a series of ruthless cruelties—committed to the fierce and learned Earl of Worcester, "Butcher of England." * With the prompt vigor and superb generalship which Edward ever displayed in war, he then cut his gory way to the force which Clarence and Warwick (though their hostility was still undeclared) had levied, with the intent to join the defeated rebels. He sent his herald, Garter King-at-arms, to summon the earl and the duke to appear before him within a certain day. The time expired; he proclaimed them traitors, and offered rewards for their apprehension! *

So sudden had been Warwick's defection—so rapid the king's movements—that the earl had not time to mature his resources, assemble his vassals, consolidate his schemes. His very preparations, upon the night on which Edward had repaid his services by such hideous ingratitude, had manned the country with armies against himself. Girt but with a scanty force collected in haste, (and which consisted merely of his retainers, in the single shire of Warwick), the march of Edward cut him off from the counties in which his name was held most dear—in which his trumpet could raise up hosts. He was disappointed in the aid he had expected from his powerful but self-interested, brother-in-law, Lord Stanley. Revenge had become more dear to him than life: life must not be hazarded, lest revenge be lost. On still marched the king; and the day that his troops entered Exeter, Warwick, the females of his family, with Clarence, and a small but armed retinue, took ship from Dartmouth, sailed for Calais, (before which town, while at anchor, Isabel was confined of her first-born)—to the earl's rage and dismay, his deputy Vauclerc fired upon his ships. Warwick then steered on towards Normandy, captured some Flemish vessels by the way, in token of defiance to the earl's old Burgundian foe—and landed at Harfleur—where he and his companions were received with royal honors by the Admiral of France, and finally took their way to the court of Louis XI., at Amboise.

"The danger is past for ever!" said King Edward, as the wine sparkled in his goblet. "Rebellion hath lost its head—and now, indeed, and for the first time a monarch, I reign alone!" †

* Stowe. Warkworth Chronicle—Cont. Croyl. Lord Worcester ordered Clapham (a squire to Lord Warwick), and nineteen others, gentlemen and yeomen, *to be impaled*, and from the horror the spectacle inspired, and the universal odium it attached to Worcester, it is to be feared that the unhappy men were still sensible to the agony of this infliction, though they appear first to have been drawn and, partially hanged;—outrage confined only to the *dead bodies* of rebels, being too common at that day to have excited the indignation which attended the sentence Worcester passed on his victims. It is in vain that some writers would seek to cleanse the memory of this learned nobleman from the stain of cruelty, by rhetorical remarks on the improbability that a cultivator of letters should be of a ruthless disposition. The general philosophy of this defence is erroneous. In ignorant ages, a man of superior acquirements is not necessarily made humane by the cultivation of his intellect; on the contrary, he too often learns to look upon the uneducated herd as things of another clay. Of this truth all history is pregnant—witness the accomplished tyrants of Greece, the profound and cruel intellect of the Italian Borgias. Richard III. and Henry VIII. were both highly educated for their age. But in the case of Tiptoft, Lord Worcester, the evidence of his cruelty is no less incontestable than that which proves his learning—the Croyland historian alone is unimpeachable. Worcester's popular name of "the Butcher" is sufficient testimony in itself. The people are often mistaken, to be sure, but can scarcely be so upon the one point—whether a man who has sate in judgment on themselves be merciful or cruel.

* One thousand pounds in money, or one hundred pounds a-year in land; an immense reward for that day.

† Before leaving England, Warwick and Clarence are generally said to have fallen in with Anthony Woodville and Lord Audley, and ordered them to execution; from which they were saved by a Dorsetshire gentleman. Carte, who, though his history is not without great mistakes, is well worth reading by those whom the character of Lord Warwick may interest, says, that the earl had "too much magnanimity to put

CHAPTER III.

The Plot of the Hostelry—The Maid and the Scholar in their Home.

THE country was still disturbed, and the adherents, whether of Henry or the earl, still rose in many an outbreak, though prevented from swelling into one common army by the extraordinary vigor not only of Edward, but of Gloucester and Hastings,—when one morning, just after the events thus rapidly related, the hostelry of Master Sancroft, in the suburban parish of Marybone, rejoiced in a motley crowd of customers and topers.

Some half score soldiers, returned in triumph from the royal camp, sate round a table placed agreeably enough in the deep recess made by the large jutting lattice; with them were mingled about as many women, strangely and gaudily clad. These last were all young; one or two, indeed, little advanced from childhood. But there was no expression of youth in their hard sinister features: coarse paint supplied the place of bloom; the very youngest had a wrinkle on her brow; their forms wanted the round and supple grace of early years. Living principally in the open air, trained from infancy to feats of activity, their muscles were sharp and prominent—their aspects had something of masculine audacity and rudeness; health itself seemed in them more loathsome than disease.

Upon those faces of bronze, vice had set its ineffable, unmistaken seal. To those eyes never had sprung the tears of compassion or woman's gentle sorrow; on those brows never had flushed the glow of modest shame; their very voices half belied their sex—harsh, and deep, and hoarse—their laughter loud and dissonant. Some amongst them were not destitute of a certain beauty, but it was a beauty of feature with a common hideousness of expression—an expression at once cunning, bold, callous, and licentious. Womanless, through the worst vices of woman—passionless, through the premature waste of passion—they stood between the sexes like foul and monstrous anomalies, made up and fashioned from the rank depravities of both. These creatures seemed to have newly arrived from some long warfaring—their shoes and the hems of their robes were covered with dust and mire—their faces were heated, and the veins in their bare, sinewy, sunburned arms were swollen by fatigue. Each had beside her on the floor a timbrel—each wore at her girdle a long knife in its sheath: well that the sheaths hid the blades, for not one—not even that which yon cold-eyed child of fifteen wore—but had on its steel the dark stain of human blood!

The presence of soldiers fresh from the scene of action had naturally brought into the hostelry several of the idle gossips of the suburb, and these stood round the table, drinking into their large ears the boasting narratives of the soldiers. At a small table, apart from the revellers, but evidently listening with attention to all the news of the hour, sate a friar, gravely discussing a mighty tankard of huffcap, and ever and anon, as he lifted his head for the purpose of drinking, glancing a wanton eye at one of the tymbesteres.

"But an' you had seen," said a trooper, who was the mouthpiece of his comrades—"an' you had seen the raptrils run when King Edward himself led the charge! Marry! it was like a cat in a rabbit burrow! Easy to see, I trow, that Earl Warwick was not amongst them! *His* men, at least, fight like devils!"

"But there was one tall fellow," said a sol-

---

them to death immediately, according to the common practice of the times, and only imprisoned them in the castle of Wardour, from whence they were soon rescued by John Thornhill, a gentleman of Dorsetshire." The whole of this story is, however, absolutely contradicted by the Warkworth Chronicle, (p. 9, edited by Mr Halliwell,) according to which authority Anthony Woodville was at that time commanding a fleet upon the Channel, which waylaid Warwick on his voyage: but the success therein attributed to the gallant Anthony, in dispersing or seizing all the earl's ships, save the one that bore the earl himself and his family, is proved to be purely fabulous, by the earl's well-attested capture of the Flemish vessels, as he passed from Calais to the coasts of Normandy, an exploit he could never have performed with a single vessel of his own. It is very probable that the story of Anthony Woodville's capture and peril at this time originates in a misadventure many years before, aud recorded in the Paston letters, as well as in the Chronicles.—In the year 1459, Anthony Woodville and his father, Lord Rivers (then zealous Lancastrians), really did fall into the hands of the Earl of March (Edward IV.), Warwick and Salisbury, aud got off with a sound "rating" upon the rude language which such "knaves' sons" and "little squires" had held to those "who were of king's blood."

dier, setting down his tankard, "who made a good fight and dour, and but for me and my comrades, would have cut his way to the king."

"Ay—ay—true! we saved his highness, and ought to have been knighted—but there's no gratitude now-a-days!"

"And who was this doughty warrior?" asked one of the bystanders, who secretly favored the rebellion.

"Why, it was said that he was Robin of Redesdale. He who fought my Lord Montagu off York."

"Our Robin!" exclaimed several voices. "Ay, he was ever a brave fellow—poor Robin!"

"'Your Robin,'" and 'poor Robin,' varlets!" cried the principal trooper. Have a care! What do you mean by your Robin?"

"Marry, sir soldier," quoth a butcher, scratching his head, and in a humble voice—"craving your pardon, and the king's, this Master Robin sojourned a short time in this hamlet, and was a kind neighbor, and mighty glib of the tongue. Don't ye mind, neighbors," he added rapidly, eager to change the conversation, "how he made us leave off when we were just about burning Adam Warner, the old nigromancer, in his den, yonder? Who else could have done that? But an' we had known Robin had been a rebel to sweet King Edward, we'd have roasted him along with the wizard!"

One of the timbrel girls, the leader of the choir, her arm round a soldier's neck, looked up at the last speech, and her eye followed the gesture of the butcher, as he pointed through the open lattice to the sombre, ruinous abode of Adam Warner.

"Was that the house ye would have burned?" she asked abruptly.

"Yes; but Robin told us the king would hang those who took on them the king's blessed privilege of burning nigromancers; and, sure enough, old Adam Warner was advanced to be wizard-in-chief to the king's own highness a week or two afterwards."

The friar had made a slight movement at the name of Warner; he now pushed his stool nearer to the principal group, and drew his hood completely over his countenance.

"Yea!" exclaimed the mechanic, whose son had been the innocent cause of the memorable siege to poor Adam's dilapidated fortress, related in the first book of this narrative—"Yea; and what did he when there? Did he not devise a horrible engine for the destruction of the poor—an engine that was to do all the work in England by the devil's help?—so that if a gentleman wanted a coat of mail, or a cloth tunic—if his dame needed a Norwich worsted—if a yeoman lacked a plough or a wagon, or his good wife a pot or a kettle, they were to go, not to the armorer, and the draper, and the tailor, and the weaver, and the wheelwright and the blacksmith,—but, hey presto! Master Warner set his imps a churning, and turned ye out mail and tunic, worsted and wagon, kettle and pot, spick and span new, from his brewage of vapor and sea-coal? Oh, have I not heard enough of the sorcerer from my brother, who works in the Chepe for Master Stokton, the mercer!—and Master Stokton was one of the worshipful deputies to whom the old nigromancer had the front to boast his devices."

"It is true," said the friar, suddenly.

"Yes, reverend father, it is true," said the mechanic, doffing his cap, and inclining his swarthy face to this unexpected witness of his veracity. A murmur of wrath and hatred was heard amongst the bystanders. The soldiers indifferently turned to their female companions. There was a brief silence; and, involuntarily, the gossips stretched over the table to catch sight of the house of so demoniac an oppressor of the poor.

"See," said the baker, "the smoke still curls from the roof-top! I heard he had come back. Old Madge, his handmaid, has bought simnel cakes of me the last week or so; nothing less than the finest wheat serves him now, I trow. However, right's right, and ——"

"Come back!" cried the fierce mechanic, "the owl hath kept close in his roost! An' it were not for the king's favor, I would soon see how the wizard liked to have fire and water brought to bear against himself!"

"Sit down, sweetheart," whispered one of the young tymbesteres to the last speaker—

"Come kiss me, my darling,
Warm kisees I trade for——"

"Avaunt!" quoth the mechanic, gruffly, and shaking off the seductive arm of the tymbestere—"Avaunt! I have neither liefe nor halfpence for thee and thine. Out on thee—a child of thy years! a rope's end to thy back were a friends best kindness!"

The girl's eyes sparkled, she instinctively put her hand to her knife; then turning to a soldier by her side, she said—"Hear you that, and sit still?"

"Thunder and wounds!" growled the soldier thus appealed to—"more respect to the sex, knave; if I don't break thy fool's costard with my sword-hilt, it is only because Red Grisell can take care of herself against twenty such lozels as thou. These honest girls have been to the wars with us; King Edward grudges no man his jolly fere. Speak up for thyself, Grisell! How many tall fellows didst thou put out of their pain, after the battle of Losecote?"

"Only five, Hal," replied the cold-eyed girl, and showing her glittering teeth with the grin of a young tigress;—"but one was a captain. I shall do better next time; it was my first battle, thou knowest!"

The more timid of the bystanders exchanged a glance of horror, and drew back. The mechanic resumed sullenly—

"I seek no quarrel with lass or lover. I am a plain, blunt man, with a wife and children, who are dear to me; and if I have a grudge to the nigromancer, it is because he glamoured my poor boy Tim. See!"—and he caught up a blue-eyed, handsome boy, who had been clinging to his side, and baring the child's arm, showed it to the spectators; there was a large scar on the limb, and it was shrunk and withered.

"It was my own fault," said the little fellow, deprecatingly.

The affectionate father silenced the sufferer with a cuff on the cheek, and resumed—"Ye note, neighbors, the day when the foul wizard took this little one in his arms: well, three weeks afterwards—that very day three weeks—as he was standing like a lamb by the fire, the good wife's caldron seethed over, without reason or rhyme, and scalded his arm till it rivelled up like a leaf in November; and if that is not glamor, why have we laws against witchcraft?"

"True—true!" groaned the chorus.

The boy, who had borne his father's blow without a murmur, now again attempted remonstrance. "The hot water went over the grey cat, too, but Master Warner never bewitched *her*, daddy."

"He takes his part!—You hear the daff laddy? He takes the old nigromancer's part—a sure sign of the witchcraft; but I'll leather it out of thee, I will!" and the mechanic again raised his weighty arm. The child did not this time await the blow; he dodged under the butcher's apron, gained the door, and disappeared. "And he teaches our own children to fly in our faces!" said the father, in a kind of whimper.

The neighbors sighed, in commiseration.

"Oh!" he exclaimed, in a fiercer tone, grinding his truth, and shaking his clenched fist towards Adam Warner's melancholy house—"I say again, if the king did not protect the vile sorcerer, I would free the land from his devilries, ere his black master could come to his help."

"The king cares not a straw for Master Warner or his inventions, my son," said a rough, loud voice. All turned, and saw the friar standing in the midst of the circle. "Know ye not, my children, that the king sent the wretch neck and crop out of the palace, for having bewitched the Earl of Warwick and his grace the Lord Clarence, so that they turned unnaturally against their own kinsman, his highness. But 'Manus malorum suos bonus breaket'—that is to say,—the fists of wicked men only whack their own bones. Ye have all heard tell of Friar Bungey, my children?"

"Ay—ay!" answered two or three in a breath—"a wizard, it's true, and a mighty one; but he never did harm to the poor, though they do say he made a quaint image of the earl, and——"

"Tut—tut!" interrupted the friar, "all Bungey did was to try to disenchant the Lord Warwick, whom yon miscreant had spellbound. Poor Bungey! he is a friend to the people; and when he found that Master Adam was making a device for their ruin, he spared no toil, I assure ye, to frustrate the inquity. Oh, how he fasted and watched! Oh, how many a time he fought, tooth and nail, with the devil in person, to get at the infernal invention! for if *he* had that invention once in his hands, he could turn it to good account, I can promise ye; and give ye rain for the green blade, and sun for the ripe sheaf. But the fiend got the better at first; and King Edward, bewitched himself for the moment, would have hanged Friar Bungey for crossing old Adam, if he had not called three times, in a loud voice—'Presto pepranxenom!' changed himself into a bird, and flown out of the window. As soon as Master Adam Warner found the field clear to himself, he employed his daughter to bewitch the Lord Hastings; he set brother against brother, and made the king and Lord George fall to loggerheads; he stirred up the rebellion, and where he would have stopped the foul fiend only knows, if your friend, Friar Bungey, who, though a wizard as you say, is only so for your benefit (and a holy priest into the bargain), had not, by aid of a good spirit, whom he conjured up in the Island of Tartary, disenchanted the king, and made him see in a dream what the villanous Warner was devising against his crown and his people,—whereon his highness sent Master Warner and his daughter back to their roost, and, helped by Friar Bungey, beat his enemies out of the kingdom. So, if ye have a mind to save your children from mischief and malice, ye may set to work with good heart, always provided that ye touch not old Adam's iron invention. Woe betide ye, if ye think to destroy *that!* Bring it safe to Friar Bungey, whom ye will find returned to the palace, and journeymen's wages will be a penny a day higher for the next ten years to come!" With these words the friar threw down his reckoning, and moved majestically to the door.

"An' I might trust you?" said Tim's father, laying hold of the friar's serge.

"Ye may—ye may!" cried the leader of the tymbesteres, starting up from the lap of her soldier, "for it is Friar Bungey himself!"

A movement of astonishment and terror was universal.

"Friar Bungey himself!" repeated the burly impostor. "Right, lassie, right; and he now goes to the palace of the Tower, to mutter good spells in King Edward's ear—spells to defeat the malignant ones, and to lower the price of beer. Wax wobiscum!"

With that salutation, more benevolent than accurate, the friar vanished from the room; the chief of the tymbesteres leaped lightly on the table, put one foot on the soldier's shoulder, and sprang through the open lattice. She found the friar in the act of mounting a sturdy mule, which had been tied to a post by the door.

"Fie, Graul Skellet! Fie, Graul!" said the conjurer. "Respect for my serge. We must not be noted together out of door in the daylight. There's a groat for thee. Vade, execrabilis,—that is, Good day to thee, pretty rogue!"

"A word, friar, a word. Wouldst thou have the old man burned, drowned, or torn piecemeal! He hath a daughter, too, who once sought to mar our trade with her gittern; a daughter, then in a kirtle that I would not have nimmed from a hedge, but whom I last saw in sarcenet and lawn, with a great lord for her fere." The tymbestere's eyes shone with malignant envy, as she added—"Graul Skellet loves not to see those, who have worn worsted and say, walk in sarcenet and lawn! Granl Skellet loves not wenches who have lords for their feres, and yet who shrink from Graul and her sisters as the sound from the leper."

"Fegs," answered the friar, impatiently, "I know nought against the daughter—a pretty lass, but too high for my kisses. And as for the father, I want not the man's life—that is, not very especially—but his model, his mechanical. He may go free, if that can be compassed; if not,—why, the model at all risks! Serve me in this."

"And thou wilt teach me the last tricks of the cards, and thy great art of making phantoms glide by on the wall?"

"Bring the model intact, and I will teach thee more, Graul;—the dead man's candle, and the charm of the newt—and I'll give thee, to boot, the caul of the parricade, that thou hast prayed me so oft for. Hum!—thou hast a girl in thy troop who hath a blinking eye that well pleases me;—but go now, and obey me. Work before play—and grace before pudding!"

The tymbestere nodded, snapped her fingers in the air, and humming no holy ditty, returned to the house through the door-way.

This short conference betrays to the reader the relations, mutually advantageous, which subsisted between the conjurer and the tymbesteres. Their troop (the mothers, perchance, of the generation we treat of) had been familiar to the friar in his old capacity of mountebank or tregetour, and in his clerical and courtly elevation, he did not disdain an ancient connection that served him well with the populace; for these grim children of vice seemed present in every place, where pastime was gay, or strife was rampant; in peace, at the merry-makings and the hostelries—in war, following the camp, and seen, at night, prowling through the battle-fields to despatch the wounded and to rifle the slain:—In merry-making, hostelry, or in camp, they could thus still spread the fame of Friar Bungey, and uphold his repute both for terrible lore and for hearty love of the commons.

Nor was this all; both tymbesteres and conjurer were fortune-tellers by profession. They could interchange the anecdotes each picked up in their different lines. The tymbestere could thus learn the secrets of gentle and courtier—the conjurer those of the artisan and mechanic.

Unconscious of the formidable dispositions of their neighbors, Sibyll and Warner were inhaling the sweet air of the early spring in their little garden. His disgrace had affected the philosopher less than might be supposed. True, that the loss of the king's favor was the deferring indefinitely,—perhaps for life,—any practical application of his adored theory; and yet, somehow or other, the theory itself consoled him. At the worst, he should find some disciple, some ingenious student, more fortunate than himself, to whom he could bequeath the secret, and who, when Adam was in his grave, would teach the world to revere his name. Meanwhile, his time was his own; he was lord of a home, though ruined and desolate; he was free, with his free thoughts; and therefore, as he paced the narrow garden, his step was lighter, his mind less absent, than when parched with feverish fear and hope, for the immediate practical success of a principle which was to be tried before the hazardous tribunal of prejudice and ignorance.

"My child," said the sage, "I feel, for the first time for years, the distinction of the seasons. I feel that we are walking in the pleasant spring. Young days come back to me like dreams; and I could almost think thy mother were once more by my side!"

Sibyll pressed her father's hand, and a soft but melancholy sigh stirred her rosy lips. She, too, felt the balm of the young year; yet her father's words broke upon sad and anxious musings. Not to youth as to age, not to loving fancy as to baffled wisdom, has seclusion charms that compensate for the passionate and active world! On coming back to the old house, on glancing round its mildewed walls, comfortless and bare, the neglected, weed-grown garden, Sibyll had shuddered in dismay. Had her ambition fallen again into its old abject state? Were all her hopes to restore her ancestral fortunes, to vindicate her dear father's fame, shrunk into this slough of actual poverty —the butterfly's wings folded back into the chrysalis shroud of torpor? The vast disparity between herself and Hastings had not struck her so forcibly at the court; here, at home, the very walls proclaimed it. When Edward had dismissed the unwelcome witnesses of his attempted crime, he had given orders that they should be conducted to their house through the most private ways. He naturally desired to create no curious comment upon their departure. Unperceived by their neighbors, Sibyll and her father had gained access by the garden gate. Old Madge received them in dismay; for she had been in the habit of visiting Sibyll weekly at the palace, and had gained, in the old familiarity subsisting, then, between maiden and nurse, some insight into her heart. She had cherished the fondest hopes for the fate of her young mistress;—and now, to labor and penury had the fate returned! The guard who accompanied them, according to Edward's orders, left some pieces of gold, which Adam rejected, but Madge secretly received and judiciously expended. And this was all their wealth. But not of toil nor of penury in themselves thought Sibyll; she thought but of Hastings—wildly, passionately, trustfully, unceasingly, of the absent Hastings. Oh! he would seek her—he would come—her reverse would but the more endear her to him! Hastings came not. She soon learned the wherefore. War threatened the land—he was at his post, at the head of armies.

Oh, with what panoply of prayer she sought to shield that beloved breast! And now the old man spoke of the blessed spring, the holiday time of lovers and of love, and the young girl, sighing, said to her mournful heart, "The world hath its sun,—where is mine?"

The peacock strutted up to his poor protectors, and spread his plumes to the gilding beams. And then Sibyll recalled the day when she had walked in that spot with Marmaduke, and he had talked of his youth, ambition, and lusty hopes, while, silent and absorbed, she had thought within herself, "could the world be open to me as to him,—I too have ambition, and it should find its goal." Now what contrast between the two—the man enriched and honored, if to-day in peril or in exile, to-morrow free to march forward still on his career—the world the country to him whose heart was bold and whose name was stainless! And she, the woman, brought back to the prison-house, scorn around her, impotent to avenge, and forbidden to fly! Wherefore?—Sibyll felt her superiority of mind, of thought, of nature—Wherefore the contrast? The success was that of man, the discomfiture that of woman. Woe to the man who precedes his age, but never yet has an age been in which genius and ambition are safe to woman!

The father and the child turned into their house; the day was declining; Adam mounted to his studious chamber, Sibyll sought the solitary servant.

"What tidings, oh, what tidings! The war, you say, is over; the great earl, his sweet daughter, safe upon the seas, but Hastings, oh, Hastings! what of him?"

"My bonnibell, my lady-bird, I have none but good tales to tell thee. I saw and spoke with a soldier who served under Lord Hastings himself; he is unscathed, he is in London. But they say that one of his bands is quartered in the suburb, and that there is a report of a rising in Hertfordshire."

"When will peace come to England and to me!" sighed Sibyll.

CHAPTER IV.

This World's Justice, and the Wisdom of our Ancestors.

The night had now commenced, and Sibyll was still listening—or, perhaps, listening not—to the soothing babble of the venerable servant. They were both seated in the little room that adjoined the hall, and their only light came through the door opening on the garden—a grey, indistinct twilight relieved by the few earliest stars. The peacock, his head under his wing, roosted on the balustrade, and the song of the nightingale, from amidst one of the neighboring copses, which studded the ground towards the chase of Marybone, came soft and distant on the serene air. The balm and freshness of spring were felt in the dews, in the skies, in the sweet breath of young herb and leaf;—through the calm of ever-watchful nature, it seemed as if you might mark, distinct and visible, minute after minute, the blessed growth of April into May.

Suddenly, Madge uttered a cry of alarm, and pointed towards the opposite wall. Sibyll, startled from her reverie, looked up, and saw something dusk and dwarf-like, perched upon the crumbling eminence. Presently this apparition leaped lightly into the garden, and the alarm of the women was lessened on seeing a young boy creep stealthily over the grass, and approach the open door.

"Heh, child!" said Madge, rising. "What wantest thou?"

"Hist, grammer, hist! Ah! the young mistress? That's well. Hist! I say again." The boy entered the room. "I'm in time to save you. In half an hour your house will be broken into, perhaps burnt. The boys are clapping their hands now at the thoughts of the bonfire. Father and all the neighbors are getting ready. Hark! hark! No, it is only the wind! This tymbesteres are to give note. When you hear their bells tinkle, the mob will meet. Run for your lives, you and the old man, and don't ever say it was poor Tim who told you this, for father wonld beat me to death. Ye can still get through the garden into the fields. Quick!"

"I will go to the master," exclaimed Madge, hurrying from the room.

The child caught Sibyll's cold hand through the dark. "And I say, mistress, if his worship *is* a wizard, don't let him punish father and mother, or poor Tim, or his little sister; though Tim was once naughty and hooted Master Warner. Many, many, many a time and oft have I seen that kind, mild face in my sleep, just as when it bent over me—while I kicked and screamed—and the poor gentleman said, 'Thinkest thou I would harm thee?' But he'll forgive me now, will he not? And when I turned the seething water over myself, and they said it was all along of the wizard, my heart pained more than the arm. But they whip me, and groan out that the devil is in me, if I don't say that the kettle upset of itself! Oh, those tymbesteres! Mistress, did you ever see them? They fright me. If you could hear how they set on all the neighbors! And their laugh—it makes the hair stand on end! But you will get away, and thank Tim too! Oh, I shall laugh then, when they find the old house empty!"

"May our dear Lord bless thee — bless thee, child," sobbed Sibyll, clasping the boy in her arms, and kissing him, while her tears bathed his cheeks.

A light gleamed on the threshold—Madge, holding a candle, appeared with Warner, his hat and cloak thrown on in haste. "What is this?" said the poor scholar. "Can it be true? Is mankind so cruel! What have I done, woe is me! what have I done to deserve this?"

"Come, dear father, quick," said Sibyll, drying her tears, and wakened, by the presence of the old man, into energy and courage. "But put thy hand on this boy's head, and bless him, for it is he who has, happily, saved us."

The boy trembled a moment as the long-bearded face turned towards him, but when he caught and recognized those meek, sweet eyes, his superstition vanished, and it was but a holy and grateful awe that thrilled his young blood, as the old man placed both withered hands over his yellow hair, and murmured—

"God shield thy youth—God make thy manhood worthy—God give thee children in thine old age with hearts like thine!"

Scarcely had the prayer ceased when the clash of timbrels, with their jingling bells, was heard in the street. Once, twice, again, and a fierce yell closed in chorus,—caught up and echoed from corner to corner, from house to house.

"Run—run!" cried the boy, turning white with terror.

"But the Eureka—my hope—my mind's child!" exclaimed Adam, suddenly, halting at the door.

"Eh—eh!" said Madge, pushing him forward. "It is too heavy to move; thou couldst not lift it. Think of thine own flesh and blood—of thy daughter—of her dead mother. Save her life if thou carest not for thine own!"

"Go, Sibyll, go—and thou, Madge—I will stay. What matters my life, it is but the servant of a thought! Perish master—perish slave!"

"Father! unless you come with me I stir not. Fly, or perish! Your fate is mine! Another minute! Oh, heaven of mercy, that roar again! We are both lost!"

"Go, sir, go; they care not for your iron—iron cannot feel. They will not touch *that!* Have not your daughter's life upon your soul!"

"Sibyll—Sibyll, forgive me! Come!" said Warner, conscience-stricken at the appeal.

Madge and the boy ran forwards—the old woman unbarred the garden-gate—Sibyll and her father went forth—the fields stretched before them calm and solitary—the boy leaped up, kissed Sibyll's pale cheek, and then bounded across the grass, and vanished.

"Loiter not, Madge. Come!" cried Sibyll.

"Nay," said the old woman, shrinking back; "they bear no grudge to me; I am too old to do ought but burden ye. I will stay, and perchance save the house and the chattels, and poor master's deft contrivance. Whist! thou knowest his heart would break if none were by to guard it."

With that the faithful servant thrust the broad pieces that yet remained of the king's gift into the gipsire Sibyll wore at her girdle, and then closed and rebarred the door before they could detain her.

"It is base to leave her," said the Scholar-gentleman.

The noble Sibyll could not refute her father. Afar they heard the trampling of feet: suddenly, a dark red light shot up into the blue air, a light from the flame of many torches.

"The Wizard—the Wizard! Death to the Wizard, who would starve the poor!" yelled forth, and was echoed by a stern hurrah.

Adam stood motionless, Sibyll by his side. "The Wizard and *his daughter!*" shrieked a sharp single voice, the voice of Graul the tymbestere.

Adam turned. "Fly, my child—they now threaten *thee.* Come—come—come;" and taking her by the hand, he hurried her across the fields, skirting the hedge, their shadows dodging, irregular, and quaint, on the starlit sward. The father had lost all thought—all care but for the daughter's life. They paused at last, out of breath and exhausted: the sounds at the distance were lulled and hushed.

They looked towards the direction of the home they had abandoned, expecting to see the flames destined to consume it reddening the sky; but all was dark,—or, rather, no light save the holy stars and the rising moon offended the majestic heaven.

"They cannot harm the poor old woman; she hath no lore. On her gray hairs has fallen not the curse of men's hate!" said Warner.

"Right, father; when they found us flown, doubtless the cruel ones dispersed. But they may search yet for thee. Lean on me, I am strong and young. Another effort, and we gain the safe coverts of the Chase."

While yet the last word hung on her lips, they saw, on the path they had left, the burst of torchlight, and heard the mob hounding on their track. But the thick copses, with their pale green just budding into life, were at hand. On they fled: the deer started from amidst the entangled fern, but stood and gazed at them without fear; the playful hares in the green alleys ceased not their nightly sports at the harmless footsteps; and when at last, in the dense thicket, they sunk down on the mossy roots of a giant oak, the nightingales overhead chanted as if in melancholy welcome. They were saved!

But in their home fierce fires glared amidst the tossing torchlight; the crowd, baffled by the strength of the door, scaled the wall, broke through the lattice-work of the hall window, and streaming through room after room, roared forth—"Death to the Wizard!" Amidst the sordid dresses of the men, the soiled and faded tinsel of the tymbesteres gleamed and sparkled. It was a scene that she fiends revelled in—dear are outrage and malice, and the excitement of turbulent passions, and the savage voices of frantic men, and the thirst of blood to those everlasting furies of a mob—under whatever name we know them, in whatever time they taint with their presence—women in whom womanhood is blasted!

Door after door was burst open with cries of disappointed rage; at last, they ascended the turret-stairs—they found a small door, barred and locked. Tim's father, a huge axe in his brawny arm, shivered the panels; the crowd rushed in,—and there, seated amongst a strange and motley litter, they found the devoted Madge. The poor old woman had collected into this place, as the stronghold of the mansion, whatever portable articles seemed to her most precious, either from value or association Sibyll's gittern (Marmaduke's gift) lay amidst a lumber of tools and implements —a faded robe of her dead mother's, treasured by Madge and Sibyll both, as a relic of holy love—a few platters and cups of pewter, the pride of old Madge's heart to keep bright and clean, odds and ends of old hangings, a battered silver brooch (a love gift to Madge herself when she was young)—these, and suchlike scraps of finery, hoards inestimable to the household memory and affection, lay confusedly heaped around the huge grim model, before which, mute and tranquil, sate the brave old woman.

The crowd halted, and stared round in superstitious terror, and dumb marvel.

The leader of the tymbesteres sprang forward—

"Where is thy master, old hag, and where the bonny maid who glamours lords, and despises us bold lasses?"

"Alack! master and the damsel have gone hours ago! I am alone in the house; what's your will?"

"The crone looks parlous witchlike!" said Tim's father, crossing himself, and somewhat retreating from her grey, unquiet eyes. And, indeed, poor Madge, with her wrinkled face, bony form, and high cap, corresponded far more with the vulgar notions of a dabbler in the black art than did Adam Warner, with his comely countenance and noble mien.

"So she doth, indeed, and verily," said a hump-backed tinker, "if we were to try a dip in the horse-pool yonder it could do no harm!"

"Away with her! away!" cried several voices at that humane suggestion.

"Nay, nay," quoth the baker, "she is a douce creature, after all, and hath dealt with me many years. I don't care what becomes of the wizard—every one knows (he added with pride) that I was one of the first to set fire to his house when Robin gainsayed it!—but right's right—burn the master, not the drudge!"

This intercession might have prevailed, but, unhappily, at that moment Graul Skellet, who had secured two stout fellows to accomplish the object so desired by Friar Bungey, laid hands on the model, and, at her shrill command, the men advanced and dislodged it from its place. At the same time, the other tymbesteres, caught by the sight of things pleasing to their wonted tastes, threw themselves, one upon the faded robe Sibyll's mother had worn in her chaste and happy youth; another, upon poor Madge's silver brooch; a third, upon the gittern.

These various attacks roused up all the spirit and wrath of the old woman: her cries of distress as she darted from one to the other, striking to the right and to the left with her feeble arms, her form trembling with passion, were at once ludicrous and piteous, and these were responded to by the shrill exclamations of the fierce tymbesteres, as they retorted scratch for scratch, and blow for blow. The spectators grew animated by the sight of actual outrage and resistance: the hump-backed tinker, whose unwholesome fancy one of the aggrieved tymbesteres had mightily warmed, hastened to the relief of his virago; and rendered furious by finding ten nails fastened suddenly on his face, he struck down the poor creature by a blow that stunned her, seized her in his arms—for deformed and weakly as the tinker was, the old woman, now sense and spirit were gone, was as light as skin and bone could be—and followed by half a score of his comrades, whooping and laughing, bore her down the stairs. Tim's father, who, whether from parental affection, or, as is more probable, from the jealous hatred and prejudice of ignorant industry, was bent upon Adam's destruction, hallooed on some of his fiercer fellows into the garden, tracked the footsteps of the fugitives by the trampled grass, and bounded over the wall in fruitless chase. But on went the more giddy of the mob, rather in sport than in cruelty, with a chorus of drunken apprentices and riotous boys, to the spot where the hump-backed tinker had dragged his passive burthen. The foul green pond near Master Sancroft's hostel reflected the glare of torches; six of the tymbesteres leaping and wheeling, with doggerel song and discordant music, gave the signal for the ordeal of the witch—

"Lake or river, dyke or ditch,
Water never drowns the witch.
Witch or wizard would ye know?—
Sink or swim, is ay or no.
Lift her, swing her, once and twice,
Lift her, swing her o'er the brim,—
Lille—lera—twice and thrice—
Ha! ha! mother, sink or swim!"

And while the last line was chanted amidst the full jolity of laughter and clamor, and clattering timbrels, there was a splash in the sullen water; the green slough on the surface parted with an oozing gurgle, and then came a dead silence.

"A murrian on the hag!—she does not even struggle!" said, at last, the hump-backed tinker.

"No, no! she cares not for water—try fire! Out with her! out!" cried Red Grisell.

"Aroint her! she is sullen!" said the tinker, and his lean fingers clutched up the dead body, and let it fall upon the margin.

"Dead!" said the baker shuddering, "we have done wrong—I told ye so! She dealt with me many a year. Poor Madge!—Right's right. She was no witch!"

"But that was the only way to try it," said the hump-backed tinker; "and if she was not a witch, why did she look like one!—I cannot abide ugly folks!"

The bystanders shook their heads. But whatever their remorse, it was diverted by a double sound: first, a loud hurrah from some of the mob who had loitered for pillage, and who now emerged from Adam's house, following two men, who, preceded by the terrible Graul, dancing before them, and tossing aloft her timbrel, bore in triumph the captured Eureka; and, secondly, the blast of a clarion at the distance, while up the street marched—horse and foot, with pike and banner—a goodly troop. The Lord Hastings in person led a royal force, by a night march, against a fresh outbreak of the rebels, not ten miles from the city, under Sir Geoffrey Gates, who had been lately arrested by the Lord Howard at Southampton—escaped—collected a disorderly body of such restless men as are always disposed to take part in civil commotion, and now menaced London itself. At the sound of the clarion the valiant mob dispersed in all directions, for even at that day mobs had an instinct of terror at the approach of the military, and a quick reaction from outrage to the fear of retaliation.

But, at the sound of martial music, the tymbesteres silenced their own instruments, and instead of flying, they darted through the crowd, each to seek the other, and unite as for counsel. Graul, pointing to Mr. Sancroft's hostelry, whispered the bearers of the Eureka to seek refuge there for the present, and to bear their trophy with the dawn to Friar Bungey, at the Tower; and then, gliding nimbly through the fugitive rioters, sprang into the centre of the circle formed by her companions.

"Ye scent the coming battle," said the archtymbestere.

"Ay—ay—ay!" answered the sisterhood.

"But we have gone miles since noon—I am faint and weary!" said one amongst them.

Red Grisell, the youngest of the band, struck her comrade on the cheek—"Faint and weary, ronion, with blood and booty in the wind!"

The tymbesteres smiled grimly on their young sister; but the leader whispered "Hush!" And they stood for a second or two with outstretched throats—with dilated nostrils—with pent breath—listening to the clarion, and the hoofs, and the rattling armor;—the human vultures foretasting their feast of carnage; then, obedient to a sign from their chieftainess, they crept lightly and rapidly into the mouth of a neighboring alley, where they cowered by the squalid huts, concealed. The troop passed on—a gallant and serried band—horse and foot about fifteen hundred men. As they filed up the thoroughfare, and the tramp of the last soldiers fell hollow on the starlit ground, the tymbesteres stole from their retreat, and, at the distance of some few hundred yards followed the procession, with long, silent, stealthy strides,—as the meaner beasts, in the instinct of hungry cunning, follow the lion for the garbage of his prey.

CHAPTER V.

The Fugitives are captured—The Tymbesterers reappear—Moonlight on the Revel of the Living—Moonlight on the Slumber of the Dead.

THE father and child made their resting-place under the giant oak. They knew not whither to fly for refuge—the day and the night had become the same to them—the night menaced with robbers, the day with the mob. If return to their home was forbidden, where in the wide world a shelter for the would-be world-improver? Yet they despaired not, their hearts failed them not. Ths majestic splendor of the night, as it deepened in its solemn calm—as the shadows of the windless trees fell larger and sharper upon the silvery earth—as the skies grew mellower and more luminous in the strengthening starlight, inspired them with the serenity of faith—for night, to the earnest soul, opens the bible of the universe, and on the leaves of Heaven is written—"God is everywhere!"

Their hands were clasped, each in each—their pale faces were upturned; they spoke not, neither were they conscious that they prayed, but their silence was thought, and the thought was worship.

Amidst the grief and solitude of the pure, there comes, at times, a strange and rapt serenity—a sleep-awake—over which the instinct of life beyond the grave glides like a noiseless dream; and ever that heaven that the soul yearns for is colored by the fancies of the fond human heart,—each fashioning the above from the desires unsatisfied below.

"There," thought the musing maiden, "cruelty and strife shall cease—there, vanish the harsh differences of life—there, those whom we have loved and lost are found, and through the Son, who tasted of mortal sorrow, we are raised to the home of the Eternal Father!"

"And there," thought the aspiring sage, "the mind, dungeoned and chained below, rushes free into the realms of space—there, from every mystery falls the veil—there, the Omniscient smiles on those who through the darkness of life have fed that lamp, the soul,—there, Thought, but the seed on earth, bursts into the flower, and ripens to the fruit!"

And on the several hope of both maid and sage the eyes of the angel stars smiled with a common promise.

At last, insenslbly, and while still musing, so that slumber but continued the reverie into visions, father and daughter slept.

The night passed away; the dawn came slow and grey; the antlers of the deer stirred above the fern; the song of the nightingale was hushed; and just as the morning star waned back, while the reddening east announced the sun, and labor and trouble resumed their realm of day, a fierce band halted before those sleeping forms.

The men had been Lancastrian soldiers, and, reduced to plunder for a living, had, under Sir Geoffrey Gates, formed the most stalwart part of the wild disorderly force whom Hilyard and Coniers had led to Olney. They had heard of the new outbreak, headed by their ancient captain Sir Geoffrey (who was supposed to have been instigated to his revolt by the gold and promises of the Lancastrian chiefs), and were on their way to join the rebels; but as war for them was but the name for booty, they felt the wonted instinct of the robber, when they caught sight of the old man and the fair maid.

Both Adam and his daughter wore, unhappily, the dresses in which they had left the court, and Sibyll's especially was that which seemed to betoken a certain rank and station.

"Awake—rouse ye!" said the captain of the band, roughly shaking the arm which encircled Sibyll's slender waist. Adam started, opened his eyes and saw himself begirt by figures in rusty armor, with savage faces peering under their steel sallets.

"How came ye hither? Yon oak drops strange acorns," qouth the chief.

"Valiant sir!" replied Adam, still seated, and drawing his gown instinctively over Sibyll's face, which nestled on his bosom, in slumber so deep and heavy, that the gruff voice had not broken it. "Valiant sir! we are forlorn and houseless—an old man and a simple girl. Some evil-minded persons invaded our home—we fled in the night—and——"

"Invaded your house! ha, it is clear," said the chief. "We know the rest."

At this moment Sibyll woke, and starting to her feet in astonishment and terror at the sight on which her eyes opened, her extreme beauty made a sensible effect upon the bravoes.

"Do not be daunted, young demoiselle," said the captain, with an air almost respectful—"It is necessary thou and Sir John should follow us, but we will treat ye well, and consult later on the ransom ye will pay us. Jock, discharge the young sumpter mule; put its load on the the black one. We have no better equipment for thee, lady—but the first haquenée we find shall replace the mule, and meanwhile, my knaves will heap their cloaks for a pillion."

"But what mean you!—you mistake us!" exclaimed Sibyll—"we are poor; we cannot ransom ourselves."

"Poor!—tut!" said the captain, pointing significantly to the costly robe of the maiden—"moreover, his worship's wealth is well known. Mount in haste—we are pressed."

And without heeding the expostulations of Sibyll and the poor scholar, the rebel put his troop into motion, and marched himself at their head, with his lieutenant.

Sibyll found the subalterns sterner than their chief; for as Warner offered to resist, one of them lifted his gisarme, with a frightful oath, and Sibyll was the first to persuade her father to submit. She mildly, however, rejected the mule, and the two captives walked together in the midst of the troop.

"*Pardie!*" said the lieutenant, "I see little help to Sir Geoffrey in these recruits, captain!"

"Fool!" said the chief, disdainfully—"if the rebellion fail, these prisoners may save our necks. Will Somers, last night, was to break into the house of Sir John Bourchier, for arms and monies, of which the knight hath a goodly store. Be sure, Sir John slinked off in the siege, and this is he and his daughter. Thou knowest he is one of the greatest knights, and the richest, whom the Yorkists boast of;—and we may name our own price for his ransom."

"But where lodge them, while we go to the battle?"

"Ned Porpustone hath a hostelry not far from the camp, and Ned is a good Lancastrian, and a man to be trusted."

"We have not searched the prisoners," said the lieutentant;—"they may have some gold in their pouches."

"Marry, when Will Somers storms a hive, little time does he leave to the bees to fly away with much honey! Natheless, thou mayst search the old knight, but civilly, and and with gentle excuses."

"And the damsel?"

"Nay! that were unmannerly, and the milder our conduct, the larger the ransom—when we have great folks to deal with."

The lieutenant accordingly fell back to search Adam's gipsire, which contained only a book and a file, and then rejoined his captain, without offering molestation to Sibyll.

The mistake made by the bravo was at least so far not wholly unfortunate, that the notion of the high quality of the captives—for Sir John Bourchier was indeed a person of considerable station and importance (a notion favored by the noble appearance of the scholar, and the delicate and high-born air of Sibyll)—procured for them all the respect compatible with the circumstances. They had not gone far before they entered a village, through which the ruffians marched with the most perfect impunity; for it was a strange feature in those civil wars, that the mass of the population except in the northern districts, remained perfectly supine and neutral: and as the little band halted at a small inn to drink, the gossips of the village collected round them, with the same kind of indolent, careless curiosity, which is now evinced, in some hamlet, at the halt of a stage-coach. Here the captain learned however, some intelligence important to his objects—viz., the night march of the troop under Lord Hastings, and the probability that the conflict was already begun. "If so," muttered the rebel, "we can see how the tide turns, before we endanger ourselves; and at the worst, our prisoners will bring something of prize-money."

While thus soliloquizing, he spied one of those cumbrous vehicles of the day called *whirlicotes*,* standing in the yard of the hostelry; and seizing upon it, *vi et armis*, in spite of all the cries and protestations of the unhappy landlord, he ordered his captives to enter, and recommenced his march. As the band proceeded farther on their way, they were joined by fresh troops, of the same class as themselves, and they pushed on gaily, till, about the hour of eight, they halted before the hostelry the captain had spoken of. It stood a little out of the high road, not very far from the village of Hadley, and the heath or chase of Gladsmoor, on which was fought, some time afterwards, the Battle of Barnet. It was a house of good aspect, and considerable size, for it was much frequented by all caravanserais and travellers from the north to the metropolis. The landlord, at heart a stanch Lancastrian, who had served in the French wars, and contrived, no one knew how, to save monies in the course of an adventurous life, gave to his hostelry the appellation and sign of the Talbot, in memory of the old hero of that name; and, hiring a tract of land, joined the occupation of a farmer to the dignity of a host. The house, which was built round a spacious quadrangle, represented the double character of its owner, one side being occupied by barns and a considerable range of stabling, while cows, oxen, and ragged colts, grouped amicably together, in a space railed off in the centre of the yard.

At another side ran a large wooden staircase, with an open gallery, propped on wooden columns, conducting to numerous chambers, after the fashion of the Tabard, in Southwark, immortalized by Chaucer. Over the archway, on entrance, ran a labyrinth of sleeping lofts, for foot passengers and muleteers, and the side facing the entrance was nearly occupied by a vast kitchen, the common hall, and the bar, with the private parlor of the host, and two or three chambers in the second story. The whirlicote jolted and rattled into the yard. Sibyll and her father were assisted out of the vehicle, and, after a few words interchanged with the host, conducted by Master Porpustone himself up the spacious stairs into a chamber, well furnished and fresh littered, with repeated assurances of safety, provided they maintained silence, and attempted no escape.

"Ye are in time," said Ned Porpustone to the Captain—"Lord Hastings made proclamation at daybreak that he gave the rebels two hours to disperse."

"Pest! I like not those proclamations. And the fellows stood their ground?"

"No; for Sir Geoffrey, like a wise soldier, *mended* the ground by retreating a mile to the left, and placing the wood between the Yorkists and himself. Hastings, by this, must have remarshalled his men. But to pass the wood is slow work, and Sir Geoffrey's cross-bows are no doubt doing damage in the covert. Come in, while your fellows snatch a morsel without; five minutes are not thrown away on filling their bellies."

"Thanks, Ned—thou art a good fellow! and if all else fail, why Sir John's ransom shall pay the reckoning. Any news of bold Robin?"

"Ay! he has 'scaped with a whole skin, and gone back to the north," answered the host, leading the way to his parlor, where a

* Whirlicotes were in use from a very early period, but only among the great, till, in the reign of Richard II., his Queen, Anne, introduced side-saddles, when the whirlicote fell out of fashion, but might be found at different hostelries on the main roads, for the accommodation of the infirm or aged.

flask of strong wine and some cold meats awaited his guest. "If Sir Geoffrey Gates can beat off the York troopers, tell him, from me, not to venture to London, but to fall back into the marches. He will be welcome there I foreguess; for every northman is either for Warwick or for Lancaster; and the two must unite now, I trow."

"But Warwick is flown!" quoth the captain.

"Tush! he has only flown, as the falcon flies when he has a heron to fight with—wheeling and soaring. Woe to the heron when the falcon swoops! But you drink not!"

"No; I must keep the head cool to-day. For Hastings is a perilous captain. Thy fist, friend!—If I fall, I leave you Sir John and his girl, to wipe off old scores; if we beat off the Yorkists, I vow to our Lady of Walsingham an image of wax, of the weight of myself." The marauder then started up, and strode to his men, who were snatching a hasty meal on the space before the hostel. He paused a moment or so, while his host whispered—

"Hastings was here before daybreak; but his men only got the sour beer; yours fight upon huff-cap."

"Up, men!—To your pikes! Dress to the right!" thundered the captain, with a sufficient pause between each sentence. "The York lozels have starved on stale beer—shall they beat huff-cap and Lancaster? Frisk and fresh—up with the Antelope * banner and long live Henry the Sixth!"

The sound of the shout that answered this harangue shook the thin walls of the chamber in which the prisoners were confined, and they heard with joy the departing tramp of the soldiers. In a short time, Master Porpustone himself, a corpulent, burly fellow, with a face by no means unprepossessing, mounted to the chamber, accompanied by a comely housekeeper, linked to him, as scandal said, by ties less irksome than Hymen's, and both bearing ample provisions, with rich pigment and lucid clary,† which they spread with great formality on an oak table before their involuntary guests.

"Eat, your worship, eat!" cried mine host, heartily. "Eat, labybird!—nothing like eating to kill time and banish care. Fortune of war, Sir John—fortune of war—never be daunted! Up to-day—down to-morrow. Come what may—York or Lancaster—still a rich man always falls on his legs. Five hundred marks or so to the captain; a noble or two, out of pure generosity, to Ned Porpustone (I scorn extortion), and you and the fair young dame may breakfast at home to-morrow, unless the captain or his favorite lieutenant is taken prisoner; and then, you see, they will buy off their necks by letting you out of the bag. Eat, I say—eat!"

"Verily," said Adam, seating himself solemnly, and preparing to obey, "I confess I'm a hungered, and the pasty hath a savory odor; but I pray thee to tell me why I am called Sir John?—Adam is my baptismal name."

"Ha! ha! good—very good, your honor—to be sure, and your father's name before you. We are all sons of Adam, and every son, I trow, has a just right and a lawful to his father's name."

With that, followed by the house-keeper, the honest landlord, chuckling heartily, rolled his goodly bulk from the chamber, which he carefully locked.

"Comprehendest thou yet, Sibyll?"

"Yes, dear sir and father—they mistake us for fugitives of mark and importance; and when they discover their error, no doubt we shall go free. Courage, dear father!"

"Me seemeth," quoth Adam, almost merrily, as the good man filled his cup from the wine flagon—"me seemeth that, if the mistake could continue, it would be no weighty misfortune—ha! ha!"—he stopped abruptly in the unwonted laughter, put down the cup—his face fell. "Ah, heaven forgive me!—and the poor Eureka and faithful Madge!"

"Oh, father! fear not; we are not without protection. Lord Hastings is returned to London—we will seek him; he will make our cruel neighbors respect thee. And Madge—poor Madge will be so happy at our return, for they could not harm her;—a woman—old and alone; no—no, man is not fierce enough for that!"

"Let us so pray; but thou eatest not, child!"

"Anon, father—anon; I am sick and weary. But, nay—nay, I am better now—better

* The antelope was one of the Lancastrian badges. The special cognizance of Henry VI. was two feathers in saltire.

† Clary was wine clarified.

Smile again, father. I am hungered, too; yes, indeed and in sooth, yes.—Ah, sweet St. Mary, give me life and strength, and hope and patience, for his dear sake!"

The stirring events which had within the last few weeks diversified the quiet life of the Scholar had somewhat roused him from his wonted abstraction, and made the actual world a more sensible and living thing than it had hitherto seemed to his mind; but now, his repast ended, the quiet of the place, (for the inn was silent and almost deserted) with the fumes of the wine—a luxury he rarely tasted—operated soothingly upon his thought and fancy, and plunged him into those reveries, so dear alike to poet and mathematician. To the thinker, the most trifling external object often suggests ideas, which, like Homer's chain, extend, link after link, from earth to heaven. The sunny motes, that in a glancing column came through the lattice, called Warner from the real day—the day of strife and blood, with thousands hard by, driving each other to the Hades—and led his scheming fancy into the ideal and abstract day—the theory of light itself; and theory suggested mechanism, and mechanism called up the memory of his oracle—old Roger Bacon; and that memory revived the great friar's hints in the Opus magus—hints which outlined the grand invention of the telescope: and so, as over some dismal precipice a bird swings itself to and fro upon the airy bough, the schoolman's mind played with its quivering fancy, and folded its calm wings above the verge of terror.

Occupied with her own dreams, Sibyll respected those of her father; and so in silence, not altogether mournful, the morning and the noon passed, and the sun was sloping westward, when a confused sound below called Sibyll's gaze to the lattice, which looked over the balustrade of the staircase, into the vast yard. She saw several armed men—their harness hewed and battered—quaffing ale or wine in haste, and heard one of them say to the landlord—

"All is lost! Sir Geoffry Gates still holds out, but it is butcher work. The troops of Lord Hastings gather round him as a net round the fish!"

Hastings!—that name!—he was at hand!—he was near!—they would be saved! Sibyll's heart beat loudly.

"And the captain?" asked Porpustone.

"Alive, when I last saw him; but we must be off. In another hour all will be hurry and skurry, flight and chase."

At this moment from one of the barns there emerged, one by one, the female vultures of the battle. The tymbesteres, who had tramped all night to the spot, had slept off their fatigue during the day, and appeared on the scene as the neighboring strife waxed low, and the dead and dying began to cumber the gory ground. Graul Skellet, tossing up her timbrel, darted to the fugitives, and grinned a ghastly grin when she heard the news—for the tymbesteres were all loyal to a king who loved women, and who had a wink and a jest for every tramping wench! The troopers tarried not, however, for further converse, but having satisfied their thirst, hurried and clattered from the yard. At the sight of the ominous tymbesteres Sibyll had drawn back, without daring to close the lattice she had opened; and the women, seating themselves on a bench, began sleeking their long hair and smoothing their garments from the scraps of straw and litter which betokened the nature of their resting-place.

"Ho, girls!" said the fat landlord, "ye will pay me for board and bed, I trust, by a show of your craft. I have two right worshipful lodgers up yonder, whose lattice looks on the yard, and whom ye may serve to divert."

Sibyll trembled, and crept to her father's side.

"And," continued the landlord, "if they like the clash of your musicals, it may bring ye a groat or so, to help ye on your journey. By the way—whither wend ye, wenches?"

"To a bonny, jolly fair," answered the sinister voice of Graul—

"Where a mighty SHOWMAN dyes
The greenery into red;
Where, presto! at the word
Lies his Fool without a head—
Where he gathers in the crowd
To the trumpet and the drum
With a jingle and a tinkle,
Graul's merry lasses come!"

As the two closing lines were caught by the rest of the tymbesteres, striking their timbrels, the crew formed themselves into a semicircle, and commenced their dance. Their movements, though wanton and fantastic, were not without a certain wild grace; and the address with which, from time to time, they cast up their instruments and caught them in descending, joined to the surprising agility with which, in the evolutions of the dance, one seemed now to chase, now to fly from, the other darting to and fro through the ranks of her companions, winding and wheeling—the chain now seemingly broken in disorder, now united link to link, as the whole force of the instruments clashed in chorus—made an exhibition inexpressibly attractive to the vulgar.

The tymbesteres, however, as may well be supposed, failed to draw Sibyll or Warner to the window; and they exchanged glances of spite and disappointment.

"Marry," quoth the landlord, after a hearty laugh at the diversion, "I do wrong to be so gay, when so many good friends perhaps are lying stark and cold. But what then? Life is short—laugh while we can!"

"Hist!" whispered his housekeeper; "art wode, Ned? Wouldst thou have it discovered that thou hast such quality birds in the cage—noble Yorkists—at the very time when Lord Hastings himself may be riding this way after the victory?"

"Always right, Meg—and I'm an ass!" answered the host, in the same undertone. "But my good nature will be the death of me some day. Poor gentlefolks, they must be unked dull, yonder!"

"If the Yorkists come hither—which we shall soon know by the scouts—we must shift Sir John and the damsel to the back of the house, over thy tap-room."

"Manage it as thou wilt, Meg—but, thou seest, they keep quiet and snug. Ho, ho, ho! that tall tymbestre is subtle enough to make an owl hold his sides with laughing. Ah! hollo, there, tymbesteres—*ribaudes*—tramps—the devil's chickens—down, down!"

The host was too late in his order. With a sudden spring, Graul, who had long fixed her eye on the open lattice of the prisoners, had wreathed herself round one of the pillars that supported the stairs, swung lightly over the balustrade—and with a faint shriek, the startled Sibyll beheld the tymbestere's hard, fierce eyes, glaring upon her through the lattice, as her long arm extended the timbrel for largess. But no sooner had Sibyll raised her face than she was recognized.

"Ho! the wizard and the wizard's daughter! Ho! the girl who glamours lords, and wears sarcenet and lawn! Ho! the nigromancer, who starves the poor!"

At the sound of their leader's cry, up sprang, up climbed the hellish sisters! One after the other, they darted through the lattice into the chamber.

"The ronions! the foul fiend has distraught them!" groaned the landlord motionless with astonishment. But the more active Meg, calling to the varlets and scullions, whom the tymbesteres had collected in the yard, to follow her, bounded up the stairs, unlocked the door, and arrived in time to throw herself between the captives and the harpies, whom Sibyll's rich super-tunic and Adam's costly gown had inflamed into all the rage of appropriation.

"What mean ye, wretches?" cried the bold Meg, purple with anger. "Do ye come for this into honest folks' hostelries, to rob their guests in broad day—noble guests—guests of mark! Oh, Sir John! Sir John! what will ye think of us?"

"Oh, Sir John! Sir John!" groaned the landlord, who had now moved his slow bulk into the room. "They shall be scourged, Sir John! They shall be put in the stocks—they shall be brent with hot iron—they——"

"Ha, ha!" interrupted the terrible Graul, "Guests of mark—noble guests, throw ye! Adam Warner, the wizard, and his daughter, whom we drove last night from their den, as many a time, sisters, and many, we have driven the rats from charnel and cave."

"Wizard! Adam! Blood of my life!" stammered the landlord—"is his name Adam, after all?"

"My name is Adam Warner," said the old man, with dignity; "no wizard—a humble scholar, and a poor gentleman, who has injured no one. Wherefore, women—if women ye are—would ye injure mine and me?"

"Faugh—wizard!" returned Graul, folding her arms. "Didst thou not send thy spawn, yonder, to spoil our mart with her gittern? Hast thou not taught her the spells to win love from the noble and young? Ho, how daintily, the young witch robes herself! Ho! laces, and satins, and we shiver with the cold, and parch with the heat—and —— doff thy tunic, minion!"

And Graul's fierce gripe was on the robe, when the landlord interposed his huge arm, and held her at bay.

"Softly, my sucking dove, softly! Clear the room, and be off!"

"Look to thyself, man. If thou harborest a wizard, against law—a wizard whom King Edward hath given up to the people—look to thy barns, they shall burn; look to thy cattle—they shall rot; look to thy secrets—they shall be told! Lancastrian, thou shalt hang! We go—we go! We have friends among the mailed men of York. We go—we will return! Woe to thee, if thou harborest the wizard and the succuba!"

With that, Graul moved slowly to the door. Host and housekeeper, varlet, groom, and scullion, made way for her, in terror; and still, as she moved, she kept her eyes on Sibyll, till her sisters, following in successive file, shut out the hideous aspect; and Meg, ordering away her gaping train, closed the door.

The host and the housekeeper then gazed gravely at each other. Sibyll lay in her father's arms breathing hard and convulsively. The old man's face bent over her in silence.

Meg drew aside her master. "You must rid the house at once of these folks. I have heard talk of yon tymbesteres; they are awsome in spite and malice. Every man to himself!"

"But the poor old gentleman, so mild—and the maid, so winsome!"

The last remark did not over please the comely Meg. She advanced at once to Adam, and said, shortly—

"Master—whether wizard or not, is no affair of a poor landlord, whose house is open to all; but ye have had food and wine—please to pay the reckoning, and God speed ye—ye are free to depart."

"We can pay you, mistress!" exclaimed Sibyll, springing up. "We have monies yet. Here—here!" and she took from her gipsire the broad pieces which poor Madge's precaution had placed therein, and which the bravoes had fortunately spared.

The sight of the gold somewhat softened the housewife.—"Lord Hastings is known to us," continued Sibyll, perceiving the impression she had made; "suffer us to rest here till he pass this way, and ye will find yourselves repaid for the kindness."

"By my troth," said the landlord, "ye are most welcome to all my poor house containeth; and as for these tymbesteres, I value them not a straw. No one can say Ned Porpustone is an ill man or inhospitable. Whoever can pay reasonably, is sure of good wine and civilty at the Talbot."

With these and many similar protestations and assurances, which were less heartily reechoed by the housewife, the landlord begged to conduct them to an apartment not so liable to molestation; and after having led them down the principal stairs, through the bar, and thence up a narrow flight of steps, deposited them in a chamber at the back of the house, and lighted a sconce therein—for it was now near the twilight. He then insisted on seeing after their evening meal, and vanished with his assistant. The worthy pair were now of the same mind; for guests known to Lord Hastings, it was worth braving the threats of the tymbesteres; especially since Lord Hastings, it seems, had just beaten the Lancastrians.

But, alas! while the active Meg was busy on the hypocras, and the worthy landlord was inspecting the savory operations of the kitchen, a vast uproar was heard without. A troop of disorderly Yorkist soldiers, who had been employed in dispersing the flying rebels, rushed helter skelter into the house, and poured into the kitchen, bearing with them the detested tymbesteres who had encountered them on their way. Among these soldiers were those who had congregated at Master Sancroft's the day before, and they were well prepared to support the cause of their griesly paramours. Lord Hastings himself had retired for the night to a farm-house nearer the field of battle than the hostel; and as in those days discipline was lax enough after a victory, the soldiers had a right to licence. Master Porpustone found himself completely at the mercy of these brawling customers, the more rude and disorderly from the remembrance of the sour beer in the morning, and Graul Skellet's assurances that Master Porpustone was a malignant Lancastrian. They laid hands on all the provisions in the house, tore the meats from the spit, devouring them half raw; set the casks running over the floors; and while they swilled and swore, and filled the place with the uproar of a hell broke loose, Graul Skellet, whom the lust for the rich garments of Sibyll still fired and stung, led her followers up the stairs towards the deserted chamber.

Mine host perceived, but did not dare openly to resist, the foray; but as he was really a good-natured knave, and as, moreover, he feared ill consequences might ensue if any friends of Lord Hastings were spoiled, outraged—nay, preadventure, murdered—in his house, he resolved, at all events, to assist the escape of his guests. Seeing the ground thus clear of the tymbesteres, he therefore stole from the riotous scene, crept up the back stairs, gained the chamber to which he had so happily removed his persecuted lodgers, and making them, in a few words, sensible that he was no longer able to protect them, and that the tymbesteres were now returned with an armed force to back their malice, conducted them safely to a wide casement only some three or four feet from the soil of the solitary garden, and bade them escape and save themselves.

"The farm," he whispered, "where they say Lord Hastings is quartered, is scarcely a mile and a half away; pass the garden wicket—leave Gladsmore Chace to the left hand,—take the path to the right, through the wood, and you will see its roof among the apple-blossoms. Our lady protect you, and say a word to my lord on behalf of poor Ned."

Scarce had he seen his guests descend into the garden, before he heard the yell of the tymbesteres, in the opposite part of the house, as they ran from room to room after their prey. He hastened to regain the kitchen; and presently the tymbesteres, breathless and panting, rushed in, and demanded their victims.

"Marry," quoth the landlord, with the self-possession of a cunning old soldier—"think ye I cumbered my house with such cattle, after pretty lasses like you had given me the inkling of what they were? No wizard shall fly away with the sign of the Talbot, if I can help it. They skulked off, I can promise ye, and did not even mount a couple of broomsticks which I handsomely offered for their ride up to London."

"Thunder and bombards!" cried a trooper, already half-drunk, and seizing Graul in his iron arms—"put the conjurer out of thine head now, and buss me, Graul—buss me!"

Then the riot became hideous: the soldiers, following their comrade's example, embraced the grim glee-woman, tearing and hauling them to and fro, one from the other, round and round, dancing, hallooing, chanting, howling, by the blaze of a mighty fire—many a rough face and hard hand smeared with blood still wet, communicating the stain to the cheeks and garb of those foul feres, and the whole revel becoming so unutterably horrible and ghastly, that even the veteran landlord fled from the spot, trembling and crossing himself:—And so, streaming athwart the lattice, and silvering over that fearful merry-making, rose the moon!

But when fatigue and drunkenness had done their work, and the soldiers fell one over the other upon the floor, the tables, the benches, into the heavy sleep of riot, Graul suddenly rose from amidst the huddled bodies, and then, silently as ghouls from a burial-ground, her sisters emerged also from their resting-piaces beside the sleepers The dying light of the fire contended but feebly with the livid rays of the moon, and played fantastically over the gleaming robes of the tymbesteres. They stood erect for a moment, listening, Graul with her finger on her lips; then they glided to the door, opened and reclosed it—darted across the yard, scaring the beasts that slept there; the watch-doy barked, but drew back, bristling and showing his fangs, as Red Grisell, undaunted, pointed her knife, and Graul flung him a red peace-sop of meat. They launched themselves through the open entrance, gained the space beyond, and scoured away to the battle field.

Meanwhile, Sibyll and her father were still under the canopy of heaven, they had scarcely passed the garden, and entered the fields, when they saw horsemen riding to and fro in all directions. Sir Geoffrey Gates, the rebel leader, had escaped; the reward of three hundred marks was set on his head, and the riders were in search of the fugitive. The human form itself had become a terror to the hunted outcasts: they crept under a thick hedge till the horsemen had disappeared, and then resumed their way. They gained the wood; but there again they halted at the sound of voices, and withdrew themselves under covert of some entangled and trampled bushes. This time it was but a party of peasants, whom curiosity had led to see the field of battle. and who were now returning home. Peasants and soldiers, both were human, and therefore to be shunned by those whom the age itself put out of the pale of law. At last the party also left the path free; and now it was full night. They pursued their way—they cleared the wood—before them lay the field of battle; and a deeper silence seemed to fall over the world! The first stars had risen, but not yet the moon. The gleam of armor from prostrate bodies, which it had mailed in vain, reflected the quiet rays: here and there flickered watchfires, where sentinels were set, but they were scattered and remote. The outcasts paused and shuddered, but there seemed no holier way for their feet; and the roof of the farmer's homestead slept on the opposite side of the field, amidst white orchard blossoms whitened still more by the stars. They went on, hand in hand—the dead, after all, were less terrible than the living. Sometimes a stern, upturned face, distorted by the last violent agony, the eyes unclosed and glazed, encountered them with its stony stare; but the weapon was powerless in the stiff hand—the menace and the insult came not from the hueless lips—persecution reposed, at last, in the lap of slaughter. They had gone midway through the field, when they heard from a spot where the corpses lay thickest piled, a faint voice calling upon God for pardon; and, suddenly, it was answered by a tone of fiercer agony—that did not pray, but curse.

By a common impulse, the gentle wanderers moved silently to the spot.

The sufferer, in prayer, was a youth scarcely passed from boyhood: his helm had been cloven, his head was bare, and his long light hair, clotted with gore, fell over his shoulders. Besides him lay a strong-built, powerful form, which writhed in torture, pierced under the arm, by a Yorkist arrow, and the shaft still projected from the wound—and the man's curse answered the boy's prayer.

"Peace to thy parting soul, brother!" said Warner, bending over the man.

"Poor sufferer!" said Sibyll, to the boy, "cheer thee; we will send succour; thou mayst live yet!"

"Water! water!—hell and torture—water, I say!" groaned the man; "one drop of water!"

It was the captain of the marauders who had captured the wanderers.

"Thine arm! lift me! move me! That evil man scares my soul from heaven!" gasped the boy.

And Adam preached penitence to the one that cursed, and Sibyll knelt down and prayed with the one that prayed.—And up rose the moon!

Lord Hastings sate, with his victorious captains,—over mead, morat, and wine—in the humble hall of the farm."

"So," said he, "we have crushed the last embers of the rebellion! This Sir Geoffrey Gates is a restless and resolute spirit; pity he escapes again for further mischief. But the House of Nevile, that over-shadowed the rising race, hath fallen at last—a waisall, brave sirs, to the new men!"

The door was thrown open, and an old soldier entered abruptly.

"My lord! my lord! Oh! my poor son! he cannot be found! The women, who ever follow the march of soldiers, will be on the ground to despatch the wounded, that they may rifle the corpses! O God! if my son—my boy—my only son——"

"I wist not, my brave Mervil, that thou hadst a son in our bands; yet I know each man by name and sight. Courage! Our wounded have been removed, and sentries are placed to guard the field!"

"Sentries! O my lord, knowest thou not that they wink at the crime that plunders the dead? Moreover, these corpse-riflers creep stealthily and unseen, as the red earth-worms, to the carcass. Give me some few of thy men—give me warrant to search the field! My son—my boy!—not sixteen summers—and his mother!"—

The man stopped and sobbed.

"Willingly!" said the gentle Hastings, "willingly! And woe to the sentries if it be as thou sayst? I will go myself, and see!—Torches there—what ho?—the good captain careth even for his dead!—Thy son! I marvel I knew him not!—Whom served he under?"

"My lord! my lord! pardon him! He is but a boy—they misled him!—he fought for the rebels. He crossed my path to-day—my arm was raised—we knew each other, and he fled from his father's sword!—Just as the strife was ended I saw him again—I saw him fall!—O mercy, mercy! do not let him perish of his wounds or by the rifler's knife, even though a rebel!"

"*Homo sum!*" quoth the noble chief, "I am man! and, even in these bloody times, Nature commands when she speaks in a father's voice! Mervil, I marked thee to-day! Thou art a brave fellow. I meant thee advancement—I give thee, instead, thy son's pardon, if he lives—ten masses if he died as a soldier's son should die, no matter under what flag—antelope or lion, pierced manfully in the breast—his feet to the foe! Come, I will search with thee!"

The boy yielded up his soul while Sibyll prayed, and her sweet voice soothed the last pang; and the man ceased to curse while Adam spoke of God's power and mercy, and his breath ebbed, gasp upon gasp, away. While thus detained, the wanderers saw not pale, fleeting figures, that had glided to the ground, and moved, gleaming, irregular, and rapid, as marsh-fed vapors, from heap to heap, of the slain. With a loud, wild cry, the robber Lancastrian half sprung to his feet, in the paroxym of the last struggle, and then fell on his face—a corpse!

The cry reached the tymbesteres, and Graul rose from a body from which she had extracted a few coins smeared with blood, and darted to the spot; and so, as Adam raised his face from contemplating the dead, whose last moments he had sought to soothe, the Alecto of the battle-field stood before him, her knife bare in her gory hand. Red Grisell, who had just left (with a spurn of wrath—for the pouch was empty) the corpse of a soldier, round whose neck she had twined her hot clasp the day before, sprang towards Sibyll: the rest of the sisterhood flocked to the place, and laughed in glee as they beheld their unexpected prey. The danger was horrible and imminent; no pity was seen in those savage eyes. The wanderers prepared for death—when, suddenly, torches flashed over the ground. A cry was heard—"See, the riflers of the dead!" Armed men bounded forward, and the startled wretches uttered a shrill unearthly scream, and fled from the spot, leaping over the carcasses, and doubling and winding, till they had vanished into the darkness of the wood.

"Provost!" said a commanding voice, "hang me up those sentinels at day-break!"

"My son! my boy! speak, Hal—speak to me. He is here—he is found!" exclaimed the old soldier, kneeling beside the corpse at Sibyll's feet.

"My lord! my beloved! my Hastings!" And Sibyll fell insensible before the chief.

CHAPTER VI.

The subtle Craft of Richard of Gloucester.

It was some weeks after the defeat of Sir Geoffrey Gates, and Edward was at Shene, with his gay court. Reclined at length within a pavilion placed before a cool fountain, in the royal gardens, and surrounded by his favorites, the king listened indolently to the music of his minstrels, and sleeked the plumage of his favorite falcon, perched upon his wrist. And scarcely would it have been possible to recognize in that lazy voluptuary the dauntless soldier, before whose lance, as deer before the hound, had so lately fled, at bloody Erpingham, the chivalry of the Lancastrian Rose; but remote from the pavilion, and in one of the deserted bowling alleys, Prince Richard and Lord Montagu walked apart, in earnest conversation. The last of these noble personages had remained inactive during the disturbances, and Edward had not seemed to entertain any suspicion of his participation in the anger and revenge of Warwick. The king took from him, it is true, the lands and earldom of Northumberland, and restored them to the Percy, but he had accompanied this act with gracious excuses, alleging the necessity of conciliating the head of an illustrious house, which had formally entered into allegiance to the dynasty of York, and bestowed upon his early favorite, in compensation, the dignity of marquis.* The politic king, in thus depriving Montagu of the wealth and the retainers of the Percy, reduced him, as a younger brother, to a comparative poverty and insignificance, which left him dependent on Edward's favor, and deprived him, as he thought, of the power

* Montagu said bitterly of this new dignity, "He takes from me the Earldom and domains of Northumberland, and makes me a Marquis, with a pie's nest to maintain it withal."—Stowe, Edw. IV.—Warkworth Chronicle.

of active mischief; at the same time, more than ever, he insisted on Montagu's society, and summoning his attendance at the court, kept his movements in watchful surveillance.

"Nay, my lord," said Richard, pursuing with much unction the conversation he had commenced, "you wrong me much, Holy Paul be my witness, if you doubt the deep sorrow I feel at the unhappy events which have led to the severence of my kinsmen! England seems to me to have lost its smile, in losing the glory of Earl Warwick's presence, and Clarence is my brother, and was my friend; and thou knowest, Montagu, thou knowest, how dear to my heart was the hope to win for my wife and lady the gentle Anne."

"Prince, said Montagu, abruptly, "though the pride of Warwick and the honor of our house may have forbidden the public revelation of the cause which fired my brother to rebellion, thou, at least, art privy to a secret ——"

"Cease!" exclaimed Richard, in great emotion, probably sincere, for his face grew livid, and its muscles were nervously convulsed. "I would not have that remembrance stirred from its dark repose. I would fain forget a brother's hasty frenzy, in the belief of his lasting penitence." He paused and turned his face, gasped for breath, and resumed—"The cause justified the father; it had justified me in the father's cause, had Warwick listened to my suit, and given me the right to deem insult to his daughter injury to myself."

"And if, my prince," returned Montagu, looking round him, and in a subdued whisper, "if yet the hand of Lady Anne were pledged to you?"

"Tempt me not—tempt me not!" crid the prince, crossing himself. Montagu continued—

"Our cause, I mean Lord Warwick's cause, is not lost, as the king deems it."

"Proceed," said Richard, casting down his eyes, while his countenace settled back into its thoughtful calm.

"I mean," renewed Montagu, "that in my brother's flight, his retainers were taken by surprise. In vain the king would confiscate his lands—he cannot confiscate men's hearts. If Warwick to-morrow set his armed heel upon the soil, trowest thou, sagacious and clear-judging prince, that the strife which would follow would be but another field of Losecote?* Thou hast heard of the honors with which King Louis has received the earl. Will that king grudge him ships and monies? And meanwhile, thinkest thou that his favorers sleep?"

"But if he land, Montagu," said Richard, who seemed to listen with an attention that awoke all the hopes of Montagu, coveting so powerful an ally—"if he land, and make open war on Edward—we must say the word boldly—what intent can he proclaim? It is not enough to say King Edward shall not reign; the earl must say also what king England should elect!"

"Prince," answered Montagu, "before I reply to that question, vouchsafe to hear my own hearty desire and wish. Though the king has deeply wronged my brother, though he has despoiled me of the lands, which were, peradventure, not too large a reward for twenty victories in his cause, and restored them to the house that ever ranked amongst the strongholds of his Lancastrian foe, yet often, when I am most resentful, the memory of my royal seigneur's past love and kindness comes over me,—above all the thought of the solemn contract between his daughter and my son;—and I feel (now the first heat of natural anger at an insult offered to my niece is somewhat cooled) that if Warwick *did* land I could almost forget my brother for my king."

"*Almost!*" repeated Richard, smiling.

"I am plain with your highness, and say but what I feel. I would even now fain trust, that by your mediation, the king may be persuaded to make such concessions and excuses, as in truth would not misbeseem him, to the father of Lady Anne, and his own kinsman; and that yet, ere it be too late, I may be spared the bitter choice between the ties of blood, and my allegiance to the king."

"But failing this hope (which I devoutly share),—and Edward, it must be owned, could scarcely trust to a letter, still less to a messenger, the confession of a crime—failing this, and your brother land, and I side with him for love of Anne, pledged to me as a bride,—what king would he ask England to elect?"

"The Duke of Clarence loves you dearly, Lord Richard," replied Montagu. "Knowest

* The battle of Erpingham, so popularly called, in contempt of the rebellious runaways.

thou not how often he hath said, 'By sweet St. George if Gloucester would join me, I would make Edward know we were all one man's sons, who should be more preferred and promoted than strangers of his wife's blood.'" *

Richard's countenance for a moment evinced disappointment; but he said drily, "Then Warwick would propose that Clarence should be king?—And the great barons, and the honest burghers, and the sturdy yeomen, would, you think, not stand aghast at the manifesto which declares not that the dynasty of York is corrupt and faulty, but that the younger son should depose the elder—that younger son, mark me! not only unknown in war, and green in council, but gay, giddy, vacillating—not subtle of wit, and resolute of deed, as he who *so* aspires should be!—Montagu—a vain dream!"—Richard paused, and then resumed, in a low tone, as to himself—"Oh! not so—not so are kings cozened from their thrones—a pretext must blind men—say they are illegitimate say they are too young—too feeble—too anything—glide into their place—and then, not war—not war. You *slay* them out—they *disappear!*" The duke's face as he muttered, took a sinister and dark expression—his eyes seemed to gaze on space. Suddenly recovering himself, as from a reverie, he turned with his wonted sleek and gracious aspect to the startled Montagu, and said, "I was but quoting from Italian history, good my lord—wise lore, but terrible, and murderous. Return we to the point. Thou seest Clarence could not reign, and as well," added the prince, with a slight sigh—"as well or better (for without vanity, I have more of a king's metal in me) might I—even *I*—aspire to my brother's crown!" Here he paused, and glanced rapidly and keenly at the marquis; but whether or not, in these words he had sought to sound Montagu, and that glance sufficed to show him it were bootless or dangerous to speak more plainly, he resumed with an altered voice—"Enough of this: Warwick will discover the idleness of such design; and if he land, his trumpets must ring to a more kindling measure. John Montagu, thinkest thou that Margaret of Anjou and the Lancastrians will not rather win thy brother to their side? *There* is the true danger to Edward—none elsewhere."

"And if so?" said Montagu, watching his listener's countenance. Richard started, and gnawed his lip. "Mark me!" continued the marquis—"I repeat that I would fain hope yet, that Edward may appease the earl; but if not, and rather than rest dishonored and aggrieved, Warwick link himself with Lancaster, and thou join him as Anne's betrothed and lord, what matters who the puppet on the throne!—we and thou shall be the rulers; or, if thou reject," added the marquis, artfully, as he supposed, exciting the jealousy of the duke—"Henry has a son—a fair, and, they say, a gallant prince—carefully tutored in the knowledged of our English laws, and who, my lord of Oxford, somewhat in the confidenee of the Lancastrians, assures me, would rejoice to forget old feuds, and call Warwick 'father,' and my niece 'Lady and Princess of Wales.'"

With all his dissimulation, Richard could ill conceal the emotions of fear—of jealousy—of dismay, which these words excited.

"Lord Oxford!" he cried, stamping his foot. "Ha! John de Vere—pestilent traitor, plottest thou thus! But we can yet seize thy person, and will have thy head."

Alarmed at this burst, and suddenly made aware that he had laid his breast too bare to the boy, whom he had thought to dazzle and seduce to his designs—Montagu said, falteringly—"But, my lord, our talk is but in confidence: at your own prayer, with your own plighted word, of prince and of kinsman, that, whatever my frankness may utter, should not pass farther. "Take," added the nobleman, with proud dignity—"take my head rather than Lord Oxford's; for I deserve death, if I reveal to one, who can betray, the loose words of another's intimacy and trust!"

"Forgive me, my cousin," said Richard, meekly; "my love to Anne transported me too far. Lord Oxford's words, as you report them, had conjured up a rival, and—but enough of this.—And now," added the prince, gravely, and with a steadiness of voice and manner that gave a certain majesty to his small stature—"now, as thou hast spoken openly, openly also will I reply. I feel the wrong to the Lady Anne as to myself; deeply, burningly, and lastingly, will it live in my mind; it may be, sooner or later, to rise to gloomy deeds, even against Edward and Edward's blood. But no, I have the king's solemn pro-

---

Hall.*

testations of repentance; his guilty passion has burned into ashes, and he now sighs—gay Edward—for a lighter fere. I cannot join with Clarence, less can I join with the Lancastrians. My birth makes me the prop of the throne of York—to guard it as a heritage (who knows?) that may descend to mine—nay, to me! And mark me well! if Warwick attempt a war of fratricide, he is lost; if, on the other hand, he can submit himself to the hands of Margaret, stained with his father's gore, the success of an hour will close in the humiliation of a life. There is a third way left, and that way thou hast piously and wisely shown. Let him, like me, resign revenge, and, not exacting a confession and a cry of Peccavi, which no king, much less King Edward the Plantagenet, can whimper forth—let him accept such overtures as his liege can make. His titles and castles shall be restored, equal possessions to those thou hast lost assigned to thee, and all my guerdon (if I can so negotiate) as all my ambition,—his daughter's hand. Muse on this, and for the peace and weal of the realm, so limit all thy schemes, my lord and cousin!"

With these words the prince pressed the hand of the marquis, and walked slowly towards the king's pavilion.

"Shame on my ripe manhood and lore of life," muttered Montagu, enraged against himself and deeply mortified. "How sentence by sentence, and step by step, yon crafty pigmy led me on, till all our projects—all our fears and hopes are revealed to him, who but views them as a foe. Anne betrothed to one, who even in fiery youth can thus beguile and dupe! —Warwick decoyed hither upon fair words, at the will of one whom Italy (boy, there thou didst forget thy fence of cunning)! has taught how the great are slain not, but *disappear!* No, even this defeat instructs me now. But right—right! the reign of Clarence is impossible, and that of Lancaster is ill-omend and portentous; and after all, my son stands nearer to the throne than any subject, in his alliance with the Lady Elizabeth. Would to heaven the king could yet——But out on me! this is no hour for musing on my own aggrandizement; rather let me fly at once, and warn Oxford, imperilled by my imprudence,—against that dark eye which hath set watch upon his life."

At that thought, which showed that Montagu, with all his worldliness, was not forgetful of one of the first duties of knight and gentleman, the marquis hastened up the alley—in the opposite direction to that taken by Gloucester—and soon found himself in the courtyard, where a goodly company were mounting their haquenées and palfreys, to enjoy a summer ride through the neighboring chase. The cold and half-slighting salutations of these minions of the hour, which now mortified the Nevile, despoiled of the possessions that had rewarded his long and brilliant services,—contrasting forcibly the reverential homage he had formerly enjoyed, stung Montagu to the quick.

"Whither ride you, brother Marquis?" said young Lord Dorset, (Elizabeth's son by her first marriage,) as Montagu called to his single squire, who was in waiting with his horse. "Some secret expedition, methinks, for I have known the day when the Lord Montagu never rode from his king's palace with less than thirty squires."

"Since my Lord Dorset prides himself on his memory," answered the scornful lord, "he may remember also the day when, if a Nevile mounted in haste, he bade the first Woodville he saw hold the stirrup."

And regarding "the brother Marquis" with a stately eye that silenced and awed retort, the long-descended Montagu passed the courtiers, and rode slowly on till out of sight of the palace; he then pushed into a hand gallop, and halted not till he had reached London, and gained the house in which, then, dwelt the Earl of Oxford, the most powerful of all the Lancastrian nobles not in exile, and who had hitherto temporized with the reigning house.

Two days afterwards the news reached Edward that Lord Oxford and Jasper of Pembroke—uncle to the boy afterwards Henry VII.—had sailed from England.

The tidings reached the king in his chamber, where he was closeted with Gloucester. The conference between them seemed to have been warm and earnest, for Edward's face was flushed, and Gloucester's brow was perturbed and sullen.

"Now heaven be praised!" cried the king, extending to Richard the letter which communicated the flight of the disaffected lords. "We have two enemies the less in our roiaulme, and many a barony the more to confiscate to our kingly wants. Ha—ha! these Lancastrians only serve to enrich us. Frowning still, Richard; smile, boy!"

"*Foi de mon âme*, Edward," said Richard, with a bitter energy, strangely at variance with his usual unctious deference to the king, "your highness's gaiety is ill-seasoned; you reject all the means to assure your throne—you rejoice in all the events that imperil it. I prayed you to lose not a moment in conciliating, if possible, the great lord whom you own you have wronged, and you replied that you would rather lose your crown than win back the arm that gave it you."

"Gave it me! an error, Richard! that crown was at once the heritage of my own birth, and the achievement of my own sword. But were it, as you say, it is not in a king's nature to bear the presence of a power more formidable than his own—to submit to a voice that commands rather than counsels; and the happiest chance that ever befel me is the exile of this earl. How, after what hath chanced, can I ever see his face again without humiliation, or he mine without resentment?"

"So you told me anon, and I answered, If that be so, and your highness shrinks from the man you have injured, beware at least that Warwick, if he may not return as a friend, come not back as an irresistible foe. If you will not conciliate, crush! Hasten by all arts to separate Clarence from Warwick. Hasten to prevent the union of the earl's popularity and Henry's rights. Keep eye upon all the Lancastrian lords, and see that none quit the realm, where they are captives, to join a camp where they can rise into leaders. And at the very moment I urge you to place strict watch upon Oxford—to send your swiftest riders to seize Jasper of Pembroke, you laugh with glee to hear that Oxford and Pembroke are gone to swell the army of your foes!"

"Better foes out of my realm than in it," answered Edward, drily.

"My liege, I say no more;" and Richard rose. "I would forestal a danger; it but remains for me to share it."

The king was touched. "Tarry yet, Richard," he said; and then, fixing his brother's eye, he continued, with a half-smile and a heightened color, "Though we know thee true and leal to us, we yet know also, Richard, but thou hast personal interest in thy counsels. Thou wouldst, by one means or another, soften or constrain the earl into giving thee the hand of Anne. Well, then, grant that Warwick and Clarence expel King Edward from his throne, they may bring a bride to console thee for the ruin of a brother."

"Thou hast no right to taunt or to suspect me, my liege," returned Richard, with a quiver in his lip. "Thou hast included me in thy meditated wrong to Warwick; and had that wrong been done——"

"Peradventure it had made thee espouse Warwick's quarrel?"

"Bluntly, yes!" exclaimed Richard, almost fiercely, and playing with his dagger. "But (he added, with a sudden change of voice), I understand and know thee better than the earl did or could. I know what in thee is but thoughtless impulse, haste of passion, the habit kings form of forgetting all things save the love or hate, the desire or anger, of a moment. Thou hast told me thyself, and with tears, of thy offence; thou hast pardoned my boy's burst of anger; I have pardoned thy evil thought; thou hast told me thyself that another face has succeeded to the brief empire of Anne's blue eye, and hast further pledged me thy kingly word, that if I can yet compass the hand of a cousin, dear to me from childhood, thou wilt confirm the union."

"It is true," said Edward. "But if thou wed thy bride, keep her aloof from the court—nay, frown not, my boy, I mean simply that I would not blush before my brother's wife!"

Richard bowed low in order to conceal the expression of his face, and went on without further notice of the explanation:

"And all this considered, Edward, I swear by Saint Paul, the holiest saint to thoughtful men, and by St. George, the noblest patron to high-born warriors, that thy crown and thine honor are as dear to me as if they were mine own. Whatever sins Richard of Gloucester may live to harbor and repent, no man shall ever say of him that he was a recreant to the honor of his country,* or slow to defend the rights of his ancestors from the treason of a vassal or the sword of a foreign foe. There-

* So Lord Bacon observes of Richard, with that discrimination, even in the strongest censure, of which profound judges of mankind are alone capable, that he was "a king jealous of the honor of the English uation."

fore, I say again, if thou reject my honest counsels—if thou suffer Warwick to unite with Lancaster and France—if the ships of Louis bear to your shores an enemy, the might of whom your reckless daring undervalues, foremost in the field in battle, nearest to your side in exile, shall Richard Plantagenet be found!"

These words, being uttered with sincerity, and conveying a promise never forfeited, were more impressive than the subtlest eloquence the wily and accomplished Gloucester ever employed as the cloak to guile, and they so affected Edward, that he threw his arms around his brother; and after one of those bursts of emotion which were frequent in one whose feelings were never deep and lasting, but easily aroused and warmly spoken, he declared himself ready to listen to and adopt all means which Richard's art could suggest for the better maintenance of their common weal and interests.

And, then, with that wondrous, if somewhat too restless and over-refining, energy which belonged to him, Richard rapidly detailed the scheme of his profound and dissimulating policy. His keen and intuitive insight into human nature had shown him the stern necessity which, against their very will, must unite Warwick with Margaret of Anjon. His conversation with Montagu had left no doubt of that peril on his penetrating mind. He foresaw that this union might be made durable and sacred by the marriage of Anne and Prince Edward; and to defeat this alliance was his first object, partly through Clarence, partly through Margaret herself.

A gentlewoman in the Duchess of Clarence's train had been arrested on the point of embarking to join her mistress. Richard had already seen and conferred with this lady, whose ambition, duplicity, and talent for intrigue, were known to him. Having secured her by promises of the most lavish dignities and rewards, he proposed that she should be permitted to join the duchess with secret messages to Isabel and the duke, warning them both, that Warwick and Margaret would forget their past feud in present sympathy, and that the rebellion against King Edward, instead of placing them on the throne, would humble them to be subordinates and aliens of the real profiters—the Lancastrtans.* He foresaw what effect these warnings would have upon the vain duke and the ambitious Isabel, whose character was known to him from childhood. He startled the king by insisting upon sending, at the same time, a trusty diplomatist to Margaret of Anjou, proffering to give the Princess Elizabeth (betrothed to Lord Montagu's son) to the young Prince Edward.* Thus, if the king, who had, as yet, no son, were to die, Margaret's son, in right of his wife, as well as in that of his own descent, would peaceably ascend the throne. "Need I say that I mean not this in sad and serious earnest," observed Richard, interrupting the astonished king—"I mean it but to amuse the Anjouite, and to deafen her ears to any overtures from Warwick. If she listen, we gain time—that time will inevitably renew irreconcilable quarrel between herself and the earl. His hot temper and desire of revenge will not brook delay. He will land, unsupported by Margaret and her partisans, and without any fixed principle of action which can strengthen force by opinion."

"You are right, Richard," said Edward, whose faithless cunning comprehended the more sagacious policy it could not originate. "All be it as you will."

"And in the meanwhile," added Richard, "watch well, but anger not, Montagu and the archbishop. It were dangerous to seem to distrust them till proof be clear—it were dull to believe them true. I go at once to fulfil my task."

CHAPTER VII.

Warwick and his Family in Exile.

WE now summon the reader on a longer if less classic journey than from Thebes to Athens, and waft him on a rapid wing from Shene to Amboise. We must suppose that the two emissaries of Gloucester have already arrived at their several destinations—the lady has reached Isabel;—the envoy, Margaret.

In one of the apartments appropriated to the earl in the royal palace, within the embrasure of a vast Gothic casement, sat Anne of Warwick; the small wicket in the window was

* COMINES, 3, c. 5; HALL; HOLLINSHED.

* *Original Letters from Harleian MSS.* Edited bv SIR H. ELLIS (Second Series).

open, and gave a view of a wide and fair garden, interspersed with thick bosquets, and regular alleys, over which the rich skies of the summer evening, a little before sunset, cast alternate light and shadow. Towards this prospect the sweet face of the Lady Anne was turned musingly. The riveted eye—the bended neck—the arms reclining on the knee—the slender fingers interlaced—gave to her whole person the character of reverie and repose.

In the same chamber were two other ladies; the one was pacing the floor with slow but uneven steps, with lips moving from time to time, as if in self-commune, with the brow contracted slightly. Her form and face took also the character of reverie, but not of repose.

The third female (the gentle and lovely mother of the other two) was seated, towards the centre of the room, before a small table, on which rested one of those religious manuscripts, full of the moralities and the marvels of cloister sanctity, which made so large a portion of the literature of the monkish ages. But her eye rested not on the Gothic letter, and the rich blazon of the holy book. With all a mother's fear, and all a mother's fondness, it glanced from Isabel to Anne—from Anne to Isabel, till at length, in one of those soft voices, so rarely heard, which makes even a stranger love the speaker, the fair countess said—

"Come hither, my child, Isabel, give me thy hand, and whisper me what hath chafed thee."

"My mother," replied the duchess, "it would become me ill to have a secret not known to thee, and yet, methinks, it would become me less to say aught to provoke thine anger."

"Anger, Isabel! who ever knew anger for those they love?"

"Pardon me, my sweet mother," said Isabel, relaxing her haughty brow, and she approached and kissed her mother's cheek.

The countess drew her gently to a seat by her side—

"And now tell me all—unless, indeed, thy Clarence hath, in some lover's hasty mood, vexed thy affection; for of the household secrets, even a mother should not question the true wife."

Isabel paused, and glanced significantly at Anne.

"Nay—see!" said the countess, smiling, though sadly—"*She*, too, hath thoughts that she will not tell to me; but they seem not such as should alarm my fears as thine do. For the moment ere I spoke to thee, *thy* brow frowned, and *her* lip smiled. She hears us not—speak on."

"Is it then true, my mother, that Margaret of Anjou is hastening hither; and can it be possible that King Louis can persuade my lord and father to meet, save in the field of battle, the arch enemy of our house?"

"Ask the earl thyself, Isabel; Lord Warwick hath no concealment from his children. Whatever he does is ever wisest, best, and knightliest—so, at least, may his children alway deem!"

Isabel's color changed, and her eye flashed. But ere she could answer, the arras was raised, and Lord Warwick entered. But no longer did the hero's mien and manner evince that cordial and tender cheerfulness, which, in all the storms of his changeful life, he had hitherto displayed when coming from power and danger, from council or from camp, to man's earthly paradise—a virtuous home.

Gloomy and absorbed, his very dress—which at that day, the Anglo-Norman deemed it a sin against self-dignity to neglect—betraying, by its disorder, that thorough change of the whole mind; that terrible internal revolution, which is made but, in strong natures, by the tyranny of a great care, or a great passion, the earl scarcely seemed to heed his countess, who rose hastily, but stopped in the timid fear of reverence of love at the sight of his stern aspect,—he threw himself abruptly on a seat, passed his hand over his face, and sighed heavily

That sigh dispelled the fear of the wife, and made her alive only to her privilege of the soother. She drew near, and, placing herself on the green rushes at his feet, took his hand and kissed it—but did not speak.

The earl's eyes fell on the lovely face looking up to him through tears, his brow softened, he drew his hand gently from hers, placed it on her head, and said, in a low voice—

"God, and our Lady bless thee, sweet wife!"

Then, looking round, he saw Isabel watching him intently, and, rising at once, he threw his arm round her waist, pressed her to his bosom, and said, "My daughter, for thee and thine, day and night have I striven and planned in vain. I cannot reward thy husband as I would—I cannot give thee, as I had hoped, a throne!"

"What title so dear to Isabel!" said the countess, "as that of Lord Warwick's daughter?"

Isabel remained cold and silent, and returned not the earl's embrace.

Warwick was, happily, too absorbed in his own feelings to notice those of his child. Moving away, he continued, as he paced the room, (his habit in emotion, which Isabel, who had many minute external traits, in common with her father, had unconsciously caught from him)—

"Till this morning, I hoped still, that my name and services, that Clarence's popular bearing and his birth of Plantagenet, would suffice to summon the English people round our standard—that the false Edward would be driven, on our landing, to fly the realm; and that, without change to the dynasty of York, Clarence, as next male heir, would ascend the throne. True, I saw all the obstacles—all the difficulties,—I was warned of them before I left England; but still I hoped. Lord Oxford has arrived—he has just left me. We have gone over the chart of the way before us, weighed the worth of every name, for and against; and, alas! I cannot but allow that all attempt to place the younger brother on the throne of the elder, would but lead to bootless slaughter, and irretrievable defeat!"

"Wherefore think you so, my lord!" asked Isabel, in evident excitement. "Your own retainers are sixty thousand; an army larger than Edward and all his lords of yesterday, can bring into the field."

"My child!" answered the earl, with that profound knowledge of his countrymen which he had rather acquired from his English heart, than from any subtlety of intellect—"armies may gain a victory, but they do not achieve a throne—unless, at least, they enforce a slavery. And it is not for me, and for Clarence, to be the violent conquerors of our countrymen; but the regenerators of a free realm, corrupted by a false man's rule."

"And what, then," exclaimed Isabel—"what do you propose, my father? Can it be possible that you can unite yourself with the abhorred Lancastrians—with the savage Anjounite, who beheaded my grandsire, Salisbury? Well do I remember your own words—'May God and St. George forget me, when I forget those grey and gory hairs!'"

Here Isabel was interrupted by a faint cry from Anne, who, unobserved by the rest, and, hitherto concealed from her father's eye by the deep embrasure of the window, had risen some moments before, and listened, with breathless attention, to the conversation between Warwick and the duchess.

"It is not true—it is not true!" exclaimed Anne passionately. "Margaret disowns the inhuman deed."

"Thou art right, Anne," said Warwick; "though I guess not how thou didst learn the error of a report so popularly believed, that till of late I never questioned its truth. King Louis assures me solemnly, that that foul act was done by the butcher Clifford against Margaret's knowledge, and when known, to her grief and anger."

"And you, who call Edward false, can believe Louis true!"

"Cease, Isabel—cease!" said the countess. "Is it thus my child can address my lord and husband! Forgive her, beloved Richard.

"Such heat in Clarence's wife misbeseems her not," answered Warwick. "And I can comprehend and pardon in my haughty Isabel a resentment which her reason must, at last, subdue; for, think not, Isabel, that it is without dread struggle and fierce agony that I can contemplate peace and league with mine ancient foe; but here two duties speak to me in voices not to be denied: my honor and my hearth, as noble and as man, demand redress—and the weal and glory of my country demand a ruler who does not degrade a warrior, nor assail a virgin, not corrupt a people by lewd pleasures, nor exhaust a land by grinding imposts; and that honor shall be vindicated, and that country shall be righted, no matter at what sacrafice of private grief and pride."

The words and the tone of the earl for a moment awed even Isabel, but after a pause, she said, sullenly, "And for this, then, Clarence hath joined your quarrel, and shared your exile!—for this,—that he may place the eternal barrier of the Lancastrian line between himself and the English throne!"

"I would fain hope," answered the earl,

calmly, "that Clarence will view our hard position more charitably than thou. If he gain not all that I could desire, should success crown our arms, he will, at least, gain much; for often and ever, did they husband, Isabel, urge me to stern measures against Edward, when I soothed him and restrained. *Mort Dieu!* how often did he complain of slight and insult from Elizabeth and her minions, of open affront from Edward, of parsimony to his wants as prince—of a life, in short, humbled and made bitter by all the indignity and the gall which scornful power can inflict on dependent pride. If he gain not the throne, he will gain, at least, the succession in thy right, to the baronies of Beauchamp, the mighty duchy and the vast heritage of York, the vice-royalty of Ireland. Never prince of the blood had wealth and honors equal to those that shall await thy lord. For the rest, I drew him not into my quarrel—long before, would he have drawn me into his; nor doth it become thee, Isabel, as child and as sister, to repent, if the husband of my daughter felt as brave men feel, without calculation of gain and profit, the insult offered to his lady's house. But, if here I overgauge his chivalry and love to me and mine, or discontent his ambition and his hopes, *Mort Dieu!* we hold him not a captive. Edward will hail his overtures of peace; let him make terms with his brother, and return."

"I will report to him what you say, my lord," said Isabel, with cold brevity; and, bending her haughty head in formal reverence, she advanced to the door. Anne sprang forward and caught her hand.

"Oh, Isabel!" she whispered; "in our father's sad and gloomy hour can you leave him thus?"—and the sweet lady burst into tears.

"Anne," retorted Isabel, bitterly, "thy heart is Lancastrian; and what, peradventure, grieves my father, hath but joy for thee."

Anne drew back, pale and trembling, and her sister swept from the room.

The earl, though he had not overheard the whispered sentences which passed between his daughters, had watched them closely, and his lip quivered with emotion, as Isabel closed the door.

"Come hither my Anne," he said, tenderly; "thou, who hast thy mother's face, never hast a harsh thought for thy father."

As Anne threw herself on Warwick's breast he continued—"And how camest tnou to learn that Margaret disowns a deed that, if done by her command, would render my union with her cause a sacriligious impiety to the dead?"

Anne colored, and nestled her head still closer to her father's bosom. Her mother regarded her confusion and her silence with an anxious eye.

The wing of the palace in which the earl's apartments were situated, was appropriated to himself and household, flanked to the left by an abutting pile containing state-chambers, never used by the austere and thrifty Louis, save on great occasions of pomp or revel; and, as we have before observed, looklng on a garden,—which was generally solitary and deserted. From this garden, while Anne yet strove for words to answer her father, and the countess yet watched her embarrassment, suddenly came the soft strain of a Provençal lute; while a low voice, rich, and modulated at once by a deep feeling and an exquisite art that would have given effect to even simpler words, breathed

THE LAY OF THE HEIR OF LANCASTER.

"His birthright but a Father's name,
A Grandsire's hero-sword;
He dwelt within the Stranger's land,
The friendless, homeless Lord!

"Yet one dear hope, too dear to tell,
Consoled the exiled man;
The Angels have their home in Heaven
And gentle thoughts in Anne."

At that name the voice of the singer trembled, and paused a moment; the earl, who at first had scarcely listened to what he deemed but the ill-seasoned gallantry of one of the royal minstrels, started in proud surprise, and Anne herself, tightening her clasp round her father's neck, burst into passionate sobs. The eye of the countess met that of her lord, but she put her finger to her lips in sign to him to listen. The song was resumed—

"Recall the single sunny time,
In childhood's April weather,
When he and thon, the boy and girl,
Roved, hand in hand, together;—

"When round thy young companion knelt
The Princes of the Isle;—
And Priest and People pray'd their God,
On England's Heir to smile."

The earl uttered a half-stifled exclamation, but the minstrel heard not the interruption, and continued—

" Methinks the sun hath never smil'd
Upon the exiled man,
Like that bright morning when the boy
Told all his soul to Anne.

" No; while his birthright but a name,
A Grandsire's hero-sword,
He would not woo the lofty maid
To love the banish'd lord.

" But when, with clarion, fife, and drum,
He claims and wins his own;
When o'er the Deluge drifts his Ark,
To rest upon a throne—

" THEN, wilt thou deign to hear the hope
That bless'd the exiled man,
When pining for his Father's crown
To deck the brows of Anne !"

The song ceased, and there was silence within the chamber, broken but by Anne's low, yet passionate weeping. The earl gently strove to disengage her arms from his neck, but she, mistaking his intention, sank on her knees, and covering her face with her hands, exclaimed—

" Pardon !—pardon !—pardon him if not me ! "

" What have I to pardon ? What hast thou concealed from me ? Can I think that thou hast met, *in secret*, one who——"

" In secret ! Never—never, father ! This is the third time only that I have heard his voice since we have been at Amboise, save when—save when——"

" Go on."

" Save when King Louis presented him to me in the revel, under the name of the Count de F——, and he asked me if I could forgive his mother for Lord Clifford's crime."

" It is, then, as the rhyme proclaimed ; and it is Edward of Lancaster, who loves and woos the daughter of Lord Warwick!"

Something in her father's voice made Anne remove her hands from her face, and look up to him with a thrill of timid joy. Upon his brow, indeed, frowned no anger—upon his lip smiled no scorn. At that moment all his haughty grief at the curse of circumstance, which drove him to his hereditary foe, had vanished. Though Montague had obtained from Oxford some glimpse of the desire which the more sagacious and temperate Lancastrians already entertained for that alliance, and though Louis had already hinted its expediency to the earl, yet, till now, Warwick himself had naturally conceived that the prince shared the enmity of his mother, and that such an union, however politic, was impossible; but now, indeed, there burst upon him the full triumph of revenge and pride. Edward of York dared to woo Anne to dishonor—Edward of Lancaster dared not even woo her as his wife till his crown was won ! To place upon the throne the very daughter the ungrateful monarch had insulted—to make her he would have humbled not only the instrument of his fall, but the successor of his purple—to unite in one glorious strife, the wrongs of the man and the pride of the father, —these were the thoughts that sparkled in the eye of the king-maker, and flushed with a fierce rapture the dark cheek, already hollowed by passion and care. He raised his daughter from the floor, and placed her in her mother's arms, but still spoke not.

" This, then, was thy secret, Anne;" whispered the countess, " and I half foreguessed it, when, last night, I knelt beside thy couch to pray, and overheard thee murmur in thy dreams."

" Sweet mother, thou forgivest me; but my father—ah, he speaks not !—One word ! Father, father, not even *his* love could console me if I angered *thee !*"

The earl, who had remained rooted to the spot, his eyes shining thoughtfully under his dark brows, and his hand slightly raised, as if piercing into the future, and mapping out its airy realm, turned quickly—

" I go to the heir of Lancaster; if this boy be bold and true—worthy of England and of thee—we will change that sad ditty of that scrannel lute into such a storm of trumpets as beseems the triumph of a conqueror, and the marriage of a prince !"

CHAPTER VIII.

How the heir of Lancaster meets the King-maker.

IN truth, the young prince, in obedience to a secret message from the artful Louis, had repaired to the court of Amboise under the name of the Count de F——. The French king had long before made himself acquainted with Prince Edward's romantic attachment to the earl's daughter, through the agent employed by Edward to transmit his portrait to Anne at Rouen; and from him, probably, came to Oxford the suggestion which that nobleman had hazarded to Montagu; and now that it became his policy seriously and earnestly to espouse the cause of his kinswoman Margaret, he saw all the advantage to his cold statecraft, which could be drawn from a boyish love. Louis had a well-founded fear of the warlike spirit, and military talents of Edward IV.; and this fear had induced him hitherto to refrain from openly espousing the cause of the Lancastrians, though it did not prevent his abetting such seditions and intrigues as could confine the attention of the martial Plantagenet to the perils of his own realm. But now that the breach between Warwick and the king had taken place—now that the earl could no longer curb the desire of the Yorkist monarch to advance his hereditary claims to the fairest provinces of France—nay, peradventure, to France itself,—while the defection of Lord Warwick gave to the Lancastrians the first fair hope of success in urging their own pretensions to the English throne—he bent all the powers of his intellect and his will towards the restoration of a natural ally, and the downfall of a dangerous foe. But he knew that Margaret and her Lancastrian favorers could not of themselves suffice to achieve a revolution—that they could only succeed under cover of the popularity and the power of Warwick, while he perceived all the art it would require to make Margaret forego her vindictive nature and long resentment, and to supple the pride of the great earl into recognizing, as a sovereign, the woman who had branded him as a traitor.

Long before Lord Oxford's arrival, Louis, with all that address which belonged to him, had gradually prepared the earl to familiarize himself to the only alternative before him, save that, indeed, of powerless sense of wrong, and obscure and lasting exile. The French king looked with more uneasiness to the scruples of Margaret; and to remove these, he trusted less to his own skill, than to her love for her only son.

His youth passed principally in Anjou—that court of minstrels—young Edward's gallant and ardent temper had become deeply imbued with the southern poetry and romance. Perhaps, the very feud between his House and Lord Warwick's, though both claimed their common descent from John of Gaunt, had tended, by the contradictions in the human heart, to endear to him the recollection of the gentle Anne. He obeyed with joy the summons of Louis, repaired to the court, was presented to Anne as the Count de F——, found himself recognized at the first glance, (for his portrait still lay upon her heart, as his remembrance in its core,) and, twice before the song we have recited, had ventured, agreeably to the sweet customs of Anjou, to address the lady of his love, under the shade of the starlit and summer copses. But, on this last occasion, he had departed from his former discretion; hitherto he had selected an hour of deeper night, and ventured but beneath the lattice of the maiden's chamber when the rest of the palace was hushed in sleep. And the fearless declaration of his rank and love now hazarded, was prompted by one who contrived to turn to grave uses the wildest whim of the minstrel, the most romantic enthusiasm of youth.

Louis had just learned from Oxford the result of his interview with Warwick. And about the same time the French king had received a letter from Margaret, announcing her departure from the Castle of Verdun for Tours, where she prayed him to meet her forthwith, and stating, that she had received from England tidings that might change all her schemes, and more than ever forbid the possibility of a reconciliation with the Earl of Warwick.

The king perceived the necessity of calling into immediate effect the aid on which he had relied, in the presence and passion of the young prince. He sought him at once—he found him in a remote part of the gardens, and overheard him breathing to himself the lay he had just composed.

"*Pasque Dieu!*" said the king, laying his hand on the young man's shoulder—"if thou wilt but repeat that song where and when I bid thee, I promise that before the month ends Lord Warwick shall pledge thee his daughter's hand; and before the year is closed thou shalt sit beside Lord Warwick's daughter in the halls of Westminster."

And the royal troubador took the counsel of the king.

The song had ceased; the minstrel emerged from the bosquets, and stood upon the sward, as, from the postern of the palace, walked with a slow step, a form which it became him not, as prince or as lover, in peace or in war, to shrink. The first stars had now risen; the light, though serene, was pale and dim. The two men—the one advancing, the other motionless—gazeed on each other in grave silence. As Count de F——, amidst the young nobles in the king's train, the earl had scarcely noticed the heir of England. He viewed him now with a different eye:—in secret complacency, for with a soldier's weakness, the soldier-baron valued men too much for their outward seeming,—he surveyed a figure already masculine and stalwart, though still in the graceful symmetry of fair eighteen.

"A youth of a goodly presence," muttered the earl, "with the dignity that commands in peace, and the sinews that can strive against hardship and death in war."

He approached, and said, calmly—"Sir minstrel, he who woes either fame or beauty may love the lute, but should wield the sword. At least, so, methinks, had the Fifth Henry said to him who boasts for his heritage the sword of Agincourt."

"O noble earl!" exclaimed the prince, touched by words far gentler than he had dared to hope, despite his bold and steadfast mien, and giving to frank and graceful emotion—"O noble earl! since thou knowest me —since my secret is told—since, in that secret, I have proclaimed a hope as dear to me as a crown, and dearer far than life, can I hope that thy rebuke but veils thy favor, and that, under Lord Warwick's eye, the grandson of Henry V. shall approve himself worthy of the blood that kindles in his veins?"

"Fair sir and prince," returned the earl, whose hardy and generous nature the emotion and fire of Edward warmed and charmed, "there are, alas! deep memories of blood and wrong—the sad deeds and wrathful words of party feud and civil war, between thy royal mother and myself; and though we may unite now against a common foe, much I fear that the Lady Margaret would brook ill a closer friendship, a nearer tie, than the exigency of the hour, between Richard Nevile and her son."

"No, sir earl; let me hope you misthink her. Hot and impetuous, but not mean and treacherous, the moment that she accepts the service of thine arm she must forget that thou hast been her foe; and if I, as my father's heir, return to England, it is in the trust that a new era will commence. Free from the passionate enmities of either faction, Yorkist and Lancastrian are but Englishmen to me. Justice to all who serve us—pardon for all who have opposed."

The prince paused, and, even in the dim light, his kingly aspect gave effect to his kingly words. "And if this resolve be such as you approve—if you, great earl, be that which even your foes proclaim, a man whose power depends less on lands and vassals—broad though the one, and numerous though the other—than on well-known love for England, her glory, and her peace, it rests with you to bury for ever in one grave the feuds of Lancaster and York! What Yorkist, who hath fought at Touton or St. Alban's, under Lord Warwick's standard, will lift sword against the husband of Lord Warwick's daughter? what Lancastrian will not forgive a Yorkist, when Lord Warwick, the kinsman of Duke Richard, becomes father to the Lancastrian heir, and bulwark to the Lancastrian throne? Oh, Warwick, if not for my sake, nor for the sake of full redress against the ingrate whom thou repentest to have placed on my father's throne, at least for the sake of England—for the healing of her bleeding wounds—for the union of her divided people, hear the grandson of Henry V., who sues to thee for thy daughter's hand!"

The royal wooer, bent his knee as he spoke —the mighty subject saw and prevented the impulse of the prince who had forgotten himself in the lover; the hand which he caught he lifted to his lips, and the next moment, in manly and soldier-like embrace, the prince's young arm was thrown over the broad shoulder of the king-maker.

CHAPTER IX.

The interview of Earl Warwick and Queen Margaret.

LOUIS hastened to meet Margaret at Tours; thither came also, her father Renè, her brother, John of Calabria, Yolante her sister, and the Count of Vaudemonte. The meeting between the queen and René was so touching as to have drawn tears to the hard eyes of Louis XI.; but, that emotion over, Margaret evinced how little affliction had humbled her high spirit, or softened her angry passions: she interrupted Louis in every argument for reconciliation with Warwick. "Not with honor to myself, and to my son," she exclaimed, "can I pardon that cruel earl—the main cause of King Henry's downfall! in vain patch up a hollow peace between us—a peace, of form and parchment! My spirit never can be contented with him, *ne* pardon!"

For several days she maintained a language which betrayed the chief cause of her own impolitic passions, that had lost her crown. Showing to Louis the letter despatched to her, proffering the hand of the Lady Elizabeth to het son, she asked "if that were not a more profitable party," * and, "if it were necessary that she should forgive—whether it were not more queenly to treat with Edward than with a two-fold rebel?"

In fact, the queen would, perhaps, have fallen into Gloucester's artful snare, despite all the arguments and even the half-menaces † of the more penetrating Louis, but for a counter-acting influence which Richard had not reckoned upon, Prince Edward, who had lingered behind Louis, arrived from Amboise, and his persuasions did more than all the representations of the crafty king. The queen loved her son with that intenseness which characterizes the one soft affection of violent natures. Never had she yet opposed his most childish whim, and now he spoke with the eloquence of one, who put his heart and his life's life into his words. At last, reluctantly, she consented to an interview with Warwick. The earl, accompanied by Oxford, arrived at Tours, and the two nobles were led into the presence of Margaret by King Louis.

The reader will picture to himself a room darkened by thick curtains drawn across the casement, for the proud woman wished not the earl to detect on her face either the ravages of years, or the emotions of offended pride. In a throne chair, placed on the dais, sate the motionless queen, her hands clasping, convulsively, the arms of the fauteuil, her features pale and rigid;—and behind the chair leant the graceful figure of her son. The person of the Lancastrian prince was little less remarkable than that of his hostile namesake, but its character was distinctly different.* Spare, like Henry V., almost to the manly defect of leanness, his proportions were slight to those which gave such portly majesty to the vast-chested Edward, but they evinced the promise of almost equal strength; the muscles hardened to iron by early exercise in arms, the sap of youth never wasted by riot and debauch: his short purple manteline trimmed with ermine, was embroidered with his grandfather's favorite device, "the silver swan"—he wore on his breast, the badge of St. George and the single ostrich plume, which made his cognzance as Prince of Wales, waved over a fair and ample forehead, on which were, even then, traced the lines of musing thought and high design; his chestnut hair curled close to his noble head, his eye shone dark and brilliant, beneath the deep-set brow, which gives to the human countenance such expression of energy and intellect:—all about him, in aspect and mien, seemed to betoken a mind riper than his years, a masculine simplicity of taste and bearing, the earnest and grave temperament, mostly allied, in youth, to pure and elevated desires, to an honorable and chivalric soul.

Below the dais stood some of the tried and gallant gentlemen who had braved exile, and tasted penury in their devotion to the House of Lancaster, and who had now flocked once

* See, for this curious passage of secret history, SIR H. FLLIS'S *Original Letters from the Harleian MSS.*, second series, vol. i., letter 42.

† Louis would have thrown over Margaret's cause, if Warwick had demanded it; he instructed MM. de Concressault and Du Plessis to assure the earl that he would aid him to the utmost to reconquer England either for the Queen Margaret or for any one else he chose (ou pour qui il voudra).—For that he loved the earl better than Margaret or her son.—BRANTE, t. ix. 276.

* "According to some of the French chroniclers, the Prince of Wales, who was one of the handsomest and most accomplished princes in Europe, was very desirous of becoming the husband of Anne Nevile," etc.—MISS STRICKLAND, *Life of Margaret of Anjou.*

more round their queen, in the hope of better days. There, were the Dukes of Exeter and Somerset—their very garments soiled and threadbare—many a day had those great lords hungered for the beggar's crust! * There, stood Sir John Fortescue, the patriarch authority of our laws, who had composed his famous treatise for the benefit of the young prince, over-fond of exercise with lancet and brand, and the recreation of knightly song. There, were Jasper of Pembroke, and Sir Henry Rous, and the Earl of Devon, and the Knight of Lytton, whose house had followed from sire to son, the fortunes of the Lancastrian Rose; † and, contrasting the sober garments of the exiles, shone the jewels and cloth of gold that decked the persons of the more prosperous foreigners, Ferri, Count of Vaudemonte, Margaret's brother, the Duke of Calabria, and the powerful form of Sir Pierre de Brezé, who had accompanied Margaret in her last disastrous campaigns, with all the devotion of a chevalier for the lofty lady adored in secret.‡

When the door opened, and gave to the eyes of those proud exiles the form of their puissant enemy, they with difficulty suppressed the murmur of their resentment, and their looks turned with sympathy and grief to the hueless face of their queen.

The earl himself was troubled—his step was less firm, his crest less haughty, his eye less serenely steadfast.

But beside him, in a dress more homely than that of the poorest exile there, and in garb and in aspect, as he lives for ever in the portraiture of Victor Hugo and our own yet greater Scott, moved Louis, popularly called "The Fell."

"Madame and cousin," said the king, "we present to you the man for whose haute courage and dread fame we have such love and respect, that we value him as much as any king, and would do as much for him as for man living,* and with my lord of Warwick, see also this noble Earl of Oxford, who, though he may have sided awhile with the enemies of your highness, comes now to pray your pardon, and to lay at your feet his sword."

Lord Oxford, (who had ever unwillingly acquiesced in the Yorkist dynasty) — more prompt than Warwick, here threw himself on his knees before Margaret, and his tears fell on her hand, as he murmured "Pardon."

"Rise, Sir John de Vere," said the queen, glancing, with a flashing eye, from Oxford to Lord Warwick. "Your pardon is right easy to purchase, for well I know that you yielded but to the time—you did not turn the time against us—you and yours have suffered much for King Henry's cause. Rise, Sir Earl."

"And," said a voice, so deep and so solemn, that it hushed the very breath of those who heard it,—"and has Margaret a pardon also for the man who did more than all others to to dethrone King Henry, and can do more than all to restore his crown?"

"Ha!" cried Margaret, rising in her passion, and casting from her the hand her son had placed upon her shoulder—"Ha!" Ownest thou thy wrongs, proud lord? Comest thou at last to kneel at Queen Margaret's feet? Look round and behold her court—some half-score brave and unhappy gentlemen, driven from their hearths and homes—their heritage the prey of knaves and varlets—their sovereign in a prison—their sovereign's wife, the sovereign's son, persecuted and hunted from the soil! And comest thou now to the forlorn majesty of sorrow to boast—'Such deeds were mine?'"

"Mother and lady," began the prince—

"Madden me not, my son. Forgiveness is for the prosperous, not for adversity and woe."

"Hear me," said the earl,—who, having once bowed his pride to the interview, had steeled himself against the passion which, in heart, he somewhat despised as a mere womans'

* Philip de Comines says he himself had seen the Dukes of Exeter and Somerset in the Low Countries in as wretched a plight as common beggars.

† Sir Robert de Lytton (whose grandfather had been Comptroller to the Household of Henry IV., and Agister of the Forests allotted to Queen Joan) was one of the most powerful knights of he time; and afterwards, according to Perkin Warbeck, one of the ministers most trusted by Henry VII, He was Lord of Lytton, in Derbyshire (where his ancestors had been settled since the Conquest), of Knebworth in Herts (the ancient seat and manor of Plantagenet de Brotherton, Earl of Norfolk and Earl-Marshal), of Myndelesden and Langley, of Standyarn, Dene, and Brekesborne, in Northamptonshire, and became, in the reign of Henry VII., Privy-Councillor, Under-Treasurer, and Keeper of the great Wardrobe.

‡ "See for the chivalrous devotion of this knight (Seneschal of Normandy) to Margaret—Miss Strickland's Life of that queen.

* ELLIS'S *Original Letters*, vol. i., letter 42, second series.

burst of inconsiderate fury—"For I have this right to be heard—that not one of these knights, your lealest and noblest friends, can say of me, that I ever stooped to gloss mine acts, or palliate bold deeds with wily words. Dear to me as comrade in arms—sacred to me as a father's head, was Richard of York, mine uncle by marriage with Lord Salisbury's sister. I speak not now of his claims by descent, (for those even king Henry could not deny), but I maintain them, even in your grace's presence, to be such as vindicate, from disloyalty and treason, me and the many true and gallant men, who upheld them through danger, by field and scaffold. Error, it might be—but the error of men who believed themselves the defenders of a just cause. Nor did I, Queen Margaret, lend myself wholly to my kinsman's quarrel, nor share one scheme that went to the dethronement of King Henry, until—pardon if I speak bluntly; it is my wont, and would be more so now, but for thy fair face and woman's form, which awe me more than if confronting the frown of Cœur de Lion, or the First great Edward—pardon me, I say, if I speak bluntly and aver, that I was not King Henry's foe until false counsellors had planned my destruction, in body and goods, land and life. In the midst of peace, at Coventry, my father and myself scarcely escaped the knife of the murderer. * In the streets of London, the very menials and hangmen employed in the service of your highness beset me unarmed ;† a little time after, and my name was attainted by an illegal Parliament. ‡ And not till after these things did Richard Duke of York ride to the Hall of Westminister, and lay his hand upon the throne; nor till after these things did I and my father Salisbury say to each other, 'The time has come when neither peace nor honor can be found for us under King Henry's reign.' Blame me, if you will, Queen Margaret; reject me, if you need not my sword; but that which I did in the gone days was such as no nobleman so outraged and *despaired*,§ would have forborne to do;—remembering that England is not the heritage of the king alone, but that safety and honor, and freedom and justice, and the *rights* of his Norman gentlemen, and his Saxon people. And rights are a mockery and a laughter if they do not justify resistance, whensoever, and by whomsoever, they are invaded and assailed."

It had been with a violent effort that Margaret had refrained from interrupting this address, which had, however, produced no inconsiderable effect upon the knightly listeners around the dais. And now, as the earl ceased, her indignation was arrested by dismay on seeing the young prince suddenly leave his post and advance to the side of Warwick.

"Right well hast thou spoken, noble earl and cousin—right well, though right plainly. And I," added the prince, "saving the presence of my queen and mother—I, the representative of my sovereign father, in his name will pledge thee a king's oblivion and pardon for the past, if thou, on thy side, acquit my princely mother of all privity to the snares against thy life and honor of which thou hast spoken, and give thy knightly word to be henceforth leal to Lancaster. Perish all memories of the past that can make walls between the souls of brave men!"

Till this moment, his arms folded in his gown, his thin, fox-like face bent to the ground, Louis had listened, silent and undisturbed. He now deemed it the moment to second the appeal of the prince. Passing his hand hypocritically over his tearless eyes, the king turned to Margaret and said—

"Joyful hour!—happy union!—May Madame la Vierge and Monsiegneur St. Martin sanctify and hallow the bond by which alone my beloved kinswoman can regain her rights and roiaulme. Amen."

Unheeding this pious ejaculation, her bosom heaving, her eyes wandering from the earl to Edward, Margaret at last gave vent to her passion.

"And is it come to this, Prince Edward of Wales, that thy mother's wrongs are not thine? Standest thou side by side with my mortal foe, who, instead of repenting treason, dares but to complain of injury? Am I fallen so low that my voice to pardon or disdain is counted but as a sough of idle air! God of my fathers, hear me! Willingly from my heart I tear the last thought and care for the

* See Hall (236), who says that Margaret had laid a snare for Salisbury and Warwick, at Warwick, and "if they had not suddenly departed their life's thread had been broken."

† HALL, FABYAN.

‡ *Parl. Rolls*, 370; W. WYR, 478.

§ Warwick's phrase:—See SIR H. ELLIS'S *Original Letters*, vol. i., second series.

pomps of earth. Hateful to me a crown for which the wearer must cringe to enemy and rebel! Away, Earl Warwick! Monstrous and unnatural seems it to the wife of captive Henry, to see thee by the side of Henry's son!"

Every eye turned in fear to the aspect of the earl, every ear listened for the answer which might be expected from his well-known heat and pride—an answer to destroy for ever the last hope of the Lancastrian line. But whether it was the very consciousness of his power to raise or to crush that fiery speaker, or those feelings natural to brave men, half of chivalry, half contempt, which kept down the natural anger by thoughts of the *sex* and sorrows of the Anjouite, or that the wonted irascibility of his temper had melted into one steady and profound passion of revenge against Edward of York, which absorbed all lesser and more trivial causes of resentment,—the earl's face, though pale as the dead, was unmoved and calm, and, with a grave and melancholy smile, he answered—

"More do I respect thee, O queen, for the hot words which show a truth rarely heard from royal lips, than hadst thou deigned to dissimulate the forgiveness and kindly charity, which sharp remembrance permits thee not to feel! No, princely Margaret, not yet can there be frank amity between thee and me! Nor do I boast the affection yon gallant gentlemen have displayed. Frankly, as thou hast spoken, do I say, that the wrongs I have suffered from another alone move me to allegiance to thyself! Let others serve thee for love of Henry—reject not my service, given but for revenge on Edward—as much, henceforth, am I his foe as formerly his friend and maker!* And if, hereafter, on the throne, thou shouldst remember and resent the former wars, at least, thou hast owed me no gratitude, and thou canst not grieve my heart, and seethe my brain, as the man whom I once loved better than a son! Thus, from thy presence I depart, chafing not at thy scornful wrath—mindful, young prince, but of *thy* just and gentle heart, and sure, in the calm of my own soul, (on which this much at least, of our destiny is reflected as on a glass,) that when, high lady, thy colder sense returns to thee, thou wilt see that the league between us *must* be made!—that thine ire, as woman, must fade before thy duties as a mother, thy affection as a wife, and thy paramount and solemn obligations to the people thou hast ruled as queen! In the dead of night, thou shalt hear the voice of Henry, in his prison, asking Margaret to set him free! The vision of thy son shall rise before thee in his bloom and promise, to demand, 'Why his mother deprives him of a crown?' and crowds of pale peasants, grinded beneath tyrannous exaction, and despairing fathers mourning for dishonored children, shall ask the christian queen, 'If God will sanction the unreasoning wrath which rejects the only instrument that can redress her people?'"

This said, the earl bowed his head and turned; but, at the first sign of his departure, there was a general movement among the the noble bystanders: Impressed by the dignity of his bearing, by the greatness of his power, and by the unquestionable truth that in rejecting him, Margaret cast away the heritage of her son—the exiles, with a common impulse, threw themselves at the queen's feet, and exclaimed, almost in the same words,

"Grace! noble queen!—Grace for the great Lord Warwick!"

"My sister," whispered John of Calabria, "thou art thy son's ruin if the earl depart!"

"*Pasque Dieu!* Vex not my kinswoman—if she prefer a convent to a throne, cross not the holy choice!" said the wily Louis, with a mocking irony on his pinched lips.

The prince alone spoke not, but stood proudly on the same spot, gazing on the earl, as he slowly moved to the door.

"Oh, Edward—Edward, my son!" exclaimed the unhappy Margaret, "If for thy sake—for thine—I must make the past a blank—speak thou for me!"

"I have spoken," said the prince, gently, "and thou didst chide me, noble mother; yet I spoke, methinks, as Henry V. had done, if of a mighty enemy he had had the power to make a noble friend?"

A short convulsive sob was heard from the throne chair; and as suddenly as it burst, it ceased. Queen Margaret rose—not a trace of that stormy emotion upon the grand and marble beauty of her face. Her voice, unnaturally calm, arrested the steps of the departing earl.

"Lord Warwick, defend this boy—restore

* Sir H. Ellis's *Original Letters*, vol. i., second series.

his rights—release his sainted father—and for years of anguish and of exile, Margaret of Anjou forgives the champion of her son!"

In an instant Prince Edward was again by the earl's side—a moment more, and the earl's proud knee bent in homage to the queen—joyful tears were in the eyes of her friends and kindred—a triumphant smile on the lips of Louis,—and Margaret's face, terrible in its stony and lock'd repose, was raised above, as if asking the All-Merciful, pardon—*for* the pardon which the human sinner had bestowed! *

CHAPTER X.

Love and Marriage—Doubts of conscience—Domestic jealousy—And household treason.

THE events that followed this tempestuous interview were such as the position of the parties necessarily compelled. The craft of Louis—the energy and love of Prince Edward—the representations of all her kindred and friends, conquered, though not without repeated struggles, Margaret's repugnance to a nearer union between Warwick and her son. The earl did not deign to appear personally in this matter. He left it, as became him, to Louis and the prince, and finally received from them the proposals, which ratified the league, and consummated the schemes of his revenge.

Upon the Very Cross† in St. Mary's Church of Angers, Lord Warwick swore without change to hold the party of King Henry. Before the same sacred symbol, King Louis and his brother, Duke of Guienne, robed in canvas, swore to sustain to their utmost the Earl of Warwick in behalf of King Henry; and Margaret recorded her oath to treat the earl as true and faithful, and never for deeds past to make him any reproach.

Then were signed the articles of marriage between Prince Edward and the Lady Anne—the latter to remain with Margaret, but the marriage not to be consummated 'till Lord Warwick had entered England and regained the realm, or most part, for King Henry'—a condition which pleased the earl, who desired to award his beloved daughter no less a dowry than a crown.

An article far more important than all to the safety of the earl, and to the permanent success of the enterprise, was one that virtually took from the fierce and unpopular Margaret the reins of government, by constituting Prince Edward, (whose qualities endeared him more and more to Warwick, and were such as promised to command the respect and love of the people), sole regent of all the realm, upon attaining his majority. For the Duke of Clarence were reserved all the lands and dignities of the Duchy of York, the right to the succession of the throne to him, and his posterity—failing male heirs to the Prince of Wales—with a private pledge of the vice-royalty of Ireland.

Margaret had attached to her consent one condition highly obnoxious to her high-spirited son, and to which he was only reconciled by the arguments of Warwick: she stipulated that he should not accompany the earl to England, nor appear there till his father was proclaimed king. In this, no doubt, she was guided by maternal fears and by some undeclared suspicion either of the good faith of Warwick, or of his means to raise a sufficient army to fulfil his promise. The brave prince wished to be himself foremost in the battles fought in his right and for his cause. But the earl contended, to the surprise and joy of Margaret, that it best behoved the prince's interests to enter England without one enemy in the field, leaving others to clear his path, free himself from all the personal hate of hostile factions, and without a drop of blood upon the sword of one heralded and announced as the peace-maker, and impartial reconciler of all feuds. So then (these high conditions settled), in the presence of the kings René and Louis, of the Earl and Countess of Warwick, and in solemn state, at Amboise, Edward of Lancaster plighted his marriage troth to his beloved and loving Anne.

It was deep night—and high revel in the Palace of Amboise crowned the ceremonies of that memorable day. The Earl of Warwick stood alone in the same chamber in which he first discovered the secret of the young Lancastrian. From the brilliant company, as-

* ELLIS'S *Original Letters from the Harleian MSS*,, letter 42.

† Miss Strickland observes upon this interview—"It does not appear that Warwick mentioned the execution of his father, the Earl of Salisbury, which is almost a confirmation of the statements of those historians who deny that he was beheaded by Margaret.

sembled in the halls of state, he had stolen unperceived away, for his great heart was full to overflowing. The part he had played for many days was over, and with it the excitement and the fever. His schemes were crowned;—the Lancastrians were won to his revenge;—the king's heir was the betrothed of his favorite child;—and the hour was visible in the distance when, by the retribution most to be desired, the father's hand should lead that child to the throne of him who would have degraded her to the dust. If victory awaited his sanguine hopes, as father to his future queen, the dignity and power of the earl became greater in in the court of Lancaster, than, even in his palmiest day, amidst the minions of ungrateful York: the sire of two lines—if Anne's posterity should fail, the crown would pass to the sons of Isabel,—in either case, from him (ill-successful in his invasion) would descend the royalty of England. Ambition, pride, revenge, might well exult in viewing the future, as mortal wisdom could discern it. The house of Nevile never seemed brightened by a more glorious star: And yet the earl was sad and heavy at heart. However he had concealed it from the eyes of others, the haughty ire of Margaret must have galled him in his deepest soul. And even, as he had that day contemplated the holy happiness in the face of Anne, a sharp pang had shot through his breast. Were those the witnesses of fair-omened spousailles? How different from the hearty greeting of his warrior-friends, was the measured courtesy of foes, who had felt and fled before his sword! If aught chanced to him, in the hazard of the field, what thought for his child could ever speak in pity from the hard and scornful eyes of the imperious Anjouite!

The mist which till then had clouded his mind, or left visible to his gaze but one stern idea of retribution, melted into air. He beheld the fearful crisis to which his life had passed — he had reached the eminence to mourn the happy gardens left behind. Gone, for ever gone, the old endearing friendships—the sweet and manly remembrances of brave companionship and early love! Who among those who had confronted war by his side, for the house of York, would hasten to clasp his hand and hail his coming, as the captain of hated Lancaster? True, could he bow his honor to proclaim the true cause of his desertion, the heart of every father would beat in sympathy with his; but less than ever could the tale that vindicated his name be told. How stoop to invoke malignant pity to the insult offered to a future queen! Dark in his grave must rest the secret no words could syllable, save by such vague and mysterious hint and comment as pass from baseless gossip into dubious history.* True, that in his change of party he was not, like Julian of Spain, an apostate to his native land. He did not meditate the subversion of his country by the foreign foe, it was but the substitution of one English monarch for another—a virtuous prince for a false and a sanguinary king.

True that the change from rose to rose had been so common amongst the greatest and the bravest, that even the most rigid could scarcely censure what the age itself had sanctioned. But what other man of his stormy day had been so conspicuous in the downfall of those he was now as conspicuously to raise? What other man had Richard of York taken so dearly to his heart—to what other man had the august father said,—"Protect my sons?" Before him seemed literally to rise the phantom of that honored prince, and with clay-cold lips to ask—"Art thou, of all the world, the doomsman of my first-born!" A groan escaped the breast of the self-tormentor, he fell on his knees, and prayed—"O pardon, thou All-seeing!—plead for me, Divine Mother! if in this I have darkly erred, taking my *heart* for my *conscience*, and mindful only of a selfish wrong! Oh, surely, no! Had Richard of York himself lived to know what I have suffered from his unworthy son—causeless insult, broken faith, public and unabashed dishonor;—yea, pardoning, serving, loving on through all, till, at the last, nothing less than the foulest taint that can light upon 'scutcheon and name was the cold, premeditated reward for untired devotion,—surely, surely Richard himself had said—'Thy honor, at last, forbids all pardon!'"

Then, in that rapidity with which the human heart, once seizing upon self-excuse, reviews, one after one, the fair apologies, the earl passed

* Hall well explains the mystery which wrapped the king's insult to a female of the House of Warwick, by the simple sentence, "the certainty was not, for both their honors, openly known!"

from the injury to himself to the mal-government of his land, and muttered over the thousand instances of cruelty and misrule which rose to his remembrance—forgetting, alas, or steeling himself to the memory, that till Edward's vices had assailed his own hearth and honor, he had been contented with lamenting them,—he had not ventured to chastise.—At length, calm and self-acquitted, he rose from his self-confession, and leaning by the open casement, drank in the reviving and gentle balm of the summer air. The state apartments he had left, formed, as we have before observed, an angle to the wing in which the chamber he had now retired to was placed. They were brilliantly illumined—their windows open to admit the fresh soft breeze of night,—and he saw, as if by daylight, distinct and gorgeous, in their gay dresses, the many revellers within. But one group caught and riveted his eye. Close by the centre window he recognized his gentle Anne, with downcast looks; he almost fancied he saw her blush, as her young bridegroom, young and beautiful as herself, whispered love's flatteries in her ear. He saw farther on, but yet near, his own sweet countess, and muttered, "After twenty years of marriage may Anne be as dear to him as *thou* art now to me!"

And still he saw, or deemed he saw, his lady's eye, after resting with tender happiness on the young pair, rove wistfully around, as if missing and searching for her partner in her mother's joy. But what form sweeps by with so haughty a majesty, then pauses by the betrothed, addresses them not, but seems to regard them with so fixed a watch? He knew by her ducal diadem, by the baudekin colors of her robe, by her unmistakable air of pride, his daughter Isabel. He did not distinguish the expression of her countenance, but an ominous thrill passed through his heart; for the *attitude* itself had an expression, and not that of a sister's sympathy and love. He turned away his face with an unquiet recollection of the altered mood of his discontented daughter. He looked again; the duchess had passed on—lost amidst the confused splendor of the revel. And high and rich swelled the merry music that invited to the stately pavon. He gazed still: his lady had left her place, the lovers, too, had vanished, and where they had stood, stood now, in close conference, his ancient enemies, Exeter and Somerset. The sudden change, from objects of love to those associated with hate, had something which touched one of these superstitions to which, in all ages, the heart, when deeply stirred, is weakly sensitive. And again, forgetful of the revel, the earl turned to the serener landscape of the grove and the moon-lit greensward, and mused, and mused, till a soft arm thrown around him, woke his reverie. For this had his lady left the revel. Divining, by the instinct born of love, the gloom of her husband, she had stolen from pomp and pleasure to his side.

"Ah! wherefore wouldst thou rob me," said the countess, "of one hour of thy presence, since so few hours remain—since when the sun, that succeeds the morrow's, shines upon these walls, the night of thine absence will have closed upon me?"

"And if that thought of parting, sad to me as thee, sufficed not, *bel'amie*, to dim the revel," answered the earl, "weetest thou not how ill the grave and solemn thoughts of one who sees before him the emprise that would change the dynasty of a realm, can suit with the careless dance and the wanton music? But, not at that moment did I think of those mightier cares, my thoughts were nearer home. Hast thou noted, sweet wife, the silent gloom, the clouded brow of Isabel, since she learned that Anne was to be the bride of the heir of Lancaster."

The mother suppressed a sigh. "We must pardon, or glance lightly over, the mood of one who loves her lord, and mourns for his baffled hopes. Well-a-day! I grieve that she admits not even me to her confidence. Ever with the favorite lady who joined her train—methinks, that new friend gives less holy counsels than a mother?"

"Ha! and yet what counsels can Isabel listen to from a comparative stranger? Even if Edward, or rather his cunning Elizabeth, had suborned this waiting-woman, our daughter never could hearken, even in an hour of anger, to the message from our dishonorer and our foe."

"Nay, but a flatterer often fosters, by praising, the erring thought. Isabel, hath something, dear lord, of thy high heart and courage, and ever from childhood, her vaulting spirit, her very character of stately beauty, have given her a conviction of destiny and power loftier than those reserved for our gentle Anne. Let us trust to time and forbearance, and hope that the affection of the generous sister will subdue the jealousy of the disappointed princess."

"Pray Heaven, indeed, that it so prove! Isabel's ascendancy over Clarence is great, and might be dangerous. Would that she consented to remain in France with thee and Anne! Her lord, at least, it seems I have convinced and satisfied. Pleased at the vast fortunes before him, the toys of vice-regal power, his lighter nature reconciles itself to the loss of a crown, which, I fear, it could never have upheld. For the more I have read his qualities in our household intimacy, the more it seems that I could scarcely have justified the imposing on England a king not worthy of so great a people. He is young yet, but how different the youth of Lancastrian Edward? In *him* what earnest and manly spirit! What heaven-born views of the duties of a king! Oh, if there be a sin in the passion that hath urged me on, let me, and me alone, atone—and may I be at least the instrument to give to England a prince whose virtues shall compensate for all!"

While yet the last word trembled upon the earl's lips, a light flashed along the floors, hitherto illumined but by the stars and the full moon. And presently Isabel, in conference with the lady whom her mother had referred to, passed into the room, on her way to her private chamber. The countenance of this female diplomatist, whose talent for intrigue Philip de Comines * has commemorated, but whose name, happily for her memory, History has concealed, was soft and winning in its expression to the ordinary glance, though the sharpness of the features, the thin compression of the lips, and the harsh dry redness of the hair, corresponded with the attributes which modern physiognomical science truly or erringly assigns to a wily and treacherous character. She bore a light in her hand, and its rays shone full on the disturbed and agitated face of the duchess. Isabel perceived at once the forms of her parents, and stopped short, in some whispered conversation, and uttered a cry almost of dismay.

"Thou leavest the revel betimes, fair daughter,' said the earl examining her countenance, with an eye somewhat stern.

"My lady," said the confidant, with a lowly reverence, "was anxious for her babe."

"Thy lady, good waiting wench," said Warwick, "needs not thy tongue to address her father. Pass on."

The gentlewoman bit her lips, but obeyed, and quitted the room. The earl approached and took Isabel's hand—it was cold as stone.

"My child," said he, tenderly, "thou dost well to retire to rest—of late thy cheek hath lost its bloom. But just now, for many causes, I was wishing thee not to brave our perilous return to England; and now, I know not whether it would make me the more uneasy, to fear for thy health if absent or thy safety if with me!"

"My lord," replied Isabel, coldly, "my duty calls me to my husband's side, and the more, since now it seems he dares the battle, but reaps not its rewards! Let Edward and Anne rest here in safety—Clarence and Isabel go to achieve the diadem and orb for others!"

"Be not bitter with thy father, girl—be not envious of thy sister!" said the earl, in grave rebuke; then, softening his tone, he added, "the women of a noble house should have no ambition of their own—their glory and their honor, they should leave, unmurmuring, in the hands of men! Mourn not if thy sister mounts the throne of him who would have branded the very name to which thou and she were born!"

"I have made no reproach, my lord. Forgive me, I pray you, if I now retire; I am sore weary, and would fain have strength and health not to be a burden to you when you depart."

The duchess bowed with proud submission, and moved on.

"Beware!" said the earl, in a low voice.

"Beware!—and of what?" said Isabel, startled.

"Of thine own heart, Isabel. Ay, go to thine infant's couch, ere thou seek thine own, and, before the sleep of Innocence, calm thyself back to womanhood."

The duchess raised her head quickly, but habitual awe of her father checked the angry answer; and kissing, with formal reverence, the hand the countess extended to her, she left the room. She gained the chamber in which was the cradle of her son, gorgeously

* COMINES, iii. 5; HALL, LINGARD, HUME, etc.

canopied with silks, inwrought with the blazoned arms of royal Clarence;—and beside the cradles sat the confidant.

The duchess drew aside the drapery, and contemplated the rosy face of the infant slumberer.

Then turning to her confidant, she said—

"Three months since, and I hoped my first-born would be a king! Away with those vain mockeries of royal birth! How suit they the destined vassal of the abhorred Lancastrian?"

"Sweet lady," said the confidant, "did I not warn thee, from the first, that this alliance, to the injury of my lord duke and this dear boy, was already imminent? I had hoped thou mightst have prevailed with the earl!"

"He heeds me not—he cares not for me!" exclaimed Isabel; "his whole love is for Anne—Anne who, without energy and pride, I scarcely have looked on as my equal! And now to my younger sister, I must bow my knee—pleased if she deign to bid me hold the skirt of her queenly robe! Never—no never!"

"Calm thyself; the courier must part this night. My Lord of Clarence is already in his chamber; he waits but thine assent to write to Edward, that he rejects not his loving messages."

The duchess walked to and fro, in great disorder.

"But to be thus secret and false to my father?"

"Doth he merit that thou shouldst sacrifice thy child to him? Reflect!—the king has no son! The English barons acknowledge not in girls a sovereign;* and, with Edward on the throne, thy son is heir-presumptive. Little chance that a male heir shall now be born to Queen Elizabeth, while from Anne and her bridegroom, a long line may spring. Besides, no matter what parchment-treaties may ordain, how can Clarence and his offspring ever be regarded by a Lancastrian king but as enemies to feed the prison or the block, when some false invention gives the seemly pretext for extirpating the lawful race."

"Cease—cease—cease!" cried Isabel, in terrible struggles with herself.

"Lady, the hour presses! And, reflect, a few lines are but words, to be confirmed or retracted as occasion suits! If Lord Warwick succeed, and King Edward lose his crown, ye can shape as ye best may your conduct to the time. But, if the earl lose the day—if again he be driven into exile—a few words now release you and yours from everlasting banishment; restore your boy to his natural heritage; deliver you from the insolence of the Anjouite, who, methinks, even dared this very day to taunt your highness——"

"She did—she did! Oh that my father had been by to hear! She bade me stand aside (that Anne might pass)—'not for the younger daughter of Lord Warwick, but for the lady admitted into the royalty of Lancaster!' Elizabeth Woodville, at least, never dared this insolence!"

"And this Margaret, the Duke of Clarence is to place on the throne which your child yonder might otherwise aspire to mount!"

Isabel clasped her hands in mute passion.

"Hark!" said the confidant, throwing open the door,—

And along the corridor came, in measured pomp, a stately procession, the chamberlain in front, announcing—"Her highness the Princess of Wales;" and Louis XI. leading the virgin bride (wife but in name and honor, till her dowry of a kingdom was made secure) to her gentle rest. The ceremonial pomp, the regal homage that attended the younger sister thus raised above herself, completed in Isabel's jealous heart the triumph of the Tempter. Her face settled into hard resolve, and she passed at once from the chamber into one near at hand, where the Duke of Clarence sate alone, the rich wines of the livery, not untasted, before him, and the ink yet wet upon a scroll he had just indited.

He turned his irresolute countenance to Isabel as she bent over him and read the letter. It was to Edward, and after briefly warning him of the meditated invasion, significantly added—"and if I may seem to share this emprise, which, *here and alone*, I cannot resist, thou shalt find me still, when the moment comes, thy affectionate brother and loyal subject."

"Well, Isabel," said the duke, "thou knowest I have delayed this, till the last hour, to please thee, for verily, lady mine, thy will is

---

* Miss Strickland (*Life of Elizabeth of York*) remarks, "How much Norman prejudice in favor of Salic law had corrupted the common, or constitutional law of England, regarding the succession." The remark involves a controversy.

my sweetest law. But now, if thy heart misgives thee——"

"It does—it does!" exclaimed the duchess, bursting into tears.

"If thy heart misgives thee," continued Clarence, who with all his weakness had much of the duplicity of his brothers, "why let it pass. Slavery to scornful Margaret—vassalage to thy sister's spouse—triumph to the House which both thou and I were taught from childhood to deem accursed,—why welcome all! so that Isabel does not weep, and our boy reproach us not in the days to come!"

For all answer, Isabel, who had seized the letter, let it drop on the table, pushed it, with averted face towards the duke, and turned back to the cradle of her child, whom she woke with her sobs, and who wailed its shrill reply in infant petulance and terror,—snatched from its slumber to the arms of the remorseful mother.

A smile of half-contemptuous joy passed over the thin lips of the she-Judas, and without speaking, she took her way to Clarence. He had sealed and bound his letter, first adding these words—"My lady and duchess, whatever her kin, has seen this letter, and approves it, for she is more a friend to York than to the earl, now he has turned Lancastrian;" and placed in a small iron coffer.

He gave the coffer, curiously clasped and locked, to the gentlewoman, with a significant glance—"Be quick or she repents! The courier waits?—his steed saddled? The instant you give it, he departs—he hath his permit to pass the gates?"

"All is prepared; ere the clock strike, he is on his way."

The confidant vanished—the duke sank in his chair, and rubbed his hands.

"Oho! father-in-law, thou deemest me too dull for a crown. I am not dull enough for thy tool. I have had the wit at least to deceive thee,—and to hide resentment beneath a smiling brow! Dullard *thou*, to believe aught less than the sovereignty of England could have bribed Clarence to thy cause!"—He turned to the table and complacently drained his goblet.

Suddenly, haggard and pale as a spectre, Isabel stood before him.

"I was mad—mad, George! The letter! the letter—it must not go!"

At that moment the clock struck. "*Bel enfant*," said the Duke, "it is too late!"

BOOK TENTH.

THE RETURN OF THE KING-MAKER.

CHAPTER I.

The Maid's hope, the Courtier's love, and the Sage's Comfort.

FAIR are thy fields, O England; fair the rural farm and the orchards in which the blossoms have ripened into laughing fruits; and fairer than all, O England, the faces of thy soft-eyed daughters.

From the field where Sibyll and her father had wandered amidst the dead, the dismal witnesses of war had vanished; and over the green pastures roved the gentle flocks. And the farm to which Hastings had led the wanderers looked upon that peaceful field through its leafy screen; and there father and daughter had found a home.

It was a lovely summer evening, and Sibyll put aside the broidery frame, at which, for the last hour, she had *not* worked; and gliding to the lattice, looked wistfully along the winding lane. The room was in the upper story, and was decorated with a care which the exterior of the house little promised, and which almost approached to elegance. The fresh green rushes that strewed the floor were intermingled with dried wild thyme and other fragrant herbs. The bare walls were hung with serge of a bright and cheerful blue; a rich *carpet de cuir* covered the oak table, on which lay musical instruments, curiously inlaid, with a few MSS., chiefly of English and Povençal poetry. The tabourets were covered with cushions of Norwich worsted, in gay colors. All was simple, it is true, yet all betokened a comfort—nay, a refinement, an evidence of wealth, very rare in the houses even of the second order of nobility.

As Sibyll gazed, her face suddenly brightened; she uttered a joyous cry—húrried from the room—descended the stairs, and passed her father, who was seated without the porch, and seemingly plunged in one of his most abstracted reveries. She kissed his brow—(he heeded her not)—bounded with light step over the sward of the orchard, and pausing by a wicket gate, listened, with throbbing heart, to the advancing sound of a horse's hoofs; nearer came the sound, and nearer. A cavalier appeared in sight, sprang from his saddle, and, leaving his palfrey to find his way to the well-known stable, sprang lightly over the little gate.

"And thou hast watched for me, Sibyll?"

The girl blushingly withdrew from the eager embrace, and said, touchingly—"My heart watchet for thee alway. Oh, shall I thank or chide thee for so much care! Thou wilt see how thy craftsmen have changed the rugged homestead into the daintiest bower!"

"Alas, my Sibyll! would that it were worthier of thy beauty, and our mutual troth! Blessings on thy trust and sweet patience; may the day soon come when I may lead thee to a nobler home; and hear knight and baron envy the bride of Hastings."

"My own lord!" said Sibyll, with grateful tears in confiding eyes; but, after a pause, she added, timidly—"Does the king still bear so stern a memory against so humble a subject?"

"The king is more worth than before, since

tidings of Lord Warwick's restless machinations in France have soured his temper. He cannot hear thy name without threats against thy father as a secret adherent of Lancaster, and accuseth thee of witching his chamberlain, —as, in truth, thou hast. The Duchess of Bedford is more than ever under the influence of friar Bungey, to whose spells and charms, and not to our good swords, she ascribes the marvellous flight of Warwick and the dispersion of our foes; and the friar, methinks, has fostered, and yet feeds Edward's suspicions of thy harmless father. The king chides himself for having suffered poor Warner to depart unscathed, and even recalls the disastrous adventure of the mechanical, and swears that, from the first, thy father was in treasonable conspiracy with Margaret. Nay, sure I am, that if I dared to wed thee while his anger lasts, he would condemn thee as a sorceress, and give me up to the secret hate of my old foes, the Woodvilles. But fie! be not so appalled, my Sibyll; Edward's passions, though fierce, are changeful, and patience will reward us both."

"Meanwhile, thou lovest me, Hastings!" said Sibyll, with great emotion. "Oh, if thou knewest how I torment myself in thine absence!—I see thee surrounded by the fairest and the loftiest, and say to myself, 'Is it possible that he can remember me?' But thou lovest me still—still—still, and ever! Dost thou not?"

And Hastings said and swore.

"And the Lady Bonville?" asked Sibyll, trying to smile archly, but with the faltering tone of jealous fear.

"I have not seen her for months," replied the noble, with a slight change of countenance. "She is at one of their western manors. They say her lord is sorely ill; and the Lady Bonville is a devout hypocrite, and plays the tender wife. But enough of such ancient and worn-out memories. Thy father—sorrows he still for his Eureka? I can learn no trace of it."

"See," said Sibyll, recalled to her filial love, and pointing to Warner as they now drew near the house, "See, he shapes another Eureka from his thoughts!"

"How fares it, dear Warner?" asked the noble, taking the scholar's hand.

"Ah!" cried the student, roused at the sight of his powerful protector. "Bringest thou tidings of IT? Thy cheerful eye tells me that—no—no—thy face changes! They have destroyed it! Oh that I could be young once more!"

"What!" said the world-wise man, astonished. "If thou hadst another youth, wouldst thou cherish the same delusion, and go again through a life of hardship, persecution, and wrong?"

"My noble son," said the philosopher, "for hours when I have felt the wrong, the persecution, and the hardship, count the days and the nights when I have felt only the hope, and the glory, and the joy! God is kinder to us all than man can know; for man looks only to the sorrow on the surface, and sees not the consolation in the deeps of the unwitnessed soul."

Sibyll had left Hastings by her father's side, and tripped lightly to the farther part of the house, inhabited by the rustic owners who supplied the homely service, to order the evening banquet—the happy banquet; for hunger gives not such flavor to the viand, nor thirst such sparkle to the wine, as the presence of a beloved guest.

And as the courtier seated himself on the rude settle, under the honey-suckles that wreathed the porch, a delicious calm stole over his sated mind. The pure soul of the student, released awhile from the tyranny of all earthly pursuit—the drudgery of a toil that, however grand, still but ministered to human and material science—had found for its only other element the contemplation of more solemn and eternal mysteries. Soaring naturally, as a bird freed from a golden cage, into the realms of heaven, he began now, with earnest and spiritual eloquence, to talk of the things and visions lately made familiar to his thoughts. Mounting from philosophy to religion, he indulged in his large ideas upon life and nature: of the stars that now came forth in heaven; of the laws that gave harmony to the universe; of the evidence of a God in the mechanism of creation; of the spark from central divinity, that, kindling in a man's soul, we call "genius;" of the eternal resurrection of the dead, which makes the very principle of being, and types, in the leaf and in the atom, the immortality of the great human race. He was sublimer, that grey old man, hunted from the circle of his kind—in his words, than ever is action in its deeds; for words can fathom truth, and deeds but blunderingly and lamely seek it.

And the sad, and gifted, and erring intellect of Hastings, rapt from its little ambition of the hour, had no answer when his heart asked, "What can courts and a king's smile give me in exchange for serene tranquillity and devoted love ?"

CHAPTER II.

The man awakes in the Sage, and the She Wolf again hath tracked the Lamb.

FROM the night in which Hastings had saved from the knives of the tymbesteres Sibyll and her father, his honor and chivalry had made him their protector. The people of the farm (a widow and her children, with the peasants in their employ) were kindly and simple folks. What safer home for the wanderers than that to which Hastings had removed them ? The influence of Sibyll over his variable heart or fancy was renewed. Again, vows were interchanged, and faith plighted. Anthony Woodville, Lord Rivers, who, however, gallant an enemy, was still more than ever, since Warwick's exile, a formidable one, and who shared his sister's dislike to Hastings, was naturally, at that time, in the fullest favor of King Edward, anxious to atone for the brief disgrace his brother-in-law had suffered during the later days of Warwick's administration. And Hastings, offended by the manners of the rival favorite, took one of the disgusts so frequent in the life of a courtier, and despite his office of chamberlain, absented himself much from his sovereign's company. Thus, in the reaction of his mind, the influence of Sibyll was greater than it otherwise might have been. His visits to the farm grew regular and frequent. The widow believed him nearly related to Sibyll, and suspected Warner to be some attainted Lancastrian, compelled to hide in secret till his pardon was obtained; and no scandal was attached to the noble's visits, nor any surprise evinced at his attentive care for all that could lend a grace to a temporary refuge unfitting the quality of his supposed kindred.

And, in her entire confidence and reverential affection, Sibyll's very pride was rather soothed than wounded, by obligations which were but proofs of love, and to which plighted troth gave her a sweet right. As for Warner,—he had hitherto seemed to regard the great lord's attentions only as a tribute to his own science, and a testimony of the interest which a statesman might naturally feel in the invention of a thing that might benefit the realm. And Hastings had been delicate in the pretexts of his visits. One time he called to relate the death of poor Madge, though he kindly concealed the manner of it, which he had discovered, but which opinion, if not law, forbade him to attempt to punish:—Drowning was but the orthodox ordeal of a suspected witch, and it was not without many scruples that the poor woman was interred in holy ground. The search for the Eureka was a pretence that sufficed for countless visits; and then, too, Hastings had counselled Adam to sell the ruined house, and undertaken the negotiation; and the new comforts of their present residence, and the expense of the maintenance, were laid to the account of the sale. Hastings had begun to consider Adam Warner as utterly blind and passive to the things that passed under his eyes; and his astonishment was great when, the morning after the visit we have just recorded, Adam suddenly lifting his eyes, and seeing the guest whispering soft tales in Sibyll's ear, rose abruptly, approached the nobleman, took him gently by the arm, led him into the garden, and thus addressed him:—

"Noble lord, you have been tender and generous in our misfortunes. The poor Eureka is lost to me and the world for ever. God's will be done ! Methinks Heaven designs thereby to rouse me to the sense of nearer duties; and I have a daughter whose name I adjure you not to sully, and whose heart I pray you not to break. Come hither no more, my Lord Hastings."

This speech, almost the only one which showed plain sense and judgment in the affairs of this life that the man of genius had ever uttered, so confounded Hastings, that he with difficulty recovered himself enough to say—

"My poor scholar, what hath so suddenly kindled suspicions which wrong thy child and me ?"

"Last eve, when ye sate together, I saw

your hand steal into hers, and suddenly I remembered the day when *I* was young and wooed her mother! And last night I slept not, and sense and memory became active for my living child, as they were wont to be only for the iron infant of my mind, and I said to myself—'Lord Hastings is King Edward's friend, and King Edward spares not maiden honor. Lord Hastings is a mighty peer, and he will not wed the dowerless and worse than nameless girl!' Be merciful! Depart—depart!"

"But," exclaimed Hastings, "if I love thy sweet Sibyll in all honesty—if I have plighted to her my troth——

"Alas!—alas!" groaned Adam.

"If I wait but my king's permission to demand her wedded hand, couldst thou forbid me the presence of my affianced?"

"She loves thee, then?" said Adam, in a tone of great anguish—"she loves thee—speak!"

"It is my pride to think it."

"Then go—go at once; come back no more till thou hast wound up thy courage to brave the sacrifice; no, not till the priest is ready at the altar—not till the bridegroom can claim the bride. And as that time will never come—never—never,—leave me to whisper to the breaking heart—'Courage;—honor and virtue are left thee yet, and thy mother from heaven looks down on a stainless child!'"

The resuscitation of the dead could scarcely have startled and awed the courtier more than this abrupt development of life and passion and energy, in a man who had hitherto seemed to sleep in the folds of his thought, as a chrysalis in its web. But as we have always seen that ever, when this strange being woke from his ideal abstraction, he awoke to honor and courage and truth,—so now, whether, as he had said, the absence of the Eureka left his mind to the sense of practical duties, or whether their common suffering had more endeared to him gentle companion, and affection sharpened reason, Adam Warner became puissant and majestic in his rights and sanctity of father; greater in his homely household character, than when, in his mania of inventor and the sublime hunger of aspiring genius, he had stolen to his daughter's couch, and waked her with the cry of "Gold!"

Before the force and power of Adam's adjuration,—his outstretched hand—the anguish, yet authority, written on his face—all the art and self-possession of the accomplished lover deserted him, as one spellbound.

He was literally without reply; till, suddenly, the sight of Sibyll, who, surprised by this singular conference, but unsuspecting its nature, now came from the house, relieved and nerved him; and his first impulse was then, as ever, worthy and noble, such as showed, though dimly, how glorious a creature he had been, if cast in a time and amidst a race, which could have *fostered the impulse into habit.*

"Brave old man." he said, kissing the hand still raised in command—"thou hast spoken as beseems thee; and my answer I will tell thy child." Then hurrying to the wondering Sibyll, he resumed. "Your father says well, that not thus, dubious and in secret, should I visit the home blest by thy beloved presence—I obey;—I leave thee, Sibyll. I go to my king, as one who hath served him long and truly, and claims his guerdon—*thee!*"

"Oh, my lord!" exclaimed Sibyll, in generous terror; "bethink thee well—remember what thou saidst but last eve. This king so fierce—my name so hated! No—no! leave me. Farewell for ever, if it be right, as what thou and my father say must be. But thy life—thy liberty—thy welfare—*they* are my happiness—thou hast no right to endanger *them!*" And she fell at his knees. He raised, and strained her to his heart; then resigning her to her father's arms, he said in a voice choked with emotion—

"Not as peer and as knight, but as man, I claim my prerogative of home and hearth! Let Edward frown—call back his gifts—banish me his court—thou art more worth than all! Look for me—sigh not—weep not—*smile* till we meet again!" He left them with these words—hastened to the stall where his steed stood, caparisoned it with his own hands, and rode with the speed of one whom passion spurs and goads, towards the Tower of London.

But as Sibyll started from her father's arms, when she heard the departing hoofs of her lover's steed,—to listen and to listen for the last sound that told of *him*, a terrible apparition, ever ominous of woe and horror, met her eye. On the other side of the orchard fence, which concealed her figure, but not her well-known face which peered above, stood the tymbestere, Graul. A shriek of terror at this recognition burst from Sibyll, as she threw herself again upon Adam's breast; but, when he looked round, to discover the cause of her alarm—Graul was gone.

CHAPTER III.

Virtuous resolves submitted to the test of Vanity and the World.

On reaching his own house, Hastings learned that the court was still at Shene. He waited but till the retinue which his rank required were equipped and ready, and reached the court, from which of late he had found so many excuses to absent himself, before night. Edward was then at the banquet and Hastings was too experienced a courtier to disturb him at such a time. In a mood unfit for companionship, he took his way to the apartments usually reserved for him, when a gentleman met him by the way, and apprized him with great respect, that the Lord Scales and Rivers had already appropriated those apartments to the principal waiting-lady of his countess,—but that other chambers, if less commodious and spacious, were at his command.

Hastings had not the supurb and more than regal pride of Warwick and Montagu, but this notice sensibly piqued and galled him.

"My apartments as Lord Chamberlain—as one of the captain-generals in the king's army, given to the waiting-lady of Sir Anthony Woodville's wife!—At whose order, sir?"

"Her highness the queen's—pardon me, my lord," and the gentleman, looking round and sinking his voice, continued—"pardon me, her highness added, 'If my Lord Chamberlain returns not ere the week ends, he may find, not only the apartment, but the office, no longer free.' My lord, we all love you—forgive my zeal, and look well if you would guard your own."

"Thanks, sir.—Is my lord of Gloucester in the palace?"

"He is—and in his chamber. He sits not long at the feast."

"Oblige me, by craving his grace's permission to wait on him at leisure—I attend his answer here."

Leaning against the wall of the corridor, Hastings gave himself up to other thoughts than those of love!—So strong is habit—so powerful vanity or ambition, once indulged, that this puny slight made a sudden revulsion in the mind of the royal favorite;—once more the agitated and brilliant court life stirred and fevered him;—that life, so wearisome when secure, became sweet when imperiled. To counteract his foes—to humble his rivals—to regain the king's countenance—to baffle, with the easy art of his skilful intellect, every hostile stratagem—such were the ideas that crossed and hurtled themselves, and Sibyll was forgotten.

The gentleman reappeared. "Prince Richard besought my lord's presence with loving welcome;" and to the Duke's apartment went Lord Hastings. Richard, clad in a loose chamber robe, which concealed the defects of his shape, rose from before a table covered with papers, and embraced Hastings with cordial affection.

"Never more gladly hail to thee, dear William. I need thy wise counsels with the king, and I have glad tidings for thine own ear."

"*Pardieu*, my prince, the king, methinks, will scarce heed the counsels of a dead man."

"Dead?"

"Ay. At court it seems men are dead—their rooms filled—their places promised or bestowed, if they come not, morn and night, to convince the king that they are alive." And Hastings, with constrained gaiety, repeated the information he had received.

"What would you, Hastings?" said the duke, shrugging his shoulders, but with some latent meaning in his tone. "Lord Rivers were nought in himself; but his lady is a mighty heiress,* and requires state, as she bestows pomp. Look round, and tell me what man ever maintained himself in power without the strong connections, the convenient dower, the acute, unseen, unsleeping woman-influence of some noble wife? How can a poor man defend his repute, his popular name, that airy but all-puissant thing we call *dignity* or *station*, against the pricks and stings of female intrigue and female gossip? But he marries, and lo, a

* Elizabeth secured to her brother, Sir Anthony, the greatest heiress in the kingdom—in the daughter of Lord Scales—a wife, by the way, who is said to have been a mere child at the time of the marriage.

host of fairy champions, who pinch the rival lozels unawares: his wife hath her army of courtpie and jupon, to array against the dames of his foes! Wherefore, my friend, while thou art unwedded, think not to cope with Lord Rivers, who hath a wife, with three sisters, two aunts and a score of she-cousins!"

"And if," replied Hastings, more and more unquiet under the duke's truthful irony,—"if I were now come to ask the king permission to wed——"

"If thou wert—and the bride elect were a lady, with power and wealth and manifold connections, and the practice of a court, thou wouldst be the mightiest lord in the kingdom since Warwick's exile."

"And if she had but youth, beauty and virtue?"

"Oh, then, my Lord Hastings, pray thy patron saint for a war—for in peace thou wouldst be lost amongst the crowd. But truce to these jests; for thou art not the man to prate of youth, virtue, and such like, in sober, earnest, amidst this work-day world, where nothing is young and nothing virtuous;—and listen to grave matters."

The duke then communicated, to Hastings the last tidings received of the machinations of Warwick. He was in high spirits; for those last tidings but reported Margaret's refusal to entertain the proposition of a nuptial alliance with the earl, though, on the other hand, the Duke of Burgundy, who was in constant correspondence with his spies, wrote word that Warwick was collecting provisions, from his own means, for more than 60,000 men; and that, with Lancaster or without, the earl was prepared to match his own family interest against the armies of Edward.

"And," said Hastings, "if all his family joined with him, what foreign king could be so formidable an invader? Maltravers and the Mowbrays, Fauconberg, Westmoreland, Fitzhugh, Stanley, Bonville, Worcester——"

"But happily," said Gloucester, "the Mowbrays have been allied also to the queen's sister; Worcester detests Warwick; Stanley always murmurs against us, a sure sign that he will fight for us; and Bonville—I have in view a trusty Yorkist to whom the retainers of *that* house shall be assigned. But of that anon. What I now wish from thy wisdom is, to aid me in rousing Edward from his lethargy: he laughs at his danger, and neither communicates with his captains nor mans his coasts. His courage makes him a dullard."

After some farther talk on these heads, and more detailed account of the preparations which Gloucester deemed necessary to urge on the king, the duke, then, moving his chair nearer to Hastings, said, with a smile,

"And now, Hastings, to thyself: it seems, that thou hast not heard the news which reached us four days since—the Lord Bonville is dead—died three months * ago at his manor house in Devon. Thy Katherine is free, and in London. Well, man, where is thy joy?"

"Time *is*—time *was!*" said Hastings, gloomily. "The day has passed when this news could rejoice me."

"Passed! nay, thy good stars themselves have fought for thee in delay. Seven goodly manors swell the fair widow's jointure; the noble dowry she brought returns to her. Her very daughter will bring thee power. Young Cecily Bonville, the heiress,† Lord Dorset demands in betrothal. The wife will be mother-in-law to thy queen's son; on the other hand, she is already aunt to the Duchess of Clarence; and George, be sure, sooner or later, will desert Warwick, and win his pardon. Powerful connections—vast possessions—a lady of immaculate name and surpassing beauty, and thy first love!—(thy hand trembles!)—thy first love—thy sole love, and thy last!"

"Prince—Prince! forbear! Even if so—in brief, Katherine loves me not!"

"Thou mistakest! I have seen her, and she loves thee not the less because her virtue so long concealed the love."

Hastings uttered an exclamation of passionate joy, but again his face darkened.

Gloucester watched him in silence; besides any motives suggested by the affection he then sincerely bore to Hastings, policy might well interest the duke in the securing to so loyal a Yorkist, the hand and the wealth of Lord

* To those who have read the Paston Letters, it will not seem strange that in that day the death of a nobleman at his country seat should be so long in reaching the metropolis—the ordinary purveyors of communication were the itinerant attendants of fairs. And a father might be ignorant for months together of the death of his son.

† Afterwards married to Dorset.

Warwick's sister; but, prudently not pressing the subject farther, he said, in an altered and careless voice, " Pardon me if I have presumed on matters on which each man judges for himself. But as, despite all obstacle, one day or other Anne Nevile *shall* be mine, it would have delighted me to know a near connection in Lord Hastings. And now, the hour grows late. I prithee let Edward find thee in his chamber."

When Hastings attended the king, he at once perceived that Edward's manner was changed to him. At first, he attributed the cause to the ill-offices of the queen and her brother; but the king soon betrayed the true source of his altered humor.

" My lord," he said, abruptly, " I am no saint, as thou knowest; but there are some ties, *par amour*, which, in my mind, become not knights and nobles about a king's person."

" My liege, I aread you not!"

"Tush, William!" replied the king, more gently, " thou hast more than once wearied me with application for the pardon of the nigromancer, Warner—the whole court is scandalized at thy love for his daughter. Thou hast absented thyself from thine office on poor pretexts! I know thee too well not to be aware that love alone can make thee neglect thy king—thy time has been spent at the knees or in the arms of this young sorceress! One word for all times—he whom a witch snares cannot be a king's true servant! I ask of thee, as a right, or as a grace—see this fair *ribaude* no more! What, man, are there not ladies enough in merry England, that thou shouldst undo thyself for so unchristian a fere?"

" My king! how can this poor maid have angered thee thus?"

" Knowest thou not"—began the king, sharply, and changing color as he eyed his favorite's mournful astonishment,—

" Ah, well!" he muttered to himself, " they have been discreet hitherto, but how long will they be so? I am in time yet. It is enough," —he added, aloud and gravely—" it is enough that our learned * Bungey holds her father as a most pestilent wizard, whose spells are muttered for Lancaster and the rebel Warwick; that the girl hath her father's unholy gifts, and I lay my command on thee, as liege king, and I pray thee, as loving friend, to see no more either child or sire! Let this suffice—and now I will hear thee on state matters."

Whatever Hastings might feel, he saw that it was no time to venture remonstrance with the king, and strove to collect his thoughts, and speak indifferently on the high interests to which Edward invited him; but he was so distracted and absent that he made but a sorry counsellor, and the king, taking pity on him, dismissed his chamberlain for the night.

Sleep came not to the couch of Hastings; his acuteness perceived that whatever Edward's superstition, and he was a devout believer in witchcraft, some more worldly motive actuated him in his resentment to poor Sibyll. But, as we need scarcely say, that neither from the abstracted Warner, nor his innocent daughter, had Hastings learned the true cause, he wearied himself with vain conjectures, and knew not that Edward involuntarily did homage to the superior chivalry of his gallant favorite, when he dreaded that, above all men, Hastings should be made aware of the guilty secret which the philosopher and his child could tell. If Hastings gave his name and rank to Sibyll, how powerful a weight would the tale of a witness now so obscure suddenly acquire!

Turning from the image of Sibyll, thus beset with thoughts of danger, embarrassment, humiliation, disgrace, ruin, Lord Hastings recalled the words of Gloucester: and the stately image of Katherine, surrounded with every memory of early passion—every attribute of present ambition—rose before him, and he slept at last, to dream not of Sibyll and the humble orchard, but of Katherine in her maiden bloom—of the trysting tree, by the Halls of Middleham—of the broken ring—of the rapture and the woe of his youth's first high-placed love.

CHAPTER IV.

The strife which Sibyll had courted, between Katherine and herself, commences in serious earnest.

HASTINGS felt relieved when, the next day, several couriers arrived with tidings so important as to merge all considerations into those of

* It will be remembered that Edward himself was a man of no learning.

state. A secret messenger from the French court threw Gloucester into one of those convuisive passions of rage, to which, with all his intellect and dissimulation, he was sometimes subject—by the news of Anne's betrothal to Prince Edward; nor did the letter from Clarence to the king, attesting the success of one of his schemes, comfort Richard for the failure of the other. A letter from Burgundy confirmed the report of the spy, announced Duke Charles's intention of sending a fleet to prevent Warwick's invasion, and rated King Edward sharply for his suppineness in not preparing suitably against so formidable a foe. The gay and reckless presumption of Edward, worthier of a knight-errant than a monarch, laughed at the word *Invasion.* "Pest on Burgundy's ships! I only wish that the earl would land!" * he said to his council. None echoed the wish! But later in the day came a third messenger with information that roused all Edward's ire; careless of each danger in the distance, he ever sprang into energy and vengeance when a foe was already in the field. And the Lord Fitzhugh (the young nobleman before seen among the rebels at Olney, and who had now succeeded to the honors of his house) had suddenlv risen in the north, at the head of a formidable rebellion. No man had so large an experience in the warfare of those districts, the temper of the people, and the inclinations of the various towns and lordships as Montagu; he was the natural chief to depute against the rebels. Some animated discussion took place as to the dependence to be placed in the marquis at such a crisis; but while the more wary held it safer, at all hazards, not to leave him unemployed, and to command his services in an expedition that would remove him from the neighborh od of his brother, should the latter land, as was expected, on the coast of Norfolk, Edward, with a blindness of conceit that seems almost incredible, believed firmly in the infatuated loyalty of the man whom he had slighted and impoverished, and whom, by his offer of his daughter to the Lancastrian Prince, he had yet more recently cozened and deluded.

Montagu was hastily summoned, and received orders to march at once to the north, levy forces and assume their command. The marquis obeyed with fewer words than were natural to him—left the presence, sprang on his horse, and as he rode from the palace, drew a letter from his bosom. "Ah, Edward!" said he, setting his teeth; "so, after the solemn betrothal of thy daughter to my son, thou wouldst have given her to thy Lancastrian enemy. Coward, to bribe his peace! —recreant, to belie thy word! I thank thee for this news, Warwick; for without that injury I feel I could never, when the hour came, have drawn sword against this faithless man,—especially for Lancaster. Ay, tremble, thou who deridest all truth and honor! He who himself betrays, cannot call vengeance, treason!"

Meanwhile, Edward departed, for farther preparations, to the Tower of London. New evidences of the mine beneath his feet here awaited the incredulous king. On the door of St. Paul's, of many of the metropolitan churches on the standard at Chepe, and on London Bridge, during the past night, had been affixed, none knew by whom, the celebrated proclamation, signed by Warwick and Clarence, (drawn up in the bold style of the earl) announcing their speedy return, containing a brief and vigorous description of the misrule of the realm, and their determination to reform all evils and redress all wrongs.* Though the proclamation named not the restoration of the Lancastrian line, (doubtless from regard for Henry's safety,) all men in the metropolis were already aware of the formidable league between Margaret and Warwick. Yet, even still, Edward smiled in contempt, for he had faith in the letter received from Clarence, and felt assured that the moment the duke and the earl landed, the former would betray his companion stealthily to the king; so, despite all these exciting subjects of grave alarm, the nightly banquet at the Tower was never merrier and more joyous. Hastings left the feast ere it deepened into revel, and, absorbed in various and profound contemplation, entered his apartment. He threw himself on a seat, and leant his face on his hands.

"Oh, no—no!" he muttered; "now, in the hour when true greatness is most seen—when prince and peer crowd around me for counsel —when noble, knight, and squire, crave permission to march in the troop of which Hastings is the leader—*now* I feel how impossible,

* Com. iii. c. 5.

* See for this proclamation, ELLIS's *Original Letters* vol. i., second series, letter 49.

how falsely fair, the dream that I could forget all—all for a life of obscurity—for a young girl's love! Love as if I had not felt its delusions to palling!—love, as if I could love again; or, if love—alas, it must be a light reflected but from memory! And Katherine is free once more!" His eye fell, as he spoke—perhaps in shame and remorse that, feeling thus now, he had felt so differently when he bade Sibyll smile till his return!

"It is the air of this accursed court which taints our best resolves!" he murmured, as an apology for himself; but scarcely was the poor excuse made, than the murmur broke into an exclamation of surprise and joy. A letter lay before him—he recognized the hand of Katherine. What years had passed since her writing had met his eye—since the lines that bade him 'farewell, and forget!' *Those* lines had been blotted with tears, and *these*, as he tore open the silk that bound them—*these*, the trace of tears, too, was on them! Yet they were but few, and in tremulous characters. They ran thus:—

"To-morrow, before noon, the Lord Hastings is prayed to visit one whose life he hath saddened by the thought and the accusation that she hath clouded and embittered his.

"KATHERINE DE BONVILLE."

Leaving Hastings to such meditations of fear or of hope, as these lines could call forth, we lead the reader to a room, not very distant from his own,—the room of the illustrious Friar Bungey.

The ex-tregetour was standing before the captured Eureka, and gazing on it with an air of serio-comic despair and rage. We say the Eureka, as comprising all the ingenious contrivances towards one single object invented by its maker, an harmonious compound of many separate details;—but the iron creature no longer deserved that superb appellation, for its various members were now disjointed and dislocated, and lay pêle mêle in multiform confusion.

By the side of the friar stood a female enveloped in a long scarlet mantle, with the hood partially drawn over the face, but still leaving visible the hard, thin, villanous lips, the stern, sharp chin, and the jaw resolute and solid as if hewed from stone.

"I tell thee, Graul," said the friar, "that thou hast had far the best of the bargain. I have put this diabolical contrivance to all manner of shapes, and have muttered over it enough Latin to have charmed a monster into civility. And the accursed thing, after nearly pinching off three fingers, and scalding me with seething water, and spluttering and sputtering enough to have terrified any man but Friar Bungey out of his skin, is *obstinatus ut mulum*—dogged as a mule: and was absolutely good for nought, till I happily thought of separating this vessel from all the rest of the gear,—and it serves now for the boiling my eggs! But by the soul of Father Merlin, whom the saints assoil, I need not have given myself all this torment, for a thing which, at best, does the work of a farthing pipkin!"

"Quick, master—the hour is late! I must go while yet the troopers, and couriers, and riders, hurrying to and fro, keep the gates from closing. What wantest thou with Graul?"

"More reverence, child!" growled the friar. "What I want of thee is briefly told; if thou hast the wit to serve me. This miserable Warner must himself expound to me the uses and trick of his malignant contrivance. Thou must find bring and him hither!"

"And if he will not expound?"

"The deputy-governor of the Tower will lend me a stone dungeon, and, if need be, the use of the brake, to unlock the dotard's tongue."

"On what plea?"

"That Adam Warner is a wizard, in the pay of Lord Warwick, whom a more mighty master like myself alone can duly examine and defeat."

"And if I bring thee the sorcerer—what wilt thou teach me in return?"

"What desirest thou most?"

Graul mused, and said—"There is war in the wind. Graul follows the camp—her trooper gets gold and booty. But the trooper is stronger than Graul; and when the trooper sleeps, it is with his knife by his side, and his sleep is light and broken, for he has wicked dreams. Give me a potion to make sleep deep, that his eyes may not open when Graul filches his gold, and his hand may be too heavy to draw the knife from its sheath!"

"Immunda—detestabilis!—thine own paramour!"

"He hath beat me with his bridal rein, he hath given a silver broad piece to Grisell—

Grisell hath sate on his knee—Graul never pardons!"

The Friar, rogue as he was, shuddered—"I cannot help thee to murder, I cannot give thee the potion; name some other reward."

"I go——"

"Nay, nay—think—pause."

"I know where Warner is hid. By this hour to-morrow night, I can place him in thy power. Say the word, and pledge me the draught."

"Well, well, *mulier abominabilis:*—that is, irresistible bonnibel,—I cannot give thee the potion; but I will teach thee an art which can make sleep heavier than the anodyne, and which wastes not like the essence, but strengthens by usage; an art thou shalt have at thy fingers' ends, and which often draws from the sleeper the darkest secrets of his heart!" *

"It is magic," said Graul, with joy.

"Ay, magic."

"I will bring thee the wizard.—But listen; he never stirs abroad, save with his daughter I must bring both."

"Nay—I want not the girl."

"But I dare not throttle her, for a great lord loves her—who would find out the deed and avenge it; and, if she be left behind, she will go to the lord, and the lord will discover what thou hast done with the Wizard, and thou wilt hang!"

"Never say, 'Hang,' to me, Graul—it is ill-mannered and ominous. Who is the lord?"

"Hastings."

"Pest!—and already he hath been searching for the thing yonder; and I have brooded over it night and day, like a hen over a chalk egg—only that the egg does not snap off the hen's claws, as that diabolism would fain snap off my digits. But the war will carry Hastings away in its whirlwind; and, in danger, the duchess is my slave, and will bear me through all. So, thou mayst bring the girl; and strangle her not; for no good ever comes of a murder,—unless indeed, it be absolutely necessary!"

"I know the men who will help me, bold *ribauds*, whom I will guerdon myself; for I want not thy coins, but thy craft. When the curfew has tolled, and the bat hunts the moth, we will bring thee the quarry——"

Graul turned—but as she gained the door—she stopped, and said abruptly, throwing back her hood—

"What age dost thou deem me?"

"Marry," quoth the Friar—"an' I had not seen thee on thy mother's knee, when she followed my stage of Tregetour—I should have guessed thee for thirty, but thou hast led too jolly a life to look still in the blossom—why speer'st thou the question?"

"Because when trooper and *ribaud* say to me—'Graul, thou art too worn and too old, to drink of our cup, and sit in the lap, to follow the young fere to the battle, and weave the blithe dance in the fair,'—I would depart from my sisters, and have a hut of my own—and a black cat without a white hair, and steal herbs by the new moon, and bones from the charnel—and curse those whom I hate—and cleave the misty air on a besom, like Mother Halkin of Edmonton. Ha—ha! Master, thou shalt present me then to the *Sabbat*. Graul has the mettle for a bonny witch!"

The Tymbestere vanished with a laugh. The friar muttered a pater-noster, for once, perchance, devoutly; and after having again deliberately scanned the *disjecta membra* of the Eureka, gravely took forth a duck's egg from his cupboard, and applied the master-agent of the machine which Warner hoped was to change the face of the globe to the only practical utility it possessed to the mountebank's comprehension!

CHAPTER V.

The meeting of Hastings and Katherine.

The next morning, while Edward was engaged in levying from his opulent citizens all the loans he could extract, knowing that gold is the sinew of war—while Worcester was manning the fortress of the Tower, in which the queen, then near her confinement, was to reside during the campaign—while Gloucester was writing commissions to captains and barons to raise men—while Sir Anthony Lord Rivers was ordering improvements in his dainty damasquine armor—and the whole Fortress Pala-

* We have before said that animal magnetism was known to Bungey, and familiar to the necromancers or rather theurgists of the middle ages.

tine was animated and alive with the stir of the coming strife—Lord Hastings escaped from the bustle, and repaired to the house of Katherine. With what motive, with what intentions, was not known clearly to himself;—perhaps, for there was bitterness in his very love for Katherine, to enjoy the retaliation due to his own wounded pride, and say to the idol of his youth, as he had said to Gloucester—"Time *is*—time *was;*"—perhaps with some remembrance of the faith due to Sibyll, wakened up the more now that Katherine seemed actually to escape from the ideal image into the real woman—to be easily wooed and won. But certainly, Sibyll's cause was not wholly lost, though greatly shaken and endangered, when Lord Hastings alighted at Lady Bonville's gate; but his face gradually grew paler, his mien less assured, as he drew near and nearer to the apartment and the presence of the widowed Katherine.

She was seated alone, and in the same room in which he had last seen her. Her deep mourning only served, by contrasting the pale and exquisite clearness of her complexion, to enhance her beauty. Hastings bowed low, and seated himself by her side in silence.

The Lady of Bonville eyed him for some moments with an unutterable expression of melancholy and tenderness. All her pride seemed to have gone; the very character of her face was changed: grave severity had become soft timidity, and stately self-control was broken into the unmistaken struggle of hope and fear.

"Hastings—*William!*" she said, in a gentle and low whisper, and at the sound of that last name from those lips, the noble felt his veins thrill and his heaat throb. "If," she continued, "the step I have taken seems to thee unwomanly and too bold, know, at least, what was my design and my excuse. There was a time" (and Katherine blushed) "when, thou knowest well, that, had this hand been mine to bestow, it would have been his who claimed the half of this ring." And Katherine took from a small crystal casket the well remembered token.

"The broken ring foretold but the broken troth," said Hastings, averting his face.

"Thy conscience rebukes thy words," replied Katherine, sadly; "I pledged my faith, if thou couldst win my father's word. What maid, and that maid a Nevile, could so forget duty and honor, as to pledge thee more? We were severed. Pass—oh, pass over that time! My father loved me dearly; but when did pride and ambition ever deign to take heed of the wild fancies of a girl's heart? Three suitors, wealthy lords,—whose alliance gave strength to my kindred, in the day when their very lives depended on their swords,—were rivals for Earl Salisbury's daughter. Earl Salisbury bade his daughter choose. Thy great friend, and my own kinsman, Duke Richard of York, himself pleaded for thy rivals. He proved to me that my disobedience,—if indeed, for the first time, a child of my house could disobey its chief—would be an eternal barrier to *thy* fortune; that while Salisbury was thy foe, he himself could not advance thy valiancy and merit; that it was with me to forward thy ambition, though I could not reward thy love; that from the hour I was another's, my mighty kinsman themselves—for they were generous—would be the first to aid the duke in thy career. Hastings, even then I would have prayed, at least, to be the bride, not of man, but God. But I was trained—as what noble demoiselle is not?—to submit wholly to a parent's welfare and his will. As a nun, I could but pray for the success of my father's cause; as a wife, I should bring to Salisbury and to York the retainers and the strongholds of a baron! I obeyed. Hear me on.—Of the three suitors for my hand, two were young and gallant—women deemed them fair and comely; and had my choice been one of these, thou mightest have deemed that a new love had chased the old. Since choice was mine, I chose the man *love* could not choose, and took this sad comfort to my heart—'*He*, the forsaken Hastings, will see, in my very choice, that I was but the slave of duty—my choice itself my penance.'"

Katherine paused, and tears dropped fast from her eyes. Hasting held his hand over his countenance, and only by the heaving of his heart wa his emotion visible. Katherine resumed:—

"Once wedded, I knew what became a wife. We met again; and to thy first disdain and anger—(which it had been dishonor in me to soothe by one word that said, 'The wife remembers the maiden's love')—to these, thy first emotions, succeeded the more cruel revenge, which would have changed sorrow and struggle to remorse and shame. And then, then—weak woman that I was—I wrapped myself in scorn and pride. Nay, I felt deep anger—was it unjust?—that thou couldst so misread, and so repay, the heart which had nothing left, save virtue, to compensate for love. And yet, yet, often when thou didst deem me most hard, most proof against memory and feeling—but why relate the trial? Heaven supported me, and if thou lovest me no longer, thou canst not despise me."

At these last words Hastings was at her feet, bending over her hand, and stifled by his emotions. Katherine gazed at him for a moment through her own tears, and then resumed:—

"But thou hadst, as *man*, consolations no woman would desire or covet. And oh, what grieved me most was, not—no, not the jealous, the wounded vanity, but it was at least this self-accusation, this remorse, that—but for one goading remembrance, of love returned and love forsaken,—thou hadst never so descended from thy younger nature, never so trifled with the solemn trust of TIME. Ah, when I have heard, or seen, or fancied one fault in thy maturer manhood, unworthy of thy bright youth, anger of myself has made me bitter and stern to thee; and if I taunted, or chid, or vexed thy pride, how little didst thou know that through the too shrewish humor spoke the too soft remembrance! For this—for this; and believing that through all, alas! my image was not replaced—when my hand was free, I was grateful that I might still—" (the lady's pale cheek grew brighter than the rose, her voice faltered, and became low and indistinct)—"I might still think it mine to atone to thee for the past. And if," she added, with a sudden and generous energy, "if in this I have bowed my pride, it is because by pride thou wert wounded; and now, at last, thou hast a just revenge."

O terrible rival for thee, lost Sibyll! Was it wonderful that, while that head drooped upon his breast, while in that enchanted change which love the softener makes in lips long scornful, eyes long proud and cold, he felt that Katherine Nevile—tender, gentle, frank without boldness, lofty without arrogance—had replaced the austere dame of Bonville, whom he half hated while he woed,—oh, was it wonderful that the soul of Hastings fled back to the old time, forgot the intervening vows, and more chill affections, and repeated only with passionate lips—"Katherine, loved still, loved ever—mine, mine at last!"

Then followed delicious silence—then vows, confessions, questions, answers—the thrilling interchange of hearts long divided, and now rushing into one. And time rolled on, till Katherine, gently breaking from her lover, said—

"And now, that thou hast the right to know and guide my projects, approve, I pray thee, my present purpose. War awaits thee, and we must part awhile!" At these words her brow darkened, and her lip quivered, "Oh, that I should have lived to mourn the day when Lord Warwick, untrue to Salisbury and to York, joined his arms with Lancaster and Margaret—the day when Katherine could blush for the brother she had deemed the glory of her house! No, no," (she continued, as Hastings interrupted her with generous excuses for the earl, and allusion to the known slights he had received),—"No, no; make not his cause the worse, by telling me that an unworthy pride, the grudge of some thwart to his policy or power, has made him forget what was due to the memory of his kinsman York, to the mangled corpse of his father Salisbury. Thinkest thou, that but for this, I could——" She stopped, but Hastings divined her thought, and guessed that, if spoken, it had run thus:—"That I could, even now, have received the homage of one who departs to meet, with banner and clarion, my brother as his foe?" The lovely sweetness of the late expression had gone from Katherine's face, and its aspect showed that her high and ancestral spirit had yielded but to one passion. She pursued—

"While this strife lasts, it becomes my widowhood, and kindred position with the earl, to retire to the convent my mother founded. To-morrow I depart."

"Alas!" said Hastings, thou speakest of the strife as if but a single field. But Warwick returns not to these shores, nor bows himself to league with Lancaster,—for a chance hazardous and desperate, as Edwards too rashly deems it. It is in vain to deny that the earl is prepared for a grave and lengthened war, and much I doubt whether Edward can resist his power; for the idolatory of the very land will swell the ranks of so dread a rebel. What if he succeed—what if we be driven into exile, as Henry's friends before us—what if the king-maker be the king-dethroner?—then, Katherine, then, once more thou wilt be at the hest of thy hostile kindred, and once more, dowered as thou art, and thy womanhood still in its richest bloom, thy hand will be lost to Hastings."

"Nay, if that be all thy fear, take with thee this pledge—that Warwick's treason to the house for which my father fell, dissolves his power over one driven to disown him as a brother,—knowing Earl Sallsbury, had he foreseen such disgrace, had disowned him as son. And if there be defeat, and flight, and exile,—wherever thou wanderest, Hastings, shall Katherine be found beside thee—Fare thee well, and our Lady shield thee; may thy lance be victorious against all foes—save one. Thou wilt forbear my——that is, *the earl!*" And Katherine, softened at that thought, sobbed aloud.

"And come triumph or defeat, I have thy pledge?" said Hastings, soothing her.

"See," said Katherine, taking the broken ring from the casket; "now, for the first time since I bore the name of Bonville, I lay this relic on my heart—art thou answered?"

CHAPTER VI.

Hastings learns what has befallen Sibyll—Repairs to the King, and encounters an old rival.

"It is destiny," said Hastings to himself, when early the next morning he was on his road to the farm.—"It is destiny—and who can resist his fate!"

"It is destiny!"—phrase of the weak human heart! "It is destiny!"—dark apology for every error! The strong and the virtuous admit *no* destiny! On earth, guides Conscience—in heaven, watches God. And Destiny is but the phantom we invoke to silence the one—to dethrone the other!

Hastings spared not his good steed. With great difficulty had he snatched a brief respite from imperious business, to accomplish the last poor duty now left to him to fulfil—to confront the maid whose heart he had seduced in vain, and say, at length, honestly and firmly—"I cannot wed thee. Forget me, and farewell."

Doubtless, his learned and ingenious mind conjured up softer words than these, and more purfled periods wherein to dress the iron truth. But in these two sentences the truth lay. He arrived at the farm—he entered the house—he felt it as a reprieve, that he met not the bounding step of the welcoming Sibyll. He sate down in the humble chamber, and waited awhile in patience—no voice was heard. The silence at length surprised and alarmed him. He proceeded farther. He was met by the widowed owner of the house, who was weeping; and her first greeting prepared him for what had chanced. "Oh, my lord, you have come to tell me they are safe—they have not fallen into the hands of their enemies—the good gentleman, so meek—the poor lady, so fair!"

Hastings stood aghast—a few sentences more explained all that he already guessed. A strange man had arrived the evening before at the house, praying Adam and his daughter to accompany him to the Lord Hastings, who had been thrown from his horse, and was now in a cottage in the neighboring lane—not hurt dangerously, but unable to be removed—and who had urgent matters to communicate. Not questioning the truth of this story, Adam and Sibyll had hurried forth, and returned no more. Alarmed by their long absence, the widow, who had first received the message from the stranger, went herself to the cottage, and found that the strory was a fable. Every search had since been made for Adam and his daughter, but in vain. The widow, confirmed in her previous belief that her lodgers had been attainted Lancastrians, could but suppose that they had been thus betrayed to their enemies. Hastings heard this with a dismay and remorse impossible to express. His only conjecture was, that the king had discovered their retreat, and taken this measure to break off the intercourse he had so sternly denounced. Full of these ideas, he hastily remounted, and stopped not till once more at the gates of the Tower. Hastening to Edward's closet, the moment he saw the king, he exclaimed, in great emotion—"My liege—my liege, do not, at this hour, when I have need of my whole energy to serve thee, do not madden my brain, and palsy my arm. This old man—the poor maid—Sibyll—Warner—speak, my liege—only tell me they are safe—promise me they shall go free, and I swear to obey thee in all else! I will thank thee in the battle-field!"

"Thou art mad, Hastings!" said the king, in great astonishment.—"Hush!" and he glanced significantly at a person who stood before several heaps of gold, ranged upon a table in the recess of the room.—"See," he whispered, "yonder is the goldsmith, who hath brought me a loan from himself and his fellows!—Pretty tales for the city thy folly will send abroad!"

But before Hastings could vent his impatient answer, this person, to Edward's still greater surprise, had advanced from his place, and forgetting all ceremony, had seized Hastings by the hem of his surcoat, exclaiming—

"My lord, lord—what new horror is this? Sibyll!—methought she was worthless, and had fled to thee!"

"Ten thousand devils!" shouted the king—"Am I ever to be tormented by that damnable wizard and his witch child? And is it, Sir Peer and Sir Goldsmith, in your king's closet that ye come, the very eve before he marches to battle, to speer and glower at each other like two madmen as ye are?"

Neither peer nor goldsmith gave way, till the courtier, naturally recovering himself the first, fell on his knee, and said, with firm, though profound respect—"Sire, if poor William Hastings has ever merited from the king one kindly thought, one generous word, forgive now whatever may displease thee in his passion or his suit, and tell him what prison contains those whom it would for ever dishonor his knighthood to know punished and endangered but for his offence."

"My lord!" answered the king, softened, but still surprised, "think you seriously that I, who but reluctantly, in this lovely month, leave my green lawns of Shene, to save a crown, could have been vexing my brain by stratagems to seize a lass—whom I swear by St. George I do not not envy thee in the least? If that does not suffice, incredulous dullard, why then take my kingly word, never before passed for so slight an occasion, that I know nothing whatsoever of thy damsel's whereabout—nor her pestilent father's—where they abode of late—where they now be—and, what is more, if any man has usurped his king's right to imprison the king's subjects, find him out, and name his punishment. Art thou convinced?"

"I am, my liege," said Hastings.

"But——" began the goldsmith.

"Holloa, you too, sir! This is too much! We have condescended to answer the man who arms three thousand retainers—"

"And I, please your highness, bring you the gold to pay them," said the trader, bluntly.

The king bit his lip, and then burst into his usual merry laugh.

"Thou art in the right, Master Alwyn. Finish counting the pieces, and then go and consult with my chamberlain—he must off with the cock-crow—but since ye seem to understand each other, he shall make thee his lieutenant of search, and I will sign any order he pleases for the recovery of the lost wisdom and the stolen beauty. Go and calm thyself, Hastings."

"I will attend you presently," my lord, said Alwyn, aside, "in your own apartment."

"Do so," said Hastings; and grateful for the king's consideration, he sought his rooms. There indeed, Alwyn soon joined him, and learned from the nobleman what filled him at once with joy and terror. Knowing that Warner and Sibyll had left the tower he had surmised that the girl's virtue had at last succumbed, and it delighted him to hear from Lord Hastings, whose word to men was never questionable, the solemn assurance of her unstained chastity. But he trembled at this mysterious disappearance, and knew not to whom to impute the snare, till the penetration of Hastings suddenly alighted near, at least to the clue. "The Duchess of Bedford," said he, "ever increasing in superstition as danger increases, may have desired to re-find so great a scholar, and reputed an astrologer and magician—if so, all is safe. On the other hand, her favorite, the friar, ever bore a jealou grudge to poor Adam, and may have soug to abstract him from her grace's search—here, there may be molestation to Adam, but surely no danger to Sibyll. Harkye, Alwyn—thou lovest the maid more worthily, and——" Hastings stopped short—for such is infirm human nature, that, though he had mentally resigned Sibyll for ever, he could not yet calmly face the thought of resigning her to a rival. "Thou lovest her," he renewed, more coldly, "and to thee, therefore, I may safely trust the search, which time, and circumstance, and a soldier's duty forbid to me. And believe—oh, believe, that I say not this from a passion which may move thy jealousy, but rather with a brother's holy love. If thou canst but see her safe, and lodged where no danger nor wrong can find her, thou hast no friend in the wide world whose service through life thou mayst command like mine."

"My lord," said Alwyn, drily, "I want no friends! Young as I am, I have lived long enough to see that friends follow fortune, but never make it! I will find this poor maid and her honored father, if I spend my last groat on the search. Get me but such an order from the king as may place the law at my control, and awe even her Grace of Bedford—and I promise the rest!"

Hastings, much relieved, deigned to press the goldsmith's reluctant hand; and, leaving him alone for a few minutes, returned with a warrant from the king, which seemed, to Alwyn, sufficiently precise and authoritative. The goldsmith then departed, and first he sought the friar, but found him not at home. Bungey had taken with him, as was his wont, the keys of his mysterious apartment. Alwyn then hastened elsewhere, to secure those experienced in such a search, and to head it in person. At the Tower, the evening was passed in bustle and excitement—the last preparations for departure. The queen, who was then far advanced towards her confinement, was, as we before said, to remain at the Tower, which was now strongly manned. Roused from her wonted apathy by the imminent dangers that awaited Edward, the night was passed by her in tears and prayers—by him, in the sound sleep of confidant valor. The next morning departed for the north the several leaders—Gloucester, Rivers, Hastings, and the king.

CHAPTER VII.

The landing of Lord Warwick, and the events that ensue thereon.

AND Charles the Bold, Duke of Burgundy, "prepared such a greate navie as lightly hath not been seene before, gathered in manner of all nations, which armie laie at the mouth of the Seyne ready to fight with the Earle of Warwick, when he should set out of his harborowe." *

But the wind fought for the Avenger. In the night came "a terrible tempest," which scattered the duke's ships "one from another, so that two of them were not in compagnie together in one place;" and when the tempest had done its work, it passed away, and the gales were fair, and the heaven was clear. When, the next day, the earl "halsed up the sales," and came in sight of Dartmouth.

It was not with an army of foreign hirelings that Lord Warwick set forth on his mighty enterprise. Scanty indeed were the troops he brought from France—for he had learned from England that "men, so much daily and hourely desired and wished so sore his arrival and return, that almost all men were in harness looking for his landyng."† As his ships neared the coast, and the banner of the Ragged Staff, worked in gold, shone in the sun, the shores swarmed with armed crowds, not to resist but to welcome. From cliff to cliff, wide and far, blazed rejoicing bonfires; and from cliff to cliff, wide and far, burst the shout, when, first of all his men, bareheaded, but, save the burgonot, in complete mail, the popular hero leapt to shore.

---

* HALL, p. 282. *Ed.* 1809.

† The popular feeling in favor of the earl is described by Hall, with somewhat more eloquence and vigor than are common with that homely chronicler—"The absence of the Earle of Warwick made the common people daily more and more to long, and be desirious to have the sight of him, and presently to behold his personage. For they judged that the sunne was clerely taken from the world when hee was absent. In such high estimation, amongst the people, was his name, that neither no one manne, they had in so much honor, neither no one persone they so much praised, or, to the clouds, so highly extolled. What shall I say? His only name sounded in every song, in the mouth of the common people, and his persone (effigies) was represented with great reverence when publique plaies or open triumphes should bee shewed or set furthe abrode in the stretes," etc. This lively passage, if not too highly colored, serves to show us the rude saturnalian kind of liberty that existed, even under a kiug so vindictive as Edward IV. Though an individual might be hanged for the jest that he would make his son heir to the crown, (viz., the grocer's shop, which bore that sign,) yet no tyranny could deal with the sentiment of the masses. In our own day, it would be less safe than in that, to make public exhibition "in plaies and triumphes," of sympathy with a man, attainted as a traitor, and in open rebellion to the crown!

"When the earle had taken land, he made a proclamation, in the name of King Henry VI., upon high paynes, commanding and charging all men apt or able to bear armor, to prepare themselves to fight against Edward, Duke of York, who had untruly usurped the croune and dignity of this realm." *

And where was Edward?—afar, following the forces of Fitzhugh and Robin of Redesdale, who, by artful retreat, drew him farther and farther northward, and left all the other quarters of the kingdom free, to send their thousands to the banners of Lancaster and Warwick. And even as the news of the earl's landing reached the king, it spread also through all the towns of the north—and all the towns in the north were in "a great rore, and made fires, and sang songs, crying—'King Henry—King Henry! a Warwicke—a Warwicke!'" But his warlike and presumptuous spirit forsook not the chief of that bloody and fatal race—the line of the English Pelops—"bespattered with kindred gore." † A messenger from Burgundy was in his tent when the news reached him." "Back, to the duke!" cried Edward; "tell me to re-collect his navy, guard the sea, scour the streams, that the earl shall not escape, nor return to France—for the doings in England, let me alone! I have ability and puissance to overcome all enemies and rebels in mine own realm." ‡

And therewith he raised his camp, abandoned the pursuit of Fitzhugh, summoned Montagu to join him, (it being now safer to hold the marquis near him, and near the axe, if his loyalty became suspected,) and marched on to meet the earl. Nor did the earl tarry from the encounter. His army, swelling as he passed—and as men read his proclamations to reform all grievances and right all wrongs—he pressed on to meet the king, while fast and fast upon Edward's rear came the troops of Fitzhugh and Hilyard; no longer flying but pursuing. The king was the more anxious to come up to Warwick, inasmuch as he relied greatly upon the treachery of Clarence, either secretly to betray or openly to desert the earl. And he knew that if he did the latter on the eve of a battle, it could not fail morally to weaken Warwick, and dishearten his army by fear that desertion should prove, as it ever does, the most contagious disease that can afflict a camp. It is probable, however, that the enthusiasm which had surrounded the earl with volunteers so numerous, had far exceeded the anticipations of the inexperienced Clarence, and would have forbid him that opportunity of betraying the earl. However this be, the rival armies drew near and nearer. The king halted in his rapid march at a small village, and took up his quarters in a fortified house, to which there was no access but by a single bridge.* Edward himself retired for a short time to his couch, for he had need of all his strength in the battle he foresaw. But scarce had he closed his eyes, when Alexander Carlile,† the serjeant of the royal minstrels, followed by Hastings and Rivers, (their jealousy laid at rest for a time in the sense of their king's danger,) rushed into his room.

"Arm, sire, arm!—Lord Montagu has thrown off the mask, and rides through thy troops, shouting, 'Long live king Henry!'"

"Ah, traitor!" cried the king, leaping from his bed. "From Warwick, hate was my due—but not from Montagu! Rivers, help buckle on my mail. Hastings, post my body-guard at the bridge. We will sell our lives dear."

Hastings vanished. Edward had scarcely hurried on his helm, cuirass, and greaves, when Gloucester entered, calm in the midst of peril.

"Your enemies are marching to seize you, brother. Hark! behind you rings the cry, 'A Fitzhugh—a Robin—death to the tyrant!' Hark! in front, 'A Montagu—a Warwick—Long live King Henry!' I come to redeem my word—to share your exile or your death. Choose either while there is yet time. Thy choice is mine!"

And while he spoke, behind, before, came the various cries near and nearer. The lion of March was in the toils.

"Now, my two-handed sword!" said Edward. "Gloucester, in this weapon learn my choice!"

But now all the principal barons and captains, still true to the king, whose crown was already lost, flocked in a body to the chamber. They fell on their knees, and with tears implored him to save himself for a happier day.

* Hall, p. 82. † Æsch. Agam. ‡ Hall, p. 283.

* Sharon Turner. Comines.
† Hearne's Fragment.

"There is yet time to escape," said D'Eyncourt—"to pass the bridge—to gain the seaport! Think not that a soldier's death will be left thee. Numbers will suffice to encumber thine arm—to seize thy person. Live not to be Warwick's prisoner—shown as a wild beast in its cage to the hooting crowd!"

"If not on thyself," exclaimed Rivers, "have pity on these loyal gentlemen, and for the sake of their lives preserve thine own. What is flight? *Warwick fled!*"

"True—*and returned!*" added Gloucester. "You are right, my lords. Come, sire, we must fly. Our rights fly not with us, but shall fight for us in absence!"

The calm WILL of this strange and terrible boy had its effect upon Edward. He suffered his brother to lead him from the chamber, grinding his teeth in impotent rage. He mounted his horse, while Rivers held the stirrup, and, with some six or seven knights and earls, rode to the bridge already occupied by Hastings and a small but determined guard.

"Come, Hastings," said the king, with a ghastly smile—"they tell us we must fly!"

"True, sire, haste—haste! I stay but to to deceive the enemy by feigning to defend the pass, and to counsel, as I best may, the faithful soldiers we leave behind."

"Brave Hastings!" said Gloucester, pressing his hand, "you do well, and I envy you the glory of this post. Come, sire."

"Ay—ay," said the king, with a sudden and fierce cry, "we go—but at least slaughtering as we go. See! yon rascal troop!—ride we through the midst! Havoc and revenge!"

He set spurs to his steed, galloped over the bridge, and, before his companions could join him, dashed alone into the very centre of the advanced guard sent to invest the fortress; and while they were yet shouting—"Where is the tyrant—where is Edward?"——

"Here!" answered a voice of thunder—"Here, rebels and faytors, in your ranks!"

This sudden and appalling reply, even more than the sweep of the gigantic sword, before which were riven sallet and mail, as the woodman's axe rives the faggot, created amongst the enemy that singular panic, which in those ages often scattered numbers before the arm and the name of one. They recoiled in confusion and dismay. Many actually threw down their arms and fled. Through a path broad and clear, amidst the forest of pikes, Gloucester and the captains followed the flashing track of the king, over the corpses, headless or limbless, that he felled as he rode.

Meanwhile, with a truer chivalry, Hastings, taking advantage of the sortie which confused and delayed the enemy, summmoned such of the loyal as were left in the fortress, advised them as the only chance of life, to affect submission to Warwick; but when the time came to remember their old allegiance,* and promising that he would not desert them, save with life, till their safety was pledged by the foe, reclosed his visor, and rode back to the front of the bridge.

And now the king and his comrades had cut their way through all barrier, but the enemy still wavered and fagged, till suddenly the cry of "Robin of Redesdale!" was heard, and sword in hand, Hilyard, followed by a troop of horse, dashed to the head of the besiegers, and, learning the king's escape, rode off in pursuit. His brief presence and sharp rebuke reanimated the falterers, and in a few minutes they gained the bridge.

"Halt, sirs," cried Hastings; "I would offer capitulation to your leader! Who is he?"

"A knight on horseback advanced from the rest.

Hastings lowered the point of his sword.

"Sir, we yield this fortress to your hands upon one condition—our men yonder are willing to submit, and shout with you for Henry VI. Pledge me your word that you and your soldiers spare their lives and do them no wrong, and we depart."

"And if I pledge it not?" said the knight.

"Then for every warrior who guards this bridge count ten dead men amongst your ranks."

"Do your worst—our bloods are up! We want life for life!—revenge for the subjects butchered by your tyrant chief! Charge! to the attack—charge! pike and bill!" The knight spurred on, the Lancastrians followed, and the knight reeled from his horse into the moat below, felled by the sword of Hastings.

For several minutes the pass was so gallantly defended that the strife seemed uncertain, though fearfully unequal, when Lord Montagu himself, hearing what had befallen, galloped to the spot, threw down his truncheon,

* SHARON TURNER, vol. iii. 289.

cried "Hold!" and the slaughter ceased. To this nobleman, Hastings repeated the terms he had proposed.

"And," said Montagu, turning with anger to the Lancastrians, who formed a detachment of Fitzhugh's force—"can Englishmen insist upon butchering Englishmen? Rather thank ye Lord Hastings, that he would spare good King Henry so many subjects' lives! The terms are granted, my lord; and your own life also, and those of your friends around you, vainly brave in a wrong cause. Depart!"

"Ah, Montagu," said Hastings, touched, and in a whisper, "what pity that so gallant a gentleman should leave a rebel's blot upon his scutcheon."

"When chiefs and suzerains are false and perjured, Lord Hastings," answered Montagu, "to obey them is not loyalty, but serfdom; and revolt is not disloyalty, but a freeman's duty. One day thou mayst know that truth, but too late!"*

Hastings made no reply—waved his hand to his fellow-defenders of the bridge, and, followed by them, went slowly and deliberately on, till clear of the murmuring and sullen foe; then putting spurs to their steeds, these faithful warriors rode fast to rejoin their king; overtook Hilyard on the way, and after a fierce skirmish, a blow from Hastings unhorsed and unhelmed the stalwart Robin, and left him so stunned as to check further pursuit. They at last reached the king, and gaining with him and his party the town of Lynn, happily found one English and two Dutch vessels on the point of sailing; without other raiment than the mail they wore—without money, the men, a few hours before hailed as sovereign, or as peers, fled from their native land as outcasts and paupers. New dangers beset them on the sea: the ships of the Easterlings, at war both with France and England, bore down upon their vessels. At the risk of drowning, they ran ashore near Alcmaer. The large ships of the Easterlings followed as far as the low water would permit, "intending at the fludde to have obtained their prey." † In this extremity, the lord of the province (Louis of Grauthuse) came aboard their vessels—protected the fugitives from the Easterlings—conducted them to the Hague—and apprised the Duke of Burgundy how his brother-in-law had lost his throne. Then were verified Lord Warwick's predictions of the faith of Burgundy! The duke, for whose alliance Edward had dishonored the man to whom he owed his crown so feared the victorious earl, that "he had rather have heard of King Edward's death than of his discomfiture."* And his first thought was to send an embassy to the kingmaker, praying the amity and alliance of the restored dynasty.

* It was in the midst of his own conspiracy against Richard of Gloucester that the head of Lord Hastings fell.

† HALL

* HALL, p. 279.

CHAPTER VIII.

What befell Adam Warner and Sibyll, when made subject to the great Friar Bungey.

WE must now return to the Tower of London—not, indeed, to its lordly halls and gilded chambers—but to the room of Friar Bungey. We must go back somwhat in time; and on the day following the departure of the king and his lords, conjure up in that strangely furnished apartment the form of the burly friar, standing before the disorganized Eureka, with Adam Warner by his side.

Graul, as we have seen, had kept her word, and Sibyll and her father, having fallen into the snare, were suddenly gagged, bound, led through by-paths to a solitary hut, where a covered wagon was in waiting, and finally, at nightfall, conducted to the Tower. The friar, whom his own repute, jolly affability, and favor with the Duchess of Bedford, made a considerable person with the authorities of the place, had already obtained from the deputy-governor an order to lodge two persons, whom his zeal for the king sought to convict of necromantic practices in favor of the rebellion, in the cells set apart for such unhappy captives. Thither the prisoners were conducted. The friar did not object to their allocation in contiguous cells; and the jailer deemed him mighty kind and charitable, when he ordered that they might be well served and fed till their examination.

He did not venture, however, to summon his captives till the departure of the king, when the Tower was, in fact, at the disposition of his powerful patroness, and when he thought he might stretch his authortiy as far as he pleased, unquestioned and unchid.

Now, therefore, on the day succeeding Edward's departure, Adam Warner was brought from his cell, and led to the chamber where the triumphant friar received him in majestic state. The moment Warner entered, he caught sight of the chaos to which his Eureka was resolved, and uttering a cry of mingled grief and joy, sprang forward to greet his profaned treasure. The friar motioned away the jailer, (whispering him to wait without), and they were left alone. Bungey listened with curious and puzzled attention to poor Adam's broken interjections of lamentation and anger, and at last, clapping him roughly on the back, said—

"Thou knowest the secret of this magical and ugly device; but in thy hands it leads only to ruin and perdition. Tell me that secret, and in *my* hands it shall turn to honor and profit. *Porkey verbey!* I am a man of few words. Do this, and thou shalt go free with thy daughter, and I will protect thee, and give thee monies, and my fatherly blessing;—refuse to do it, and thou shalt go from thy snug cell into a black dungeon full of newts and rats, where thou shalt rot till thy nails are like bird's talon's, and thy skin shrivelled up into mummy, and covered with hair like Tebuchadnezzar!"

"Miserable varlet! Give *thee* my secret—give *thee* my fame—my life. Never! I scorn and spit at thy malice!"

The friar's face grew convulsed with rage—"Wretch!" he roared forth, "darest thou unslip thy houndlike malignity upon great Bungey?—Knowest thou not that he could bid the walls open and close upon thee—that he could set yon serpents to coil round thy limbs, and yon lizard to gnaw out thine entrails? Despise not my mercy, and descend to plain sense. What good didst thou ever reap from thy engine?—why shouldst thou lose liberty—nay, life—if I will, for a thing that has cursed thee with man's horror and hate?"

"Art thou Christian and friar to ask me why? Were not Christians themselves hunted by wild beasts, and burned at the stake, and boiled in the caldron for their belief? Knave, whatever is holiest, men ever persecute! Read thy bible!"

"Read the bible?" exclaimed Bungey, in pious horror at such a proposition—"Ah! blasphemer, now I have thee!—Thou art a heretic and Lollard. Hollo—there!"

The friar stamped his foot—the door opened, but to his astonishment and dismay appeared, not the grim jailer, but the Duchess of Bedford herself, preceded by Nicholas Alwyn.

"I told your grace truly—see lady!" cried the goldsmith—"Vile impostor, where hast thou hidden this wise man's daughter?"

The friar turned his dull, bead-like eyes in vacant consternation, from Nicholas to Adam, from Adam to the duchess.

"Sir friar," said Jacquetta, mildly—for she wished to conciliate the rival seers—"what means this over-zealous violation of law? Is it true, as Master Alwyn affirms, that thou hast stolen away and seducted this venerable sage and his daughter—a maid I deemed worthy of a post in my own household?"

"Daughter and lady," said the friar, sullenly, "this ill faytor, I have reason to know, has been practising spells for Lord Warwick and the enemy. I did but summon him hither that my art might undo his charms; and as for his daughter, it seemed more merciful to let her attend him, than to leave her alone and unfriended, specially," added the friar, with a grin—"since the poor lord she hath witched is gone to the wars."

"It is true then, wretch, that thou or thy caitiffs have dared to lay hands on a maiden of birth and blood!" exclaimed Alywn. "Tremble!—see, here, the warrant signed by the king, offering a reward for thy detection, empowering me to give thee up to the laws. By St. Dunstan! but for thy friar's frock, thou shouldst hang."

"Tut—tut, Master Goldsmith!" said the duchess, haughtily—"lower thy tone. This holy man is under my protection, and his fault was but over-zeal. What were this sage's devices and spells?"

"Marry!" said the friar, gruffly—"that is what your grace just hindreth my knowing. But he cannot deny that he is a pestilent astrologer, and sends word to the rebels what hours are lucky or fatal for battle and assault."

"Ha!" said the duchess, "he is an astrologer! true, and came nearer to the alchemist's truth than any multiplier that ever served me! My own astrologer is just dead—why died he at such a time? Peace—peace! be there peace between two so learned men! Forgive thy brother, Master Warner!"

Adam had hitherto disdained all participation in this dialogue. In fact, he had returned to the Eureka, and was silently examining if any loss of the vital parts, had occurred in its melancholy dismemberment. But now he turned round, and said, "Lady, leave the lore of the stars to their great Maker. I forgive this man, and thank your grace for your justice. I claim these poor fragments, and crave your leave to suffer me to depart with my device and my child."

"No—no!" said the duchess, seizing his hand. "Hist! whatever Lord Warwick paid thee, I will double. No time now for alchemy; but for the horoscope, it is the veriest season. I name thee my special astrologer!"

"Accept—accept!" whispered Alwyn; "for your daughter's sake—for your own—nay, for the Eureka's!"

Adam bowed his head, and groaned forth—"But I go not hence—no, not a foot—unless *this* goes with me. Cruel wretch, how he hath deformed it!"

"And now," cried Alwyn, eagerly, "this wronged and unhappy maiden?"

"Go! be it thine to release and bring her to our presence, good Alwyn," said the duchess; she shall lodge with her father, and receive all honor. Follow me, Master Warner!"

No sooner, however, did the friar perceive that Alwyn had gone in search of the jailer, than he arrested the steps of the duchess, and said, with the air of a much-injured man—

"May it please your grace to remember, that unless the greater magician have all power, and aid in thwarting the lesser, the lesser can prevail; and therefore, if your grace finds, when too late, that Lord Warwick's or Lord Fitzhugh's arms prosper—that woe and disaster befall the king—say not it was the fault of Friar Bungey!—such things may be! Nathless I shall still sweat, and watch, and toil; and if, despite your unhappy favor and encouragement to this hostile sorcerer, the king *should* beat his enemies, why then, Friar Bungey is not so powerless as your grace holds him. I have said—*Porkey verbey!—Vigilabo et conabo—et perspirabo—et hungerabo—pro vos et vestros, Amen!*"

The Duchess was struck by this eloquent appeal; but more and more convinced of the dread science of Adam, by the evident apprehensions of the redoubted Bungey, and firmly persuaded that she could bribe or induce the former to turn a science that would otherwise be hostile into salutary account, she contented herself with a few words of conciliation and compliment, and summoning the attendants who had followed her, bade them take up the various members of the Eureka (for Adam clearly demonstrated that he would not depart without them), and conducted the philosopher to a lofty chamber, fitted up for the defunct astrologer.

Hither, in a short time, Alwyn had the happiness of leading Sibyll, and witnessing the delighted reunion of the child and father. And then after he had learned the brief details of their abduction, he related how, baffled in all attempt to trace their clue, he had convinced himself that either the duchess or Bungey was the author of the snare, returned to the Tower shown the king's warrant, learned that an old man and a young female had indeed been admitted into the fortress, and hurried at once to the duchess, who, surprised at his narration and complaint, and anxious to regain the services of Warner, had accompanied him at once to the friar.

"And though," added the goldsmith, "I could indeed procure you lodgings more welcome to ye elsewhere, yet it is well to win the friendship of the duchess, and royalty is ever an ill foe.—How came ye to quit the palace?"

Sibyll changed countenance, and her father answered gravely—"We incurred the king's displeasure, and the excuse was the popular hatred of me and the Eureka."

"Heaven made the people, and the devil makes three-fourths of what is popular!" bluntly said the man of the Middle Class, ever against both extremes.

"And how?" asked Sibyll—"how, honored and true friend, didst thou obtain the king's warrant, and learn the snare into which we had fallen?"

This time it was Alwyn who changed countenance. He mused a moment, and then frankly answering—"Thou must thank Lord

Hastings," gave the explanation already known to the reader.

But the grateful tears this relation called forth from Sibyll—her clasped hands—her evident emotion of delight and love so pained poor Alwyn, that he rose abruptly, and took his leave.

And now, the Eureka was a luxury as peremptorily forbid to the astrologer, as it had been to the alchemist! Again the true science was despised, and the false cultivated and honored. Condemned to calculations, which no man (however wise) in that age, held altogether delusive, and which yet Adam Warner studied with very qualified belief—it happened by some of those coincidences, which have from time to time appeared to confirm the credulous in judicial astrology, that Adam's predictions became fulfilled. The duchess was prepared for the first tidings—that Edward's foes fled before him. She was next prepared for the very day in which Warwick landed, and then her respect for the astrologer became strangely mingled with suspicion and terror, when she found that he proceeded to foretell but ominous and evil events;—and when, at last, still in corroboration of the unhappily too faithful horoscope, came the news of the king's flight, and the earl's march upon London, she fled to Friar Bungey in dismay. And Friar Bungey said—

"Did I not warn you, daughter? Had you suffered me to——"

"True—true!" interrupted the duchess. "*Now* take, hang, rack, drown, or burn your horrible rival, if you will, but undo the charm, and save us from the earl?"

The friar's eyes twinkled, but to the first thought of spite and vengeance succeeded another;—if he who had made the famous waxen effigies of the Earl of Warwick, were now to be found guilty of some atrocious and positive violence upon Master Adam Warner, might not the earl be glad of so good an excuse to put an end to himself?—

"Daughter," said the friar at that reflection, and shaking his head mysteriously and sadly —"daughter, it is too late."

The duchess, in great despair, flew to the queen. Hitherto she had concealed from her royal daughter the employment she had given to Adam; for Elizabeth, who had, herself, suffered from the popular belief in Jacquetta's sorceries, had of late earnestly besought her to lay aside all practices that could be called into question. Now, however, when she confessed to the agitated and distracted queen the retaining of Adam Warner, and his fatal predictions, Elizabeth, who, from discretion and pride, had carefully hidden from her mother (too vehement to keep a secret) that offence in the king the memory of which had made Warner peculiarly obnoxious to him, exclaimed, "Unhappy mother, thou hast employed the very man my fated husband would the most carefully have banished from the palace—the very man who could blast his name."

The duchess was aghast and thunderstricken.

"If ever I forsake Friar Bungey again!" she muttered—"OH, THE GREAT MAN!"

But events which demand a detailed recital now rapidly pressing on, gave the duchess not even the time to seek further explanation of Elizabeth's words, much less to determine the doubt that rose in her enlightened mind whether Adam's spells might not be yet unravelled by the timely execution of the sorcerer!

CHAPTER IX.

The Deliberations of Mayor and Council, while Lord Warwick marches upon London.

It was a clear and bright day in the first week of October, 1470, when the various scouts employed by the mayor and council of London came back to the Guild, at which that worshipful corporation were assembled — their steeds blown and jaded, themselves panting and breathless—to announce the rapid march of the Earl of Warwick. The lord mayor of that year, Richard Lee, grocer and citizen, sat in the venerable hall in a huge leather chair, over which a pall of velvet had been thrown in haste, clad in his robes of state, and surrounded by his aldermen and the magnates of the city. To the personal love which the greater part of the body bore to the young and courteous king, was added the terror which the corporation justly entertained of the Lancastrian faction.

They remembered the dreadful excesses

which Margaret had permitted to her army in the year 1461—what time, to use the expression of the old historian, "the wealth of London looked pale;" and how grudgingly she had been restrained from condemning her revolted metropolis to the horrors of sack and pillage. And the bearing of this august representation of the trade and power of London was not, at the first, unworthy of the high influence it had obtained. The agitation and disorder of the hour had introduced into the assembly several of the more active and accredited citizens, not of right belonging to it; but they sat, in silent discipline and order, on long benches, beyond the table crowded by the corporate officers. Foremost among these, and remarkable by the firmness and intelligence of his countenance, and the earnest self-possession with which he listened to his seniors, was Nicholas Alwyn, summoned to the council from his great influence with the apprentices and younger freemen of the city.

As the last scout announced his news, and was gravely dismissed,

The lord mayor rose; and, being, perhaps, a better educated man than many of the haughtiest barons, and having more at stake than most of them, his manner and language had a dignity and earnestness which might have reflected honor on the higher court of parliament.

"Brethren and citizens," he said with the decided brevity of one who felt it no time for many words, "in two hours we shall hear the clarions of Lord Warwick at our gates; in two hours we shall be summoned to give entrance to an army assembled in the name of King Henry. I have done my duty—I have manned the walls—I have marshalled what soldiers we can command. I have sent to the deputy-governor of the Tower——"

"And what answer gives he, my lord mayor?" interrupted Humfrey Heyford.

"None to depend upon. He answers that Edward IV., in abdicating the kingdom, has left him no power to resist; and that between force and force, king and king, might makes right."

A deep breath, like a groan, went through the assembly.

Up rose Master John Stokton, the mercer. He rose, trembling from limb to limb.

"Worshipful, my lord mayor," said he, "it seems to me that our first duty is to look to our own selves!"

Despite the gravity of the emergence, a laugh burst forth and was at once silenced, at this frank avowal.

"Yes," continued the mercer, turning round and striking the table with his fist, in the action of a nervous man—"yes—for King Edward has set us the example. A stout and a dauntless champion, whose whole youth has been war, King Edward has fled from the kingdom—King Edward takes care of himself—it is our duty to do the same!"

Strange though it may seem, this homely selfishness went at once through the assembly, like a flash of conviction. There was a burst of applause, and as it ceased, the sullen explosion of a bombard (or cannon) from the city wall, announced that the warder had caught the first glimpse of the approaching army.

Master Stokton started as if the shot had gone near to himself, and dropped at once into his seat, ejaculating, "The Lord have mercy upon us!" There was a pause of a moment, and then several of the corporation rose simultaneously. The mayor, preserving his dignity, fixed on the sheriff.

"Few words, my lord, and I have done," said Richard Gardyner—"there is no fighting without men. The troops at the Tower are not to be counted on. The populace are all with Lord Warwick, even though he brought the devil at his back. If you hold out, look to rape and plunder before sunset to-morrow. If ye yield, go forth in a body, and the earl is not the man to suffer one Englishman to be injured in life or health who once trusts to his good faith. My say is said."

"Worshipful, my lord," said a thin, cadaverous alderman, who rose next—"This is a judgment of the Lord and his saints. The Lollards and heretics have been too much suffered to run at large, and the wrath of Heaven is upon us."

An impatient murmuring attested the unwillingness of the larger part of the audience to listen further; but an approving buzz from the elder citizens announced that the fanaticism was not without its favorers. Thus stimulated and encouraged, the orator continued; and concluded an harangue, interrupted more stormily than all that had preceded, by an exhortation to leave the city to its fate, and to march in a body to the New Prison, draw forth five suspected Lollards, and burn them at Smithfield, in order to appease the Almighty and divert the tempest!

This subject of controversy, once started, might have delayed the audience till the ragged staves of the Warwickers drove them forth from their hall, but for the sagacity and promptitude of the mayor.

"Brethren," he said, "it matters not to me, whether the counsel suggested be good or bad, on the main; but this have I heard,—there is small safety in death-bed repentance. It is too late now, to do through fear of the devil, what we omitted to do through zeal for the church. The sole question is, 'Fight or make terms.' Ye say we lack men—verily, yes, while no leaders are found! Walworth, my predecessor, saved London from Wat Tyler. Men were wanting *then* till the mayor and his fellow citizens marched forth to Mile End. It may be the same now. Agree to fight, and we'll try it—what say you, Nicholas Alwyn?—you know the temper of our young men."

Thus called upon, Alwyn rose, and such was the good name he had already acquired, that every murmur hushed into eager silence.

"My lord mayor," he said, "there is a proverb in my country, which says, 'Fish swim best that's bred in the sea;' which means, I take it, that men do best what they are trained for! Lord Warwick and his men are trained for fighting. Few of the fish about London Bridge are bred in *that* sea! Cry 'London to the rescue!'—put on hauberk and helm, and you will have crowns enough to crack around you. What follows?—Master Stokton hath said it: pillage and rape for the city—gibbet and cord for mayor and aldermen. Do I say this, loving the house of Lancaster? No; as Heaven shall judge me, I think that the policy King Edward hath chosen, and which costs him his crown to-day, ought to make the house of York dear to burgess and trader. He hath sought to break up the iron rule of the great barons—and never peace to England till that be done. He has failed; but for a day. He has yielded for the time; so must we. 'There's a time to squint, and a time to look even.' I advice that we march out to the earl—that we make honorable terms for the city—that we take advantage of one faction to gain what we have not gained with the other—that we fight for our profit, not with swords where we shall be worsted, but in council and parliament, by speech and petition. New power is ever gentle and douce. What matters to us York or Lancaster?—all we want is good laws. Get the best we can from Lancaster—and when King Edward returns, as return he will, let him bid higher than Henry for our love. Worshipful my lords and brethren, while barons and knaves go to loggerheads, honest men get their own. Time grows under us like grass. York and Lancaster may pull down each other—and what is left?—Why, three things that thrive in all weather—London, Industry, and the People! We have fallen on a rough time. Well, what says the proverb? 'Boil stones in butter, and you may sup the broth.' I have done."

This characteristic harangue, which was fortunate enough to accord with the selfishness of each one, and yet give the many excuse of sound sense and policy to all, was the more decisive in its effect, inasmuch as the young Alwyn, from his own determined courage, and his avowed distaste to the Lancaster faction, had been expected to favor warlike counsels. The mayor himself, who was faithfully and personally attached to Edward, with a deep sigh, gave way to the feeling of the assembly. And the resolution being once come to, Henry Lee was the first to give it whatever advantage could be derived from prompt and speedy action.

"Go we forth at once," said he—"go as becomes us, in our robes of state, and with the insignia of the city. Never be it said that the guardians of the city of London could neither defend with spirit, nor make terms with honor. We give entrance to Lord Warwick. Well, then, it must be our own free act. Come! Officers of our court, advance."

"Stay a bit—stay a bit," whispered Stokton, digging sharp claws into Alwyn's arm—"let them go first,—a word with you, cunning Nick—a word."

Master Stokton, despite the tremor of his nerves, was a man of such wealth and substance, that Alwyn might well take the request, thus familiarly made, as a compliment not to be received discourteously; moreover, he had his own reasons for hanging back from a procession which his rank in the city did not require him to join.

While, therefore, the mayor and the other dignitaries left the hall, with as much state and order as if not going to meet an invading army, but to join a holiday festival, Nicholas and Stokton lingered behind.

"Master Alwyn," said Stokton, then, with a sly wink of his eye, "you have this day done yourself great credit; you will rise—I have my eye on you! I have a daughter—I have a daughter! Aha! a lad like you may come to great things!"

"I am much bounden to you, Master Stokton," returned Alwyn, somewhat abstractedly—"but what's your will?"

"My will!—hum, I say, Nicholas what's your advice? Quite right not to go to blows. Odds costards! that mayor is a very tiger! But don't you think it would be wiser not to join this procession? Edward IV., an' he ever come back, has a long memory He deals at my ware, too—a good customer at a mercer's; and, Lord! how much money he owes the city!—hum—I would not seem ungrateful."

"But if you go not out with the rest, there be other mercers who will have King *Henry's* countenance and favor; and it is easy to see that a new court will make vast consumption in mercery."

Master Stokton looked puzzled.

"That were a hugeous pity, good Nicholas; and, certes, there is Wat Smith in Eastgate, who would cheat that good King Henry, poor man! which were a shame to the city; but, on the other hand, the Yorkists mostly pay on the nail, (except King Edward, God save him!) and the Lancastrians are as poor as mice. Moreover, King Henry is a meek man, and does not avenge—King Edward a hot and a stern man, and may call it treason to go with the Red Rose! I wish I knew how to decide! I have a daughter—an only daughter—a buxom lass, and well dowered. I would I had a sharp son-in-law to advise me!"

"Master Stokton, in one word, then—He never goes far wrong who can run with the hare and hunt with the hounds. Good day to you, I have business elsewhere."

So saying, Nicholas, rather hastily, shook off the mercer's quivering fingers, and hastened out of the hall.

"Verily," murmured the disconsolate Stokton, "run with the hare, quotha!—that is, go with King Edward; but hunt with the hounds—that is, go with King Henry. Odds costards! it's not so easily done by a plain man, not bred in the north. I'd best go—home, and do nothing!"

With that, musing and bewildered, the poor man sneaked out, and was soon lost amidst the murmuring, gathering, and swaying crowds, many amongst which were as much perplexed as himself.

In the meanwhile, with his cloak muffled carefully round his face, and with a long, stealthy, gliding stride, Alwyn made his way through the streets, gained the river, entered a boat in waiting for him, and arrived at last at the palace of the Tower.

CHAPTER X.

The triumphal entry of the Earl—The royal captive in the tower—The meeting between King-maker and King.

ALL in the chambers of the metropolitan fortress exhibited the greatest confusion and dismay. The sentinels, it is true, were still at their posts, men-at-arms at the outworks, the bombards were loaded, the flag of Edward IV. still waved aloft from the battlements; but the officers of the fortress and the captains of its soldiery were, some assembled in the old hall, pale with fear, and wrangling with each other—some had fled, none knew whither—some had gone avowedly and openly to join the invading army.

Through this tumultuous and feeble force, Nicholas Alwyn was conducted by a single faithful servitor of the queen's (by whom he was expected); and one glance of his quick eye, as he passed along, convinced him of the justice of his counsels. He arrived at last, by a long and winding stair, at one of the loftiest chambers, in one of the loftiest towers, usually appropriated to the subordinate officers of the household.

And there, standing by the open casement, commanding some extended view of the noisy and crowded scene beyond, both on stream and land, he saw the queen of the fugitive monarch. By her side was the Lady Scrope, her most familiar friend and confidant—her three infant children, Elizabeth, Mary, and Cecily—grouped around her knees, playing with each other, and unconscious of the terrors of the times; and apart from the rest stood the Duchess of bedford, conferring eagerly with Friar Bungey, whom she had summoned in haste, to know if this art could not yet prevail over enemies merely mortal.

The servitor announced Alwyn, and retired; the queen turned—"What news, Master Alwyn? Quick! What tidings from the lord mayor?"

"Gracious my queen and lady," said Alwyn, falling on his knees—"you have but one course to pursue. Below yon casement lies your barge—to the right, see the round grey tower of Westminster Sanctuary; you have time yet, and but time!"

The old Duchess of Bedford turned her sharp, bright, grey eyes from the pale and trembing friar, to the goldsmith, but was silent. The queen stood aghast!—"Mean you," she faltered at last, "that the city of London forsakes the king?—shame on the cravens!"

"Not cravens, my lady and queen," said Alwyn, rising. "He must have iron nails that stratches a bear—and the white bear above all. The king has fled—the barons have fled—the soldiers have fled—the captains have fled—the citizens of London alone fly not; but there is nothing, save life and property, left to guard."

"Is this thy boasted influence with the commons, and youths of the city?"

"My humble influence, may it please your grace, (I say it now openly, and I will say it a year hence, when King Edward will hold his court in these halls once again—my influence, such as it is, has been used to save lives, which resistance would waste in vain. Alack, alack! 'No gaping against an oven,' gracious lady! Your barge is below—Again I say, there is yet time—when the bell tolls the next hour, that time will be past!"

"Then Jesu defend these children!" said Elizabeth, bending over her infants, and weeping bitterly—"I will go!"

"Hold!" said the Duchess of Bedford, "men desert us—but do the spirits also forsake?—Speak, friar! canst thou yet do aught for us?—and if not, thinkest thou it is the right hour to yield and fly?"

"Daughter," said the friar, whose terror might have moved pity—"as I said before, thank yourself. This Warner, this—in short, the lesser magician, hath been aided and cockered to countervail the greater, as I forewarned. Fly! run! fly! Verily and indeed, it is the properest of all times to save ourselves; and the stars and the book, and my familiar, all call out—'off and away!'"

"'Fore heaven!" exclaimed Alwyn, who had hitherto been dumb with astonishment at this singular interlude—"sith he who hath shipped the devil, must make the best of him, thou art for once an honest man, and a wise counsellor. Hark! the second gun! The earl is at the gates of the city!"

The queen lingered no longer—she caught her youngest child in her arms; the Lady Scrope followed with the two others.—"Come, follow quick, Master Alwyn," said the duchess, who, now that she was compelled to abandon the world of prediction and soothsaying, became thoroughly the sagacious, plotting, ready woman of this life—"Come, your face and name will be of service to us, an' we meet with obstruction."

Before Alwyn could reply, the door was thrown open, and several of the officers of the household rushed pêle-mêle into the royal presence.

"Gracious queen!" cried many voices at once, each with a different sentence of fear and warning—"Fly!—We cannot depend on the soldiers—the populace are up—they shout for King Henry—Dr. Godard is preaching against you at St. Paul's Cross—Sir Geoffrey Gates has come out of the sanctuary, and with him all the miscreants and outlaws—the mayor is now with the rebels! Fly!—the sanctuary—the sanctuary!"

"And who amongst you is of highest rank?" asked the duchess, calmly; for Elizabeth, completely overwhelmed, seemed incapable of speech or movement.

"I, Giles de Malvoisin, knight banneret," said an old warrior, armed cap-a-pie, who had fought in France under the hero Talbot.

"Then, sir," said the duchess, with majesty, "to your hands I confide the eldest daughter of your king. Lead on!—we follow you. Elizabeth, lean on me."

With this, supporting Elizabeth, and leading her second grandchild, the duchess left the chamber.

The friar followed amidst the crowd, for well he knew that if the soldiers of Warwick once caught hold of him, he had fared about as happily as the fox amidst the dogs; and Alwyn, forgotten in the general confusion, hastened to Adam's chamber.

The old man, blessing any cause that induced his patroness to dispense with his astrological labors, and restored him to the care of his Eureka, was calmly and quietly employed in repairing the mischief effected by the bungling friar. And Sibyll, who at the first alarm had flown to his retreat, joyfully hailed the entrance of the friendly goldsmith.

Alwyn was, indeed, perplexed what to advise for the principal sanctuary would, no doubt, be crowded by ruffians of the worst character; and the better lodgments which that place, a little town in itself,* contained, be already pre-occupied by the Yorkists of rank; and the smaller sanctuaries were still more liable to the same objection. Moreover, if Adam should be recognized by any of the rabble that would meet them by the way, his fate, by the summary malice of a mob, was certain. After all, the Tower would be free from the populace: and as soon as, by a few rapid questions, Alwyn learned from Sibyll that she had reason to hope her father would find protection with Lord Warwick, and called to mind that Marmaduke Nevile was necessarily in the earl's train, he advised them to remain quiet and concealed in their apartments, and promised to see and provide for them the moment the Tower was yielded up to the new government.

The counsel suited both Sibyll and Warner. Indeed, the philosopher could not very easily have been induced to separate himself again from the beloved Eureka; and Sibyll was more occupied at that hour with thoughts and prayers for the beloved Hastings,—afar—a wanderer and an exile,—than with the turbulent events amidst which her lot was cast.

In the storms of a revolution which convulsed a kingdom and hurried to the dust a throne, Love saw but a single object—Science but its tranquil toil. Beyond the realm of men lies ever with its joy and sorrow. its vicissitude and change, the domain of the human heart. In the revolution, the toy of the scholar was restored to him; in the revolution, the maiden mourned her lover. In the movement of the mass, each unit hath its separate passion. The blast that rocks the tree, shakes a different world in every leaf!

* The Sanctuary of Westminster was fortified.

CHAPTER XI.

The Tower in commotion.

On quitting the Tower, Alwyn regained the boat, and took his way to the city; and here, whatever credit that worthy and excellent personage may lose in certain eyes, his historian is bound to confess that his anxiety for Sibyll did not entirely distract his attention from interest or ambition. To become the head of his class, to rise to the first honors of his beloved city of London, had become to Nicholas Alwyn a hope and aspiration which made as much a part of his being as glory to a warrior, power to a king, an Eureka to a scholar; and, though more mechanically than with any sordid calculation or self-seeking, Nicholas Alwyn repaired to his Ware in the Chepe. The streets, when he landed, already presented a different appearance from the disorder and tumult noticeable when he had before passed them. The citizens had now decided what course to adopt; and though the shops, or rather booths, were carefully closed, streamers of silk, cloth of arras and gold, were hung from the upper casements; the balconies were crowded with holiday gazers; the fickle populace (the same herd that had hooted the meek Henry, when led to the Tower) were now shouting, "A Warwick!" "A Clarance!" and pouring throng after throng, to gaze upon the army, which, with the mayor and aldermen, had already entered the city. Having seen to the security of his costly goods, and praised his apprentices duly for their care of his interests, and their abstinence from joining the crowd, Nicholas then repaired to the upper story of his house, set forth from his casements and balcony the richest stuffs he possessed. However, there was his own shrewd, sarcastic smile on his firm lips, as he said to his apprentices, "When these are done with, lay them carefully by against Edward of York's re-entry!"

Meanwhile, preceded by trumpets, drums, and heralds, the Earl of Warwick and his royal son-in-law rode into the shouting city. Behind came the litter of the Duchess of Clarence, attended by the Earl of Oxford, Lord Fitzhugh, the Lords Stanley and Shrewsbury, Sir Robert de Lytton, and a princely cortège of knights, squires, and nobles; while, file upon file, rank upon rank, followed the long march of the unresisted armament.

Warwick clad in complete armor of Milan steel—save the helmet, which was borne behind him by his squire,—mounted on his own noble Saladin, preserved upon a countenance so well suited to command the admiration of a populace, the same character as heretofore, of manly majesty and lofty frankness. But to a nearer and more searching gaze than was likely to be bent upon him in such an hour, the dark deep traces of care, anxiety, and passion might have been detected in the lines which now thickly intersected the forehead, once so smooth and furrowless; and his kingly eye, not looking, as of old, right forward as he moved, cast unquiet, searching glances about him and around, as he bowed his bare head from side to side of the welcoming thousands.

A far greater change to outward appearance, was visible in the fair young face of the Duke of Clarence. His complexion, usually sanguine and blooming, like his elder brother's was now little less pale than that of Richard. A sullen, moody, discontented expression, which not all the heartiness of the greetings he received could dispel, contrasted forcibly with the good-humored laughing recklessness, which had once drawn a "God bless him!" from all on whom rested his light-blue joyous eye. He was unarmed, save by a corslet richly embossed with gold. His short mantle-line of crimson velvet, his hosen of white cloth laced with gold, and his low horsemen's boots of Spanish leather curiously carved and broidered, with long golden spurs, his plumed and jewelled cap, his white charger with housings enriched with pearls and blazing with cloth of gold, his broad collar of precious stones, with the order of St. George; his general's truncheon raised aloft, and his Plantagenet banner borne by the herald over his royal head, caught the eyes of the crowd, only the more to rivet them on an aspect ill fitting the triumph of a bloodless victory. At his left hand, where the breadth of the streets permitted, rode Henry Lee, the mayor, uttering no word unless appealed to, and then answering but with childing reverence and monosyllables.

A narrow winding in the streets, which left Warwick and Clarence alone side by side, gave the former the opportunity he had desired.

"How, prince and son," he said in a hollow whisper—"is it with this brow of care that thou saddenest our conquest, and enterest the capital we gain without a blow?"

"By St. George!" answered Clarence, sullenly, and in the same tone; "thinkest thou it chafes not the son of Richard of York, after such toils and bloodshed, to minister to the dethronement of his kin and the restoration of the foe of his race?"

"Thou shouldst have thought of that before," returned Warwick, but with sadness and pity in the reproach.

"Ay, before Edward of Lancaster was made my lord and brother," retorted Clarence, bitterly.

"Hush!" said the earl, "and calm thy brow. Not thus didst thou speak at Amboise; either thou wert then less frank, or more generous. But regrets are vain: we have raised the whirlwind, and must rule it."

And with that, in the action of a man who would escape his own thoughts, Warwick made his black steed demivolte; and the crowd shouted again the louder, at the earl's gallant horsemanship, and Clarence's dazzling collar of jewels.

While thus the procession of the victors, the nominal object of all this mighty and sudden revolution—of this stir and uproar—of these shining arms and flaunting banners—of this heaven or hell in the deep passions of men—still remained in his prison chamber of the Tower a true type of the thing factions contend for; absent, insignificant, unheeded, and, save by a few of the leaders and fanatical priests, absolutely forgotten!

To this solitary chamber we are now transported; yet solitary is a word of doubtful propriety—for though the royal captive was alone, so far as the human species make up a man's companionship and solace—though the faithful gentlemen, Manning, Bedle, and Allerton, had, on the news of Warwick's landing, been thrust from his chamber, and were now in the ranks of his new and strange defenders, yet power and jealousy had not left his captivity all forsaken. There was still the starling in its cage, and the fat, asthmatic spaniel still wagged its tail at the sound of its master's voice, or the rustle of his long gown. And still from the ivory crucifix gleamed the sad and holy face of the God—present alway—and who, by faith and patience, linketh evermore grief to joy,—but earth to heaven.

The august prisoner had not been so utterly cut off from all knowledge of the outer life as to be ignorant of some unwonted and important stir in the fortress and the city. The squire who had brought him his morning meal had been so agitated as to excite the captive's attention, and had then owned that the Earl of Warwick had proclaimed Henry king, and was on his march to London. But neither the squire nor any of the officers of the Tower dared release the illustrious captive, nor even remove him as yet to the state apartments vacated by Elizabeth. They knew not what might be the pleasure of the stout earl or the Duke of Clarence, and feared over-officiousness might be their worst crime. But naturally imagining that Henry's first command, at the new position of things, might be for liberty, and perplexed whether to yield or refuse, they absented themselves from his summons, and left the whole Tower in which he was placed actually deserted.

From his casement the king could see, however, the commotion, and the crowds upon the wharf and river, with the gleam of arms and banners;—and hear the sounds of "A Warwick!" "A Clarence!" "Long live good Henry VI.!" A strange combination of names, which disturbed and amazed him much! But by degrees, the unwonted excitement of perplexity and surprise settled back into the calm serenity of his most gentle mind and temper. That trust in an all-directing Providence, to which he had schooled himself, had, (if we may so say with reverence) driven his beautiful soul into the opposite error, so fatal to the affairs of life; the error that deadens and benumbs the energy of free will and the noble alertness of active duty. Why strain and strive for the things of this world? God would order all for the best. Alas, God hath placed us in this world, each, from king to peasant, with nerves, and hearts, and blood, and passions, to struggle with our kind; and, no matter how heavenly the goal, to labor with the million in the race!

"Forsooth," murmured the king, as his hands clasped behind him, he paced slowly to and fro the floor, "this ill world seemeth but a feather blown about by the winds, and never to be at rest. Hark! Warwick and King Henry—the lion and the lamb! Alack, and we are fallen on no Paradise, where such union were not a miracle! Foolish bird!"—and with a pitying smile upon that face whose holy sweetness might have disarmed a fiend, he paused before the cage and contemplated his fellow-captive—"Foolish bird, the uneasiness and turmoil without have reached even to thee. Thou beatest thy wings against the wires—thou turnest thy bright eyes to mine restlessly. Why? Pantest thou to be free, silly one, that the hawk may swoop on its defenceless prey? Better, perhaps, the cage for thee, and the prison for thy master. Well—out if thou wilt! Here at least thou art safe!" and opening the cage the starling flew to his bosom, and nestled there, with its small, clear voice mimicking the human sound.

"Poor Henry—poor Henry! Wicked men—poor Henry!"

The king bowed his meek head over his favorite, and the fat spaniel, jealous of the monopolized caress, came waddling towards its master, with a fond whine, and looked up at him with eyes that expressed more of faith and love than Edward of York, the ever wooing and ever wooed, had read in the gaze of woman.

With these companions, and with thoughts growing more and more composed and rapt from all that had roused and vexed his interest in the forenoon, Henry remained till the hour had long passed for his evening meal. Surprised at last by a negligence which (to do his jailers justice) had never before occurred, ane finding no response to his hand-bell—no attendant in the anteroom—the outer doors locked as usual—but the sentinel's tread in the court below, hushed and still, a cold thrill for a moment shot through his blood. 'Was he left for hunger to do its silent work!' Slowly he bent his way from the outer rooms back to his chamber; and, as he passed the casement again he heard, though far in the distance, through the dim air of the deepening twilight, the cry of "Long live King Henry!"

This devotion without—this neglect within, was a wonderous contrast! Meanwhile the spaniel, with that instinct of fidelity which divines the wants of the master, had moved, snuffling and smelling, round and round the chambers, till it stopped and scratched at a cupboard in the ante-room, and then with a joyful bark flew back to the king, and taking the hem of his gown between his teeth, led him towards the spot it had discovered; and there, in truth, a few of those small cakes, usually served up for the night's livery, had been carelessly left. They sufficed for the day's food, and the king, the dog, and the starling, shared them peacefully together. This done, Henry carefully replaced his bird in its cage, bade the dog creep to the hearth and lie still; passed on to his little oratory, with the relics of cross and saint strewed around the solemn image,—and in prayer forgot the world!

Meanwhile darkness set in: the streets had grown deserted, save where in some nooks and by lanes gathered groups of the soldiery; but for the most part, the discipline in which Warwick held his army, had dismissed those stern loiterers to the various quarters provided for them, and little remained to remind the peaceful citizens that a throne had been uprooted, and a revolution consummated, that eventful day. It was at this time that a tall man, closely wrapped in his large horseman's cloak, passed alone through the streets, and gained the Tower. At the sound of his voice by the great gate, the sentinel started in alarm; a few moments more, and all left to guard the fortress were gathered around him. From these he singled out one of the squires who usually attended Henry, and bade him light his steps to the king's chamber. As in that chamber Henry rose from his kness, he saw the broad red light of a torch flickering under the chinks of the threshold; he heard the slow tread of approaching footsteps, the spaniel uttered a low growl, its eyes are sparkling,—the door opened, and the torch borne behind by the squire, and raised aloft so that its glare threw a broad light over the whole chamber, brought into full view the dark and haughty countenance of the Earl of Warwick.

The squire, at a gesture from the earl, lighted the sconces on the wall, the tapers on the table, and quickly vanished. King-maker and king were alone! At the first sight of Warwick, Henry had turned pale, and receded a few paces, with one hand uplifted in adjuration or command, while with the other he veiled his eyes—whether that his startled movement came from the weakness of bodily nerves, much shattered by sickness and confinement, or from the sudden emotions called forth by the aspect of one who had wrought him calamities so dire. But the craven's terror in the presence of a living foe was, with all his meekness, all his holy abhorrence of wrath and warfare, as unknown to that royal heart as to the high blood of his Hero-sire. And so, after a brief pause, and a thought that took the shape of prayer, not for safety from peril, but for grace to forgive the past, Henry VI. advanced to Warwick, who still stood dumb by the threshold, combating with his own mingled and turbulent emotions of pride and shame, and said, in a voice majestic even from its very mildness—

"What tale of new woe and evil hath the Earl of Salisbury and Warwick come to announce to the poor captive who was once a king?"

"Forgive me! Forgiveness, Henry, my lord—Forgiveness!" exclaimed Warwick, falling on his knee. The meek reproach—the touching words—the mien and visage altered, since last beheld, from manhood into age—the grey hairs and bended form of the king, went at once to that proud heart; and as the earl bent over the wan, thin hand resigned to his lips, a tear upon its surface outsparkled all the jewels that it wore.

"Yet no," continued the earl, (impatient, as proud men are, to hurry from repentance to atonement, for the one is of humiliation and the other of pride),—"yet no, my liege—not now do I crave thy pardon. No; but when begirt, in the halls of thine ancestors, with the peers of England, the victorious banner of St. George waving above the throne which thy servant hath rebuilt—then, when the trumpets are sounding thy rights without the answer of a foe—then, when from shore to shore of fair England the shout of thy people echoes to the vault of heaven—*then* will Warwick kneel again to King Henry, and sue for the pardon he hath not ignobly won!"

"Alack, sir," said the king, with accents of

mournful, yet half-reproving kindness, "it was not amidst trumps and banners that the Son of God set mankind the examplar and pattern of charity to foes. When thy hand struck the spurs from my heel—when thou didst parade me through the hooting crowd to this solitary cell, *then*, Warwick, I forgave thee, and prayed to heaven for pardon for *thee*, if thou didst wrong me—*for myself*, if a kings fault had deserved a subject's harshness. Rise, sir earl; our God is a jealous God, and the attitude of worship is for Him alone."

Warwick rose from his knee; and the king, perceiving and compassionating the struggle which shook the strong man's breast, laid his hand on the earl's shoulder, and said—"Peace be with thee!—thou hast done me no real harm. I have been as happy in these walls as in the green parks of Windsor; happier than in the halls of state, or in the midst of wrangling armies. What tidings now?"

"My liege, is it possible that you know not that Edward is a fugutive and a beggar, and that Heaven hath permitted me to avenge at once your injuries and my own. This day, without a blow, I have regained your city of London; its streets are manned with my army. From the council of peers, and warriors, and prelates, assembled at my house, I have stolen hither alone and in secret, that I might be the first to hail your grace's restoration to the throne of Henry V."

The king's face so little changed at this intelligence, that its calm sadness almost enraged the impetuous Warwick, and with difficulty he restrained from giving utterance to the thought —'He is not worthy of a throne who cares so little to possess it.'

"Well-a-day?" said Henry, sighing, "Heaven, then, hath sore trials yet in store for mine old age! Tray—Tray!" and stooping, he gently patted his dog, who kept watch at his feet, still glaring suspiciously at Warwick—"We are both too old for the chase now!—Will you be seated, my lord?"

"Trust me," said the earl, as he obeyed the command, having first set chair and footstool for the king, who listened to him with downcast eyes and his head drooping on his bosom —"trust me, your later days, my liege, will be free from the storms of your youth. All chance of Edward's hostility is expired. Your aliance, though I seem boastful so to speak—your alliance with one in whom the people can confide for some skill in war, and some more profound experience of the habits and tempers of your subjects than your former councillors could possess, will leave your honored leisure free for the holy meditations it affects; and your glory, as your safety, shall be the care of men who can awe this rebellious world.'

"Alliance!" said the king, who had caught but that one word. "Of what speakest thou, sir earl?"

"These missives will explain all, my liege. This letter from my lady the Queen Margaret, and this from your gracious son, the Prince of Wales."

"Edward! my Edward!" exclaimed the king, with a father's burst of emotion. "Thou hast seen him, then?—bears he his health well?—is he of cheer and heart?"

"He is strong and fair, and full of promise, and brave as his grandsire's sword."

"And knows he—knows he well, that we all are the potter's clay in the lands of God'?"

"My liege," said Warwick, embarrassed, "he has as much devotion as befits a Christian knight and a goodly prince."

"Ah!" sighed the king, "ye men of arms have strange thoughts on these matters;" and cutting the silk of the letters, he turned from the warrior. Shading his face with his hand, the earl darted his keen glance on the features of the king, as, drawing near to the table, the latter read the communications which announced his new connection with his ancient foe.

But Henry was at first so affected by the sight of Margaret's well-known hand, that he thrice put down her letter, and wiped the moisture from his eyes.

"My poor Margaret, how thou hast suffered!" he murmured; "these very characters are less firm and bold than they were. Well—well!" and at last he betook himself resolutely to the task: Once or twice his countenance changed, and he uttered an exclamation of surprise. But the proposition of a marriage between Prince Edward and the Lady Anne did not revolt his forgiving mind, as it had the haughty and stern temper of his consort. And when he had concluded his son's epistle, full of the ardor of his love and the spirit of his yoath, the king passed his left hand over his brow, and then extending his right to Warwick, said, in accents which trembled with emotion—"Serve *my* son—since he is *thine*, too;—give peace to his distracted kingdom—repair my errors—press not hard upon those who contend against us, and Jesu and his Saints will bless this bond!"

The earl's object, perhaps, in seeking a meeting with Henry, so private and unwitnessed, had been, that none, not even his brother, might hearken to the reproaches he anticipated to receive, or say hereafter that he heard Warwick, returned as victor and avenger to his native land, descend, in the hour of triumph, to extenuation and excuse. So affronted, imperilled, or to use his own strong word, "so *despaired*," had he been in the former rule of Henry, that his intellect, which however vigorous in his calmer moods, was liable to be obscured and dulled by his passions, had half-confounded the gentle king with his ferocious wife and stern councillors, and he had thought he never could have humbled himself to the *man*, even so far as knighthood's submission to Margaret's sex had allowed him to the woman. But the sweetness of Henry's manners and disposition—the saint-like dignity which he had manifested throughout this painful interview, and the touching grace and trustful generosity of his last words—words which consummated the earl's large projects of ambition and revenge, had that effect upon Warwick which the preaching of some holy man, dwelling upon the patient sanctity of the Saviour, had of old on a grim Crusader, all incapable himself of practising such meek excellence, and yet all-moved and penetrated by its loveliness in another, and, like such Crusader, the representation of all mildest and most forgiving singularly stirred up in the warrior's mind images precisely the reverse—images of armed valor and stern vindication, as if where the Cross was planted, sprang from the earth the standard and the war-horse!

"Perish your foes! May war and storm scatter them as the chaff!—My liege, my royal master," continued the earl, in a deep, low, faltering voice. "Why knew I not thy holy and princely heart before? Why stood so many between Warwick's devotion and a king so worthy to command it? How poor, beside thy great-hearted fortitude and thy Christian heroism, seems the savage valor of false Edward! Shame upon one who can betray the trust thou hast placed in him. Never will I!—Never! I swear it! No! though all England desert thee, I will stand alone with my breast of mail before thy throne! Oh, would that my triumph had been less peaceful and less bloodless!—would that a hundred battle-fields were yet left to prove how deeply—deeply in his heart of hearts—Warwick feels the forgiveness of his king!"

"Not so—not so—not so—not *battle-fields*, Warwick!" said Henry. "Ask not to serve the king by shedding one subject's blood."

"Your pious will be obeyed!" replied Warwick. "We will see if mercy can effect in others what thy pardon effects in me. And now my, my liege, no longer must these walls confine thee. The chambers of the palace await their sovereign. What ho, there!"—and going to the door, he threw it open, and agreeably to the orders he had given below, all the officers left in the fortress stood crowded together in the small ante-room, bareheaded, with tapers in their hands, to conduct the monarch to the halls of his conquered foe.

At the sudden sight of the earl, these men, struck involuntarily and at once by the grandeur of his person and his animated aspect, burst forth with the rude retainer's cry, "A Warwick! a Warwick!"

"Silence!" thundered the earl's deep voice. "Who names the subject in the sovereign's presence? Behold your king!"

The men, abashed by the reproof, bowed their heads and sank on their knees, as Warwick took a taper from the table, to lead the way from the prison.

Then Henry turned slowly, and gazed with a lingering eye upon the walls, which even sorrow and solitude had endeared. The little oratory—the crucifix—the relics—the embers burning low on the hearth—the rude timepiece—all took to his thoughtful eye an almost human aspect of melancholy and omen; and the bird, roused, whether by the glare of the lights, or the recent shout of the men, opened its bright eyes and fluttering restlessly to and fro, shrilled out its favorite sentence—"Poor Henry!—poor Henry—wicked men!—who would be a king?"

"Thou hearest it, Warwick?" said Henry, shaking his head.

"Could an eagle speak, it would have another cry than the starling," returned the earl, with a proud smile.

"Why, look you," said the king, once more releasing the bird, which settled on his wrist, "the eagle had broken his heart in the narrow cage—the eagle had been no comforter for a captive; it is these gentler ones that love and soothe us best in our adversities. Tray, Tray, fawn not *now*, sirrah, or I shall think thou hast been false in thy fondness heretofore! Cousin, I attend you."

And with his bird on his wrist, his dog at his heels, Henry VI. followed the earl to the illuminated hall of Edward, where the table was spread for the royal repast, and where his old friends, Manning, Bedle, and Allerton, stood weeping for joy; while from the gallery raised aloft, the musicians gave forth the rough and stirring melody which had gradually fallen out of usage, but which was once the Norman's national air, and which the warlike Margaret of Anjou had retaught to her minstrels—"THE BATTLE HYMN OF ROLLO."

BOOK ELEVENTH.

THE NEW POSITION OF THE KING-MAKER.

CHAPTER I.

Wherein Master Adam Warner is notably commended and advanced—and Greatness says to Wisdom, "Thy Destiny be Mine, Amen."

THE Chronicles inform us, that two or three days after the entrance of Warwick and Clarence—viz., on the 6th of October—those two leaders, accompanied by the Lords Shrewsbury, Stanley, and a numerous and noble train, visited the Tower in formal state, and escorted the king, robed in blue velvet, the crown on his head, to public thanksgivings at St. Paul's, and thence to the Bishop's Palace,* where he continued chiefly to reside.

The proclamation that announced the change of dynasty was received with apparent acquiescence through the length and breadth of the kingdom, and the restoration of the Lancastrian line seemed yet the more firm and solid by the magnanimous forbearance of Warwick and his councils. Not one execution that could be termed the act of a private revenge, stained with blood the second reign of the peaceful Henry. One only head fell on the scaffold—that of the Earl of Worcester.† This solitary execution, which was regarded by all classes as a due concession to justice—only yet more illustrated the general mildness of the new rule.

It was in the earliest days of this sudden Restoration, that Alwyn found the occasion to serve his friends in the Tower. Warwick was eager to conciliate all the citizens, who, whether frankly or grudgingly, had supported his cause; and, amongst these, he was soon informed of the part taken in the Guildhall by the rising goldsmith. He sent for Alwyn to his house in Warwick lane, and after complimenting him on his advance in life and repute, since Nicholas had waited on him with baubles for his embassy to France, he offered him the special rank of goldsmith to the king.

The wary, yet honest, trader paused a moment in some embarrassment before he answered—

"My good lord, you are noble and gracious eno' to understand and forgive me when I say that I have had, in the upstart of my fortunes, the countenance of the late King Edward and his queen; and though the public weal made me advise my fellow-citizens not to resist your entry, I would not, at least, have it said that my desertion had benefited my private fortunes."

Warwick colored, and his lip curled. "Tush, man, assume not virtues which do not exist amongst the sons of trade, nor, much I trow, amongst the sons of Adam. I read thy mind. Thou thinkest it unsafe openly to commit thyself to the new state. Fear not—we are firm."

"Nay, my lord," returned Alwyn, "it is not so. But there are many better citizens

* Not to the Palace at Westminster, as some historians, preferring the French to the English authorities, have asserted that palace was out of repair.

† Lord Warwick himself did not sit in judgment on Worcester. He was tried and condemned by Lord Oxford. Though some old offences in his Irish Government were alleged against him, the cruelties which rendered him so odious were of recent date. He had (as we before took occasion to relate) impaled twenty persons after Warwick's flight into France. The Warkworth Chronicle says, "he was ever afterwardes greatly behated among the people for this *disordynate dethe* that he used, contrary to the laws of the lande."

than I, who remember that the Yorkists were ever friends to commerce. And you will find that only by great tenderness to our crafts you can win the heart of London, though you have passed its gates."

"I shall be just to all men," answered the earl, drily; "but if the flat-caps are false, there are eno' of bonnets of steel to watch over the Red Rose!"

"Your are said, my lord," returned Alwyn bluntly, to "love the barons, the knights, the gentry, the yeomen, and the peasants, but to despise the traders—I fear me, that report in this is true."

"I love not the trader spirit, man—the spirit that cheats, and cringes, and haggles, and splits straws for pence, and roasts eggs by other men's blazing rafters. Edward of York, forsooth, was a great trader! It was a sorry hour for England, when such as ye, Nick Alwyn, left your green villages for loom and booth. But thus far have I spoken to you as a brave fellow, and of the north countree. I have no time to waste on words. Wilt thou accept mine offer, or name another boon, in my power? The man who hath served me, *wrongs me,—till I have served him again!*"

"My lord, yes; I will name such a boon;—safety, and if you will, some grace and honor, to a learned scholar now in the Tower—one Adam Warner, whom——"

"Now in the Tower! Adam Warner! And wanting a friend, I no more an exile! That is my affair, not thine. Grace, honor—ay, to his heart's content. And his noble daughter? *Mort Dieu!* she shall choose her bridegroom among the best of England. Is she, too, in the fortress?"

"Yes," said Alwyn, briefly, not liking the last part of the earl's speech.

The earl rang the bell on his table. "Send hither Sir Marmaduke Nevile."

Alwyn saw his former rival enter, and heard the earl commission him to accompany, with a fitting train, his own litter to the Tower. And you, Alwyn, go with your foster-brother, and pray Master Warner and his daughter to be my guests for their own pleasure. Come hither, my rude Northman—come. I see I shall have many secret foes in this city—wilt not thou at least be Warwick's open friend?"

Alwyn found it hard to resist the charm of the earl's manner and voice, but, convinced in his own mind that the age was against Warwick, and that commerce and London would be little advantaged by the earl's rule, the trading spirit prevailed in his breast.

"Gracious my lord," he said, bending his knee in no servile homage—"he who befriends my order, commands me."

The proud noble bit his lip, and with a silent wave of his hand, dismissed the foster-brothers.

"Thou art but a churl at best, Nick," said Marmaduke, as the door closed on the young men. "Many a baron would have sold his father's hall for such words from the earl's lip."

"Let barons sell their free conduct for fair words. I keep myself unshackled, to join that cause which best fills the market, and reforms the law. But tell me, I pray thee, sir knight, what makes Warner and his daughter so dear to your lord?"

"What! know you not?—and has she not told you,—Ah—what was I about to say?"

"Can there be a secret between the earl and the scholar?" asked Alwyn, in wonder.

"If there be, it is our place to respect it," returned the Nevile, adjusting his manteline—"and now we must command the litter."

In spite of all the more urgent and harassing affairs that pressed upon him, the earl found an early time to attend to his guests. His welcome to Sibyll was more than courteous—it was paternal. As she approached him, timidly, and with a downcast eye, he advanced, placed his hand upon her head—

"The Holy Mother ever have thee in her charge, child!—This is a father's kiss, young mistress," added the earl, pressing his lips to her forehead—"and in this kiss, remember that I pledge to thee care for thy fortunes, honor for thy name—my heart to do thee service—my arm to shield from wrong!—Brave scholar, thy lot has become interwoven with my own—prosperous is now my destiny—my destiny be thine! Amen!"

He turned then to Warner, and without further reference to a past, which so galled his proud spirit, he made the scholar explain to him the nature of his labors. In the mind of every man who has passed much of his life in successful action, there is a certain, if we may so say, untaught *mathesis*,—but especially among those who have been bred to the art of war. A great soldier is a great mechanic—a great mathematician, though he may know it not; and Warwick, therefore, better than many a scholar, comprehended the principle upon which Adam founded his experiments. But though he caught also a glimpse of the vast results which such experiments in themselves were calculated to effect, his strong common sense perceived yet more clearly that the time was not ripe for such startling inventions.

"My friend," he said, "I comprehend thee passably. It is clear to me, that if thou canst succeed in making the elements do the work of man with equal precision, but with far greater force and rapidity, thou must multiply eventually, and, by multiplying, cheapen, all the products of industry—that thou must give to this country the market of the world,—and that thine would be the true alchemy that turneth all to gold."

"Mighty intellect—thou graspest the truth!" exclaimed Adam.

"But," pursued the earl, with a mixture of prejudice and judgment, "grant thee success to the full, and thou wouldst turn this bold land of yeomanry and manhood into one community of griping traders and sickly artisans. *Mort Dieu!* we are over-commerced as it is—the bow is already deserted for the ell measure. The town populations are ever the most worthless in war. England is begirt with mailed foes; and if by one process she were to accumulate treasure and lose soldiers, she would but tempt invasion and emasculate defenders. Verily, I avise and implore thee to turn thy wit and scholarship to a manlier occupation!"

"My life knows no other object—kill my labor and thou destroyest me," said Adam, in a voice of gloomy despair. Alas, it seemed that, whatever the changes of power, no change could better the hopes of science in an age of iron!

Warwick was moved. "Well," he said, after a pause, "be happy in thine own way. I will do my best, at least, to protect thee. To-morrow resume thy labors; but this day, at least, thou must feast with me."

And at his banquet that day, among the knights and barons, and the abbots and the warriors, Adam sate on the dais, near the earl, and Sibyll at "the mess" of the ladies of the Duchess of Clarence. And ere the feast broke up, Warwick thus addressed his company:—

"My friends,—Though I, and most of us reared in the lap of war, have little other clerkship than sufficed our bold fathers before us, yet in the free towns of Italy and the Rhine—yea, and in France, under her politic king—we may see that a day is dawning wherein new knowledge will teach many marvels to our wiser sons. Wherefore it is good that a state should foster men who devote laborious nights and weary days to the advancement of arts and letters, for the glory of our common land. A worthy gentleman, now at this board, hath deeply meditated contrivances which may make our English artisans excel the Flemish loons, who now fatten upon our industry to the impoverishment of the realm. And, above all, he also purposes to complete an invention which may render our ship craft the most notable in Europe. Of this I say no more at the present; but I commend our guest, Master Adam Warner, to your good service, and pray you especially, worshipful sirs of the church now present, to shield his good name from that charge which most paineth and endangereth honest men. For ye wot well that the commons, from ignorance, would impute all to witchcraft that passeth their understanding, Not," added the earl, crossing himself, "that witchcraft does not horribly infect the land, and hath been largely practised by Jacquetta of Bedford, and her confederates, Bungey and others. But our cause needeth no such aid; and all that Master Warner purposes is in behalf of the people, and in conformity with holy church. So this waisall to his health and house."

This characteristic address being received with respect, though with less applause than usually greeted the speeches of the great earl, Warwick added, in a softer and more earnest tone, "And in the fair demoiselle, his daughter, I pray you to acknowledge the dear friend of my beloved lady and child, Anne, Princess of Wales; and for the sake of her highness, and in her name, I arrogate to myself a share with Master Warner in this young donzell's guardianship and charge. Know ye, my gallant gentles and fair squires, that he who can succeed in achieving either by leal love or bold deeds as best befit a wooer, the grace of my young ward, shall claim from my hand a knight's fee, with as much of my best land as a bull's hide can cover; and when Heaven shall grant safe passage to the Princess Anne and her noble spouse, we will hold at Smithfield a tourney in honor of St. George and our ladies, wherein, *pardie*, I myself would be sorely tempted to provoke my jealous countess, and break a lance for the fame of the demoiselle whose fair face is married to a noble heart.'

That evening, in the galliard, many an admiring eye turned to Sibyll, and many a young gallant, recalling the earl's words, sighed to win her grace. There had been a time when such honor and such homage would have, indeed, been welcome; but now, ONE saw them not, and they were valueless. All that, in her earlier girlhood, Sibyll's ambition had coveted when musing on the brilliant world, seemed now well nigh fulfilled—her father protected by the first noble of the land, and that not with the degrading condescension of the Duchess of Bedford, but as Power alone should protect Genius—honored while it honors;—her gentle birth recognized;—her position elevated;—fair fortunes smiling, after such rude trials;—and all won without servility or abasement. But her ambition having once exhausted itself in a diviner passion, all excitement seemed poor and spiritless compared to the lonely waiting at the humble farm for the voice and step of Hastings. Nay, but for her father's sake, she could almost have loathed the pleasure, and the pomp, and the admiration, and the homage, which seemed to insult the reverses of the wandering exile.

The earl had designed to place Sibyll among Isabel's ladies, but the haughty air of the duchess chilled the poor girl; and, pleading the excuse that her father's health required her constant attendance, she prayed permission to rest with Warner wherever he might be lodged. Adam himself, now that the Duchess of Bedford and Friar Bungey were no longer in the Tower, entreated permission to return to the place where he had worked the most successfully upon the beloved Eureka, and, as the Tower seemed a safer residence than any private home could be, from popular prejudice and assault, Warkick kindly ordered apartments, far more commodious than they had yet occupied, to be appropriated to the father and daughter. Several attendants were assigned to them, and never was man of letters or science more honored now than the poor scholar, who, till then, had been so persecuted and despised!

Who shall tell Adam's serene delight. Alchemy and astrology at rest—no imperious duchess—no hateful Bungey—his free mind left to its congenial labors! And Sibyll, when they met, strove to wear a cheerful brow, praying him only never to speak to her of Hastings. The good old man, relapsing into his wonted mechanical existence, hoped she had forgotten a girl's evanescent fancy.

But the peculiar distinction showed by the earl to Warner, confirmed the reports circulated by Bungey—"that he was, indeed, a fearful nigromancer, who had much helped the earl in his emprise." The earl's address to his guests in behalf both of Warner and Sibyll—the high state accorded to the student, reached even the sanctuary; for the fugitives there easily contrived to learn all the gossip of the city. Judge of the effect the tale produced upon the envious Bungey—judge of the representations it enabled him to make to the credulous duchess! It was clear now to Jacquetta, as the sun in noonday, that Warwick rewarded the evil-predicting astrologer for much dark and secret service, which Bungey, had she listened to him, might have frustrated; and she promised the friar that, if ever again she had the power, Warner and the Eureka should be placed at his sole mercy and discretion.

The friar himself, however, growing very weary of the dulness of the sanctuary, and covetous of the advantages enjoyed by Adam began to meditate acquiescence in the fashion of the day, and a transfer of his allegiance to the party in power. Emboldened by the clemency of the victors—learning that no rewards for his own apprehension had been offered—hoping that the stout earl would forget or forgive the old offence of the waxen effigies—and aware of the comparative security his friar's gown and cowl afforded him, he resolved one day to venture forth from his retreat. He even flattered himself that he could cajole Adam—whom he really believed the possessor of some high and weird secrets, but whom otherwise he despised as a very weak creature—into forgiving his past brutalities, and soliciting the earl to take him into favor.

At dusk, then, and by the aid of one of the subalterns of the Tower, whom he had formerly made his friend, the friar got admittance into Warner's chamber. Now it so chanced that Adam, having his own superstitions, had lately taken it into his head that all the various disasters which had befallen the Eureka, together with all the little blemishes and defects that yet marred its construction, were owing to the want of the diamond bathed in the mystic moonbeams, which his German authority had long so emphatically prescribed—and now that a monthly stipend far exceeding his wants was at his disposal—and that it became him to do all possible honor to the earl's patronage, he resolved that the diamond should be no longer absent from the operations it was to influence. He obtained one of passable size and sparkle, exposed it the due number of nights to the new moon, and had already prepared its place in the Eureka, and was contemplating it with solemn joy, when Bungey entered.

"Mighty brother," said the friar, bowing to the ground, "be merciful as thou art strong! Verily thou hast proved thyself the magician, and I but a poor wretch in comparison—for lo! thou art rich and honored, and I poor and proscribed! Deign to forgive thine enemy, and take him as thy slave by right of conquest. Oh, Cogsbones!—oh, Gemini! what a jewel thou hast got!"

"Depart! Thou disturbest me, said Adam, oblivious, in his absorption, of the exact reasons for his repugnance, but feeling indistinctly that something very loathsome and hateful was at his elbow, and, as he spoke, he fitted the diamond into its socket.

"What!—a jewel!—a diamond!—in the—in the—in the—MECHANICAL!" faltered the friar, in profound astonishment, his mouth watering at the sight. If the Eureka were to be envied before—how much more enviable now! "If ever I get thee again, O ugly talisman!" he muttered to himself, "I shall know where to look for something better than a pot to boil eggs!"

"Depart I say!" repeated Adam turning round at last, and shuddering as he now clearly recognized the friar, and recalled his malignity. "Dearest thou molest me still?"

The friar abjectly fell on his knees, and, after a long exordium of penitent excuses entreated the scholar to intercede in his favor with the earl.

"I want not all *thy* honors and advancement, great Adam—I want only to serve thee, trim thy furnace, and hand thee thy tools, and work out my apprenticeship under thee, master. As for the earl, he will listen to thee, I know, if thou tellest him that I had the trust of his foe, the duchess; that I can give him all her closest secrets; that I——"

"Avaunt! Thou art worse than I deemed thee, wretch! Cruel and ignorant I knew thee—and now, mean and perfidious! *I* work with *thee!* I commend to the earl a living disgrace to the name of scholar! Never! If thou wantest bread and alms, those I can give, as a Christian gives to want; but trust, and honor, and learned repute, and noble toils, those are not for the impostor and the traitor. There—there—there!" And he ran to a closet, took out a handful of small coins, thrust them into the friar's hands, and, pushing him to the door, called to his servants to see his visitor to the gates. The friar turned round with a scowl. He did not dare to utter a threat, but he vowed a vow in his soul, and went his way.

It chanced, some days after this, that Adam, in one of his musing rambles about the precincts of the Tower, which (since it was not then inhabited as a palace) was all free to his rare and desultory warderings, came by some workmen employed in repairing a bombard; and, as whatever was of mechanical art always woke his interest, he paused, and pointed out to them a very simple improvement which would necessarily tend to make the balls go farther and more direct to their object.

The principal workman, struck with his remarks, ran to one of the officers of the Tower; the officer came to listen to the learned man, and then went to the Earl of Warwick to declare that Master Warner had the most wonderful comprehension of military mechanism. The earl sent for Warner, seized at once upon the very simple truth he suggested as to the proper width of the bore, and holding him in higher esteem than he had ever done before, placed some new cannon he was constructing under his superintendence. As this care occupied but little of his time, Warner was glad to show gratitude to the earl, looking upon the destructive engines simply as mechanical contrivances, and wholly unconscious of the new terror he gave to his name.

Soon did the indignant and conscience-stricken Duchess of Bedford hear, in the Sanctuary, that the fell wizard she had saved from the clutches of Bungey was preparing the most dreadful, infallible, and murtherous instruments of war, against the possible return of her son-in-law !

Leaving Adam to his dreams, and his toils, and his horrible reputation, we return to the world upon the surface—the Life of Action.

CHAPTER II.

The Prosperity of the Outer Show.—The Cares of the Inner Man.

THE position of the king-maker was, to a superficial observer, such as might gratify to the utmost the ambition and the pride of man. He had driven from the land one of the most gorgeous princes, and one of the boldest warriors that ever sate upon a throne. He had changed a dynasty without a blow. In the alliances of his daughters, whatever chanced, it seemed certain that by one or the other, his posterity would be the kings of England.

The easiness of his victory appeared to prove of itself that the hearts of the people were with him; and the parliament that he hastened to summon, confirmed by law, the revolution achieved by a bloodless sword.*

Nor was there aught abroad which menaced disturbance to the peace at home. Letters from the Countess of Warwick and Lady Anne announced their triumphant entry at Paris, where Margaret of Anjou was received with honors never before rendered but to a Queen of France.

A solemn embassy, meanwhile, was preparing to proceed from Paris to London, to congratulate Henry, and establish a permanent treaty of peace and commerce.† While Charles of Burgundy himself, (the only ally left to Edward), supplicated for the continuance of amicable relations with England; stating that they were formed with the country, not with any special person who might wear the crown;* and forbade his subjects by proclamation, to join any enterprise for the recovery of his throne, which Edward might attempt.

The conduct of Warwick, whom the parlia ment had declared, conjointly with Clarence, protector of the realm during the minority of the Prince of Wales, was worthy of the triumph he had obtained. He exhibited now a greater genius for government than he had yet displayed. For all his passions were nerved to the utmost, to consummate his victory, and sharpen his faculties. He united mildness towards the defeated faction, with a firmness which repelled all attempt at insurrection.†

In contrast to the splendor that surrounded his daughter Anne, all accounts spoke of the humiliation to which Charles subjected the exiled king, and in the Sanctuary, amidst homicides and felons, the wife of the earl's defeated foe gave birth to a male child, baptized and christened (says the chronicler), "as the son of a common man." For the Avenger and his children were regal authority and gorgeous pomp—for the Fugitive and his offspring were the bread of the exile, or the refuge of the outlaw.

But still the earl's prosperity was hollow—the statue of brass stood on limbs of clay.—The position of a man with the name of subject, but the authority of king, was an unpopular anomaly in England. In the principal trading towns had been long growing up that animosity towards the aristocracy, of which Henry VII. availed himself to raise a despotism, (and which, even in our day, causes the main disputes of faction); but the recent revolution was one in which the towns *had had no share.* It was a revolution made by the representatives of the barons, and his followers. It was connected with no advancement of the middle class—it seemed to the men of commerce but the violence of a turbulent and disappointed nobility. The very name given to Warwick's supporters was unpopular in the towns. They were not called the Lancastrians, or the friends of King Henry—they were styled then, and still are so, by the old Chronicler, "*The Lords' Party.*" Most of whatever was still feudal—the haughtiest of the magnates—the rudest of the yeomanry—the most warlike of the knights—gave to Warwick the sanction of

* LINGARD, HUME, etc.

† RYMER, xi., 283—690.

* HUME—COMINES.

† HABINGTON.

their allegiance; and this sanction was displeasing to the intelligence of the towns.

Classes in all times have a keen instinct of their own class-interests. The revolution which the earl had affected was the triumph of aristocracy, its natural results would tend to strengthen certainly the moral, and probably the constitutional, power already possessed by that martial order. The new parliament was their creature—Henry VI. was a cipher—his son a boy with unknown character, and according to vulgar scandal, of doubtful legitimacy, seemingly bound hand and foot in the trammels of the archbaron's mighty house—the earl himself had never scrupled to evince a distaste to the change in society which was slowly converting an agricultural into a trading population.

It may be observed, too, that a middle class as rarely unites itself with the idols of the populace as with the chiefs of a seignorie. The brute attachment of the peasants and the mobs to the gorgeous and lavish earl, seemed to the burgesses the sign of a barbaric clanship, opposed to that advance in civilization towards which they half unconsciously struggled.

And here we must rapidly glance at what, as far as a statesman may foresee, would have been the probable result of Warwick's ascendancy, if durable and effectual. If attached, by prejudice and birth, to the aristocracy, he was yet, by reputation and habit, attached also to the popular party—that party more popular than the middle class—the majority—the masses:—his whole life had been one struggle against despotism in the crown. Though far from entertaining such schemes as in similar circumstances might have occurred to the deep sagacity of an Italian patrician for the interest of his order, no doubt his policy would have tended to this one aim—the limitation of the monarchy by the strength of an aristocracy endeared to the agricultural population, owing to that population its own powers of defence, with the wants and grievances of that population thoroughly familiar, and willing to satisfy the one and redress the other: in short, the great baron would have secured and promoted liberty according to the notions of a seigneur and a Norman, by making the king but the first nobleman of the realm.

Had the policy lasted long enough to succeed, the subsequent despotism, which changed a limited into an absolute monarchy under the Tudors, would have been prevented, with all the sanguinary reaction, in which the Stuarts were the sufferers. The earl's family, and his own "large father-like heart," had ever been opposed to religious persecution; and timely toleration to the Lollards might have prevented the long-delayed revenge of their posterity—the Puritans. Gradually, perhaps, might the system he represented (of the whole consequences of which he was unconscious) have changed monarchic into aristocratic government, resting, however, upon broad and popular institutions; but no doubt, also, the middle, or rather the commercial class, with all the blessings that attend their power, would have risen much more slowly than when made as they were already, partially under Edward IV., and more systematically under Henry VII., the instrument for destroying feudal aristocracy, and thereby establishing, for a long and fearful interval, the arbitrary rule of the single tyrant. Warwick's dislike to the commercial biasses of Edward was, in fact, not a patrician prejudice alone. It required no great sagacity to perceive that Edward had designed to raise up a class that, though powerful when employed against the barons, would long be impotent agatnst the encroachments of the crown; and the earl viewed that class not only as foes to his own order, but as tools for the destruction of the ancient liberties.

Without presuming to decide which policy, upon the whole, would have been the happier for England—the one that based a despotism on the middle class, or the one that founded an aristocracy upon popular affection, it was clear to the more enlightened burgesses of the great towns, that between Edward of York and the Earl of Warwick a vast principle was at stake, and the commercial king seemed to them a more natural ally than the feudal baron; and equally clear is it to us, now, that the true spirit of the age fought for the false Edward, and against the honest earl.

Warwick did not, however, apprehend any serious results from the passive distaste of the trading towns. His martial spirit led him to despise the least martial part of the population. He knew that the towns would not rise in arms, so long as their charters were respected; and that slow undermining hostility which exists only in opinion, his intellect, so vigorous in immediate dangers, was not far-sighted enough to comprehend. More direct cause for apprehension would there have been to a suspicious mind in the demeanor of the earl's colleague in the Protectorate—the Duke of Clarence. It was obviously Warwick's policy to satisfy this weak but ambitious person. The duke was, as before agreed, declared heir to the vast possessions of the house of York. He was invested with the Lieutenancy of Ireland, but delayed his departure to his government till the arrival of the Prince of Wales. The personal honors accorded him in the meanwhile were those due to a sovereign; but still the duke's brow was moody, though if the earl noticed it, Clarence rallied into seeming cheerfulness, and reiterated pledges of faith and friendship.

The manner of Isabel to her father was varying and uncertain: at one time hard and cold; at another, as if in the reaction of secret remorse, she would throw herself into his arms, and pray him, weepingly, to forgive her wayward humors. But the curse of the earl's position was that which he had foreseen before quitting Amboise, and which, more or less, attends upon those who, from whatever cause, suddenly desert the party with which all their associatians, whether of fame or friendship, have been interwoven. His vengeance against one had comprehended many still dear to him. He was not only separated from his old companions in arms, but he had driven their most eminent into exile. He stood alone amongst men whom the habits of an active life had indissolubly connected, in his mind, with recollections of wrath and wrong. Amidst that princely company which begirt him, he hailed no familiar face. Even many of those who most detested Edward, (or rather the Woodvilles), recoiled from so startling a desertion to the Lancastrian foe. It was a heavy blow to a heart already bruised and sore, when the fiery Raoul de Fulke, who had so idolized Warwick, that, despite his own high lineage, he had worn his badge upon his breast, sought him at the dead of night, and thus said—

"Lord of Salisbury and Warwick, I once offered to serve thee as a vassal, if thou wouldst wrestle with lewd Edward for the crown which only a manly brow should wear; and hadst thou now returned, as Henry of Lancaster returned of old, to gripe the sceptre of the Norman with a conqueror's hand, I had been the first to cry, 'Long live King Richard—namesake and emulator of Cœur de Lion!' But to place upon the throne yon monk-puppet, and to call on brave hearts to worship a patterer of aves and a counter of beads—to fix the succession of England in the adulterous offspring of Margaret,* the butcher-harlot—to give the power of the realm to the men against whom thou thyself hast often led me to strive with lance and battle-axe, is to open a path which leads but to dishonor, and thither Raoul de Fulke follows not even the steps of the Lord of Warwick. Interrupt me not—speak not! As thou to Edward, so I now to thee, forswear allegiance, and I bid thee farewell for ever!"

"I pardon thee," answered Warwick; "and if ever thou art wronged as I have been, thy heart will avenge me.—Go!"

But when this haughty visitor was gone, the earl covered his face with his hands, and groaned aloud. A defection perhaps even more severely felt came next. Katherine de Bonville had been the earl's favorite sister: he wrote to her at the convent to which she had retired, praying her affectionately to come to London, "and cheer his vexed spirit, and learn the true cause, not to be told by letter, which had moved him to things once farthest from his thought." The messenger came back—the letter unopened—for Katherine had left the convent, and fled into Burgundy, distrustful, as it seemed to Warwick, of her own brother. The nature of this lion-hearted man was, as we have seen, singularly kindly, frank, and affectionate; and now in the most critical, the most anxious, the most tortured period of his life, confidence and affection were forbidden

* One of the greatest obstacles to the cause of the Red Rose, was the popular belief that the young prince was not Henry's son. Had that belief not been widely spread and firmly maintained, the lords who arbitrated between Henry VI. and Richard Duke of York, in October, 1460, could scarcely have come to the resolution to set aside the Prince of Wales altogether, to accord Henry the crown for his life, and declare the Duke of York his heir. Ten years previously, (in November, 1450,) before the young prince was born or thought of, and the proposition was really just and reasonable, it was moved in the House of Commons to declare Richard Duke of York next heir to Henry, which, *at least*, by birthright, he certainly was; but the motion met with little favor, and the mover was sent to the Tower.

to him. What had he not given for one hour of the soothing company of his wife, the only being in the world to whom his pride could have communicated the grief of his heart, or the doubts of his conscience! Alas! never on earth should he hear that soft voice again! Anne, too, the gentle, child-like Anne, was afar—but *she* was happy—a basker in the brief sunshine, and blind to the darkening clouds. His elder child, with her changeful moods, added but to his disquiet and unhappiness. Next to Edward, Warwick, of all the House of York, had loved Clarence, though a closer and more domestic intimacy had weakened the affection, by lessening the esteem. But looking farther into the future, he now saw in this alliance the seeds of many a rankling sorrow. The nearer Anne and her spouse to power and fame, the more bitter the jealousy of Clarence and his wife. Thus, in the very connections which seemed most to strengthen his house, lay all which must destroy the hallowed unity and peace of family and home.

The Archbishop of York had prudently taken no part whatever in the measures that had changed the dynasty—he came now to reap the fruits: did homage to Henry VI., received the Chancellor's seals, and recommenced intrigues for the Cardinal's hat. But between the bold warrior and the wily priest, there could be but little of the endearment of brotherly confidence and love. With Montagu alone could the earl confer in cordiality and unreserve; and their similar position, and certain points of agreement in their characters, now more clearly brought out and manifest, served to make their friendship for each other firmer and more tender, in the estrangement of all other ties, than ever it had been before. But the marquis was soon compelled to depart from London, to his post as warden of the northern marches; for Warwick had not the rash presumption of Edward, and neglected no precaution against the return of the dethroned king.

So there, alone, in pomp and in power, vengeance consummated, ambition gratified, but love denied—with an aching heart and a fearless front—amidst old foes made prosperous, and old friends alienated and ruined—stood the king-maker! and, day by day, the ultimely streaks of grey showed more and more, amidst the raven curls of the strong man.

CHAPTER III.

Farther Views into the Heart of Man, and the Conditions of Power.

But woe to any man who is called to power with exaggerated expectations of his ability to do good! Woe to the man whom the populace have esteemed a popular champion, and who is suddenly made the guardian of law! The Commons of England had not bewailed the exile of the good earl simply for love of his groaning table, and admiration of his huge battle-axe—it was not merely either in pity, or from fame, that his "name had sounded in every song"—and that, to use the strong expression of the chronicler, the people "judged that the sun was clearly taken from the world when he was absent."

They knew him as one who had ever sought to correct the abuses of power—to repair the wrongs of the poor; who, even in war, had forbidden his knights to slay the common men. He was regarded, therefore, as a reformer; and wonderful, indeed, were the things, proportioned to his fame and his popularity, which he was expected to accomplish; and his thorough knowledge of the English character, and experience of every class—especially the lowest as the highest—conjoined with the vigor of his robust understanding, unquestionably enabled him, from the very first, to put a stop to the lawless violences which had disgraced the rule of Edward. The infamous spoliations of the royal purveyors ceased—the robber-like excesses of the ruder barons and gentry were severely punished—the country felt that a strong hand held the reins of power.

But what is justice, when men ask miracles! The peasant and mechanic were astonished that wages were not doubled—that bread was not to be had for asking—that the disparities of life remained the same, the rich still rich, the poor still poor. In the first days of the revolution, Sir Geoffrey Gates, the freebooter, little comprehending the earl's merciful policy, and anxious naturally to turn a victory into its accustomed fruit of rapine and pillage, placed himself at the head of an armed mob, marched from Kent to the suburbs of London, and, joined by some of the miscreants from the different Sanctuaries, burned and pillaged, ravished and slew. The earl quelled this insurrection with spirit and ease,* and great was the praise he received thereby. But all-pervading is the sympathy the poor feel for the poor! And when even the refuse of the populace once felt the sword of Warwick, some portion of the popular enthusiasm must have silently deserted him.

Robert Hilyard, who had borne so large a share in the restoration of the Lancastrians, now fixed his home in the metropolis; and anxious as ever to turn the current to the popular profit, he saw, with rage and disappointment, that as yet no party but the nobles had really triumphed. He had longed to achieve a revolution that might be called the people's; and he had abetted one that was called "the Lord's doing." The affection he had felt for Warwick arose principally from his regarding him as an instrument to prepare society for the more democratic changes he panted to effect; and, lo! he himself had been the instrument to strenghen the aristocracy. Society resettled after the storm—the noble retained his armies—the damagogue had lost his mobs! Although, through England were scattered the principles which were ultimately to destroy feudalism—to humble the fierce barons into silken lords—to reform the church—to ripen into a commonwealth, through the representative system—the principles were but in the germ; and when Hilyard mingled with the traders or the artisans of London, and sought, to form a party which might comprehend something of steady policy and definite object, he found himself regarded as a visionary fanatic by some, as a dangerous dare-devil by the rest. Strange to say, Warwick was the only man who listened to him with attention; the man behind the age, and the man before the age, ever have some inch of ground in common: both desired to increase liberty; both honestly and ardently loved the masses; but each in the spirit of his order: Warwick defended freedom as against the throne, Hilyard as against the barons. Still, notwithstanding their differences, each was so convinced of the integrity of the other, that it wanted only a foe in the field to unite them as before. The natural ally of the popular baron was the leader of the populace.

Some minor, but still serious, griefs added to the embarrassment of the earl's position. Margaret's jealousy had bound him to defer all rewards to lords and others, and encumbered with a provisional counsel all great acts of government, all grants of offices, lands, or benefits.* And who knows not the expectations of men after a successful revolution! The royal exchequer was so empty, that even the ordinary household was suspended; † and as ready money was then prodigiously scarce, the mighty revenues of Warwick barely sufficed to pay the expenses of the expedition, which, at his own cost, had restored the Lancastrians line. Hard position, both to generosity and to prudence, to put off and apologize to just claims and valiant service!

With intense, wearying, tortured anxiety, did the earl await the coming of Margaret and her son. The conditions imposed on him in their absence crippled all his resources. Several even of the Lancastrian nobles held aloof while they saw no authority but Warwick's. Above all, he relied upon the effect that the young Prince of Wales's presence, his beauty, his graciousness, his frank spirit—mild as his father's, bold as his grandsire's—would create upon all that inert and neutral mass of the public, the affection of which, once gained, makes the solid strength of a government. The very appearance of that prince would at once dispel the slander on his birth. His resemblance to his heroic grandfather would suffice to win him all the hearts by which, in absence, he was regarded as a stranger, a dubious alien. How often did the earl groan forth—"If the prince were but here, all were won!"

Henry was worse than a cipher—he was an eternal embarrassment. His good intentions, his scrupulous piety, made him ever ready to interfere. The church had got hold of him already, and prompted him to issue proclamations against the disguised Lollards, which would have lost him, at one stroke, half his subjects. This Warwick prevented, to the great discontent of the honest prince. The moment required all the prestige that an imposing presence and a splendid court could bestow. And Henry, glad of the poverty of his exchequer, deemed it a sin to make a parade of earthly glory. "Heaven will punish

* Hall, Habington.

* Sharon Turner.

† See Ellis's *Original Letters*, from Harleian MSS., second series, vol. i., letter 42.

me again," said he, meekly, "if, just delivered from a dungeon, I gild my unworthy self with all the vanities of perishable power."

There was not a department which the chill of this poor king's virtue did not somewhat benumb. The gay youths, who had revelled in the alluring court of Edward IV., heard with disdainful mockery, the grave lectures of Henry on the length of their lovelocks and the beakers of their shoes. The brave warriors presented to him for praise were entertained with homilies on the guilt of war. Even poor Adam was molested and invaded by Henry's pious apprehensions that he was seeking, by vain knowledge, to be superior to the will of Providence.

Yet, albeit perpetually irritating and chafing the impetuous spirit of the earl, the earl, strange to say, loved the king more and more. This perfect innocence, this absence from guile and self-seeking, in the midst of an age never excelled for fraud, falsehood, and selfish simulation, moved Warwick's admiration as well as pity. Whatever contrasted Edward IV. had a charm for him. He schooled his hot temper, and softened his deep voice, in that holy presence; and the intimate persuasion of the hollowness of all worldly greatness, which worldly greatness itself had forced upon the earl's mind, made something congenial between the meek saint and the fiery warrior. For the hundredth time groaned Warwick, as he quitted Henry's presence—

"Would that my gallant son-in-law were come! his spirit will soon learn how to govern, then Warwick may be needed no more! I am weary—sore weary of the task of ruling men!"

"Holy St. Thomas!" bluntly exclaimed Marmaduke, to whom these sad words were said—"whenever you visit the king, you come back—pardon me, my lord—half unmanned. He would make a monk of you!"

"Ah!" said Warwick, thoughtfully—"there have been greater marvels than that. Our boldest fathers often died the meekest shavelings. An' I had ruled this realm as long as Henry,—nay, an' this same life I lead now were to continue two years, with its broil and fever, I could well conceive the sweetness of the cloister and repose. How sits the wind? Against them still—against them still! I cannot bear this suspense!"

The winds had ever seemed malignant to Margaret of Anjou, but never more than now. So long a continuance of stormy and adverse weather was never known in the memory of man; and we believe that it has scarcely its parallel in history.

The earl's promise to restore King Henry was fulfilled in October. From November to the following April, Margaret with the young and royal pair, and the Countess of Warwick, lay at the sea-side, waiting for a wind.* Thrice, in defiance of all warnings from the mariners of Harfleur did she put to sea, and thrice was she driven back on the coast of Normandy—her ships much damaged. Her friends protested that this malice of the elements was caused by sorcery †—a belief which gained ground in England, exhilarated the Duchess of Bedford, and gave new fame to Bungey who arrogated all the merit, and whose weather wisdom, indeed, had here borne out his predictions. Many besought Margaret not to tempt Providence, nor to trust the sea; but the queen was firm to her purpose, and her son laughed at omens—yet still the vessels could only leave the harbor to be driven back upon the land.

Day after day, the first question of Warwick, when the sun rose, was, "How sets the wind?" Night after night, ere he retired to rest—"Ill sets the wind!" sighed the earl. The gales that forbade the coming of the royal party, sped to the unwilling lingerers—courier after courier—envoy after envoy, and at length Warwick, unable to bear the sickening suspense at distance, went himself to Dover,‡ and from its white cliffs looked, hour by hour, for the sails which were to bear 'Lancaster and its fortunes.' The actual watch grew more intolerable than the distant expectation, and the earl sorrowfully departed to his castle of Warwick, at which Isabel and Clarence then were. Alas! where the old smile of home?

CHAPTER IV.

The Return of Edward of York.

AND the winds still blew, and storm was on the tide, and Margaret came not; when, in the

* FABYAN, 502.
† HALL. *Warkworth Chronicle.*
‡ HALL.

gusty month of March, the fishermen of the Humber beheld a single ship, without flag or pennon, and sorely stripped and rivelled by adverse blasts, gallantly struggling towards the shore. The vessel was not of English build, and resembled, in its bulk and fashion, those employed by the Easterlings in their trade;—half merchantman, half war-ship.

The villagers of Ravenspur—the creek of which, the vessel now rapidly made to—imagining that it was some trading craft in distress, grouped round the banks, and some put out their boats. But the vessel held on its way, and, as the water was swelled by the tide, and unusually deep, silently cast anchor close ashore, a quarter of a mile from the crowd.

The first who leapt on land, was a knight of lofty stature, and in complete armor, richly inlaid with gold arabesques. To him succeeded another, also in mail, and, though well-built and fair-proportioned, of less imposing presence. And then, one by one, the womb of the dark ship gave forth a number of armed soldiers, infinitely larger than it could have been supposed to contain, till the knight, who first landed, stood the centre of a group of five hundred men. Then, were lowered from the vessel, barbed and caparisoned, some five score horses; and, finally, the sailors and rowers, armed but with steel caps and short swords, came on shore, till not a man was left on board.

"Now praise," said the chief knight, "to God and St. George, that we have escaped the water! and not with invisible winds, but with bodily foes must our war be waged."

"*Beau sire*," cried one knight who had debarked immediately after the speaker, and who seemed, from his bearing and equipment, of higher rank than those that followed—"beau sire, this is a slight army to reconquer a king's realm! Pray Heaven, that our bold companions have also escaped the deep!"

"Why verily, we are not eno,' at the best, to spare one man," said the chief knight gaily, but, lo! we are not without welcomers." And he pointed to the crowd of villagers who now slowly neared the warlike group, but halting at a little distance, continued to gaze at them in some anxiety and alarm.

"Ho there! good fellows!" cried the leader, striding towards the throng—"what name give you to this village?"

"Ravenspur, please your worship," answered one of the peasants."

"Ravenspur — hear you that, lords and friends? Accept the omen! On this spot landed, from exile, Henry of Bolingbroke, known, afterwards, in our annals as King Henry IV.! Bare is the soil of corn and of trees—it disdains meaner fruit; it *grows kings!* Hark!"— The sound of a bugle was heard at a little distance, and in a few moments, a troop of about a hundred men were seen rising above an undulation in the ground, and as the two bands recognized each other, a shout of joy was given and returned.

As this new reinforcement advanced, the peasantry and fishermen, attracted by curiosity and encouraged by the peaceable demeanor of the debarkers, drew nearer, and mingled with the first comers.

"What manner of men, be ye, and what want ye?" asked one of the bystanders, who seemed of better nurturing than the rest, and who, indeed, was a small franklin.

No answer was returned by those he more immediately addressed, but the chief knight heard the question, and suddenly unbuckling his helmet, and giving it to one of those beside him, he turned to the crowd a countenance of singular beaury, at once animated and majestic, and said, in a loud voice, "We are Englishmen, like you, and we come here to claim our rights. Ye seem tall fellows and honest. Standard-bearer, unfurl our flag!" And, as the ensign suddenly displayed the device of a sun, in a field azure, the chief continued, "March under this banner, and for every day ye serve, ye shall have a month's hire."

"Marry!" quoth the franklin, with a suspicious, sinister look, "these be big words. And who are you, sir knight, who would levy men in King Henry's kingdom?"

"Your knees, fellows!" cried the second knight. "Behold your true liege and suzerain, Edward IV.! Long live King Edward!"

The soldiers caught up the cry, and it was re-echoed lustily by the smaller detachment that now reached the spot; but no answer came from the crowd. They looked at each other in dismay, and retreated rapidly from their place amongst the troops. In fact the whole of the neighboring district was devoted to Warwick, and many of the peasantry about had joined the former rising under Sir John

Coniers. The franklin alone retreated not with the rest; he was a bluff, plain, bold fellow, with good English blood in his veins. And when the shout ceased, he said, shortly, "We, hereabouts, know no king but King Henry. We fear you would impose upon us. We cannot believe that a great lord like him you call Edward IV. would land, with a handful of men, to encounter the armies of Lord Warwick. We forewarn you to get into your ship, and go back as fast as ye came, for the stomach of England is sick of brawls and blows; and what ye devise is treason!"

Forth from the new detachment stepped a youth of small stature, not in armor, and with many a weather stain on his gorgeous dress. He laid his hand upon the franklin's shoulder, "Honest and plain-dealing fellow," said he, "you are right: pardon the foolish outburst of these brave men, who cannot forget as yet that their chief has worn the crown. We come back not to disturb this realm, nor to affect aught against King Henry, whom the saints have favored. No, by St. Paul, we come but back to claim our lands unjustly forfeit. My noble brother here is not king of England, since the people will it not, but he *is* Duke of York, and he will be contented if assured of the style and lands our father left him. For me, called Richard of Gloucester, I ask nothing, but leave to spend my manhood where I have spent my youth, under the eyes of my renowned godfather, Richard Nevile, Earl of Warwick. So report of us. Whither leads yon road?"

"To York," said the franklin, softened, despite his judgment, by the irresistible suavity of the voice that addressed him.

"Thither will we go, my lord duke and brother, with your leave," said Prince Richard, "peaceably and as petitioners. God save ye, friends and countrymen, pray for us, that King Henry and the parliament may do us justice. We are not over rich now, but better times may come. Largess!" and filling both hands with coins from his gipsire, he tossed the bounty among the peasants.

"*Mille tonnere!* What means he with this humble talk of King Henry and the parliament?" whispered Edward to the Lord Say, while the crowd scrambled for the largess, and Richard smilingly mingled amongst them, and conferred with the franklin.

"Let him alone, I pray you, my liege; I guess his wise design. And now for our ships. What orders for the master?"

"For the other vessels let them sail or anchor as they list. But for the bark that has borne Edward king of England to the land of his ancestors there is no return!"

The royal adventurer then beckoned the Flemish master of the ship, who, with every sailor aboard, had debarked, and the loose dresses of the mariners made a strong contrast to the mail of the warriors with whom they mingled.

"Friend!" said Edward, in French, "thou hast said that thou wilt share my fortunes, and that thy good fellows are no less free of courage and leal in trust."

"It is so, sire. Not a man who has gazed on thy face, and heard thy voice, but longs to serve one on whose brow Nature has written *king*."

"And trust me," said Edward, "no prince of my blood shall be dearer to me than you and yours, my friends in danger and in need. And sith it be so, the ship that hath borne such hearts and such hopes should, in sooth, know no meaner freight. Is all prepared?"

"Yes, sire, as you ordered. The train is laid for the brennen."

"Up, then, with the fiery signal, and let it tell, from cliff to cliff, from town to town, that Edward the Plantagenet, once returned to England, leaves it but for the grave!"

The master bowed, and smiled grimly. The sailors, who had been prepared for the burning, arranged before between the master and the prince, and whose careless hearts Edward had thoroughly won to his person and his cause, followed the former towards the ship, and stood silently grouped around the shore. The soldiers, less inforned, gazed idly on, and Richard now regained Edward's side.

"Reflect," he said, as he drew him apart, "that, when on this spot landed Henry of Bolingbroke, he *gave not out that he was marching to the throne of Richard II.* He professed but to claim his duchy—and men were influenced by justice, till they became agents of ambition. This be your policy:—with two thousand men you are but Dukeof York; with ten thousand men you are King of England! In passing hither, I met with many, and sounding the temper of the district, I find it not ripe to share your hazard. The world soon ripens when it hath to hail success!"

"O young boy's smooth face!—O old man's deep brain!" said Edward, admiringly—"what a king hadst *thou* made!"

A sudden flush passed over the prince's pale cheek, and, ere it died away, a flaming torch was hurled aloft in the air—it fell whirling into into the ship—a moment, and a loud crash—a moment, and a mighty blaze! Up sprung from the deck, along the sails, the sheeted fire—

"A giant beard of flame."*

It reddened the coast—the skies from far and near;—it glowed on the faces and the steel of the scanty army—it was seen, miles away, by the warders of many a castle manned with the troops of Lancaster;—it brought the steed from the stall, the courier to the selle;—it sped, as of old the beacon fire that announced to Clytemnestra the return of the Argive king. From post to post rode the fiery news, till it reached Lord Warwick in his hall, King Henry in his palace, Elizabeth in her sanctuary. The iron step of the dauntless Edward was once more pressed upon the soil of England.

CHAPTER V.

The Progress of the Plantagenet.

A FEW words suffice to explain the formidable arrival we have just announced. Though the Duke of Burgundy had, by public proclamation, forbidden his subjects to aid the exiled Edward; yet, whether moved by the entreaties of his wife, or wearied by the remonstances of his brother-in-law, he at length privately gave the dethroned monarch 50,000 florins to find troops for himself, and secretly hired Flemish and Dutch vessels to convey him to England.† But, so small was the force to which the bold Edward trusted his fortunes, that it almost seemed as if Burgundy sent him forth to his destruction. He sailed from the coast of Zealand: the winds, if less unmanageable than those that blew off the seaport where Margaret and her armament awaited a favoring breeze, were still adverse. Scared from the coast of Norfolk by the vigilance of Warwick and Oxford, who had filled that district with armed men, storm and tempest drove him at last to Humber Head, where we have seen him land, and whence we pursue his steps.

The little band set out upon its march, and halted for the night at a small village two miles inland. Some of the men were then sent out on horseback, for news of the other vessels, that bore the remnant of the invading force. These had, fortunately, effected a landing in various places; and, before daybreak, Anthony Woodville, and the rest of the troops, had joined the leader of an enterprise that seemed but the rashness of despair, for its utmost force, including the few sailors allured to the adventurer's standard, was about two thousand men.* Close and anxious was the consultation then held. Each of the several detachments reported alike of the sullen indifference of the population, which each had sought to excite in favor of Edward. Light riders † were dispatched in various directions, still farther to sound the neighborhood. All returned ere noon, some bruised and maltreated by the stones and staves of the rustics, and not a voice had been heard to echo the cry—"Long live King Edward!" The profound sagacity of Gloucester's guileful counsel was then unanimously recognized. Richard dispatched a secret letter to Clarence; and it was resolved immediately to proceed to York, and to publish everywhere along the road that the fugitive had returned but to claim his private heritage, and remonstrate with the parliament which had awarded the Duchy of York to Clarence, his younger brother.

"Such a power," saith the Chronicle, "hath justice ever among men, that all, moved by mercy or compassion, began either to favor or not to resist him." And so, wearing the Lancastrian Prince of Wales's cognizance of the ostrich feather, crying out as they marched—"Long live King Henry," the hardy liars, four days after their debarkation, arrived at the gates of York.

Here, not till after much delay and negotiation, Edward was admitted only as Duke of

---

* Φλογὸς μεγαν πωγωνα.
Æsch. Agam., 314.

† COMINES. HALL. LINGARD. S. TURNER.

* Fifteen hundred, according to the Croyland historian.

† HALL.

York, and upon condition that he would swear to be a faithful and loyal servant to King Henry; and at the gate by which he was to enter, Edward actually took that oath, "a priest being bye to say mass in the mass tyme, receiving the body of our Blessed Saviour!" *

Edward tarried not long in York; he pushed forward. Two great nobles guarded those districts—Montagu; and the Earl of Northumberland, to whom Edward had restored his lands and titles, and who, on condition of retaining them, had re-entered the service of Lancaster. This last, a true server of the times, who had sided with all parties, now judged it discreet to remain neutral. † But Edward must pass within a few miles of Pontefract Castle, where Montagu lay with a force that could destroy him at a blow. Edward was prepared for the assault, but trusted to deceive the marquis, as he had deceived the citizens of York; the more for the strong personal love Montagu had ever shown him. If not, he was prepared equally to die in the field, rather than eat again the bitter bread of the exile. But to his inconceivable joy and astonishment, Montagu, like Northumberland, lay idle and supine. Edward and his little troop threaded safely the formidable pass.

Alas! Montagu had that day received a formal order from the Duke of Clarence, as co-protector of the realm,‡ to suffer Edward to march on, provided his force was small, and he had taken the oaths to Henry, and assumed but the title of Duke of York, "for your brother the earl hath had compunctious visitings, and would fain forgive what hath passed, for my father's sake, and unite all factions by Edward's voluntary abdication of the throne—at all hazards, I am on my way northward, and you will not fight till I come." The marquis, who knew the conscientious doubts which Warwick had entertained in his darker hours, who had no right to disobey the co-protector, who knew no reason to suspect Lord Warwick's son-in-law, and who, moreover, was by no means anxious to be, himself, the executioner of Edward whom he had once so truly loved, —though a little marvelling at Warwick's softness, yet did not discredit the letter, and the less regarded the free passage he left to the returned exiles, from contempt for the smallness of their numbers, and his persuasion that if the earl saw fit to alter his counsels, Edward was still more in his power the farther he advanced amidst a hostile population, and towards the armies which the Lords Exeter and Oxford were already mustering.

But that free passage was everything to Edward! It made men think that Montagu, as well as Northumberland, favored his enterprise; that the hazard was less rash and hopeless than it had seemed; that Edward counted upon finding his most powerful allies among those falsely supposed to be his enemies. The popularity Edward had artfully acquired amongst the captains of Warwick's own troops, on the march to Middleham, now bested him. Many of them were knights and gentlemen residing in the very districts through which he passed. They did not join him, but they did not oppose. Then, rapidly flocked to "the Sun of York,"—first, the adventurers and condottieri, who in civil war adopt any side for pay; next came the disappointed, the ambitious, and the needy. The hesitating began to resolve, the neutral to take a part. From the state of petitioners supplicating a pardon, every league the Yorkists marched advanced them to the dignity of assertors of a cause. Doncaster first, then Nottingham, then Leicester—true to the town spirit we have before described—opened their gates to the trader prince.

Oxford and Exeter reached Newark with their force. Edward marched on them at

---

* HALL.

† This is the most favorable interpretation of his conduct; according to some he was in correspondence with Edward, who showed his letters.

‡ Our historians have puzzled their brains in ingenious conjectures of the cause of Montagu's fatal supineness at this juncture, and have passed over the only probable solution of the mystery, which is to be found simply enough stated thus in Stowe's Chronicle: —"The Marquess Montacute would have fought with King Edward, but that *he had received letters from the Duke of Clarence that he should not fight till hee came.*" This explanation is borne out by the Warkworth Chronicler and others, who, in an evident mistake of the person addressed, state that Clarence wrote word *to Warwick* not to fight till he came. Clarence could not have written so to Warwick, who, according to all authorities, was mustering his troops near London, and not in the way to fight Edward; nor could Clarence have had authority to issue such commands to his colleague, nor would his colleague have attended to them, since we have the amplest testimony that Warwick was urging all his captains to attack Edward at once. The duke's order was, therefore, clearly addressed to Montagu.

once. Deceived as to his numbers, they took panic and fled. When once the foe flies, friends ever start up from the very earth! Hereditary partisans—gentlemen, knights, and nobles—now flocked fast round the adventurer. Then came Lovell, and Cromwell, and D'Eyncourt, ever true to York; and Stanley, never true to any cause. Then came, the brave knights Parr and Norris, and De Burgh; and no less than three thousand retainers belonging to Lord Hastings—the new man—obeyed the summons of his couriers and joined their chief at Liecester.

Edward of March, who had landed at Ravenspur with a handful of brigands, now saw a king's army under his banner.* Then, the audacious perjurer threw away the mask; then, forth went—not the prayer of the attainted Duke of York—but the proclamation of the indignant king. England now beheld *two* sovereigns, equal in their armies. It was no longer a rebellion to be crushed; it was a dynasty to be decided.

CHAPTER VI.

Lord Warwick, with the Foe in the Field and the Traitor at the Hearth.

EVERY precaution which human wisdom could foresee, had Lord Warwick taken to guard against invasion, or to crush it at the onset.† All the coasts on which it was most probable Edward would land had been strongly guarded. And if the Humber had been left without regular troops, it was because prudence might calculate that the very spot where Edward did land was the very last he would have selected—unless guided by fate to his destruction—in the midst of an unfriendly population, and in face of the armies of Northumberland and of Montagu. The moment the earl heard of Edward's reception at York—far from the weakness which the false Clarence (already in correspondence with Gloucester) imputed to him—he despatched to Montagu, by Marmaduke Nevile, peremptory orders to intercept Edward's path, and give him battle before he could advance farther towards the centre of the island. We shall explain presently why this messenger did not reach the marquis. But Clarence was some hours before him in his intelligence and his measures.

When the earl next heard that Edward had passed Pontefract with impunity, and had reached Doncaster, he flew first to London, to arrange for its defence; consigned the care of Henry to the Archbishop of York, mustered a force already quartered in the neighborhood of the metropolis, and then marched rapidly back towards the Coventry, where he had left Clarence with seven thousand men; while he dispatched new messengers to Montagu and Northumberland, severely rebuking the former for his supineness, and ordering him to march in all haste to attack Edward in the rear. The earl's activity, promptitude, and all-provident generalship, form a mournful contrast to the errors, the pusillanimity, and the treachery of others, which hitherto, as we have seen, made all his wisest schemes abortive. Despite Clarence's sullenness, Warwick had discovered no reason, as yet, to doubt his good faith. The oath he had taken—not only to Henry, in London, but to Warwick, at Amboise—had been the strongest which can bind man to man. If the duke had not gained all he had hoped, he had still much to lose and much to dread by desertion to Edward. He had been the loudest in bold assertions when he heard of the invasion; and above all, Isabel, whose influence over Clarence, at that time, the earl overrated, had, at the tidings of so imminent a danger to her father, forgot all her displeasure and recovered all her tenderness.

During Warwick's brief absence, Isabel had, indeed, exerted her utmost power to repair her former wrongs, and induce Clarence to be faithful to his oath. Although her inconsistency and irresolution had much weakened her

---

* The perplexity and confusion which involve the annals of this period may be guessed by this—that two historians, eminent for research, (Lingard and Sharon Turner,) differ so widely as to the numbers who had now joined Edward, that Lingard asserts that at Nottingham he was at the head of fifty or sixty thousand men; and Turner gives him, at the most, between six and seven thousand. The latter seems nearer to the truth. We must here regret, that Turner's partiality to the House of York induces him to slur over Edward's detestable perjury at York, and to accumulate all rhetorical arts to command admiration for his progress—to the prejudice of the salutary moral horror we ought to feel for the atrocious perfidy and violation of oath to which he owed the first impunity that secured the after triumph.

† HALL.

influence with the duke, for natures like his are governed but by the ascendancy of a steady and tranquil will, yet still she so far prevailed, that the duke had despatched to Richard a secret courier, informing him that he had finally resolved not to desert his father-in-law.

This letter reached Gloucester as the invaders were on their march to Conventry, before the strong walls of which, the Duke of Clarence lay encamped. Richard, after some intent and silent reflection, beckoned to him his familiar Catesby.

"Marmaduke Nevile, whom our scouts seized on his way to Pontefract, is safe and in the rear?"

"Yes, my lord; prisoners but encumber us; shall I give orders to the provost to end his captivity?"

"Ever ready, Catesby!" said the duke, with a fell smile. "No—harkye, Clarence vacillates; if he hold firm to Warwick, and the two forces fight honestly against us, we are lost; on the other hand, if Clarence join us, his defection will bring not only the men he commands, all of whom are the retainers of the York lands and duchy, and therefore free from peculiar bias to the earl, and easily lured back to their proper chief; but it will set an example that will create such distrust and panic amongst the enemy, and give such hope of fresh desertions to our own men, as will open to us the keys of the metropolis. But Clarence, I say, vacillates; look you, here is his letter from Amboise to King Edward; see, his duchess, Warwick's very daughter, approves the promise it contains! If this letter reach Warwick, and Clarence knows it is in hand, George will have no option but to join us. He will never dare to face the earl, his pledge to Edward once revealed——"

"Most true; a very legal subtlety, my lord," said the lawyer Catesby, admiringly.

"You can serve us in this. Fall back; join Sir Marmaduke; affect to sympathize with him; affect to side with the earl; affect to make terms for Warwick's amity and favor; affect to betray us; affect to have stolen this letter. Give it to young Nevile, artfully effect his escape, as if against our knowledge, and commend him to lose not an hour—a moment—in gaining the earl, and giving him so important a forewarning of the meditated treason of his son-in-law."

"I will do all: I comprehend: but how will the duke learn in time that the letter is on its way to Warwick?"

"I will see the duke, in his own tent."

"And how shall I effect Sir Marmaduke's escape?"

"Send hither the officer who guards the prisoner; I will give him orders to obey thee in all things."

The invaders marched on. The earl, meanwhile, had reached Warwick,—hastened thence, to throw himself into the stronger fortifications of the neighboring Coventy, without the walls of which Clarence was still encamped; Edward advanced on the town of Warwick thus vacated; and Richard, at night, rode alone to the camp of Clarence.*

The next day, the earl was employed in giving orders to his lieutenants to march forth, join the troops of his son-in-law, who were a mile from the walls, and advance upon Edward, who had that morning quitted Warwick town—when, suddenly, Sir Marmaduke Nevile rushed into his presence, and, faltering out—"Beware, beware!" placed in his hands the fatal letter which Clarence had despatched from Amboise.

Never did blow more ruthless fall upon man's heart! Clarence's perfidy—*that* might be disdained, but the closing lines, which revealed a daughter's treachery—words cannot express the father's anguish.

The letter dropped from his hand, a stupor seized his senses, and, ere yet recovered, pale men hurried into his presence to relate how, amidst joyous trumpets and streaming banners, Richard of Gloucester had lead the Duke of Clarence to the brotherly embrace of Edward.†

Breaking from these messengers of evil news, that could not now surprise, the earl strode on, alone, to his daughter's chamber.

He placed the letter in her hands, and folding his arms, said—"What sayest thou of this, Isabel of Clarence?"

* HALL, and others.

† HALL. The chronicler adds—"It was no marvell that the Duke of Clarence, with so small persuasion and less exhorting, turned from the Earl of Warwick's party, for, as you have heard before, *this marchindise* was labored, conducted, and concluded by a damsell, when the duke was in the French Court, to the earl's utter confusion." Hume makes a notable mistake in deferring the date of Clarence's desertion to the Battle of Barnet.

The terror, the shame, the remorse, that seized upon the wretched lady—the death-like lips—the suppressed shriek—the momentary torpor, succeeded by the impulse which made her fall at her father's feet, and clasp his knees—told the earl, if he had before doubted, that the letter lied not—that Isabel had known and sanctioned its contents.

He gazed on her (as she grovelled at his feet) with a look that her eyes did well to shun.

"Curse me not—curse me not!"—cried Isabel, awed by his very silence. "It was but a brief frenzy. Evil counsel—evil passion! I was maddened that my boy had lost a crown. I repented—I repented—Clarence shall yet be true. He hath promised it—vowed it to me;—hath written to Gloucester to retract all—to——"

"Woman!—Clarence is in Edward's camp!"

Isabel started to her feet, and uttered a shriek so wild and despairing, that at least it gave to her father's lacerated heart the miserable solace of believing the *last* treason had not been shared. A softer expression—one of pity, if not of pardon—stole over his dark face.

"I curse thee not," he said, "I rebuke thee not. Thy sin hath its own penance. Ill omen broods on the hearth of the household traitor! never more shalt thou see holy love in a husband's smile. His kiss shall have the taint of Judas. From his arms thou shalt start with horror, as from those of thy wronged father's betrayer—perchance his deathsman! Ill omen broods on the cradle of the child for whom a mother's ambition was but a daughter's perfidy. Woe to thee, wife and mother! Even my forgiveness cannot avert thy doom!"

"Kill me—kill me!" exclaimed Isabel, springing towards him; but seeing his face averted, his arms folded on his breast—that noble breast, never again her shelter—she fell lifeless on the floor.*

The earl looked round, to see that none were by to witness his weakness, took her gently in his arms, laid her on her couch, and, bending over her a moment, prayed God to pardon her.

He then hastily left the room—ordered her handmaids and her litter, and while she was yet unconscious, the gates of the town opened, and forth through the arch went the closed and curtained vehicle which bore the ill-fated duchess to the new home her husband had made with her father's foe! The earl watched it from the casement of his tower, and said to himself,—

"I had been unmanned had I known her within the same walls. Now for ever I dismiss her memory and her crime. Treachery hath done its worst, and my soul is proof against all storms!"

At night came messengers from Clarence and Edward, who had returned to Warwick town, with offers of *pardon* to the earl—with promises of favor, power, and grace. To Edward, the earl deigned no answer; to the messenger of Clarence he gave this—"Tell thy master, I had liefer be always like myself, than like a false and a perjured duke, and that I am determined never to leave the war till I have lost my own life, or utterly extinguished and put down my foes."*

After this terrible defection, neither his remaining forces, nor the panic amongst them which the duke's desertion had occasioned, nor the mighty interests involved in the success of his arms, nor the irretrievable advantage which even an engagement of equivocal result with the earl in person, would give to Edward, justified Warwick in gratifying the anticipations of the enemy,—that his valor and wrath would urge him into immediate and imprudent battle.

Edward, after the vain bravado of marching up to the walls of Coventry, moved on towards London. Thither the earl sent Marmaduke, enjoining the Archbishop of York and the lord mayor but to hold out the city for three

* As our narrative does not embrace the future fate of the Duchess of Clarence, the reader will pardon us if we remind him that her firstborn (who bore his illustrious grandfather's tittle of Earl of Warwick), was cast into prison, on the accession of Henry VII., and afterwards beheaded by that king. By birth he was the rightful heir to the throne. The ill-fated Isabel died young (five years after the date at which our tale has arrived). One of her female attendants was tried and executed on the charge of having poisoned her. Clarence lost no time in seeking to supply her place. He solicited the hand of Mary of Burgundy, sole daughter and heir of Charles the Bold. Edward's jealousy and fear forbade him to listen to an alliance that might, as Lingard observes, enable Clarence "to employ the power of Burgundy to win the crown of England;" and hence arose those dissensions which ended in the secret murder of the perjured duke.

* HALL,

days, and he would come to their aid with such a force as would ensure lasting triumph. For, indeed, already were hurrying to his banner, Montagu, burning to retrieve his error—Oxford and Exeter, recovered from, and chafing at, their past alarm. Thither his nephew, Fitzhugh, led the earl's own clansmen of Middleham; thither were spurring Somerset from the west, * and Sir Thomas Dymoke from Lincolnshire, and the Knight of Lytton, with his hardy retainers, from the Peak. Bold Hilyard waited not far from London, with a host of mingled yeomen and bravos, reduced, as before, to discipline under his own sturdy energies, and the military craft of Sir John Coniers. If London would but hold out till these forces could unite, Edward's destruction was still inevitable.

* Most historians state that Somerset was then in London; but Sharon Turner quotes Harleian MSS., 38, to show that he had left the metropolis "to raise an army from the western counties," and ranks him amongst the generals at the battle of Barnet.

BOOK TWELFTH.

THE BATTLE OF BARNET.

CHAPTER I.

A King in his City hopes to Recover his Realm—A Woman in her chamber fears to Forfeit Her Own.

EDWARD and his army reached St. Albans. Great commotion—great joy were in the Sanctuary of Westminster! The Jerusalem Chamber, therein, was made the high council hall of the friends of York. Great commotion, great terror were in the city of London—timid Master Stokton had been elected mayor; horribly frightened either to side with an Edward or a Henry, timid Master Stokton feigned or fell ill, Sir Thomas Cook, a wealthy and influential citizen, and a member of the House of Commons, had been appointed deputy in his stead. Sir Thomos Cook took fright also, and ran away.* The power of the city thus fell into the hands of Ursewike, the Recorder, a zealous Yorkist. Great commotion, great scorn, were in the breasts of the populace, as the Archbishop of York, hoping thereby to rekindle their loyalty, placed King Henry on horseback, and paraded him through the streets, from Chepeside to Walbrook, from Walbrook to St. Paul's; for the news of Edward's arrival, and the sudden agitation and excitement it produced on his enfeebled frame, had brought upon the poor king one of the epileptic attacks to which he had been subject from childhood, and which made the cause of his frequent imbecility; and, just recovered from such a fit—his eyes vacant—his face haggard—his head drooping, the spectacle of such an antagonist to the vigorous Edward, moved only pity in the few, and ridicule in the many.

* FABYAN.

Two thousand Yorkist gentlemen were in the various Sanctuaries; aided and headed by the Earl of Essex, they came forth armed and clamorous, scouring the streets, and shouting, "King Edward!" with impunity. Edward's popularity in London was heightened amongst the merchants by prudent reminiscences of the vast debts he had incurred, which his victory only could ever enable him to repay to his good citizens.* The women, always, in such a moment, active partisans, and useful, deserted their hearths to canvas all strong arms and stout hearts for the handsome woman-lover.† The Yorkist Archbishop of Canterbury did his best with the ecclesiastics,—the Yorkist Recorder his best with the flat-caps. Alwyn, true to his anti-feudal principles, animated all the young freemen to support the merchant king—the favorer of commerce—*the man of his age!* The city authorities began to yield to their own and the general metropolitan predilections. But still the Archbishop of York had six thousand soldiers at his disposal, and London could be yet saved to Warwick, if the prelate acted with energy, and zeal, and good faith. That such was his first intention is clear, from his appeal to the public loyalty in King Henry's procession; but when he perceived how little effect that pageant had produced—when, on re-entering the Bishop of London's palace, he saw before him the guileless, helpless puppet of contending factions, gasping for breath, scarcely able to articulate, the heartless prelate turned away, with a muttered ejaculation of contempt:—

"Clarence had not deserted," said he to himself, "unless he saw greater profit with

* COMINES. † Ibid.

King Edward!" And then he began to commune with himself, and to commune with his brother-prelate of Canterbury; and in the midst of all this commune arrived Catesby, charged with messages to the archbishop from Edward—messages full of promise and affection on the one hand—of menace and revenge upon the other. Brief,—Warwick's cup of bitterness had not yet been filled; that night the archbishop and the mayor of London met, and the Tower was surrendered to Edward's friends;—the next day Edward and his army entered, amidst the shouts of the populace—rode to St. Paul's where the archbishop* met him, leading Henry by the hand, again a captive; thence Edward proceeded to Westminster Abbey, and, fresh from his atrocious perjury at York, offered thanksgivings for its success. The Sanctuary yielded up its royal fugitives, and, in joy and in pomp, Edward led his wife and her new-born babe, with Jacquetta and his elder children, to Baynard's Castle.

The next morning (the third day), true to his promise, Warwick marched towards London with the mighty armament he had now collected. Treason had done its work—the metropolis was surrendered, and King Henry in the Tower.

"These things considered," says the chronicler, "the earl saw that all calculations of necessity were brought to this end,—that they must now be committed to the hazard and chance of one battle." † He halted, therefore, at St. Alban's, to rest his troops; and marching thence towards Barnet, pitched his tents on the upland ground, then called the Heath or Chase of Gladsmoor, and waited the coming foe.

Nor did Edward linger long from that stern meeting. Entering London on the 11th of April, he prepared to quit it on the 13th. Besides the force he had brought with him he had now recruits in his partisans from the Sanctuaries and other hiding-places in the metropolis, while London furnished him, from her high-spirited youths, a gallant troop of bow and billmen, whom Alwyn had enlisted, and to whom Edward willingly appointed, as captain, Alwyn himself;—who had atoned for his submission to Henry's restoration by such signal activity on behalf of the young king, whom he associated with the interests of his class, and the weal of the great commercial city, which some years afterwards rewarded his affection by electing him to her chief magistracy.*

It was on that very day, the 13th of April, some hours before the departure of the York army, that Lord Hastings entered the Tower, to give orders relative to the removal of the unhappy Henry, whom Edward had resolved to take with him on his march.

And as he had so ordered, and was about to return, Alwyn, emerging from one of the interior courts, approached him in much agitation, and said thus—"Pardon me, my lord, if in so grave an hour I recall your attention to one you may haply have forgotten."

"Ah, the poor maiden; but you told me, in the hurried words that we have already interchanged, that she was safe and well."

"Safe, my lord—not well. Oh, hear me. I depart to battle for your cause and your king's. A gentleman in your train has advised me that you are married to a noble dame in the foreign land. If so, this girl whom I have loved so long and truly, may yet forget you—may yet be mine. Oh, give me that hope, to make me a braver soldier."

"But," said Hastings, embarrassed, and with a changing countenance, "but time presses, and I know not where the demoiselle——"

"She is here," interrupted Alwyn; "here, within these walls—in yonder court-yard. I have just left her. *You*, whom she loves, forgot her! *I*, whom she disdains, remembered. I went to see to her safety—to counsel her to rest here for the present, whatever betides: and, at every word I said, she broke in upon me but with one name—that name was thine! And when stung, and in the impulse of the moment, I exclaimed,—'He deserves not this devotion. They tell me, Sibyll, that Lord Hastings has found a wife in exile'—oh, that look! that cry! they haunt me still. 'Prove

* SHARON TURNER. It is a comfort to think that this archbishop was, two years afterwards, first robbed, and then imprisoned by Edward IV., nor did he recover his liberty till a few weeks before his death, in 1476 (five years subsequently to the battle of Barnet.)

† HALL.

* Nicholas Alwyn, the representative of that generation which aided the commercial and antifeudal policy of Edward IV. and Richard III., and welcomed its consummation under their Tudor successor, rose to be Lord Mayor of London in the fifteenth year of the reign of Henry VII.—FABYAN.

it—prove it, Alwyn,' she cried, 'And—' I interrupted, 'and thou couldst yet, for thy father's sake, be true wife to me?'"

"Her answer, Alwyn?"

"It was this—'For my father's sake, only, then, could I live on; and—' her sobs stopped her speech, till she cried again, "I believe it not! thou hast deceived me. Only from his lips will I hear the sentence.' Go to her, manfully and frankly, as becomes you, high lord—go! It is but a single sentence thou hast to say, and thy heart will be the lighter, and thine arm the stronger, for those honest words."

Hastings pulled his cap over his brow, and stood a moment as if in reflection; he then said, "Show me the way; thou art right. It is due to her and to thee; and as, by this hour to-morrow, my soul may stand before the judgment seat, that poor child's pardon may take one sin from the large account."

CHAPTER II.

Sharp is the kiss of the Falcon's beak.

HASTINGS stood in the presence of the girl to whom he had pledged his troth. They were alone; but in the next chamber might be heard the peculiar sound made by the mechanism of the Eureka. Happy and lifeless mechanism, which moves, and toils, and strives on, to change the destiny of millions, but hath neither ear, nor eye, nor sense, nor heart—the avenues of pain to man! She had—yes, literally—she had recognized her lover's step upon the stair, she had awakened at once from that dull and icy lethargy with which the words of Alwyn had chained life and soul. She sprang forward as Hastings entered—she threw herself, in delirious joy, upon his bosom. "Thou art come—thou art! It is not true—not true. Heaven bless thee!—thou art come!" But sudden as the movement, was the recoil. Drawing herself back, she gazed steadilly on his face, and said—"Lord Hastings, they tell me thy hand is another's. *Is* it true?"

"Hear me!" answered the nobleman. "When first I——"

"Oh, God!—oh, God! he answers not—he falters. Speak! Is it true?"

"It is true. I am wedded to another."

Sibyll did not fall to the ground, nor faint, nor give vent to noisy passion. But the rich color which before had been varying and fitful, deserted her cheek, and left it of an ashen whiteness; the lips, too, grew tightly compressed, and her small fingers, interlaced, were clasped with strained and convulsive energy, so that the quivering of the very arms was perceptible. In all else she seemed composed, as she said, "I thank you, my lord, for the simple truth—no more is needed. Heaven bless you and yours! Farewell!"

"Stay!—you shall—you must hear me on. Thou knowest how dearly in youth I loved Katherine Nevile. In manhood the memory of that love haunted me, but beneath thy sweet smile I deemed it, at last, effaced;—I left thee to seek the king, and demand his assent to our union. I speak not of obstacles that then arose;—in the midst of them I learned Katherine was lone and widowed—was free. At her own summons, I sought her presence, and learned that she had loved me ever—loved me still. The intoxication of my early dream returned—reverse and exile followed close—Katherine left her state, her fortunes, her native land, and followed the banished man, and so memory, and gratitude, and destiny concurred, and the mistress of my youth became my wife. None other could have replaced thy image—none other have made me forget the faith I pledged thee. The thought of thee has still pursued me—will pursue me to the last. I dare not say *now* that I love thee still, but yet——" He paused, but rapidly resumed, "Enough, enough—dear art thou to me, and honored—dearer, more honored than a sister. Thank Heaven, at least, and thine own virtue, my falsehood leaves thee pure and stainless. Thy hand may yet bless a worthier man. If our cause triumphs, thy fortunes, thy father's fate, shall be my fondest care. Never—never will my sleep be sweet, and my conscience laid to rest, till I hear thee say, as honored wife—perchance, as blessed and blessing mother—'False one, I am happy!'"

A cold smile, at these last words, flitted over the girl's face—the smile of a broken heart—but it vanished, and with that strange mixture of sweetness and pride—mild and forgiving, yet still spirited and firm—which belonged to her character, she nerved herself to the last and saddest effort to preserve dignity and conceal despair. "Farther words, my lord, are idle—I am rightly punished for a proud folly. Let not woman love above her state. Think no more of my destiny."

"No, no," interrupted the remorseful lord, "thy destiny must haunt me till thou hast chosen one with a better right to protect thee."

At the repetition of that implied desire to transfer *her* also to another—a noble indignation came to mar the calm for she had hitherto not vainly struggled. "Oh, man!" she exclaimed, with passion, "does thy deceit give me the right to deceive another? I—I wed! —I—I—vow at the altar—a love dead, dead for ever—dead as my own heart! Why dost thou mock me with the hollow phrase, 'Thou art pure and stainless?' Is the virginity of the soul still left? Do the tears I have shed for thee—doth the thrill of my heart, when I heard thy voice—doth the plighted kiss that burns, burns now into my brow, and on my lips—do these, these leave me free to carry to a new affection the cinders and ashes of a soul thou hast ravaged and deflowered? Oh, coarse and rude belief of men,—that nought is lost if the mere form be pure! The freshness of the first feelings, the bloom of the sinless thought, the sigh, the blush of the devotion—never, never felt but once! these, these make the true dower a maiden should bring to the hearth to which she comes as wife. Oh, taunt!—Oh, insult! to speak to me of happiness—of the altar! Thou never knewest, lord, how I really loved thee!" And for the first time, a violent gush of tears came to relieve her heart.

Hastings was almost equally overcome. Well experienced as he was in those partings, when maids reproach and gallants pray for pardon, but still sigh—"Farewell,"—he had now no words to answer that burst of uncontrollable agony, and he felt at once humbled and relieved, when Sibyll again, with one of those struggles which exhaust years of life, and almost leave us callous to all after trial, pressed back the scalding tears, and said, with unnatural sweetness—"Pardon me, my lord—I meant not to reproach—the words escaped me —think of them no more. I would fain, at least, part from you now, as I had once hoped to part from you at the last hour of life—without one memory of bitterness and anger, so that my conscience, whatever its other griefs, might say—'My lips never belied my heart—my words never pained him!' And now then, Lord Hastings, in all charity we part. Farewell, for ever, and for ever! Thou hast wedded one who loves thee, doubtless, as tenderly as I had done. Ah! cherish that affection! There are times even in thy career when a little love is sweeter than much fame. If thou thinkest I have aught to pardon thee, now with my whole heart I pray, as while life is mine that prayer shall be murmured—'Heaven forgive this man, as I do! Heaven make his home the home of peace, and breathe into those now near and dear to him the love and the faith that I once——'" She stopped, for the words choked her, and, hiding her face, held out her hand, in sign of charity and of farewell.

"Ah! if I dared pray like thee," murmured Hastings, pressing his lips upon that burning hand, "how should I weary Heaven to repair, by countless blessings, the wrong which I have done thee. And Heaven will—oh, it surely will!"—he pressed the hand to his heart, dropped it, and was gone.

In the court-yard he was accosted by Alwyn—

"Thou hast been frank, my lord?"

"I have."

"And she bears it, and——"

"See how *she* forgives, and how *I* suffer!" said Hastings, turning his face towards his rival; and Alwyn saw that the tears were rolling down his cheeks—"Question me no more."

There was a long silence—they quitted the precincts of the Tower, and were at the riverside. Hastings, waving his hand to Alwyn, was about to enter the boat which was to bear him to the war-council assembled at Baynard's Castle, when the trader stopped him, and said anxiously—

"Think you not, for the present, the Tower, is the safest asylum for Sibyll and her father? If we fail and Warwick returns, they are protected by the earl; if we triumph, thou wilt eusure their safety from all foes?"

"Surely:—in either case, their present home is the most secure."

The two men then parted; and not long afterwards, Hastings, who led the on-guard, was on his way towards Barnet: with him also went the foot volunteers under Alwyn. The army of York was on its march. Gloucester, to whose vigilance and energy were left the final preparations, was necessarily the last of the generals to quit the city. And suddenly, while his steed was at the gate of Baynard's Castle, he entered, armed *cap-à-pie*, into the chamber where the Duchess of Bedford sate with her grandchildren: "Madame," said he, "I have a grace to demand from you which will, methinks, not be displeasing. My lieutenants report to me that an alarm has spread amongst my men—a religious horror of some fearful bombards and guns which have been devised by a sorcerer in Lord Warwick's pay. Your famous Friar Bungey has been piously amongst them, promising, however, that the mists which now creep over the earth shall last through the night and the early morrow; and if he deceive us not, we may post our men so as to elude the hostile artillery. But, sith the friar is so noted and influential, and sith there is a strong fancy that the winds which have driven back Margaret obeyed his charm, the soldiers clamor out for him to attend us, and, on the very field itself, counteract the spells of the Lancastrian nigromancer. The good friar, more accustomed to fight with fiends than men, is daunted, and resists. As much may depend on his showing us good will, and making our fellows suppose we have the best of the witch-craft, I pray you to command his attendance, and cheer up his courage. He waits without."

"A most notable—a most wise advice, beloved Richard!" cried the duchess. "Friar Bungey is, indeed, a potent man. I will win him at once to your will;" and the duchess hurried from the room.

The friar's bodily fears, quieted at last by assurances that he should be posted in a place of perfect safety during the battle, and his avarice excited by promises of the amplest rewards, he consented to accompany the troops upon one stipulation—viz., that the atrocious wizard, who had so often baffled his best spells—the very wizard who had superintended the accursed bombards, and predicted Edward's previous defeat and flight, (together with the diobolical invention, in which all the malice and strength of his sorcery were centered,) might, according to Jacquetta's former promise, be delivered forthwith to his mercy and accompany him to the very spot, where he was to dispel and counteract the Lancastrian nigromancer's enchantments. The duchess, too glad to purchase the friar's acquiescence on such cheap terms, and to whose superstitious horror for Adam's lore in the black art, was now added a purely political motive for desiring him to be made away with—inasmuch as in the Sanctuary she had, at last, extorted from Elizabeth the dark secret which might make him a very dangerous witness against the interests and honor of Edward—readily and joyfully consented to this proposition.

A strong guard was at once despatched to the Tower with the friar himself, followed by a covered wagon, which was to serve for conveyance to Bungey and his victim.

In the meanwhile, Sibyll, after remaining for some time in the chamber which Hastings had abandoned to her solitary woe, had passed to the room in which her father held mute commune with his Eureka.

The machine was now thoroughly completed;—improved and perfected, to the utmost art the inventor ever could attain. Thinking that the prejudice against it might have arisen from its uncouth appearance, the poor philosopher had sought now to give it a gracious and imposing appearance. He had painted and gilt it with his own hands—it looked bright and gaudy in its gay hues; its outward form was worthy of the precious and propitious jewel which lay hidden in its centre.

"See, child—see!" said Adam; "is it not beautiful and comely?"

"My dear father, yes!" answered the poor girl, as still she sought to smile; then, after a short silence, she continued—"Father, of late, methinks, I have too much forgotten thee; pardon me, if so. Henceforth, I have no care in life but thee—henceforth let me ever, when thou toilest, come and sit by thy side. I would not be alone!—*I dare not!* Father—father! God shield thy harmless life! I have nothing to love under heaven but thee!"

The good man turned wistfully, and raised, with tremulous hands, the sad face that had pressed itself on his bosom. Gazing thereon mournfully, he said—"Some new grief hath chanced to thee, my child. Methought I heard another voice besides thine in yonder room. Ah! has Lord Hastings——"

"Father, spare me!—thou wert too right—

thou didst judge too wisely—Lord Hastings *is* wedded to another! But see, I can smile still—I am calm. My heart will not break so long as it hath thee to love and pray for!"

She wound her arms round him as she spoke, and he roused himself from his world out of earth again. Though he could bring no comfort, there was something, at least, to the forlorn one, in his words of love—in his tears of pity.

They sat down together, side by side, as the evening darkened. The Eureka forgotten in the hour of its perfection! They noted not the torches which flashed below, reddened at intervals the walls of their chamber, and gave a glow to the gay gilding and bright hues of the gaudy model. Yet those torches flickered round the litter that was to convey Henry the Peaceful to the battle-field, which was to decide the dynasty of his realm! The torches vanished, and forth from the dark fortress went the captive king.

Night succeeded to eve, when again the red glare shot upward on the Eureka, playing with fantastic smile on its quaint aspect—steps and voices, and the clatter of arms, sounded in the yard, on the stairs, in the adjoining chamber—and suddenly the door was flung open, and, followed by some half score soldiers, strode in the terrible friar.

"Aha, Master Adam! who is the greater nigromancer now? Seize him!—Away! And help you, Master Sergeant, to bear this piece of the foul fiend's cunning devising. Ho, ho! see you how it is tricked out and furbished up all for the battle, I warrant ye!"

The soldiers had already seized upon Adam, who, stupefied by astonishment rather than fear, uttered no sound, and attempted no struggle. But it was in vain they sought to tear from him Sibyll's clinging and protecting arms. A supernatural strength, inspired by a kind of superstition that no harm could chance to him while she was by, animated her slight form; and fierce though the soldiers were, they shrunk from actual and brutal violence to one thus young and fair. Those small hands clung so firmly, that it seemed that nothing but the edge of the sword could sever the child's clasp from the father's neck.

"Harm him not—harm him at your peril, friar!" she cried, with flashing eyes. "Tear him from me, and if King Edward win the day, Lord Hastings shall have thy life; if Lord Warwick, thy days are numbered, too. Beware, and avaunt!"

The friar was startled. He had forgotten Lord Hastings in the zest of his revenge. He feared that, if Sibyll were left behind, the tale she might tell would indeed bring on him a powerful foe in the daughter's lover—on the other hand, should Lord Warwick get the better, what vengeance would await her appeal to the great protector of her father! He resolved, therefore, on the instant, to take Sibyll as well as her father; and if the fortune of the day allowed him to rid himself of Warner, a good occasion might equally occur to dispose for ever of the testimony of Sibyll. He had already formed a cunning calculation in desiring Warner's company; for while, should Edward triumph, the sacrifice of the hated Warner was resolved upon, yet, should the earl get the better, he could make a merit to Warner that he (the friar) had not only spared, but saved, his life, in making him his companion. It was in harmony with this double policy that the friar mildly answered to Sibyll—

"Tush, my daughter! Perhaps if your father be true to King Edward, and aid my skill instead of obstructing it, he may be none the worse for the journey he must take; and if thou likest to go with him, there's room in the vehicle, and the more the merrier. Harm them not soldiers—no doubt they will follow quietly."

As he said this, the men, after first crossing themselves, had already hoisted up the Eureka; and when Adam saw it borne from the room, he instinctly followed the bearers. Sibyll, relieved by the thought that, for weal or for woe, she should, at least, share her father's fate, and scarce foreboding much positive danger from the party which contained Hastings and Alwyn, attempted no further remonstrance.

The Eureka was placed in the enormous vehicle—it served as a barrier between the friar and his prisoners.

The friar himself, as soon as the wagon was in motion, addressed himself civilly enough to his fellow-travellers, and assured them there was nothing to fear, unless Adam thought fit to disturb his incantations. The captives answered not his address, but nestled close to each other, interchanging, at intervals, words of comfort, and recoiling as far as possible from the ex-tregetour, who, having taken a more congenial companion, in the shape of a great leathern bottle, finally sunk into the silent and complacent doze which usually rewards the libations to the Bromian god.

The vehicle, with many other baggage-wagons in the rear of the army, in that memorable night-march, moved mournfully on; the night continued wrapped in fog and mist, agreeably to the weatherwise predictions of the friar; the rumbling groan of the vehicle, the tramp of the soldiers, the dull rattle of their arms, with now and then the neigh of some knight's steed in the distance, were the only sounds that broke the silence, till once, as they neared their destination, Sibyll started from her father's bosom, and sudderingly thought she recognized the hoarse chant and the tinkling bells of the ominous tymbesteres.

CHAPTER III.

A Pause.

In the profound darkness of the night, and the thick fog, Edward had stationed his men at a venture upon the heath at Gladsmoor,* and hastily environed the camp with palisades and trenches. He had intended to have rested immediately in front of the foe, but, in the darkness, mistook the extent of the hostile line, and his men were ranged only opposite to the *left* side of the earl's force (towards Hadley), leaving the right unopposed. Most fortunate for Edward was this mistake; for Warwick's artillery, and the new and deadly bombards he had constructed, were placed in the *right* of the earl's army; and the provident earl, naturally supposing Edward's left was there opposed to him, ordered his gunners to cannonade all night. Edward, "as the flashes of the guns illumined by fits the gloom of midnight, saw the advantage of his unintentional error; and to prevent Warwick from discovering it, reiterated his orders for the most profound silence."† Thus even his very blunders favored Edward more than the wisest precautions had served his hated foe.

Raw, cold, and dismal dawned the morning of the fourteenth of April, the Easter Sabbath. In the fortunes of that day were involved those of all the persons who hitherto in the course of this narrative, may have seemed to move in separate orbits from the fiery star of Warwick. Now, in this crowning hour, the vast and gigantic destiny of the great earl comprehended all upon which its darkness or its light had fallen; not only the luxurious Edward, the perjured Clarence, the haughty Margaret, her gallant son, the gentle Anne, the remorseful Isabel, the dark guile of Gloucester, the rising fortunes of the gifted Hastings,—but on the hazard of that die rested the hopes of Hilyard, and the interests of the trader, Alwyn, and the permanence of that frank, chivalric, hardy, still half Norman race, of which Nicholas Alwyn and his Saxon class were the rival antagonistic principle, and Marmaduke Nevile the ordinary type. Dragged inexorably into the whirlpool of that mighty fate, were even the very lives of the simple Scholar—of his obscure and devoted child. Here, into this gory ocean, all scattered rivulets and streams had hastened to merge at last.

But grander and more awful than all individual interests were those assigned to the fortunes of this battle, so memorable in the English annals;—the ruin or triumph of a dynasty;—the fall of that warlike baronage, of which Richard Nevile was the personation—the crowning flower—the greatest representative and the last—associated with memories of turbulence and excess it is true, but with the proudest and grandest achievements in our early history—with all such liberty as had been yet achieved since the Norman Conquest—with all such glory as had made the island famous,—here with Runnymede, and there with Cressy!—the rise of a crafty, plotting, imperious Despotism, based upon the growing sympathy of craftsmen and traders, and ripening on the one hand to the Tudor tyranny, the Republican reaction under the Stuarts, the slavery, and the civil war—but, on the other hand, to the concentration of all the vigor and life of genius into a single and strong government, the graces, the arts, the letters of a polished court, the freedom, the energy, the

* Edward "had the greater number of men."—Hall, p. 296.

† Sharon Turner.

resources of a commercial population, destined to rise above the tyranny at which it had first connived, and give to the emancipated Saxon the markets of the world.

Upon the victory of that day, all these contending interests—this vast alternative in the future—swayed and trembled. Out, then, upon that vulgar craving of those who comprehend neither the vast truths of life, nor the grandeur of ideal art, and who ask from poet or narrator, the poor and petty morality of "Poetical Justice"—a justice existing not in our work-day world—a justice existing not in the sombre page of history—a justice existing not in the loftier conceptions of men whose genius has grappled with the engimas which art and poetry only can foreshadow and divine:—unknown to us in the street and the market—unknown to us on the scaffold of the patriot, or amidst the flames of the martyr—unknown to us in the Lear and the Hamlet—in the Agamemnon and the Prometheus. Millions upon millions, ages upon ages, are entered but as items in the vast account in which the recording angel sums up the unerring justice of God to man.

Raw, cold, and dismal, dawned the morning of the fourteenth of April. And on that very day Margaret and her son, and the wife and daughter of Lord Warwick, landed, at last, on the shores of England. * Come they for joy, or for woe—for victory, or despair? The issue of this day's fight on the Heath of Gladsmoor will decide. Prank thy halls, O Westminster, for the triumph of the Lancastrian king—or open thou, O Grave, to receive the saint-like Henry and his noble son. The king-maker goes before ye saint-like father and noble son, to prepare your thrones amongst the living, or your mansions amongst the dead!

CHAPTER IV.

The Battle.

Raw, cold, and dismal, dawned the morning of the fourteenth of April. The heavy mist still covered both armies, but their hum and stir was already heard through the gloaming, the neighing of steeds, and the clangour of mail. Occasionally a movement of either force made dim forms, seming gigantic through the vapor, indistinctly visible to the antagonist army; and there was something ghastly and unearthlike in these omnious shapes, suddenly seen, and suddenly vanishing, amidst the sullen atmosphere. By this time, Warwick had discovered the mistake of his gunners; for, to the right of the earl, the silence of the Yorkists was still unbroken, while abruptly from the thick gloom to the left broke the hoarse mutter, and low growl of the awakening war. Not a moment was lost by the earl in repairing the error of the night: his artillery wheeled rapidly from the right wing, and, sudden as a storm of lightening, the fire from the cannon flashed through the dun and heavy vapor: and, not far from the very spot where Hasting was marshalling the wing entrusted to his command, made a deep chasm in the serried ranks. Death had begun his feast!

At that moment, however, from the centre of the Yorkist army, arose, scarcely drowned by the explosion, that deep-toned shout of enthusiasm, which, he who has once heard it, coming, as it were, from the one heart of an armed multitude, will ever recall as the most kindling and glorious sound which ever quickened the pulse and thrilled the blood,—for along that part of the army now rode King Edward. His mail was polished as a mirror, but otherwise unadorned, resembling that which now invests his effigies at the Tower,* and the housings of his steed were spangled with silver suns, for the silver sun was the cognizance on all his banners. His head was bare, and through the hazy atmosphere the gold of his rich locks seemed literally to shine. Followed by his body squire, with his helm and lance, and the lords in his immediate staff, his truncheon in his hand, he passed slowly along the steady line, till, halting where he deemed his voice could be farthest heard, he reined in, and lifting his hand, the shout of the soldiery was hushed,—though still while he spoke from Warwick's archers came the arrowy shower, and still the gloom was pierced and the hush interrupted by the flash and the roar of the bombards.

* Margaret landed at Weymouth—Lady Warwick, at Portsmouth.

* The suit of armor, however, which the visitor to the Royal Armory ia expected to believe King Edward could have worn, is infiuitely too small for such credulity. Edward's height was six feet two inches.

"Englishmen and friends," said the martial chief, "to bold deeds go but few words. Before you is the foe! From Ravenspur to London I have marched—treason flying from my sword, loyalty gathering to my standard. With but two thousand men, on the fourteenth of March, I entered England—on the fourteenth of April, fifty thousand is my muster-roll. Who shall say, then, that I am not king when one month mans a monarch's army from his subjects' love? And well know ye, now, that my cause is yours and England's! Those against us are men who would rule in despite of law—barons whom I gorged with favors, and who would reduce this fair realm of King, Lords, and Commons, to be the appanage and property of one man's measureless ambition—the park, forsooth, the homestead to Lord Warwick's private House! Ye gentlemen and knights of England, let them and their rabble prosper, and your properties will be despoiled—your lives insecure—all law struck dead. What differs Richard of Warwick from Jack Cade, save that if his name is nobler, so is his treason greater? Commoners and soldiers of England—freemen, however humble—what do these rebels lord (who would rule in the name of Lancaster) desire? To reduce you to villeins and to bondsmen, as your forefathers were to them. Ye owe freedom from the barons to the just laws of my sires your kings. Gentlemen and knights, commoners and soldiers, Edward IV. upon his throne, will not profit by a victory more than you. This is no war of dainty chivalry—it is a war of true men against false. No quarter! Spare not either knight or hilding! Warwick, forsooth, will not smite the Commons. Truly not—the rabble are his friends. I say to you ——" and Edward, pausing in the excitement and sanguinary fury of his tiger nature—the soldiers, heated like himself to the thirst of blood, saw his eyes sparkle, and his teeth gnash, as he added in a deeper and lower, but not less audible voice, "I say to you, SLAY ALL! * What heel spares the viper's brood?"

"We will—we will!" was the horrid answer, which came hissing and muttered forth from morion and cap of steel.

"Hark! to their bombards!" resumed Edward. "The enemy would fight from afar, for they excel us in their archers and gunners. Upon them, then—hand to hand, and man to man! Advance banners—sound trumpets! Sir Oliver, my basinet! Soldiers, if my standard falls, look for the plume upon your king's helmet! Charge!"

* HALL.

Then, with a shout wilder and louder than before, on through the hail of the arrows—on through the glare of the bombards—rather with a rush than in a march, advanced Edward's centre against the array of Somerset. But from a part of the encampment where the circumvallation seemed strongest, a small body of men moved not with the general body.

To the left of the churchyard of Hadley, at this day, the visitor may notice a low wall; on the other side of that wall is a garden, then but a rude eminence on Gladsmoor Heath. On that spot a troop in complete armour, upon destriers pawing impatiently, surrounded a man upon a sorry palfrey, and in a gown of blue—the color of royalty and of servitude,—that man, was Henry the Sixth. In the same space stood Friar Bungey, his foot on the Eureka, muttering incantations, that the mists he had foretold,* and which had protected the Yorkists from the midnight guns, might yet last, to the confusion of the foe. And near him, under a gaunt, leafless tree, a rope round his neck, was Adam Warner—Sibyll, still faithful to his side, nor shuddering at the arrows and the guns—her whole fear concentrated upon the sole life for which her own was prized. Upon this eminence, then, these lookers-on stood aloof. And the meek ears of Henry heard through the fog the inexplicable sullen, jarring, clash,—steel had met steel.

"Holy Father!" exclaimed the kingly saint, "and this is the Easter Sabbath, thy most solemn day of peace!"

"Be silent," thundered the friar, "thou disturbest my spells. *Barabbarara—Santhinoa—Foggibus increscebo—confusio inimicis—Garabbora vapor et mistes!*"

We must now rapidly survey the dispositions of the army under Warwick. In the right wing, the command was entrusted to the Earl

* Lest the reader should suppose that the importance of Friar Bungey upon this bloody day has been exaggerated by the narrator, we must cite the testimony of sober Alderman Fabyan:—"Of the mists and other impediments which fell upon the Lords' party, by reason of the incantations wrought by Friar Bungey, as the fame went, me list not to write."

of Oxford and the Marquis of Montagu. The former, who led the cavalry of that division, was stationed in the van; the latter, according to his usual habit—surrounded by a strong body-guard of knights, and a prodigious number of squires as aide-de-camps—remained at the rear, and directed thence, by his orders, the general movement! In this wing the greater number were Lancastrian, jealous of Warwick, and only consenting to the generalship of Montagu, because shared by their favorite hero, Oxford. In the mid-space, lay the chief strength of the bowmen, with a goodly number of pikes and bills, under the Duke of Somerset; and this division also was principally Lancastrian, and shared the jealousy of Oxford's soldiery. The left wing, composed for the most of Warwick's yeomanry and retainers, was commanded by the Duke of Exeter, conjointly with the earl himself. Both armies kept a considerable body in reserve, and Warwick, besides this resource, had selected from his own retainers a band of picked archers, whom he had skilfully placed in the outskirts of a wood that then stretched from Wrotham Park to the column that now commemorates the battle of Barnet, on the high northern road. He had guarded these last-mentioned archers (where exposed in front to Edward's horsemen) by strong tall barricades, leaving only such an opening as would allow one horseman, at a time, to pass, and defending by a formidable line of pikes this narrow opening left for communication, and to admit to a place of refuge in case of need. These dispositions made, and ere yet Edward had advanced on Somerset, the earl rode to the front of the wing under his special command, and, agreeably to the custom of the time, observed by his royal foe, harangued the troops. Here were placed those who loved him as a father, and venerated him as something superior to mortal man—here the retainers, who had grown up with him from his childhood—who had followed him to his first fields of war—who had lived under the shelter of his many castles, and fed in that rude equality of a more primæval age, which he loved still to maintain, at the lavish board. And now Lord Warwick's coal-black steed halted, motionless in the van.

His squire behind bore his helmet, overshadowed as the eagle of Monthermer, the outstretched wings of which spread wide into sable plumes: and as the earl's noble face turned full and calm upon the bristling lines, there arose, not the vulgar uproar that greeted the aspect of the young Edward. By one of those strange sympathies which pass through multitudes, and seize them with a common feeling, the whole body of those adoring vassals became suddenly aware of the change which a year had made in the face of their chief and father. They saw the grey flakes in his Jove-like curls—the furrows in that lofty brow—the hollows in that bronzed and manly visage, which had seemed to their rude admiration to wear the stamp of the two-fold Divinity—Beneficence and Valor. A thrill of tenderness and awe shot through the veins of every one—tears of devotions rushed into man ya hardy eye. No—*there*, was not the ruthless captain addressing his hireling butchers; it *was* the chief and father rallying gratitude, and love, and reverence, to the crisis of his stormy fate.

"My friends, my followers, and my children," said the earl, "the field we have entered is one from which there is no retreat; here must your leader conquer, or here die. It is not a parchment pedigree—it is not a name, derived from the ashes of dead men, that make the only charter of a king. We Englishmen were but slaves, if, in giving crown and sceptre to a mortal like ourselves, we asked not in return the kingly virtues. Beset, of old, by evil counsellors, the reign of Henry VI. was obscured, and the weal of the realm endangered. Mine own wrongs seemed to me great, but the disasters of my country not less. I deemed that in the race of York, England would know a wiser and happier rule. What was, in this, mine error ye partly know. A prince dissolved in luxurious vices—a nobility degraded by minions and blood-suckers—a people plundered by purveyors, and a land disturbed by brawl and riot. But ye know not all: God makes man's hearth man's altar—our hearths were polluted—our wives and daughters were viewed as harlots—and lechery ruled the realm. A king's word should be fast as the pillars of the world. What man ever trusted Edward and was not deceived? Even now the unknightly liar stands in arms with the weight of perjury on his soul. In his father's town of York, ye know that he took, three short weeks since, solemn oath of fealty to King Henry. And now King Henry is his captive, and King Henry's holy crown upon his traitor's head—'traitors' calls he Us? What name, then, rank enough for him? Edward gave the promise of a brave man, and I served him. He proved a base, a false, a licentious, and a cruel king, and I forsook him; may all free hearts in all free lands so serve kings when they become tyrants!

"Ye fight against a cruel and torcious usurper, whose bold hand cannot sanctify a black heart—ye fight not only for King Henry, the meek and the godly—ye fight not for him alone, but for his young and princely son, the grandchild of Henry of Agincourt, who, old men tell me, has that hero's face, and who, I know, has that hero's frank and royal and noble soul—ye fight for the freedom of your land, for the honor of your women, for what is better than any king's cause—for justice and mercy—for truth and manhood's virtues against corruption in the laws, slaughter by the scaffold, falsehood in a ruler's lips, and shameless harlotry in the councils of ruthless power. The order I have ever given in war, I give now;—we war against the leaders of evil, not against the hapless tools—we war against our oppressors, not against our misguided brethren. Strike down every plumed crest, but when the strife is over, spare every common man! Hark! while I speak, I hear the march of your foe! Up standards!—blow trumpets! And now, as I brace my basinet, may God grant us all a glorious victory, or a glorious grave. On, my merry men! show these London loons the stout hearts of Warwickshire and Yorkshire. On, my merry men! A Warwick! A Warwick!"

As he ended, he swung lightly over his head the terrible battle-axe which had smitten down, as the grass before the reaper, the chivalry of many a field; and ere the last blast of the trumpets died, the troops of Warwick and of Gloucester met, and mingled hand to hand.

Although the earl had, on discovering the position of the enemy, moved some of his artillery from his right wing, yet there still lay the great number and strength of his force. And there, therefore, Montagu, rolling troop on troop to the aid of Oxford, pressed so overpoweringly upon the soldiers under Hastings, that the battle very soon wore a most unfavorable aspect for the Yorkists. It seemed, indeed, that the success which had always hitherto attended the military movements of Montagu, was destined for a crowning triumph. Stationed, as we have said, in the rear, with his light-armed squires, upon fleet steeds, around him, he moved the springs of the battle with the calm sagacity which at that moment no chief in either army possessed. Hastings was thoroughly outflanked, and though his men fought with great valor, they could not resist the weight of superior numbers.

In the midst of the carnage in the centre, Edward reined in his steed, as he heard the cry of victory in the gale—

"By heaven!" he exclaimed, "our men at the left are cravens—they fly! they fly!—Ride to Lord Hastings, Sir Humphrey Bourchier, bid him defile hither what men are left him; and now, ere our fellows are well aware what hath chanced yonder, charge we, knights and gentlemen, on, on!—break Somerset's line; on, on, to the heart of the rebel earl!"

Then, visor closed, lance in rest, Edward and his cavalry dashed through the arches and billmen of Somerset; clad in complete mail, impervious to the weapons of the infantry, they slaughtered as they rode, and their way was marked by corpses and streams of blood. Fiercest and fellest of all, was Edward himself; when his lance shivered, and he drew his knotty mace from its sling by his saddle bow, woe to all who attempted to stop his path. Vain alike steel helmet or leathern cap, jerkin or coat of mail. In vain Somerset threw himself into the mêlée. The instant Edward and his cavalry had made a path through the lines for his foot soldiery, the fortunes of the day were half retrieved. It was no rapid passage, pierced and reclosed, that he desired to effect, it was the wedge in the oak of war. There, rooted in the very midst of Somerset's troops, doubling on each side, passing on but to return again, where helm could be crashed and man overthrown, the mighty strength of Edward widened the breach more and more, till faster and faster poured in his bands, and the centre of Warwick's army seemed to reel and whirl round the broadening gap through its ranks—as the waves round some chasm in a maëlstrom.

But in the interval, the hard-pressed troops commanded by Hastings were scattered and dispersed; driven from the field, they fled in numbers through the town of Barnet; many halted not till they reached London, where they spread the news of the earl's victory and Edward's ruin.*

Through the mist, Friar Bungey discerned the fugitive Yorkists under Hastings, and heard their cries of despair: Through the mist, Sibyll saw, close beneath the entrenchments which protected the space on which they stood, an armed horseman with the well-known crest of Hastings on his helmet, and, with lifted visor, calling his men to the return, in the loud voice of rage and scorn. And then, she herself sprang forwards, and forgetting his past cruelty in his present danger, cried his name—weak cry, lost in the roar of war! But the friar, now fearing he had taken the wrong side, began to turn from his spells, to address the most abject apologies to Adam, to assure him that he would have been slaughtered at the Tower, but for the friar's interruption; and that the rope round his neck was but an insignificant ceremony due to the prejudices of the soldiers. "Alas, Great Man," he concluded; "I see still that thou art mightier than I am; thy charms, though silent, are more potent than mine, though my lungs crack beneath them! *Confusio Inimicis Taralorolu,*—I mean no harm to the earl,—*Garrabora, mistes et nubes;*—Lord, what will become of me!"

Meanwhile, Hastings, with a small body of horse who being composed of knights and squires, specially singled out for the sword, fought with the pride of disdainful gentlemen, and the fury of desperate soldiers—finding it impossible to lure back the fugitives, hewed their own way through Oxford's ranks, to the centre, where they brought fresh aid to the terrible arm of Edward.

CHAPTER V.

The Battle.

THE mist still continued so thick that Montagu was unable to discern the general prospects of the field. But, calm and resolute in his post, amidst the arrows which whirled round him, and often struck, blunted, against his Milan mail, the marquis received the reports of his aide-de-camps (may that modern world be pardoned!) as one after one, they emerged through the fog to his side.

"Well," he said, as one of these, messengers now spurred to the spot, "we have beaten off Hastings and his hirelings; but I see not 'the Silver Star' of Lord Oxford's banner."*

"Lord Oxford, my lord, has followed the enemy he routed to the farthest verge of the heath."

"Saints help us! Is Oxford thus headstrong? He will ruin all if he be decoyed from the field! Ride back, sir! Yet—hold!"—as another of the aide-de-camps appeared. "What news from Lord Warwick's wing?"

"Sore beset, bold marquis. Gloucester's line seems countless; it already outflanks the earl. The duke himself seems inspired by hell! Twice has his slight arm braved even the earl's battle-axe, which spared the boy but smote to the dust his comrades!"

"Well, and what of the centre, sir?" as a third form now arrived.

"There, rages Edward in person. He hath pierced into the midst. But Somerset still holds on gallantly!"

Montagu turned to the first aide-de-camp.

"Ride, sir! Quick! This to Oxford—No pursuit! Bid him haste, with all his men, to the left wing, and smite Gloucester in the rear. Ride, ride—for life and victory! If he come but in time, the day is ours!" †

The aide-de-camp darted off, and the mist swallowed up horse and horesman.

"Sound trumpets to the return!" said the marquis;—then, after a moment's musing—"Though Oxford hath drawn off our main force of cavalry, we have still some stout lances left, and Warwick must be strengthened. On to the earl! *Laissez aller!* A Montagu! a Montagu!" And lance in rest, the marquis, and the knights immediately around him, and hitherto not personally engaged, descended the hillock at a hand gallop, and were met by a troop outnumbering their own, and commanded by the Lords D'Eyencourt and Say.

* SHARON TURNER.

* The Silver Star of the De Veres had its origin in a tradition that one of their ancestors, when fighting in the Holy Land, saw a falling star descend on his shield. Fatal to men, nobler even than the De Veres, was that silver falling star.

† FABYAN.

At this time, Warwick was indeed in the the same danger that had routed the troops of Hastings; for, by a similar position, the strength of the hostile numbers being arrayed with Gloucester, the duke's troops had almost entirely surrounded him. * And Gloucester himself wondrously approved the trust that had consigned to his stripling arm the flower of the Yorkist army. Through the mists, the blood-red manteline he wore over his mail, the grinning teeth of the boar's head which crested his helmet, flashed and gleamed wherever his presence was most needed to encourage the flagging or spur on the fierce. And there seemed to both armies something ghastly and preternatural in the savage strength of this small, slight figure thus startingly caparisoned, and which was heard evermore uttering its sharp war-cry—"Gloucester, to the onslaught! Down with the rebels, down!"

Nor did this daring personage disdain, in the midst of his fury, to increase the effect of valor by the art of a brain that never ceased to scheme on the follies of mankind. "See! see!" he cried, as he shot meteor-like from rank to rank. "See—these are no natural vapors! Yonder the mighty friar, who delayed the sails of Margaret, chants his spells to the Powers that ride the gale. Fear not the bombards—their enchanted balls swerve from the brave! The dark legions of Air fight for us! For the hour is come when the fiend shall rend his prey!" And fiendlike seemed the form thus screeching forth its predictions from under the grim headgear; and then darting and disappearing amidst the sea of pikes, cleaving its path of blood!

But still the untiring might of Warwick defied the press of numbers that swept round him, tide upon tide. Through the mists, his black armor, black plume, black steed, gloomed forth like one thundercloud in the midst of a dismal heaven. The noble charger bore along that mighty rider, animating, guiding all, with as much ease and lightness as the racer bears its puny weight; the steed itself was scarce less terrible to encounter than the sweep of the rider's axe. Protected from arrow and lance by a coat of steel, the long chaffron or pike which projected from its barbed frontal dropped with gore as it scoured along. No line of men, however serried, could resist the charge of that horse and horseman. And vain even Gloucester's dauntless presence and thrilling battle cry, when the stout earl was seen looming through the vapor, and his cheerful shout was heard, "My merry men, fight on!"

For a third time, Gloucester, spurring forth from his recoiling and shrinking followers, bending low over his saddle bow, covered by his shield, and with the tenth lance (his favorite weapon, because the one in which skill best supplied strength) he had borne that day, launched himself upon the vast bulk of his tremenduous foe. With that dogged energy—that rapid calculation which made the basis of his character, and which ever clove through all obstacles at the one that, if destroyed, destroyed the rest,—in that, his first great battle, as in his last at Bosworth, he singled out the leader, and rushed upon the giant as the mastiff on the horns and dewlap of the bull. Warwick, in the broad space which his arm had made around him in the carnage, reined in as he saw the foe, and recognized the griesly cognizance and scarlet mantle of his godson. And even in that moment, with all his heated blood, and his remembered wrong, and his imminent peril, his generous and lion heart felt a glow of admiration at the valor of the boy he had trained to arms—of the son of the beloved York. "His father little thought," muttered the earl, "that that arm should win glory against his old friend's life!" And as the half-uttered word died on his lips, the well-poised lance of Gloucester struck full upon his bassinet, and, despite the earl's horsemanship and his strength, made him reel in his saddle, while the prince shot by, and suddenly wheeling round, cast away the shivered lance, and assailed him sword in hand.

"Back, Richard—boy, back!" said the earl, in a voice that sounded hollow through his helmet—"It is not against thee that my wrongs call for blood—pass on!"

"Not so, Lord Warwick," answered Richard, in a sobered, and almost solemn voice, dropping for the moment the point of his sword, and raising, his visor, that he might be the better heard,—"On the field of battle all memories, sweet in peace, must die! St. Paul be my judge, that even in this hour I love you well; but I love renown and glory more. On the edge of my sword sit power and royalty, and

* Sharon Turner.

what high souls prize most—ambition: these would nerve me against mine own brother's breast, were that breast my barrier to an illustrious future. Thou hast given thy daughter to another! I smite the father, to regain my bride. Lay on, and spare not!—for he who hates thee most would prove not so fell a foe as the man who sees his fortunes made or marred—his love crushed or yet crowned, as this day's battle closes in triumph or defeat.—Rebel, defend thyself!"

No time was left for further speech; for as Richard's sword descended, two of Gloucester's followers, Parr and Milwater by name, dashed from the halting lines at the distance, and bore down to their young prince's aid. At the same moment, Sir Marmaduke Nevile and the Lord Fitzhugh spurred from the opposite line; and thus encouraged, the band on either side came boldly forward, and the melée grew fierce and general. But still Richard's sword singled out the earl, and still the earl, parrying his blows, dealt his own upon meaner heads. Crushed by one swoop of the axe, fell Milwater to the earth—down, as again it swung on high, fell Sir Humphrey Bourchier, who had just arrived to Gloucester with messages from Edward, never uttered in the world below. Before Marmaduke's lance fell Sir Thomas Parr; and these three corpses making a barrier between Gloucester and the earl, the duke turned fiercely upon Marmaduke, while the earl, wheeling round, charged into the midst of the hostile line, which scattered to the right and left.

"On! my merry men, on!" rang once more through the heavy air. "They give way—the London tailors,—on!" and on dashed, with their joyous cry, the merry men of Yorkshire and Warwick, the warrior-yeomen! Separated thus from his great foe, Gloucester, after unhorsing Marmaduke, galloped off to sustain that part of his following which began to waver and retreat before the rush of Warwick and his chivalry.

This, in truth, was the regiment recruited from the loyalty of London, and little accustomed, we trow, were the worthy heroes of Cockaigne, to the discipline of arms, nor trained to that stubborn resistance which makes, under skilful leaders, the English *peasants* the most enduring soldiery that the world has known since the day when the Roman sentinel perished amidst the falling columns and lava floods,* rather than, though society itself dissolved, forsake his post unbidden. "St. Thomas defend us!" muttered a worthy tailor, who in the flush of his valor, when safe in the Chepe, had consented to bear the rank of lieutenant—"it is not reasonable to expect men of pith and substance to be crushed into jellies, and carved into subtleties by horse-hoofs and pole-axes. Right about face! Fly!"—and throwing down his sword and shield, the lieutenant fairly took to his heels as he saw the charging column, headed by the raven steed of Warwick, come giant-like through the fog.

The terror of one man is contagious, and the Londoners actually turned their backs, when Nicholas Alwyn cried, in his shrill voice and northern accent, "Out on you! What will the girls say of us in East-gate and the Chepe?—Hurrah for the bold hearts of London!—Round me, stout 'prentices! let the boys shame the men! This shaft for Cockaigne!" And as the troop turned irresolute, and Alwyn's arrow left his bow, they saw a horseman by the side of Warwick reel in the saddle and fall at once to the earth, and so great evidently was the rank of the fallen man, that even Warwick reined in, and the charge halted midway in its career. It was no less a person than the Duke of Exeter whom Alwyn's shaft had disabled for the field. This incident, coupled with the hearty address of the stout goldsmith, served to reanimate the flaggers, and Gloucester, by a circuitous route, reaching their line a moment after, they dressed their ranks, and a flight of arrows followed their loud "Hurrah for London Town!"

But the charge of Warwick had only halted, and (while the wounded Exeter was borne back by his squires to the rear) it dashed into the midst of the Londoners, threw their whole line into confusion, and drove them, despite all the efforts of Gloucester, far back along the plain. This well-timed exploit served to extricate the earl from the main danger of his position; and hastening to improve his advantage, he sent forthwith to command the reserved forces under Lord St. John, the Knight

* At Pompeii.

of Lytton, Sir John Coniers, Dymoke, and Robert Hilyard, to bear down to his aid.

At this time Edward had succeeded, after a most stubborn fight, in effecting a terrible breach through Somerset's wing; and the fogs continued still so dense and mirk, that his foe itself, for Somerset had prudently drawn back to re-form his disordered squadron, seemed vanished from the field. Halting now, as through the dim atmosphere came from different quarters the many battle-cries of that feudal-day, by which alone he could well estimate the strength or weakness of those in the distance, his calmer genius as a general cooled, for a time, his individual ferocity of knight and soldier. He took his helmet from his brow, to listen with greater certainty; and the lords and riders round him were well content to take breath and pause from the weary slaughter.

The cry of "Gloucester to the *onslaught!*" was heard no more. Feebler and feebler, scatteringly as it were, and here and there, the note had changed into "Gloucester to the *rescue!*"

Farther off, rose, mingled and blent together, the opposing shouts—"A Montagu!—a Montagu!"—"Strike for D'Eyncourt and King Edward!"—"A Say—a Say!"

"Ha!" said Edward, thoughtfully, "bold Gloucester fails—Montagu is bearing on to Warwick's aid—Say and D'Eyncourt stop his path. Our doom looks dark! Ride, Hastings—ride! retrieve thy laurels, and bring up the reserve under Clarence. But harkye, leave not his side—he may desert again! Ho! ho! Again, 'Gloucester to the rescue!' Ah! how lustily sounds the cry of 'Warwick!' By the flaming sword of St. Michael, we will slacken that haughty shout, or be evermore dumb ourself, ere the day be an hour nearer to the eternal judgment!"

Deliberately Edward rebraced his helmet, and settled himself in his saddle, and with his knights riding close each to each, that they might not lose themselves in the darkness, regained his infantry and led them on to the quarter where the war now raged fiercest, round the black steed of Warwick and the blood-red manteline of the fiery Richard.

CHAPTER VI.

The Battle.

It was now scarcely eight in the morning, though the battle had endured three hours; and as yet victory so inclined to the earl, that nought but some dire mischance could turn the scale. Montagu had cut his way to Warwick, Somerset had re-established his array. The fresh vigor brought by the earl's reserve had well nigh completed his advantage over Gloucester's wing. The new infantry under Hilyard, the unexhausted riders under Sir John Coniers and his knightly compeers, were dealing fearful havoc, as they cleared the plain; and Gloucester, fighting inch by inch, no longer outnumbering but outnumbered, was driven nearer and nearer towards the town, when suddenly a pale, sickly, and ghost-like ray of sunshine, rather resembling the watery gleam of a waning moon than the radiance of the Lord of Light, broke through the mists, and showed to the earl's eager troops the banner and badges of a new array hurrying to to the spot. "Behold," cried the young Lord Fitzhugh, "the standard and the badge of the Usurper—a silver sun! Edward himself is delivered into our hands! Upon them—bill and pike, lance and brand, shaft and bolt!—Upon them, and crown the day!"

The same fatal error was shared by Hilyard, as he caught sight of the advancing troop, with their silvery cognizance. He gave the word, and every arrow left its string. At the same moment, as both horse and foot assailed the fancied foe, the momentary beam vanished from the heaven, the two forces mingled in the sullen mists, when, after a brief conflict, a sudden and horrible cry of "*Treason! Treason!*" resounded from either band. The shinning star of Oxford, returning from the pursuit, had been mistaken for Edward's cognizance of the sun.* Friend was slaughtering friend, and when the error was detected, each believed the other had deserted to the foe. In vain, here Montagu and Warwick, and there Oxford and his captains sought to dispel the confusion, and unite those whose blood had been fired against each other. While yet in doubt, confusion and dismay, rushed full into the centre Edward of York himself, with

* CONT. CROYL., 555; FABYAN, HABINGTON, HUME, S. TURNER.

his knights and riders; and his tossing banners, scarcely even yet distinguished from Oxford's starry ensigns, added to the general incertitude and panic. Loud in the midst rose Edward's trumpet-voice, while *through* the midst, like one crest of foam upon a roaring sea, danced his plume of snow.

Hark! again, again—near and nearer—the tramp of steeds, the clash of steel, the whiz and hiss of arrows, the shout of "Hastings to the onslaught!" Fresh, and panting for glory and for blood, came on King Edward's large reserve: from all the scattered parts of the field spurred the Yorkist knights, where the uproar, so much mightier than before, told them that the crisis of the war was come. Thither, as vultures to the carcase, they flocked and wheeled; thither D'Eyncourt, and Lovell, and Cromwell's bloody sword, and Say's knotted mace; and thither, again rallying his late half-beaten myrmidons, the grim Gloucester, his helmet bruised and dinted, but the boar's teeth still gnashing wrath and horror from the griesly crest. But direst and most hateful of all in the eyes of the yet undaunted earl, thither, plainly visible, riding scarcely a yard before him, with the cognizance of Clare wrought on his gay mantle, and in all the pomp and bravery of a holiday suit, came the perjured Clarence. Conflict now it could scarce be called: as well might the Dane have rolled back the sea from his footstool, as Warwick and his disordered troop (often and aye, dazzled here by Oxford's star, there by Edward's sun, dealing random blows against each other) have resisted the general whirl and torrent of the surrounding foe. To add to the rout, Somerset and the onguard of his wing had been marching towards the earl at the very time that the cry of "treason" had struck their ears, and Edward's charge was made: these men, nearly all Lancastrians, and ever doubting Montagu, if not Warwick, with the example of Clarence and the Archbishop of York fresh before them, lost heart at once—Somerset himself headed the flight of his force.

"All is lost!" said Montagu, as side by side with Warwick the brothers fronted the foe, and for one moment stayed the rush.

"Not yet," returned the earl; "a band of my northern archers still guard yon wood—I know them—they will fight to the last gasp! Thither then, with what men we may. You so marshal our soldiers, and I will make good the retreat. Where is Sir Marmaduke Nevile?"

"Here!"

"Horsed again, young cousin!—I give thee a perilous commission. Take the path down the hill; the mists thicken in the hollows, and may hide thee. Overtake Somerset—he hath fled westward, and tell him, from me, if he can yet rally but one troop of horse—but one—and charge Edward suddenly in the rear, he will yet redeem all. If he refuse, the ruin of his king, and the slaughter of the brave men he deserts, be on his head! Swift,—*à tout bride*, Marmaduke. Yet one word," added the earl, in a whisper—"if you fail with Somerset come not back, make to the Sanctuary. *You* are too young to die, cousin! Away!—keep to the hollows of the chase."

As the knight vanished, Warwick turned to his comrades.—"Bold nephew Fitzhugh, and ye brave riders, round me—so, we are fifty knights! Haste thou, Montagu, to the wood!—the wood!"

So noble in that hero age was the Individual, MAN, even amidst the multitudes massed by war, that history vies with romance in showing how far a single sword could redress the scale of war. While Montagu, with rapid dexterity, and a voice yet promising victory, drew back the remnant of the lines, and in serried order retreated to the outskirts of the wood, Warwick and his band of knights protected the movement from the countless horsemen who darted forth from Edward's swarming and momently thickening ranks. Now dividing and charging singly—now rejoining—and breast to breast, they served to divert and perplex and harass the eager enemy. And never in all his wars, in all the former might of his indomitable arm, had Warwick so excelled the martial chivalry of his age, as in that eventful and crowning hour. Thrice almost alone, he penetrated into the very centre of Edward's body-guard, literally felling to the earth all before him. Then perished by his battle-axe Lord Cromwell, and the redoubted Lord of Say—then, no longer sparing even the old affection, Gloucester was hurled to the ground. The last time he penetrated even to Edward himself, smiting down the king's standard-bearer, unhorsing Hastings, who threw himself on his path; and Edward, setting his teeth in stern joy as he saw him, rose in his stirrups, and for a moment the mace of the king, the axe of the earl, met as thunder encounters thunder; but then a hundred knights rushed into the rescue, and robbed the baffled avenger of his prey. Thus charging and retreating, driving back, with each charge, far and farther the mighty multitude hounding on to the lion's death, this great chief and his devoted knights, though terribly reduced in number, succeeded at last in covering Montagu's skilful retreat; and when they gained the outskirts of the wood, and dashed through the narrow opening between the barricades, the Yorkshire archers approved their Lord's trust, and, shouting as to a marriage feast, hailed his coming.

But few, alas! of his fellow-horsemen had survived that marvellous enterprise of valor and despair. Of the fifty knights who had shared its perils, eleven only gained the wood; and, though in this number the most eminent (save Sir John Coniers, either slain or fled,) might be found—their horses, more exposed than themselves, were for the most part wounded and unfit for further service. At this time the sun again, and suddenly as before, broke forth—not now with a feeble glimmer, but a broad and almost a cheerful beam, which sufficed to give a fuller view, than the day had yet afforded, of the state and prospects of the field.

To the right and to the left, what remained of the cavalry of Warwick were seen flying fast—gone the lances of Oxford, the bills of Somerset. Exeter, pierced by the shaft of Alwyn, was lying cold and insensible, remote from the contest, and deserted even by his squires.

In front of the archers, and such men as Montagu had saved from the sword, halted the immense and murmuring multitude of Edward, their thousand banners glittering in the sudden sun; for, as Edward beheld the last wrecks of his foe, stationed near the covert, his desire of consummating victory and revenge made him cautions, and, fearing an ambush, he had abruptly halted.

When the scanty followers of the earl thus beheld the immense force arrayed for their destruction, and saw the extent of their danger and their loss—here the handful, there the multitude—a simultaneous exclamation of terror and dismay broke from their ranks.

"Children!" cried Warwick, "droop not! Henry, at Agincourt, had worse odds than we!"

But the murmur among the archers, the lealest part of the earl's retainers, continued, till there stepped forth their captain, a grey old man, but still sinewy and unbent, the iron relic of a hundred battles.

"Back to your men, Mark Forester!" said the earl, sternly.

The old man obeyed not. He came on to Warwick, and fell on his knees beside his stirrup.

"Fly, my lord, escape is possible for you and your riders. Fly through the wood, we will screen your path with our bodies. Your children, father of your followers, your children, of Middleham, ask no better fate than to die for you! Is it not so?" and the old man, rising, turned to those in hearing. They answered by a general acclamation.

"Mark Forester speaks well," said Montagu. "On you depends the last hope of Lancaster. We may yet join Oxford and Somerset! This way, through the wood—come!" and he laid his hand on the earl's rein.

"Knights and sirs," said the earl dismounting, and partially raising his visor as he turned to the horsemen, "let those who will, fly with Lord Montagu! Let those who, in a just cause, never despair of victory, nor, even at the worst, fear to face their Maker, fresh from the glorious death of heroes, dismount with me!" Every knight sprang from his steed, Montagu the first. "Comrades!" continued the earl, then addressing the retainers, "when the children fight for a father's honor, the father flies not from the peril into which he has drawn the children. What to me were life, stained by the blood of mine own beloved retainers, basely deserted by their chief? Edward has proclaimed that he will spare *none*. Fool! he gives us, then, the superhuman mightiness of despair! To your bows!—one shaft—if it pierce the joints of the tyrant's mail—one shaft may scatter yon army to the winds! Sir Marmaduke has gone to rally noble Somerset and his riders—if we make good our defence one little hour—the foe may be yet smitten in the rear, and the day retrieved! Courage and heart then!" Here the earl lifted his visor to the farthest bar, and showed his cheerful face—"Is this the face of a man who thinks all hope is gone?"

In this interval, the sudden sunshine revealed to King Henry, where he stood, the dispersion of his friends. To the rear of the palisades, which protected the spot where he was placed, already grouped "the lookers-on, and no fighters," * as the chronicler words it, who, as the guns slackened, ventured forth to learn the news, and who now, filling the churchyard of Hadley, strove hard to catch a peep of Henry the saint, or of Bungey the sorcerer. Mingled with these, gleamed the robes of the tymbesteres, pressing nearer and nearer to the barriers, as wolves, in the instinct of blood, come nearer and nearer round the circling watch-fire of some northern travellers. At this time the friar, turning to one of the guards who stood near him, said, "The mists are needed no more now—King Edward hath got the day—eh?"

"Certes, great master," quoth the guard, "nothing now lack's to the king's triumph, except the death of the earl."

"Infamous nigromancer, hear that!" cried Bungey to Adam. "What now avail thy bombards and thy talisman! Hark ye!—tell me the secret of the last—of the damnable engine under my feet, and I may spare thy life."

Adam shrugged his soldiers in impatient disdain; "Unless I gave thee my science, my secret were profitless to thee. Villian and numbscull, do thy worst."

The friar made a sign to a soldier who stood behind Adam, and the soldier silently drew the end of the rope which girded the Scholar's neck round a bough of the leafless tree. "Hold!" whispered the friar, "not till I give the word.—the earl may recover himself yet," he added to himself. And therewith he began once more to vociferate his incantations. Meanwhile, the eyes of Sibyll had turned for a moment from her father; for the burst of sunshine, lighting up the valley below, had suddenly given to her eyes, in the distance, the gable-ends of the old farm-house, with the wintry orchard,—no longer, alas! smiling with starry blossoms. Far remote from the battle-field was that abode of peace—that once happy home, where she had watched the coming of the false one!

Loftier and holier were the thoughts of the fated king. He had turned his face from the field, and his eyes were fixed upon the tower of the church behind. And while he so gazed, the knoll from the belfry began solemnly to chime. It was now near the hour of the Sabbath prayers, and amidst horror and carnage, still the holy custom was not suspended.

"Hark!" said the king, mournfully—"That chime summons many a soul to God!"

While thus the scene on the eminence of Hadley, Edward, surrounded by Hastings, Gloucester, and his principal captains, took advantage of the unexpected sunshine, to scan the foe and its position, with the eye of his intuitive genius for all that can slaughter man. "This day," he said, "brings no victory, assures no crown, if Warwick escape alive. To you, Lovell and Ratcliffe, I entrust two hundred knights;—your sole care—the head of the rebel earl!"

"And Montagu?" said Ratcliffe.

"Montagu? Nay—poor Montagu, I loved him as well once, as my own mother's son; and Montagu," he muttered to himself, "I never wronged, and therefore him I can forgive! Spare the marquis.—I mislike that wood; they must have more force within than that handful on the skirts betrays. Come hither, D'Eyncourt."

And a few minutes afterwards, Warwick and his men saw two parties of horse leave the main body—one for the right hand, one the left—followed by long detachments of pikes, which they protected; and then the central array marched slowly and steadily on towards the scanty foe. The design was obvious—to surround on all sides the enemy, driven to its last desperate bay. But Montagu and his brother had not been idle in the breathing pause; they had planted the greater portion of the archers skilfully among the trees. They had placed their pikemen on the verge of the barricades, made by sharp stakes and fallen timber, and where their rampart was unguarded by the pass which had been left free for the horsemen, Hilyard and his stoutest fellows took their post, filling the gap with breasts of iron.

And now, as with horns and clarions—with a sea of plumes, and spears, and pennons, the multitudinous deathsmen came on, Warwick, towering in the front, not one feather on his eagle crest despoiled or shorn, stood, dismounted, his visor still raised, by his renowned

* Hall.

steed. Some of the men had by Warwick's order removed the mail from the destrier's breast; and the noble animal, relieved from the weight, seemed as unexhausted as its rider; save where the champed foam had bespecked its glossy hide, not a hair was turned; and the onguard of the Yorkists heard its fiery snort, as they moved slowly on. This figure of horse and horsemen stood prominently forth, amidst the little band. And Lovell, riding by Ratcliffe's side, whispered—"Beshrew me, I would rather King Edward had asked for mine own head, than that gallant earl's!"

"Tush, youth," said the inexorable Ratcliffe—"I care not of what steps the ladder of mine ambition may be made!"

While they were thus speaking, Warwick, turning to Montagu and his knights, said—

"Our sole hope is in the courage of our men. And, as at Touton, when I gave the throne to yon false man, I slew, with my own hand, my noble Malech, to show that on that spot I would win or die, and by that sacrifice so fired the soldiers, that we turned the day—so now—oh, gentlemen, in another hour ye would jeer me, for my hand fails; this hand that the poor beast hath so often fed from! Saladin, last of thy race, serve me now in death as in life. Not for my sake, oh noblest steed that ever bore a knight—not for mine this offering!"

He kissed the destrier on his frontal, and Saladin, as if conscious of the coming blow, bent his proud crest humbly, and licked his lord's steel-clad hand. So associated together had been horse and horseman, that had it been a human sacrifice, the bystanders could not have been more moved. And when, covering the charger's eyes with one hand, the earl's dagger descended, bright and rapid—a groan went through the ranks. But the effect was unspeakable! The men knew at once, that to them, and them alone, their lord entrusted his fortunes and his life—they were nerved to more than mortal daring. No escape for Warwick—why, then, in Warwick's person they lived and died! Upon foe as upon friend, the sacrifice produced all that could tend to strengthen the last refuge of despair. Even Edward, where he rode in the van, beheld and knew the meaning of the deed. Victorious Touton rushed back upon his memory with a thrill of strange terror and remorse.

"He will die as he has lived," said Gloucester, with admiration. "If I live for such a field, God grant me such a death!"

As the words left the duke's lips, and Warwick, one foot on his dumb friend's corpse, gave the mandate, a murderous discharge from the archers in the covert, rattled against the line of the Yorkists, and the foe, still advancing, stepped over a hundred corpses to the conflict. Despite the vast preponderance of numbers, the skill of Warwick's archers, the strength of his position, the obstacle to the cavalry made by the barricades, rendered the attack perilous in the extreme. But the orders of Edward were prompt and vigorous. He cared not for the waste of life, and as one rank fell, another rushed on. High before the barricades, stood Montagu, Warwick, and the rest of that indomitable chivalry, the flower of the ancient Norman heroism. As idly beat the waves upon a rock as the ranks of Edward upon that serried front of steel. The sun still shone in heaven, and still Edward's conquest was unassured. Nay, if Marmaduke could yet bring back the troops of Somerset upon the rear of the foe, Montagu and the earl felt that the victory might be for them. And often the earl paused, to harken for the cry of "Somerset" on the gale, and often Montagu raised his visor to look for the banners and the spears of the Lancastrian duke. And ever, as the earl listened and Montagu scanned the field, larger and larger seemed to spread the armament of Edward. The regiment which boasted the stubborn energy of Alwyn was now in movement, and, encouraged by the young Saxon's hardihood, the Londoners marched on, unawed by the massacre of their predecessors.

But Alwyn, avoiding the quarter defended by the knighis, defiled a little towards the left. where his quick eye inured to the northern fogs, had detected the weakness of the barricade in the spot where Hilyard was stationed; and this pass Alwyn (discarding the bow) resolved to attempt at the point of the pike—the weapon answering to our modern bayonet. The first rush which he headed was so impetuous as to effect an entry. The weight of the numbers behind urged on the foremost, and Hilyard had not sufficient space for the sweep of the two-handed sword which had done good work that day. While here the conflict became fierce and doubtful, the right wing led by D'Eyncourt had pierced the wood, and, surprised to discover no ambush, fell upon the archers in the rear. The scene was now inexpressibly terrific; cries and groans, and the ineffable roar and yell of human passion resounded demon-like through the shade of the leafless trees. And at this moment, the provident and rapid generalship of Edward had moved up one of his heavy bombards. Warwick and Montagu, the most of the knights, were called from the barricades to aid the archers thus assailed behind, but an instant before that defence was shattered into air by explosion of the bombard.

In another minute horse and foot rushed through the opening. And amidst all the din was heard the voice of Edward, "Strike! and spare not; we win the day!" "We win the day! — victory! — victory!" repeated the troops behind; rank caught the sound from rank—and file from file—it reached the captive Henry, and he paused in prayer; it reached the ruthless friar, and he gave the sign to the hireling at his shoulder; it reached the priest as he entered, unmoved, the church of Hadley. And the bell, changing its note into a quicker and sweeter chime, invited the living to prepare for death, and the soul to rise above the cruelty, and the falsehood, and the pleasure and the pomp, and the wisdom and the glory of the world! And suddenly, as the chime ceased, there was heard, from the eminence hard by, a shriek of agony—a female shriek—drowned by the roar of a bombard in the field below.

On pressed the Yorkists through the pass forced by Alwyn. "Yield, thee, stout fellow," said the bold trader to Hilyard, whose dogged energy, resembling his own, moved his admiration, and in whom, by the accent in which Robin called his men, he recognized a north countryman;—"Yield, and I will see that thou goest safe in life and limb—look round—ye are beaten."

"Fool!" answered Hilyard, setting his teeth—"the People are never beaten!" And as the words left his lips, the shot from the recharged bombard shattered him piecemeal.

"On for London, and the crown!" cried Alwyn—"the citizens *are* the people!"

At this time, through the general crowd of the Yorkists, Rathcliffe and Lovell, at the head of their appointed knights, galloped forward to accomplish their crowning mission.

Behind the column which still commemorates "the great battle" of that day, stretches now a trilateral patch of pasture land, which faces a small house. At that time this space was rough forest ground, and where now, in the hedge, rise two small trees, types of the diminutive offspring of our niggard and ignoble civilization, rose then two huge oaks, coeval with the warriors of the Norman Conquest. They grew close together, yet, though their roots interlaced—though their branches mingled, one had not taken nourishment from the other. They stood, equal in height and grandeur, the twin giants of the wood. Before these trees, whose ample trunks protected them from the falchions in the rear, Warwick and Montagu took their last post. In front rose, literally, mounds of the slain, whether of foe or friend; for round the two brothers to the last had gathered the brunt of war, and they towered now, almost solitary in valor's sublime despair, amidst the wrecks of battle, and against the irresistible march of fate. As side by side they had gained this spot, and the vulgar assailants drew back, leaving the bodies of the dead their last defence from death, they turned their visors to each other, as for one latest farewell on earth.

"Forgive me, Richard!" said Montagu—"forgive me thy death;—had I not so blindly believed in Clarence's fatal order, the savage Edward had never passed alive through the pass of Pontefract."

"Blame not thyself," replied Warwick. "We are but the instruments of a wiser Will. God assoil thee, brother mine. We leave this world to tyranny and vice. Christ receive our souls!"

For a moment their hands clasped, and then all was grim silence.

Wide and far, behind and before, in the gleam of the sun, stretched the victorious armament, and that breathing pause sufficed to show the grandeur of their resistance—the grandest of all spectacles, even in its hopeless extremity—the defiance of brave hearts to the brute force of the Many. Where they stood they were visible to thousands, but not a man stirred against them. The memory of Warwick's past achievements—the consciousness of his feats that day—all the splendor of his fortunes and his name, made the mean fear to strike, and the brave ashamed to murder. The gallant D'Eyncourt sprung from his steed, and advanced to the spot. His followers did the same.

"Yield, my lords—yield! Ye have done all that men could do."

"Yield, Montagu," whispered Warwick. "Edward can harm not thee. Life has sweets; so they say, at least."

"Not with power and glory gone. We yield not, Sir Knight," answered the marquis, in a calm tone.

"Then die! and make room for the new men whom ye so have scorned!" exclaimed a fierce voice; and Ratcliffe, who had neared the spot, dismounted, and hallooed on his bloodhounds.

Seven points might the shadow have traversed on the dial, and before Warwick's axe, and Montagu's sword, seven souls had gone to judgment. In that brief crisis, amidst the general torpor and stupefaction and awe of the bystanders, round one little spot centered still a war.

But numbers rushed on numbers, as the fury of conflict urged on the lukewarm; Montagu was beaten to his knee—Warwick covered him with his body—a hundred axes resounded on the earl's stooping casque—a hundred blades gleamed round the joints of his harness: —a simultaneous cry was heard:—over the mounds of the slain, through the press into the shadow of the oaks, dashed Gloucester's charger. The conflict had ceased—the executioners stood mute in a half-circle. Side by side, axe and sword still griped in their iron hands, lay Montagu and Warwick.

The young duke, his visor raised, contemplated the fallen foes in silence. Then dismounting, he unbraced with his own hand the earl's helmet. Revived for a moment by the air, the hero's eyes unclosed, his lips moved, he raised, with a feeble effort, the gory battle-axe, and the armed crowd rocoiled in terror. But the earl's soul, dimly conscious, and about to part, had escaped from that scene of strife—its later thoughts of wrath and vengeance—to more gentle memories, to such memories as fade the last from true and manly hearts!

"Wife!—child!" murmured the earl, indistinctly. "Anne—Anne!—Dear ones, God comfort ye!" And with these words the breath went—the head fell heavily on its mother earth—the face set, calm and undistorted as the face of a soldier should be, when a brave death has been worthy of a brave life.

"So," muttered the dark and musing Gloucester, nnconscious of the throng; "so perishes the Race of Iron! Low lies the last Baron who could control the throne and command the people. The Age of Force expires with knighthood and deeds of arms. And over this dead great man I see the New Cycle dawn. Happy, henceforth, he who can plot, and scheme, and fawn, and smile!" Waking with a start, from his reverie, the splendid dissimulator said, as in sad reproof—"Ye have been over-hasty, knights and gentlemen. The House of York is mighty enough to have spared such noble foes. Sound trumpets! Fall in file! Way, there—way! King Edward comes! Long live the King!"

CHAPTER VII.

The Last Pilgrims in the Long Procession to the Common Bourne.

THE king and his royal brothers, immediately after the victory rode back to London to announce their triumph. The foot soldiers still stayed behind to recruit themselves after the sore fatigue; and towards the eminence by Hadley Church, the peasants and villagers of the district had pressed in awe and in wonder; for on that spot had Henry (now sadly led back to a prison, never again to unclose to his living form) stood to watch the destruction of the host gathered in his name—and to that spot the corpses of Warwick and Montagu were removed, while a bier was prepared to convey their remains to London *—and on

* The bodies of Montagu and the earl were exhibited bareheaded at St. Paul's church for three days, "that no pretences of their being alive might stir up any rebellion afterwards; they were then carried down to the Priory of Bisham, in Berkshire, where, among their ancestors by the mother's side (the Earls of Salisbury), the two unquiet brothers rest in one tomb. The large river of blood, divided now into many streams, runs so

that spot had the renowned friar conjured the mists — exorcised the enchanted guns — and defeated the horrible machinations of the Lancastrian wizard.

And towards the spot, and through the crowd, a young Yorkist captain passed with a prisoner he had captured, and whom he was leading to the tent of Lord Hastings, the only one of the commanders from whom mercy might be hoped, and who had tarried behind the king and his royal brothers to make preparations for the removal of the mighty dead.

"Keep close to me, Sir Marmaduke," said the Yorkist; "we must look to Hastings to appease the king; and, if he hope not to win your pardon, he may at least, after such a victory, aid one foe to fly."

"Care not for me, Alwyn," said the knight; "when Somerset was deaf, save to his own fears,—I came back to die by my chieftain's side, alas, too late—too late! Better now death than life! What kin, kith, ambition, love, were to other men, was Lord Warwick's smile to me!"

Alwyn kindly respected his prisoner's honest emotion, and took advantage of it to lead him away from the spot where he saw knights and warriors thickest grouped, in soldier-like awe and sadness, round the Hero-Brothers. He pushed through a humbler crowd of peasants, and citizens, and women with babes at their breast; and suddenly, saw a troop of timbrel women dancing round a leafless tree, and chanting some wild, but mirthful and joyous doggerel.

"What obscene and ill-seasoned revelry is this!" said the trader to a gaping yeoman.

"They are but dancing, poor girls, round the wicked wizard, whom Friar Bungey caused to be strangled,—and his witch daughter."

A chill foreboding seized upon Alwyn; he darted forward, scattering peasant and tymbestere, with his yet bloody sword. His feet stumbled against some broken fragments; it was the poor Eureka, shattered, at last, for the sake of the diamond! Valueless to the great friar, since the science of the owner could not pass to his executioner—valueless, the mechanism and the invention, the labor and the genius, but the superstition, and the folly, and the delusion, *had* their value, and the impostor who destroyed the engine clutched the jewel!

From the leafless tree was suspended the the dead body of a man; beneath, lay a female, dead too; but whether by the hand of man or the mercy of Heaven there was no sign to tell. Scholar and Child, Knowledge and Innocence, alike were cold; the grim Age had devoured them as it devours ever those before, as behind, its march—and confounds, in one common doom, the too guileless and the too wise!

"Why crowd ye thus, knaves?" said a commanding voice.

"Ha, Lord Hastings!—approach, behold!" exclaimed Alwyn.

"Ha—ha!" shouted Graul, as she led her sisters from the spot, wheeling and screaming, and tossing up their timbrels—"Ha! the witch and her lover!—Ha—ha! Foul is fair! —Ha—ha! Witchcraft and death go together, as thou mayst learn at the last, sleek wooer."

And, peradventure, when, long years afterwards, accusations of witchcraft, wantonness, and treason, resounded in the ears of Hastings, and, at the signal of Gloucester, rushed in the armed doomsmen, those ominous words echoed back upon his soul!

At that very hour the gates of the Tower were thrown open to the multitude. Fresh from his victory, Edward and his brothers had gone to render thankgivings at St. Paul's, (they were devout—those three Plantagents!) thence to Baynard's Castle, to escort the queen and her children once more to the Tower. And, now, the sound of trumpets stilled the joyous uproar of the multitude, for, in the balcony of the casement that loooked towards the chapel, the herald had just announced that King Edward would show himself to the people. On every inch of the court-yard, climbing up wall and palisade, soldier, citizen, thief, harlot,—age, childhood, all the various conditions and epochs of multiform life, swayed, clung, murmured, moved, jostled, trampled;—the beings of the little hour!

High from the battlements against the westering beam floated Edward's conquering flag —a sun shining to the sun. Again, and a third time, rang the trumpets, and on the balcony, his crown upon his head, but his form

small they are hardly observed as they flow by."[1]—*Sic transit gloria mundi!*

[1] HABINGTON'S *Life of Edward IV.*, one of the most eloquent compositions in the language, though incorrect as a history.

still sheathed in armor, stood the king. What mattered to the crowd his falseness and his perfidy—his licentiousness and cruelty? All vices ever vanish in success! Hurrah for King Edward! THE MAN OF THE AGE suited the age, had valor for its war and cunning for its peace, and the sympathy of the age was with him! So there stood the king;—at his right hand, Elizabeth, with her infant boy (the heir of England) in her arms—the proud face of the duchess seen over the queen's shoulder. By Elizabeth's side was the Duke of Gloucester, leaning on his sword, and at the left of Edward, the perjured Clarence bowed his fair head to the joyous throng! At the sight of the victorious king, of the lovely queen, and, above all, of the young male heir, who promised length of days to the line of York, the crowd burst forth with a hearty cry—"Long live the king and the king's son!" Mechanically Elizabeth turned her moistened eyes from Edward to Edward's brother, and suddenly, as with a mother's prophetic instinct, clasped her infant closer to her bosom, when she caught the glittering and fatal eye of Richard Duke of Gloueester (York's young hero of the day, Warwick's grim avenger in the future), fixed upon that harmless life—destined to interpose a feeble obstacle between the ambition of a ruthless intellect and the heritage of the English throne!

NOTES.

I.

THE Badge of the Bear and ragged Staff was so celebrated in the fifteenth century, that the following extract from a letter addressed by Mr. Courthope, Rouge Croix, to the author, will no doubt interest the reader, and the author is happy in the opportunity afforded of expressing his acknowledgements for the courteous attention with which Mr. Courthope has honored his inquiries:—

"*College of Arms.*

"As regards the badge of Richard Nevile, Earl of Warwick—viz., the Bear and Staff I agree with you, certainly, as to the probability of his having sometimes used the whole badge, and sometimes the *staff* only, which accords precisely with the way in which the Bear and Staff are set forth in the Rous Roll to the early Earls (Warwick), before the Conquest. We, there, find them figured with the staff upon their shields, and the bear at their feet, and the staff alone is introduced as a quartering upon their shields.

"The story of the origin of these badges is as follows:

"Arth, or Arthgal, is reputed to have been the first Earl of Warwick, and being one of the knights of King Arthur's Round Table, it behoved him to have a cognizance; and Arth or Narth signifying in British the same as Ursus in Latin, he took the bear for such cognizance: his successor, Morvidus, Earl of Warwick, in single combat, overcame a mighty giant (who had encountered him with a tree pulled up from the root, the boughts of which had been torn from it), and in token of his success, assumed the ragged staff. You will thus see that the origins of the two were different, which would render the bearing of them separately not unlikely, and you will likewise infer that both came through the Beauchamps. I do not find the ragged staff ever attributed to the Neviles before the match with Beauchamp.

"As regards the crest or cognizance of Nevile, the Pied Bull has been the cognizance of that family from a very early time, and the Bull's head its crest, and both the one and the other may have been used by the King-maker, and by his brother, the Marquis Montagu; the said bull appears at the feet of Richard Nevile in the Rous Roll, accompanied by the Eagle of Monthermer; the crests on either side of him are those of Montagu and Nevile: besides these two crests, both of which the Marquis Montagu may have used, he certainly did use the Gryphon, issuant out of a ducal coronet, as this appears alone for his crest, on his garter plate, as a crest for Montagu, he having given the arms of that family precedence over his paternal coat of Nevile; the King-maker, likewise, upon his seal, gives the precedence to Montagu and Monthermer, and they alone appear upon his shield.

II.

Hume, Rapin, and Carte, all dismiss the story of Edward's actual imprisonment at Middleham, while Lingard, Sharon Turner, and others, adopt it implicitly. And yet, though Lingard has successfully grappled with some of Hume's objections, he has left others wholly unanswered. Hume states that no such fact is mentioned in Edward's subseqeunt proclamation against Clarence and Warwick. Lingard answers, after correcting an immaterial error in Hume's dates, —"that the proclamation ought not to have mentioned it, because it was confined to the enumeration of offences only committed after the general amnesty in 1469." And then, surely with some inconsistency, quotes the attainder of Clarence many years afterwards, in which the king enumerates it among his offences, "as jeoparding the king's royal estate, person, and life, in strait warde, putting him thereby from all his libertye after procuring great commotions." But it is clear that if the amnesty hindered Edward from charging Warwick with this imprisonment only one year after it was granted, it would, *a fortiori*, hinder him from charging Clarence with it *nine* years after. Most probable is it that this article of accusation does not refer to any imprisonment, real or supposed, at Middleham, in 1469, but to Clarence's invasion of England in 1470, when Edward's state, personne, and life were indeed jeopardized by his narrow escape from the fortified house, where he might fairly be called, "in straite warde;" especially as the words, "after procuring great commotions," could not apply to the date of the supposed detention in Middleham, when, instead of procuring commotions, Clarence had helped Warwick to allay them, but *do* properly apply to his subsequent rebellion in 1470. Finally, Edward's charges against his brother, as Lingard, himself, has observed elsewhere, are not proofs, and that king never scrupled at any falsehood to serve his turn. Nothing, in short, can be more improbable than this tale of Edward's captivity—there was no object in it. At the very time it is said to have taken place, Warwick is absolutely engaged in warfare against the king's foes. The moment Edward leaves Middleham, instead of escaping to London, he goes carelessly and openly to York, to judge and execute the very captain of the rebels whom Warwich has subdued, and in the very midst of Warwick's armies! Far from appearing to harbor the natural resentment so vindictive a king must have felt (had so great an indignity been offered to him)—almost immediately after he leaves York, he takes the Nevile family into greater power than ever, confers new dignities upon Warwick, and betroths his eldest daughter to Warwick's nephew. On the whole, then, perhaps some such view of the king's visit to Middleham, which has been takeu in this narrative, may be considered not the least probable compromise of the disputed and contradictory evidence on the subject.

END OF "THE LAST OF THE BARONS."

RIENZI,

THE LAST OF THE TRIBUNES.

DEDICATION OF RIENZI.

TO

ALESSANDRO MANZONI,

As to the Genius of the Place, are Dedicated,

THESE FRUITS,

Gathered on the Soil of Italian Fiction.

PREFACE TO THE FIRST EDITION OF RIENZI.

I BEGAN this tale two years ago at Rome. On removing to Naples, I threw it aside for "The Last Days of Pompeii," which required more than "Rienzi" the advantage of residence within reach of the scenes described. The fate of the Roman Tribune continued, however, to haunt and impress me, and, some time after "Pompeii," was published, I renewed my earlier undertaking. I regarded the completion of these volumes, indeed, as a kind of duty;—for having had occasion to read the original authorities from which modern historians have drawn their accounts of the life of Rienzi, I was led to believe that a very remarkable man had been superficially judged, and a very important period crudely examined.* And this belief was sufficiently strong to induce me at first to meditate a more serious work upon the life and times of Rienzi.† Various reasons concurred against this project—and I renounced the biography to commence the fiction. I have still, however, adhered, with a greater fidelity than is customary in Romance, to all the leading events of the public life of the Roman Tribune; and the Reader will perhaps find in these pages a more full and detailed account of the rise and fall of Rienzi, than in any English work of which I am aware. I have, it is true, taken a view of his character different in some respects from that of Gibbon or Sismondi. But it is a view, in all its main features, which I believe (and think I could prove) myself to be warranted in taking, not less by the facts of History than the laws of Fiction. In the meanwhile, as I have given the facts from which I have drawn my interpretation of the principal agent, the reader has sufficient data for his own judgment. In the picture of the Roman Populace, as in that of the Roman Nobles of the fourteenth century, I follow literally the descriptions left to us;—they are not flattering, but they are faithful, likenesses.

Preserving generally the real chronology of Rienzi's life, the plot of this work extends over a space of some years, and embraces the variety of characters necessary to a true delineation of events. The story, therefore, cannot have precisely that order of interest found in fictions strictly and genuinely *dramatic*, in which (to my judgment at least) the time ought to be as limited as possible, and the characters as few;—no new character of importance to the catastrophe being admissible towards the end of the work. If I may use the word Epic in its most modest and unassuming acceptation, this Fiction, in short, though indulging in dramatic situations, belongs, as a whole, rather to the Epic than the Dramatic school.

* See Appendix, Nos. I. and II.

† I have adopted the termination of *Rienzi* instead of *Rienzo*, as being more familiar to the general reader.—But the latter is perhaps the more accurate reading, since the name was a popular corruption from Lorenzo.

I cannot conclude without rendering the tribute of my praise and homage to the versatile and gifted Author of the beautiful Tragedy of Rienzi. Considering that our hero be the same—considering that we had the same materials from which to choose our several stories—I trust that I shall be found to have little, if at all, trespassed upon ground previously occupied. With the single exception of a love-intrigue between a relative of Rienzi and one of the antagonist party, which makes the plot of Miss Metford's Tragedy, and is little more than an episode in my Romance, having slight effect on the conduct and none on the fate of the hero, I am not aware of any resemblance between the two works; and even *this* coincidence I could easily have removed, had I deemed it the least advisable:—but it would be almost discreditable if I had *nothing* that resembled a performance possessing so much it were an honor to imitate.

In fact, the prodigal materials of the story—the rich and exuberant complexities of Rienzi's character—joined to the advantage possessed by the Novelist of embracing all that the Dramatist must reject*—are sufficient to prevent Dramatist and Novelist from interfering with each other.

London, December 1, 1835.

PREFACE TO THE PRESENT EDITION, 1848.

From the time of its first appearance, "Rienzi" has had the good fortune to rank high amongst my most popular works—though its interest is rather drawn from a faithful narration of historical facts, than from the inventions of fancy. And the success of this experiment confirms me in my belief, that the true mode of employing history in the service of romance, is to study diligently the materials *as* history; conform to such views of the facts as the Author would adopt, if he related them in the dry character of historian; and obtain that warmer interest which fiction bestows, by tracing the causes of the facts in the characters and emotions of the personages of the time. The events of his work are thus already shaped to his hand—the characters already created—what remains for him, is the inner, not outer, history of man—the chronicle of the human heart; and it is by this that he introduces a new harmony between character and event, and adds the completer solution of what is actual and true, by those speculations of what is natural and probable, which are out of the province of history, but belong especially to the philosophy of romance. And—if it be permitted the tale-teller to come reverently for instruction in his art to the mightiest teacher of all, who, whether in the page or on the scene, would give to airy fancies the breath and the form of life,—such, we may observe, is the lesson the humblest craftsman in historical romance may glean from the Historical Plays of Shakespeare. Necessarily, Shakespeare consulted history according to the imperfect lights, and from the popular authorities, of his age; and I do not say, therefore, that as an historian we can rely upon Shakespeare as correct. But to that in which he believed he rigidly adhered; nor did he seek, as lesser artists (such as Victor Hugo and his disciples) seek now, to turn perforce the Historical into the Poetical, but leaving history as he found it, to call forth from its arid prose the flower of the latent poem. Nay, even in the more imaginative plays which he has founded upon novels and legends popular in his time, it is curious and instructive to see how little he has altered the original ground-work—taking for granted the main materials of the story, and reserving all his matchless resources of wisdom and invention, to illustrate from mental analysis, the creations whose outline he was content to borrow. He receives, as a literal fact not to be altered, the somewhat incredible assertion of the novelist, that the pure and delicate and high-born Venetian loves the swarthy Moor—and that Romeo fresh from his "woes for Rosaline," becomes suddenly enamoured of Juliet: He found the Improbable and employed his art to make it truthful.

That "Rienzi" should have attracted pe-

* Thus the slender space permitted to the Dramatist does not allow Miss Mitford to be very faithful to facts; to distinguish between Rienzi's earlier and his later period of power; or to detail the true, but somewhat intricate causes of his rise, his splendor, and his fall.

culiar attention in Italy, is of course to be attributed to the choice of the subject rather than to the skill of the Author. It has been translated into the Italian language by eminent writers; and the authorities for the new view of Rienzi's times and character which the Author deemed himself warranted to take, have been compared with his text by careful critics and illustrious scholars, in those states in which the work has been permitted to circulate.* I may say, I trust without unworthy pride, that the result has confirmed the accuracy of delineations which English readers relying only on the brilliant but disparaging account in Gibbon deemed too favorable; and has tended to restore the great Tribune to his long forgotten claims to the love and reverence of the Italian land. Nor, if I may trust to the assurances that have reached me from many now engaged in the aim of political regeneration, has the effect of that revival of the honors due to a national hero, leading to the ennobling study of great examples, been wholly without its influence upon the rising generation of Italian youth, and thereby upon those stirring events which have recently drawn the eyes of Europe to the men and the lands beyond the Alps.

In preparing for the press this edition of a work illustrative of the exertions of a Roman, in advance of his time, for the political freedom of his country, and of those struggles between contending principles, of which Italy was the most stirring field in Middle Ages, it is not out of place or season to add a few sober words, whether as a student of the Italian Past, or as an observer, with some experience of the social elements of Italy as it now exists, upon the state of affairs in that country.

It is nothing new to see the Papal Church in the capacity of a popular reformer, and in contra-position to the despotic potentates of the several states, as well as to the German Emperor, who nominally inherits the sceptre of the Cæsars. Such was its common character under its more illustrious Pontiffs; and the old Republics of Italy grew up under the shadow of the Papal throne, harboring ever two factions—the one for the Emperor, the one for the Pope—the latter the more naturally allied to Italian independence. On the modern stage, we almost see the repetition of many an ancient drama. But the past should teach us to doubt the continuous and steadfast progress of any single line of policy under a principality so constituted as that of the Papal Church—a principality in which no race can be perpetuated, in which no objects can be permament; in which the successor is chosen by a select ecclesiastical synod, under a variety of foreign as well as of national influences; in which the chief usually ascends the throne at an age that ill adapts his mind to the idea of human progress, and the active direction of mundane affairs;—a principality in which the peculiar sanctity that wraps the person of the Sovereign exonerates him from the healthful liabilities of a power purely temporal, and directly accountable to Man. A reforming Pope is a lucky accident, and dull indeed must be the brain which believes in the possibility of a long succession of reforming Popes, or which can regard as other than precarious and unstable the discordant combination of a constitutional government with an infallible head.

It is as true as it is trite that political freedom is not the growth of a day—it is not a flower without a stalk, and it must gradually develop itself from amidst the unfolding leaves of kindred institutions.

In one respect, the Austrian domination, fairly considered, has been beneficial to the States over which it has been directly exercised, and may be even said to have unconsciously schooled them to the capacity for freedom. In those States the personal rights which depend on impartial and incorrupt administration of the law, are infinitely more secure than in most of the Courts of Italy. Bribery, which shamfully predominates in the judicature of certain Principalities, is as unknown in the juridical courts of Austrian Italy as in England. The Emperor himself is often involved in legal disputes with a subject, and justice is as free and as firm for the humblest suitor, as if his antagonist were his equal. Austria, indeed but holds together the motley and inharmonious members of its vast domain on either side the Alps, by a general character of paternal mildness and forbearance in all that great circle of good government which lies without the one principle of constitutional liberty.

* In the Papal States, I believe, it was neither, prudently nor effectually, proscribed.

It asks but of its subjects to submit to be well governed—without agitating the question "how and by what means that government is carried on." For every man, except the politician, the innovator, Austria is no harsh stepmother. But it is obviously clear that the better in other respects the administration of a state it does but foster the more the desire for that political security, which is only found in constitutional freedom: the reverence paid to personal rights, but begets the passion for political; and under a mild despotism are already half matured the germs of a popular constitution. But it is still a grave question whether Italy is ripe for self-government—and whether, were it possible that the Austrian domination could be shaken off—the very passions so excited, the very bloodshed so poured forth, would not ultimately place the larger portion of Italy under auspices less favorable to the sure growth of freedom, than those which silently brighten under the sway of of the German Cæsar.

The two kingdoms, at the opposite extremes of Italy, to which circumstances and nature seem to assign the man ascendancy, are Naples and Sardinia. Looking to the former, it is impossible to discover on the face of the earth a country more adapted for commercial prosperity. Nature formed it as the garden of Europe, and the mart of the Mediterranean. Its soils and climate could unite the products of the East with those of the Western Hemisphere. The rich island of Sicily should be the great corn granary of the modern nations as it was of the ancient; the figs, the olives, the oranges, of both the Sicilies, under skilful cultivation, should equal the produce of Spain and the Orient, and the harbors of the kingdom (the keys to three-quarters of the globe) should be crowded with the sails and busy with the life of commerce. But, in the character of its population, Naples has been invariably in the rear of Italian progress; it caught but partial inspiration from the free Republics, or even the wise Tyrannies, of the Middle Ages; the theatre of frequent revolutions without fruit; and all rational enthusiasm created by that insurrection, which has lately bestowed on Naples the boon of a representative system, cannot but be tempered by the conviction that of all the States in Italy, this is the one which least warrants the belief of permanence to political freedom, or of capacity to retain with vigor what may be seized by passion.*

Far otherwise is it, with Sardinia. Many years since, the writer of these pages ventured to predict that the time must come when Sardinia would lead the van of Italian civilization, and take proud place amongst the greater nations of Europe. In the great portion of this population there is visible the new blood of a young race; it is not, as with other Italian states, a worn-out stock; you do not see there a people fallen, proud of the past, and lazy amidst ruins, but a people rising, practical, industrious, active; there, in a word, is an eager youth to be formed to mature development, not a decrepit age to be restored to bloom and muscle. Progress is the great characteristic of the Sandinian state. Leave it for five years; visit it agaiu, and you behold improvement. When you enter the kingdom and find, by the very skirts of its admirable roads, a raised footpath for the passengers and travellers from town to town, you become suddenly aware that you are in a land where close attention to the humbler classes is within the duties of a government. As you pass on from the more purely Italian part of the population,—from Genoese country into that of Piedmont,—the difference between a new people and an old, on which I have dwelt, becomes visible in the improved cultivation of the soil, the better habitations of the laborer, the neater aspect of the towns, the greater activity in the thoroughfares. To the extraordinary virtues

---

* If the electoral Chamber in the new Neapolitan Constitution, give a fair share of members to the Island of Sicily, it will be rich in the inevitable elements of discord, and nothing save a wisdom and moderation, which cannot soberly be anticipated, can prevent the ultimate separation of the island from the dominion of Naples. Nature has set the ocean between the two countries—but differences in character, in degre and quality of civilization—national jealousies, historical memories, have trebled the space of the seas that roll between them.—More easy to unite under one free Parliament, Spain with Flanders; or re-annex to England its old domains of Aquitaine and Normandy—than to unite in one Council Chamber *truly* popular, the passions, interests, and prejudices of Sicily and Naples.—Time will show. And now, in May, 1849—Time has already shown the impracticability of the first scheme proposed for cordial union between Naples and Sicily, and has rendered it utterly impossible, by mutual recollections of hatred, bequeathed by a cival war of singular barbarism, that Naples should permanently retain Sicily by any other hold than the brute force of conquest.

of the King, as King, justice is scarcely done, whether in England or abroad. Certainly, despite his recent concessions, Charles Albert is not and cannot be at heart, much of a constitutional reformer; and his strong religious tendencies, which, perhaps unjustly, have procured him in philosophical quarters the character of a bigot, may link him more than his political, with the cause of the Father of his Church. But he is nobly and pre-eminently national, careful of the prosperity and jealous of the honor of his own state, while conscientiously desirous of the independence of Italy. His attention to business, is indefatigable. Nothing escapes his vigilance. Over all departments of the kingdom is the eye of a man ever anxious to improve. Already the silk manufactures of Sardinia almost rival those of Lyons: in their own departments the tradesmen of Turin exhibit an artistic elegance and elaborate finish, scarcely exceeded in the wares of London and Paris.

The King's internal regulations are admirable; his laws, administered with the most impartial justice—his forts and defences are in that order, without which, at least on the Continent, no land is safe—his army is the most perfect in Italy. His wise genius extends itself to the elegant as to the useful arts — an encouragement that shames England, and even France, is bestowed upon the School for Painters, which has become one of the ornaments of his illustrious reign. The character of the main part of the population, and the geographical position of his country, assist the monarch and must force on himself, or his successors, in the career of improvement so signally begun. In the character of the people, the vigor of the Northman ennobles the ardor and fancy of the West. In the position of the country, the public mind is brought into constant communication with the new ideas in the free lands of Europe. Civilization sets in direct currents towards the streets and marts of Turin. Whatever the result of the present crisis in Italy, no power and no chance which statesman can predict, can preclude Sardinia from ultimately heading all that is best in Italy. The King may improve his present position, or peculiar prejudices, inseparable perhaps from the heritage of absolute monarchy, and which the raw and rude councils of an Electoral Chamber, newly called into life, must often irritate and alarm, may check his own progress towards the master throne of the Ausonian land. But the people themselves, sooner or later, will do the work of the King. And in now looking round Italy for a race worthy of Rienzi, and able to accomplish his proud dreams, I see but one for which the time is ripe or ripening, and I place the hopes of Italy in the men of Piedmont and Sardinia.

LONDON,
February 14, 1848.

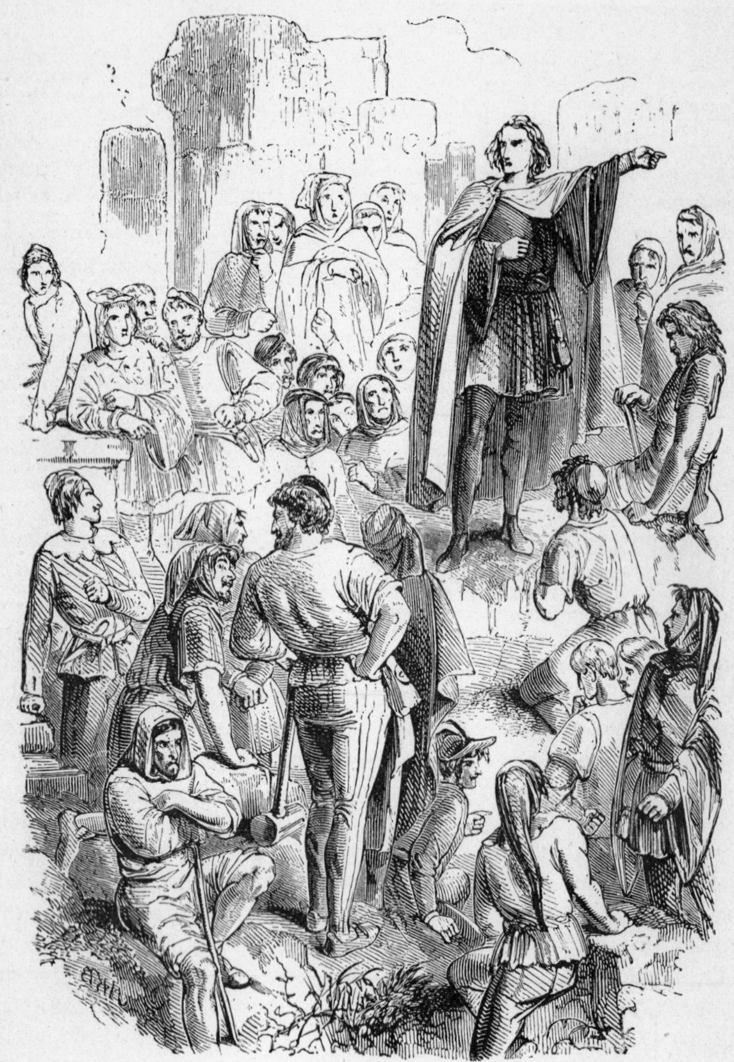

RIENZI.

BOOK FIRST.

THE TIME, THE PLACE, AND THE MEN.

"Fu da sua gioventudine nutricato di latte di eloquenza; buono grammatico, megliore rettorico, autorista buono .. . . Oh, come spesso diceva, 'Dove sono questi buoni Romani? Dov'è loro somma giustizia? Poterommi trovare in tempo che questi fioriscano?' Era bell 'omo . . . Accadde che uno suo frate fu ucciso, e non ne fu fatta vendetta di sua morte: non lo poteò aiutare; pensa lungo mano vendicare 'l sangua di suo frate; pensa lunga mano dirizzare la cittate di Roma male guidata."—*Vita di Cola di Rienzi.* Ed. 1828. Forli.

"From his youth he was nourished with the milk of eloquence; a good grammarian, a better rhetorician, well versed in the writings of authors . . . Oh, how often would he say, 'Where are those good Romans? Where is their supreme justice? Shall I ever behold such times as those in which they flourished?' He was a handsome man . . . It happened that a brother of his was slain, and no retribution was made for his death: he could not help him; long did he ponder how to avenge his brother's blood; long did he ponder how to direct the unguided state of Rome."—*Life of Cola di Rienzi.*

CHAPTER I.

The Brothers.

THE celebrated name which forms the title to this work will sufficiently apprise the reader that it is in the earlier half of the fourteenth century that my story opens.

It was on a summer evening that two youths might be seen walking beside the banks of the Tiber, not far from that part of its winding course which sweeps by the base of Mount Avantine. The path they had selected was remote and tranquil. It was only at a distance that were seen the scattered and squalid houses that bordered the river, from amidst which rose, dark and frequent, the high roof and enormous towers which marked the fortified mansion of some Roman baron. On one side of the river, behind the cottages of the fishermen, soared Mount Janiculum, dark with massive foliage from which gleamed at frequent intervals, the gray walls of many a castellated palace, and the spires and columns of a hundred churches; on the other side, the deserted Aventine rose abrupt and steep covered with thick brushwood; while, on the height, from concealed but numerous convents, rolled, not unmusically, along the quiet landscape and the rippling waves the sound of the holy bell.

Of the young men introduced in this scene, the elder, who might have somewwat passed his twentieth year, was of a tall and even commanding stature; and there was that in his presence remarkable and almost noble, despite the homeliness of his garb, which consisted of the long, loose gown and the plain tunic, both of dark-grey serge, which distinguished, at that time, the dress of the humbler scholars who frequented the monasteries for such rude knowledge as then yielded a scanty return for intense toil. His countenance was handsome, and would have been rather gay than thoughtful in its expression, but for that vague and abstracted dreaminess of eye which so usually denotes a propensity to revery and contemplation, and betrays that the past or the future is more congenial to the mind than the enjoyment and action of the present hour.

The younger, who was yet a boy, had nothing striking in his appearance or countenance, unless an expression of great sweetness and gentleness could be so called; and there was something almost feminine in the tender deference with which he appeared to listen to his companion. His dress was that usually worn by the humbler classes, though somewhat neater, perhaps, and newer; and the fond vanity of a mother might be detected in the care with which the long and silky ringlets had been smoothed and parted as they escaped from his cap and flowed midway down his shoulders.

As they thus sauntered on, beside the whispering reeds of the river, each with his arm round the form of his comrade, there was a grace in the bearing, in the youth, and in the evident affection of the brothers—for such their connection—which elevated the lowliness of their apparent condition.

"Dear brother," said the elder, "I cannot express to thee how I enjoy those evening hours. To you alone I feel as if I were not a mere visionary and idler when I talk of the uncertain future, and build up my palaces of the air. Our parents listen to me as if I were uttering fine things out of a book; and my dear mother, Heaven bless her! wipes her eyes, and says, 'Hark, what a scholar he is!' As for the monks, if I ever dare look from my Livy, and cry, 'Thus should Rome be again!' they stare, and gape, and frown, as though I had broached an heresy. But you, sweet brother, though you share not my studies, sympathize so kindly with all their results—you seem so to approve my wild schemes, and to encourage my ambitious hopes—that sometimes I forget our birth, our fortunes, and think and dare as if no blood save that of the Teuton Emperor flowed through our veins."

"Methinks, dear Cola," said the younger brother, "that Nature played us an unfair trick—to you she transmitted the royal soul, derived from our father's parentage; and to me only the quiet and lowly spirit of my mother's humble lineage."

"Nay," answered Cola, quickly, "you would then have the brighter share,—for I should have but the Barbarian origin, and you the Roman. Time was, when to be a simple Roman was to be nobler than a northern king.—Well, well, we may live to see great changes!"

"I shall live to see thee a great man, and that will content me," said the younger, smiling affectionately; "a great scholar all confess you to be already: our mother predicts your fortunes every time she hears of your welcome visits to the Colonna."

"The Colonna!" said Cola, with a bitter smile; "the Colonna—the pedants!—They affect, dull souls, the knowledge of the past, play the patron, and misquote Latin over their cups! They are pleased to welcome me at their board, because the Roman doctors call me learned, and because Nature gave me a wild wit, which to them is pleasanter than the stale jests of a hired buffoon. Yes, they would advance my fortunes—but how? by some place in the public offices, which would fill a dishonored coffer, by wringing, yet more sternly, the hard earned coins from our famishing citizens! If there be a vile thing in the world, it is a plebeian, advanced by patricians, not for the purpose of righting his own order, but for playing the pandor to the worst interests of theirs. He who is of the people but makes himself a traitor to his birth, if he furnishes the excuse for these tyrant hypocrites to lift up their hands and cry—'See what liberty exists in Rome, when *we*, the patricians, thus elevate a plebeian!' Did they ever elevate a plebeian if he sympathized with plebeians? No, brother; should I be lifted above our condition, I will be raised by the arms of my country men, and not upon their necks."

"All I hope, is, Cola, that you will not, in your zeal for your fellow-citizens, forget how dear you are to us. No greatness could ever reconcile me to the thought that it brought you danger."

"And *I* could laugh at all danger, if it led to greatness. But greatness—greatness! Vain dream! Let us keep it for our *night* sleep. Enough of *my* plans; now, dearest brother, of yours."

And, with the sanguine and cheerful elasticity which belonged to him, the young Cola, dismissing all wilder thoughts, bent his mind to listen, and to enter into, the humbler projects of his brother. The new boat and the holiday dress, and the cot removed to a quarter more secure from the oppression of the barons, and such distant pictures of love as a dark eye and a merry lip conjure up to the vague sentiments of a boy;—to schemes and aspirations of which such objects made the limit, did the scholar listen, with a relaxed brow and a tender smile; and often, in later life, did that conversation occur to him, when he shrank from asking his own heart which ambition was the wiser.

"And then," continued the younger brother,

"by degrees I might save enough to purchase such a vessel as that which we now see, laden, doubtless, with corn and merchandise, bringing —oh, such a good return—that I could fill your room with books, and never hear you complain that you were not rich enough to purchase some crumbling old monkish manuscript. Ah, that would make me so happy!" Cola smiled as he pressed his brother closer to his breast.

"Dear boy," said he, "may it rather be mine to provide for your wishes! Yet methinks the masters of yon vessel have no enviable possession see how anxiously the men look round, and behind, and before: peaceful traders though they be, they fear, it seems, even in this city (once the emporium of the civilized world), some pirate in pursuit; and ere the voyage be over, they may find that pirate in a Roman noble. Alas, to what are we reduced!"

The vessel thus referred to was speeding rapidly down the river, and some three or four armed men on deck were indeed intently surveying the quiet banks on either side, as if anticipating a foe. The bark soon, however, glided out of sight, and the brothers fell back upon those themes which require only the future for a text to become attractive to the young.

At length, as the evening darkened, they remembered that it was past the usual hour in which they returned home, and they began to retrace their steps.

"Stay," said Cola, abruptly, "how our talk has beguiled me! Father Uberto promised me a rare manuscript, which the good friar confesses hath puzzled the whole convent. I was to seek his cell for it this evening. Tarry here a few minutes, it is but half-way up the Aventine. I shall soon return."

"Can I not accompany you?"

"Nay," returned Cola, with considerate kindness, "you have borne toil all the day, and must be wearied; my labors, of the body, at least, have been light enough. You are delicate, too, and seem fatigued already; the rest will refresh you. I shall not be long."

The boy acquiesced, though he rather wished to accompany his brother; but he was of a meek and yielding temper, and seldom resisted the lightest command of those he loved. He sat him down on a little bank by the river-side, and the firm step and towering form of his brother were soon hid him from his gaze by the thick and melancholy foliage.

At first he sat very quietly, enjoying the cool air, and thinking over all the stories of ancient Rome that his brother had told him in their walk. At length he recollected that his little sister, Irene, had begged him to bring her home some flowers; and, gathering such as he could find at hand (and many a flower grew, wild and clustering, over that desolate spot), he again seated himself, and began weaving them into one of those garlands for which the southern peasantry still retain their ancient affection, and something of their classic skill.

While the boy was thus engaged, the tramp of horses and the loud shouting of men were heard at the distance. They came near, and nearer.

"Some baron's procession, perhaps, returning from a feast," thought the boy. "It will be a pretty sight—their white plumes and scarlet mantles! I love to see such sights, but I will just move out of their way."

So, still mechanically platting his garland, but with eyes turned towards the quarter of the expected procession, the young Roman moved yet nearer towards the river.

Presently the train came in view,—a gallant company, in truth; horsemen in front, riding two abreast, where the path permitted, their steeds caparisoned superbly, their plumes waving gaily, and the gleam of their corselets glittering through the shades of the dusky twilight. A large and miscellaneous crowd, all armed, some with pikes and mail, others with less warlike or worse fashioned weapons, followed the cavaliers; and high above plume and pike floated the blood-red banner of the Orsini, with the motto and device (in which was ostentatiously displayed the Guelfic badge of the keys of St. Peter) wrought in burnished gold. A momentary fear crossed the boy's mind, for at that time, and in that city, a nobleman begirt with his swordsmen was more dreaded than a wild beast by the plebeians; but it was already too late to fly—the train were upon him.

"Ho, boy!" cried the leader of the horsemen, Martino di Porto, one of the great House of the Orsini; "hast thou seen a boat pass up the river?—But thou must have seen it—how long since?"

"I saw a large boat about half an hour ago," answered the boy, terrified by the rough voice and imperious bearing of the cavalier.

"Sailing right a-head, with a green flag at the stern?"

"The same, noble sir."

"On, then! we will stop her course ere the moon rise," said the baron. "On!—let the boy go with us, lest he prove traitor, and alarm the Colonna."

"An Orsini, an Orsini!" shouted the multitude; "on, on!" and, despite the prayers and remonstrances of the boy, he was placed in the thickest of the crowd, and borne, or rather dragged along with the rest—frightened, breathless, almost weeping, with his poor little garland still hanging on his arm, while a sling was thrust into his unwilling hand. Still he felt, through all his alarm, a kind of childish curiosity to see the result of the pursuit.

By the loud and eager conversation of those about him, he learned that the vessel he had seen contained a supply of corn destined to a fortress up the river held by the Colonna, then at deadly feud with the Orsini; and it was the objeet of the expedition in which the boy had been thus lucklessly entrained to intercept the provision, and divert it to the garrison of Martino di Porto. This news somewhat increased his consternation, for the boy belonged to a family that claimed the patronage of the Colonna.

Anxiously and tearfully he looked with every moment up the steep ascent of the Aventine; but his guardian, his protector, still delayed his appearance.

They had now proceeded some way, when a winding in the road brought suddenly before them the object of their pursuit, as, seen by the light of the earliest stars, it scudded rapidly down the stream.

"Now, the Saints be blest!" quoth the chief; "she is ours!"

"Hold!" said a captain (a German) riding next to Martino, in a half whisper; "I hear sounds which I like not, by yonder trees—hark! the neigh of a horse!—by my faith, too, there is the gleam of a corselet."

"Push on, my masters," cried Martino; "the heron shall not balk the eagle—push on!"

With renewed shouts, those on foot pushed forward, till, as they had nearly gained the copse referred to by the German, a small compact body of horsemen, armed cap-à-pié, dashed from amid the trees, and, with spears in their rests, charged into the ranks of the pursuers.

"A Colonna! a Colonna!" "An Orsini! an Orsini!" were shouts loudly and fiercely interchanged. Martino di Porto, a man of great bulk and ferocity, and his cavaliers, who were chiefly German Mercenaries, met the encounter unshaken. "Beware the bear's hug," cried the Orsini, as down went his antagonist, rider and steed, before his lance.

The contest was short and fierce; the complete armor of the horsemen protected them on either side from wounds,—not so unscathed fared the half-arm foot-followers of the Orsini, as they pressed, each pushed on by the other, against the Colonna. After a shower of stones and darts, which fell but as hailstones against the thick mail of the horsemen, they closed in, and by their number, obstructed the movements of the steeds, while the spear, sword, and battle-axe of their opponents made ruthless havoc amongst their undisciplined ranks. And Martino, who cared little how many of his mere mob were butchered, seeing that his foes were for the moment embarrassed by the wild rush and gathering circle of his foot train (for the place of conflict, though wider than the previous road, was confined and narrow), made a sign to some of his horsemen, and was about to ride forward towards the boat, now nearly out of sight, when a bugle at some distance was answered by one of his enemy at hand; and the shout of "Colonna to the rescue!" was echoed afar off. A few moments brought in view a numerous train of horses at full speed, with the banners of Colonna waving gallantly in the front.

"A plague on the wizards! who would have imagined they had divined us so craftily!" muttered Martino! "we must not abide these odds;" and the hand he had first raised for advance, now gave the signal of retreat.

Serried breast to breast and in complete order, the horsemen of Martino turned to fly; the foot rabble who had come for spoil remained but for slaughter. They endeavored to imitate their leaders; but how could they all elude the rushing chargers and sharp lances of their antagonists, whose blood was heated by the affray, and who regarded the lives at their mercy as a boy regards the wasp's nest he destroys. The crowd dispersing in all directions,—some, indeed, escaped up the hills, where the footing was impracticable to the horses; some plunged into the river and swam across to the opposite bank,—those less cool or experienced, who fled right onwards, served, by clogging the way of their enemy, to facilitate the flight of their leaders, but fell themselves, corpse upon corpse, butchered in the unrelenting and unreristed pursuit.

"No quarter to the ruffians—every Orsini slain is a robber the less—strike for God, the Emperor, and the Colonna!" such were the shouts which rung the knell of the dismayed and falling fugitives. Among those who fled onward, in the very path most accessible to the cavalry, was the young brother of Cola, so innocently mixed with the affray. Fast he fled, dizzy with terror—poor boy, scarce before ever parted from his parents' or his brother's side!—the trees glided past him—the banks receded;—on the sped, and fast behind came the tramp of the hoofs—the shouts—the curses—the fierce laughter of the foe, as they bounded over the dead and the dying in their path. He was now at the spot in which his brother had left him; hastily he glanced behind, and saw the couched lance and horrent crest of the horseman close at his rear; despairingly he looked up, and, behold! his brother bursting through the tangled brakes that clothed the mountain, and bounding to his succor.

"Save me! save me, brother!" he shrieked aloud, and the shriek reached Cola's ear;—the snort of the fiery charger breathed hot upon him;—a moment more, and with one wild shrill cry of "Mercy, mercy" he fell to the ground—a corpse: the lance of the pursuer passing through and through him, from back to breast, and nailing him on the very sod where he had sate, full of young life and careless hope, not an hour ago.

The horseman plucked forth his spear and passed on in pursuit of new victims; his comrades following. Cola had descended,—was on the spot,—kneeling by his murdered brother. Presently, to the sound of horn and trumpet, came by a nobler company than most of those hitherto engaged; who had been, indeed, but the advanced-guard of the Colonna. At their head rode a man in years, whose long white hair escaped from his plumed cap and mingled with his venerable beard. "How is this?" said the chief, reining in his steed, "young Rienzi!"

The youth looked up, as he heard that voice, and then flung himself before the steed of the old noble, and, clasping his hands, cried out in a scarce articulate tone: "It is my brother, noble Stephen,—a boy, a mere child!—the best—the mildest! See how his blood dabbles the grass;—back, back—your horse's hoofs are in the stream! Justice, my Lord, justice!—you are a great man."

"Who slew him? an Orsini, doubtless; you shall have justice."

"Thanks, thanks," murmured Rienzi, as he tottered once more to his brother's side, turned the boy's face from the grass, and strove wildly to feel the pulse of his heart; he drew back his hand hastily, for it was crimsoned with blood, and lifting that hand on high, shrieked out again, "Justice! justice!"

The group round the old Stephen Colonna, hardened as they were in such scenes, were affected by the sight. A handsome boy, whose tears ran fast down his cheeks, and who rode his palfrey close by the side of the Colonna, drew forth his sword. "My Lord," said he, half sobbing, "an Orsini only could have butchered a harmless lad like this; let us lose not a moment,—let us on after the ruffians."

"No, Adrian, no!" cried Stephen laying his hand on the boy's shoulder; "your zeal is to be lauded, but we must beware an ambush. Our men have ventured too far—what ho, there!—sound a return."

The bugles, in a few minutes, brought back the pursuers,—among them, the horseman whose spear had been so fatally misused. He was the leader of those engaged in the conflict with Martino di Porto; and the gold wrought into his armor, with the gorgeous trappings of his charger, betokened his rank.

"Thanks, my son, thanks," said the old Colonna to this cavalier, "you have done well and bravely. But tell me, knowest thou, for thou hast an eagle eye, which of the Orsini slew this poor boy?—a foul deed; his family, too, our clients!"

"Who? yon lad?" replied the horseman, lifting the helmet from his head, and wiping his heated brow; "say you so! how came he, then, with Martino's rascals? I fear me the mistake hath cost him dear. I could but suppose him of the Orsini rabble, and so—and so—"

"*You* slew him!" cried Rienzi, in a voice of thunder, starting from the ground. "Justice! then, my Lord Stephen, justice! you promised me justice, and I will have it!"

"My poor youth," said the old man, compassionately, "you should have had justice against the Orsini; but see you not this has been an error? I do not wonder you are too grieved to listen to reason now. We must make this up to you."

"And let this pay for masses for the boy's soul; I grieve me much for the accident," said the younger Colonna, flinging down a purse of gold. "Ay, see us at the palace next week, young Cola—next week. My father, we had best return towards the boat; its safeguard may require us yet."

"Right, Gianni; stay, some two of you, and see to the poor lad's corpse;—a grievous accident! how could it chance?"

The company passed back the way they came, two of the common soldiers alone remaining, except the boy Adrian, who lingered behind a few moments, striving to console Rienzi, who, as one bereft of sense, remained motionless, gazing on the proud array as it swept along, and muttering to himself, "Justice, justice! I will have it yet."

The loud voice of the elder Colonna summoned Adrian, reluctantly and weeping, away. "Let me be your brother," said the gallant boy, affectionately pressing the scholar's hand to his heart; "I want a brother like you."

Rienzi made no reply; he did not heed or hear him—dark and stern thoughts, thoughts in which were the germ of a mighty revolution, were at his heart. He woke from them with a start, as the soldiers were now arranging their bucklers so as to make a kind of bier for the corpse, and then burst into tears as he fiercely motioned them away, and clasped the clay to his breast till he was literally soaked with the oozing blood.

The poor child's garland had not dropped from his arm even when he fell, and, entangled by his dress, it still clung around him. It was a sight that recalled to Cola all the gentleness, the kind heart, and winning graces of his only brother—his only friend! It was a sight that seemed to make yet more inhuman the untimely and unmerited fate of that innocent boy. "My brother! my brother!" groaned the survivor! "how shall I meet our mother?—how shall I meet even night and solitude again?—so young, so harmless! See ye, sirs, he was but too gentle. And they will not give us justice, because his murderer was a noble and a Colonna. And this gold, too—gold for a brother's blood! Will they not"—and the young man's eyes glared like fire—"will they not give us justice? Time shall show!" So saying, he bent his head over the corpse; his lips muttered, as with some prayer or invocation; and then rising, his face was as pale as the dead beside him,—but it was no longer pale with *grief!*

From that bloody clay, and that inward prayer, Cola di Rienzi rose a new being. With his young brother died his own youth. But for that event, the future liberator of Rome might have been but a dreamer, a scholar, a poet; the peaceful rival of Petrarch; a man of thoughts, not deeds. But from that, all his faculties, energies, fancies, genius, became concentrated into a single point; and patriotism, before a vision, leapt into the life and vigor of a passion, lastingly kindled, stubbornly hardened, and awfully consecrated,—by revenge!

CHAPTER II.

An Historical Survey—Not to be passed over, except by those who dislike to understand what they read.

YEARS had passed away, and the death of the Roman boy, amidst more noble and less excusable slaughter, was soon forgotten,—forgotten almost by the parents of the slain, in the growing fame and fortunes of their eldest son,—forgotten and forgiven never by that son himself. But, between that prologue of blood, and the political drama which ensues,—between the fading interest, as it were, of a dream, and the more busy, actual, and continuous excitements of sterner life,—this may be the most fitting time to place before the reader a short and rapid outline of the state and circumstances of that city in which the principal scenes of this story are laid:—an outline necessary, perhaps, to many, for a full comprehension of the motives of the actors, and the vicissitudes of the plot.

Despite the miscellaneous and mongrel tribes that had forced their settlements in the City of the Cæsars, the Roman population retained an inordinate notion of their own supremacy over the rest of the world; and, degenerated from the iron virtues of the Republic, possessed all the insolent and unruly turbulence which characterized the *Plebs* of the ancient Forum. Amongst a ferocious, yet not a brave populace, the nobles supported themselves less as sagacious tyrants than as relentless banditti. The popes had struggled in vain against these stubborn and stern patricians. Their state derided, their command defied, their persons publicly outraged, the pontiff-sovereigns of the rest of Europe resided, at the Vatican, as prisoners under terror of execution. When, thirty-eight years before the date of the events we are about to witness, a Frenchman, under the name of Clement V., had ascended the chair of St. Peter, the new pope, with more prudence than valor, had deserted Rome for the tranquil retreat of Avignon; and the luxurious town of a foreign province became the court of the Roman pontiff, and the throne of the Christian Church.

Thus deprived of even the nominal check of the papal presence, the power of the nobles might be said to have no limits, save their own caprice, or their mutual jealousies and feuds. Though arrogating through fabulous genealogies their descent from the ancient Romans, they were, in reality, for the most part, the sons of the bolder barbarians of the North; and, contaminated by the craft of Italy, rather than imbued with its national affections, they retained the disdain of their foreign ancestors for a conquered soil and a degenerate people. While the rest of Italy, especially in Florence, in Venice, and in Milan, was fast and far advancing beyond the other states of Europe in civilization and in art, the Romans appeared rather to recede than to improve;—unblest by laws, unvisited by art, strangers at once to the chivalry of a warlike, and the graces of a peaceful, people. But they still possessed the sense and desire of liberty, and, by ferocious paroxysms and desperate struggles, sought to vindicate for their city the title it still assumed of "the Metropolis of the World." For the last two centuries they had known various revolutions,—brief, often bloody, and always unsuccessful. Still, there was the empty pageant of a popular form of government. The Thirteen quarters of the city named each a chief; and the assembly of these magistrates, called Caporini, by theory possessed an authority they had neither the power nor the courage to exert. Still there was the proud name of Senator; but, at the present time, the office was confined to one or to two persons, sometimes elected by the pope, sometimes by the nobles. The authority attached to the name seems to have had no definite limit; it was that of a stern dictator, or an indolent puppet, according as he who held it had the power to enforce the dignity he assumed. It was never conceded but to nobles, and it was by the nobles that all the outrages were committed. Private enmity alone was gratified whenever public justice was invoked: and the vindication of order was but the execution of revenge.

Holding their palaces as the castles and fortresses of princes, each asserting his own independency of all authority of law, and planting fortifications, and claiming principalities in the patrimonial territories of the Church, the barons of Rome made their state still more secure, and still more odious, by the maintenance of troops of foreign (chiefly of German) mercenaries, at once braver in disposition, more disciplined in service, and more skilful in arms, than even the freest Italians of that time. Thus they united the judicial and military force, not for the protection, but for the ruin of Rome. Of these barons, the most powerful were the Orsini and Colonna; their feuds were hereditary and incessant, and every day witnessed the fruits of their lawless warfare, in bloodshed, in rape, and in conflagration. The flattery or the friendship of Petrarch, too credulously believed by modern historians, has invested the Colonna, especially of the date now entered upon, with an elegance and a dignity not their own. Outrage, fraud, and assassination, a sordid avarice in securing lucrative offices to themselves, an insolent oppression of their citizens, and the most dastardly cringing to power superior to their own (with but few exceptions), mark the character of the first family of Rome. But, wealthier than the rest of the barons, they were, therefore, more luxurious, and, perhaps, more intellectual; and their pride was flattered in being patrons of those arts of which they could never have become the professors. From these multipled oppressors the Roman citizens turned with fond and impatient regret to their ignorant and dark notions of departed liberty and greatness. They confounded the times of the Empire with those of the Republic; and often looked to the Teutonic king, who obtained his election from beyond the Alps, but his *title* of emperor from the Romans, as the deserter of his legitimate trust and proper home; vainly imagining that, if both the Emperor and the Pontiff fixed their residence in Rome, Liberty and Law would again seek their natural shelter beneath the resuscitated majesty of the Roman people.

The absence of the pope and the papal court served greatly to impoverish the citizens; and they had suffered yet more visibly by the depredations of hordes of robbers, numerous and unsparing, who infested Romagna, obstructing all the public ways, and were, sometimes secretly, sometimes openly, protected by the barons, who often recruited their banditti garrisons by banditti soldiers.

But besides the lesser and ignobler robbers, there had risen in Italy a far more formidable description of free-booters. A German, who assumed the lofty title of the Duke Werner, had, a few years prior to the period we approach, enlisted and organized a considerable force, styled "The Great Company," with which he besieged cities and invaded states, without any object less shameless than that of pillage. His example was soon imitated: numerous "Companies," similarly constituted, devastated the distracted and divided land. They appeared, suddenly raised, as if by magic, before the walls of a city, and demanded immense sums as the purchase of peace. Neither tyrant nor commonwealth maintained a force sufficient to resist them; and if other northern mercenaries were engaged to oppose them, it was only to recruit the standards of the freebooters with deserters. Mercenary fought not mercenary—nor German, German: and greater pay, and more unbridled rapine, made the tents of the "Companies" far more attractive than the regulated stipends of a city, or the dull fortress and impoverished coffers of a chief. Werner, the most implacable and ferocious of all these adventurers, and who had so openly gloried in his enormities as to wear upon his breast a silver plate, engraved with the words, "Enemy to God, to Pity, and to Mercy," had not long since ravaged Romagna with fire and sword. But, whether induced by money, or unable to control the fierce spirits he had raised, he afterwards led the bulk of his company back to Germany. Small detachments, however, remained, scattered throughout the land, waiting only an able leader once more to re-unite them: amongst those who appeared most fitted for that destiny was Walter de Montreal, a Knight of St. John, and gentleman of Provence, whose valor and military genius had already, though yet young, raised his name into dreaded celebrity; and whose ambition, experience, and sagacity, relieved by certain chivalric and noble qualities, were suited to enterprises far greater and more important than the violent depredations of the atrocious Werner. From these scourges, no state had suffered more grievously than Rome. The patrimonial territories of the pope,—in part wrested from him by petty tyrants, in part laid waste by these foreign robbers,—yielded but a scanty supply to the necessities of Clement VI., the most accomplished gentleman and the most graceful voluptuary of his time; and the good father had devised a plan, whereby to enrich at once the Romans and their pontiff.

Nearly fifty years before the time we enter upon, in order both to replenish the papal coffers and pacify the starving Romans, Boniface VIII. had instituted the Festival of the Jubilee, or Holy Year; in fact, a revival of a Pagan ceremonial. A plenary indulgence was promised to every Catholic who, in that year, and in the first year of every succeeding century, should visit the churches of St. Peter and St. Paul. An immense concourse of pilgrims, from every part of Christendom, had attested the wisdom of the invention; "and two priests stood night and day, with rakes in their hands, to collect without counting the heaps of gold and silver that were poured on the altar of St. Paul." *

It is not to be wondered at that this most lucrative festival should, ere the next century was half expired, appear to a discreet pontiff

* Gibbon, vol. xii. c. 59.

to be too long postponed. And both pope and city agreed in thinking it might well bear a less distant renewal. Accordingly, Clement VI. had proclaimed, under the name of the *Mosaic* Jubilee, a second Holy Year for 1350 —viz., three years distant from that date at which, in the next chapter, my narrative will commence. This circumstance had a great effect in whetting the popular indignation against the barons, and preparing the events I shall relate; for the roads were, as I before said, infested by the banditti, the creatures and allies of the barons. And if the roads were not cleared, the pilgrims might not attend. It was the object of the pope's vicar, Raimond, bishop of Orvietto (bad politician and good canonist), to seek, by every means, to remove all impediment between the offerings of devotion and the treasury of St. Peter.

Such, in brief, was the state of Rome at the period we are about to examine. Her ancient mantle of renown still, in the eyes of Italy and of Europe, cloaked her ruins. In name, at least, she was still the queen of the earth; and from her hands came the crown of the emperor of the north, and the keys of the father of the church. Her situation was precisely that which presented a vast and glittering triumph to bold ambition,—an inspiring, if mournful, spectacle to determined patriotism,—and a fitting stage for that more august tragedy which seeks its incidents, selects its actors, and shapes its moral, amidst the vicissitudes and crimes of nations.

CHAPTER III.

The Brawl.

On an evening in April, 1347, and in one of those wide spaces in which Modern and Ancient Rome seemed blent together—equally desolate and equally in ruins—a miscellaneous and indignant populace were assembled. That morning the house of a Roman jeweller had been forcibly entered and pillaged by the soldiers of Martino di Porto, with a daring effrontery which surpassed even the ordinary licence of the barons. The sympathy and sensation throughout the city were deep and ominous.

"Never will I submit to this tyranny!"

"Nor I!"

"Nor I!"

"Nor by the bones of St. Peter, will I!"

"And what, my friends, is this tyranny to which you will not submit?" said a young nobleman, addressing himself to the crowd of citizens who, heated, angry, half-armed, and with the vehement gestures of Italian passion, were now sweeping down the long and narrow street that led to the gloomy quarter occupied by the Orsini.

"Ah, my lord!" cried two or three of the citizens in a breath, "you will right us—you will see justice done to us—you are a Colonna."

"Ha, ha, ha!" laughed scornfully one man of gigantic frame, and wielding on high a huge hammer, indicative of his trade. "Justice and Colonna! body of God! those names are not often found together."

"Down with him! down with him! he is an Orsinist,—down with him!" cried at least ten of the throng: but no hand was raised against the giant.

"He speaks the truth," said a second voice, firmly.

"Ay, that doth he," said a third, knitting his brows, and unsheating his knife, "and we will abide by it. The Orsini are tyrants—and the Colonnas are, at the best, as bad."

"Thou liest in thy teeth, ruffian!" cried the young noble, advancing into the press and confronting the last asperser of the Colonna.

Before the flashing eye and menacing gesture of the cavalier, the worthy brawler retreated some steps, so as to leave an open space between the towering form of the smith, and the small, slender, but vigorous frame of the young noble.

Taught from their birth to despise the courage of the plebeians, even while careless of much reputation as to their own, the patricians of Rome were not unaccustomed to the rude fellowship of these brawls; nor was it unoften that the mere presence of a noble sufficed to scatter whole crowds, that had the moment before been breathing vengeance against his order and his house.

Waving his hand, therefore, to the smith, and utterly unheeding either his brandished weapon or his vast stature, the young Adrian di Castello, a distant kinsman of the Colonna, haughtily bade him give way.

"To your homes, friends! and know," he added, with some dignity, "that ye wrong us much, if ye imagine we share the evil-doings of the Orsini, or are pandering solely to our own passions in the feud between their house and ours. May the Holy Mother so judge me," continued he, devoutly lifting up his eyes, "as I now with truth declare, that it is for your wrongs, and for the wrongs of Rome that I have drawn this sword against the Orsini."

"So say all the tyrants," rejoined the smith, hardily, as he leant his hammer against a fragment of stone—some remnant of ancient Rome—"they never fight against each other, but it is for our good. One Colonna cuts me the throat of Orsini's baker—it is for our good! another Colonna seizes on the daughter of Orsini's tailor—it is for our good! *our* good—yes, for the good of the people!—the good of the bakers and tailors, eh?"

"Fellow," said the young nobleman, gravely, "if a Colonna did thus, he did wrong; but the holiest cause may have bad supporters."

"Yes, the holy Church itself is propped on very indifferent columns," answered the smith, in a rude witicism on the affection of the pope for the Colonna.

"He blasphemes! the smith blasphemes!" cried the partisans of that powerful house. "A Colonna, a Colonna!"

"An Orsini, an Orsini!" was no less promptly the counter cry.

"THE PEOPLE!" shouted the smith, waving his formidable weapon far above the heads of the group.

In an instant the whole throng, who had at first united against the aggression of one man, were divided by the hereditary wrath of faction. At the cry of Orsini, several new partisans hurried to the spot; the friends of the Colonna drew themselves on one side—the defenders of the Orsini on the other—and the few who agreed with the smith that both factions were equally odious and the people was the sole legitimate cry in a popular commotion, would have withdrawn themselves from the approaching *mêlée*, if the smith himself, who was looked upon by them as an authority of great influence, had not—whether from resentment at the haughty bearing of the young Colonna, or from that appetite of contest not uncommon in men of a bulk and force which assure them in all personal affrays the lofty pleasure of superiority—if, I say, the smith himself had not, after a pause of indecision, retired among the Orsini, and entrained, by his example, the alliance of his friends with the favorers of that faction.

In popular commotions, each man is whirled along with the herd, often half against his own approbation or assent. The few words of peace by which Adrian di Castello commenced an address to his friends were drowned amidst their shouts. Proud to find in their ranks one of the most beloved, and one of the noblest of that name, the partisans of the Colonna placed him in their front, and charged impetuously on their foes. Adrian, however, who had acquired from circumstances something of that chivalrous code which he certainly could not have owed to his Roman birth, disdained at first to assault men among whom he recognized no equal, either in rank or the practice of arms. He contented himself with putting aside the few strokes that were aimed at him in the gathering confusion of the conflict—few; for those who recognized him, even amidst the bitterest partisans of the Orsini, were not willing to expose themselves to the danger and odium of spilling the blood of a man, who, in addition to his great birth and the terrible power of his connections, was possessed of a personal popularity, which he owed rather to a comparison with the vices of his relatives than to any remarkable virtues hitherto displayed by himself. The smith alone, who had as yet taken no active part in the fray, seemed to gather himself up in determined opposition as the cavalier now advanced within a few steps of him.

"Did we not tell thee," quoth the giant, frowning, "that the Colonna were, not less than the Orsini, the foes of the people? Look at thy followers and clients: are they not cutting the throats of humble men by way of vengeance for the crime of a great one? But that is the way one patrician always scourges the insolence of another. He lays the rod on the backs of the people, and then cries, 'See how just I am!'"

"I do not answer thee now," answered Adrian; "but if thou regrettest with me this waste of blood, join with me in attempting to prevent it."

"I—not I! let the blood of the slaves flow

to-day: the time is fast coming when it shall be washed away by the blood of the lords."

"Away, ruffian!" said Adrian, seeking no further parley, and touching the smith with the flat side of his sword. In an instant the hammer of the smith swung in the air, and, but for the active spring of the young noble, would infallibly have crushed him to the earth. Ere the smith could gain time for a second blow, Adrian's sword passed twice through his right arm, and the weapon fell heavily to the ground.

"Slay him, slay him!" cried several of the clients of the Colonna, now pressing, dastard-like, round the disarmed and disabled smith.

"Ay, slay him!" said, in tolerable Italian, but with a barbarous accent, one man, half-clad in armor, who had but just joined the group, and who was one of those wild German bandits whom the Colonna held in their pay; "He belongs to a horrible gang of miscreants sworn against all order and peace. He is one of Rienzi's followers, and, bless the Three Kings! raves about the People."

"Thou sayest right, barbarian," said the sturdy smith, in a loud voice, and tearing aside the vest from his breast with his left hand; "come all—Colonna and Orsini—dig to this heart with your sharp blades, and when you have reached the centre, you will find there the object of your common hatred—'Rienzi and the People!'"

As he uttered these words, in language that would have seemed above his station (if a certain glow and exaggeration of phrase and sentiment were not common, when excited, to all the Romans), the loudness of his voice rose above the noise immediately round him, and stilled, for an instant, the general din; and when, at last, the words, "Rienzi and the People" rang forth, they penetrated midway through the increasing crowd, and were answered as by an echo, with a hundred voices—"Rienzi and the People!"

But whatever impression the words of the mechanic made on others, it was equally visible in the young Colonna. At the name of Rienzi the glow of excitement vanished from his cheek; he started back, muttered to himself, and for a moment seemed, even in the midst of that stirring commotion, to be lost in a moody and distant revery. He recovered, as the shout died away; and saying to the smith, in a low tone, "Friend, I am sorry for thy wound; but seek me on the morrow, and thou shalt find thou hast wronged me;" he beckoned to the German to follow him, and threaded his way through the crowd, which generally gave back as he advanced. For the bitterest hatred to the order of the nobles was at that time in Rome mingled with a servile respect for their persons, and a mysterious awe of their uncontrollable power.

As Adrian passed through that part of the crowd in which the fray had not yet commenced, the murmurs that followed him were not those which many of his race could have heard.

"A Colonna," said one.

"Yet no ravisher," said another, laughing wildly.

"Nor murtherer," muttered a third, pressing his hand to his breast. "'Tis not against *him* that my father's blood cries aloud."

"Bless him," said a fourth, "for as yet no man curses him!"

"Ah, God help us!" said an old man, with a long gray beard, leaning on his staff: "the serpent's young yet; the fangs will show by and by."

"For shame, father! he is a comely youth, and not proud in the least. What a smile he hath!" quoth a fair matron, who kept on the outskirt of the *mêlée*.

"Farewell to a man's honor when a noble smiles on his wife!" was the answer.

"Nay," said Luigi, a jolly butcher, with a roguish eye, "what a man can win fairly from maid or wife, that let him do, whether plebeian or noble—that's my morality; but when an ugly old patrician finds fair words will not win fair looks, and carries me off a dame on the back of a German boar, with a stab in the side for comfort to the spouse,—then, I say, he is a wicked man, and an adulterer."

While such were the comments and the murmurs that followed the noble, very different were the looks and words that attended the German soldier.

Equally, nay, with even greater promptitude, did the crowd make way at his armed and heavy tread; but not with looks of reverence:—the eye glared as he approached; but the cheek grew pale—the head bowed—the lip quivered; each man felt a shudder of hate and fear, as recognizing a dread and mortal foe

And well and wrathfully did the fierce mercenary note the signs of the general aversion. He pushed on rudely—half-smiling in contempt, half-frowning in revenge, as he looked from side to side; and his long, matted, light hair, tawny-colored moustache, and brawny front, contrasted strongly with the dark eyes, raven locks, and slender frames of the Italians.

"May Lucifer double damn those Cerman cut-throats!" muttered, between his grinded teeth, one of the citizens.

"Amen!" answered, heartily, another.

"Hush!" said a third, timorously looking round; "If one of them hear thee, thou art a lost man."

"Oh, Rome! Rome! to what art thou fallen!" said bitterly one citizen, clothed in black, and of a higher seeming than the rest; "when thou shudderest in thy streets at the tread of a hired barbarian!"

"Hark to one of our learned men, and rich citizens!" said the butcher, reverently.

"'Tis a friend of Rienzi's," quoth another of the group, lifting his cap.

With downcast eyes, and a face in which grief, shame, and wrath, were visibly expressed, Pandulfo di Guido, a citizen of birth and repute, swept slowly through the crowd, and disappeared.

Meanwhile, Adrian, having gained a street which, though in the neighborhood of the crowd, was empty and desolate, turned to his fierce comrade. "Rodolf!" said he, "mark!—no violence to the citizens. Return to the crowd, collect the friends of our house, withdraw them from the scene; let not the Colonna be blamed for this day's violence; and assure our followers, in my name, that I swear, by the kighthood I received at the Emperor's hands, that by my sword shall Martino di Porto be punished for his outrage. Fain would I, in person, allay the tumult, but my presence only seems to sanction it. Go—thou hast weight with them all."

"Ay, Signor, the weight of blows!" answered the grim soldier. "But the command is hard; I would fain let their puddle-blood flow an hour or two longer. Yet, pardon me; in obeying thy orders, do I obey those of my master, thy kinsman? It is old Stephen Colonna,—who seldom spares blood or treasure, God bless him—(save his own!)—whose money I hold, and to whose hests I am sworn."

"Diavolo!" muttered the cavalier and the angry spot was on his cheek; but with the habitual self-control of the Italian nobles, he smothered his rising choler, and said aloud, with calmness, but dignity,—

"Do as I bid thee; check this tumult,—make *us* the forbearing party. Let all be still within one hour hence, and call on me to-morrow for thy reward; be this purse an earnest of my future thanks. As for my kinsman, whom I command thee to name more reverently, 'tis in his name I speak. Hark! the din increases—the contest swells—go—lose not another moment."

Somewhat awed by the quiet firmness of the patrician, Rodolf nodded, without answer, slid the money into his bosom, and stalked away into the thickest of the throng. But, even ere he arrived, a sudden reaction had taken place.

The young cavalier, left alone in that spot, followed with his eyes the receding form of the mercenary, as the sun, now setting, shone slant upon his glittering casque, and said bitterly to himself—"Unfortunate city, fountain of all mighty memories—fallen queen of a thousand nations—how art thou decrowned and spoiled by thy recreant and apostate children! Thy nobles divided against themselves—thy people cursing thy nobles—thy priests, who should sow peace, planting discord—the father of thy church deserting thy stately walls, his home a refuge, his mitre a fief, his court a Gallic village—and we! we, of the haughtiest blood of Rome—we, the sons of Cæsars, and of the lineage of demigods, guarding an insolent and abhorred state by the swords of hirelings, who mock our cowardice while they receive our pay,—who keep our citizens slaves, and lord it over their very masters in return! Oh, that we, the hereditary chiefs of Rome, could but feel—oh, that we could but find, our only legitimate safeguard, in the grateful hearts of our countrymen!"

So deeply did the young Adrian feel the galling truth of all he uttered, that the indignant tears rolled down his cheeks as he spoke. He felt no shame as he dashed them away; for that weakness which weeps for a fallen race is the tenderness not of women but of angels.

As he turned slowly to quit the spot, his

steps were suddenly arrested by a loud shout: "Rienzi! Rienzi!" smote the air. From the walls of the Capitol to the bed of the glittering Tiber, that name echoed far and wide; and, as the shout died away, it was swallowed up in a silence so profound, so universal, so breathless, that you might have imagined that death itself had fallen over the city. And now, at the extreme end of the crowd, and elevated above their level, on vast fragments of stone which had been dragged from the ruins of Rome in one of the late frequent tumults between contending factions, to serve as a barricade for citizens against citizens,—on these silent memorials of the past grandeur, the present misery, of Rome, stood that extraordinary man, who, above all his race, was the most penetrated with the glories of the one time, with the degradation of the other.

From the distance at which he stood from the scene, Adrian could only distinguish the dark outline of Rienzi's form; he could only hear the faint sound of his mighty voice; he could only perceive, in the subdued yet waving sea of human beings that spread around, their heads bared in the last rays of the sun, the unutterable effect which an eloquence described by contemporaries almost as miraculous,—but in reality less so from the genius of the man than the sympathy of the audience,—created in all, who drank into their hearts and souls the stream of its burning thoughts.

It was but for a short time that that form was visible to the earnest eye, that that voice at intervals reached the straining ear, of Adrian di Castello; but that time sufficed to produce all the effect which Adrian himself had desired.

Another shout, more earnest, more prolonged than the first—a shout in which spoke the release of swelling thoughts, of intense excitement—betokened the close of the harangue; and then you might see, after a minute's pause, the crowd breaking in all directions and pouring down the avenues in various knots and groups, each testifying the strong and lasting impression made upon the multitude by that address. Every cheek was flushed—every tongue spoke: the animation of the orator had passed, like a living spirit, into the breasts of the audience. He had thundered against the disorders of the patricians, yet, by a word, he had disarmed the anger of the plebeians—he had preached freedom, yet he had opposed license. He had calmed the present, by a promise of the future. He had chid their quarrels, yet had supported their cause. He had mastered the revenge of to-day, by a solemn assurance that there should come justice for the morrow. So great may be the power, so mighty the eloquence, so formidable the genius, of one man,—without arms, without rank, without sword or ermine, who addresses himself to a people that is oppressed!

CHAPTER IV.

An Adventure.

Avoiding the broken streams of the dispersed crowd, Adrian Colonna strode rapidly down one of the narrow streets leading to his palace, which was situated at no inconsiderable distance from the place in which the late contest had occurred. The education of his life made him feel a profound interest, not only in the divisions and disputes of his country, but also in the scene he had just witnessed, and the authority exercised by Rienzi.

An orphan of a younger, but opulent branch of the Colonna, Adrian had been brought up under the care and guardianship of his kinsman, that astute, yet valiant Stephen Colonna, who, of all the nobles of Rome, was the most powerful, alike from the favor of the pope, and the number of armed hirelings whom his wealth enabled him to maintain. Adrian had early manifested what in that age was considered an extraordinary disposition towards intellectual pursuits, and had acquired much of the little that was then known of the ancient language and the ancient history of his country.

Though Adrian was but a boy at the time in which, first presented to the reader, he witnessed the emotions of Rienzi at the death of his brother, his kind heart had been penetrated with sympathy for Cola's affliction, and shame for the apathy of his kinsmen at the result of their own feuds. He had earnestly sought the friendship of Rienzi, and, despite his years, had become aware of the power and energy of his character. But though Rienzi, after a short time, had appeared to think no more of his brother's death—though he again entered the halls of the Colonna, and shared their disdainful hospitalities, he maintained a certain distance and reserve of manner, which even Adrian could only partially overcome. He rejected every offer of service, favor, or promotion; and any unwonted proof of kindness from Adrian seemed, instead of making him more familiar, to offend him into colder distance. The easy humor and conversational vivacity which had first rendered him a welcome guest with those who passed their lives between fighting and feasting, had changed into a vein ironical, cynical, and severe. But the dull barons were equally amused at his wit, and Adrian was almost the only one who detected the serpent couched beneath the smile.

Often Rienzi sat at the feast, silent, but observant, as if watching every look, weighing every word, taking gauge and measurement of the intellect, policy, temperament, of every guest; and when he had seemed to satisfy himself, his spirits would rise, his words flow, and while his dazzling but bitter wit lit up the revel, none saw that the unmirthful flash was the token of the coming storm. But all the while, he neglected no occasion to mix with the humbler citizens, to stir up their minds, to inflame their imaginations, to kindle their emulation, with pictures of the present and with legends of the past. He grew in popularity and repute, and was yet more in power with the herd, because in favor with the nobles. Perhaps it was for that reason that he had continued the guest of the Colonna.

When, six years before the present date, the Capitol of the Cæsars witnessed the triumph of Petrarch, the scholastic fame of the young Rienzi had attracted the friendship of the poet,—a friendship that continued, with slight interruption, to the last, through careers so widely different; and afterwards, one among the Roman Deputies to Avignon, he had been conjoined with Petrarch * to supplicate Clement VI. to remove the Holy See from Avignon to Rome. It was in this mission that, for the first time, he evinced his extraordinary powers of eloquence and persuasion. The pontiff, indeed, more desirous of ease than glory, was not convinced by the arguments, but he was enchanted with the pleader; and Rienzi returned to Rome, loaded with honors and clothed with the dignity of high and responsible office. No longer the inactive scholar, the gay companion, he rose at once to pre-eminence above all his fellow-citizens. Never before had authority been borne with so austere an integrity, so uncorrupt a zeal. He had sought to impregnate his colleagues with the same loftiness of principle—he had failed. Now secure in his footing, he had begun openly to appeal to the people; and already a new spirit seemed to animate the populace of Rome.

While these were the fortunes of Rienzi, Adrian had been long separated from him, and absent from Rome.

The Colonna were staunch supporters of the imperial party, and Adrian di Castello had received and obeyed an invitation to the Emperor's court. Under that monarch he had initiated himself in arms, and, among the knights of Germany, he had learned to temper the natural Italian shrewdness with the chivalry of northern valor.

In leaving Bavaria, he had sojourned a short time in the solitude of one of his estates by the fairest lake of northern Italy; and thence, with a mind improved alike by action and study, had visited many of the free Italian states, imbibed sentiments less prejudiced than those of his order, and acquired an early reputation for himself while inly marking the characters and deeds of others. In him, the best qualities of the Italian noble were united. Passionately addicted to the cultivation of letters, subtle and profound in policy, gentle and bland of manner, dignifying a love of pleasure with a certain elevation of taste, he yet possessed a gallantry of conduct, and purity of honor, and an aversion from cruelty, which were then very rarely found in the Italian temperament, and which even the Chivalry of the North, while maintaining among themselves, usually abandoned the moment they came into contact with the systematic craft and disdain of honesty, which made the character of the ferocious. yet wily, South. With these qualities he combined, indeed, the soft-

* According to the modern historians; but it seems more probable that Rienzi's mission to Avignon was posterior to that of Petrarch. However this be, it was at Avignon that Petrarch and Rienzi became most intimate, as Petrarch himself observes in one of his letters.

er passions of his countrymen,—he adored Beauty, and he made a deity of Love.

He had but a few weeks returned to his native city, whither his reputation had already preceded him, and where his early affection for letters and gentleness of bearing were still remembered. He returned to find the position of Rienzi far more altered than his own. Adrian had not yet sought the scholar. He wished first to judge with his own eyes, and at a distance, of the motives and object of his conduct; for partly he caught the suspicions which his own order entertained of Rienzi, and partly he shared in the trustful enthusiasm of the people.

"Certainly," said he now to himself, as he walked musingly onward, "certainly, no man has it more in his power to reform our diseased state, to heal our divisions, to awaken our citizens to the recollections of ancestral virtue. But that very power, how dangerous is it! Have I not seen, in the free states of Italy, men, called into authority for the sake of preserving the people, honest themselves at first, and then, drunk with the sudden rank, betraying the very cause which had exalted them? True, those men were chiefs and nobles; but are plebeians less human? Howbeit I have heard and seen enough from afar,—I will now approach, and examine the man himself."

While thus soliloquizing, Adrian but little noted the various passengers, who, more and more rarely as the evening waned, hastened homeward. Among these were two females, who now alone shared with Adrian the long and gloomy street into which he had entered. The moon was already bright in the heavens, and, as the women passed the cavalier with a light and quick step, the younger one turned back and regarded him by the clear light with an eager, yet timid glance.

"Why dost thou tremble, my pretty one!" said her companion, who might have told some five-and-forty years, and whose garb and voice bespoke her of inferior rank to the younger female. "The streets seem quiet enough now, and, the Virgin be praised! we are not so far from home either."

"Oh! Benedetta, it is *he!* it is the young signor—it is Adrian!"

"That is fortunate," said the nurse, for such was her condition, "since they say he is as bold as a Northman: and as the Palazzo Colonna is not very far from hence, we shall be within reach of his aid should we want it: that is to say, sweet one, if you will walk a little slower than you have yet done."

The young lady slackened her pace, and sighed.

"He is certainly very handsome," quoth the nurse: "but thou must not think more of him; he is too far above thee for marriage, and for aught else, thou art too honest, and thy brother too proud—"

"And thou, Benedetta, art too quick with thy tongue. How canst thou talk thus, when thou knowest he hath never, since, at least, I was a mere child, even addressed me: nay, he scarce knows of my very existence. He, the Lord Adrian di Castello, dream of the poor Irene! the mere thought is madness!"

"Then why," said the nurse, briskly, "dost thou dream of *him?*"

Her companion sighed again more deeply than at first.

"Holy St. Catherine!" continued Benedetta, "if there were but one man in the world, I would die single ere I would think of him, until, at least, he had kissed my hand twice, and left it my own fault if if were not my lips instead."

The young lady still replied not.

"But how didst thou contrive to love him?" asked the nurse. "Thou canst not have seen him very often! it is but some four or five weeks since his return to Rome."

"Oh, how dull art thou?" answered the fair Irene. "Have I not told thee again and again, that I loved him six years ago?"

"When thou hadst told but thy tenth year, and a doll would have been thy most suitable lover! As I am a Christian, Signora, thou hast made good use of thy time.

"And during his absence," continued the girl, fondly, yet sadly, "did I not hear him spoken of, and was not the mere sound of his name like a love-gift that bade me remember? And when they praised him, have I not rejoiced? and when they blamed him, have I not resented? and when they said that his lance was victorious in the tourney, did I not weep with pride? and when they whispered that his vows were welcome in the bower, wept I not as fervently with grief? Have not the six years of his absence been a dream, and was not his return a waking into light—a morn-

pressed too heavily upon him, to slide from his left arm, and standing over her form, while sheltered from behind by the wall which he had so warily gained, he contented himself with parrying the blows hastily aimed at him, without attempting to retaliate. Few of the Romans, however, accustomed to such desultory warfare, were then well and dexterously practised in the use of arms; and the science Adrian had acquired in the schools of the martial north, befriended him now, even against such odds. It is true, indeed, that the followers of Orsini did not share the fury of their lord; partly afraid of the consequence to themselves should the blood of so high-born a signor be spilt by their hands, partly embarrassed with the apprehension that they should see themselves suddenly beset with the ruthless hirelings so close within hearing, they struck but aimless and random blows, looking every moment behind and aside, and rather prepared for flight than slaughter. Echoing the cry of "Colonna," poor Benedetta fled at the first clash of swords. She ran down the dreary street still shrieking that cry, and passed the very portals of Stephen's palace (where some grim forms yet loitered) without arresting her steps there, so great were her confusion and terror.

Meanwhile, the two armed men, whom Adrian had descried, proceeded leisurely up the street. The one was of a rude and common mould, his arms and his complexion testified his calling and race; and by the great respect he paid to his companion, it was evident that that companion was no native of Italy. For the brigands of the north, while they served the vices of the southern, scarce affected to disguise their contempt for his cowardice.

The companion of the brigand was a man of a martial, yet easy air. He wore no helmet, but a cap of crimson velvet, set off with a white plume; on his mantle, or surcoat, which was of scarlet, was wrought a broad white cross, both at back and breast; and so brilliant was the polish of his corselet, that, as from time to time the mantle waved aside and exposed it to the moonbeams, it glittered like light itself.

"Nay, Rodolf," said he, "if thou hast so good a lot of it here with that hoary schemer, Heaven forbid that I should wish to draw thee back again to our merry band. But tell me—this Rienzi—thinkest thou he has any solid and formidable power?"

"Pshaw! noble chieftain, not a whit of it. He pleases the mob; but as for the nobles, they laugh at him; and, as for the soldiers, he has no money!"

"He pleases the mob, then!"

"Ay, that doth he; and when he speaks aloud to them, all the roar of Rome is hushed."

"Humph!—when nobles are hated, and soldiers are bought, a mob may, in any hour, become the master. An honest people and a weak mob,—a corrupt people and a strong mob," said the other, rather to himself than to his comrade, and scarce, perhaps, conscious of the eternal truth of his aphorism. "He is no mere brawler, this Rienzi, I suspect—I must see to it. Hark! what noise is that? By the Holy Sepulchre, it is the ring of our own metal!"

"And that cry—'a Colonna!'" exclaimed Rodolf. "Pardon me, master,—I must away to the rescue!"

"Ay, it is the duty of thy hire; run;—yet stay, I will accompany thee, gratis for once, and from pure passion for mischief. By this hand, there is no music like clashing steel!"

Still Adrian continued gallantly and unwounded to defend himself, though his arm now grew tired, his breath well-nigh spent, and his eyes began to wink and reel beneath the glare of the tossing torches. Orsini himself, exhausted by his fury, had paused for an instant, fronting his foe with a heaving breast and savage looks, when, suddenly, his followers exclaimed, "Fly! fly!—the bandits approach—we are surrounded!"—and two of the servitors, without further parley, took fairly to their heels. The other five remained irresolute, and waiting but the command of their master, when he of the white plume, whom I have just described, thrust himself into the *mêlée*.

"What! gentles," said he, "have ye finished already? Nay, let us not mar the sport; begin again, I beseech you. What are the odds? Ho! six to one!—nay, no wonder that ye have waited for fairer play. See, we two will take the weaker side. Now then, let us begin again."

"Insolent!" cried the Orsini. "Knowest thou him whom thou addressest thus arrogantly?—I am Martino di Porto. Who art thou?"

"Walter de Montreal, gentleman of Provence, and Knight of St. John!" answered the other, carelessly.

At that redoubted name—the name of one of the boldest warriors, and of the most accomplished freebooter of his time—even Martino's cheek grew pale, and his followers uttered a cry of terror.

"And this, my comrade," continued the Knight, "for we may as well complete the introduction, is probably better known to you than I am, gentles of Rome; and you doubtless recognize in him Rodolf of Saxony, a brave man and a true, where he is properly paid for his services."

"Signor," said Adrian to his enemy, who, aghast and dumb, remained staring vacantly at the two new-comers, "you are now in my power. See, our own people, too, are approaching."

And, indeed, from the palace of Stephen Colonna, torches began to blaze, and armed men were seen rapidly advancing to the spot.

"Go home in peace, and if, to-morrow, or any day more suitable to thee, thou wilt meet me alone, and lance to lance, as is the wont of the knights of the empire; or with band to band, and man for man, as is rather the Roman custom; I will not fail thee—there is my gage."

"Nobly spoken," said Montreal; "and, if ye choose the latter, by your leave, I will be one of the party."

Martino answered not; he took up the glove, thrust it in his bosom, and strode hastily away; only, when he had got some paces down the street, he turned back, and, shaking his clenched hand at Adrian, exclaimed, in a voice trembling with impotent rage—"Faithful to death!"

The words made one of the mottoes of the Orsini; and, and whatever its earlier signification, had long passed into a current proverb, to signify their hatred to the Colonna.

Adrian, now engaged in raising, and attempting to revive Irene, who was still insensible, disdainfully left it to Montreal to reply.

"I doubt not, Signor," said the latter, cooly, "that thou wilt be faithful to Death: for Death, God wot, is the only contract which men, however ingenious, are unable to break or evade."

"Pardon me, gentle Knight," said Adrian, looking up from his charge, "if I do not yet give myself wholly to gratitude. I have learned enough of knighthood to feel thou wilt acknowledge that my first duty is here—"

"Oh, a lady, then, was the cause of the quarrel! I need not ask who was in the right, when a man brings to the rivalry such odds as yon caitiff."

"Thou mistakest a little, Sir Knight,—it is but a lamb I have rescued from the wolf."

"For thy own table! Be it so!" returned the knight, gaily.

Adrian smiled gravely, and shook his head in denial. In truth, he was somewhat embarrassed by his situation. Though habitually gallant, he was not willing to expose to misconstruction the disinterestedness of his late conduct, and (for it was his policy to conciliate popularity) to sully the credit which his bravery would give him among the citizens, by conveying Irene (whose beauty, too, as yet, he had scarcely noted) to his own dwelling; and yet, in her present situation, there was no alternative. She evinced no sign of life. He knew not her home, nor parentage. Benedetta had vanished. He could not leave her in the streets; he could not resign her to the care of another; and, as she lay now upon his breast, he felt her already endeared to him by that sense of protection which is so grateful to the human heart. He briefly, therefore, explained to those now gathered round him, his present situation, and the cause of the past conflict; and bade the torch-bearers precede him to his home.

"You, Sir Knight," added he, turning to Montreal, "if not already more pleasantly lodged, will, I trust, deign to be my guest?"

"Thanks, Signor," answered Montreal, maliciously, "but I, also, perhaps, have my own affairs to watch over. Adieu! I shall seek you at the earliest occasion. Fair night, and gentle dreams!

'Robers Bertrams qui estoit tors
Mais à ceval estoit mult fors
Cil avoit o lui grans effors
Multi ot 'homes per lui mors.'"*

* "An ill-favored man, but a stout horseman, was Robert Bertram. Great deeds were his, and many a man died by his hand."

And, muttering this rugged chant from the old "Roman de Rou," the Provençal, followed by Rodolf, pursued his way.

The vast extent of Rome, and the thinness of its population, left many of the streets utterly deserted. The principal nobles were thus enabled to possess themselves of a wide range of buildings, which they fortified, partly against each other, partly against the people; their numerous relatives and clients lived around them, forming, as it were, petty courts and cities in themselves.

Almost opposite to the principal palace of the Colonna (occupied by his powerful kinsman, Stephen) was the mansion of Adrian. Heavily swung back the massive gates at his approach; he ascended the broad staircase, and bore his charge into an apartment which his tastes had decorated in a fashion not as yet common in that age. Ancient statues and busts were arranged around; the pictured arras of Lombardy decorated the walls, and covered the massive seats.

"What ho! Lights here, and wine!" cried the Seneschal.

"Leave us alone," said Adrian, gazing passionately on the pale cheek of Irene, as he now, by the clear light, beheld all its beauty; and a sweet yet burning hope crept into his heart.

CHAPTER V.

The Description of a Conspirator, and the dawn of the Conspiracy.

ALONE, by a table covered with various papers, sat a man in the prime of life. The chamber was low and long; many antique and disfigured bas-reliefs and torsos were placed around the wall, interspersed, here and there, with the short sword and close casque, time-worn relics of the prowess of ancient Rome. Right above the table at which he sate, the moonlight streamed through a high and narrow casement, deep sunk in the massy wall. In a niche to the right of this window, guarded by a sliding door, which was now partially drawn aside—but which, by its solid substance, and the sheet of iron with which it was plated, testified how valuable, in the eyes of the owner, was the treasure it protected—were ranged some thirty or forty volumes, then deemed no inconsiderable library; and being, for the most part, the laborious copies in manuscript by the hand of the owner, from immortal originals.

Leaning his cheek on his hand, his brow somewhat knit, his lip slightly compressed, that personage indulged in meditations far other than the indolent dreams of scholars. As the high and still moonlight shone upon his countenance, it gave an additional and solemn dignity to features which were naturally of a grave and majestic cast. Thick and auburn hair, the color of which, not common to the Romans, was ascribed to his descent from the Teuton emperor, clustered in large curls above a high and expansive forehead; and even the present thoughtful compression of the brow could not mar the aspect of latent power, which it derived from that great breadth between the eyes, in which the Grecian sculptors of old so admirably conveyed the expression of authority, and the silent energy of command. But his features were not cast in the Grecian, still less in the Teuton mould. The iron jaw, the aquiline nose, the somewhat sunken cheek, strikingly recalled the character of the hard Roman race, and might not inaptly have suggested to a painter a mode for the younger Brutus.

The marked outline of the face, and the short, firm upper lip, were not concealed by the beard and mustachios usually then worn; and in the faded portrait of the person now described, still extant at Rome, may be traced a certain resemblance to the popular pictures of Napoleon; not indeed in the features, which are more stern and prominent in the portrait of the Roman, but in that peculiar expression of concentrated and tranquil power which so nearly realizes the ideal of intellectual majesty. Though still young, the personal advantages most peculiar to youth,—the bloom and glow, the rounded cheek in which care has not yet ploughed its lines, the full unsunken eye, and the slender delicacy of frame,—these are not the characteristics of that solitary student. And, though considered by his contemporaries as eminently handsome, the judgment was propably formed less from the more vulgar claims to such distinction, than from the height of the stature, and advantage at that time more esteemed than at present, and that nobler order of beauty which cultivated genius and commanding character usually stamp upon even homely features;—the more rare in an age so rugged.

The character of Rienzi (for the youth presented to the reader in the first chapter of this history is now again before him in maturer years) had acquired greater hardness and energy with each stepping-stone to power. There was a circumstance attendant on his birth which had, probably, exercised great and early influence on his ambition. Though his parents were in humble circumstances, and of lowly calling, his father was the natural son of the Emperor, Henry VII.; * and it was the pride of the parents that probably gave to Rienzi the unwonted advantages of education. This pride transmitted to himself,—his descent from royalty dinned into his ear, infused into his thoughts, from his cradle,—made him, even in his earliest youth, deem himself the equal of the Roman signors, and half unconsciously aspire to be their superior. But, as the literature of Rome was unfolded to his eager eye and ambitious heart, he became imbued with that pride of country which is nobler than the pride of birth; and, save when stung by allusions to his origin, he unaffectedly valued himself more on being a Roman plebeian than the descendant of a Teuton king. His brother's death, and the vicissitudes he himself had already undergone, deepened the earnest and solemn qualities of his character; and, at length, all the faculties of a very uncommon intellect were concentrated into one object—which borrowed from a mind strongly and mystically religious, as well as patriotic, a sacred aspect, and grew at once a duty and a passion.

"Yes," said Rienzi, breaking suddenly from his revery, "yes, the day is at hand when Rome shall rise again from her ashes; Justice shall dethrone Oppression; men shall walk safe in their ancient Forum. We will rouse from his forgotten tomb the indomitable soul of Cato! There shall be a *people* once more in Rome! And I—I shall be the instrument of that triumph—the restorer of my race! mine shall be the first voice to swell the battle-cry of freedom—mine the first hand to rear her banner—yes, from the height of my own soul as from a mountain, I see already rising the liberties and the grandeur of the New Rome; and on the corner-stone of the mighty fabric posterity shall read my name."

Uttering these lofty boasts, the whole person of the speaker seemed instinct with his ambition. He strode the gloomy chamber with light and rapid steps, as if on air; his breast heaved, his eyes glowed. He felt that love itself can scarcely bestow a repture equal to that which is felt, in his first virgin enthusiasm, by a patriot who knows himself *sincere!*

There was a slight knock at the door, and a servitor, in the rich liveries worn by the pope's officials,* presented himself.

"Signor," said he, "my Lord, the Bishop of Orvietto, is without."

"Ha! that is fortunate. Lights there!—My Lord, this is an honor which I can estimate better than express."

"Tut, tut! my good friend," said the Bishop, entering, and seating himself familiarly, "no ceremonies between the servants of the Church; and never, I ween well, had she greater need of true friends than now. These unholy tumults, these licentious contentions, in the very shrines and city of St. Peter, are sufficient to scandalize all Christendom."

"And so will it be," said Rienzi, "until his Holiness himself shall be graciously persuaded to fix his residence in the seat of his predecessors, and curb with a strong arm the excessses of the nobles."

"Alas, man!" said the Bishop, "thou knowest that these words are but as wind; for were the Pope to fulfil thy wishes, and remove from Avignon to Rome, by the blood of St. Peter! he would not curb the nobles, but the nobles would curb him. Thou knowest well that until his blessed predecessor, of pious memory, conceived the wise design of escaping to Avignon, the Father of the Christian world was but like many other fathers in their old age, controlled and guarded by his rebellious children. Recollectest thou not

* De Sade supposes that the *mother* of Rienzi was the daughter of an illegitimate son of Henry VII., supporting his opinion from a MS. in the Vatican. But, according to the contemporaneous biographer, Rienzi, in addressing Charles, king of Bohemia claims the relationship from his father. "Di vostro legnaggio sono—figlio di bastardo d'Enrico imperatore," etc. A more recent writer, il Padre Gabrini, cites an inscription in support of this descent: "Nicolaus Tribunus . . . *Laurentii Teutonici* Filius," etc.

* Not the present hideous habiliments, which are said to have been the invention of Michael Angelo.

how the noble Boniface himself, a man of great heart, and nerves of iron, was kept in thraldom by the ancestors of the Orsini—his entrances and exits made but at their will—so that, like a caged eagle, he beat himself against his bars and died? Verily, thou talkest of the memories of Rome--these are not the memories that are very attractive to popes."

"Well," said Rienzi, laughing gently, and drawing his seat nearer to the Bishop's, "my Lord has certainly the best of the argument at present; and I must own, that strong, licentious, and unhallowed as the order of nobility was then, it is yet more so now."

"Even I," rejoined Raimond, coloring as he spoke, "though Vicar of the Pope, and representative of his spiritual authority, was, but three days ago, subjected to a coarse affront from that very Stephen Colonna, who has ever received such favor and tenderness from the Holy See. His servitors jostled mine in the open streets, and I myself—I, the delegate of the sire of kings—was forced to draw aside to the wall, and wait until the hoary insolent swept by. Nor were blaspheming words wanting to complete the insult. "'Pardon, Lord Bishop,' said he, as he passed me; 'but this world, thou knowest, must necessarily take precedence of the other.'"

"Dared he so high?" said Rienzi, shading his face with his hand, as a very peculiar smile—scarcely itself joyous, thongh it made others gay, and which completely changed the character of his face, naturally grave even to sternness—played round his lips. Then it is time for thee, holy father, as for us, to——"

"To what?" interrupted the Bishop, quickly. "Can we affect aught! Dismiss thy enthusiastic dreamings—descend to the real earth—look soberly round us. Against men so powerful, what *can* we do?"

"My Lord," answered Rienzi, gravely, "it is the misfortune of signors of your rank never to know the people, or the accurate signs of the time. As those who pass over the heights of mountains see the clouds sweep below, veiling the plains and valleys from their gaze, while they, only a little above the level, survey the movements and the homes of men; even so from your lofty eminence ye behold but the indistinct and sullen vapors—while from my humbler station I see the preparations of the shepherds, to shelter themselves and herds from the storm which those clouds betoken. Despair not, my Lord; endurance goes but to a certain limit—to that limit it is already stretched; Rome waits but the occasion (it will soon come, but not suddenly) to rise simultaneously against her oppressors."

The great secret of eloquence is to be in earnest—the great secret of Rienzi's eloquence was in the mightiness of his enthusiasm. He never spoke as one who doubted of success. Perhaps, like most men who undertake high and great actions, he himself was never thoroughly aware of the obstacles in his way. He saw the end, bright and clear, and overleaped, in the vision of his soul, the crosses and the length of the path; thus the deep convictions of his own mind stamped themselves irresistibly upon others. He seemed less to promise than to prophesy.

The Bishop of Orvietto, not over wise, yet a man of cool temperament and much worldly experience, was forcibly impressed by the energy of his companion; perhaps, indeed, the more so, inasmuch as his own pride and his own passions were also enlisted against the arrogance and license of the nobles. He paused ere he replied to Rienzi.

"But is it," he asked, at length, "only the plebeians who will rise? Thou knowest how they are caitiff and uncertain."

"My Lord," answered Rienzi, "judge by one fact, how strongly I am surrounded by friends of no common class: thou knowest how loudly I speak against the nobles—I cite them by their name—I beard the Savelli, the Orsini, the Colonna, in their very hearing. Thinkest thou that they forgive me? thinkest thou that, were only the plebeians my safeguard and my favorers, they would not seize me by open force,—that I had not long ere this found a gag in their dungeons, or been swallowed up in the eternal dumbness of the grave? Observe," continued he, as, reading the Vicar's countenance, he perceived the impression he had made—"observe, that, throughout the whole world, a great revolution has begun. The barbaric darkness of centuries has been broken; the KNOWLEDGE which made men as demigods in the past time has been called from her urn; a Power, subtler than brute force, and mightier than armed men, is at work; we have begun once more to do homage to the Royalty of Mind. Yes, that same Power which, a few years ago, crowned Petrarch in the Capitol, when it witnessed, after the silence of twelve centuries, the glories of a TRIUMPH,—which heaped upon a man of obscure birth, and unknown in arms, the same honors given of old to emperors and the vanquishers of kings,—which united in one act of homage even the rival houses of Colonna and Orsini,—which made the haughtiest patricians emulous to bear the train, to touch but the purple robe, of the son of the Florentine plebeian,—which still draws the eyes of Europe to the lowly cottage of Vaucluse,—which gives to the humble student the all-acknowledged licence to admonish tyranny, and approach, with haughty prayers, even the Father of the Church;—yes, that same Power, which, working silently throughout Italy, murmurs under the solid base of the Venetian oligarchy;* which, beyond the Alps, has wakened into visible and sudden life in Spain, in Germany, in Flanders; and which, even in that barbarous Isle, conquered by the Norman sword ruled by the bravest of living kings,† hasroused a spirit, Norman cannot break—kings to rule over must rule by—yes, that same power is everywhere abroad: it speaks, it conquers in the voice even of him who is before you; it unites in his cause all on whom but one glimmering of light has burst, all in whom one generous desire can be kindled! Know, Lord Vicar, that there is not a man in Rome, save our oppressors themselves—not a man who has learned one syllable of our ancient tongue—whose heart and sword are not with me. The peaceful cultivators of letters—the proud nobles of the second order—the rising race, wiser than their slothful sires; above all, my Lord, the humbler ministers of religion, priest and monks, whom luxury hath not blinded, pomp hath not deafened, to the monstrous outrage to Christianity daily and nightly perpetrated in the Christian Capital; these,—all these,—are linked with the merchant and the artisan in one indissoluble bond, waiting but the signal to fall or to conquer, to live freemen, or to die martyrs, with Rienzi and their country!"

"Sayest thou so in truth?" said the Bishop, startled, and half rising. "Prove but thy words, and thou shalt not find the ministers of God are less eager than their lay brethren for the happiness of men."

"What I say," rejoined Rienzi, in a cooler tone, "that can I show; but I may only prove it to those who will be with us."

"Fear me not," answered Raimond: "I know well the secret mind of his Holiness, whose delegate and representative I am; and could he see but the legitimate and natural limit set to the power of the patricians, who, in their arrogance, have set at nought the authority of the Church itself, be sure that he would smile on the hand that drew the line. Nay, so certain of this am I, that if ye succeed, I, his responsible but unworthy vicar, will myself sanction the success. But beware of crude attempts; the Church must not be weakened by linking itself to failure."

"Right, my Lord," answered Rienzi; "and in this, the policy of religion is that of freedom. Judge of my prudence by my long delay. He who can see all around him impatient—himself not less so—and yet suppress the signal, and bide the hour, is not likely to lose his cause by rashness."

"More, then, of this anon," said the Bishop, resettling himself in his seat. "As thy plans mature, fear not to communicate with me. Believe that Rome has no firmer friend than he who, ordained to preserve order, finds himself impotent against aggression. Meanwhile, to the object of my present visit, which links itself, in some measure, perhaps, with the topics on which we have conversed. . . Thou knowest that when his Holiness intrusted thee with thy present office, he bade thee also announce his beneficent intention of granting a general Jubilee at Rome for the year 1350—a most admirable design for two reasons, sufficiently apparent to thyself: first, that every Christian soul that may undertake the pilgrimage to Rome on that occasion, may thus obtain a general remission of sins; and secondly, because, to speak carnally, the concourse of pilgrims so assembled, usually, by the donations and offerings their piety suggests, very materially add to the revenues of the Holy See: at

* It was about eight years afterwards that the long-smothered hate of the Venetian people to that wisest and most vigilant of all oligarchies, the Sparta of Italy, broke out in the conspiracy under Marino Faliero.

† Edward III., in whose reign opinions far more popular than those of the following century began to work. The Civil Wars threw back the action into the blood. It was indeed an age throughout the world which put forth abundant blossoms, but crude and unripened fruit;—a singular leap, followed by as singular a pause.

this time, by the way, is no very flourishing condition. This thou knowest, dear Rienzi."

Rienzi bowed his head in assent, and the prelate continued—

"Well, it is with the greatest grief that his Holiness perceives that his pious intentions are likely to be frustrated: for so fierce and numerous are now the brigands in the public approaches to Rome, that, verily, the boldest pilgrim may tremble a little to undertake the journey; and those who do so venture will, probably, be composed of the poorest of the Christian community, — men who, bringing with them neither gold, nor silver, nor precious offerings, will have little to fear from the rapacity of the brigands. Hence arise two consequences: on the one hand, the rich—whom, Heaven knows, and the Gospel has, indeed, expressly declared, have the most need of a remission of sins—will be deprived of this glorious occasion for absolution; and, on the other hand, the coffers of the Church will be impiously defrauded of that wealth which it would otherwise doubtless obtain from the zeal of her children."

"Nothing can be more logically manifest, my Lord," said Rienzi.

The Vicar continued—"Now, in letters received five days since from his Holiness, he bade me expose these fearful consequences to Christianity to the various patricians who are legitimately fiefs of the Church, and command their resolute combination against the marauders of the road. With these have I conferred, and vainly."

"For by the aid, and from the troops, of those very brigands, these patricians have fortified their palaces against each other," added Rienzi.

"Exactly for that reason," rejoined the Bishop. "Nay, Stephen Colonna himself had the audacity to confess it. Utterly unmoved by the loss to so many precious souls, and, I may add, to the papal treasury, which ought to be little less dear to right-discerning men, they refuse to advance a step against the bandits. Now, then, hearken the second mandate of his Holiness:—'Failing the nobles,' saith he, in his prophetic sagacity, 'confer with Cola di Rienzi. He is a bold man, and a pious, and, thou tellest me, of great weight with the people; and say to him, that if his wit can devise the method for extirpating these sons of Bolial, and rendering a safe passage along the public ways, largely, indeed, will he merit at our hands,—lasting will be the gratitude we shall owe to him; and whatever succor thou, and the servants of our See, can render to him, let it not be stinted.'"

"Said his Holiness thus!" exclaimed Rienzi. "I ask no more—the gratitude is mine that he hath thought thus of his servant, and intrusted me with this charge; at once I accept it—at once I pledge myself to success. Let us, my Lord, let us, then clearly understand the limits ordained to my discretion. To curb the brigands without the walls, I must have authority over those within. If I undertake, at peril of my life, to clear all the avenues to Rome of the robbers who now infest it, shall I have full licence for conduct bold, peremptory, and severe?"

"Such conduct the very nature of the charge demands," replied Raimond.

"Ay—even though it be exercised against the arch offenders—against the supporters of the brigands—against the haughtiest of the nobles themselves?"

The Bishop paused, and looked hard in the face of the speaker. "I repeat," said he, at length, sinking his voice, and with a significant tone, "in these bold attempts, success is the sole sanction. *Succeed*, and we will excuse thee all—even to the——"

"Death of a Colonna or an Orsini, should justice demand it; and provided it be according to the law, and only incurred by the violation of the law!" added Rienzi, firmly.

The Bishop did not reply in words, but a slight motion of his head was sufficient answer to Rienzi.

"My Lord," said he, "from this time, then, all is well; I date the revolution—the restoration of order, of the state—from this hour, this very conference. Till now, knowing that justice must ever wink upon great offenders, I had hesitated, through fear lest thou and his Holiness might deem it severity, and blame him who replaces the law, because he smites the violators of law. Now I judge ye more rightly. Your hand, my Lord."

The Bishop extended his hand; Rienzi grasped it firmly, and then raised it respectfully to his lips. Both felt that the compact was sealed.

This conference, so long in recital, was

short in the reality; but its object was already finished, and the Bishop rose to depart. The outer portal of the house was opened, the numerous servitors of the Bishop held on high their torches, and he had just turned from Rienzi, who had attended him to the gate, when a female passed hastily through the Prelate's train, and starting as she beheld Rienzi, flung herself at his feet.

"Oh, hasten, Sir! hasten, for the love of God, hasten! or the young Signora is lost for ever!"

"The Signora!—Heaven and earth, Benedetta, of whom do you speak?—of my sister—of Irene? is she not within?"

"Oh, Sir—the Orsini—the Orsini!"

"What of them?—speak, woman!"

Here, breathlessly, and with many a break, Benedetta recounted to Rienzi, in whom the reader has already recognized the brother of Irene, so far of the adventure with Martino di Porto as she had witnessed: of the termination and result of the contest she knew nought.

Rienzi listened in silence; but the deadly paleness of his countenance, and the writhing of the nether lip, testified the emotions to which he gave no audible vent.

"You hear, my Lord Bishop—you hear," said he, when Benedetta had concluded; and turning to the Bishop, whose departure the narrative had delayed—"you hear to what outrage the citizens of Rome are subjected. My hat and sword! instantly! My lord forgive my abruptness."

"Whither art thou bent, then?" asked Raimond.

"Whither—whither!—Ay, I forgot, my Lord, you have no sister. Perhaps, too, you had no brother?—No, no; one victim at least I will live to save. Whither, you ask me?—to the palace of Martino di Porto."

"To an Orsini *alone*, and for justice?"

"Alone, and for *justice!*—No!" shouted Rienzi, in a loud voice, as he seized his sword, now brought to him by one of his servants, and rushed from the house; "but one man is sufficient for *revenge!*"

The Bishop paused for a moment's deliberation. "He must not be lost," muttered he, "as he well may be, if exposed thus solitary to the wolf's rage. What ho!" he cried aloud; "advance the torches!—quick, quick! We ourself—we, the Vicar of the Pope—will see to this. Calm yourselves, good people; your young Signora shall be restored. On! to the palace of Martino di Porto!"

CHAPTER VI.

Irene in the Palace of Arian di Castello.

As the Cyprian gazed on the image in which he had embodied a youth of dreams, what time the living hues flushed slowly beneath the marble,—so gazed the young and passionate Adrian upon the form reclined before him, reawakening gradually to life. And, if the beauty of that face were not of the loftiest or the most dazzling order, if its soft and quiet character might be outshone by many, of loveliness less really perfect, yet never was there a countenance that, to some eyes, would have seemed more charming, and never one in which more eloquently was wrought that ineffable and virgin expression which Italian art seeks for in its models,—in which modesty is the outward, and tenderness the latent expression; the bloom of youth, both of form and heart, ere the first frail and delicate freshness of either is brushed away: and when even love itself, the only unquiet visitant that should be known at such an age, is but a sentiment, and not a passion!

"Benedetta!" murmured Irene, at length opening her eyes, unconsciously, upon him who knelt beside her,—eyes of that uncertain, that most liquid hue, on which you might gaze for years and never learn the secret of the color, so changed it with the dilating pupil, —darkening in the shade, and brightening into azure in the light:

"Benedetta," said Irene, "where art thou? Oh, Benedetta! I have had such a dream."

"And I, too, such a vision!" thought Adrian

"Where am I?" cried Irene, rising from the couch. "This room—these hangings—Holy Virgin! do I dream still!—and you! Heavens!—it is the Lord Adrian di Castello!"

"Is that a name thou hast been taught to fear?" said Adrian; "if so I will forswear it.

If Irene now blushed deeply, it was not in that wild delight with which her romantic heart might have foretold that she would listen to the first words of homage from Adrian di Cas tello. Bewildered and confused,—terrified at the strangeness of the place and shrinking even from the thought of finding herself alone with one who for years had been present to her fancies,—alarm and distress were the emotions she felt the most, and which most were impressed upon her speaking countenance; and as Adrian now drew nearer to her, despite the gentleness of his voice and the respect of his looks, her fears, not the less strong that they were vague, increased upon her: she retreated to the further end of the room, looked wildly round her, and then, covering her face with her hands, burst into a paroxysm of tears.

Moved himself by these tears, and divining her thoughts, Adrian forgot for a moment all the more daring wishes he had formed.

"Fear not, sweet lady," said he, earnestly: "recollect thyself, I beseech thee; no peril, no evil can reach thee here; it was this hand that saved thee from the outrage of the Orsini—this roof is but the shelter of a friend! Tell me, then, fair wonder, thy name and residence, and I will summon my servitors, and guard thee to thy home at once."

Perhaps the relief of tears, even more than Adrian's words, restored Irene to herself, and enabled her to comprehend her novel situation; and as her senses, thus cleared, told her what she owed to him whom her dreams had so long imaged as the ideal of all excellence, she recovered her self-possession, and uttered her thanks with a grace not the less winning, if it still partook of embarrassment.

"Thank me not," answered Adrian, passionately. "I have touched thy hand—I am repaid. Repaid! nay, all gratitude—all homage is for me to render!"

Blushing again, but with far different emotions than before, Irene, after a momentary pause, replied, "Yet, my Lord, I must consider it a debt the more weighty that you speak of it so lightly. And now, complete the obligation. I do not see my companion—suffer her to accompany me home; it is but a short way hence."

"Blessed, then, is the air that I have breathed so unconsciously!" said Adrian. "But thy companion, dear lady, is not here. She fled, I imagine, in the confusion of the conflict; and not knowing thy name, nor being able, in thy then state, to learn it from thy lips, it was my happy necessity to convey thee hither;—but I will be thy companion. Nay, why that timid glance? my people, also, shall attend us."

"My thanks, noble Lord, are of little worth; my brother, who is not unknown to thee, will thank thee more fittingly. May I depart?" and Irene, as she spoke, was already at the door.

"Art thou so eager to leave me?" answered Adrian, sadly. "Alas! when thou hast departed from my eyes, it will seem as if the moon had left the night!—but it is happiness to obey thy wishes, even though they tear thee from me."

A slight smile parted Irene's lips, and Adrian's heart beat audibly to himself, as he drew from that smile, and those downcast eyes, no unfavorable omen.

Reluctantly and slowly he turned towards the door, and summoned his attendants. "But," said he, as they stood on the lofty staircase, "thou sayest, sweet lady, that thy brother's name is not unknown to me. Heaven grant that he be, indeed, a friend of the Colonna!"

"His boast," answered Irene, evasively; "the boast of Cola di Rienzi is, to be a friend to the friends of Rome."

"Holy Virgin of Ara Cœli!—is thy brother that extraordinary man?" exclaimed Adrian, as he foresaw, at the mention of that name, a barrier to his sudden passion. "Alas! in a Colonna, in a noble, he will see no merit; even though thy fortunate deliverer, sweet maiden, sought to be his early friend!"

"Thou wrongest him much, my Lord," returned Irene, warmly; "he is a man above all others to sympathize with thy generous valor, even had it been exerted in defence of the humblest woman in Rome,—how much more, then, when in protection of his sister!"

"The times are, indeed, diseased," answered Adrian, thoughtfully, as they now found themselves in the open street, "when men who alike mourn for the woes of their country are yet suspicious of each other; when to be a patrician is to be regarded as an enemy to the people; when to be termed the friend of the people is to be considered a foe to the patricians: but come what may, oh! let me hope, dear lady, that no doubts, no divisions, shall banish from *thy* breast one gentle memory of me!"

"Ah! little, little do you know me!" began Irene, and stopped suddenly short.

"Speak! speak again!—of what music has this envious silence deprived my soul! Thou wilt not, then, forget me? And," continued Adrian, "we shall meet again? It is to Rienzi's house we are bound now; to-morrow I shall visit my old companion,—to-morrow I shall see thee. Will it not be so?"

In Irene's silence was her answer.

"And as thou hast told me thy brother's name, make it sweet to my ear, and add to it thine own."

"They call me Irene."

"Irene, Irene!—let me repeat it. It is a soft name, and dwells upon the lips as if loath to leave them—a fitting name for one like thee."

Thus making his welcome court to Irene, in that flowered and glowing language which, if more peculiar to that age and to the gallantry of the south, is also the language in which the poetry of youthful passion would, in all times and lands, utter its rich extravagance, could heart speak to heart, Adrian conveyed homeward his beautiful charge, taking, however, the most circuitous and lengthened route; an artifice which Irene either perceived not, or silently forgave. They were now within sight of the street in which Rienzi dwelt, when a party of men, bearing torches, came unexpectedly upon them. It was the train of the Bishop of Orvietto, returning from the palace of Martino di Porto, and in their way (accompanied by Rienzi) to that of Adrian. They had learned at the former, without an interview with the Orsini, from the retainers in the court below, the fortune of the conflict, and the name of Irene's champion; and, despite Adrian's general reputation for gallantry, Rienzi knew enough of his character, and the nobleness of his temper, to feel assured that Irene was safe in his protection. Alas! in that very safety to the person is often the most danger to the heart. Woman never so dangerously loves, as when he who loves her, for her sake, subdues himself.

Clasped to her brother's breast, Irene bade him thank her deliverer; and Rienzi, with that fascinating frankness which sits so well on those usually reserved, and which all who would rule the hearts of their fellow-men must at times command, advanced to the young Colonna, and poured forth his gratitude and praise.

"We have been severved too long,—we must know each other again," replied Adrian. "I shall seek thee, ere long, be assured."

Turning to take his leave of Irene, he conveyed her hand to his lips, and pressing it, as it dropped from his clasp, was he deceived in thinking that those delicate fingers lightly, involuntarily, returned the pressure?

CHAPTER VII.

Upon Love and Lovers.

If, in adopting the legendary love-tale of Romeo and Juliet, Shakespeare had changed the scene in which it is cast for a more northern clime, we may doubt whether the art of Shakespeare himself could have reconciled us at once to the suddenness and the strength of Juliet's passion. And, even as it is, perhaps there are few of our rational and sober-minded islanders who would not honestly confess, if fairly questioned, that they deem the romance and fervor of those ill-starred lovers of Verona exaggerated and over-drawn. Yet, in Italy, the picture of that affection born of a night—but "strong as death"—is one to which the veriest common-places of life would afford parallels without number. As in different ages, so in different climes, love varies wonderfully in the shapes it takes. And even at this day, beneath Italian skies, many a simple girl would feel as Juliet, and many a homely gallant would rival the extravagance of Romeo. Long suits in that sunny land, wherin as whereof, I now write, are unknown. In no other land, perhaps, is there found so commonly the love at first sight, which in France is a jest, and in England a doubt; in no other land, too, is love, though so suddenly conceived, more faithfully preserved. That which is ripened in fancy comes at once to passion, yet is embalmed through all time by sentiment. And this must be my and their excuse, if the love of Adrian seem too prematurely formed, and that of Irene too romantically conceived;—it is the excuse which they take from the air and sun, from the customs of their ancestors, from the soft contagion of example.

But while they yielded to the dictates of their hearts, it was with a certain though secret sadness—a presentiment that had, perhaps, its charm, though it was of cross and evil. Born of so proud a race, Adrian could scarcely dream of marriage with the sister of a plebeian; and Irene, unconscious of the future glory of her brother, could hardly have cherished any hope, save that of being loved. Yet these adverse circumstances, which, in the harder, the more prudent, the more self-denying, perhaps the more virtuous minds, that are formed beneath the northern skies, would have been an inducement to wrestle against love so placed, only contributed to feed and to strengthen *theirs* by an opposition which has ever its attraction for romance. They found frequent, though short, opportunities of meeting—not quite alone, but only in the conniving presence of Benedetta: sometimes in the public gardens, sometimes amidst the vast and deserted ruins by which the house of Rienzi was surrounded. They surrendered themselves, without much question of the future, to the excitement—the elysium—of the hour: they lived but from day to day; *their* future was the next time they should meet; beyond that epoch, the very mists of their youthful love closed in obscurity and shadow which they sought not to penetrate: and as yet they had not arrived at that period of affection when there was danger of their fall,—their love had not passed the golden portal where Heaven ceases and Earth begins. Everything for them was the poetry, the vagueness, the refinement,—not the power, the concentration, the mortality,—of desire! The look — the whisper—the brief pressure of the hand,—at most, the first kisses of love, rare and few,—these marked the human limits of that sentiment which filled them with a new life, which elevated them as with a new soul.

The roving tendencies of Adrian were at once fixed and centered; the dreams of his tender mistress had awakened to a life dreaming still, but "rounded with a *truth.*" All that earnestness, and energy, and fervor of emotion, which, in her brother, broke forth in the schemes of patriotism and the aspirations of power, were, in Irene, softened down into one object of existence, one concentration of soul,—and that was love. Yet, in this range of thought and action, so apparently limited, there was in reality, no less boundless a sphere than in the wide space of her brother's many-pathed ambition. Not the less had she the power and scope for all the loftiest capacities granted to our clay. Equal was her enthusiasm for her idol; equal, had she been equally tried, would have been her generosity, her devotion:—greater, be sure, her courage; more inalienable her worship; more unsullied by selfish purposes and sordid views. Time, change, misfortune, ingratitude, would have left *her* the same! What state could fall, what liberty decay, if the zeal of man's noisy patriotism were as pure as the silent loyalty of a woman's love?

In them everything *was young!*—the heart unchilled, unblighted,—that fulness and luxuriance of life's life which has in it something of divine. At that age, when it seems as if we could never die, how deathless, how flushed and mighty as with the youngness of a god, is all that our hearts create! Our own youth is like that of the earth itself, when it peopled the woods and waters with divinities; when life ran riot, and yet only gave birth to beauty;—all its shapes, of poetry,—all its airs, the melodies of Arcady and Olympus! The Golden Age never leaves the world: it exists still, and shall exist, till love, health, poetry, are no more; but only for the young!

If I now dwell, though but for a moment, on this interude in a drama calling forth more masculine passions than that of love, it is because I foresee that the occasion will but rarely recur. If I linger on the description of Irene and her hidden affection, rather than wait for circumstances to portray them better than the author's words can, it is because I foresee that that loving and lovely image must continue to the last rather a shadow than a portrait,—thrown in the background, as is the real destiny of such natures, by bolder figures and more gorgeous colors; a something whose presence is rather felt than seen, and whose very harmony with the whole consists in its retiring and subdued repose.

CHAPTER VIII.

The Enthusiastic Man judged by the Discreet Man.

"THOU wrongest me," said Rienzi, warmly, to Adrian, as they sat alone, towards the close of a long conference; "I do not play the part of a mere demagogue; I wish not to stir the great deeps in order that my lees of fortune may rise to the surface. So long have I brooded over the past, that it seems to me as if I had become a part of it—as if I had no separate existence. I have coined my whole soul into one master passion,—and its end is the restoration of Rome."

"But by what means?"

"My Lord! my Lord! there is but one way to restore the greatness of a people—it is an appeal to the people themselves. It is not in the power of princes and barons to make a state permanently glorious; they raise themselves, but they raise not the people with them. All great regenerations are the universal movement of the mass."

"Nay," answered Adrian, "then have we read history differently. To me, all great regenerations seem to have been the work of the few, and tacitly accepted by the multitude. But let us not dispute after the manner of the schools. Thou sayest loudly that a vast crisis is at hand; that the Good Estate (*buono stato*) shall be established. How? where are your arms?—your soldiers? Are the nobles less strong than heretofore? is the mob more bold, more constant? Heaven knows that I speak not with the prejudices of my order—I weep for the debasement of my country! I am a Roman, and in that name I forget that I am a noble. But I tremble at the storm you would raise so hazardously. If your insurrection succeed, it will be violent: it will be purchased by blood—by the blood of all the loftiest names of Rome. You will aim at a second expulsion of the Tarquins; but it will be more like a second proscription of Sylla. Massacres and disorders never pave the way to peace. If, on the other hand, you fail, the chains of Rome are rivetted for ever: an ineffectual struggle to escape is but an excuse for additional tortures to the slave."

"And what, then, would the Lord Adrian have us do?" said Rienzi, with that peculiar and sarcastic smile which has before been noted. "Shall we wait till the Colonna and Orsini quarrel no more? shall we ask the Colonna for liberty, and the Orsini for justice? My Lord, we cannot appeal to the nobles against the nobles. We must not ask them to moderate their power; we must restore to ourselves that power. There may be danger in the attempt—but we attempt it amongst the monuments of the Forum: and if we fall—we shall perish worthy of our sires! Ye have high descent, and sounding titles, and wide lands, and you talk of *your* ancestral honors! We, too,—we plebeians of Rome,—we have *ours!* Our fathers were freemen! where is our heritage? not sold—not given away: but stolen from us, now by fraud, now by force—filched from us in our sleep; or wrung from us with fierce hands, amidst our cries and struggles. My Lord, we but ask that lawful heritage to be restored to us: to us—nay, to you it is the same; your liberty, alike, is gone. Can you dwell in your father's house, without towers, and fortresses, and the bought swords of bravos? can you walk in the streets at dark without arms and followers? True, *you*, a noble, may retaliate; though *we* dare not. You, in your turn, may terrify and outrage others; but does licence compensate for liberty? They have given you pomp and power—but the safety of equal laws were a better gift. Oh, were I you—were I Stephen Colonna himself, I should pant, ay, thirstily as I do now, for that free air which comes not through bars and bulwarks against my fellow-citizens, but in the open space of Heaven—safe, because protected by the silent Providence of Law, and not by the lean fears and hollow-eyed suspicions which are the comrades of a hated power. The tyrant thinks he is free, because he commands slaves: the meanest peasant in a free state is more free than he is. Oh, my Lord, that you—the brave, the generous, the enlightened—you, almost alone amidst your order, in the knowledge that we *had* a country—oh, would that you who can sympathize with our sufferings, would strike with us for their redress!"

"Thou wilt war against Stephen Colonna, my kinsman; and though I have seen him but little, nor, truth to say, esteem him much, yet he is the boast of our house,—how can I join thee?"

"His life will be safe, his possessions safe, his rank safe. What do we war against? His power to do wrong to others."

"Should he discover that thou hast force beyond words, he would be less merciful to *thee*."

"And has he not discovered that? Do not

the shouts of the people tell him that I am a man whom he should fear? Does he—the cautious, the wily, the profound—does he build fortresses, and erect towers, and not see from his battlements the mighty fabric that I, too, have erected?"

"You! where, Rienzi?"

"In the hearts of Rome! Does he not see?" continued Rienzi. "No, no; he—all, all his tribe are blind. Is it not so?"

"Of a certainty, my kinsman has no belief in your power, else he would have crushed you long ere this. Nay, it was but three days ago that he said, gravely, he would rather *you* addressed the populace than the best priest in Christendom; for that other orators inflamed the crowd, and no man so stilled and dispersed them as you did."

"And I called *him* profound! Does not Heaven hush the air most when most it prepares the storm? Ay, my Lord, I understand. Stephen Colonna despises me. I have been"—(here, as he continued, a deep blush mantled over his cheek)—"you remember it—at his palace in my younger days, and pleased him with witty tales and light apophthegms. Nay—ha! ha!—he would call me, I think, sometimes, in gay compliment, his jester,—his buffoon! I have brooked his insult; I have even bowed to his applause. I would undergo the same penance, stoop to the same shame, for the same motive, and in the same cause. What did I desire to effect? Can you tell me? No! I will whisper it, then, to you: it was—the contempt of Stephen Colonna. Under that contempt I was protected, till protection became no longer necessary. I desired not to be thought formidable by the partricians, in order that, quietly and unsuspected, I might make my way amongst the people. I have done so; I now throw aside the mask. Face to face with Stephen Colonna, I could tell him, this very hour, that I brave his anger; that I laugh at his dungeons and armed men. But if he think me the same Rienzi as of old, let him; I can wait my hour."

"Yet," said Adrian, waiving an answer to the haughty language of his companion, "tell me, what dost thou ask for the people, in order to avoid an appeal to their passions?—ignorant and capricious as they are, thou canst not appeal to their reason."

"I ask full justice and safety for all men. I will be contented with no less a compromise. I ask the nobles to dismantle their fortresses; to disband their armed retainers; to acknowledge no impunity for crime in high lineage; to claim no protection save in the courts of the common law."

"Vain desire!" said Adrian. "Ask what may yet be granted."

"Ha—ha!" replied Rienzi, laughing bitterly, "did I not tell you it was a vain dream to ask for law and justice at the hands of the great? Can you blame me, then, that I ask it elsewhere?" Then, suddenly changing his tone and manner, he added with great solemnity—"Waking life hath false and vain dreams; but sleep is sometimes a mighty prophet. By sleep it is that Heaven mysteriously communes with its creatures, and guides and sustains its earthly agents in the path to which its providence leads them on."

Adrian made no reply. This was not the first time he had noted that Rienzi's strong intellect was strangely conjoined with a deep and mystical superstition. And this yet more inclined the young noble, who, though sufficiently devout, yielded but little to the wilder credulities of the time, to doubt the success of the schemer's projects. In this he erred greatly, though his error was that of the worldly wise. For nothing ever so inspires human daring, as the fond belief that it is the agent of a Diviner Wisdom. Revenge and patriotism, united in one man of genius and ambition—such are the Archimedian levers that find, in FANATICISM, the spot *out* of the world by which to move the world. The prudent man may direct a state; but it is the enthusiast who regenerates it,—or ruins.

CHAPTER IX.

"When the People saw this Picture, every one Marvelled."

BEFORE the market-place, and at the foot of the Capitol, an immense crowd was assembled. Each man sought to push before his neighbor; each struggled to gain access to one particular spot, round which the crowd was wedged thick and dense.

"Corpo di Dio!" said a man of huge stature, pressing onward, like some bulky ship, casting the noisy waves right and left from its prow, "this is hot work; but for what, in the holy Mother's name, do ye crowd so! See you not, Sir Ribald, that my right arm is disabled, swathed, and bandaged, so that I cannot help myself better than a baby? and yet you push against me as if I were an old wall!"

"Ah, Cecco del Vecchio!—what, man! we must make way for you—you are too small and tender to bustle through a crowd! Come, I will protect you!" said a dwarf of some four feet high, glancing up at the giant.

"Faith," said the grim smith, looking round on the mob, who laughed loud at the dwarf's proffer, "we all do want protection, big and small. What do you laugh for, ye apes?—ay, you don't understand parables."

"And yet it is a parable we are come to gaze upon," said one of the mob, with a slight sneer.

"Pleasant day to you, Signor Baroncelli," answered Cecco del Vecchio; "you are a good man, and love the people; it makes one's heart smile to see you. What's all this pother for?"

"Why the Pope's Notary hath set up a great picture in the market-place, and the gapers say it relates to Rome; so they are melting their brains out, this hot day, to guess at the riddle."

"Ho! ho!" said the smith, pushing on so vigorously that he left the speaker suddenly in the rear; "if Cola di Rienzi hath aught in the matter, I would break through stone rocks to get to it."

"Much good will a dead daub do us," said Baroncelli sourly, and turning to his neighbors; but no man listened to him, and he, a would-be demagogue, gnawed his lip in envy.

Amidst half-awed groans and curses from the men whom he jostled aside, and open objurgations and shrill cries from the women, to whose robes and head-gear he showed as little respect, the sturdy smith won his way to a space fenced round by chains, in the centre of which was placed a huge picture.

"How came it hither?" cried one; "I was first at the market."

"We found it here at day-break," said a vender of fruit: "no one was by."

"But why do you fancy Rienzi had a hand in it?"

"Why, who else could?" answered twenty voices.

"True! Who else?" echoed the gaunt smith. "I dare be sworn the good man spent the whole night in painting it himself. Blood of St. Peter! but it is mighty fine! What is it about?"

"That's the riddle," said a meditative fish-woman; "if I could make it out, I should die happy."

"It is something about liberty and taxes, no doubt," said Luigi, the butcher, leaning over the chains. "Ah, if Rienzi were minded, every poor man would have his bit of meat in his pot."

"And as much bread as he could eat," added a pale baker.

"Chut! bread and meat—everybody has that now!—but what wine the poor folks drink! One has no encouragement to take pains with one's vineyard," said a vine-dresser.

"Ho, hollo!—long life to Pandulfo di Guido! make way for master Pandulfo; he is a learned man; he is a friend of the great Notary's; he will tell us all about the picture; make way, there—make way!"

Slowly and modestly, Pandulfo di Guido, a quiet, wealthy, and honest man of letters, whom nought save the violence of the times could have roused from his tranquil home, or his studious closet, passed to the chains. He looked long and hard at the picture, which was bright with new, and yet moist colors, and exhibited somewhat of the reviving art, which, though hard and harsh in its features, was about that time visible, and, carried to a far higher degree, we yet gaze upon in the paintings of Perugino, who flourished during the succeeding generation. The people pressed round the learned man, with open mouths; now turning their eyes to the picture, now to Pandulfo.

"Know you not," at length said Pandulfo, "the easy and palpable meaning of this design? Behold how the painter has presented to you a vast and stormy sea—mark how its waves—"

"Speak louder—louder!" shouted the impatient crowd.

"Hush!" cried those in the immediate vicinity of Pandulfo, "the worthy Signor is perfectly audible!"

Meanwhile, some of the more witty, pushing towards a stall in the market-place, bore from it a rough table, from which they besought Pandulfo to address the people. The pale citizen, with some pain and shame, for he was no practised spokesman, was obliged to assent; but when he cast his eyes over the vast and breathless crowd, his own deep sympathy with their cause inspired and emboldened him. A light broke from his eyes; his voice swelled into power; and his head, usually buried in his breast, became erect and commanding in its air.

"You see before you in the picture" (he began again) "a mighty and tempestuous sea: upon its waves you behold five ships; four of them are already wrecks,—their masts are broken, the waves are dashing through the rent planks, they are past all aid and hope: on each of these ships lies the corpse of a woman. See you not, in the wan face and livid limbs, how faithfully the limner hath painted the hues and loathsomeness of death? Below each of these ships is a word that applies the metaphor to truth. Yonder, you see the name of Carthage; the other three are Troy, Jerusalem, and Babylon. To these four is one common inscription. 'To exhaustion were we brought by injustice!' Turn now your eyes to the middle of the sea,—there you behold the fifth ship, tossed amidst the waves, her mast broken, her rudder gone, her sails shivered, but not yet a wreck like the rest, though she soon may be. On her deck kneels a female, clothed in mourning; mark the woe upon her countenance,—how cunningly the artist has conveyed its depth and desolation: she stretches out her arms in prayer, she implores your and Heaven's assistance. Mark now the superscription—'This is Rome!'—Yes, it is your country that addresses you in this emblem!"

The crowd waved to and fro, and a deep murmur crept gathering over the silence which they had hitherto kept.

"Now," continued Pandulfo, "turn your gaze to the right of the picture, and you will behold the cause of the tempest,—you will see why the fifth vessel is thus perilled, and her sisters are thus wrecked. Mark, four different kinds of animals, who, from their horrid jaws, send forth the winds and storms which torture and rack the sea. The first are the lions, the wolves, the bears. These, the inscription tells you, are the lawless and savage signors of the state. The next are the dogs and swine,—these are the evil counsellors and parasites. Thirdly, you behold the dragons and the foxes,—and these are false judges and notaries, and they who sell justice. Fourthly, in the hares, the goats, the apes, that assist in creating the storm, you perceive, by the inscription, the emblems of the popular thieves and homicides, ravishers and spoliators. Are ye bewildered still, O Romans! or have ye mastered the riddle of the picture?"

Far in their massive palaces the Savelli and Orsini heard the echo of the shouts that answered the question of Pandulfo.

"Are ye, then, without hope!" resumed the scholar, as the shout ceased, and hushing, with the first sound of his voice, the ejaculations and speeches which each man had turned to utter to his neighbor. "Are ye without hope? Doth the picture which shows your tribulation, promise you no redemption? Behold, above that angry sea, the heavens open, and the majesty of God descends gloriously, as to judgment: and, from the rays that surround the Spirit of God extend two flaming swords, and on those swords stand, in wrath, but in deliverance, the two patron saints—the two mighty guardians of your city! People of Rome, farewell! the parable is finished." *

CHAPTER X.

A Rough Spirit Raised, which may Hereafter Rend the Wizard.

WHILE thus animated was the scene around the Capitol, *within* one of the apartments of the palace sat the agent and prime cause of that excitement. In the company of his quiet scribes, Rienzi appeared absorbed in the patient details of his avocation. While the murmur and the hum, the shout and the tramp of multitudes, rolled to his chamber, he seemed not to heed them, nor to rouse himself a moment from his task. With the

* "M. Sismondi attributes to Rienzi a fine oration at the showing of the picture, in which he thundered against the vices of the patricians. The contemporary biographer of Rienzi says nothing of this harangue. But, apparently (since history has its liberties as well as fiction), M. Sismondi has thought it convenient to confound two occasions very distinct in themselves

unbroken regularity of an automaton, he continued to enter in his large book, and with the clear and beautiful characters of the period, those damning figures which taught him, better than declamations, the frauds practised on the people, and armed him with that weapon of plain fact which it is so difficult for abuse to parry.

"Page 2, Vol. B.," said he, in the tranquil voice of business, to the clerks; "see there, the profits of the salt duty; department No. 3—very well. Page 9, Vol. D.—what is the account rendered by Vescobaldi, the collector? What! twelve thousand florins?—no more?—unconscionable rascal!" (Here was a loud shout without of 'Pandulfo!—long live Pandulfo!') "Pastrucci, my friend, your head wanders; you are listening to the noise without—please to amuse yourself with the calculation I entrusted to you. Santi, what is the entry given in by Antonio Tralli?"

A slight tap was heard at the door, and Pandulfo entered.

The clerks continued their labor, though they looked up hastily at the pale and respectable visitor, whose name, to their great astonishment, had thus become a popular cry.

"Ah, my friend," said Rienzi, calmly enough in voice, but his hands trembled with ill-suppressed emotion, "you would speak to me alone, eh? well, well,—this way." Thus saying, he led the citizen into a small cabinet in the rear of the room of office, carefully shut the door, and then giving himself up to the natural impatience of his character, seized Pandulfo by the hand: "Speak!" cried he: "do they take the interpretation?—have you made it plain and palpable enough?—has it sunk deep into their souls?"

"Oh, by St. Peter! yes!" returned the citizen, whose spirits were elevated by his recent discovery that he, too, was an orator—a luxurious pleasure for a timid man. "They swallowed every word of the interpretation; they are moved to the marrow—you might lead them this very hour to battle, and find them heroes. As for the sturdy smith—"

"What! Cecco del Vecchio?" interrupted Rienzi; "ah, his heart is wrought in bronze—what did he?"

"Why, he caught me by the hem of my robe as I descended my rostrum, (oh! would you could have seen me!—*per fede* I had caught your mantle!—I was a second *you!*) and said, weeping like a child, 'Ah, Signor, I am but a poor man, and of little worth; but if every drop of blood in this body were a life, I would give it for my country!'"

"Brave soul," said Rienzi, with emotion; "would Rome had but fifty such! No man hath done us more good among his own class than Cecco del Vecchio."

"They feel a protection in his very size," said Pandulfo. "It is something to hear such big words from such a big fellow."

"Were there *any* voices lifted in disapprobation of the picture and its sentiment?"

"None."

"The time is nearly ripe, then—a few suns more and the fruit must be gathered. The Aventine,—the Lateran,—and then *the solitary trumpet!*" Thus saying, Rienzi, with folded arms and downcast eyes, seemed sunk into a reverie.

"By the way," said Pandulfo, "I had almost forgot to tell thee, that the crowd would have poured themselves hither, so impatient were they to see thee; but I bade Cecco del Vecchio mount the rostrum, and tell them, in his blunt way, that it would be unseemly at the present time, when thou wert engaged in the Capitol on civil and holy affairs, to rush in so great a body into thy presence. Did I not right?"

"Most right, my Pandulfo."

"But Cecco del Vecchio says he must come and kiss thy hand; and thou mayst expect him here the moment he can escape unobserved from the crowd."

"He is welcome!" said Rienzi, half mechanically, for he was still absorbed in thought.

"And, lo! here he is,"—as one of the scribes announced the visit of the smith.

"Let him be admitted!" said Rienzi, seating himself composedly.

When the huge smith found himself in the presence of Rienzi, it amused Pandulfo to perceive the wonderful influences of mind over matter. That fierce and sturdy giant, who, in all popular commotions, towered above his tribe, with thews of stone, and nerves of iron, the rallying point and bulwark of the rest,—stood now coloring and trembling before the intellect, which (so had the eloquent spirit of Rienzi waked and fanned the spark which, till then, had lain dormant in that rough bosom) might almost be said to have created his own. And he, indeed, who first arouses in the bondsman the sense and soul of freedom, comes as near as is permitted to man, nearer than the philosopher, nearer even than the poet, to the great creative attribute of God!—But, if the breast be uneducated, the gift may curse the giver; and he who passes at once from the slave to the freeman may pass as rapidly from the freeman to the ruffian.

"Approach, my friend," said Rienzi, after a moment's pause; "I know all that thou hast done, and wouldst do, for Rome! Thou art worthy of her best days, and thou art born to share in their return."

The smith dropped at the feet of Rienzi, who held out his hand to raise him, which Cecco del Vecchio seized, and reverentially kissed.

"This kiss does not betray," said Rienzi, smiling; "but rise, my friend,—this posture is only due to God and his saints!"

"He is a saint who helps us at need!" said the smith, bluntly, "and that no man has done as thou hast. But when," he added, sinking his voice, and fixing his eyes hard on Rienzi, as one may do who waits a signal to strike a blow, "when—when shall we make the great effort?"

"Thou hast spoken to all the brave men in thy neighborhood,—are they well prepared?"

"To live or die, as Rienzi bids them!"

"I must have the list—the number—names—houses and callings, this night."

"Thou shalt."

"Each man must sign his name or mark with his own hand."

"It shall be done."

"Then, harkye! attend Pandulfo di Guido at his house this evening, at sunset. He shall instruct thee where to meet this night some brave hearts;—thou art worthy to be ranked amongst them. Thou wilt not fail!"

"By the holy Stairs! I will count every minute till then," said the smith, his swarthy face lighted with pride at the confidence shown him.

"Meanwhile, watch all your neighbors; let no man flag or grow faint-hearted,—none of thy friends must be branded as a traitor!"

"I will cut his throat, were he my own mother's son, if I find one pledged man flinch!" said the fierce smith.

"Ha, ha!" rejoined Rienzi, with that strange laugh which belonged to him; "a miracle! a miracle! The Picture speaks now!"

It was already nearly dusk when Rienzi left the Capitol. The broad space before its walls was empty and deserted, and wrapping his mantle closely round him, he walked musingly on.

"I have almost climbed the height," thought he, "and now the precipice yawns before me. If I fail, what a fall! The last hope of my country falls with me. Never will a noble rise against the nobles. Never will another plebeian have the opportunities and the power that I have! Rome is bound up with me—with a single life. The liberties of all time are fixed to a reed that a wind may uproot. But oh, Providence! hast thou not reserved and marked me for great deeds? How, step by step, have I been led on to this solemn enterprise! How has each hour prepared its successor! And yet what danger! *if* the inconstant people, made cowardly by long thraldom, do but waver in the crisis, I am swept away!"

As he spoke, he raised his eyes, and lo, before him, the first star of twilight shone calmly down upon the crumbling remnants of the Tarpeian Rock. It was no favoring omen, and Rienzi's heart beat quicker as that dark and ruined mass frowned thus suddenly on his gaze.

"Dread monument," thought he, "of what dark catastrophes, to what unknown schemes, hast thou been the witness! To how many enterprises, on which history is dumb, hast thou set the seal! How know we whether they were criminal or just? How know we whether he, thus doomed as a traitor, would not, if successful, have been immortalized as a deliverer? If I fall, who will write my chronicle? One of the people? alas! blinded and ignorant, they furnish forth no minds that can appeal to posterity. One of the patrician? in what colors shall I then be painted! No tomb will rise for me amidst the wrecks; no hand scatter flowers upon my grave!"

Thus meditating on the verge of that mighty enterprise to which he had devoted himself, Rienzi pursued his way. He gained the Tiber, and paused for a few moments beside its legendary stream, over which the purple and star-lit heaven shone deeply down. He crossed the bridge which leads to the quarter of the Trastevere, whose haughty inhabitants yet boast themselves the sole true descendants of the ancient Romans. Here his step grew quicker and more light; brighter, if less solemn, thoughts crowded upon his breast; and ambition, lulled for a moment, left his strained and over-labored mind to the reign of a softer passion.

CHAPTER XI.

Nina di Raselli.

"I TELL you, Lucia, I do not love those stuffs; they do not become me. Saw you ever so poor a dye?—this purple, indeed! that crimson! Why did you let the man leave them? Let him take them elsewhere to-morrow. They may suit the signoras on the other side the Tiber, who imagine everything Venetian must be perfect; but I, Lucia, *I* see with my own eyes, and judge from my own mind."

"Ah, dear lady," said the serving-maid, "if you were, as you doubtless will be, some time or other, a grand signora, how worthily you would wear the honors! Santa Cecila! no other dame in Rome would be looked at while the Lady Nina were by!"

"Would we not teach them what pomp was?" answered Nina. "Oh! what festivals would we hold! Saw you not from the gallery the revels given last week by the Lady Giulia Savelli?"

"Ay, signora; and when you walked up the hall in your silver and pearl tissue, there ran such a murmur through the gallery; every one cried, "The Savelli have entertained an angel!"

"Pish! Lucia; no flattery, girl."

"It is naked truth, lady. But that *was* a revel, was it not? There was grandeur!—fifty servitors in scarlet and gold! and the music playing all the while. The minstrels were sent for from Bergamo. Did not that festival please you? Ah, I warrant many were the fine speeches made to you that day!"

"Heigho!—no, there was one voice wanting, and all the music was marred. But, girl, were *I* the Lady Giulia, I would not have been contented with a poor revel."

"How, poor! Why all the nobles say it outdid the proudest marriage-feast of the Colonna. Nay, a Neapolitan who sat next me, and who had served under the young Queen Joanna, at her marriage, says, that even Naples was outshone."

"That may be. I know nought of Naples; but I know what *my* court should have been, were I what—what I am not, and may never be! The banquet vessels should have been of gold; the cups jewelled to the brim; not an inch of the rude pavement should have been visible; all should have glowed with cloth of gold. The fountain in the court should have showered up the perfumes of the East; my pages should not have been rough youths, blushing at their own uncouthness, but fair boys, who had not told their twelfth year, culled from the daintiest palaces of Rome: and, as for the music, oh, Lucia!—each musician should have worn a chaplet, and deserved it; and he who played best should have had a reward, to inspire all the rest—a rose from me. Saw you, too, the Lady Giulia's robe? What colors? they might have put out the sun at noonday!—yellow, and blue, and orange, and scarlet! Oh, sweet Saints!—but my eyes ached all the next day!"

"Doubtless, the Lady Giulia lacks your skill in the mixture of colors," said the complaisant waiting-woman.

"And then, too, what a mien!—no royalty in it! She moved along the hall, so that her train well nigh tripped her every moment; and then she said, with a foolish laugh, 'These holyday robes are but troublesome luxuries.' Troth, for the great there should be no holyday robes; 'tis for myself, not for others, that I would attire! Every day should have its new robe, more gorgeous than the last;—every day should be a holyday!"

"Methought," said Lucia, "that the Lord Giovanni Orsini seemed very devoted to my Lady."

"He! the bear!"

"Bear, he may be! but he has a costly skin. His riches are untold."

"And the fool knows not how to spend them."

"Was not that the young Lord Adrian who spoke to you just by the columns, where the music played?"

"It might be,—I forget."

"Yet, I hear that few ladies forget when Lord Adrian di Castello woos them."

"There was but one man whose company seemed to me worth the recollection," answered Nina, unheeding the insinuation of the artful hand-maid.

"And who was he?" asked Lucia.

"The old scholar from Avignon!"

"What! he with the gray beard? Oh, Signora!"

"Yes," said Nina, with a grave and sad voice; "when he spoke, the whole scene vanished from my eyes,—for he spoke to me of HIM!"

As she said this, the Signora sighed deeply, and the tears gathered to her eyes.

The waiting-woman raised her lips in disdain, and her looks in wonder; but she did not dare to venture a reply.

"Open the lattice," said Nina, after a pause, "and give me yon paper. Not that, girl—but the verses sent me yesterday. What! art thou Italian, and dost thou not know, by instinct that I spoke of the rhyme of Petrarch?"

Seated by the open casement, through which the moonlight stole soft and sheen, with one lamp beside her, from which she seemed to shade her eyes, though in reality she sought to hide her countenance from Lucia, the young Signora appeared absorbed in one of those tender sonnets which then turned the brains and inflamed the hearts of Italy.*

Born of an impoverished house which, though boasting its descent from a consular race of Rome, scarcely at that day maintained a rank amongst the inferior order of nobility, Nina di Raselli was the spoiled child—the idol of the tyrant—of her parents. The energetic and self-willed character of her mind made her rule where she should have obeyed; and as in all ages dispositions can conquer custom, she had, though in a clime and land where the young and unmarried of her sex are usually chained and fettered, assumed, and by assuming won, the prerogative of independence. She possessed, it is true, more learning and more genius than generally fell to the share of women in that day; and enough of both to be deemed a miracle by her parents;—she had, also, what they valued more, a surpassing beauty; and, what they feared more, an indomitable haughtiness;—a haughtiness mixed with a thousand soft and endearing qualities where she loved; and which, indeed, where she loved, seemed to vanish.

At once vain yet high-minded, resolute yet impassioned, there was a gorgeous magnificence in her very vanity and splendor,—an ideality in her waywardness: her defects made a part of her brilliancy; without them she would have seemed less woman; and, knowing her, you would have compared all women by her standard. Softer qualities beside her seemed not more charming, but more insipid. She had no vulgar ambition, for she had obstinately refused many alliances which the daughter of Raselli could scarcely have hoped to form. The untutored minds and savage power of the Roman nobles seemed to her imagination, which was full of the *poetry* of rank, its luxury and its graces, as something barbarious and revolting, at once to be dreaded and despised. She had, therefore, passed her twentieth year unmarried, but not without love. The faults, themselves, of her character, elevated that ideal of love which she had formed. She required some being round whom all her vainer qualities could rally; she felt that where she loved she must adore; she demanded no common idol before which to humble so strong and imperious a mind. Unlike women of gentler mould, who desire, for a short period, to exercise the caprices of sweet empire,—when she loved she must cease to command; and pride, at once, he humbled to devotion. So rare were the qualities that could attract her; so imperiously did her haughtiness require that those qualities should be above her own, yet of the same order; that her love elevated its object like a god. Accustomed to despise, she felt all the luxury it is to venerate!

And if it were her lot to be united with one thus loved, her nature was that which might become elevated by the nature that it gazed on. For her beauty—Reader, shouldst thou ever go to Rome, thou wilt see in the Capitol the picture of the Cumæan Sibyl, which, often copied, no copy can even faintly represent. I

* Although it is true that the love sonnets of Petrarch were not then, as now, the most esteemed of his works, yet it has been a great, though a common error, to represent them as little known and coldly admired. Their effect was, in reality prodigious and universal. Every ballad-singer sung them in the streets, and (says Filippo Villani), "Gravissimi nesciebant abstinere"—"Even the gravest could not abstain from them."

beseech thee, mistake not this sibyl for another, for the Roman galleries abound in sibyls.* The sibyl I speak of is dark, and the face has an Eastern cast: the robe and turban, gorgeous though they be, grow dim before the rich, but transparent roses of the cheek; the hair would be black, save for that golden glow which mellows it to a hue and lustre never seen but in the south, and even in the south most rare; the features, not Grecian, are yet faultless; the mouth, the brow, the ripe and exquisite contour, all are human and voluptuous; the expression, the aspect, is something more; the form is, perhaps, too full for the perfection of loveliness, for the delicacy of Athenian models; but the luxuriant fault has a majesty. Gaze long upon that picture: it charms, yet commands, the eye. While you gaze, you call back five centuries. You see before you the breathing image of Nina di Raselli!

But it was not those ingenious and elaborate conceits in which Petrarch, great Poet though he be, has so often mistaken pedantry for passion, that absorbed at that moment the attention of the beautiful Nina. Her eyes rested not on the page, but on the garden that stretched below the casement. Over the old fruit-trees and hanging vines fell the moonshine: and in the centre of the green, but half-neglected sward, the waters of a small and circular fountain, whose perfect proportions spoke of days long passed, played and sparkled in the starlight. The scene was still and beautiful; but neither of its stillness nor its beauty thought Nina: towards one, the gloomiest and most rugged, spot in the whole garden, turned her gaze; there, the trees stood densely massed together, and shut from view the low but heavy wall which encircled the mansion of Raselli. The boughs on those trees stirred gently, but Nina saw them wave; and now from the copse emerged, slowly and cautiously a solitary figure, whose shadow threw itself, long and dark, over the sward. It approached the window, and a low voice breathed Nina's name.

"Quick, Lucia!" cried she, breathlessly, turning to her handmaid: "quick! the rope-ladder! it is he! he is come! How slow you are! haste, girl, he may be discovered! There,—O joy,—O joy!—My lover! my hero! my Rienzi!'

"It is you!" said Rienzi, as, now entering the chamber, he wound his arms round her half-averted form, "and what is night to others is day to me!"

The first sweet moments of welcome were over; and Rienzi was seated at the feet of his mistress: his head rested on her knees—his face looking up to hers—their hands clasped each in each.

"And for me thou bravest these dangers!" said the lover; "the shame of discovery, the wrath of thy parents!"

"But what are my perils to thine? Oh, Heaven! if my father found thee here thou wouldst die!"

"He would think it then so great a humiliation, that thou, beautiful Nina, who mightest match with the haughiest names of Rome, shouldst waste thy love on a plebeian—even though the grandson of an emperor!"

The proud heart of Nina could sympathize well with the wounded pride of her lover: she detected the soreness which lurked beneath his answer, carelessly as it was uttered.

"Hast thou not told me," she said, "of that great Marius, who was no noble, but from whom the loftiest Colonna would rejoice to claim his descent? and do I not know in thee one who shall yet eclipse the power of Marius, unsullied by his vices?"

"Delicious flattery! sweet prophet!" said Rienzi, with a melancholy smile; "never were thy supporting promises of the future more welcome to me than now; for to thee I will say what I would utter to none else—my soul half sinks beneath the mighty burthen I have heaped upon it. I want new courage as the dread hour approaches; and from thy words and looks I drink it."

"Oh!" answered Nina, blushing as she spoke, "glorious is indeed the lot which I have bought by my love for thee: glorious to share thy schemes, to cheer thee in doubt, to whisper hope to thee in danger."

"And give grace to me in triumph!" added Rienzi, passionately. "Ah! should the future ever place upon these brows the laurel-wreath due to one who has saved his country,

* The sibyl referred to is the well-known one by Domenichino. As a mere work of art, that by Guercino, called the Persian sibyl, in the same collection, is perhaps superior; but in beauty, in character, there is no comparison.

what joy, what recompence, to lay it at thy feet! Perhaps, in those long and solitary hours of languor and exhaustion which fill up the interstices of time,—the dull space for sober thought between the epochs of exciting action, — perhaps I should have failed and flagged, and renounced even my dreams for Rome, had they not been linked also with my dreams for thee!—had I not pictured to myself the hour when my fate should elevate me beyond my birth; when thy sire would deem it no disgrace to give thee to my arms; when thou, too shouldst stand amidst the dames of Rome, more honored, as more beautifnl, than all; and when I should see that pomp, which my own soul disdains,* made dear and grateful to me because associated with thee! Yes, it is these thoughts that have inspired me, when sterner ones have shrunk back appalled from the spectres that surround their goal. And oh! my Nina, sacred, strong, enduring must be, indeed, the love which lives in the same pure and elevated air as that which sustains my hopes of liberty and fame!"

This was the language which, more even than the vows of fidelity and the dear adulation which springs from the heart's exuberance, had bound the proud and vain soul of Nina to the chains that it so willingly wore. Perhaps, indeed, in the absence of Rienzi, her weaker nature pictured to herself the triumph of humbling the high-born signoras, and eclipsing the barbarous magnificence of the chiefs of Rome; but in his presence, and listening to his more elevated and generous ambition, as yet all unsullied by one private feeling save the hope of her, her higher sympathies were enlisted with his schemes, her mind aspired to raise itself to the height of his, and she thought less of her own rise than of his glory. It was sweet to her pride to be the sole confidant of his most secret thoughts, as of his most hardy undertakings; to see bared before her that intricate and plotting spirit; to be admitted even to the knowledge of its doubt and weakness, as of its heriosm and power.

Nothing could be more contrasted than the loves of Rienzi and Nina, and those of Adrian and Irene: in the latter, all were the dreams, the phantasies, the extravagance, of youth; they never talked of the futnre; they mingled no other aspirations with those of love. Ambition, glory, the world's high objects, were nothing to them when together; their love had swallowed up the world, and left nothing visible beneath the sun, save itself. But the passion of Nina and *her* lover was that of more complicated natures and more mature years: it was made up of a thousand feelings, each naturally severed from each, but compelled into one focus by the mighty concentration of love; their talk was of the world; it was from the world that they drew the aliment which sustained it; it was of the future they spoke and thought; of its dreams and imagined glories they made themselves a home and altar; their love had in it more of the Intellectual than that of Adrian and Irene; it was more fitted for this hard earth; it had in it, also, more of the leaven of the later and iron days, and less of poetry and the first golden age.

"And must thou leave me now?" said Nina, her cheek no more averted from his lips, nor her form from his parting embrace. "The moon is high yet; it is but a little hour thou hast given me."

"An hour! Alas!" said Rienzi, "it is near upon midnight—our friends await me."

"Go, then, my soul's best half! go; Nina shall not detain thee one moment from those higher objects which make thee so dear to Nina When—when shall we meet again!"

"Not," said Rienzi, proudly, and with all his soul upon his brow, "not thus, by stealth! no! nor as I thus have met thee, the obscure and contemned bondsman! When next thou seest me, it shall be at the head of the sons of Rome! her champion! her restorer! or ——" said he, sinking his voice—

"There is no *or!* interrupted Nina, weaving her arms round him, and catching his enthusiasm; "thou hast uttered thine own destiny!"

"One kiss more!—farewell!—the tenth day from the morrow shines upon the restoration of Rome!"

---

* "Quem semper abhorrui sicut cenum" is the expression used by Rienzi, in his letter to his friend at Avignon, and which was probably sincere. Men rarely act according to the bias of their own tastes.

CHAPTER XII.

The Strange adventures that befel Walter de Montreal.

It was upon that same evening, and while the earliest stars yet shone over the city, that Walter de Montreal, returning, alone, to the convent then associated with the church of Santa Marià del Priorata (both of which belonged to the Knights of the Hospital, and in the first of which Montreal had taken his lodgment), paused amidst the ruins and desolation which lay around his path. Though little skilled in the classic memories and associations of the spot, he could not but be impressed with the surrounding witnesses of departed empire; the vast skeleton, as it were, of the dead giantess.

"Now," thought he, as he gazed around upon the roofless columns and shattered walls, everywhere visible, over which the starlight shone, ghastly and transparent, backed by the frowning and embattled fortresses of the Frangipani, half hid by the dark foliage that sprung up amidst the very fanes and palaces of old—Nature exulting over the frailer Art; "now," thought he, "bookmen would be inspired, by this scene, with fantastic and dreaming visions of the past. But to me these monuments of high ambition and royal splendor create only images of the future. Rome may yet be, with her seven-hilled diadem, as Rome has been before, the prize of the strongest hand and the boldest warrior,—revived, not by her own degenerate sons, but the infused blood of a new race. William the Bastard could scarce have found the hardy Englishers so easy a conquest as Walter the Well-born may find these eunuch Romans. And which conquest were the more glorious, —the barbarous Isle, or the Metropolis of the World? Short step from the general to the podesta—shorter step from the podesta to the king!"

While thus revolving his wild, yet not altogether chimerical, ambition, a quick light step was heard amidst the long herbage, and, looking up, Montreal perceived the figure of a tall female descending from that part of the hill then covered by many convents, towards the base of the Aventine. She supported her steps with a long staff, and moved with such elasticity and erectness, that now, as her face became visible by the starlight, it was surprising to perceive that it was the face of one advanced in years,—a harsh, proud countenance, withered, and deeply wrinkled, but not without a certain regularity of outline.

"Merciful Virgin!" cried Montreal, starting back as the face gleamed upon him: "is it possible? It is she!—it is——"

He sprung forward, and stood right before the old woman, who seemed equally surprised, though more dismayed, at the sight of Montreal.

"I have sought thee for years," said the Knight, first breaking the silence; "years, long years,—thy conscience can tell thee why."

"*Mine*, man of blood!" cried the female, trembling with rage or fear; "darest *thou* talk of conscience? *Thou*, the dishonorer—the robber—the professional homicide! *Thou*, disgrace to knighthood and to birth! *Thou*, with the cross of chastity and of peace upon thy breast! *Thou* talk of conscience, hypocrite!—thou?"

"Lady—lady!" said Montreal, deprecatingly, and almost quailing beneath the fiery passion of that feeble woman, "I have sinned against thee and thine. But remember all my excuses!—early love—fatal obstacles—rash vow—irresistible temptation! Perhaps," he added, in a more haughty tone, "perhaps, yet, I may have the power to atone my error, and wring, with mailed hand, from the successor of St. Peter, who hath power to loose as to bind——"

"Perjured and abandoned!" interrupted the female; "dost thou dream that violence can purchase absolution, or that thou canst ever atone the past?—a noble name disgraced, a father's broken heart and dying curse! Yes, that curse, I hear it now! it rings upon me thrillingly, as when I watched the expiring clay! it cleaves to thee—it pursues thee—it shall pierce thee through thy corselet—it shall smite thee in the meridian of thy power! Genius wasted—ambition blasted—penitence deferred—a life of brawls, and a death of shame—thy destruction the offspring of thy crime!—To this, to this, an old man's curse hath doomed thee!—AND THOU ART DOOMED!"

These words were rather shrieked than spoken: and the flashing eye, the lifted hand, the dilated form of the speaker—the hour—the solitude of the ruins around—all conspired to give to the fearful execration the character of prophecy. The warrior, against whose undaunted breast a hundred spears had shivered in vain, fell appalled and humbled to the ground. He seized the hem of his fierce denouncer's robe, and cried, in a choked and hollow voice, "Spare me! spare me!"

"Spare thee!" said the unrelenting crone: "hast *thou* ever spared man in thy hatred, or woman in thy lust? Ah, grovel in the dust! —crouch—crouch!—wild beast as thou art! whose sleek skin and beautiful hues have taught the unwary to be blind to the talons that rend, and the grinders that devour;—crouch, that the foot of the old and impotent may spurn thee!"

"Hag!" cried Montreal, in the reaction of of sudden fury and maddened pride, springing up to the full height of his stat re. "Hag! thou hast passed the limits to which, remembering who thou art, my forbearance gave thee licence. I had well-nigh forgot that thou hadst assumed my part—*I* am the Accuser! Woman! the boy!—shrink not! uivocate not! lie not!—thou wert the thief!"

"I was. Thou taughtest me the lesson how to steal a——"

"Render—restore him!" interrupted Montreal, stamping on the ground with such force that the splinters of the marble fragments on which he stood shivered under his armed heel.

The woman little heeded a violence at which the fiercest warrior of Italy might have trembled; but she did not make an immediate answer. The character of her countenance altered from passion into an expression of grave, intent, and melancholy thought. At length she replied to Montreal; whose hand had wandered to his dagger-hilt, with the instinct of long habit, whenever enraged or thwarted, rather than from any design of blood; which, stern and vindictive as he was, he would have been incapable of forming against any woman,—much less against the one then before him.

"Walter de Montreal," said she, in a voice so calm that it almost sounded like that of compassion, "the boy, I think, has never known brother or sister: the only child of a once haughty and lordly race, on both sides, though now on both dishonored—nay, why so impatient? thou wilt soon learn the worst—the boy is dead!"

"Dead!" repeated Montreal, recoiling and growing pale; "dead!—no, no—say not that! He has a mother,—you know he has!—a fond, meekhearted, anxious, hoping mother!—no!—no, he is not dead!"

"Thou canst feel, then, for a mother?" said the old woman, seemingly touched by the tone of the Provençal. "Yet, bethink thee; is it not better that the grave should save him from a life of riot, of bloodshed, and of crime? Better to sleep with God than to wake with the fiends!"

"Dead!" echoed Montreal; "dead!—the pretty one!—so young!—those eyes—the mother's eyes—closed so soon?"

"Hast thou aught else to say? Thy sight scares my very womanhood from my soul!—let me be gone."

"Dead!—may I believe thee? or dost thou mock me? Thou hast uttered *thy* curse, hearken to *my* warning:—If thou hast lied in this, thy last hour shall dismay thee, and thy death-bed shall be the death-bed of despair!"

"Thy lips," replied the female, with a scornful smile, "are better adapted lewd vows to unhappy maidens, than for the denunciations which sound solemn only when coming from the good. Farewell!"

'Stay! inexorable woman! stay!—where sleeps he? Masses shall be sung! priests shall pray!—the sins of the father shall not be isited on that young head!"

"At Florence!" returned the woman, hastily. "But no stone records the departed one! —The dead boy had no name!"

Waiting for no further questionings, the woman now passed on,—pursued her way;—and the long herbage, and the winding descent, soon snatched her ill-omened apparition from the desolate landscape.

Montreal, thus alone, sunk with a deep and heavy sigh upon the ground, covered his face with his hands, and burst into an agony of grief; his chest heaved, his whole frame trembled, and he wept and sobbed aloud, with all the fearful vehemence of a man whose passions are strong and fierce, but to whom the violence of grief alone is novel and unfamiliar.

He remained thus, prostrate and unmanned, for a considerable time, growing slowly and gradually more calm as tears relieved his emotion; and, at length, rather indulging a gloomy reverie than a passionate grief. The moon was high and the hour late when he arose, and then few traces of the past excitement remained upon his countenance; for Walter de Montreal was not of that mould in which woe can force a settlement, or to which any affliction can bring the continued and habitual melancholy that darkens those who feel more enduringly, though with emotions less stormy. His were the elements of the true Franc character, though carried to excess: his sternest and his deepest qualities were mingled with fickleness and caprice; his profound sagacity often frustrated by a whim; his towering ambition deserted for some frivolous temptation; and his elastic, sanguine, and high-spirited nature, faithful only to the desire of military glory, to the poetry of a daring and stormy life, and to the susceptibilities of that tender passion without whose colorings no portrait of chivalry is complete, and in which he was capable of a sentiment, a tenderness, and a loyal devotion, which could hardly have been supposed compatible with his reckless levity and his undisciplined career.

"Well," said he, as he rose slowly, folded his mantle round him, and resumed his way, "it was not for *myself* I grieved thus. But the pang is past, and the worst is known. Now, then, back to those things that never die —restless projects and daring schemes. That hag's curse keeps my blood cold still, and this solitude has something in it weird and awful. Ha!—what sudden light is that?"

The light which caught Montreal's eye broke forth almost like a star, scarcely larger, indeed, but more red and intense in its ray, Of itself it was nothing uncommon, and might have shone either from convent or cottage. But it streamed from a part of the Aventine which contained no habitations of the living, but only the empty ruins and shattered porticoes, of which even the names and memories of the ancient inhabitants were dead. Aware of this, Montreal felt a slight awe (as the beam threw its steady light over the dreary landscape); for he was not without the knightly superstitions of the age, and it was now the witching hour consecrated to ghost and spirit. But fear, whether of this world or the next, could not long daunt the mind of the hardy freebooter; and, after a short hesitation, he resolved to make a digression from his way, and ascertain the cause of the phenomenon. Unconsciously, the martial tread of the barbarian passed over the site of the famed, or infamous, Temple of Isis, which had once witnessed those wildest orgies commemorated by Juvenal; and came at last to a thick and dark copse, from an opening in the centre of which gleamed the mysterious light. Penetrating the gloomy foliage, the knight now found himself before a large ruin, gray and roofless, from within which came, indistinct and muffled, the sound of voices.

Through a rent in the wall, forming a kind of casement, and about ten feet from the ground, the light now broke over the matted and rank soil, embedded, as it were, in vast masses of shade, and streaming through a mouldering portico hard at hand. The Provençal stood, though he knew it not, on the very place once consecrated by the Temple: the Portico and the Library of Liberty (the first public library instituted in Rome). The wall of the ruin was covered with innumerable creepers and wild brushwood, and it required but little agility on the part of Montreal, by the help of these, to raise himself to the height of the aperture, and, concealed by the luxuriant foliage, to gaze within. He saw a table, lighted with tapers, in the centre of which was a crucifix; a dagger, unsheathed; an open scroll, which the event proved to be of sacred character; and a brazen bowl. About a hundred men, in cloaks, and with black vizards, stood motionless around; and one, taller than the rest, without disguise or mask—whose pale brow and stern features seemed by that light yet paler and yet more stern—appeared to be concluding some address to his companions.

"Yes," said he, "in the church of the Lateran I will make the last appeal to the people. Supported by the Vicar of the Pope, myself an officer of the Pontiff, it will be seen that Religion and Liberty—the heroes and the martyrs—are united in one cause. After that time, words are idle; action must begin. By this crucifix I pledge my faith, on this blade I devote my life, to the regeneration of Rome! And you (then no need for mask or mantle)! when the solitary trump is heard, when the solitary horseman is seen,—*you*, swear to rally round the standard of the Republic, and resist —with heart and hand, with life and soul, in defiance of death, and in hope of redemption —the arms of the oppressor!"

"We swear—we swear!" exclaimed every voice: and, crowding toward cross and weapon, the tapers were obscured by the intervening throng, and Montreal could not perceive the ceremony, nor hear the muttered formula of the oath: but he could guess that the rite then common to conspiracies—and which required each conspirator to shed some drops of his own blood, in token that life itself was devoted to the enterprise—had not been omitted, when, the group again receding, the same figure as before had addressed the meeting, holding on high the bowl with both hands,—while from the left arm, which was bared, the blood weltered slowly, and trickled, drop by drop, upon the ground,—said, in a solemn voice and up-turned eyes:

"Amidst the ruins of thy temple, O Liberty! we, Romans, dedicate to thee this libation! We, befriended and inspired by no unreal and fabled idols, but by the Lord of Hosts, and Him, who, descending to earth, appealed not to emperors and to princes, but to the fisherman and the peasant,—giving to the lowly and the poor the mission of Revelation." Then, turning suddenly to his companions, as his features, singularly varying in their character and expression, brightened, from solemn awe, into a martial and kindling enthusiasm, he cried aloud, "Death to the Tyranny! Life to the Republic!" The effect of the transition was startling. Each man, as by an involuntary and irresistible impulse, laid his hand upon his sword. as he echoed the sentiment; some, indeed, drew forth their blades, as if for instant action.

"I have seen enow: they will break up anon," said Montreal to himself: "and I would rather face an army of thousands, than even half-a-dozen enthusiasts, so inflamed,—and I thus detected." And, with this thought, he dropped on the ground, and glided away, as, once again, through the still midnight air, broke upon his ear the muffled shout—"DEATH TO THE TYRANNY!—LIFE TO THE REPUBLIC!"

BOOK SECOND.

THE REVOLUTION.

"Ogni Lascivia, ogni male, nulla giustizia, nullo freno. Non c'era piu remedia, ogni persona periva. Allora Cola di Rienzi," &c.—*Vita di Cola di Rienzi*, lib, i. chap. 2.

"Every kind of lewdness, every form of evil: no justice, no restraint. Remedy there was none; perdition fell on all. Then Cola di Rienzi," &c.—*Life of Cola di Rienzi.*

CHAPTER I.

The Knight of Provence, and his Proposal.

It was nearly noon as Adrian entered the gates of the palace of Stephen Colonna. The palaces of the nobles were not then as we see them now, receptacles for the immortal canvas of Italian, and the imperishable sculpture of Grecian Art; but still to this day are retained the massive walls, and barred windows, and spacious courts, which at that time protected their rude retainers. High above the gates rose a lofty and solid tower, whose height commanded a wide view of the mutilated remains of Rome: the gate itself was adorned and strengthened on either side by columns of granite, whose Doric capitals betrayed the sacrilege that had torn them from one of the many temples that had formerly crowded the sacred Forum. From the same spoils came, too, the vast fragments of travertine which made the walls of the outer court. So common at that day were these barbarous appropriations of the most precious monuments of art, that the columns and domes of earlier Rome were regarded by all classes but as quarries, from which every man was free to gather the materials, whether for his castle or his cottage,—a wantonness of outrage far greater than the Goths', to whom a later age would fain have attributed all the disgrace, and which, more perhaps than even heavier offences, excited the classical indignation of Petrarch, and made him sympathize with Rienzi in his hopes of Rome. Still may you see the churches of that or even earlier dates, of the most shapeless architecture, built on the sites, and from the marbles, consecrating (rather than consecrated by) the names of Venus, of Jupiter, of Minerva. The palace of the Prince of the Orsini, duke of Gravina, is yet reared above the graceful arches (still visible) of the theatre of Marcellus; then a fortress of the Savelli.

As Adrian passed the court, a heavy wagon blocked up the way, laden with huge marbles, dug from the unexhausted mine of the Golden House of Nero: they were intended for an additional tower, by which Stephen Colonna proposed yet more to strengthen the tasteless and barbarous edifice in which the old noble maintained the dignity of outraging the law.

The friend of Petrarch and the pupil of Rienzi sighed deeply as he passed this vehicle of new spoliations, and as a pillar of fluted alabaster, rolling carelessly from the wagon, fell with a loud crash upon the pavement. At the foot of the stairs grouped some dozen of the bandits whom the old Colonna entertained: they were playing at dice upon an ancient tomb, the clear and deep inscription on which (so different from the slovenly character of the later empire) bespoke it a memorial of the most powerful age of Rome, and which, now empty even of ashes, and upset, served for a table to these foreign savages, and was strewn, even at that early hour, with fragments of meat and flasks of wine. They scarcely stirred, they scarcely looked up, as the young noble passed them; and the fierce oaths and loud ejaculations, uttered in a northern *patois*, grated harsh upon his ear, as he mounted, with a slow step, the lofty and unclean stairs.

He came into a vast ante-chamber, which was half filled with the higher class of the patrician's retainers: some five or six pages, chosen from the inferior noblesse, congregated by a narrow and deep sunk casement, were discussing the grave matters of gallantry and intrigue; three petty chieftains of the band below, with their corselets donned, and their swords and casques beside them, were sitting, stolid and silent, at a table, in the middle of the room, and might have been taken for automatons, save for the solemn regularity with which they ever and anon lifted to their moustachioed lips their several goblets, and then, with a complacent grunt, re-settled to their contemplations. Striking was the contrast which their northern phlegm presented to a crowd of Italian clients, and petitioners, and parasites, who walked restlessly to and fro, talking loudly to each other, with all the vehement gestures and varying physiognomy of southern vivacity. There was a general stir and sensation as Adrian broke upon this miscellaneous company. The bandit captains nodded their heads mechanically; the pages bowed, and admired the fashion of his plume and hose; the clients, and petitioners, and parasites, crowded round him, each with a separate request for interest with his potent kinsman. Great need had Adrian of his wonted urbanity and address, in extricating himself from their grasp; and painfully did he win, at last, the low and narrow door, at which stood a tall servitor, who admitted or rejected the applicants, according to his interest or caprice.

"Is the Baron alone?" asked Adrian.

"Why, no, my Lord: a foreign signor is with him—but to you he is of course visible."

"Well, you may admit me. I would inquire of his health."

The servitor opened the door — through whose aperture peered many a jealous and wistful eye—and consigned Adrian to the guidance of a page, who, older and of greater esteem than the loiterers in the ante-room, was the especial henchman of the Lord of the Castle. Passing another but empty chamber, vast and dreary, Adrian found himself in a small cabinet, and in the presence of his kinsman.

Before a table, bearing the implements of writing, sate the old Colonna: a robe of rich furs and velvet hung loose upon his tall and stately frame; from a round skull-cap, of comforting warmth and crimson hue, a few grey locks descended, and mixed with a long and reverent beard. The countenance of the aged noble, who had long passed his eightieth year, still retained the traces of a comeliness for which in earlier manhood he was remarkable. His eyes, if deep-sunken, were still keen and lively, and sparkled with all the fire of youth; his mouth curved upward in a pleasant, though half-satiric, smile; and his appearance on the whole was prepossessing and commanding, indicating rather the high blood, the shrewd wit, and the gallant valor of the patrician, than his craft, hypocrisy, and habitual but disdainful spirit of opression.

Stephen Colonna, without being absolutely a hero, was indeed far braver than most of the Romans, though he held fast to the Italian maxim—never to fight an enemy while it is possible to cheat him. Two faults, however, marred the effect of his sagacity: a supreme insolence of disposition, and a profound belief in the lights of his experience. He was incapable of analogy. What had never happened in his time, he was perfectly persuaded never could happen. Thus, though generally esteemed an able diplomatist, he had the cunning of the intriguant, and not the providence of a statesman. If, however, pride made him arrogant in prosperity, it supported him in misfortune. And in the earlier vicissitudes of a life which had partly been consumed in exile, he had developed many noble qualities of fortitude, endurance, and real greatness of soul; which showed that his failings were rather acquired by circumstance than derived from nature. His numerous and high-born race were proud of their chief; and with justice; for he was the ablest and most honored, not only of the direct branch of the Colonna, but also, perhaps, of all the more powerful barons.

Seated at the same table with Stephen Colonna was a man of noble presence, of about three or four and thirty years of age, in whom Adrian instantly recognized Walter de Montreal. This celebrated knight was scarcely of the personal appearance which might have corresponded with the terror his name generally excited. His face was handsome, almost to the extreme of womanish delicacy. His fair hair waved long and freely over a white and unwrinkled forehead: the life of a camp and the suns of Italy had but little embrowned his clear and healthful complexion, which retained much of the bloom of youth. His features were aquiline and regular; his eyes, of a light hazel, were, large, bright, and penetrating; and a short, but curled beard and moutachio, trimmed with soldier-like precision, and very little darker than the hair, gave indeed a martial expression to his comely countenance, but rather the expression which might have suited the hero of courts and tournaments, than the chief of a brigand's camp. The aspect, manner, and bearing, of the Provençal were those which captivate rather than awe,—blending, as they did, a certain military frankness with the easy and graceful dignity of one conscious of gentle birth, and accustomed to mix, on equal terms, with the great and noble.

His form happily contrasted and elevated the character of a countenance which required strength and stature to free its uncommon beauty from the charge of effeminacy, being of great height and remarkable muscular power, without the least approach to clumsy and unwieldy bulk: it erred, indeed, rather to the side of leanness than flesh,—at once rebust and slender. But the chief personal distinction of this warrior, the most redoubted lance of Italy, was an air and carriage of chivalric and heroic grace, greatly set off at this time by his splendid dress, which was of brown velvet sown with pearls, over which hung the surcoat worn by the Knights of the Hospital, whereon was wrought, in white, the eight-pointed cross that made the badge of his order. The Knight's attitude was that of earnest conversation, bending slightly forward towards the Colonna, and resting both his hands—which (according to the usual distinction of the old Norman race,* from whom, though born in Provence, Montreal boasted his descent) were small and delicate, the fingers being covered with jewels, as was the fashion of the day—upon the golden hilt of an enormons sword, on the sheath of which was elaborately wrought the silver lilies that made the device of the Provençal Brotherhood of Jerusalem.

"Good morrow, fair kinsman!" said Stephen. "Seat thyself, I pray; and know in this knightly visitor the celebrated Sieur de Montreal."

"Ah, my Lord," said Montreal, smiling, as he saluted Adrian; "and how is my lady at home?"

"You mistake, Sir Knight," quoth Stephen; "my young kinsman is not yet married: 'faith, as Pope Boniface remarked, when he lay stretched on a sick bed, and his confessor talked to him about Abraham's bosom, 'that is a pleasure the greater for being deferred.'"

"The Signor will pardon my mistake," returned Montreal.

"But not," said Adrian, "the neglect of Sir Walter in not ascertaining the fact in person. My thanks to him, noble kinsman, are greater than you weet of; and he promised to visit me, that he might receive them at leisure."

"I assure you, Signor," answered Montreal, "that I have not forgotten the invitation; but so weighty hitherto have been my affairs at Rome, that I have been obliged to parley with my impatience to better our acquaintance."

"Oh, ye knew each other before?" said Stephen. "And how?"

"My Lord, there is a damsel in the case!" replied Montreal. "Excuse my silence."

"Ah, Adrian, Adrian! when will you learn my continence!" said Stephen, solemnly stroking his grey beard. "What an example I set you! But a truce to this light conversation,—let us resume our theme. You must know, Adrian, that it is to the brave band of my guest I am indebted for those valiant gentlemen below, who keep Rome so quiet, though my poor habitation so noisy. He has called to proffer more assistance, if need be; and to advise me on the affairs of Northern Italy. Continue, I pray thee, Sir Knight; I have no disguises from my kinsman."

"Thou seest," said Montreal, fixing his penetrating eyes on Adrian, "thou seest, doubtless, my Lord, that Italy at this moment presents to us a remarkable spectacle. It is a

* Small hands and feet, however disproportioned to the rest of the person, were at that time deemed no less a distinction of the well-born, than they have been in a more refined age. Many readers will remember the pain occasioned to Petrarch by his tight shoes. The supposed beauty of this peculiarity is more derived from the feudal than the classic time.

contest between two opposing powers, which shall destroy the other. The one power is that of the unruly and turbulent, people—a power which they call 'Liberty;' the other power is that of the chiefs and princes—a power which they more appropriately call 'Order.' Between these parties the cities of Italy are divided. In Florence, in Genoa, in Pisa, for instance, is established a Free State —a Republic, God wot! and a more riotous, unhappy state of government, cannot well be imagined.

"That is perfectly true," quoth Stephen; "they banished my own first cousin from Genoa."

"A perpetual strife, in short," continued Montreal, "between the great families; an alternation of prosecutions, and confiscations, and banishments: to-day, the Guelfs proscribe the Ghibellines—to-morrow, the Ghibellines drive out the Guelfs. This may be liberty, but it is the liberty of the strong against the weak. In the other cities, as Milan, as Verona, as Bologna, the people are under the rule of one man,—who calls himself a prince, and whom his enemies call a tyrant. Having more force than any other citizen, he preserves a firm government; having more constant demand on his intellect and energies than the other citizens, he also preserves a wise one. These two orders of government are enlisted against each other: whenever the people in the one rebel against their prince, the people of the other—that is, the Free States—send arms and money to their assistance."

"You hear, Adrian, how wicked those last are," quoth Stephen.

"Now it seems to me," continued Montreal, "that this contest must end some time or other. All Italy must become republican or monarchical. It is easy to predict which will be the result."

"Yes, Liberty must conquer in the end!" said Adrian, warmly.

"Pardon me, young Lord; my opinion is entirely the reverse. You perceive that these republics are commercial,—are traders; they esteem wealth, they despise valor, they cultivate all trades save that of the armorer. Accordingly, how do they maintain themselves in war? By their own citizens? Not a whit of it! Either they send to some foreign chief, and promise, if he grant them his protection, the principality of the city for five or ten years in return; or else they borrow from some hardy adventurer, like myself, as many troops as they can afford to pay for. It is not so, Lord Adrian?"

Adrian nodded his reluctant assent.

"Well, then, it is the fault of the foreign chief if he do not make his power permanent; as has been already done in States once free by the Visconti and the Scala: or else it is the fault of the captain of the mercenaries if he do not convert his brigands into senators, and himself into a king. These are events so natural, that one day or other they will occur throughout all Italy. And all Italy will then become monarchical. Now it seems to me the interest of all the powerful families—your own, at Rome, as that of the Visconti, at Milan—to expedite this epoch, and to check, while you yet may with ease, that rebellious contagion amongst the people which is now rapidly spreading, and which ends in the fever of licence to them, but in the corruption of death to you. In these free States, the nobles are the first to suffer: first your privileges, then your property, are swept away. Nay, in Florence, as ye well know, my Lords, no noble is even capable of holding the meanest office in the State!"

"Villains!" cried Colonna, "they violate the first law of nature!"

"At this moment," resumed Montreal, who, engrossed with his subject, little heeded the interruptions he received from the holy indignation of the Baron: "at this moment, there are many—the wisest, perhaps, in the free States—who desire to renew the old Lombard leagues, in defence of their common freedom everywhere, and against whomsoever shall aspire to be prince. Fortunately, the deadly jealousies between these merchant States—the base plebeian jealousies—more of trade than of glory—interpose at present an irresistible obstacle to this design; and Florence, the most stirring and the most esteemed of all, is happily so reduced by reverses of commerce as to be utterly unable to follow out so great an undertaking. Now, then, is the time for us, my Lords; while these obstacles are so great for our foes, now is the time for us to form and cement a counter-league between all the princes of Italy. To you, noble Stephen, I have come, as your rank demands,—alone, of all the barons of Rome,—to propose to you this honorable union. Observe what advantages it proffers to your house. The popes have abandoned Rome for ever; there is no counter-poise to your ambition,—there need be none to your power. You see before you the examples of Visconti and Taddeo di Pepoli. You may found in Rome, the first city of Italy, a supreme and uncontrolled principality, subjugate utterly your weaker rivals,—the Savelli, the Malatesta, the Orsini, and leave to your sons' sons an hereditary kingdom that may aspire once more, perhaps, to the empire of the world."

Stephen shaded his face with his hand as he answered: "But this, noble Montreal, requires means:—money and men."

"Of the last, you can command from me enow—my small company, the best disciplined, can (whenever I please) swell to the most numerous in Italy: in the first, noble Baron, the rich House of Colonna cannot fail; and even a mortgage on its vast estates may be well repaid when you have possessed yourselves of the whole revenues of Rome. You see," continued Montreal, turning to Adrian, in whose youth he expected a more warm ally than in his hoary kinsmàn: "you see, at a glance, how feasible is this project, and what a mighty field it opens to your House."

"Sir Walter de Montreal," said Adrian, rising from his seat, and giving vent to the indignation he had with difficulty suppressed, "I grieve much that, beneath the roof of the first citizen of Rome, a stranger should attempt thus calmly, and without interruption, to excite the ambition of emulating the execrated celebrity of a Visconti or a Pepoli. Speak, my Lord! (turning to Stephen)—speak, noble kinsman! and tell this Knight of Provence, that if by a Colonna the ancient grandeur of Rome cannot be restored, it shall not be, at least, by a Colonna that her last wrecks of liberty shall be swept away."

"How now, Adrian!—how now, sweet kinsman!" said Stephen, thus suddenly appealed to, "calm thyself. I pr'ythee. Noble Sir Walter, he is young—young, and hasty—he means not to offend thee."

"Of that I am persuaded," returned Montreal, coldly, but with great and courteous command of temper. "He speaks from the impulse of the moment,—a praiseworthy fault in youth. It was mine at his age, and many a time have I nearly lost my life for the rashness. Nay, Signor, nay!—touch not your sword so meaningly, as if you fancied I intimated a threat; far from me such presumption. I have learned sufficient caution, believe me, in the wars, not wantonly to draw against me a blade which I have seen wielded against such odds."

Touched, despite himself, by the courtesy of the Knight, and the allusion to a scene in which, perhaps, his life had been preserved by Montreal, Adrian extended his hand to the latter.

"I was to blame for my haste," said he, frankly; "but know, my very heat," he added more gravely, "that your project will find no friends among the Colonna. Nay, in the presence of my noble kinsman, I dare to tell you, that could even his high sanction lend itself to such a scheme, the best hearts of his house would desert him; and I myself, his kinsman, would man yonder castle against so unnatural an ambition!"

A slight and scarce perceptible cloud passed over Montreal's countenance at these words; and he bit his lip ere he replied:

"Yet if the Orsini be less scrupulous, their first exertion of power would be heard in the crashing house of the Colonna."

"Know you," returned Adrian, "that one of our mottoes is this haughty address to the Romans,—'If we fall, ye fall also?' And better that fate, than a rise upon the wrecks of our native city."

"Well, well, well!" said Montreal, re-seating himself, "I see that I must leave Rome to herself,—the League must thrive without her aid. I did but jest, touching the Orsini, for they have not the power that would make their efforts safe. Let us sweep, then, our past conference from our recollection. It is the nineteenth, I think, Lord Colonna, on which you propose to repair to Cornetto, with your friends and retainers, and on which you have invited my attendance?"

"It is on that day, Sir Knight," replied the Baron, evidently much relieved by the turn the conversation had assumed. "The fact is, that we have been so charged with indifference to the interests of the good people, that I strain a point in this expedition to contradict the assertion; and we propose, therefore, to escort and protect, against the robbers of the road, a convoy of corn to Corneto. In truth, I may add another reason, besides fear of the robbers that makes me desire as numerous a train as possible. I wish to show my enemies, and the people generally, the solid and growing power of my house; the display of such an armed band as I hope to levy, will be a magnificent occasion to strike awe into the riotous and refactory. Adrian, you will collect your servitors, I trust, on that day; we would not be without you."

"And as we ride along, fair Signor," said Montreal, inclining to Adrian, "we will find at least one subject on which we can agree: all brave men and true knights have one comtopic,—and its name is Woman. You must make me acquainted with the names of the fairest dames of Rome; and we will discuss old adventures in the Parliament of Love, and hope for new. By the way, I suppose, Lord Adrian, you, with the rest of your countrymen, are Petrarch-stricken?"

"Do you not share our enthusiasm, slur not so your gallantry, I pray you."

"Come, we must not again disagree; but, by my halidame, I think one troubadour roundel worth all that Petrarch ever wrote. He has but borrowed from our knightly poesy, to disguise it, like a carpet coxcomb."

"Well," said Adrian, gaily, "for every line of the troubadours that you quote, I will cite you another. I will forgive you for injustice to Petrarch, if you are just to the troubadours."

"Just!" cried Montreal, with real enthusiasm: "I am of the land, nay the very blood of the troubadour! But we grow too light for your noble kinsman; and it is time for me to bid you, for the present, farewell. My Lord Colonna, peace be with you; farewell, Sir Adrian,—brother mine in knighthood,—remember your challenge."

And with an easy and careless grace the Knight of St. John took his leave. The old Baron, making a dumb sign of excuse to Adrian, followed Montreal into the adjoining room.

"Sir Knight!" said he, "Sir Knight!" as he closed the door upon Adrian, and then drew Montreal to the recess of the casement, —'a word in your ear. Think not I slight your offer, but these young men must be managed; the plot is great—noble—grateful to my heart; but it requires time and caution. I have many of my house, scrupulous as yon hot-skull, to win over; the way is pleasant, but must be sounded well and carefully; you understand?"

From under his bent brows, Montreal darted one keen glance at Stephen, and then answered:

"My friendship for you dictated my offer. The League may stand without the Colonna, beware a time when the Colonna cannot stand without the Legue. My Lord, look well around you; there are more freemen—ay, bold and stirring ones, too—in Rome, than you imagine Beware Rienzi! Adieu, we meet soon again."

Thus saying, Montreal departed, soliloquizing as he passed with his careless step through the crowded ante-room:

"I shall fail here!—these caitiff nobles have neither the courage to be great, nor the wisdom to be honest. Let them fall!—I may find an adventurer from the people, an adventurer like myself, worth them all."

No sooner had Stephen returned to Adrian than he flung his arms affectionately round his ward, who was preparing his pride for some sharp rebuke for his petulance.

"Nobly feigned,—admirable, admirable!" cried the baron; "you have learned the true art of a statesman at the Emperor's court. I always thought you would—always said it. You saw the dilemma I was in, thus taken by surprise by that barbarian's mad scheme; afraid to refuse,—more afraid to accept. You extricated me with consummate address: that passion,—so natural to your age,—was a famous feint; drew off the attack; gave me time to breathe; allowed me to play with the savage. But we must not offend him, you know: all my retainers would desert me, or sell me to the Orsini, or cut my throat, if he but held up his finger. Oh! it was admirably managed, Adrian—admirably!"

"Thank Heaven!" said Adrian, with some difficulty recovering the breath which his astonishment had taken away, "you do not think of embracing that black proposition?"

"Think of it! no, indeed!" said Stephen, throwing himself back on his chair. "Why, do you not know my age, boy? Hard on my ninetieth year, I should be a fool indeed to throw myself into such a whirl of turbulence and agitation. I want to keep what I have, not risk it by grasping more. Am I not the beloved of the pope? shall I hazard his excommunication? Am I not the most powerful of the nobles? should I be more if I were king? At my age to talk to me of such stuff!—the man's an idiot. Besides," added the old man, sinking his voice, and looking fearfully round, "if I were a king, my sons might poison me for the succession. They are good lads, Adrian, very! But such a temptation!—I would not throw it in their way; these grey hairs have experience! Tyrants don't die a natural death; no, no! Plague on the Knight, say I; he has already cast me into a cold sweat."

Adrian gazed on the working features of the old man, whose selfishness thus preserved him from crime. He listened to his concluding words—full of the dark truth of the times; and as the high and pure ambition of Rienzi flashed upon him in contrast, he felt that he could not blame its fervor, or wonder at its excess.

"And then, too," resumed the Baron, speaking more deliberately as he recovered his self-possession, "this man, by way of a warning, shows me at a glance, his whole ignorance of the state. What think you? he has mingled with the mob, and taken their rank breath for power; yes, he thinks words are soldiers, and bade me—me, Stephen Colonna—beware—of whom, think you? No, you will never guess!—of that speech-maker, Rienzi! my own old jesting guest! Ha! ha! ha!—the ignorance of these barbarians! ha! ha! ha!" and the old man laughed till the tears ran down his cheeks.

"Yet many of the nobles fear that same Rienzi," said Adrian, gravely.

"Ah! let them, let them!—they have not our experience—our knowledge of the world, Adrian. Tut, man,—when did declamation ever overthrow castles, and conquer soldiery? I like Rienzi to harangue the mob about old Rome, and such stuff; it gives them something to think of and prate about, and so all their fierceness evaporates in words; they might burn a house if they did not hear a speech. But, now I am on that score, I must own the pedant has grown impudent in his new office; here, here,—I received this paper ere I rose to-day. I hear a similar insolence has been shown to all the nobles. Read it, will you," and the Colonna put a scroll into his kinsman's hand.

"I have received the like," said Adrian, glancing at it. "It is a request of Rienzi's to attend at the Church of St. John of Lateran, to hear explained the inscription on a Table just discovered. It bears, he saith, the most intimate connection with the welfare and state of Rome."

"Very entertaining, I dare to say, to professors and bookmen. Pardon me, kinsman; I forgot your taste for these things; and my son, Gianni, too, shares your fantasy. Well, well! it is innocent enough! Go—the man talks well."

"Will you not attend, too?"

"I—my dear boy—I!" said the old Colonna, opening his eyes in such astonishment that Adrian could not help laughing at the simplicity of his own question.

CHAPTER II.

The Interview, and the Doubt.

As Adrian turned from the palace of his guardian, and bent his way in the direction of the Forum, he came somewhat unexpectedly upon Raimond, bishop of Orvietto, who, mounted upon a low palfrey, and accompanied by some three or four of his waiting-men, halted abruptly when he recognized the young noble.

"Ah, my son! it is seldom that I see thee: how fares it with thee?—well? So, so! I rejoice to hear it. Alas! what a state of society is ours, when compared to the tranquil pleasures of Avignon! There, all men who, like us, are fond of the same pursuits, the same studies, *deliciæ musarum*, hum! hum! (the Bishop was proud of an occasional quotation, right or wrong), are brought easily and naturally together. But here we scarcely dare stir out of our houses, save upon great occasions. But, talking of great occasions, and the Muses, reminds me of our good Rienzi's invitation to the Lateran: of course you will attend; 'tis a mighty knotty piece of Latin he proposes to solve—so I hear, at least; very interesting to us, my son,—very!"

"It is to-morrow," answered Adrian. "Yes, assuredly; I will be there."

"And, harkye, my son," said the Bishop, resting his hand affectionately on Adrian's shoulder, "I have reason to hope that he will remind our poor citizens of the Jubilee for the year Fifty, and stir them towards clearing the road of the brigands: a necessary injunction, and one to be heeded timeously; for who will come here for absolution when he stands a chance of rushing unannealed upon purgatory by the way? You have heard Reinzi,—ay? quite a Cicero—quite! Well, Heaven bless you, my son! you will not fail?"

"Nay, not I."

"Yet, stay—a word with you: just suggest to all whom you may meet the advisability of a full meeting; it looks well for the city to show respect to letters."

"To say nothing of the Jubilee," added Adrian, smiling.

"Ah, to say nothing of the Jubilee—very good! Adieu for the present!" And the Bishop, resettling himself on his saddle, ambled solemnly on to visit his various friends, and press them to the meeting.

Meanwhile, Adrian continued his course till he had passed the Capitol, the Arch of Severus, the crumbling columns of the fane of Jupiter, and found himself amidst the long grass, the whispering reeds, and the neglected vines, that wave over the now-vanished pomp of the Golden House of Nero. Seating himself on a fallen pillar—by that spot where the traveller descends to the (so called) Baths of Livia—he looked impatiently to the sun, as to blame it for the slowness of its march.

Not long, however, had he to wait before a light step was heard crushing the fragrant grass; and presently through the arching vines gleamed a face that might well have seemed the nymph, the goddess of the scene.

"My beautiful! my Irene!—how shall I thank thee!"

It was long before the delighted lover suffered himself to observe upon Irene's face a sadness that did not usually cloud it in his presence. Her voice, too, trembled; her words seemed constrained and cold.

"Have I offended thee?" he asked; "or what less misfortune hath occurred?"

Irene raised her eyes to her lover's, and said, looking at him earnestly, "Tell me, my Lord, in sober and simple truth, tell me, would it grieve thee much were this to be our last meeting?"

Paler than the marble at his feet grew the dark cheek of Adrian. It was some moments ere he could reply, and he did so then with a forced smile and a quivering lip.

"Jest not so, Irene! Last!—that is not a word for us!"

"But hear me, my Lord——"

"Why so cold?—call me Adrian!—friend! —lover! or be dumb!"

"Well, then, my soul's soul! my all of hope! my life's life!" exclaimed Irene, passionately, "hear me! I fear that we stand at this moment upon some gulf whose depth I see not, but which may divide us for ever! Thou knowest the real nature of my brother, and dost not misread him as many do. Long has he planned, and schemed, and communed with himself, and feeling his way amidst the people, prepared the path to some great design. But now——(thou wilt not betray—thou wilt not injure him?—he is *thy* friend?)"

"And thy brother! I will give my life for his! Say on!"

"But now, then," resumed Irene, "the time for that enterprise, whatever it be, is coming fast. I know not of its exact nature, but I know that it is against the nobles—against thy order—against thy house itself! If it succeed—oh, Adrian! thou thyself mayst not be free from danger; and my name, at least, will be coupled with the name of thy foes. If it fail,—my brother, my bold brother, is swept away! He will fall a victim to revenge or justice, call it as you will. Your kinsman may be his judge—his executioner; and I—even if I should yet live to mourn over the boast and glory of my humble line—could I permit myself to love, to see, one in whose veins flowed the blood of his destroyer? Oh! I am wretched—wretched! these thoughts make me well-nigh mad!" and, wringing her hands bitterly, Irene sobbed aloud.

Adrian himself was struck forcibly by the picture thus presented to him, although the alternative it embraced had often before forced itself dimly on his mind. It was true, however, that, not seeing the schemes of Rienzi backed by any physical power, and never yet having witnessed the mighty force of a moral revolution, he did not conceive that any rise to which he might instigate the people could be permanently successful: and, as for his punishment, in that city, where all justice was the slave of interest, Adrian knew himself powerful enough to obtain forgiveness even for the greatest of all crimes—armed insurrection against the nobles. As these thoughts recurred to him, he gained the courage to console and cheer Irene. But his efforts were only partially successful. Awakened by her fears to that consideration of the future which hitherto she had forgotten, Irene, for the first time, seemed deaf to the charmer's voice.

"Alas!" said she, sadly, "even at the best, what can this love, that we have so blindly encouraged—what can it end in? Thou must not wed with one like me; and I! how foolish I have been!"

"Recall thy senses then, Irene," said Adrian, proudly, partly perhaps in anger, partly in his experience of the sex. "Love another, and more wisely, if thou wilt; cancel thy vows with me, and continue to think it a crime to love, and a folly to be true!"

"Cruel!" said Irene, falteringly, and in her turn alarmed. "Dost thou speak in earnest?"

"Tell me, ere I answer you, tell me this: come death, come anguish, come a whole life of sorrow, as the end of this love, wouldst thou yet repent that thou hast loved? If so, thou knowest not the love that I feel for thee."

"Never! never can I repent!" said Irene, falling upon Adrian's neck; "forgive me!"

"But is there, in truth," said Adrian, a little while after this lover-like quarrel and reconciliation, "is there, in truth, so marked a difference between thy brother's past and his present bearing? How knowest thou that the time for action is so near?"

"Because now he sits closeted whole nights with all ranks of men; he shuts up his books,—he reads no more,—but, when alone, walks to and fro his chamber muttering to himself. Sometimes he pauses before the calendar, which of late he has fixed with his own hand against the wall, and passes his finger over the letters, till he comes to some chosen date, and then he plays with his sword and smiles. But two night since, arms, too, in great number were brought to the house; and I heard the chief of the men who brought them, a grim giant, known well amongst the people, say, as he wiped his brow,—'These will see work soon!'"

"Arms! Are you sure of that?" said Adrian, anxiously. "Nay, then, there is more in these schemes than I imagined! But (observing Irene's gaze bent fearfully on him as his voice changed, he added, more gaily)—but come what may, believe me,—my beautiful! my adored! that while I live, thy brother shall not suffer from the wrath he may provoke,—nor I, though he forget our ancient friendship, cease to love thee less."

"Signora! Signora! child! it is time! we must go!" said the shrill voice of Benedetta, now peering through the foliage. "The working men pass home this way; I see them approaching."

The lovers parted; for the first time the serpent had penetrated into their Eden,—they had conversed, they had thought of other things than Love.

CHAPTER III.

The Situation of a Popular Patrician in Times of Popular Discontent.—Scene of the Lateran.

THE situation of a Patrician who honestly loves the people is, in those evil times, when power oppresses and freedom struggles,—when the two divisions of men are wrestling against each other,—the most irksome and perplexing that destiny can possibly contrive. Shall he take part with the nobles?—he betrays his conscience! With the people?—he deserts his friends. But that consequence of the last alternative is not the sole—nor, perhaps, to a strong mind, the most severe. All men are swayed and chained by public opinion—it is the public judge; but puplic opinion is not the same for all ranks. The public opinion that excites or deters the plebeian, is the opinion of the plebeians,—of those whom he sees, and meets, and knows; of those with whom he is brought in contact,—those with whom he has mixed from childhood,—those whose praises are daily heard,—whose censure frowns upon him with every hour.* So,

---

*** It is the same in still smaller divisions. The public opinion for lawyers is that of lawyers; of soldiers**

also, the public opinion of the great is the opinion of *their* equals,—of those whom birth and accident cast for ever in their way. This distinction is full of important practical deductions; it is one which, more than most maxims, should never be forgotten by a politician who desires to be profound. It is, then, an ordeal terrible to pass—which few plebeians ever pass, which it is therefore unjust to expect patricians to cross unfalteringly—the ordeal of opposing the public opinion which exists for *them*. They cannot help doubting their own judgment,—they cannot help thinking the voice of wisdom or of virtue speaks in those sounds which have been deemed oracles from their cradle. In the tribunal of Sectarian Prejudice they imagine they recognize the court of the Universal Conscience. Another powerful antidote to the activity of a patrician so placed, is in the certainty that to the last the motives of such activity will be alike misconstrued by the aristocracy he deserts and the people he joins. It seems so unnatural in a man to fly in the face of his own order, that the world is willing to suppose any clue to the mystery save that of honest conviction or lofty patriotism. "Ambition!" says one. "Disappointment!" cries another. "Some private grudge!" hints a third. "Mob-courting vanity!" sneers a fourth. The people admire at first, but suspect afterwards. The moment he thwarts a popular wish, there is no redemption for him: he is accused of having acted the hypocrite,—of having worn the sheep's fleece: and now, say they,—"See! the wolf's teeth peep out!" Is he familiar with the people?—it is cajolery! Is he distant,—it is pride! What, then sustains a man in such a situation, following his own conscience, with his eyes opened to all the perils of the path? Away with the cant of public opinion,—away with the poor delusion of posthumous justice; he will offend the first, he will never obtain the last. What sustains him? HIS OWN SOUL! A man thoroughly great has a certain contempt for his kind while he aids them: their weal or woe are all; their applause—their blame—are nothing to him. He walks forth from the circle of birth and habit; he is deaf to the little motives of little men. High, through the widest space his orbit may describe, he holds on his course to guide or to enlighten; but the noises below reach him not! Until the wheel is broken,—until the dark void swallow up the star,—it makes melody, night and day, to its own ear: thirsting for no sound from the earth it illumines, anxious for no companionship in the path through which it rolls, conscious of its own glory, and contented, therefore, to be *alone!*

But minds of this order are rare. All ages cannot produce them. They are exceptions to the ordinary and human virtue, which is influenced and regulated by external circumstance. At a time when even to be merely susceptible to the voice of fame was a great pre-eminence in moral energies over the rest of mankind, it would be impossible that any one should ever have formed the conception of that more refined and metaphysical sentiment, that purer excitement to high deeds—that glory in one's own heart, which is so immeasurably above the desire of a renown that lackeys the heels of others. In fact, before we can dispense with the world, we must, by a long and severe novitiate—by the probation of much thought, and much sorrow—by deep and sad conviction of the vanity of all that the world can give us, have raised ourselves—not in the fervor of an hour, but habitually—*above* the world: and abstraction—an idealism—which, in our wiser age, how few even of the wisest, can attain! Yet, till we are thus fortunate, we know not the true divinity of contemplation, nor the all-sufficing mightiness of conscience; nor can we retreat with solemn footsteps into that Holy of Holies in our own souls, wherein we know, and feel, how much our nature is capable of the self-existence of a God!

But to return to the things and thoughts of earth. Those considerations, and those links of circumstance, which, in a similar situation have changed so many honest and courageous minds, changed also the mind of Adrian. He

that of the army: of scholars, it is that of men of literature and science. And to the susceptible amongst the latter, the hostile criticism of learning has been more stinging than the severest moral censures of the vulgar. Many a man has done a great act, or composed a great work, solely to please the two or three persons constantly present to him. Their voice was *his* public opinion. The public opinion that operated on Bishop, the murderer, was the opinion of the Burkers, his comrades. Did that condemn him? No! He knew no other public opinion till he came to be hanged, and caught the loathing eyes, and heard the hissing execrations of the crowd below his gibbet.

felt in a false position. His reason and conscience shared in the schemes of Rienzi, and his natural hardihood and love of enterprise would have led him actively to share the danger of their execution. But this, all his associations, his friendships, his private and household ties, loudly forbade. Against his order, against his house, against the companions of his youth, how could he plot secretly, or act sternly? By the goal to which he was impelled by patriotism, stood hypocrisy and ingratitude. Who would believe him the honest champion of his country who was a traitor to his friends? Thus, indeed,

> "The native hue of resolution
> Was sicklied o'er with the pale cast of thought!"

And he who should have been by nature a leader of the time became only its spectator. Yet Adrian endeavored to console himself for his present passiveness in a conviction of the policy of his conduct. He who takes no share in the commencement of civil revolutions, can often become, with the most effect, a mediator between the passions and the parties subsequently formed. Perhaps, under Adrian's circumstances, delay was really the part of a prudent statesman; the very position which cripples at the first, often gives authority before the end. Clear from the excesses, and saved from the jealousies, of rival factions, all men are willing to look with complaisance and respect to a new actor in a turbulent drama; his moderation may make him trusted by the people; his rank enable him to be a fitting mediator with the nobles; and thus the qualities that would have rendered him a martyr at one period of the Revolution, raise him perhaps into a saviour at another.

Silent, therefore, and passive, Adrian waited the progress of events. If the projects of Rienzi failed, he might, by that inactivity, the better preserve the people from new chains, and their champion from death. If those projects succeeded, he might equally save his house from the popular wrath—and, advocating liberty, check disorder. Such, at least, were his hopes; and thus did the Italian sagacity and caution of his character control and pacify the enthusiasm of youth and courage.

The sun shone, calm and cloudless, upon the vast concourse gathered before the broad space that surrounds the Church of St. John of Lateran. Partly by curiosity—partly by the desire of the Bishop of Orvietto—partly because it was an occasion in which they could display the pomp of their retinues—many of the principal Barons of Rome had gathered to this spot.

On one of the steps ascending to the church, with his mantle folded round him, stood Walter de Montreal, gazing on the various parties that, one after another, swept through the lane which the soldiers of the Church preserved unimpeded, in the middle of the crowd, for the access of the principal nobles. He watched with interest, though with his usual carelessness of air and roving glance, the different marks and looks of welcome given by the populace to the different personages of note. Banners and penons preceded each Signor, and, as they waved aloft, the witticisms or nicknames—the brief works of praise or censure, that imply so much—which passed to and fro among that lively crowd, were treasured carefully in his recollection.

"Make way, there!—way for my Lord Martino Orsini—Baron di Porto!"

"Peace, minion!—draw back! way for the Signor Adrian Colonna, Baron di Castello, and Knight of the Empire."

And at those two rival shouts, you saw waving on high the golden bear of the Orsini, with the motto—"Beware my embrace!" and the solitary column on an azure ground, of the Colonna, with Adrian's especial device—"Sad, but strong." The train of Martino Orsini was much more numerous than that of Adrian, which last consisted but of ten servitors. But Adrian's men attracted far greater admiration amongst the crowd, and pleased more the experienced eye of the warlike Knight of St. John. Their arms were polished like mirrors; their height was to an inch the same; their march was regular and sedate; their mien erect; they looked neither to the right nor left; they betrayed that ineffable discipline—that harmony of order—which Adrian had learned to impart to his men during his own apprenticeship of arms. But the disorderly train of the Lord of Porto was composed of men of all heights. Their arms were ill-polished and ill-fashioned, and they pressed confusedly on each other; they laughed and spoke aloud; and in their mien and bearing expressed all the insolence of men who despised alike the master they served and the people they awed. The two bands coming unexpectedly on each other through this narrow defile, the jealousy of the two houses presently declared itself. Each pressed forward for the precedence; and, as the quiet regularity of Adrian's train, and even its compact paucity of numbers, enabled it to pass before the servitors of his rival, the populace set up a loud shout—"A Colonna for ever!"—"Let the Bear dance after the Column!"

"On, ye knaves!" said Orsini aloud to his men. "How have ye suffered this affront?" And passing himself to the head of his men, he would have advanced through the midst of his rival's train, had not a tall guard, in the Pope's livery, placed his baton in the way.

"Pardon, Lord! we have the Vicar's express commands to suffer no struggling of the different trains one with another."

"Knave! dost thou bandy words with me?" said the fierce Orsini; and with his sword he clove the baton in two.

"In the Vicar's name, I command you to fall back!" said the sturdy guard, now placing his huge bulk in the very front of the noble's path.

"It is Cecco del Vecchio!" cried those of the populace, who were near enough to perceive the interruption and its cause.

"Ay," said one, "the good Vicar has put many of the stoutest fellows in the Pope's livery, in order the better to keep peace. He could have chosen none better than Cecco."

"But he must not fall!" cried another, as Orsini, glaring on the smith, drew back his sword as if to plunge it through his bosom.

"Shame—shame! shall the Pope be thus insulted in his own city?" cried several voices. "Down with the sacrilegious—down!" And, as if by a preconcerted plan, a whole body of the mob broke at once through the lane, and swept like a torrent over Orsini and his jostled and ill-assorted train. Orsini himself was thrown on the ground with violence, and trampled upon by a hundred footsteps; his men, huddled and struggling as much against themselves as against the mob, were scattered and overset; and when, by a great effort of the guards, headed by the smith himself, order was again restored, and the line reformed, Orsini, well nigh choked with his rage and humiliation, and greatly bruised by the rude assaults he had received, could scarcely stir from the ground. The officers of the Pope raised him, and when he was on his legs, he looked wildly around for his sword, which, falling from his hand, had been kicked amongst the crowd, and seeing it not, he said, between his ground teeth, to Cecco del Vecchio—

"Fellow, thy neck shall answer this outrage, or may God desert me!" and passed along through the space; while a half-suppressed and exultant hoot from the bystanders followed his path.

"Way there!" cried the smith, "for the Lord Martino di Porto, and may all the people know that he has threatened to take my life for the discharge of my duty in obedience to the Pope's Vicar!"

"He dare not!" shouted out a thousand voices; "the people can protect their own!"

This scene had not been lost on the Provençal, who well knew how to construe the wind by the direction of straws, and saw at once, by the boldness of the populace, that they themselves were conscious of a coming tempest. "*Par Dieu,*" said he, as he saluted Adrian, who, gravely, and without looking behind, had now won the steps of the church, "yon tall fellow has a brave heart, and many friends, too. What think you," he added, in a low whisper, "is not this scene a proof that the nobles are less safe than they wot of?"

"The beast begins to kick against the spur, Sir Knight," answered Adrian; "a wise horseman should, in such a case, take care how he pull the rein too tight, lest the beast should rear, and he be overthrown—yet that is the policy thou wouldst recommend."

"You mistake," returned Montreal, "my wish was to give Rome one sovereign instead of many tyrants,—but hark! what means that bell?"

"The ceremony is about to begin," answered Adrian. "Shall we enter the church together?"

Seldom had a temple consecrated to God witnessed so singular a spectacle as that which now animated the solemn space of the Lateran.

In the centre of the church, seats were raised in an amphitheatre, at the far end of which was a scaffolding, a little higher than the rest; below this spot, but high enough to be in sight of all the concourse, was placed a vast table of iron, on which was graven an ancient inscription, and bearing in its centre a clear and prominent device, presently to be explained.

The seats were covered with cloth and rich tapestry. In the rear of the church was drawn a purple curtain. Around the amphitheatre were the officers of the Church, in the party-colored liveries of the Pope. To the right of the scaffold sate Raimond, Bishop of Orvietto, in his robes of state. On the benches round him you saw all the marked personages of Rome—the judges, the men of letters, the nobles, from the lofty rank of the Savelli to the inferior grade of a Raselli. The space beyond the amphitheatre was filled with the people, who now poured fast in, stream after stream: all the while rang, clear and loud, the great bell of the church.

At length, as Adrian and Montreal seated themselves at a little distance from Raimond, the bell suddenly ceased—the murmurs of the people were stilled—the purple curtain was withdrawn, and Rienzi came forth with slow and majestic steps. He came—but not in his usual sombre and plain attire. Over his broad breast he wore a vest of dazzling whiteness—a long robe, in the ample fashion of the toga, descended to his feet and swept the floor. On his head he wore a fold of white cloth, in the centre of which shone a golden crown. But the crown was divided, or cloven, as it were, by the mystic ornament of a silver sword, which, attracting the universal attention, testified at once that this strange garb was worn, not from the vanity of display, but for the sake of presenting to the concourse—in the person of the citizen—a type and emblem of that state of the city on which he was about to descant.

"Faith," whispered one of the old nobles to his neighbor, "the plebeian assumes it bravely."

"It will be rare sport," said a second. "I trust the good man will put some jests in his discourse."

"What showman's tricks are these?" said a third.

"He is certainly crazed!" said a fourth.

"How handsome he is!" said the women, mixed with the populace.

"This is a man who has learned the people by heart," observed Montreal to Adrian "He knows he must speak to the eye, in order to win the mind: a knave,—a wise knave!"

And now Rienzi had ascended the scaffold: and as he looked long and steadfastly around the meeting, the high and thoughtful repose of his majestic countenance, its deep and solemn gravity, hushed all the murmurs, and made its effect equally felt by the sneering nobles as the impatient populace.

"Signors of Rome," said he, at length, "and ye, friends, and citizens, you have heard why we are met together this day; and you, my Lord Bishop of Orvietto,—and ye, fellow laborers with me in the field of letters,—ye, too, are aware that it is upon some matter relative to that ancient Rome, the rise and the decline of whose past power and glories we have spent our youth in endeavoring to comprehend. But this, believe me, is no vain enigma of erudition, useful but to the studious,—referring but to the dead. Let the Past perish!—let darkness shroud it!—let it sleep for ever over the crumbling temples and desolate tombs of its forgotten sons,—if it cannot afford us, from its disburied secrets, a guide for the Present and the Future. What, my Lords, ye have thought that it was for the sake of antiquity alone that we have wasted our nights and days in studying what antiquity can teach us! You are mistaken; it is nothing to know what we have been, unless it is with the desire of knowing that which we ought to be. Our ancestors are mere dust and ashes, save when they speak to our posterity; and then their voices resound, not from the earth below, but the heaven above. There is an eloquence in Memory, because it is the nurse of Hope. There is a sanctity in the Past, but only because of the chronicles it retains,—chronicles of the progress of mankind,—stepping-stones in civilization, in liberty, and in knowledge. Our fathers forbid us to recede,—they teach us what is our rightful heritage,—they bid us reclaim, they bid us augment, that heritage,—preserve their virtues, and avoid their errors. These are the true uses of the Past. Like the sacred edifice in which we are,—it is a tomb upon which to rear a temple. I see that you marvel at this long beginning; ye look to each other—ye ask to what it tends. Behold this broad plate of iron; upon it is graven an inscription but lately disinterred from the heaps of stone and ruin, which—O shame to Rome!—were once the palaces of empire, and the arches of triumphant power. The device in the centre of the table, which you behold, conveys the act of the Roman Senators,—who are conferring upon Vespasian the imperial authority. It is this inscription which I have invited you to hear read! It specifies the very terms and limits of the authority thus conferred. To the Emperor was confided the power of making laws and alliances with whatsoever nation,—of increasing, or of diminishing the limits of towns and districts,—of—mark this, my Lords! exalting men to the rank of dukes and kings,—ay, and of deposing and degrading them;—of making cities, and of unmaking; in short, of all of the attributes of imperial power. Yes, to that Emperor was confided this vast authority; but, by whom? Heed—listen, I pray you—let not a word be lost;—by whom, I say? By the Roman Senate! What was the Roman Senate? The Representative of the Roman People!"

"I knew he would come to that!" said the smith, who stood at the door with his fellows, but to whose ear, clear and distinct, rolled the silver voice of Rienzi.

"Brave fellow! and this, too, in the hearing of the Lords!"

"Ay, you see what the people were, and we should never have known this but for him."

"Peace, fellows;" said the officer to those of the crowd, from whom came these whispered sentences.

Rienzi continued.—"Yes, it is the people who intrusted this power—to the people, therefore, it belongs!—Did the haughty Emperor arrogate the crown? Could he assume the authority of himself? Was it born with him? Did he derive it, my Lord Barons, from the possession of towered castles—of lofty lineage? No! all-powerful as he was, he had no right to one atom of that power, save from the voice and trust of the Roman people. Such, O my countrymen! such was even at that day, when Liberty was but the shadow of her former self,—such was the acknowledged prerogative of your fathers! All power was the gift of the people. What have ye to give now? Who, who, I say,—what single person, what petty chief, asks *you* for the authority he assumes? His senate is his sword; his chart of licence is written, not with ink, but blood. The people!—there is *no* people! Oh! would to God that we might disentomb the spirit of the Past as easily as her records!"

"If I were your kinsman," whispered Montreal to Adrian, "I would give this man short breathing-time between his peroration and confession."

"What is your Emperor?" continued Rienzi; "a stranger! What the great head of your Church?—an exile! Ye are without your lawful chiefs; and why? Because ye are *not* without your law-defying tyrants! The licence of your nobles, their discords, their dissensions, have driven our Holy Father from the heritage of St. Peter;—they have bathed your streets in your own blood; they have wasted the wealth of your labors on private quarrels and the maintenance of hireling ruffians! Your forces are exhausted against yourselves. You have made a mockery of your country, once the mistress of the world. You have steeped her lips in gall—ye have set a crown of thorns upon her head! What, my Lords!" cried he, turning sharply round towards the Savelli and Orsini, who, endeavoring to shake off the thrill which the fiery eloquence of Rienzi had stricken to their hearts, now, by contemptuous gestures and scornful smiles, testified the displeasure they did not dare loudly to utter in the presence of the Vicar and the people.—"What! even while I speak—not the sanctity of this place restrains you! I am an humble man—a citizen of Rome;—but I have this distinction: I have raised against myself many foes and scoffers for that which I have done for Rome. I am hated because I love my country; I am despised, because I would exalt her. I retaliate—I shall be avenged. Three traitors in your own palaces shall betray you: their names are—Luxury, Envy, and Dissension!"

"There he had them on the hip!"

"Ha, ha! by the Holy Cross, that was good!"

"I would go to the hangman for such another keen stroke as that!"

"It is a shame if *we* are cowards, when one man is thus brave," said the smith.

"This is the man we have always wanted!"

"Silence!" proclaimed the officer.

"O Romans!" resumed Rienzi, passionately—"awake! I conjure you! Let this memorial of your former power—your ancient liberties—sink deep into your souls. In a propitious hour, if ye seize it,—in an evil one, if ye suffer the golden opportunity to escape, —has this record of the past been unfolded to your eyes. Recollect that the Jubilee approaches."

The Bishop of Orvietto smiled, and bowed approvingly; the people, the citizens, the inferior nobles, noted well those signs of encouragement; and, to their minds, the Pope himself, in the person of his Vicar, looked benignly on the daring of Rienzi.

"The Jubilee approaches,—the eyes of all Christendom will be directed hither. Here, where, from all quarters of the globe, men come for peace, shall they find discord?—seeking absolution, shall they perceive but crime? In the centre of God's dominion, shall they weep at your weakness?—in the seat of the martyred saints, shall they shudder at your vices?—in the fountain and source of Christ's law, shall they find all law unknown? You were the glory of the world—will you be its by-word? You were its example—will you be its warning? Rise, while it is yet time!—clear your roads from the bandits that infest them!—your walls from the hirelings that they harbor! Banish these civil discords, or the men—how proud, how great, soever—who maintain them! Pluck the scales from the hand of Fraud!—the sword from the hand of Violence!—the balance and the sword are the ancient attributes of Justice!—restore them to *her* again! This be your high task, —these be your great ends! Deem any man who opposes them a traitor to his country. Gain a victory greater than those of the Cæsars —a victory over yourselves! Let the pilgrims of the world behold the resurrection of Rome! Make one epoch of the Jubilee of Religion and the Restoration of Law! Lay the sacrifice of your vanquished passions—the first-fruits of your renovated liberties—upon the very altar that these walls contain! and never! oh, never! since the world began, shall men have made a more grateful offering to their God!"

So intense was the sensation these words created in the audience—so breathless and overpowered did they leave the souls which they took by storm—that Rienzi had descended the scaffold, and already disappeared behind the curtain from which he had emerged, ere the crowd were fully aware that he had ceased.

The singularity of this sudden apparition—robed in mysterious splendor, and vanishing the moment its errand was fulfilled—gave additional effect to the words it had uttered. The whole character of that bold address became invested with a something preternatural and inspired; to the minds of the vulgar, the mortal was converted into the oracle; and, marvelling at the unhesitating courage with which their idol had rebuked and conjured the haughty barons,—each of whom they regarded in the light of sanctioned executioners, whose anger could be made manifest at once by the gibbet or the axe,—the people could not but superstitiously imagine that nothing less than authority from above could have gifted their leader with such hardihood, and preserved him from the danger it incurred. In fact, it was in this very courage of Rienzi that his safety consisted; he was placed in those circumstances where audacity is prudence. Had he been less bold, the nobles would have been more severe; but so great a licence of speech in an officer of the Holy See, they naturally imagined, was not unauthorized by the assent of the Pope, as well as by the approbation of the people. Those who did not (like Stephen Colonna) despise words as wind, shrank back from the task of punishing one whose voice might be the mere echo of the wishes of the pontiff. The dissensions of the nobles among each other, were no less favorable to Rienzi. He attacked a body, the members of which had no union.

"It is not *my* duty to slay him!" said one.

"I am not the representative of the barons!" said another.

"If Stephen Colonna heeds him not, it would be absurd, as well as dangerous, in a meaner man to make himself the champion of the order!" said a third.

The Colonna smiled approval, when Rienzi denounced an Orsini—an Orsini laughed aloud, when the eloquence burst over a Colonna. The lesser nobles were well pleased to hear attacks upon both: while, on the other hand, the Bishop, by the long impunity of Rienzi, had taken courage to sanction the conduct of his fellow-officer. He affected, indeed, at times, to blame the excess of his fervor, but it was always accompanied by the praises of his honesty; and the approbation of the Pope's Vicar confirmed the impression of the nobles as to the approbation of the Pope. Thus, from the very rashness of his enthusiasm had grown his security and success.

Still, however, when the barons had a little recovered from the stupor into which Rienzi had cast them, they looked round to each other; and their looks confessed their sense of the insolence of the orator, and the affront offered to themselves.

"*Per fede!*" quoth Reginaldo di Orsini, "this is past bearing,—the plebeian has gone too far!"

"Look at the populace below! how they murmur and gape,—and how their eyes sparkle—and what looks they bend at us?" said Luca di Savelli to his mortal enemy, Castruccio Malatesta: the sense of a common danger united in one moment, but only *for* a moment, the enmity of years.

"Diavolo!" muttered Raselli (Nina's father) to a baron, equally poor, "but the clerk has truth in his lips. 'Tis a pity he is not noble."

"What a clever brain marred!" said a Florentine merchant. "That man might be something, if he were sufficiently rich."

Adrian and Montreal were silent: the first seemed lost in thought,—the last was watching the various effects produced upon the audience.

"Silence!" proclaimed the officers. "Silence, for my Lord Vicar."

At this announcement, every eye turned to Raimond, who, rising with much clerical importance, thus addressed the assembly:—

"Although, Barons and Citizens of Rome, my well-beloved flock, and children,—I, no more than yourselves, anticipated the exact nature of the address ye have just heard,—and, albeit, I cannot feel unalloyed contentment at the manner, nor, I may say, at the whole matter of that fervent exhortation—*yet* (laying great emphasis on the last word), I cannot suffer you to depart without adding to the prayers of our Holy Father's servant, those, also, of His Holiness's spiritual representative. It is true! the Jubilee approaches! The Jubilee approaches —and yet our roads, even to the gates of Rome, are infested with murderous and godless ruffians! What pilgrim can venture across the Apennines to worship at the altars of St. Peter? The Jubilee approaches: what scandal shall it be to Rome if these shrines be without pilgrims—if the timid recoil from, if the bold fall victims to, the dangers of the way! Wherefore, I pray you all, citizens and chiefs alike,—I pray you all to lay aside those unhappy dissensions which have so long consumed the strength of our sacred city; and, uniting with each other in the ties of amity and brotherhood, to form a blessed league against the marauders of the road. I see amongst you, my Lords, many of the boasts and pillars of the state; but, alas! I think with grief and dismay on the causeless and idle hatred that has grown up between you!—a scandal to our city, and reflecting, let me add, my Lords, no honor on your faith as Christians, nor on your dignity as defenders of the Church."

Amongst the inferior nobles—along the seats of the judges and the men of letters—through the vast concourse of the people—ran a loud murmur of approbation at these words. The greater barons looked proudly, but not contemptuously, at the countenance of the prelate, and preserved a strict and unrevealing silence.

"In this holy spot," continued the Bishop, "let me beseech you to bury those fruitless animosities which have already cost enough of blood and treasure; and let us quit these walls with one common determination to evince our courage and display our chivalry only against our universal foes;—those ruffians who lay waste our fields, and infest our public ways,—the foes alike of the people we should protect, and the God whom we should serve!"

The Bishop resumed his seat; the nobles looked at each other without reply; the people began to whisper loudly among themselves; when, after a short pause, Adrian di Castello rose.

"Pardon me, my Lords, and you, reverend Father, if I, inexperienced in years and of little mark or dignity amongst you, presume to be the first to embrace the proposal we have just heard. Willingly do I renounce all ancient cause of enmity with any of my compeers. Fortunately for me, my long absence from Rome has swept from my remembrance the feuds and rivalries familiar to my early youth; and in this noble conclave I see but one man (glancing at Martino di Porto, who sat sullenly looking down) against whom I have, at any time, deemed it a duty to draw my sword; the gage that I once cast to that noble is yet, I rejoice to think, unredeemed. I withdraw it. Henceforth my only foes shall be the foes of Rome!"

"Nobly spoken!" said the Bishop, aloud.

"And," continued Adrian, casting down his glove amongst the nobles, "I throw, my Lords, the gage, thus resumed, amongst you all, in challenge to a wider rivalry, and a more noble field. I invite any man to vie with me in the zeal that he shall show to restore tranquillity to our roads, and order to our state. It is a contest in which, if I be vanquised with reluctance, I will yield the prize without envy. In ten days from this time, reverend Father, I will raise forty horsemen-at-arms, ready to obey whatever orders shall be agreed upon for the security of the Roman state. And you, O Romans, dismiss, I pray you, from your minds, those eloquent invectives against your fellow-citizens which ye have lately heard. All of us, of what rank soever, may have shared in the excesses of these unhappy times; let us endeavor, not to avenge nor to imitate, but to reform and to unite. And may the people hereafter find, that the true boast of a partrician is, that his power the better enables him to serve his country."

"Brave words!" quoth the smith, sneeringly.

"If they were all like him!" said the smith's neighbor.

"He has helped the nobles out of a dilemma," said Pandulfo.

"He has shown gray wit under young hairs," said an aged Malatesta.

"You have turned the tide, but not stemmed it, noble Adrian," whispered the ever-boding Montreal, as, amidst the murmurs of the general approbation, the young Colonna resumed his seat.

"How mean you?" said Adrian.

"That your soft words, like all patrician conciliations, have come too late."

Not another noble stirred, though they felt, perhaps, disposed to join in the general feeling of amnesty, and appeared, by signs and whispers, to applaud the speech of Adrian. They were too habituated to the ungracefulness of an unlettered pride, to bow themselves to address conciliating language either to the people or their foes. And Raimond, glancing round, and not willing that their unseemly silence should be long remarked, rose at once, to give it the best construction in his power.

"My son, thou hast spoken as a patriot and a Christian; by the approving silence of your peers we all feel that they share your sentiments. Break we up the meeting—its end is obtained. The manner of our proceeding against the leagued robbers of the road requires maturer consideration elsewhere. This day shall be an epoch in our history."

"It shall," quoth Cecco del Vecchio, gruffly, between his teeth.

"Children, my blessing upon you all!" concluded the Vicar, spreading his arms.

And in a few minutes more the crowd poured from the church. The different servitors and flag-bearers ranged themselves on the steps without, each train anxious for their master's precedence; and the nobles, gravely collecting in small knots, in the which was no mixture of rival blood, followed the crowd down the aisles. Soon rose again the din, and the noise, and the wrangling, and the oaths, of the hostile bands, as, with pain and labor, the Vicar's officers marshalled them in "order most disorderly."

But so true were Montreal's words to Adrian, that the populace already half forgot the young noble's generous appeal, and were only bitterly commenting on the ungracious silence of his brother Lords. What, too, to them was this crusade against the robbers of the road? They blamed the good Bishop for not saying boldly to the nobles—"*Ye* are the first robbers we must march against!" The popular discontents had gone far beyond palliatives; they had arrived at that point when the people longed less for reform that change. There are times when a revolution cannot be warded off; it must come—come alike by resistance or by concession. Wo to that race in which a revolution produces no fruits!—in which the thunderbolt smites the high place, but does not purify the air! To suffer in vain is often the lot of the noblest individuals; but when a People suffer in vain, let them curse themselves!

CHAPTER IV.

The Ambitious Citizen, and the Ambitious Soldier.

THE Bishop of Orvieto lingered last, to confer with Rienzi, who awaited him in the recesses of the Lateran. Raimond had the penetration not to be seduced into believing that the late scene could effect any reformation amongst the nobles, heal their divisions, or lead them actively against the infestors of the Campagna. But as he detailed to Rienzi all that had occurred subsequent to the departure of that hero of the scene, he concluded with saying:—

"You will perceive from this, one good result will be produced: the first armed dissension—the first fray among the nobles—will seem like a breach of promise; and, to the people and to the Pope, a reasonable excuse for despairing of all amendment amongst the Barons,—an excuse which will sanction the efforts of the first, and the approval of the last."

"For such a fray we shall not long wait," answered Rienzi.

"I believe the prophecy," answered Raimond, smiling; "at present all runs well. Go you with us homeward?"

"Nay, I think it better to tarry here till the crowd is entirely dispersed; for if they were to see me, in their present excitement, they might insist on some rash and hasty enterprise. Besides, my Lord," added Rienzi, "with an ignorant people, however honest and enthusiastic, this rule must be rigidly observed—stale not your presence by custom. Never may men like me, who have no external rank, appear amongst the crowd, save on those occasions when the mind is itself a rank."

"That is true, as you have no train," answered Raimond, thinking of his own well-liveried menials. "Adieu, then! we shall meet soon."

"Ay, at Philippi, my Lord. Reverend Father, your blessing!"

It was some time subsequent to this conference that Rienzi quitted the sacred edifice. As he stood on the steps of the church—now silent and deserted—the hour that precedes the brief twilight of the South lent its magic to the view. There he beheld the sweeping arches of the mighty Aqueduct extending far along the scene, and backed by the distant and purpled hills. Before—to the right—rose the gate which took its Roman name from the Cœlian Mount, at whose declivity it yet stands. Beyond—from the height of the steps—he saw the villages scattered through the gray Campagna, whitening in the sloped sun; and in the furthest distance the mountain shadows began to darken over the roofs of the ancient Tusculum, and the second Alban * city, which yet rises, in desolate neglect, above the vanished palaces of Pompey and Domitian.

The Roman stood absorbed and motionless for some moments, gazing on the scene, and inhaling the sweet balm of the mellow air. It was the soft spring-time—the season of flowers, and green leaves, and whispering winds—the pastoral May of Italia's poets: but hushed was the voice of song on the banks of the Tiber—the reeds gave music no more. From the sacred Mount in which Saturn held his home, the Dryad and the Nymph, and Italy's native Sylvan, were gone for ever. Rienzi's original nature—its enthusiasm—its veneration for the past—its love of the beautiful and the great—that very attachment to the graces and pomp which give so florid a character to the harsh realities of life, and which power afterwards too luxuriantly developed; the exuberance of thoughts and fancies, which poured itself from his lips in so brilliant and inexhaustible a flood—all bespoke those intellectual and imaginative biasses, which, in calmer times, might have raised him in literature to a more indisputable eminence than that to which action can ever lead; and something of such consciousness crossed his spirit at that moment.

"Happier had it been for me," thought he, "had I never looked out from my own heart upon the world. I had all within me that makes contentment of the present, because I had that which can make me forget the present. I had the power to re-people—to create: the legends and dreams of old—the divine faculty of verse, in which the beautiful superfluities of the heart can pour themselves—these were mine! Petrarch chose wisely

* The first Alba—the Alba Longa—whose origin Fable ascribes to Ascanius, was destroyed by Tullus Hostilius. The second Alba, or modern Albano, was erected on the plain below the ancient town, a little before the time of Nero.

for himself! To address the world, but from without the world; to persuade—to excite—to command,—for these are the aim and glory of ambition;—but to shun its tumult, and its toil! His the quiet cell which he fills with the shapes of beauty—the solitude, from which he can banish the evil times whereon we are fallen,—but in which he can dream back the great hearts and the glorious epochs of the past. For me—to what cares I am wedded! to what labors I am bound! what instruments I must use! what disguises I must assume! to tricks and artifice I must bow my pride! base are my enemies—uncertain my friends; and verily, in this struggle with blinded and mean men, the soul itself becomes warped and dwarfish. Patient and darkling, the Means creep through caves and the soiling mire, to gain at last the light which is the End."

In these reflections there was a truth, the whole gloom and sadness of which the Roman had not yet experienced. However august be the object we propose to ourselves, every less worthy path we take to insure it distorts the mental sight of our ambition; and the means, by degrees, abase the end to their own standard. This is the true misfortune of a man nobler than his age—that the instruments he must use soil himself: half he reforms his times; but half, too, the times will corrupt the reformer. His own craft undermines his safety;—the people, whom he himself accustoms to a false excitement, perpetually crave it; and when their ruler ceases to seduce their fancy, he falls their victim. The reform he makes by these means is hollow and momentary—it is swept away with himself: it was but the trick—the show—the wasted genius of a conjuror: the curtain falls—the magic is over—the cup and balls are kicked aside. Better one slow step in enlightenment,—which being made by the reason of a whole people, cannot recede,—than these sudden flashes in the depth of the general night, which the darkness, by contrast doubly dark, swallows up everlastingly again!

As, slowly and musingly, Rienzi turned to quit the church, he felt a light touch upon his shoulder.

"Fair evening to you, Sir Scholar," said a frank voice.

"To you, I return the courtesy," answered Rienzi, gazing upon the person who thus suddenly accosted him, and in whose white cross and martial bearing the reader recognizes the Knight of St. John.

"You know me not, I think?" said Montreal; "but that matters little, we may easily commence our acquaintance: for me, indeed, I am fortunate enough to have made myself already acquainted with you."

"Possibly we have met elsewhere, at the house of one of those nobles to whose rank you seem to belong?"

"Belong! no, not exactly!" returned Montreal, proudly. "High-born and great as your magnates deem themselves, I would not, while the mountains can yield one free spot for my footstep, change my place in the world's many grades for theirs. To the brave, there is but one sort of plebeian, and that is the coward. But you, sage Rienzi," continued the Knight, in a gayer tone, "I have seen in more stirring scenes than the hall of a Roman Baron."

Rienzi glanced keenly at Montreal, who met his eye with an open brow.

"Yes!" resumed the Knight—"but let us walk on; suffer me for a few moments to be your companion. Yes! I have listened to you—the other eve, when you addressed the populace, and to-day, when you rebuked the nobles; and at midnight, too, not long since, when (your ear, fair Sir!—lower, it is a secret!)—at midnight, too, when you administered the oath of brotherhood to the bold conspirators, on the ruined Aventine!"

As he concluded, the Knight drew himself aside to watch, upon Rienzi's countenance, the effect which his words might produce.

A slight tremor passed over the frame of the conspirator—for so, unless the conspiracy succeed, would Rienzi be termed, by others than Montreal: he turned abruptly round to confront the Knight, and placed his hand involuntarily on his sword, but presently relinquished the grasp.

"Ha!" said the Roman, slowly, "if this be true, fall Rome! There is treason even among the free!"

"No treason, brave Sir!" answered Montreal; "I possess thy secret—but none have betrayed it to me."

"And is it as friend or foe that thou hast learned it?"

"That as it may be," returned Montreal, carelessly. "Enough at present, that I could send thee to the gibbet, if I said but the word,—to show my power to be thy foe; enough, that I have not done it, to prove my disposition to be thy friend."

"Thou mistakest, stranger! that man does not live who could shed my blood in the streets of Rome! The gibbet! Little dost thou know of the power which surrounds Rienzi."

These words were said with some scorn and bitterness; but, after a moment's pause, Rienzi resumed, more calmly:—

"By the cross on thy mantle, thou belongest to one of the proudest orders of knighthood: thou art a foreigner, and a cavalier. What generous sympathies can convert thee into a friend of the Roman people?"

"Cola di Rienzi," returned Montreal, "the sympathies that unite us are those which unite all men who, by their own efforts, rise above the herd. True, I was born noble—but powerless and poor: at my beck now move, from city to city, the armed instruments of authority: my breath is the law of thousands. This empire I have not inherited; I won it by a cool brain and a fearless arm. Know me for Walter de Montreal; is it not a name that speaks a spirit kindred to thine own? Is not ambition a common sentiment between us? I do not marshal soldiers for gain only, though men have termed me avaricious—nor butcher peasants for the love of blood, though men have called me cruel. Arms and wealth are the sinews of power; it is power that I desire;—thou, bold Rienzi, strugglest thou not for the same? Is it the rank breath of the garlic-chewing mob—is it the whispered envy of schoolmen—is it the hollow mouthing of boys who call thee patriot and freeman, words to trick the ear—that will content thee? These are but *thy* instruments to *power*. Have I spoken truly?"

Whatever distaste Rienzi might conceive at this speech he masked effectually. "Certes," said he, "it would be in vain, renowned Captain, to deny that I seek but that power of which thou speakest. But what union can there be between the ambition of a Roman citizen and the leader of paid armies that take their cause only according to their hire—to-day, fight for liberty in Florence—to-morrow, for tyranny in Bologna? Pardon my frankness; for in this age that is deemed no disgrace which I impute to thy armies. Valor and generalship are held to consecrate any cause they distinguish; and he who is the master of princes, may be well honored by them as their equal."

"We are entering into a less deserted quarter of the town," said the Knight; "is there no secret place—no Aventine—in this direction, where we can confer?"

"Hush!" replied Rienzi, cautiously looking round. "I thank thee, noble Montreal, for the hint; nor may it be well for us to be seen together. Wilt thou deign to follow me to my home, by the Palatine Bridge?* there we can converse undisturbed and secure."

"Be it so," said Montreal, falling back.

With a quick and hurried step, Rienzi passed through the town, in which, wherever he was discovered, the scattered citizens saluted him with marked respect; and, turning through a labyrinth of dark alleys, as if to shun the more public thoroughfares, arrived at length at a broad space near the river. The first stars of night shone down on the ancient temple of Fortuna Virilis, which the chances of Time had already converted into the Church of St. Mary of Egypt; and facing the twice-hallowed edifice stood the house of Rienzi.

"It is a fair omen to have my mansion facing the ancient Temple of Fortune," said Rienzi, smiling, as Montreal followed the Roman into the chamber I have already described.

"Yet Valor need never pray to Fortune," said the Knight; "the first commands the last."

Long was the conference between these two men, the most enterprising of their age. Meanwhile, let me make the reader somewhat better acquainted with the character and designs of Montreal, than the hurry of events has yet permitted him to become.

Walter de Montreal, generally known in the chronicles of Italy by the designation of Fra Moreale, had passed into Italy—a bold adventurer, worthy to become a successor of those roving Normans (from one of the most eminent of whom, by the mother's side, he claimed

* The picturesque ruins shown at this day as having once been the habitation of the celebrated Cola di Rienzi, were long asserted by the antiquarians to have belonged to another Cola or Nicola. I believe, however, that the dispute has been lately decided; and, indeed, no one but an antiquary, and that a Roman one, could suppose that there were two Colas to whom the inscription on the house would apply.

descent) who had formerly played so strange a part in the chivalric errantry of Europe,—realizing the fables of Amadis and Palmerin—(each knight, in himself a host), winning territories and oversetting thrones; acknowledging no laws save those of knighthood; never confounding themselves with the tribe amongst which they settled; incapable of becoming citizens, and scarcely contented with aspiring to be kings. At that time, Italy was the India of all those well-born and penniless adventurers who, like Montreal, had inflamed their imagination by the ballads and legends of the Roberts and the Godfreys of old; who had trained themselves from youth to manage the barb, and bear, through the heats of summer, the weight of arms; and who, passing into an effeminate and distracted land, had only to exhibit bravery in order to command wealth. It was considered no disgrace for some powerful chieftain to collect together a band of these hardy aliens,—to subsist amidst the mountains on booty and pillage,—to make war upon tyrant or republic, as interest suggested, and to sell, at enormous stipends, the immunities of peace. Sometimes they hired themselves to one state to protect it against the other; and the next year beheld them in the field against their former employers. These bands of Northern stipendiaries assumed, therefore, a civil, as well as a military, importance; they were as indispensable to the safety of one state as they were destructive to the security of all. But five years before the present date, the Florentine Republic had hired the services of a celebrated leader of these foreign soldiers,—Gualtier, duke of Athens.

By acclamation, the people themselves had elected that warrior to the state of prince, or tyrant, of their state; before the year was completed, they revolted against his cruelties, or rather against his exactions,—for, despite all the boasts of their historians, they felt an attack on their purses more deeply than an assault on their liberties,—they had chased him from their city, and once more proclaimed themselves a Republic. The bravest, and most favored of the soldiers of the Duke of Athens had been Walter de Montreal; he had shared the rise and the downfall of his chief. Amongst popular commotions, the acute and observant mind of the Knight of St. John had learned no mean civil experience; he had learned to sound a people—to know how far they would endure—to construe the signs of revolution—to be a reader of the times. After the downfall of the Duke of Athens, as a Free Companion, in other words a Freebooter, Montreal had augmented under the fierce Werner his riches and his renown. At present without employment worthy his spirit of enterprise and intrigue, the disordered and chiefless state of Rome had attracted him thither. In the league he had proposed to Colonna—in the suggestions he had made to the vanity of that Signor—his own object was to render his services indispensable—to constitute himself the head of the soldiery whom his proposed designs would render necessary to the ambition of the Colonna, could it be excited—and, in the vastness of his hardy genius for enterprise, he probably foresaw that the command of such a force would be, in reality, the command of Rome;—a counter-revolution might easily unseat the Colonna and elect himself to the principality.

It had sometimes been the custom of Roman,-as of other Italian, States, to prefer for a chief magistrate, under the title of *Podesta*, a foreigner to a native. And Montreal hoped that he might possibly become to Rome what the Duke of Athens had been to Florence—an ambition he knew well enough to be above the gentleman of Provençe, but not above the leader of an army. But, as we have already seen, his sagacity perceived at once that he could not move the aged head of the patricians to those hardy and perilous measures which were necessary to the attainment of supreme power. Contented with his present station, and taught moderation by his age and his past reverses, Stephen Colonna was not the man to risk a scaffold from the hope to gain a throne. The contempt which the old patrician professed for the people, and their idol, also taught the deep-feeling Montreal that, if the Colonna possessed not the ambition, neither did he possess the policy, requisite for empire. The Knight found his caution against Rienzi in vain, and he turned to Rienzi himself. Little cared the Knight of St. John which party were uppermost—prince or people—so that his own objects were attained; in fact, he had studied the humors of a people, not in order to serve, but to rule them; and, believing all men actuated by a similar ambition, he imagined that, whether a demagogue or a patrician reigned, the people were equally to be victims, and that the cry of "Order" on the one hand, or of "Liberty" on the other, was but the mere pretext by which the energy of one man sought to justify his ambition over the herd. Deeming himself one of the most honorable spirits of his age, he believed in no honor which *he* was unable to feel; and, sceptic in virtue, was therefore credulous of vice.

But the boldness of his own nature inclined him, perhaps, rather to the adventurous Rienzi than to the self-complacent Colonna; and he considered that to the safety of the first he and his armed minions might be even more necessary than to that of the last. At present his main object was to learn from Rienzi the exact strength which he possesssed, and how far he was prepared for any actual revolt.

The acute Roman took care, on the one hand, how he betrayed to the Knight more than he yet knew, or he disgusted him by apparent reserve on the other. Crafty as Montreal was, he possessed not that wonderful art of mastering others which was so pre-eminently the gift of the eloquent and profound Rienzi, and the difference between the grades of their intellect was visible in their present conference.

"I see," said Rienzi, "that amidst all the events which have lately smiled upon my ambition, none is so favorable as that which assures me of your countenance and friendship. In truth, I require some armed alliance. Would you believe it, our friends, so bold in private meetings, yet shrink from a public explosion. They fear not the partricians, but the soldiery of the partricians; for it is the remarkable feature in the Italian courage, that they have no terror for each other, but the casque and sword of a foreign hireling make them quail like deer."

"They will welcome gladly, then, the assurance that such hirelings shall be in their service—not against them; and as many as you desire for the revolution, so many shall you receive."

"But the pay and the conditions," said Rienzi, with his dry, sarcastic smile. "How shall we arrange the first, and what shall we hold to be the second?"

"That is an affair easily concluded," replied Montreal. "For me, to tell you frankly, the glory and excitement of so great a revulsion would alone suffice. I like to fell myself necessary to the completion of high events. For my men it is otherwise. Your first act will be to seize the revenues of the state. Well, whatever they amount to, the product of the first year, great or small, shall be divided amongst us. You the one half, I and my men the other half."

"It is much," said Rienzi, gravely, and as if in calculation,—"but Rome cannot purchase her liberties too dearly. So be it then decided."

"Amen!—and now, then, what is your force? for these eighty or a hundred signors of the Aventine,—worthy men, doubtless,—scarce suffice for a revolt!"

Gazing cautiously round the room, the Roman placed his hand on Montreal's arm—

"Between you and me, it requires time to cement it. We shall be unable to stir these five weeks. I have too rashly anticipated the period. The corn is indeed cut, but I must now, by private adjuration and address, bind up the scattered sheaves."

"Five weeks," repeated Montreal; "that is far longer than I anticipated."

"What I desire," continued Rienzi, fixing his searching eyes upon Montreal, "is, that, in the meanwhile, we should preserve a profound calm,—we should remove every suspicion. I shall bury myself in my studies, and convoke no more meetings."

"Well—"

"And for yourself, noble Knight, might I venture to dictate, I would pray you to mix with the nobles—to profess for me and for the people the profoundest contempt—and to contribute to rock them yet more in the cradle of their false security. Meanwhile, you could quietly withdraw as many of the armed mercenaries as you influence from Rome, and leave the nobles without their only defenders Collecting these hardy warriors in the recesses of the mountains, a day's march from hence, we may be able to summon them at need, and they shall appear at our gates, and in the midst of our rising—hailed as deliverers by the nobles, but in reality allies with the people. In the confusion and despair of our enemies at discovering their mistake, they will fly from the city."

"And its revenues and its empire will become the appanage of the hardy soldier and the intriguing demagogue!" cried Montreal, with a laugh.

"Sir Knight, the division shall be equal."

"Agreed!"

"And now, noble Montreal, a flask of our best vintage!" said Rienzi, changing his tone.

"You know the Provençals," answered Montreal, gaily.

The wine was brought, the conversation became free and familiar, and Montreal, whose craft was acquired, and whose frankness was natural, unwittingly committed his secret projects and ambition more nakedly to Rienzi than he had designed to do. They parted apparently the best of friends.

"By the way," said Rienzi, as they drained the last goblet, "Stephen Colonna betakes him to Corneto, with a convoy of corn, on the 19th. Will it not be as well if you join him? You can take that opportunity to whisper discontent to the mercenaries that accompany him on his mission, and induce them to our plan."

"I thought of that before," returned Montreal; "it shall be done. For the present, farewell!"

"'His barb, and his sword,
And his lady, the peerless,
Are all that are prized
By Orlando the fearless.

"'Success to the Norman,
The darling of story;
His glory is pleasure—
His pleasure is glory.'"

Chanting this rude ditty as he resumed his mantle, the Knight waved his hand to Rienzi, and departed.

Rienzi watched the receding form of his guest with an expression of hate and fear upon his countenance. "Give that man the power," he muttered, "and he may be a second Totila.* Methinks I see, in his griping and ferocious nature,—through all the gloss of its gaiety and knightly grace,—the very personification of our old Gothic foes. I trust I have lulled him! Verily, two suns could no more blaze in one hemisphere, than Walter de Montreal and Cola di Rienzi live in the same city. The star-seers tell us that we feel a secret and uncontrollable antipathy to those whose astral influences destine them to work us evil; such antipathy do I feel for yon fair-faced homicide. Cross not my path, Montreal!—cross not my path!"

With this soliloquy Rienzi turned within, and, retiring to his apartment, was seen no more that night.

* Innocent VI., some years afterwards, proclaimed Montreal to be *worse* than Totila.

CHAPTER V.

The procession of the Barons.—The beginning of the end.

It was the morning of the 19th of May, the air was brisk and clear, and the sun, which had just risen, shone cheerily upon the glittering casques and spears of a gallant procession of armed horsemen, sweeping through the long and principal street of Rome. The neighing of the horses, the ringing of the hoofs, the dazzle of the armor, and the tossing to and fro of the standards, adorned with the proud insignia of the Colonna, presented one of the gay and brilliant spectacles peculiar to the middle ages.

At the head of the troop, on a stout palfrey, rode Stephen Colonna. At his right was the Knight of Provençe, curbing, with an easy hand, a slight, but fiery steed of the Arab race: behind him followed two squires, the one leading his war-horse, the other bearing his lance and helmet. At the left of Stephen Colonna rode Adrian, grave and silent, and replying only by monosyllables to the gay bavardage of the Knight of Provençe. A considerable number of the flower of the Roman nobles followed the old Baron; and the train was closed by a serried troop of foreign horsemen, completely armed.

There was no crowd in the street,—the citizens looked with seeming apathy at the procession from their half-closed shops.

"Have these Romans no passion for shows?" asked Montreal; "if they could be more easily amused they would be more easily governed."

"Oh, Rienzi, and such buffoons, amuse them. We do better,—we terrify!" replied Stephen.

"What sings the troubadour, Lord Adrian?" said Montreal.

"'Smiles, false smiles, should form the school
For those who rise, and those who rule:
The brave they trick, the fair subdue,
Kings deceive, and States undo.
Smiles, false smiles!

"'Frowns, true frowns, ourselves betray,
The brave arouse, the fair dismay,
Sting the pride, which blood must heal,
Mix the bowl, and point the steel.
Frowns, true frowns!"

"The lay is of France, Signor; yet methinks it brings its wisdom from Italy;—for the serpent smile is your countrymen's proper distinction, and the frown ill becomes them."

"Sir Knight," replied Adrian, sharply, and incensed at the taunt, "you foreigners have taught us how to frown:—a virtue sometimes."

"But not wisdom, unless the hand could maintain what the brow menaced," returned Montreal, with haughtiness; for he had much of the Franc vivacity which often overcame his prudence; and he had conceived a secret pique against Adrian since their interview at Stephen's palace.

"Sir Knight," answered Adrian, coloring, "our conversation may lead to warmer words than I would desire to have with one who has rendered me so gallant a service."

"Nay, then, let us go back to the troubadours," said Montreal, indifferently. "Forgive me if I do not think highly, in general, of Italian honor, or Italian valro; *your* valor I acknowledge, for I have witnessed it, and valor and honor go together,—let that suffice!"

As Adrian was about to answer, his eye fell suddenly on the burly form of Cecco del Vecchio, who was leaning his bare and brawny arms over his anvil, and gazing, with a smile, upon the group. There was something in that smile which turned the current of Adrian's thoughts, and which he could not contemplate without an unaccountable misgiving.

"A strong villain, that," said Montreal, also eyeing the smith. "I should like to enlist him. Fellow!" cried he, aloud, "you have an arm that were as fit to wield the sword as to fashion it. Desert your anvil, and follow the fortunes of Fra Moreale!"

The smith nodded his head. "Signor Cavalier," said he, gravely, "we poor men have no passion for war; we want not to kill others—we desire only ourselves to live,—if you will let us!"

"By the Holy Mother, a slavish answer! But you Romans——"

"*Are* slaves!" interrupted the smith, turning away to the interior of his forge.

"The dog is mutinous!" said the old Colonna. And as the band swept on, the rude foreigners, encouraged by their leaders, had each some taunt or jest, uttered in a barbarous attempt at the southern *patois*, for the lazy giant, as he again appeared in front of his forge, leaning on his anvil as before, and betraying no sign of attention to his insultors, save by a heightened glow of his swarthy visage;—and so the gallant procession passed through the streets, and quitted the Eternal City.

There was a long interval of deep silence—of general calm — throughout the whole of Rome: the shops were still but half-opened; no man betook himself to his business; it was like the commencement of some holyday, when indolence precedes enjoyment.

About noon, a few small knots of men might be seen scattered about the streets, whispering to each other, but soon dispersing; and every now and then, a single passenger, generally habited in the long robes used by the men of letters, or in the more sombre garb of monks, passed hurriedly up the street towards the Church of St. Mary of Egypt, once the Temple of Fortune. Then, again, all was solitary and deserted. Suddenly, there was heard *the sound of a single trumpet!* It swelled—it gathered on the ear. Cecco del Vecchio looked up from his anvil! *A solitary horseman* paced slowly by the forge, and wound a long loud blast of the trumpet suspended round his neck, as he passed through the middle of the street. Then might you see a crowd, suddenly, and as by magic, appear emerging from every corner; the street became thronged with multitudes; but it was only by the tramp of their feet, and an indistinct and low murmur, that they broke the silence. Again the horseman wound his trump, and when the note ceased, he cried aloud—"Friends and Romans! to-morrow, at dawn of day, let each man find himself unarmed before the Church of St. Angelo. Cola di Rienzi convenes the Romans to provide for the good state of Rome." A shout, that seemed to shake the bases of the seven hills, broke forth at the end of this brief exhortation; the horseman rode slowly on, and the crowd followed.—This was the commencement of the Revolution!

CHAPTER VI.

The Conspirator becomes the Magistrate.

AT midnight, when the rest of the city seemed hushed in rest, lights were streaming from the windows of the Church of St. Angelo. Breaking from its echoing aisles, the long and solemn notes of sacred music stole at frequent intervals upon the air. Rienzi was praying within the church; thirty masses consumed the hours from night till morn, and all the sanction of religion was invoked to consecrate the enterpise of liberty.* The sun had long risen, and the crowd had long been assembled before the church door, and in vast streams along every street that led to it,—when the bell of the church tolled out long and merrily; and as it ceased, the voices of the choristers within chanted the following hymn, in which were somewhat strikingly, though barbarously, blended, the spirit of the classic patriotism with the fervor of religious zeal:—

THE ROMAN HYMN OF LIBERTY.

Let the mountains exult around! †
On her seven-hill'd throne renown'd,
Once more old Rome is crown'd!
Jubilate!

Sing out, O Vale and Wave!
Look up from each laurell'd grave,
Bright dust of the deathless brave!
Jubilate!

Pale Vision, what art thou?—Lo,
From Time's dark deeps,
Like a Wind, It sweeps,
Like a wind, when the tempests blow!

A shadowy form—as a giant ghost—
It stands in the midst of the armed host!
The dead man's shroud on Its awful limbs;
And the gloom of Its presence the day-light dims:
And the trembling world looks on aghast—
All hail to the SOUL OF THE MIGHTY PAST!
Hail! all hail!

As we speak—as we hallow—It moves, It breathes;
From its clouded crest bud the laurel wreaths—
As a Sun that leaps up from the arms of Night,
The shadow takes shape, and the gloom takes light.
Hail! all hail!

The SOUL OF THE PAST, again,
To its ancient home,
In the hearts of Rome,
Hath come to resume its reign!

O Fame, with a prophet's voice,
Bid the ends of the Earth rejoice!
Wherever the Proud are Strong,
And Right is oppress'd by Wrong;—
Wherever the day dim shines
Through the cell where the captive pines;—
Go forth with a trumpet's sound!
And tell to the Nations round—
On the Hills which the Heroes trod—
In the shrines of the Saints of God—
In the Cæsars' hall, and the Martyrs' prison—
That the slumber is broke, and the Sleeper arisen!
That the reign of the Goth and the Vandal is o'er:
And Earth feels the tread of THE ROMAN once more!

As the hymn ended, the gate of the church opened; the crowd gave way on either side, and, preceded by three of the young nobles of the inferior order, bearing standards of allegorical design, depicting the triumph of Liberty, Justice, and Concord, forth issued Rienzi, clad in complete armor, the hemlet alone excepted. His face was pale with watching and intense excitement—but stern, grave, and solemnly composed; and its expressicn so repelled any vociferous and vulgar burst of feeling, that those who beheld it hushed the shout on their lips, and stilled, by a simultaneous cry of reproof, the gratulations of the crowd behind. Side by side with Rienzi moved Raimond, Bishop of Orvietto: and behind, marching two by two, followed a hundred men-at-arms. In complete silence the procession began its way, until, as it approached the Capitol, the awe of the crowd gradually vanished, and thousands upon thousands of voices rent the air with shouts of exultation and joy.

Arrived at the foot of the great staircase, which then made the principal ascent to the square of the Capitol, the procession halted; and as the crowd filled up that vast space in front—adorned and hallowed by many of the most majestic columns of the temples of old—

---

* In fact, I apprehend that if ever the life of Cola di Rienzi shall be written by a hand worthy of the task, it will be shown that a strong religious feeling was blended with the political enthusiasm of the people,—the religious feeling of a premature and crude reformation, the legacy of Arnold of Brescia. It was not, however, one excited against the priests, but favored by them. The principal conventual orders declared for the Revolution.

† "Exultent in circuito Vestro Montes," etc.—Let the mountains exult around! So begins Rienzi's letter to the Senate and Roman people; preserved by Hocsemius.

Rienzi addressed the Populace, whom he had suddenly elevated into a People.

He depicted forcibly the servitude and misery of the citizens—the utter absence of all law—the want even of common security to life and property. He declared that, undaunted by the peril he incurred, he devoted his life to the regeneration of their common country; and he solemnly appealed to the people to assist the enterprise, and at once to sanction and consolidate the Revolution by an established code of law and a Constitutional Assembly. He then ordered the chart and outline of the Constitution he proposed, to be read by the Herald to the multitude.

It created,—or rather revived, with new privileges and powers,—a Representative Assembly of Councillors. It proclaimed, as its first law, one that seems simple enough to our happier times, but never hitherto executed at Rome: Every wilful homicide, of whatever rank, was to be punished by death. It enacted, that no private noble or citizen should be suffered to maintain fortifications and garrisons in the city or the country; that the gates and bridges of the State should be under the control of whomsoever should be elected Chief Magistrate. It forbade all harbor of brigands, mercenaries, and robbers, on payment of a thousand marks of silver; and it made the Barons who possessed the neighboring territories responsible for the safety of the roads, and the transport of merchandise. It took under the protection of the State the widow and the orphan. It appointed, in each of the quarters of the city, an armed militia, whom the tolling of the bell of the Capitol, at any hour, was to assemble to the protection of the State. It ordained, that in each harbor of the coast, a vessel should be stationed, for the safeguard of commerce. It decreed the sum of one hundred florins to the heirs of every man who died in the defence of Rome; and it devoted the public revenues to the service and protection of the State.

Such, moderate at once and effectual, was the outline of the New Constitution; and it may amuse the reader to consider how great must have been the previous disorders of the city, when the common and elementary provisions of civilization and security made the character of the code proposed, and the limit of a popular revolution.

The most rapturous shouts followed this sketch of the New Constitution: and, amidst the clamor, up rose the huge form of Cecco del Vecchio. Despite his condition, he was a man of great importance at the present crisis: his zeal and his courage, and, perhaps, still more, his brute passion and stubborn prejudice, had made him popular. The lower order of mechanics looked to him as their head and representative; out, then, he spake loud and fearlessly,—speaking well, because his mind was full of what he had to say.

"Countrymen and Citizens!—This New Constitution meets with your approbation—so it ought. But what are good laws, if we do not have good men to execute them? Who can execute a law so well as the man who designs it? If you ask me to give you a notion how to make a good shield, and my notion pleases you, would you ask me, or another smith, to make it for you? If you ask another, he may make a good shield, but it would not be the same as that which I should have made, and the description of which contented you. Cola di Rienzi has proposed a Code of Law that shall be our shield. Who should see that the shield become what he proposes, but Cola di Rienzi? Romans! I suggest that Cola di Rienzi be intrusted by the people with the authority, by whatsoever name he pleases, of carrying the New Constitution into effect;—and whatever be the means, we, the People, will bear him harmless."

"Long life to Rienzi!—long live Cecco del Vecchio! He hath spoken well!—none but the Law-maker shall be the Governor!"

Such were the acclamations which greeted the ambitious heart of the Scholar. The voice of the people invested him with the supreme power. He had created a Commonwealth—to become, if he desired it, a Despot.

CHAPTER VII.

Looking after the Halter when the Mare is stolen.

WHILE such were the events at Rome, a servitor of Stephen Colonna was already on his way to Corneto. The astonishment with which the old Baron received the intelligence may be easily imagined. He lost not a moment in convening his troop; and, while in all the bustle of departure, the Knight of St. John abruptly entered his presence. His mien had lost its usual frank composure.

"How is this?" said he, hastily; "a revolt?—Rienzi sovereign of Rome?—can the news be believed?"

"It is too true!" said Colonna, with a bitter smile. "Where shall we hang him on our return?"

"Talk not so wildly, Sir Baron," replied Montreal, discourteously; "Rienzi is stronger than you think for. I know what men are, and you only know what noblemen are! Where is your kinsman, Adrian?"

"Hs is here, noble Montreal," said Stephen, shrugging his shoulders, with a half-disdainful smile at the rebuke, which he thought it more prudent not to resent; "he is here!—see him enter!"

"You have heard the news?" exclaimed Montreal.

"I have."

"And despise the revolution?"

"I fear it!"

"Then you have some sense in you. But this is none of my affair: I will not interrupt your consultations. Adieu for the present!" and, ere Stephen could prevent him, the Knight had quitted the chamber.

"What means this demagogue?" Montreal muttered to himself. "Would he trick me?—has he got rid of my presence in order to monopolize all the profit of the enterprise? I fear me so!—the cunning Roman! We northern warriors could never compete with the intellect of these Italians but for their cowardice. But what shall be done? I have already bid Rodolf communicate with the brigands, and they are on the eve of departure from their present lord. Well! let it be so! Better that I should first break the power of the Barons, and then make my own terms, sword in hand, with the plebeian. And if I fail in this,—sweet Adeline! I shall see thee again!—that is some comfort!—and Louis of Hungary will bid high for the arm and brain of Walter de Montreal. What, ho! Rodolf!" he exclaimed aloud, as the sturdy form of the trooper, half-armed and half-intoxicated, reeled along the court-yard. "Knave! art thou drunk at this hour?"

"Drunk or sober," answered Rodolf, bending low, "I am at thy bidding."

"Well said!—are thy friends ripe for the saddle?"

"Eighty of them already tired of idleness and the dull air of Rome, will fly wherever Sir Walter de Montreal wishes."

"Hasten, then,—bid them mount; we go not hence with the Colonna—we leave while they are yet talking! Bid my squires attend me!"

And when Stephen Colonna was settling himself on his palfrey, he heard, for the first time, that the Knight of Provence, Rodolf the trooper, and eighty of the stipendiaries, had already departed,—whither, none knew.

"To precede us to Rome! gallant barbarian!" said Colonna. "Sirs, on!"

CHAPTER VIII.

The Attack—The Retreat—The Election—And the Adhesion.

ARRIVING at Rome, the company of the Colonna found the gates barred, and the walls manned. Stephen bade advance his trumpeters, with one of his captains, imperiously to demand admittance.

"We have orders," replied the chief of the town-guard, "to admit none who bear arms, flags, or trumpets. Let the Lords Colonna dismiss their train, and they are welcome."

"Whose are these insolent mandates?" asked the captain.

"Those of the Lord Bishop of Orvietto and Cola di Rienzi, joint protectors of the Buono Stato." *

The captain of the Colonna returned to his chief with these tidings. The rage of Stephen was indescribable. "Go back," he cried, as soon as he could summon voice, "and say, that, if the gates are not forthwith opened to me and mine, the blood of the plebeians be on their own head. As for Raimond, Vicars of the Pope have high spiritual authority, none temporal. Let him prescribe a fast, and he shall be obeyed; but, for the rash Rienzi, say that Stephen Colonna will seek him in the Capital to-morrow, for the purpose of throwing him out of the highest window."

These messages the envoy failed not to deliver.

* Good Estate.

The captain of the Romans was equally stern in his reply.

"Declare to your Lord," said he, "that Rome holds him and his as rebels and traitors; and that the moment you regain your troop, our archers receive our command to draw their bows—in the name of the Pope, the City, and the Liberator."

This threat was executed to the letter; and ere the old Baron had time to draw up his men in the best array, the gates were thrown open, and a well-armed, if undisciplined, multitude poured forth, with fierce shouts, clashing their arms, and advancing the azure banners of the Roman State. So desperate their charge, and so great their numbers, that the Barons, after a short and tumultuous conflict, were driven back, and chased by their pursuers for more than a mile from the walls of the city.

As soon as the Barons recovered their disorder and dismay, a hasty council was held, at which various and contradictory opinions were loudly urged. Some were for departing on the instant to Palestrina, which belonged to the Colonna, and possessed an almost inaccessible fortress. Others were for dispersing, and entering peaceably, and in detached parties, through the other gates. Stephen Colonna—himself incensed and disturbed from his usual self-command—was unable to preserve his authority; Luca di Savelli,* a timid, though treacherous and subtle man, already turned his horse's head, and summoned his men to follow him to his castle in Romagna, when the old Colonna bethought himself of a method by which to keep his band from a disunion that he had the sense to perceive would prove fatal to the common cause. He proposed that they should at once repair to Palestrina, and there fortify themselves; while one of the chiefs should be selected to enter Rome alone, and apparently submissive, to examine the strength of Rienzi; and with the discretionary power to resist if possible,—or to make the best terms he could for the admission of the rest.

"And who," asked Savelli, sneeringly, "will undertake this dangerous mission? Who, unarmed and alone, will expose himself to the rage of the fiercest populace of Italy, and the caprice of a demagogue in the first flush of his power?"

The Barons and the Captains looked at each other in silence. Savelli laughed.

Hitherto Adrian had taken no part in the conference, and but little in the previous contest. He now came to the support of his kinsman.

"Signors!" said he, "I will undertake this mission,—but on mine own account, independently of yours;—free to act as I may think best, for the dignity of a Roman noble, and the interests of a Roman citizen; free to raise my standard on mine own tower, or to yield fealty to the new estate."

"Well said!" cried the old Colonna, hastily. "Heaven forbid we should enter Rome as foes, if to enter it as friends be yet allowed us! What say ye, gentles?"

"A more worthy choice could not be selected," said Savelli; "but I should scarce deem it possible that a Colonna could think there was an option between resistance and fealty to this upstart revolution."

"Of that, Signor, I will judge for myself; if you demand an agent for yourselves, choose another. I announce to ye frankly, that I have seen enough of other states to think the recent condition of Rome demanded some redress. Whether Rienzi and Raimond be worthy of the task they have assumed, I know not."

Savelli was silent. The old Colonna seized the word.

"To Palestrina, then!—are ye all agreed on this? At the worst, or at the best, we should not be divided! On this condition alone I hazard the safety of my kinsman!"

The Barons murmured a little among themselves;—the expediency of Stephen's proposition was evident, and they at length assented to it.

Adrian saw them depart, and then, attended only by his 'squire, slowly rode towards a more distant entrance into the city. On arriving at the gates, his name was demanded—he gave it freely.

"Enter, my Lord," said the warder, "our orders were to admit all that came unarmed and unattended. But to the Lord Adrian di Castello, alone, we had a special injunction to give the honors due to a citizen and a friend."

* The more correct orthography were Luca di Savello, but the one in the text is preserved as more familiar to the English reader.

Adrian, a little touched by this implied recollection of friendship, now rode through a long line of armed citizens, who saluted him respectfully as he passed, and, as he returned the salutation with courtesy, a loud and approving shout followed his horse's steps.

So, save by one attendant, alone, and in peace, the young patrician proceeded leisurely through the long streets, empty and deserted,—for nearly one half of the inhabitants were assembled at the walls, and nearly the other half were engaged in a more peaceful duty,—until, penetrating the interior, the wide and elevated space of the Capitol broke upon his sight. The sun was slowly setting over an immense multitude that overspread the spot, and high above a scaffold raised in the centre, shone, to the western ray, the great Gonfalon of Rome, studded with silver stars.

Adrian reined in his steed. "This," thought he, "is scarcely the hour thus publicly to confer with Rienzi; yet fain would I, mingled with the crowd, judge how far his power is supported, and in what manner it is borne." Musing a little, he withdrew into one of the obscurer streets, then wholly deserted, surrendered his horse to his 'squire, and, borrowing of the latter his morion and long mantle, passed to one of the more private entrances of the Capitol, and, enveloped in his cloak, stood—one of the crowd—intent upon all that followed.

"And what," he asked of a plainly dressed citizen, "is the cause of this assembly?"

"Heard you not the proclamation?" returned the other in some surprise. "Do you not know that the Council of the City and the Guilds of the Artisans have passed a vote to proffer to Rienzi the title of king of Rome?"

The Knight of the Emperor, to whom belonged that august dignity, drew back in dismay.

"And," resumed the citizen, "this assembly of all the lesser Barons, Councillors, and Artificers, is convened to hear the answer."

"Of course it will be assent?"

"I know not—there are strange rumors; hitherto the Liberator has concealed his sentiments."

At that instant a loud flourish of martial music announced the approach of Rienzi. The crowd tumultuously divided, and presently, from the Palace of the Capitol to the scaffold passed Rienzi, still in complete armor, save the helmet, and with him, in all the pomp of his episcopal robes, Raimond of Orvietto.

As soon as Rienzi had ascended the platform, and was thus made visible to the whole concourse, no words can suffice to paint the enthusiasm of the scene—the shouts, the gestures, the tears, the sobs, the wild laughter, in which the sympathy of those lively and susceptible children of the South broke forth. The windows and balconies of the Palace were thronged with the wives and daughters of the lesser Barons and more opulent citizens; and Adrian, with a slight start, beheld amongst them,—pale — agitated—tearful, — the lovely face of his Irene—a face that even thus would have out-shone all present, but for one by her side, whose beauty the emotion of the hour only served to embellish. The dark, large, and flashing eyes of Nina di Raselli, just bedewed, were fixed proudly on the hero of her choice: and pride, even more than joy, gave a richer carnation to her cheek, and the presence of a queen to her noble and rounded form. The setting sun poured its full glory over the spot; the bared heads—the animated faces of the crowd—the gray and vast mass of the Capitol; and, not far from the side of Rienzi, it brought into a strange and startling light the sculptured form of a colossal Lion of Basalt,* which gave its name to a staircase leading to the Capitol. It was an old Egyptian relic,—vast, worn, and grim; some symbol of a vanished creed, to whose face the sculptor had imparted something of the aspect of the human countenance. And this producing the effect probably sought, gave at all times a mystic, preternatural, and fearful expression to the stern features, and to that solemn and hushed repose, which is so peculiarly the secret of Egyptian sculpture. The awe which this colossal and frowning image was calculated to convey, was felt yet more deeply by the vulgar, because "the Staircase of the Lion" was the wonted place of the state executions, as of the state ceremonies. And

* The existent Capitol is very different from the building at the time of Rienzi; and the reader must not suppose that the present staircase, designed by Michael Angelo, at the base of which are two marble lions, removed by Pius IV. from the Church of St. Stephen del Cacco, was the staircase of the Lion of Basalt, which bears so stern a connection with the history of Rienzi. That mute witness of dark deeds is no more.

seldom did the stoutest citizen forget to cross himself, or feel unchilled with a certain terror, whenever, passing by the place, he caught, suddenly fixed upon him, the stony gaze and ominous grin of that old monster from the cities of the Nile.

It was some minutes before the feelings of the assembly allowed Rienzi to be heard. But when, at length, the last shout closed with a simultaneous cry of "Long live Rienzi! Deliverer and King of Rome!" he raised his hand impatiently, and the curiosity of the crowd procured a sudden silence.

"Deliverer of Rome, my countrymen!" said he. "Yes! change not that title—I am too ambitious to be a King! Preserve your obedience to your Pontiff—your allegiance to your Emperor—but be faithful to your own liberties. Ye have a right to your ancient constitution; but that constitution needed not a king. Emulous of the name of Brutus, I am above the titles of a Tarquin! Romans, awake! awake! be inspired with a nobler love of liberty than that which, if it dethrones the tyrant of to-day, would madly risk the danger of tyranny for to-morrow! Rome wants still a liberator—never an usurper!—Take away yon bauble!"

There was a pause; the crowd were deeply affected—but they uttered no shouts; they looked anxiously for a reply from their councillors, or popular leaders.

"Signor," said Pandulfo di Guido, who was one of the Caporioni, "your answer is worthy of your fame. But, in order to enforce the law, Rome must endow you with a legal title—if not that of King, deign to accept that of Dictator or of Consul."

"Long live the Consul Rienzi!" cried several voices.

Rienzi waved his hand for silence.

"Pandulfo di Guido! and you, honored Councillors of Rome! such title is at once too august for my merits, and too inapplicable to my functions. I am one of the people—the people are my charge; the nobles can protect themselves. Dictator and Consul are the appellations of patricians. No," he continued after a short pause, "if ye deem it necessary, for the preservation of order, that your fellow-citizen should be intrusted with a formal title and a recognized power, be it so; but let it be such as may attest the nature of our new institutions, the wisdom of the people, and the moderation of their leaders. Once, my countrymen, the people elected, for the protectors of their rights and the guardians of their freedom, certain officers responsible to the people,—chosen from the people,—provident *for* the people. Their power was great, but it was delegated: a dignity, but a trust. The name of these officers was that of Tribune. Such is the title that conceded, not by clamor alone, but in the full Parliament of the people, and accompanied *by* such Parliament, ruling *with* such Parliament,—such is the title I will gratefully accept." *

The speech, the sentiments of Rienzi were rendered far more impressive by a manner of earnest and deep sincerity; and some of the Romans, despite their corruption, felt a momentary exultation iu the forbearance of their chief. "Long live the Tribune of Rome!" was shouted, but less loud than the cry of "Live the King!" And the vulgar almost thought the revolution was incomplete, because the loftier title was not assumed. To a degenerate and embruted people, liberty seems too plain a thing, if unadorned by the pomp of the very despotism they would dethrone. Revenge is their desire, rather than Release; and the greater the new power they create, the greater seems their revenge against the old. Still all that was most respected, intelligent, and powerful amongst the assembly, were delighted at a temperance which they foresaw would free Rome from a thousand dangers, whether from the Emperor or the Pontiff. And their delight was yet increased, when Rienzi added, so soon as returning silence permitted—"And since we have been equal laborers in the same cause, whatever honors be awarded to me, should be extended also to the Vicar of the Pope, Raimond, Lord Bishop of Orvietto. Remember, that both Church and State are properly the rulers of the people, only because their benefactors.—Long live the

* Gibbon and Sismondi alike (neither of whom appears to have consulted with much attention the original documents preserved by Hocsemius), say nothing of the Representative Parliament, which it was almost Rienzi's first public act to institute or model. Six days from the memorable 19th of May, he addressed the people of Viterbo in a letter yet extant. He summons them to elect and send two syndics, or ambassadors, to the general Parliament.

first Vicar of a Pope that was ever also the Liberator of a State!"

Whether or not Rienzi was only actuated by patriotism in his moderation, certain it is, that his sagacity was at least equal to his virtue; and perhaps nothing could have cemented the revolution more strongly, than thus obtaining for a colleague the Vicar, and Representative of the Pontifical power: it borrowed, for the time, the sanction of the Pope himself—thus made to share the responsibility of the revolution, without monopolizing the power of the State.

While the crowd hailed the proposition of Rienzi; while their shouts yet filled the air; while Raimond, somewhat taken by surprise, sought by signs and gestures to convey at once his gratitude and his humility, the Tribune-Elect, casting his eyes around, perceived many hitherto attracted by curiosity, and whom, from their rank and weight, it was desirable to secure in the first heat of the public enthusiasm. Accordingly, as soon as Raimond had uttered a short and pompous harangue,—in which his eager acceptance of the honor proposed him was ludicrously contrasted by his embarrassed desire not to involve himself or the Pope in any untoward consequences that might ensue,—Rienzi motioned to two heralds that stood behind upon the platform, and one of these advancing, proclaimed—"That as it was desirable that all hitherto neuter should now profess themselves friends or foes, so they were invited to take at once the oath of obedience to the laws, and subscription to the Buono Stato."

So great was the popular fervor, and so much had it been refined and deepened in its tone by the addresses of Rienzi, that even the most indifferent had caught the contagion: and no man liked to be seen shrinking from the rest: so that the most neutral, knowing themselves the most marked, were the most entrapped into allegiance to the Buono Stato. The first who advanced to the platform and took the oath was the Signor di Raselli, the father of Nina.—Others of the lesser nobility followed his example.

The presence of the Pope's Vicar induced the aristocratic; the fear of the people urged the selfish; the encouragement of shouts and gratulations excited the vain. The space between Adrian and Rienzi was made clear. The young noble suddenly felt the eyes of the Tribune were upon him; he felt that those eyes recognized and called upon him—he colored—he breathed short. The noble forbearance of Rienzi had touched him to the heart;—the applause—the pageant—the enthusiasm of the scene, intoxicated—confused him.—He lifted his eyes and saw before him the sister of the Tribune—the lady of his love! His indecision—his pause—continued, when Raimond, observing him, and obedient to a whisper from Rienzi, artfully cried aloud—"Room for the Lord Adrian di Castello! a Colonna! a Colonna!" Retreat was cut off. Mechanically, and as if in a dream, Adrian ascended to the platform; and to complete the triumph of the Tribune, the sun's last ray beheld the flower of the Colonna—the best and bravest of the Barons of Rome—confessing his authority, and subscribing to his laws!

BOOK THIRD.

THE FREEDOM WITHOUT LAW.

"Ben furo avventurosi i cavalieri
Ch' erano a quella età, che nei valloni,
Nelle scure spelonche e boschi fieri,
Tane di serpi, d'orsi e di leoni,
Trovavan quel che nei palazai altieri
Appena or trovar pon giudici buoni;
Donne che nella lor più fresca etade
Sien degne di aver titol di beltade."

ARIOSTO, *Orl. Fur.* can. xiii. 1.

CHAPTER I.

The Return of Walter de Montreal to his Fortress.

WHEN Walter de Montreal and his mercenaries quitted Corneto, they made the best of their way to Rome; arriving there, long before the Barons, they met with a similar reception at the gates, but Montreal prudently forbore all attack and menace, and contented himself with sending his trusty Rodolf into the city to seek Rienzi, and to crave permission to enter with his troop. Rodolf returned in a shorter time than was anticipated. "Well," said Montreal impatiently, "you have the order I suppose. Shall we bid them open the gates?"

"Bid them open our graves," replied the Saxon, bluntly. "I trust my next heraldry will be to a more friendly court."

"How! what mean you?"

"Briefly this:—I found the new governor, or whatever his title, in the palace of the Capitol, surrounded by guards and councillors, and in a suit of the finest armor I ever saw out of Milan."

"Pest on his armor! give us his answer."

"'Tell Walter de Montreal,' said he, then, if you will have it, 'that Rome is no longer a den of thieves; tell him, that if he enters, he must abide a trial——'"

"A trial!" cried Montreal, grinding his teeth.

"'For participation in the evil doings of Werner and his freebooters.'"

"Ha!"

"'Tell him, moreover, that Rome declares war against all robbers, whether in tent or tower, and that we order him in forty-eight hours to quit the territories of the Church.'"

"He thinks, then, not only to deceive, but to menace me? Well, proceed."

"That was all his reply to you; to me, however, he vouchsafed a caution still more obliging. 'Hark ye, friend,' said he, 'for every German bandit found in Rome after to-morrow, our welcome will be cord and gibbet! Begone.'"

"Enough! enough!" cried Montreal, coloring with rage and shame. "Rodolf, you have a skilful eye in these matters, how many Northmen would it take to give that same gibbet to the upstart?"

Rodolf scratched his huge head, and seemed awhile lost in calculation; at length he said, "You, Captain, must be the best judge, when I tell you, that twenty thousand Romans are the least of his force; so I heard by the way; and this evening he is to accept the crown, and depose the Emperor."

"Ha, ha!" laughed Montreal, "is he so mad? then he will want not our aid to hang himself. My friends, let us wait the result. At present neither barons nor people seem likely to fill our coffers. Let us across the country to Terracina. Thank the saints," and Montreal (who was not without a strange kind of devotion,—indeed he deemed that virtue essential to chivalry) crossed himself piously, "the free companions are never long without quarters!"

"Hurrah for the Knight of St. John!" cried the mercenaries. "And hurrah for fair Provençe and bold Germany!" added the Knight, as he waved his hand on high, struck spurs into his already wearied horse, and breaking out into his favorite song,

> "His steed and his sword,
> And his lady the peerless," etc.,

Montreal, with his troop, struck gallantly across the Campagna.

The Knight of St. John soon, however, fell into an absorbed and moody reverie; and his followers imitating the silence of their chief, in a few minutes the clatter of their arms and the jingle of their spurs, alone disturbed the stillness of the wide and gloomy plains across which they made towards Terracina. Montreal was recalling with bitter resentment his conference with Rienzi; and, proud of his own sagacity and talent for scheming, he was humbled and vexed at the discovery that he had been duped by a wilier intriguer. His ambitious designs on Rome, too, were crossed, and even crushed for the moment, by the very means to which he had looked for their execution. He had seen enough of the Barons to feel assured that while Stephen Colonna lived, the head of the order, he was not likely to obtain that mastery in the state which, if leagued with a more ambitious or a less timid and less potent signor, might reward his aid in expelling Rienzi. Under all circumstances, he deemed it advisable to remain aloof. Should Rienzi grow strong, Montreal might make the advantageous terms he desired with the Barons; should Rienzi's power decay, his pride, necessarily humbled, might drive him to seek the assistance, and submit to the proposals, of Montreal. The ambition of the Provençal, though vast and daring, was not of a consistent and persevering nature. Action and enterprise were dearer to him, as yet, than the rewards which they proffered; and if baffled in one quarter, he turned himself, with the true spirit of the knight-errant, to any other field for his achievements. Louis, king of Hungary, stern, war-like, implacable, seeking vengeance for the murder of his brother, the ill-fated husband of Joanna, (the beautiful and guilty Queen of Naples—the Mary Stuart of Italy,) had already prepared himself to subject the garden of Campania to the Hungarian yoke.

Already his bastard brother had entered Italy—already some of the Neapolitan states had declared in his favor—already promises had been held out by the northern monarch to the scattered Companies—and already those fierce mercenaries gathered menacingly round the frontiers of that Eden of Italy, attracted, as vultures to the carcass, by the preparation of war and the hope of plunder. Such was the field to which the bold mind of Montreal now turned its thoughts; and his soldiers had joyfully conjectured his design when they had heard him fix Terracina as their bourne. Provident of every resource, and refining his audacious and unprincipled valor by a sagacity which promised, when years had more matured and sobered his restless chivalry, to rank him among the most dangerous enemies Italy had ever known, on the first sign of Louis's warlike intentions, Montreal had seized and fortified a strong castle on that delicious coast beyond Terracina, by which lies the celebrated pass once held by Fabius against Hannibal, and which Nature has so favored for war as for peace, that a handful of armed men might stop the march of an army. The possession of such a fortress on the very frontiers of Naples, gave Montreal an importance of which he trusted to avail himself with the Hungarian king: and now, thwarted in his more grand and aspiring projects upon Rome, his sanguine, active, and elastic spirit congratulated itself upon the resource it had secured.

The band halted at nightfall on this side the Pontine Marshes, seizing without scruple some huts and sheds, from which they ejected the miserable tenants, and slaughtering with no greater ceremony the swine, cattle, and poultry of a neighboring farm. Shortly after sunrise they crossed those fatal swamps which had already been partially drained by Boniface VIII.; and Montreal, refreshed by sleep, reconciled to his late mortification by the advantages opened to him in the approaching war with Naples, and rejoicing as he approached a home which held one who alone divided his heart with ambition, had resumed all the gaiety which belonged to his Gallic birth and his reckless habits. And that deadly but consecrated road, where yet may be seen the labors of Augustus, in the canal which had witnessed the Voyage so humorously described by Horace, echoed with the loud laughter and frequent snatches of wild song by which the barbarian robbers enlivened their rapid march.

It was noon when the company entered upon that romantic pass I have before referred to—the ancient Lantulæ. High to the left rose steep and lofty rocks, then covered by the prodigal verdure, and the countless flowers, of the closing May; while to the right the sea, gentle as a lake, and blue as heaven, rippled musically at their feet. Montreal, who largely possessed the poetry of his land, which is so eminently allied with a love of nature, might at another time have enjoyed the beauty of the scene; but at that moment less external and more household images were busy within him.

Abruptly ascending where a winding path up the mountain offered a rough and painful road to their horses' feet, the band at length arrived before a strong fortress of gray stone, whose towers were concealed by the lofty foliage, until they emerged sullenly and suddenly from the laughing verdure. The sound of the bugle, the pennon of the knight, the rapid watchword, produced a loud shout of welcome from a score or two of grim soldiery on the walls; the portcullis was raised, and Montreal, throwing himself hastily from his panting steed, sprung across the threshold of a jutting porch, and traversed a huge hall, when a lady—young, fair, and richly dressed—met him with a step equally swift, and fell breathless and overjoyed into his arms.

"My Walter! my dear, dear Walter; welcome—ten thousand welcomes!"

"Adeline, my beautiful—my adored—I see thee again!"

Such were the greetings interchanged as Montreal pressed his lady to his heart, kissing away her tears, and lifting her face to his, while he gazed on its delicate bloom with all the wistful anxiety of affection after absence.

"Fairest," said he, tenderly, "thou hast pined, thou hast lost roundness and color since we parted. Come, come, thou art too gentle, or too foolish, for a soldier's love."

"Ah, Walter!" replied Adeline, clinging to him, "now thou art returned, and I shall be well. Thou wilt not leave me again a long, long time."

"Sweet one, no;" and flinging his arm round her waist, the lovers—for alas! they were not wedded!—retired to the more private chambers of the castle.

CHAPTER II.

The Life of Love and War.—The Messenger of Peace.—The Joust.

Girt with his soldiery, secure in his feudal hold, enchanted with the beauty of the earth, sky, and sea around, and passionately adoring his Adeline, Montreal for awhile forgot all his more stirring projects and his ruder occupations. His nature was capable of great tenderness, as of great ferocity; and his heart smote him when he looked at the fair cheek of his lady, and saw that even his presence did not suffice to bring back the smile and the fresh hues of old. Often he cursed that fatal oath of his knightly order which forbade him to wed, though with one more than his equal; and remorse embittered his happiest hours. That gentle lady in that robber hold, severed from all she had been taught most to prize—mother, friends, and fair fame—only loved her seducer the more intensely; only the more concentrated upon one object all the womanly and tender feelings denied every other and less sinful vent. But she felt her shame, though she sought to conceal it, and a yet more gnawing grief than even that of shame contributed to prey upon her spirits and undermine her health. Yet, withal, in Montreal's presence she was happy, even in regret; and in her declining health she had at least a consolation in the hope to die while his love was undiminished. Sometimes they made short excursions, for the disturbed state of the country forbade them to wander far from the castle, through the sunny woods, and along the glassy sea, which make the charm of that delicious scenery; and that mixture of the savage with the tender, the wild escort, the tent in some green glade in the woods at noon, the lute and voice of Adeline, with the fierce soldiers grouped and listening at the distance, might have well suited the verse of Ariosto, and harmonized singularly with that strange, disordered, yet chivalric time, in which the Classic South became the seat of the Northern Romance. Still, however, Montreal maintained his secret intercourse with the Hungarian king, and, plunged in new projects, willingly forsook for the present all his designs on Rome. Yet deemed he that his more august ambition was only delayed, and, bright in the more distant prospects of his adventurous career, rose the Capitol of Rome and shone the sceptre of the Cæsars.

One day, as Montreal, with a small troop in attendance, passed on horseback near the walls of Terracina, the gates were suddenly thrown open, and a numerous throng issued forth, preceded by a singular figure, whose steps they followed bareheaded and with loud blessings; a train of monks closed the procession, chanting a hymn, of which the concluding words were as follows:—

Beauteous on the mountains—lo,
The feet of him glad tidings gladly bringing;
The flowers along his pathway grow,
And voices, heard aloft, to angel harps are singing:
And strife and slaughter cease
Before thy blessed way, Young Messenger of Peace!
O'er the mount, and through the moor,
Glide thy holy steps secure.
Day and night no fear thou knowest,
Lonely—but with God thou goest.
Where the Heathen rage the fiercest,
Through the armed throng thou piercest.
For thy coat of mail, bedight
In thy spotless robe of white.
For the sinful sword—thy hand
Bearing bright the silver wand:
Through the camp and through the court,
Through the bandit's gloomy fort,
On the mission of the dove,
Speeds the minister of love;
By a word the wildest taming,
And the world to Christ reclaiming:
While, as once the waters trod
By the footsteps of thy God,
War, and wrath, and rapine cease,
Hush'd round thy charmed path, O Messenger of Peace!

The stranger to whom these honors were paid was a young, unbearded man, clothed in white wrought with silver; he was unarmed and barefooted: in his hand he held a tall silver wand. Montreal and his party halted in astonishment and wonder, and the Knight, spurring his horse toward the crowd, confronted the stranger.

"How, friend," quoth the Provençal, "is thine a new order of pilgrims, or what especial holiness has won thee this homage?"

"Back, back," cried some of the bolder of the crowd, "let not the robber dare arrest the Messenger of Peace."

Montreal waved his hand disdainfully.

"I speak not to you, good sirs, and the worthy friars in your rear know full well that I never injured herald or palmer."

The monks, ceasing from their hymn, advanced hastily to the spot; and indeed the devotion of Montreal had ever induced him to purchase the goodwill of whatever monastery neighbored his wandering home.

"My son," said the eldest of the brethren, "this is a strange spectacle, and a sacred: and when thou learnest all, thou wilt rather give the messenger a passport of safety from the unthinking courage of thy friends than intercept his path of peace."

"Ye puzzle still more my simple brain," said Montreal, impatiently, "let the youth speak for himself; I perceive that on his mantle are the arms of Rome blended with other quarterings, which are a mystery to me,—though sufficiently versed in heraldic art as befits a noble and a knight."

"Signor," said the youth, gravely, "know in me the messenger of Cola di Rienzi, Tribune of Rome, charged with letters to many a baron and prince in the ways between Rome and Naples. The arms wrought upon my mantle are those of the Pontiff, the City, and the Tribune."

"Umph; thou must have bold nerves to traverse the Campagna with no other weapon than that stick of silver!"

"Thou art mistaken, Sir Knight," replied the youth, boldly, "and judgest of the present by the past; know that not a single robber now lurks within the Campagna, the arms of the Tribune have rendered every road around the city as secure as the broadest street of the city itself."

"Thou tellest me wonders."

"Through the forest—and in the fortress, —through the wildest solitudes, —through the most populous towns,—have my comrades borne this silver wand unmolested and unscathed; wherever we pass along, thousands hail us, and tears of joy bless the messengers of him who hath expelled the brigand from his hold, the tyrant from his castle, and ensured the gains of the merchant and the hut of the peasant."

"*Pardieu*," said Montreal, with a stern smile, "I ought to be thankful for the preference shown to me; I have not yet received the commands, nor felt the vengeance, of the Tribune; yet, methinks, my humble castle lies just within the patrimony of St. Peter."

"Pardon me, Signor Cavalier," said the youth; "but do I address the renowned Knight of St. John, warrior of the Cross, yet leader of banditti?"

"Boy, you are bold; I am Walter de Montreal."

"I am bound, then, Sir Knight, to your castle."

"Take care how thou reach it before me, or thou standest a fair chance of a quick exit. How now, my friends!" seeing that the crowd at these words gathered closer round the messenger, "Think ye that I, who have my mate in kings, would find a victim in an unarmed boy? Fie! give way—give way. Young man, follow me homeward; you are safe in my castle as in your mother's arms." So saying, Montreal, with great dignity and deliberate gravity, rode slowly towards his castle, his soldiers, wondering, at a little distance, and the white-robed messenger following with the crowd, who refused to depart; so great was their enthusiasm, that they even ascended to the gates of the dreaded castle, and insisted on waiting without until the return of the youth assured them of his safety.

Montreal, who, however lawless elsewhere, strictly preserved the rights of the meanest boor in his immediate neighborhood, and rather affected popularity with the poor, bade the crowd enter the court-yard, ordered his servitors to provide them with wine and refreshment, regaled the good monks in his great hall, and then led the way to a small room, where he received the messenger.

"This," said the youth, "will best explain my mission," as he placed a letter before Montreal.

The Knight cut the silk with his dagger, and read the epistle with great composure.

"Your Tribune," said he, when he had finished it, "has learned the laconic style of power very soon. He orders me to render this castle, and vacate the Papal Territory within ten days. He is obliging; I must have breathing time to consider the proposal; be seated, I pray you, young sir. Forgive me, but I should have imagained that your lord had enough upon his hands with his Roman barons, to make him a little more indulgent to us foreign visitors. Stephen Colonna——"

"Is returned to Rome, and has taken the oath of allegiance; the Savelli, the Orsini, the Frangipani, have all subscribed their submission to the *Buono Stato*."

"How!" cried Montreal, in great surprise.

"Not only have they returned, but they have submitted to the dispersion of all their mercenaries, and the dismantling of all their fortifications. The iron of the Orsini palace now barricades the Capitol, and the stone-work of the Colonna and the Savelli has added new battlements to the gates of the Lateran and St. Laurence."

"Wonderful man!" said Montreal, with reluctant admiration. "By what means was this effected?"

"A stern command and a strong force to back it. At the first sound of the great bell, twenty thousand Romans rise in arms. What to such an army are the brigands of an Orsini or a Colonna?—Sir Knight, your valor and renown make even Rome admire you; and I, a Roman, bid you beware."

"Well, I thank thee—thy news, friend, robs me of breath. So the Barons submit, then?"

"Yes: on the first day, one of the Colonna, the Lord Adrian, took the oath; within a week, Stephen, assured of safe conduct, left Palestrina, with Savelli in his train; the Orsini followed—even Martino di Porto has silently succumbed."

"The Tribune—but is that his dignity—methought he was to be king——"

"He was offered, and he refused, the title. His present rank, which arrogates no patrician honors, went far to conciliate the nobles."

"A wise knave!—I beg pardon, a sagacious prince!—Well, then, the Tribune lords it mightily, I suppose, over the great Roman names?"

"Pardon me—he enforces impartial justice from peasant or patrician; but he preserves to the nobles all their just privileges and legal rank."

"Ha!—and the vain puppets, so they keep

the semblance, scarce miss the substance—I understand. But this shows genius—the Tribune is unwed, I think. Does he look among the Colonna for a wife?"

"Sir Knight, the Tribune is already married; within three days after his ascension to power, he won and bore home the daughter of the Baron di Raselli."

"Raselli! no great name; he might have done better."

"But it is said," resumed the youth, smiling, "that the Tribune will shortly be allied to the Colonna, through his fair sister the Signora Irene. The Baron di Castello woos her."

"What, Adrian Colonna! Enough! you have convinced me that a man who contents the people and awes or conciliates the nobles is born for empire. My answer to this letter I will send myself. For your news, Sir Messenger, accept this jewel," and the knight took from his finger a gem of some price. "Nay, shrink not, it was as freely given to me as it is now to thee."

The youth, who had been agreeably surprised, and impressed, by the manner of the renowned freebooter, and who was not a little astonished himself with the ease and familiarity with which he had been relating to Fra Moreale, in his own fortress, the news of Rome, bowed low as he accepted the gift.

The astute Provençal, who saw the evident impression he had made, perceived also that it might be of advantage in delaying the measures he might deem it expedient to adopt. "Assure the Tribune," said he, on dismissing the messenger, "shouldst thou return ere my letter arrive, that I admire his genius, hail his power, and will not fail to consider as favorably as I may of his demand."

"Better," said the messenger, warmly (he was of good blood, and gentle bearing),—"better ten tyrants for our enemy, than one Montreal."

"An enemy! believe me, sir, I seek no enmity with princes who know how to govern, or a people that has the wisdom at once to rule and to obey."

The whole of that day, however, Montreal remained thoughtful and uneasy; he despatched trusty messengers to the Governor of Aquila (who was then in correspondence with Louis of Hungary), to Naples, and to Rome:—the last charged with a letter to the Tribune, which, without absolutely compromising himself, affected submission, and demanded only a longer leisure for the preparations of departure. But, at the same time, fresh fortifications were added to the castle, ample provisions were laid in, and night and day, spies and scouts were stationed along the pass, and in the town of Terracina. Montreal was precisely the chief who prepared most for war when most he pretended peace.

One morning, the fifth from the appearance of the Roman messenger, Montreal, after narrowly surveying his outworks and his stores, and feeling satisfied that he could hold out at least a month's siege, repaired, with a gayer countenance than he had lately worn, to the chamber of Adeline.

The lady was seated by the casement of the tower, from which might be seen the glorious landscape of woods, and vales, and orange groves—a strange garden for such a palace! As she leant her face upon her hand, with her profile slightly turned to Montreal, there was something ineffably graceful in the bend of her neck,—the small head so expressive of gentle blood,—with the locks parted in front in that simple fashion which modern times have so happily revived. But the expression of the half-averted face, the abstracted intentness of the gaze, and the profound stillness of the attitude, were so sad and mournful, that Montreal's purposed greeting of gallantry and gladness died upon his lips. He approached in silence, and laid his hand upon her shoulder.

Adeline turned, and taking the hand in hers, pressed it to her heart, and smiled away all her sadness. "Dearest," said Montreal, "couldst thou know how much any shadow of grief on thy bright face darkens my heart, thou wouldst never grieve. But no wonder that in these rude walls—no female of equal rank near thee, and such mirth as Montreal can summon to his halls, grating to thy ear—no wonder that thou repentest thee of thy choice."

"Ah, no—no, Walter, I never repent. I did but think of our child as you entered. Alas! he was our only child! How fair he was, Walter; how he resembled thee!"

"Nay, he had thine eyes and brow," replied the Knight, with a faltering voice, and turning away his head.

"Walter," resumed the lady, sighing, "do you remember?—this is his birthday. He is ten years old to-day. We have loved each other eleven years, and thou hast not tired yet of thy poor Adeline."

"As well might the saints weary of paradise," replied Montreal, with an enamoured tenderness, which changed into softness the whole character of his heroic countenance.

"Could I think so, I should indeed be blest!" answered Adeline. "But a little while longer, and the few charms I yet possess must fade; and what other claim have I on thee?"

"All claim;—the memory of thy first blushes—thy first kiss—of thy devoted sacrifices—of thy patient wanderings—of thy uncomplaining love! Ah, Adeline, we are of Provence, not of Italy; and when did Knight of Provence avoid his foe, or forsake his love? But enough, dearest, of home and melancholy for to-day. I come to bid thee forth. I have sent on the servitors to pitch our tent beside the sea,—we will enjoy the orange blossoms while we may. Ere another week pass over us, we may have sterner pastime and closer confines."

"How, dearest Walter! thou dost not apprehend danger?"

"Thou speakest, lady-bird," said Montreal, laughing, "as if danger were novelty; methinks by this time, thou shouldst know it as the atmosphere we breathe."

"Ah, Walter, is this to last for ever? Thou art now rich and renowned; canst thou not abandon this career of strife?"

"Now, out on thee, Adeline. What are riches and renown but the means to power! And for strife, the shield of warriors was my cradle—pray the saints it may be my bier! These wild and wizard extremes of life—from the bower to the tent—from the cavern to the palace—to-day a wandering exile, tomorrow the equal of kings—make the true element of the chivalry of my Norman sires. Normandy taught me war, and sweet Provence love. Kiss me, dear Adeline; and now let thy handmaids attire thee. Forget not thy lute, sweet one. We will rouse the echoes with the songs of Provence."

The ductile temper of Adeline yielded easily to the gaiety of her lord; and the party soon sallied from the castle towards the spot in which Montreal had designed their resting-place during the heats of day. But already prepared for all surprise, the castle was left strictly guarded, and besides the domestic servitors of the castle, a detachment of ten soldiers, completely armed, accompanied the lovers. Montreal himself wore his corselet, and his 'squires followed with his helmet and lance. Beyond the narrow defile at the base of the castle, the road at that day opened into a broad patch of verdure, circled on all sides, save that open to the sea, by wood, interspersed with myrtle and orange, and a wilderness of ordorous shrubs. In this space, and sheltered by the broad spreading and classic *fagus* (so improperly translated into the English *beech*), a gay pavilion was prepared, which commanded the view of the sparkling sea;—shaded from the sun, but open to the gentle breeze. This was poor Adeline's favorite recreation, if recreation it might be called. She rejoiced to escape from the gloomy walls of her castellated prison, and to enjoy the sunshine and the sweets of that vuluptuous climate without the fatigue which of late all exercise occasioned her. It was a gallantry on the part of Montreal, who foresaw how short an interval might elapse before the troops of Rienzi besieged his walls; and who was himself no less at home in the bower than in the field.

As they reclined within the pavilion—the lover and his lady,—of the attendants without, some lounged idly on the beach; some prepared the awning of a pleasure-boat against the decline of the sun; some, in a ruder tent, out of sight in the wood, arranged the mid-day repast; while the strings of the lute, touched by Montreal himself with a careless skill, gave their music to the dreamy stillness of the noon.

While thus employed, one of the Montreal's scouts arrived breathless and heated at the tent.

"Captain," said he, "a company of thirty lances completely armed, with a long retinue of 'squires and pages, have just quitted Terracina. Their banners bear the two-fold insignia of Rome and the Colonna."

"Ho!" said Montreal, gaily, "such a troop is a welcome addition to our company; send our 'squire hither."

The 'squire appeared.

"Hie thee on thy steed towards the procession thou wilt meet with in the pass, (nay, sweet lady mine, no forbiddal!) seek the chief, and say that the good Knight Walter de Montreal sends him greeting, and prays him, in passing our proper territory, to rest awhile with us a welcome guest; and—stay,—add, that if to while an hour or so in gentle pastime be acceptable to him, Walter de Montreal would rejoice to break a lance with him, or any knight in his train, in honor of our respective ladies. Hie thee quick!"

"Walter, Walter," began Adeline, who had that keen and delicate sensitiveness to her situation, which her reckless lord often wantonly forgot; "Walter, dear Walter, canst thou think it honor to——"

"Hush thee, sweet *Fleur de lis!* Thou hast not seen pastime this many a day; I long to convince thee that thou art still the fairest lady in Italy—ay, and of Christendom. But these Italians are craven knights, and thou needst not fear that my proffer will be accepted. But in truth, lady mine, I rejoice for graver objects, that chance throws a Roman noble, perhaps a Colonna, in my way;—women understand not these matters; and aught concerning Rome touches us home at this moment."

With that the Knight frowned, as was his wont in thought, and Adeline ventured to say no more, but retired to the interior division of the pavilion.

Meanwhile the 'squire approached the procession that had now reached the middle of the pass. And a stately and gallant company it was:—if the complete harness of the soldiery seemed to attest a warlike purpose, it was contradicted on the other hand by a numerous train of unarmed 'squires and pages gorgeously attired, while the splendid blazon of two heralds preceding the standard-bearers, proclaimed their object as peaceful, and their path as sacred. It required but a glance at the company to tell the leader. Arrayed in a breast-plate of steel, wrought profusedly with gold arabesques, over which was a mantel of dark green velvet, bordered with pearls, while above his long dark locks waved a black ostrich plume in a high Macedonian cap, such as, I believe, is now worn by the Grand Master of the order of St. Constantine, rode in the front of the party, a young cavalier, distinguished from his immediate comrades, partly by his graceful presence and partly by his splendid dress.

The 'squire approached respectfully, and dismounting, delivered himself of his charge. The young cavalier smiled, as he answered, "Bear back to Sir Walter de Montreal the greeting of Adrian Colonna, Baron di Castello, and say, that the solemn object of my present journey will scarce permit me to encounter the formidable lance of so celebrated a knight; and I regret this the more, inasmuch as I may not yield to any dame the palm of my liege lady's beauty. I must live in hope of a happier occasion. For the rest, I will cheerfully abide for some few hours the guest of so courteous a host."

The 'squire bowed low. "My master," said he, hesitatingly, "will grieve much to miss so noble an opponent. But my message refers to all this knightly and gallant train; and if the Lord Adrian di Castello deems himself forbidden the joust by the object of his present journey, surely one of his comrades will be his proxy with my master."

Out and quickly spoke a young noble by the side of Adrian, Riccardo Annibaldi, who afterwards did good service both to the Tribune and to Rome, and whose valor brought him, in later life, to an untimely end.

"By the Lord Adrian's permission," cried he, "I will break a lance with——"

"Hush! Annibaldi," interrupted Adrian. "And you, Sir 'Squire, know, that Adrian di Castello permits no proxy in arms. Avise the Knight of St. John that we accept his hospitality, and if, after some converse on graver matters, he should still desire so light an entertainment, I will forget that I am the ambassador to Naples, and remember only that I am a Knight of the Empire. You have your answer."

The 'squire with much ceremony made his obeisance, remounted his steed, and returned in a half-gallop to his master.

"Forgive me, dear Annibaldi," said Adrian, "that I balked your valor; and believe me that I never more longed to break a lance against any man than I do against this boasting Frenchman. But bethink you, that though to us, brought up in the dainty laws of chivalry, Walter de Montreal is the famous Knight of Provence, to the Tribune of Rome, whose grave mission we now fulfil, he is but the mercenary captain of a Free Company. Grievously in his eyes should we sully our dignity by so wanton and irrelevant a holiday conflict with a declared and professional brigand."

"For all that," said Annibaldi, "the brigand ought not to boast that a Roman knight shunned a Provençal lance."

"Cease, I pray thee!" said Adrian, impatiently. In fact, the young Colonna, already chafed bitterly against his discreet and dignified rejection of Montreal's proffer, and recollecting with much pique the disparaging manner in which the Provençal had spoken of the Roman chivalry, as well as a certain tone of superiority, which in all warlike matters Montreal had assumed over him,—he now felt his cheek burn, and his lip quiver. Highly skilled in the martial accomplishments of his time, he had a natural and excusable desire to prove that he was at least no unworthy antagonist even of the best lance in Italy; and, added to this, the gallantry of the age made him feel it a sort of treason to his mistress to forego any means of asserting her perfections.

It was, therefore, with considerable irritation that Adrian, as the pavilion of Montreal became visible, perceived the 'squire returning to him. And the reader will judge how much this was increased when the latter, once more dismounting, accosted him thus:

"My master, the Knight of St. John, on hearing the courteous answer of the Lord Adrian di Castello, bids me say, that lest the graver converse the Lord Adrian refers to should mar gentle and friendly sport, he ventures respectfully to suggest, that the tilt should preface the converse. The sod before the tent is so soft and smooth, that even a fall could be attended with *no danger* to knight or steed."

"By our Lady!" cried Adrian and Annibaldi in a breath, "but thy last words are discourteous; and" (proceeded Adrian, recovering himself) "since thy master will have it so, let him look to his horse's girths. I will not gainsay his fancy."

Montreal, who had thus insisted upon the exhibition, partly, it may be, from the gay and ruffling bravado, common still amongst his brave countrymen; partly because he was curious of exhibiting before those who might soon be his open foes his singular and unrivalled address in arms, was yet more moved to it on learning the name of the leader of the Roman Company; for his vain and haughty spirit, however it had disguised resentment at the time, had by no means forgiven certain warm expressions of Adrian in the palace of Stephen Colonna, and in the unfortunate journey to Corneto. While Adrian, halting at the entrance of the defile, aided by his 'squires, indignantly, but carefully, indued the rest of his armor, and saw, himself, to the girths, stirrup-leathers, and various buckles in the caparison of his noble charger, Montreal in great glee kissed his lady, who, though too soft to be angry, was deeply vexed, (and yet her vexation half forgotten in fear for his safety,) snatched up her scarf of blue, which he threw over his breastplate, and completed his array with the indifference of a man certain of victory. He was destined, however, to one disadvantage, and that the greatest; his armor and lance had been brought from the castle—not his war-horse. His palfrey was too slight to bear the great weight of his armor, nor amongst his troop was there one horse that for power and bone could match with Adrian's. He chose, however, the strongest that was at hand, and a loud shout from his wild followers testified their admiration when he sprung unaided from the ground into the saddle—a rare and difficult feat of agility in a man completely arrayed in the ponderous armor which issued at that day from the forges of Milan, and was worn far more weighty in Italy than any other part of Europe. While both companies grouped slowly, and mingled in a kind of circle round the green turf, and the Roman heralds, with bustling importance, attempted to marshal the spectators into order, Montreal rode his charger round the sward, forcing it into various caracoles, and exhibiting, with the vanity that belonged to him, his exquisite and practised horsemanship.

At length, Adrian, his visor down, rode slowly into the green space, amidst the cheers of his party. The two Knights, at either end, gravely fronted each other; they made the courtesies with their lances, which, in friendly and sportive encounters, were customary; and, as they thus paused for the signal of encounter, the Italians trembled for the honor of their chief: Montreal's stately height and girth of chest forming a strong contrast, even in armor, to the form of his opponent, which was rather under the middle standard, and though firmly knit, slightly and slenderly built. But to that perfection was skill in arms brought in those times, that great strength and size were far from being either the absolute requisites, or even the usual attributes, of the more celebrated knights; in fact, so much was effected by the power and the management of the steed, that a light weight in the rider was often rather to his advantage than his prejudice: and, even at a later period, the most accomplished victors in the tourney, the French Bayard and the English Sydney, were far from remarkable either for bulk or stature.

Whatever the superiority of Montreal in physical power, was, in much, counterbalanced by the inferiority of his horse, which, though a thick-built and strong Calabrian, had neither the blood, bone, nor practised discipline of the northern charger of the Roman. The shining coat of the latter, coal black, was set off by a scarlet cloth wrought in gold; the neck and shoulders were clad in scales of mail; and from the forehead projected a long point, like the horn of an unicorn, while on its crest waved a tall plume of scarlet and white feathers. As the mission of Adrian to Naples was that of pomp and ceremony to a court of great splendor, so his array and retinue were befitting the occasion and the passion for show that belonged to the time; and the very bridle of his horse, which was three inches broad, was decorated with gold, and even jewels. The Knight himself was clad in mail, which had tested the finest art of the celebrated Ludovico of Milan; and, altogether, his appearance was unusually gallant and splendid, and seemed still more so beside the plain but brightly polished and artfully flexile armor of Montreal (adorned only with his lady's scarf), and the common and rude mail of his charger. This contrast, however, was not welcome to the Provençal, whose vanity was especially indulged in warlike equipments; and who, had he foreseen the "pastime" that awaited him, would have outshone even the Colonna.

The trumpeters of either party gave a short blast—the Knights remained erect as statues of iron; a second, and each slightly bent over his saddle-bow; a third, and with spears couched, slackened reins, and at full speed, on they rushed, and fiercely they met midway. With the reckless arrogance which belonged to him, Montreal had imagined, that at the first touch of his lance Adrian would have been unhorsed; but to his great surprise the young Roman remained firm, and amidst the shouts of his party, passed on to the other end of the lists. Montreal himself was rudely shaken, but lost neither seat nor stirrup.

"This can be no carpet knight," muttered Montreal between his teeth, as, this time, he summoned all his skill for a second encounter; while Adrian, aware of the great superiority of his charger, resolved to bring it to bear against his opponent. Accordingly, when the Knights again rushed forward, Adrian, covering himself well with his buckler, directed his care less against the combatant, whom he felt no lance wielded by mortal hand was likely to dislodge, than against the less noble animal he bestrode. The shock of Montreal's charge was like an avalanche—his lance shivered into a thousand pieces, Adrian lost both stirrups, and but for the strong iron bows which guarded the saddle in front and rear, would have been fairly unhorsed; as it was, he was almost doubled back by the encounter, and his ears rung and his eyes reeled, so that for a moment or two he almost lost all consciousness. But his steed had well repaid its nurture and discipline. Just as the combatants closed, the animal, rearing on high, pressed forward with its mighty crest against its opponent with a force so irresistible as to drive back Montreal's horse several paces: while Adrian's lance, poised with exquisite skill, striking against the Provençal's helmet, somewhat rudely diverted the Knight's attention for the moment from his rein. Montreal, drawing the curb too tightly in the suddenness of his recovery, the horse reared on end; and, receiving at that instant, full upon his breastplate, the sharp horn and mailed crest of Adrian's charger—fell back over its rider upon the sward. Montreal disencumbered himself in great rage and shame, as a faint cry from his pavilion reached his ear, and redoubled his mortification. He rose with a lightness which astonished the beholders; for so heavy was the armor worn at that day, that few knights once stretched upon the ground could rise without assistance; and drawing his sword, cried out fiercely—"On foot, on foot!—the fall was not mine, but this accursed beast's, that I must needs for my sins raise to the rank of a charger. Come on——"

"Nay Sir Knight," said Adrian, drawing

off his gauntlets and unbuckling his helmet, which he threw on the ground, "I come to thee a guest and a friend; but to fight on foot is the encounter of mortal foes. Did I accept thy offer, my defeat would but stain thy knighthood."

Montreal, whose passion had beguiled him for the moment, sullenly acquiesced in this reasoning. Adrian hastened to soothe his antagonist. "For the rest," said he, "I cannot pretend to the prize. Your lance lost me my stirrups—mine left you unshaken. You say right; the defeat, if any, was that of your steed."

"We may meet again when I am more equally horsed," said Montreal, still chafing.

"Now, our Lady forbid!" exclaimed Adrian, with so devout an earnestness that the bystanders could not refrain from laughing; and even Montreal, grimly and half-reluctantly, joined in the merriment. The courtesy of his foe, however, conciliated and touched the more frank and soldierly qualities of his nature, and composing himself, he replied:—

"Signor di Castello, I rest your debtor for a courtesy that I have but little imitated. Howbeit, if thou wouldst bind me to thee for ever, thou wilt suffer me to send for my own charger, and afford me a chance to retrieve mine honor. With that steed, or with one equal to thine, which seems to me of the English breed, I will gage all I possess, lands, castle, and gold, sword and spurs, to maintain this pass, one by one, against all thy train."

Fortunately, perhaps, for Adrian, ere he could reply, Riccardo Annibaldi cried, with great warmth, "Sir Knight, I have with me two steeds well practised in the tourney; take thy choice, and accept in me a champion of the Roman against the French chivalry;—there is my gage."

"Signor," replied Montreal, with ill-suppressed delight, "thy proffer shows so gallant and free a spirit, that it were foul sin in me to balk it. I accept thy gage, and whichever of thy steeds thou rejectest, in God's name bring it hither, and let us waste no words before action."

Adrian, who felt that hitherto the Romans had been more favored by fortune than merit, vainly endeavored to prevent this second hazard. But Annibaldi was greatly chafed, and his high rank rendered it impolitic in Adrian to offend him by peremptory prohibition; the Colonna reluctantly, therefore, yielded his assent to the engagement. Annibaldi's steeds were led to the spot, the one a noble roan, the other a bay, of somewhat less breeding and bone, but still of great strength and price. Montreal finding the choice pressed upon him, gallantly selected the latter and less excellent.

Annibaldi was soon arrayed for the encounter, and Adrian gave the word to the trumpeters. The Roman was of a stature almost equal to that of Montreal, and though some years younger, seemed, in his armor, nearly of the same thews and girth, so that the present antagonists appeared at the first glance more evenly matched than the last. But this time Montreal, well horsed, inspired to the utmost by shame and pride, felt himself a match for an army; and he met the young Baron with such prowess, that while the very plume on his casque seemed scarcely stirred, the Italian was thrown several paces from his steed, and it was not till some moments after his visor was removed by his 'squires that he recovered his senses. This event restored Montreal to all his natural gaiety of humor, and effectually raised the spirits of his followers, who had felt much humbled by the previous encounter.

He himself assisted Annibaldi to rise with great courtesy, and a profusion of compliments, which the proud Roman took in stern silence, and then led the way to the pavilion, loudly ordering the banquet to be spread. Annibaldi, however, loitered behind, and Adrian, who penetrated his thoughts, and who saw that over their cups a quarrel between the Provençal and his friend was likely to ensue, drawing him aside, said:—"Methinks, dear Annibaldi, it would be better if you, with the chief of our following, were to proceed onward to Fondi, where I will join you at sunset. My 'squires, and some eight lances, will suffice for my safeguard here; and, to say truth, I desire a few private words with our strange host, in the hope that he may be peaceably induced to withdraw from hence without the help of our Roman troops, who have enough elsewhere to feed their valor."

Annibaldi pressed his companion's hand: "I understand thee," he replied with a slight blush, "and indeed, I could but ill brook the complacent triumph of the barbarian. I accept thy offer."

CHAPTER III.

The Conversation between the Roman and the Provençal.—Adeline's History.—The Moon-lit Sea.—The Lute and the Song.

As soon as Annibaldi, with the greater part of the retinue, was gone, Adrian, divesting himself of his heavy greaves, entered alone the pavilion of the Knight of St. John. Montreal has already doffed all his armor, save the breastplate, and he now stepped forward to welcome his guest with the winning and easy grace which better suited his birth than his profession. He received Adrian's excuses for the absence of Annibaldi and the other knights of his train with a smile which seemed to prove how readily he divined the cause, and conducted him to the other and more private division of the pavilion in which the repast (rendered acceptable by the late exercise of guest and host) was prepared; and here Adrian for the first time discovered Adeline. Long inurement to the various and roving life of her lover, joined to a certain pride which she derived from conscious, though forfeited, rank, gave to the outward manner of that beautiful lady an ease and freedom which often concealed, even from Montreal, her sensitiveness to her unhappy situation. At times, indeed, when alone with Montreal, whom she loved with all the devotion of romance, she was sensible only to the charm of a presence which consoled her for all things; but in his frequent absence, or on the admission of any stranger, the illusion vanished—the reality returned. Poor lady! Nature had not formed, education had not reared, habit had not reconciled, her to the breath of shame!

The young Colonna was much struck by her beauty, and more by her gentle and high-born grace. Like her lord she appeared younger than she was; time seemed to spare a bloom which an experienced eye might have told was destined to an early grave; and there was something almost girlish in the lightness of her form—the braided luxuriance of her rich auburn hair, and the color that went and came, not only with every moment, but almost with every word. The contrast between her and Montreal became them both—it was the contrast of devoted reliance and protecting strength: each looked fairer in the presence of the other; and as Adrian sate down to the well-laden board, he thought he had never seen a pair more formed for the poetic legends of their native Troubadours.

Montreal conversed gaily upon a thousand matters—pressed the wine flasks—and selected for his guest the most delicate portions of the delicious *spicola* of the neighboring sea, and the rich flesh of the wild boar of the Pontine Marshes.

"Tell me," said Montreal, as their hunger was now appeased—"tell me, noble Adrian, how fares your kinsman, Signor Stephen? A brave old man for his years."

"He bears him as the youngest of us," answered Adrian.

"Late events must have shocked him a little," said Montreal, with an arch smile. "Ah, you look grave—yet commend my foresight; —I was the first who prophesied to thy kinsman the rise of Cola di Rienzi; he seems a great man—never more great than in conciliating the Colonna and the Orsini."

"The Tribune," returned Adrian, evasively, "is certainly a man of extraordinary genius. And now, seeing him command, my only wonder is how he ever brooked to obey—majesty seems a very part of him."

"Men who win power, easily put on its harness, dignity," answered Montreal; "and if I hear aright—(pledge me to your lady's health) —the Tribune, if not himself nobly born, will soon be nobly connected."

"He is already married to a Raselli, an old Roman house," replied Adrian.

"You evade my pursuit,—*Le doulx soupir! le doulx soupir!* as the old Cabestan has it" —said Montreal, laughing. "Well, you have pledged me one cup to your lady, pledge another to the fair Irene, the Tribune's sister—always provided they two are not one.—You smile and shake your head."

"I do not disguise from you, Sir Knight," answered Adrian, "that when my present embassy is over, I trust the alliance between the Tribune and a Colonna will go far towards the benefit of both."

"I have heard rightly, then," said Montreal, in a grave and thoughtful tone. "Rienzi's power must, indeed, be great."

"Of that my mission is a proof. Are you aware, Signor de Montreal, that Louis, King of Hungary——"

"How! what of him?"

"Has referred the decision of the feud between himself and Joanna of Naples, respecting the death of her royal spouse, his brother, to the fiat of the Tribune? This is the first time, methinks, since the death of Constantine, that so great a confidence and so high a charge were ever intrusted to a Roman!"

"By all the saints in the calendar," cried Montreal, crossing himself, "this news is indeed amazing! The fierce Louis of Hungary waive the right of the sword, and choose other umpire than the field of battle!"

"And this," continued Adrian, in a significant tone, "this it was which induced me to obey your courteous summons. I know, brave Montreal, that you hold intercourse with Louis. Louis has given to the Tribune the best pledge of his amity and alliance; will you do wisely if you——"

"Wage war with the Hungarian's ally," interrupted Montreal. "This you were about to add; the same thought crossed myself. My Lord, pardon me—Italians sometimes invent what they wish. On the honor of a Knight of the Empire, these tidings are the naked truth?"

"By my honor, and on the Cross," answered Adrian, drawing himself up; "and in proof thereof, I am now bound to Naples to settle with the Queen the preliminaries of the appointed trial."

"Two crowned heads before the tribunal of a plebeian, and one a defendant against the charge of murther!" muttered Montreal; "the news might well amaze me!"

He remained musing and silent a little while, till looking up, he caught Adeline's tender gaze fixed upon him with that deep solicitude with which she watched the outward effect of schemes and projects she was too soft to desire to know, and too innocent to share.

"Lady mine," said the Provençal, fondly, "how sayest thou? must we abandon our mountain castle, and these wild woodland scenes, for the dull walls of a city? I fear me so.—The Lady Adeline," he continued, turning to Adrian, "is of a singular bias; she hates the gay crowds of streets and thoroughfares, and esteems no palace like the solitary outlaw's hold. Yet, methinks, she might outshine all the faces of Italy,—thy mistress, Lord Adrian, of course, excepted."

"It is an exception which only a lover, and that too a betrothed lover, would dare to make," replied Adrian, gallantly.

"Nay," said Adeline, in a voice singularly sweet and clear, "nay, I know well at what price to value my lord's flattery, and Signor di Castello's courtesy. But you are bound, Sir Knight, to a court, that, if fame speak true, boasts in its Queen the very miracle and mould of beauty."

"It is some years since I saw the Queen of Naples," answered Adrian; "and I little dreamed then, when I gazed upon that angel face, that I should live to hear her accused of the foulest murther that ever stained even Italian royalty."

"And, as if resolved to prove her guilt," said Montreal, "ere long be sure she will marry the very man who did the deed. Of this I have certain proof."

Thus conversing, the Knights wore away the daylight, and beheld from the open tent the sun cast his setting glow over the purple sea. Adeline had long retired from the board, and they now saw her seated with her handmaids on a mound by the beach; while the sound of her lute faintly reached their ears. As Montreal caught the air, he turned from the converse, and sighing, half shaded his face with his hand. Somehow or other the two Knights had worn away all the little jealousy or pique which they had conceived against each other at Rome. Both imbued with the soldier-like spirit of the age, their contest in the morning had served to inspire them with that strange kind of respect, and even cordiality, which one brave man even still (how much more at that day!) feels for another, whose courage he has proved while vindicating his own. It is like the discovery of a congenial sentiment hitherto latent; and, in a life of camps, often establishes sudden and lasting friendship in the very lap of enmity. This feeling had been ripened by their subsequent familiar intercourse, and was increased on Adrian's side by the feeling, that in convincing Montreal of the policy of withdrawing from the Roman territories, he had obtained an advantage that well repaid whatever danger and delay he had undergone.

The sigh, and the altered manner of Montreal, did not escape Adrian, and he naturally connected it with something relating to her whose music had been its evident cause.

"Yon lovely dame," said he, gently, "touches the lute with an exquisite and fairy hand, and that plaintive air seems to my ear as of the minstrelsy of Provence."

"It is the air I taught her," said Montreal, sadly, "married as it is to indifferent words, with which I first wooed a heart that should never have given itself to me! Ay, young Colonna, many a night has my boat been moored beneath the starlit Sorgia that washes her proud father's halls, and my voice awaked the stillness of the waving sedges with a soldier's serenade. Sweet memories! bitter fruit!"

"Why bitter? ye love each other still."

"But I am vowed to celibacy, and Adeline de Courval is leman where she should be wedded dame. Methinks I fret at that thought even more than she,—dear Adeline!"

"Your lady, as all would guess, is then nobly born?"

"She is," answered Montreal, with a deep and evident feeling which, save in love, rarely, if ever, crossed his hardy breast. "She is! our tale is a brief one:—we loved each other as children: Her family was wealthier than mine: We were separated. I was given to understand that she abandoned me. I despaired, and in despair I took the cross of St. John. Chance threw us again together. I learned that her love was undecayed. Poor child!—she was even then, sir, but a child! I, wild—reckless—and not unskilled, perhaps, in the arts that woo and win. She could not resist my suit or her own affection!—We fled. In those words you see the thread of my after history. My sword and my Adeline were all my fortune. Society frowned on us. The Church threatened my soul. The Grand Master my life. I became a knight of fortune. Fate and my right hand favored me. I have made those who scorned me tremble at my name. That name shall yet blaze, a star or a meteor, in the front of troubled nations, and I may yet win by force from the Pontiff the dispensation refused to my prayers. On the same day, I may offer Adeline the diadem and the ring.—Eno' of this;—you marked Adeline's cheek!—Seems it not delicate? I like not that changeful flush,—and she moves languidly,—*her* step that was so blithe!"

"Change of scene and the mild south will soon restore her health," said Adrian; "and in your peculiar life she is so little brought in contact with others, especially of her own sex, that I trust she is but seldom made aware of whatever is painful in her situation. And woman's love, Montreal, as we both have learned, is a robe that wraps her from many a storm!"

"You speak kindly," returned the Knight; "but you know not all our cause of grief. Adeline's father, a proud sieur, died,—they said of a broken heart,—but old men die of many other diseases than that! The mother, a dame who boasted her descent from princes, bore the matter more sternly than the sire; clamored for revenge,—which was odd, for she is as religious as a Dominican, and revenge is not Christian in a woman, though it is knightly in a man!—Well, my Lord, we had one boy, our only child; he was Adeline's solace in my absence,—his pretty ways were worth the world to her! She loved him so, that, but he had her eyes and looked like her when he slept, I should have been jealous! He grew up in our wild life, strong and comely; the young rogue, he would have been a brave knight! My evil stars led me to Milan, where I had business with the Visconti. One bright morning in June, our boy was stolen; verily that June was like a December to us!"

"Stolen!—how?—by whom?"

"The first question is answered easily,—the boy was with his nurse in the court-yard, the idle wench left him for but a minute or two—so she avers—to fetch him some childish toy; when she returned he was gone; not a trace left, save his pretty cap with the plume in it! Poor Adeline, many a time have I found her kissing that relic till it was wet with tears!"

"A strange fortune, in truth. But what interest could——"

"I will tell you," interrupted Montreal, "the only conjecture I could form;—Adeline's mother, on learning we had a son, sent to Adeline a letter, that well nigh broke her heart, reproaching her for her love to me, and so forth, as if that had made her the vilest of the sex. She bade her take compassion on her child, and not bring him up to a robber's life,—so was she pleased to style the bold career of Walter de Montreal. She offered to rear the child in her own dull halls, and fit him, no doubt, for a shaven pate and a monk's cowl. She chafed much that a mother would not part with her treasure! She alone, partly in revenge, partly in silly compassion for Adeline's child, partly, it may be, from some pious fanaticism, could, it so seemed to me, have robbed us of our boy. On inquiry, I learned from the nurse—who, but that she was of the same sex as Adeline, should have tasted my dagger,—that in their walks, a woman of advanced years, but seemingly of humble rank, (that might be disguise!) had often stopped, and caressed and admired the child. I repaired at once to France, sought the old castle of De Courval;—it had passed to the next heir, and the old widow was gone, none knew whither, but, it was conjectured, to take the veil in some remote convent."

"And you never saw her since?"

"Yes, at Rome," answered Montreal, turning pale; "when last there I chanced suddenly upon her: and then at length I learned my boy's fate, and the truth of my own surmise; she confessed to the theft—and my child was dead! I have not dared to tell Adeline of this; it seems to me as if it would be like plucking the shaft from the wounded side—and she would die at once, bereft of the uncertainty that rankles within her. She has still a hope—it comforts her; though my heart bleeds when I think on its vanity. Let this pass, my Colonna."

And Montreal started to his feet as if he strove, by a strong effort, to shake off the weakness that had crept over him in his narration.

"Think no more of it. Life is short—its thorns are many—let us not neglect any of its flowers. This is piety and wisdom too. Nature that meant me to struggle and to toil, gave me, happily, the sanguine heart and the elastic soul of France; and I have lived long enough to own that to die young is not an evil. Come, Lord Adrian, let us join my lady ere you part, if part you must; the moon will be up soon, and Fondi is but a short journey hence. You know that though I admire not your Petrarch, you with more courtesy laud our Provençal ballads, and you must hear Adeline sing one that you may prize them the more. The race of the Troubadours is dead, but the minstrelsy survives the minstrel!"

Adrian, who scarce knew what comfort to administer to the affliction of his companion, was somewhat relieved by the change in his mood, though his more grave and sensitive nature was a little startled at its suddenness. But, as we have before seen, Montreal's spirit (and this made perhaps its fascination) was as a varying and changeful sky; the gayest sunshine, and the fiercest storm swept over it in rapid alternation; and elements of singular might and grandeur, which, properly directed and concentrated, would have made him the blessing and glory of his time, were wielded with a boyish levity, roused into war and desolation, or lulled into repose and smoothness, with all the suddenness of chance, and all the fickleness of caprice.

Sauntering down to the beach, the music of Adeline's lute sounded more distinctly in their ears, and involuntarily they hushed their steps upon the rich and odorous turf, as in a voice, though not powerful, marvellously sweet and clear, and well adapted to the simple fashion of the words and melody, she sang the following stanzas:—

LAY OF THE LADY OF PROVENCE.

1.

Ah, why art thou sad, my heart? Why
Darksome and lonely?
Frowns the face of the happy sky
Over thee only?
Ah me, ah me!
Render to joy the earth!
Grief shuns, not envies, Mirth;
But leave one quiet spot,
Where Mirth may enter not,
To sigh, Ah me!—
Ah me!

2.

As a bird, though the sky be clear,
Feels the storm lower:
My soul bodes the tempest near
In the sunny hour;
Ah me, ah me!
Be glad while yet we may!
I bid thee, my heart, be gay;
And still I know not why,—
Thou answerest with a sigh,
(Fond heart!) Ah me!—
Ah me!

3.

As this twilight o'er the skies,
Doubt brings the sorrow;
Who knows when the daylight dies,
What waits the morrow?
Ah me, ah me!
Be blithe, be blithe, my lute,
Thy strings will soon be mute;
Be blithe—hark! while it dies,
The note forewarning, sighs
Its last—Ah me!
Ah me!

"My own Adeline—my sweetest night-bird," half-whispered Montreal, and softly approaching, he threw himself at his lady's feet—"thy song is too sad for this golden eve."

"No sound ever went to the heart," said Adrian, "whose arrow was not feathered by sadness. True sentiment, Montreal, is twin with melancholy, though not with gloom."

The lady looked softly and approvingly up at Adrian's face; she was pleased with its expression; she was pleased yet more with words of which women rather than men would acknowledge the truth. Adrian returned the look with one of deep and eloquent sympathy and respect; in fact, the short story he had heard from Montreal had interested him deeply in her; and never to the brilliant queen, to whose court he was bound, did his manner wear so chivalric and earnest a homage as it did to that lone and ill-fated lady on the twilight shores of Terracina.

Adeline blushed slightly and sighed; and then, to break the awkwardness of a pause which had stolen over them, as Montreal, unheeding the last remark of Adrian, was tuning the strings of the lute, she said—"Of course the Signor di Castello shares the universal enthusiasm for Petrarch?"

"Ay," cried Montreal; "my lady is Petrarch mad, like the rest of them: but all I know is, that never did belted knight and honest lover woo in such fantastic and tortured strains."

"In Italy," answered Adrian, "common language is exaggeration;—but even your own Troubadour poetry might tell you that love, ever seeking a new language of its own, cannot but often run into what to all but lovers seems distortion and conceit."

"Come, dear Signor," said Montreal, placing the lute in Adrian's hands, "let Adeline be the umpire between us, which music—yours or mine—can woo the more blandly."

"Ah," said Adrian, laughing; "I fear me, Sir Knight, you have already bribed the umpire."

Montreal's eyes and Adeline's met, and in that gaze Adeline forgot all her sorrows.

With a practised and skilful hand, Adrian touched the strings; and selecting a song which was less elaborate than those mostly in vogue amongst his countrymen, though still conceived in the Italian spirit, and in accordance with the sentiment he had previously expressed to Adeline, he sang as follows:—

LOVE'S EXCUSE FOR SADNESS.

Chide not, beloved, if oft with thee
  I feel not rapture wholly;
For aye the heart that's fill'd with love,
  Runs o'er in melancholy.
To streams that glide in noon, the shade
  From summer skies is given;
So, if my breast reflects the cloud,
  'Tis but the cloud of heaven!
Thine image glass'd within my soul,
  So well the mirror keepeth;
That, chide me not, if with the *light*
  The *shadow* also sleepeth.

"And now," said Adrian, as he concluded, "the lute is to you: I but prelude your prize."

The Provençal laughed, and shook his head. —"With any other umpire, I had had my lute broken on my own head, for my conceit in provoking such a rival; but I must not shrink from a contest I have myself provoked, even though in one day *twice* defeated." And with that, in a deep and exquisitely melodious voice, which wanted only more scientific culture to have challenged any competition, the Knight of St. John poured forth

THE LAY OF THE TROUBADOUR.

1.

Gentle river, the moonbeam is hush'd on thy tide,
On thy pathway of light to my lady I glide.
My boat, where the stream laves the castle, I moor,—
All at rest save the maid and her young Troubadour!
  As the stars to the waters that bore
    My bark, to my spirit thou art;
  Heaving yet, see it bound to the shore,
    So moor'd to thy beauty my heart,—
      Bel' amie, bel' amie, bel' amie!

2.

Wilt thou fly from the world? It hath wealth for the vain;
But Love breaks his bond when there's gold in the chain:
Wilt thou fly from the world? It hath courts for the proud;—
But Love, born in caves, pines to death in the crowd.
  Were this bosom thy world, dearest one,
    Thy world could not fail to be bright;
  For thou shouldst thyself be its sun,
    And what spot could be dim in thy light—
      Bel' amie, bel' amie, bel' amie?

3.

The rich and the great woo thee, dearest; and poor,
Though his fathers were princes, thy young Troubadour!
But his heart never quail'd save to thee, his adored,—
There's no guile in his lute, and no stain on his sword.
  Ah, I reck not what sorrows I know,
    Could I still on thy solace confide;
  And I care not, though earth be my foe,
    If thy soft heart be found by my side,—
      Bel' amie, bel' amie, bel' amie!

4.

The maiden she blush'd, and the maiden she sighed,
Not a cloud in the sky, not a gale on the tide;
But though tempest had raged on the wave and the wind,
That castle, methinks, had been still left behind!
Sweet lily, though bow'd by the blast,
(To this bosom transplanted) since then,
Wouldst thou change, could we call the past,
To the rock from thy garden again—
Bel' amie, bel' amie, bel amie?

Thus they alternated the time with converse and song, as the wooded hills threw their sharp, long shadows over the sea; while from many a mound of waking flowers, and many a copse of citron and orange, relieved by the dark and solemn aloe, stole the summer breeze, laden with mingled odors; and, over the seas, colored by the slow-fading hues of purple and rose, that the sun had long bequeated to the twilight, flitted the gay fire-flies that sparkle along that enchanted coast. At length, the moon slowly rose above the dark forest-steeps, gleaming on the gay pavilion and glittering pennon of Montreal,—on the verdant sward,—the polished mail of the soldiers, stretched on the grass in various groups, half-shaded by oaks and cypress, and the war-steeds grazing peaceably together—a wild mixture of the Pastoral and the Iron time.

Adrian, reluctantly reminded of his journey, rose to depart.

"I fear," said he to Adeline, "that I have already detained you too late in the night air: but selfishness is little considerate."

"Nay, you see we are prudent," said Adeline, pointing to Montreal's mantle, which his provident hand had long since drawn around her form; "but if you must part, farewell, and success attend you!"

"We may meet again, I trust," said Adrian.

Adeline sighed gently; and the Colonna, gazing on her face by the moonlight, to which it was slightly raised, was painfully struck by its almost transparent delicacy. Moved by his compassion, ere he mounted his steed, he drew Montreal aside,—"Forgive me if I seem presumptuous," said he; "but to one so noble this wild life is scarce a fitting career. I know that, in our time, War consecrates all his children; but surely a settled rank in the court of the Emperor, or an honorable reconciliation with your knightly brethren, were better——"

"Than a Tartar camp, and a brigand's castle," interrupted Montreal, with some impatience. "This you were about to say—you are mistaken. Society thrust me from her bosom; let society take the fruit it hath sown. 'A fixed rank,' say you? some subaltern office, to fight at other men's command! You know me not: Walter de Montreal was not formed to obey. War when I will, and rest when I list, is the motto of my escutcheon. Ambition proffers me rewards you wot not of; and I am of the mould as of the race of those whose swords have conquered thrones. For the rest, your news of the alliance of Louis of Hungary with your Tribune makes it necessary for the friend of Louis to withdraw from all feud with Rome. Ere the week expire, the owl and the bat may seek refuge in yon gray turrets."

"But your lady?"

"Is inured to change.—God help her, and temper the rough wind to the lamb!"

"Enough, Sir Knight: but should you desire a sure refuge at Rome for one so gentle and so highborn, by the right hand of a knight, I promise a safe roof and an honored home to the Lady Adeline."

Montreal pressed the offered hand to his heart; then plucking his own hastily away, drew it across his eyes, and joined Adeline, in a silence that showed he dared not trust himself to speak. In a few moments Adrian and his train were on the march; but still the young Colonna turned back, to gaze once more on his wild host and that lovely lady, as they themselves lingered on the moonlit sward, while the sea rippled mournfully on their ears.

It was not many months after that date, that the name of Fra Moreale scattered terror and dismay throughout the fair Campania. The right hand of the Hungarian king, in his invasion of Naples, he was chosen afterwards vicar (or vice-gerent) of Louis in Aversa; and fame and fate seemed to lead him triumphantly along that ambitious career which he had elected, whether bounded by the scaffold or the throne.

BOOK FOURTH.

THE TRIUMPH AND THE POMP.

"Allora fama e paura di si buono reggimento, passa in ogni terra."—*Vita di Cola di Rienzi*, lib. i. cap. 21.

"Then the fame and the fear of that so good government passed into every land."—*Life of Cola di Rienzi.*

CHAPTER I.

The Boy Angelo—The Dream of Nina Fulfilled.

THE thread of my story transports us back to Rome. It was in a small chamber, in a ruinous mansion by the base of Mount Aventine, that a young boy sate, one evening, with a woman of a tall and stately form, but somewhat bowed both by infirmity and years. The boy was of a fair and comely presence; and there was that in his bold, frank, undaunted carriage, which made him appear older than he was.

The old woman, seated in the recess of the deep window, was apparently occupied with a Bible that lay open on her knees; but ever and anon she lifted her eyes, and gazed on her young companion with a sad and anxious expression.

"Dame," said the boy, who was busily employed in hewing out a sword of wood, "I would you had seen the show to-day. Why, every day is a show at Rome now! It is show enough to see the Tribune himself on his white steed—(oh, it is so beautiful!)—with his white robes all studded with jewels. But to-day, as I have just been telling you, the Lady Nina took notice of me, as I stood on the stairs of the Capitol: you know, dame, I had donned my best blue velvet doublet."

"And she called you a fair boy, and asked if you would be her little page; and this has turned thy brain, silly urchin that thou art——"

"But the words are the least: if you saw the Lady Nina, you would own that a smile from her might turn the wisest head in Italy. Oh, how I should like to serve the Tribune! All the lads of my age are mad for him. How they will stare, and envy me at school to-morrow! You know too, dame, that though I was not always brought up at Rome, I am Roman. Every Roman loves Rienzi."

"Ay, for the hour: the cry will soon change. This vanity of thine, Angelo, vexes my old heart. I would thou wert humbler."

"Bastards have their own name to win," said the boy, coloring deeply. "They twit me in the teeth, because I cannot say who my father and mother were."

"They need not," returned the dame, hastily. "Thou comest of noble blood and long descent, though, as I have told thee often, I know not the exact names of thy parents. But what art thou shaping that tough sapling of oak into?"

"A sword, dame, to assist the Tribune against the robbers."

"Alas! I fear me, like all those who seek power in Italy, he is more likely to enlist robbers than to assail them."

"Why, la you there, you live so shut up, that you know and hear nothing, or you would have learned that even that fiercest of all the robbers, Fra Moreale, has at length yielded to the Tribune, and fled from his castle, like a rat from a falling house."

"How, how!" cried the dame; "what say you? Has this plebeian, whom you call the Tribune—has he boldly thrown the gage to that dread warrior? and has Montreal left the Roman territory?"

"Ay, it is the talk of the town. But Fra

Moreale seems as much a bugbear to you as to e'er a mother in Rome. Did he ever wrong you, dame?"

"Yes!" exclaimed the old woman, with so abrupt a fierceness, that even that hardy boy was startled.

"I wish I could meet him, then," said he, after a pause, as he flourished his mimic weapon.

"Now Heaven forbid! He is a man ever to be shunned by thee, whether for peace or war. Say again this good Tribune holds no terms with the Free Lances."

"Say it again—why all Rome knows it."

"He is pious, too, I have heard; and they do bruit it that he sees visions, and is comforted from above," said the woman, speaking to herself. Then turning to Angelo, she continued,—"Thou wouldst like greatly to accept the Lady Nina's proffer?"

"Ah, that I should, dame, if you could spare me."

"Child," replied the matron, solemnly, "my sand is nearly run, and my wish is to see thee placed with one who will nurture thy young years, and save thee from a life of licence. That done, I may fulfil my vow, and devote the desolate remnant of my years to God. I will think more of this, my child. Not under such a plébeian's roof shouldst thou have lodged, nor from a stranger's board been fed: but at Rome, my last relative worthy of the trust is dead;—and at the worst, obscure honesty is better than gaudy crime. Thy spirit troubles me already. Back, my child; I must to my closet, and watch and pray."

Thus saying, the old woman, repelling the advance, and silencing the muttered and confused words, of the boy—half affectionate as they were, yet half tetchy and wayward—glided from the chamber.

The boy looked abstractedly at the closing door, and then said to himself—"The dame is always talking riddles: I wonder if she know more of me than she tells, or if she is any way akin to me. I hope not, for I don't love her much; nor, for that matter, anything else. I wish she would place me with the Tribune's lady, and then we'll see who among the lads will call Angelo Villani bastard."

With that the boy fell to work again at his sword with redoubled vigor. In fact, the cold manner of this female, his sole nurse, companion, substitute for parent, had repelled his affections without subduing his temper; and though not originally of evil disposition, Angelo Villani was already insolent, cunning, and revengeful; but not, on the other hand, without a quick susceptibility to kindness as to affront, a natural acuteness of understanding, and a great indifference to fear. Brought up in quiet affluence rather than luxury, and living much with his protector, whom he knew but by the name of Ursula, his bearing was graceful, and his air that of the well-born. And it was his carriage, perhaps, rather than his countenance, which, though handsome, was more distinguished for intelligence than beauty, which had attracted the notice of the Tribune's bride. His education was that of one reared for some scholastic profession. He was not only taught to read and write, but had been even instructed in the rudiments of Latin. He did not, however, incline to these studies half so fondly as to the games of his companions, or the shows or riots in the street, into all of which he managed to thrust himself, and from which he had always the happy dexterity to return safe and unscathed.

The next morning Ursula entered the young Angelo's chamber. "Wear again thy blue doublet to-day," said she; "I would have thee look thy best. Thou shalt go with me to the palace."

"What, to-day?" cried the boy joyfully, half leaping from his bed. "Dear dame Ursula, shall I really then belong to the train of the great Tribune's lady?"

"Yes; and leave the old woman to die alone! Your joy becomes you,—but ingratitude is in your blood. Ingratitude! Oh, it has burned my heart into ashes—and yours, boy, can no longer find a feul in the dry crumbling cinders."

"Dear dame, you are always so biting. You know you said you wished to retire into a convent, and I was too troublesome a charge for you. But you delight in rebuking me, justly or unjustly."

"My task is over," said Ursula, with a deep-drawn sigh.

The boy answered not; and the old woman retired with a heavy step, and, it may be, a heavier heart. When he joined her in their common apartment, he observed what his joy had previously blinded him to—that Ursula did not wear her usual plain and sober dress. The gold chain, rarely assumed then by women not of noble birth—though, in the other sex, affected also by public functionaries and wealthy merchants—glittered upon a robe of the rich flowered stuffs of Venice, and the clasps that confined the vest at the throat and waist were adorned with jewels of no common price.

Angelo's eye was struck by the change, but he felt a more manly pride in remarking that the old lady became it well. Her air and mien were indeed those of one to whom such garments were habitual; and they seemed that day more than usually austere and stately.

She smoothed the boy's ringlets, drew his short mantle more gracefully over his shoulder, and then placed in his belt a poniard whose handle was richly studded, and a purse well filled with florins.

"Learn to use both discreetly," said she; "and, whether I live or die, you will never require to wield the poniard to procure the gold."

"This, then," cried Angelo, enchanted, "is a real poniard to fight the robbers with! Ah, with this I should not fear *Fra Moreale*, who wronged thee so. I trust I may yet avenge thee, though thou didst rate me so just now for ingratitude."

"I *am* avenged. Nourish not such thoughts, my son, they are sinful; at least I fear so. Draw to the board and eat; we will go betimes, as petitioners should do."

Angelo had soon finished his morning meal, and sallying with Ursula to the porch, he saw, to his surprise, four of those servitors who then usually attended persons of distinction, and who were to be hired in every city, for the convenience of strangers or the holyday ostentation of the gayer citizens.

"How grand we are to-day!" said he, clapping his hands with an eagerness which Ursula failed not to reprove.

"It is not for vain show," she added, "which true nobility can well dispense with, but that we may the more readily gain admittance to the palace. These princes of yesterday are not easy of audience to the over humble."

"Oh! but you are wrong this time," said the boy. "The Tribune gives audience to all men, the poorest as the richest. Nay, there is not a ragged boor, or a bare-footed friar, who does not win access to him sooner than the proudest baron. That's why the people love him so. And he devotes one day of the week to receiving the widows and the orphans;—and you know, dame, I am an orphan."

Ursula, already occupied with her own thoughts, did not answer, and scarcely heard, the boy; but leaning on his young arm, and preceded by the footmen to clear the way, passed slowly towards the palace of the Capitol.

A wonderful thing would it have been to a more observant eye, to note the change which two or three short months of the stern but salutary and wise rule of the Tribune had effected in the streets of Rome. You no longer beheld the gaunt and mail-clad forms of foreign mercenaries stalking through the vistas, or grouped in lazy insolence before the embattled porches of some gloomy palace. The shops, that in many quarters had been closed for years, were again open, glittering with wares and bustling with trade. The thoroughfares, formerly either silent as death, or crossed by some affrighted and solitary passenger with quick steps, and eyes that searched every corner,—or resounding with the roar of a pauper rabble, or the open feuds of savage nobles, now exhibited the regular, and wholesome, and mingled streams of civilized life, whether bound to pleasure or to commerce. Carts and wagons laden with goods which had passed in safety by the dismantled holds of the robbers of the Campagna, rattled cheerfully over the pathways. "Never, perhaps," —to use the translation adapted from the Italian authorities, by a modern and by no means a partial historian *—"Never, perhaps, has the energy and effect of a single mind been more remarkably felt than in the sudden reformation of Rome by the Tribune Rienzi. A den of robbers was converted to the discipline of a camp or convent. 'In this time,' says the historian, † 'did the woods begin to rejoice that they were no longer infested with robbers; the oxen began to plough; the pilgrims visited the sanctuaries; ‡ the roads and inns were replenished with travellers: trade,

* Gibbon.

† Vita di Cola di Rienzi, lib. i. c. 9.

‡ Gibbon: the words in the original are "*li pellegrini cominciaro a fere la cerca per la santuaria.*"

plenty, and good faith, were restored in the markets; and a purse of gold might be exposed without danger in the midst of the highways.'"

Amidst all these evidences of comfort and security to the people—some dark and discontented countenances might be seen mingled in the crowd, and whenever one who wore the livery of the Colonna or the Orisini felt himslf jostled by the throng, a fierce hand moved involuntarily to the sword-belt, and a half-suppressed oath was ended with an indignant sigh. Here and there too,—contrasting the redecorated, refurnished, and smiling shops—heaps of rubbish before the gate of some haughty mansion testified the abasement of fortifications which the owner impotently resented as a sacrilege. Through such streets and such throngs did the party we accompany wend their way, till they found themselves amidst crowds assembled before the entrance of the Capitol. The officers there stationed kept, however, so discreet and dexterous an order, that they were not long detained; and now in the broad place or court of that memorable building, they saw the open doors of the great justice-hall, guarded but by a single sentinel, and in which, for six hours daily, did the Tribune hold his court, for "patient to hear, swift to redress, inexorable to punish, his tribunal was always accessible to the poor and stranger." *

Not, however, to that hall did the party bend its way, but to the entrance which admitted to the private apartments of the palace. And here the pomp, the gaud, the more than regal magnificence, of the residence of the Tribune, strongly contrasted the patriarchal simplicity which marked his justice court.

Even Ursula, not unaccustomed, of yore, to the luxurious state of Italian and French principalities, seemed roused into surprise at the hall crowded with retainers in costly liveries, the marble and gilded columns wreathed with flowers, and the gorgeous banners wrought with the blended arms of the Republican City and the Pontifical See, which blazed aloft and around.

Scarce knowing whom to address in such an assemblage, Ursula was relieved from her perplexity by an officer attired in a suit of crimson and gold, who, with a grave and formal decorum, which indeed reigned throughout the whole retinue, demanded, respectfully, whom she sought? "The Signora Nina!" replied Ursula, drawing up her stately person, with a natural, though somewhat antiquated, dignity. There was something foreign in the accent, which influenced the officer's answer.

"To-day, madam, I fear that the Signora receives only the Roman ladies. To-morrow is that appointed for all foreign dames of distinction."

Ursula, with a slight impatience of tone, replied—

"My business is of that nature which is welcome on any day, at palaces. I come, Signor, to lay certain presents at the Signora's feet which I trust she will deign to accept."

"And say, Signor," added the boy, abruptly, "that Angelo Villani, whom the Lady Nina honored yesterday with her notice, is no stranger but a Roman; and comes, as she bade him, to proffer to the Signora his homage and devotion."

The grave officer could not refrain a smile at the pert, yet not ungraceful, boldness of the boy.

"I remember me, Master Angelo Villani," he replied, "that the Lady Nina spoke to you by the great staircase. Madam, I will do your errand. Please to follow me to an apartment more fitting your sex and seeming."

With that the officer led the way across the hall to a broad staircase of white marble, along the centre of which were laid those rich Eastern carpets which at that day, when rushes strewed the chambers of an English monarch, were already common to the greater luxury of Italian palaces. Opening a door at the first flight, he ushered Ursula and her young charge into a lofty ante-chamber, hung with arras of wrought velvets; while over the opposite door, through which the officer now vanished, were blazoned the armorial bearings which the Tribune so constantly introduced in all his pomp, not more from the love of show, than from his politic desire to mingle with the keys of the Pontiff the heraldic insignia of the Republic.

"Philip of Valois is not housed like this man!" muttered Ursula. "If this last, I shall have done better for my charge than I recked of."

The officer soon returned, and led them

* Gibbon.

across an apartment of vast extent, which was indeed the great reception chamber of the palace. Four-and-twenty columns of the Oriental alabaster which had attested the spoils of the later emperors, and had been disinterred from forgotten ruins, to grace the palace of the Reviver of the old Republic, supported the light roof, which, half Gothic, half classic, in its architecture, was inlaid with gilded and purple mosaics. The tesselated floor was covered in the centre with cloth of gold, the walls were clothed, at intervals, with the same gorgeous hangings, relieved by panels freshly painted in the most glowing colors, with mystic and symbolical designs. At the upper end of this royal chamber, two steps ascended to the place of the Tribune's throne, above which was the canopy wrought with the eternal armorial bearings of the Pontiff and the City.

Traversing this apartment, the officer opened the door at its extremity, which admitted to a small chamber, crowded with pages in rich dresses of silver and blue velvet. There were few amongst them elder than Angelo; and, from their general beauty, they seemed the very flower and blossom of the city.

Short time had Angelo to gaze on his comrades that were to be:—another minute, and he and his protectress were in the presence of the Tribune's bride.

The chamber was not large—but it was large enough to prove that the beautiful daughter of Raselli had realized her visions of vanity and splendor.

It was an apartment that mocked description—it seemed a cabinet for the gems of the world. The daylight, shaded by high and deep-set casements of stained glass, streamed in a purple and mellow hue over all that the art of that day boasted most precious, or regal luxury held most dear. The candelabras of the silver workmanship of Florence; the carpets and stuffs of the East; the draperies of Venice and Genoa; paintings like the illuminated missals, wrought in gold, and those lost colors of blue and crimson; antique marbles, which spoke of the bright days of Athens; tables of disinterred mosaics, their freshness preserved as by magic; censers of gold that steamed with the odors of Araby, yet so subdued as not to deaden the healthier scent of flowers, which blushed in every corner from their marble and alabaster vases; a small and spirit-like fountain, which seemed to gush from among wreaths of roses, diffusing in its diamond and fairy spray, a scarce felt coolness to the air;—all these, and such as these, which it were vain work to detail, congregated in the richest luxuriance, harmonized with the most exquisite taste, uniting the ancient arts with the modern, amazed and intoxicated the sense of the beholder. It was not so much the cost, nor the luxury, that made the character of the chamber; it was a certain gorgeous and almost sublime phantasy,—so that it seemed rather the fabled retreat of an enchantress, at whose word genii ransacked the earth, and fairies arranged the produce, than the grosser splendor of an earthly queen. Behind the piled cushions upon which Nina half-reclined, stood four girls, beautiful as nymphs, with fans of the rarest feathers, and at her feet lay one older than the rest, whose lute, though now silent, attested her legitimate occupation.

But, had the room in itself seemed somewhat too fantastic and over-charged in its prodigal ornaments, the form and face of Nina would at once have rendered all appropriate; so completely did she seem the natural Spirit of the Place; so wonderfully did her beauty, elated as it now was with contented love, gratified vanity, exultant hope, body forth the brightest vision that ever floated before the eyes of Tasso, when he wrought into one immortal shape the glory of the Enchantress with the allurements of the Woman.

Nina half rose as she saw Ursula, whose sedate and mournful features involuntarily testified her surprise and admiration at a loveliness so rare and striking, but who, undazzled by the splendor around, soon recovered her wonted self-composure, and seated herself on the cushion to which Nina pointed, while the young visitor remained standing, and spell-bound by childish wonder, in the centre of the apartment. Nina recognized him with a smile.

"Ah, my pretty boy, whose quick eye and bold air caught my fancy yesterday! Have you come to accept my offer? Is it you, madam, who claim this fair child?"

"Lady," replied Ursula, "my business here is brief: by a train of events, needless to weary you with narrating, this boy from his infancy fell to my charge—a weighty and anxious trust to one whose thoughts are beyond the barrier of life. I have reared him as became a youth of gentle blood; for on both sides, lady, he is noble, though an orphan, motherless and sireless."

"Poor child!" said Nina, compassionately.

"Growing now," continued Ursula, "oppressed by years, and desirous only to make my peace with Heaven, I journeyed hither some months since, in the design to place the boy with a relation of mine; and, that trust fulfilled, to take the vows in the City of the Apostle. Alas! I found my kinsman dead, and a baron of wild and dissolute character was his heir. Here remaining, perplexed and anxious, it seemed to me the voice of Providence when, yester-evening, the child told me you had been pleased to honor him with your notice. Like the rest of Rome, he has already learned enthusiasm for the Tribune—devotion to the Tribune's bride. Will you, in truth, admit him of your household? He will not dishonor your protection by his blood, nor, I trust, by his bearing."

"I would take his face for his guarantee, madam, even without so distinguished a recommendation as your own. Is he Roman? His name then must be known to me."

"Pardon me, lady," replied Ursula: "he bears the name of Angelo Villani—not that of his sire or mother. The honor of a noble house for ever condemns his parentage to rest unknown. He is the offspring of a love unsanctioned by the church."

"He is the more to be loved, then, and to be pitied—victim of sin not his own!" answered Nina, with moistened eyes, as she saw the deep and burning blush that covered the boy's cheeks. "With the Tribune's reign commences a new era of nobility, when rank and knighthood shall be won by a man's own merit—not that of his ancestors. Fear not, madam: in my house he shall know no slight."

Ursula was moved from her pride by the kindness of Nina: she approached with involuntary reverence, and kissed the Signora's hand—

"May our Lady reward your noble heart!" said she: "and now my mission is ended, and my earthly goal is won. Add only, lady, to your inestimable favors one more. These jewels"—and Ursula drew from her robe a casket, touched the spring, and the lid flying back, discovered jewels of great size and the most brilliant water,—"these jewels," she continued, laying the casket at Nina's feet, "once belonging to the princely house of Thoulouse, are valueless to me and mine. Suffer me to think that they are transferred to one whose queenly brow will give them a lustre it cannot borrow."

"How!" said Nina, coloring very deeply; "think you, madam, my kindness can be bought? What woman's kindness ever was? Nay, nay—take back the gifts, or I shall pray you to take back your boy."

Ursula was astonished and confounded: to her experience such abstinence was a novelty, and she scarcely knew how to meet it. Nina perceived her embarrassment with a haughty and triumphant smile, and then, regaining her former courtesy of demeanor, said, with a grave sweetness—

"The Tribune's hands are clean,—the Tribune's wife must not be suspected. Rather, madam, should I press upon *you* some token of exchange for the fair charge you have committed to me. Your jewels hereafter may profit the boy in his career: reserve them for one who needs them."

"No, lady," said Ursula, rising and lifting her eyes to heaven;—"they shall buy masses for his mother's soul; for him I shall reserve a competence when his years require it. Lady, accept the thanks of a wretched and desolate heart. Fare you well!"

She turned to quit the room, but with so faltering and weak a step, that Nina, touched and affected, sprung up, and with her own hand guided the old woman across the room, whispering comfort and soothing to her; while, as they reached the door, the boy rushed forward, and, clasping Ursula's robes, sobbed out —"Dear dame, not one farewell for your little Angelo! Forgive him all he has cost you! Now, for the first time, I feel how wayward and thankless I have been."

The old woman caught him in her arms, and kissed him passionately; when the boy, as if a thought suddenly struck him, drew forth the purse she had given him, and said, in a choked and scarce articulate voice,—"And let this, dearest dame, go in masses for my poor *father's* soul; for *he* is dead too, you know!"

These words seemed to freeze at once all

the tenderer emotions of Ursula. She put back the boy with the same chilling and stern severity of aspect and manner which had so often before repressed him: and recovering her self-possession, at once quitted the apartment without saying another word. Nina, surprised, but still pitying her sorrow and respecting her age, followed her steps across the pages' ante-room and the reception chamber, even to the foot of the stairs,—a condescension the haughtiest princess of Rome could not have won from her; and returning, saddened and thoughtful, she took the boy's hand, and affectionately kissed his forehead.

"Poor boy!" she said, "it seems as if Providence had made me select thee yesterday from the crowd, and thus conducted thee to thy proper refuge. For to whom should come the friendlest and the orphans of Rome, but to the palace of Rome's first Magistrate?" Turning then to her attendants, she gave them instructions as to the personal comforts of her new charge, which evinced that if power had ministered to her vanity, it had not steeled her heart. Angelo Villani lived to repay her *well!*

She retained the boy in her presence, and conversing with him familiarly, she was more and more pleased with his bold spirit and frank manner. Their conversation was however interrupted, as the day advanced, by the arrival of several ladies of the Roman nobility. And then it was that Nina's virtues receded into shade, and her faults appeared. She could not resist the woman's triumph over those arrogant signoras who now cringed in homage where they had once slighted with disdain. She affected the manner of, she demanded respect due to, a queen. And by many of those dexterous arts which the sex know so well, she contrived to render her very courtesy a humiliation to her haughty guests. Her commanding beauty and her graceful intellect saved her, indeed, from the vulgar insolence of the upstart; but yet more keenly stung the pride, by forbidding to those she mortified the retaliation of contempt. Hers were the covert taunt—the smiling affront—the sarcasm in the mask of compliment—the careless exaction of respect in trifles, which could not outwardly be resented, but which could not inly be forgiven.

"Fair day to the Signora Colonna," said she to the proud wife of the proud Stephen; "we passed your palace yesterday. How fair it now seems, relieved from those gloomy battlements which it must often have saddened you to gaze upon. Signora (turning to one of the Orsini), your lord has high favor with the Tribune, who destines him to great command. His fortunes are secured, and we rejoice at it; for no man more loyally serves the state. Have you seen, fair Lady of Frangipani, the last verses of Petrarch in honor of my lord?—they rest yonder. May we so far venture as to request you to point out their beauties to the Signora di Savelli? We rejoice, noble Lady of Malatesta, to observe that your eyesight is so well restored. The last time we met, though we stood next to you in the revels of the Lady Giulia, you seemed scarce to distinguish us from the pillar by which we stood!"

"Must this insolence be endured!" whispered the Signora Frangipani to the Signora Malatesta.

"Hush, hush; if ever it be *our* day again!"

CHAPTER II.

The Blessing of a Councillor whose Interests and Heart are Our Own.—The Straws thrown Upward,—Do they Portend a Storm.

It was later that day than usual, when Rienzi returned from his tribunal to the apartments of the palace. As he traversed the reception hall, his countenance was much flushed; his teeth were set firmly, like a man who has taken a strong resolution from which he will not be moved; and his brow was dark with that settled and fearful frown which the describers of his personal appearance have not failed to notice as the characteristic of an anger the more deadly because invariably just. Close at his heels followed the Bishop of Orvietto and the aged Stephen Colonna. "I tell you, my Lords," said Rienzi, "that ye plead in vain. Rome knows no distinction between ranks. The law is blind to the agent—lynx-eyed to the deed."

"Yet," said Raimond, hesitatingly, "bethink thee, Tribune; the nephew of two cardinals, and himself once a senator."

Rienzi halted abruptly, and faced his companions. "My Lord Bishop," said he, "does not this make the crime more inexcusable? Look you, thus it reads:—A vessel from Avignon to Naples, charged with the revenues of Provence to Queen Joanna, on whose cause, mark you, we now hold solemn council, is wrecked at the mouth of the Tiber; with that, Martino di Porto—a noble, as you say—the holder of that fortress whence he derives his title,—doubly bound by gentle blood and by immediate neighborbood to succor the oppressed—falls upon the vessel with his troops (what hath the rebel with armed troops?)—and pillages the vessel like a common robber. He is apprehended—brought to my tribunal—receives fair trial—is condemned to die. Such is the law;—what more would ye have?"

"Mercy," said the Colonna.

Rienzi folded his arms, and laughed disdainfully. "I never heard my Lord Colonna plead for mercy when a peasant had stolen the bread that was to feed his famishing children."

"Between a peasant and a prince, Tribune, *I*, for one, recognize a distinction:—the bright blood of an Orsini is not to be shed like that of a base plebeian——"

"Which, I remember me," said Rienzi, in a low voice, "you deemed small matter enough when my boy-brother fell beneath the wanton spear of your proud son. Wake not that memory, I warn you; let it sleep.—For shame, old Colonna—for shame; so near the grave, where the worm levels all flesh, and preaching, with those gray hairs, the uncharitable distinction between man and man. Is there not distinction enough at the best? Does not one wear purple, and the other rags? Hath not one ease, and the other toil? Doth not the one banquet while the other starves? Do I nourish any mad scheme to level the ranks which society renders a necessary evil? No. I war no more with Dives than with Lazarus. But before Man's judgment-seat, as before God's, Lazarus and Dives are made equal. No more."

Colonna drew his robe round him with great haughtiness, and bit his lip in silence. Raimond interposed.

"All this is true, Tribune. But," and he drew Rienzi aside, "you know we must be politic as well as just. Nephew to two Cardinals, what enmity will not this provoke at Avignon."

"Vex not yourself, holy Raimond, I will answer it to the Pontiff." While they spoke the bell tolled heavily and loudly.

Colonna started.

"Great Tribune," said he, with a slight sneer, "deign to pause ere it be too late. I know not that I ever before bent to you a suppliant; and I ask you now to spare mine own foe. Stephen Colonna prays Cola di Rienzi to spare the life of an Orsini."

"I understand thy taunt, old Lord," said Rienzi, calmly, "but I resent it not. You are foe to the Orsini, yet you plead for him—it sounds generous; but hark you,—you are more a friend to your order than a foe to your rival. You cannot bear that one, great enough to have contended with you, should perish like a thief. I give full praise to such noble forgiveness; but I am no noble, and I do not sympathize with it. One word more;—if this were the sole act of fraud and violence that this bandit baron had committed, your prayers should plead for him; but is not his life notorious? Has he not been from boyhood the terror and disgrace of Rome? How many matrons violated, merchants pillaged, peaceful men stilettoed in the daylight, rise in dark witness against the prisoner? And for such a man do I live to hear an aged prince and a pope's vicar plead for mercy?—Fie, fie! But I will be even with ye. The next *poor* man whom the law sentences to death, for your sake will I pardon."

Raimond again drew aside the Tribune, while Colonna struggled to suppress his rage.

"My friend," said the Bishop, "the nobles will feel this as an insult to their whole order; the very pleading of Orsini's worst foe must convince thee of this. Martino's blood will seal their reconciliation with each other, and they will be as one man against thee."

"Be it so: with God and the People on my side, I will dare, though a Roman, to be just. The bell ceases—you are already too late." So saying, Rienzi threw open the casement; and by the staircase of the Lion rose a gibbet from which swung with a creaking sound, arrayed in his patrician robes, the yet palpitating corpse of Martino di Porto.

"Behold!" said the Tribune, sternly, "thus die all robbers. For *traitors*, the same law has the axe and the scaffold!"

Raimond drew back and turned pale. Not

so the veteran noble. Tears of wounded pride started from his eyes; he approached, leaning on his staff, to Rienzi, touched him on his shoulder, and said,—

"Tribune, a judge has lived to envy his victim!"

Rienzi turned with an equal pride to the Baron.

"We forgive idle words in the aged. My Lord, have you done with us?—we would be alone."

"Give me thy arm, Raimond," said Stephen. "Tribune—farewell. Forget that the Colonna sued thee,—an easy task, methinks; for, wise as you are, you forget what every one else can remember."

"Ay, my Lord, what?"

"Birth, Tribune, birth—that's all!"

"The Signor Colonna has taken up my old calling, and turned a wit," returned Rienzi, with an indifferent and easy tone.

Then following Raimond and Stephen with his eyes, till the door closed upon them, he muttered, "Insolent! were it not for Adrian, thy gray beard should not bear thee harmless. Birth! what Colonna would not boast himself, if he could, the grandson of an emperor?—Old man, there is danger in thee which must be watched." With that he turned musingly towards the casement, and again that griesly spectacle of death met his eye. The people below, assembled in large concourse, rejoiced at the execution of one whose whole life had been infamy and rapine—but who had seemed beyond justice—with all the fierce clamor that marks the exultation of the rabble over a crushed foe. And where Rienzi stood, he heard their shouts of "Long live the Tribuue, the just judge, Rome's liberator!" But at that time other thoughts deafened his senses to the popular enthusiasm.

"My poor brother!" he said, with tears in his eyes, "it was owing to this man's crimes—and to a crime almost similar to that for which he has now suffered—that thou wert entrained to the slaughter; and they who had no pity for the lamb, clamor for compassion to the wolf! Ah, wert thou living now, how these proud heads would bend to thee; though dead, thou wert not worthy of a thought. God rest thy gentle soul, and keep my ambition pure as it was when we walked at twilight, side by side together!"

The Tribune shut the casement, and turning away sought the chamber of Nina. On hearing his step without, she had already risen from the couch, her eyes sparkling, her bosom heaving; and as he entered, she threw herself on his neck, and murmured as she nestled to his breast,—"Ah, the hours since we parted!"

It was a singular thing to see that proud lady, proud of her beauty, her station, her new honors;—whose gorgeous vanity was already the talk of Rome, and the reproach to Rienzi, how suddenly and miraculously she seemed changed in his presence! Blushing and timid, all pride in herself seemed merged in her proud love for him. No woman ever loved to the full extent of the passion, who did not venerate where she loved, and who did not feel humbled (delighted in that humility) by her exaggerated and overwhelming estimate of the superiority of the object of her worship.

And it might be the consciousness of this distinction between himself and all other created things, which continued to increase the love of the Tribune to his bride, to blind him to her failings towards others, and to indulge her in a magnificence of parade, which, though to a certain point politic to assume, was carried to an extent which if it did not conspire to produce his downfall, has served the Romans with an excuse for their own cowardice and desertion, and historians with a plausible explanation of causes they had not the industry to fathom. Rienzi returned his wife's caresses with an equal affection, and bending down to her beautiful face, the sight was sufficient to chase from his brow the emotions, whether severe or sad, which had lately darkened its broad expanse.

"Thou hast not been abroad this morning, Nina!"

"No, the heat was oppressive. But nevertheless, Cola, I have not lacked company—half the matronage of Rome has crowded the palace."

"Ah, I warrant it.—But yon boy, is he not a new face?"

"Hush, Cola, speak to him kindly, I entreat: of his story anon. Angelo, approach. You see your new master, the Tribune of Rome."

Angelo approached with a timidity not his wont, for an air of majesty was at all times natural to Rienzi, and since his power it had naturally taken a graver and austerer aspect, which impressed those who approached him, even the ambassadors of princes, with a certain involuntary awe. The Tribune smiled at the effect he saw he had produced, and being by temper fond of children, and affable to all but the great, he hastened to dispel it. He took the child affectionately in his arms, kissed him, and bade him welcome.

"May we have a son as fair!" he whispered to Nina, who blushed, and turned away.

"Thy name, my little friend?"

"Angelo Villani."

"A Tuscan name. There is a man of letters at Florence, doubtless writing our annals from hearsay at this moment, called Villani. Perhaps akin to thee?"

"I have no kin," said the boy, bluntly; "and therefore I shall the better love the Signora and honor you, if you will let me. I am Roman — all the Roman boys honor Rienzi."

"Do they, my brave lad?" said the Tribune, coloring with pleasure; "that is a good omen of my continued prosperity." He put down the boy, and threw himself on the cushions, while Nina placed herself on a kind of low stool beside him.

"Let us be alone," said he; and Nina motioned to the attendant maidens to withdraw.

"Take my new page with you," said she; "he is yet, perhaps, too fresh from home to enjoy the company of his giddy brethren."

When they were alone, Nina proceeded to narrate to Rienzi the adventure of the morning; but though he seemed outwardly to listen, his gaze was on vacancy, and he was evidently abstracted and self-absorbed. At length, as she concluded, he said, "Well, Nina, you have acted as ever, kindly and nobly. Let us to other themes. I am in danger."

"Danger!" echoed Nina, turning pale.

"Why, the word must not appal you—you have a spirit like mine, that scorns fear; and, for that reason, Nina, in all Rome you are my only confidant. It was not only to glad me with thy beauty, but to cheer me with thy counsel, to support me with thy valor, that Heaven gave me thee as a helpmate."

"Now, our Lady bless thee for those words!" said Nina, kissing the hand that hung over her shoulder; "and if I started at the word danger, it was but the woman's thought of thee,—an unworthy thought, my Cola, for glory and danger go together. And I am as ready to share the last as the first. If the hour of trial ever come, none of thy friends shall be so faithful to thy side as this weak form but undaunted heart."

"I know it, my own Nina; I know it," said Rienzi, rising, and pacing the chamber with large and rapid strides. "Now listen to me. Thou knowest that to govern in safety, it is my policy as my pride to govern justly. To govern justly is an awful thing, when mighty barons are the culprits. Nina, for an open and audacious robbery, our court has sentenced Martin of the Orsini, the Lord of Porto, to death. His corse swings now on the Staircase of the Lion."

"A dreadful doom!" said Nina, shuddering.

"True; but by his death thousands of poor and honest men may live in peace. It is not that which troubles me: the Barons resent the deed, as an insult to them that law should touch a noble. They will rise—they will rebel. I foresee the storm—not the spell to allay it."

Nina paused a moment,—"They have taken," she then said, "a solemn oath on the Eucharist not to bear arms against thee."

"Perjury is a light addition to theft and murder," answered Rienzi, with his sarcastic smile.

"But the people are faithful."

"Yes, but in a civil war (which the saints forefend!) those combatants are the stanchest who have no home but their armor, no calling but the sword. The trader will not leave his trade at the toll of a bell every day; but the Barons' soldiery are ready at all hours."

"To be strong," said Nina,—who, summoned to the councils of her lord, showed an intellect not unworthy of the honor,—"to be strong in dangerous times, authority must *seem* strong. By showing no fear, you may prevent the cause of fear."

"My own thought!" returned Rienzi, quickly. "You know that half my power with these Barons is drawn from the homage rendered to me by foreign states. When from every city in Italy the ambassadors of crowned princes seek the alliance of the Tribune, they must veil their resentment at the rise of the Plebeian. On the other hand, to be strong abroad I must seem strong at home: the vast design I have planned, and, as by a miracle, begun to execute, will fail at once if it seem abroad to be intrusted to an unsteady and fluctuating power. That design (continued Rienzi, pausing, and placing his hand on a marble bust of the young Augustus) is greater than his, whose profound yet icy soul united Italy in subjection,—for it would unite Italy in freedom;—yes! could we but form one great federative league of all the States of Italy, each governed by its own laws, but united for mutual and common protection against the Attilas of the North, with Rome for their Metropolis and their Mother, this age and this brain would have wrought an enterprise which men should quote till the sound of the last trump!"

"I know thy divine scheme," said Nina, catching his enthusiasm; "and what if there be danger in attaining it? Have we not mastered the greatest danger in the first step?"

"Right, Nina, right! Heaven (and the Tribune, who ever recognized, in his own fortunes, the agency of the hand above, crossed himself reverently) will preserve him to whom it hath vouchsafed such lofty visions of the future redemption of the Land of the true Church, and the liberty and advancement of its children! This I trust: already many of the cities of Tuscany have entered into treaties for the formation of this league; nor from a single tyrant, save John di Vico, have I received aught but fair words and flattering promises. The time seems ripe for the grand stroke of all."

"And what is that?" demanded Nina, wonderingly.

"Defiance to all foreign interference. By what right does a synod of stranger princes give Rome a king in some Teuton Emperor? Rome's people alone should choose Rome's governor;—and shall we cross the Alps to render the title of our master to the descendants of the Goth?"

Nina was silent: the custom of choosing the sovereign by a diet beyond the Rhine, reserving only the ceremony of his subsequent coronation for the mock assent of the Romans, however degrading to that people, and however hostile to all notions of substantial independence, was so unquestioned at that time, that Rienzi's daring suggestion left her amazed and breathless, prepared as she was for any scheme, however extravagantly bold.

"How!" said she, after a long pause; "do I understand aright? Can you mean defiance to the Emperor?"

"Why, listen: at this moment there are two pretenders to the throne of Rome—to the imperial crown of Italy—a Bohemian and a Bavarian. To their election our assent—Rome's assent—is not requisite—not asked. Can we be called free—can we boast ourselves republican—when a stranger and a Barbarian is thus thrust upon our necks? No, we will be free in reality as in name. Besides, (continued the Tribune, in a calmer tone,) this seems to me politic as well as daring. The people incessantly demand wonders from me: how can I more nobly dazzle, more virtuously win them, than by asserting their inalienable right to choose their own rulers? The daring will awe the Barons, and foreigners themselves; it will give a startling example to all Italy; it will be the first brand of an universal blaze. It shall be done, and with a pomp that befits the deed!"

"Cola," said Nina, hesitatingly, "your eagle spirit often ascends where mine flags to follow; yet be not over bold."

"Nay, did you not, a moment since, preach a different doctrine? To be strong, was I not to seem strong?"

"May fate preserve you!" said Nina, with a foreboding sigh.

"Fate," cried Rienzi; "there is *no* fate! Between the thought and the success, God is the only agent; and (he added with a voice of deep solemnity) I shall not be deserted. Visions by night, even while thine arms are around me; omens and impulses, stirring and divine, by day, even in the midst of the living crowd—encourage my path, and point my goal. Now, even now, a voice seems to whisper in my ear—'Pause not; tremble not; waver not;—for the eye of the All-Seeing is upon thee, and the hand of the All-Powerful shall protect!'"

As Rienzi thus spoke, his face grew pale, his hair seemed to bristle, his tall and proud form trembled visibly, and presently he sunk down on a seat, and covered his face with his hands.

An awe crept over Nina, though not unaccustomed to such strange and preternatural emotions, which appeared yet the more singular in one who in common life was so calm, stately, and self-possessed. But with every increase of prosperity and power, those emotions seemed to increase in their fervor, as if in such increase the devout and overwrought superstition of the Tribune recognized additional proof of a mysterious guardianship mightier than the valor or art of man.

She approached fearfully, and threw her arms around him, but without speaking.

Ere yet the Tribune had well recovered himself, a slight tap at the door was heard, and the sound seemed at once to recall his self-possession.

"Enter," he said, lifting his face, to which the wonted color slowly returned.

An officer, half-opening the door, announced that the person he had sent for waited his leisure.

"I come!—Core of my heart," (he whispered to Nina), "we will sup alone to-night, and will converse more on these matters:" so saying, with somewhat less than his usual loftiness of mien, he left the room, and sought his cabinet, which lay at the other side of the reception chamber. Here he found Cecco del Vecchio.

"How, my bold fellow," said the Tribune, assuming with wonderful ease that air of friendly equality which he always adopted with those of the lower class, and which made a striking contrast with the majesty, no less natural, which marked his manner to the great. "How now, my Cecco! Thou bearest thyself bravely, I see, during these sickly heats; we laborers—for both of us labor, Cecco—are too busy to fall ill as the idle do, in the summer, or the autumn, of Roman skies. I sent for thee, Cecco, because I would know how thy fellow-craftsmen are like to take the Orsini's execution."

"Oh! Tribune," replied the artificer, who, now familiarized with Rienzi, had lost much of his earlier awe of him, and who regarded the Tribune's power as partly his own creation; "they are already out of their honest wits, at your courage in punishing the great men as you would the small."

"So;—I am repaid! But hark you, Cecco, it will bring, perhaps, hot work upon us. Every Baron will dread lest it be his turn next, and dread will make them bold, like rats in despair. We may have to fight for the Good Estate."

"With all my heart, Tribune," answered Cecco, gruffly. "I, for one, am no craven."

"Then keep the same spirit in all your meetings with the artificers. I fight for the people. The people at a pinch must fight with me."

"They will," replied Cecco; "they will!"

"Cecco, this city is under the spiritual dominion of the Pontiff—so be it—it is an honor, not a burthen. But the *temporal* dominion, my friend, should be with Romans only. Is it not a disgrace to Republican Rome, that while we now speak, certain barbarians, whom we never heard of, should be deciding beyond the Alps on the merits of two sovereigns, whom we never saw? Is not this a thing to be resisted? An Italian city,—what hath it to do with a Bohemian Emperor?"

"Little eno', St. Paul knows!" said Cecco

"Should it not be a claim questioned?"

"I think so!" replied the smith.

"And if found an outrage on our ancient laws, should it not be a claim resisted?"

"Not a doubt of it."

"Well, go to! The archives assure me that never was Emperor lawfully crowned but by the free votes of the people. *We* never chose Bohemian or Bavarian."

"But, on the contrary, whenever these Northmen come hither to be crowned, we try to drive them away with stones and curses,—for we are a people, Tribune, that love our liberties."

"Go back to your friends—see—address them, say that your Tribune will demand of these pretenders to Rome the right to her throne. Let them not be mazed or startled, but support me when the occasion comes."

"I am glad of this," quoth the huge smith; "for our friends have grown a little unruly of late, and say——"

"What do they say?"

"That it is true you have expelled the banditti, and curb the Barons, and administer justice fairly;—"

"Is not that miracle enough for the space of some two or three short months?"

"Why, they say it would have been more than enough in a noble; but you, being raised from the people, and having such gifts and so forth, might do yet more. It is now three weeks since they have had any new thing to talk about; but Orsini's execution to-day will cheer them a bit."

"Well, Cecco, well," said the Tribune, rising, "they shall have more anon to feed their mouths with. So you think they love me not quite so well as they did some three weeks back?"

"I say not so," answered Cecco. "But we Romans are an impatient people."

"Alas, yes!"

"However, they will no doubt stick close enough to you; provided, Tribune, you don't put any new tax upon them."

"Ha! But if, in order to be free, it be necessary to fight—if to fight, it be necessary to have soldiers, why then the soldiers must be paid:—won't the people contribute something to their own liberties;—to just laws, and safe lives?"

"I don't know," returned the smith, scratching his head as if a little puzzled; "but I know that poor men won't be overtaxed. They say they are better off with you than with the Barons before, and therefore they love you. But men in business, Tribune, poor men with families, must look to their bellies. Only one man in ten goes to law—only one man in twenty is butchered by a Baron's brigand; but every man eats, and drinks, and feels a tax."

"This cannot be your reasoning, Cecco!" said Rienzi, gravely.

"Why, Tribune, I am an honest man, but I have a large family to rear."

"Enough; enough!" said the Tribune, quickly; and then he added abstractedly as to himself, but aloud,—"Methinks we have been too lavish; these shows and spectacles should cease."

"What!" cried Cecco; "what, Tribune!—would you deny the poor fellows a holiday. They work hard enough, and their only pleasure is seeing your fine shows and processions; and then they go home and say,—'See, *our* man beats all the Barons! what state he keeps!'"

"Ah! they blame not my splendor, then!"

"Blame it; no! Without it they would be ashamed of you, and think the *Buono Stato* but a shabby concern."

"You speak bluntly, Cecco, but perhaps wisely. The saints keep you! Fail not to remember what I told you!"

"No, no. It is a shame to have an Emperor thrust upon us;—so it is. Good evening, Tribune."

Left alone, the Tribune remained for some time plunged in gloomy and foreboding thoughts.

"I am in the midst of a magician's spell," said he; "if I desist, the fiends tear me to pieces. What I have begun, that must I conclude. But this rude man shows me too well with what tools I work. For *me* failure is nothing. I have already climbed to a greatness which might render giddy many a born prince's brain. But with my fall—Rome, Italy, Peace, Justice, Civilization—all fall back into the abyss of ages!"

He rose; and after once or twice pacing his apartment, in which from many a column gleamed upon him the marble effigies of the great of old, he opened the casement to inhale the air of the now declining day.

The Place of the Capitol was deserted save by the tread of the single sentinel. But still, dark and fearful, hung from the tall gibbet the clay of the robber noble; and the colossal shape of the Egytian lion rose hard by, sharp and dark in the breathless atmosphere.

"Dread statue!" thought Rienzi, "how many unwhispered and solemn rites hast thou witnessed by thy native Nile, ere the Roman's hand transferred thee hither—the antique witness of Roman crimes! Strange! but when I look upon thee I feel as if thou hadst some mystic influence over my own fortunes. Beside thee was I hailed the republican Lord of Rome; beside thee are my palace, my tribunal, the place of my justice, my triumphs, and my pomp:—to thee my eyes turn from my bed of state: and if fated to die in power and peace, thou mayst be the last object my eyes will mark! Or if myself a victim——"—he paused—shrank from the thought presented to him—turned to a recess of the chamber—drew aside a curtain, that veiled a crucifix and a small table, on which lay a Bible and the monastic emblems of the skull and cross-bones—emblems, indeed grave and irresistible, of the nothingness of power, and the uncertainty of life. Before these sacred monitors, whether to humble or to elevate, knelt that proud and aspiring man; and when he rose, it was with a lighter step and more cheerful mien than he had worn that day.

CHAPTER III.

The Actor Unmasked.

"IN intoxication," says the proverb, "men betray their real characters." There is a no less honest and truth-revealing intoxication in prosperity, than in wine. The varnish of power brings forth at once the defects and the beauties of the human portrait.

The unprecedented and almost miraculous rise of Rienzi from the rank of the Pontiff's official to the Lord of Rome, would have been accompanied with a yet greater miracle, if it had not somewhat dazzled and seduced the object it elevated. When, as in well-ordered states and tranquil times, men rise slowly, step by step, they accustom themselves to their growing fortunes. But the leap of an hour from a citizen to a prince—from the victim of oppression to the dispenser of justice—is a transition so sudden as to render dizzy the most sober brain. And, perhaps, in proportion to the imagination, the enthusiasm, the genius of the man, will the suddenness be dangerous—excite too extravagant a hope—and lead to too chimerical an ambition. The qualities that made him rise, hurry him to his fall; and victory at the Marengo of his fortunes, urges him to destruction at its Moscow.

In his greatness Rienzi did not so much acquire new qualities, as develop in brighter light and deeper shadow those which he had always exhibited. On the one hand he was just—resolute—the friend of the oppressed—the terror of the oppressor. His wonderful intellect illumined everything it touched. By rooting out abuse, and by searching examination and wise arrangement, he had trebled the revenues of the city without imposing a single new tax. Faithful to his idol of liberty, he had not been betrayed by the wish of the people into despotic authority; but had, as we have seen, formally revived, and established with new powers, the Parliamentary Council of the city. However extensive his own authority, he referred its exercise to the people; in their name he alone declared himself to govern, and he never executed any signal action without submitting to them its reasons or its justification. No less faithful to his desire to restore prosperity as well as freedom to Rome, he had seized the first dazzling epoch of his power to propose that great federative league with the Italian States which would, as he rightly said, have raised Rome to the indisputable head of European nations. Under his rule trade was secure, literature was welcome, art began to rise.

On the other hand, the prosperity which made more apparent his justice, his integrity, his patriotism, his virtues, and his genius, brought out no less glaringly his arrogant consciousness of superiority, his love of display, and the wild and daring insolence of his ambition. Though too just to avenge himself by retaliating on the particians their own violence, though, in his troubled and stormy tribuneship, not one unmerited or illegal execution of baron or citizen could be alleged against him, even by his enemies; yet sharing, less excusably, the weakness of Nina, he could not deny his proud heart the pleasure of humiliating those who had ridiculed him as a buffoon, despised him as a plebeian, and who, even now slaves to his face, were cynics behind his back. "They stood before him while he sate," says his biographer; "all these Barons, bareheaded; their hands crossed on their breasts; their looks downcast;—oh, how frightened they were!"—a picture more disgraceful to the servile cowardice of the nobles than the haughty sternness of the Tribune. It might be that he deemed it policy to break the spirit of his foes, and to awe those whom it was a vain hope to conciliate.

For his pomp there was a greater excuse: it was the custom of the time; it was the insignia and witness of power; and when the modern historian taunts him with not imitating the simplicity of an ancient tribune, the sneer betrays an ignorance of the spirit of the age, and the vain people whom the chief magistrate was to govern. No doubt his gorgeous festivals, his solemn possessions, set off and ennobled—if parade can so be ennobled—by a refined and magnificent richness of imagination, associated always with popular emblems, and designed to convey the idea of rejoicing for Liberty Restored, and to assert the state and majesty of Rome Revived—no doubt these spectacles, however otherwise judged in a more enlightened age and by closet sages, served greatly to augment the importance of the Tribune abroad, and to dazzle the pride of a fickle and ostentatious populace. And taste grew refined, luxury called labor into requisition, and foreigners from all states were attracted by the splendor of a court over which presided, under republican names, two sovereigns,* young and brilliant, the one renowned for his genius, the other eminent for her beauty. It was, indeed, a dazzling and royal dream in the long night of Rome, spoiled of her Pontiff and his voluptuous train—that holyday reign of Cola di Rienzi! And often afterwards it was recalled with a sigh, not only by the poor for its justice, the merchant for its security, but the gallant for its splendor, and the poet for its ideal and intellectual grace!

As if to show that it was not to gratify the more vulgar appetite and desire, in the midst of all his pomp, when the board groaned with the delicacies of every clime, when the wine most freely circled, the Tribune himself preserved a temperate and even rigid abstinence.† While the apartments of state and the chamber of his bride were adorned with a profuse luxury and cost, to his own private rooms he transported precisely the same furniture which had been familiar to him in his obscurer life. The books, the busts, the reliefs, the arms which had inspired him heretofore with the visions of the past, were endeared by associations which he did not care to forego.

But that which constituted the most singular feature of his character, and which still wraps all around him in a certain mystery, was his religious enthusiasm. The daring but wild doctrines of Arnold of Brescia, who, two centuries anterior, had preached reform, but inculcated mysticism, still lingered in Rome, and had in earlier youth deeply colored the mind of Rienzi; and as I have before observed, his youthful propensity to dreamy thought, the melancholy death of his brother, his own various but successful fortunes, had all contributed to nurse the more zealous and solemn aspirations of this remarkable man. Like Arnold of Brescia, his faith bore a strong resemblance to the intense fanaticism of our own Puritans of the Civil War, as if similar political circumstances conduced to similar religious sentiments. He believed himself inspired by awful and mightly commune with beings of the better world. Saints and angels ministered to his dreams; and without this, the more profound and hallowed enthusiasm, he might never have been sufficiently emboldened by mere human patriotism, to his unprecedented enterprise: it was the secret of much of his greatness,—many of his errors. Like all men who are thus self-deluded by a vain but not inglorious superstition, united with, and colored by, earthly ambition, it is impossible to say how far he was the visionary, and how far at times he dared to be the impostor. In the ceremonies of his pageants, in the ornaments of his person, were invariably introduced mystic and figurative emblems. In times of danger he publicly professed to have been cheered and directed by divine dreams, and on many occasions the prophetic warnings he announced having been singularly verified by the event, his influence with the people was strengthened by a belief in the favor and intercourse of Heaven. Thus, delusion of self might tempt and conduce to imposition on others, and he might not scruple to avail himself of the advantage of seeming what he believed himself to be. Yet, no doubt this intoxicating credulity pushed him into extravagance unworthy of, and strangely contrasted by, his soberer intellect, and made him disproportion his vast ends to his unsteady means, by the proud fallacy, that where man failed, God would interpose. Cola de Rienzi was no faultless hero of romance. In him lay, in conflicting prodigality, the richest and most opposite elements of character; strong sense, visionary superstition, an eloquence and energy that mastered all he approached, a blind enthusiasm that mastered himself; luxury and abstinence, sternness and susceptibility, pride to the great, humility to the low; the most devoted patriotism and the most avid desire of personal power. As few men undertake great and des-

* Rienzi, speaking in one of his letters of his great enterprise, refers it to the ardor of youth. The exact date of his birth is unknown; but he was certainly a young man at the time now referred to. His portrait in the Museo Barberino, from which his description has been already taken in the first book of this work, represents him as beardless, and, as far as one can judge, somewhere above thirty—old enough, to be sure, to have a beard; and seven years afterwards he wore a long one, which greatly displeased his *naive* biographer, who seems to consider it a sort of crime. The head is very remarkable for its stern beauty, and little, if at all, inferior to that of Napoleon; to which, as I before remarked, it has some resemblance in expression, if not in feature.

† Vita di Cola di Rienzi.—The biographer praises the abstinence of the *Tribune*.

perate designs without strong animal spirits, so it may be observed, that with most who have risen to eminence over the herd, there is an aptness, at times, to a wild mirth and an elasticity of humor which often astonish the more sober and regulated minds, that are "the commoners of life." And the theatrical grandeur of Napoleon, the severe dignity of Cromwell, are strangely contrasted by a frequent, nor always seasonable buffoonery, which it is hard to reconcile with the ideal of their characters, or the gloomy and portentous interest of their careers. And this, equally a trait in the temperament of Rienzi, distinguished his hours of relaxation, and contributed to that marvellous versatility with which his harder nature accommodated itself to all humors and all men.. Often from his austere judgment-seat he passed to the social board an altered man; and even the sullen Barons who reluctantly attended his feasts, forgot his public greatness in his familiar wit; albeit this reckless humor could not always refrain from seeking its subject in the mortification of his crest-fallen foes—a pleasure it would have been wiser and more generous to forego. And perhaps it was, in part, the prompting of this sarcastic and unbridled humor that made him often love to astonish as well as to awe. But even this gaiety, if so it may be called, taking an appearance of familiar frankness, served much to ingratiate him with the lower orders; and, if a fault in the prince, was a virtue in the demagogue.

To these various characteristics, now fully developed, the reader must add a genius of designs so bold, of conceptions so gigantic and august, conjoined with that more minute and ordinary ability which masters details; that with a brave, noble, intelligent, devoted people to back his projects, the accession of the Tribune would have been the close of the thraldom of Italy, and the abrupt limit of the dark age of Europe. With such a people, his faults would have been insensibly checked, his more unwholesome power have received a sufficient curb. Experience familiarizing him with power, would have gradually weaned him from extravagance in its display; and the active and masculine energy of his intellect would have found field for the more restless spirits, as his justice gave shelter to the more tranquil. Faults he had, but whether those faults or the faults of the people, were to prepare his downfal, is yet to be seen.

Meanwhile, amidst a discontented nobility and a fickle populace, urged on by the danger of repose to the danger of enterprise; partly blinded by his outward power, partly impelled by the fear of internal weakness; at once made sanguine by his genius and his fanaticism, and uneasy by the expectations of the crowd,—he threw himself headlong into the gulf of the rushing Time, and surrendered his lofty spirit to no other guidance than a conviction of its natural bouyancy and its heaven-directed haven.

CHAPTER IV.

The Enemy's Camp.

WHILE Rienzi was preparing, in concert, perhaps, with the ambassadors of the brave Tuscan States, whose pride of country and love of liberty were well fitted to comprehend, and even share them, his schemes for the emancipation from all foreign yoke of the Ancient Queen, and the Everlasting Garden of the World; the Barons, in restless secrecy, were revolving projects for the restoration of their own power.

One morning, the heads of the Savelli, the Orsini, and the Frangipani, met at the disfortified palace of Stephen Colonna. Their conference was warm and earnest—now resolute, now wavering, in its object—as indignation or fear prevailed.

"You have heard," said Luca di Savelli, in in his usual soft and womanly voice, "that the Tribune has proclaimed, that, the day after to-morrow, he will take the order of knighthood, and watch the night before in the church of the Lateran: He has honored me with a request to attend his vigil."

"Yes, yes, the knave. What means this new fantasy?" said the brutal Prince of the Orsini.

"Unless it be to have the cavalier's right to challenge a noble," said old Colonna, "I cannot conjecture. Will Rome never grow weary of this madman?"

"Rome is the more mad of the two," said Luca di Savelli; "but methinks, in his wildness, the Tribune hath committed one error of which we may well avail ourselves at Avignon."

"Ah," cried the old Colonna, "that must be our game; passive here, let us fight at Avignon."

"In a word then, he hath ordered that his bath shall be prepared in the holy porphyry vase in which once bathed the Emperor Constantine."

"Profanation! profanation!" cried Stephen. "This is enough to excuse a bull of excommunication. The Pope shall hear of it. I will despatch a courier forthwith."

"Better wait and see the ceremony," said the Savelli; "some greater folly will close the pomp, be assured."

"Hark ye, my masters," said the grim Lord of the Orsini; "ye are for delay and caution; I for promptness and daring; my kinsman's blood calls aloud, and brooks no parley."

"And what do?" said the soft-voiced Savelli; "fight without soldiers, against twenty thousand infuriated Romans? not I."

Orsini sunk his voice into a meaning whisper. "In Venice," said he, "this upstart might be mastered without an army. Think you in Rome no man wears a stiletto?"

"Hush," said Stephen, who was of far nobler and better nature than his compeers, and who, justifying to himself all other resistance to the Tribune, felt his conscience rise against assassination; "this must not be—your zeal transports you."

"Besides, whom can we employ? scarce a German left in the city; and to whisper this to a Roman were to exchange places with poor Martino—Heaven take him, for he's nearer heaven than ever he was before," said the Savelli.

"Jest me no jests," cried the Orsini, fiercely. "Jests on such a subject! By St. Francis, I would, since thou lovest such wit, thou hadst it all to thyself; and, methinks, at the Tribune's board I have seen thee laugh at his rude humor, as if thou didst not require a cord to choke thee."

"Better to laugh then to tremble," returned the Savelli.

"How! darest thou say I tremble?" cried the Baron.

"Hush, hush," said the veteran Colonna, with impatient dignity. "We are not now in such holiday times as to quarrel amongst ourselves. Forbear, my lords."

"Your greater prudence, Signor," said the sarcastic Savelli, "arises from your greater safety. Your house is about to shelter itself under the Tribune's; and, when the Lord Adrian returns from Naples, the innkeeper's son will be brother to your kinsman."

"You might spare me that taunt," said the old noble, with some emotion. "Heaven knows how bitterly I have chafed at the thought; yet I would Adrian were with us. His word goes far to moderate the Tribune, and to guide my own course, for my passion beguiles my reason; and since his departure methinks we have been the more sullen without being the more strong. Let this pass. If my own son had wed the Tribune's sister, I would yet strike a blow for the old constitution as becomes a noble, if I but saw that the blow would not cut off my own head."

Savelli, who had been whispering apart with Rinaldo Frangipani, now said—

"Noble Prince, listen to me. You are bound by your kinsman's approaching connection, your venerable age, and your intimacy with the Pontiff, to a greater caution than we are. Leave to us the management of the enterprise, and be assured of our discretion."

A young boy, Stefanello, who afterwards succeeded to the representation of the direct line of the Colonna, and whom the reader will once again encounter ere our tale be closed, was playing by his grandsire's knees. He looked sharply up at Savelli, and said, "My grandfather is too wise, and you are too timid. Frangipani is too yielding, and Orsini is too like a vexed bull. I wish I were a year or two older."

"And what would you do, my pretty censurer?" said the smooth Savelli, biting his smiling lip.

"Stab the Tribune with my own stiletto, and then hey for Palestrina!"

"The egg will hatch a brave serpent," quoth the Savelli. "Yet why so bitter against the Tribune, my cockatrice?"

"Because he allowed an insolent mercer to arrest my uncle Agapet for debt. The debt had been owed these ten years; and though it is said that no house in Rome has owed more money than the Colonna, this is the first time I ever heard of a rascally creditor being allowed to claim his debt unless with doffed cap and bended knee. And I say that I would not live to be a Baron, if such upstart insolence is to be put upon me."

"My child," said old Stephen, laughing heartily, "I see our noble order will be safe enough in your hands."

"And," continued the child, emboldened by the applause he received, "if I had time after pricking the Tribune, I would fain have a second stroke at——"

"Whom?" said the Savelli, observing the boy pause.

"My cousin Adrian. Shame on him, for dreaming to make one a wife whose birth would scarce fit her for a Colonna's leman!"

"Go play, my child—go play," said the old Colonna, as he pushed the boy from him.

"Enough of this babble," cried the Orsini, rudely. "Tell me, old lord; just as I entered, I saw an old friend (one of your former mercenaries) quit the palace—may I crave his errand?"

"Ah, yes; a messenger from Fra Moreale. I wrote to the Knight, reproving him for his desertion on our ill-starred return from Corneto, and intimating that five hundred lances would be highly paid for just now."

"Ah," said Savelli; "and what is his answer!"

"O, wily and evasive: He is profuse in compliments and good wishes; but says he is under fealty to the Hungarian king, whose cause is before Rienzi's tribunal; that he cannot desert his present standard; that he fears Rome is so evenly balanced between patricians and the people, that whatever party would permanently be uppermost must call in a podesta; and this character alone the Provençal insinuates would suit him."

"Montreal our Podesta?" cried the Orsini.

"And why not?" said Savelli; "as good a well-born Podesta as a low-born Tribune? But I trust we may do without either. Colonna, has this messenger from Fra Moreale left the city?"

"I suppose so."

"No," said Orsini; "I met him at the gate, and knew him of old: it is Rodolf, the Saxon (once a hireling of the Colonna), who has made some widows among my clients in the good old day. He is a little disguised now; however, I recognized and accosted him, for I thought he was one who might yet become a friend, and I bade him await me at my palace."

"You did well," said the Savelli, musing, and his eyes met those of Orsini. Shortly afterwards a conference, in which much was said and nothing settled, was broken up; but Luca di Savelli, loitering at the porch, prayed the Frangipani, and the other Barons, to adjourn to the Orsini's palace.

"The old Colonna," said he, "is well-nigh in his dotage. We shall come to a quick determination without him, and we can secure his proxy in his son."

And this was a true prophecy, for half-an-hour's consultation with Rodolf of Saxony sufficed to ripen thought into enterprise.

CHAPTER V.

The Night and its Incidents.

WITH the following twilight, Rome was summoned to the commencement of the most magnificent spectacle the Imperial City had witnessed since the fall of the Cæsars. It had been a singular privilege, arrogated by the people of Rome, to confer upon their citizens the order of knighthood. Twenty years before, a Colonna and an Orsini had received this popular honor. Rienzi, who designed it as the prelude to a more important ceremony, claimed from the Romans a similar distinction. From the Capitol to the Lateran swept, in long procession, all that Rome boasted of noble, of fair, and brave. First went horsemen without number, and from all the neighboring parts of Italy, in apparel that well befitted the occasion. Trumpeters, and musicians of all kinds, followed, and the trumpets were of silver; youths bearing the harness of the knightly war-steed, wrought with gold, preceded the march of the loftiest matronage of Rome, whose love for show and it may be whose admiration for triumphant fame, (which to women sanctions many offences), made them forget the humbled greatness of their lords: amidst them Nina and Irene, outshining all the rest; then came the Tribune and the Pontiff's Vicar, surrounded by all the great Signors of the city, smothering alike resentment, revenge, and scorn, and struggling who should approach nearest to the monarch of the day. The high-hearted old Colonna alone remained aloof, following at a little distance, and in a garb studiously plain. But his age, his rank, his former renown in war and state, did not suffice to draw to his gray locks and high-born mien a single one of the shouts that attended the meanest lord on whom the great Tribune smiled. Savelli followed nearest to Rienzi, the most obsequious of the courtly band; immediately before the Tribune came two men; the one bore a drawn sword, the other the *pendone*, or standard usually assigned to royalty. The Tribune himself was clothed in a long robe of white satin, whose snowy dazzle (*miri candoris*) is peculiarly dwelt on by the historian, richly decorated with gold; while on his breast were many of those mystic symbols I have before alluded to, the exact meaning of which was perhaps known only to the wearer. In his dark eye, and on that large tranquil brow, in which thought seemed to sleep, as sleeps a storm, there might be detected a mind abstracted from the pomp around; but ever and anon he roused himself, and conversed partially with Raimond or Savelli.

"This is a quaint game," said the Orsini, falling back to the old Colonna: "but it may end tragically."

"Methinks it may," said the old man, "if the Tribune overhear thee."

Orsini grew pale. "How—nay—nay, even if he did, he never resents words, but professes to laugh at our spoken rage. It was but the other day that some knave told him what one of the Annibaldi said of him—words for which a true cavalier would have drawn the speaker's life's blood; and he sent for the Annibaldi, and said, 'My friend, receive this purse of gold,—court wits should be paid.'"

"Did Annibaldi take the gold?"

"Why, no; the Tribune was pleased with his spirit, and made him sup with him; and Annibaldi says he never spent a merrier evening, and no longer wonders that his kinsman, Riccardo, loves the buffoon so."

Arrived now at the Lateran, Luca di Savelli fell also back, and whispered to Orsini; the Frangipani, and some other of the nobles, exchanged meaning looks; Rienzi, entering the sacred edifice in which, according to custom, he was to pass the night watching his armor, bade the crowd farewell, and summoned them the next morning, "To hear things that might, he trusted, be acceptable to heaven and earth."

The immense multitude received this intimation with curiosity and gladness, while those who had been in some measure prepared by Cecco del Vecchio, hailed it as an omen of their Tribune's unflagging resolution. The concourse dispersed with singular order and quietness; it was recorded as a remarkable fact, that in so great a crowd, composed of men of all parties, none exhibited licence or indulged in quarrel. Some of the barons and cavaliers, among whom was Luca di Savelli, whose sleek urbanity and sarcastic humor found favor with the Tribune, and a few subordinate pages and attendants, alone remained; and, save a single sentinel at the porch, that broad space before the Palace, the Basilica and Fount of Constantine, soon presented a silent and desolate void to the melancholy moonlight. Within the church, according to the usage of the time and rite, the descendant of the Teuton kings received the order of the Santo Spirito. His pride, or some superstition equally weak, though more excusable, led him to bathe in the porphyry vase which an absurd legend consecrated to Constantine; and this, as Savelli predicted, cost him dear. These appointed ceremonies concluded, his arms were placed in that part of the church, within the columns of St. John. And here his state bed was prepared.*

The attendant barons, pages, and chamberlains, retired out of sight to a small side chapel in the edifice; and Rienzi was left alone. A single lamp, placed beside his bed, contended with the mournful rays of the moon, that cast through, the long casements, over aisle and pillar, its "dim religious light." The sanctity of the place, the solemnity of the hour, and the solitary silence round, were well calculated to deepen the high-wrought and earnest mood of that son of fortune. Many and high fancies swept over his mind—now of worldly aspirations, now of more august but visionary belief, till at length, wearied with his own reflections, he cast himself on the bed. It was an omen which graver history has not neg-

* In a more northern country, the eve of knighthood would have been spent without sleeping. In Italy, the ceremony of watching the armor does not appear to have been so rigidly observed.

lected to record, that the moment he pressed the bed, new prepared for the occasion, part of it sank under him: he himself was affected by the accident, and sprung forth, turning pale and muttering; but, as if ashamed of his weakness, after a moment's pause, again composed himself to rest, and drew the drapery round him.

The moonbeams grew fainter and more faint as the time proceeded, and the sharp distinction between light and shade faded fast from the marble floor; when from behind a column at the furthest verge of the building, a strange shadow suddenly crossed the sickly light—it crept on—it moved, but without an echo,—from pillar to pillar it fitted—it rested at last behind the column nearest to the Tribune's bed—it remained stationary.

The shades gathered darker and darker round; the stillness seemed to deepen; the moon was gone; and, save from the struggling ray of the lamp beside Rienzi, the blankness of night closed over the solemn and ghostly scene.

In one of the side chapels, as I have before said, which, in the many alterations the church has undergone, is probably long since destroyed, were Savelli and the few attendants retained by the Tribune. Savelli alone slept not; he remained sitting erect, breathless and listening, while the tall lights in the chapel rendered yet mcre impressive the rapid changes of his countenance.

"Now pray Heaven," said he, "the knave miscarry not! Such an occasion may never again occur! He has a strong arm and a dexterous hand, doubtless; but the other is a powerful man. The deed once done, I care not whether the doer escape or not; if not, why we must stab him! Dead men tell no tales. At the worst, who can avenge Rienzi? There is no other Rienzi! Ourselves and the Frangipani seize the Aventine, the Colonna and the Orsini the other quarters of the city; and without the master-spirit, we may laugh at the mad populace. But if discovered;——" and Savelli, who, fortunately for his foes, had not nerves equal to his will, covered his face and shuddered;—"I think I hear a noise!—no—is it the wind?—tush, it must be old Vico de Scotto, turning in his shell of mail!—silent—I like not that silence! No cry—no sound! Can the ruffian have played us false? or could he not scale the casement? It is but a child's effort;—or did the sentry spy him?"

Time passed on: the first ray of daylight slowly gleamed, when he thought he heard the door of the church close. Savelli's suspense became intolerable: he stole from the chapel, and came in sight of the Tribune's bed—all was silent.

"Perhaps the silence of death," said Savelli, as he crept back.

Meanwhile the Tribune, vainly endeavoring to close his eyes, was rendered yet more watchful by the uneasy position he was obliged to assume—for the part of the bed towards the pillow having given way, while the rest remained solid, he had inverted the legitimate order of lying, and drawn himself up as he might best accommodate his limbs, towards the foot of the bed. The light of the lamp, though shaded by the draperies, was thus opposite to him. Impatient of his wakefulness, he at last thought it was this dull and flickering light which scared away the slumber, and was about to rise, to remove it further from him, when he saw the curtain at the other end of the bed gently lifted: he remained quiet and alarmed;—ere he could draw a second breath, a dark figure interposed between the light and the bed; and he felt that a stroke was aimed against that part of the couch, which, but for the accident that had seemed to him ominous, would have given his breast to the knife. Rienzi waited not a second and better-directed blow; as the assassin yet stooped, groping in the uncertain light, he threw on him all the weight and power of his large and muscular frame, wrenched the stiletto from the bravo's hand, and dashing him on the bed, placed his knee on his breast.—The stiletto rose—gleamed—descended—the murtherer swerved aside, and it pierced only his right arm. The Tribune raised, for a deadlier blow, the revengeful blade.

The assassin thus foiled was a man used to all form and shape of danger, and he did not now lose his presence of mind.

"Hold!" said he; "if you kill me, you will die yourself. Spare me, and I will save *you*."

"Miscreant!"

"Hush—not so loud, or you will disturb your attendants, and some of them may do what I have failed to execute. Spare me, I say, and I will reveal that which were worth more than my life; but call not—speak not aloud, I warn you!"

The Tribune felt his heart stand still: in that lonely place, afar from his idolizing people—his devoted guards—with but loathing barons, or, it might be, faithless menials, within call, might not the baffled murtherer give a wholesome warning?—and those words and that doubt seemed suddenly to reverse their respective positions, and leave the conqueror still in the assassin's power.

"Thou thinkest to deceive me," said he, but in a voice whispered and uncertain, which showed the ruffian the advantage he had gained: "thou wouldst that I might release thee without summoning my attendants, that thou mightst a second time attempt my life."

"Thou hast disabled my right arm, and disarmed me of my only weapon"

"How camest thou hither?"

"By connivance."

"Whence this attempt?"

"The dictation of others."

"If I pardon thee——"

"Thou shalt know all!"

"Rise," said the Tribune, releasing his prisoner, but with great caution, and still grasping his shoulder with one hand, while the other pointed the dagger at his throat.

"Did my sentry admit thee? There is but one entrance to the church, methinks."

"He did not; follow me, and I will tell thee more."

"Dog! thou hast accomplices?"

"If I have, thou hast the knife at my throat."

"Wouldst thou escape?"

"I cannot, or I would."

Rienzi looked hard, by the dull light of the lamp, at the assassin. His rugged and coarse countenance, rude garb, and barbarian speech, seemed to him proof sufficient that he was but the hireling of others; and it might be wise to brave one danger present and certain, to prevent much danger future and unforeseen. Rienzi, too, was armed, strong, active, in the prime of life;—and at the worst, there was no part of the building whence his voice would not reach those within the chapel,—if they could be depended upon.

"Show me then thy place and means of entrance," said he; "and if I but suspect thee as we move—thou diest. Take up the lamp."

The ruffian nodded; with his left hand took up the lamp as he was ordered; and with Rienzi's grasp on his shoulder, while the wound from his right arm dropped gore as he passed, he moved noiselessly along the church—gained the altar—to the left of which was a small room for the use or retirement of the priest. To this he made his way. Rienzi's heart misgave him a moment.

"Beware," he whispered, "the least sign of fraud, and thou art the first victim!"

The assassin nodded again, and proceeded. They entered the room; and then the Tribune's strange guide pointed to an open casement. "Behold my entrance," said he; "and, if you permit me, my egress——"

"The frog gets not out of the well so easily as he came in, friend," returned Rienzi, smiling. "And now, if I am not to call my guards, what am I to do with thee!"

"Let me go, and I will seek thee to-morrow; and if thou payest me handsomely, and promisest not to harm limb or life, I will put thine enemies and my employers in thy power."

Rienzi could not refrain from a slight laugh at the proposition, but composing himself, replied—"And what if I call my attendants, and give thee to their charge?"

"Thou givest me to those very enemies and employers; and in despair lest I betray them, ere the day dawn they cut my throat—or thine."

"Methinks, knave, I have seen thee before."

"Thou hast. I blush not for name or country. I am Rodolf of Saxony!"

"I remember me;—servitor of Walter de Montreal. He, then, is thy instigator!"

"Roman, no! That noble Knight scorns other weapon than the open sword, and his own hand slays his own foes. Your pitiful, miserable, dastard Italians, alone employ the courage, and hire the arm, of others."

Rienzi remained silent. He had released hold of his prisoner, and stood facing him; every now and then regarding his countenance, and again relapsing into thought. At length, casting his eyes round the small chamber thus singularly tenanted, he observed a kind of closet, in which the priests' robes, and some articles used in the sacred service, were contained. It suggested at once an escape from his dilemma; he pointed to it—

"There, Rodolf of Saxony, shalt thou pass

some part of this night—a small penance for thy meditated crime; and to-morrow, as thou lookest for life, thou wilt reveal all."

"Hark ye, Tribune," returned the Saxon, doggedly; "my liberty is in your power, but neither my tongue nor my life. If I consent to be caged in that hole, you must swear on the crossed hilt of the dagger that you now hold, that, on confession of all I know, you pardon and set me free. My employers are enough to glut your rage an' you were a tiger. If you do not swear this——"

"Ah, my modest friend!—the alternative?"

"I brain myself against the stone wall! Better such a death than the rack!"

"Fool, I want not revenge against such as thou. Be honest, and I swear that, twelve hours after thy confession, thou shalt stand safe and unscatched without the walls of Rome. So help me our Lord and his saints."

"I am content!—*Donner und Hagel*, I have lived long enough to care only for my own life, and the great captain's next to it;—for the rest, I reck not if ye southerns cut each other's throats, and make all Italy one grave."

With this benevolent speech, Rodolf entered the closet; but ere Rienzi could close the door, he stepped forth again—

"Hold," said he: "this blood flows fast. Help me to bandage it, or I shall bleed to death ere my confession."

"*Per fede*," said the Tribune, his strange humor enjoying the man's cool audacity; "but, considering the service thou wouldst have rendered me, thou art the most pleasant, forbearing, unabashed, good fellow, I have seen this many a year. Give us thine own belt. I little thought my first eve of knighthood would have been so charitably spent!"

"Methinks these robes would make a better bandage," said Rodolf, pointing to the priests' gear suspended from the wall.

"Silence, knave," said the Tribune, frowning; "no sacrilege! Yet, as thou takest such dainty care of thyself, thou shalt have mine own scarf to accommodate thee."

With that the Tribune, placing his dagger on the ground, while he cautiously guarded it with his foot, bound up the wounded limb, for which condescension Rodolf gave him short thanks; resumed his weapon and lamp; closed the door; drew over it the long, heavy bolt without, and returned to his couch, deeply and indignantly musing over the treason he had so fortunately escaped.

At the first gray streak of dawn he went out of the great door of the church, called the sentry, who was one of his own guard, and bade him privately, and now ere the world was astir, convey the prisoner to one of the private dungeons of the Capitol. "Be silent," said he: "utter not a word of this to any one; be obedient, and thou shalt be promoted. This done, find out the councillor, Pandulfo di Guido, and bid him seek me here ere the crowd assemble."

He then, making the sentinel doff his heavy shoes of iron, led him across the church, resigned Rodolf to his care, saw them depart, and in a few minutes afterwards his voice was heard by the inmates of the neighboring chapel; and he was soon surrounded by his train.

He was already standing on the floor, wrapped in a large gown lined with furs; and his piercing eye scanned carefully the face of each man that approached. Two of the Barons of the Frangipani family exhibited some tokens of confusion and embarrassment, from which they speedily recovered at the frank salutation of the Tribune.

But all the art of Savelli could not prevent his features from betraying to the most indifferent eye the terror of his soul;—and, when he felt the penetrating gaze of Rienzi upon him, he trembled in every joint. Rienzi alone did not, however, seem to notice his disorder; and when Vico di Scotto, an old knight, from whose hands he received his sword, asked him how he had passed the night, he replied, cheerfully—

"Well, well—my brave friend! Over a maiden knight some good angel always watches. Signor Luca di Savelli, I fear you have slept but ill: you seem pale. No matter! —our banquet to-day will soon brighten the current of your gay blood."

"Blood, Tribune!" said di Scotto, who was innocent of the plot: "thou sayest blood, and lo! on the floor are large gouts of it not yet dry."

"Now, out on thee, old hero, for betraying my awkwardness! I pricked myself with my own dagger in unrobing. Thank Heaven it hath no poison in its blade!"

The Frangipani exchanged looks,—Luca di

Savelli clung to a column for support,—and the rest of the attendants seemed grave and surprised.

"Think not of it, my masters," said Rienzi: "it is a good omen, and a true prophecy. It implies that he who girds on his sword for the good of the state, must be ready to spill his blood for it: that am I. No more of this—a mere scratch: it gave more blood than I recked of from so slight a puncture, and saves the leech the trouble of the lancet. How brightly breaks the day! We must prepare to meet our fellow-citizens—they will be here anon. Ha, my Pandulfo—welcome!—thou, my old friend, shalt buckle on this mantle!"

And while Pandulfo was engaged in the task, the Tribune whispered a few words in his ear, which, by the smile on his countenance, seemed to the attendants one of the familiar jests with which Rienzi distinguished his intercourse with his more confidential intimates.

CHAPTER VI.

The celebrated Citation.

THE bell of the great Lateran church sounded shrill and loud, as the mighty multitude, greater even than that of the preceding night, swept on. The appointed officers made way with difficulty for the barons and ambassadors, and scarcely were those noble visitors admitted ere the crowd closed in their ranks, poured headlong into the church, and took the way to the chapel of Boniface VIII. There, filling every cranny, and blocking up the entrance, the more fortunate of the press beheld the Tribune surrounded by the splendid court his genius had collected, and his fortune had subdued. At length, as the solemn and holy music began to swell through the edifice, preluding the celebration of the mass, the Tribune stepped forth, and the hush of the music was increased by the universal and dead silence of the audience. His height, his air, his countenance were such as always command the attention of crowds; and at this time they received every adjunct from the interest of the occasion, and that peculiar look of intent yet suppressed fervor, which is, perhaps, the sole gift of the eloquent that Nature alone can give.

"Be it known," said he, slowly and deliberately, "in virtue of that authority, power, and jurisdiction, which the Roman people, in general parliament, have assigned to us, and which the Sovereign Pontiff hath confirmed, that we, not ungrateful of the gift and grace of the Holy Spirit—whose soldier we now are—nor of the favor of the Roman people, declare, that Rome, capital of the world, and base of the Christian church; and that every City, State, and People of Italy, are henceforth free. By that freedom, and in the same consecrated authority, we proclaim, that the election, jurisdiction, and monarchy of the Roman empire appertain to Rome and Rome's people, and the whole of Italy. We cite, then, and summon personally, the illustrious princes, Louis Duke of Bavaria, and Charles King of Bohemia, who would style themselves Emperors of Italy, to appear before us, or the other magistrates of Rome, to plead and to prove their claim between this day and the Day of Pentecost. We cite also, and within the same term, the Duke of Saxony, the Prince of Brandenburg, and whosoever else, potentate, prince, or prelate, asserts the right of Elector to the imperial throne—a right that, we find it chronicled from ancient and immemorial time, appertaineth only to the Roman people—and this in vindication of our civil liberties, without derogation of the spiritual power of the Church, the Pontiff, and the Sacred College.* Herald, proclaim the cita-

---

* "Il tutto senza derogare all' autorità della Chiesa del Papa e del Sacro Collegio." So concludes this extraordinary citation, this bold and wonderful assertion of the classic independence of Italy, in the most feudal time of the fourteenth century. The anonymous biographer of Rienzi declares that the Tribune cited also the Pope and the Cardinals to reside in Rome. De Sade powerfully and incontrovertibly refutes this addition to the daring or the extravagance of Rienzi. Gibbon, however, who has rendered the rest of the citation in terms more abrupt and discourteous than he was warranted by any authority, copies the biographer's blunder, and sneers at De Sade, as using arguments "rather of decency than of weight." Without wearying the reader with all the arguments of the learned Abbé, it may be sufficient to give the first two.

1. All the other contemporaneous historians that have treated of this event, G. Villani, Hocsemius, the Vatican MSS. and other chroniclers, relating the citation of the Emperor and Electors, say nothing of that of the Pope and Cardinals; and the Pope (Clement VI.), in his subsequent accusations of Rienzi, while very bitter against his citation of the Emperor, is wholly silent on what would have been to the Pontiff

tion, at the greater and more formal length, as written and entrusted to your hands, without the Lateran."

As Rienzi concluded this bold proclamation of the liberties of Italy, the Tuscan ambassadors, and those of some other of the free states, murmured low approbation. The ambassadors of those States that affected the party of the Emperor looked at each other in silent amaze and consternation. The Roman Barons remained with mute lips and downcast eyes; only over the aged face of Stephen Colonna settled a smile, half of scorn, half of exultation. But the great mass of the citizens were caught by words that opened so grand a prospect as the emancipation of all Italy, and their reverence of the Tribune's power and fortune was almost that due to a supernatural being; so that they did not pause to calculate the means which were to correspond with the boast.

While his eye roved over the crowd, the gorgeous assemblage near him, the devoted throng beyond;—as on his ear boomed the murmur of thousands and ten thousands, in the space without, from before the Palace of Constantine (Palace now his own!) sworn to devote life and fortune to his cause; in the flush of prosperity that yet had known no check; in the zenith of power, as yet unconscious of reverse, the heart of the Tribune swelled proudly: visions of mighty fame and limitless dominion,—fame and dominion, once his beloved Rome's, and by him to be restored, rushed before his intoxicated gaze; and in the delirious and passionate aspirations of the moment, he turned his sword alternately to the three quarters of the then known globe, and said, in an abstracted voice, as a man in a dream, "In the right of the Roman people *this* too is mine!" *

Low though the voice, the wild boast was heard by all around as distinctly as if borne to them in thunder. And vain it were to describe the various sensations it excited; the extravagance would have moved the derision of his foes, the grief of his friends, but for the manner of the speaker, which, solemn and commanding, hushed for the moment even reason and hatred themselves in awe; afterwards remembered and repeated, void of the spell they had borrowed from the utterer, the words met the cold condemnation of the well-judging; but at that moment all things seemed possible to the hero of the people. He spoke as one inspired—they trembled and believed; and, as rapt from the spectacle, he stood a moment silent, his arm still extended—his dark dilating eye fixed upon space—his lip parted—his proud head towering and erect above the herd,—his own enthusiasm kindled that of the more humble and distant spectators; and there was a deep murmur begun by one, echoed by the rest, "The Lord is with Italy and Rienzi!"

The Tribune turned, he saw the Pope's Vicar astonished, bewildered, rising to speak. His sense and foresight returned to him at once, and, resolved to drown the dangerous disavowal of the Papal authority for this hardihood, which was ready to burst from Raimond's lips, he motioned quickly to the musicians, and the solemn and ringing chant of the sacred ceremony prevented the Bishop of Orvietto all occasion of self-exoneration or reply.

The moment the ceremony was over, Rienzi touched the Bishop, and whispered, "We will explain this to your liking. You feast with us at the Lateran.—Your arm." Nor did he leave the good Bishop's arm, nor trust him to other companionship, until to the stormy sound of horn and trumpet, drum and cymbal, and amidst such a concourse as might have hailed, on the same spot, the legendary baptism of Constantine, the Tribune and his nobles entered the great gates of the Lateran, then the Palace of the World.

Thus ended that remarkable ceremony and that proud challenge of the Northern Powers, in behalf of the Italian liberties, which, had it been afterwards successful, would have been

---

the much greater offence of citing himself and the Cardinals.

2. The literal act of this citation, as published formally in the Lateran, is extant in Hocsemius, (whence is borrowed, though not at all its length, the speech in the text of our present tale;) and in this document the Pope and his Cardinals are *not* named in the summons.

Gibbon's whole account of Rienzi is superficial and unfair. To the cold and sneering scepticism, which so often deforms the gigantic work of that great writer, allowing nothing for that sincere and urgent enthusiasm which, whether of liberty or religion, is the most common parent of daring action, the great Roman seems but an ambitious and fantastic madman. In Gibbon's hands what would Cromwell have been? what Vane? what Hampden? The pedant, Julian, with his dirty person and pompous affectation, was Gibbon's ideal of a great man.

* "Questo e mio."

deemed a sublime daring; which, unsuccessful, has been construed by the vulgar into a frantic insolence; but which, calmly considering all the circumstances that urged on the Tribune, and all the power that surrounded him, was not, perhaps, altogether so imprudent as it seemed. And, even accepting that imprudence in the extremest sense,—by the more penetrating judge of the higher order of character, it will probably be considered as the magnificent folly of a bold nature, excited at once by position and prosperity, by religious credulities, by patriotic aspirings, by scholastic visions too suddenly transferred from revery to action, beyond that wise and earthward policy which sharpens the weapon ere it casts the gauntlet.

CHAPTER VII.

The Festival.

THE Festival of that day was far the most sumptuous hitherto known. The hint of Cecco del Vecchio, which so well depicted the character of his fellow-citizens, as yet it exists, though not to such excess, in their love of holyday pomp and gorgeous show, was not lost upon Rienzi. One instance of the universal banqueting (intended, indeed, rather for the people than the higher ranks) may illustrate the more than royal profusion that prevailed. From morn till eve, streams of wine flowed like a fountain from the nostrils of the Horse of the great Equestrian Statue of Constantine. The mighty halls of the Lateran palace, open to all ranks, were prodigally spread; and the games, sports, and buffooneries of the time, were in ample requisition. Apart, the Tribunessa, as Nina was rather unclassically entitled, entertained the dames of Rome; while the Tribune had so effectually silenced Raimond, that the good Bishop shared his peculiar table—the only one admitted to that honor. As the eye ranged each saloon and hall—it beheld the space lined with all the nobility and knighthood—the wealth and strength—the learning and the beauty—of the Italian metropolis; mingled with ambassadors and noble strangers, even from beyond the Alps; *—envoys not only of the free states that had welcomed the rise of the Tribune, but of the high-born and haughty tyrants who had first derided his arrogance, and now cringed to his power.

There, were not only the ambassadors of Florence, of Sienna, of Arezzo (which last subjected its government to the Tribune), of Todi, of Spoleto, and of countless other lesser towns and states, but of the dark and terrible Visconti, prince of Milan; of Obizzo of Ferrara, and the tyrant rulers of Verona and Bologna; even the proud and sagacious Malatesta, lord of Rimini, whose arm afterwards broke for awhile the power of Montreal, at the head of his Great Company, had deputed his representative in his most honored noble. John di Vico, the worst and most malignant despot of his day, who had sternly defied the arms of the Tribune, now subdued and humbled, was there in person; and the ambassadors of Hungary and of Naples mingled with those of Bavaria and Bohemia, whose sovereigns that day had been cited to the Roman Judgment Court. The nodding of plumes, the glitter of jewels and cloth of gold, the rustling of silks and jingle of golden spurs, the waving of banners from the roof, the sounds of minstrelsy from the galleries above, all presented a picture of such power and state—a court and chivalry of such show—as the greatest of the feudal kings might have beheld with a sparkling eye and a swelling heart. But at that moment the cause and lord of all that splendor, recovered from his late exhilaration, sat moody and abstracted, remembering with a thoughtful brow the adventure of the past night, and sensible that amongst his gaudiest revellers lurked his intended murtherers. Amidst the swell of the minstrelsy and the pomp of the crowd, he felt that treason scowled beside him; and the image of the skeleton obtruding, as of old, its grim thought of death upon the feast, darkened the ruby of the wine, and chilled the glitter of the scene.

It was while the feast was loudest that Rienzi's page was seen gliding through the banquet, and whispering several of the nobles; each bowed low, but changed color as he received the message.

"My Lord Savelli," said Orsini, himself trembling, "bear yourself more bravely. This must be meant in honor, not revenge. I suppose your summons corresponds with mine."

---

* The simple and credulous biographer of Rienzi declares his fame to have reached the ears of the Soldan of Babylon.

"He—he—asks—asks—me to supper at the Capitol; a fri—endly meeting—(pest on his friendship!)—after the noise of the day."

"The words addressed also to me!" said Orsini, turning to one of the Frangipani.

Those who received the summons soon broke from the feast, and collected in a group, eagerly conferring. Some were for flight, but flight was confession; their number, rank, long and consecrated impunity, reassured them, and they resolved to obey. The old Colonna, the sole innocent Baron of the invited guests, was also the only one who refused the invitation. "Tush!" said he, peevishly; "here is feasting enough for one day! Tell the Tribune that ere he sups I hope to be asleep. Gray hairs cannot encounter all this fever of festivity."

As Rienzi rose to depart, which he did early, for the banquet took place while yet morning, Raimond, eager to escape and confer with some of his spiritual friends, as to the report he should make to the Pontiff, was beginning his expressions of farewell, when the merciless Tribune said to him gravely—

"My Lord, we want you on urgent business at the Capitol. A prisoner—a trial—perhaps (he added with his portentous and prophetic frown) an *execution* waits us! Come."

"Verily, Tribune," stammered the good Bishop, "this is a strange time for execution!"

"Last night was a time yet more strange.—Come."

There was something in the way in which the final word was pronounced, that Raimond could not resist. He sighed, muttered, twitched his robes, and followed the Tribune. As he passed through the halls, the company rose on all sides. Rienzi repaid their salutations with smiles and whispers of frank courtesy and winning address. Young as he yet was, and of a handsome and noble presence, that took every advantage from splendid attire, and yet more from an appearance of intellectual command in his brow and eye, which the less cultivated signors of that dark age necessarily wanted—he glittered through the court as one worthy to form, and fitted to preside over, it; and his supposed descent from the Teuton Emperor, which, since his greatness, was universally bruited and believed abroad, seemed undeniably visible to the foreign lords in the majesty of his mien and the easy blandness of his address

"My Lord Prefect," said he to a dark and sullen personage in black velvet, the powerful and arrogant John di Vico, prefect of Rome, "we are rejoiced to find so noble a guest at Rome: we must repay the courtesy by surprising you in your own palace ere long;—nor will you, Signor (as he turned to the envoy from Tivoli), refuse us a shelter amidst your groves and waterfalls ere the vintage be gathered. Methinks Rome, united with sweet Tivoli, grows reconciled to the Muses. Your suit is carried, Master Venoni: the council recognizes its justice; but I reserved the news for this holyday—you do not blame me, I trust." This was whispered, with a half-affectionate frankness, to a worthy citizen, who, finding himself amidst so many of the great, would have shrunk from the notice of the Tribune; but it was the policy of Rienzi to pay an especial and marked attention to those engaged in commercial pursuits. As, after tarrying a moment or two with the merchant, he passed on, the tall person of the old Colonna caught his eye—

"Signor," said he, with a profound inclination of his head, but with a slight emphasis of tone, "you will not fail us this evening."

"Tribune—" began the Colonna.

"We receive no excuse," interrupted the Tribune, hastily, and passed on.

He halted for a few moments before a small group of men plainly attired, who were watching him with intense interest; for they, too, were scholars, and in Rienzi's rise they saw another evidence of that wonderful and sudden power which intellect had begun to assume over brute force. With these, as if abruptly mingled with congenial spirits, the Tribune relaxed all the gravity of his brow. Happier, perhaps, his living career—more unequivocal his posthumous renown—had his objects as his tastes been theirs!

"Ah, *carissime!*" said he to one, whose arm he drew within his own,—"and how proceeds thy interpretation of the old marbles?—half unravelled? I rejoice to hear it! Confer with me as of old, I pray thee. To-morrow—no, nor the day after, but next week—we will have a tranquil evening. Dear poet, your ode transported me to the days of Horace; yet, methinks, we do wrong to reject the vernacular for the Latin. You shake your head? Well, Petrarch thinks with you: his great epic moves with the stride of a giant—so I hear from his friend and envoy,—and here he is. My Lælius, is that not your name with Petrarch? How shall I express my delight at his comforting, his inspiring letter? Alas! he overrates not my intentions, but my power. Of this hereafter."

A slight shade darkened the Tribune's brow at these words: but moving on, a long line of nobles and princes on either side, he regained his self-possession, and the dignity he had dropped with his former equals. Thus he passed through the crowd, and gradually disappeared.

"He bears him bravely," said one, as the revellers reseated themselves. "Noticed you the *we*—the style royal?"

"But it must be owned that he lords it well," said the ambassador of the Visconti: "less pride would be cringing to his haughty court."

"Why," said a professor of Bologna, "why is the Tribune called proud? I see no pride in him."

"Nor I," said a wealthy jeweller.

While these, and yet more contradictory, comments followed the exit of the Tribune, he passed into the saloon, where Nina presided; and here his fair person and silver tongue ("*Suavis colorataeque sententiæ*," according to the description of Petrarch) won him a more general favor with the matrons than he experienced with their lords, and not a little contrasted the formal and nervous compliments of the good Bishop, who served him on such occasions with an excellent foil.

But as soon as these ceremonies were done, and Rienzi mounted his horse, his manner changed at once into a stern and ominous severity.

"Vicar," said he abruptly, to the Bishop, "we might well need your presence. Learn that at the Capitol now sits the Council in judgment upon an assassin. Last night, but for Heaven's mercy, I should have fallen a victim to a hireling's dagger. Knew you aught of this?"

And he turned so sharply on the Bishop, that the poor canonist nearly dropped from his horse in surprise and terror.

"I!—" said he.

Rienzi smiled—"No, good my Lord Bishop! I see you are of no murtherer's mould. But to continue:—that I might not appear to act in mine own cause, I ordered the prisoner to be tried in my absence. In his trial (you marked the letter brought me at our banquet?)——"

"Ay, and you changed color."

"Well I might: in his trial, I say, he has confessed that nine of the loftiest lords of Rome were his instigators. *They sup with me to-night!*—Vicar, forwards!"

BOOK FIFTH.

THE CRISIS.

"Questo ha acceso 'l fuoco e la flamma laquale non la par spotegnere."—*Vit. di Col. di Rienzi*, lib. cap. 29.

"He has kindled fire and flames which he will not be able to extinguish."—*Life of Cola di Rienzi.*

CHAPTER I.

The Judgment of the Tribune.

THE brief words of the Tribune to Stephen Colonna, though they sharpened the rage of the proud old noble, where such as he did not on reflection deem it prudent to disobey. Accordingly, at the appointed hour, he found himself in one of the halls of the Capitol, with a gallant party of his peers. Rienzi received them with more than his usual graciousness.

They sate down to the splendid board in secret uneasiness and alarm, as they saw that, with the exception of Stephen Colonna, none, save the conspirators, had been invited to the banquet. Rienzi, regardless of their silence and abstraction, was more than usually gay—the old Colonna more than usually sullen.

"We fear we have but ill pleased you, my Lord Colonna, by our summons. Once, methinks, we might more easily provoke you to a smile."

"Situations are changed, Tribune, since you were my guest."

"Why, scarcely so. I have risen, but you have not fallen. Ye walk the streets day and night in security and peace; your lives are safe from the robber, and your palaces no longer need bars and battlements to shield you from your fellow-citizens. I have risen, but *we all* have risen—from barbarous disorder into civilized life! My Lord Gianni Colonna, whom we have made Captain over Campagna, you will not refuse a cup to the Buono Stato;—nor think we mistrust your valor, when we say, that we rejoice Rome hath no enemies to attest your generalship."

"Methinks," quoth the old Colonna, bluntly, "we shall have enemies enough from Bohemia and Bavaria, ere the next harvest be green."

"And, if so," replied the Tribune, calmly, "foreign foes are better than civil strife."

"Ay, if we have money in the treasury; which is but little likely, if we have many more such holydays."

"You are ungracious, my Lord," said the Tribune; "and, besides, you are more uncomplimentary to Rome than to ourselves. What citizen would not part with gold to buy fame and liberty?"

"I know very few in Rome that would," answered the Baron. "But tell me, Tribune, you who are a notable casuist, which is the best for a state—that its governor should be overthrifty or over-lavish?"

"I refer the question to my friend, Luca di Savelli," replied Rienzi. "He is a grand philosopher, and I wot well could explain a much knottier riddle, which we will presently submit to his acumen."

The Barons, who had been much embarrassed by the bold speech of the old Colonna, all turned their eyes to Savelli, who answered with more composure than was anticipated.

"The question admits a double reply. He who is *born* a ruler, and maintains a foreign army, governing by fear, should be penurious. He who is *made* ruler, who courts the people, and would reign by love, must win their affection by generosity, and dazzle their fancies by pomp. Such, I believe, is the usual maxim in

Italy, which is rife in all experience of state wisdom."

The Barons unanimously applauded the discreet reply of Savelli, excepting only the old Colonna.

"Yet pardon me, Tribune," said Stephen, "if I depart from the courtier-like decision of our friend, and opine, though with all due respect, that even a friar's coarse serge,* the parade of humility, would better become thee, than this gaudy pomp, the parade of pride!" So saying, he touched the large loose sleeve fringed with gold, of the Tribune's purple robe.

"Hush, father!" said Gianni, Colonna's son, coloring at the unprovoked rudeness and dangerous candor of the veteran.

"Nay, it matters not," said the Tribune, with affected indifference, though his lip quivered and his eye shot fire; and then, after a pause, he resumed with an awful smile—"If the Colonna love the serge of the friar, he may see enough of it ere we part. And now, my Lord Savelli, for my question, which I pray you listen to; it demands all your wit. Is it best for a State's Ruler to be over-forgiving, or over-just? Take breath to answer: you look faint—you grow pale—you tremble—you cover your face! Traitor and assassin, your conscience betrays you! My Lords, relieve your accomplice, and take up the answer."

"Nay, if we are discovered," said the Orsini, rising in despair, "we will not fall unavenged—die, tyrant!"

He rushed to the place where Rienzi stood—for the Tribune also rose,—and made a thrust at his breast with his dagger: the steel pierced the purple robe, yet glanced harmlessly away—and the Tribune regarded the disappointed murderer with a scornful smile.

"Till yesternight, I never dreamt that under the robe of state I should need the secret corselet," said he. "My Lords, you have taught me a dark lesson, and I thank ye."

So saying, he clapped his hands, and suddenly the folding doors at the end of the hall flew open, and discovered the saloon of the Council hung with a silk of a blood-red, relieved by rays of white—the emblem of crime and death. At a long table sate the councillors in their robes; at the bar stood a ruffian form, which the banqueters too well recognized.

"Bid Rodolf of Saxony approach!" said the Tribune.

And led by two guards, the robber entered the hall.

"Wretch, *you* then betrayed us!" said one of the Frangipani.

"Rodolph of Saxony goes ever to the highest bidder," returned the miscreant, with a horrid grin. "You gave me gold, and I would have slain your foe; your foe defeated me; he gives me life, and life in a greater boon than gold!"

"Ye confess your crime, my Lords! Silent? dumb! Where is your wit, Savelli? Where your pride, Rinaldo di Orsini? Gianni Colonna, is your chivalry come to this?"

"Oh!" continued Rienzi, with deep and passionate bitterness; "oh, my Lords, will nothing conciliate you—not to me, but to Rome? What hath been my sin against you and yours? Disbanded ruffians (such as your accuser)—dismantled fortresses—impartial law—what man, in all the wild revolutions of Italy, sprung from the people, ever yielded less to their licence? Not a coin of your coffers touched by wanton power,—not a hair of your heads harmed by private revenge. You, Gianni Colonna, loaded with honors, intrusted with command—you, Alphonso di Frangipani, endowed with new principalities,—did the Tribune remember one insult he received from you as the Plebeian? You accuse my pride;—was it my fault that ye cringed and and fawned upon my power,—flattery on your lips, poison at your hearts? No, *I* have not offended you; let the world know that in me you aimed at liberty, justice, law, order, the restored grandeur, the renovated rights of Rome! At these, the Abstract and the Immortal—not at this frail form, ye struck;—by the divinity of these ye are defeated;—for the outraged majesty of these,—criminals and victims,—ye must die!"

With these words, uttered with the tone and air that would have become the loftiest spirit of the ancient city, Rienzi, with a majestic step, swept from the chamber into the Hall of Council.*

* "Vestimenta da Bizoco," was the phrase used by Colonna; a phrase borrowed from certain heretics (*bizocchi*) who affected extreme austerity; afterwards the word passed into a proverb.—See the comments of Zefirino Re, in Vit. di Cola di Rienzi.

* The guilt of the Barons in their designed assassina-

All that night the conspirators remained within that room, the doors locked and guarded; the banquet unremoved, and its splendor strangely contrasting the mood of the guests.

The utter prostration and despair of these dastard criminals—so unlike the knightly nobles of France and England, has been painted by the historian in odious and withering colors. The old Colonna alone sustained his impetuous and imperious character. He strode to and fro the room like a lion in his cage, uttering loud threats of resentment and defiance; and beating at the door with his clenched hands, demanding egress, and proclaiming the vengence of the Pontiff.

The dawn came, slow and grey upon that agonized assembly: and just as the last star faded from the melancholy horizon, and by the wan and comfortless heaven, they regarded each other's faces, almost spectral with anxiety and fear, the great bell of the Capital sounded the notes in which they well recognized the chime of death! It was then that the door opened, and a drear and gloomy procession of cordeliers, one to each Baron, entered the apartment! At that spectacle, we are told, the terror of the conspirators was so great, that it froze up the very power of speech.* The greater part at length, deeming all hope over, resigned themselves to their ghostly confessors. But when the friar appointed to Stephen approached that passionate old man, he waved his hand impatiently, and said—"Tease me not! tease me not!"

"Nay, son, prepare for the awful hour."

"Son, indeed!" quoth the Baron, "I am old enough to be thy grandsire; and for the rest, tell him who sent thee, that I neither am prepared for death, nor will prepare! I have made up my mind to live these twenty years, and longer too;—if I catch not my death with the cold of this accursed night."

Just at that moment a cry that almost seemed to rend the Capitol asunder was heard, as, with one voice, the multitude below yelled forth—

tion of Rienzi, though hastily slurred over by Gibbon, and other modern writers, is clearly attested by Muratori, the Bolognese Chronicle, etc.—*They even confessed the crime.* (See Cron. Estens: Muratori, tom. xviii. p. 442).

* "Diventarono si gelati che non poteano favellare."

"Death to the conspirators!—death! death!"

While this the scene in that hall, the Tribune issued from his chamber, in which he had been closeted with his wife and sister. The noble spirit of the one, the tears and grief of the other (who saw at one fell stroke perish the house of her betrothed), had not worked without effect upon a temper, stern and just indeed, but naturally averse from blood; and a heart capable of the loftiest species of revenge.

He entered the Council, still sitting with a calm brow, and even a cheerful eye.

"Pandulfo di Guido," he said, turning to that citizen, "you are right; you spoke as a wise man and a patriot, when you said that to cut off with one blow, however merited, the noblest heads of Rome, would endanger the State, sully our purple with an indelible stain, and unite the nobility of Italy against us."

"Such, Tribune, was my argument, though the Council have decided otherwise"

"Hearken to the shouts of the populace, you cannot appease their honest warmth," said the demagouge Baroncelli.

Many of the Council murmured applause.

"Friends," said the Tribune, with a solemn and earnest aspect, "let not Posterity say that Liberty loves blood; let us for once adopt the example and imitate the mercy of our great Redeemer! We have triumphed—let us forbear; we are saved—let us forgive!"

The speech of the Tribune was supported by Pandulfo, and others of the more mild and moderate policy; and after a short but animated discussion, the influence of Rienzi prevailed, and the sentence of death was revoked but by a small majority.

"And now," said Rienzi, "let us be more than just; let us be generous. Speak—and boldly. Do any of ye think that I have been over-hard, over-haughty with these stubborn spirits?—I read your answer in your brows!—I have! Do any of ye think this error of mine may have stirred them to their dark revenge? Do any of you deem that they partake, as we do, of human nature,—that they are sensible to kindness, that they are softened by generosity,—that they can be tamed and disarmed by such vengeance as is dictated to noble foes by Christian laws?"

"I think," said Pandulfo, after a pause,

"that it will not be in human nature, if the men you pardon, thus offending and thus convicted, again attempt your life!"

"Methinks," said Rienzi, "we must do even more than pardon. The first great Cæsar, when he did not crush a foe, strove to convert him to a friend——"

"And perished by the attempt," said Baroncelli, abruptly.

Rienzi started and changed color.

"If you would save these wretched prisoners, better not wait till the fury of the mob become ungovernable," whispered Pandulfo.

The Tribune roused himself from his revery.

"Pandulfo," said he, in the same tone, "my heart misgives me—the brood of serpents are in my hand—I do not strangle them—they may sting me to death, in return for my mercy—it is their instinct! No matter: it shall not be said that the Roman Tribune bought with so many lives his own safety: nor shall it be written upon my grave-stone, 'Here lies the coward, who did not dare forgive.' What, ho! there, officers, unclose the doors! My masters, let us acquaint the prisoners with their sentence."

With that, Rienzi seated himself on the chair of state, at the head of the table, and the sun, now risen, cast its rays over the blood-red walls, in which the Barons, marshalled in order into the chamber, thought to read their fate.

"My Lords," said the Tribune, "ye have offended the laws of God and man; but God teaches man the quality of mercy. Learn at last, that I bear a charmed life. Nor is he whom, for high purposes, Heaven hath raised from the cottage to the popular throne, without invisible aid and spiritual protection. If hereditary monarchs are deemed sacred, how much more one in whose power the divine hand hath writ its witness! Yes, over him who lives but for his country, whose greatness is his country's gift, whose life is his country's liberty, watch the souls of the just, and the unsleeping eyes of the sworded seraphim! Taught by your late failure and your present peril, bid your anger against me cease; respect the laws, revere the freedom of your city, and think that no state presents a nobler spectacle than men born as ye are—a partrician and illustrious order—using your power to protect your city, your wealth to nurture its arts, your chivalry to protect its laws! Take back your swords—and the first man who strikes against the liberties of Rome, let *him* be your victim; even though that victim be the Tribune. Your cause has been tried—your sentence is pronounced. Renew your oath to forbear all hostility, private or public, against the government and the magistrates of Rome, and ye are pardoned—ye are free!"

Amazed, bewildered, the Barons mechanically bent the knee: the friars who had received their confessions, administered the appointed oath; and while, with white lips, they muttered the solemn words, they heard below the roar of the multitude for their blood.

This ceremony ended, the Tribune passed into the banquet-hall, which conducted to a balcony, whence he was accustomed to address the people; and never, perhaps, was his wonderful mastery over the passions of an audience (*ad persuadendum efficax dictator, quoque dulcis ac lepidus*)* more greatly needed or more eminently shown, than on that day; for the fury of the people was at its height, and it was long ere he succeeded in turning it aside. Before he concluded, however, every wave of the wild sea lay hushed.—The orator lived to stand on the same spot, to plead for a life nobler than those he now saved,—and to plead unheard and in vain!

As soon as the Tribune saw the favorable moment had arrived, the Barons were admitted into the balcony:—in the presence of the breathless thousands, they solemnly pledged themselves to protect the Good Estate. And thus the morning which seemed to dawn upon their execution witnessed their reconciliation with the people.

The crowd dispersed, the majority soothed and pleased;—the more sagacious, vexed and dissatisfied.

"He has but increased the smoke and the flame which he was not able to extinguish," growled Cecco del Vecchio; and the smith's appropriate saying passed into a proverb and a prophecy.

Meanwhile, the Tribune, conscious at least that he had taken the more generous course, broke up the Council, and retired to the chamber where Nina and his sister waited him.

* Petrarch of Rienzi.

These beautiful young women had conceived for each other the tenderest affection. And their differing characters, both of mind and feature, seemed by contrast to heighten the charms of both; as in a skilful jewellery, the pearl and diamond borrow beauty from each other.

And as Irene now turned her pale countenance and streaming eyes from the bosom to which she had clung for support, the timid sister, anxious, doubtful, wistful;—the proud wife, sanguine and assured, as if never diffident of the intentions nor of the power of her Rienzi:—the contrast would have furnished to a painter no unworthy incarnation of the Love that hopeth, and the Love that feareth, all things.

"Be cheered, my sweet sister," said the Tribune, first caught by Irene's imploring look; "not a hair on the heads of those who boast the name of him thou lovest so well is injured. —Thank Heaven," as his sister, with a low cry, rushed into his arms, "that it was against my life they conspired! Had it been another Roman's, mercy might have been a crime! Dearest, may Adrian love thee half as well as I; and yet, my sister and my child, none can know thy soft soul like he who watched over it since its first blossom expanded to the sun. My poor brother! had he lived, your counsel had been his; and methinks his gentle spirit often whispers away the sternness which, otherwise, would harden over mine. Nina, my queen, my inspirer, my monitor—ever thus let thy heart, masculine in my distress, be woman's in my power; and be to me, with Irene, upon earth, what my brother is in heaven!"

The Tribune, exhausted by the trials of the night, retired for a few hours to rest; and as Nina, encircling him with her arms, watched over his noble countenance—care hushed, ambition laid at rest, its serenity had something almost of sublime. And tears of that delicious pride, which woman sheds for the hero of her dreams, stood heavy in the wife's eyes, as she rejoiced more, in the deep stillness of her heart, at the prerogative, alone hers, of sharing his solitary hours, than in all the rank to which his destiny had raised her, and which her nature fitted her at once to adorn and to enjoy. In that calm and lonely hour she beguiled her heart by waking dreams, vainer than the sleeper's; and pictured to herself the long career of glory, the august decline of peace, which were to await her lord.

And while she thus watched and thus dreamed, the cloud, as yet no bigger than a man's hand, darkened the horizon of a fate whose sunshine was well-nigh past!

CHAPTER II.

The Flight.

FRETTING his proud heart, as a steed frets on the bit, old Colonna regained his palace. To him, innocent of the proposed crime of his kin and compeers, the whole scene of the night and morning presented but one feature of insult and degradation. Scarce was he in his palace, ere he ordered couriers, in whom he knew he could confide, to be in preparation for his summons. "This to Avignon," said he to himself, as he concluded an epistle to the Pontiff.—"We will see whether the friendship of the great house of the Colonna will outweigh the frantic support of the rabble's puppet.—This to Palestrina,—the rock is inaccessible!—This to John di Vico, he may be relied upon, traitor though he be!—This to Naples; the Colonna will disown the Tribune's ambassador, if he throw not up the trust and hasten hither, not a lover but a soldier!—And may this find Walter de Montreal! Ah, a precious messenger he sent us, but I will forgive all—all, for a thousand lances." And as with trembling hands he twined the silk round his letters, he bade his pages invite to his board, next day, all the signors who had been implicated with him on the previous night.

The Barons came—far more enraged at the disgrace of pardon, than grateful for the boon of mercy. Their fears combined with their pride; and the shouts of the mob, the whine of the cordeliers, still ringing in their ears, they deemed united resistance the only course left to protect their lives and avenge their affront.

To them the public pardon of the Tribune seemed only a disguise to private revenge. All they believed was, that Rienzi did not dare to destroy them in the face of day; forgetfulness and forgiveness appeared to them as the means designed to lull their vigilance, while abasing their pride: and the knowledge of crime detected forbade them all hope of safety. The hand of their own assassin might be armed against them, or they might be ruined singly, one by one, as was the common tyrant-craft of that day. Singularly enough, Luca di Savelli was the most urgent for immediate rebellion. The fear of death made the coward brave.

Unable even to conceive the romantic generosity of the Tribune, the Barons were yet more alarmed when, the next day, Rienzi, summoning them one by one to a private audience, presented them with gifts, and bade them forget the past: excused himself rather than them, and augmented their offices and honors.

In the Quixotism of a heart to which royalty was natural, he thought that there was no medium course; and that the enmity he would not silence by death, he could crush by confidence and favors. Such conduct from a born king to hereditary inferiors might have been successful; but the generosity of one who has abruptly risen over his lords is but the ostentation of insult. Rienzi in this, and, perhaps, in forgiveness itself, committed a fatal error of *policy*, which the dark sagacity of a Visconti, or, in later times, of a Borgia, would never have perpetrated. But it was the error of a bright and a great mind.

Nina was seated in the grand saloon of the palace—it was the day of reception for the Roman ladies.

The attendance was so much less numerous than usual that it startled her, and she thought there was a coldness and restraint in the manner of the visitors present, which somewhat stung her vanity.

"I trust we have not offended the Signora Colonna," she said to the Lady of Gianni, Stephen's son. "She was wont to grace our halls, and we miss much her stately presence."

"Madam, my Lord's mother is unwell!"

"Is she so? We will send for her more welcome news. Methinks we are deserted today."

As she spoke, she carelessly dropped her handkerchief—the haughty dame of the Colonna bent not—not a hand stirred; and the Tribunessa looked for a moment surprised and disconcerted. Her eye roving over the throng, she perceived several, whom she knew as the wives of Rienzi's foes, whispering together with meaning glances, and more than one malicious sneer at her mortification was apparent. She recovered herself instantly, and said to the Signora Frangipani, with a smile, "May we be a partaker of your mirth? You seem to have chanced on some gay thought, which it were a sin not to share freely."

The lady she addressed colored slightly, and replied, "We were thinking, madam, that had the Tribune been present, his vow of knighthood would have been called into requisition."

"And how, Signora?"

"It would have been his pleasing duty, madam, to succor the distressed." And the Signora glanced significantly on the kerchief still on the floor.

"You designed me, then, this slight, Signoras," said Nina, rising with great majesty. "I know not whether your Lords are equally bold to the Tribune; but this I know, that the Tribune's wife can in future forgive your absence. Four centuries ago, a Frangipani might well have stooped to a Raselli; today, the dame of a Roman Baron might acknowledge a superior in the wife of the first magistrate of Rome. I compel not your courtesy, nor seek it."

"We have gone too far," whispered one of the ladies to her neighbor. "Perhaps the enterprise may not succeed; and then——"

Further remark was cut short by the sudden entrance of the Tribune. He entered with great haste, and on his brow was that dark frown which none ever saw unquailing.

"How, fair matrons!" said he, looking round the room with a rapid glance, "ye have not deserted us yet? By the blessed cross, your Lords pay a compliment to our honor, to leave us such lovely hostages, or else, God's truth, they are ungrateful husbands. So, madam," turning sharp round to the wife of Gianni Colonna, "your husband is fled to Palestrina; yours, Signora Orsini, to Marino; yours with him, fair bride of Frangipani,—ye came hither to——. But *ye* are sacred even from a word!"

The Tribune paused a moment, evidently striving to suppress his emotion, as he observed the terror he had excited—his eye fell upon Nina, who, forgetting her previous vexation, regarded him with anxious amazement. "Yes," said he to her, "you alone, perhaps, of this fair assemblage, know not that the nobles whom I lately released from the headsman's gripe are a second time forsworn. They have left home in the dead of the night, and already the Heralds proclaim them traitors and rebels. *Rienzi forgives no more!*"

"Tribune," exclaimed the Signora Frangipani, who had more bold blood in her veins than her whole house, "were I of thine own sex, I would cast the words, Traitor and Rebel, given to my Lord, in thine own teeth!—Proud man, the Pontiff soon will fulfil that office!"

"Your Lord is blest with a dove, fair one," said the Tribune, scornfully. "Ladies, fear not, while Rienzi lives, the wife even of his worst foe is safe and honored. The crowd will be here anon; our guards shall attend ye home in safety, or this palace may be your shelter—for, I warn ye, that your Lords have rushed into a great peril. And ere many days be past, the streets of Rome may be as rivers of blood."

"We accept your offer, Tribune," said the Signora Frangipani, who was touched, and, in spite of herself, awed by the Tribune's manner. And as she spoke, she dropped on one knee, picked up the kerchief, and, presenting it respectfully to Nina, said, "Madam, forgive me. I alone of these present respect you more in danger than in pride."

"And I," returned Nina, as she leaned in graceful confidence on Rienzi's arm, "I reply, that if there be danger, the more need of pride."

All that day and all that night rang the great bell of the Capitol. But on the following daybreak, the assemblage was thin and scattered; there was a great fear stricken into the hearts of the people, by the flight of the Barons, and they bitterly and loudly upbraided Rienzi for sparing them to this opportunity of mischief. That day the rumors continued; the murmurers for the most part remained within their houses, or assembled in listless and discontented troops. The next day dawned; the same lethargy prevailed. The Tribune summoned his Council (which was a Representative assembly).

"Shall we go forth as we are," said he, "with such few as will follow the Roman standard!"

"No," replied Pandulfo, who, by nature timid, was yet well acquainted with the disposition of the people, and therefore a sagacious counsellor. "Let us hold back; let us wait till the rebels commit themselves by some odious outrage, and then hatred will unite the waverers, and resentment lead them."

This counsel prevailed; the event proved its wisdom. To give excuse and dignity to the delay, messengers were sent to Marino, whither the chief part of the Barons had fled, and which was strongly fortified, demanding their immediate return.

On the day on which the haughty refusal of the insurgents was brought to Rienzi, came fugitives from all parts of the Campagna. Houses burned—convents and vineyards pillaged—cattle and horses seized—attested the warfare practised by the Barons, and animated the drooping Romans, by showing the mercies they might expect for themselves. That evening, of their own accord, the Romans rushed into the place of the Capitol:—Rinaldo Orsini had seized a fortress in the immediate neighborhood of Rome, and had set fire to a tower, the flames of which were visible to the city. The tenant of the tower, a noble lady, old and widowed, was burnt alive. Then rose the wild clamor—the mighty wrath—the headlong fury. The hour for action had arrived.*

CHAPTER III.

The Battle.

"I HAVE dreamed a dream," cried Rienzi, leaping from his bead. "The lion-hearted Boniface, foe and victim of the Colonna, hath appeared to me, and promised victory.† Nina, prepare the laurel-wreath: this day victory shall be ours!"

"Oh, Rienzi! to-day?"

"Yes! hearken to the bell—hearken to the trumpet. Nay, I hear even now the impatient hoofs of my white war-steed! One kiss, Nina, ere I arm for victory,—stay—comfort poor Irene; let me not see her—she weeps that my foes are akin to her betrothed; I can-

* "Ardea terre, arse la Castelluzza e case, *e uomini.* Non si schifo di ardere una nobile donna Vedova, veterana, in una torre. Per tale crudeltade li Romani furo più irati," etc.—*Vita di C. di Rienzi*, lib. i. cap. 20.

† "In questa notte mi è apparito Santo Bonifacio Papa," etc.—*Vit. di Col. Rien.* cap. 32.

not brook her tears; I watched her in her cradle. To-day, I must have no weakness on my soul! Knaves, twice perjured!—wolves, never to be tamed!—shall I meet ye at last sword to sword? Away, sweet Nina, to Irene, quick! Adrian is at Naples, and were he in Rome, her lover is sacred, though fifty times a Colonna."

With that, the Tribune passed into his wardrobe, where his pages and gentlemen attended with his armor. "I hear, by our spies," said he, "that they will be at our gates ere noon—four thousand foot, seven hundred horsemen. We will give them a hearty welcome, my masters. How, Angelo Villani, my pretty page, what do you out of your lady's service?"

"I would fain see a warrior arm for Rome," said the boy, with a boy's energy.

"Bless thee, my child; there spoke one of Rome's true sons!"

"And the Signora has promised me that I shall go with her guard to the gates, to hear the news——"

"And report the victory?—thou shalt. But they must not let thee come within shaft-shot. What! my Pandulfo, thou in mail?"

"Rome requires every man," said the citizen, whose weak nerves were strung by the contagion of the general enthusiasm.

"She doth—and once more I am proud to be a Roman. Now, gentles, the Dalmaticum:* I would that every foe should know Rienzi; and, by the Lord of Hosts, fighting at the head of the imperial people, I have a right to the imperial robe. Are the friars prepared? Our march to the gates shall be preceded by a solemn hymn—so fought our sires."

"Tribune, John di Vico is arrived with a hundred horse to support the Good Estate."

"He hath!—The Lord has delivered us then of a foe, and given our dungeons a traitor!—Bring hither yon casket, Angelo.—So—Hark thee! Pandulfo, read this letter."

The citizens read, with surprise and consternation, the answer of the wily Prefect to the Colonna's epistle.

"He promises the Baron to desert to him in the battle, with the Prefect's banner," said Pandulfo. "What is to be done?"

* A robe or mantle of white, borne by Rienzi; at one time belonging to the sacerdotal office, afterwards an emblem of empire.

"What!—take my signet—here—see him lodged forthwith in the prison of the Capitol. Bid his train leave Rome, and if found acting with the Barons, warn them that their Lord dies. Go—see to it without a moment's delay. Meanwhile to the chapel—we will hear mass."

Within an hour the Roman army—vast, miscellaneous—old men and boys, mingled with the vigor of life, were on their march to the Gate of San Lorenzo; of their number, which amounted to twenty thousand foot, not one-sixth could be deemed men-at-arms; but the cavalry were well equipped, and consisted of the lesser Barons and the more opulent citizens. At the head of these rode the Tribune in complete armor, and wearing on his casque a wreath of oak and olive leaves, wrought in silver. Before him waved the great gonfalon of Rome, while in front of this multitudinous array marched a procession of monks, of the order of St. Francis, (for the ecclesiastical body of Rome went chiefly with the popular spirit, and its enthusiastic leader,)—slowly chanting the following hymn, which was made inexpressibly startling and imposing at the close of each stanza, by the clash of arms, the blast of trumpets, and the deep roll of the drum; which formed, as it were, a martial chorus to the song:—

ROMAN WAR-SONG.

1.

March, march for your hearths and your altars!
Cursed to all time be the dastard that falters,
Never on earth may his sins be forgiven
Death on his soul, shut the portals of heaven!
A curse on his heart, and a curse on his brain!—
Who strikes not for Rome, shall to Rome be her Cain!
  Breeze fill our banners, sun gild our spears,
  Spirito Santo, Cavaliers! *
    Blow, trumpets, blow,
    Blow, trumpets, blow,
      Gaily to glory we come;
    Like a king in his pomp,
      To the blast of the tromp,
      And the roar of the mighty drum!
  Breeze fill our banners, sun gild our spears.
  Spirito Santo, Cavaliers!

2.

March, march for your Freedom and Laws!
Earth is your witness—all Earth's is your cause!

* Rienzi's word of battle was *Spirito Santo Cavaliere*, *i.e.*, Cavalier in the singular number. The plural number has been employed in the text, as somewhat more animated, and therefore better adapted to the kind of poetry into the service of which the watchword has been pressed.

Seraph and saint from their glory shall heed ye,
The angel that smote the Assyrian shall lead ye;
To the Christ of the Cross man is never so holy
As in braving the proud in defence of the lowly!
Breeze fill our banners, sun gild our spears,
Spirito Santo, Cavaliers!
Blow, trumpets, blow,
Blow, trumpets, blow,
Gaily to glory we come;
Like a king in his pomp,
To the blast of the tromp,
And the roar of the mighty drum!
Breeze fill our banners, sun gild our spears,
Spirito Santo, Cavaliers!

3.

March, march! ye are sons of the Roman,
The sound of whose step was as fate to the foeman!
Whose realm, save the air and the wave, had no wall,
As he strode through the world like a lord in his hall;
Though your fame hath sunk down to the night of the grave,
It shall rise from the field like the sun from the wave.
Breeze fill our banners, sun gild our spears,
Spirito Santo, Cavaliers!
Blow, trumpets, blow,
Blow, trumpets, blow,
Gaily to glory we come;
Like a king in his pomp,
To the blast of the tromp,
And the roar of the mighty drum!
Breeze fill our banners, sun gild our spears,
Spirito Santo, Cavaliers!

In this order they reached the wide waste that ruin and devastation left within the gates, and, marshalled in long lines on either side, extending far down the vistaed streets, and leaving a broad space in the centre, awaited the order of their leader.

"Throw open the gates, and admit the foe!" cried Rienzi, with a loud voice; as the trumpets of the Barons announced their approach.

Meanwhile the insurgent Patricians, who had marched that morning from a place called the Monument, four miles distant, came gallantly and boldly on.

With old Stephen, whose great height, gaunt frame, and lordly air, showed well in his gorgeous mail, rode his sons,—the Frangipani and the Savelli, and Giordano Orsini, brother to Rinaldo.

"To-day the tyrant shall perish!" said the proud Baron; "and the flag of the Colonna shall wave from the Capitol."

"The flag of the Bear," said Giordano Orsini, angrily.—"The victory will not be *yours* alone, my Lord!"

"Our house ever took precedence in Rome," replied the Colonna haughtily.

"Never, while one stone of the palaces of the Orsini stands upon another."

"Hush!" said Luca di Savelli; "are ye dividing the skin while the lion lives? We shall have fierce work to-day."

"Not so," said the old Colonna; "John di Vico will turn, with his Romans, at the first onset, and some of the malcontents within have promised to open the gates.—How, knave?" as a scout rode up breathless to the Baron. "What tidings?"

"The gates are opened—not a spear gleams from the walls!"

"Did I not tell ye, Lords?" said the Colonna, turning round triumphantly. "Methinks we shall win Rome without a single blow.—Grandson, where now are thy silly forebodings?" This was said to Pietro, one of his grandsons—the first-born of Gianni—a comely youth, not two weeks wedded, who made no reply. "My little Pietro here," continued the Baron, speaking to his comrades, "is so new a bridegroom, that last night he dreamed of his bride; and deems it, poor lad, a portent."

"She was in deep mourning, and glided from my arms, uttering, 'Woe, woe, to the Colonna!'" said the young man, solemnly.

"I have lived nearly ninety years," replied the old man, "and I may have dreamed, therefore, some forty thousand dreams; of which, two came true, and the rest were false. Judge, then, what chances are in favor of the science!"

Thus conversing, they approached within bow-shot of the gates, which were still open. All was silent as death. The army, which was composed chiefly of foreign mercenaries, halted in deliberation—when, lo!—a torch was suddenly cast on high over the walls; it gleamed a moment—and then hissed in the miry pool below.

"It is the signal of our friends within, as agreed on," cried old Colonna. "Pietro, advance with your company!" The young nobleman closed his visor, put himself at the head of the band under his command; and, with his lance in his rest, rode in a half gallop to the gates. The morning had been clouded and overcast, and the sun, appearing only at intervals, now broke out in a bright stream of light—as it glittered on the waving plume and shining mail of the young horseman, disappearing under the gloomy arch, several paces in advance of his troop. On swept his followers—forward went the cavalry headed by Gianni Colonna, Pietro's father.—There was a minute's silence, broken only by the clatter of the arms, and tramp of hoofs,—when from within the walls rose the abrupt cry—"Rome, the Tribune, and the People! *Spirito Santo, Cavaliers!*" The main body halted aghast. Suddenly Gianni Colonna was seen flying backward from the gate at full speed.

"My son, my son!" he cried, "they have murdered him;"—he halted abrupt and irresolute, then adding, "But I will avenge!" wheeled round, and spurred again through the arch,—when a huge machine of iron, shaped as a portcullis, suddenly descended upon the unhappy father, and crushed man and horse to the ground—one blent, mangled, bloody mass.

The old Colonna saw, and scarce believed his eyes; and ere his troop recovered its stupor, the machine rose, and over the corpse dashed the Popular Armament. Thousands upon thousands, they came on; a wild, clamorous, roaring stream. They poured on all sides upon their enemies, who drawn up in steady discipline, and clad in complete mail, received and broke their charge.

"Revenge, and the Colonna!"—"The Bear and the Orsini!"—"Charity and the Frangipani!"* "Strike for the Snake† and the Savelli!" were then heard on high, mingled with the German and hoarse shout, "Full purses, and the Three Kings of Cologne." The Romans, rather ferocious than disciplined, fell butchered in crowds round the ranks of the mercenaries: but as one fell, another succeeded; and still burst with undiminished fervor the counter cry of "Rome, the Tribune, and the People!—*Spirito Santo, Cavaliers!*" Exposed to every shaft and every sword by his emblematic diadem and his imperial robe, the fierce Rienzi led on each assault, wielding an enormous battle-axe, for the use of which the Italians were celebrated, and which he regarded as a national weapon. Inspired by every darker and sterner instinct of his nature, his blood heated, his passions aroused, fighting as a citizen for liberty, as a monarch for his crown, his daring seemed to the astonished foe as that of one frantic; his preservation that of one inspired: now here, now there; wherever flagged his own, or failed the opposing, force, glittered his white robe, and rose his bloody battle-axe; but his fury seemed rather directed against the chiefs than the herd; and still where his charger wheeled was heard his voice, "Where is a Colonna?"—"Defiance to the Orsini!"—"*Spirito Santo, Cavaliers!*" Three times was the sally led from the gate; three times were the Romans beaten back; and on the third, the gonfalon, borne before the Tribune, was cloven to the ground. Then, for the first time, he seemed amazed and alarmed, and, raising his eyes to heaven, he exclaimed, "O Lord, hast thou then forsaken me?" With that, taking heart, once more he waved his arm, and again led forward his wild array.

At eve the battle ceased. Of the Barons who had been the main object of the Tribune's assault, the pride and boast was broken. Of the princely line of the Colonna, three lay dead. Giordano Orsini was mortally wounded; the fierce Rinaldo had not shared the conflict. Of the Frangipani, the haughtiest signors were no more; and Luca, the dastard head of the Savelli, had long since saved himself by flight. On the other hand, the slaughter of the citizens had been prodigious;—the ground was swamped with blood—and over heaps of slain, (steeds and riders,) the twilight star beheld Rienzi and the Romans returning victors from the pursuit. Shouts of rejoicing followed the Tribune's panting steed through the arch; and just as he entered the space within, crowds of those whose infirmities, sex, or years, had not allowed them to share the conflict,—women, and children, and drivelling age, mingled with the bare feet and dark robes of monks and friars, apprised of the victory, were prepared to hail his triumph.

Rienzi reined his steed by the corpse of the boy Colonna, which lay half immersed in a pool of water, and close by it, removed from the arch where he had fallen, lay that of Gianni Colonna—(that Gianni Colonna whose spear had dismissed his brother's gentle spirit). He glanced over the slain, as the melancholy

* Who had taken their motto from some fabled ancestor who had broke bread with a beggar in a time of famine.

† The Lion was, however, the animal usually arrogated by the heraldic vanity of the Savelli.

Hesperus played upon the bloody pool and the gory corselet, with a breast heaved with many emotions; and turning, he saw the young Angelo, who, with some of Nina's guard, had repaired to the spot, and had now approached the Tribune.

"Child," said Rienzi, pointing to the dead, "*blessed art thou who hast no blood of kindred to avenge!*—to him who hath, sooner or later comes the hour; and an awful hour it is!"

The words sank deep into Angelo's heart, and in after life became words of fate to the speaker and the listener.

Ere Rienzi had well recovered himself, and as were heard around him the shrieks of the widows and mothers of the slain—the groans of the dying—the exhortations of the friars—mingled with sounds of joy and triumph—a cry was raised by the women and stragglers on the battle-field without, of "The foe!—the foe!"

"To your swords," cried the Tribune; "fall back in order;—yet they cannot be so bold!"

The tramp of horses, the blast of a trumpet, were heard; and presently, at full speed, some thirty horsemen dashed through the gate.

"Your bows," exclaimed the Tribune, advancing;—"yet hold—the leader is unarmed—it is our own banner. By our Lady, it is our ambassador of Naples, the Lord Adrian di Castello!"

Panting—breathless—covered with dust—Adrian halted at the pool red with the blood of his kindred—and their pale faces, set in death, glared upon him.

"Too late—alas! alas!—dread fate!—unhappy Rome!"

"They fell into the pit they themselves had digged," said the Tribune, in a firm but hollow voice.—"Noble Adrian, would thy counsels had prevented this!"

"Away, proud man—away!" said Adrian, impatiently waving his hand,—"thou shouldst protect the lives of Romans, and——oh, Gianni!—Pietro!—could not birth, renown, and thy green years, poor boy—could not these save ye?"

"Pardon him, my friends," said the Tribune to the crowd,—"his grief is natural, and he knows not all their guilt.—Back, I pray ye—leave him to our ministering."

It might have fared ill for Adrian, but for the Tribune's brief speech. And as the young Lord, dismounting, now bent over his kinsmen—the Tribune also surrendering his charger to his 'squires, approached, and, despite Adrian's reluctance and aversion, drew him aside,—

"Young friend," said he, mournfully, "my heart bleeds for you; yet bethink thee, the wrath of the crowd is fresh upon them: be prudent."

"Prudent!"

"Hush—by my honor, these men were not worthy of your name. Twice perjured—once assassins—twice rebels—listen to me!"

"Tribune, I ask no other construing of what I see—they might have died justly, or been butchered foully. But there is no peace between the executioner of my race and me."

"Will *you*, too, be forsworn? Thine oath!—Come, come, I hear not these words. Be composed—retire—and if, three days hence, you impute any other blame to me than that of unwise lenity, I absolve you from your oath, and you are free to be my foe. The crowd gape and gaze upon us—a minute more, and I may not avail to save you."

The feelings of the young patrician were such as utterly baffle description. He had never been much amongst his house, nor ever received more than common courtesy at their hands. But lineage is lineage still! And there, in the fatal hazard of war, lay the tree and sapling, the prime and hope of his race. He felt there was no answer to the Tribune, the very place of their death proved they had fallen in an assault upon their countrymen. He sympathized not with their cause, but their fate. And rage, revenge alike forbidden—his heart was the more softened to the shock and paralysis of grief. He did not therefore speak, but continued to gaze upon the dead, while large and unheeded tears flowed down his cheeks, and his attitude of dejection and sorrow was so moving, that the crowd, at first indignant, now felt for his affliction. At length his mind seemed made up. He turned to Rienzi, and said, falteringly, "Tribune, I blame you not, nor accuse. If you have been rash in this, God will have blood for blood. I wage no war with you—you say right, my oath prevents me; and if you govern well, I can still remember that I am Roman. But—but—look to that bleeding clay—we meet no more!—your sister—God be with her!—between her and me flows a dark gulf!" The young noble paused some moments, choked by his emotions, and then continued, "These papers discharge me of my mission. Standard-bearers, lay down the banner of the Republic. Tribune, speak not—I would be calm—calm. And so farewell to Rome." With a hurried glance towards the dead, he sprung upon his steed, and, followed by his train, vanished through the arch.

The Tribune had not attempted to detain him—had not interrupted him. He felt that the young noble had thought—acted as became him best. He followed him with his eyes.

"And thus," said he gloomily, "Fate plucks from me my noblest friend and my justest counsellor—a better man Rome never lost!"

Such is the eternal doom of disordered states. The mediator between rank and rank,—the kindly noble—the dispassionate patriot—the first to act—the most hailed in action—darkly vanishes from the scene. Fiercer and more unscrupulous spirits alone stalk the field; and no neutral and harmonizing link remains between hate and hate,—until exhaustion, sick with horrors, succeeds to frenzy, and despotism is welcomed as repose!

CHAPTER IV.

The Hollowness of the Base.

THE rapid and busy march of state events has led us long away from the sister of the Tribune and the betrothed of Adrian. And the sweet thoughts and gentle day-dreams of that fair and enamored girl, however full to *her* of an interest beyond all the storms and perils of ambition, are not so readily adapted to narration:—their soft monotony a few words can paint. They knew but one image, they tended to but one prospect. Shrinking from the glare of her brother's court, and eclipsed, when she forced herself to appear, by the more matured and dazzling beauty, and all-commanding presence, of Nina,—to her the pomp and crowd seemed an unreal pageant, from which she retired to the *truth of life*,—the hopes and musings of her own heart. Poor girl! with all the soft and tender nature of her dead brother, and none of the stern genius and the prodigal ambition,—the eye-fatiguing ostentation and fervor of the living—she was but ill-fitted for the unquiet but splendid region to which she was thus suddenly transferred.

With all her affection for Rienzi, she could not conquer a certain fear which, conjoined with the difference of sex and age, forbade her to be communicative with him upon the subject most upon her heart.

As the absence of Adrian at the Neapolitan Court passed the anticipated date (for at no Court then, with a throne fiercely disputed, did the Tribune require a nobler or more intelligent representative,—and intrigues and counter-intrigues delayed his departure from week to week), she grew uneasy and alarmed. Like many, themselves unseen, inactive, the spectators of the scene, she saw involuntarily further into the time than the deeper intellect either of the Tribune or Nina; and the dangerous discontent of the nobles was visible and audible to her in looks and whispers, which reached not acuter or more suspected ears and eyes. Anxiously, restlessly, did she long for the return of Adrian, not from selfish motives alone, but from well-founded apprehensions for her brother. With Adrian di Castello, alike a noble and a patriot, each party had found a mediator, and his presence grew daily more needed, till at length the conspiracy of the Barons had broken out. From that hour she scarcely dared to hope; her calm sense, unblinded by the high-wrought genius which, as too often happens, made the Tribune see harsh realities through a false and brilliant light, perceived that the Rubicon was passed; and through all the events that followed she could behold but two images—danger to her brother, separation from her betrothed.

With Nina alone could her full heart confer; for Nina, with all the differences of character, was a woman who loved. And this united them. In the earlier power of Rienzi, many of their happiest hours had been passed together, remote from the gaudy crowd, alone and unrestrained, in the summer nights, on the moonlit balconies, in that interchange of thought, sympathy, and consolation, which to two impassioned and guileless women makes the most intetesting occupation and the most effectual solace. But of late, this intercourse had been much marred. From the morning in which the Barons had received their pardon, to that on which they had marched on Rome, had been one succession of fierce excitements. Every face Irene saw was clouded and overcast—all gaiety was suspended—bustling and anxious councillors, or armed soldiers, had for days been the only visitors of the palace. Rienzi had been seen but for short moments: his brow wrapt in care. Nina had been more fond, more caressing than ever, but in those caresses there seemed a mournful and ominous compassion. The attempts at comfort and hope were succeeded by a sickly smile and broken words; and Irene was prepared, by the presentiments of her own heart, for the stroke that fell—victory was to her brother—his foe was crushed—Rome was free—but the lofty house of the Colonnas had lost its stateliest props, and Adrian was gone for ever!—She did not blame him; she could not blame her brother; each had acted as became his several station. She was the poor sacrifice of events and fate—the Iphigenia to the Winds which were to bear the bark of Rome to the haven, or, it might be, to whelm it in the abyss. She was stunned by the blow; she did not even weep or complain; she bowed to the storm that swept over her, and it passed. For two days she neither took food nor rest; she shut herself up; she asked only the boon of solitude: but on the third morning she recovered as by a miracle, for, on the third morning, the following letter was left at the palace:—

"IRENE,—Ere this you have learned my deep cause of grief; you feel that to a Colonna Rome can no longer be a home, nor Rome's Tribune be a brother. While I write these words honor but feebly supports me: all the hopes I had formed, all the prospects I had pictured, all the love I bore and bear thee, rush upon my heart, and I can only feel that I am wretched. Irene, Irene, your sweet face rises before me, and in those beloved eyes I read that I am forgiven,—I am understood; and dearly as I know thou lovest me, thou wouldst rather I were lost to thee, rather I were in the grave with my kinsmen, than know I lived the reproach of my order, the recreant of my name. Ah! why was I a Colonna? why did Fortune make me noble, and nature and circumstance attach me to the people? I am barred alike from love and from revenge; all my revenge falls upon thee and me. Adored! we are perhaps separated for ever; but, by all the happiness I have known by thy side—by all the rapture of which I dreamed—by that delicious hour which first gave thee to my gaze, when I watched the soft soul returning to thine eyes and lip—by thy first blushing confession of love—by our first kiss—by our last farewell—I swear to be faithful to thee to the last. None other shall ever chase thine image from my heart. And now, when Hope seems over, Faith becomes doubly sacred; and thou, my beautiful, wilt thou not remember me? wilt thou not feel as if we were the betrothed of Heaven? In the legends of the North we are told of the knight who, returning from the Holy Land, found his mistress (believing his death) the bride of Heaven, and he built a hermitage by the convent where she dwelt; and, though they never saw each other more, their souls were faithful unto death. Even so, Irene, be we to each other—dead to all else—betrothed in memory—to be wedded above!

"And yet, yet ere I close, one hope dawns upon me. Thy brother's career, bright and lofty, may be but as a falling star; should darkness swallow it, should his power cease, should his throne be broken, and Rome know no more her Tribune; shouldst thou no longer have a brother in the judge and destroyer of my house; shouldst thou be stricken from pomp and state; shouldst thou be friendless, kindredless, alone—then, without a stain on mine honor, without the shame and odium of receiving power and happiness from hands yet red with the blood of my race, I may claim thee as my own. Honor ceases to command when thou ceasest to be great. I dare not too fondly indulge this dream, perchance it is a sin in both. But it must be whispered, that thou mayest know all thy Adrian, all his weakness and his strength. My own loved, my ever loved, loved more fondly now when loved despairingly, farewell! May angels heal thy sorrow, and guard *me* from sin, that ***hereafter*** at least we may meet again!"

"He loves me—he loves me still!" said the maiden, weeping at last; "and I am blest once more!"

With that letter pressed to her heart she recovered outwardly from the depth of her affliction; she met her brother with a smile, and Nina with embraces; and if still she pined and sorrowed, it was in that "concealment" which is the "worm i' the bud."

Meanwhile, after the first flush of victory, lamentation succeeded to joy in Rome; so great had been the slaughter that the private grief was large enough to swallow up all public triumph; and many of the mourners blamed even their defender for the swords of the assailant, "*Roma fu terribilmente vedovata.*" * The numerous funerals deeply affected the Tribune; and, in proportion to his sympathy with his people, grew his stern indignation against the Barons. Like all men whose religion is intense, passionate, and zealous, the Tribune had little toleration for those crimes which went to the root of religion. Perjury was to him the most base and inexpiable of offences, and the slain Barons had been twice perjured: in the bitterness of his wrath he forbade their families for some days to lament over their remains; and it was only in private and in secret that he permitted them to be interred in their ancestral vaults: an excess of vengeance which sullied his laurels, but which was scarcely inconsistent with the stern patriotism of his character. Impatient to finish what he had begun, anxious to march at once to Marino, where the insurgents collected their shattered force, he summoned his Council, and represented the certainty of victory, and its result in the complete restoration of peace. But pay was due to the soldiery; they already murmured; the treasury was emptied, it was necessary to fill it by raising a new tax.

Among the councillors were some whose families had suffered greviously in the battle—they lent a lukewarm attention to propositions of continued strife. Others, among whom was Pandulfo, timid but well-meaning, aware that grief and terror even of their own triumph had produced reaction amongst the people, declared that they would not venture to propose a new tax. A third party, headed by Baroncelli—a demagouge whose ambition was without principle—but who, by pandering to the worst passions of the populace, by a sturdy coarseness of nature with which they sympathized—and by that affectation of advancing what we now term the "movement," which often gives to the fiercest fool an advantage over the most prudent statesman, had quietly acquired a great influence with the lower ranks—offered a more bold opposition. They dared even to blame the proud Tribune for the gorgeous extravagance they had themselves been the first to recommend—and half insinuated sinister and treacherous motives in his acquittal of the Barons from the accusation of Rodolf. In the very Parliament which the Tribune had revived and remodelled for the support of freedom—freedom was abandoned. His fiery eloquence met with a gloomy silence, and finally, the votes were against his propositions for the new tax and the march to Marino. Rienzi broke up the Council in haste and disorder. As he left the hall, a letter was put into his hands; he read it, and remained for some moments as one thunderstruck. He then summoned the Captain of his Guards, and ordered a band of fifty horsemen to be prepared for his commands; he repaired to Nina's apartment, he found her alone, and stood for some moments gazing upon her so intently that she was awed and chilled from all attempt at speech. At length he said, abruptly—

"We must part."

"Part!"

"Yes, Nina—your guard is preparing; you have relations, I have friends, at Florence. Florence must be your home."

"Cola,——"

"Look not on me thus.—In power, in state, in safety—you were my ornament and counsellor. *Now* you but embarrass me. And——"

"Oh, Cola, speak not thus! What hath chanced? Be not so cold—frown not—turn not away! Am I not something more to thee than the partner of joyous hours—the minion of love? Am I not thy wife, Cola—not thy leman?"

"Too dear—too dear to me," muttered the Tribune; "with thee by my side I shall be but half a Roman. Nina, the base slaves whom I myself made free desert me.—Now, in the very hour in which I might sweep away for ever all obstacles to the regeneration of Rome—now, when one conquest points the path to complete success—now when the land is visible, my fortune suddenly leaves me in the midst of the seas! There is greater danger now than in the rage of the Barons—

* "Rome was terribly widowed."

the Barons are fled; it is the People who are becoming traitors to Rome and to me."

"And wouldst thou have *me* traitor also! No, Cola; in death itself Nina shall be beside thee. Life and honor are reflected but from thee, and the stroke that slays the substance, shall destroy the humble shadow. I will not part from thee."

"Nina," said the Tribune, contending with strong and convulsive emotion—"it may be literally of *death* that you speak.—Go! leave one who can no longer protect you or Rome!"

"Never—Never."

"You are resolved?"

"I am."

"Be it so," said the Tribune, with deep sadness in his tone. "Arm thyself for the worst."

"There is no *worst* with thee, Cola!

"Come to my arms, brave woman; thy words rebuke my weakness. But my sister! —if *I* fall, *you*, Nina, will not survive—your beauty a prey to the most lustful heart and the strongest hand. *We* will have the same tomb on the wrecks of Roman liberty. But Irene is of weaker mould; poor child, I have robbed her of a lover, and now——"

"You are right; let Irene go. And in truth we may well disguise from her the real cause of her departure. Change of scene were best for her grief; and under all circumstances would seem decorum to the curious. I will see and prepare her."

"Do so, sweetheart. I would gladly be a moment alone with thought. But remember, she must part to-day—our sands run low."

As the door closed on Nina, the Tribune took out the letter and again read it deliberately. "So the Pope's Legate left Sienna:—prayed that Republic to withdraw its auxiliary troops from Rome—proclaimed me a rebel and a heretic;—thence repaired to Marino;—now in council with the Barons. Why, have my dreams belied me, then—false as the waking things that flatter and betray by day? In such peril will the people forsake me and themselves? Army of saints and martyrs, shades of heroes and patriots, have ye abandoned for ever your ancient home? No, no, I was not raised to perish thus; I will defeat them yet—and leave my name a legacy to Rome; a warning to the oppressor—an example to the free!"

CHAPTER V.

The Rottenness of the Edifice.

THE kindly skill of Nina induced Irene to believe that it was but the tender consideration of her brother to change a scene embittered by her own thoughts, and in which the notoriety of her engagement with Adrian exposed her to all that could mortify and embarrass, that led to the proposition of her visit to Florence. Its suddenness was ascribed to the occasion of an unexpected mission to Florence (for a loan of arms and money), which thus gave her a safe and honored escort. —Passively she submitted to what she herself deemed a relief; and it was agreed that she should for a while be the guest of a relation of Nina's, who was the abbess of one of the wealthiest of the Florentine convents: the idea of monastic seclusion was welcome to the bruised heart and wearied spirit.

But though not apprised of the immediate peril of Rienzi, it was with deep sadness and gloomy forebodings that she returned his embrace and parting blessing; and when at length alone in her litter, and beyond the gates of Rome, she repented a departure to which the chance of danger gave the appearance of desertion.

Meanwhile, as the declining day closed around the litter and its troop, more turbulent actors in the drama demand our audience. The traders and artisans of Rome at that time, and especially during the popular government of Rienzi, held weekly meetings in each of the thirteen quarters of the city. And in the most democratic of these, Cecco del Vecchio was an oracle and leader. It was at that assembly, over which the smith presided, that the murmurs that preceded the earthquake were heard.

"So," cried one of the company—Luigi, the goodly butcher,—"they say he wanted to put a new tax on us; and that is the reason he broke up the Council to-day, because, good men, they were honest, and had bowels for the people: it is a shame and a sin that the treasury should be empty."

"I told him," said the smith, "to beware how he taxed the people. Poor men won't be taxed. But as he does not follow my advice, he must take the consequence—the horse runs from one hand, the halter remains in the other."

"Take *your* advice, Cecco! I warrant me his stomach is too high for that now. Why he has grown as proud as a pope."

"For all that, he is a great man," said one of the party. "He gave us laws—he rid the Campagna of robbers—filled the streets with merchants, and the shops with wares—defeated the boldest lords and fiercest soldiery of Italy——"

"And now wants to tax the people!—that's all the thanks we get for helping him," said the grumbling Cecco. "What would he have been without us?—we that make, can unmake."

"But," continued the advocate, seeing that he had his supporters—"but then he taxes us for our own liberties."

"Who strikes at them now?" asked the butcher.

"Why the Barons are daily mustering new strength at Marino."

"Marino is not Rome," said Luigi, the butcher. "Let's wait till they come to our gates again—we know how to receive them. Though, for the matter of that, I think we have had enough fighting—my two poor brothers had each a stab too much for them. Why won't the Tribune, if he *be* a great man, let us have peace? All we want now is quiet."

"Ah!" said a seller of horse-harness. "Let him make it up with the Barons. They were good customers, after all."

"For my part," said a merry-looking fellow, who had been a grave-digger in bad times, and had now opened a stall of wares for the living, "I could forgive him all, but bathing in the holy vase of porphyry."

"Ah, that was a bad job," said several, shaking their heads.

"And the knighthood was but a silly show, an' it were not for the wine from the horse's nostrils—*that* had some sense in it."

"My masters," said Cecco, "the folly was in not beheading the Barons when he had them all in the net; and so Messere Baroncelli says. (Ah, Baroncelli is an honest man, and follows no half measures!) It was a sort of treason to the people not to do so. Why, but for that, we should never have lost so many tall fellows by the gate of San Lorenzo."

"True, true, it was a shame; some say the Barons bought him."

"And then," said another, "those poor Lords Colonna—boy and man—they were the best of the family, save the Castello. I vow I pitied them."

"But to the point," said one of the crowd, *the richest* of the set; "*the tax is the thing*. The ingratitude to tax *us*.—Let him dare to do it!"

"Oh, he will not dare, for I hear that the Pope's bristles are up at last; so he will only have *us* to depend upon!"

The door was thrown upon—a man rushed in open-mouthed—

"Masters, masters, the Pope's legate has arrived at Rome, and sent for the Tribune, who has just left his presence."

Ere his auditors had recovered their surprise, the sound of trumpets made them rush forth; they saw Rienzi sweep by with his usual cavalcade, and in his proud array. The twilight was advancing, and torch-bearers preceded his way. Upon his countenance was deep calm, but it was not the calm of contentment. He passed on, and the street was again desolate. Meanwhile Rienzi reached the Capitol in silence, and mounted to the apartments of the palace, where Nina, pale and breathless, awaited his return.

"Well, well, thou smilest! No—it is that dread smile, worse than frowns. Speak, beloved, speak! What said the Cardinal?"

"Little thou wilt love to hear. He spoke at first high and solemnly, about the crime of declaring the Romans free; next about the treason of asserting that the election of the King of Rome was in the hands of the Romans."

"Well—thy answer."

"That which became Rome's Tribune: I reasserted each right, and proved it. The Cardinal passed to other charges."

"What?"

"The blood of the Barons by San Lorenzo —blood only shed in our own defence against perjured assailants; this is in reality the main crime. The Colonna have the Pope's ear. Furthermore, the sacrilege—yes, the sacrilege (come laugh, Nina, laugh!) of bathing in a vase of porphyry used by Constantine while yet a heathen."

"Can it be! What saidst thou?"

"I laughed. 'Cardinal,' quoth I, 'what was not too good for a heathen is not too good for a Christian Catholic!' And verily the sour

Frenchman looked as if I had smote him on the hip. When he had done, I asked him, in my turn, 'Is it alleged against me that I have wronged one man in my judgment-court?'—Silence. 'Is it said that I have broken one law of the state?'—Silence. 'Is it even whispered that trade does not flourish—that life is not safe—that abroad or at home the Roman name is not honored, to that point which no former rule can parallel?'—Silence. 'Then,' said I, 'Lord Cardinal, I demand thy thanks, not thy censure.' The Frenchman looked, and looked, and trembled, and shrunk, and then out he spoke. 'I have but one mission to fulfil, on the part of the Pontiff—resign at once thy Tribuneship, or the Church inflicts upon thee its solemn curse.'"

"How—how?" said Nina, turning very pale; "what is it that awaits thee?"

"Excommunication!"

This awful sentence, by which the spiritual arm had so often stricken down the fiercest foe, came to Nina's ear as a knell. She covered her face with her hands. Rienzi paced the room with rapid strides. "The curse!" he muttered; "the Church's curse—for me—for ME!"

"Oh, Cola! didst thou not seek to pacify this stern——"

"Pacify! Death and dishonor! Pacify! 'Cardinal,' I said, and I felt his soul shrivel at my gaze, 'my power I received from the people—to the people alone I render it. For my soul, man's word cannot scathe it. Thou, haughty priest, thou thyself art the accursed, if, puppet and tool of low cabals and exiled tyrants, thou breathest but a breath in the name of the Lord of Justice, for the cause of the oppressor, and against the rights of the oppressed.' With that I left him, and now——"

"Ay, now—now what will happen? Excommunication! In the metropolis of the Church, too—the superstition of the people! Oh, Cola!"

"If," muttered Rienzi, "my conscience condemned me of one crime—if I had stained my hands in one just man's blood—if I had broken one law I myself had framed—if I had taken bribes, or wronged the poor, or scorned the orphan, or shut my heart to the widow—then, then—but no! Lord, *thou* wilt not desert me!"

"But *man* may!" thought Nina mournfully, as she perceived that one of Rienzi's dark fits of fanatical and mystical revery was growing over him—fits which he suffered no living eye, not even Nina's, to witness when they gathered to their height. And now, indeed, after a short interval of muttered soliloquy, in which his face worked so that the veins on his temples swelled like cords, he abruptly left the room, and sought the private oratory connected with his closet. Over the emotions there indulged let us draw the veil. Who shall describe those awful and mysterious moments, when man, with all his fiery passions, turbulent thoughts, wild hopes, and despondent fears, demands the solitary audience of his Maker?

It was long after this conference with Nina, and the midnight bell had long tolled, when Rienzi stood alone, upon one of the balconies of the palace, to cool, in the starry air, the fever that yet lingered on his exhausted frame. The night was exceedingly calm, the air clear, but chill, for it was now December. He gazed intently upon those solemn orbs to which our wild credulity has referred the prophecies of our doom.

"Vain science!" thought the Tribune, "and gloomy fantasy, that man's fate is preordained — irrevocable — unchangeable, from the moment of his birth! Yet, were the dream not baseless, fain would I know which of yon stately lights is my natal star,—which images—which reflects—my career in life, and the memory I shall leave in death." As this thought crossed him, and his gaze was still fixed above, he saw, as if made suddenly more distinct than the stars around it, that rapid and fiery comet which in the winter of 1347 dismayed the superstitions of those who recognized in the stranger of the heavens the omen of disaster and of woe. He recoiled as it met his eye, and muttered to himself, "Is such indeed my type! or, if the legendary lore speak true, and these strange fires portend nations ruined and rulers overthrown, does it foretell my fate? I will think no more."* As his eyes fell, they rested upon the Colossal Lion of Basalt in the place below, the starlight investing its gray and towering form with a more ghostly whiteness; and then it was, that

* Alas! if by the Romans associated with the fall of Rienzi, that comet was by the rest of Europe connected with the more dire calamity of the Great Plague that so soon afterwards ensued.

he perceived two figures in black robes lingering by the pedestal which supported the statue, and apparently engaged in some occupation which he could not guess. A fear shot through his veins, for he had never been able to divest himself of the vague idea that there was some solemn and appointed connection between his fate and that old Lion of Basalt. Somewhat relieved, he heard his sentry challenge the intruders; and as they came forward to the light, he perceived that they wore the garments of monks.

"Molest us not, son," said one of them to the sentry. "By order of the Legate of the Holy Father we affix to this public monument of justice and of wrath, the bull of excommunication against a heretic and rebel. Woe to the Accursed of the Church!"

CHAPTER IV.

The Fall of the Temple.

It was as a thunderbolt in a serene day—the reverse of the Tribune in the zenith of his power, in the abasement of his foe; when, with but a handful of brave Romans, determined to be free, he might have crushed for ever the antagonist power to the Roman liberties—have secured the rights of his country, and filled up the measure of his own renown. Such a reverse was the very mockery of Fate, who bore him through disaster, to abandon him in the sunniest noon of his prosperity.

The next morning not a soul was to be seen in the streets; the shops were shut—the churches closed; the city was as under an interdict. The awful curse of the papal excommunication upon the chief magistrate of the Pontifical City, seemed to freeze up all the arteries of life. The Legate himself, affecting fear of his life, had fled to Monte Fiascone, where he was joined by the Barons immediately after the publication of the edict. The curse worked best in the absence of the execrator.

Towards evening a few persons might be seen traversing the broad space of the Capitol, crossing themselves, as the bull, placarded on the Lion, met their eyes, and disappearing within the doors of the great palace. By and by, a few anxious groups collected in the streets, but they soon dispersed. It was a paralysis of all intercourse and commune. That spiritual and unarmed authority, which, like the invisible hand of God, desolated the market-place, and humbled the crowned head, no physical force could rally against or resist. Yet, through the universal awe, one conviction touched the multitude—it was for them that their Tribune was thus blasted in the midst of his glories! The words of the Brand recorded against him on wall and column detailed his offences:—rebellion in asserting the liberties of Rome—heresy in purifying ecclesiastical abuses;—and, to serve for a miserable covert to the rest, it was sacrilege for bathing in the porphyry vase of Constantine! They felt the conviction; they sighed—they shuddered—and, in his vast palace, save a few attached and devoted hearts, the Tribune was alone!

The staunchest of his Tuscan soldiery were gone with Irene. The rest of his force, save a few remaining guards, was the paid Roman militia, composed of citizens; who, long discontented by the delay of their stipends, now seized on the excuse of the excommunication to remain passive, but grumbling, in their homes.

On the third day, a new incident broke upon the death-like lethargy of the city; a hundred and fifty mercenaries, with Pepin of Minorbino, a Neapolitan, half noble, half bandit (a creature of Montreal's), at their head, entered the city, seized upon the fortresses of the Colonna, and sent a herald through the city, proclaiming, in the name of the Cardinal Legate, the reward of ten thousand florins for the head of Cola di Rienzi.

Then, swelled on high, shrill but not inspiring as of old, the great bell of the Capitol—the people, listless, disheartened, awed by the spiritual fear of the papal authority, (yet greater, in such events, since the removal of the see,) came unarmed to the Capitol; and there, by the Place of the Lion, stood the Tribune. His 'squires, below the step, held his war-horse, his helm, and the same battle-axe which had blazed in the van of victorious war.

Beside him were a few of his guard, his attendants, and two or three of the principal citizens.

He stood bareheaded and erect, gazing upon the abashed and unarmed crowd with a look of bitter scorn, mingled with deep compassion; and, as the bell ceased its toil, and the throng remained hushed and listening, he thus spoke:—

"Ye come, then, once again! Come ye as slaves or freemen? A handful of armed men are in your walls: will ye who chased from your gates the haughtiest knights—the most practised battle-men of Rome, succumb now to one hundred and fifty hirelings and strangers? Will ye arm for your Tribune? You are silent!—be it so. Will you arm for *your own* liberties—*your own* Rome? Silent still! By the saints that reign on the thrones of the heathen gods! are ye thus fallen from your birthright? Have you no arms for your own defence? Romans, hear me! Have I wronged you?—if so, by *your* hands let me die: and then, with knives yet reeking with my blood, go forward against the robber who is but the herald of your slavery; and I die honored, grateful, and avenged. You weep! Great God! you weep! Ay, and I could weep, too—that I should live to speak of liberty in vain to Romans—Weep! is this an hour for tears? Weep now, and your tears shall ripen harvests of crime, and license, and despotism, to come! Romans, arm! follow me at once to the Place of the Colonna: expel this ruffian—expel your enemy (no matter what afterwards you do to me):" he paused; no ardor was kindled by his words—"or," he continued, "I abandon you to your fate." There was a long, low, general murmur; at length it became shaped into speech, and many voices cried simultaneously: "The Pope's bull!—Thou art a man accursed!"

"What!" cried the Tribune; "and is it *ye* who forsake me, ye for whose cause alone man dares to hurl against me the thunders of his God? Is it not for *you* that I am declared heretic and rebel! What are my imputed crimes? That I have *made* Rome and *asserted* Italy to be free; that I have subdued the proud Magnates, who were the scourge both of Pope and People. And you—you upbraid me with what I have dared and done for you! Men, *with* you I would have fought, *for* you I would have perished. You forsake yourselves in forsaking me, and since I no longer rule over brave men, I resign my power to the tyrant you prefer. Seven months I have ruled over you, prosperous in commerce, stainless in justice—victorious in the field:—I have shown you what Rome could be; and, since I abdicate the government ye gave me, when I am gone, strike for your own freedom! It matters nothing who is the chief of a brave and great people. Prove that Rome hath many a Rienzi, but of brighter fortunes."

"I would he had not sought to tax us," said Cecco del Vecchio, who was the very personification of the vulgar feeling: "and that he had beheaded the Barons!"

"Ay!" cried the ex-gravedigger; "but that blessed porphyry vase!"

"And why should we get our throats cut," said Luigi, the butcher, "like my two brothers?—Heaven rest them!"

On the face of the general multitude there was a common expression of irresolution and shame, many wept and groaned, none (save the aforesaid grumblers) *accused;* none upbraided, but none seemed disposed to arm. It was one of those listless panics, those strange fits of indifference and lethargy which often seize upon a people who make liberty a matter of impulse and caprice, to whom it has become a catchword, who have not long enjoyed all its rational, and sound, and practical, and blessed results; who have been affrayed by the storms that herald its dawn;—a people such as is common to the south: such as even the north has known; such as, had Cromwell lived a year longer, even England might have seen; and, indeed, in some measure, such a reaction from popular enthusiasm to popular indifference England *did* see, when her children madly surrendered the fruits of a bloody war, without reserve, without foresight, to the lewd pensioner of Louis, and the royal murderer of Sydney. To such prostation of soul, such blindness of intellect, even the noblest people will be subjected, when liberty, which should be the growth of ages, spreading its roots through the strata of a thousand customs, is raised, the exotic of an hour, and (like the Tree and Dryad of ancient fable) flourishes and withers with the single spirit that protects it.

"Oh, Heaven, that I were a man!" exclaimed Angelo, who stood behind Rienzi.

"Hear him, hear the boy," cried the Tribune; "out of the mouths of babes speaketh wisdom! He wishes that he were a man, as ye are men, that he might do as ye should do. Mark me,—I ride with these faithful few through the quarter of the Colonna, before the fortress of your foe. Three times before that fortress shall my trumpets sound; if at the third blast ye come not, armed as befits ye—I say not all, but three, but two, but *one* hundred of ye—I break up my wand of office, and the world shall say one hundred and fifty robbers quelled the soul of Rome, and crushed her magistrate and her laws!"

With those words he descended the stairs, and mounted his charger; the populace gave way in silence, and their Tribune and his slender train passed slowly on, and gradually vanished from the view of the increasing crowd.

The Romans remained on the place, and after a pause, the demagogue Baroncelli, who saw an opening to his ambition, addressed them. Though not an eloquent nor gifted man, he had the art of uttering the most popular commonplaces. And he knew the weak side of his audience, in their vanity, indolence, and arrogant pride.

"Look you, my masters," said he, leaping up to the Place of the Lion; "the Tribune talks bravely—he always did—but the monkey used the cat for his chestnuts; he wants to thrust your paws into the fire; you will not be so silly as to let him. The saints bless us! but the Tribune, good man, gets a palace and has banquets, and bathes in a porphyry vase; the more shame on him!—in which San Sylvester christened the Emperor Constantine: all this is worth fighting for; but you, my masters, what do *you* get except hard blows, and a stare at a holyday spectacle? Why, if you beat these fellows, you will have another tax on the wine: *that* will be *your* reward!"

"Hark!" cried Cecco, "there sounds the trumpet,—a pity he wanted to tax us!"

"True," cried Baroncelli, "there sounds the trumpet; a *silver* trumpet, by the Lord! Next week, if you help him out of the scrape, he'll have a golden one. But go—why don't you move, my friends?—'tis but one hundred and fifty mercenaries. True, they are devils to fight, clad in armor from top to toe; but what then?—if they do cut some four or five hundred throats you'll beat them at last, and the Tribune will sup the merrier."

"There sounds the second blast," said the butcher. "If my old mother had not lost two of us already, 'tis odds, but I'd strike a blow for the bold Tribune."

"You had better put more quicksilver in you," continued Baroncelli, "or you will be too late. And what a pity that will be!—If you believe the Tribune, he is the only man that can save Rome. What, you, the finest people in the world—you, not able to save yourselves!—you, bound up with one man—you, not able to dictate to the Colonna and Orsini! Why, who beat the Barons at San Lorenzo? Was it not you? Ah! you got the buffets, and the Tribune the *moneta!* Tush, my friends, let the man go; I warrant there are plenty as good as he to be bought a cheaper bargain. And, hark! there is the third blast; it is too late now!"

As the trumpet from the distance sent forth its long and melancholy note, it was as the last warning of the parting genius of the place; and when silence swallowed up the sound, a gloom fell over the whole assembly. They began to regret, to repent, when regret and repentance availed no more. The buffoonery of Baroncelli became suddenly displeasing; and the orator had the mortification of seeing his audience disperse in all directions, just as he was about to inform them what great things he himself could do on their behalf.

Meanwhile the Tribune, passing unscathed through the dangerous quarter of the enemy, who, dismayed at his approach, shrunk within their fortress, proceeded to the Castle of St. Angelo, whither Nina had already preceded him; and which he entered to find that proud lady with a smile for his safety,—without a tear for his reverse.

CHAPTER VII.

The Successors of an Unsuccessful Revolution.—Who is to Blame—The Forsaken One or the Forsakers?

Cheerfully broke the winter sun over the streets of Rome, as the army of the Barons swept along them. The Cardinal Legate at the head; the old Colonna (no longer haughty and erect, but bowed, and broken-hearted at the loss of his sons) at his right hand;—the sleek smile of Luca Savelli—the black frown of Rinalo Orsini, were seen close behind. A long but barbarous array it was; made up chiefly of foreign hirelings; nor did the procession resemble the return of exiled citizens, but the march of invading foes.

"My Lord Colonna," said the Cardinal Legate, a small withered man, by birth a Frenchman, and full of the bitterest prejudices against the Romans, who had in a former mission very ill received him, as was their wont with foreign ecclesiastics; "this Pepin, whom Montreal has deputed at your orders, hath done us indeed good service."

The old Lord bowed, but made no answer. His strong intellect was already broken, and there was dotage in his glassy eye. The Cardinal muttered, "He hears me not; sorrow hath brought him to second childhood!" and looking back, motioned to Luca Savelli to approach.

"Luca," said the Legate, "it was fortunate that the Hungarian's black banner detained the Provençal at Aversa. Had he entered Rome, we might have found Rienzi's successor worse than the Tribune himself. Montreal," he added, with a slight emphasis and a curled lip, "is a gentleman, and a Frenchman. This Pepin, who is his delegate, we must bribe, or menace to our will."

"Assuredly," answered Savelli, "it is not a difficult task: for Montreal calculated on a more stubborn contest, which he himself would have found leisure to close——"

"As Podesta, or Prince of Rome! the modest man! We Frenchmen have a due sense of our own merits; but this sudden victory surprises him as it doth us, Luca; and we shall wrest the prey from Pepin, ere Montreal can come to his help! But Rienzi must die. He is still, I hear, shut up in St. Angelo. The Orsini shall storm him there ere the day be much older. To-day we possess the Capitol—annul all the rebel's laws—break up his ridiculous parliament, and put all the government of the city under three senators—Rinaldo Orsini, Colonna, and myself; you, my Lord, I trust, we shall fitly provide for."

"Oh! I am rewarded enough by returning to my palace; and a descent on the Jewellers' quarter will soon build up its fortifications. Luca Savelli is not an ambitious man. He wants but to live in peace."

The Cardinal smiled sourly, and took the turn towards the Capitol.

In the front space the usual gapers were assembled. "Make way! make way! knaves!" cried the guards, trampling on either side the crowd, who accustomed to the sedate and courteous order of Rienzi's guard, fell back too slowly for many of them to escape severe injury from the pikes of the soldiers and the hoofs of the horses. Our friend, Luigi, the butcher, was one of these, and the surliness of the Roman blood was past boiling heat when he received in his ample stomach the blunt end of a German's pike. "There, Roman," said the rude mercenary, in his barbarous attempt at Italian, "make way for your betters; you have had enough crowds and shows of late, in all conscience."

"Betters!" gulped out the poor butcher; "a Roman has no betters; and if I had not lost two brothers by San Lorenzo, I would——"

"The dog is mutinous," said one of the followers of the Orsini, succeeding the German who had passed on, "and talks of San Lorenzo!"

"Oh!" said another Orsinist, who rode abreast, "I remember him of old. He was one of Rienzi's gang."

"Was he?" said the other, sternly; "then we cannot begin salutary examples too soon;" and, offended at something swaggering and insolent in the butcher's look, the Orsinist coolly thrust him through the heart with his pike, and rode on over his body.

"Shame! Shame!" "Murder! Murder!" cried the crowd: and they began to press, in the passion of the moment, round the fierce guards.

The Legate heard the cry, and saw the rush: he turned pale. "The rascals rebel again!" he faltered.

"No, your Eminence—no," said Luca; "but it may be as well to infuse a wholesome terror; they are all unarmed; let me bid the guards disperse them. A word will do it."

The Cardinal assented; the word was given; and, in a few minutes, the soldiery, who still smarted under the vindictive memory of defeat from an undisciplined multitude, scattered the crowd down the streets without scruple or mercy—riding over some, spearing others—filling the air with shrieks and yells, and strewing the ground with almost as many men as a few days before would have sufficed to have guarded Rome, and preserved the constitution! Through this wild, tumultuous scene, and over the bodies of its victims, rode the Legate and his train, to receive in the Hall of the Capitol the allegiance of the citizens, and to proclaim the return of the oppressors.

As they dismounted at the stairs, a placard in large letters struck the eye of the Legate. It was placed upon the pedestal of the Lion of Basalt, covering the very place that had been occupied by the bull of excommunication. The words were few, and ran thus:

"TREMBLE! RIENZI SHALL RETURN!"

"How! what means this mummery!" cried the Legate, trembling already, and looking round to the nobles.

"Please your Eminence," said one of the councillors, who had come from the Capitol to meet the Legate, "we saw it at day-break, the ink yet moist, as we entered the Hall. We deemed it best to leave it for your Eminence to deal with."

"*You* deemed! Who are *you* then?"

"One of the members of the Council, your Eminence, and a stanch opponent of the Tribune, as is well known, when he wanted the new tax——"

"Council—trash! No more councils now! Order is restored at last. The Orsini and the Colonna will look to you in future. Resist a tax, did you? Well, that was right when proposed by a tyrant; but *I* warn you, friend, to take care how you resist the tax *we* shall impose. Happy if your city can buy its peace with the Church on any terms:—and his Holiness is short of the florins."

The discomfited councillor shrank back

"Tear off yon insolent placard. Nay, hold! fix over it our proclamation of ten thousand florins for the heretic's head! *Ten* thousand? methinks that is too much *now*—we will alter the cipher. Meanwhile Rinaldo Orsini, Lord Senator, march thy soldiers to St. Angelo; let us see if the heretic can stand a siege."

"It needs not, your Eminence," said the councillor, again officiously bustling up; "St. Angelo is surrendered. The Tribune, his wife, and one page, escaped last night, it is said, in disguise."

"Ha!" said the old Colonna, whose dulled sense had at length arrived at the conclusion that something extraordinary arrested the progress of his friends! "What is the matter? What is that placard? Will no one tell me the words? My old eyes are dim."

As he uttered the questions, in the shrill and piercing treble of age, a voice replied in a loud and deep tone—none knew whence it came; the crowd was reduced to a few stragglers, chiefly friars in cowl and serge, whose curiosity nought could daunt, and whose garb ensured them safety—the soldiers closed the rear: a voice, I say, came, startling the color from many a cheek—in answer to the Colonna, saying:

"TREMBLE! RIENZI SHALL RETURN!"

BOOK SIXTH.

THE PLAGUE.

"Erano gli anni della fruttifera Incarnazione del Figliuolo di Dio al numero pervenuti d mille trecento quarant'otto, quando nell' egregia citta di Fiorenza oltre ad ogni altra Italica bellissima, pervenne la mortifera pestilenza."—BOCCACCIO, *Introduzione al Decamerone.*

"The years of the fructiferous incarnation of the Son of God had reached the number of one thousand three hundred and forty-eight, when into the illustrious city of Florence, beautiful beyond every other in Italy, entered the death-fraught pestilence."—*Introduction to the Decameron.*

CHAPTER I.

The Retreat of the Love.

By the borders of one of the fairest lakes of Northern Italy stood the favorite mansion of Adrian di Castello, to which in his softer and less patriotic moments his imagination had often and fondly turned; and thither the young nobleman, dismissing his more courtly and distinguished companions in the Neapolitan embassy, retired after his ill-starred return to Rome. Most of those thus dismissed joined the Barons; the young Annibaldi, whose daring and ambitious nature had attached him strongly to the Tribune, maintained a neutral ground; he betook himself to his castle in the Campagna, and did not return to Rome till the expulsion of Rienzi."

The retreat of Irene's lover was one well fitted to feed his melancholy reveries. Without being absolutely a fortress, it was sufficiently strong to resist any assault of the mountain robbers or petty tyrants in the vicinity; while, built by some former lord from the materials of the half-ruined villas of the ancient Romans, its marbled columns and tesselated pavements relieved with a wild grace the gray stone walls and massive towers of feudal masonry. Rising from a green eminence gently sloping to the lake, the stately pile cast its shadow far and dark over the beautiful waters; by its side, from the high and wooded mountains on the background, broke a waterfall, in irregular and sinuous course—now hid by the foliage, now gleaming in the light, and collecting itself at last in a broad basin—beside which a little fountain, inscribed with half-obliterated letters, attested the departed elegance of the classic age—some memento of lord and poet whose very names were lost; thence descending through mosses and lichen, and odorous herbs, a brief, sheeted stream bore its surplus into the lake. And there, amidst the sturdier and bolder foliage of the North, grew, wild and picturesque, many a tree transplanted, in ages back, from the sunnier East; not blighted nor stunted in that golden clime, which fosters almost every produce of nature as with a mother's care. The place was remote and solitary. The roads that conducted to it from the distant towns were tangled, intricate, mountainous, and beset by robbers. A few cottages, and a small convent, a quarter of a league up the verdant margin, were the nearest habitations; and save by some occasional pilgrim or some bewildered traveller, the loneliness of the mansion was rarely invaded. It was precisely the spot which proffered rest to a man weary of the world, and indulged the memories which grow in rank luxuriance over the wrecks of passion. And he whose mind, at once gentle and self-dependent, can endure solitude, might have ransacked all earth for a more fair and undisturbed retreat.

But not to such a solitude had the earlier dreams of Adrian dedicated the place. Here had he thought—should one bright being have presided—here should love have found its haven: and hither, when love at length admitted of intrusion, hither might wealth and congenial culture have invited all the gentler and better spirits which had begun to move over the troubled face of Italy, promising a second and younger empire of poesy, and lore, and art. To the graceful and romantic but somewhat pensive and inert, temperament of the young noble, more adapted to calm and civilized than stormy and barbarous times, ambition proffered no reward so grateful as lettered leisure and intellectual repose. His youth colored by the influence of Petrarch, his manhood had dreamed of a happier Vaucluse not untenanted by a Laura. The visions which had connected the scene with the image of Irene made the place still haunted by her shade; and time and absence only ministering to his impassioned meditations, deepened his melancloly and increased his love.

In this lone retreat—which even in describing from memory, for these eyes have seen, these feet have trodden, this heart yet yearneth for, the spot—which even, I say, in thus describing, seems to me (and haply also to the gentle reader) a grateful and welcome transit from the storms of action and the vicissitudes of ambition, so long engrossing the narrative;—in this lone retreat Adrian passed the winter, which visits with so mild a change that intoxicating clime. The roar of the world without was borne but in faint and indistinct murmurings to his ear. He learned only imperfectly, and with many contradictions, the news which broke like a thunderbolt over Italy, that the singular and aspiring man—himself a revolution—who had excited the interest of all Europe, the brightest hopes of the enthusiastic, the profusest adulation of the great, the deepest terror of the despot, the wildest aspirations of all free spirits, had been suddenly stricken from his state, his name branded and his head proscribed. This event, which happened at the end of December, reached Adrian, through a wandering pilgrim, at the commencement of March, somewhat more than two months after the date; the March of that awful year 1348, which saw Europe, and Itally especially, desolated by the direst pestilence which history has recorded, accursed alike by the numbers and the celebrity of its victims, and yet strangely connected with some not unpleasing images by the grace of Boccaccio and the eloquence of Petrarch.

The pilgrim who informed Adrian of the revolution at Rome was unable to give him any clue to the present fate of Rienzi or his family. It was only known that the Tribune and his wife had escaped, none knew whither; many guessed that they were already dead, victims to the numerous robbers who immediately on the fall of the Tribune settled back to their former habits, sparing neither age nor sex, wealth nor poverty. As all relating to the ex-Tribune was matter of eager interest, the pilgrim had also learned that, previous to the fall of Rienzi, his sister had left Rome, but it was not known to what place she had been conveyed.

The news utterly roused Adrian from his dreaming life. Irene was then in the condition his letter dared to picture—severed from her brother, fallen from her rank, desolate and friendless. "Now," said the generous and high-hearted lover, "she may be mine without a disgrace to my name. Whatever Rienzi's faults, she is not implicated in them. *Her* hands are not red with my kinsman's blood; nor can men say that Adrian di Castello allies himself with a House whose power is built upon the ruins of the Colonnas. The Colonna are restored—again triumphant—Rienzi is nothing—distress and misfortune unite me at once to her on whom they fall!"

But how were these romantic resolutions to be executed—Irene's dwelling-place unknown? He resolved himself to repair to Rome and make the necessary inquiries: accordingly he summoned his retainers:—blithe tidings to them, those of travel! The mail left the armory—the banner the hall—and after two days of animated bustle, the fountain by which Adrian had passed so many hours of revery was haunted only by the birds of the returning spring; and the nightly lamp no longer cast its solitary ray from his turret chamber over the bosom of the deserted lake.

CHAPTER II.

The Seeker.

It was a bright, oppressive, sultry morning

when a solitary horseman was seen winding that unequalled road, from whose height, amidst fig-trees, vines, and olives, the traveller beholds gradually break upon his gaze the enchanting valley of the Arno, and the spires and domes of Florence. But not with the traveller's customary eye of admiration and delight passed that solitary horseman, and not upon the usual activity, and mirth, and animation of the Tuscan life, broke that noon day sun. All was silent, void, and hushed; and even in the light of heaven there seemed a sicklied and ghastly glare. The cottages by the road-side were some shut up and closed, some open, but seemingly inmateless. The plough stood still, the distaff plied not: horse and man had a dreary holiday. There was a darker curse upon the land than the curse of Cain! Now and then a single figure, usually clad in the gloomy robe of a friar, crossed the road, lifting towards the traveller a livid and amazed stare, and then hurried on, and vanished beneath some roof, whence issued a faint and dying moan, which but for the exceeding stillness around could scarcely have pierced the threshold. As the traveller neared the city, the scene became less solitary, yet more dread. There might be seen carts and litters, thick awnings wrapped closely round them, containing those who sought safety in flight, forgetful that the Plague was everywhere! And while these gloomy vehicles, conducted by horses, gaunt, shadowy skeletons, crawling heavily along, passed by, like hearses of the dead, sometimes a cry burst the silence in which they moved, and the traveller's steed darted aside, as some wretch, on whom the disease had broke forth, was dropped from the vehicle by the selfish inhumanity of his comrades, and left to perish by the way. Hard by the gate a wagon paused, and a man with a mask threw out its contents in a green slimy ditch that bordered the road. These were garments and robes of all kind and value; the broidered mantle of the gallant, the hood and veil of my lady, and the rags of the peasant. While glancing at the labor of the masker, the cavalier beheld a herd of swine, gaunt and half famished, run to the spot in the hopes of food, and the traveller shuddered to think *what* food they might have anticipated! But ere he reached the gate, those of the animals that had been busiest rooting at the infectious heap, dropped down dead amongst their fellows.*

"Ho, ho," said the masker, and his hollow voice sounded yet more hollow through his vizard,—"comest thou here to die, stranger? See, thy brave mantle of triple-pile and golden broidery will not save thee from the gavocciolo.† Ride on, ride on;—to-day fit morsel for thy lady's kiss, to-morrow too foul for the rat and worm!"

Replying not to this hideous welcome, Adrian, for it was he, pursued his way. The gates stood wide open: this was the most appalling sign of all, for, at first, the most jealous precaution had been taken against the ingress of strangers. Now all care, all foresight, all vigilance, were vain. And thrice nine warders had died at that single post, and the officers to appoint their successors were dead too! Law and Police, and the Tribunals of Health, and the Boards of Safety, Death had stopped them all! And the Plague killed art itself, social union, the harmony and mechanism of civilization, as if they had been bone and flesh!

So, mute and solitary, went on the lover, in his quest of love, resolved to find and to save his betrothed, and guided (that faithful and loyal knight!) through the Wilderness of Horror by the blessed hope of that strange passion, noblest of all when noble, basest of all when base! He came into a broad and spacious square lined with palaces, the usual haunt of the best and most graceful nobility of Italy. The stranger was alone now, and the tramp of his gallant steed sounded ghastly and fearful in his own ears, when just as he turned the corner of one of the streets that led from it, he saw a woman steal forth with a child in her arms, while another, yet in infancy, clung to her robe. She held a large bunch of flowers to her nostrils (the fancied and favorite mode to prevent infection), and muttered to the children, who were moaning with hunger,—"Yes, yes, you shall have food! Plenty of food now for the stirring forth. But oh, *that stirring forth!*"—and she peered about and round, lest any of the diseased might be near.

"My friend," said he, "can you direct me to the convent of ——"

"Away, man, away!" shrieked the woman.

---

* The same spectacle greeted, and is recorded by, Boccaccio.

† The tumor that made the fatal symptom.

"Alas!" said Adrian, with a mournful smile, "can you not see that I am not, as yet, one to *spread* contagion?"

But the woman, unheeding him, fled on; when, after a few paces, she was arrested by the child that clung to her.

"Mother, mother!" it cried, "I am sick—I cannot stir."

The woman halted, tore aside the child's robe, saw under the arm the fatal tumor, and, deserting her own flesh, fled with a shriek along the square. The shriek rang long in Adrian's ears, though not aware of the unnatural cause;—the *mother feared not for her infant, but herself*. The voice of Nature was no more heeded in that charnel city than it is in the tomb itself! Adrian rode on at a brisker pace, and came at length before a stately church; its doors were wide open, and he saw within a company of monks (the church had no other worshippers, and they were masked) gathered round the altar, and chanting the *Miserere Domine;*—the ministers of God, in a city hitherto boasting the devoutest population in Italy, without a flock!

The young Cavalier paused before the door, and waited till the service was done, and the monks descended the steps into the street.

"Holy fathers," said he then, "may I pray your goodness to tell me my nearest way to the convent Santa Maria de' Pazzi?"

"Son," said one of these featureless spectres, for so they seemed in their shroud-like robes, and uncouth vizards,—"son, pass on your way, and God be with you. Robbers or revellers may now fill the holy cloisters you speak of. The abbess is dead; and many a sister sleeps with her. And the nuns have fled from the contagion."

Adrian half fell from his horse, and, as he still remained rooted to the spot, the dark procession swept on, hymning in solemn dirge through the desolate street the monastic chaunt—

"By the Mother and the Son,
Death endured and mercy won:
Spare us, sinners though we be;
Miserere Domine!"

Recovering from his stupor, Adrian regained the brethren, and, as they closed the burthen of their song, again accosted them.

"Holy fathers, dismiss me not thus. Perchance the one I seek may yet be heard of at the convent. Tell me which way to shape my course."

"Disturb us not, son," said the monk who spoke before. "It is an ill omen for thee to break thus upon the invocations of the ministers of Heaven."

"Pardon, pardon! I will do ample penance, pay many masses; but I seek a dear friend—the way—the way——"

"To the right, till you gain the first bridge. Beyond the third bridge, on the river side, you will find the convent," said another monk, moved by the earnestness of Adrian.

"Bless you, holy father," faltered forth the Cavalier, and spurred his steed in the direction given. The friars heeded him not, but again resumed their dirge. Mingled with the sound of his horse's hoofs on the clattering pavement, came to the rider's ear the imploring line—

"Miserere Domine!"

Impatient, sick at heart, desperate, Adrian flew through the street at the full speed of his horse. He passed the market-place—it was empty as the desert;—the gloomy and barricadoed streets, in which the counter cries of Guelf and Ghibeline had so often cheered on the Chivalry and Rank of Florence. Now huddled together in vault and pit, lay Guelf and Ghibeline, knightly spurs and beggar's crutch. To that silence the roar even of civil strife would have been a blessing! The first bridge, the river side, the second, the third bridge, all were gained, and Adrian at last reined his steed before the walls of the convent. He fastened his steed to the porch, in which the door stood ajar, half torn from its hinges, traversed the court, gained the opposite door that admitted to the main building, came to the jealous grating, now no more a barrier from the profane world, and as he there paused a moment to recover breath and nerve, wild laughter and loud song, interrupted and mixed with oaths, startled his ear. He pushed aside the great door, entered, and, led by the sounds, came to the refectory. In that meeting-place of the severe and mortified maids of heaven, he now beheld gathered round the upper table, used of yore by the abbess, a strange, disorderly, ruffian herd, who at first glance seemed indeed of all ranks, for some wore serge, or even rags, others were tricked out in all the bravery of satin and velvet, plume and mantle. But a second glance sufficed to indicate that the companions were much of the same degree, and that the finery of the more showy was but the spoil rent from unguarded palaces or tenantless bazars; for under plumed hats, looped with jewels, were grim, unwashed, unshaven faces, over which hung the long locks which the professed brethren of the sharp knife and hireling arm had just begun to assume, serving them often instead of a mask. Amidst these savage revellers, were many women, young and middle aged, foul and fair, and Adrian piously shuddered to see amongst the loose robes and uncovered necks of the professional harlots the saintly habit and beaded rosary of nuns. Flasks of wine, ample viands, gold and silver vessels, mostly consecrated to holy rites, strewed the board. As the young Roman paused spell-bound at the threshold, the man who acted as president of the revel, a huge, swarthy ruffian, with a deep scar over his face, which, traversing the whole of the left cheek and upper lip, gave his large features an aspect preternaturally hideous, called out to him—

"Come in, man—come in! Why stand you there amazed and dumb? We are hospitable revellers, and give all men welcome. Here are wine and women. My Lord Bishop's wine, and my Lady Abbess's women!

"Sing hey, sing ho, for the royal DEATH,
That scatters a host with a single breath;
That opens the prison to spoil the palace,
And rids honest necks from the hangman's malice.
Here's a health to the Plague! Let the mighty ones dread,
The poor never lived till the wealthy were dead.
A health to the Plague! may She ever as now
Loose the rogue from his chain and the nun from her vow:
To the jailer a sword, to the captive a key,
Hurrah for Earth's Curse—'tis a blessing to me!"

Ere this fearful stave was concluded, Adrian, sensible that in such orgies there was no chance of prosecuting his inquiries, left the desecrated chamber and fled, scarcely drawing breath, so great was the terror that seized him, till he stood once more in the court amidst the hot, sickly, stagnant sunlight, that seemed a fit atmosphere for the scenes on which it fell. He resolved, however, not to desert the place without making another effort at inquiry; and while he stood without the court, musing and doubtful, he saw a small chapel hard by, through whose long casement gleamed faintly, and dimmed by the noon-day, the light of tapers. He turned towards its porch, entered, and saw beside the sanctuary a single nun kneeling in prayer. In the narrow aisle, upon a long table, (at either end of which burned the tall dismal tapers whose rays had attracted him,) the drapery of several shrouds showed him the half-distinct outline of human figures hushed in death. Adrian himself, impressed by the sadness and sanctity of the place, and the touching sight of that solitary and unselfish watcher of the dead, knelt down and intensely prayed.

As he rose, somewhat relieved from the burthen at his heart, the nun rose also, and started to perceive him.

"Unhappy man!" said she, in a voice which, low, faint, and solemn, sounded as a ghost's—"what fatality brings thee hither? Seest thou not thou art in the presence of clay which the Plague hath touched—thou breathest the air which destroys! Hence! and search throughout all the desolation for one spot where the Dark Visitor hath not come!"

"Holy maiden," answered Adrian, "the danger you hazard does not appal me;—I seek one whose life is dearer than my own."

"Thou needest say no more to tell me thou art newly come to Florence! Here son forsakes his father, and mother deserts her child. When life is most hopeless, these worms of a day cling to it as if it were the salvation of immortality! But for me alone, death has no horror. Long severed from the world, I have seen my sisterhood perish—the house of God desecrated—its altar overthrown, and I care not to survive,—the last whom the Pestilence leaves at once unperjured and alive."

The nun paused a few moments, and then, looking earnestly at the healthful countenance and unbroken frame of Adrian, sighed heavily—"Stranger, why fly you not?" she said. "Thou mightst as well search the crowded vaults and rotten corruption of the dead, as search the city for one living."

"Sister, and bride of the blessed Redeemer!" returned the Roman, clasping his hands—"one word I implore thee. Thou art, methinks, of the sisterhood of yon dismantled convent; tell me, knowest thou if Irene di Gabrini,*—guest

* The family name of Rienzi was Gabrini.

of the late Abbess, sister of the fallen Tribune of Rome,—be yet amongst the living?"

"Art thou her brother, then?" said the nun. "Art thou that fallen Sun of the Morning?"

"I am her betrothed," replied Adrian, sadly. "Speak."

"Oh, flesh, flesh! how art thou victor to the last, even amidst the triumps hand in the lazar-house of corruption!" said the nun. "Vain man! think not of such carnal ties; make thy peace with heaven, for thy days are surely numbered!"

"Woman!" cried Adrian, impatiently—"talk not to me of myself, nor rail against ties whose holiness thou canst not know. I ask thee again, as thou thyself hopest for mercy and for pardon, is Irene living?"

The nun was awed by the energy of the young lover, and after a moment, which seemed to him an age of agonized suspense, she replied—

"The maiden thou speakest of died not with the general death. In the dispersion of the few remaining, she left the convent—I know not whither; but she had friends in Florence—their names I cannot tell thee."

"Now bless thee, holy sister! bless thee! How long since she left the convent?"

"Four days have passed since the robber and the harlot have seized the house of Santa Maria," replied the nun, groaning: "and they were quick successors to the sisterhood."

"Four days!—and thou canst give me no clue?"

"None—yet stay, young man!"—and the nun, approaching, lowered her voice to a hissing whisper—"Ask the *Becchini*." *

Adrian started aside, crossed himself hastily, and quitted the convent without answer. He returned to his horse, and rode back into the silenced heart of the city. Tavern and hotel these were no more; but the palaces of dead princes were free to the living stranger. He entered one—a spacious and splendid mansion. In the stables he found forage still in the manger; but the horses, at that time in the Italian cities a proof of rank as well as wealth, were gone with the hands that fed them. The high-born Knight assumed the office of groom, took off the heavy harness, fastened his steed to the rack, and as the wearied animal, unconscious of the surrounding horrors, fell eagerly upon its meal, its young lord turned away, and muttered, "Faithful servant, and sole companion! may the pestilence that spareth neither beast nor man, spare thee! and mayst thou bear me hence with a lighter heart!"

A spacious hall, hung with arms and banners—a wide flight of marble stairs, whose walls were painted in the stiff outlines and gorgeous colors of the day, conducted to vast chambers, hung with velvets and cloth of gold, but silent as the tomb. He threw himself upon the cushions which were piled in the centre of the room, for he had ridden far that morning, and for many days before, and he was wearied and exhausted, body and limb; but he could not rest. Impatience, anxiety, hope, and fear, gnawed his heart and fevered his veins, and, after a brief unsatisfactory attempt to sober his own thoughts, and devise some plan of search more certain than that which chance might afford him, he rose, and traversed the apartments, in the acknowledged hope which chance alone could suggest.

It was easy to see that he had made his resting-place in the home of one of the princes of the land; and the splendor of all around him far outshone the barbarous and rude magnificence of the less civilized and wealthy Romans. Here, lay the lute as last touched—the gilded and illumined volume as last conned; there, were seats drawn familiarly together, as when lady and gallant had interchanged whispers last.

"And such," thought Adrian,—"such desolation may soon swallow up the vestige of the unwelcomed guest, as of the vanished lord!"

At length he entered a saloon, in which was a table still spread with wine-flasks, goblets of glass, and one of silver, withered flowers, half-mouldy fruits, and viands. At one side the arras, folding-doors opened to a broad flight of stairs, that descended to a little garden at the back of the house, in which a fountain still played sparkling and livingly—the only thing, save the stranger, living there! On the steps lay a crimson mantle, and by it a lady's

* According to the usual custom of Florence, the dead were borne to their resting-place on biers, supported by citizens of equal rank; but a new trade was created by the plague, and men of the lowest dregs of the populace, bribed by immense payment, discharged the office of transporting the remains of the victims. These were called Becchini.

glove. The relics seemed to speak to the lover's heart of a lover's last wooing and last farewell. He groaned aloud, and feeling he should have need of all of his strength, filled one of the goblets from a half-emptied flask of Cyprus wine. He drained the draught—it revived him. "Now," he said, "once more to my task!—I will sally forth," when suddenly he heard heavy steps along the rooms he had quitted—they approached—they entered; and Adrian beheld two huge and ill-omened forms stalk into the chamber. They were wrapped in black homely draperies, their arms were bare, and they wore large shapeless masks, which descended to the breast, leaving only access to sight and breath in three small and circular apertures. The Colonna half drew his sword, for the forms and aspects of these visitors were not such as men think to look upon in safety.

"Oh!" said one, "the palace has a new guest to-day. Fear us not, stranger; there is room,—ay, and wealth enough for all men now in Florence! Per Bacco! but there is still one goblet of silver left—how comes that? So saying, the man seized the cup which Adrian had just drained, and thrust it into his breast. He then turned to Adrian, whose hand was still upon his hilt, and said, with a laugh which came chocked and muffled through his vizard—"Oh, we cut no throats, Signor; the Invisible spares us that trouble. We are honest men, state officers, and come but to see if the cart should halt here to-night."

"Ye are then——"

"Becchini!"

Adrian's blood ran cold. The Becchinio continued—"And keep you this house while you rest at Florence, Signor?"

"Yes, if the rightful lord claim it not."

"Ha! ha! 'Rightful lord!' The Plague is Lord of all now! Why, I have known three gallant companies tenant this palace the last week, and have buried them all—all! It is a pleasant house enough, and gives good custom! Are you alone?"

"At present, yes."

"Show us where you sleep, that we may know where to come for you. You won't want us these three days, I see."

"Ye are pleasant welcomers!" said Adrian;—"but listen to me. Can ye find the living as well as bury the dead? I seek one in this city who, if you discover her, shall be worth to you a year of burials!"

"No, no! that is out of our line. As well look for a dropped sand on the beach, as for a living being amongst closed houses and yawning vaults; but if you will pay the poor grave-diggers beforehand, I promise you, you shall have the first of a new charnel-house;—it will be finished just about your time."

"There!" said Adrian, flinging the wretches a few pieces of gold—"there! and if you would do me a kinder service, leave me, at least while living; or I may save you that trouble." And he turned from the room.

The Becchino who had been spokesman followed him. "You are generous, Signor, stay; you will want fresher food than these filthy fragments. I will supply thee of the best, while—while thou wantest it. And hark, —whom wishest thou that I should seek?"

This question arrested Adrian's departure. He detailed the name, and all the particulars he could suggest of Irene; and, with sickened heart, described the hair, features, and stature of that lovely and hallowed image, which might furnish a theme to the poet, and now gave a clue to the grave-digger.

The unhallowed apparition shook his head when Adrian had concluded. "Full five hundred such descriptions did I hear in the first days of the Plague, when there were still such things as mistress and lover; but it is a dainty catalogue, Signor, and it will be a pride to the poor Becchino to discover or even to bury so many charms! I will do my best; meanwhile, I can recommend you, if in a hurry, to make the best use of your time, to many a pretty face and comely shape——"

"Out, fiend!" muttered Adrian: "fool to waste time with such as thou!"

The laugh of the grave-digger followed his steps.

All that day did Adrian wander through the city, but search and question were alike unavailing; all whom he encountered and interrogated seemed to regard him as a madman, and these were indeed of no kind likely to advance his object. Wild troops of disordered, drunken revellers, processions of monks, or here and there, scattered individuals gliding rapidly along, and shunning all approach or speech, made the only haunters of the dismal streets, till the sun sunk, lurid and yellow, behind the hills, and Darkness closed around the noiseless pathway of the Pestilence.

CHAPTER III.

The Flowers amidst the Tombs.

ADRIAN found that the Becchino had taken care that famine should not forestall the plague; the banquet of the dead was removed, and fresh viands and wines of all kinds,—for there was plenty then in Florence!—spread the table. He partook of the refreshment, though but sparingly, and shrinking from repose in beds beneath whose gorgeous hangings Death had been so lately busy, carefully closed door and window, wrapped himself in his mantle, and found his resting-place on the cushions of the chamber in which he had supped. Fatigue cast him into an unquiet slumber, from which he was suddenly awakened by the roll of a cart below, and the jingle of bells. He listened, as the cart proceeded slowly from door to door, and at length its sound died away in the distance. He slept no more that night!

The sun had not long risen ere he renewed his labors; and it was yet early when, just as he passed a church, two ladies richly dressed came from the porch, and seemed through their vizards to regard the young Cavalier with earnest attention. The gaze arrested him also, when one of the ladies said, "Fair sir, you are over-bold: you wear no mask; neither do you smell to flowers."

"Lady, I wear no mask, for I would be seen: I search these miserable places for one in whose life I live."

"He is young, comely, evidently noble, and the plague hath not touched him: he will serve our purpose well," whispered one of the ladies to the other.

"You echo my own thoughts," returned her companion; and then turning to Adrian, she said, "You seek one you are not wedded to, if you seek so fondly?"

"It is true."

"Young and fair, with dark hair and neck of snow; I will conduct you to her."

"Signora!"

"Follow us!"

"Know you whom I am, and whom I seek?"

"Yes."

"Can you in truth tell me aught of Irene?"

"I can: follow me."

"To her?"

"Yes, yes: follow us!"

The ladies moved on as if impatient of further parley. Amazed, doubtful, and, as if in a dream, Adrian followed them. Their dress, manner, and the pure Tuscan of the one who had addressed him, indicated them of birth and station; but all else was a riddle which he could not solve.

They arrived at one of the bridges, where a litter and a servant on horseback holding a palfrey by the bridle were in attendance. The ladies entered the litter, and she who had before spoken bade Adrian follow on the palfrey.

"But tell me——" he began.

"No questions, Cavalier," said she, impatiently; "follow the living in silence, or remain with the dead, as you list."

With that the litter proceeded, and Adrian mounted the palfrey wonderingly, and followed his strange conductors, who moved on at a tolerably brisk pace. They crossed the bridge, left the river on one side, and, soon ascending a gentle acclivity, the trees and flowers of the country began to succeed dull walls and empty streets. After proceeding thus somewhat less than half an hour, they turned up a green lane remote from the road, and came suddenly upon the porticoes of a fair and stately palace. Here the ladies descended from their litter; and Adrian, who had vainly sought to extract speech from the attendant, also dismounted, and following them across a spacious court, filled on either side with vases of flowers and orange-trees, and then through a wide hall in the farther side of the quadrangle, found himself in one of the loveliest spots eye ever saw or poet ever sung. It was a garden plot of the most emerald verdure, bosquets of laurel and of myrtle opened on either side into vistas half overhung with clematis and rose, through whose arcades the prospect closed with statues and gushing fountains; in front, the lawn was bounded by rows of vases on marble pedestals filled with flowers; and broad and gradual flights of steps of the whitest marble led from terrace to terrace, each adorned with statues and fountains, half way down a high but softly sloping and verdant hill. Beyond, spread in wide, various, and luxurious landscape, the vineyards and olive-groves, the villas and villages, of the Vale of Arno, intersected by the silver river, while the city, in all its calm, but without its horror, raised its roofs and spires to the sun. Birds of every hue and song, some free, some in net-work of golden wire, warbled round; and upon the centre of the sward reclined four ladies unmasked and richly dressed, the eldest of whom seemed scarcely more than twenty; and five cavaliers, young and handsome, whose jewelled vests and golden chains attested their degree. Wines and fruits were on a low table beside; and musical instruments, chess-boards, and gammon-tables, lay scattered all about. So fair a group, and so graceful a scene, Adrian never beheld but once, and that was in the midst of the ghastly pestilence of Italy!—such group and such scene our closet indolence may yet revive in the pages of the bright Boccaccio!

On seeing Adrian and his companions approach, the party rose instantly; and one of the ladies, who wore upon her head a wreath of laurel-leaves, stepping before the rest, exclaimed, "Well done, my Mariana! welcome back, my fair subjects. And you, sir, welcome hither."

The two guides of the Colonna had by this time removed their masks; and the one who had accosted him, shaking her long and raven ringlets over a bright, laughing eye, and a cheek to whose native olive now rose a slight blush, turned to him ere he could reply to the welcome he had received.

"Signor Cavalier," said she, "you now see to what I have decoyed you. Own that this is pleasanter than the sights and sounds of the city we have left. You gaze on me in surprise. See, my Queen, how speechless the marvel of your court has made our new gallant; I assure you he could talk quickly enough when he had only us to confer with: nay, I was forced to impose silence on him."

"Oh! then you have not yet informed him of the custom and origin of the court he enters?" quoth she of the laurel wreath.

"No, my Queen; I thought all description given in such a spot as our poor Florence now is would fail of its object. My task is done, I resign him to your grace!"

So saying the lady tripped lightly away, and began coquettishly sleeking her locks in the smooth mirror of a marble basin, whose waters trickled over the margin upon the grass below, ever and anon glancing archly towards the stranger, and sufficiently at hand to overhear all that was said.

"In the first place, Signor, permit us to inquire," said the lady who bore the appellation of Queen, "thy name, rank, and birthplace."

"Madam," returned Adrian, "I came hither little dreaming to answer questions respecting myself; but what it pleases you to ask, it must please me to reply to. My name is Adrian di Castello, one of the Roman house of the Colonna."

"A noble column of a noble house!" answered the Queen. "For us, respecting whom your curiosity may perhaps be aroused, know that we six ladies of Florence, deserted by or deprived of our kin and protectors, formed the resolution to retire to this palace, where, if death comes, it comes stripped of half its horrors; and as the learned tell us that sadness engenders the awful malady, so you see us sworn foes to sadness. Six cavaliers of our acquaintance agreed to join us. We pass our days, whether many or few, in whatever diversions we can find or invent. Music and the dance, merry tales and lively songs, with such slight change of scene as from sward to shade, from alley to fountain, fill up our time, and prepare us for peaceful sleep and happy dreams. Each lady is by turns Queen of our fairy court, as is my lot this day. One law forms the code of our constitution—that nothing sad shall be admitted. We would live as if yonder city were not, and as if (added the fair Queen, with a slight sigh) youth, grace, and beauty, could endure for ever. One of our knights madly left us for a day, promising to return; we have seen him no more: we will not guess what hath chanced to him. It became necessary to fill up his place; we drew lots who should seek his substitute; it fell upon the ladies who have—not, I trust, to your displeasure—brought you hither. Fair sir, my explanation is made."

"Alas, lovely Queen," said Adrian, wrestling strongly, but vainly, with the bitter disappointment he felt—"I cannot be one of your happy circle; I am in myself a violation of your law. I am filled with but one sad and anxious thought, to which all mirth would seem impiety. I am a seeker amongst the living and the dead for one being of whose fate I am uncertain; and it was only by the words that fell from my fair conductor, that I have been decoyed hither from my mournful task. Suffer me, gracious lady, to return to Florence."

The Queen looked in mute vexation towards the dark-eyed Mariana, who returned the glance by one equally expressive, and then suddenly stepping up to Adrian, she said,—

"But, Signor, if I should still keep my promise, if I should be able to satisfy thee of the health and safety of—of Irene."

"Irene!" echoed Adrian in surprise, forgetful at the moment that he had before revealed the name of her he sought—"Irene—Irene di Gabrini, sister of the once renowned Rienzi!"

"The same," replied Mariana, quickly; "I knew her, as I told you. Nay, Signor, I do not deceive thee. It is true that I cannot bring thee to her; but better as it is,—she went away many days ago to one of the towns of Lombardy, which, they say, the Pestilence has not yet pierced. Now, noble sir, is not your heart lightened? and will you so soon be a deserter from the Court of Loveliness; and perhaps," she added, with a soft look from her large dark eyes, "of Love?"

"Dare I, in truth, believe you, Lady?" said Adrian, all delighted, yet still half doubting.

"Would I deceive a true lover, as methinks you are? Be assured. Nay, Queen, receive your subject."

The Queen extended her hand to Adrian, and led him to the group that still stood on the grass at a little distance. They welcomed him as a brother, and soon forgave his abstracted courtesies, in compliment to his good mien and illustrious name.

The Queen clapped her hands, and the party again ranged themselves on the sward. Each lady beside each gallant. "You, Mariana, if not fatigued," said the Queen, "shall take the lute and silence these noisy grass-hoppers, which chirp about us with as much pretension as if they were nightingales. Sing, sweet subject, sing; and let it be the song our dear friend, Signor Visdomini,* made for a kind of inaugural anthem to such as we admitted to our court."

* I know not if this be the same Visdomini who, three years afterwards, with one of the Medici, conducted so gallant a reinforcement to Scarperia, then besieged by Visconti d'Oleggio.

Mariana, who had reclined herself by the side of Adrian, took up the lute, and, after a short prelude, sung the words thus imperfectly translated:—

THE SONG OF THE FLORENTINE LADY.

Enjoy the more the smiles of noon
If doubtful be the morrow;
And know the Fort of Life is soon
Betray'd to Death by Sorrow!

Death claims us all—then, Grief, away!
We'll own no meaner master;
The clouds that darken round the day
But bring the night the faster.

Love—feast—be merry while on earth,
Such, Grave, should be thy moral!
Ev'n Death himself is friends with Mirth,
And veils the tomb with laurel.*

While gazing on the eyes I love,
New life to mine is given—
If joy the lot of saints above,
Joy fits us best for Heaven.

To this song, which was much applauded, succeeded those light and witty tales in which the Italian novelists furnished Voltaire and Marmontel with a model—each, in his or her turn, taking up the discourse, and with an equal dexterity avoiding every lugubrious image or mournful reflection that might remind those graceful idlers of the vicinity of Death. At any other time the temper and accomplishments of the young Lord di Castello would have fitted him to enjoy and to shine in that Arcadian court. But now he in vain sought to dispel the gloom from his brow, and the anxious thought from his heart. He revolved the intelligence he had received, wondered, guessed, hoped, and dreaded still; and if for a moment his mind returned to the scene about him, his nature, too truly poetical for the false sentiment of the place, asked itself in what, save the polished exterior and the graceful circumstance, the mirth that he now so reluctantly witnessed differed from the brutal revels in the convent of Santa Maria—each alike in its motive, though so differing in the manner—equally callous and equally selfish, coining horror into enjoyment. The fair Mariana, whose partner had been reft from her, as the Queen had related, was in no mind to lose the new one she had gained. She pressed upon him from time to time the wine-flask and

* At that time, in Italy, the laurel was frequently planted over the dead.

the fruits; and in those unmeaning courtesies her hand gently lingered upon his. At length, the hour arrived when the companions retired to the Palace, during the fiercer heats of noon—to come forth again in the declining sun, to sup by the side of the fountain, to dance, to sing, and to make merry by torchlight and the stars till the hour of rest. But Adrian, not willing to continue the entertainment, no sooner found himself in the apartment to which he was conducted, than he resolved to effect a silent escape, as under all circumstances the shortest, and not perhaps the least courteous, farewell left to him. Accordingly, when all seemed quiet and hushed in the repose common to the inhabitants of the South during that hour, he left his apartment, descended the stairs, passed the outer court, and was already at the gate, when he heard himself called by a voice that spoke vexation and alarm. He turned to behold Mariana.

"Why, how now, Signor di Castello, is our company so unpleasing, is our music so jarring, are our brows so wrinkled, that you should fly as the traveller flies from the witches he surprises at Benevonto? Nay, you cannot mean to leave us yet?"

"Fair dame," returned the cavalier, somewhat disconcerted, "it is in vain that I seek to rally my mournful spirits, or to fit myself for the court to which nothing sad should come. Your laws hang abou me like a culprit —better timely flight than harsh expulsion."

As he spoke he moved on, and would have passed the gate, but Mariana caught his arm.

"Nay," said she, softly: "are there no eyes of dark light, and no neck of wintry snow, that can compensate to thee for the absent one? Tarry and forget, as doubtless in absence even *thou* art forgotten!"

"Lady," answered Adrian, with great gravity, not unmixed with an ill-suppressed disdain, "I have not sojourned long enough amidst the sights and sounds of woe, to blunt my heart and spirit into callousness to all around. Enjoy, if thou canst, and gather the rank roses of the sepulchre; but to me, haunted still by funeral images, Beauty fails to bring delight, and Love—even *holy* love—seems darkened by the Shadow of Death. Pardon me, and farewell."

"Go, then," said the Florentine, stung and enraged at his coldness; "go and find your mistress amidst the associations on which it pleases your philosophy to dwell. I did but deceive thee, blind fool! as I had hoped for thine own good, when I told thee Irene—(was that her name?)—was gone from Florence. Of her I know nought, and heard nought, save from thee. Go back and search the vault, and see whether thou lovest her still!"

CHAPTER IV.

We Obtain what we Seek, and Know it Not.

In the fiercest heat of the day, and on foot, Adrian returned to Florence. As he approached the city, all that festive and gallant scene he had quitted seemed to him like a dream; a vision of the gardens and bowers of an enchantress, from which he woke abruptly as a criminal may wake on the morning of his doom to see the scaffold and the deathsman; —so much did each silent and lonely step into the funeral city bring back his bewildered thoughts at once to life and to death. The parting words of Mariana sounded like a knell at his heart. And now as he passed on—the heat of the day, the lurid atmosphere, long fatigue, alternate exhaustion and excitement, combining with the sickness of disappointment, the fretting consciousness of precious moments irretrievably lost, and his utter despair of forming any systematic mode of search—fever began rapidly to burn through his veins. His temples felt oppressed as with the weight of a mountain; his lips parched with intolerable thirst; his strength seemed suddenly to desert him; and it was with pain and labor that he dragged one languid limb after the other.

"I feel it," thought he, with the loathing nausea and shivering dread with which nature struggles ever against death; "I feel it upon me—the Devouring and the Viewless—I shall perish, and without saving her; nor shall even one grave contain us!"

But these thoughts served rapidly to augument the disease which began to prey upon him; and ere he reached the interior of the city, even thought itself forsook him. The images of men and houses grew indistinct and shadowy before his eyes; the burning pavement became unsteady and reeling beneath his feet; delirium gathered over him, and he went on his way muttering broken and incoherent words; the few who met fled from him in dismay. Even the monks, still continuing their solemn and sad processions, passed with a murmnred *bene vobis* to the other side from that on which his steps swerved and faltered. And from a booth at the corner of a street, four Becchini, drinking together, fixed upon him from their black masks the gaze that vultures fix upon some dying wanderer of the desert. Still he crept on, stretching out his arms like a man in the dark, and seeking with the vague sense that yet struggled against the gathering delirium, to find out the mansion in which he had fixed his home; though many as fair to live, and as meet to die in, stood with open portals before and beside his path.

"Irene, Irene!" he cried, sometimes in a muttered and low tone, sometimes in a wild and piercing shriek, "where art thou? Where! I come to snatch thee from them! they shall not have thee, the foul and ugly fiends! Pah! how the air smells of dead flesh! Irene, Irene! we will away to mine own palace and the heavenly lake—Irene!"

While thus benighted, and thus exclaiming, two females suddenly emerged from a neighboring house, masked and mantled.

"Vain Wisdom!" said the taller and slighter of the two, whose mantle, it is here necessary to observe, was of a deep blue, richly broidered with silver, of a shape and a color not common in Florence, but usual in Rome, where the dress of ladies of the higher rank was singularly bright in hue and ample in fold—thus differing from the simpler and more slender draperies of the Tuscan fashion—"Vain wisdom, to fly a relentless and certain doom!"

"Why, thou wouldst not have us hold the same home wlth three of the dead in the next chamber—strangers too to us—when Florence has so many empty halls? Trust me we shall not walk far ere we suit ourselves with a safer lodgment."

"Hitherto, indeed, we have been miraculously preserved," sighed the other, whose voice and shape were those of extreme youth; "yet would that we knew where to fly—what mount, what wood, what cavern, held my brother and his faithful Nina! I am sick with horrors!"

"Irene, Irene! Well then, if thou art at Milan or some Lombard town, why do I linger here? To horse, to horse! Oh, no! no!—not the horse with the bells! not the death-cart." With a cry, a shriek, louder than the loudest of the sick man's, broke that young female away from her companion. It seemed as if a single step took her to the side of Adrian. She caught his arm—she looked in his face—she met his unconscious eyes bright with a fearful fire. "It has seized him!"—(she then said in a deep but calm tone)—the Plague!"

"Away, away! are you mad?" cried her companion; "hence, hence,—touch me not now thou hast touched him—go!—here we part!"

"Help me to bear him somewhere, see, he faints, he droops, he falls!—help me, dear Signora, for pity, for the love of God!"

But, wholly possessed by the selfish fear which overcame all humanity in that miserable time, the elder woman, though naturally kind, pitiful, and benevolent, fled rapidly away, and soon vanished. Thus left alone with Adrian, who had now in the fierceness of the fever that preyed within him, fallen on the ground, the strength and nerve of that young girl did not forsake her. See tore off the heavy mantle which encumbered her arms, and cast it from her; and then, lifting up the face of her lover—for who but Irene was that weak woman, thus shrinking from the contagion of death?—she supported him on her breast, and called aloud and again for help. At length the Becchini, in the booth before noticed, (hardened in their profession, and who, thus hardened, better than the most cautious, escaped the pestilence), lazily approached—"Quicker, quicker, for Christ's love!" said Irene. "I have much gold; I will reward you well; help me to bear him under the nearest roof."

"Leave him to us, young lady: we have had our eyes upon him," said one of the grave-diggers. "We'll do our duty to him, first and last."

"No—no! touch not his head—that is my care. There, I will help you; so,—now then,—but be gentle!"

Assisted by these portentous officers, Irene, who would not release her hold, but seemed to watch over the beloved eyes and lips, (set and closed as they were), as if to look back the soul from parting, bore Adrian into a neighboring house, and laid him on a bed; from which Irene (preserving as only women do, in such times, the presence of mind and vigilant providence which make so sublime a contrast with their keen suceptibilities) caused them first to cast off the draperies and clothing, which might retain additional infection. She then dispatched them for new furniture, and for whatsoever leech money might yet bribe to a duty, now chiefly abandoned to those heroic Brotherhoods who, however vilified in modern judgment by the crimes of some unworthy members, were yet, in the dark times, the best, the bravest, and the holiest agents, to whom God ever delegated the power to resist the oppressor—to feed the hungry—to minister to woe; and who, alone amidst that fiery Pestilence, (loosed, as it were, a demon from the abyss, to shiver into atoms all that binds the world to Virtue and to Law), seemed to awaken, as by the sound of an angel's trumpet, to that noblest Chivalry of the Cross—whose faith is the scorn of self—whose hope is beyond the Lazar-house—whose feet, already winged for immortality, trample, with a conquerer's march, upon the graves of Death !

While this the ministry and the office of love,—along that street in which Adrian and Irene had met at last—came singing, reeling, roaring, the dissolute and abandoned crew who had fixed their quarters in the Convent of Santa Maria de' Pazzi, their bravo chief at their head, and a nun, (no longer in nun's garments) upon either arm. "A health to the Plague !" shouted the ruffian: "A health to the Plague !" echoed his frantic Bacchanals.

"A health to the Plague, may she ever, as now,
Loose the rogue from his chain, and the nun from her vow;
To the jailer a sword—to the captive a key,
Hurrah for Earth's Curse ! 'tis a blessing to me."

"Holla !" cried the chief, stopping ; "here, Margherita; here 's a brave cloak for thee, my girl: silver enow on it to fill thy purse, if it ever grow empty; which it may, if ever the Plague grow slack."

"Nay," said the girl, who, amidst all the havoc of debauch, retained much of youth and beauty in her form and face; nay, Guidoito; perhaps it has infection."

"Pooh, child, silver never infects. Clap it on, clap it on. Besides, fate is fate, and when it is thine hour there will be other means besides the *gavocciolo*."

So saying, he seized the mantle, threw it roughly over her shoulders, and dragged her on as before, half pleased with the finery, half frightened with the danger; while gradually died away, along the lurid air and the mournful streets, the chant of that most miserable mirth.

CHAPTER V.

The Error.

For three days, the fatal three days, did Adrian remain bereft of strength and sense. But he was not smitten by the scourge which his devoted and generous nurse had anticipated. It was a fierce and dangerous fever, brought on by the great fatigue, restlessness, and terrible agitation he had undergone.

No professional mediciner could be found to attend him; but a good friar, better perhaps skilled in the healing art than many who claimed its monopoly, visited him daily. And in the long and frequent absences to which his other and numerous duties compelled the monk, there was one ever at hand to smooth the pillow, to wipe the brow, to listen to the moan, to watch the sleep. And even in that dismal office, when, in the frenzy of the sufferer, her name, coupled with terms of passionate endearment, broke from his lips, a thrill of strange pleasure crossed the heart of the betrothed, which she chid as if it were a crime. But even the most unearthly love is selfish in the rapture of being loved ! Words cannot tell, heart cannot divine, the mingled emotions that broke over her when, in some of these incoherent ravings, she dimly understood that *for her* the city had been sought, the death dared, the danger incurred. And as then bending passionately to kiss that burning brow, her tears fell fast over the idol of her youth, the fountains from which they gushed were those, fathomless and countless, which a life could not weep away. Not an impulse of the human and the woman heart that was not stirred; the adoring gratitude, the meek wonder thus to *be* loved, while deeming it so simple a merit thus *to* love;—as if all sacrifice *in* her were a thing of course,—*to* her a virtue nature could not paragon, worlds could not repay ! And there he lay, the victim to his own fearless faith, helpless—dependent upon her—a thing between life and death, to thank, to serve—to be proud of, yet protect, to compassionate, yet revere—the saver, to be saved! Never seemed one object to demand at once from a single heart so many and so profound emotions; the romantic enthusiasm of the girl—the fond idolatry of the bride—the watchful providence of the mother over her child.

And strange to say, with all the excitement of that lonely watch, scarcely stirring from his side, taking food only that her strength might not fail her,—unable to close her eyes,—though, from the same cause, she would fain have taken rest, when slumber fell upon her charge—with all such wear and tear of frame and heart, she seemed wonderfully supported. And the holy man marvelled, in each visit, to see the cheek of the nurse still fresh, and her eye still bright. In her own superstition she thought and felt that Heaven gifted her with a preternatural power to be true to so sacred a charge; and in this fancy she did not wholly err:—for Heaven *did* gift her with that diviner power, when it planted in so soft a heart the enduring might and energy of Affection! The friar had visited the sick man late on the third night, and administered to him a strong sedative. "This night," said he to Irene, "will be the crisis should he awaken, as I trust he may, with a returning consciousness, and a calm pulse, he will live; if not, young daughter, prepare for the worst. But should you note any turn in the disease, that may excite alarm, or require my attendance, this scroll will inform you where I am, if God spare me still, at each hour of the night and morning."

The monk retired, and Irene resumed her watch.

The sleep of Adrian was at first broken and interrupted—his features, his exclamations, his gestures, all evinced great agony, whether mental or bodily: it seemed, as perhaps it was, a fierce and doubtful struggle between life and death for the conquest of the sleeper. Patient, silent, breathing but by long-drawn gasps, Irene sate at the bed-head. The lamp was removed to the further end of the chamber, and its ray shaded by the draperies, did not suffice to give to her gaze more than the outline of the countenance she watched. In that awful suspense, all the thoughts that hitherto had stirred her mind lay hushed and mute. She was only sensible to that unutterable fear which few of us have been happy enough not to know. That crushing weight under which we can scarcely breathe or move, the avalanche over us, freezing and suspended, which we cannot escape from, beneath which, every moment, we may be buried and overwhelmed. The whole destiny of life was in the chances of that single night! It was just as Adrian at last seemed to glide into a deeper and serener slumber, that the bells of the death-cart broke with their boding knell the palpable silence of the streets. Now hushed, now revived, as the cart stopped for its gloomy passengers, and coming nearer and nearer after every pause. At length she heard the heavy wheels stop under the very casement, and a voice deep and muffled calling aloud, "Bring out the dead!" She rose, and with a noiseless, step passed to secure the door, when the dull lamp gleamed upon the dark and shrouded form of the Becchini.

"You have not marked the door, nor set out the body," said one gruffly; "but this is the *third night!* He is ready for us."

"Hush, he sleeps—away, quick, it is not the Plague that seized him."

"Not the Plague?" growled the Becchino in a disappointed tone; "I thought no other illness dared encroach upon the rights of the gavocciolo!"

"Go—here's money; leave us."

And the grisly carrier sullenly withdrew. The cart moved on, the bell renewed its summons, till slowly and faintly the dreadful larum died in the distance.

Shading the lamp with her hand, Irene stole to the bed side, fearful that the sound and the intrusion had disturbed the slumberer. But his face was still locked, as in a vice, with that iron sleep. He stirred not—the breath scarcely passed his lips—she felt his pulse, as the wan hand lay on the coverlid—there was a slight beat—she was contented—removed the light, and, retiring to a corner of the room, placed the little cross suspended round her neck upon the table, and prayed, in her intense suffering, to Him who had known death, and who—Son of Heaven though he was, and Sovereign of the Seraphim—had also prayed, in his earthly travail, that the cup might pass away.

The Morning broke, not, as in the North, slowly and through shadow, but with the sudden glory with which in those climates Day leaps upon earth—like a giant from his sleep. A sudden smile—a burnished glow—and night had vanished. Adrian still slept; not a muscle seemed to have stirred; the sleep was even heavier than before; the silence became a burthen upon the air. Now, in that exceeding torpor so like unto death, the solitary watcher became alarmed and terrified. Time passed—morning glided to noon—still not a sound nor motion. The sun was midway in Heaven—the Friar came not. And now again touching Adrian's pulse, she felt no flutter—she gazed on him, appalled and confounded; surely nought living could be so still and pale. "Was it indeed sleep, might it not be——" She turned away, sick and frozen; her tongue clove to her lips. Why did the father tarry?—she would go to him—she would learn the worst—she could forbear no longer. She glanced over the scroll the Monk had left her: "From sunrise," it said, "I shall be at the Convent of the Dominicans. Death has stricken many of the brethren." The Convent was at some distance, but she knew the spot, and fear would wing her steps. She gave one wistful look at the sleeper and rushed from the house. "I shall see thee again presently," she murmured. Alas! what hope can calculate beyond the moment? And who shall claim the tenure of '*The Again?*'

It was not many minutes after Irene had left the room, ere, with a long sigh, Adrian opened his eyes—an altered and another man; the fever was gone, the reviving pulse beat low indeed, but calm. His mind was once more master of his body, and, though weak and feeble, the danger was past, and life and intellect regained.

"I have slept long," he muttered, "and oh, such dreams! And me thonght I saw Irene, but could not speak to her, and while I attempted to grasp her, her face changed, her form dilated, and I was in the clutch of the foul grave-digger. It is late—the sun is high—I must be up and stirring. Irene is in Lombardy. No, no; that was a lie, a wicked lie; she is at Florence, I must renew my search"

As this duty came to his remembrance, he rose from the bed—he was amazed at his own debility: at first he conld not stand without support from the wall; by degrees, however, he so far regained the mastery of his limbs as to walk, though with effort and pain. A ravening hunger preyed upon him, he found some scanty and iight food in the chamber, which he devoured eagerly. And with scarce less eagerness laved his enfeebled form and haggard face wlth the water that stood at hand. He now felt refreshed and invigorated, and began to indue his garmemts, which he found thrown on a heap beside the bed. He gazed with surprise and a kind of self-compassion upon his emaciated hands and shrunken limbs, and began now to comprehend that he must have had some severe hut unconscious illness. "Alone, too," thought he; "no one near to tend me! Nature my only nurse! But alas! alas! how long a time may thus have been wasted, and my adored Irene——quick, quick, not a moment more will I lose."

He soon found himself in the open street; the air revived him; and that morning had sprung up the blessed breeze, the first known for weeks. He wandered on very slowly and feebly till he came to a broad square, from which, in the vista, might be seen of one the principal gates of Florence, and the fig-trees and olive-groves beyond. It was then that a Pilgrim of tall stature approached towards him as from the gate; his hood was thrown back, and gave to view a countenance of great but sad command; a face, in whose high features, massive brow, and proud, unshrinking gaze, shaded by an expression of melancholy more stern than soft, Nature seemed to have written majesty, and Fate disaster. As in that silent and dreary place, these two, the only tenants of the street, now encountered, Adrian stopped abruptly, and said in a startled and doubting voice: "Do I dream still, or do I behold Rienzi?"

The Pilgrim paused also, as he heard the name, and gazing long on the attenuated features of the young lord, said: "I am he that was Rienzi! and you, pale shadow, is it in this grave of Italy that I meet with the gay and high Colonna? Alas, young friend," he added, in a more relaxed and kindly voice, "hath the Plague not spared the flower of the Roman nobles? Come, I, the cruel and the harsh Tribune, *I* will be thy nurse: he who might have been my brother, shall yet claim from me a brother's care."

With these words he wound his arm tenderly round Adrian; and the young noble, touched by his compassion, and agitated by the surprise, leaned upon Rienzi's breast in silence.

"Poor youth," resumed the Tribune, for so, since rather fallen than deposed, he may yet be called; "I ever loved the young, (my brother died young;) and you more than most. What fatality brought thee hither?"

"Irene!" replied Adrian falteringly.

"Is it so, really? Art thou a Colonna, and yet prize the fallen? The same duty has brought me also to the city of Death. From the furthest south—over the mountains of the robber—through the fastnesses of my foes—through the towns in which the herald proclaimed in my ear the price of my head—I have passed hither, on foot and alone, safe under the wings of the Almighty One. Young man, thou shouldst have left this task to one who bears a wizard's life, and whom Heaven and Earth yet reserve for an appointed end!"

The Tribune said this in a deep and inward voice; and in his raised eye and solemn brow might be seen how much his reverses had deepened his fanaticism, and added even to the sanguineness of his hopes.

"But," asked Adrian, withdrawing gently from Rienzi's arm, "thou knowest, then, where Irene is to be found; let us go together. Lose not a moment in this talk; time is of inestimable value, and a moment in this city is often but the border to eternity."

"Right," said Rienzi, awakening to his object. "Bur fear not, I *have dreamt* that I shall save her, the gem and darling of my house. Fear not, *I* have no fear."

"Know you where to seek?" said Adrian, impatiently; "the Convent holds far other guests."

"Ha! so said my dream!"

"Talk not now of dreams," said the lover; "but if you have no other guide; let us part at once in quest of her. I will take yonder street, you take the opposite, and at sunset let us meet in the same spot."

"Rash man!" said the Tribune, with great solemnity; "scoff not at the visions which Heaven makes a parable to its Chosen. Thou seekest counsel of thy human wisdom; I, less presumptuous, follow the hand of the mysterious Providence, moving even now before my gaze as a pillar of light through the wilderness of dread. Ay, meet we here at sunset, and prove whose guide is the most unerring. If my dream tell me true, I shall see my sister living, ere the sun reach yonder hill, and by a church dedicated to St. Mark."

The grave earnestness with which Rienzi spoke impressed Adrian with a hope which his reason would not acknowledge. He saw him depart with that proud and stately step to which his sweeping garments gave a yet more imposing dignity, and then passed up the street to the right hand. He had not got half way when he felt himself pulled by the mantle. He turned, and saw the shapeless mask of a Becchino.

"I feared you were sped, and that another had cheated me of my office," said the grave-digger, "seeing that you returned not to the old Prince's palace. You don't know me from the rest of us I see, but I am the one you told to seek ——"

"Irene!"

"Yes, Irene di Gabrini; you promised ample reward."

"You shall have it."

"Follow me."

The Becchino strode on, and soon arrived at a manison. He knocked twice at the porter's entrance, an old woman cautiously opened the door. "Fear not, good aunt," said the grave-digger; "this is the young Lord I spoke to thee of. Thou sayest thou hadst two ladies in the palace, who alone survived of all the lodgers, and their names were Bianca de Medici, and—what was the other?"

"Ireni di· Gabrini, a Roman lady. But I told thee this was the fourth day they left the house, terrified by the deaths within it."

"Thou didst so: and was there anything remarkable in the dress of the Signora di Gabrini?"

"Yes, I have told thee: a blue mantle, such as I have rarely seen, wrought with silver."

"Was the broidery that of stars, silver stars," exclaimed Adrian, "with a sun in the centre?"

"It was."

"Alas! alas! the arms of the Tribune's family! I remember how I praised the mantle the first day she wore it—the day on which we were betrothed!" And the lover at once conjectured the secret sentiment which had induced Irene to retain thus carefully a robe so endeared by association.

"You know no more of your lodgers?"

"Nothing."

"And is this all you have learned, knave?" cried Adrian.

"Patience. I must bring you from proof to proof, and link to link, in order to win my reward. Follow Signor."

The Becchino then passing through the several lanes and streets, arrived at another house of less magnificent size and architecture. Again he tapped thrice at the parlor door, and this time came forth a man withered, old and palsied, whom death seemed to disdain to strike.

"Signor Astuccio," said the Becchino, "pardon me; but I told thee I might trouble thee again. This is the gentleman who wants to know, what is often best unknown—but that's not my affair. Did a lady—young and beautiful—with dark hair, and of a slender form, enter this house, stricken with the first symptom of the Plague, three days since?"

"Ay, thou knowest that well enough; and thou knowest still better, that she has departed these two days: it was quick work with her, quicker than with most?"

"Did she wear anything remarkable?"

"Yes, troublesome man: a blue cloak, with stars of silver."

"Couldst thou guess aught of her previous circumstances?"

"No, save that she raved much about the nunnery of Santa Maria de' Pazzi, and bravos, and sacrilege."

"Are you satisfied Signor?" asked the grave-digger, with an air of triumph, turning to Adrian. "But no, I will satisfy thee better, if thou hast courage. Wilt thou follow?"

"I comprehend thee; lead on. Courage! What is there on earth now to fear?"

Muttering to himself, "Ay, leave me alone. I have a head worth something; I ask no gentleman to go by my word; I will make his own eyes the judge of what my trouble is worth," the grave-digger now led the way through one of the gates a little out of the city. And here, under a shed, sat six of his ghastly and ill-omened brethren, with spades and pick-axes at their feet.

His guide now turned round to Adrian, whose face was set, and resolute in despair.

"Fair Signor," said he, with some touch of lingering compassion, "wouldst thou really convince thine own eyes and heart?—the sight may appal, the contagion may destroy, thee,—if, indeed, as it seems to me, Death has not already written '*mine*' upon thee."

"Raven of bode and woe!" answered Adrian, "seest thou not that all I shrink from is thy voice and aspect? Show me her I seek, living or dead."

"I will show her to you, then," said the Becchino, sullenly, "such as two nights since she was committed to my charge. Line and lineament may already be swept away, for the Plague hath a rapid besom; but I have left that upon her by which you will know the Becchino is no liar. Bring hither the torches, comrades, and lift the door. Never stare; it's the gentleman's whim, and he'll pay it well."

Turning to the right while Adrian mechanically followed his conductors, a spectacle whose dire philosophy crushes as with a wheel all the pride of mortal man—the spectacle of that vault in which earth hides all that on earth flourished, rejoiced, exulted—awaited his eye!

The Becchini lifted a ponderous grate, lowered their torches (scarcely needed, for through the aperture rushed, with a hideous glare, the light of the burning sun,) and motioned to Adrian to advance. He stood upon the summit of the abyss and gazed below.

* * * * *
* * * * *

It was a large deep and circular space, like the bottom of an exhausted well. In niches cut into the walls of earth around, lay, duly coffined, those who had been the earliest victims of the plague, when the Becchino's market was not yet glutted, and priest followed, and friend mourned the dead. But on the floor below, *there* was the loathsome horror! Huddled and matted together—some naked, some in shrouds already black and rotten—lay the later guests, the unshriven and unblest! The torches, the sun, streamed broad and red over Corruption in all its stages, from the pale blue tint and swollen shape, to the moistened undistinguishable mass, or the riddled bones, where yet clung, in strips and tatters, the black and mangled flesh. In many, the face remained almost perfect, while the rest of the body was but bone; the long hair, the human face, surmounting the grisly skeleton. There was the infant, still on the mother's breast; there was the lover, stretched across the dainty limbs of his adored! The rats, (for they clustered in numbers to that feast,) disturbed, not scared, sate up from their horrid meal as the light glimmered over them, and thousands of them lay round, stark, and dead, poisoned by that they fed on! There, too, the wild satire of the grave-diggers had cast, though stripped of their gold and jewels, the emblems that spoke of departed rank;—the broken wand of the Councillor; the General's baton; the Priestly Mitre! The foul and livid exhalations gathered like flesh itself, fungous and putrid, upon the walls, and the *——

* * * * *

* * * * *

But who shall detail the ineffable and unimaginable horrors that reigned over the Palace where the Great King received the prisoners whom the sword of the Pestilence had subdued?

But through all that crowded court—crowded with beauty and with birth, with the strength of the young and the honors of the old, and the valor of the brave, and the wisdom of the learned, and the wit of the scorner, and the piety of the faithful—only one figure attracted Adrian's eye. Apart from the rest, a late comer,—the long locks streaming far and dark over arm and breast—lay a female, the face turned partially aside, the little seen not recognizable even by the mother of the dead,—but wrapped round in that fatal mantle, on which, though blackened and tarnished, was yet visible the starry heraldry assumed by those who claimed the name of the proud Tribune of Rome, Adrian saw no more—he fell back into the arms of the grave-diggers: when he recovered, he was still without the gates of Florence—reclined upon a green mound—his guide stood beside him—holding his steed by the bridle as it grazed patiently on the neglected grass. The other brethren of the axe had resumed their seat under the shed.

"So, you have revived! Ah! I thought it was only the effluvia; few stand it as we do. And so, as your search is over, deeming you would now be quitting Florence if you have any sense left to you, I went for your good horse. I have fed him since your departure from the palace. Indeed I fancied he would be my perquisite, but there are plenty as good. Come, young sir, mount. I feel a pity for you, I know not why, except that you are the only one I have met for weeks, who seem to care for another more than for yourself. I hope you are satisfied now that I showed some brains, eh! in your service; and as I have kept my promise, you'll keep yours."

"Friend," said Adrian, "here is gold enough to make thee rich; here, too, is a jewel that merchants will tell thee princes might vie to purchase. Thou seemest honest, despite thy calling, or thou mightest have robbed and murdered me long since. Do me one favor more."

"By my poor mother's soul, yes."

"Take yon—yon clay from that fearful place. Inter it in some quiet and remote spot—apart—alone! You promise me?—you swear it?—it is well! And now help me on my horse. Farewell Italy, and if I die not with this stroke, may I die as befits at once honor and despair—with trumpet and banner round me—in a well-fought field against a worthy foe!—Save a knightly death, nothing is left to live for!"

* The description in the text is borrowed from the famous waxwork model [of the interior of the Charnel-house] at Florence.

BOOK SEVENTH.

THE PRISON.

"Fu rinchiuso in una torre grossa e larga; avea libri assai, suo Tito Livic sue storie di Roma, la Bibbia."—*Vit. di Cola di Rienzi*, lib. ii. c. 13.

"He was immured in a high and spacious tower; he had books enough, his Titus Livius, his histories of Rome, the Bible," etc.

CHAPTER I.

Avignon.—The Two Pages.—The Stranger Beauty.

THERE is this difference between the drama of Shakspeare, and that of almost every other master of the same art; that in the first, the catastrophe is rarely produced by one single cause—one simple and continuous chain of events. Various and complicated agencies work out the final end. Unfettered by the rules of time and place, each time, each place depicted, presents us with its appropriate change of action, or of actors. Sometimes the interest seems to halt, to turn aside, to bring us unawares upon objects hitherto unnoticed, or upon qualities of the characters hitherto hinted at, not developed. But, in reality, the pause in the action is but to collect, to gather up, and to grasp, all the varieties of circumstance that conduce to the Great Result: and the art of fiction is only deserted for the fidelity of history. Whoever seeks to place before the world the true representation of a man's life and times, and, enlarging the Dramatic into the Epic, extends his narrative over the vicissitudes of years, will find himself unconsciously, in this, the imitator of Shakspeare. New characters, each conducive to the end—new scenes, each leading to the last, rise before him as he proceeds, sometimes seeming to the reader to delay, even while they advance, the dread catastrophe. The sacrificial procession sweeps along, swelled by new comers, losing many that first joined it; before, at last, the same as a whole, but differing in it components, the crowd reach the fated bourn of the Altar and the Victim!

It is five years after the date of the events I have recorded, and my story conveys us to the Papal Court at Avignon—that tranquil seat of power, to which the successors of St. Peter had transplanted the luxury, the pomp, and the vices, of the Imperial City. Secure from the fraud or violence of a powerful and barbarous nobility, the courtiers of the See surrendered themselves to a holyday of delight,—their repose was devoted to enjoyment, and Avignon presented, at that day, perhaps the gayest and most voluptuous society of Europe. The elegance of Clement VI. had diffused an air of literary refinement over the grosser pleasures of the place, and the spirit of Petrarch still continued to work its way through the councils of faction and the orgies of debauch.

Innocent VI. had lately succeeded Clement, and whatever his own claims to learning,* he, at least, appreciated knowledge and intellect in others; so that the graceful pedantry of the time continued to mix itself with the pursuit of pleasure. The corruption which reigned through the whole place was too confirmed to yield to the example of Innocent, himself a man of simple habits and exemplary life. Though, like his predecessor, obedient to the policy of France, Innocent possessed a hard and

* Matteo Villani (lib. iii. cap. 44) says, that Innocent VI. had not much pretension to learning. He is reported, however, by other authorities, cited by Zefirino Re, to have been "eccellente canonista." He had been a professor in theUniversity of Toulouse.

extended ambition. Deeply concerned for the interests of the Church, he formed the project of confirming and re-establishing her shaken dominion in Italy; and he regarded the tyrants of the various states as the principal obstacles to his ecclesiastical ambition. Nor was this the policy of Innocent VI. alone. With such exceptions as peculiar circumstances necessarily occasioned, the Papal See was, upon the whole, friendly to the political liberties of Italy. The Republics of the Middle Ages grew up under the shadow of the Church: and there, as elsewhere, it was found, contrary to a vulgar opinion, that Religion, however prostituted perverted, served for the general protection of civil freedom,—raised the lowly, and resisted the oppressor.

At this period there appeared at Avignon a lady of singular and matchless beauty, she had come with a slender but well appointed retinue from Florence, but declared herself of Neapolitan birth; the widow of a noble of the brilliant court of the unfortunate Jane. Her name was Cesarini. Arrived at a place where, even in the cidadel of Christianity, Venus retained her ancient empire, where Love made the prime business of life, and to be beautiful was to be of power; the Signora Cesarini had scarcely appeared in public before she saw at her feet half the rank and gallantry of Avignon. Her female attendants were beset with bribes and billets; and nightly, beneath her lattice, was heard the plaintive serenade. She entered largely into the gay dissipation of the town, and her charms shared the celebrity of the hour with the verse of Petrarch. But though she frowned on none, none could claim the monopoly of her smiles. Her fair fame was as yet umblemished; but if any might presume beyond the rest, she seemed to have selected rather from ambition than love, and Giles, the warlike Cardinal d'Albornoz, all powerful at the sacred court, already foreboded the hour of his triumph.

It was late noon, and in the antechamber of the fair Signora waited two of that fraternity of pages, fair and richly clad, who, at that day, furnished the favorite attendants to rank of either sex.

"By my troth," cried one of these young servitors, pushing from him the dice with which himself and his companion had sought to beguile their leisure, "this is but dull work! and the best part of the day is gone. Our lady is late."

"And I have donned my new velvet mantle," replied the other, compassionately eyeing his finery.

"Chut, Giacomo," said his comrade, yawning; "a truce with thy conceit.—What news abroad, I wonder? Has his Holiness come to his senses yet?"

"His senses! what, is he mad then?" quoth Giacomo, in a serious and astonished whisper.

"I think he is; if, being Pope, he does not discover that he may at length lay aside mask and hood. 'Continent Cardinal—lewd Pope,' is the old motto, you know; something must be the matter with the good man's brain if he continue to live like a hermit."

"Oh, I have you! but faith, his Holiness has proxies eno. The bishops take care to prevent women, Heaven bless them! going out of fashion; and Albornoz does not maintain your proverb, touching the Cardinals."

"True, but Giles is a warrior,—a cardinal in the church, but a soldier in the city."

"Will he carry the fort here, think you Angelo?"

"Why, fort is female, but ——"

"But what?"

"The Signora's brow is made for power, rather than love, fair as it is. She sees in Albornoz the prince, and not the lover. With what a step she sweeps the floor! it disdains even the cloth of gold!"

"Hark!" cried Giacomo, hastening to the lattice, "hear you the hoofs below? Ah, a gallant company!"

"Returned from hawking," answered Angelo, regarding wistfully the cavalcade, as it swept the narrow street. "Plumes waving, steeds curvetting—see how yon handsome cavalier presses close to that dame!"

"His mantle is the color of mine," sighed Giacomo.

As the gay procession paced slowly on, till hidden by the winding street, and as the sound of laughter and the tramp of horses was yet faintly heard, there frowned right before the straining gaze of the pages, a dark massive tower of the mighty masonry of the eleventh century: the sun gleamed sadly on its vast and dismal surface, which was only here and there relieved by loopholes and narrow slits, rather than casements. It was a striking contrast to the gaiety around, the glittering shops, and the gaudy train that had just filled the space below. This contrast the young men seemed involuntarily to feel; they drew back, and looked at each other.

"I know your thoughts, Giacomo," said Angelo, the handsomer and elder of the two. "You think yon tower affords but a gloomy lodgment?"

"And I thank my stars that made me not high enough to require so grand a cage," rejoined Giacomo.

"Yet," observed Angelo, "it holds one, who in birth was not our superior."

"Do tell me something of that strange man," said Giacomo, regaining his seat; "you are Roman and should know."

"Yes!" answered Angelo, haughtily drawing himself up. "I *am* Roman! and I should be unworthy my birth, if I had not already learned what honor is due to the name of Cola di Rienzi."

"Yet your fellow-Romans nearly stoned him I fancy," muttered Giacomo. "Honor seems to lie more in kicks than money. Can you tell me," continued the page in a louder key, "can you tell me if it be true, that Rienzi appeared at Prague before the Emperor, and prophesied that the late Pope and all the Cardinals should be murdered, and a new Italian Pope elected, who should endue the Emperor with a golden crown, as Sovereign of Sicilia, Calabria, and Apulia,* and himself with a crown of silver, as King of Rome, and all Italy? And ——

"Hush!" interrupted Angelo, impatiently. "Listen to me, and you shall know the exact story. On *last* leaving Rome (thou knowest that, after his fall, he was present at the Jubilee in disguise) the Tribune——" here Angelo, pausing, looked round, and then with a flushed cheek and raised voice resumed, "Yes, the *Tribune*, that *was* and *shall* be—travelled in disguise, as a pilgrim, over mountain and forest, night and day, exposed to rain and storm, no shelter but the cave,—he who had been, they say, the very spoilt one of Luxury. Arrived at length in Bohemia, he disclosed himself to a Florentine in Prague, and through his aid obtained audience of the Emperor Charles."

* An absurd fable, adopted by certain historians.

"A prudent man, the Emperor!" said Giacomo, "close-fisted as a miser. He makes conquests by bargain, and goes to market for laurels,—as I have heard my brother say, who was under him."

"True; but I have also heard that he likes bookmen and scholars—is wise and temperate, and much is yet hoped from him in Italy! Before the Emperor, I say, came Rienzi. 'Know, great Prince,' said he, 'that I am that Rienzi to whom God gave to govern Rome, in peace, with justice, and to freedom. I curbed the nobles, I purged corruption, I amended law. The powerful prosecuted me—pride and envy have chased me from my dominions. Great as you are, fallen as I am, I too have wielded the sceptre and might have worn a crown. Know, too, that I am illegitimately of your lineage: my father the son of Henry VII.;* the blood of the Teuton rolls in my veins; mean as were my earlier fortunes, and humble my earlier name! From you, O King, I seek protection, and I demand justice." †

"A bold speech, and one from equal to equal," said Giacomo; "surely you swell us out the words."

"Not a whit; they were written down by the Emperor's scribe, and every Roman who has once heard knows them by heart: once every Roman was the equal to a king, and Rienzi maintained our dignity in asserting his own."

Giacomo, who discreetly avoided quarrels, knew the weak side of his friend; and though in his heart he thought the Romans as good-for-nothing a set of turbulent dastards as all Italy might furnish, he merely picked a straw from his mantle, and said, in rather an impatient tone, "Humph! proceed! did the Emperor dismiss him?"

"Not so: Charles was truck with his bearing and his spirit; received him graciously, and entertained him hospitably. He remained some time at Prague, and astonished all the learned with his knowledge and eloquence." ‡

* Uncle to the Emperor of Charles.

† See, for this speech, "the Anonymous Biographer," lib. ii. cap. 12.

‡ His Italian contemporary delights in representing this remarkable man as another Crichton. "Disputava," he says of him when at Prague, "disputava con Mastri di teologia; molto diceva, parlava cose meravigliose .... abbair fea ogni persona."—"He disputed with Masters of theology—he spoke much, he discoursed things wonderful — he astonished every one."

"But if so honored at Prague, how comes he a prisoner at Avignon?"

"Giacomo," said Angelo, thoughtfully, "there are some men whom we, of another mind and mould, can rarely comprehend, and never fathom. And of such men I have observed that a supreme confidence in their own fortunes or their own souls, is the most common feature. Thus impressed, and thus buoyed, they rush into danger with a seeming madness, and from danger soar to greatness, or sink to death. So with Rienzi; dissatisfied with empty courtesies, and weary of playing the pedant, since once he had played the prince;—some say of his own accord, (though others relate that he was surrendered to the Pope's legate by Charles), he left the Emperor's court, and without arms, without money, betook himself at once to Avignon!"

"Madness indeed!"

"Yet, perhaps his only course, under all circumstances," resumed the elder page. "Once before his fall, and once during his absence from Rome, he had been excommunicated by the Pope's legate. He was accused of heresy—the ban was still on him. It was necessary that he should clear himself. How was the poor exile to do so? No powerful friend stood up for the friend of the people. No courtier vindicated one who had trampled on the neck of the nobles. His own genius was his only friend; on that only could he reply. He sought Avignon, to free himself from the accusations against him; and, doubtless, he hoped that there was but one step from his acquittal to his restoration. Besides, it is certain that the Emperor had been applied to, formally to surrender Rienzi. He had the choice before him; for to that sooner or later it must come—to go free, or to go in bonds—as a criminal, or as a Roman. He chose the latter. Wherever he passed along, the people rose in every town, in every hamlet. The name of the great Tribune was honored throughout all Italy. They besought him not to rush into the very den of peril.—they implored him to save himself for that country which he had sought to raise. 'I go to vindicate myself, and fo triumph,' was the Tribune's answer. Solemn honors were paid in the cities through which he passed;* and I am told that never ambassador, prince, or baron, entered Avignon with so long a train as that which followed into these very walls the steps of Cola di Rienzi."

"And on his arrival?"

"He demanded an audience, that he might refute the charges against him. He flung down the gage to the proud cardinals who had excommunicated him. He besought a trial."

"And what said the Pope?"

"Nothing—by word. Yon tower was his answer!"

"A rough one!"

"But there have been longer roads than that from the prison to the palace, and God made not men like Rienzi for the dungeon and the chain."

As Angelo said this with a loud voice, and with all the enthusiasm with which the fame of the fallen Tribune had inspired the youth of Rome, he heard a sigh behind him. He turned in some confusion, and at the door which admitted to the chamber occupied by the Signora Cesarini, stood a female of noble presence. Attired in the richest garments, gold and gems were dull to the lustre of her dark eyes, and as she now stood, erect and commanding, never seemed brow more made for the regal crown—never did human beauty more fully consummate the ideal of a heroine and a queen.

"Pardon me, Signora," said Angelo, hesitatingly; "I spoke loud, I disturbed you; but I am Roman, and my theme was——"

"Rienzi!" said the lady, approaching; "a fit one to stir a Roman heart. Nay—no excuses: they would sound ill on thy generous lips. Ah, if—" the Signora paused suddenly, and sighed again; then in an altered and graver tone she resumed—"If fate restore Rienzi to his proper fortunes, he shall know what thou deemest of him."

"If you, lady, who are of Naples," said Angelo, with meaning emphasis, "speak thus of a fallen exile, what must I have felt who acknowledged a sovereign?"

"Rienzi is not of Rome alone—he is of Italy—of the world," returned Signora. "And you, Angelo, who have had the boldness to speak of one thus fallen, have proved with what loyalty you can serve those who have the fortune to own you."

As she spoke, the Signora looked at the

* "Per tutto la via li furo fatti solenni onori," etc.—*Vit. di Col. di Rienzi*, lib. ii. cap. 13.

page's downcast and blushing face long and wistfully, with the gaze of one accustomed to read the soul in the countenance.

"Men are often deceived," said she, sadly, yet with a half smile; "but women rarely,—save in love. Would that Rome were filled with such as you! Enough! Hark! Is that the sound of hoofs in the court below?"

"Madam," said Giacomo, bringing his mantle gallantly over his shoulder, "I see the servitors of Monsignore the Cardinal d'Albornoz.—It is the Cardinal himself."

"It is well!" said the Signora, with a brightening eye; "I await him!" With these words she withdrew by the door through which she had surprised the Roman page.

CHAPTER II.

The Character of a Warrior Priest.—An Interview.—The Intrigue and Counter-intrigue of Courts.

GILES, (or Egidio,*) Cardinal d'Albornoz, was one of the most remarkable men of that remarkable time, so prodigal of genius. Boasting his descent from the royal houses of Aragon and Leon, he had early entered the church, and yet almost a youth, attained the archbishopric of Toledo. But no peaceful career, however brilliant, sufficed to his ambition. He could not content himself with the honors of the church, unless they were the honors of a church militant. In the war against the Moors, no Spaniard had more highly distinguished himself; and Alphonso XI. king of Castile, had insisted on receiving from the hand of the martial priest the badge of knighthood. After the death of Alphonso, who was strongly attached to him, Albornoz repaired to Avignon, and obtained from Clement VI. the cardinal's hat. With Innocent he continued in high favor, and now, constantly in the councils of the Pope, rumors of war-like preparation, under the banners of Albornoz, for the recovery of the papal dominions from the various tyrants that usurped them, were already circulated through the court.† Bold, sagacious, enterprising, and cold-hearted,—with the valor of the knight, and the cunning of the priest,—such was the character of Giles, Cardinal d'Albornoz.

Leaving his attendant gentlemen in the antechamber, Albornoz was ushered into the apartment of the Signora Cesarini. In person, the Cardinal was about the middle height; the dark complexion of Spain had faded by thought, and the wear of ambitious schemes, into a sallow but hardy hue; his brow was deeply furrowed, and though not yet passed the prime of life, Albornoz might seem to have entered age, but for the firmness of his step, the slender elasticity of his frame, and an eye which had acquired calmness and depth from thought, without losing any of the brilliancy of youth.

"Beautiful Signora," said the Cardinal, bending over the hand of the Cesarini with a grace which betokened more of the prince than of the priest "the commands of his Holiness have detained me, I fear, beyond the hour in which you vouchsafed to appoint my homage, but my heart has been with you since we parted.

"The Cardinal d'Albornoz," replied the Signora, gently withdrawing her hand, and seating herself, "has so many demands on his time, from the duties of his rank and renown, that methinks to divert his attention for a few moments to less noble thoughts is a kind of treason to his fame."

"Ah, Lady," replied the Cardinal, "never was my ambition so nobly directed as it is now. And it were a prouder lot to be at thy feet than on the throne of St. Peter."

A momentary blush passed over the cheek of the Signora, yet it seemed the blush of indignation as much as of vanity; it was succeeded by an extreme paleness. She paused before she replied; and then fixing her large and haughty eyes on the enamoured Spaniard, she said, in a low voice,

"My Lord Cardinal, I do not affect to misunderstand your words; neither do I place them to the account of a general gallantry. I am

---

* Egidio is the proper Italian equivalent to the French name Gilles,—but the Cardinal is generally called, by the writers of that day, Gilio d'Albornoz.

† It is a characteristic anecdote of this bold Churchman, that Urban V. one day demanded an account of the sums spent in his military expedition against the Italian tyrants. The Cardinal presented to the Pope a wagon, filled with the keys of the cities and fortresses he had taken. "This is my account," said he; "you perceive how I have invested your money." The Pope embraced him, and gave him no further trouble about his accounts.

vain enough to believe you imagine you speak truly when you say you love me."

"Imagine!" echoed the Spaniard.

"Listen to me," continued the Signora. "She whom the Cardinal Albornoz honors with his love has a right to demand of him its proofs. In the papal court, whose power like his?—I require you to exercise it for me.

"Speak, dearest Lady; have your estates been seized by the barbarians of these lawless times? Hath any dared to injure you? Lands and titles, are these thy wish?—my power is thy slave."

"Cardinal, no! there is one thing dearer to an Italian and a woman than wealth or station—it is revenge!"

The Cardinal drew back from the flashing eye that was bent upon him, but the spirit of her speech touched a congenial chord.

"There," said he, after a little hesitation, "there spake high descent. Revenge is the luxury of the well-born. Let serfs and churls forgive an injury. Proceed, Lady."

"Hast thou heard the last news from Rome?" asked the Signora.

"Surely," replied the Cardinal, in some surprise, "we were poor statesmen to be ignorant of the condition of the capital of the papal dominions; and my heart mourns for that unfortunate city. But wherefore wouldst thou question me of Rome?—thou art—"

"Roman! Know, my Lord, that I have a purpose in calling myself of Naples. To your discretion I intrust my secret—I am of Rome! Tell me of her state."

"Fairest one," returned the Cardinal, "I should have known that that brow and presence were not of the light *Campania*. My reason should have told me that they bore the stamp of the Empress of the World. The state of Rome," continued Albornoz, in a graver tone, "is briefly told. Thou knowest that after the fall of the able but insolent Rienzi, Pepin, count of Minorbino, (a creature of Montreal's), who had assisted in expelling him, would have betrayed Rome to Montreal, but he was neither strong enough nor wise enough, and the Barons chased him as he had chased the Tribune. Some time afterwards a new demagogue, John Cerroni, was installed in the Capitol. He once more expelled the nobles; new revolutions ensued—the Barons were recalled. The weak successor of Rienzi summoned the people to arms—in vain: in terror and despair he abdicated his power, and left the city a prey to the interminable feuds of the Orsini, the Colonna, and the savelli."

"Thus much I know, my Lord; but when his Holiness succeeded to the chair of Clement VI.——"

"Then," said Albornoz, and a slight frown darkened his sallow brow, "then came the blacker part of the history. Two senators were elected in concert by the Pope."

"Their names?"

"Bertoldo Orsini, and one of the Colonna. A few weeks afterwards, the high price of provisions stung the rascal stomachs of the mob—they rose, they clamored, they armed, they besieged the Capitol——"

"Well, well,' cried the Signora, clasping her hands, aud betokening in every feature her interest in the narration.

"Colonna only escaped death by a vile disguise; Bertoldo Orsini was stoned."

"Stoned!—there fell one!"

"Yes, Lady, one of a great house; the least drop of whose blood were worth an ocean of plebeian puddle. At present, all is disorder, misrule, anarchy, at Rome. The contests of the nobles shake the city to the centre; and prince and people, wearied of so many experiments to establish a government, have now no governor but the fear of the sword. Such, fair madam, is the state of Rome. Sigh not, it occupies now our care. It shall be remedied; and I, madam, may be the happy instrument of restoring peace to your native city."

"There is but one way of restoring peace to Rome," answered the Signora, abruptly, "and that is—The restoration of Rienzi!"

The Cardinal started. "Madam," said he, "do I hear aright?—are you not nobly born?—can you desire the rise of a plebeian? Did you not speak of revenge, and now you ask for mercy?"

"Lord Cardinal," said the beautiful Signora, earnestly, "I do not ask for mercy: such a word is not for the lips of one who demands justice. Nobly born I am—ay, and from a stock to whose long descent from the patricians of ancient Rome the high line of Aragon itself would be of yesterday. Nay, I would not offend you, Monsignore; your greatness is not borrowed from pedigrees and tombstones—your greatness is your own achieving: would you speak honestly, my Lord, you would own that you are proud only of *your own* laurels, and that in your heart, you laugh at the stately fools who trick themselves out in the mouldering finery of the dead!"

"Muse! prophetess! you speak aright," said the high-spirited Cardinal, with unwonted energy; "and your voice is like that of the Fame I dreamed of in my youth. Speak on, Speak ever!"

"Such," continued the Signora, "such as your pride, is the just pride of Rienzi. Proud that he is the workman of his own great renown. In such as the Tribune of Rome we acknowledge the founders of noble lineage. Ancestry makes not them—they make ancestry. Enough of this. I am of noble race, it is true; but my house, and those of many, have been crushed and broken beneath the yoke of the Orsini and Colonna—it is against them I desire revenge. But I am better than an Italian lady—I am a Roman woman—I weep tears of blood for the disorders of my unhappy country. I mourn that even you, my Lord,—yes, that a barbarian, however eminent and however great, should mourn for Rome. I desire to restore her fortunes."

"But Rienze would only restore his own."

"Not so, my Lord Cardinal; not so. Ambitious and proud he may be—great souls are so—but he has never had one wish divorced from the welfare of Rome. But put aside all thoughts of his interests—it is not of these I speak. You desire to re-establish the papal power in Rome. Your senators have failed to do it. Demagogues fail—Rienzi alone can succeed; he alone can command the turbulent passions of the Barons—he alone can sway the capricious and fickle mob. Release, restore Rienzi, and through Rienzi the Pope regains Rome!"

The Cardinal did not answer for some moments. Buried as in a revery, he sate motionless, shading his face with his hand. Perhaps he secretly owned there was a wiser policy in the suggestions of the Signora than he cared openly to confess. Lifting his head, at length, from his bosom, he fixed his eyes upon the Signora's watchful countenance, and, with a forced smile, said,

"Pardon me, madam; but while we play the politicians, forget not that I am thy adorer. Sagacious may be thy councils, yet wherefore are they urged? Why this anxious interest for Rienzi? If by releasing him the Church may gain an ally, am I sure that Giles d'Albornoz will not raise a rival?"

"My lord," said the Signora, half rising, "you are my suitor; but your rank does not tempt me—your gold cannot buy. If you love me, I have a right to command your services to whatsoever task I would require—it is the law of chivalry. If ever I yield to the addresses of mortal lover, it will be to the man who restores to my native land her hero and her savior."

"Fair patriot," said the Cardinal, "your words encourage my hope, yet they half damp my ambition; for fain would I desire that love and not service should alone give me the treasure that I ask. But hear me, sweet lady; you over-rate my power: I cannot deliver Rienzi—he is accused of rebellion, he is excommunicated for heresy. His acquittal rests with himself."

"You can procure his trial?"

"Perhaps, Lady."

"That *is* his acquittal. And a private audience of his Holiness?"

"Doubtless."

"*That* is his restoration! Behold all I ask?"

"And then, sweet Roman, it will be *mine* to ask," said the Cardinal, passionately, dropping on his knee, and taking the Signora's hand. For one moment, that proud lady felt that she was woman—she blushed, she trembled; but it was not (could the Cardinal have read that heart) with passion or with weakness; it was with terror and with shame. Passively she surrendered her hand to the Cardinal, who covered it with kisses.

"Thus inspired," said Albornoz, rising, "I will not doubt of success. To-morrow I wait on thee again."

He pressed her hand to his heart—the lady felt it not. He sighed his farewell—she did not hear it. Lingeringly he gazed; and slowly he departed. But it was some moments before, recalled to herself, the Signora felt that she was alone.

"Alone!" she cried, half aloud, and with wild emphasis—"alone! Oh, what have I undergone—what have I said! Unfaithful, even in thought to *him!* Oh, never! never! I, that have felt the kiss of his hallowing lips

—that have slept on his kingly heart—I !—holy Mother, befriend and strengthen me !" she continued, as, weeping bitterly, she sunk upon her knees: and for some moments she was lost in prayer. Then, rising composed, but deadly pale, and with the tears rolling heavily down her cheeks, the Signora passed slowly to the casement; she threw it open, and bent forward; the air of the declining day came softly on her temples; it cooled, it mitigated, the fever that preyed within. Dark and huge before her frowned, in its gloomy shadow, the tower in which Rienzi was confined; she gazed at it long and wistfully, and then, turning away, drew from the folds of her robe a small and sharp dagger. "Let me save him for glory !" she murmured; "and *this* shall save me from dishonor !"

CHAPTER III.

Holy Men.—Sagacious Deliberations.—Just Resolves.—And Sordid Motives to all.

ENAMORED of the beauty, and almost equally so of the lofty spirit, of the Signora Cesarini, as was the warlike Cardinal of Spain, love with him was not so master a passion as that ambition of complete success in all the active designs of life, which had hitherto animated his character and signalized his career. Musing, as he left the Signora, on her wish for the restoration of the Roman Tribune, his experienced and profound intellect ran swiftly through whatever advantages to his own political designs might result from that restoration. We have seen that it was the intention of the new Pontiff to attempt the recovery of the patrimonial territories, now torn from him by the gripe of able and disaffected tyrants. With this view, a military force was already in preparation, and the Cardinal was already secretly nominated the chief. But the force was very inadquate to the enterprise; and Albornoz depended much upon the moral strength of the cause in bringing recruits to his standard in his progress through the Italian states. The wonderful rise of Rienzi had excited an extraordinary enthusiasm in his favor through all the free populations of Italy. And this had been yet more kindled and inflamed by the influential eloquence of Petrarch who, at that time, possessed of a power greater than ever, before or since, (not even excepting the Sage of Ferney), wielded by a single literary man, had put forth his boldest genius in behalf of the Roman Tribune. Such a companion as Rienzi in the camp of the Cardinal might be a magnet of attraction to the youth and enterprise of Italy. On nearing Rome, he might himself judge how far it would be advisable to reinstate Rienzi as a delegate of the papal power. And, in the meanwhile, the Roman's influence might be serviceable, whether to awe the rebellious nobles or conciliate the stubborn people. On the other hand, the Cardinal was shrewd enough to perceive that no possible good could arise from Rienzi's present confinement. With every month it excited deeper and more universal sympathy. To his lonely dungeon turned half the hearts of republican Italy. Literature had leagued its new and sudden, and therefore mighty and even disproportioned, power with his cause; and the Pope, without daring to be his judge, incurred the odium of being his jailer. "A popular prisoner," said the sagacious Cardinal to himself, "is the most dangerous of guests. Restore him as your servant, or destroy him as your foe ! In this case I see no alternative but acquittal or the knife !" In these reflections that able plotter, deep in the Machiavelism of the age, divorced the lover from the statesman.

Recurring now to the former character, he felt some disagreeable and uneasy forebodings at the earnest interest of his mistress. Fain would he have attributed, either to some fantasy of patriotism or some purpose of revenge, the anxiety of the Cesarini; and there was much in her stern and haughty character which favored that belief. But he was forced to acknowledge to himself some jealous apprehension of a sinister and latent motive, which touched his vanity and alarmed his love. "Howbeit," he thought, as he turned from his unwilling fear, "I can play with her at her own weapons; I can obtain the release of Rienzi, and claim my reward. If denied, the hand that opened the dungeon can again rivet the chain. In her anxiety is my power !"

These thoughts the Cardinal was still revolving in his palace, when he was suddenly summoned to attend the Pontiff.

The pontifical palace no longer exhibited

the gorgeous yet graceful luxury of Clement VI., and the sarcastic Cardinal smiled to himself at the quiet gloom of the ante-chambers. "He thinks to set an example—this poor native of Limoges!" thought Albornoz; "and has but the mortification of finding himself eclipsed by the poorest bishop. He humbles himself, and fancies that the humility will be contagious."

His Holiness was seated before a small and rude table bestrewed with papers, his face buried in his hands; the room was simply furnished, and in a small niche beside the casement was an ivory crucifix; below, the death's head and cross-bones, which most monks then introduced with a purpose similar to that of the ancients by the like ornaments,—mementos of the shortness of life, and therefore admonitions to make the best of it! On the ground lay a map of the Patrimonial Territory, with the fortesses in especial, distinctly and prominently marked. The Pope gently lifted up his head as the Cardinal was announced, and discovered a plain but sensible and somewhat interesting countenance. "My son!" said he, with a kindly courtesy to the lowly salutation of the proud Spaniard, "scarcely wouldst thou imagine, after our long conference this morning, that new cares would so soon demand the assistance of thy counsels. Verily, the wreath of thorns stings sharp under the triple crown; and I sometimes long for the quiet abode of my old professor's chair in Toulouse: my station is of pain and toil."

"God tempers the wind to the shorn lamb," observed the Cardinal, with pious and compassionate gravity.

Innocent could scarcely refrain a smile as he replied, "The lamb that carries the cross must have the strength of a lion. Since we parted, my son, I have had painful intelligence; our couriers have arrived from the Campagna —the heathen rage furiously—the force of John di Vico has augmented fearfully, and the most redoubted adventurer of Europe has enlisted under his banner."

"Does his Holiness," cried the Cardinal, anxiously, "speak of Fra Moreale, the Knight of St. John?"

"Of no less a warrior," returned the Pontiff. "I dread the vast ambition of that wild adventurer."

"Your Holiness hath cause," said the Cardinal, drily.

"Some letters of his have fallen into the hands of the servants of the Church; they are here: read them, my son."

Albornoz received and deliberately scanned the letters; this done, he replaced them on the table, and remained for a few moments silent and absorbed.

"What think you, my son?" said the Pope, at length, with an impatient and even peevish tone.

"I think that with Montreal's hot genius and John di Vico's frigid villany, your Holiness my live to envy, if not the quiet, at least the revenue of the Professor's chair."

"How, Cardinal, said the Pope, hastily, and with an angry flush on his pale brow. The Cardinal quietly proceeded.

"By these letters it seems that Montreal has written to all the commanders of free lances throughout Italy offering the highest pay of a soldier to every man who will join his standard, combined with the richest plunder of a brigand. He meditates great schemes then!—I know the man!"

"Well,—and our course?"

"Is plain," said the Cardinal, loftily, and with an eye that flashed with a soldier's fire. "Not a moment is to be lost! Thy son should at once take the field. Up with the Banner of the Church!"

"But are we strong enough? our numbers are few. Zeal slackens! the piety of the Baldwins is no more!"

"Your Holiness knows well," said the Cardinal, "that for the multitude of men there are two watchwords of war—Liberty and Religion. If Religion begins to fail, we must employ the profaner word. 'Up with the Banner of the Church—and down with the tyrants!' We will proclaim equal laws and free governments;* and, God willing, our camp shall prosper better with those promises than the tents of Montreal with the more vulgar shout of 'Pay and Rapine.'"

"Giles d'Albornoz," said the Pope, emphatically; and, warmed by the spirit of the

* In correcting the pages of this work, in the year 1847. . . . strange coincidences between the present policy of the Roman Church and that by which in the 14th century it recovered both spiritual and temporal power cannot fail to suggest themselves.

Cardinal, he dropped the wonted etiquette of phrase, "I trust implicitly to you. Now the right hand of the Church—hereafter, perhaps, its head. Too well I feel that the lot has fallen on a lowly place. My successor must requite my deficiencies."

No changeing hue, no brightening glance, betrayed to the searching eye of the Pope whatever emotion these words had called up in the breast of the ambitious Cardinal. He bowed his proud head humbly as he answered, "Pray Heaven that Innocent VI. may long live to guide the Church to glory. For Giles d'Albornoz, less priest than soldier, the din of the camp, the breath of the war-steed, suggest the only aspirations which he ever dares indulge. But has your Holiness imparted to your servant all that——"

"Nay," interrupted Innocent, "I have yet intelligence equally ominous. This John di Vico,—pest go with him!—who still styles himself (the excommunicated ruffian!) Prefect of Rome, has so filled that unhappy city with his emissaries, that we have well-nigh lost the seat of the Apostle. Rome, long in anarchy, seems now in open rebellion. The nobles—sons of Belial!—it is true, are once more humbled; but how? One Baroncelli a new demagogue, the fiercest—the most bloody that the fiend ever helped—has arisen—is invested by the mob with power, and uses it to butcher the people and insult the Pontiff. Wearied of the crimes of this man, (which are not even decorated by ability), the shout of the people day and night along the streets is for 'Rienzi the Tribune.'"

"Ha!" said the Cardinal, "Rienzi's faults then are forgotten in Rome, and there is felt for him the same enthusiasm in that city as in the rest of Italy?"

"Alas! it is so."

'It is well, I have thought of this: Rienzi can accompany my progress—"

"My son! the rebel, the heretic—"

"By your Holiness's absolution will become a quiet subject and 'orthodox Catholic," said Albornoz. "Men are good or bad as they suit our purpose. What matters a virtue that is useless, or a crime that is useful, to us? The army of the Church proceeds against tyrants—it proclaims everywhere to the Papal towns the restoration of their popular constitutions. Sees not your Holiness that the acquittal of Rienzi, the popular darling, will be hailed an earnest of your sincerity?—sees not your Holiness that his name will fight for us?—sees not your Holiness that the great demagouge Rienzi must be used to extinguish the little demagouge Baroncelli? We must regain the Romans, whether of the city or whether in the seven towns of John di Vico. When they hear Rienzi is in our camp, trust me, we shall have a multitude of deserters from the tyrants—trust me, we shall hear no more of Baroncelli."

"Ever sagacious," said the Pope, musingly; "it is true, we can use this man: but with caution. His genius is formidable——'

"And therefore must be conciliated if we acquit, we must make him ours. My experience has taught me this, when you cannot slay a demagogue by law, crush him with honors. He must be no longer Tribune of the People. Give him the Patrician title of *Senator*, and he is then the Lieutenant of the Pope!"

"I will see to this my son—your suggestions please, but alarm me: he shall at least be examined;—but if he be found a heretic——"

"Should, I humbly advise, be declared a saint."

The Pope bent his brow for a moment, but the effort was too much for him, and after a moment's struggle, he fairly laughed aloud.

"Go to, my son," and he affectionately patting the Cardinal's sallow cheek. "Go to,—If the world heard thee, what would it say?"

"That Giles d'Albornoz had just enough religion to remember that the State is a Church, but not too much to forget that the Church is a State."

With these words the conference ended. That very evening the Pope decreed that Rienzi should be permitted the trial he had demanded.

CHAPTER IV.

The Lady and the Page.

It wanted three hours of midnight, when Albornoz, resuming his character of gallant, despatched to the Signora Cesarini the following billet.

"Your commands are obeyed. Rienzi will receive an examination on his faith. It is well that he should be prepared. It may suit your purpose, as to which I am so faintly enlightened, to appear to the prisoner what you are—the obtainer of this grace. See how implicitly one noble heart can trust another! I send by the bearer an order that will admit one of your servitors to the prisoner's cell. Be it, if you will, your task to announce to him the new crisis of his fate. Ah! madam, may fortune be so favorable to me, and grant me the same intercessor—from thy lips my sentence is to come."

As Albornoz finished this epistle, he summoned his confidential attendant, a Spanish gentleman, who saw nothing in his noble birth that should prevent his fulfilling the various hests of the Cardinal.

"Alvarez," said he, "these to the Signora Cesarini by another hand; thou art unknown to her household. Repair to the state tower; this to the Governor admits thee. Mark who is admitted to the prisoner Cola di Rienzi: Know his name, examine whence he comes. Be keen, Alvarez. Learn by what motive the Cesarini interests herself in the prisoner's fate. All too of herself, birth, fortunes, lineage, would be welcome intelligence. Thou comprehendest me? It is well. One caution—thou hast no mission from, no connection with, me. Thou art an officer of the prison, or of the Pope,—what thou wilt. Give me the rosary; light the lamp before the crucifix; place yon hair-shirt beneath those arms. I would have it appear as if *meant* to be hidden! Tell Gomez that the Dominican preacher is to be admitted."

"Those friars have zeal," continued the Cardinal to himself, as, after executing his orders, Alvarez withdrew. "They would burn a man—but only on the Bible? They are worth conciliating, if the triple crown be really worth the winning; were it mine, I would add the eagle's plume to it."

And plunged into the aspiring future, this bold man forgot even the object of his passion. In real life, after a certain age, ambitious men love indeed; but it is only as an interlude. And indeed with most men, life has more absorbing though not more frequent concerns than those of love. Love is the business of the idle, but the idleness of the busy.

The Cesarini was alone when the Cardinal's messenger arrived, and he was scarcely dismissed with a few lines, expressive of a gratitude which seemed to bear down all those guards with which the coldness of the Signora usually fenced her pride, before the page Angelo was summoned to her presence.

The room was dark with the shades of the gathering night when the youth entered, and he discerned but dimly the outline of the Signora's stately form; but by the tone of her voice, he perceived that she was deeply agitated.

"Angelo," said she, as he approached, "Angelo—" and her voice failed her. She paused as for breath and again proceeded. "You alone have served us faithfully; you alone shared our escape, our wanderings, our exile—you alone know my secret—you of my train alone are Roman!—Roman! it was once a great name Angelo, the name has fallen; but it is only because the nature of the Roman Race fell first. Haughty they are, but fickle; fierce, but dastard; vehement in promise, but rotten in their faith. You are a Roman, and though I have proved your truth, your very birth makes me afraid of falsehood."

"Madam," said the page, "I was but a child when you admitted me of your service, and I am yet only on the verge of manhood. But boy though I yet be, I would brave the stoutest lance of knight, or freebooter, in defence of the faith of Angelo Villani, to his liege Lady and his native land."

"Alas! alas!" said the Signora, bitterly, "such has been the *words* of thousands of thy race. What have been their deeds? But I will trust thee, as I have trusted ever. I know that thou are covetous of honor, that thou hast youth's comely and bright ambition."

"I am an orphan and a bastard," said Angelo, bluntly! "And circumstance stings me sharply on to action; I would win my own name."

"Thou shalt," said the Signora. "We shall live yet to reward thee. And now be quick. Bring hither one of thy page's suits,—mantle and head-gear. Quick, I say, and whisper not to a soul what I have asked of thee."

CHAPTER V.

The Inmate of the Tower.

THE night slowly advanced, and in the highest chamber of that dark and rugged tower which fronted the windows of the Cesarini's palace sate a solitary prisoner. A single lamp burned before him on a table of stone, and threw its rays over an open Bible; and those stern but fantastic legends of the prowess of ancient Rome, which the genius of Livy has dignified into history.* A chain hung pendent from the vaults of the tower, and confined the captive; but so as to leave his limbs at sufficient liberty to measure at will the greater part of the cell. Green and damp were the mighty stones of the walls. and through a narrow aperture, high out of reach, came the moonlight, and slept in long shadow over the rude floor. A bed at one corner completed the furniture of the room. Such for months had been the abode of the conqueror of the haughtiest Barons, and the luxurious dictator of the stateliest city of the world!

Care, and travel, and time, and adversity, had wrought their change in the person of Rienzi. The proportions of his frame had enlarged from the compact strength of earlier manhood, the clear paleness of his cheek was bespread with a hectic and deceitful glow. Even in his present studies, intent as they seemed, and genial though the lecture to a mind enthusiastic even to fanaticism, his eyes could not rivet themselves as of yore steadily to the page. The charm was gone from the letters. Every now and then he moved restlessly, started, re-settled himself, and muttered broken exclamations like a man in an anxious dream. Anon, his gaze impatiently turned upward, about, around, and there was a strange and wandering fire in those large deep eyes, which might have thrilled the beholder with a vague and unaccountable awe.

Angelo had in the main correctly narrated the more recent adventures of Rienzi after his fall. He had first with Nina and Angelo betaken himself to Naples, and found a fallacious and brief favor with Louis, king of Hungary; that harsh but honorable monarch had refused to yield his illustrious guest to the demand of Clement, but had plainly declared his inability to shelter him in safety. Maintaining secret intercourse with his partisans at Rome, the fugitive then sought a refuge with the Eremites, sequestered in the lone recesses of the Monte Maiella, where in solitude and thought he had passed a whole year, save the time consumed in his visit to and return from Florence. Taking advantage of the Jubilee in Rome, he had then, disguised as a pilgrim, traversed the vales and mountains still rich in the melancholy ruins of ancient Rome, and entering the city, his restless and ambitious spirit indulged in new but vain conspiracies!* Excommunicated a second time by the Cardinal di Ceccano, and again a fugitive, he shook the dust from his feet as he left the city, and raising his hands towards those walls, in which are yet traced the witness of the Tarquins, cried aloud—"Honored as thy prince—persecuted as thy victim—Rome, Rome, thou shalt yet receive me as thy conquerer!"

Still disguised as a pilgrim, he passed unmolested through Italy into the Court of the Emperor Charles of Bohemia, where the page, who had probably witnessed, had rightly narrated, his reception. It is doubtful, however, whether the conduct of the Emperor, had been as chivalrous as appears by Angelo's relation, or whether he had not delivered Rienzi to the Pontiff's emissaries. At all events it is certain, that from Prague to Avignon, the path of the fallen Tribune had been as one triumph. His strange adventures—his unbroken spirit—the new power that intellect daily and wonderfully excited over the minds of the rising generation—the eloquence of Petrarch and the common sympathy of the vulgar for fallen greatness,—all conspired to make Rienzi the hero of the age. Not a town through which he passed which would not have risked a siege for his protection—not a house that would not have sheltered him—not a hand that would not have struck in his defence. Refusing all offers of aid, disdaining all occasion of escape inspired by his indomitable hope, and his unalloyed belief ln the brightness of his own destinies, the Tribune sought Avignon—and found a dungeon!

* "Avea libri assai, sue Tito Livio, sue norie di Roma la Bibbia et altri libri assai, non finava di studiare."—*Vit. di Col. Rienzi*, lib. ii. cap. 13. See translation to motto to Book VII. p. 202.

* Rainald, Ann. 1350. N. 4, E. 5.

These, his external adventures, are briefly and easily told; but who shall tell what passed within?"—who narrate the fearful history of the heart?—who paint the rapid changes of emotion and of thought—the indignant grief—the stern dejection—the haughty disappointment that saddened while it never destroyed the resolve of that great soul? Who can say what must have been endured, what meditated, in the hermitage of Maiella;—on the lonely hills of the perished empire it had been his dream to restore;—in the Courts of Barbarian Kings;—and above all, on returning obscure and disguised, amidst the crowds of the Christian world, to the seat of his former power? What elements of memory, and in what a wild and fiery brain! What reflections to be conned in the dungeons of Avignon, by a man who had pushed into all the fervor of fanaticism—four passions, a single one of which has, in excess, sufficed to wreck the strongest reason—passions, which in themselves it is most difficult to combine,—the dreamer—the aspirant—the very nympholept of Freedom, yet of Power—of Knowledge, yet of Religion!

"Ay," muttered the prisoner, "ay, these texts are comforting—comforting. The righteous are not always oppressed." With a long sigh he deliberately put aside the Bible, kissed it with great reverence, remained silent, and musing for some minutes; and then as a slight noise was heard at one corner of the cell, said softly, "Ah, my friends, my comrades, the rats! it is their hour—I am glad I put aside the bread for them!" His eye brightened as it now detected those strange and unsocial animals venturing forth through a hole in the wall, and, darkening the moonshine on the floor, steal fearlessly towards him. He flung some fragments of bread to them, and for some moments watched their gambols with a smile. "Manchino, the white-faced rascal, he beats all the rest—ha, ha! he is a superior wretch—he commands the tribe, and will venture the first into the trap. How will he bite against the steel, the fine fellow! while all the ignobler herd will gaze at him afar off, and quake and fear, and never help. Yet if united, they might gnaw the trap and release their leader! Ah, ye are base vermin, ye eat my bread. yet if death came upon me, ye would riot on my carcass. Away!" and clapping his hands, the chain round him clanked harshly, and the noisome co-mates of his dungeon vanished in an instant.

That singular and eccentric humor which marked Rienzi, and which had seemed a buffoonery to the stolid sullenness of the Roman nobles, still retained its old expression in his countenance, and he laughed loud as he saw the vermin hurry back to their hiding-place.

"A little noise and the clank of a chain—fie, how ye imitate mankind!" Again he sank into silence, and then heavily and listlessly drawing towards him the animated tales of Livy, said, "An hour to midnight!—waking dreams are better than sleep. Well, history tells us how men have risen—ay, and nations too—after sadder falls than that of Rienzi or of Rome!"

In a few minutes, he was apparently absorbed in the lecture; so intent indeed, was he in the task, that he did not hear the steps which wound the spiral stairs that conducted to his cell, and it was not till the wards harshly grated beneath the huge key, and the door creaked on its hinges, that Rienzi, in amaze at intrusion at so unwonted an hour, lifted his eyes. The door had reclosed on the dungeon, and by the lonely and pale lamp he beheld a figure leaning, as for support, against the wall. The figure was wrapped from head to foot in the long cloak of the day, which, aided by a broad hat, shaded by plumes, concealed even the features of the visitor.

Rienzi gazed long and wistfully.

"Speak," he said at length, putting his hand to his brow. "Methinks either long solitude has bewildered me, or, sweet sir, your apparition dazzles. I know you not—am I sure?—" and Rienzi's hair bristled while he slowly rose—"Am I sure that it is living man who stands before me? Angels have entered the prison-house before now. Alas! an angel's comfort never was more needed."

The stranger answered not, but the captive saw that his heart heaved even beneath his cloak; loud sobs choked his voice; at length, as by a violent effort, he sprung forward, and sunk at the Tribune's feet. The disguising hat, the long mantle fell to the ground—it was the face of a woman that look upward through passionate and glazing tears—the arms of a woman that clasped the prisoner's knees! Rienzi gazed mute and motionless as stone.

"Powers and Saints of Heaven!" he murmured at last, "do ye tempt me further!—is it?—no, no—yet speak!"

"Beloved—adored!—do you not know me?"

"It is—it is!" shrieked Rienzi wildly, "it is my Nina—my wife—my ——" His voice forsook him. Clasped in each other's arms, the unfortunates for some moments seemed to have lost even the sense of delight at their reunion. It was as an unconscious and deep trance, through which something *like* a dream only faintly and indistinctively stirs.

At length recovered—at length restored, the first broken exclamations, the first wild caresses of joy over—Nina lifted her head from her husband's bosom, and gazed sadly on his countenance—"Oh, what thou hast known since we parted!—what, since that hour when, borne on by thy bold heart and wild destiny, thou didst leave me in the Imperial Court, to seek again the diadem and find the chain! Ah! why did I heed thy commands?—why suffer thee to depart alone? How often in thy progress hitherward, in doubt, in danger, might this bosom have been thy resting-place, and this voice have whispered comfort to thy soul? Thou art well, my lord—My Cola! Thy pulse beats quicker than of old—thy brow is furrowed. Ah! tell me thou art well!"

"Well," said Rienzi, mechanically. "Methinks so!—the mind diseased blunts all sense of bodily decay. Well—yes! And thou—thou, at least, art not changed, save to maturer beauty. The glory of the laural-wreath has not faded from thy brow. Thou shalt yet—" then breaking off abruptly—"Rome—tell me of Rome! And thou—how camest thou hither? Ah! perhaps my doom is sealed, and in their mercy they have vouchsafed that I should see thee once more before the deathsman blinds me. I remember, it is the grace vouchsafed to malefactors. When *I* was a lord of life and death, I too permitted the meanest criminal to say farewell to those he loved."

"No—not so, Cola,!" exclaimed Nina, putting her hand before his mouth. "I bring thee more auspicious tidings. To-morrow thou art to be heard. The favor of the Court is propitiated. Thou wilt be acquitted."

"Ha! speak again."

"Thou wilt be heard, my Cola—thou must be acquitted!"

"And Rome be free!—Great God, I thank Thee?"

The Tribune sank on his knees, and never had his heart, in his youngest and purest hour, poured forth thanksgiving more fervent, yet less selfish. When he rose again, the whole man seemed changed. His eye had resumed its earlier expressions of deep and serene command. Majesty sate upon his brow. The sorrows of the exile were forgotten. In his sanguine and rapid thoughts, he stood once more the guardian of his country,—and its sovereign!

Nina gazed upon him with that intense and devoted worship, which steeped her vainer and her harder qualities in all the fondness of the softest women. "Such," thought she, "was his look eight years ago, when he left my maiden chamber, full of the mighty schemes which liberated Rome—such his look, when at the dawning sun he towered amidst the crouching Barons, and kneeling population of the city he had made his throne!"

"Yes, Nina!" said Rienzi, as he turned and caught her eye. "My soul tells me that my hour is at hand, If they try me openly, they dare not convict—if they acquit me, they dare not but restore. To-morrow, saidst thou, to-morrow?"

"To-morrow, Rienzi; be prepared!"

"I am—for triumph! But tell me what happy chance brought thee to Avignon?"

"*Chance*, Cola!" said Nina, with reproachful tenderness. "Could I know that thou wert in the dungeons of the Pontiff, and linger in idle security at Prague? Even at the Emperor's Court thou hadst thy partisans and favorers. Gold was easily procured. I repaired to Florence—disguised my name—and came hither to plot, to scheme, to win thy liberty, or to die with thee. Ah! did not thy heart tell thee that morning and night the eyes of thy faithful Nina gazed upon this gloomy tower; and that one friend, humble though she be, never could forsake thee!"

"Sweet Nina! Yet—yet—at Avignon power yields not to beauty without reward. Remember, there is a worse death than the pause of life."

Nina turned pale. "Fear not," she said, with a low but determined voice; "fear not, that men's lips should say Rienzi's wife delivered him. None in this corrupted Court know that I am thy wife."

"Woman," said the Tribune, sternly; "thy lips elude the answer I would seek. In our degenerate time and land, thy sex and ours forget too basely what foulness writes a leprosy in the smallest stain upon a matron's honor. That thy heart would never wrong me, I believe; but if thy weakness, thy fear of my death should wrong me, thou art a bitterer foe to Rienzi than the swords of the Colonna. Nina, speak!"

"Oh, that my soul could speak," answered Nina, "Thy words are music to me, and not a thought of mine but echoes them. Could I touch this hand, could I meet that eye, and not know that death were dearer to thee than shame? Rienzi, when last we parted, in sadness, yet in hope, what were thy words to me?"

"I remember them well," returned the Tribune: "'I leave thee,' I said, 'to keep alive at the Emperor's Court, by thy genius, the Creat Cause. Thou hast youth and beauty —and courts have lawless and ruffian suitors. I give thee no caution; it were beneath thee and me. But I leave thee the power of death.' And with that, Nina——"

"Thy hands tremblingly placed in mine this dagger.' I live—need I say more?"

"My noble and beloved Nina, it is enough. Keep the dagger yet."

"Yes; till we meet in the Capitol of Rome!"

A slight tap was heard at the door; Nina regained in an instant her disguise.

"It is on the stroke of midnight," said the jailer, appearing at the threshold.

"I come," said Nina.

"And thou hast to prepare thy thoughts," she wispered to Rienzi: "arm all thy glorious intellect. Alas! is it again we part? How my heart sinks!"

The presence of the jailer at the threshold broke the bitterness of parting by abridging it. The false page pressed her lips on the prisoner's hand, and left the cell.

The jailer, lingering behind for a moment, placed a parchment on the table. It was the summons from the court appointed for the trial of the Tribune.

CHAPTER VI.

The Scent does not Lie.—The Priest and the Soldier.

On descending the stairs, Nina was met by Alvarez.

"Fair page," said the Spaniard, gaily, "thy name, thou tellest me, is Villani?—Angelo Villani—why I know thy kinsman, methinks. Vouchsafe, young master, to enter this chamber, and drink a night-cup to thy lady's health; I would fain learn tidings of my old friends."

"At another time," answered the false Angelo, drawing the cloak closer round her face; it is late—I am hurried."

"Nay," said the Spaniard, "you escape me not so easily;" and he caught firm hold of the page's shoulder.

"Unhand me, sir!" said Nina, haughtily, and almost weeping, for her strong nerves were yet unstrung. "Jailer, at thy peril—unbar the gates."

"So hot," sald Alvarez, surprised at so great a waste of dignity in a page; "nay, I meant not to offend thee. May I wait on thy pageship to-morrow?"

"Ay, to-morrow," said Nina eager to escape.

"And meanwhile," said Alvarez, "I will accompany thee home—we can confer by the way."

So saying, without regarding the protestations of the supposed page, he passed with Nina into the open air. "Your lady," said he carelessly, "is wondrous fair; her lightest will is law to the greatest noble of Avignon. Methinks she is of Naples—is it so? Art thou dumb, sweet youth?"

The page did not answer, but with a step so rapid that it almost put the slow Spaniard out of breath, hastened along the narrow space between the tower and the palace of the Signora Cesarini, nor could all the efforts of Alvarez draw forth a single syllable from his reluctant companion, till they reached the gates of the palace, and he found himself discourteously left without the walls.

"A plague on the boy!" said he, biting his lips; "if the Cardinal thrive as well as his servant, by're Lady, Monsignore is a happy man!"

By no means pleased with the prospect of an interview with Albornoz, who, like most able men, valued the talents of those he employed exactly in proportion to their success, the Spaniard slowly returned home. With the licence accorded to him, he entered the Cardinal's chamber somewhat abruptly, and perceived him in earnest conversation with a Cavalier, whose long moustache curled upward, and the bright cuirass worn underneath his mantle, seemed to betoken him of martial profession. Pleased with the respite, Alvarez hastily withdrew: and, in fact, the Cardinal's thoughts at that moment, and for that night, were bent upon other subjects than those of love.

The interruption served, however, to shorten the conversation between Albornoz and his guest. The latter rose.

"I think," said he, buckling on a short and broad rapier, which he laid aside during the interview,—"I think, my Lord Cardinal, you encourage me to consider that our negotiation stands a fair chance of a prosperous close. Ten thousand florins, and my brother quits Viterbo, and launches the thunderbolt of the Company on the lands of Rimini. On your part——"

"On my part it is agreed," said the Cardinal, "that the army of the Church interferes not with the course of your brother's arms—there is peace between us. One warrior understands another!"

"And the word of Giles d'Albornoz, son of the royal race of Arragon, is a guarantee for the faith of a Cardinal," replied the Cavalier, with a smile. "It is, my Lord, in your *former* quality that we treat.

"There is my right hand," answered Albornoz, too politic to heed the insinuation. The Cavalier raised it respectfully to his lips, and his armed tread was soon heard descending the stairs.

"Victory," cried Albornoz, tossing his arms aloof; "Victory, now thou art mine!"

"With that he rose hastily, deposited his papers in an iron chest, and opening a concealed door behind the arras, entered a chamber that rather resembled a monk's cell than the apartment of a prince. Over a mean pallet hung a sword, a dagger, and a rude image of the Virgin. Without summoning Alvarez, the Cardinal unrobed, and in a few moments was asleep.

———

CHAPTER VII.

Vaucluse and its Genius Loci.—Old Acquaintance Renewed.

THE next day at early noon the Cavalier, whom our last chapter presented to the reader, was seen mounted on a strong Norman horse, winding his way slowly along a green and pleasant path some miles from Avignon. At length he found himself in a wild and romantic valley, through which wandered that delightful river whose name the verse of Petrarch has given to so beloved a fame. Sheltered by rocks, and in this part winding through the greenest banks, enamelled with a thousand wild flowers and water-weeds, went the crystal Sorgia. Advancing farther, the landscape assumed a more sombre and sterile aspect. The valley seemed enclosed or shut in by fantastic rocks of a thousand shapes, down which dashed and glittered a thousand rivulets. And, in the very wildest of the scene, the ground suddenly opened into a quaint and cultivated garden, through which, amidst a profusion of foliage, was seen a small and lonely mansion,—the hermitage of the place. The horseman was in the valley of the Vaucluse; and before his eye lay the garden and the house of PETRARCH! Carelessly, however, his eye scanned the consecrated spot; and unconsciously it rested, for a moment, upon a solitary figure seated musingly by the margin of the river. A large dog at the side of the noonday idler barked at the horseman as he rode on. "A brave animal and a deep bay!" though the traveller; to him the dog seemed an object much more interesting than its master. And so,—as the crowd of little men pass unheeding and unmoved, those in whom Posterity shall acknowledge the landmarks of their age,—the horseman turned his glance from the Poet!

Thrice blessed name! Immortal Florentine! * not as the lover, nor even as the poet, do I bow before thy consecrated memory—venerating thee as one it were a sacrilege to introduce in this unworthy page—save by name and as a shadow; but as the first who ever asserted to people and to prince the august majesty of Letters; who claimed to Genius

* I need scarcely say that it is his origin, not his actual birth, which entitles us to term Petrarch a Florentine.

the prerogative to influence states, to control opinion, to hold an empire over the hearts of men; and prepare events by animating passion, and guiding thought! What, (though but feebly felt and dimly seen)—what do we yet owe to Thee if Knowledge be not a Power; if MIND be a Prophet and a Fate, foretelling and foredooming the things to come! From the greatest to the least of us, to whom the pen is at once a sceptre and a sword, the low-born Florentine has been the arch-messenger to smoothe the way and prepare the welcome. Yes! even the meanest of the aftercomers—even he now vents his gratitude,—is thine everlasting debtor! Thine, how largely is the honor, if his labors, humble though they be, find an audience wherever literature is known; preaching in remotest lands the moral of forgotten revolutions, and scattering in the palace and in the market-place the seeds that shall ripen into fruit when the hand of the sower shall be dust, and his very name, perhaps, be lost! For few, alas! are they, whose *names* may outlive the grave; but the *thoughts* of every man who writes, are made undying;—others appropriate, advance, exalt them; and millions of minds unknown, undreamt of, are required to produce the immortality of one!

Indulging meditations very different from those which the idea of Petrarch awakens in a later time, the Cavalier pursued his path.

The valley was long left behind, and the way grew more and more faintly traced, until it terminated in a wood, through whose tangled boughs the sunlight broke playfully. At length, the wood opened into a wide glade, from which rose a precipitous ascent, crowned with the ruins of an old castle. The traveller dismounted, led his horse up the ascent, and, gaining the ruins, left his steed within one of the roofless chambers, overgrown with the longest grass and a profusion of wild shrubs; thence ascending, with some toil, a narrow and broken staircase, he found himself in a small room, less decayed than the rest, of which the roof and floor were yet whole.

Stretched on the ground in his cloak, and leaning his head thoughtfully on his hand, was a man of tall stature, and middle age. He lifted himself on his arm with great alacrity as the Cavalier entered.

"Well, Brettone, I have counted the hours—what tidings?"

"Albornoz consents."

"Glad news! Thou givest me new life. *Pardieu*, I shall breakfast all the better for this, my brother. Hast thou remembered that I am famishing?"

Brettone drew from beneath his cloak a sufficiently huge flask of wine, and a small panier, tolerably well filled; the inmate of the tower threw himself upon the provant with great devotion. And both the soldiers, for such they were, stretched at length on the ground, regaled themselves with considerable zest, talking hastily and familiarly between every mouthful.

"I say, Brettone, thou playest unfairly; thou hast already devoured more than half the pasty: push it hitherward. And so the Cardinal consents! What manner of man is he? Able as they say?"

"Quick, sharp, and earnest, with an eye of fire, few words, and comes to the point."

"Unlike a priest then;—a good brigand spoilt. What hast thou heard of the force he heads? Ho, not so fast with the wine."

"Scanty at present.—He relies on recruits throughout Italy."

"What his designs for Rome? There, my brother, there tends my secret soul! As for these petty towns and petty tyrants, I care not how they fall, or by whom. But the Pope must not return to Rome. Rome must be mine. The city of a new empire, the conquest of a new Attila! There, every circumstance combines in my favor!—the absence of the Pope, the weakness of the middle class, the poverty of the populace, the imbecile though ferocious barbarism of the Barons, have long concurred to render Rome the most facile, while the most glorious conquest!"

"My brother, pray Heaven your ambition do not wreck you at last; you are ever losing sight of the land. Surely with the immense wealth we are acquiring, we may——"

"Aspire to be something greater than Free Companions, generals to-day, and adventurers to-morrow. Rememberest thou, how the Norman sword won Sicily, and how the bastard William converted on the field of Hastings his baton into a sceptre. I tell thee, Brettone, that this loose Italy has crowns on the hedge that a dexterous hand may carry off at the point of the lance. My course is taken, I will form the fairest army in Italy, and with it I will win a throne in the Capitol. Fool that I was six years ago!—Instead of deputing that mad dolt Pepin of Minorbino, had I myself deserted the Hungarian, and repaired with my soldiery to Rome, the fall of Rienzi would have been followed by the rise of Montreal. Pepin was outwitted, and threw away the prey after he had hunted it down. The lion shall not again trust the chase to the jackal!"

"Walter, thou speakest of the fate of Rienzi, let it warn thee!"

"Rienzi!" replied Montreal; "I know the man! In peaceful times or with an honest people, he would have founded a great dynasty. But he dreamt of laws and liberty for men who despise the first and will not protect the last. We, of a harder race, know that a new throne must be built by the feudal and not the civil system; and into the city we must transport the camp. It is by the multitude that the proud Tribune gained power,—by the multitude he lost it; it is by the sword that I will win it, and by the sword will I keep it!"

"Rienzi was too cruel, he should not have incensed the Barons," said Brettone, about to finish the flask, when the strong hand of his brother plucked it from him, and anticipated the design.

"Pooh," said Montreal, finishing the draught with a long sigh, "he was not cruel enough. He sought only to be just, and not to distinguish between noble and peasant. He should have distinguished? He should have exterminated the nobles root and branch. But this no Italian can do. This is reserved for me."

"Thou wouldst not butcher all the best blood of Rome?"

"Butcher! No, but I would seize their lands, and endow with them a new nobility, the hardy and fierce nobility of the North, who well know how to guard their prince, and *will* guard him, as the fountain of their own power. Enough of this now. And talking of Rienzi—rots he still in his dungeon?"

"Why, this morning, ere I left, I heard strange news. The town was astir, groups in every corner. They said that Rienzi's trial was to be to-day, and from the names of the judges chosen, it is suspected that acquittal is already determined on."

"Ha! thou shouldst have told me of this before."

"Should he be restored to Rome, would it militate against thy plans?"

"Humph! I know not—deep thought and dexterous management would be needed. I would fain not leave this spot till I hear what is decided on."

"Surely, Walter, it would have been wiser and safer to have stayed with thy soldiery, and intrusted me with the absolute conduct of this affair."

"Not so," answered Montreal; "thou art a bold fellow enough, and a cunning——but my head in these matters is better than thine. Besides," continued the Knight, lowering his voice, and shading his face, "I had vowed a pilgrimage to the beloved river, and the old trysting-place. Ah me!——But all this, Brettone, thou understandest not—let it pass. As for my safety, since we have come to this amnesty with Albornoz, I fear but little danger even if discovered: besides, I want the florins. There are those in this country, Germans, who could eat an Italian army at a meal, whom I would fain engage, and their leaders want earnest-money—the griping knaves!—How are the Cardinal's florins to be paid?"

"Half now—half when thy troops are before Rimini!"

"Rimini! the thought whets my sword. Rememberest thou how that accursed Malatesta drove me from Aversa,* broke up my camp, and made me render to him all my booty? There fell the work of years! But for that my banner would now be floating over St. Angelo. I will pay back the debt with fire and sword, ere the summer has shed its leaves."

The fair countenance of Montreal grew terrible as he uttered these words; his hands griped the handle of his sword, and his strong frame heaved visibly; tokens of the fierce and unsparing passions, by the aid of which a life of rapine and revenge had corrupted a nature originally full no less of the mercy than the courage of Provençal chivalry.

Such was the fearful man who now (the

* This Malatesta, a signior of illustrious family, was one of the most skilful warriors in Italy. He and his brother Galeotte had been raised to the joint-tyranny of Rimini by the voice of its citizens. After being long the foes of the Church, they were ultimately named as its captains by the Cardinal Albornoz.

wildness of his youth sobered, and his ambition hardened and concentered) was the rival with Rienzi for the mastery of Rome.

CHAPTER VIII.

The Crowd.—The Trial.—The Verdict.—The Soldier and the Page.

It was on the following evening that a considerable crowd had gathered in the streets of Avignon. It was the second day of the examination of Rienzi, and with every moment was expected the announcement of the verdict. Amongst the foreigners of all countries assembled in that seat of the Papal splendor, the interest was intense. The Italians, even of the highest rank were in favor of the Tribune, the French against him. As for the good townspeople of Avignon themselves, they felt but little excitement in anything that did not bring money into their pockets; and if it had been put to the secret vote, no doubt there would have been a vast majority for burning the prisoner as a marketable speculation!

Amongst the crowd was a tall man in a plain and rusty suit of armor, but with an air of knightly bearing, which somewhat belied the coarseness of his mail; he wore no helmet, but a small morion of black leather, with a long projecting shade, much used by wayfarers in the hot climate of the south. A black patch covered nearly the whole of one cheek, and altogether he bore the appearance of a grim soldier, with whom war had dealt harshly, both in purse and person.

Many were the jests at the shabby swordsman's expense, with which that lively population amused their impatience; and though the shade of the morion concealed his eyes, an arch and merry smile about the corners of his mouth showed that he could take a jest at himself.

"Well," said one of the crowd, (a rich Milanese,) "I am of a state that *was* free, and I trust the People's man will have justice shown him."

"Amen," said a grave Florentine.

"They say," whispered a young student from Paris, to a learned doctor of laws, with whom he abode, "that his defence has been a masterpiece."

"He hath taken no degrees," replied the doctor, doubtingly. "Ho, friend, why dost thou push me so? thou hast rent my robe."

This was said to a minstrel, or jongleur, who, with a small lute slung round him, was making his way, with great earnestness, through the throng.

"I beg pardon, worthy sir," said the minstrel; "but this is a scene to be sung of! Centuries hence; ay, and in lands remote, legend and song will tell the fortunes of Cola di Rienzi, the friend of Petrarch and the Tribune of Rome!"

The young French student turned quickly round to the minstrel, with a glow, on his pale face; not sharing the general sentiments of his countrymen against Rienzi, he felt that it was an era in the world when a minstrel spoke thus of the heroes of intellect—not of war.

At this time the tall soldier was tapped impatiently on the back.

"I pray thee, great sir," said a sharp and imperious voice, "to withdraw that tall bulk of thine a little on one side—I cannot see through thee; and I would fain my eyes were among the first to catch a glimpse of Rienzi as he passes from the court."

"Fair sir page," replied the soldier, good-humoredly, as he made way for Angelo Villani, "thou wilt not always find that way in the world is won by commanding the strong. When thou art older thou wilt beard the weak, and the strong thou wilt wheedle."

"I must change my nature, then," answered Angelo, (who was of somewhat small stature, and not yet come to his full growth,) trying still to raise himself above the heads of the crowd.

The soldier looked at him approvingly; and as he looked he sighed, and his lips worked with some strange emotion.

"Thou speakest well," said he, after a pause. "Pardon me the rudeness of the question; but art thou of Italy?—thy tongue savors of the Roman dialect; yet I have seen lineaments like thine on this side the Alps."

"It may be, good fellow" said the page, haughtily; "but I thank Heaven that I am of Rome."

At this moment a loud shout burst from that part of the crowd nearest the court. The sound of trumpets again hushed the throng into deep and breathless silence, while the

Pope's guards, ranged along the space conducting from the court, drew themselves up more erect, and fell a step or two back upon the crowd.

As the trumpet ceased, the voice of a herald was heard, but it did not penetrate within several yards of the spot where Angelo and the soldier stood; and it was only by a mighty shout that in a moment circled through, and was echoed back by, the wide multitude—by the waving of kerchiefs from the windows—by broken ejaculations, which were caught up from lip to lip, that the page knew that Rienzi was acquitted.

"I would I could see his face!" sighed the page, querulously.

"And thou shalt," said the soldier; and he caught up the boy in his arms, and pressed on with the strength of a giant, parting the living stream from right to left, as he took his way to a place near the guards, and by which Rienzi was sure to pass.

The page, half-pleased, half-indignant, struggled a little, but finding it in vain, consented tacitly to what he felt an outrage on his dignity.

"Never mind," said the soldier, "thou art the first I ever willingly raised above myself; and I do it now for the sake of thy fair face, which reminds me of one I loved.

But these last words were spoken low, and the boy, in his anxiety to see the hero of Rome, did not hear or heed them. Presently Rienzi came by; two gentlemen, of the Pope's own following, walked by his side. He moved slowly, amidst the greetings and clamor of the crowd, looking neither to the right nor the left. His bearings was firm and collected, and, save by the flush of his cheek, there was no external sign of joy or excitement. Flowers dropped from every balcony on his path; and just when he came to a broader space, where the ground was somewhat higher, and where he was in fuller view of the houses around, he paused,—and, uncovering, acknowledged the homage he had received, with a look,—a gesture—which each who beheld never forgot. It haunted even that gay and thoughtless court, when the last tale of Rienzi's life reached their ears. And Angelo, clinging then round that soldier's neck, recalled—but we must not anticipate.

It was not, however, to the dark tower that Rienzi returned. His home was prepared at the palace of the Cardinal d'Albornoz. The next day he was admitted to the Pope's presence, and on the evening of that day he was proclaimed Senator of Rome.

Meanwhile the soldier had placed Angelo on the ground; and as the page faltered out no courteous thanks, he interrupted him in a sad and kind voice, the tone of which struck the page forcibly, so little did it suit the rough and homely appearance of the man.

"We part," he said, "as strangers, fair boy; and since thou sayest thou art of Rome, there is no reason why my heart should have warmed to thee as it has done; yet if ever thou wantest a friend,—seek him"—and the soldier's voice sunk into a whisper—"in Walter de Montreal."

Ere the page recovered his surprise at that redoubted name, which his earliest childhood had been taught to dread, the Knight of St. John had vanished amongst the crowd.

CHAPTER IX.

Albornoz and Nina.

BUT the eyes which, above all others, thirsted for a glimpse of the released captive were forbidden that delight. Alone in her chamber, Nina awaited the result of the trial. She heard the shouts, the exclamations, the tramp of hundreds along the streets; she felt that the victory was won; and, her heart long overcharged, she burst into passionate tears. The return of Angelo soon acquainted her with all that had passed; but it somewhat chilled her joy to find Rienzi was the guest of the dreaded Cardinal. That shock, in which certainty, however happy, replaces suspense, had so powerful an effect on her frame, joined to her loathing fear of a visit from the Cardinal, that she became for three days alarmingly ill; and it was only on the fifth day from that which saw Rienzi endowed with the rank of Senator of Rome, that she was recovered sufficiently to admit Albornoz to her presence.

The Cardinal had sent daily to inquire after her health, and his inquiries, to her alarmed mind, had appeared to insinuate a pretension to the right to make them. Meanwhile Albornoz had had enough to divert and occupy his thoughts. Having bought off the formidable Montreal from the service of John de Vico, one of the ablest and fiercest enemies of the Church, he resolved to march to the territories of that tyrant as expeditiously as possible, and so not to allow him time to obtain the assistance of any other band of the mercenary adventurers, who found Italy the market for their valor. Occupied with raising troops, procuring money, corresponding with the various free states, and establishing alliances in aid of his ulterior and more ambitious projects at the court of Avignon, the Cardinal waited with tolerable resignation the time when he might claim from the Signora Cesarini the reward to which he deemed himself entitled. Meanwhile he had held his first conversations with Rienzi, and, under the semblance of courtesy to the acquitted Tribune, Albornoz had received him as his guest, in order to make himself master of the character and disposition of one in whom he sought a minister and a tool. That miraculous and magic art, attested by the historians of the time, which Rienzi possessed over every one with whom he came into contact, however various in temper, station, or opinions, had not deserted him in his interview with the Pontiff. So faithfully had he described the true condition of Rome, so logically had he traced the causes and the remedies of the evils she endured, so sanguinely had he spoken of his own capacities for administering her affairs, and so brilliantly had he painted the prospects which that administration opened to the weal of the Church, and the interest of the Pope, that Innocent, though a keen and shrewd, and somewhat sceptical calculator of human chances, was entirely fascinated by the eloquence of the Roman.

"Is this the man," he is reported to have said, "whom for twelve months we have treated as a prisoner and a criminal? Would that it were on his shoulders only that the Christian empire reposed!"

At the close of the interview he had, with every mark of favor and distinction, conferred upon Rienzi the rank of Senator, which, in fact, was that of Viceroy of Rome, and had willingly acceded to all the projects which the enterprising Rienzi had once more formed—not only for recovering the territories of the Church, but for extending the dictatorial sway of the Seven-hilled, City over the old dependencies of Italy.

Albornoz, to whom the Pope retailed this conversation was somewhat jealous of the favor the new Senator had so suddenly acquired, and immediately on his return home sought an interview with his guest. In his heart, the Lord Cardinal, emphatically a man of action and business, regarded Rienzi as one rather cunning than wise—rather fortunate than great—a mixture of the pedant and the demagogue. But after a long and scrutinizing conversation with the new Senator, even he yielded to the spell of his enchanting and master intellect. Reluctantly Albornoz confessed to himself that Rienzi's rise was not the thing of chance; yet more reluctantly he perceived that the Senator was one whom he might treat with as an equal, but could not rule as a minion. And he entertained serious doubts whether it would be wise to reinstate him in a power which he evinced the capacity to wield and the genius to extend. Still, however, he did not repent the share he had taken in Rienzi's acquittal. His presence in a camp so thinly peopled was a matter greately to be desired. And through his influence, the Cardinal more than ever trusted to enlist the Romans in favor of his enterprise for the recovery of the territory of St. Peter!

Rienzi, who panted once more to behold his Nina, endeared to him by trial and absence, as by fresh bridals, was not however able to discover the name she had assumed at Avignon; and his residence with the Cardinal closely but respectfully watched as he was, forbade Nina all opportunity of corresponding with him. Some half bantering hints which Albornoz had dropped upon the interest taken in his welfare by the most celebrated beauty of Avignon, had filled him with a vague alarm which he trembled to acknowledge even to himself. But the * *volto sciolto* which, in common with all Italian politicians, concealed whatever were his *pensieri stretti*—enabled him to baffle completely the jealous and lynx-like observation of the Cardinal. Nor had Alvarez been better enabled to satisfy the curiosity of his master. He had indeed sought the page of Villani, but the imperious manner of that wayward and haughty boy had cut short all attempts at cross-examination. And all he could ascertain was, that the real An-

* *Volto sciolto, pensieri stretti*—the countenance open, the thoughts restrained.

gelo Villani was not the Angelo Villani who had visited Rienzi.

Trusting at last that he should learn all, and inflamed by such passion and such hope as he was capable of feeling, Albornoz now took his way to the Cesarini's palace.

He was ushered with due state into the apartment of the Signora. He found her pale, and with the traces of illness upon her noble and statuelike features. She rose as he entered; and when he approached, she half bent her knee, and raised his hand to her lips. Surprised and delighted at a reception so new, the Cardinal hastened to prevent the condescension; retaining both her hands, he attempted gently to draw them to his heart.

"Fairest!" he whispered, "couldst thou know how I have mourned thy illness—and yet it has but left thee more lovely, as the rain only brightens the flower. Ah! happy if I have promoted thy lightest wish, and if in thine eyes I may henceforth seek at once an angel to guide me and a paradise to reward."

Nina, releasing her hand, waved it gently, and motioned the Cardinal to a seat. Seating herself at a little distance, she then spoke with great gravity and downcast eyes.

"My Lord, it is your intercession, joined to his own innocence, that has released from yonder tower the elected governor of the people of Rome. But freedom is the least of the generous gifts you have conferred; there is a greater in a fair name vindicated, and rightful honor re-bestowed. For this, I rest ever your debtor; for this, if I bear children, they shall be taught to bless your name; for this the historian who recalls the deeds of this age, and the fortunes of Cola di Rienzi, shall add a new chaplet to the wreaths you have already won. Lord Cardinal, I may have erred. I may have offended you—you may accuse me of woman's artifice. Speak not, wonder not, hear me out. I have but one excuse, when I say that I held justified any means short of dishonor, to save the life and restore the fortunes of Cola di Rienzi. Know, my Lord, that she who now addresses you is his wife."

The Cardinal remained motionless and silent. But his sallow countenance grew flushed from the brow to the neck, and his thin lips quivered for a moment, and then broke into a withering and bitter smile. At length he rose from his seat, very slowly, and said, in a voice trembling with passion,

"It is well, madam. Giles d'Albornoz has been, then, a puppet in the hands, a stepping-stone in the rise, of the plebeian demagogue of Rome. You but played upon me for your own purposes; and nothing short of a Cardinal of Spain, and a Prince of the royal blood of Aragon, was meet to be the instrument of a mountebank's juggle! Madam, yourself and your husband might justly be accused of ambition——"

"Cease, my Lord," said Nina, with unspeakable dignity; "whatever offence has been committed against you was mine alone. Till after our last interview, Rienzi knew not even of my presence at Avignon."

"At our last interview, Lady, (you do well to recall it!) methinks there was a hinted and implied contract. I have fulfilled my part—I claim yours. Mark me! I do not forego that claim. As easily as I rend this glove can I rend the parchment which proclaims thy husband 'the Senator of Rome.' The dungeon is not death, and its door will open *twice*."

"My Lord—my Lord!" cried Nina, sick with terror, "wrong not so your noble nature, your great name, your sacred rank, your chivalric blood. You are of the knightly race of Spain, yours not the sullen, low, and inexorable vices that stain the petty tyrants of this unhappy land. You are no Visconti—no Castracani—you cannot stain your laurels with revenge upon a woman. Hear me," she continued, and she fell abruptly at his feet; "men dupe, deceive our sex—and for selfish purposes; they are pardoned—even by their victims. Did *I* deceive you with a false hope? Well—what my object?—what my excuse? My husband's liberty—my land's salvation! Woman,—my Lord, alas, your sex too rarely understand her weakness or her greatness! Erring—all human as she is to others—God gifts her with a thousand virtues to the one she loves! It is from that love that she alone drinks her nobler nature. For the hero of her worship she has the meekness of the dove—the devotion of the saint; for his safety in peril, for his rescue in misfortune, her vain sense imbibes the sagacity of the serpent—her weak heart, the courage of the lioness! It is this which, in absence, made me mask my face in smiles, that the friends of the houseless exile might not despair of his fate—it is this which brought me through forests beset with robbers, to watch the stars upon yon solitary tower—it was this which led my steps to the revels of your hated court—this which made me seek a deliverer in the noblest of its chiefs—it is this which has at last opened the dungeon door to the prisoner now within your halls; and this, Lord Cardinal," added Nina, rising, and folding her arms upon her heart—"this, if your anger seeks a victim, will inspire me to die without a groan,—but without dishonor!"

Albornoz remained rooted to the ground. Amazement—emotion—admiration—all busy at his heart. He gazed at Nina's flashing eyes and heaving bosom as a warrior of old upon a prophetess inspired. His eyes were riveted to hers as by a spell. He tried to speak, but his voice failed him. Nina continued:

"Yes, my Lord; these are no idle words! If you seek revenge, it is in your power. Undo what you have done. Give Rienzi back to the dungeon, or to disgrace, and you are avenged; but not on *him*. All the hearts of Italy shall become to him a second Nina! I am the guilty one, and I the sufferer. Hear me swear—in that instant which sees new wrong to Rienzi, this hand is my executioner.—My Lord, I supplicate you no longer!"

Albornoz continued deeply moved. Nina but rightly judged him, when she distinguished the aspiring Spaniard from the barbarous and unrelenting voluptuaries of Italy. Despite the profligacy that stained his sacred robe—despite all the acquired and increasing callousness of a hard, scheming, and sceptical man, cast amidst the worst natures of the worst of times—there lingered yet in his soul much of the knightly honor of his race and country. High thoughts and daring spirits touched a congenial string in his heart, and not the less, in that he had but rarely met them in his experience of camps and courts. For the first time in his life, he felt that he had seen the woman who could have contented him even with wedlock, and taught him the proud and faithful love of which the minstrels of Spain had sung. He sighed, and still gazing on Nina, approached her, almost reverentially; he knelt and kissed the hem of her robe. "Lady," he said, "I would I could believe that you have altogether read my nature aright, but I were indeed lost to all honor, and unworthy of gentle birth, if I still harbored a single thought against the peace and virtue of one like thee. Sweet heroine,"—he continued—"so lovely, yet so pure—so haughty, and yet so soft—thou hast opened to me the brightest page these eyes have ever scanned in the blotted volume of mankind. Mayest thou have such happiness as life can give; but souls such as thine make their nest like the eagle, upon rocks and amidst the storms. Fear me no more—think of me no more—unless hereafter, when thou hearest men speak of Giles d'Albornoz, thou mayest say in thine own heart,"—and here the Cardinal's lip curled with scorn—"he did not renounce every feeling worthy of a man, when Ambition and Fate endued him with the surplice of the priest."

The Spaniard was gone before Nina could reply.

BOOK EIGHTH.

THE GRAND COMPANY.

Montreal nourrissolt de plus vastes projets.... il donnoit à sa compagnie un gouvernement régulier....Par cette discipline il faisoit régner l'abondance dans son camp; les gens de guerre ne parloient, en Italie, que des richesses qu'on acquéroit à son service."
—SISMONDI, *Hist. des Republiques Italiennes*, tom. vi. c. 42.

" Montreal cherished more vast designs....he subjected his company to a regular system of government....By means of this discipline he kept his camp abundantly supplied, and military adventurers in Italy talked of nothing but the wealth won in his service."
SISMONDI'S *Hist of Ital. Republics*.

CHAPTER I.

The Encampment.

It was a most lovely day, in the very glow and meridian of an Italian summer, when a small band of horsemen were seen winding a hill which commanded one of the fairest landscapes of Tuscany. At their head was a cavalier in a complete suit of chain armor, the links of which were so fine, that they resembled a delicate and curious network, but so strongly compacted, that they would have resisted spear or sword no less effectually than the heaviest corselet, while adapting themselves exactly and with ease to every movement of the light and graceful shape of the rider. He wore a hat of dark green velvet shaded by long plumes, while of two squires behind, the one bore his helmet and lance, the other led a strong war-horse, completely cased in plates of mail, which seemed, however, scarcely to encumber its proud and agile paces. The countenance of the cavalier was comely, but strongly marked, and darkened, by long exposure to the suns of many climes, to a deep bronze hue: a few raven ringlets escaped from beneath his hat down a cheek closely shaven. The expression of his features was grave and composed even to sadness; nor could all the loveliness of the unrivalled scene before him dispel the quiet and settled melancholy of his eyes. Besides the squires, ten horsemen, armed cap-à-pié, attended the knight; and the low and murmured conversation they carried on at intervals, as well as their long fair hair, large stature, thick short beards, and the studied and accurate equipment of their arms and steeds, bespoke them of a hardier and more warlike race than the children of the south. The cavalcade was closed with a man almost of gigantic height bearing a banner richly decorated, wherein was wrought a column, with the inscription, "ALONE AMIDST RUINS." Fair indeed was the prospect which with every step expanded yet more widely its various beauty. Right before stretched a long vale, now covered with green woodlands glittering in the yellow sunlight, now opening into narrow plains bordered by hillocks, from whose mosses of all hues grew fantastic and odorous shrubs; while, winding amidst them, a broad and silver stream broke into light at frequent intervals, snatched by wood and hillock from the eye, only to steal upon it again, in sudden and bright surprise. The opposite slope of gentle mountains, as well as that which the horsemen now descended, was covered with vineyards, trained in alleys and arcades: and the clustering grape laughed from every leafy and glossy covert, as gaily as when the Fauns held a holiday in the shade. The eye of the Cavalier roved listlessly over this enchanting prospect, sleeping in the rosiest light of a Tuscan heaven, and then became fixed with a more earnest attention on the gray and frowning walls of a distant castle, which, high upon the steepest of the opposite mountains, overlooked the valley.

"Behold," he muttered to himself, "how every Eden in Italy hath its curse! Wherever the land smiles fairest, be sure to find the brigand's tent and the tyrant's castle!"

Scarce had these thoughts passed his mind, ere the shrill and sudden blast of a bugle that sounded close amongst the vineyards by the side of the path startled the whole group. The cavalcade halted abruptly. The leader made a gesture to the squire who led his war-horse. The noble and practised animal remained perfectly still, save by champing its bit restlessly, and moving its quick ear to and fro, as aware of a coming danger,—while the squire, unencumbered by the heavy armor of the Germans, plunged into the thicket and disappeared. He returned in a few minutes, already heated and breathless.

"We must be on our guard," he whispered; "I see the glimmer of steel through the vine leaves."

"Our ground is unhappily chosen," said the Knight, hastily bracing on his helmet and leaping on his charger; and waving his hand towards a broader space in the road, which would permit the horsemen more room to act in union, with his small band he made hastily to the spot—the armor of the soldiers rattling heavily as two by two they proceeded on.

The space to which the Cavalier had pointed was a green semicircle of several yards in extent, backed by tangled copses of brushwood sloping down to the vale below. They reached it in safety; they drew up breast to breast in the form of a cresent: every visor closed save that of the Knight, who looked anxiously and keenly round the landscape.

"Hast thou heard, Giulio," he said, to his favorite squire, (the only Italian of the band,) "whether any brigands have been seen lately in these parts?"

"No, my Lord; on the contrary, I am told that every lance hath left the country to join the Grand Company of Fra Moreale. The love of his pay and plunder has drawn away the mercenaries of every Tuscan Signor."

As he ceased speaking, the bugle sounded again from nearly the same spot as before; it was answered by a brief and martial note from the very rear of the horsemen At the same moment, from the thickets behind, broke the gleam of mail and spears. One after another, rank after rank, from the copse behind them, emerged men-at-arms, while suddenly, from the vines in front, still greater numbers poured forth with loud and fierce shouts.

"For God, for the Emperor, and for the Colonna!" cried the Knight, closing his visor; and the little band, closely serried, the lance in every rest, broke upon the rush of the enemy in front. A score or so, borne to the ground by the charge, cleared a path for the horsemen, and, without waiting the assault of the rest, the Knight wheeled his charger and led the way down the hill, almost at full gallop, despite the roughness of the descent: a flight of arrows despatched after them fell idly on their iron mail.

"If they have no horse," cried the Knight, "we are saved!"

And, indeed, the enemy seemed scarcely to think of pursuing them; but (gathered on the brow of a hill) appeared contented to watch their flight.

Suddenly a curve in the road brought them before a broad and wide patch of waste land, which formed almost a level surface, interrupting the descent of the mountain. On the commencement of this waste, drawn up in still array, the sunlight broke on the breastplates of a long line of horsemen, whom the sinuosities of the road had hitherto concealed from the Knight and his party.

The little troop halted abruptly—retreat—advance alike cut off: gazing first at the foe before them, they remained still as a cloud, every eye was then turned towards the Knight.

"An thou wouldst, my Lord," said the leader of the Northmen, perceiving the irresolution of their chief, "we will fight to the last. You are the only Italian I ever knew whom I would willingly die for!"

This rude profession was received with a sympathetic murmur from the rest, and the soldiers drew closer around the Knight. "Nay, my brave fellows," said the Colonna, lifting his visor, "it is not in so inglorious a field, after such various fortunes, that we are doomed to perish. If these be brigands, as we must suppose, we can yet purchase our way. If the troops of some Signor, we are strangers to the feud in which he is engaged. Give me yon banner—I will ride on to them."

"Nay, my Lord," said Giulio; "such marauders do not always spare a flag of truce. There is danger——"

"For that reason your leader braves it. Quick!"

The Knight took the banner, and rode deliberately up to the horseman. On approaching, his warlike eye could not but admire the perfect caparison of their arms, the strength and beauty of their steeds, and the steady discipline of their long and glittering line.

As he rode up, and his gorgeous banner gleamed in the noonlight, the soldiers saluted him. It was a good omen, and he hailed it as such. "Fair sirs," said the Knight. "I come, at once herald and leader of the little band who have just escaped the unlooked-for assault of armed men on yonder hill—and, claiming aid, as knight from knight, and soldier from soldier, I place my troop under the protection of your leader. Suffer me to see him."

"Sir Knight," answered one, who seemed the captain of the band, "sorry am I to detain one of your gallant bearing, and still more so, on recognizing the device of one of the most potent houses of Italy. But our orders are strict, and we must bring all armed men to the camp of our General."

"Long absent from my native land, I knew not," replied the Knight, "that there was war in Tuscany. Permit me to crave the name of the general whom you speak of, and that of the foe against whom ye march."

The Captain smiled slightly.

"Walter de Montreal is the General of the Great Company, and Florence his present foe."

"We have fallen, then, into friendly, if fierce, hands," replied the Knight, after a moment's pause. To Sir Walter de Montreal I am known of old. Permit me to return to my companions, and acquaint them that if accident has made us prisoners, it is, at least, only to the most skilful warrior of his day that we are condemned to yield."

The Italian then turned his horse to join his comrades.

"A fair Knight and a bold presence," said the Captain of the Companions to his neighbor, "though I scarce think it is the party we are ordered to intercept. Praised be the Virgin, however, his men seem from the North. Them, perhaps we may hope to enlist."

The Knight now, with his comrades, rejoined the troop. And, on receiving their parole not to attempt escape, a detachment of thirty horsemen were despatched to conduct the prisoners to the encampment of the Great Company.

Turning from the main road, the Knight found himself conducted into a narrow defile between the hills, which, succeded by a gloomy track of wild forest-land brought the party at length into a full and abrupt view of a wide plain, covered with the tents of what, for Italian warfare, was considered a mighty army. A stream, over which rude and hasty bridges had been formed from the neighboring timber, alone separated the horsemen from the encampment.

"A noble sight!" said the captive Cavalier, with enthusiasm, as he reined in his steed, and gazed upon the wild and warlike streets of canvass, traversing each other in vistas broad and regular.

One of the captains of the Great Company who rode beside him, smiled complacently.

"There are few masters of the martial art who equal Fra Moreale," said he; "and savage, reckless, and gathered from all parts and all countries—from cavern and from market-place, from prison and from palace, as are his troops, he has reduced them already into a discipline which might shame even the soldiery of the Empire."

The knight made no reply; but, spurring his horse over one of the rugged bridges, soon found himself amidst the encampment. But that part at which he entered little merited the praises bestowed upon the discipline of the army. A more unruly and disorderly array, the Cavalier, accustomed to the stern regularity of English, French, and German discipline, thought he had never beheld: here and there, fierce, unshaven, half-naked brigands might be seen, driving before them the cattle which they had just collected by predatory excursions. Sometimes a knot of dissolute women stood — chattering, scolding, gesticulating—collected round groups of wild shagged Northmen, who, despite the bright purity of the summer-noon, were already engaged in deep potations. Oaths, and laughter, and drunken merriment, and fierce brawl, rang from side to side; and ever and anon some hasty conflict with drawn knives was begun and finished by the fiery and savage bravoes of Calabria or the Apennines, before the very eyes and almost in the very path of the troop. Tumblers, and mountebanks, and jugglers, and Jew pedlers, were exhibiting their tricks or their wares at every interval, apparently well inured to the lawless and turbulent market in which they exercised their several callings. Despite the protection of the horsemen who accompanied them, the prisoners were not allowed to pass without molestation. Groups of urchins, squalid, fierce, and ragged, seemed to start from the ground, and surrounded their horses like swarms of bees, uttering the most discordant cries; and, with the gestures of savages, rather demanding than beseeching money, which, when granted, seemed only to render them more insatiable. While, sometimes mingled with the rest, were seen the bright eyes and olive cheek, and half-pleading, half-laughing smile of girls, whose extreme youth, scarce emerged from childhood, rendered doubly striking, their utter and unredeemed abandonment.

"You did not exaggerate the decorum of the Grand Company?" cried the Knight, gravely, to his new acquaintance.

"Signor," replied the other, "you must not judge of the kernel by the shell. We are scarcely yet arrived at the camp. These are the outskirts, occupied rather by the rabble than the soldiers. Twenty thousand men from the sink, it must be owned, of every town in Italy, follow the camp, to fight if necessary, but rather for plunder, and for forage:—such you now behold. Presently you will see those of another stamp."

The Knight's heart swelled high. "And to such men is Italy given up!" thought he. His revery was broken by a loud burst of applause from some convivialists hard by. He turned, and under a long tent, and round a board covered with wine and viands, sate some thirty or forty bravoes. A ragged minstrel, or jongleur, with an immense beard and mustachios, was tuning, with no inconsiderable skill, a lute which had acccompanied him in all his wanderings—and suddenly changing its notes into a wild and warlike meloldy, he commenced in a loud and deep voice the following song:—

THE PRAISE OF THE GRAND COMPANY

1.

Ho, dark one from the golden South,
Ho, fair one from the North;
Ho, coat of mail and spear of sheen—
Ho, wherefore ride ye forth?
"We come from mount, we come from cave,
We come across the sea,
In long array, in bright array,
To Montreal's Companiè."
Oh, the merry, merry band,
Light heart, and heavy hand—
Oh, the Lances of the Free!

2.

Ho, Princes of the castled height—
Ho, Burghers of the town;
Apulia's strength, Romagna's pride,
And Tusca's old renown!
Why quail ye thus? why pale ye thus?
What spectre do ye see?
"The blood-red flag, and trampling march,
Of Montreal's Companiè."
Oh, the sunshine of your life—
Oh, the thunders of your strife!
Wild Lances of the Free!

3.

Ho, scutcheons o'er the vaulted tomb
Where Norman valor sleeps,
Why shake ye so? why quake ye so?
What wind the trophy sweeps?
"We shake without a breath—below,
The dead are stirred to see,
The Norman's fame revived again
In Montreal's Companiè."
Since Roger won his crown,
Who hath equalled your renown,
Brave Lances of the Free?

4.

Ho, ye who seek to win a name,
Where deeds are bravest done—
Ho, ye who wish to pile a heap,
Where gold is lightest won;
Ho, ye who loathe the stagnant life,
Or shun the law's decree,
Belt on the brand, and spur the steed,
To Montreal's Companiè.
And the maid shall share her rest,
And the miser share his chest,
With the Lances of the Free!
The Free!
The Free!
Oh! the Lances of the Free!

Then suddenly, as if inspired to a wilder flight by his own minstrelsy, the jongleur, sweeping his hand over the chords, broke forth into an air admirably expressive of the picture which his words, running into a rude, but lively and stirring doggerel, attempted to paint.

THE MARCH OF THE GRAND COMPANY.

Tirà, tiralà—trumpet and drum—
Rising bright o'er the height of the mountain they come !
German, and Hun, and the Islandrie,
Who routed the Frenchman at Famed Cressiè,
Wherein the rose changed its hue with the *fleur-de-lis;*
With the Roman, and Lombard, and Piedmontese,
And the dark-haired son of the southern seas.
Tirà, Tiralà—more near and near
Down the steep—see them sweep;—rank by rank they appear !
With the Cloud of the Crowd hanging dark at their rear—
Serried, and steadied, and orderliè,
Like the course—like the force—of a marching sea !
Open your gates, and out with your gold,
For the blood must be spilt, or the ransom be told !
Woe, Burghers, woe ! Behold them led
By the stoutest arm and the wisest head,
With the snow-white cross on the cloth of red;—
With the eagle eye, and the lion port,
His barb for a throne, and his camp for a court:
Sovereign and scourge of the land is he—
The kingly Knight of the Companiè !
Hurrah—hurrah—hurrah !
Hurrah for the army—hurrah for its lord—
Hurrah for the gold that is got by the sword—
Hurrah—hurrah—hurrah !
For the Lances of the Free !

Shouted by the full chorus of those desperate boon companions, and caught up and re-echoed from side to side, near and far, as the familiar and well-known words of the burthen reached the ears of more distant groups or stragglers, the effect of this fierce and licentious minstrelsy was indiscribable. It was impossible not to feel the zest which that daring life imparted to its daring followers, and even the gallant and stately Knight who listened to it, reproved himself for an involuntary thrill of sympathy and pleasure.

He turned with some impatience and irritation to his companion, who had taken a part in the chorus, and said, "Sir, to the ears of an Italian noble, conscious of the miseries of his country, this ditty is not welcome. I pray you, let us proceed.'"

"I humbly crave your pardon, Signor," said the Free Companion; but really so attractive is the life led by Free Lances, under Fra Moreale, that sometimes we forget the ——but pardon me—we will on."

A few moments more, and bounding over a narrow circumvallation, the party found themselves in a quarter, animated indeed, but of a wholly different character of animation. Long lines of armed men were drawn up on either side of a path, conducting to a large marquee, placed upon a little hillock, surmounted by a blue flag, and up this path armed soldiers were passing to and fro with great order, but with a pleased and complacent expression upon their swarthy features. Some that repaired to the marquee were bearing packets and bales upon their shoulders—those that returned seemed to have got rid of their burthens, but every now and then, impatiently opening their hands, appeared counting and recounting to themselves the coins contained therein.

The Knight looked inquiringly at his companion.

"It is the marquee of the merchants," said the captain; "they have free admission to the camp, and their property and persons are rigidly respected. They purchase each soldier's share of the plunder at fair prices, and either party is contented with the bargain."

"It seems, then, that there in some kind of rude justice observed amongst you," said the Knight.

"Rude ! *Diavolo !* Not a town in Italy but would be glad of such even justice, and such impartial laws. Yonder lie the tents of the judges, appointed to try all offences of soldier against soldier. To the right, the tent with the golden ball contains the treasurer of the army. Fra Moreale incurs no arrears with his soldiery."

It was, indeed, by these means that the Knight of St. Jonn had collected the best equipped and the best contented force in Italy. Every day brought him recruits. Nothing was spoken of amongst the mercenaries of Italy but the wealth acquired in his service, and every warrior in the pay of Republic or of Tyrant sighed for the lawless standard of Fra Moreale. Already had exaggerated tales of the fortunes to be made in the ranks of the Great Company passed the Alps; and, even now, the Knight, penetrating farther into the camp, beheld from many a tent the proud banners and armorial blazon of German nobility and Galliç knighthood.

"You see," said the Free Companion, pointing to these insignia, "We are not without our different ranks in our wild city. And while we speak, many a golden spur is speeding hitherward from the North !"

All now in the quarter they had entered was still and solemn; only afar came the mingled hum, or the sudden shout of the pandemonium in the rear, mellowed by distance to a not unpleasing sound. An occasional soldier, crossing their path, stalked silently and stealthily to some neighboring tent, and seemed scarcely to regard their approach.

"Behold! we are before the General's pavilion," said the Free Lance.

Blazoned with purple and gold, the tent of Montreal lay a little apart from the rest. A brooklet from the stream they had crossed murmured gratefully on the ear, and a tall and wide-spreading beech cast its shadow over the gorgeous canvass.

While his troop waited without, the Knight was conducted at once to the presence of the formidable adventurer.

CHAPTER II.

Adrian once more the Guest of Montreal.

MONTREAL was sitting at the head of a table, surrounded by men, some military, some civil, and whom he called his councillors, and with whom he apparently debated all his projects. These men, drawn from various cities, were intimately acquainted with the internal affairs of the several states to which they belonged. They could tell to a fraction the force of a signor, the wealth of a merchant, the power of a mob. And thus, in his lawless camp, Montreal presided, not more as a general than a statesmen. Such knowledge was invaluable to the chief of the Great Company. It enabled him to calculate exactly the time to attack a foe, aud the sum to demand for a suppression of hostilities. He knew what parties to deal with—where to importune—where to forbear. And it usually happened that, by some secret intrigue, the appearance of Montreal's banner before the walls of a city was the signal for some sedition or some broil within. It may be that he thus also promoted an ulterior, as well as his present, policy.

The divan were in full consultation when an officer entered, and whispered a few words in Montreal's ear. His eyes brightened. "Admit him," he said hastily. "Messires," he added to his councillors, rubbing his hands, "I think our net has caught our bird. Let us see."

At this moment the drapery was lifted and the Knight admitted.

"How!" muttered Montreal, changing color, and in evident disappointment. "Am I to be ever thus balked?"

"Sir Walter de Montreal," said the prisoner, "I am once more your guest. In these altered features you perhaps scarcely recognize Adrian di Castello."

"Pardon me, noble Signor," said Montreal, rising with great courtesy: "the mistake of my varlets disturbed my recollection for a moment.—I rejoice once more to press a hand that has won so many laurels since last we parted. Your renown has been grateful to my ears. Ho!" continued the chieftain, clapping his hands, "see to the refreshment and repose of this noble Cavalier and his attendants. Lord Adrian, I will join you presently."

Adrian withdrew. Montreal, forgetful of his councillors, traversed his tent with hasty strides; then summoning the officer who had admitted Adrian, he said, "Count Landau still keeps the pass?"

"Yes, General!"

"Hie thee fast back, then—the ambuscade must tarry till nightfall. We have trapped the wrong fox."

The officer departed, and shortly afterwards Montreal broke up the divan. He sought Adrian, who was lodged in a tent beside his own.

"My Lord," said Montreal, "it is true that my men had orders to stop every one on the roads towards Florence. I am at war with that city. Yet I expected a very different prisoner from you. Need I add, that you and your men are free?"

"I accept the courtesy, noble Montreal, as frankly as it is rendered. May I hope hereafter to repay it? Meanwhile permit me, without any disrespect, to say that had I learned the Grand Company was in this direction, I should have altered my course. I had heard that your arms were bent (somewhat to my mind more nobly) against Malatesta, the tyrant of Rimini!"

"They were so. He *was* my foe; he *is* my tributary. We conquered him. He paid us the price of his liberty. We marched by Asciano upon Sienna. For sixteen thousand florins we spared that city; and we now hang like a thunderbolt over Florence, which dared to send her puny aid to the defence of Rimini. Our marches are forced and rapid and our camp in this plain but just pitched."

"I hear that the Grand Company is allied with Albornoz, and that its General is secretly the soldier of the Church. Is it so?"

"Ay — Albornoz and I understand one another," replied Montreal, carelessly; "and not the less so that we have a mutual foe; whom both are sworn to crush, in Visconti, the archbishop of Milan."

"Visconti! the most potent of the Italian princes. That he has justly incurred the wrath of the Church I know—and I can readily understand that Innocent has revoked the pardon which the intrigues of the Archbishop purchased from Clement VI. But I do not see clearly why Montreal should willingly provoke so dark and terrible a foe."

Montreal smiled sternly. "Know you not," he said, "the vast ambition of that Visconti? By the Holy Sepulchre, he is precisely the enemy my soul leaps to meet! He has a genius worthy to cope with Montreal's. I have made myself master of his secret plans—they are gigantic! In a word, the Archbishop designs the conquest of all Italy. His enormous wealth purchases the corrupt—his dark sagacity ensnares the credulous—his daring valor awes the weak. Every enemy he humbles—every ally he enslaves. This is precisely the Prince whose progress Walter de Montreal must arrest. For this (he said in a whisper as to himself) is precisely the Prince who, if suffered to extend his power, will frustrate the plans and break the force of Walter de Montreal."

Adrian was silent, and for the first time a suspicion of the real nature of the Provençal's designs crossed his breast.

"But, noble Montreal," resumed the Colonna, "give me, if your knowledge serves, as no doubt it does,—give me the latest tidings of my native city. I am Roman, and Rome is ever in my thoughts."

"And well she may," replied Montreal, quickly. "Thou knowest that Albornoz, as Legate of the Pontiff, led the army of the Church into the Papal Territories. He took with him Cola di Rienzi. Arrived at Monte Fiascona, crowds of Romans of all ranks hastened thither to render homage to the Tribune. The Legate was forgotten in the popularity of his companion. Whether or not Albornoz grew jealous—for he is proud as Lucifer,—of the respect paid to the Tribune, or whether he feared the restoration of his power, I cannot tell. But he detained him in his camp, and refused to yield him to all the solicitations and all the deputations of the Romans. Artfully, however, he fulfilled one of the real objects of Rienzi's release. Through his means he formally regained the allegiance of Rome to the Church, and by the attraction of his presence swelled his camp with Roman recruits. Marching to Viterbo, Rienzi distinguished himself greatly in deeds of arms against the tyrant* John di Vico. Nay, he fought as one worthy of belonging to the Grand Company. This increased the zeal of the Romans; and the city disgorged half its inhabitants to attend the person of the bold Tribune. To the entreaties of these worthy citizens (perhaps the very men who had before shut up their darling in St. Angelo) the crafty Legate merely replied, 'Arm against John di Vico—conquer the tyrants of the Territory—re-establish the patrimony of St. Peter, and Rienzi shall then be proclaimed Senator, and return to Rome.'"

"These words inspired the Romans with so great a zeal, that they willingly lent their aid to the Legate. Aquapendente, Bolzena yielded, John di Vico was half reduced and half-terrified into submission, and Gabrielli, the tyrant of Agobbio, has since succumbed. The glory is to the Cardinal, but the merit with Rienzi."

"And now?"

"Albornoz continued to entertain the Senator-Tribune with great splendor and fair words, but not a word about restoring him to Rome. Wearied with this suspense, I have learned by secret intelligence that Rienzi has left the camp, and betaken himself with few attendants to Florence, where he has friends, who will provide him with arms and money to enter Rome."

"Ah then! now I guess," said Adrian, with a half smile, "for whom I was mistaken!"

Montreal blushed slightly. "Fairly conjectured!" said he.

"Meanwhile, at Rome," continued the Provençal—"at Rome, your worthy House, and that of the Orsini, being elected to the supreme power, quarrelled among themselves, and could not keep the authority they had

* Vit. di Col. di Rienzi.

won. Francesco Baroncelli,* a new demagogue, a humbler imitator of Rienzi, rose upon the ruins of the peace broken by the nobles, obtained the title of Tribune, and carried about the very insignia used by his predecessor. But less wise than Rienzi, he took the antipapal party. And the Legate was thus enabled to play the papal demagogue against the usurper. Baroncelli was a weak man, his sons committed every excess in mimicry of the high-born tyrants of Padua and Milan. Virgins violated and matrons dishonored, somewhat contrasted the solemn and majestic decorum of Rienzi's rule;—in fine, Baroncelli fell massacred by the people. And now, if you ask what rules Rome, I answer, 'It is the hope of Rienzi.'"

"A strange man, and various fortunes. What will be the end of both!"

"Swift murder to the first, and eternal fame to the last," answered Montreal, calmly. "Rienzi will be restored; that brave phœnix will wing its way through storm and cloud to its own funeral pyre: I foresee, I compassionate, I admire.—And then," added Montreal, "I look *beyond!*"

"But wherefore feel you so certain that, if restored, Rienzi must fall?"

"Is it not clear to every eye, save his, whose ambition blinds? How can mortal genius, however great, rule that most depraved people by popular means? The Barons—(you know their indomitable ferocity)—wedded to abuse, and loathing every semblance to law; the Barons, humbled for a moment, will watch their occasion, and rise. The people will again desert. Or else, grown wise in one respect by experience, the new Senator will see that popular favor has a loud voice, but a recreant arm. He will, like the Barons, surround himself by foreign swords. A detachment from the Grand Company will be his courtiers; they will be his masters! To pay them the people must be taxed. Then the idol is execrated. No Italian hand can govern these hardy demons of the north; they will mutiny and fall away. A new demagogue wlll lead on the people, and Rienzi will be the victim. Mark my prophecy!"

"And then the '*beyond*' to which you look?"

"Utter prostration of Rome, for new and long ages; God makes not two Rienzis; *or*," said Montreal, proudly, "the infusion of a new life into the worn-out and diseased frame,—the foundation of a new dynasty. Verily, when I look around me, I believe that the Ruler of nations designs the restoration of the South by the irruptions of the North; and that out of the old Franc and Germanic race will be built up the thrones of the future world!"

As Montreal thus spoke, leaning on his great war-sword, with his fair and heroic features—so different, in their frank, bold, fearless expression, from the dark and wily intellect that characterises the lineaments of the South—eloquent at once with enthusiasm and thought—he might have seemed no unfitting representative of the genius of that northern chivalry of which he spake. And Adrian half fancied that he saw before him one of the old Gothic scourges of the Western World.

Their conversation was here interrupted by the sound of a trumpet and presently an officer entering, announced the arrival of ambassadors from Florence.

"Again you must pardon me, noble Adrian," said Montreal, "and let me claim you as my guest at least for to-night. Here you may rest secure, and on parting, my men shall attend you to the frontiers of whatsoever territory you design to visit."

---

* This Baroncelli, who has been introduced to the reader in a former portion of this work, is called by Matteo Villani "a man of vile birth and little learning —he had been a Notary of the Capitol."

In the midst of the armed dissensions between the Barons, which followed the expulsion of Rienzi, Baroncelli contrived to make himself Master of the Capitol, and of what was considered an auxiliary of no common importance—viz., the *Great Bell*, by whose alarum Rienzi had so often summoned to arms the Roman people. Baroncelli was crowned Tribune, clothed in a robe of gold brocade, and invested with the crozier-sceptre of Rienzi. At first, his cruelty against the great took the appearance of protection to the humble; but the excesses of his sons (not exaggerated in the text), and his own brutal but bold ferocity, soon made him execrated by the people, to whom he owed his elevation. He had the folly to declare against the Pope; and this it really was that mainly induced Innocent to restore and oppose to their New Demagogue, the former and more illustrious Tribune. Baroncelli, like Rienzi, was excommunicated; and in his instance, also, the curse of the Church was the immediate cause of his downfall. In attempting flight he was massacred by the mob, December, 1353. Some, however, have maintained that he was slain in combat with Rienzi; and others, by a confusion of dates, have made him succeed to Rienzi on the *death* of the latter.—*Matteo Villani*, lib. iii. cap. 78. *Osservaz. Stor. di Zefirino Re. MS. Vat. Rip. dal Bzovio*, ann. 1353. N. 2.

Adrian, not sorry to see more of a man so celebrated, accepted the invitation.

Left alone, he leaned his head upon his hand, and soon became lost in his reflections.

CHAPTER III.

Faithful and Ill-fated Love.—The Aspirations Survive the Affections.

SINCE that fearful hour in which Adrian Colonna had gazed upon the lifeless form of his adored Irene, the young Roman had undergone the usual vicissitudes of a wandering and adventurous life in those exciting times. His country seemed no longer dear to him. His very rank precluded him from the post he once aspired to take in restoring the liberties of Rome; and he felt that if ever such a revolution could be consummated, it was reserved for one in whose birth and habits the people could feel sympathy and kindred, and who could lift his hand in their behalf without becoming the apostate of his order and the judge of his own House. He had travelled through various courts, and served with renown in various fields. Beloved and honored wheresoever he fixed a temporary home, no change of scene had removed his melancholy—no new ties had chased away the memory of the Lost. In that era of passionate and poetical romance, which Petrarch represented rather than created, Love had already begun to assume a more tender and sacred character than it had hitherto known, it had gradually imbibed the divine spirit which it derives from Christianity, and which associates its sorrows on earth with the visions and hopes of heaven. To him who relies upon immortality, fidelity to the dead is easy; because death cannot extinguish hope, and the soul of the mourner is already half in the world to come. It is an age that desponds of a future life—representing death as an eternal separation—in which, if men grieve awhile for the dead, they hasten to reconcile themselves to the living.

For true is the old aphorism, that love exists not without hope. And all that romantic worship which the Hermit of Vaucluse felt, or feigned, for Laura, found its temple in the desolate heart of Adrian Colonna. He was emphatically the Lover of *his time!* Often as, in his pilgrimage from land to land, he passed the walls of some quiet and lonely convent, he seriously meditated the solemn vows, and internally resolved that the cloister should receive his maturer age. The absence of years had, however, in some degree restored the dimmed and shattered affection for his fatherland, and he desired once more to visit the city in which he had first beheld Irene. "Perhaps," he thought, "time may have wrought some unlooked-for change; and I may yet assist to restore my country."

But with this lingering patriotism no ambition was mingled. In that heated stage of action, in which the desire for power seemed to stir through every breast, and Italy had become the El Dorado of wealth, or the Utopia of empire, to thousands of valiant arms and plotting minds, there was at least one breast that felt the true philosophy of the Hermit. Adrian's nature, though gallant and masculine, was singularly imbued with that elegance of temperament which recoils from rude contact, and to which a lettered and cultivated indolence is the supremest luxury. His education, his experience, and his intellect, had placed him far in advance of his age, and he looked with a high contempt on the coarse villanies and base tricks by which Italian ambition sought its road to power. The rise and fall of Rienzi, who, whatever his failings, was at least the purest and most honorable of the self-raised princes of the age, had conspired to make him despond of the success of noble, as he recoiled from that of selfish aspirations. And the dreamy melancholy which resulted from his ill-starred love, yet more tended to wean him from the stale and hackneyed pursuits of the world. His character was full of beauty and of poetry—not the less so in that it found not a vent for its emotions in the actual occupation of the poet! Pent within, those emotions diffused themselves over all his thoughts and colored his whole soul. Sometimes, in the blessed abstraction of his visions, he pictured to himself the lot he might have chosen had Irene lived, and fate united them—far from the turbulent and vulgar roar of Rome—but amidst some yet unpolluted solitude of the bright Italian soil. Before his eye there rose the lovely landscape—the palace by the borders of the waveless lake—the vineyards in the valley—the dark forests waving from the hill —and that home, the resort and refuge of all the minstrelsy and love of Italy, brightened by the "Lampeggiar dell' angelico riso,"* that makes a paradise in the face we love. Often, seduced by such dreams to complete oblivion of his loss, the young wanderer started from the ideal bliss to behold around him the solitary waste of way—or the moonlit tents of war —or, worse than all, the crowds and revels of a foreign court.

Whether or not such fancies now, for a moment, allured his meditations, conjured up, perhaps, by the name of Irene's brother, which never sounded in his ears but to awaken ten thousand associations, the Colonna remained thoughtful and absorbed, until he was disturbed by his own squire, who, accompanied by Montreal's servitors, ushered in his solitary but ample repast. Flasks of the richest Florentine wines—viands prepared with all the art which, alas, Italy has now lost!—goblets and salvers of gold and silver, prodigally wrought with barbaric gems—attested the princely luxury which reigned in the camp of the the Grand Company. But Adrian saw in all only the spoliation of his degraded country, and felt the splendor almost as an insult. His lonely meal soon concluded, he became impatient of the monotony of his tent; and, tempted by the cool air of descending eve, sauntered carelessly forth. He bent his steps by the side of the brooklet that curved, snakelike and sparkling, by Montreal's tent; and finding a spot somewhat solitary and apart from the warlike tenements around, flung himself by the margin of the stream.

The last rays of the sun quivered on the wave that danced musically over its stony bed; and amidst a little copse on the opposite bank broke the brief and momentary song of such of the bolder habitants of that purple air as the din of the camp had not scared from their green retreat. The clouds lay motionless to the west, in that sky, so darkly and intensely blue, never seen but over the landscapes that a Claude or a Rosa, loved to paint; and dim and delicious rose hues gathered over the gray peaks of the distant Apennines. From afar floated the hum of the camp, broken by the neigh of returning steeds; the blast of an occasional bugle; and, at regular intervals, by the armed tramp of the neighboring sentry. And opposite to the left of the copse—upon a rising ground, matted with reeds, moss, and waving shrubs—were the ruins of some old Etruscan building, whose name had perished, whose very uses were unknown.

The scene was so calm and lovely, as Adrian gazed upon it, that it was scarcely possible tc imagine it at that very hour the haunt of fierce and banded robbers, among most of whom the very soul of man was embruted, and to all of whom murder or rapine made the habitual occupation of life.

Still buried in his reveries, and carelessly dropping stones into the noisy rivulet Adrian was aroused by the sound of steps.

"A fair spot to listen to the lute and the ballads of Provence," said the voice of Montreal, as the Knight of St. John threw himself on the turf beside the young Colonna.

"You retain, then, your ancient love of your national melodies," said Adrian.

"Ay, I have not yet survived *all* my youth," answered Montreal, with a slight sigh. "But somehow or other, the strains that once pleased my fancy now go too directly to my heart. So, though I still welcome jongleur and minstrel, I bid them sing their *newest* conceits. I cannot wish ever again to hear the poetry I heard when *I was young!*"

"Pardon me," said Adrian, with great interest, "but fain would I have dared, though a secret apprehension prevented me hitherto,—fain would I have dared to question you of that lovely lady, with whom, seven years ago, we gazed at moonlight upon the odorous orange-groves and rosy waters of Terracina."

Montreal turned away his face; he laid his hand on Adrian's arm, and murmured, in a deep and hoarse tone, "I am alone now!"

Adrian pressed his hand in silence. He felt no light shock at thus learning the death of one so gentle, so lovely, and so ill-fated.

"The vows of my knighthood," continued Montreal, "which precluded Adeline the rights of wedlock—the shame of her house—the angry grief of her mother—the wild vicissitudes of my life, so exposed to peril—the loss of her son—all preyed silently on her frame. She did not die (die is too harsh a word!), but she drooped away, and glided into heaven. Even as on a summer's morn some soft dream fleets across us, growing less and

* "The splendor of the angel smile—PETRARCH.

less distinct, until it fades, as it were, into light, and we awaken — so faded Adeline's parting spirit, till the daylight of God broke upon it."

Montreal paused a moment, and then resumed: "These thoughts make the boldest of us weak sometimes, and we Provençals are foolish in these matters !—God wot, she was very dear to me !"

The Knight bent down and crossed himself devoutly, his lips muttered a prayer. Strange as it my seem to our more enlightened age, so martial a garb did morality then wear that this man, at whose word towns had blazed and torrents of blood had flowed, neither adjudged himself, nor was adjudged by the majority of his contemporaries, a criminal. His order, half monastic, half warlike, was emblematic of himself. He trampled upon man, yet humbled himself to God; nor had all his acquaintance with the refining scepticism of Italy shaken the sturdy and simple faith of the bold Provençal. So far from recognizing any want of harmony between his calling and his creed, he held that man no true chevalier who was not as devout to the Cross as relentless with the sword.

"And you have no child save the one you lost ?" asked Adrian, when he observed the wonted composure of Montreal once more returning.

"None!" said Montreal, as his brow darkened. "No love-begotten heir of mine will succeed to the fortunes I trust yet to build. Never on earth shall I see upon the face of her child the likeness of Adeline! Yet, at Avignon, I saw a boy I would have claimed; for methought she must have looked her soul into his eyes, they were so like hers! Well, well! the Provence tree hath other branches; and some unborn nephew must be—what? The stars have not yet decided! But ambition is now the only thing in the world left me to love."

"So differently operates the same misfortune upon different characters," thought the Colonna. "To me, crowns became valueless when I could no longer dream of placing them on Irene's brow !"

The similarity of their fates, however, attracted Adrian strongly towards his host; and the two Knights conversed together with more friendship and unreserve than they had hitherto done. At length Montreal said, "By the way, I have not inquired you destination."

"I am bound to Rome," said Adrian; "and the intelligence I have learned from you incites me thitherward yet more eagerly. If Rienzi return, I may mediate successfully, perchance, between the Tribune-Senator and the nobles; and if I find my cousin. young Stefanello, now the head of our house, more tractable than his sires, I shall not despair of conciliating the less powerful Barons. Rome wants repose; and whoever governs, if he govern but with justice, ought to be supported both by prince and plebeian !"

Montreal listened with great attention, and then muttered to himself, "No, it cannot be ?' He mused a little while, shading his brow with his hand, before he said aloud, "To Rome you are bound. Well, we shall meet soon amidst its ruins. Know, by the way, that my object here is already won: these Florentine merchants have acceded to my terms; they have purchased a two years' peace; to-morrow the camp breaks up, and the Grand Company march to Lombardy. There, if my schemes prosper, and the Venetians pay my price, I league the rascals (under Landau, my Lieutenant) with the Sea-City, in defiance of the Visconti, and shall pass my autumn in peace amidst the pomps of Rome."

"Sir Walter de Montreal," said Adrian, "your frankness perhaps makes me presumptuous; but when I hear you talk, like a huxtering trader, of selling alike your friendship and your forbearance; I ask myself, 'Is this the great Knight of St. John; and have men spoken of him fairly, when they assert the sole stain on his laurels to be his avarice ?'

Montreal bit his lip; nevertheless, he answered calmly, "My frankness has brought its own penance, Lord Adrian. However, I cannot wholly leave so honored a guest under an impression which I feel to be plausible, but not just. No, brave Colonna; report wrongs me. I value Gold, for Gold is the Architect of Power ! It fills the camp—it storms the city—it buys the market-place—it raises the palace—it founds the throne. I value Gold, it is the means necessary to my end !"

"And that end——"

"Is—no matter what," said the Knight coldly. "Let us to our tents the dews fall heavily, and the *malaria* floats over these houseless waters."

The pair rose;—yet, fascinated by the beauty of the hour, they lingered for a moment by the brook. The earliest stars shone over its crisping wavelets, and a delicious breeze murmured gently amidst the glossy herbage."

"Thus gazing," said Montreal, softly, "we reverse tne old Medusan fable the poets tell us of, and look and muse ourselves *out* of stone. A little while, and it was the *sunlight* that gilded the wave—it now shines as brightly and glides as gaily beneath the *stars;* even so rolls the stream of time: one luminary succeeds the other equally welcome—equally illumining—equally evanescent!—You see, the poetry of Provence still lives beneath my mail!"

Adrian early sought his couch; but his own thoughts and the sounds of loud mirth that broke from Montreal's tent, where the chief feasted the captains of his band, a revel from which he had the delicacy to excuse the Roman noble, kept the Colonna long awake; and he had scarcely fallen into an unquiet slumber, when yet more discordant sounds again invaded his repose. At the earliest dawn the wide armament was astir—the creaking of cordage—the tramp of men—loud orders and louder oaths—the slow rolling of baggage-wains—and the clank of the armorers, announced the removal of the camp, and the approaching departure of the Grand Company.

Ere Adrian was yet attired, Montreal entered his tent.

"I have appointed," he said, "five score lances under a trusty leader, to occompany you, noble Adrian, to the borders of Romagna; they wait your leisure. In another hour I depart; the on-guard are already in motion."

Adrian would fain have declined the proffered escort; but he saw that it would only offend the pride of the chief. Who soon retired. Hastily Adrian endued his arms—the air of the fresh morning, and the glad sun rising gorgeously from the hills, revived his wearied spirit. He repaired to Montreal's tent, and found him alone, the implements of writing before him, and a triumphant smile upon his countenance.

"Fortune showers new favors on me!" he said, gaily. "Yesterday the Florentines spared me the trouble of a siege: and to-day (even since I last saw you—a few minutes since) puts your new Senator of Rome into my power."

"How! have your bands then arrested Rienzi?"

"Not so—better still! The Tribune changed his plan, and repaired to Perugia, where my brothers now abide—sought them—they have supplied him with money and soldiers enough to brave the perils of the way, and to defy the swords of the Barons. So writes my good brother Arimbaldo, a man of letters, whom the Tribune thinks rightly he has decoyed with old tales of Roman greatness, and mighty promises of grateful advancement. You find me hastily expressing my content at the arrangement. My brothers themselves will accompany the Senator-Tribune to the walls of the Capitol."

"Still, I see not how this places Rienzi in your power."

"No! His soldiers are my creatures—his comrades my brothers—his creditor myself! Let him rule Rome then—the time soon comes when the Vice-Regent must yield to——"

"The Chief of the Grand Company," interrupted Adrian, with a shudder, which the bold Montreal was too engrossed with the unconcealed excitement of his own thoughts to notice. "No, Knight of Provence, basely have we succumbed to domestic tyrants: but never, I trust, will Romans be so vile as to wear the yoke of a foreign usurper."

Montreal looked hard at Adrian, and smiled sternly.

"You mistake me," said he; "and it will be time enough for you to play the Brutus when I assume the Cæsar. Meanwhile we are but host and guest. Let us change the theme."

Nevertheless this, their latter conference, threw a chill over both during the short time the Knights remained together, and they parted with a formality which was ill-suited to their friendly intercourse of the night before. Montreal felt he had incautiously revealed himself, but caution was no part of his character, whenever he found himself at the head of an army, and at the full tide of fortune; and at that moment, so confident was he of the success of his wildest schemes, that he recked little whom he offended, or whom alarmed.

Slowly, with his strange and ferocious escort, Adrian renewed his way. Winding up a steep ascent that led from the plain,—when he reached the summit, the curve in the road showed him the whole army on its march;—the gonfalons waving—the armor flashing in the sun, line after line, like a river of steel, and the whole plain bristling with the array of that moving war;—while the solemn tread of the armed thousands fell subdued and stifled at times by martial and exulting music. As they swept on, Adrian descried at length the stately and towering form of Montreal upon a black charger, distinguished even at that distance from the rest, not more by his gorgeous armor than his lofty stature. So swept he on in the pride of his array—in the flush of his hopes—the head of a mighty armament—the terror of Italy—the hero that was—the monarch that might be!

BOOK NINTH.

THE RETURN.

"Allora la sua venuta fu a Roma sentita; Romani si apparecchiavano a riceverlo con letizia... furo fatti archi trionfali," etc., etc.—*Vita di Col. di Rienzi*, lib. ii. c. 17.

"Then the fame of his coming was felt at Rome; the Romans made ready to receive him with gladness... triumphal arches were erected," etc., etc.—*Life of Cola di Rienzi.*

CHAPTER I.

The Triumphal Entrance.

ALL Rome was astir!—from St. Angelo to the Capitol, windows, balconies, roofs, were crowded with animated thousands. Only here and there, in the sullen quarters of the Colonna, the Orsini, and the Savelli, reigned a death-like solitude and a dreary gloom. In those fortifications, rather than streets, not even the accustomed tread of the barbarian sentinel was heard. The gates closed—the casements barred—the grim silence around—attested the absence of the Barons. They had left the city so soon as they had learned the certain approach of Rienzi. In the villages and castles of the Campagna, surrounded by their mercenaries, they awaited the hour when the people, weary of their idol, should welcome back even those ferocious Iconoclasts.

With these exceptions, all Rome was astir! Triumphal arches of drapery, wrought with gold and silver, raised at every principal vista, were inscribed with mottoes of welcome and rejoicing. At frequent intervals stood youths and maidens, with baskets of flowers and laurels. High above the assembled multitudes—from the proud tower of Hadrian—from the turrets of the Capitol—from the spires of the sacred buildings dedicated to Apostle and to Saint—floated banners as for a victory. Rome once more opened her arms to receive her Tribune!

Mingled with the crowd—disguised by his large mantle—hidden by the pressure of the throng—his person, indeed, forgotten by most—and, in the confusion of the moment, heeded by none—stood Adrian Colonna! He had not been able to conquer his interest for the brother of Irene. Solitary amidst his fellow-citizens, he stood—the only one of the proud race of Colonna who witnessed the triumph of the darling of the people.

"They say he has grown large in his prison," said one of the bystanders; "he was lean enough when he came by day-break out of the Church of St. Angelo!"

"Ay," said another, a litte man with a shrewd, restless eye, "they say truly; I saw him take leave of the Legate."

Every eye was turned to the last speaker; he became at once a personage of importance. "Yes," continued the little man with an elated and pompous air, "as soon, d'ye see, as he had prevailed on Messere Brettone, and Messere Arimbaldo, the brothers of Fra Moreale, to accompany him from Perugia to Monte Fiascone, he went at once to the Legate d'Albornoz, who was standing in the open air conversing with his captains. A crowd followed. I was one of them; and the Tribune nodded at me—ay, that did he!—and so, with his scarlet cloak, and his scarlet cap, he faced the proud Cardinal with a pride greater than his own. 'Monsignore,' said he, 'though you accord me neither money nor arms, to meet the dangers of the road and brave the ambush of the Barons, I am prepared to depart. Senator of Rome, his Holiness hath made me: according to custom, I pray you, Monsignore, forthwith to confirm the rank.' I would you could have seen how the proud Spaniard stared, and blushed, and frowned; but he bit his lip, and said little."

"And confirmed Rienzi Senator?"

"Yes; and blessed him, and bade him depart."

"Senator," said a stalwart but gray-haired giant with folded arms; "I like not a title that has been borne by a patrician. I fear me, in the new title he will forget the old."

"Fie, Cecco del Vecchio, you were always a grumbler!" said a merchant of cloth, whose commodity the ceremonial had put in great request. "Fie!—for my part, I think Senator a less new-fangled title than Tribune. I hope there will be feasting enow, at last. Rome has been long dull. A sad time for trade, I warrant me!"

The artisan grinned scornfully. He was one of those who distinguished between the middle class and the working, and he loathed a merchant as much as he did a noble. "The day wears," said the little man; "he must be here anon. The Senator's lady, and all his train, have gone forth to meet him these two hours."

Scarce were these words uttered, when the crowd to the right swayed restlessly; and presently a horseman rode rapidly through the street. "Way there! Keep back! Way—make way for the Most Illustrious the Senator of Rome!"

The crowd became hushed—then murmuring—then hushed again. From balcony and casement stretched the neck of every gazer. The tramp of steeds was heard at a distance—the sound of clarion and trumpet;—then, gleaming through the distant curve of the streets, was seen the wave of the gonfalons—then, the glitter of spears—and then from the whole multitude, as from one voice, arose the shout,—"He comes! he comes!"

Adrian shrunk yet more backward amongst the throng; and, leaning against the wall of one of the houses, contemplated the approaching pageant.

First came, six abreast, the procession of Roman horsemen who had gone forth to meet the Senator, bearing boughs of olive in their hands; each hundred preceded by banners, inscribed with the words, "Liberty and Peace restored." As these passed the group by Adrian, each more popular citizen of the cavalcade was recognized, and received with loud shouts. By the garb and equipment of the horsemen, Adrian saw that they belonged chiefly to the traders of Rome; a race who, he well knew, unless strangely altered, valued liberty only as a commercial speculation. "A vain support these," thought the Colonna;—"What next?" On, then, came in glittering armor the German mercenaries, hired by the the gold of the Brothers of Provence, in number two hundred and fifty, and previously in the pay of Malatesta of Rimini;—tall, stern, sedate, disciplined,—eyeing the crowd with a look, half of barbarian wonder, half of insolent disdain. No shout of gratulation welcomed these sturdy strangers; it was evident that their aspect cast a chill over the assembly.

"Shame!" growled Cecco del Vecchio, audibly. "Has the people's friend need of the swords which guard an Orsini or a Malatesta?—shame!"

No voice this time silenced the huge malcontent.

"His only real defence against the Barons," thought Adrian, "if he pay them well! But their number is not sufficient?"

Next came two hundred fantassins, or foot-soldiers, of Tuscany, with the corselets and arms of the heavy-armed soldiery—a gallant company, and whose cheerfull looks and familiar bearing appeared to sympathize with the crowd. And in truth they did so,—for they were Tuscans, and therefore lovers of freedom. In them, too, the Romans seemed to recognize natural and legitimate allies,—and there was a general cry of "Vivano i bravi Toscani!"

"Poor defence!" thought the more sagacious Colonna; "the Barons can awe, and the mob corrupt them."

Next came a file of trumpeters and standard-bearers;—and now the sound of the music was drowned by shouts, which seemed to rise simultaneously as from every quarter of the city;—Rienzi! Rienzi!—Welcome, welcome!—Liberty and Rienzi! Rienzi and the Good Estate!" Flowers dropped on his path, kerchiefs and banners waved from every house;—tears might be seen coursing, unheeded, down bearded cheeks;—youth and age were kneeling together, with uplifted hands, invoking blessings on the head of the Restored.

On he came, the Senator-Tribune—"*the Phœnix to his pyre!*"

Robed in scarlet, that literally blazed with gold, his proud head bared in the sun, and bending to the saddle bow, Rienzi passed slowly through the throng. Not in the flush of that hour were visible, on his glorious countenance, the signs of disease and care: the very enlargement of his proportions gave a greater majesty to his mien. Hope sparkled in his eye—triumph and empire sat upon his brow. The crowd could not contain themselves; they pressed forward, each upon each. anxious to catch the glance of his eye, to touch the hem of his robe. He himself was deeply affected by their joy. He halted; with faltering and broken words, he attempted to address them. "I am repaid," he said,—"repaid for all;—may I live to make you happy!"

The crowd parted again—the Senator moved on—again the crowd closed in. Behind the Tribune, to their excited imagination, seemed to move the very goddess of ancient Rome.

Upon a steed, caparisoned with cloth of gold;—in snow-white robes, studded with gems that flashed back the day,—came the beautiful and regal Nina. The memory of her pride, her ostentation, all forgotten in that moment, she was scarce less welcome, scarce less idolized, than her lord. And her smile all radiant with joy—her lip quivering with proud and elate emotion,—never had she seemed at once so born alike for love and for command;—a Zenobia passing through the pomp of Rome,—not a captive, but a queen.

But not upon that stately form riveted the gaze of Adrian—pale, breathless, trembling, he clung to the walls against which he learned. Was it a dream? Had the dead revived? Or was it his own—his living Irene—whose soft and melancholy loveliness shone sadly by the side of Nina—a star beside the moon? The pageant faded from his eyes—all grew dim and dark. For a moment he was insensible. When he recovered, the crowd was hurrying along, confused and blent with the mighty stream that followed the procession. Through the moving multitude he caught the graceful form of Irene, again snatched by the closing standards of the procession from his view. His blood rushed back from his heart through every vein. He was as a man who for years had been in a fearful trance, and who is suddenly awakened to the light of heaven.

One of that mighty throng remained motionless with Adrian. It was Cecco del Vecchio.

"*He did not see me*," muttered the smith to himself; "*old friends are forgotten now!* Well, well, Cecco del Vecchio hates tyrants still—no matter what their name, nor how smoothly they are disguised. He did not see ME! Umph!"

CHAPTER II.

The Masquerade.

THE acute reader has already learned, without the absolute intervention of the author as narrator, the incidents occurring to Rienzi in the interval between his acquittal at Avignon and his return to Rome. As the impression made by Nina upon the softer and better nature of Albornoz died away, he naturally began to consider his guest—as the profound politicians of that day ever considered men—a piece upon the great Chess-Board, to be moved, advanced, or sacrificed, as best suited the scheme in view. His purpose accomplished, in the recovery of the patrimonial territory, the submission of John di Vico, and the fall and death of the Demagogue Baroncelli, the Cardinal deemed it far from advisable to restore to Rome, and with so high a dignity, the able and ambitious Rienzi. Before the daring Roman, even his own great spirit quailed; and he was wholly unable to conceive or to calculate the policy that might be adopted by the new Senator, when once more Lord of Rome. Without affecting to detain, he therefore declined to assist in restoring him.

And Rienzi thus saw himself within an easy march of Rome, without one soldier to protect him against the Barons by the way. But Heaven had decreed that no *single* man, however gifted, or however powerful, should long counteract or master the destinies of Rienzi: and perhaps in no more glittering scene of his life did he evince so dexterous and subtle an intellect as he now did in extricating himself from the wiles of the Cardinal. Repairing to Perugia, he had, as we have seen, procured, through the brothers of Montreal, men and money for his return. But the Knight of St. John was greatly mistaken, if he imagined that Rienzi was not thoroughly aware of the perilous and treacherous tenure of the support he had received. His keen eye read at a glance the aims and the characters of the brothers of Montreal—he knew that while affecting to serve him, they designed to control—that, made the debtor of the grasping and aspiring Montreal, and surrounded by the troops conducted by Montreal's brethren, he was in the midst of a net which, if not broken, would soon involve fortune and life itself in its fatal and deadly meshes. But, confident in the resources and promptitude of his own genius, he yet sanguinely trusted to make those *his* puppets, who dreamed tha he was their own; and, with empire for the stake, he cared not how crafty the antagonists he was compelled to engage.

Meanwhile, uniting to all his rasher and all his nobler qualities, a profound dissimulation, he appeared to trust implicitly to his Provençal companions; and his first act on entering the Capitol, after the triumphal procession, was to reward with the highest dignities in his gift, Messere Arimbaldo and Messere Brettone de Montreal!

High feasting was there that night in the halls of the Capitol; but dearer to Rienzi than all the pomp of the day, were the smiles of Nina. Her proud and admiring eyes, swimming with delicious tears, fixed upon his countenance, she but felt that they were re-united, and that the hours, however brilliantly illumined, were hastening to that moment, when, after so desolate and dark an absence, they might once more be alone.

Far other the thoughts of Adrian Colonna, as he sate alone in the dreary palace in the yet more dreary quarter of his haughty race. Irene then was alive,—he had been deceived by some strange error,—she had escaped the devouring pestilence; and something in the pale sadness of her gentle features, even in that day of triumph, told him he was still remembered. But as his mind by degrees calmed itself from its first wild and tumultuous rapture, he could not help asking himself the question whether they were not still to be divided! Stefanello Colonna, the grandson of the old Stephen, and (by the death of his sire and brother) the youthful head of that powerful House, had already raised his standard against the Senator. Fortifying himself in the almost impregnable fastness of Palestrina, he had assembled around him all the retainers of his family, and his lawless soldiery now ravaged the neighboring plains far and wide.

Adrian foresaw that the lapse of a few days would suffice to bring the Colonna and the Senator to open war. Could he take part against those of his own blood? The very circumstance of his love for Irene would yet more rob such a proceeding of all appearance of disinterested patriotism, and yet more deeply and irremediably stain his knightly fame, wherever the sympathy of his equals was enlisted with the cause of the Colonna. On the other hand, not only his love for the Senator's sister, but his own secret inclinations and honest convictions, were on the side of one who alone seemed to him possessed of the desire and the genius to repress the disorders of his fallen city. Long meditating, he feared no alternative was left him but in the same cruel neutrality to which he had been before condemned; but he resolved at least to make the attempt—rendered favorable and dignified by his birth and reputation—to reconcile the contending parties. To effect this, he saw that he must begin with his haughty cousin. He was well aware that were it known that he had first obtained an interview with Rienzi—did it appear as if he were charged with overtures from the Senator—although Stefanello himself might be inclined to yield to his representations, the insolent and ferocious Barons who surrounded him would not deign to listen to the envoy of the People's chosen one; and instead of being honored as an intercessor, he should be suspected as a traitor. He determined, then, to depart for Palestrina; but (and his heart beat audibly) would it not be possible first to obtain an interview with Irene? It was no easy enterprise, surrounded as she was, but he resolved to adventure it. He summoned Giulio.

"The Senator holds a festival this evening—think you that the assemblage will be numerons?"

"I hear," answered Giulio, "that the banquet given to the Ambassadors and Signors to-day is to be followed to-morrow by a mask, to which all ranks are admitted. By Bacchus,*

* Still a common Roman expletive.

if the Tribune only invited nobles, the smallest closet in the Capitol would suffice to receive his maskers. I suppose a mask has been resolved on in order to disguise the quality of the visitors."

Adrian mused a moment; and the result of his revery was a determination to delay for another sun his departure to Palestrina—to take advantage of the nature of the revel, and to join the masquerade.

That species of entertainment, though unusual at that season of the year, had been preferred by Rienzi, partly and ostensibly because it was one in which all his numerous and motley supporters could be best received; but chiefly and secretly because it afforded himself and his confidential friends the occasion to mix unsuspected amongst the throng, and learn more of the real anticipation of the Romans with respect to his policy and his strength, than could well be gathered from the enthusiasm of a public spectacle.

The following night was beautifully serene and clear. The better to accommodate the numerous guests, and to take advantage of the warm and moonlit freshness of the air, the open court of the Capitol, with the Place of the Lion, (as well as the state apartments within,) was devoted to the festival.

As Adrian entered the festive court with the rush of the throng, it chanced that in the eager impatience of some maskers, more vehement than the rest, his vizard was deranged. He hastily replaced it; but not before one of the guests had recognized his countenance.

From courtesy, Rienzi and his family remained at first unmasked. They stood at the head of the stairs to which the old Egyptian Lion gave the name. The lights shone over that Colossal Monument—which, torn from its antique home, had witnessed, in its grim repose, the rise and lapse of countless generations, and the dark and stormy revolutions of avenging fate. It was an ill omen, often afterwards remarked, that the place of that state festival was the place also of the state executions. But at that moment, as group after group pressed forward to win smile and word from the celebrated man, whose fortunes had been the theme of Europe, or to bend in homage to the lustrious loveliness of Nina, no omen and no warning clouded the universal gladness.

Behind Nina, well contented to shrink from the gaze of the throng, and to feel her softer beauty eclipsed by the dazzling and gorgeous charms of her brother's wife, stood Irene. Amidst the crowd on her alone Adrian fixed his eyes. The years which had flown over the fair brow of the girl of sixteen—then animated by, yet trembling beneath, the first wild breath of Love;—youth in every vein—passion and childish tenderness in every thought, had not marred, but they had changed, the character of Irene's beauty. Her cheek, no longer varying with every instant, was settled into a delicate and thoughtful paleness—her form more rounded to the proportions of Roman beauty, had assumed an air of dignified and calm repose. No longer did the restless eye wander in search of some imagined object; no longer did the lip quiver into smiles at some untold hope or half-unconscious recollection. A grave and mournful expression gave to her face (still how sweet!) a gravity beyond her years. The bloom, the flush, the April of the heart, was gone; but yet neither time, nor sorrow, nor blighted love, had stolen from her countenance its rare and angelic softness—nor that inexpressible and virgin modesty of form and aspect, which, contrasting the bolder beauties of Italy, had more than aught else distinguished to Adrian, from all other women, the idol of his heart. And feeding his gaze upon those dark deep eyes, which spoke of thought far away and busy with the past, Adrian felt again and again that he was not forgotten! Hovering near her, but suffering the crowd to press one after another before him, he did not perceive that he had attracted the eagle eye of the Senator.

In fact, as one of the maskers passed Rienzi, he whispered, "Beware, a Colonna is among the masks! beneath the reveller's domino has often lurked the assassin's dagger. Yonder stands your foe—mark him!"

These words were the first sharp and thrilling intimation of the perils into which he had rushed, that the Tribune-Senator had received since his return. He changed color slightly; and for some minutes the courtly smile and ready greeting with which he had hitherto delighted every guest, gave way to a moody abstraction.

"Why stands yon strange man so mute and

motionless?" whispered he to Nina. "He speaks to none—he approaches us not—a churl, a churl!—he must be seen to."

"Doubtless, some German or English barbarian," answered Nina. "Let not, my Lord, so slight a cloud dim your merriment."

"You are right, dearest; we have friends here; we are well girt. And, by my father's ashes, I feel that I must accustom myself to danger. Nina, let us move on; methinks we might now mix among the maskers—masked ourselves."

The music played loud and cheerily as the Senator and his party mingled with the throng.

But still his eye turned ever towards the gray domino of Adrian, and he perceived that it followed his steps. Approaching the private entrance of the Capitol, he for a few moments lost sight of his unwelcome pursuer: but just as he entered, turning abruptly, Rienzi perceived him close at his side—the next moment the stranger had vanished amidst the throng. But that moment had sufficed to Adrian—he had reached Irene. "Adrian Colonna (he whispered) waits thee beside the Lion."

In absorption of his own reflections, Rienzi fortunately did not notice the sudden paleness and agitation of his sister. Entered within his palace, he called for wine—the draught revived his spirits—he listened smilingly to the sparkling remarks of Nina; and enduing his mask and disguise, said, with his wonted cheerfulness, "Now for Truth—strange that in festivals it should only speak behind a vizard! My sweet sister, thou hast lost thine old smile, and I would rather see that than—Ha! has Irene vanished?"

"Only, I suppose, to change her dress, my Cola, and mingle with the revellers," answered Nina. "Let my smile atone for hers."

Rienzi kissed the bright brow of his wife as she clung fondly to his bosom. "Thy smile is the sunlight," said he; "but this girl disturbs me. Methinks *now* at least, she might wear a gladder aspect

"Is there nothing of love beneath my fair sister's gloom?" answered Nina. "Do you not call to mind how she loved Adrian Colonna?"

"Does that fantasy hold still?" returned Rienzi, musingly. "Well, and she is fit bride for a monarch."

"Yet it were an alliance that would, better than one with monarchs, strengthen thy power at Rome!"

"Ay, were it possible; but that haughty race!—Perchance this very masker that so haunted our steps was but her lover. I will look to this. Let us forth, my Nina. Am I well cloaked?"

"Excellently well—and I?"

"The sun behind a cloud."

"Ah, let us not tarry long; what hour of revel like that when thy hand in mine, this head upon thy bosom, we forget the sorrows we have known, and even the triumphs we have shared?"

Meanwhile, Irene, confused and lost amidst a transport of emotion, already disguised and masked, was threading her way through the crowd back to the staircase of the Lion. With the absence of the Senator that spot had comparatively been deserted. Music and the dance attracted the maskers to another quarter of the wide space. And Irene now approaching, beheld the moonlight fall over the statue, and a solitary figure leaning against the pedestal. She paused, the figure approached, and again she heard the voice of her early love.

"Oh, Irene! recognized even in this disguise," said Adrian, seizing her trembling hand; "have I lived to gaze again upon that form—to touch this hand? Did not these eyes behold thee lifeless in that fearful vault, which I shudder to recall? By what miracle wert thou raised again? By what means did Heaven spare to this earth one that it seemed already to have placed amongst its angels?"

"Was this, indeed, thy belief?" said Irene, falteringly, but with an accent eloquent of joy. "Thou didst not then willingly desert me? Unjust that I was, I wronged thy noble nature, and deemed that my brother's fall, my humble lineage, thy brilliant fate, had made thee renounce Irene."

"Unjust indeed!" answered the lover. "But surely I saw thee amongst the dead!—thy cloak, with the silver stars—who else wore the arms of the Roman Tribune?"

"Was it but that cloak then, which, dropped in the streets, was probably assumed by some more ill-fated victim; was it *that* sight alone, that made thee so soon despair? Ah! Adrian," continued Irene, tenderly, but with reproach; "not even when I saw *thee* seemingly lifeless on the couch by which I had watched three days and nights, not even then did *I* despair!"

"What, then, my vision did not deceive me! It was you who watched by my bed in that grim hour, whose love guarded, whose care preserved me! And I, wretch that I was!——"

"Nay," answered Irene, "your thought was natural. Heaven seemed to endow me with superhuman strength, whilst I was necessary to thee. But judge of my dismay. I left thee to seek the good friar who attended thee as thy leech; I returned, and found thee not. Heart-sick and terrified, I searched the desolate city in vain. Strong as I was while hope supported me, I sunk beneath fear.—And my brother found me senseless, and stretched on the ground, by the church of St. Mark."

"The church of St. Mark!—so foretold his dream!"

"He had told me he had met thee; we searched for thee in vain; at length we heard that thou hadst left the city, and—and—I rejoiced, Adrian, but I repined!"

For some minutes the young lovers surrendered themselves to the delight of reunion, while new explanations carried forth new transports.

"And now," murmured Irene, "now that we have met——" she paused, and her mask concealed her blushes.

"Now that we have met," said Adrian, filling up the silence, "wouldst thou say further, 'that we should not part?' Trust me, dearest, that is the hope that animates my heart. It was but to enjoy these brief bright moments with thee, that I delayed my departure to Palestrina. Could I but hope to bring my young cousin into amity with thy brother, no barrier would prevent our union. Willingly I forget the past—the death of my unhappy kinsmen, (victims, it is true, to their own faults;) and, perhaps, amidst all the crowds that hailed his return, none more appeciated the great and lofty qualities of Cola di Rienzi, than did Adrian Colonna."

"If this be so," said Irene, "let me hope the best; meanwhile, it is enough of comfort and of happiness to know, that we love each other as of old. Ah, Adrian, I am sadly changed; and often have I thought it a thing beyond my dreams, that thou shouldst see me again and love me still."

"Fairer art thou and lovelier than ever," answered Adrian, passionately; "and time, which has ripened thy bloom, has taught me more deeply to feel thy value. Farewell, Irene, I linger here no longer; thou wilt, I trust, hear soon of my success with my House, and ere the week be over I may return to claim thy hand in the face of day."

The lovers parted; Adrian lingered on the spot, and Irene hastened to bury her emotion and her raptures in her own slumber.

As her form vanished, and the young Colonna slowly turned away, a tall mask strode abruptly towards him.

"Thou art a Colonna," it said, "and in the power of the Senator. Dost thou tremble?"

"If I be a Colonna, rude masker," answered Adrian, coldly, "thou shouldst know the old proverb, 'He who stirs the column, shall rue the fall.'"

The stranger laughed aloud, and then lifting his mask, Adrian saw that it was the Senator who stood before him.

"My Lord Adrian di Castello," said Rienzi, resuming all his gravity, "is it as friend or foe that you have honored our revels this night?"

"Senator of Rome," answered Adrian, with equal stateliness, "I partake of no man's hospitality but as a friend. A foe, at least to you, I trust never justly to be esteemed."

"I would," rejoined Rienzi, "that I could apply to myself unreservedly that most flattering speech. Are these friendly feelings entertained towards me as the governor of the Roman people, or as the brother of the woman who has listened to to your vows?"

Adrian, who when the Senator had unmasked had followed his example, felt at these words that his eye quailed beneath Rienzi's. However, he recovered himself with the wonted readiness of an Italian, and replied laconically.

"As both."

"Both!" echoed Rienzi. "Then, indeed, noble Adrian, you are welcome hither. And yet, methinks, if you conceived there was no cause for enmity between us, you would have wooed the sister of Cola di Rienzi in a guise more worthy of your birth; and, permit me to add, of that station which God, destiny, and my country, have accorded unto *me*. You dare not, young Colonna, meditate dishonor to the sister of the Senator of Rome. High-born as you are, she is your equal."

"Were I the Emperor, whose simple knight I but am, your sister were my equal," answered Adrian, warmly. "Rienzi, I grieve that I am discovered to you yet. I had trusted that, as a mediator between the Barons and yourself, I might first have won your confidence, and then claimed my reward. Know that with to-morrow's dawn I depart for Palestrina, seeking to reconcile my young cousin to the choice of the People and the Pontiff. Various reasons, which I need not now detail, would have made me wish to undertake this heraldry of peace without previous communication with you. But since we *have* met, intrust me with any terms of conciliation, and I pledge you the right hand, not of a Roman noble—alas! the *prisca fides* has departed from that pledge!—but of a Knight of the Imperial Court, that I will not betray your confidence."

Rienzi, accustomed to read the human countenance, had kept his eyes intently fixed upon Adrian while he spoke; when the Colonna concluded, he pressed the proffered hand, and said, with that familiar and winning sweetness which at times was so peculiar to his manner.

"I trust you, Adrian, from my soul. You were mine early friend in calmer, perchance happier, years. And never did river reflect the stars more clearly, than your heart then mirrored back the truth. I trust you!"

While thus speaking, he had mechanically led back the Colonna to the statue of the Lion; there pausing, he resumed:

"Know that I have this morning despatched my delegate to your cousin Stefanello. With all due courtesy, I have apprised him of my return to Rome, and invited hither his honored presence. Forgetting all ancient feuds, mine own past exile, I have assured him, here, the station and dignity due to the head of the Colonna. All that I ask in return is obedience to the law. Years and reverses have abated my younger pride, and though I may yet preserve the sternness of the Judge, none shall hereafter complain of the insolence of the Tribune."

"I would," answered Adrian, "that your mission to Stefanello had been delayed a day; I would fain have forestalled its purport. Howbeit, you increase my desire of departure, should I yet succeed in obtaining an honorable and peaceful reconciliation, it is not in disguise that I will woo your sister."

"And never did Colonna," replied Rienzi, loftily, "bring to his House a maiden whose alliance more gratified ambition. I still see, as I have seen ever, in mine own projects, and mine own destinies, the chart of the new Roman Empire!"

"Be not too sanguine yet, brave Rienzi," replied Adrian, laying his hand on the Lion of Basalt: "bethink thee on how many scheming brains this dumb image of stone hath looked down from its pedestal—schemes of sand, and schemers of dust. Thou hast enough, at present, for the employ of all thine energy—not to extend thy power, but to preserve thyself. For, trust me, never stood human greatness on so wild and dark a precipice!"

"Thou art honest," said the Senator; "and these are the first words of doubt, and yet of sympathy, I have heard in Rome. But the People love me, the Barons have fled from Rome, the Pontiff approves, and the swords of the Northmen guard the avenues of the Capitol. But these are nought; in mine own honesty are my spear and buckler. Oh, never," continued Rienzi, kindling with his enthusiasm, "never since the days of the old Republic, did Roman dream a purer and brighter aspiration, than that which animates and supports me now. Peace restored—law established—art, letters, intellect, dawning upon the night of time; the Patricians, no longer bandits of rapine, but the guard of order; the People ennobled from a mob, brave to protect, enlightened to guide, themselves. Then, not by the violence of arms, but by the majesty of her moral power, shall the Mother of Nations claim the obedience of her children. Thus dreaming and thus hoping, shall I tremble or despond? No, Adrian Colonna, come weal or woe, I abide, unshrinking and unawed, by the chances of my doom!"

So much did the manner and the tone of the Senator exalt his language, that even the sober sense of Adrian was enchanted and subdued. He kissed the hand he held, and said earnestly,

"A doom that I will deem it my boast to share—a career that it will be my glory to sooth. If I succeed in my present mission——"

"You are my brother!" said Rienzi.

"If I fail?"

"You may equally claim that alliance. You pause—you change color."

"Can I desert my house?"

"Young Lord," said Rienzi, loftily, "say rather can you desert your country? If you doubt my honesty, if you fear my ambition, desist from your task, rob me not of a single foe. But if you believe that I have the will and the power to serve the State—if you recognize, even in the reverses and calamities I have known and mastered, the protecting hand of the Saviour of Nations—if those reverses were but the mercies of Him who chasteneth—necessary, it may be, to correct my earlier daring and sharpen yet more my intellect—if, in a word, thou believest me one whom, whatever be his faults, God hath preserved for the sake of Rome, forget that you are a Colonna—remember only that you are a Roman!"

"You have conquered me, strange and commanding spirit," said Adrian, in a low voice, completely carried away; "and whatever the conduct of my kindred, I am yours and Rome's. Farewell."

CHAPTER III.

Adrian's Adventures at Palestrina.

It was yet noon when Adrian beheld before him the lofty mountains that shelter Palestrina, the *Præneste* of the ancient world. Back to a period before Romulus existed, in the earliest ages of that mysterious civilization which in Italy preceded the birth of Rome, could be traced the existence and the power of that rocky city. Eight dependent towns owned its sway and its wealth; its position, and the strength of those mighty walls, in whose ruins may yet be traced the masonry of the remote Pelasgi, had long braved the ambition of the neighboring Rome. From that very citadel, the Mural Crown* of the mountain, had waved the standard of Marius; and up the road which Adrian's scanty troop slowly wound, had echoed the march of the murtherous Sylla, on his return from the Mithridatic war. Below, where the city spread towards the plain, were yet seen the shattered and roofless columns of the once celebrated Temple of Fortune; and still the immemorial olives clustered gray and mournfully around the ruins.

A more formidable hold the Barons of Rome could not have selected; and as Adrian's military eye scanned the steep ascent and the rugged walls, he felt that with ordinary skill it might defy for months all the power of the Roman Senator. Below, in the fertile valley, dismantled cottages and trampled harvests attested the violence and rapine of the insurgent Barons; at that very moment were seen, in the old plain of the warlike Hernici, troops of armed men, driving before them herds of sheep and cattle, collected in their lawless incursions. In sight of that *Præneste*, which had been the favorite retreat of the luxurious Lords of Rome in its most polished day, the Age of Iron seemed renewed.

The banner of the Colonna, borne by Adrian's troop, obtained ready admittance at the Porta del Sole. As he passed up the irregular and narrow streets that ascended to the citadel, groups of foreign mercenaries,—half-ragged, half-tawdry knots of abandoned women,—mixed here and there with the liveries of the Colonna, stood loitering amidst the ruins of ancient fanes and palaces, or basked lazily in the sun, upon terraces, through which, from amidst weeds and grass, glowed the imperishable hues of the rich mosaics, which had made the pride of that lettered and graceful nobility, of whom savage freebooters were now the heirs.

The contrast between the Past and Present forcibly occurred to Adrian, as he passed along; and, despite his order, he felt as if Civilization itself were enlisted against his House upon the side of Rienzi.

Leaving his train in the court of the citadel, Adrian demanded admission to the presence of his cousin. He had left Stefanello a child on his departure from Rome, and there could therefore be but a slight and unfamiliar acquaintance betwixt them, despite their kindred.

Peals of laughter came upon his ear, as he followed one of Stefanello's gentlemen through

* Hence, apparently, its Greek name of Stephane. Palestrina is yet one of the many proofs which the vicinity of Rome affords of the old Greek civilization of Italy.

a winding passage that led to the principal chamber. The door was thrown open, and Adrian found himself in a rude hall, to which some appearance of hasty state and attempted comfort had been given. Costly arras imperfectly clothed the stone walls, and the rich seats and decorated tables, which the growing civilization of the northern cities of Italy had already introduced into the palaces of Italian nobles, strangely contrasted the rough pavement, spread with heaps of armor negligently piled around. At the farther end of the apartment, Adrian shudderingly perceived, set in due and exact order, the implements of torture.

Stefanello Colonna, with two other Barons indolently reclined on seats drawn around a table, in the recess of a deep casement, from which might still be seen the same glorious landscape, bounded by the dim spires of Rome, which Hannibal and Pyrrhus had ascended that very citadel to survey!

Stefanello himself, in the first bloom of youth, bore already on his beardless countenance those traces usaully the work of the passions and vices of maturest manhood. His features were cast in the mould of the old Stephen's; in their clear, sharp, high bred outline might be noticed that regular and graceful symmetry, which blood, in men as in animals, will sometimes entail through generations; but the features were wasted and meagre. His brows were knit as in an eternal frown; his thin and bloodless lips wore that insolent contempt which seems so peculiarly cold and unlovely in early youth; and the deep and livid hollows round his eyes spoke of habitual excess and premature exhaustion. By him sat (reconciled by hatred to one another) the hereditary foes of his race; the soft, but cunning and astute features of Luca di Savelli, contrasted with the broad frame and ferocious countenance of the Prince of the Orsini.

The young head of the Colonna rose with some cordiality to receive his cousin. "Welcome," he said, "dear Adrian; you are arrived in time to assist us with your well-known military skill. Think you not we shall stand a long siege, if the insolent plebeian dare adventure it? You know our friends, the Orsini and the Savelli? Thanks to St. Peter, or Peter's delegate, we have now happily meaner throats to cut than those of each other!"

Thus saying, Stefanello again threw himself listlessly on his seat, and the shrill, woman's voice of Savelli took part in the dialogue.

"I would, noble Signor, that you had come a few hours earlier: we are still making merry at the recollection—he, he, he!"

"Ah, excellent," cried Stefanello, joining in the laugh; "our cousin has had a loss. Know Adrian, that this base fellow, whom the Pope has had the impudence to create Senator, dared but yesterday to send us a varlet, whom he called—by our Lady!—his *ambassador!*"

"Would you could have seen his mantle, Signor Adrian!" chimed in Savelli; "purple velvet, as I live, decorated in gold, with the arms of Rome: we soon spoiled his finery.

"What!" exclaimed Adrian, "you did not break the laws of all nobility and knighthood?—you offered no insult to a herald!"

"Herald," sayest thou!" cried Stefanello, frowning till his eyes were scarce visible. "It is for Princes and Barons alone to employ heralds. An' I had had my will, I would have sent back the minion's head to the usurper."

"What did ye then?" asked Adrian, coldly.

"Bade our swineherds dip the fellow in the ditch, and gave him a night's lodging in a dungeon to dry himself withal."

"And this morning—he, he, he!" added the Savelli, "we had him before us, and drew his teeth, one by one;—I would you could have heard the fellow mumble out for mercy!"

Adrian rose hastily, and struck the table fiercely with his gauntlet.

"Stefanello Colonna," said he, coloring with noble rage, "answer me: did you dare to inflict this indelible disgrace upon the name we jointly bear? Tell me at least, that you protested against this foul treason to all the laws of civilization and of honor. You answer not. House of the Colonna, can such be thy representative!"

"To me these words!" said Stefanello, trembling with passion. "Beware! Methinks *thou* art the traitor, leagued perhaps with yon rascal mob. Well do I remember that thou, the betrothed of the Demagogue's sister, didst not join with my uncle and my father of old, but didst basely leave the city to her plebeian tyrant."

"That did he!" said the fierce Orsini, approaching Adrian menacingly, while the gentle cowardice of Savelli sought in vain to pluck him back by the mantle—"that did he! and but for thy presence, Stefanello——"

"Coward and blusterer!" interrupted Adrian, fairly beside himself with indignation and shame, and dashing his gauntlet in the very face of the advancing Orsini—"wouldst thou threaten one who has maintained, in every list of Europe, and against the stoutest Chivalry of the North, the honor of Rome, which thy deeds the while disgraced? By this gage, I spit upon and defy thee. With lance and with brand, on horse and on foot, I maintain against thee and all thy line, that thou art no knight to have thus maltreated, in thy strongholds, a peaceful and unarmed herald. Yes, even here, on the spot of thy disgrace, I challenge thee to arms!"

"To the court below! Follow me," said Orsini, sullenly, and striding towards the threshold. "What, ho there! my helmet and breast-plate!"

"Stay, noble Orsini," said Stefanello. "The insult offered to thee is my quarrel—mine was the deed—and against me speaks this degenerate scion of our line. Adrian di Castello—sometimes called Colonna—surrender your sword: you are my prisoner!"

"Oh!" said Adrian, grinding his teeth, "that my ancestral blood did not flow through thy veins—else—but enough! Me! your equal, and the favored Knight of the Emperor, whose advent now brightens the frontiers of Italy!—me—you dare not detain. For your friends, I shall meet them yet perhaps, ere many days are over, where none shall separate our swords. Till then, remember, Orsini, that it is against no unpractised arm that thou wilt have to redeem thine honor!"

Adrian, his drawn sword in his hand, strode towards the door, and passed the Orsini, who stood, lowering and irresolute, in the centre of the apartment.

Savelli whispered Stefanello. "He says, 'Ere many days be past!' Be sure, dear Signor, that he goes to join Rienzi. Remember the alliance he once sought with the Tribune's sister may be renewed. Beware of him! Ought he to leave the castle? The name of a Colonna, associated with the mob, would distract and divide half our strength."

"Fear me not," returned Stefanello, with a malignant smile. "Ere you spoke, I had determined!"

The young Colonna lifted the arras from the wall, opened a door, and passed into a low hall, in which sate twenty mercenaries.

"Quick!" said he. "Seize and disarm yon stranger in the green mantle—but slay him not. Bid the guard below find dungeons for his train. Quick! ere he reach the gate."

Adrian had gained the open hall below—his train and steed were in sight in the court—when suddenly the soldiers of the Colonna, rushing through another passage than that which he had passed, surrounded and interrupted his retreat.

"Yield thee, Adrian di Castello," cried Stefanello from the summit of the stairs; "or your blood be on your own head."

Three steps did Adrian make through the press, and three of his enemies fell beneath his sword. "To the rescue!" he shouted to his band, and already these bold and daring troopers had gained the hall. Presently the alarm bell tolled loud—the court swarmed with soldiers. Oppressed by numbers, beat down rather than subdued, Adrian's little train was soon secured, and the flower of the Colonna, wounded, breathless, disarmed, but still uttering loud defiance, was a prisoner in the fortress of his kinsman.

CHAPTER IV.

The Position of the Senator.—The Work of Years.—The Rewards of Ambition.

THE indignation of Rienzi may readily be conceived, on the return of his herald mutilated and dishonored. His temper, so naturally stern, was rendered yet more hard by the remembrance of his wrongs and trials; and the result which attended his overtures of conciliation to Stefanello Colonna stung him to the soul.

The bell of the Capitol tolled to arms within ten minutes after the return of the herald. The great gonfalon of Rome was unfurled on the highest tower; and the very evening after Adrian's arrest, the forces of the Senator, headed by Rienzi in person, were on the road to Palestrina. The troopers of the Barons had, however, made incursions as far as Tivoli with the supposed connivance of the inhabi tants, and Rienzi halted at that beautiful spot to raise recruits, and receive the allegiance of the suspected, while his soldiers with Arimbaldo and Brettone at their head, went in search of the marauders. The brothers of Montreal returned late at night with the intelligence, that the troopers of the Barons had secured themselves amidst the recesses of the wood of Pantano.

The red spot mounted to Rienzi's brow. He gazed hard at Brettone, who stated the news to him, and a natural suspicion shot across his mind.

"How!—escaped!" he said. "Is it possible? Enough of such idle skirmishes with these lordly robbers. Will the hour ever come when I shall meet them hand to hand? Brettone," and the brother of Montreal felt the dark eye of Rienzi pierce to his very heart; "Brettone!" said he, with an abrupt change of voice, "are your men to be *trusted?* Is there no connivance with the Barons?"

"How!" said Brettone, sullenly, but somewhat confused.

"How me no hows!" quoth the Tribune-Senator, fiercely. "I know that thou art a valiant Captain of valiant men. Thou and thy brother Arimbaldo have served me well, and I have rewarded ye well! Have I not! Speak!"

"Senator," answered Arimbaldo, taking up the word, "you have kept your word to us. You have raised us to the highest rank your power could bestow, and this has amply atoned our humble services."

"I am glad ye allow thus much," said the Tribune.

Arimbaldo proceeded somewhat more loftily "I trust, my Lord, you do not doubt us?"

"Arimbaldo," replied Rienzi, in a voice of deep, but half-suppressed emotion; "you are a lettered man, and you have seemed to share my projects for the regeneration of our common kind. *You* ought not to betray me. There is something in unison between *us.* But, chide me not, I am surrounded by treason, and the very air I breathe seems poison to my lips."

There was a pathos mingled with Rienzi's words which touched the milder brother of Montreal. He bowed in silence. Rienzi surveyed him wistfully, and sighed. Then, changing the conversation, he spoke of their intended siege of Palestrina, and shortly afterwards retired to rest.

Left alone, the brothers regarded each other for some moments in silence. "Brettone," said Arimbaldo at length, in a whispered voice, "my heart misgives me. I like not Walter's ambitious schemes. With our own countrymen we are frank and loyal, why play the traitor with this high-souled Roman?" *

"Tush!" said Brettone. "Our brother's hand of iron alone can sway this turbulent people; and if Rienzi be betrayed, so also are his enemies, the Barons. No more of this! I have tidings from Montreal; he will be in Rome in a few days."

"And then?"

"Rienzi, weakened by the Barons (for he must not conquer)—the Barons, weakened by Rienzi—our Northmen seize the Capitol, and the soldiery, now scattered throughout Italy, will fly to the standard of the Great Captain. Montreal must be first Podesta, then King, of Rome."

Arimbaldo moved restlessly in his seat, and the brethren conferred no more on their projects.

The situation of Rienzi was precisely that which tends the most to sour and to harden the fairest nature. With an intellect capable of the grandest designs, a heart that beat with the loftiest emotions, elevated to the sunny pinnacle of power and surrounded by loud-tongued adulators, he knew not among men a single breast in which he could confide. He was as one on a steep ascent, whose footing crumbles, while every bough at which he grasps seems to rot at his touch. He found the people more than ever eloquent in his favor, but while they shouted raptures as he passed, not a man was capable of *making a sacrifice for him!* The liberty of a state is never achieved by a single individual; if not the people—if not the greater number—a zealous and fervent minority, at least, must go hand in hand with him. Rome demanded sacrifices in all who sought the Roman regeneration—sacrifices of time, ease, and money. The crowd fol-

---

* The anonymous biographer of Rienzi makes the following just remark: "Sono li tedeschi, come discendon de la Alemagna, semplici, puri, senza fraude, come si allocano tra' taliani, diventano mastri coduti, viziosi, che sentono ogni malizia."—*Vit. de Col. di Rienzi*, lib. ii. cap. 16.

lowed the procession of the Senator, but not a single Roman devoted his life, *unpaid*, to his standard; not a single coin was subscribed in the defence of freedom. Against him were arrayed the most powerful and the most ferocious Barons of Italy; each of whom could maintain, at his own cost, a little army of practised warriors. With Rienzi were traders and artificers, who were willing to enjoy the fruits of liberty, but not to labor at the soil; who demanded, in return for empty shouts, peace and riches; and who expected that one man was to effect in a day what would be cheaply purchased by the struggle of a generation. All their dark and rude notion of a reformed state was to live unbutchered by the Barons and untaxed by their governors. Rome, I say, gave to her Senator not a free arm, nor a voluntary florin. * Well aware of the danger which surrounds the ruler who defends his state by foreign swords, the fondest wish, and the most visionary dream of Rienzi, was to revive amongst his Romans, in their first enthusiasm at his return, an organized and voluntary force, who, in protecting him, would protect themselves:—not, as before, in his first power, a *nominal* force of twenty thousand men, who at any hour might yield (as they did yield) to one hundred and fifty; but a regular, well disciplined, and trusty body, numerous enough to resist aggression, not numerous enough to become themselves the aggressors.

Hitherto all his private endeavors, his public exhortations, had failed; the crowd listened shouted—saw him quit the city to meet their tyrants, and retured to their shops saying to each other, "What a great man!"

The character of Rienzi has chiefly received for its judges men of the closet, who speculate upon human beings as if they were machines; who gauge the great, not by their merit, but their success; and who have censured or sneered at the Tribune, where they should have condemned the People! Had but one-half the spirit been found in Rome which ran through a single vein of Cola di Rienzi, the august Republic, if not the majestic empire, of Rome, might be existing now! Turning from the people, the Senator saw his rude and savage troops, accustomed to the licence of a tyrant's camp, and under commanders in whom it was ruin really to confide—whom it was equal ruin openly to distrust. Hemned in on every side by dangers, his character daily grew more restless, vigilant, and stern; and still, with all the aims of the patriot, he felt all the curses of the tyrant. Without the rough and hardening career which, through a life of warfare, had brought Cromwell to a similar power—with more of grace and intellectual softness in his composition, he resembled that yet greater man in some points of character—in his religious enthusiasm; his rigid justice, often forced by circumstance into severity, but never wantonly cruel or blood-thirsty; in his singular pride of country; and his mysterious command over the minds of others. But he resembled the giant Englishman far more in circumstance than original nature, and that circumstance assimilated their characters at the close of their several careers. Like Cromwell, beset by secret or open foes, the assassin's dagger ever gleamed before his eyes; and his stout heart, unawed by real, trembled at imagined, terrors. The countenance changing suddenly from red to white—the blood-shot, restless eye, belying the composed majesty of mien—the muttering lips—the broken slumber—the secret corselet,—these to both were the rewards of Power!

The elasticity of youth had left the Tribune! His frame, which had endured so many shocks, had contracted a painful disease in the dungeon at Avignon *—his high soul still supported him, but the nerves gave way. Tears came readily into his eyes, and often, like Cromwell, he was thought to weep from hypocrisy, when in truth it was the hysterie of over-wrought and irritable emotion. In all his former life singularly temperate, † he now fled from his goading thoughts to the beguiling excitement of wine. He drank deep, though its effects were never visible upon him except in a freer and wilder mood, and the indulgence of that racy humor, half-mirthful, half-bitter, for which his younger day had been

* This plain fact is thoroughly borne of by every authority.

* "Dicea che ne la prigione era stato ascarmato.—*Vit. di Col. di Rienzi*, lib. ii. cap. 18.

† "Solea prima esser sobrio, temperato, astinente, ora è diventato distemperatissimo bevitore," etc.—*Ibid.*

"At first he used to be sober, temperate, abstinent; now he is become the most intemperate drinker, etc.—*Life of Cola di Rienzi*.

distinguished. Now the mirth had more loudness, but the bitterness more gall.

Such were the characteristics of Rienzi at his return to power—made more apparent with every day. Nina he still loved with the same tenderness, and, if possible, she adored him more than ever: but, the zest and freshness of triumphant ambition gone, somehow or other, their intercourse together had not its old charm. Formerly they talked constantly of the *future*—of the bright days in store for them. Now, with a sharp and uneasy pang, Rienzi turned from all thought of that "gay to-morrow." There was no "gay to-morrow" for him! Dark and thorny as was the present hour, all beyond seemed yet less cheering and more ominous. Still he had some moments, brief but brilliant, when, forgetting the iron race amongst whom he was thrown, he plunged into scholastic reveries of the worshipped Past, and half-fancied that he was of a people worthy of his genius and his devotion, Like most men who have been preserved through great dangers, he continued with increasing fondness to nourish a credulous belief in the grandeur of his own destiny. He could not imagine that he had been so delivered, and for no end! He was the Elected, and therefore the Instrument, of Heaven. And thus, that Bible which in his loneliness, his wanderings, and his prison, had been his solace and support, was more than ever needed in his greatness.

It was another cause of sorrow and chargin to one who, amidst such circumstances of public danger, required so peculiarly the support and sympathy of private friends,—that he found he had incurred amongst his old coadjutors the common penalty of absence. A few were dead; others wearied with the storms of public life, and chilled in their ardor by the turbulent revolutions to which, in every effort for her amelioration, Rome had been subjected, had retired,—some altogether from the city, some from all participation in political affairs. In his halls, the Tribune-Senator was surrounded by unfamiliar faces, and a new generation. Of the heads of the popular party, most were animated by a stern dislike to the Pontifical domination, and looked with suspicion and repugnance upon one who, if he governed for the People, had been trusted and honored by the Pope. Rienzi was not a man to forget former friends, however lowly, and had already found time to seek an interview with Cecco del Vecchio. But the stern Republican had received him with coldness. His foreign mercenaries, and the title of Senator, were things that the artisan could not digest. With his usual bluntness, he had said so Rienzi.

"As for the last," answered the Tribune, affably, "names do not alter natures. When I forget that to be delegate to the Pontiff is to be the guardian of his flock, forsake me. As for the first, let me but see five hundred Romans sworn to stand armed day and night for the defence of Rome, and I dismiss the Northmen."

Cecco del Vecchio was unsoftened; honest, but uneducated—impracticable, and by nature a malcontent, he felt as if he were no longer necessary to the Senator, and this offended his pride. Strange as it may seem, the sullen artisan bore, too, a secret grudge against Rienzi, for not having seen and selected him from a crowd of thousands on the day of his triumphal entry. Such are the small offences which produce deep danger to the great!

The artisans still held their meetings, and Cecco del Vecchio's voice was heard loud in grumbling forebodings. But what wounded Rienzi yet more than the alineation of the rest, was the confused and altered manner of his old friend and familiar, Pandulfo di Guido. Missing that popular citizen among those who daily offered their homage at the Capitol, he had sent for him, and sought in vain to revive their ancient intimacy. Pandulfo affected great respect, but not all the condescension of the Senator could conquer his distance and his restraint. In fact, Pandulfo had learned to form ambitious projects of his own; and but for the return of Rienzi, Pandulfo di Guido felt that he might now, with greater safety, and indeed with some connivance from the Barons, have been the Tribune of the People. The facility to rise into popular eminence which a disordered and corrupt state, unblest by a regular constitution, offers to ambition, breeds the jealousy and the rivalship which destroy union, and rot away the ties of party.

Such was the situation of Rienzi, and yet, wonderful to say, he seemed to be adored by the multitude; and law and liberty, life and death, were in his hands!

Of all those who attended his person, Angelo, Villani was the most favored; that youth who had accompanied Rienzi in his long exile, had also, at the wish of Nina, attended him from Avignon, through his sojourn in the camp of Albornoz. His zeal, intelligence, and frank and evident affection, blinded the Senator to the faults of his character, and established him more and more in the gratitude of Rienzi. He loved to feel that one faithful heart beat near him, and the page, raised to the rank of his chamberlain, always attended his person, and slept in his ante-chamber.

Retiring that night at Tivilo, to the apartment prepared for him, the Senator sat down by the open casement ,through which were seen waving in the starlight, the dark pines that crowned the hills, while the stillness of the hour gave to his ear the dash of the waterfalls heard above the regular and measured tread of the sentinels below. Leaning his cheek upon his hand, Rienzi long surrendered himself to gloomy thought, and, when he looked up, he saw the bright blue eye of Villani fixed in anxious sympathy on his countenance.

"Is my Lord unwell?" asked the young chamberlain, hesitating.

"Not so, my Angelo; but somewhat sick at heart. Methinks, for a September night, the air is chill!"

"Angelo," resumed Rienzi, who had already acquired that uneasy curiosity which belongs to an uncertain power,—"Angelo, bring me hither yon writing implements; hast thou heard aught what the men say of our probable success against Palestrina?"

"Would my Lord wish to learn all their gossip, whether it please or not?" answered Villani.

"If I studied only to hear what pleased me, Angelo, I should never have returned to Rome."

"Why, then, I heard a constable of the Northmen say, meaningly, that the place will not be carried.

"Humph! And what said the captains of my Roman Legion?"

"My Lord, I have heard it whispered that they fear defeat less than they do the revenge of the Barons, if they are successful."

"And with such tools the living race of Europe and misjudging posterity will deem that the workman is to shape out the Ideal and the Perfect! Bring me yon Bible."

As Angelo reverently brought to Rienzi the sacred book, he said,

"Just before I left my companions below, there was a rumor that the Lord Adrian Colonna had been imprisoned by his kinsman."

"I too heard, and I believe, as much," returned Rienzi; "these Barons would gibbet their own children in irons, if there were any chance of the shackles growing rusty for want of prey. But the wicked shall be brought low, and their strong places shall be made desolate."

"I would, my Lord," said Villani, that our Northmen had other captains than these Provençals."

"Why?" asked Rienzi, abruptly.

"Have the creatures of the Captain of the Grand Company ever held faith with any man whom it suited the avarice or the ambition of Montreal to betray? Was he not, a few months ago, the right arm of John di Vico, and did he not sell his services to John di Vico's enemy, the Cardinal Albornoz? These warriors barter men as cattle."

"Thou describest Montreal rightly: a dangerous and an awful man. But methinks his brothers are of a duller and meaner kind; they dare not the crimes of the Robber Captain. Howbeit, Angelo, thou hast touched a string that will make discord with sleep tonight. Fair youth, thy young eyes have need of slumber; withdraw, and when thou hearest men envy Rienzi, think that——"

"God never made Genius to be envied!" interrupted Villani, with an energy that overcame his respect. "We envy not the sun, but rather the valleys that ripen beneath his beams."

"Verily, if I be the sun," said Rienzi, with a bitter and melancholy smile, "I long for night,—and come it will, to the human as to the celestial Pilgrim!—Thank Heaven, at least, that our ambition cannot make us immortal!"

CHAPTER V.

The Biter Bit.

THE next morning, when Rienzi descended to the room where his captains awaited him, his quick eye perceived that a cloud still lowered upon the brow of Messere Brettone. Arimbaldo, sheltered by the recess of the rude casement, shunned his eye.

"A fair morning, gentles," said Rienzi; 'the Sun laughs upon your enterprise. I have messengers from Rome betimes—fresh troops will join us ere noon."

"I am glad, Senator," answered Brettone, "that you have tidings which will counteract the ill of those I have to narrate to thee. The soldiers murmur loudly—their pay is due to them; and, I fear me, that without money they will not march to Palestrina."

"As they will," returned Rienzi, carelessly. "It is but a few days since they entered Rome; pay did they receive in advance—if they demand more, the Colonna and Orsini may outbid me. Draw off your soldiers, Sir Knight, and farewell."

Brettone's countenance fell—it was his object to get Rienzi more and more in his power and he wished not to suffer him to gain that strength which would accrue to him from the fall of Palestrina: the indifference of the Senator foiled and entrapped him in his own net.

"That must not be," said the brother of Montreal, after a confused silence; "we cannot leave you thus to your enemies—the soldiers demand pay——"

"And should have it," said Rienzi. "I know these mercenaries—it is ever with them, mutiny or money. I will throw myself on my Romans, and triumph—or fall, if so Heaven decrees, with them. Acquaint your constables with my resolve."

Scarce were these words spoken, ere, as previously concerted with Brettone, the chief constable of the mercenaries, appeared at the door. "Senator," said he, with a rough semblance of aspect, "Your orders to march have reached me, I have sought to marshal my men—but——"

"I know what thou wouldst say, friend, interrupted Rienzi, waving his hand: "Messere Brettone will give you my reply. Another time, Sir Captain, more ceremony with the Senator of Rome—you may withdraw."

The unforseen dignity of Rienzi rebuked and abashed the constable; he looked at Brettone, who motioned him to depart. He closed the door and withdrew.

"What is to be done?" said Brettone.

"Sir Knight," replied Rienzi, gravely, "let us understand each other. Would you serve me or not? If the first, you are not my equal, but subordinate—and you must obey and not dictate; if the last, my debt to you shall be discharged, and the world is wide enough for both."

"We have declared allegiance to you," answered Brettone, "and it shall be given."

"One caution before I re-accept your fealty," replied Rienzi, very slowly. "For an open foe, I have my sword—for a traitor, mark me, Rome has the axe; of the first I have no fear; for the last, no mercy."

"These are not words that should pass between friends," said Brettone, turning pale with suppressed emotion.

"Friends!—ye are my friends, then!—your hands! Friends, so ye are!—and shall prove it! Dear Arimbaldo, thou, like myself, art book-learned,—a clerkly soldier. Dost thou remember how in the Roman history it is told that the Treasury lacked money for the soldiers? The Consul convened the Nobles. 'Ye,' said he, 'that have the offices and dignity should be the first to pay for them.' Ye heed me, my friends; the nobles took the hint, they found the money—the army was paid. This example is not lost on you. I have made you the leaders of my force, Rome hath showered her honors on you. Your generosity shall commence the example which the Roman shall thus learn of strangers. Ye gaze at me, *my friends!* I read your noble souls—and thank ye beforehand. Ye have the dignity and the office; ye have also the wealth!—pay the hirelings, pay them!" *

Had a thunderbolt fallen at the feet of Brettone, he could not have been more astounded than at this simple suggestion of Rienzi's. He lifted his eyes to the Senator's face, and saw there that smile which he had already, bold as he was, learned to dread. He felt himself fairly sunk in the pit he had digged for another. There was that in the Senator-Tribune's brow that told him to refuse was to declare open war, and the moment was not ripe for that.

"Ye accede," said Rienzi; "ye have done well."

The Senator clapped his hands—his guard appeared.

* See the anonymous biograhpher, lib. ii. cap. 19.

"Summon the head constables of the soldiery."

The brothers still remained dumb.

The constables entered.

"My friends," said Rienzi, Messere Brettone and Messere Arimbaldo have my directions to divide amongst your force a thousand florins. This evening we encamp beneath Palestrina."

The constables withdrew in visible surprise. Rienzi gazed a moment on the brothers, chuckling within himself—for his sarcastic humor enjoyed his triumph. "You lament not your devotion, *my friends!*"

"No," said Brettone, rousing himself; "the sum but trivially swells our debt."

"Frankly said—your hands once more!—the good people of Tivoli expect me in the Piazza—they require some admonitions. Adieu till noon."

When the door closed on Rienzi, Brettone struck the handle of his sword fiercely—"The Roman laughs at us," said he. "But let Walter de Montreal once appear in Rome, and the proud jester shall pay us dearly for this."

"Hush!" said Arimbaldo, "walls have ears, and that imp of Satan, young Villani, seems to me ever at our heels!"

"A thousand florins! I trust his heart hath as many drops," growled the chafed Brettone, unheeding his brother.

The soldiers were paid—the army marched—the eloquence of the Senator had augmented his force by volunteers from Tivoli, and wild and half armed peasantry joined his standard from the Campagna and the neighboring mountains.

Palestrina was beseiged: Rienzi continued dexterously to watch the brothers of Montreal. Under pretext of imparting to the Italian volunteers the advantage of their military science, he separated them from their mercenaries, and assigned to them the command of the less disciplined Italians, with whom, he believed, they could not venture to tamper. He himself assumed the lead of the Northmen—and, despite themselves, they were fascinated by his artful, yet dignified affability, and the personal courage he displayed in some sallies of the besieged Barons. But as the huntsmen upon all the subtlest windings of their prey,—so pressed the relentless and speeding Fates upon Cola di Rienzi!

CHAPTER VI.

The Events Gather to the End.

WHILE this the state of the camp of the besiegers, Luca di Savelli and Stefanello Colonna were closeted with a stranger, who had privately entered Palestrina on the night before the Romans pitched their tents beneath its walls. This visitor, who might have somewhat passed his fortieth year, yet retained, scarcely diminished, the uncommon beauty of form and countenance for which his youth had been remarkable. But it was no longer that character of beauty which has been described in his first introduction to the reader. It was no longer the almost woman delicacy of feature and complexion, or the highborn polish, and graceful suavity of manner, which distinguished Walter de Montreal: a life of vicissitude and war had at length done its work. His bearing was now abrupt and imperious, as that of one accustomed to rule wild spirits, and he had exchanged the grace of persuasion for the sternness of command. His athletic form had grown more spare and sinewy, and instead of the brow half shaded by fair and clustering curls, his forehead, though yet but slightly wrinkled, was completely bald at the temples; and by its unwonted height, increased the dignity and manliness of his aspect. The bloom of his complexion was faded, less by outward exposure than inward thought, into a bronzed and settled paleness; and his features seemed more marked and prominent, as the flesh had somewhat sunk from the contour of the cheek. Yet the change suited the change of age and circumstance; and if the Provençal now less realized the idea of the brave and fair knight-errant, he but looked the more what the knight-errant had become—the sagacious counsellor and the mighty leader.

"You must be aware," said Montreal, continuing a discourse which appeared to have made great impression on his companions, "that in this contest between yourselves and the Senator, I alone hold the balance. Rienzi is utterly in my power—my brothers, the leaders of his army; myself, his creditor. It rests with me to secure him on the throne, or to send him to the scaffold. I have but to give the order, and the Grand Company enter Rome; but without their agency, methinks if you keep faith with me, our purpose can be effected."

"In the meanwhile, Palestrina is besieged by your brothers!" said Stefanello, sharply.

"But they have my order to waste their time before its walls. Do you not see, by this very siege, fruitless, as, if I will, it shall be, Rienzi loses fame abroad, and popularity in Rome."

"Sir Knight," said Luca di Savelli, you speak as a man versed in the profound policy of the times; and under all the circumstances which menace us, your proposal seems but fitting and reasonable. On the one hand, you undertake to restore us and the other Barons to Rome; and to give Rienzi to the Staircase of the Lion——"

"Not so, not so," replied Montreal, quickly. "I will consent either so to subdue and cripple his power, as to render him a puppet in our hands, a mere shadow of authority—or, if his proud spirit chafe at its cage, to give it once more liberty amongst the wilds of Germany. I would fetter or banish him, but not destroy; unless (added Montreal, after a moment's pause) fate absolutely drives us to it. Power should not demand victims; but to secure it, victims may be necessary."

"I understand your refinements," said Luca di Savelli, with his icy smile, "and am satisfied. The Barons once restored, our palaces once more manned, and I am willing to take the chance of the Senator's longevity. This service you promise to effect?"

"I do."

"And, in return you demand our assent to your enjoying the rank of Podesta for five years?"

"You say right."

"I, for one, accede to the terms," said the Saville: "there is my hand; I am wearied of these brawls, even amongst ourselves, and think that a Foreign Ruler may best enforce order: the more especially, if like you, Sir Knight, one whose birth and renown are such as to make him comprehend the difference between Barons and Plebeians."

"For my part," said Stefanello, "I feel that we have but a choice of evils—I like not a foreign Podesta; but I like a plebeian Senator still less;—there too is my hand, Sir Knight."

"Noble Signors," said Montreal, after a short pause, and turning his piercing gaze from one to the other with great deliberation, "our compact is sealed; one word by way of codicil. Walter de Montreal is no Count Pepin of Minorbino! Once before, little dreaming, I own, that the victory would be so facile, I entrusted your cause and mine to a deputy; your cause he promoted, mine he lost. He drove out the Tribune, and then suffered the Barons to banish himself. This time I see to my own affairs; and, mark you, I have learned in the Grand Company one lesson; viz., never to pardon spy or deserter, of whatever rank. Your forgiveness for the hint. Let us change the theme. So ye detain in your fortress my old friend the Baron di Castello?"

"Ay," said Luca di Savelli; for Stefanello, stung by Montreal's threat, which he dared not openly resent, preserved a sullen silence; "Ay, he is one noble the less to the Senator's council."

"You act wisely. I know his views and temper; at present dangerous to our interests. Yet use him well, I entreat you; he may hereafter serve us. And now, my Lords, my eyes are weary, suffer me to retire. Pleasant dreams of the New Revolution to us all!"

"By your leave, noble Montreal, we will attend you to your couch," said Luca di Savelli.

"By my troth, and ye shall not. I am no Tribune to have great Signors for my pages; but a plain gentleman, and a hardy soldier: your attendants will conduct me to whatever chamber your hospitality assigns to one who could sleep soundly beneath the rudest hedge under your open skies."

Savelli, however, insisted on conducting the Podesta that was to be, to his apartment. He then returned to Stefanello, whom he found pacing the saloon with long and disordered strides.

"What have we done, Savelli?" said he, quickly; "sold our city to a barbarian!"

"Sold!" said Savelli; "to my mind it is the other part of the contract in which we have played our share. We have bought, Colonna, not sold—bought our lives from yon army; bought our power, our fortunes, our castles, from the Demagogue Senator; bought, what is better than all, triumph and revenge. Tush, Colonna, see you not that if we had balked this great warrior, we had perished? Leagued with the Senator, the Grand Company would have marched to Rome; and, whether Montreal assisted or murdered Rienzi, (for methinks he is a Romulus, who would brook no Remus), *we* had equally been undone. *Now*, we have have made our own terms, and our shares are equal. Nay, the first steps to be taken are in our favor. Rienzi is to be snared, and *we* are to enter Rome."

"And then the Provençal is to be Despot of the city."

"Podesta, if you please. Podestas who offend the people are often banished, and sometimes stoned—Podestas who insult the nobles are often stilettoed, and sometimes poisoned," said Savilli. "'Sufficient for the day is the evil thereof.' Meanwhile, say nothing to the bear, Orsini. Such men mar all wisdom. Come, cheer thee, Stefanello."

"Luca di Savelli, you have not such a stake in Rome as I have," said the young Lord, haughtily; "no Podesta can take from *you* the rank of the first Signor of the Italian metropolis!"

"An you had said so to the Orsini, there would have been drawing of swords," said Savelli. "But cheer thee, I say; is not our first care to destroy Rienzi, and then, between the death of one foe and the rise of another, are there not such preventives as Ezzlino da Romano has taught to wary men? Cheer thee, I say; and, next year, if we but hold together, Stefanello Colonna and Luca di Savelli will be joint Senators of Rome, and these great men food for worms!"

While thus conferred the Barons, Montreal, ere he retired to rest, stood gazing from the open lattice of his chamber over the landscape below, which slept in the autumnal moonlight, while at a distance gleamed, pale and steady, the lights round the encampment of the besiegers.

"Wide plains and broad valleys," thought the warrior, "soon shall ye repose in peace beneath a new sway, against which no petty tyrant shall dare rebel. And ye, white walls of canvass, even while I gaze—*ye* admonish me how realms are won. Even as, of old, from the Nomad tents was built by the stately Babylon,* that 'was not till the Assyrian founded it for them that dwell in the wilderness;' so by the new Ishmaelites of Europe shall a race, undreamt of now, be founded; and the camp of yesterday, be the city of tomorrow. Verily, when, for one soft offence, the Pontiff thrust me from the bosom of the Church, little guessed he what enemy he raised to Rome! How solemn is the night!—how still the heavens and earth!—the very stars are as hushed, as if intent on the events that are to pass below! So solemn and so still feels mine own spirit, and an awe unknown till now warns me that I approach the crisis of my daring fate!"

* Isaiah, c. xxii.

BOOK TENTH.

THE LION OF BASALT.

"Ora voglio contare la morte del Tribuno."—*Vit. di Col. di Rienzi*, lib. ii. cap. 24.

"Now will I narrate the death of the Tribune."—*Life of Cola di Rienzi*

CHAPTER I.

The Conjunction of Hostile Planets in the House of Death.

On the fourth day of the siege, and after beating back to those almost impregnable walls the soldiery of the Barons, headed by the Prince of the Orsini, the Senator returned to his tent, where despatches from Rome awaited him. He ran his eye hastily over them, till he came to the last; yet each contained news that might have longer delayed the eye of a man less inured to danger. From one he learned that Albornoz, whose blessing had confirmed to him the rank of Senator, had received with special favor the messengers of the Orsini and Colonna. He knew that the Cardinal, whose views connected him with the Roman Patricians, desired his downfall; but he feared not Albornoz: perhaps in his secret heart he wished that any open aggression from the Pontiff's Legate might throw him wholly on the people.

He learned further, that, short as had been his absence, Pandulfo di Guido had twice addressed the populace, not in favor of the Senator, but in artful regrets of the loss to the trade of Rome in the absence of her wealthiest nobles.

"For this, then, he has deserted me," said Rienzi to himself. "Let him beware!"

The tidings contained in the next touched him home: Walter de Montreal had openly arrived in Rome. The grasping and lawless bandit, whose rapine filled with a robber's booty every bank in Europe—whose Company was the army of a King—whose ambition, vast, unprincipled, and profound, he so well knew—whose brothers were in his camp—their treason already more than suspected;—Walter de Montreal was in Rome!

The Senator remained perfectly aghast at this new peril; and then said, setting his teeth as in a vice,

"Wild tiger, thou art in the Lion's den!" Then pausing, he broke out again, "One false step, Walter de Montreal, and all the mailed hands of the Grand Company shall not pluck thee from the abyss! But what can I do? Return to Rome—the plans of Montreal unpenetrated—no accusation against him! On what pretence can I with honor raise the siege? To leave Palestrina, is to give a triumph to the Barons—to abandon Adrian, to degrade my cause. Yet, while away from Rome, every hour breeds treason and danger. Pandulfo, Albornoz, Montreal—all are at work against me. A keen and trusty spy, now; ha, ha, well thought of—Villani!—What, ho—Angelo Villani!"

The young chamberlain appeared.

"I think," said Rienzi, "to have often heard, that thou art an orphan?"

"True, my Lord; the old Augustine nun who reared my boyhood, has told me again and again that my parents are dead. Both noble, my Lord; but I am the child of shame. And I say it often, and think of it ever, in order to make Angelo Villani remember that he has a name to win."

"Young man, serve me as you have served,

and if I live you shall have no need to call yourself an orphan. Mark me! I want a friend—the Senator of Rome wants a friend—only one friend—gentle Heaven! only one!"

Angelo sank on his knee, and kissed the mantle of his Lord.

"Say a follower. I am too mean to be Rienzi's friend."

"To mean!—go to!—there is nothing mean before God, unless it be a base soul under high titles. With me, boy, there is but one nobility, and Nature signs its charter. Listen: thou hearest daily of Walter de Montreal, brother to these Provençals—great captain of great robbers?"

"Ay, and I have seen him, my Lord."

"Well, then, he is in Rome. Some daring thought—some well-supported and deep-schemed villany, could alone make that bandit venture openly into an Italian city, whose territories he ravaged by fire and sword a few months back. But his brothers have lent me money—assisted my return;—for their own ends, it is true: but the seeming obligation gives them real power. These Northern swordsmen would cut my throat if the Great Captain bade them. He counts on my supposed weakness. I know him of old. I suspect—nay I read, his projects; but I cannot prove them. Without proof, I cannot desert Palestrina in order to accuse and seize him. Thou art shrewd, thoughtful, acute;—couldst thou go to Rome?—watch day and night his movements—see if he receive messengers from Albornoz or the Barons—if he confer with Pandulfo di Guido;—watch his lodgment, I say, night and day. He affects no concealment; your task will be less difficult than it seems. Apprise the Signora of all you learn. Give me your news daily. Will you undertake this mission!"

"I will, my Lord."

"To horse, then, quick!—and mind—save the wife of my bosom, I have no confidant in Rome."

CHAPTER II.

Montreal at Rome.—His Reception of Angelo Villani.

THE danger that threatened Rienzi by the arrival of Montreal was indeed formidable. The Knight of St. John, having marched his army into Lombardy, had placed it at the disposal of the Venetian State in its war with the Archbishop of Milan. For this service he received an immense sum; while he provided winter quarters for his troop, for whom he proposed ample work in the ensuing spring. Leaving Palestrina secretly and in disguise, with but a slender train, which met him at Tivoli, Montreal repaired to Rome. His ostensible object was, partly to congratulate the Senator on his return, partly to receive the money's lent to Rienzi by his brother.

His secret object we have partly seen; but not contented with the support of the Barons, he trusted, by the corrupting means of his enormous wealth, to form a third party in support of his own ulterior designs. Wealth, indeed, in that age and in that land, was scarcely less the purchaser of diadems than it had been in the later days of the Roman Empire. And in many a city torn by hereditary feuds, the hatred of faction rose to that extent, that a foreign tyrant, willing and able to expel one party, might obtain at least the temporary submission of the other. His after-success was greatly in proportion of his power to maintain his state by a force which was independent of the citizens, and by a treasury which did not require the odious recruit of taxes. But more avaricious than ambitious, more cruel than firm, it was by griping exaction, or unnecessary bloodshed, that such usurpers usually fell.

Montreal, who had scanned the frequent revolutions of the time with a calm and investigating eye, trusted that he should be enabled to avoid both these errors: and, as the reader has already seen, he had formed the profound and sagacious project of consolidating his usurpation by an utterly new race of nobles, who, serving him by the feudal tenure of the North, and ever ready to protect him, because in so doing they protected their own interests, should assist to erect, not the rotten and unsupported fabric of a single tyranny, but the strong fortress of a new, hardy, and compact Aristocratic State. Thus had the great dynasties of the North been founded; in which a King, though seemingly curbed by the Barons, was in reality supported by common interest, whether against a subdued population or a foreign invasion.

Such were the vast schemes—extending

into yet wider fields of glory and conquest, bounded only by the Alps—with which the Captain of the Grand Company beheld the columns and arches of the Seven-hilled City.

No fear disturbed the long current of his thoughts. His brothers were the leaders of Rienzi's hireling army—that army were his creatures. Over Rienzi himself he assumed the right of a creditor. Thus against one party he deemed himself secure. For the friends of the Pope, he had supported himself with private, though cautious, letters from Albornoz, who had desired only to make use of him for the return of the Roman Barons; and with the heads of the latter we have already witnessed his negotiations. Thus was he fitted, as he thought, to examine, to tamper with all parties, and to select from each the materials necessary for his own objects.

The open appearance of Montreal excited in Rome no inconsiderable sensation. The friends of the Barons gave out that Rienzi was in league with the Grand Company; and that he was to sell the imperial city to the plunder and pillage of Barbarian robbers. The effrontery with which Montreal (against whom, more than once, the Pontiff had thundered his bulls) appeared in the Metropolitan City of the Church, was made yet more insolent by the recollection of that stern justice which had led the Tribune to declare open war against all the robbers of Italy: and this audacity was linked with the obvious reflection, that the brothers of the bold Provençal were the instruments of Rienzi's return. So quickly spread suspicion through the city, that Montreal's presence alone would in a few weeks have sufficed to ruin the Senator. Meanwhile, the natural boldness of Montreal silenced every whisper of prudence; and, blinded by the dazzle of his hopes, the Knight of St. John, as if to give double importance to his coming, took up his residence in a sumptuous palace, and his retinue rivalled, in the splendor of garb and pomp, the display of Rienzi himself in his earlier and more brilliant power.

Amidst the growing excitement, Angelo Villani arrived at Rome. The character of this young man had been formed by his peculiar circumstances. He possessed qualities which often mark the Illegitimate as with a common stamp. He was insolent—like most of those who hold a doubtful rank; and while ashamed of his bastardy, was arrogant of the supposed nobility of his unknown parentage. The universal ferment and agitation of Italy at that day rendered ambition the most common of all the passions, and thus ambition, in all its many shades and varieties, forces itself into delineations of character in this history. Though not for Angelo Villani were the dreams of the more lofty and generous order of that sublime infirmity, he was strongly incited by the desire and resolve to *rise*. He had warm affections and grateful impulses; and his fidelity to his patron had been carried to a virtue: but from his irregulated and desultory education, and the reckless profligacy of those with whom, in ante-chambers and guard-rooms, much of his youth had been passed, he had neither high principles nor an enlightened honor. Like most Italians, cunning and shrewd, he scrupled not at any deceit that served a purpose or a friend. His strong attachment to Rienzi had been unconsciously increased by the gratification of pride and vanity, flattered by the favor of so celebrated a man. Both self-interest and attachment urged him to every effort to promote the views and safety of one at once his benefactor and patron; and on undertakiug his present mission, his only thought was to fulfil it with the most complete success. Far more brave and daring than was common with the Italians, something of the hardihood of an Ultra-Montane race gave nerve and vigor to his craft; and from what his art suggested, his courage never shrunk.

When Rienzi had first detailed to him the objects of his present task, he instantly called to mind his adventure with the tall soldier in the crowd at Avignon. "If ever thou wantest a friend, seek him in Walter de Montreal," were words that had often rung in his ear, and they now recurred to him with prophetic distinctness. He had no doubt that it was Montreal himself whom he had seen. Why the Great Captain should have taken this interest in him, Angelo little cared to conjecture. Most probably it was but a crafty pretence—one of the common means by which the Chief of the Grand Company attracted to himself the youths of Italy, as well as the warriors of the North. He only thought now how he could turn the Knight's promise to account. What more easy than to present himself to

Montreal—remind him of the words—enter his service—and thus effectually watch his conduct? The office of spy was not that which would have pleased every mind, but it shocked not the fastidiousness of Angelo Villani; and the fearful hatred with which his patron had often spoken of the avaricious and barbarian robber—the scourge of his native land,—had infected the young man, who had much of the arrogant and mock patriotism of the Romans, with a similar sentiment. More vindictive even than grateful, he bore, too, a secret grudge against Montreal's brothers, whose rough address had often wounded his pride: and, above all, his early recollections of the fear and execration in which Ursula seemed ever to hold the terrible Fra Moreale, impressed him with a vague belief of some ancient wrong to himself or his race, perpetrated by the Provençal, which he was not ill-pleased to have the occasion to avenge. In truth, the words of Ursula, mystic and dark as they were in their denunciation, had left upon Villani's boyish impressions an unaccountable feeling of antipathy and hatred to the man it was now his object to betray. For the rest, every device seemed to him decorous and justifiable, so that it saved his master, served his country, and advanced himself.

Montreal was alone in his chamber when it was anounced to him that a young Italian craved an audience. Professionally open to access, he forthwith gave admission to the applicant.

The Knight of St. John instantly recognized the page he had encountered at Avignon; and when Angelo Villani said, with easy boldness, "I have come to remind Sir Walter de Montreal of a promise——"

The Knight interrupted him with cordial frankness—"Thou needest not —I remember it. Dost thou now require my friendship?"

"I do, noble Signor!" answered Angelo; "I know not where else to seek a patron."

"Canst thou read and write? I fear me not."

"I have been taught those arts," replied Villani."

"It is well. Is thy birth gentle?"

"It is."

"Better still;—thy name?"

"Angelo Villani."

"I take thy blue eyes and low broad brow," said Montreal, with a slight sigh, "in pledge of thy truth. Henceforth, Angelo Villani, thou art in the list of my secretaries. Another time thou shalt tell me more of thyself. Thy service dates from this day. For the rest, no man ever wanted wealth who served Walter de Montreal; nor advancement, if he served him faithfully. My closet, through yonder door, is thy waiting room. Ask for, and send hither, Lusignan of Lyons; he is my chief scribe, and will see to thy comforts, and instruct thee in thy business."

Angelo withdrew—Montreal's eye followed him.

"A strange likeness!" said he, musingly and sadly; "my heart leaps to that boy!"

CHAPTER III.

Montreal's Banquet.

Some few days after the date of the last chapter, Rienzi received news from Rome, which seemed to produce in him a joyous and elated excitement. His troops still lay before Palestrina, and still the banners of the Barons waved over its unconquered walls. In truth, the Italians employed half their time in brawls amongst themselves; the Velletritrani had feuds with the people of Tivoli, and the Romans were still afraid of conquering the Barons;—"The hornet," said they, "stings worse after he is dead; and neither an Orsini, a Savelli, nor a Colonna, was ever known to forgive."

Again and again had the captains of his army assured the indignant Senator that the fortress was impregnable, and that time and money were idly wasted upon the siege. Rienzi knew better, but he concealed his thoughts.

He now summoned to his tent the brothers of Provence, and announced to them his intention of returning instantly to Rome. "The mercenaries shall continue the siege under our Lieutenant, and you, with my Roman Legion, shall accompany me. Your brother, Sir Walter, and I, both want your presence; we have affairs to arrange between us. After a few days I shall raise recruits in the city, and return."

This was what the brothers desired; they

approved, with evident joy, the Senator's proposition.

Rienzi next sent for the lieutenant of his body-guard, the same Riccardo Annibaldi whom the reader will remember in the earlier part of this work, as the antagonist of Montreal's lance. This young man—one of the few nobles who espoused the cause of the Senator—had evinced great courage and military ability, and promised fair (should Fate spare his life *) to become one of the best Captains of his time.

"Dear Annibaldi," said Rienzi; "at length I can fulfil the project on which we have privately conferred. I take with me to Rome the two Provençal Captains—I leave you chief of the army. Palestrina will yield now—eh!—ha, ha, ha!—Palestrina will yield now!"

"By my right hand, I think so, Senator," replied Annibaldi. "These foreigners have hitherto only stirred up quarrels amongst ourselves, and if not cowards are certainly traitors!"

"Hush, hush, hush! Traitors! The learned Arimbaldo, the brave Brettone, traitors! Fie on it! No, no; they are very excellent, honorable men, but not lucky in the camp;—not lucky in the camp;—better speed to them in the city! And now to busiuess."

The Senator then detailed to Annibaldi the plan he himself had formed for taking the town, and the military skill of Annibaldi at once recognized its feasibility.

With his Roman troop, and Montreal's brothers, one at either hand, Renzi then departed to Rome.

That night Montreal gave a banquet to Pandulfo di Guido, and to certain of the principal citizens, whom one by one he had already sounded, and found hollow at heart to the cause of the Senator.

Pandulfo sate at the right hand of the Knight of St. John, and Montreal lavished upon him the most courteous attentions.

"Pledge me in this—it is from the Vale of Chiana, near Monte Pulciano," said Montreal. "I think I have heard bookmen say (you know, Signor Pandulfo, we ought all to be bookmen now!) that the site was renowned of old. In truth the wine hath a racy flavor."

"I hear," said Bruttini, one of the lesser Barons, (a staunch friend of the Colonna), "that in this respect the innkeeper's son has put his book-learning to some use: he knows every place where the wine grows richest.'

"What! the Senator is turned wine-bibber!" said Montreal, quaffing a vast goblet full;" "that must unfit him for business—'tis a pity."

"Verily, yes," said Pandulfo; "a man at the head of a state should be temperate—*I* never drink wine unmixed."

"Ah," whispered Montreal, "if your calm good sense ruled Rome, then, indeed, the metropolis of Italy might taste of peace. Signor Vivaldi,"—and the host turned towards a wealthy draper,—"these disturbances are bad for trade."

"Very, very!" groaned the draper.

"The Barons are your best customers," quoth the minor noble.

"Much, much!" said the draper.

"'Tis a pity that they are thus roughly expelled," said Montreal, in a melancholy tone. "Would it not be possible, if the Senator (*I* drink his health) were less rash—less zealous, rather,—to unite free institutions with the return of the Barons?—*such* should be the task of a truly wise statesman!"

"It surely might be possible," returned Vivaldi; "the Savelli alone spend more with me than all the rest of Rome."

"I know not of it be possible," said Bruttini; "but I do know that is an outrage to all decorum that an innkeeper's son should be enabled to make a solitude of the palaces of Rome."

"It certainly seems to indicate too vulgar a desire of mob favor," said Montreal. "However, I trust we shall harmonize all these differences. Rienzi, perhaps,—nay, doubtless, *means* well!"

"I would," said Vivaldi, who had received his cue, "That we might form a mixed constitution—Plebeians and Patricians, each in their separate order,"

"But," said Montreal, gravely, "so new an experiment would demand great physical force."

"Why, true; but we might call in an umpire—a foreigner who had no interest in either

* It appears that this was the same Annibaldi who was afterwards slain in an affray:—Petrarch lauds his valor and laments his fate.

faction—who might protect the new Buono Stato; a Podesta, as we have done before—Brancaleone, for instance. How well and wisely he ruled! that was a golden age for Rome. A Podesta for ever!—that's my theory."

"You need not seek far for the president of your council," said Montreal smiling at Pandulfo; "a citizen at once popular well-born, and wealthy, may be found at my right hand."

Pandulfo hemmed and colored.

Montreal proceeded. "A committee of trades might furnish an honorable employment to Signor Vivaldi; and the treatment of all foreign affairs—the employment of armies, etc., might be left to the Barons, with a more open competition, Signor di Bruttini, to the Barons of the second order than has hitherto been conceded to their birth and importance. Sirs, will you taste the Malvoisie?"

"Still," said Vivaldi, after a pause—(Vivaldi anticipated at least the supplying with cloth the whole of the Grand Company)—"still, such a moderate and well-digested constitution would never be acceded to by Rienzi."

"Why should it? what need of Rienzi?" exclaimed Bruttini. "Rienzi may take another trip to Bohemia."

"Gently, gently," said Montreal; "I do not despair. All open violence against the Senator would strengthen his power. No, no, humble him—admit the Barons, and then insist on your own terms. Between the two factions you might then establish a fitting balance. And in order to keep your new constitution from the encroachment of either extreme, there *are* warriors and knights, too, who for a certain rank in the great city of Rome would maintain horse and foot at its service. We Ultra-Montanes are often harshly judged; we are wanderers and Ishmaelites, solely because we have no honorable place of rest. Now, if *I*——"

"Ay, if you, noble Montreal!" said Vivaldi.

The company remained hushed in breathless attention, when suddenly there was heard—deep, solemn, muffled,—the great bell of the Capitol!

"Hark!" said Vivaldi, the bell: "it tolls for execution: an unwonted hour!"

"Sure, the Senator has not returned!" exclaimed Pandulfo di Guido, turning pale.

"No, no," quoth Bruttini, "it is but a robber, caught two nights ago in Romagna. I heard that he was to die to-night."

At the word "robber," Montreal changed countenance slightly. The wine circulated—the bell continued to toll—its suddenness over, it ceased to alarm. Conversation flowed again.

"What were you saying, Sir Knight?" said Vivaldi.

"Why, let me think on't;—oh, speaking of the necessity of supporting a new state by force, I said that if *I*——"

"Ah, that was it!" quoth Bruttini, thumping the table.

"If *I* were summoned to your aid—*summoned*, mind ye, and absolved by the Pope's Legate of my former sins—(they weigh heavily on me, gentles)—I would myself guard your city from foreign foe and civil disturbance, with my gallant swordsmen. Not a Roman citizen should contribute a 'danaro' to the cost."

"*Viva Fra Moreale!*" cried Bruttini; and the shout was echoed by all the boon companions.

"Enough for me," continued Montreal, "to expiate my offences. Ye know, gentlemen, my order is vowed to God and the Church—a warrior-monk am I! Enough for me to expiate my offences, I say, in the defence of the Holy City. Yet I, too, have my private and more earthly views,—who is above them? I —— the bell changes its note!"

"It is but the change that preludes execution—the poor robber is about to die!"

Montreal crossed himself, and resumed:—"I am a knight and a noble," said he proudly; "the profession I have followed is that of arms; but—I will not disguise it—mine equals have regarded me as one who has stained his scutcheon by too reckless a pursuit of glory and of gain. I wish to reconcile myself with my order—to purchase a new name to vindicate myself to the Grand Master and the Pontiff. I have had hints, gentles,—hints, that I might best promote my interest by restoring order to the Papal metropolis. The Legate Albornoz (here is his letter) recommends me to keep watch upon the Senator."

"Surely," interrupted Pandulfo, "I hear steps below."

"The mob going to the robber's execution," said Bruttini; "proceed, Sir Knight!"

"And," continued Montreal, surveying his audience before he proceeded farther, "what think ye—(I do but ask your opinion, wiser than mine)—what think ye, as a fitting precaution against too arbitrary a power in the Senator—what think ye of the return of the Colonna, and the bold Barons of Palestrina?"

"Here's to their health!" cried Vivaldi, rising.

As by a sudden impulse, the company rose. "To the health of the besieged Barons!" was shouted aloud.

"Next, what if—(I do but humbly suggest) —what if you gave the Senator a colleague?— it is no affront to him. It was but as yesterday that one of the Colonna, who was Senator, received a colleague in Bertoldo Orsini."

"A most wise precaution," cried Vivaldi. "And where a colleague like Pandulfo di Guido?"

"*Viva Pandulfo di Guido!*" cried the guests, and again their goblets were drained to the bottom.

"And if in this I can assist ye by fair words with the Senator (ye know he owes me moneys —my brothers have served him), commanded Walter de Montreal."

"And if fair words fail?" said Vivaldi.

"The Grand Company—(heed me, *ye* are the counsellors)—the Grand Company is accustomed to forced marches!"

"*Viva Fra Moreale!* cried Bruttini and Vivaldi, simultaneously. "A health to all, my friends;" continued Bruttini; "a health to to the Barons, Rome's old friends; to Pandulfo di Guido, the Senator's new colleague; and to Fra Moreale, Rome's new Podesta."

"The bell has ceased," said Vivaldi, putting down his goblet.

"Heaven have mercy on the robber!" added Bruttini.

Scarce had he spoken, ere three taps were heard at the door—the guests looked at each other in dumb amaze.

"New guests!" said Montreal. "I asked some trusty friends to join us this evening. By my faith they are welcome! Enter!"

The door opened slowly; three by three entered, in complete armor, the guards of the Senator. On they marched, regular and speechless. They surrounded the festive board—they filled the spacious hall, and the lights of the banquet were reflected upon their corselets as on a wall of steel.

Not a syllable was uttered by the feasters, they were as if turned to stone. Presently the guards gave way, and Rienzi himself appeared. He approached the table, and folding his arms, turned his gaze deliberately from guest to guest, til at last, his eyes rested on Montreal, who had also risen, and who alone of the party had recovered the amaze of the moment.

And there, as these two men, each so celebrated, so proud, able, and ambitious, stood, front to front—it was literarlly as if the rival Spirits of Force and Intellect, Order and Strife, of the Falchion and the Fasces—the Antagonist Principles by which empires are ruled and empires are overthrown, had met together, incarnate and opposed. They stood, both silent,—as if fascinated by each other's gaze,—loftier in stature, and nobler in presence than all around.

Montreal spoke first, and with a forced smile.

"Senator of Rome!—dare I believe that my poor banquet tempts thee, and may I trust that these armed men are a graceful compliment to one to whom arms have been a pastime?"

Rienzi answered not, but waved his hand to his guards. Montreal was seized on the instant. Again he surveyed the guests—as a bird from the rattle-snake—shrunk Pandulfo di Guido, trembling, motionless, aghast, from the glittering eye of the Senator. Slowly Rienzi raised his fatal hand towards the unhappy citizen—Pandulfo saw,—felt his doom, —shrieked, and fell senseless in the arms of the soldiers.

One other and rapid glance cast the Senator round the board, and then, with a disdainful smile, as if anxious for no meaner prey, turned away. Not a breath had hitherto passed his lips—all had been dumb show—and his grim silence had imparted a more freezing terror to his unguessed-for apparition. Only, when he reached the door, he turned back, gazed upon the Knight of St. John's bold and undaunted face, and said, almost in a whisper, "Walter de Montreal!—you heard the death-knell!"

CHAPTER IV.

The Sentence of Walter de Montreal.

In silence the Captain of the Grand Company was borne to the prison of the Capitol. In the same building lodged the rivals for the government of Rome; the one occupied the prison, the other the palace. The guards forebore the ceremony of fetters, and leaving a lamp on the table, Montreal perceived he was not alone,—his brothers had preceded him.

"Ye are happily met," said the Knight of St. John; "we have passed together pleasanter nights than this is likely to be."

"Can you jest, Walter?" said Arimbaldo, half-weeping. "Know you not that our doom is fixed? Death scowls upon us."

"Death!" repeated Montreal, and for the first time his countenance changed; perhaps for the first time in his life he felt the thrill and agony of fear.

"Death!" he repeated again. "Impossible! He dare not, Brettone; the soldiers, the Northmen!—they will mutiny, they will pluck us back from the grasp of the headsman!"

"Cast from you so vain a hope," said Brettone sullenly: "the soldiers are encamped at Palestrina."

"How! Dolt—fool! Came you then to Rome *alone!* Are we *alone* with this dread man?

"*You* are the dolt! Why came you hither?" answered the brother.

"Why, indeed! but that I knew thou wast the Captain of the army; and—but thou said'st right—the folly is mine, to have played against the crafty Tribune so unequal a brain as thine. Enough! Reproaches are idle. When were ye arrested?"

"At dusk—the instant we entered the gates of Rome. Rienzi entered privately."

"Humph! What can he know against me? Who can have betrayed me? My secretaries are tried—all trustworthy—except that youth, and he so seemingly zealous—that Angelo Villani!"

"Villani! Angelo Villani!" cried the brothers in a breath. "Hast thou confided aught to him?"

"Why, I fear he must have seen—at least in part—my correspondence with you, and with the Barons—he was among my scribes. Know you aught of him?"

"Walter, Heaven hath demented you!" returned Brettone. "Angelo Villani is the favorite menial of the Senator."

"Those eyes deceived me, then," muttered Montreal, solemnly and shuddering; "and, as if *her* ghost had returned to earth, God smites me from the grave!"

There was a long silence. At length Montreal, whose bold and sanguine temper was never long clouded, spoke again.

"Are the Senator's coffers full?—But that is impossible."

"Bare as a Dominican's."

"We are saved, then. He shall name his price for our heads. Money must be more useful to him than blood."

And as if with that thought all further meditation were rendered unnecessary, Montreal doffed his mantle, uttered a short prayer, and flung himself on a pallet in a corner of the cell.

"I have slept on worse beds," said the Knight, stretching himself; and in a few minutes he was fast asleep.

The brothers listened to his deep-drawn, but regular breathing, with envy and wonder, but they were in no mood to converse. Still and speechless, they sate like statues beside the sleeper. Time passed on, and the first cold air of the hour that succeeds to midnight crept through the bars of their cell. The bolts crashed, the door opened, six men-at-arms entered, passed the brothers, and one of them touched Montreal.

"Ha!" said he, still sleeping, but turning round. "Ha! said he, in the soft Provençal tongue, "sweet Adeline, we will not rise yet—it is so long since we met!"

"What says he?" muttered the guard, shaking Montreal roughly. The Knight sprang up at once and his hand grasped the head of his bed as for his sword. He stared round bewildered, rubbed his eyes, and then gazing on the guard, became alive to the present.

"Ye are early risers in the Capitol," said he. "What want ye of me?"

"*It* waits you!"

"*It!*" What!" said Montreal.

"The rack!" replied the soldier, with a malignant scowl.

The Great Captain said not a word. He

looked for one moment at the six swordsmen, as if measuring his single strength against theirs. His eye then wandered round the room. The rudest bar of iron would have been dearer to him than he had ever yet found the proofest steel of Milan. He completed his survey with a sigh, threw his mantle over his shoulders, nodded at his brethren, and followed the guard.

In a hall of the Capitol, hung with the ominous silk of white rays on a blood-red ground, sate Rienzi and his councillors. Across a recess was drawn a black curtain.

"Walter de Montreal," said a small man at the foot of the table, 'Knight of the illustrious order of St. John of Jerusalem——"

"And Captain of the Grand Company!" added the prisoner, in a firm voice.

"You stand accused of divers counts: robbery and murder, in Tuscany, Romagna, and Apulia——"

"For robbery and murder, brave men, and belted Knights," said Montreal, drawing himself up, "would use the words 'war and victory.' To those charges I plead guilty! Proceed."

"You are next accused of treasonable conspiracy against the liberties of Rome for the restoration of the proscribed Barons—and of traitorous correspondence with Stefanello Colonna at Palestrina."

"My accuser?"

"Step forth, Angelo Villani!"

"*You* are my betrayer, then?" said Montreal steadily. "I deserved this. I beseech you, Senator of Rome, let this young man retire. I confess my correspondence with the Colonna, and my desire to restore the Barons."

Rienzi motioned to Villani, who bowed and withdrew.

"There rests only then for you, Walter de Montreal, to relate, fully and faithfully, the details of your conspiracy."

"That is impossible," replied Montreal, carelessly.

"And why?"

"Because, doing as I please with my own life, I will not betray the lives of others."

"Bethink thee—thou wouldst have betrayed the life of thy judge!"

"Not betrayed—thou didst not trust me."

"The law, Walter de Montreal, hath sharp inquisitors—behold!"

The black curtain was drawn aside, and the eye of Montreal rested on the executioner and the rack! His proud breast heaved indignantly.

"Senator of Rome," said he, "these instruments are for serfs and villains. I have been a warrior and a leader; life and death have been in my hands—I have used them as I listed; but to mine equal and my foe, I never proffered the insult of the rack."

"Sir Walter de Montreal," returned the Senator, gravely, but with some courteous respect, "your answer is that which rises naturally to the lips of brave men. But learn from me, whom fortune had made thy judge, that no more for serf and villain, than for knight and noble, are such instruments and engines of law, or the tests of truth. I yielded but to the desire of these reverend councillors, to test thy nerves. But, wert thou the meanest peasant of the Campagna, before my judgment-seat thou needst not apprehend the torture. Walter de Montreal, amongst the Princes of Italy thou hast known, amongst the Roman Barons thou wouldst have aided, is there one who could make that boast?"

"I desired only," said Montreal, with some hesitation, "to unite the Barons *with* thee; nor did I intrigue against thy *life!*"

Rienzi frowned—"Enough," he said, hastily. "Knight of St. John, I *know* thy secret projects, subterfuge and evasion neither befit nor avail thee. If thou didst not intrigue against my life, thou didst intrigue against the life of Rome. Thou hast but one favor left to demand on earth, it is the manner of thy death."

Montreal's lip worked convulsively.

"Senator," said he, in a low voice, "may I crave audience with thee *alone* for one minute?"

The councillors looked up.

"My Lord," whispered the eldest of them, "doubtless he hath concealed weapons—trust him not."

"Prisoner," returned Rienzi, after a moment's pause; "if thou seekest for mercy thy request is idle, and before my coadjutors I have no secret; speak out what thou hast to say!"

"Yet listen to me," said the prisoner, folding his arms; "it concerns not my life, but Rome's welfare."

"Then," said Rienzi, in an altered tone, "thy request is granted. Thou mayst add to thy guilt the design of the assassin, but for Rome I would dare greater danger."

So saying, he motioned to the councillors, who slowly withdrew by the door which had admitted Villani, while the guards retired to the farthest extremity of the hall."

"Now, Walter de Montreal, be brief, for thy time is short."

"Senator," said Montreal, "my life can but little profit you: men will say that you destroyed your creditor in order to cancel your debt. Fix a sum upon my life, estimate it at the price of a monarch's; every florin shall be paid to you, and your treasury will be filled for five years to come. If the '*Buono Stato*' depends on your government, what I have asked, your solicitude for Rome will not permit you to refuse."

"You mistake me, bold robber," said Rienzi sternly; "your *treason* I could guard against, and therefore forgive; your ambition, never! Mark me, I know you! Place your hand on your heart and say whether, could we change places, you, as Rienzi, would suffer all the gold of earth to purchase the life of Walter de Montreal? For men's reading of my conduct, that must I bear; for mine own reading, mine eyes must be purged from corruption. I am answerable to God for the trust of Rome. And Rome trembles while the head of the Grand Company lives in the plotting brain and the daring heart of Walter de Montreal. Man—wealthy, great, and subtle as you are, your hours are numbered; with the rise of the sun you die!"

Montreal's eyes fixed upon the Senator's face, saw hope was over; his pride and his fortitude returned to him.

"We have wasted words," said he. "I played for a great stake, I have lost, and must pay the forfeit! I am prepared. On the threshold of the Unknown World, the dark spirit of prophecy rushes into us. Lord Senator, I go before thee to announce—that in Heaven or in Hell—ere many days be over, room must be given to one mightier than I am!"

As he spoke, his form dilated, his eye glared; and Rienzi, cowering as never had he cowered before, shrunk back, and shaded his face with his hand.

"The manner of your death?" he asked, in a hallow voice.

"The axe: it is that which befits knight and warrior. For thee, Senator, Fate hath a less noble death."

"Robber, be dumb!" cried Rienzi, passionately; "Guards, bear back the prisoner. At sunrise, Montreal——"

"*Sets* the sun of the scourge of Italy," said the Knight, bitterly. "Be it so. One request more; the Knights of St. John claim affinity with the Augustine order; grant me an Augustine confessor."

"It is granted; and in return for thy denunciations, I, who can give thee no earthly mercy, will implore the Judge of all for pardon to thy soul!"

"Senator, I have done with man's mediation. My brethren? Their deaths are not necessary to thy safety or thy revenge!"

Rienzi mused a moment: "No," said he, "dangerous tools they were, but without the workman they may rust unharming. They served me once, too. Prisoner, their lives are spared."

CHAPTER V.

The Discovery.

THE Council was broken up—Rienzi hastened to his own apartments. Meeting Villani by the way, he pressed the youth's hand affectionately. "You have saved Rome and me from great peril," said he; "the saints reward you!" Without tarrying for Villani's answer he hurried on. Nina, anxious and perturbed awaited him in their chamber.

"Not a-bed yet?" said he: "fie, Nina, even thy beauty will not stand these vigils."

"I could not rest till I had seen thee. I hear (all Rome has heard it ere this) that thou hast seized Walter de Montreal, and that he will perish by the headsman."

"The first robber that ever died so brave a death," returned Rienzi, slowly unrobing himself.

"Cola, I have never crossed your schemes, —your policy, even by a suggestion. Enough for me to triumph in their success, to mourn for their failure. Now, I ask thee one request —spare me the life of this man."

"Nina——"

"Hear me,—for thee I speak! Despite his crimes, his valor and his genius have gained him admirers, even amongst his foes. Many a prince, many a state that secretly rejoices at his fall, will affect horror against his judge. Hear me farther; his brothers aided your return; the world will term you ungrateful. His brothers lent you moneys, the world—(out on it!)—will term you——"

"Hold!" interrupted the Senator. "All that thou sayest, my mind forestalled. But thou knowest me—to thee I have no disguise. No compact can bind Montreal's faith—no mercy win his gratitude. Before his red right hand truth and justice are swept away. If I condemn Montreal I incur disgrace and risk danger—granted. If I release him, ere the first showers of April, the chargers of the Northmen will neigh in the halls of the Capitol. Which shall I hazard in this alternative, myself or Rome? Ask me no more—to bed, to bed!"

"Couldst thou read my forebodings, Cola, mystic—gloomy—unaccountable?"

"Forebodings!—I have mine," answered Rienzi, sadly, gazing on space, as if his thoughts peopled it with spectres. Then, raising his eyes to Heaven, he said with that fanatical energy which made much both of his strength and weakness—"Lord, mine at least not the sin of Saul! the Amalekite shall not be saved!"

While Rienzi enjoyed a short, troubled, and restless sleep, over which Nina watched—unslumbering, anxious, tearful, and oppressed with dark and terrible forewarnings—the accuser was more happy than the judge. The last thoughts that floated before the young mind of Angelo Villani, ere wrapped in sleep, were bright and sanguine. He felt no honorable remorse that he had entrapped the confidence of another—he felt only that his scheme had prospered, that his mission had been fulfilled. The grateful words of Rienzi rang in his ear, and hopes of fortune and power, beneath the sway of the Roman Senator, lulled him into slumber, and colored all his dreams.

Scarce, however, had he been two hours asleep, ere he was wakened by one of the attendants of the palace, himself half awake. "Pardon me, Messere Villani," said he "but there is a messenger below from the good Sister Ursula; he bids thee haste instantly to the Convent—she is sick unto death, and has tidings that crave thy immediate presence."

Angelo, whose morbid susceptibility as to his parentage was ever excited by vague but ambitious hopes—started up, dressed hurriedly, and joining the messenger below, repaired to the Convent. In the Court of the Capitol, and by the Staircase of the Lion, was already heard the noise of the workmen, and looking back, Villani beheld the scaffold, hung with black—sleeping cloudlike in the gray light of dawn—at the same time, the bell of the Capitol tolled heavily. A pang shot athwart him. He hurried on;—despite the immature earliness of the hour, he met groups of either sex, hastening along the streets to witness the execution of the redoubted Captain of the Grand Company. The Convent of the Augustines was at the farthest extremity of that city, even then so extensive, and the red light upon the hill tops already heralded the rising sun, ere the young man reached the venerable porch. His name obtained him instant admittance.

"Heaven grant," said an old Nun, who conducted him through a long and winding passage, "that thou mayst bring comfort to the sick sister, she has pined for thee grievously since matins."

In a cell set apart for the reception of visitors (from the outward world), to such of the Sisterhood as received the necessary dispensation, sate the aged Nun. Angelo had only seen her once since his return to Rome, and since then disease had made rapid havoc on her form and features. And now, in her shroudlike garments and attenuated frame, she seemed by the morning light as a spectre whom day had surprised above the earth. She approached the youth, however, with a motion more elastic and rapid than seemed possible to her worn and ghastly form. "Thou art come," she said. "Well, well! This morning after matins, my confessor, an Augustine, who alone knows the secrets of my life, took me aside, and told me that Walter de Montreal had been seized by the Senator—that he was adjudged to die, and that one of the Augustine brotherhood had been sent for to attend his last hours—is it so?"

"Thou wert told aright," said Angelo, won

the city; and, as he boasted, was the only chief in Italy who reigned in his palace guarded only by his citizens.

Despite his perilous situation—despite his suspicions, and his fears, no wanton cruelty stained his stern justice—Montreal and Pandulfo di Guido were the only state victims he demanded. If, according to the dark Machiavelism of Italian wisdom, the death of those enemies was impolitic, it was not in the act, but the mode of doing it. A prince of Bologna, or of Milan would have avoided the sympathy excited by the scaffold, and the drug or the dagger would have been the safer substitute for the axe. But with all his faults, real and imputed, no single act of that foul and murtherous policy, which made the science of the more fortunate prince of Italy, ever advanced the ambition or promoted the security of the Last of the Roman Tribunes. Whatever his errors, he lived and died as became a man, who dreamed the vain but glorious dream, that in a corrupt and dastard populace he could revive the genius of the old Republic.

Of all who attended on the Senator, the most assiduous and the most honored was still Angelo Villani. Promoted to a high civil station, Rienzi felt it as a return of youth, to find one person entitled to his gratitude;—he loved and confided in the youth as a son. Villani was never absent from his side, except in intercourse with the various popular leaders in the various quarters of the city; and in this intercourse his zeal was indefatigable—it seemed even to prey upon his health; and Rienzi chid him fondly, whenever starting from his own reveries, he beheld the abstracted eye and the livid paleness which had succeeded the sparkle and bloom of youth.

Such chiding the young man answered only by the same unvarying words.

"Senator, I have a great trust to fulfil;"—and at these words he smiled.

One day Villani, while with the Senator, said rather abruptly, "Do you remember, my Lord, that before Viterbo, I acquitted myself so in arms, that even the Cardinal d'Albornoz was pleased to notice me?"

"I remember your valor well, Angelo; but why the question!"

"My Lord, Bellini, the Captain of the Guard of the Capitol is dangerously ill."

"I know it."

"Whom can my Lord trust at the post?"

"Why, the Lieutenant."

"What!—a soldier that has served under the Orsini!"

"True. Well! there is Tommaso Filangieri."

"An excellent man; but is he not kin by blood to Pandulfo di Guido?"

"Ay—is he so? It must be thought of. Hast *thou* any friend to name!" said the Senator, smiling, "Methinks thy cavils point that way."

"My Lord," replied Villani, coloring; "I am too young, perhaps; but the post is one that demands fidelity more than it does years. Shall I own it?—My tastes are rather to serve thee with my sword than with my pen."

"Wilt thou, indeed, accept the office? It is of less dignity and emolument than the one you hold; and you are full young to lead these stubborn spirits."

"Senator, I led taller men than they are to the assault of Viterbo. But, be it as seems best to your superior wisdom. Whatever you do, I pray you to be cautious. If you select a traitor to the command of the Capitol Guard!—I tremble at the thought!"

"By my faith, thou dost turn pale at it, dear boy; thy affection is a sweet drop in a bitter draught. Whom can I choose better than thee?—thou shalt have the post, at least during Bellini's illness. I will attend to it to-day. The business, too, will less fatigue thy young mind than that which now employs thee. Thou art over-labored in our cause."

"Senator, I can but repeat my usual answer—I have a great trust to fulfil!"

CHAPTER VII.

The Tax.

These formidable conspiracies quelled, the Barons nearly subdued, and three parts of the Papal territory re-united to Rome, Rienzi now deemed he might safely execute one of his favorite projects for the preservation of the liberties of his native city; and this was to raise and organize in each quarter of Rome a Roman Legion. Armed in the defence of their own institutions, he thus trusted to establish amongst her own citizens the only soldiery requisite for Rome.

But so base were the tools with which this great man was condemned to work out his noble schemes, that none could be found to serve their own country, without a pay equal to that demanded by foreign hirelings. With the insolence so peculiar to a race that has once been great, each Roman said, "Am I not better than a German?—Pay me, then, accordingly."

The Senator smothered his disgust—he had learned at last to know that the age of the Catos was no more. From a daring enthusiast, experience had converted him into a practical statesman. The Legions were necessary to Rome—they were formed—gallant their appearance and faultless their caparisons. How were they to be paid? There was but one means to maintain Rome—Rome must be taxed. A gabelle was put upon wine and salt.

The Proclamation ran thus:—

"Romans! raised to the rank of your Senator, my whole thought has been for your liberties and welfare; already treason defeated in the City, our banners triumphant without, attest the favor with which the Diety regards men who seek to unite liberty with law. Let us set an example to Italy and the World! Let us prove that the Roman sword can guard the Roman Forum! In each Rione of the City is provided a Legion of the Citizens, collected from the traders and artisans of the town; they allege that they cannot leave their callings without remuneration. Your Senator calls upon you willingly to assist in your own defence. He has given you liberty; he has restored to you peace, your oppressors are scattered over the earth. He asks you now to preserve the treasures you have gained. To be free, you must sacrifice something; for freedom, what sacrifice too great? Confident of your support, I at length, for the first time, exert the right entrusted to me by office—and for Rome's salvation I tax the Romans!"

Then followed the announcement of the gabelle.

The Proclamation was set up in the public thoroughfares. Round one of the placards a crowd assembled. Their gestures were vehement and unguarded—their eyes sparkled—they conversed low, but eagerly.

"He dares to tax us, then! Why, the Barons or the Pope could not do more than that!"

"Shame! shame!" cried a gaunt female; "we, who were his friends! How are our little ones to get bread?"

"He should have seized the Popes money!" quoth an honest wine-vender.

"Ah! Pandulfo di Guido would have maintained an army at his own cost. He was a rich man. What insolence in the innkeeper's son to be a Senator!"

"We are not Romans if we suffer this!" said a deserter from Palestrina.

"Fellow-citizens!" exclaimed gruffly a tall man, who had hitherto been making a clerk read to him the particulars of the tax imposed, and whose heavy brain at length understood that wine was to be made dearer—"Fellow-citizens, we must have a new revolution! This is indeed gratitude! What have we benefited by restoring this man! Are we always to be ground to the dust? To pay—pay—pay! Is that all we are fit for?"

"Hark to Cecco del Vecchio!"

"No, no; not now," growled the smith. "To-night the artificers have a special meeting. We 'll see—we 'll see!"

A young man, muffled in a cloak, who had not been before observed, touched the smith.

"Whoever storms the Capitol the day after to-morrow at the dawn," he whispered, "shall find the guards absent!"

He was gone before the smith could look round.

The same night Rienzi, retiring to rest, said to Angelo Villani—"A bold but necessary measure this of mine! How do the people take it?"

"They murmur a little, but seem to recognize the necessity. Cecco del Vecchio *was* the loudest grumbler, but is now the loudest approver."

"The man is rough; he once deserted me;—but then that fatal excommunication! He and the Romans learned a bitter lesson in that desertion, and experience has, I trust, taught them to be honest. Well, if this tax be raised quietly, in two years Rome will be again the Queen of Italy;—her army manned—her Republic formed; and then—then——"

"Then what, Senator?"

"Why then, my Angelo, Cola di Rienzi may

die in peace! There is a want which a profound experience of power and pomp brings at last to us—a want gnawing as that of hunger, wearing as that of sleep!—*my Angelo, it is the want to die!*"

"My Lord, I would give this right hand," cried Villani earnestly, "to hear you say you were attached to life!"

"You are a good youth, Angelo!" said Rienzi, as he passed to Nina's chamber; and in her smile and wistful tenderness, forgot for awhile—that he was a great man!

CHAPTER VIII.

The Threshold of the Event.

THE next morning the Senator of Rome held high Court in the Capitol. From Florence, from Padua, from Pisa, even from Milan, (the dominion of the Visconti), from Genoa, from Naples,—came Ambassadors to welcome his return, or to thank him for having freed Italy from the freebooter De Montreal. Venice alone, who held in her pay the Grand Company, stood aloof. Never had Rienzi seemed more prosperous and more powerful, and never had he exhibited a more easy and cheerful majesty of demeanor.

Scarce was the audience over, when a messenger arrived from Palestrina. The town had surrendered, the Colonna had departed, and the standard of the Senator waved from the walls of the last hold of the rebellious Barons. Rome might now at length consider herself free, and not a foe seemed left to menace the repose of Rienzi.

The Court dissolved. The Senator, elated and joyous, repaired towards his private apartments, previous to the banquet given to the Ambassadors. Villani met him with his wonted sombre aspect.

"No sadness to-day, my Angelo," said the Senator, gaily; "Palestrina is ours!"

"I am glad to hear such news, and to see my Lord of so fair a mien," answered Angelo. "Does he not now desire life?"

"Till Roman virtue revives, perhaps—yes! But thus are we fools of Fortune;—to-day glad—to-morrow dejected."

"To-morrow," repeated Villani, mechanically; "Ay—to-morrow perhaps dejected."

"Thou playest with my words, boy," said Rienzi, half angrily, as he turned away.

But Villani heeded not the displeasure of his Lord.

The banquet was thronged and brilliant; and Rienzi that day, without an effort, played the courteous host.

Milanese, Paduan, Pisan, Neapolitan, vied with each other in attracting the smiles of the potent Senator. Prodigal were their compliments—lavish their promises of support. No monarch in Italy seemed more securely throned.

The banquet was over (as usual on state occasions) at an early hour; and Rienzi, somewhat heated with wine, strolled forth alone from the Capitol. Bending his solitary steps towards the Palatine, he saw the pale and veil-like mists that succeed the sunset, gather over the wild grass which waves above the the Palace of the Cæsars. On a mound of ruins (column and arch overthrown) he stood, with folded arms, musing and intent. In the distance lay the melancholy tombs of the Campagna, and the circling hills, crested with the purple hues soon to melt beneath the starlight. Not a breeze stirred the dark cypress and unwaving pine. There was something awful in the stillness of the skies, hushing the desolate grandeur of the earth below. Many and mingled were the thoughts that swept over Rienzi's breast; memory was busy at his heart. How often, in his youth, had he trodden the same spot!—what visions had he nursed!—what hopes conceived! In the turbulence of his later life, Memory had long slept; but at that hour, she re-asserted her shadowy reign with a despotism that seemed prophetic. He was wandering—a boy, with his young brother, hand in hand, by the river side at eve: anon he saw a pale face and gory side, and once more uttered his imprecations of revenge! His first successes, his virgin triumphs, his secret love, his fame, his power, his reverses, the hermitage of Maiella, the dungeon of Avignon, the triumphal return to Rome,—all swept across his breast with a distinctness as if he were living those scenes again!—and *now!*—he shrunk from the *present*, and descended the hill. The moon, already risen, shed her light over the Forum, as he passed through its mingled ruins. By the Temple of Jupiter, two figures suddenly emerged; the moonlight fell upon their faces, and Rienzi recognized Cecco del Vecchio and Angelo Villani. They saw him not; but, eagerly conversing, disappeared by the arch of Trajan.

"Villani! ever active in my service!" thought the Senator; "methinks this morning I spoke to him harshly—it was churlish in me!"

He re-entered the Place of the Capitol—he stood by the staircase of the Lion; there was a red stain upon the pavement, unobliterated since Montreal's execution, and the Senator drew himself aside with an inward shudder. Was it the ghastly and spectral light of the Moon, or did the face of that old Egyptian Monster wear an aspect that was as of life? The stony eyeballs seemed bent upon him with a malignant scowl; and as he passed on, and looked behind, they appeared almost preternaturally to follow his steps. A chill, he knew not why, sunk into his heart. He hastened to regain his palace. The sentinels made way for him.

"Senator," said one of them, doubtingly, "Messere Angelo Villani is our new captain—we are to obey his orders?"

"Assuredly," returned the Senator, passing on. The man lingered uneasily, as if he would have spoken, but Rienzi observed it not. Seeking his chamber, he found Nina and Irene waiting for him. His heart yearned to his wife. Care and toil had of late driven her from his thoughts, and he felt it remorsefully, as he gazed upon her noble face, softened by the solicitude of untiring and anxious love.

"Sweetest," said he, winding his arms around her tenderly; "thy lips never chide me, but thine eyes sometimes do! We have been apart too long. Brighter days dawn upon us, when I shall have leisure to thank thee for all thy care. And you, my fair sister, you smile on me!—ah, you have heard that your lover, ere this, is released by the cession of Palestrina, and to-morrow's sun will see him at your feet. Despite all the cares of the day, I remembered thee, my Irene, and sent a messenger to bring back the blush to that pale cheek. Come, come, we shall be happy again!" And with that domestic fondness common to him, when harsher thoughts permitted, he sate himself beside the two persons dearest to his hearth and heart.

"So happy—if we could have many hours like this!" murmured Nina, sinking on his breast. "Yet sometimes I wish——"

"And I too," interrupted Rienzi; "for I read thy woman's thought—*I* too sometimes wish fate had placed us in the lowlier valleys of life! But it may come yet! Irene wedded to Adrian—Rome married to Liberty—and then, Nina, methinks you and I would find some quiet hermitage, and talk over old gauds and triumphs, as of a summer's dream. Beautiful, kiss me! Couldst thou resign these pomps?"

"For a desert with *thee*, Cola!"

"Let me reflect," resumed Rienzi; "is not to-day the seventh of October? Yes! on the seventh, be it noted, my foes yielded to my power! Seven! my fated number, whether ominous of good or evil! Seven months did I reign as Tribune—seven * years was I absent as an exile; to-morrow, that sees me without an enemy, completes my seventh week of return!"

"And seven was the number of the crowns the Roman Convents and the Roman Council awarded thee, after the ceremony which gave thee the knighthood of *Santo Spirito!*" † said Nina, adding, with woman's tender wit, "the brightest association of all!"

"Follies seem these thoughts to others, and to philosophy, in truth, they are so," said Rienzi; "but all my life long, omen and type and shadow have linked themselves to action and event: and the atmosphere of other men hath not been mine. Life itself a riddle, why should riddles amaze us? *The Future!*—what mystery in the very word! Had we lived all *through* the Past, since Time was, our profoundest experience of a thousand ages could not give us a guess of the events that wait the very moment we are about to enter! Thus deserted by reason, what wonder that we recur to the Imagination, on which, by dream and

* There was the lapse of one year between the release of Rienzi from Avignon, and his triumphal return to Rome: a year chiefly spent in the campaign of Albornoz.

† This superstition had an excuse in strange historical coincidences; and the number seven was indeed to Rienzi what the 3rd of September was to Cromwell. The ceremony of the seven crowns which he received after his knighthood, on the nature of which ridiculous ignorance has been shown by many recent writers. was, in fact, principally a religious and typical donation, (symbolical of the gifts of the Holy Spirit,) conferred by the heads of convents—and that part of the ceremony which was political, was republican, not regal.

symbol, God sometimes paints the likeness of things to come? Who can endure to leave the Future all unguessed, and sit tamely down to groan under the fardel of the Present? No, no! that which the foolish-wise call Fanaticism, belongs to the same part of us as Hope. Each but carries us onward—from a barren strand to a glorious, if unbounded sea. Each is the yearning for the GREAT BEYOND. which attests our immortality. Each has its visions and chimeras—some false, but *some* true! Verily, a man who becomes great is often but made so by a kind of sorcery in his own soul—a Pythia which prophesies that he *shall* be great—and so renders the life one effort to fulfil the warning! Is this folly?—it were so, if all things stopped at the grave! But perhaps the very sharpeniug, and exercising, and elevating the faculties here—though but for a bootless end *on* earth—may be designed to fit the soul, thus quickened and ennobled, to some high destiny *beyond* the earth! Who can tell? not I!——Let us pray!"

While the Senator was thus employed, Rome in her various quarters presented less holy and quiet scenes.

In the fortress of the Orsini lights flitted to and fro, through the gratings of the great court. Angelo Villani might be seen stealing from the postern-gate. Another hour, and the Moon was high in heaven; toward the ruins of the Colosseum, men, whose dress bespoke them of the lowest rank, were seen creeping from lanes and alleys, two by two; from these ruins glided again the form of the son of Montreal. Later yet—the Moon is sinking—a gray light breaking in the East—and the gates of Rome, by St. John of Lateran, are open! Villani is conversing with the sentries! The Moon has set—the mountains are dim with a mournful and chilling haze—Villani is before the palace of the Capitol—the *only* soldier there! Where are the Roman legions that were to guard alike the freedom and the deliverer of Rome?

CHAPTER THE LAST.

The Close of the Chase.

IT was the morning of the 8th of October, 1354. Rienzi, who rose betimes, stirred restlessly in his bed. "It is yet early," he said to Nina, whose soft arm was round his neck; "none of my people seem to be astir. Howbeit, *my* day begins before *theirs*."

"Rest yet, my Cola; you want sleep."

"No; I feel feverish, and this old pain in the side torments me. I have letters to write."

"Let me be your secretary, dearest," said Nina.

Rienzi smiled affectionately as he rose; he repaired to his closet adjoining his sleeping apartment, and used the bath, as was his wont. Then dressing himself, he returned to Nina, who, already loosely robed, sate by the writing-table, ready for her office of love.

"How still are all things!" said Rienzi. "What a cool and delicious prelude, in these early hours, to the toilsome day."

Leaning over his wife, he then dictated different letters, interrupting the task at times by such observations as crossed his mind.

"So, now to Annibaldi! By the way, young Adrian should join us to-day; how I rejoice for Irene's sake!"

"Dear sister—yes! she loves,—if any, Cola, can so love,—as we do."

"Well, but to your task, my fair scribe. Ha! what noise is that? I hear an armed step—the stairs creak—some one shouts my name."

Rienzi flew to his sword! the door was thrown rudely open, and a figure in complete armor appeared within the chamber.

"How! what means this?" said Rienzi, standing before Nina, with his drawn sword.

The intruder lifted his visor—it was Adrian Colonna.

"Fly, Rienzi!—hasten, Signora? Thank Heaven, I can save ye yet! Myself and train released by the capture of Palestrina, the pain of my wound detained me last night at Tivoli. The town was filled with armed men—not *thine*, Senator. I heard rumors that alarmed me. I resolved to proceed onward I reached Rome, the gates of the city were wide open!"

"How!"

"Your guard gone. Presently I came upon a band of the retainers of the Savelli. My insignia, as a Colonna, misled them. I learned that this very hour some of your enemies are within the city, the rest are on their march—the people themselves arm against you. In the obscurer streets I passed through, the mob were already forming. They took me for thy foe, and shouted. I came hither—thy sentries have vanished. The private door below is unbarred and open. Not a soul seems left in thy palace. Haste—save thyself?—Where is Irene?"

"The Capitol deserted!—impossible!" cried Rienzi. He strode across the chambers to the ante-room, where his night-guard usually waited—it was empty! He passed hastily to Villani's room—it was untenanted! He would have passed farther, but the doors were secured without. It was evident that all egress had been cut off, save by the private door below,—and *that* had been left open to admit his murderers!

He returned to his room--Nina had already gone to rouse and prepare Irene, whose chamber was on the other side, within one of their own.

"Quick, Senator!" said Adrian. "Methinks there is yet time. We must make across to the Tiber. I have stationed my faithful squires and Northmen there. A boat waits us.

"Hark!" interrupted Rienzi, whose senses had of late been preternaturally quickened. "I hear a distant shout—a familiar shout, 'Viva 'l Popolo!' Why, so say I! These must be friends."

"Deceive not thyself; thou hast scarce a friend at Rome."

"Hist!" said Rienzi in a whisper; "save Nina—save Irene. I cannot accompany thee."

"Art thou mad?"

"No! but fearless. Besides, did I accompany, I might but destroy you all. Were I found with you, you would be massacred with me. Without me ye are safe. Yes, even the Senator's wife and sister have provoked no revenge. Save them, noble Colonna! Cola di Rienzi puts his trust in God alone!"

By this time Nina had returned, Irene with her. Afar was heard the tramp—steady—slow—gathering—of the fatal multitude.

"Now, Cola," said Nina, with a bold and cheerful air, and she took her husband's arm, while Adrian had already found his charge in Irene.

"Yes, *now*, Nina!" said Rienzi; at length we part! If this is my last hour—*in* my last hour I pray God to bless and shield thee! for verily, thou hast been my exceeding solace—provident as a parent, tender as a child, the smile of my hearth, the—the——"

Rienzi was almost unmanned. Emotions, deep, conflicting, unspeakably fond and grateful, literally choked his speech.

"What!" cried Nina, clinging to his breast, and parting her hair from her eyes, as she sought his averted face. "Part!—never! This is my place—all Rome shall not tear me from it!"

Adrian, in despair, seized her hand, and attempted to drag her thence.

"Touch me not, sir!" said Nina, waving her arm with angry majesty, while her eyes sparkled as a lioness, whom the huntsmen would sever from her young. "I am the wife of Cola di Rienzi, the great Senator of Rome, and by his side will I live and die!"

"Take her hence: quick!—quick! I hear the crowd advancing."

Irene tore herself from Adrian, and fell at the feet of Rienzi—she clasped his knees.

"Come, my brother, come! Why lose these precious moments? Rome forbids you to cast away a life in which her very self is bound up."

"Right, Irene; Rome is bound up with me, and we will rise or fall together!—no more!"

"You destroy us all!" said Adrian, with generous and impatient warmth. "A few minutes more, and we are lost. Rash man! it is not to fall by an infuriate mob that you have been preserved from so many dangers."

"I believe it," said the Senator, as his tall form seemed to dilate as with the greatness of his own soul. "I shall triumph yet! Never shall mine enemies—never shall posterity say that a *second* time Rienzi abandoned Rome! Hark! 'Viva 'l Popolo!' still the cry of 'THE PEOPLE.' That cry scares none but tyrants! I shall triumph and survive!"

"And I with thee!" said Nina, firmly. Rienzi paused a moment, gazed on his wife, passionately clasped her to his heart, kissed her again and again, and then said, "Nina, I command thee,—Go!"

"Never!"

He paused. Irene's face drowned in tears, met his eyes.

"We will all perish with you," said his sister; "you only, Adrian, *you* leave us!"

"Be it so," said the Knight, sadly; "we will

all remain," and he desisted at once from further effort.

There was a dead but short pause, broken but by a convulsive sob from Irene. The tramp of the raging thousands sounded fearfully distinct. Rienzi seemed lost in thought —then lifting his head he said calmly, "Ye have triumphed—I join ye—I but collect these papers, and follow you. Quick, Adrian—save them!" and he pointed meaningly to Nina.

Waiting no other hint, the young Colonna seized Nina in his strong grasp—with his left hand he supported Irene, who with terror and excitement was almost insensible. Rienzi relieved him of the lighter load—he took his sister in his arms, and descended the winding stairs. Nina remained passive—she heard her husband's step behind, it was enough for her —she but turned once to thank him with her eyes. A tall Northman clad in armor stood at the open door. Rienzi placed Irene, now perfectly lifeless, in the soldier's arms, and kissed her pale cheek in silence.

"Quick, my Lord," said the Northman, "on all sides they come!" So saying, he bounded down the descent with his burthen. Adrian followed with Nina, the Senator paused one moment, turned back, and was in his room ere Adrian was aware that he had vanished.

Hastily he drew the coverlid from his bed, fastened it to the casement bars, and by its aid dropped (at a distance of several feet) into the balcony below. "I will not die like a rat," said he, "in the trap they have set for me! The whole shall, at least, see and hear me."

This was the work of a moment.

Menwhile, Nina had scarcely proceeded six paces, before she discovered that she was alone with Adrian.

"Ha! Cola!" she cried, "where is he? he has gone!"

"Take heart, Lady, he has returned but for some secret papers he has forgotten. He will follow us anon."

"Let us wait, then."

"Lady," said Adrian, grinding his teeth, "hear you not the crowd?—on, on!" and he flew with a swifter step. Nina struggled in his grasp—Love gave her strength of despair. With a wild laugh she broke from him. She flew back—the door was closed—but unbarred —her trembling hands lingered a moment round the spring. She opened it, drew the heavy bolt across the panels, and frustrated all attempts from Adrian to regain her. She was on the stairs,—she was in the room. Rienzi was gone! She fled, shrieking his name, through the State Chambers—all was desolate. She found the doors opening on the various passages that admitted to the rooms below barred without. Breathless and gasping, she returned to the chamber. She hurried to the casement—she perceived the method by which he had descended below—her brave heart told her of his brave design;—she saw they were separated,—"But the same roof holds us," she cried, joyously, "and our fate shall be the same!" With that thought she sank in mute patience on the floor.

Forming the generous resolve not to abandon the faithful and devoted pair without another effort, Adrian had followed Nina, but too late—the door was closed against his efforts. The crowd marched on—he heard their cry change on a sudden—it was no longer "LIVE THE PEOPLE!" but, "DEATH TO THE TRAITOR!" His attendant had already disappeared, and waking now only to the danger of Irene, the Colonna in bitter grief turned away, lightly sped down the descent, and hastened to the river side, where the boat and his band awaited him.

The balcony on which Rienzi had alighted was that from which he had been accustomed to address the people—it communicated with a vast hall used on solemn occasions for State festivals—and on either side were square projecting towers, whose grated casements looked into the balcony. One of these towers was devoted to the armory, the other contained the prison of Brettone, the brother of Montreal. Beyond the latter tower was the general prison of the Capitol. For then the prison and the palace were in awful neighborhood!

The windows of the Hall were yet open—and Rienzi passed into it from the balcony—the witness of the yesterday's banquet was still there—the wine, yet undried, crimsoned the floor, and gobblets of gold and silver shone from the recesses. He proceeded at once to the armory, and selected from the various suits that which he himself had worn when, nearly eight years ago, he had chased the Barons from the gates of Rome. He arrayed himself in the mail, leaving only his head uncovered; and then taking, in his right hand, from the wall, the great Gonfalon of Rome, returned once more to the hall. Not a man encountered him. In that vast building, save the prisoners, and the faithful Nina, whose presence he knew not of—the Senator was alone.

On they came, no longer in measured order, as stream after stream—from lane, from alley, from palace and from hovel—the raging sea received new additions. On they came—their passions excited by their numbers—women and men, children and malignant age—in all the awful array of aroused, released, unresisted physical strength and brutal wrath; "Death to the traitor—death to the tyrant—death to him who has taxed the people!"—"*Mora l' traditore che ha fatta la gabella!—Mora!*" Such was the cry of the people—such the crime of the Senator! They broke over the low palisades of the Capitol—they filled with one sudden rush the vast space;—a moment before so desolate,—now swarming with human beings athirst for blood!

Suddenly came a dead silence, and on the balcony above stood Rienzi—his head was bared and the morning sun shone over that lordly brow, and his hair grown gray before its time, in the service of that maddening multitude. Pale and erect he stood—neither fear, nor anger, nor menace—but deep grief and high resolve—upon his features! A momentary shame—a momentary awe seized the crowd.

He pointed to the Gonfalon, wrought with the Republican motto and arms of Rome, and thus he began:—

"I too am a Roman and a Citizen; hear me!"

"Hear him not! hear him not! his false tongue can charm away our senses!" cried a voice louder than his own; and Rienzi recognized Cecco del Vecchio.

"Hear him not! down with the tyrant!" cried a more shrill and youthful tone; and by the side of the artisan stood Angelo Villani.

"Hear him not! death to the death-giver!" cried a voice close at hand, and from the grating of the neighboring prison glared near upon him, as the eye of a tiger, the vengeful gaze of the brother of Montreal.

Then from Earth to Heaven rose the roar—"Down with the tyrant—down with him who taxed the people!"

A shower of stones rattled on the mail of the Senator,—still he stirred not. No changing muscle betokened fear. His persuasion of his own wonderful powers of eloquence, if he could but be heard, inspired him yet with hope; he stood collected in his own indignant, but determined thoughts;—but the knowledge of that very eloquence was now his deadliest foe. The leaders of the multitude trembled lest he *should* be heard; "*and doubtless*," says the contemporaneous biographer, "*had he but spoken he would have changed them all, and the work been marred.*"

The soldiers of the Barons had already mixed themselves with the throng—more deadly weapons than stones aided the wrath of the multitude—darts and arrows darkened the air; and now a voice was heard shrieking, "Way for the torches!" And red in the sunlight the torches tossed and waved, and danced to and fro, above the heads of the crowd, as if the fiends were let loose amongst the mob! And what place in hell *hath* fiends like those a mad mob can furnish? Straw, and wood, and litter, were piled hastily round the great doors of the Capitol, and the smoke curled suddenly up, beating back the rush of the assailants.

Rienzi was no longer visible, an arrow had pierced his hand—the right had that supported the flag of Rome—the right hand that had given a constitution to the Republic. He retired from the storm into the desolate hall.

He sat down;—and tears, springing from no weak and woman source, but tears from the loftiest fountain of emotion—tears that befit a warrior when his own troops desert him—a patriot when his countrymen rush to their own doom—a father when his children rebel against his love,—tears such as these forced themselves from his eyes and relieved,—but *they changed*, his heart!

"Enough, enough!" he said, presently rising and dashing the drops scornfully away; "I have risked, dared, toiled enough for this dastard and degenerate race. I will yet baffle their malice—I renounce the thought of which they are so little worthy!—Let Rome perish!—I feel, at last, that I am nobler than my country!—she deserves not so high a sacrifice!"

With that feeling, Death lost all the nobleness of aspect it had before presented to him,

Rienzi fell from the vices of the People. The Tribune was a victim to ignorant cowardice—the Senator, a victim to ferocious avarice. It is this which modern historians have failed to represent. Gibbon records rightly, that the Count of Minorbino entered Rome with one hundred and fifty soldiers, and barricadoed the quarter of the Colonna—that the bell of the Capitol sounded—that Rienzi addressed the People—that they were silent and inactive—and that Rienzi then abdicated the government. But for this he calls *Rienzi* "pusillanimous." Is not that epithet to be applied to *the People?* Rienzi invoked them to move against the Robber—the People refused to obey. Rienzi wished to fight—the People refused to stir. It was not the cause of Rienzi alone which demanded their exertions—it was the cause of the People—*theirs*, not his, the shame, if one hundred and fifty foreign solders mastered Rome overthrew their liberties and restored their tyrants! Whatever Rienzi's sins, whatever his unpopularity, *their* freedom, *their* laws, *their* republic, were at stake; and these they surrendered to one hundred and fifty hirelings! This is the fact that damns them! But Rienzi was not unpopular when he addressed and conjured them: they found no fault with him. "The sighs and the groans of the People," says Sismondi, justly, "replied to his,"—they could weep, but they would not fight. This strange apathy the modern historians have not accounted for, yet the principal cause was obvious—Rienzi was *excommunicated!* * In stating the fact, these writers have seemed to think that excommunication in Rome, in the fourteenth century, produced no effect!—the effect it did produce I have endeavored in these pages to convey.

The causes of the second fall and final murder of Rienzi are equally misstated by modern narrators. It was from no fault of his—no injustice, no cruelty, no extravagance—it was not from the execution of Montreal, nor that of Pandulfo di Guido—*it was from a gabelle on wine and salt that he fell.* To preserve Rome from the tyrants it was necessary to maintain an armed force; (to pay the force a tax was necessary;) the tax was imposed—and the multitude joined with the tyrants, and their cry was, "Perish the traitor *who has made the gabelle!*" This was their only charge—this the only crime that their passions and their fury could cite against him.

The faults of Rienzi are sufficiently visible, and I have not unsparingly shown them; but we must judge men, not according as they approach perfection, but according as their good or bad qualities preponderate—their talents or their weaknesses—the benefits they effected, the evil they wrought. For a man who rose to so great a power, Rienzi's faults were singularly few—*crimes* he committed none. He is almost the only man who ever rose from the rank of a citizen to a power equal to that of monarchs without a single act of violence or treachery. When *in* power, he was vain, ostentatious, and imprudent,—always an enthusiast—often a fanatic; but his very faults had greatness of soul, and his very fanaticism at once supported his enthusiastic daring, and proved his earnest honesty. It is evident that no heinous charge could be brought against him even by his enemies, for all the accusations to which he was subjected, when excommunicated, exiled, fallen, were for two offences which Petrarch rightly deemed the proofs of his virtue and his glory: first, for declaring Rome to be free; secondly, for pretending that the Romans had a right of choice in the election of the Roman Emperor.* Stern, just, and inflexible, as he was when Tribune, his fault was never that of *wanton* cruelty. The accusation against him, made by the gentle Petrarch, indeed, was that he was not determined enough—that he did not consummate the revolution by exterminating the patrician tyrants. When Senator, he was, without sufficient ground, accused of avarice in the otherwise just and necessary execution of Montreal.† It was natural enough that his enemies and the vulgar should suppose that he executed a creditor to get rid of a debt; but it was inexcusable in later, and wiser, and fairer writers to repeat so grave a calumny, without at least adding the obvious suggestion, that the avarice of Rienzi could have been much better gratified by sparing than by destroying the life of one of the richest subjects in Europe. Montreal, we may be quite sure, would have purchased his life at an immeasurably higher price than the paltry sum lent to Rienzi by his brothers. And this is not a probable hypothesis, but a certain fact, for we are expressly told that Montreal, "knowing the Tribune was in want of money, offered Rienzi, that if he would let him go, he, Montreal, would furnish him not only with twenty thousand florins, (four times the amount of Rienzi's debt to him,) but with as many soldiers and as much money as he pleased." This offer Rienzi did not attend to. Would he have rejected it had avarice been his motive? And what cul-

* And this curse I apprehend to have been the more effective in the instance of Rienzi, from a fact that it would be interesting and easy to establish: viz., that he owed his rise as much to religious as to civil causes. He aimed evidently to be a religious Reformer. All his devices, ceremonies, and watchwords, were of a religious character. The monks took part with his enterprise, and joined in the revolution. His letters are full of mystical fanaticism. His references to ancient heroes of Rome are always mingled with invocations to her Christian Saints. The Bible, at that time little read by the public civilians of Italy, is constantly in his hands, and his addresses studded with texts. His very garments were adorned with sacred and mysterious emblems. No doubt, the ceremony of his Knighthood, which Gibbon ridicules as an act of mere vanity, was but another of his religious extravagances; for he peculiarly dedicated his Knighthood to the service of the Santo Spirito; and his bathing in the vase of Constantine was quite of a piece, not with the vanity of the Tribune, but with the extravagance of the Fanatic. In fact, they tried hard to prove him a heretic; but he escaped a charge under the mild Innocent, which a century or two before, or a century or two afterwards, would have sufficed to have sent a dozen Rienzis to the stake. I have dwelt the more upon this point, because, if it be shown that religious causes operated with those of liberty, we throw a new light upon the whole of that most extraordinary revolution, and its suddenness is infinitely less striking. The deep impression Rienzi produced upon that populace was thus stamped with the spirit of the religious enthusiast more than that of the classical demagogue. And, as in the time of Cromwell, the desire for temporal liberty was warmed and colored by the presence of a holier and more spiritual fervor:—"The Good Estate" (*Buono Stato*) of Rienzi reminds us a little of the Good Cause of General Cromwell.

* The charge of heresy was dropped.

† Gibbon, in mentioning the execution of Montreal, omits to state that Montreal was more than suspected of conspiracy and treason to restore the Colonna. Matthew Villani records it as a common belief that such truly was the offence of the Provençal. The biographer of Rienzi gives additional evidence of the fact. Gibbon's knowledge of this time was superficial. As one instance of this, he strangely enough represents Montreal as the head of the *first* Free Company that desolated Italy: he took that error from the Père du Cerceau.

pable injustice, to mention the vague calumny without citing the practical contradiction! When Gibbon tells us, also, that "the *most* virtuous citizen of Rome, meaning Pandulfo, or Pandolficcio di Guido,* was sacrificed to his jealousy, he a little exaggerates the expression bestowed upon Pandulfo, which is that of "virtuoso assai;" and that expression, too, used by a man who styles the robber Montreal "eccellente uomo —di quale fama suono per tutta la Italia di virtude" † —(so good a moral critic was the writer!) but he also altogether waves all mention of the probabilities that are sufficiently apparent, of the scheming of Pandulfo to supplant Rienzi, and to obtain the "Signoria del Popolo." Still, however, if the death of Pandulfo may be considered a blot on the memory of Rienzi, it does not appear that it was this which led to his own fate. The cry of the mob surrounding his palace was not, "Perish him who executed Pandulfo," it was—and this again and again must be carefully noted—it was nothing more nor less than, "*Perish him who has made the gabelle!*"

Gibbon sneers at the military skill and courage of Rienzi. For this sneer there is no cause. His first attempts, his first rise, attested sufficiently his daring and brave spirit; in every danger he was present—never shrinking from a foe so long as he was supported by the People. He distinguished himself at Viterbo when in the camp of Albornoz, in several feats of arms,‡ and his end was that of a hero. So much for his courage; as to his military skill, it would be excusable enough if Rienzi—the eloquent and gifted student, called from the closet and the rostrum to assume the command of an army—should have been deficient in the art of war; yet, somehow or other, upon the whole, his arms prospered. He defeated the chivalry of Rome at her gates; and if he did not, after his victory, march to Marino, for which his biographer § and Gibbon blame him, the reason is sufficiently clear—"Volea pecunia per soldati"—*he wanted money for the soldiers!* On his return as Senator, it must be remembered that he had to besiege Palestrina, which was considered even by the ancient Romans almost impregnable by position; but during the few weeks he was in power, Palestrina yielded—all his open enemies were defeated —the tyrants expelled—Rome free; and this without support from any party, Papal or Popular, or, as Gibbon well expresses it, "suspected by the People—abandoned by the Prince."

On regarding what Rienzi did, we must look to his means, to the difficulties that surrounded him, to the scantiness of his resources. We see a man without rank, wealth, or friends, raising himself to the head of a popular government in the metropolis of the Church —in the City of the Empire. We see him reject any title save that of a popular magistrate—establish at one stroke a free constitution—a new code of law. We see him first expel, then subdue, the fiercest aristocracy in Europe—conquer the most stubborn banditti, rule impartially the most turbulent people, embruted by the violence, and sunk in the corruption of centuries. We see him restore trade—establish order—create civilization as by a miracle—receive from crowned heads homage and congratulation—outwit, conciliate, or awe, the wiliest priesthood of the Papal Diplomacy—and raise his native city at once to sudden yet acknowledged eminence over every other state, its superior in arts, wealth, and civilization;—we ask what errors we are to weigh in the opposite balance, and we find an unnecessary ostentation, a fanatical extravagance, and a certain insolent sternness. But what are such offences —what the splendor of a banquet, or the ceremony of Knighthood, or a few arrogant words, compared with the vices of almost every prince who was his contemporary? This is the way to judge character: we must compare men with men, and not with ideals of what men should be. We look to the amazing benefits Rienzi conferred upon his country. We ask his means, and see but his own abilities. His treasury becomes impoverished—his enemies revolt—the Church takes advantage of his weakness—he is excommunicated—the soldiers refuse to fight—the People refuse to assist —the Barons ravage the country—the ways are closed, the provisions are cut off from Rome.* A handful of banditti enter the city—Rienzi proposes to resist them —the People desert—he abdicates. Rapine, Famine, Massacre, ensue—they who deserted, regret, repent—yet he is still unassisted, alone—now an exile, now a prisoner, his own genius saves him from every peril, and restores him to greatness. He returns, the Pope's Legate refuses him arms—the People refuse him money. He re-establishes law and order, expels the tyrants, renounces his former faults †—is prudent, wary, provident—reigns a few weeks—taxes the People, in support of the People, and is torn to pieces! One day of the rule that followed is sufficient to vindicate his reign and avenge his memory—and for centuries afterwards, whenever that wretched and degenerate populace dreamed of glory or sighed for justice, they

---

* Matthew Villani speaks of him as a wise and good citizen, of great repute among the People—and this, it seems, he really was.

† "An excellent man whose fame for valor resounded throughout all Italy."

‡ Vit. di Col. di Rienzi, lib. ii. cap. 14.

§ In this the anonymous writer compares him gravely to Hannibal, who knew how to conquer, but not how to use his conquest.

* "Allora le strade furo chiuse, li massari de la terre non portavano grano, ogni die nasceva nuovo rumore."—*Vit. di Col. di Rienzi*, lib. i. cap. 37.

† This, the second period of his power, has been represented by Gibbon and others as that of his principal faults, and he is evidently at this time no favorite with his contemporaneous biographer; but looking to what he *did*, we find amazing dexterity, prudence, and energy in the most difficult crisis, and *none of his earlier faults*. It is true, that he does not show the same brilliant extravagance which, I suspect, dazzled his contemporaries, more than his sounder qualities; but we find that in a few weeks he had conquered all his powerful enemies—that his eloquence was as great as ever—his promptitude greater—his diligence indefatigable—his foresight unslumbering. "He alone," says the biographer, "carried on the affairs of Rome, but his officials were slothful and cold." This too, tortured by a painful disease—already—though yet young—broken and infirm. The only charges against him, as Senator, were the deaths of Montreal and Pandulfo di Guido, the imposition of the gabelle, and the renunciation of his former habits of rigid abstinence, for indulgence in wine and feasting. Of the first charges, the reader has already been enabled to form a judgment. To the last, alas! the reader must extend indulgence, and for it he may find excuse. We must compassionate even more than condemn the man to whom excitement has become nature, and who resorts to the physical stimulus or the momentary Lethe, when the mental exhilarations of hope, youth, and glory, begin to desert him. His alleged intemperance, however, which the Romans (a peculiarly sober people) might perhaps exaggerate, and for which he gave the excuse of a thirst produced by disease contracted in the dungeon of Avignon—evidently and confessedly did not in the least diminsh his attention to business, which, according to his biograher, was at that time greater than ever.

recalled the bright vision of their own victim, and deplored the fate of Cola di Rienzi. That he was not a tyrant is clear in this—when he was dead, he was bitterly regretted. The People never regret a tyrant! From the unpopularity that springs from other faults there is often a re-action; but there is no re-action in the populace towards their betrayer or oppressor. A thousand biographies cannot decide upon the faults or merits of a ruler like the one fact, whether he is beloved or hated ten years after he is dead. But if the ruler has been murdered by the People, and is then regretted by them, their repentance is his acquittal.

I have said that the moral of the Tribune's life, and of this fiction, is not the stale and unprofitable moral that warns the ambition of an individual:—More vast, more solemn, and more useful, it addresses itself to nations. If I judge not erringly, it proclaims that, to be great and free, a People must trust not to individuals but themselves—that there is no sudden leap from servitude to liberty—that it is to institutions, not to men, that they must look for reforms that last beyond the hour—that their own passions are the real despots they should subdue, their own reason the true regenerator of abuses. With a calm and a noble people, the individual ambition of a citizen can never effect evil:—to be impatient of chains, is not to be worthy of freedom—to murder a magistrate is not to ameliorate the laws.* The People write their own condemnation whenever they use characters of blood; and theirs alone the madness and the crime, if they crown a tyrant or butcher a victim.

* Rienzi was murdered because the Romans had been in the habit of murdering whenever they were displeased. They had, very shortly before, stoned one magistrate, and torn to pieces another. By the same causes and the same career a People may be made to resemble the bravo whose hand wanders to his knife at the smallest affront, and if to-day he poniards the enemy who assaults him, to-morrow he strikes the friend who would restrain.

APPENDIX II.

A WORD UPON THE WORK BY PERE DU CERCEAU AND PERE BRUMOY, ENTITLED "CONJURATION DE NICOLAS GABRINI, DIT DE RIENZI, TYRAN DE ROME."

SHORTLY after the Romance of "Rienzi" first appeared, a translation of the biography compiled by Cerceau and Brumoy was published by Mr. Whittaker. The translator, in a short and courteous advertisement, observes, "That it has always been considered as a work of authority; and even Gibbon appears to have relied on it without further research:" *......that, "as a record of facts, therefore, the work will, it is presumed, be acceptable to the public." The translator has fulfilled his duty with accuracy, elegance, and spirit,—and he must forgive me, if, in justice to History and Rienzi, I point out a very few from amongst a great many reasons, why the joint labor of the two worthy Jesuits cannot be considered either a work of authority, or a record of facts. The translator observes in his preface, "that the general outline (of Du Cerceau's work) was *probably* furnished by an Italian life written by a contemporary of Rienzi." The fact, however, is, that Du Cerceau's book is little more than a wretched paraphrase of that very Italian life mentioned by the translator,—full of blunders, from ignorance of the peculiar and antiquated dialect in which the original is written, and of assumptions by the Jesuit himself, which rest upon no authority whatever. I will first show, in support of this assertion, what the Italians themselves think of the work of Fathers Brumoy and Du Cerceau. The Signor Zefirino Re, who has proved himself singularly and minutely acquainted with the history of that time, and whose notes to the "Life of Rienzi" are characterized by acknowledged acuteness and research, thus describes the manner in which the two Jesuits compounded this valuable "record of facts."

"Father Du Cerceau for his work made use of a French translation of the life by the Italian contemporary printed in Bracciano, 1624, executed by Father Sanadon, another Jesuit, from whom he received the MS. This proves that Du Cerceau knew little of our 'volgar lingua' of the fourteenth century. But the errors into which he has run show, that even that little was unknown to his guide, and still less to Father Brumoy, (however learned and reputed the latter might be in *French* literature,) who, after the death of Du Cerceau, supplied the deficiencies in the first pages of the author's MS., which were, I know not how, lost; and in this part are found the more striking errors in the work, which shall be noticed in the proper place; in the meantime, one specimen will suffice. In the third chapter, book i., Cola, addressing the Romans, says, 'Che lo giubileo si appressima, che se la gente, la quale verrà al giubileo, li trova sproveduti di annona, le pietre (per metatesi sta scritto le preite) ne porteranno da Roma per rabbia di fame, e le pietre non basteranno a tanta moltitudine. Il francese traduce. Le jubilé approche, et vous n'avez ni provisions, ni vivres; les etrangers....trouveront votre ville denué de tout. Ne comptez point sur les secours des gens d'Eglise; ils sortiront de la ville, s'ils n'y trouvent de quoi subsister: et d'ailleurs pourroient-ils suffire à la multitude innombrable, que se trouvera dans vos murs?'" * "Buon Dio!" exclaims the learned Zefirino, "Buon Dio! le pietre prese per tanta gente di chiesa!" †

Another blunder little less extraordinary occurs in Chapter vi., in which the ordinances of Rienzi's Buono Stato are recited.

It is set forth as the third ordinance:—"Che nulla casa di Roma sia data per terra per alcuna cagione, ma

* Here, however, he does injustice to Gibbon.

* The English translator could not fail to adopt the Frenchman's ludicrous mistake.

† See Preface to Zefirino Re's edition of the "Life of Rienzi," p. 9, note on Du Cerceau.

vada in commune;" which simply means, that the houses of delinquents should in no instance be razed, but added to the community or confiscated. This law being intended partly to meet the barbarous violences with which the excesses and quarrels of the Barons had half dismantled Rome, and principally to repeal some old penal laws by which the houses of a certain class of offenders might be destroyed; but the French translator construes it, "*Que nulle maison de Rome ne saroit donnee en propre*, pour quelque raison que ce pût être; mais que les revenus en appartiendroient au public!" *

But enough of the blunders arising from ignorance. —I must now be permitted to set before the reader a few of the graver offences of wilful assumption and preposterous invention.

When Rienzi condemned some of the Barons to death, the Père thus writes: I take the recent translation published by Mr. Whittaker:—

"The next day the Tribune, resolving more than ever to rid himself of his prisoners, ordered tapestries of two colors, red and white, to be laid over the place whereon he held his councils, and which he had made choice of to be the theatre of this bloody tragedy, as the extraordinary tapestry seemed to declare. He afterwards sent a cordelier to every one of the prisoners to administer the sacraments, and then ordered the Capitol bell to be tolled. At that fatal sound and the sight of the confessors, the Lords no longer doubted of sentence of death being passed upon them. They all confessed except the old Colonna, and many received the communion. In the meanwhile the people, naturally prompt to attend, when their first impetuosity had time to calm, could not without pity behold the dismal preparations which were making. The sight of the bloody color in the tapestry shocked them. On this first impression they joined in opinion in relation to so many illustrious heads now going to be sacrificed, and lamented more their unhappy catastrophe, as no crime had been proved upon them to render them worthy of such barbarous treatment. Above all, the unfortunate Stephen Colonna, whose birth, age, and affable behavior, commanded respect, excited a particular compassion. An universal silence and sorrow reigned among them. Those who were nearest Rienzi discovered an alteration. They took the opportunity of imploring his mercy towards the prisoners in terms the most affecting and moving."

Will it be believed, that in the original from which the Père Du Cerceau borrows or rather imagines this touching recital, there is not a single syllable about the pity of the people, nor their shock at the bloody colors of the tapestry, nor their particular compassion for the unfortunate Stephen Colonna?—in fine, the *People* are not even mentioned at all. All that is said is, "Some Roman citizens, (alcuni cittadini Romani,) considering the judgment Rienzi was about to make, interposed with soft and caressing words, and at last changed the opinion of the Tribune;" all the rest is the pure fiction of the ingenious Frenchman! Again, Du Cerceau describing the appearance of the Barons at this fatal moment, says, "Notwithstanding the grief and despair visible in their countenances, *they showed a noble indignation, generally attendant on innocence in the hour of death.*" What says the authority from which alone, except his own, the good Father could take his account? Why, not a word about this noble indignation, or this parade of innocence! The original says simply, that "*the Barons were so frozen with terror that they were unable to speak*," (diventaso si gelati che non poteano favellare;) "that the greater part humbled themselves, (e prese penitenza e comunione;) that when Rienzi addressed them, "*all* the Barons (come dannati) stood in sadness." * Du Cerceau then proceeds to state, that "although he (Rienzi) was grieved at heart to behold his victims snatched from him, he endeavored to make a merit of it in the eyes of the People." *There is not a word of this in the original!*

So, when Rienzi, on a later occasion, placed the Prefect John di Vico in prison, this Jesuit says, "*To put a gloss upon this action* before the eyes of the people, Rienzi *gave out that* the Governor, John di Vico, keeping a correspondence with the conspirators, came with no other view than to betray the Romans." And if this scribbler who pretends to have consulted the Vatican MSS., had looked at the most ordinary authorities, he would have seen that John di Vico *did* come with that view. (See for Di Vico's secret correspondence with the Barons, La Cron. Bologn. p. 406; and La Cron. Est. p. 444).

Again, in the battle between the Barons and the Romans at the gates, Du Cerceau thus describes the conduct of the Tribune:—"The Tribune, amidst his troops, knew so little of what had passed, that seeing at a distance one of his standards fall, he looked upon all as lost, and, casting up his eyes to heaven full of despair, cried out, 'O God, will you then forsake me?' But no sooner was he informed of the entire defeat of his enemies, than his dread and cowardice even turned to boldness and arrogance."

Now in the original all that is said of this is "That it is true that the standard of the Tribune fell—the Tribune astonished, (or if you please, dismayed, *sbigottio*,) stood with his eyes raised to heaven, and could find no other words than, 'O God hast thou betrayed me?'" This evinced, perpaps, alarm or consternation at the fall of his standard—a consternation natural, not to a coward, but a fanatic, at such an event. But not a word is said about Rienzi's cowardice in the action itself; it is not stated when the accident happened—nothing bears out the implication that the Tribune was remote from the contest, and knew little of what passed. And if this ignorant Frenchman had *consulted any other contemporaneous historian whatever*, he would have found it asserted by them all, that the fight was conducted with great valor, both by the Roman populace and their leader on the one side, and the Barons on the other.—G. Vill. lib. xii. cap. 105; Cron. Sen. tom. xv. Murat. p. 119; Cron. Est. p. 444. Yet Gibbon rests his own sarcasm on the Tribune's courage solely on the baseless exaggeration of this Père Du Cerceau.

So little, indeed, did this French pretender know of the history of the time and place he treats of, that he imagines the Stephen Colonna who was killed in the battle above-mentioned was the *old* Stephen Colonna, and is very pathetic about his "venerable appearance," etc. This error, with regard to a man so eminent as Stephan Colonna the elder, is inexcusable: for, had the priest turned over the other pages of the very collection in which he found the biography he deforms, he would have learned that old Stephen Colonna was

* The English translator makes this law unintelligible:—"That no family of Rome shall appropriate to their own use what they think fit, but that the revenues shall appertain to the public"!!!—The revenues of what?

* See Vita di Col. di Rienzi, lib. i. cap. 29.

alive some time after that battle.—[Cron. Sen. Murat. tom. xv. p. 121.]

Again, just before Rienzi's expulsion from the office of Tribune, Du Cerceau, translating in his headlong way the old biographer's account of the causes of Rienzi's loss of popularity, says, "He shut himself up in his palace, and his presence was known only by the rigorous punishments which he caused his agents to inflict upon the innocent." Not a word of this in the original!

Again, after the expulsion, Du Cerceau says, that the Barons seized upon the "immense riches" he had amassed,—the words in the original are, "grandi ornamenti,' which are very different things from immense riches. But the most remarkable sins of commission are in this person's account of the second rise and fall of Rienzi under the title of Senator. Of this I shall give but one instance:—

"The Senator, who perceived it, became only the more cruel. His jealousies produced only fresh murders. In the continual dread he was in, that the general discontent would terminate in some secret attempt upon his person, he determined to intimidate the most enterprising, by sacrificing sometimes one, sometimes another, and chiefly those whose riches rendered them the more guilty in his eyes. Numbers were sent every day to the Capitol prison. Happy were those who could get off with the confiscation of their estates."

Of these grave charges there is not a syllable in the original! And so much for the work of Père Cerceau and Père Brumoy, by virtue of which, historians have written of the life and times of Rienzi, and upon the figments of which, the most remarkable man in an age crowded with great characters is judged by the general reader!

I must be pardoned for this criticism, which might not have been necessary, had not the work to which it relates, in the English translation quoted from, (a translation that has no faults but those of the French original,) been actually received as an historical and indisputable authority, and opposed with a triumphant air to some passages in my own narrative which were literally taken from the authentic records of the time.

END OF "RIENZI, THE LAST OF THE TRIBUNES."